Lonely in the Heart of the World

MINDI MELTZ

LONELY IN THE HEART OF THE WORLD
by MINDI MELTZ

LOGOSOPHIA

Logosophia, LLC

Logosophia, LLC
90 Oteen Church Road
Asheville, NC 28805
www.logosophiabooks.com

First Edition

Library of Congress-in-Publication Data

Meltz, Mindi
Lonely in the Heart of the World

ISBN 978-0-9815757-4-2

Cover design and layout by Susan Yost
Cover art by Brian Mashburn
Calligraphy and illuminated lettering by Krys Crimi
Back cover and interior art by Chiwa

This book is dedicated to my father, who taught me the
languages of water, silence, and unconditional love.

The mass illusion of this mind
connecting reality with lost time,
going back where the silver river runs,
remembering when we danced upon the sun,
and the golden painted ponies, they raced upon the land,
and the brothers and the sisters, they joined the gypsy band,
and the crocodile he slept well into the day,
and the kookaburra she wept, for she had something to say:

She said kookaburra kookaburra coo coo, what have I done?
Kookaburra kookaburra coo coo, I'm the only one.
Kookaburra kookaburra coo coo, my family left me here.
Kookaburra kookaburra coo coo, I'm alone, I fear.

Well the flamingo he stood upon his webbed paw.
He said Kookaburra, why are you crying?
Is there no one left at all?
And the kookaburra looked up with a tear upon her cheek.
This standing, wise flamingo was a soul she sought to seek.
And the sky he opened up, where an eagle-bird did soar,
and he swept across the mountains, to love the earth once more.

Kookaburra kookaburra coo coo, I see it all so clear.
Kookaburra kookaburra coo coo, your family is right here.
Kookaburra kookaburra coo coo, wipe your tears away.
Kookaburra kookaburra coo coo, we are here to stay.

Well the blue heron, he waltzed along the oceanside
to the song of a banjo-violin and tears no longer cried.
And the dolphin, she thought, without a single word,
about everything and nothing and how walking is absurd.
And the kookaburra she smiled. She turned her frown away.
And her eyes they changed to laughter; she had one last thing to say:

She said, kookaburra kookaburra coo coo, coo coo beh-da beh-dam doo da…
Kookaburra kookaburra coo coo, coo da-n-doo da-n-doo dee da…
Kookaburra kookaburra coo coo, sah endoo endah dah-n-dah dee da…
Kookaburra kookaburra coo coo, coo coo coo…

"Nothing of the Sort" by Utah Green

Without

onely wasn't always her name. There was a time before the wind first called her that. She lived as someone created her ~ an imagined life. She had never yet felt even her own touch. She stood inside the tower, facing out, and the glass around her drank the light.

The formless wind slammed against it, without breaking, without pain.

She did not know then where the wind was or where it came from. She could not yet understand the language it spoke of the things beyond her round, high room: the shape of the rocky island around the tower, the churning of the salt and sea around the island, the changing textures of a faraway shore, the cries of the City. She heard only the muffled thump of the wind's blasts against the glass's curve, and beneath that the hollow drone of infinity.

The day her father did not come, she never thought to call out to him, for she had never thought beyond this room. She sat still and tried to remember the stories he had told her, and what would happen next.

Sometimes the wind hissed outward, and sometimes it sucked inward. Sometimes it wound like a soft ribbon around the tower, and at other times it came battering and beating as if the tower were the only thing that stood in its way, and she did not know whether it raced toward something in the future or away from something in the past.

She did not yet know what she was.

"Someone will rescue me," she remembered, whispering it. "Love will come."

She tried to draw comfort from her father's promise, but she did not understand what it meant. Her own voice in the silence horrified her. Though she stood at the top of the tower and faced out, still she saw nothing but herself. For the glass was not a window but a mirror, and the mirror surrounded her.

What did you mean, when you imagined a princess?

Not someone who would rule one day as queen; no one with any power.

"Princess!" you cried out as children, when your eyes could still track the movement of light off a worm path into the wilderness beyond, and you meant that anything was possible.

"*Princess*," you giggled in the locker room when you were older, and you meant someone who wanted too much, who expected more than she had been taught to hope for.

"Princess," you sneered when you were older still, and you meant a kind of beauty that could never apply to yourselves, a beauty which seemed foolish now that childhood was over.

"Princess," you muttered, shaking your heads years later, and mistaking habit for wisdom you laughed at the very idea of innocence: nobody was ever that good or that guileless, and your age—if nothing else—had taught you that much.

But of course the truth is that there was a god once, who destroyed the old, beautiful world—and then he was sad, because the new world he made disappointed him, and he did not know how to reclaim what he had lost. So he locked his daughter up high in a circle of glass, in order to preserve her. He kept her apart from you, so she would never know what he had done.

In her he saw what he had intended from the very beginning. He told her she was his goddess and would live forever. *Princess*, he called her. For he did not want to endanger her with something so human, so specific, so partial as a name.

"You're too old for this," you say to your son, taking the toy sword from his hand. "Do your homework."

So the boy, somewhere in some house, bends his body into the chair, and takes the tiny sword of the pen in his hand instead. Inside, his body still swings with the rhythm of the movement he was making. He stares at the numbers and questions written on the square paper on the square desk. And he thinks about the shape of girls.

You go down the stairs, unaware of increasing your closeness to the earth. You do not touch your wife.

Once there was a story about beauty, and the heroism it took to live such beauty.

But that story is no longer told in the City.

So now you—man and woman, in some house somewhere—sit on different couches and watch the TV, because you want to know about the world.

But what *is* this world?

You think the City is reality. You think this is the world. You would say the story begins here, where all the people are.

The City is made of rectangles, and what the rectangles are made of is no longer recognizable and has no name. It is hard and shiny, and it does not change with the weather. Also the City is made of people, and all of your thoughts and feelings, and your belief in a god who fed you on promises.

The City smells like fuel and trash and sterilization. It sounds like alarms and curses and motors, sudden stops and the songless hum of machines. It tastes like black metal dust, and it feels like nothing.

The even ground in the City makes your bones clatter dryly against each other when you walk. The lights stay on all night. You step out of buildings and into cars, and then suddenly you are somewhere else, and you cannot remember what you were thinking of, and then you get out of the cars and step into buildings. And you cannot remember how your bodies did that. You all have jobs, and your jobs have nothing to do with living, and yet you need them to survive.

The City is never dark and never quiet. In the offices, in the schools, in the cars, you must sit tight and never move; yet at the same time, there is never any stillness.

It goes on like this. Comfort is bright lights, crowds, the inside of a car, big rooms up high. Excitement is loud noise, the idea of sex, and anything new. Happiness is a new Thing, and sorrow is being without It. The arms of the City do not embrace its people, but reach outward in ever-expanding roads, clawing desperately at the Earth.

This is the world, you think.

You do not ask yourselves what planet you live on. You do not ask yourselves where you are. You do not ask yourselves if this story is real.

But if you could look down from the sky, you would see how small the City actually is. It would not look real. It would look like a clumsy child's drawing: amidst richly hued hills that change with the light, the City would seem to break into those curves with a flatness that hollows your belly out to look at, leaving a plain of shattered pieces defined only by grey, thickened lines.

The god who drew this City believed he could re-make the world. He thought his drawing was realistic, more realistic than reality. He was wrong, but he was so powerful that even this ridiculous drawing could begin to destroy everything around it in only a hundred years.

You do not ask yourselves what lies beyond the City. You do not want to know because you are afraid of what you have forgotten, and because you miss it so much, it might hurt to remember.

Yet suppose that only a day's walk from the City (though no one walks any more) surged the sea. Suppose that across that sea—whose lengths could not be counted in days and nights—pulsed this tiny island, and on the island stood a glass tower. Suppose that in the top of the tower lived the fairy tale you had forgotten, that dream you had stuffed away. Suppose she was still alive.

Now the woman in the tower, who knew only that she was younger than her father, and older than she had once been, began to hear the soft, heavy echo of her own heart in her ears. At first it terrified her, like something creeping up on her from inside. But once she got used to it, she began to trust it, and then she listened to it, and then suddenly she felt attached to it. She tried to locate it, sensing that this sound kept her alive—afraid that, if she forgot it for an instant, it might stop. Wouldn't it ever tire? She had never thought about this before; she had never thought about anything ending.

But now her father's coming had ended.

For as long as she could remember, this god who was her father had been her only company. Every day he had come to the tower.

"This is the sun, and this is the moon," he would tell her, though it was not the real sun and moon, but a dream of these things that he played out for her, with his magic, on the round glass walls. "These are the eagles, and these are the deepest forests. These are the green lakes, and these are the deer—see them running!" The Princess had watched it all. She had seen the water and the fields, the focused opening and closing of flowers. She had watched her father's dreams with him in the glass, wanting to be near him, wanting to go wherever he went—though as he spoke his voice receded and fell quieter, and often he seemed to forget she was there. She had watched the landscapes unfold before her, and the distant, wandering animals.

"When will we feel that meadow, that sky?" she had asked her father once. "When will we go there?"

But her father had shaken his head. "Someday," he said, "he will come and rescue you, and he will take you there. I cannot."

"Who will come?" she had cried, for she had heard this promise before and could not understand it—this idea of someone else besides themselves.

"The one from the green water, who walks in the tops of the trees…" he had murmured, but his voice came even softer then, so that she could barely hear it. And she did not know if he was telling the truth, for when he dreamed that place in the glass for her—where carpets of green lay over the water so thick they seemed like meadows you could run across, and giant trees made a rhythm in space like music, and long-necked birds with masked faces fanned their wings in a hot, weighted stillness—he would cease to speak to her at all, and he would hold his face in his hands sometimes and whisper a word she did not know:

Lost.

Her father's eyes were a sharp and painful blue. Later she would remember how, when she asked him questions like these, they seemed to answer her with surprise—the pupils filling them like greater and greater unknowns—and something else she did not want to see there, a tightness she would learn later (from other eyes) was the pinched crease of pain.

His hair was clean and yellow, like her own, but there was a rougher tangle of hair growing beneath his mouth and over his cheeks, like the faces of the animals she saw in his dreams, and she liked to touch that. His hands were warm.

But on this day he did not come. Nor the next, nor the next.

He would never come again.

The first feeling she could identify, beneath the sound of her heart, was an absence of feeling—the strain of a dull weight in her gut, like a slow falling of loose grey sand.

You would begin the story with the City, as if the City *were* the world. But I will not begin it there. I will begin with the real world, which is at once a body and a dream.

This body is familiar to you, and yet it is not human. It does not begin head on top. It begins with the womb, which is the sea, and the womb is not a piece of the body, but rather the body is held and changed within the sea—the rest of the body constantly born and born again from those hungry waters of creation.

From out of the sea come the sands, and the sands are the face of the world, constantly changing expression beneath the moods of the sea. Then come the fields and the deserts, which are the sad, quiet feet of the world, and at the same time its flesh, and at the same time its lungs of wind. Then come the forests, forever digesting themselves, which are its belly. Then rise the breasts of the mountains—hundreds of breasts, rising and rising, and at the same time deepening, their valleys rich and scented, their slopes falling so fast that the light weeps over them. And these highest peaks, cold and eerily peaceful, sharply braving the sky—these are the mind of the world.

The trees its boundless arms. The grass its nerves. The hot springs its lusty mouths. The rivers its arteries and veins, running everywhere, not only through the soil and stone but through the air as rain and mist and snow. The parts of this body are not arranged like your body seems to be, and they are constantly changing. Yet you remember. You remember the path this nameless goddess will walk, from the womb of the sea across the fields and the desert, through the forested mountains and into the sky—this path that will also carry her all the way back again, on the other side of her dream. You remember.

You remember, almost, that the City was built upon what once was the heart of the world. Maybe that's why the City feels so important.

Yet you cannot remember any more the landscape of that heart, before the City was made.

The Princess in the tower also remembered the world, though she did not know how. The bed she had slept in forever was not made of glass, nor of otherworldly magic. Where did it come from—this crinkly softness that, had she understood it, would have felt like real autumn leaves from some real, living forest floor? How was it that the pillow she laid her head upon to dream felt so deliciously slippery; what else has the texture of silver, if silver were a sensation, but the feathers of real birds? It seemed she slept upon the depth of water and the softness of rotting earth, and that she covered herself with the thickness of clouds or meadow grass. If this were true, where had these things come from, and how was she able to recognize them? Yet older than time seemed this bed to her, and more familiar than dreams, and more comforting than death.

Though her father had told her that her body was unimportant, that she was a goddess and did not need the things the animals needed, she began to wonder about it now that he was gone. What were the little impressions, like empty pools, inside her hands for? Why did her elbows bend, and her wrists, so that if she brought her fingertips together she could form a circle? She lifted one foot into the air, then the other. What was this for: the roundness of the boneless belly? The undulation of a foot's sole? Her breast felt cool with the heart hot beneath it. She lost her fingers in the folds of the dress. A sudden spiral of sensation made her close her eyes.

Maybe the Princess had always known her father would leave her. Maybe that's why she had cried sometimes, though she cannot remember that now, or what it felt like.

"He will come for you," her father had said, "after I am gone." Hadn't he said that? But it brought her no comfort now.

The wind did not blow every day, and on the days it did not blow the Princess in the tower felt safer, and tried not to think of anything. But on other days it beat about the tower continuously. Sleeping, she would fall into the sound, the pillows of its gusts engulfing her, but then she would jolt awake suddenly as its movement seemed to double back behind her, bucking like a trapped beast. Its crude shoves jarred her out of oblivion, and she rose from the bed and paced. The future seemed to be rushing toward her through invisible space, coming and coming at a faster speed than she could understand. She could hear it, outside, and it was here already, and yet it was not.

The absence of her father—her aloneness without him—was so loud it hummed. It was so loud she had to cover her ears.

Circling her glass room, she replayed the love story in her mind—the one her father had dreamed out for her, over and over on the glass wall. The man on the white horse rescued the woman from the great teeth, the great jaws, the great darkness below the water, below the earth…She knew it might take a long time, because the man always had to battle so many demons before reaching the woman. But in the meantime she slept with her feet curled tight beneath her on the bed, unable to see through the glass floor, imagining what might lie below.

Over and over, she tried to remember the end of the story. She tried to understand what love *was*, and what happened when the faces of the man and the woman finally drew close, and blurred, and spoke.

Please rescue me, she prayed. She thought of the beautiful white horse, and wondered why it was necessary in order for love to happen, and though she did not know what a horse was, she wished she had one of her own.

She missed her father. She missed his dreams, which had made so much sense at the time, and had been her only reality. She did not yet have a language for the things she felt inside when she thought of her father and lived in his absence, day after day, or when she tried to remember the last time he had come to the tower, and what had happened, and why. The hours she spent curled like a question mark on her side, her knees digging into her forehead, what she felt—no, she would not remember those times later. She would refuse to ever think of those hours again.

But the wind would name her *Lonely*, all the same. We are not named for just anything. We are named for what sets us apart.

In those foggy glass walls wrapping round and round her, she began to dream dreams her father had not taught her. Waves of color in a sea of lights, colors running in and out of doors, tensing and releasing, bringing pain and pleasure at once. She did not understand what she was seeing— that it was people, that it was crowds and masses of so many people she could never see all of their faces in her lifetime. She saw straight lines for the first time, and they were terrifying, like a neck snapped and broken. She saw buildings made of lines that lasted longer than stone, that stretched higher than the sky, built on layers of waste. She saw those masses trudging through a maze of hard, greenless hallways whose walls hemmed them close.

And then the nightmares began.

No, we are not named for just anything. We are named for what separates us from others.

Now the glass, emptied of dreams, was nothing but a mirror, dreamless and merciless, on all sides.

She saw the wilderness in her own eyes, and she saw that her eyes were not like her father's, but very dark, despite her pale face and yellow hair. She knew then that something inside her was not like him, and maybe that was why he had finally left her.

Because later she would never be sure if her dreams changed before or after her father was gone. Could it be that he stopped coming because she was not the *Princess* that he called her after all—not inside herself, where her own dreams were made?

But she had to rise now—she had to—and did not know why. She was a goddess, her father had told her, and she did not need food, and she did not need water, and she did not need touch, and nothing could ever happen to her. Yet this movement began inside her body, lurched forward in her empty gut. A bright space in her mind; a wind in her mouth. She must rise and exist today, and every day, for some reason she did not yet know. She paced again around the room. Her face was reflected so many times over, it lost its meaning. The Princess fell to her knees and poured her vision into the glass.

"Ya!" she called out, trying to be brave. Wasn't there anything beyond herself?

It seemed then that her father's face appeared behind her, but before she could be sure, it changed.

It became a new face, youthful and elegant, with brave eyes that leaped right over her confusion and into the abyss of her—right into that place from which the unknown came. She felt sure it was the man with the white horse, whose image seemed now to kneel down behind her, whose face now tilted toward hers, his lips smiling and parted against her neck. She closed her eyes and shivered, and when she opened them he was gone.

"Come back!"

She would never forget that face. She knew the struggling shine inside his eyes belonged to her, and that he, too, was frightened by the heartbeat in his ears. She knew by the tremor in his smooth jaw that he was lonely too, and that his lips had opened to take her in. She felt his loneliness in her hips; she felt it in her heart falling like a silent avalanche between her ribs; she felt it seize up the muscles of her thighs. She ran her fingertips over her scalp, her cheeks, the wetness of her mouth.

She kept staring at that mirror all day, but he never came back. She stared until the image of her own face overcame her, and she fell asleep on the cold glass floor.

In her dreams, a terrible old woman was chasing her around and around the glass room, and she herself could never take a different path than that same repeating circle, and she could never get out. And the princess had never seen another woman, but the broken crazy shuffle of this old woman behind her was familiar—and the worst nightmare she had ever had.

She kept dreaming, on and on after that, and her dreams ran together, and when her mind finally swam toward waking, she could not remember them. She remembered only the smell of them, like bodies hot in the darkness, putrid with sweat and cramped tight and still for too long. She remembered someone crying gently below her, the cry echoing up through endless angles of stone and glass. She thought it was someone very young.

When she woke for real, she was lying on the floor, and it was night. She breathed in, and she could smell her own body for the first time, sweet and alive. She rolled over onto her back, looked up at the glass, and saw through it for the first time to the stars.

She was not afraid. She did not feel lost or insignificant. She felt, in a way, as if she were still looking at her reflection, but as if her being were somehow far bigger and more wonderful than she had ever realized.

The sky looked rich and somber, with every color fallen and merged inside it, as if when colors died they all returned to the night to decompose into this fertile blackness. And through it came the white pricks of the stars, sharp as pain—faraway beams of no-color. Clouds spread across in smears of silver, each one silent and serious, cushioning the beauty of the stars as if to keep them from bursting.

Then she saw that the sky surrounded her, and was everywhere. She stood up. She turned around and around looking at the sky, whose black was so shiny it seemed to hold a brightness deep within, like a singing in the silence or a smile through tears. She spun around, just on the verge of dancing. Then she went to the glass, because the mirror had finally become not a dreamscape or a mirror but a window, and through that window where she'd seen reflected her mysterious lover's face, she now saw a mountain.

She could not tell how far away it was, because she had not yet learned distance, beyond the distance of wall to wall. She could not imagine a distance such as this. From here its peaks were merely a calm, cryptic pattern, glowing faintly white. But the mountain made her feel that her life extended somewhere beyond her. She thought she might understand, for the first time, for just a moment, what her father meant when he told her she was immortal.

She looked at the mountain all night and never grew sleepy. She pressed herself as close as she could right up to the glass, staring out. The longer she looked at that delicate, eloquent line of the mountain's edge against the sky, the more it started to look like something written, a pattern in some language that she was ever on the tantalizing brink of remembering. She knew for the first time what loneliness was, and she knew that whatever was written there was the answer to that loneliness. The world itself was her mirror, and she herself was the world, and everything was possible.

As her vision followed the rivers of snow downward, and along the patterns of stone and tree so far away that they were only shades of each other, her hands drifted unconsciously over her own peaks and valleys, the patterns of her own body that she had never before explored. When the dawn came, she felt tense and desperate in a way she did not understand. She pressed her bare limbs against the glass; she pressed her face to that image; she cried out to it and licked it hungrily with her tongue.

But when she touched the glass it shocked her, like a deathly silence that cut right through her bones. She jumped back and looked at her knees. They were red, and when she touched them, they were cold. She looked back up and saw her own face, and the mountain was gone.

Then a scream began, and the scream must be coming from her. Inside the scream were all the sounds she had never heard, as if she held inside her all the world that she had never seen: gulls and rain and laughter and wind, waves breaking and fire crackling, coyotes and thunder. As she screamed, her breath hit the glass hard. The image of her face collapsed slowly inward. The mountain appeared again where a hole opened in the glass before her, as if reflecting the widening cavern of her own open mouth.

For it was not glass after all, but ice.

In the City, there are the familiar square ceilings, the familiar angry lights. There are the signs and the words, the suits and the high-heeled shoes. There is the dog waiting outside on the concrete, his head in his paws, sniffing half-heartedly at the passing feet.

You sit in your rows of desks, raising your hands. Some of you want desperately to be seen; others want to disappear.

"Who created this world?" asks the teacher. "Who made the City and gave us all the things we need, and made us all-powerful, so that we should never suffer again?"

"Hanum," you answer. "Hanum created the world."

"Are there other gods in this world?"

"There is only one god: Hanum."

In the stores, in the malls, in the catalogs, the idea of a Princess persists: Hanum's unattainable, mythical daughter. On a clothing label, on a bottle of shampoo, on a box of ready-made health crackers or a can of fruit. She shows up in commercials, on the hood of a car or drinking a soda.

The image is everywhere, and yet no one speaks of it. The hunger that creates this image is not taught in schools, and the worship of this image is silent. You do not name her in the churches, and yet she is the reason you go.

In the schools, in the lunchroom, you laugh. Maybe someone betrays his innocence by speaking of the Princess in the Tower as if she is real. And you laugh, using your vulgarest words to express your contempt, your embarrassment.

Of course you do not believe in that image any more. That kind of beauty. Skin as smooth as still water and flushed like the first hesitant color in a pale winter dawn. Yellow-white hair shining down her shoulders like a memory of childhood sunlight, brighter somehow than the sun you see today. Eyes deep as galaxies, lips forever new. Her body at once proud and yielding, like a sapling grown without cover in an open field, her bones strong and her curves definite but muted beneath a hazy gown of changing silver....

In the schools you only say, "Hanum created the world."

"And why do we seem sometimes to suffer?" asks the teacher. "Why do bad things happen?"

"Because of the Witch," you say. "A woman from the old world, who tricked Hanum into marrying her. She fights the magic he made. She wants to take the world back into chaos, into wilderness."

For something is wrong. Once Hanum walked among you, and magic was made before your eyes, and the purpose of things explained. Roads had a destination, and the City Center, where food and energy come from, was open to everyone and understood by all. But now life is done out of habit, and no one remembers exactly why. Money, the magic current of the City, gets dammed up in certain buildings and does not reach everyone. Some people do not live in buildings at all but on the streets. Some people are not functioning properly.

Behind the schools, skipping class, you give the Witch another name, a name you dare not speak in public: *Dark Goddess.* You whisper that She killed Hanum, after all.

And the Princess in the Tower is only a symbol now, though women still wear fake faces over their real faces in their effort to look as they imagine she looked, for they cannot believe that such beauty—that kind of beauty that unfolds from a body out of pure, raw life—is naturally possible. She is chaste, and they are not. She has no needs, and they do. She is beautiful, and they are formless, constantly aging despite Hanum's dream of everlasting life. In your manufactured world, you have never seen beauty that is not fake, and so you no longer believe in it.

The City is full of contradictions. It is shameful to make love to any one person more than once or to miss anyone after they have said goodbye. Yet it is forbidden to lust after anyone but the person who is bound and promised to stay by your side.

Families are sacred, and yet no one has a family. No one wants to be anywhere near the people who bore them or remembers where they came from.

Animals are the only ones who love unconditionally, but they are not prioritized in emergencies, and in a pinch they are thrown away.

Everyone tries to be different, but everyone is different in the same way.

Drugs are forbidden, but they are easier to get than love.

Every woman, when she wakes in the morning, imagines for a split second that she is the Princess. She imagines she is that passive perfection of which all men dream. Or she imagines that the god Hanum comes for her alone, and what it would feel like to make love to a god.

Every man, in the moment of waking, before he remembers his life, imagines that he is the one to claim that Princess from the old stories—that he is the hero who will take her in his arms, the light of her redeeming eyes focused upon him.

But none of you remember, as you trudge through your days, that you imagined or longed for such things when you woke.

Nor do you realize that everyone else longed for them, too.

Now the wind came hurtling in.

The Princess whirled away from it, curled into a ball, and whimpered. The scent of her own body flamed stronger, and it was calling to her, and she did not understand what it was saying, and she wanted it to stop. For it was something her father had never mentioned—this body. Here it had turned the glass to ice and melted it. She did not trust it. There was something wrong. Something was coming for her—in the wind, in the pounding of her heart—and it did not feel like rescue.

She lifted her head and opened her eyes. The wind filled the room, and now the room was cold and meant nothing any more.

She crawled to the hole and poked her head out, and as the dazzling freshness of the air sparked against her face for the first time, she saw the rocky island around the tower, and—down below—the old woman from her nightmare.

Surely it was the Witch her father had always warned her about, who guarded this tower and who kept her from leaving! She stood there right at the bottom, her grey form turned toward the sea.

The Princess stared at the Witch in shock while the wind spun dizzily around her head, and the Witch did not move, did not turn her head. The girl was afraid to see that face. But finally she gathered her courage and cried, "Let me out!" Her voice shook her, so that she reeled back and hit her head on the ice, but the old, gray woman did not seem to hear.

Why? the wind asked, and she understood its voice for the first time. It was so cold. She could not connect its force with the echoes she had heard from inside the tower, when it had blown around harmlessly like a distant philosophy of life. She pressed her hands to her ears and pursed her lips, which felt dry and bruised now.

Why leave? the wind repeated carelessly.

"Because I'm lonely in here," she murmured, as if to herself, but the wind whispered back.

What do you want, then?

"I want love." The girl let her breath out hot in the face of the wind as if to blow it away, though its ability to speak to her—the only time anyone had ever spoken to her besides her father—unsettled her. She closed her eyes and let the wind touch her for a moment, helpless to the pleasure of it. Even when it beat against her in violence, it felt good to be touched.

"Hey!" She waited for the Witch to turn around. She was ready. "Can't you hear me? I want to get out now! You can't keep me here."

It was only a dream, said the wind.

No. The girl tried to ignore the wind now, panicking as she looked out hungrily across the sea. Distance. Space. It made her mind buckle.

The Witch did not move. The girl looked down for what seemed like a long, long time. The space around her head was terrible, but to turn back into the room seemed worse.

At last the wind nudged her again. It would not leave her alone. *So who are you, that you think yourself worthy of love?*

She shivered up and down her spine, and could not seem to stop. "I don't have to prove myself to you," she said to the wind. "I'm the daughter of a god. Who are *you,* to ask me such questions?"

The wind laughed, in a way that was at once cruel and kind.

I do not need to prove myself, or name myself.

"Why not?"

Because there is nothing I am seeking, and nothing that I want.

The girl sensed perhaps a judgment in this, and responded a little defensively, "Well, it's not that I want so much. I've been trapped in a tower all my life, and I ask for love. Is that so much to ask? I'm lonely, is all."

Then I will call you Lonely, since that is what you call yourself. Lonely shall be your name.

Lonely began to cry. It was an easy thing, and it melted her down into herself, where she found comfort in the hollow of her own chest. "But I don't want to be lonely," she sniffed, missing her father.

I'll be your friend, said the wind, but Lonely thought she heard mockery in its tone.

"I don't want you!" she cried. "Leave me alone."

But the wind is in charge of the path voices take, and finally it whipped the girl's voice down to the old woman's ears. The woman turned, very slowly, her stooped back rising and her bent head following. Not moving her eyes, she lifted toward Lonely a crumpled, nightmare face, and in that face Lonely saw—though she would later forget—the same sorrow she'd seen every day of her life in her father's eyes. But something in these eyes wasn't right.

The Witch said, without expression, her voice creaking as if she sucked her breath in instead of letting it out when she spoke, "Your father is dead."

The wind stopped.

"Why?" said Lonely. She had heard of death, but she didn't think it was possible. Not for herself and her father, who were gods, and needed nothing.

But the old woman did not speak again. Her hair webbed her face in the wind as she turned back to the sea. There was an old chair there at the foot of the tower, made of driftwood and bones, and the old woman fell down into it and dropped her face in her hands, as if exhausted by the four words she had spoken. Yet Lonely felt certain that she must be a powerful witch, because she did not seem to suffer from the cold, and all around her there was nothing but grey barren rock and grey churning sea and grey heartless wind.

Inside the room Lonely paced until she was dizzy. She screamed and breathed against the frozen door, but it was thicker than the walls and she only melted it a little, turning it slippery with small rivers of water that freed themselves and ran to the floor like tears. She caught them and touched them to her tongue, and then she beat the door with her fists. She punched it until her skin broke, and then she curled up at the foot of it with her knuckles in her mouth, tasting her first taste: the salty, mineral taste of blood. In that taste she sensed, vaguely, what death was. But still she did not understand where her father had gone.

She dreamed a white bird flew into her room through the hole she had screamed into the wall. He perched on her chest, his feet so thin and light, like spider webs, that she barely felt him. Tenderly, so that it did not hurt her at all, he pierced her breast bone with his long beak, and pulled out her wild, throbbing heart. He dropped it into his feet, upturned like hands, as he lifted off her chest into the air. He flew with it to the frozen door, where, glowing like an ember in his grasp, it melted a hole big enough for her body. Then he came back down to where she lay, and held her heart out to her. She reached for it with trembling hands, saying, "Thank you."

The bird said, "It was already there. I only wanted to show you." He looked at her in a way that was familiar, then flew up into the open sky above her.

Waking was like spinning upward, as if she were a leaf that spun in the spiral of the bird's wake.

When she opens her eyes, she is only a puddle of glassy limbs down on the windy stone, with the wide universe open around her.

There is no tower.

But there are people below the tower, within the sea, of whom no one ever, ever speaks.

And on this night they cry out, with a cry that makes no sound but shakes the earth under the waters, and makes the waters rise a little, and the ground tremble beneath the buildings of the City.

No one is hurt, but in a factory where Things are manufactured, glass breaks and chemicals are knocked together which start a fire—and the fire burns up part of several buildings before it is put out. And you do not think about what fire is or where it comes from, and the men who work with the chemicals do not wonder about the magic they are using, or what it means to handle such power.

But the tremors, even after they end, make you uneasy in a way you have no words for, as if the foundations of reality itself are unsafe.

Maybe there is more to this world than you remember. Maybe there are still goddesses turning under the sea, and gods in the sky who toss the rain sadly from hand to hand—hoping that someone will once again pray for it, will dance for it, will cry for it, will need it to grow food. Maybe there are people who still live real lives outside of the City—in the desert, in the forest, in the mountains, and even in places that do not exist any more.

Because you still dream, in the City. Only you will not admit to it, so your dreams cannot help you. No one has time to sleep, in the City. No one has time to stop.

But the dreams still come. Someone—did you not realize this?—someone has been keeping them alive for you.

Fire

I changed my mind ~ I want to go back is Lonely's first thought about waking. The sense of space around her in the darkness ~ something she cannot define, something whose boundaries she cannot imagine ~ is awful to her.

This is life, says the wind. No, I don't want it, I want to go back. Again she draws her body into a ball.

All the dreams she did not understand, the nightmares that came for her after her father died—always a darkness has lurked around the safe boundaries of her world. There was so much she took for granted. The bed. The shape of space. The comfortable warmth. The comfortable beauty. The only love she had.

If only she had never woken. She did not mean to make this choice. Or did she? To stay, too, was impossible.

But nothing more happens now. The rhythm of the little waves, at once feminine and deep, feels like a new heartbeat near her own. One that carries on without her, whether she wills it or not.

Lonely sits up.

At least the universe is easier to meet for the first time at night. The darkness makes it fade quickly into the near distance, where her mind can rest in the intimate plunk of wavelets falling. Though sometimes a big wave hisses, or the darkness rushes at her in a sudden breeze, for the most part the air feels calmer down here than out her window up high. But not far away looms the outline of the Witch's chair.

Lonely watches the back of that chair, making sure it doesn't move, making sure that face stays hidden behind it. A thin thread of moon curls like an old woman's hair between the clouds, just beginning, but Lonely does not see it. Everything around her is slow and quiet but something is picking up speed inside her chest. Something hot runs through her, deafening, and she does not fit herself suddenly—she twists away from herself. She does not know what this is, this feeling—

fear, says the wind helpfully.

Lonely glances back up at the chair, silhouetted against the paler mass of the sea that swirls up to it. She feels vulnerable. She took her height for granted in the tower. She struggles to stand up now, but her head spins, and she falls back down on one knee.

I want to go back, she thinks again, her heart tensing.

come down, the rocks say. *don't be afraid. we'll hold you.*

She maneuvers her body down close to the rocks, gripping them hard and not taking her eyes off the chair. Their cold sears into her breasts and thighs, but she remembers she is a goddess, and it cannot hurt her. The cold is only the way the rocks speak to her, turning her body white and hard, strong and stern. She realizes that nothing is going to happen until she makes it happen.

So she stands and walks toward the chair, her feet silently folding over the uneven ground. The cold vibrates upward through her soles to her core, so that by the time she reaches the old woman, she feels split open, her muscles shaking.

She comes around the side of the chair, listening to her heartbeat running, waiting for the rush of that face turning toward her.

But the old woman does not turn her face away from the sea. In the darkness, that face is less frightening; it is only stark, and full of peaks and shadow, like the stones. The body that meditates under those black folds of cloth is difficult to differentiate from the ragged landscape around it. Lonely cannot see where the woman's hands are; she cannot see where the shadow of a limb could burst out from, or where the cloth ends and the ocean begins.

"Why do you trap me here?" Lonely asks.

There is no answer, so she forces herself to continue around, to stand in front of the chair, between the Witch and the sea.

Now the Witch raises her eyes, but those eyes do not register Lonely. Lonely sees only the ocean there, much bigger than she.

"Just like a child," the Witch says in a tired whisper, her voice like the voice of the wind when you've been alone for too long and it begins to sound human. "Just like a child, you think everything is about you."

"There's no one else here!" Lonely cries, though she's relieved to hear the woman's voice. "Just me and you." She wraps her arms around herself, cupping her body's own warmth against her. The wind whistles.

"That's what you think." The Witch sighs and, to Lonely's relief, closes her giant eyes.

"Why did you trap me in the tower?" Lonely tries again.

"I! What could I do?" She draws a breath in, and then her voice escapes a little from whatever it's caught beneath, but there is no tone to it, no blood warming it, no feeling. "Your father trapped you. He thought that would save him." She sighs again, as if the words exhaust her.

Lonely does not believe her. "Why did he die?" she asks, trying to say the word confidently like she understands what it means, like she does not feel this thing: fear.

The Witch's eyes snap open and she grins a wicked grin that makes Lonely shrink into herself, because there is something inside this woman that Lonely thinks she can never understand, and that can never understand her. And at the same time she stares past Lonely, so that Lonely cannot help but glance behind herself into that rocking, churning mystery, afraid.

"Because he was not all god," the Witch hisses triumphantly. "Because he's human, too, just like me. Just like you. Someday you'll be old and ugly like me, Princess. And those nightmares will get you, like his nightmares got him."

Then suddenly, like the wind bursting forth, the Witch grabs Lonely's wrists and binds them in the quick claws of her fingers. "I always wondered what you felt like," she says. "But you feel like me. I can feel your heartbeat." Lonely pulls back but the Witch won't let go. "I know your heart. You're afraid of being alone, and ending up just like me. Your fear is your fate. Your fear is your fate…!" The Witch looks up as if pleading, and in this moment it is the silent pleading that Lonely hears, more than the words. A long moment passes as the wind circles them, watching without eyes, hearing without ears. The first pain that Lonely feels—the first pain in her whole life that she can name—is not her own. It feels like her father's pain, but closer to her body.

"Please," she says finally, her heart drenched and heavy. "Let me go. I want to get off this island. I want to live, and I want to find love."

The Witch lets go of her wrists and presses her face into her own hands.

"There is no such thing," she murmurs.

"There is," says Lonely. "There is someone just for me. Someone who was going to come and rescue me. My father told me."

"Who?" The old woman looks up suspiciously, her hands outspread in the air.

"A Prince he knew long ago. Someone who was meant for me. Someone from a green, quiet place where birds walk on water and people live in—in trees. There was a white horse—My father told me!"

The old woman's eyes are somewhere else. She seems almost to be smiling. Suddenly, Lonely glimpses someone else in her face—someone beautiful, someone young. But then she lowers her head and growls,

"So where is he? Why hasn't he come?"

"I don't know." It's true. She is supposed to stay and wait for him. Didn't her father tell her to wait? That her love would come for her? But how long? Now the tower is gone. And she could not wait there any longer. There were the nightmares, the white bird, the scent of her own body, her own heartbeat coming and coming, and the wind….

She stands there desperate, watching the old woman, not knowing what to do or where to go, feeling that she cannot turn around knowing that this awful presence watches her. The older woman is shaped so differently from Lonely. Lonely knows nothing of aging, but she sees that this body has become less and less human over time, and more and more a part of the stone and wind and sea, her shape craggy and uneven with the black dress catching around it, her voice rising sharp and falling hazy. In the dark the older woman looks rooted in the eerie bone chair with its wily curves and gleaming white spokes above her head.

"Go," the Witch says. "I cannot bear to feel you near me." She drops her head and murmurs on like the sea, like the mind whirling around within itself, like Lonely's own mind spinning alone in that tower for so many years. "He will betray you. He will ask you to give up everything for him. Then he will see his humanness inside you, and he will be afraid. So he will leave you. Then nothing…nothing…."

Lonely thinks, *There is something sweeter beyond all this. Far away from this island, away from this woman with her empty voice, away from the memory of the tower, there is a high mountain kissed by the sun, and in its valleys are wide fields of flowers. And in those flowers a face….* It is that mountain that holds the answer, though she cannot see it now. She is sure of it.

"I'm leaving here," she says, making her voice brave.

The Witch looks up. "Thirteen moons," she says.

"What?"

"Up there." The Witch points, without looking. "The other earth, the ghost earth! White ghost that pulls the seas. Grows round and belly-full—grows pregnant—and then she loses everything! What happens to the full moon's child? What happened? Suddenly she is gone! Suddenly a thin sliver again! Don't you see?"

Lonely nods, terrified, not understanding at all. But she sees the sliver of light in the black sky behind the woman.

"When the moon dies for the thirteenth time, when she's lost her child again, and has nothing, come back to me then with proof! Find your love, bring back proof that he loves you, bring back proof that he will love you forever!"

Lonely stares.

"Isn't that what you want? Isn't it? To know you will never be left again?"

"But what is the proof?" whispers Lonely, who does not even know what love is, but wants it.

The Witch leans back, and the great chair—which looks so much heavier than she—tips back with her, its front legs floating in the air. "Ah, I don't know," she answers. "I don't know." With an echo, as if the very stone, deep down, is hollow, she lets the chair fall forward again. "You don't know it, but we are trapped on this island forever. Whatever happens to you when you leave it—" She stops, shakes her head. "You will think you have escaped this. You will think you have found the real world, and that it is more real than this one—but you are still trapped here with me. Only the proof of that love will break this world open and free us, yes? Isn't that the story? Isn't it? I want to see it, Princess." She looks greedily, hungrily, toward Lonely's eyes, but those eyes still do not see Lonely, and those eyes water blackly, like mouths. Suddenly Lonely sees their darkness. She sees that they are not like her father's eyes—that glass blue—but like her own. What does it mean?

"Don't think promises are enough. I do not want to hear his promises. Promises are not proof. If you fail, you will find yourself here, again. Thirteen moons. You will wake up in exactly the same place. Like you never left. Like the happiness you found in the great big world was only a dream. I tell you."

"But there is no more tower," Lonely whimpers, and though she knows it is true—though she can see the emptiness behind the witch's head—she is afraid now to believe it.

The Witch laughs. "Oh, but that was only a silly thing—a little dream your father made to comfort himself. What lies below this island is real, and it is what killed him, and it is what will kill me, and when you wake up here again, that is where you will be."

Lonely feels her jaw freeze, feels her stomach drop. *Fear.* She remembers the dreams her father dreamed. The monsters below. "Why?" she cries, restless in her own terror. "Why are you bringing me back here, if you hate me, if you don't even want me?"

The Witch drops her head and shakes it as if to shake off sleep, muttering,

"*I'm* not doing anything. Oh, Goddess, there is nothing I can do any more."

"I thought you were powerful," Lonely says loudly, trying again for courage, "sitting out here in the cold wind, but now I see you are only a crazy old woman. You have no power over me. My father loved me, and his love will guide me."

To her surprise, the Witch does not scream or lunge at her or do anything in response to this. She considers Lonely for a moment as if trying to remember something. "Your ancestors are many gods," she says at last. "You have the sea gods in you, and the earth gods and the fire gods, and the sky gods. You have all of them. Most of all you have the ideals of air, like him. But you are also human, like me. Humanness is that dark, fifth element, that nobody ever remembers until it is too late."

"I don't care! I don't understand. How do I get off this island? How do I get to the mountain?"

"Just go. I am tired of talking. I am so tired."

"No!" cries Lonely, who is still learning about wanting, and cannot bear the feeling of it. "You have to tell me how!"

Suddenly the Witch shoots up from her chair with the impossible strength of a fish leaping out of water. Her face is inches from Lonely's and her breath smells like salt, and her whirling eyes threaten to suck Lonely in and drown her.

"I'll tell you once more," she says, and for the first time Lonely notices the way she speaks words—differently from the way she herself speaks them or her father spoke them, as if they are slightly foreign to her, "and then I am done with you. Again you trap yourself, blaming someone else! There was no frozen door! There is no one holding you to this island! Do you understand? I do not care! I tell you, I do not care."

"But you told me—"

"It is up to you now, Princess. It is up to you." Such insistence in her eyes, such sincere, tearful fury—and Lonely will not understand it for a long time to come.

"But there *was* a tower," sulks Lonely, and will not back away though she trembles under the woman's blind gaze. "The door *was* frozen shut. It *was.*"

"Then how did your father get in?"

Lonely thinks for a moment. "He was a magician?"

The witch seems to think on this also. "Yes," she nods after a moment.

"So it's not real? You won't really bring me back here?"

But the witch laughs. "You named yourself Lonely," she says. "And I tell you, Princess, you'll bring yourself back."

Then she pushes Lonely into the sea.

The dream god Sky never dreams his own dreams, until one night he does.

One night as the darkness turns toward him, something makes him draw in his breath sharply—his own breath, which he can hear, suddenly, in the blackness, as if he were more than a dream, as if his human body floats out here alone in the freezing night.

But Sky is not human, not any more. He is only dreams, and his people, now, are only white birds floating over a still lake at the top of the world, where no one can ever reach them.

Every night he hovers, nothing but idea, outside someone's mind. He waits until the flashing lights—sometimes painful in their frenzy, their frantic knots—go out. He waits until breath is deep and singular, sure and steady as if breathing were the only thing that person has to do. He waits for the opening in the darkness of the finally peaceful mind. He waits for that question—not desperate, not heavy, but only curious—about what else life could be besides suffering.

Every night Sky raps at the window of someone's mind, calls out in a whisper. The darkness turns toward him: a subtle shifting he can feel, softer and more vulnerable than the beginning of the world. That darkness turns toward him, like an eye.

Every night, for the sake of the people in the City—for their dreams, though they will not remember them in the morning, though they will not believe them, though his people, who have already died once, are dying again for the lack of that belief—Sky surrenders, and becomes what is needed.

Sometimes a gruff roar opens inside him, a roar that expands his shoulders into massive form and steels his jaw and thickens his skin with coarse black hair.

Sometimes the darkness feels like water, and he slips inside it with fins waving, skin full of rainbows.

Sometimes his body becomes three simple segments—one for the head, one for the heart, and one for desire—and he greets the dark human mind with the terror of too many legs and too many eyes.

Whatever is needed. It is not he who decides what creature he will become, but the mind itself. The need decides. Someone else's need, to recover the animal within the soul—the animal that knows the way home. Even Sky himself does not know this. He is only a vehicle.

But on this night the darkness recognizes him. It turns and looks at him through a cold, familiar window.

There is something wrong. As if he is the one dreaming, as if someone else entered *his* dream—but that is not possible, because he never sleeps. He holds the vigil for his lost people. He keeps the dreams alive. He can never sleep.

But it feels like his own dream. Which is not possible, because to dream one has to want. And he does not want anything. He is not human like that any more.

Yet he is not becoming any animal this time—only himself. It's just like a dream, the way he tries to claw his way out of it, the way the walls of it seem made of some unyielding yet ever-stretching cloth, the way he cannot get his voice out of his body, or find his hands.

And—he will always remember it—this darkness is a woman.

The soft breasts in which a child might nestle his head and sleep.

The mother arms, reaching.

The little girl who was lost forever, whom he could not save.

The beautiful woman he was too young to save, who laughed at his simple, handmade spear, and walked willingly away with her captor.

The tears that were not cried, the water-soft heart, the warm caves inside woman where all is broken and forgiven. That place he was never admitted to, before everything was lost.

And the ultimate darkness. That mystery, where man gives something of himself that he can never get back.

It's all locked up there, where he hid it away inside himself, inside some high doorless room of his mind. But now he sees that the room is so fragile, made of glass, and if he moves—if he even breathes too hard—it might break.

And she is calling to him, her mouth stretched wide, and she is pounding on the glass walls, trying to get into his dream.

For the first time in the hundred years since the City was made, this dream god—this bird-boy of the sky—feels an ache in his feet, and longs to wrap them around the body of the Earth. He feels it there, pulsing against his soles, like a heart, and he remembers.

He cannot look away from her, though he shivers inside himself with the effort.

"Why did the people of the Old World believe in so many gods?" a student asks. "Why were they so afraid of these gods and goddesses of water, who would throw up the sea or hold back the rains?"

"Long ago," you explain, "these things mattered to people. People got their food from the sea, and from land fed by the rain. But we don't need those things now, of course."

"But why did they have to have a god for everything? A goddess for the river, a god for the wind, a god for a stone…."

"Because they had no control, then, over the elements, the way we do now. They wanted to pretend that someone did. They wanted to believe the changes of the weather and the seasons had meaning. So they made up gods."

When you were young, and desperate for your own manhood, perhaps you stole away in the night, borrowed a car, and went out into the wilderness in search of your destiny. Maybe you braved starvation, the elements, and the spirits and gods of the old world, of whom your friends still whispered. Maybe you even dug into the ancient caves, or the ancient lakes, in search of the old riches—in search of something you could not name and yet needed then, in order to prove you were real.

"Did you see any ghosts?" your friends joked when you returned. "Did you get attacked by any demon women in the desert, who tried to eat you up?"

You knew they were only jealous, but you did not answer them, because the answer was yes, and you were ashamed.

Sometimes, now, your family takes a trip into the country—for the scenic views, the distant images of mountains. But you stay inside your car, with the air conditioning on. You have a vacation home built on a mountaintop, a place you like to go to get away from the messes you've made, so you can look back on all that ugliness from a distance and imagine it beautiful. The house is so big that you almost never have to go outside. You have everything you need inside that house—like a little city in there, with entertaining images and entertaining food and entertaining sounds.

"Don't you have to be careful out there?" friends ask you when you return. "I've heard there are still people living out there in the mountains—primitive people. Who knows if they might steal one of your children away when you aren't looking?"

"Oh, but I'm told they're harmless," you answer confidently. "Very simple people—they have no modern technologies at all. They're more afraid of us than we are of them. We never even saw one. The more we develop the mountain, the less we'll hear of them. Or they will finally come down into the City, like everyone else before them—if they're even still out there."

Your own children, too young yet for bars, steal their liquor and make fires in alleyways. In the rest of the City, the only memory anyone has of fire is electric ranges, toasters, microwaves, heaters. Teenagers and homeless people are the only ones who still know the power of this element—the way standing around those flames and drinking that heat can make them feel alive inside again. But they cannot think what to do with such power.

"I've seen the wilderness," a boy boasts to a girl. "I've walked the desert and climbed the mountains. I've even sailed into the sea. This here—" He takes a jewel from his pocket and drops it into her palm. "This is the eye of a dragon."

She looks down at it, then fast at his eyes, not wanting to look foolish, wondering whether or not to laugh. He is grinning, and she gives him a hesitant smile. The flames are hot near her belly, the crowd is loud around her, and she wants desperately to ask if they are real—the dragons, the gods, the goddesses, the magic that catches in her throat sometimes that she has no name for, that hurts.

But she doesn't know if he, or you, or anyone is telling the truth.

Listen.

I know you don't remember who I am, and you do not know if you can trust me.

I can barely remember myself.

And yet I know you, and I know the stories. I am telling them now to remind you. I am telling them to find you. Always, I am listening for your listening. I am echoing between you and your heart.

For the City was built on the Heart of the World, and I am trying to find my way home.

1ˢᵗ MOON

The smooth white bird, with the slim neck as long as his body, flies from an island in the sea, back over the land, and up. With ten flaps of his wings he has reached the edges of the waves. With five flaps he has crossed the brief sands and the golden meadows, and the whole of the City he covers with four flaps more. With twelve flaps he crosses the desert. With nine flaps he rises up the flanks of emerald mountains, his vision set, as always, on the highest high, the farthest far. He disappears into clouds and is gone.

Somewhere in the recesses of those mountains the bird crossed over without looking down, in a place no one knows about—not even the people who still live in the mountains—on a mountain rounder and lower than that piercing white peak of Lonely's dreams, there is a garden where prayers are grown.

The women who live there are goddesses, and that means that they do not hunger or suffer the way humans do, and they have no bodies that define them. It is their job to communicate between the elements and the people, and to embody the very world the humans long for.

They can take the form of women. And they do, in order to make their prayers. In human form, they pray for humans, so that their prayers become real. To manifest anything, they must become it.

Likewise the form of the garden in which they pray, in which their rituals are held—that, too, is the form of a woman. At its base, the vagina: flowers the colors of fire, their layered mouths hanging open in invitation to the hungry bees, their velvet petals falling to the ground in piles of extravagant bliss. Above that, the round sunroom of the womb, its glass tinted rose, filled with deep cushions of silk.

Then the belly of the garden, where food is grown—not for the goddesses themselves, who do not eat, but spirit food for manifesting healthy crops everywhere, and for praying that the people will learn once again to draw their nourishment from the land.

The heart of the garden, a breathing green place. The walls made not of stone but of interlacing shrub and ivy, so that when sunlight breaks in, it breaks the thicket open. In its center a fountain, whose waters connect all parts of the garden together. And then above the heart, the throat: a bridge of wooden boards over an underground room of echoes, a room full of string and wind instruments which they play upon when they wish to give voice to the voiceless or to pray in song. Breezes pluck through a thicket of reeds above it.

A river runs through the garden from head to toe, and that river is the garden's spine. And that river connects everything. Not only the head to the womb and the heart to the vagina, but the top of the world to the bottom. The goddesses hold the end of this river like the end of a rope, and at the other end—far away in the ocean, in the bottom of the world—the Dark Goddess holds the other end. Even though that rope is frayed almost to breaking now—most of the water held in a reservoir for the City's use, with only the smallest trickles escaping to the sea—the river has secret passageways that the City has not yet closed. Together the Dark Goddess and these Bright Goddesses on the mountaintop listen to the vibrations and changes of the world through that river that runs between them, and wait for the world to awaken again.

One night the Bright Goddesses look into the pool of the fountain and see the face of the Dark Goddess, just as old as she ever was, her eyes focused eternally inward, and through her very self to the other side. She speaks for the first time in many years. She says,

"She has left the tower. She is gone. New Moon, I have lost her again."

In the uppermost mind of the garden, there is only stillness and calm space.

And in the center of that space stands a single giant oak, in whose branches the birds gather to bring messages and intuitions from the the City below and the spirit realm above.

It is in this quietest, most enlightened of spaces, beneath this gentle tree, that someone not quite boy and not quite man, not quite human and not quite god, so often comes to meditate and try to be at peace with himself.

But it doesn't work.

For from the mind of the garden, this boy-man they call Dragon can also creep to the edge and look over the rock wall to the rest of the garden—the shape of woman stretching out below. He sees the goddesses in their human form, making prayers. He sees them kneeling in circles, their long hair brushing their knees. He sees them dancing, calling out in soft wails, calling to the souls of women far below to remember themselves, to remember their bodies, remember their power. He sees them caressing each other, sending prayers of healing to human women through their motions and their murmured songs.

He sees these things in secret, with one hand moving fast, the other gripping the stone. The goddesses who raised him, who have touched and caressed and loved him all his life—they do not touch him now that he is almost a man. They do not come near him in their human form.

Often, to comfort his loneliness, they have appeared to him as other, easier things. A crystal of sound from the flute of some bird's voice, a shadow across the fountain's pool, the yellow of a flower splashing in its own light, the design of mist floating in the remnants of early morning and stepping down from the cold shelf of the air to almost press warm against him. A column of sunlight, the dust within it spiraling dizzily.

But Dragon watches them when they are women: when they are flesh and skin, abundant with curve and lip and the hidden in-between. He has smelled them, like the weighty soil where flowers grow. He has watched them when they toss open their faces to the sky, their throats naked, to call down its power, and when they lay their hands between their own breasts or each others', speaking to the hearts of the world, and when one of them lies down in the petals or the beds of lush moss and receives the others' healing touch.

Day after day, he traces the inner walls of the garden that has nurtured his life since childhood. The sound of the river rushes continuously through him. He wanders through heart-shaped leaves that tickle his shoulders, and the bees rub their bellies in nectar that will carry the longing of one flower to another. He rests his face in a bundle of blossoms, plain pink and whiskered in the center but wild with sweetness, and breathes in and in and in, his body almost heavier than he can manage. Loneliness crawls over him like ants. All his life he will feel the presence of woman in the life of nature: delicate things that ripple in the wind, and the roaring release of water, and the round, secretive earth, and the wings that tear into song.

All around him, forever, lies the hidden presence of the goddess, disguised in busy, unpredictable beauty, unresponsive to his heat, oblivious to his desire.

On this day, as he sits in the heart of the garden with his head in his hands, he hears someone walking. He hears the crunch of leaves underfoot, a sound the goddesses never make. He looks up. Just like a heart, some days this central garden is misty and dark, and other days it is shining and full of new growth. This evening it seems uncertain under a slow cloudy sky, the fountain's song dulled and the ivy's leaves bowed in a thick humid air. The oldest goddess of the garden, the one who first lifted him in her arms when she found him outside the gate at six years old, is walking toward him. She is older than he has ever seen her, just like a human being would be old—not desirable at all but frightening in the weakness of her step, the falling of her face toward death.

He stands up trembling. "Are you all right?"

She smiles and nods, sitting down beside where he was sitting, and the fountain mists her cheek. "I am the same as always. Only I wanted to come to you in this form, so you could understand how old I really am. In fact, I am older even than this. There is no human form that could express my age. And yet today I feel human. I feel the pain of a human being, for having to say what I must say to you."

"You're going to send me away," says Dragon. And in this moment—though in other, desperate moments he has torn at those vines and scratched at these walls, swearing he would leave them, cursing them for ignoring him, for leaving him alone among them like this—at this moment, he feels only a hard fury in the center of his chest, to know that his third mother in a row is abandoning him. He feels it as if he always expected it. He feels that fury, very calm, very sure, in the center of his chest—and he holds onto it like a secret weapon, as if it makes him strong, as if somehow he will be able to tear it out and win after all. Only later will he realize that fury is useless.

"We love you," says the old woman now.

"And what will I do?" says Dragon evenly, thinking himself calm, thinking himself a man. He can feel the muscles in his face twitching. "Where will I go?"

She closes her eyes and breathes a slow, careful breath out. "Listen to the river, Dragon. It flows out of this garden, and through the forest and the fields, all the way through the desert and to the sea. Into it we lay all of our love, all of our prayers, and send them down to the people. We do not know what will happen to our prayers, or how they will be used. We only give them. In this way, we give you to the world."

"Why—?" But Dragon stops, something choking his voice that he does not want the old woman to hear. He stares at her hard, and her eyes finally open as if he willed them to.

"It is not right for you to stay here longer," she says more firmly. "You distract the women from their prayers with your desire. Even when I speak your name to them, I feel that womanhood begin to simmer, as if some humanness begins to form inside them. We work for the world, not for ourselves; we put all of our energy into prayer. But human beings are fascinated with the body itself. Human men glorify the beauty of the female body in a different way. I fear that in the presence of your longing, we may become attached to our own human forms and the feelings they give us."

"Then why did you take me in? Why am I here?" he roars at her, lunging up to loom above her, raging in response to these women who he knows can feel his power, and whom he can never, ever touch. He forgets all his calm. "Why?"

She doesn't pull back, doesn't react. She looks at the wrinkled hands in her lap, and he looks at them, too, and feels afraid. "It was arrogant of me," she answers softly. "Twelve years ago I took you in. I thought we could raise a boy among us. I thought we could teach you a sensitivity that so many men do not know. I thought perhaps you could share that with the world. Maybe you still will. But it isn't up to me. We are torturing you now, though we do not mean to."

Her gentleness weakens him. He sits down beside her again, longing for her touch—not the touch that draws out his forbidden fire, but the touch of Mother, the touch he will never have again. "But am I a god?" he whispers.

She looks away from him, into the shadows of the ivy. "I think you are part god." She pauses. "These days, gods and humans mingle. But humans do not believe in gods any more, and so they do not recognize them when they see them. And the gods long for the love of humans, so they sneak among them, and pretend to be them. But it is forbidden, Dragon." She looks back at him suddenly. "Sometimes a human woman might give birth to a child that is half a god, and everyone else—though they claim not to believe in gods, you understand—feels somehow that he is something Other. There is a terrible suspicion around him. Then perhaps the mother wants to hide him, or even destroy him, because if the people find out, they will fear and hate her. They will think she must have traveled into the wilderness, and done wild things that they do not believe a woman should do. Especially if the father was a god of fire. Do you understand?"

Dragon shakes his head, the stone of fury hardening inside him again.

"What I believe is that one day everyone will be a different mix of god and human. One day, everyone will have at least a little humanness in them, and everyone will die. But death isn't the hardest part of being half-human, Dragon. The hardest part is to learn how to use and control the god power in you, when so much of you is human, and longing to fulfill your needs. This desire you feel is human, and it makes you weak. But that same fire is so much power, Dragon, and magic too. You do not even know it yet, but one day you must learn how to use it wisely."

Dragon looks into her eyes, clenching his jaw, and all his need is in him—insistent, definite, more real to him than anything in this world.

"What you long for here…" She shakes her head, looks down again at her hands. "These bodies you see, Dragon, this ecstasy—it is all illusion. It is all a dream of the real world below. Now you will go from here, and you will enter that real world. What could be more wonderful?"

She looks up at him then, for he curves toward her as he rises, baring his teeth, the shape of his body clinging for a last hopeless moment to the empty space around her. He tears the robe they dressed him in down the center, its white edges floating away from his hard fast limbs. He feels his head smoldering above his body as he walks away with nothing in his big hands, his nakedness a furious rebellion against her rejection. *See me*, say his swinging arms as he walks away. *I* am *a god, with nothing to sustain me but passion.* He strides through the belly of the garden, through the rose-tinted womb, through the lower chamber of bliss and desire, and comes to the doorway he entered when he was six years old. With a howl, he breaks down the door. He bursts in a shower of petals through the lowermost gateway of the Garden, through which man both enters and leaves—entering as a seed, and exiting as a birth into this world.

Her father's eyes so blue—a painful, skyward blue. Hair on his face, like an animal's hair, hiding his expression.

Lonely remembers her father sitting on the end of the bed, his voice the only sound. She remembers the assurance of his weight, and sleeping against his warm arm, and waking to his dreams that flickered across the glass like fire. She remembers the sound of his voice reciting to her the stories of the world, a sound she felt as a comforting vibration in her belly.

He used to say to her, "Princess, I give you this blessing. We are magic, you and I. And I tell you, little goddess, you will never hunger. You will never thirst. You are blessed."

She did not know about hunger or thirst. In his words she felt the comfort of their togetherness, of their one world together, the only world she knew. But she shivered at the sound of the word "never": a cold impossibility. She felt the loneliness of that word in her body.

"But why do you look that way?" she asked him once, or maybe it was a thousand times. She meant the pinch around his eyes, the tightness of his lips, the thing that was wrong that she could not name.

"Because," he said, and then stopped. She remembers waiting through that moment, feeling him already leave her. There were places in her father's eyes that she wanted to go but could not reach. Her father's sorrow was all around her, all the time, heavier than her whole being. Always when they watched the dreams of the green water, he would whisper that word: *Lost*.

"Because I am tired," he answered her finally, and would say no more. But then he wrapped his arm around her and held her close.

And that was enough, then.

Now she is alone. Now she walks beneath the sea, breathing water. Her feet spin like paddles, and water floods her ears with silence.

She waves her arms about but the water slurs their motion. Everything she tries to do happens slowly. She isn't sure if she's moving forward—or anywhere. She cannot feel her body, and she does not know if it's because she is dreaming or only terribly cold.

Maybe time floats by. As in the tower, there is no difference between day and night. Living things shoot around her face in bursts of bubble and light, or maybe she is only watching her own thoughts explode inside her mind.

The sea weighs her down and buoys her up. It freezes her and bobs her along. It carries her faithfully and forgets her at the same time. She doesn't yet know what anger is, but when the fish pass by with their heartless eyes glinting black at her, a heat burns helplessly in her cold limbs and she claws the water in slow motion and curses the Witch with words that are only mouthfuls of darkness. The water follows her hands, easy and invisible, trapping her. She presses against it and it is nothing, falling away. She tries to turn, to move—but she is only trying, going nowhere.

When sunlight, first clear and then blinding, tumbles down in pieces through the creased layers above her, somehow inside herself she becomes lighter and begins to float upward. Her face emerges like an old memory from the blank surface of the sea, and she gazes out at great distances of light and sky. She sees now that loneliness is made of eternity, and though she does not yet know the word for sorrow, she sinks below again, and keeps sinking.

The light thins and disintegrates. Something brushes her, disturbingly soft. She no longer knows that she is cold; the darkness feels hot and close as easily as it feels empty and far. She keeps sinking. She thinks of her father. She remembers the look in his eyes, and there is this sense of finality, as if he was wrong about something, and he knew it all along. But she does not know what. She thinks she remembers that he loved her.

Now Lonely is walking at the bottom of the sea, and because she is a goddess, she can breathe underwater, and because she is a goddess, she needs nothing. She will keep walking forever; she does not care. She has no choice, because her heart is so heavy, or the sea is so heavy upon it, weighing her down. She hears voices now, crying. Perhaps one of them is her own. Sometimes the darkness takes form, wrestling with itself. Sometimes it is red as blood, or blue as ice, and sometimes it throbs inside her mind, wailing and sobbing, until she feels her skull will burst open. Then sometimes she feels nothing again, and does not know if her eyes are open or closed.

The nightmares return, the same ones from the tower. More real than her father's dreams. They go like this:

Animals hold each other down, tear each other apart, eat each other in mouthfuls of raw flesh. Men stomp toward her with heavy boots and sharp weapons. When she sees them, she knows that they, too, have killed. They killed those women, instead of rescuing them, and they will kill her. Their bodies hunch darkly; again and again their eyes claim her with brutal certainty. She cannot understand their faces but she can see every muscle in their metal fists. And then all at once they leap upon her with a hollow explosion that is almost like sound, and she screams but cannot hear herself, and she breathes in water.

But she keeps on walking, through the nightmares, because she has no choice. There is almost a comfort now in having reached the very bottom. She can sink no further. She feels how the water supports her. She feels a warmth against the soles of her feet, as if she is walking on light.

Someone takes her hand.

She shoots upward, too fast, and cries out soundlessly. The water rushes by her, ripping off her numbness layer by layer until she can feel the cold again like a song against her skin—flickering behind her elbows and knees, pouring over her forehead and down her nose—and she can hear the water roaring in her ears, and she can taste the salt in her mouth, and by the time her head bursts again into the light and the pale weightless air, she is choking and coughing.

"Hold onto me," says a woman, and Lonely reaches around a body like a planet of warmth inside a universe of cold. She wraps her arms around the squeaky-wet skin, her arms making a circle the way arms do, thinking just barely, "oh, so that's why they're shaped…," as she presses her head to a pillow of silver hair and rests.

The wind, beginning everywhere and nowhere, beginning in dissonance, in restlessness, in the discomfort that moves toward change—beginning where layers of warmth and cold slide across each other, beginning where the earth's rhythm is uneven, where there is question—twirls up over the disturbed sea, flies across the grey meadow of the waves, and then over the treeless land.

Songless, it breaks against the towering corners of the office buildings. Over the factory, it makes beauty out of smoke. It tallies in a bit of clothing, but is squeezed out by frantic smoothing hands. It invites the bound hair to dance, but the head escapes inside a glass door that keeps winds out.

It rushes up the straight line of one street and down another, and swerves into fields, into desert—where the bodies of trees no longer hold the world together, where nothing holds or stops or meets it. It rushes as if seeking, as if panicked, as if lonely, as if driven by the same desperation that drives you to violence—the desperation of knowing that you can do anything, that nothing will stop you, that nothing you do matters. It makes a chaos of dust in its path.

But what makes you hopeless is knowing that the wind is not desperate, or lonely, or seeking, after all. It is only the wind.

Dragon skids down the mountain, wild with the feel of his own new nakedness, both terrifying and delicious. His breath comes in quick, furious hisses as he swings from ledge to ledge, scraping himself raw. His body plummets through pain, uncaring. Everything makes him angry. Each twisted thicket, each blade of stone, each slippery slide of mud, seems to want nothing but to thwart his passage, confuse him, swallow him into its lonely abyss. He grabs and tears, stumbling, rolling, and falling downward all night, racing into gravity, wracked with emotion but unbeaten by it, moving too fast to see it—too fast for it to catch him.

By dawn he has reached the bottom of the mountain and started walking. He has already forgotten who he was the night before, the evil grip of his own shadow, the way he ripped trees from the earth and tore them to pieces just to prove he existed. The way he ground the flowers into the earth with his bitter feet, the way he chased the deer through their own thick wave of terror, baring his teeth, meaning to wrestle down the body of the doe and rape her.

Today he is holy. Today he walks tall and strong, and tries to breathe the way they taught him, up and down the length of him, and the soles of his feet meditate against the earth with each step, and he looks upon his own soul with awe.

He walks to the west, in the direction of the sea. To the north of the river lies the City, and the nothing all around it. But Dragon veers the other way, away from the main body of the river, across the desert toward a high cliff wall to the south that he remembers. Once he passes near a road, and another time he has to cross one. He crouches in the brush, the muscles of his arms wound around his knees, shivering at the smell. The cars passing mean nothing to him: they have no life, no form, no answer to his need. They are only blurs of wind that interrupt his journey. He waits impatiently for a space of stillness and then runs across the unfeeling pavement, his feet burning. The housing development he passes in the distance, at the end of one of these roads, likewise means nothing to him. It looks like a pile of debris on the land, and he is unaware of its relationship to people. The noise of traffic fogs his mind, so that he cannot concentrate on anything but his single idea—not even a desire but the only idea he can think of—to reach the caves of his infanthood. The further he walks to the south, the more that noise—a noise he could not define and cannot remember once it is gone—fades behind him. This part of the desert has not yet been reached by the City. Dragon keeps walking, following his instincts now.

As he walks his body stretches taller, his spine lengthening within him. His voice drops into his chest and waits in the darkness of his lungs like a coiled serpent. He feels the big muscles of his thighs swinging, hard with power, his walk carrying the weight of his heart now like it's nothing. His hands hang curled at his sides. His penis, thick and heavy, bounces off to one side, and sometimes points ahead as if leading him insistently onward. Sometimes he stops and yells into the silence. He yells his own name, to hear it come back to him.

Naked, he has not yet imagined new clothing. He has not yet imagined the different costumes he could appear in, the identities he could take. His dark skin drinks the sun and does not sweat. Food and water are unknown to him. But the cries of the birds as they call for their mates are familiar.

The desert lies down under him, surrendered and bare. The desert is nothing but a song about absence. Once it held the ocean, but the ocean retreated and left it behind. It was the bottom of the ocean, and now it is the bottom of no thing, the empty space around a thing that is gone. Dragon doesn't know about the ocean, but he knows about loss. He keeps on walking through the blur of the sunlight and reaches for the ghosts of water though he does not thirst.

When he reaches the high cliff he walks alongside it, east to west with the sun. The canyon is so wide that in the afternoon he cannot see the other end of it through the haze of dust. As the afternoon yawns into evening, the dust surrounds him more thickly in the increasing wind, and he no longer knows direction, but only his own movement. He feels he is walking in place, and he walks harder, pounding his own form into the nothingness like a sharp mold into clay.

He presses closer to the cliff wall and climbs up along a ridge, seeking the highest point, the most dangerous route. He walks along the narrowest ledge just to feel the challenge of death swinging below him, and he throws stones into the nothingness, so hard he almost loses his balance.

There is a smell that tells him he's close: an obscene, sulfuric smell mixed with ashes. He presses himself closer to the cliff wall, searching its stubble with his hands for a memory. Without seeing them, he finds the caves he was first raised in. He sits down in the cold air that blows from the mouth of the biggest cave, its opening eroded but still hiding him from the wind. He curls his knees to his chest, making himself small like a boy.

The stone around him swirls with color—ages worth of color, colors echoing the many phases of the sun's retreat into night. This day's sun has already set, and the desert night is coming for him.

By starlight as the wind clears, he draws pictures of the dragons on his skin with shards of red sandstone. He tries to make their eyes but the mere dust of the stone cannot make them as bright as his memory of them. He presses a blade of the stone harder against his skin in frustration, and blood blooms around it.

Dragon was given his name by the goddesses who found him, because they knew he was raised by dragons. It was a dragon who left him at their gate, and in the morning they saw her tracks—tracks that had not been seen in this world for longer than any human could remember.

Someone—perhaps his birth mother, in an agonized fury at either her god lover or herself—had cast him into that cave as an infant, sobbing, "Go! Go back to that fire."

He had lain in the total blackness of that cave, listening to the long drops of water from faraway lands come trailing through the earth and hurtling down to the stone. Somewhere in the distance, he heard steam. Then he began to yelp and whine and scream, as if his voice itself were fire that would burn his fate to ashes. The dragons came, sliding their heavy leather feet against the cold stone, slowly swirling their endless tails around the sculpted curves of tunnels, surrounding him without speaking, gazing at him with diamond eyes. He grew quiet, but was not afraid, and when the white flames came leaping from their throats, they did not burn him, though they turned his skin blacker. In fact, the dragons cradled him in a nest of fire, lifting him off the cold floor, their flames meeting beneath him in a ring. They carried him deeper into their cave, deeper into the earth, where the stone was always wet and warm, and the fire was always soft and slippery against his skin, and the damp round walls were always lit, patterned with shadows like a moving echo of these most ancient monsters.

The dragons raised the boy for six years. And he loved them. But in the end, they could not keep him either.

Now Dragon presses the sharp stone into his skin, seeking pain, seeking some trace of humanness in his blood. He knows the wounds will heal over before the end of the night, easy and smooth, as if they were never there— and he hates this sign of inhumanness in himself, as his first mother must have hated it.

Having lived all his life in the Garden or the caves, he does not recognize Coyote when Coyote comes running across the night, his footsteps hot and immediate, much closer than the distant memory of dragons. Coyote runs from side to side across Dragon's vision, veering constantly closer. He does not look at Dragon but Dragon sees him smile.

"You called me?" Coyote says.

"No," says Dragon, sullen, trying not to look.

"Then who are you calling, with your sweet-smelling blood?"

"I don't know."

"You don't know? But your blood makes me hungry, and so I come."

Dragon watches Coyote tap the earth lightly, testingly, with his sly nose. "I don't care."

"Whom do you cry for then, not caring, from your bleeding eyes?"

Dragon sniffs. "My mother."

"Who is your mother?" Coyote swings closer, his path like a pendulum before Dragon's vision, zeroing in tighter and tighter toward a single point.

"Leave me alone."

"Who is your mother?"

"A woman! A woman who hated me because I shamed her, because I was too much a god."

"Who is your mother?" Coyote repeats more quietly.

Dragon is silent.

"Who?"

"She was a dragon," Dragon sighs, more quietly now because he feels somehow that his rage doesn't matter, that it isn't even real. "She gave me up because I was not one of her kind and she could not care for me."

"*Who* is your mother?" Only a whisper now. A hiss.

Dragon tries not to cry. He grits his teeth, holding the bloody stone in his hand. "She was a goddess who cast me out of her garden. Because I was too much a human being."

"Whom do you cry for, then?" Coyote barks. "Whom do you call?"

Dragon says nothing, only bows his head, and is about to begin again the drawing upon his flesh.

But suddenly Coyote leaps forward at a single point between Dragon's eyes, gripping the boy's spirit in his teeth.

"Who are you?" he snarls, his eyes swirling. "Are you a man? Who are you, spilling your own blood, not caring? Your actions have consequences. Your blood calls and I come."

Dragon shakes him off, shakes himself awake. He lies on his back, breathing hard up at the naked stars. Coyote's voice is like a flame inside his skull.

The next day he washes his body with dust. The wounds are gone but the memory of Coyote is alive and fierce within him. He turns away from the rainbow caves. There was no reason to come here. He keeps walking into the calm morning.

He feels smooth and strong and his mind is clear. But his penis swells again, and aches all through him. He does not touch it. He lets his erection move him forward into the hot day, flaunting his frustration to the empty wind. The sand burns his feet. Sweat comes now, and traces the muscles of his chest, making him itch. As he walks into the afternoon, zigzagging dizzily across red and gold, he sees the bare desert before him rise sometimes into soft hills, draped here and there with swaths of tiny yellow flowers, and folding around his vision like flesh—as if the desert begins to evolve into a body before it reaches the sea.

The sight of those hills, close and intimate around him, is what finally brings him down.

Maybe you know, though no one admits it, and you do not know how you know, that Hanum's wife killed him. It seems to you that the preacher hints at it in his sermons. Children are whispering about it in the schools. You shake your heads about it in silence, but thrilled shivers run through you as you pause at your work and stare out the window. At home, you will not look at each other for days, for fear that your eyes will betray the merest thought of it.

"How did she do it?" wonder two young girls in an attic, who have pledged to be friends for life. "She put a spell on him," says one, smiling wickedly. "Maybe she drowned him in the sea," says the other, dreaming shyly into a corner.

But at night, whether you live in families or alone, whether you fell asleep in someone's arms or wrapped only in bleached sheets, your pillow is wet; you stare down your shadows with wide eyes in the space between midnight and dawn. What will happen, if your god is dead? Perhaps the Princess is real after all. Will she save you? But how could she, when she is only a girl? Why did beauty seem so important once; can beauty feed you, or undo your loneliness, or make you strong? You never believed in it, you tell yourself.

Money, the measure of reality's certainty, plummets in value. You reach into your pocket and finger it. It is so thin.

There is a secret place in this world, but I cannot tell you where it is yet, and I cannot tell you how I know.

In that place there is a girl named Mira, who is not crazy. And no one else there is crazy either.

Mira can see everything that happens there, though no one can see her vision, which is enclosed in layers of numbness inside her mind. She can hide here in this place as well as anywhere. People might think she is here inside her body, for example, but she is not.

Mira could tell you: that man who screamed and screamed for so many years was only angry because he did not want to go to sleep. Hanum was trying to make him go to sleep, trying to dull his body and make him forget his spirit, and he did not want that. That was why he screamed. That was the only reason.

And that one who is afraid—*paranoia,* Hanum called it. That's because there are things to be afraid of in this world. Mira knows. Weapons in the hands of anger. Careless bodies. Loud noise and machines faster than animals can run. Everybody wants something from you. People have secret aims, and they will use you to achieve them. Who could live with eyes and ears open, and not be afraid all the time?

And that woman who raves about gods and dragons—couldn't they be real? If they were not real, why would everyone be so afraid of what she's saying? Why would they need to lock her up for saying it?

And the one who *isolates*—maybe he needs to be alone. Maybe he needs space to think. Mira herself could never think with people all around her, digging and pulling at her with their needing eyes and hearts and minds. She would lose herself.

This is where they've all been kept for so many years, in case you wondered—all the people who spoke the truth about the City, the people who did not believe in that reality. The ones who screamed the loudest have already been put to sleep: the one with *panic attacks*, who felt the walls were too tight, the *hysterical* one, who kept worrying that something was happening to her daughter, somewhere left behind with the man who almost killed her.

Deep down, in this secret place, Mira closes her eyes now. Closing her eyes makes no sound, so no one knows if she is asleep or awake. *Mira*. Maybe that is her name, because that is what the others call her, and what her mother called her. Her father, in his desperate whispers, called her *Mia*. Her sister, a long time ago when they understood one another, called her *Miri*. But secretly, Mira calls herself *Mirr*. She likes the sound of *Mirr*, like a murmur, like the hum of the wind through the meadow…

Sometimes Mirr still dreams of me. She feels my horn when she closes her eyes, a light spiraling up from between her own eyes. (As a child, she was surprised at her ability to move instantly into a dream like that, even without meaning to, even without going to sleep. Now she knows that everything is a dream, and everything is real, so that sleeping and waking are no longer separate for her.) Sometimes she can see that horn spiraling up from every mind in the room—every mind called crazy, every mind spinning and spinning, a whirlpool of unruly spirit.

She knows the old woman killed the man who trapped them here. She knows she killed him with the same poison with which he put them all to sleep. But it does not matter, because they're still here, and they're still sleeping.

Mira also knows there is another woman, both young and old, kneeling before her now, even though she has not opened her eyes. Mira feels this woman surround her with love without touching her, and she knows this woman is the soul of the River Yora, which she used to see from the cliff as a little girl. She is afraid to open her eyes. But the image of the spiraling horn, the light between madness and heaven, snaps into oblivion in her mind, and she feels hoof-beats in her stomach, and she feels she will be sick, for she does not know that the running inside her is her own.

Without opening her eyes or her mouth, she says to this beautiful woman, this spirit of the river, *You have to get out of here.*

☽

Lonely wakes on a beach, her dress like a jellyfish around her and the sand smeared across her, grating inside the crevices of her body. The riot of waves hitting the shore seems like nothing to do with the silent realm she has emerged from. She lifts her head and struggles up on one elbow. The other woman is braced above her, her body half over her, and she starts backward with a gasp as Lonely comes up—both of them startled as if they had just woken together in someone else's dream.

Lonely breathes in. She has never noticed air before.

Her eyes take in the light. The woman's body curves and swells like the water, and her pale skin is wet. Two beads of water tremble on her clavicle, catching the light; Lonely is breathless for a moment with the beauty of them, and then she remembers to breathe in again, and the air she breathes becomes space to hold this beauty. She looks up at the woman's face, at her huge eyes with their grey-green darkness and feverish light.

"Who are you?" asks Lonely, breathing out.

The soft woman backs away, and as she does so, her gown flows toward the sea as if made of water. Lonely can see her rolling breasts like unshelled eggs under the rivulets falling from her shoulders. But her eyes, too, seem to retreat.

"I do not know," she answers.

Lonely stares at her.

"Yora," the woman says suddenly, as if remembering now. "My name is Yora." Her voice is deep and dark to match her eyes, its halting awkwardness belying its richness. "You are strong," she says then. "You could have died, but you kept walking."

Lonely opens her mouth to speak. She tries to remember.

"Did you know you were strong?"

"No," says Lonely.

"We are both free now, and I must go," says Yora, her voice turning windy and distant. "Is there anything you need?"

"I need—" begins Lonely, but stops. What is need? She is lost. But she remembers the Witch, the sobbing face in a frame of driftwood and bone. "Love," she says quickly, to cover the memory. "I need to find love."

"Ah," says Yora, and her eyes turn away like the eyes of the fishes into darkness. "That is true," she says. "It seems everyone wants that."

"Where is it?" asks Lonely.

"Beyond the beach lie fields, and beyond the fields lies a desert, and beyond that lies the forest," Yora's faraway voice chants, like a prophecy, like a story already told, "and beyond that, the mountain—"

"Yes, the mountain!" cries Lonely, for she remembers suddenly the peak she saw from her tower of dreaming. It seems long ago but she's sure that it was real, that it means something, and since love is what she longs for, it must mean something about love. There is nothing higher, nothing more beautiful, than that mountain. In this image, somehow, she has already seen her prince's face.

"All I can tell you," continues Yora, "is do not ever enter the City. You cannot find love there. You will lose yourself there."

"What is the City?" Lonely asks.

Yora smiles a smile without joy, and does not answer. "And be careful of desire," she says instead.

"I desire nothing," says Lonely, "except love." For she remembers her father's promises.

"But once you begin to feel the pleasures of the body, you will feel desire. The more you desire, the more you will become human, the more you will become mortal. Eat once, and you will always be hungry. Trust me, for I have seen what it brings. Only suffering."

Lonely still doesn't know what hunger is, though she wonders if she feels it now, looking into Yora's tender eyes. "Don't go," she pleads.

But Yora stands, the dress of water gushing across her, like a flood of tears unleashed in full. "I, too, must keep moving," she answers. "But look." She motions with her arm past Lonely. "Take this with you, my gift to you. Someone to carry you, because you have no shoes."

Lonely turns around and sees, before a wash of open hills—so much closer than the image of the familiar mountain, which she sees also, distant and wreathed in mist—a horse.

A white horse, just like she always secretly dreamed of having for her own—with no prince riding it. It is white, but its belly is shaggy and dirty with the sand that clings to it. Its ankles are wet. It snorts, eyeing Lonely nervously, and sends a rough shiver from its shoulders to its flanks. She hears Yora's sad voice behind her.

"He has been a friend to me. But I cannot take him with me now, and there is no need for anyone to carry me. Because I am nothing…."

Lonely turns back, and Yora, sighing as if with relief, is gone.

She must have been a goddess. Perhaps she turned into water. Perhaps she shifted into some other realm or someone else's imagination. But what Lonely is, Lonely herself is not sure. She knows only that she can never escape this question, now, of her own life.

Dragon passes through an arch, rounds a corner, and is confronted with leering stone formations: awkward round-headed giants, curvaceous loops, strange bubbles of hardened sand. He falls to his knees without knowing why. The cliffside is pink, and successive U's and arches lead into a labyrinth of smooth, interlocking caves. As his eyes close halfway, he can see only the searing line between their shadows and the unforgiving sunlight.

He is masturbating. He hadn't meant to. He'd thought he would seat and arrange himself carefully on this hard earth and bring stillness up through the stone, let the windows of stone within stone draw his focus inward to a place beyond himself, and bring him peace. He's done it before. But there is no peace now. As soon as his knees touch the rock, his right hand is moving fast. When he finally touches that forbidden pillar of longing his blood rushes so fast to the sensation that he feels as if he will explode instantly. He pulls his dry hand harder against the skin, and he cannot move his hand fast enough—cannot get fast enough to the release that he knows won't be enough even when it comes.

But he is so accustomed to shame that when he sees a movement in the cave above him, he stops immediately. He falls forward on his hands and grips the stone to keep them still, gasping as he sees a woman crawl from a dark entrance. She is smaller than the goddesses, her skin brushed thickly with dusk and darker than his own, and when she emerges halfway into the last band of sunlight, she is still dark. But her eyes shine out from that darkness, laughing. She grips the small full fruits of her breasts in her hands as if she will toss them to him, then slides her hands luxuriously down the rumpled brown cloth that lies across her thin thighs. She plays her fingers around in that soft mess of darkness and cloth, then presses them deeper between her legs.

"Come on," she breathes, smiling. "Why stop?" Her words seem lit from within, each one wet and bright and caught like dew in the air. Her nipples are lavender within paler pools of skin more tender than a butterfly's wing.

Dragon is breathing so hard he feels he will choke.

"Come on," she says again, "I'll do it with you." And she lies back against the stone, unfurling her spine into a light, graceful arch, and as her lips part her legs part too, and her fingers press deeper into the crumpled brown cloth and beneath it. He cannot see the place beneath it, between her quick, dark, dusty legs. But the cloth splits open around her thigh and he can see the shape of her buttock curving smooth against the stone. When she licks her lips and grips one breast with her other hand, pulling it so hard that her nails press into the flesh, accentuating its impossible softness, he moves his hand again, and with one thrust he is already coming. His quiet cries grate against the dry air as he doubles over to the ground in dizzy relief.

He remains there with his forehead resting on the stone, his body shaking, feeling the tears still in him—deeper in than that frothy excitement, and harder to release. When he finally raises his eyes, hopeful and afraid, the woman is gone. He tells himself he will go after her, but then drops his head and succumbs to an equally desperate exhaustion.

Yora has no body.

She has no feet that take direction. She has no lungs that take their share of oxygen. She has no eyes that have to witness or ears that have to listen. She has no hands that can love or hurt, give or take. No voice that speaks an opinion. No, she renounces these things. Not because she is a goddess, but because she is nothing. She is a drop in the sea. The drop is not the sea, nor is it separate from the sea. In the white steady roar of water, she attempts to lose her memory and her mind.

She will not make decisions. She will not think. She will not act.

Water of the sea is everywhere even, everywhere moving, everywhere. Light comes and goes on its surface, but does not attach itself to any part. It breaks into shape, but then the shape is lost, with no parts that made it whole. The sound is continuous, like sleep.

The day that Lonely left the tower, Yora left a prison of her own. She did not consciously decide it. She had no purpose in leaving. She only discovered herself no longer able to stay, and she discovered this by the fact that she was already leaving, flowing into the sea and away. The little girl Mira—the only one she would miss, the only one from whom Yora received more than she gave—wanted to go with Yora but was afraid. So she sent her soul along with Yora in another form. *Say I am male,* the soul had said to Yora, *not female. Say I am just an animal, nothing more. That is the only way I can be safe.*

But Yora cannot be responsible for this soul or its love for her. She cannot be responsible for anyone anymore. So she gave it away.

The sea is death. But it is not stillness; it is not peace. Yora lays herself down in nothingness, but the nothingness itself keeps moving, and by giving up her will she only allows another, larger will to take over. It feels easier, but it is not. She is still moving over the earth. She is not gone, after all.

Instead, like a ghost, she evaporates into the sky. It does not happen all at once. She is pressed and changed, hot and cold, but she does not feel it. She is accustomed to these influences, and to not feeling anything on her own. Perhaps days, moons, or years pass. She is only moisture in the sky. She cannot be seen. She is too far up to be felt. She lies suspended in whiteness.

Delilah crouches behind the inner lip of the cave and hunts Dragon with her eyes. She breathes in, scraping her bare skin against the stone beneath her on purpose, imagining his penis now lying still and innocent beneath him. It feels like so long since she held one. She wants to hold it in her hands and her mouth—engulf it, devour it. She wants to revel and play in the design of man himself.

No one has come through these arches for months, and no one has ever come on foot, with nothing on his back and nothing in his hands. Eventually someone always comes, and it is always a man, for only men dare travel into these outer realms of wilderness. Or if women dare, perhaps they are not allowed. But Delilah neither knows nor cares about the women.

The men come seeking the jewels of the mountains: riches beneath the desert sands, remnants of dragon eyes and scales, whatever is new and precious and brings the hope of wealth—some fulfillment they cannot imagine but dream of day and night. Soon, Delilah knows, they will come from the west with concrete in their wake, building a new road that will turn the whole world into City. This new road will cut right through the ancient purple ridge that separates the City from the desert, that runs halfway from the sea to the mountains. Lovers she's taken in the past have told her of its coming. But for now they take the older roads, around the end of the ridge to the east, and where the roads end they drive their vehicles over the sand, heading toward the old caves where the dragons were said to have lived, though they'll claim not to believe in such things. The men's instincts, smarter and more focused than their minds, frequently lead them near Delilah's caves. Thrusting points and deep caverns of stone arrest their eyes, and the insistence of the sun begins to weigh them to the ground, where the sand luxuriates under their touch. Delilah knows it is not jewels they really want, not riches they really need. She knows the road-builders are only following orders, from someone they no longer remember, and that they do not know where the new road is going. For these greedy, stupid men she would have contempt, except that whatever it is they do need is also what she needs. She has only to remind them.

Usually, the months that pass without human contact make her wary when she first sees them. She has to walk beside them for a little while first, or sit at their fire, to get used to the sound of their voices again.

But this one felt so easy. She could almost have climbed right down and opened to him, without speaking. Maybe it was his own obvious desire, the way he lay it down like that right outside her door. Maybe it's a certain helpless surprise in him, that makes her trust him. She shouldn't have allowed him to see where she lives, but there he was, and she could not help it.

She won't need to talk to him, won't need to sit beside him and listen to him boast of his adventures in order to feel comfortable. But she does need to watch him first, to make sure she's in control. Now she waits, breathes, tries to catch up with herself inside. Each time, she must go through this remembering: the feel of her own body coming near to another.

For just a moment, she must crawl back into her darkness and lie on the cold stone in there, her fingers whispering over her own breasts, the little pleats of her ribs, her hard belly. She feels good today, her body sharp and strong. No pain, no weakness. She opens and closes her knees, staring up at the stone turning color in a sunset-tinted shadow, thinking of the boy outside. It's spring. The flowers are opening their depths with ridiculous abandon, the animals going crazy—so desperate for each other they don't care who or what sees them. Yesterday she saw two coyotes fucking in broad daylight, the female looking at her lazily as she stood there and took it from behind, tongue dripping out as if to mock Delilah's own longing.

A bat flickers across her vision, not even solid. Delilah turns her head to watch it disappear into an opening of paling light, and feels the weight of her own need. Her fingers play anxiously in the wetness that rises from her—a ridiculous surplus of wetness in a waterless land, the decadence of her own body surprising her. She watched the boy coming across the flat desert beyond. He was like a vision with his desire leading him, his fists heavy and beautiful against his hips. She thought he was a sun god, with his clenched, red-black body, his shoulders angled and shining, his chest lined too perfectly like stone just recently broken. Some pendant in the center of his chest flashed in the sun, blinding her. She rolls over and slides to the edge to look at him again. She follows the indented path of his spine, dipping between the hard banks of his muscles like surrender.

Now. She will go down to him. But something holds her back a moment longer. Something about this one makes her nervous. She shouldn't have let him see where she comes from, even though he could never fit between the stones that form the entrance to her cave. She shouldn't have revealed herself so carelessly. There is no reason to feel uneasy—no one has ever come back looking for her later on. Once is enough with a "demon goddess," after all. But still.

A snake who slept inside her cave today now flows across the floor and over her lap, heading to the outer stones that will still remember sun in the evening. He pauses to take in the warmth of her flesh. Delilah sighs, her breath heavy in her throat. She doesn't want the boy to leave. She doesn't want to miss her chance. She's watching him as the snake twines around her, climbing the slope of her neck with his invisible limbs. She shivers, resisting helplessness, but it comes over her too fast to stop. The snake slips his head through her hair and flicks his feather tongue against the underside of her chin.

The evening comes but it isn't fully cold yet. Darkness lifts like dust from the earth, intimate and hazy. Delilah inches down the crook of the stone like a spider. She can feel the boy's hot breath suspended in the air, and she knows he's at least part mortal. She can feel that intensity of humanness, that densest form of aliveness—the very top of the food chain. Now she crawls on her hands and knees. Above her the rest of the bats release themselves suddenly like smoke from the cave, their silence fluttering above her, their musky mammalian heat blooming into the sky.

She leans close to the boy's sleeping form and blows the hair away from the nape of his neck. She crawls forward, brushing her lower lip, and then lightly, her tongue, downward along his spine. The lower half of his body rests in sand, and as she moves forward off the stone, her palms press into a softness that is difficult to resist. It pulls her closer. She drops her lips to the indentation of his tail bone and breathes in. She can taste the sharp edge of his sweat. He bucks underneath her in a panic of surprise.

When he flips over, her little body traps his big one through sheer novelty. She feels him freeze, his breath pummeling her in gasps as he turns and faces upward. The pressure of it makes her cry out, falling between his thighs and gripping them hard. She nuzzles his penis like a familiar animal with her nose and lips, feeling the terror of his unfamiliar breath and taking it in. She teases him with her tongue, holding him captive with her tiny wet touch. She is not afraid of men. What can they do to her? She isn't afraid of a fight, and not one will ever know her enough to take anything from her. The things she fears are things they cannot give her.

This one doesn't seem to know what to do. The animal of him bounces against her tongue. He cries a strange, high cry, as if swept into a river that fills his mouth and steals his breath, and then he expands into a frenzy of limbs. He is everywhere trying to get into her—she feels his teeth for one wild moment, she feels unconscious fingers like Coyote's laughter near her hungry places, she feels herself lifted and turned and held suddenly beneath him inside the envelope of his arms. He stands over her on his hands and knees and she lies haphazardly, her legs tangled in his, watching him to see what will happen next.

"Who are you?" he hisses.

She smiles. His face hangs over her. His eyes, furious, pin her to the earth, and she enjoys being pinned, but is tormented by the empty air between them. A cool breeze slips in, brightening her wet places. She can feel her breasts pressing against space, her nipples biting the nothingness. She taps his erection with one finger, and it presses against her hand with a life of its own. His chest is hairless and shiny as a mirror. His lips are full and proud and they pout as they hang open. He stares.

It's strange, as if he's paralyzed by his own desire. Delilah rolls onto her belly and slips out from under him, and he stays there, frozen. But she hears his knees grate against the sand as she stands up and walks away, swinging her small hips. She looks back and licks her lips as she walks. It's so easy to seduce, her own desire undulating through her body. She sees the expression return to his face.

When she hears him coming after her, she runs. She runs across the hot sand in the darkness, laughing as the stars spill over her, the thrill and the fear and the fastness of his coming knocking her down. The expectation of oblivion is on her so fast, her mind already goes blank. Desire beats against her skin, a voiceless wind. She lands on her hands and knees and closes her eyes. In the moment before the weight of his body throws her belly-down into the ground, her psyche releases every emotion she doesn't want to remember, knowing that the force of his entrance will eclipse everything.

He fills her up. All her focus is there, at the deep point inside where his desire now suddenly, intensely reaches her—and pulls back and then reaches her again, and again. Sex is simply this: friction. Two opposing forces rubbing in opposite directions, drawing ecstasy from their opposition, and the sensation of a place inside that cannot physically be felt without the touch of the other. Desire has tormented Delilah for many moons, but she could not locate its source within her body. It was a tiny, focused softness, too soft to make sense to her as anything but a nameless frustration—a place that never touches air, never touches anything but itself, and which she cannot feel until the knowing arrow of another body comes in from nowhere and pinpoints it exactly. *That* touch, at her very center. *That* place. That was what she needed to feel. Now she can let out her breath.

She feels the life returning to her body. Suddenly she can see the sky again and enjoy the simple grit of sand against her belly.

She doesn't know whether it's his masculinity or simply satisfaction that equalizes her somehow, so that she feels steady and calm for those few moments, as solid as earth. In those too-brief moments of not needing, not wanting—before he comes far, far too soon, and then collapses, shriveling and shrinking out of her inch by inch—she feels that life is a loving kindness, and that growing old will not be so bad, and that everyone she's lost is inside her somehow, not lost at all.

But what is love? Where will you find it? How will you know it if you do? How will it know you?

The wind sails around Lonely's face, sticky with the scent of the sea, asking questions with its emptiness. Lonely feels cold as she lays her bare arms across the horse's back and leans hesitantly into his stiff damp fur, into his hard flesh, into his shifting, nervous strength. He does not move. The wind buffets her in soft puffs, as if despite its difficult questions it is attending to her, pressing her face and skin, molding her and the horse carefully together.

Then she looks up at the horse's eyes, small on the sides of his long, silent head, and they glimmer at her, pupils wide. She touches his warm nodding face, cups her hand under his great breathing nostrils. He shivers again.

"What should I do?" she cries in a low voice. "Do I get on?" She misses Yora already, but the horse is better than no one. He seems to ignore her, sniffing the sand and then turning his great neck to look vaguely back toward the sea. He stands tense, his eyes wide, as she grips his warm body and starts to climb up him. She balances her weight and looks off into the cold morning dunes, into the foggy possibility of the world.

"Go," she whispers, and the horse doesn't move. He stands still and endures the wind, glancing back again at the sea. He whimpers.

"Go," she says again, louder. They cannot stay here. She feels sure of that now.

The horse lurches a little as he begins, and Lonely hangs on, feeling all the effort and weight of his muscles roll beneath her hands. In shock and confusion she feels the horse's body come alive beneath her. Balancing on the tail of her spine, she rides a movement beyond her control past grey ages of sand and onward into newborn green.

The vision of the world breaks through her in waves. As the horse heaves them up onto the dune, his hooves sinking awkwardly in sand, she looks down to see little beach plants, their simple leaves like cups of hope. Their humble smallness gives her strength, drawing her spirit downward from the memory of a tall, cold tower. When she sees them she thinks she might survive, after all.

While the horse pauses to explore them with his heavy square nose, Lonely sits high and easy, feeling the brightness of her shoulders in the smooth air.

Welcome, Lonely, the wind breathes. *This is the world.* She doesn't even mind the name now, because it has a lilt to it that sounds pretty.

And this is only just the edge of the world. She can feel how the world begins here, dashing off before her into wild distances and heights, and how the sea—like the nothingness before the world—still swirls darkly behind her.

The wind threads a restless line between nothing and beginning, rushing in directionless fits, chasing its tail over the wrinkled slopes of sand.

When the fields finally spread out before her, Lonely spreads her own arms, laughing. Her fingers swim in space. The sky makes her head hurt. Above her the sun blazes with a confidence she has never known. She can smell its sweetness beaming in the grasses. The light smiles inside her skin, pressing her hair with a weight that burns but does not hurt.

A bird explodes out of the golden grasses beneath the horse's feet, and then a hundred birds lift up before her, where just now there was nothing. Their beating wings palpitate in the air. Lonely can hear their music, like twisted cords of light. She leans forward into possibility, unconsciously seeking to increase the pleasure of her own body against the body of the horse. Freedom balloons upward from the roots of her, rolling with the rhythm of the horse, shocking her, making her gasp.

She looks down at the animal that carries her. She places her hand on his shoulders and feels the bones turn beneath his skin. She wonders what guides him forward. She wonders where forward is. She wishes she could look into his eyes. His head sways from side to side. Sometimes he flicks it into the air, at the wind.

In a house in the City, you sit staring at a wall. You are supposed to be doing something. Cleaning up from breakfast, maybe.

Breakfast was pieces of sugar floating in milk. But the sugar was not pleasurable, or reminiscent of love. It did not come from flowers. Nor was the milk fulfilling, or reminiscent of the comfort of mothers, and it did not even come from anything that could be called alive.

Anyway, you are not thinking of breakfast. Breakfast is only something that is done in the morning, because that is what is done. You are not thinking of anything. It is becoming more and more difficult to think, and you do not know why. Maybe it is the sound of the machines that run the house, though those sounds have always been there: never ceasing, never changing. At times there will be a click, a brief whirring rise, and the hum will begin. There is always some machine humming. Over this sound, you cannot hear the songs of the birds outside, or the sound of your own breath or your own footsteps—much less your heartbeat. And yet it is a quiet sound.

You stare blankly at a magazine open in front of you on the table. You cannot feel those bright colors. You cannot feel that world they portray of magic and ever-greater excitement. Pictures of the Princess in the Tower. All women want to look like her. Blonde and slim and innocent.

Last night your husband beat you when you told him the rumors you heard, that Hanum is dead. Then you realized he'd heard those rumors too, but did not want to hear. You know he is afraid he will lose his job; the road construction must continue, and things must go on as they did before. But you're afraid you can feel the god's death in the hum of the machines. As if this is all that remains.

The hum of the refrigerator. It is impossible for you to describe—even if you wanted to—this toneless sound. It does not sound like anything. It does not remind anyone of anything. It does not change or communicate anything. It does not respond to anything. It is the loneliest sound you have ever heard. It is the only thing you have ever heard, and yet you are not listening to it now; it is there all the time, and you are hardly even aware of it.

If Hanum is dead, still the Princess must live on in that tower. At least you can think on that, when the days grow too weary, and the nights too unanswered. You never stopped believing. Yet sometimes you're not sure what it is that you believe, now that you so badly need something to hold onto. There is no life in that image. It's just an image. It does not reach out to you. It never leaves that tower, out in some nowhere sea. Something is wrong! Anguish you cannot define, inside this numb, well-dressed body. Suppose someone rescued that princess: would she save everyone then? But no one ever will. No man you know would do such a thing.

You're cold, so you turn the knob on the wall. A new hum rises up, plateaus, and continues. The heat comes on, from somewhere. Not heat from the sun, not the heat of the body. What is it? What is this house made of? Where are you? But you do not ask such questions. The heat comes up through the floor, through the dust, a sickly ghost. It does not soothe you. It makes you restless and irritable. You pace. If it gets too hot, you can turn on the cold. But it does not matter. You wear sweaters indoors in the summer, shorts indoors in the winter. And nothing answers the restlessness inside you. You can change your environment in any way you please, and yet no matter what you do, you hate it. Maybe you almost welcome your endless discomfort, for at least it is a feeling you can identify. Cold. Hot. Cold. Hot. Cold.

Oh, if only you would stop and notice even for a moment; if only you would wonder, how did you know you were cold? What does it mean to be cold?

But you cannot remember, because it ended before you were born, a time when a house was heated by a living, breathing fire at its heart that could keep people company all night. For fires are dangerous, aren't they? How could one live inside a house?

No, you cannot remember a time when houses had souls.

For a few precious moments, the boy's body is like a sleep that surrounds and dissolves Delilah's mind. Grains of sand roll imperceptibly over her lips. The desert air contracts into cold night, but she is safe inside the oblivion of flesh—flesh in place of food, in place of love, in place of self.

Then suddenly she needs to breathe. He must weigh twice as much as she does. She strains against him to turn around, resenting the effort it takes. She heaves him away; he is soft and sluggish with the expenditure of life force. He clings to her as he rolls, his eyes opening.

She closes hers. She doesn't want to look at him yet.

She tries to ignore a familiar ache in her uterus that tightened even as she relaxed, as if to deny her the rare pleasure she'd captured. She was holding the bleeding in, trying to keep it from touching him. A long time ago, only the first day of her period was painful. Now it is every day, and sometimes even when she's not bleeding. And though the pain has always come, every moon, even when she lived in the City, now she feels some other sickness creeping in too. It's something she doesn't recognize, that turns her unrecognizable to herself. Now she is someone who feels tired nearly all the time, who cries out, sometimes, when she moves.

It seems she must look at this boy after all, because he isn't saying anything, and that makes her uneasy. The look in his eyes startles her. She wants, already, to run—but he is so close, it feels dangerous to do so.

"You're bleeding," he says.

Unprepared for this bluntness, Delilah starts. "So?" she snaps.

"Does it hurt?"

She stares at him, dragging herself backward with her free arm. "No."

"What is your name?"

"Delilah." She doesn't want to know his. But he tells her anyway.

"They call me Dragon."

"Who does?"

He hesitates. "The women who kept me."

Delilah laughs, in spite of herself. "Kept you? Like a pet?"

"I don't know," Dragon answers, his breath audible and heavy.

"So what's your power, god-man?" she says, feeling her own power respond to his desire, remembering his hard hands swinging as he walked across the desert. She's annoyed now at this strange vulnerability, and wants something that she cannot name.

"What do you mean?"

"You're part god, aren't you? I can tell. What can you do?"

"I don't know." He looks at the sky, draws his red eyebrows together, scowls. "You're right. I *am* a god. What can I do?" He looks back at her. "What can you do?"

She laughs again, or tries to. "I'm human. I can bleed. That's my power." She meant to do away with that pity in his eyes, but her joke makes it worse.

"If you're bleeding, does that mean you're going to die someday?" he asks gently.

She stares at him, again. Is it his godness that makes him unrepulsed by the smear of blood she's left on his body? She tries not to care. But it repulses her that he doesn't. Suddenly he raises himself up on one elbow and cups her face in the other hand, in a gesture so intimate it freezes her. "Delilah," he says, "isn't it hard, being human? I try not to want this... I try not to."

"It's not hard for me," she says, turning away with relief. "It's hard for you, because you're part god." Partly just to quiet him, she climbs onto his rising hardness, laughs, and grabs his lips in her own. She rubs violently against him, weakening him instantly, and her brief moment of fear wafts away without a trace into the desert infinity. He grips her breasts and molds them into the longings of his hands, and she rides him while he plays with her body, surrounding him with her hunger and rolling him inside her until she fills it. She cries out just to hear herself—a singer, a dancer, someone with power. She hears his gasps and pushes at him harder, just to hear the way his will breaks—to hear a kind of helplessness in his voice which she would never and could never allow herself.

She doesn't fully come but it's good enough. She has one of those deep, inner pseudo-orgasms that never peak but only roll slowly into nonexistent heights, beyond her capacity to experience. She buckles over him, forgetting the dance, hovering on the edge of pain. When he's done, she's more sore than satisfied, but the pain ends her hunger just as well.

While he sleeps, she walks naked around the night, lifting her arms like lazy wings. Some pains force her to be still, but this one she feels in her womb at the dark moon is eased by movement. The bats come tickling around her with their lovely, inaudible sounds—glimpses of darkness within darkness, ideas she cannot hold to. She feels them calling, feels them hearing her presence as their calls bounce back. She walks round and round, her hands slicing the silence, forgetting, forgetting. But when she lies down on the earth and closes her eyes, she still knows exactly which direction he lies in. She knows the infinity of this place like the map of her own body.

From what other men have told her, she knows there is a rumor, far off where she came from, that she is a demon goddess, a dangerous enchantress able to survive alone in the desert for years. But she isn't. Nothing has ever been more clear to her than that she is human and nothing more. Her secret is only that she doesn't care about what other people care about, or need it. She does have one friend, though, and that friend is a god, though she never knows when she'll see him again. Without him she would surely have died. She misses him all the time, especially now, when her humanness seems to haunt her more and more in the form of headaches, backaches, sleeplessness, exhaustion. She's eaten almost nothing but meat for ten years. Maybe whatever magic Moon gave her is finally wearing off. Maybe her body is finally starting to give in to the reality of a place in which survival ought to have been impossible.

He would know what to do. Sometimes in those hours of strange madness before dawn, lying awake after the hunt, she whispers to the bats and begs them to send a message to Moon, wherever he is. But they do not travel more than a half a night's walk from her cave.

Maybe she can't sleep because she feels that terrible grey noise coming. Maybe the City is finally coming for her after all these precious years she's escaped it. Pain creeps up from the roots of her body the way the road sneaks out across the desert, the concrete hardening layer by layer and inch by inch. Delilah has lived in the desert for seven years but she is only human, after all. No power in a human being can win against the City—against that grey noise, that grey dust, that blur of directionless motion that overpowers the mind.

She lies still for a long time—too long—and tries not to think about why her heart weighs heavier inside her, as it always seems to after sex. Without meaning to, she falls asleep for moments at a time, and in her dreams she is tiptoeing around Dragon, picking up the pieces of herself that scattered when he entered her. They glow in the dark, and when she looks at them closely, they are scorpions, their ancient bodies resembling crustaceans from the deep sea which Delilah has never seen.

Just before dawn she hears coyotes laughing, and she jumps up and looks with scorn at Dragon's sleeping form. She's restless now, and hungry for the hunt. But soon the sun will rise, and at the same time she is so tired—always more so at this time of the moon. When the eerie, faceless smile of that moon sets far away over the City which she will never, ever go back to, she returns to her cave. The cave entrance is small, just big enough for her little black form. All her life, wherever she is, she has found spaces to hide in, where she can find safety in the peaceful apathy of darkness. To recover from the chill that's crept into her, she buries herself beneath layers of animal skins, disappearing beneath them. Her womb relaxes a little. The base of her spine aches with a vague, rhythmic pulse. She feels each step downward into sleep, her mind resting beneath the weight of the skins, and she dreams wild-animal dreams.

The horse carries Lonely all day through space.

She does not know how to guide him, and so must surrender to his nervous whims. Frequently, he pauses to nibble, then bolts forward again, trots a short way, then twists his neck as if to watch for someone behind them. Yet she barely notices. There is too much wonder all around her.

For a time, she forgets the mountain, though the sound of the sea recedes behind her. The grasses give in to the wind with absolute trust; they stroke her bare feet, tender and curious, as she rides through them, like a worshipful populace who have long awaited her coming. She cannot help the pleasure of her skin against them. Is it godness or humanness that feels this, like color blooming in the body—wetly, slowly exploding? Her throat trembles as she breathes.

Is this love? she thinks, overwhelmed, and the sun smiles, a contraction of brightness in the air.

You can have anything you want, says the wind, making a sudden crescendo to match her passion, and she believes it. She does not notice its contradictions. She is too much astounded by her own joy.

The day expands, and the heat of the sun clings to her face. Lonely is young and full of divinity—she is invincible. The rasping love song of crickets leaps inside the grasses.

I want you, they call to each other. *Take me.* Back and forth they call, and her body memorizes their voices. She closes her eyes and imagines her prince riding toward her. She imagines the relief of his knowing, his answers—the way he will finally find her and everything will make sense. *Take me, take me, take me....*

When the horse finally stops and swings his head to the ground to graze, Lonely shifts on his back, surprised, and finds her body still pulsing with his rhythm. She remembers her aloneness. In the near distance, naked sky meets the hills, and she cannot see what lies beyond them.

I want you, I want you.

Impatient, she slides off.

Now the sunlight grays just slightly, the wind blows colder, and the meadow turns serious as she begins to walk upon it. Her hips feel dizzy and heavy as they swing over her own two feet again. The crickets' rhythm feels like almost the same thing as her heartbeat now. She wanders aimlessly, touching her own body, confused.

I am the earth, says the earth. *I am always with you. You cannot leave me.*

Lonely doesn't know if this is good or bad. The earth is not as soft as the touch of the grasses would have had her imagine. It is bony and dry, like something very old, and sometimes it is spiny, and hurts.

She leaves her horse behind her, not thinking, leaving him in his communion with the grass. She does not yet understand such space. She does not think to keep things with her, or know that a thing can be lost. She does not know whether or not she needs the horse, or whether or not he needs her. He is like the sun and the grass and the birds to her: a sensation, a wonder, knowable by its immediate touch but without future or past or meaning.

Lonely does not see that crack of white in the sky now, the waxing moon rising above the far mountain—though it sees her, and its light touches her head with the echo of longing and the foreshadow of memories she does not yet have but is making, as she stares back at the sun melting into the hills they have come through. She can no longer hear the sea. The cricket-song beats in her, intimate and close.

The sun falls and falls into the hills, and Lonely watches, fascinated. It is like a fire that, when it hits the earth, somehow does not burn it, but instead spills over it in an agony of color. Somehow it gives up its fire, gives up its hunger, and surrenders to the deep knowing solidity of the one Earth. Lonely hopes that love is like this surrender: the way the sun surrenders itself to earth, which makes it dissolve into sky and disappear. Then its memory fades from blood red to a paler pink, like blood flushed beneath white skin, and then to grey, and then to blue darkness reflecting the jewel of the earth. She imagines it falling into the cold sea, falling through darkness until somehow—she cannot yet imagine how—from its falling it begins to rise.

The beauty of it thrills her, and because she understands this beauty, it seems to her that she will find love at any moment now. It seems to her that at any moment, she will somehow arrive.

The horse whinnies—a sound like a high anxious wind.

Lonely looks over and sees him, his tail flowing. The air is silver and eerie, and she feels hints of death riding inside it that she has not felt before. She remembers night on the island, the old woman's face stiff and certain before her like fate. Fearful, she runs toward the horse, who lowers his head and allows her to climb on.

They walk on as one being up the hill. Moonlight undresses the darkness before her and parts the grasses. Her body rolls against the moving horse. She closes her eyes and leans forward again, an unnamed urgency tensing her legs as the horse heaves upward, his mane brushing her forehead.

When she opens her eyes, her breath is heavy, and she casts her gaze over the edge of a high cliff, and sees below her the thousand stars of The City.

When Delilah first came to the desert, she did not look back. She was hold-ing Moon's hand, and she felt calm inside for the first time she could remem-ber. On her back she carried her school backpack, filled with four T-shirts, two pairs of jeans, two sweatshirts, a big knife and a small knife, and a roll of twine. In her right hand she carried a single jug of water. Her muscles were strong from working out and fighting, except for her left shoulder, which was still weak from what had happened the year before—when they took Mira away. But she wasn't thinking about that. She kept her mind blank.

They crossed over that purple ridge, a sacred boundary, and Delilah started breathing again. Moon was playing his flute as they walked, and it felt so good that she started laughing, and then she started crying and couldn't stop. It was awful. She felt the way she'd felt the first time she gave herself an orgasm—as if she'd just broken something inside herself that could never be mended, and that she had not even known was there. She didn't know about crying; she didn't know how to be someone who cried; and she didn't know how to stop it either, so she cried through gritted teeth, hissing and swallow-ing, choking back angry, animal sounds.

But they kept walking, and Moon was cool, his eyes gentle and averted, and her crying finally stopped as they entered into clear hazeless sunlight, and then veiled themselves in pure shining darkness, and curled up to sleep in a silence that made her feel, for the first time, safe. Moon held her in his familiar arms. She knew he would take care of her. He had a magic bow and arrow he would give her, and a little marijuana. In her dreams she felt her mind open up into the possibility of actually living. She could not remember ever dreaming before. But now it seemed like she could, in fact, become someone who dreamed. All the things she had to fight before—and all the people who did not understand her—didn't matter now.

After Moon went away, she wasn't afraid. He had taught her how to hunt, how to survive. She didn't let herself think about whether or not he would ever come back. She was alone, and she owned her solitude in a way she had never owned anything in her life. No one had ever let her own something this big before. She could not perceive the ends of it. The power of it dizzied her.

The silence won her trust almost instantly, the way no person ever had or would. The more she loved the silence, the more she spoke into it with her own voice and felt it listening, and the more the creatures of the silence began to trust her back.

Raven. Coyote. Serpent. Tarantula. Desert owl. They watched her with their hungry, independent eyes from the horizon, and left the gifts of their tracks in the sand outside her cave in the morning. She started to sleep dur-ing the day like they did, and wake in the cool night to follow them, and after a while she no longer felt she had to apologize for her presence. She had never felt tenderness for anyone before, until she met these animals. She had never felt humbled by anything, until the big desert silence flattened out her mind and glowed around her voice and woke her every night with its clap of nothingness. The dusty winds scoured her body and emptied her out. For the first time she did not feel angry any more. And that lasted for many moons.

Then something began to itch at her from inside. She had a rhythm now, with the animals. She had even learned how to preserve meat by drying it in the wind, and had soaked and scraped and dried a piece of leather, in the hopes of learning to make wraps to keep herself warm when the winter came. Most importantly, she had in her power the greatest human gift: the ability to make fire. It was something she had learned as a young child from other children in the ghetto whose families were secretly the survivors of other peoples—peoples who actually knew what life was and what kept it going. Even in the City, all her life she had made fires—because it comforted her, and because sometimes fire was the only thing that seemed to recognize her. She knew stones that made fire. She knew how to use sticks to make fire. Fire was her kin; she could see where it hid and draw it out. As long as she could make fire, she could survive.

And yet that very fire itched at her from within now. When the snakes came through her cave to enter their winter sleeping quarters, some of them passed right over her warm body, and after the passing of that slow caress she could not sleep. This was the only thing that frightened her: that flesh hunger, and not being able to fill it. The lack of human touch made her feverish, as if her body were leaving itself, seeking beyond itself for some other. She could feel her life force leaking from her, making her clumsy. She hated herself for this weakness, but the fear was greater than the hatred. It was a fear she could not name—would not name. She rolled restlessly against her animal skins during the hot day, trying to soothe herself with their friction and their illusion of living contact.

Delilah did not miss love or good food because she had not had them where she came from. She did not miss things because things had never done anything for her. But she missed touch. In the City it was the one thing that had come easily, and it was the only thing that had made her feel alive.

Delilah wasn't like other girls. She never had been. When, after almost a year of desperation, she finally saw the first man riding across the desert in an all-terrain vehicle, she felt no fear at all. She followed the tire tracks until he stopped, wearing frayed jeans she'd cut to the tops of her thighs, and then she met him at the entrance to the cave he planned to plunder. She told him she could show him the way. Inside the cave, when she could not see his face and knew that she was finally in control, she took off her shirt and met his hands with her small, pointed breasts when he reached forward in the darkness to find the flashlight he had dropped.

Over the years they came more and more frequently, in bigger and bigger vehicles. She hated them, but she needed them too. She made sure she always found them, and that they could never find her.

In the tower Lonely dreamed of the City, but they were her own dreams, not ones her father gave her—and she does not trust those dreams.

She doesn't understand, exactly, what she is seeing now. She still sees it at such a distance. But there are movements among the lights. There are echoes. Longing pours fast up her throat, filling her mouth. The nightmares lurk in the back of her mind.

The people are here. This is where the people live. The others.

Now she sees that even the lights move, in rivers, from here as slow as a lullaby. Smoke, a continuous foul breath, spins upward as if from unseen mouths. The City's shapes are jagged like a mass of broken teeth, and it wants her. It cannot be avoided. How the City shines! There is at once so much life and death—packed together in such frenzy—that Lonely can feel it pawing into her gut, surrounding her before she can fight it, turning her stomach over and over with excitement, delirium and colors pounded hard and fast together into blackness.

And those lights! Is each one a soul? Is each one another human being, as wild and complex as her own great, mysterious life seems to her?

Her father did not dream this place for her, no. Her father, certainly, did not want her here. She wonders if her father even knew that such a place existed. Did he foresee the hunger this would cause her—how those lights would call to her loneliness like a bold and frightening promise amidst the suddenly empty, too-quiet beauty of the fields?

Lonely wraps her arms around the horse's neck. She doesn't understand him or know why he is hers, but she clings to his warmth to keep from falling into the abyss that pulls her. She remembers Yora's words, and knows that Yora warned her against becoming human. Yet how could she not find an end to loneliness, among so many people?

The cliff is steep below her but in places the slope has crumbled, making treacherous, winding trails downward. She urges the horse onward, thrusting her body against his and squeezing him with her legs.

But the horse will not budge.

"Come on," says Lonely impatiently, "You don't understand. I need people. We have to get down there, we have to." She begins to cry. She is so lonely. It is unbearable, to be so lonely. Always before she had her father. Always before she was safe. There were no questions. There was no longing. It isn't fair that he left her, with no explanation of what was to come, no way to ease the loneliness in his absence. "Please," she says to the horse.

She cannot hear any noise; it seems the City is silent from this distance. Yet when she speaks she can barely hear her own voice. For there are a thousand noises, which must have grown closer as she rode toward them, but so gradually that she did not notice them. Still they are so dim and low, they are all a blur, so that she is not aware of any one sound until she tries to speak and finds her voice drowned by the din of this noise so crowded and huge it sounds like silence.

When the horse still doesn't move, she slides onto the ground. She knows she can go on without him. She stands there, hating her own hesitation. *Only thirteen moons,* she remembers suddenly, winding her fingers restlessly into the horse's mane. Here is where all the people live. *Go.*

But she does not go. She stands still, her feet chilled against the earth.

Then she is startled to see someone running toward her out of the corner of her eye.

"Oh no!" she cries, without knowing why.

But it's only a dog, and now he's come up to her, his breath hot on her legs, and he is grinning up at her with kind, sudden eyes. The horse backs up.

"Where did you come from?" breathes Lonely, kneeling to press her hand along the dog's happy head. "Do you come from people?"

The dog is at once hefty and lean, like a wolf. *i come from Wild, and i come from people,* he says, speaking with his friendly, shaking presence, his controlled beastliness, the mild force of his weight against her.

"Tell me about people," Lonely whispers. She has never seen a dog before but some expressions are like a universal language, easy to recognize: the excitement in the wagging of a tail, the encouragement in an open mouth and lolling tongue, the trust in full open eyes. "Tell me something about this place."

i belong to people. i am their angel. without me, they have no connection to Wild. without me, they do not remember what it feels like to be Loved perfectly.

"Does someone care for you?" Lonely asks, feeling now the fur's mat and tangle, the bare places where wounded skin has healed roughly.

i am here to Love, he repeats. *i am their angel. i am their guide.*

"But don't you, too, need to be loved?"

yes, so that they learn how to love. i believe in them! i know they can love! i love them! He is so excited, his messages fast and panting.

Lonely understands him without wondering how, and she feels his love—

feels it all over her as he bounds around her. She has so many questions she
wants to ask the dog, who knows everything of people, and who is the first
other being she has met since Yora and the horse.

"Why is it so loud?" she asks him. "Why can't I hear myself?"

the people all screaming, all screaming at once.

"But why?"

they cannot hear each other. they scream and scream. but they are not listening.

"What are they saying?"

i do not know. but the dogs, too, are barking, crying.

"Why?"

*they are locked up. they are tied up in the cold. all they want is to Love. maybe people,
too, cry for that.*

"But why don't they love each other?" Lonely asks desperately, feeling
more and more confused. There is something wrong in what the dog is saying. But he does not answer now, only rolls his face against her hand, and
rolls over onto his back, asking for touch.

Lonely pets him for a long time, and then he runs back down the hill to
the people he is in this life to love, and Lonely does not follow. Still squatting
on the ground, she glances over at the horse, who has kept a wary distance.

"What about you?" she asks, fascinated by something she hadn't thought
about before, feeling newly connected to life through the dog's conversation.
"Why are you with me?"

The horse looks at her, his eyes close together from the front, and his
big bulk seems to tremble but he does not speak—at least not in a way that
Lonely can understand. But Lonely feels suddenly that she cannot leave him.

At once afraid of entering the City alone and afraid to leave it, she curls
up in the grass, hoping to sleep and dream some dream that will help her.
Maybe the white bird will return to her. The wind ripples against her face,
as if unable to relax.

"What is this place?" she whispers, but the wind gives no answer.

To comfort herself she listens to the intimate shuffle of moles inside the
ground, clambering sightless through their simple, damp darkness. With her
head against the earth she fills herself with close, obvious noises, trying to think
clearly amid the din of the abyss. She can hear a moth shifting inside its chrysalis, and she imagines each wrinkle of its tight, brand new wings, immersing
her mind in detail until it spins into stillness. She leaps with relief into sleep.

But she does not dream. Not yet, not out here in wide open space with her
mind hanging off the edge of the world, without her father's dreams to guide
her. For the first time, her body takes sleep for the sake of rest and forgetting—
to clear away the day and make way for a new one. So much has happened.

Sometime later she wakes afraid, to the sound of a shriek far below. She sees the familiar night sky—the same one she gazed upon from her tower—but around her the hills creep and rise, threatening to drown her in their depths. Space looms, and for the first time she does not trust it. *What have I done?* She thinks, rising up to clutch her knees to her chest—the careless joy she felt the day before astounding her. Panicking, she looks for the horse, wanting to get up higher. But he is gone.

"Horse!" she cries, immediately on her feet, forgetting the City.

Then she sees him, wandering down the slope along the edge of the valley, his nose to the ground. He is not moving fast, nor moving into the City. *He is searching for the earth*, is the first thing she thinks, absurdly.

She trails behind him, afraid to go deeper into the depths of the valleys, afraid to lose sight of the moon or the stars. But, as always, he seems to know where he is going. He walks over the other side of a ridge, sniffing the air, sniffing the ground, and into a low cover of trees. They can no longer see the City. On this side of the ridge, the earth smells different—secret and dense. They enter the brush and it scratches and tears at Lonely, and she fights it, terrified, crying "Wait!" She hears a sound coming closer, and it sounds like something alive.

Then suddenly there is the horse, and a stream flowing before him. Now Lonely remembers the sound of water. She remembers Yora, and she stumbles to the water's side. The only light that can be found in the valley runs there, in the stream—runs in shy ribbons away, always away, but always there is more of it coming. The water is so simple in its downward motion, fleeting and glowing, its music alive and jubilant like incongruent life in a desolate world.

Lonely kneels before it and drinks with the horse—just to connect with the water, just to remember Yora and the feeling of her warm body and kind eyes.

But the water is cold, colder than the cold wind on the island where the tower stood. It slams against her insides like something solid and wakes her as if she had still been sleeping.

Why are you so cold? she asks the water with her mouth.

because i come from places, says the stream. *and i am going places, and i never stop. because once i was solid, and once i was air, and will be again. you do not know this story yet.*

But Lonely doesn't care about the story because suddenly she is so thirsty. The water brightens and fills every cell in her brain, making her mind float easy, and it swells inside her organs as if before they were only flaccid shapes that lay dormant and lifeless, but now suddenly know purpose. She tastes in that water the blood-wet taste of the earth and the dizzy height of the mountain. She feels the parts of her body begin to connect and talk to one another.

She lifts her head from the water and sees the lush green that nestles all along the length of the nourishing stream.

Yora. Yora with her moist, vulnerable skin and her eyes weighted from within by an overheavy love. Remembering her, Lonely wants at once to be held by her and to hold her, to be rescued by that love and to rescue Yora from it. Where did Yora come from, and what other landscapes lay behind her reticent eyes? There is so much Lonely does not know, so much still to be found.

Comforted by the continuous sound of the water, she sleeps again on the hard ground, easily becoming dirty, hungering against the soil for some sense of companionship in the earth. The horse sleeps standing over her, as if protecting her. Inside the cricket song, the heartbeat of the meadow, and buoyed up by the shuffling song of the stream, she dreams of the City. She dreams it is a giant insect, and she understands that its call is one of desire—a desperate call for the Other, for the ideal mate it longs for out in the darkness that it can never find. But like an insect, its mind is so cold: she can feel its coldness encasing her, heartless, freezing her body and trapping her like the ice-glass tower.

When she wakes again at dawn, she listens for a long time to the story of the stream, and though she does not understand everything it says, she understands that it is coming from that mountain.

The City may hold all the people in the world, but her lover is a god. Her father said so. She decides she will find him on that high mountain, because the mountain is beautiful.

But she does not know that one day she will return to the City, when she is no longer able to make such choices.

In the morning the horse wakes early and grazes in the sun. He is careful in his movements, knowing that he is something simple and humble now, whom the earth speaks to and remembers. He did not know that, in this new life, he would be hungry. He did not know, before, this need to eat and eat, and never be filled. The earth seems to bounce beneath the weight of his hooves, and the sun sizzles over his back, baring him to the world. The grass smells like home.

He did not know that a body could feel this way.

Say I am male, the soul told the spirit of the river. *Not female. Not female.*

When Lonely comes toward him, the horse snorts at her and hops a few paces sideways, his nerves snapping. Though he knows her now—though he will not leave her—he feels a nameless terror in her presence. It isn't that she is dangerous, but rather something about her careless fragility, the lazy openness of her body as she moves through space, that fills him with foreboding. He doesn't want to carry her like that, rising up from his body into the air. He wants to stay here, alone, in the safety of the anonymous meadow.

His heartbeat slows a little when she crouches low on the ground and speaks to him in her soft windy voice. He catches that voice in the cup of his ear, to keep track of it. He is safe in his big maleness, but he is afraid of himself, too. It would be easier, perhaps, to surrender. He shivers with confusion.

The grass makes sense, with its sharp green song for his mouth. It means only one thing. And the wind makes sense, carrying messages of warning or fear. Fear is a constant spirit that hovers around the horse's life. It is a sensor in his body, that he obeys always. He fears the mountain that he feels Lonely yearning toward. He fears what she will ask of him today. He fears her gaze as she sits and stares at him.

When she rises again and climbs on top of him, he rears a little, but says nothing. He raises his head into the wind and jerks his body restlessly. He wants to run but cannot find the courage to do so. To stay still is terrible, and yet to burst out into the wind is also too much to bear.

Not knowing what else to do, the horse lowers his head and keeps pulling at the grasses, bringing their airy freshness into his mouth. The grass tastes safe. Lonely's voice is thin and high. He flicks his ears, catching it and batting it away from him. Her weight sinks into him and bends his spine, which tingles up and down with her warmth. He feels his own strength, and for a moment it comforts him. Yes, he is this now. Only this animal. He is safe. He keeps eating as the morning brightens. The grasses are the first of spring; they speak to his senses of a new world.

After a while her weight also begins to comfort him—this softness weighing him down like a heavy sunlight. That weight centers him. Her patience comforts him. He lifts his head and again considers the wind, her presence, and the meadow. He does not like the smells from the land ahead of him: empty smells, bare and burning and ghost-ridden. But they are better than the scent of the City, which was deadly.

He feels the heat of her body hungering forward, feels her press forward, feels himself moved forward as if he were a part of her. What else can he do? He lurches in a stumbling way, his head hanging down, uncertain. What is this, the urgency he feels within her body? Was there some purpose he had once, some calling to love something more than the grass and the wind? He feels her thighs press him, and though they are slim and light, their certainty moves him.

"I trust you," he hears her say. "I know you know the way."

At the same time her body moves, and it says, *We are going to the mountain. We are going through the desert. We are going onward, toward the sun.*

The horse finds himself moving, a held tension finally released. The wildness of the meadow focuses in his strong limbs. And he carries her forward with a sense of relief now, the frame of her body channeling his own body forth the way the earth around the stream, with the will of its solid banks, gives the water its motion, its shape, and its freedom.

Dragon sketches soft shapes in the late afternoon across the stone maze where Delilah lives. She's chosen to live inside this cliff, he has learned, because it opens out on the other side to a tiny spring, that rises up from some unknown depth of earth. He likes to stay near it, playing his breath over its pink surface and listening to its small, sticky sound, for he knows that even if she avoids him by tunneling into secret, narrow caves, she'll always have to return to the water. Usually she sleeps all through the day, and will not come until dusk. But he'll see her eventually. And she is not going to make him leave. He belongs to the desert too. He was born here.

He imagines her scooping the water, greedy and careless, her mouth slurping wet, the water running down her neck and soaking spots of her T-shirt against her skin. She wears a T-shirt now—something he has never seen before. She will not bare her breasts for him again. But the cloth of it is so helpless and soft, torn around her shoulders, and with little holes worn through it beneath her neck. Her hair is cropped short, ragged from the edge of the rusty knife she used to cut it, and its jagged edges leave her features sharp and bare, her smile twisting her face into a surprise of beauty as she turns toward him. Her naked neck dips helplessly into the quick points of her shoulders. He remembers this as he waits for her. He can imagine the muscles in her thin legs as she kneels and the mist of rough hair along them that darkens her already dark skin. Her feet are bare. The ragged threads of her cut-off jeans contrast with the dry smooth sheen of her thigh. Her hips are thin, her body narrow and wiry like some lonely child's, but when he touched her she was soft—softer than any part of him, a softness that hid between her sharp bones, that wanted to yield to him.

He hurls his drawing stone into space and lies on his back, letting the cooling breeze lick the sweat from his chest. He pictures for the hundredth time the insistent redness of her nipples shouting from the slippery darkness of her shiny body, feels her claws in his skin.

"You can't stay," she'd hissed at him when he stepped in front of her on the second night, blocking her path. She was climbing down from her cave, her body instinctual and wary, but he could tell she had not expected him to be there still, and that his power in surprising her made her mad. "You don't get to keep coming back for more. That's not how it works."

He had gripped her waist then and leaned over her little frame, feeling his desire so strong it almost knocked him off balance. "What should I do?" he asked her. "What should I do with this feeling?" His voice was slow and careful and deep, like a hand that reached down into her darkness and lifted a jewel, examined it carefully, felt it pulse in his fingers.

He felt her stiffen. He felt her fury but also her confusion. Her "no" was tiny then, and he knew she did not mean it. He reached behind her and gripped her ass in his fingers, feeling his own strength, feeling her flesh squeeze deliciously in his hand like a fruit that he could burst. If she were still wearing the little leather skirt, he could have slipped his fingers right up inside. But the denim was tight. He fit one finger beneath it, felt the misty heat radiating from her source. He ground her roughly against him. He could not stop himself—her body, the ecstasy of it, forced his hands. He ripped the cloth from her breasts and overcame her mouth with his, the sound of the ripping cloth arousing him so much he thought he would come immediately. His legs were weak with the memory of what his body remembered from the night before, and the memory of the goddesses was gone—everything was gone but her heat, and that place that would welcome him.

But then his foot caught fire. When he jumped back, releasing her, he saw a scorpion standing tall in the sand, lifting its spiral tail and small, wrestler's arms in challenge.

"What—?" he cried. For it hurt, and she had done it to him, somehow. He had sensed this from the beginning: the desert was in league with her. And he needed her. He needed her not to hurt him.

She was looking downward, stretching and releasing the torn cloth of her shirt impatiently. He didn't understand how so much distance had inserted itself between them in only a moment. "Fuck you," she said. "I only have two T-shirts left."

Dragon did not hear her. "You made that thing sting me."

Delilah laughed. "Don't be ridiculous. You're the god. I don't make anything do anything."

"But you did," he insisted. He was afraid. This girl seemed the opposite of the soft-tongued women whose paradise he had left behind. Look what she had made him do! He felt suddenly that to step toward her again was to leave them behind forever. And despite his desire he could not move. He felt the scorpion's hatred inside his skin. He knew that she would tear him to pieces. And who was he—that demon who had grabbed at her, unthinking and wild?

"I want you gone," she said, her voice dry and unkind. "Go back where you come from." Then she turned and walked away, swinging her tiny hips as if she were huge, as if she were waves and waves of fat, luxurious flesh.

"*Delilah!*" he yelled, but she did not turn around. Her words had made him so angry that, when he called her name again, it came out as fire. At first he did not understand what had happened. The flames stood in the air and blinded him. When they disappeared, the air was bowed and foggy with heat, and Delilah still had not turned around. His mouth was so dry he started coughing, but the tension in his body was relieved. He pawed the air as she continued to leave him, trying to understand if what he had seen was real.

That's what I can do, he thinks now. *I can make fire.* To avoid trying to understand it, to avoid realizing that he doesn't know how to make it again, he thinks about love. He thinks he loves Delilah, and that fire is love. The scorpion was Delilah's defense, an obstacle for him to overcome. And though he does not know how to love, the practice of those long hours forcing himself to be patient with the still loneliness of flowers, forcing himself to breathe as the goddesses moved around him, keep him now from madness.

Tired of waiting, he gets up and wanders the desert with no direction, turning constantly to keep her caves in view, testing their angles in different perspectives in his memory. He doesn't care whether it is day or night. Loneliness is like a sickness that weighs down his limbs and makes breathing difficult. Still, he feels the smallest sense of satisfaction, simply to know of her existence.

High on the cliffside, giant saguaros make a forest of hard sentinels, and he feels their presence in the wind—feels that the whole world is watching him, its silence the challenge of possibility. His soul is the heat that lifts off the earth and bends the air into form.

Coyote appears, running the other way. When he glances back once, Dragon imagines a look of disdain. Is he looking at Dragon, or beyond him, to Delilah's caves? Coyote mocked him for crying for his mother. *What kind of man are you,* he might be saying now, *that you let women control you?*

Dragon clenches his fists and turns back, squinting. The patterns of her caves swirl like a dangerous, frozen storm of pink fire, striking new hues in the changing sun, casting shadows thick as blood. Afternoon in the desert is a long story about shadow: giant shadows marching over giant stones, marching a path of silence. When he listens to that silence he believes he can hear Delilah's soul turning deep within her, slower than her fast body and full of a wonder she will not speak of. It scrapes a little against her insides, like something dry and thirsty. He doesn't know, after all, how he feels about her. What does he want from her? What is she doing to him? He should leave. He should escape this tricky landscape of hope and death, which distorts his mind and turns him into some evil creature of reasonless lust. But where would he go?

He lived here once, but that was long ago. He lived inside the earth then, for by then the dragons almost never emerged. It was too dangerous. They were the very last of their kind, and they had held out for hundreds of years, undiscovered. They meditated inside those caves, and ate nothing but the fire from each others' mouths, and they never saw the sun. Dragon was one of them, and he remembered nothing of day and night, or of the world. They made the light with their eyes, with their fire. They made the darkness with their absence when they curled up to sleep. At each moment, the dragons made and re-made the only world there was for the boy who loved them.

But now he walks alone on skin legs, human, and Coyote's challenge pushes at his mind.

He likes the idea of clothing. Delilah is less vulnerable, more sure of herself, inside her clothes; they raise her a level above him by hiding her from him. Dragon walks and tries to imagine himself into a costume that suits him. What does a man wear? He remembers the flow of the long robes the goddesses wore, how that flow carried them and made their walk easy. He wants that ease, but he wants the power of his legs, too, and their hard decision. He wants his penis free to rise, and he wants Delilah to look at it when it rises for her. But at the same time, he wants to hide it, so she will not have such power over him. He wants to tempt her. He wants her to want him.

He closes his eyes while he walks, because there are no obstacles before him. He imagines the dragons, whose skin was rainbows—whose scales, sometimes, were eyes. It is one of those eyes that hangs over his heart now, one of his dragon mother's million eyes, that he will keep forever for his heart to see by. This he will not cover. The area of his heart he must leave bare.

Maybe he will walk then in a split skirt, a skirt that encloses each leg as he strides forward, and hangs loose below his groin. Maybe each leg of this garment will flare out around the ankle, so he will have the graceful flare of a skirt to carry him. This cloth will be sleek and tough like the skin of dragons, and rainbowed like their changing light, except that for Dragon the colors come through only in the redder colors of fire. Only the wisest, oldest dragons could achieve the colors of the hottest flame: the blue flame that turns to spirit. And Dragon did not live with them long enough to ever know that part of fire.

Maybe gold bracelets will ring his wrists, spiraling power around his hungry hands. And he wants something on his head: a crown, a round channel to draw up the energy the way the goddesses taught him, so that one day he will

learn to bring the power of that fire up into his mind. One day it will no longer torment him, but connect him with the sky. The crown must be gold, too,
for gold is kin to him: gold is nothing more than dragons' blood hardened.

He opens his eyes and the costume is real. He laughs out loud. Yes, he is
a god! He can do anything. He can make things appear by imagining them.

What now? He stalks the desert restlessly, wishing Coyote would come
back and see him. He walks until he tires himself, and then he searches for
shade, not because he can be burned by the sun but because he burns from
inside. Across from the cliff wall, a long walk away, the desert suddenly grows
lush in a pathway of colorful cacti and arched, hanging trees with leaves like
rain—a ribbon of life in touch with a ghost of water far below the earth.
Here and there it bubbles to the surface, making small, miraculous oases
where coyotes and rabbits alike come to drink. It runs parallel to the cliffside,
between it and the terraced ledges of sandstone that rise higher and higher
and are backed by a distant ridge in the north, a long purple spine spanning
the horizon. He walks under the sun until he arrives at that river of green,
then winds his way between the cacti where Delilah probably never goes, her
bare human feet too vulnerable to the spines that litter the sand.

Under a gentle bowed tree that breathes a shroud of cooling vapor, Dragon
sits down, resting himself on the cold relief of stone. He closes his eyes. Just
inside the gate to the Garden, before the palace of woman's pleasure, lies
a simpler, darker, first room, and there grows another great oak, with roots
that travel beneath the entire garden and far out into the flowers and forest
beyond. Around its base grow hundreds of ferns, their furry heads—Dragon
knows—just now rising in their tight spirals. One goddess, sweet and shy,
once knelt with Dragon among those ferns, showing him their ancient shapes
like tiny human spines unfurling. She explained to him the way his desire—
his life force—when he learned to focus it, would unspiral up the length of
him like the growth of those primitive ferns, filling him with spirit, so that he
could meet the world with all his being, whole and clear.

Now he imagines meditating with Delilah, the amazing mystery of her
darkness pressed wet against the hard sun of his rising, her legs around him.
They would unfurl together like the ferns. He knows she needs that as much
as he does. Together they will raise up their fire into something purer, something calm and brilliant like the eyes of the goddesses…

But this time, his imagination does not make the image real. He struggles
with the memory of her body—more fantastic, more painfully pleasurable
than he had ever imagined a woman's body would be. He wishes for water
suddenly, that it might try to soothe him, the way the goddesses tried to
soothe him, though they always failed.

He opens his eyes. The cacti, purple and yellow and green, clench their unattainable water in swollen leaves, and they bristle cruelly at him. Twisted mesquite trees lean over, their leaves thin and spare, and littler trees thrust up under them, their stems crisscrossed like cages. Dragon sees the terror with which the things of the desert hoard their meager water inside themselves, and the beauty this hoarding brings. The silence of the desert, to which the long shadows march, is a song whose words become clear as he leans dizzily against the trunk of the tree—words about a longing for water, the absence of water, the spaces that water leaves behind. Water pumps through the deep silence of the tree, and through his body from his heart down through his limbs, down into his penis, into his feet, back to his heart again.

This place will make him stronger. This place will make him a man, and he will win Delilah in the end. He opens his mouth and makes a hissing sound. He wants the fire to come again. He wants to feel that power that can come from him—a power he never knew he owned. But the fire will not come now. He stands up and hurls a stone against stone, breathing harshly. He wants to have some effect. Who is he? What belongs to him?

Stumbling and angry, not thinking, he searches for water. When some instinct inside him finally finds it, it is rich and exuberant, lacing the happy stones with its nourishment—so much fuller and more alive than the tiny pool that Delilah drinks from, which is just enough to sustain her life. It is almost a real river here, wider and deeper than even the stream in the Garden. He kneels and kisses it with his lips, dazzled by its cold freedom, and afraid. If he lay down inside it, what then? What would happen to him? He gropes at it with his hands, but there is nothing to hold onto. Instead it holds him—pulls him inward like a depthless mouth—with its motion. He feels there is something for him inside it. Some gift there tantalizes him, glittering like a woman's smile, but he does not know how to get in.

Yet he is calmer now. He glances back into the far shadows where Delilah's caves are hidden from view, enfolded in the trickster curves of desert cliffsides. He aches, suddenly, to know that she must live so far from these living things, for something tells him she cannot bear to be anywhere near this nourishing river of love.

Moon, exhausted from vomiting up the poison he drank, his skin pale from long hours in used basement air, his eyes nearly extinguished from the low after the high, floats through the prettier streets of the City and listens to conversations outside parked cars.

"Good morning. What a lovely day!"

"Yes, I hear it's going to be a hot one."

He doesn't mind the sick feeling in his body. At least it is something. It makes him feel more human, for once—human like the only person he has ever loved.

Last night he dreamed of a frog in muddy, sick waters. He could hear the sound, underwater, of its delicate skin trying to breathe—a sound like paper tongues flapping in the wind. It was that grotesque sound that finally woke him, vomiting. He knows what the dream means, but it doesn't matter.

He likes it that he looks too ragged, too far gone to be spoken to. People turn their faces away. He doesn't feel like talking to anyone. He just walks and listens, trying to understand.

People talk about the weather all the time, like it's important. But they don't act like it's important. There is something hard between them and the lifeless ground. They do not lift their arms and open their mouths when the wind blows, or pray when the clouds gather round, or seek the other worlds when fog settles in. Instead, they stand by their cars, saying the same thing they said yesterday.

"Beautiful day, isn't it?"

"Gorgeous!"

But it's the same as yesterday. Every day is the same: the sun in an empty sky, and hot. There is no other kind of weather in the City any more. Maybe the sky here is different, after a hundred years of smog coating it, or maybe the west winds that brought the weather have abandoned it, or maybe Hanum somehow engineered it this way. But every single day has been sunny and cloudless for as long as the youngest generation can remember.

The people have nothing else to say. Don't they have any other kind of weather inside of them? *Yes,* Moon thinks, *and no one wants to admit it.* But why be ashamed? Why be ashamed of the somber face of winter—that wordless stillness, the different shapes of trees when they lose their flesh of green? Why be ashamed of the passion of thunder, or the mystery of mist?

A horn blares, and Moon jumps to the side. Tires squeal angrily against pavement. He'd forgotten: this is where cars go, the road. Only cars here, not people. There are people inside the cars, but nobody remembers that. A person in one car honks and steers her car hard in front of another, as if the other car is only a car with nothing inside it. Are they real bodies inside those cars? They cannot feel the wind or touch the things they pass. They cannot see details. They twitch a single muscle in the ankle or the wrist, and the machine does whatever they want to do.

But inside the cars are vulnerable bodies, and inside the thoughts are longings that no one speaks. Moon knows that.

He stops and turns his flute over in his hands. No one remembers any more. No one remembers anything but sun and fake smiling; they've forgotten the beautiful darkness inside.

No one cries now. No one remembers the rain.

Delilah skips from shadow to shadow beneath the lithe, jagged pines. She feels their breathing, their ever-running blood. Their bristly tops sweep the sky, mirroring the tattered grey clouds that skid over them in the evening wind. The drone of that wind is like an eerie sleep through the heads of the pines, a foggy, disorienting sound.

How can there be a pine forest here, she'd asked Moon years ago, *on this cliff above the desert? How can it be winter up here, when below us the earth is bare and burned by the sun?*

Because we're in someone else's dream, he had said. *Nothing makes sense in this world. Or if it does, we do not understand it.*

Whose dream? Who dreams us?

No one knows. Most people don't even know they're in a dream.

Is it because you're a god that you know?

No. He'd laughed. *Anyone who's paid attention to their dreams can tell that life is only another one.*

Why don't you ever tell me your dreams?

Because. They don't mean anything.

But you must know who's dreaming us. You know everything. Tell me. I want out of this dream.

No you don't. He was serious now. *And I don't know. I don't want to know.*

No. You're right. Me neither.

But Delilah climbs the cliff above her caves and enters this forest again and again because of her dreams, and she survives because of those dreams. The dreams tell her what animal to hunt—what animal has decided, for whatever reason she doesn't pretend to understand, that it needs to become a part of her. It is always this wind through the tops of the pines, wailing like a witch's prayer, that reminds her of her dream, even if down in the desert she could remember nothing but a shuffling darkness or a sudden movement opening in space. Sometimes even when she remembers the dream, the animal appears like a riddle, giving her a pathway to follow or an abstract pattern, which she doesn't understand until she recognizes it in the retreating tail of a rabbit or the blurred fan of a grouse's wings.

She never kills predators, because she feels herself to be one of them. Nor does she kill in the desert, where among the bats, lizards, snakes, foxes, scorpions, owls, ravens, vultures, and all the other creatures people mistrust and fear, she has for the first time in her life come to feel at home. She kills only up here in the pine forest, where Moon first taught her to hunt.

It's spring now, but at night the iron-cold shadows of the pines, split in silence by white swords of moonlight, make her feel like it's winter all year round. Sap runs through the lean, straight trunks in passionate rivers no matter what the season, and as Delilah crouches and encircles one of them with her arm to steady herself, she feels its spirit writhe gleefully like a wiry muscle up into the sky. Pines are the only trees she has ever known well, and she understands them, for unlike other plants, they feel as if they are constantly moving, as if they themselves are hunters or guardians of the hunt and the hunted. Their seeds germinate only at the touch of fire.

The pines own this forest. In this part of it, nothing else grows beneath them but silence, and they cast their shadowy winter dreams upon a bed of their own red needles, nearly as soft under running feet as the desert sand.

On the prickly desert floor, Delilah wears her old sneakers, their toes split open and curling upwards. But in the forest she wears strips of leather she made herself, cut to fit her feet. They're tied simply and held clumsily, but they hold, and they allow her feet to move silently, feeling every detail without getting cut. She rises from the ground, listening. Her shoulders, always curled a little inward like the cave she sleeps in, ache, and she rolls them around impatiently, trying to shake off that nameless tension. She tiptoes at a run between the trunks, her bare feet inside the leather so calloused she does not feel the sharp points of the needles, only the silence that cushions them. She doesn't know where she is going but she cannot stay still for long, and as always, it is pure need that propels her forward into the unknown.

An owl calls, his voice the black hole of a question, observing her. Delilah stops and calls back in her owl voice—a different voice, one she does not recognize as part of her own limited self. *Now I am also an owl*, her call says. *I am also a hunter; let me share your space.*

And yet tonight is different. Tonight she's unsteady. She doesn't know tonight what she is seeking.

Delilah never begged when she lived in the City; she only stole. And it's not like begging now, the way she creeps through the pine forest longing for food, though tonight she feels helpless in a way she has not felt before. *It's like*…. She struggles to imagine, as she always does, how she would explain it to Moon, who is perhaps the only person she will ever see as worthy of explaining anything to.

But no, she wouldn't explain it to Moon after all, because it makes her sound selfish and jealous, and she doesn't like to sound that way in front of Moon, because he is so good. Yes, she knows now: this helplessness is like the way she felt as a child when her father was still alive, when she walked into the kitchen late one night to get a glass of water and found her little sister Mira still up, talking in a hushed voice with her father like a grown-up. Delilah had stopped, instinctively ashamed, and their father had leaned back and taken his hands from Mira's small lap, so that Delilah could see he'd been holding her hands in his. Mira had blanked her eyes to Delilah, revealing nothing. And Delilah had felt—what had she felt? Her father never told her his secrets. Her father barely spoke to her at all. She supposed he thought her too impulsive, too wild, too driven by desire to sit still and absorb such wisdom. But to Mira he gave everything, and Mira kept it all hidden within herself, never sharing those secrets with Delilah, until she became as foreign and indecipherable to Delilah as their father himself. It was as if their father gradually translated Mira's entire being into another language, until Delilah could not understand her at all.

Helpless. In fact, when hunting through her dreams like this, trying to understand the hidden ways of her prey, Delilah feels the way she always did, no matter what age, no matter how fierce she could be with anyone else, when she stood in the presence of her sister. Even once it became clear that Mira was completely mad—screaming whenever she was put in a car, not speaking to anyone, murmuring to plants—Delilah continued to feel vulnerable whenever she approached her little sister, as if she herself were the younger one. It was a feeling of inexplicable awe and longing that infuriated her, as every one of her attempts to soothe or talk to Mira was rejected.

"Hoah," Delilah huffs to herself in the darkness, trying to ground herself with the sound of her own voice. It unnerves her the way she gets lost in thoughts sometimes, the way her past still walks beside her constantly, and tries to talk to her. She loses her focus, spaces out—something she never used to do. Too many years speaking to no one but bats—that must be it.

Often Delilah cannot remember her dream until she comes to the pine forest and hears the wind, but this evening she remembered the animal clearly when she awoke. Pausing and turning from side to side, she closes her eyes now and listens, hopeful that another, truer memory will surface—some dream beneath that dream. For the animal she dreamed of she cannot kill. She knew this when Moon took her hunting for the first time, and this animal was the first animal they spotted, standing alone in a clearing. He motioned with his head and waited for her to take aim, but she sat there with the bow resting in her lap, frozen.

"*Now*," he whispered, but she said, out loud, "No," and her voice resounded in space.

The deer bounded with graceful, slow-motion leaps into the forest beyond.

"Not that one," she gasped, snatching her breath back from the clutches of a terror she could not explain.

"Why?" said Moon. "She was looking at me. She knew."

"No," said Delilah, still staring at the empty clearing, "I mean not deer. Not any deer. I won't kill that animal."

"Why not?"

"I don't know." She said it with conviction, as if the terror of the unknown was reason in itself.

"You're crazy, Lil," he said, but he was laughing, and he didn't ask any more questions, which was why she loved him. Nothing angered him, and he never pressed.

Later she knew, not suddenly but gradually—with a realization she managed to deny to herself for long enough that when it finally hit her its potency was faded and less painful—that animal reminded her of Mira. It was the deer's silence, its sweetness, its feet light on the earth and its body thin and easily disappearing, but most of all its eyes, eyes that shamed her with their impossible compassion. Furthermore, Delilah knew that this feeling would always make her tremble when she hunted any animal—this sense that she was hunting Mira's kindred. She felt, ridiculous as it would sound to say out loud, that her people were the predators and Mira's were the prey, and that was why she had never been able to approach her little sister without feeling ashamed of herself, as if without even trying she would push Mira away with her own hunger, her own clumsy, ignorant humanness.

But the feeling was strongest with deer. Now in the darkness she remembers the deer's watery eyes in her dream last night. "I won't," she says out loud, the image of the deer so real inside her that she almost speaks her sister's name. *Mira. Miri.* But she refuses. She would rather starve.

"There must be someone else," she whispers. Sometimes it overwhelms her to think how many animals must die in her lifetime to sustain her. She knows Mira used to feel the same, which was why she stopped eating meat, stopped eating almost entirely before she was taken away. But Delilah does not have that kind of self-control. In her memory, she has never had self-control of any kind. She cannot put off what she wants. Desire fills her, animates her, defines her, tells her where to go and what to do next in any given situation. With her whole body she desires meat. She doesn't care for vegetables and she has no patience for stalking plants, which are even more hidden and mysterious to her than the animals. Occasionally she eats a little of the tough cacti, whose flesh she mashes into pulp. In the autumn sometimes she finds pomegranates, whose juice is like blood.

She keeps moving. The deer's eyes in her mind are like the round glowing call of the owl: singular, dark, and deep.

Then she turns away from the sound and faces the long silence before her, and something happens that has not happened in the seven years since she came to the desert, not once. She misses her sister. The feeling roars up behind her heart like the oceanic wind, threatening to break her apart.

"Fuck this," she says to the silence, her voice determined and challenging. The whole night is the deer's eye, murky and alive. She feels as if the deer is hunting her. She runs again and keeps on running, making a loop back to the open cliff, back to the safety of the desert.

She has meat left still from the boar she killed a week ago. She will not kill tonight. Not if it means looking into those eyes.

She skitters down the cliff face, spidery and swift, the motions of her hands abrupt with frustration. Her whole body hurts. Cramps in her legs. A pinched nerve in her neck. Her eyes hurt. Tension binds her shoulders. Pain. It comes like this, from nowhere, and she growls with it, furious.

She takes a faster, steeper route than usual, having nothing to carry back with her. There is no landscape to separate the forest from the desert, or the desert from the fields, or the fields from the sea. Reality shifts suddenly, and one finds oneself suddenly in a different place.

Maybe, Moon had said once, *we are in the dream of a person who travels only by car, or by something even faster, so that they have no sense of the transition between places. Maybe we live in a dismembered world, a world dreamed by a mind that has forgotten the connections between things.*

Delilah had not understood what he meant then, but she remembered how her sister used to scream like an animal in the car. How she would look out the window with her little head jerking fast back and forth as if her eyes could not make sense of the images beyond a terrifying blur, how she would shrink and cringe at each other car that passed so close, and how as the ton-heavy mass of machinery hurtled her forward at a faster and faster speed, her scream would crescendo and then suddenly break off—though her mouth still hung open—as if the car moved so fast she had lost her voice somewhere far behind her.

That's how Delilah's sister was. Things that everyone else took for granted, she saw as alien. As if she belonged somewhere else.

That night, Dragon makes the fire again after all, as he did the morning Delilah turned from him and he called her name. This time it keeps burning, living on nothing.

It happens while he's meditating. He sits before Delilah's caves, willing himself to breathe in the pink sandstone scent that he now associates with her and to sit quietly with the memory of her presence. As the women of the Garden taught him, he breathes his desire upward through his spine, into his belly, his rib cage, his heart, his throat, his mind.

Once, he had asked them where the energy would go, and would it leave him finally—would he finally have relief. But they could not tell him this. They could not explain. They could only promise him that, with continued practice, he would find a new way to use this energy and that it would no longer torment and control him.

He has always struggled with the meditation, but he continues to believe in it. He has never been able to bring it all the way up to his head. Usually by the time it reaches his heart, the fire down below—as if raging on its own brighter and brighter—draws all his energy and thoughts back down with its magnetism, repeatedly, until he finally gives in to it, his disappointment lost in the ecstasy of familiar release.

But today, perhaps because he's been with a woman now, even if only once, he is able to hold the fire hovering for longer and longer in his heart, though not any higher. It burns, and his chest burns, until he wants to scream, but he can't, because he can't bring it up to his throat. He feels so much love for Delilah—or what he thinks must be love—that it's as if his heart itself is straining with the need for release. She is gone, and he cannot tell her. Then his heart seems to explode, and he coughs, and fire shoots out of his mouth, as if he really were born from dragons.

As he watches the single flame twist eerily over the sand, all alone with nothing to feed it, yet alive, he feels the same sweet release as if he had really come, and then filling that emptiness he feels a power he has never known before. It makes him want to try again and again, so that when that first little flame dies into the twilight, he breathes in hard and closes his eyes, lifting his chest and willing the energy of his passion to rise up inside him once more.

"I am a god!" he cries out loud. "I am a god of fire!"

By the time night surrounds him, a full and many-tongued fire rages neatly before him, and it keeps burning all on its own. Delilah has appeared from nowhere, emerging out of the darkness around it with her quick eyes. *This is my power!* he thinks fiercely, and he waits for her wonder, her admiration.

He watches her eyes move with the fire, and he feels certain of the hunger it makes in her, but she only says, low and angry, "You're still here."

"Come sit with me," he says, ignoring his own strange terror. "Please." He knows his fire will win her. It has to. He watches her eyes, the way her chin jerks back a little as she swallows. She's wearing a big button-down shirt, its collar falling back loosely around her neck and shoulders. He doesn't know what men's clothing looks like but he knows that shirt does not belong to her; its bigness makes her look vulnerable. "I made this fire," he says. "I made it for you."

She seems to consider, though she doesn't come any closer. "How is it burning?" But there is no question in her voice, only a slight growl beneath the flatness of it. Her curiosity seems to him milder than is appropriate for such a feat. His fire is burning with nothing to fuel it, with nothing to feed its hunger, like the fire of dragons!

"I made it," he says again, his breath catching in his own wonder. "With magic."

She nods once. He feels that perhaps he is not the first person to do magic in her presence, or the first god she has known. She is holding something in her fist, clutching it and bringing it to her mouth, where she rips off a bite and begins to chew. Eating. Hunger. Something he has never known. All his magic suddenly feels like nothing at all compared to her unattainable humanness.

"Don't you like fire?" he asks, a little desperately. She crouches now, outside the ring of the fire's light, where he can barely see the whites of her eyes. Her knees poke through the frayed holes in her jeans.

She doesn't say anything. She rips the piece of meat she was chewing and tosses one half to a fox who moves in a careful half-circle behind her, engaged in a low dance of silence against the earth. The fox's ears are bigger than her face, smart and alert, and her eyes wink open at Dragon, shaped like big glowing seeds. She is slim and wavering, a piece of elegant feminine magic that Delilah seems to have conjured up from nowhere, but when Dragon looks back at Delilah, the fox disappears, her tail erasing her into the darkness like a wisp of smoke.

Dragon thinks of Coyote, wonders about the animals of the desert, wonders if they are testing him.

"What kind of meat are you eating?" he asks her.

"Boar."

"How did you kill a wild boar?"

"With a dagger, this one. Look, I don't live here because I like conversation. Why are you here? You want another fuck, is that it? Okay. One more, and then go."

Dragons wants her, but he doesn't know how to answer such a question. He does not like the word she used, and her forwardness makes him hesitate.

"You should be more careful with that power," he says.

She looks at him sharply, but says nothing. He watches as pieces of her fall accidentally into the light: in this moment the damp little stones of her collar bone, in the next moment—as she turns to toss the fox a last morsel—the boyish turn of her ankle. He isn't used to seeing a woman so careless with her body. Her ease is mesmerizing. It feels as if she might fall into his arms almost accidentally, if he were close enough. But no, when she turns back to him he remembers she is not careless at all. She is careful and precise. She won't let him that close.

"I just want you to come over here," he tries. "By this fire I made for you."

But that makes her stand up again. She chews on her meat and stares into the fire, avoiding his eyes, one hip thrust outward.

"Don't you like me?" Dragon cries.

Now her lips purse into a saucy squiggle as she considers him. Her eyes laugh in a way that makes him remember her touch, her easy wetness. There is something constantly seductive about those eyes, the way the pupils float up in them like flames from some low darkness, the way they sparkle like that below her crooked, mocking eyebrows. Her voice is too deep for someone so small: husky and confident. Dangerous.

"I understand you," she allows finally.

"What do you understand?"

"That you want to fuck, for example, but you don't think it's…right, or something."

Dragon leans back so the firelight can dream over his chest. She does want him, he thinks, but she does not love him. And he does not trust her. The moment he sees her, she makes this brutal urgency rise up in his body. With the goddesses, it wasn't their fault that he felt this way. The goddesses taught him the meditations. They tried to love him. But Delilah has no boundaries. What she did to him that night is unstoppable and immediate. It could happen again and again. He sees himself spiraling into a darkness from which there could be no return, and where no love could ever reach him.

Yet she needs him. In his heart, he feels almost certain of this. He could pull her out of that darkness.

"Where do you come from?" he asks slowly, when she still doesn't move. Maybe if she talks, he will begin to come closer to her, and she will trust him. "Where did you come from, before the desert?"

"It doesn't matter. I can never go back."

"Neither can I." He looks at her meaningfully, hoping she'll remember what she said to him before, about going back where he came from—the unfairness of that demand.

"The City," she says, after a long pause.

"What is the City?"

"It's where human beings are kept."

"Kept?" He's feeling cruel, wanting to turn the knives of each careless thing she said back into her. "Like pets?"

"Like slaves," she says firmly. He sees he cannot hurt her that way, the way she hurts him. She is too hard. She squats again now, letting her legs open to the fire, casually inviting. There is a tiny hole in the crotch of her jeans. All he can see there is blackness. He watches her. He wants her to look at his body. He wants her to love that part of him, that important bulge in the costume he made.

"So—you escaped? From slavery?"

"I hope so."

"Do you have a mother?" Where that came from, he doesn't know. He feels dizzy with the longing she makes in him, like a curse of desperation she lays over him. He needs to get inside her. He needs to understand her.

"Somewhere."

"Don't you care where?"

"Not really."

"Do you have—a father?" What does this mean? Something else he has never asked himself.

"Dead."

He hesitates. "What *is* death? I mean—"

"I don't know, I haven't been there," she interrupts, her voice impatient, almost bitter, as if death is a place someone went without her and didn't invite her along.

She is never going to look at him. He lays his body closer to the ground, holding himself up on one elbow. He wants to press her body against his, rub it on himself like warm honey. He can feel the power in his arms, the way they will melt her against him.

"Delilah," he says with difficulty, unable to move. "Come here."

She shakes her head, still not looking at him, and makes a sound that seems like laughter, but he isn't sure.

How can she understand him? She is the opposite of him. How long has she lived here alone, without company, without words, without touch?

"Aren't you lonely?" he asks.

"None of your business, and no."

They are silent for a moment while he thinks, but his thoughts are caught between his legs, weighted down by this endless urgency. He closes his eyes, anxiously closing his mind around the memory of those serene white faces, that cool fountain, those guileless flowers. He tries to hold onto the images but they're all catching on fire. The white gowns aflame, the petals aflame.

When he finally opens his eyes again, breathing a little harder, it's because he cannot believe she is still there, not telling him to leave, but still staring into his fire. In her waiting there, in her long silence, he tries to believe he hears something like kindness, or at least interest.

"Why do you live out here?" he asks softly.

She shrugs. "Things are simpler."

"What do you mean? Please. I want you to talk to me. I want—" But he stops himself.

She turns her face away, so that it is hidden in shadow. He hears her sigh, or did he imagine it? "I guess you don't know unless you've grown up in the City," she says. "But you could have anything there. There was too much. I started to hate it—how easy it was to get things, to have things, and none of it mattered."

She looks right at him now and lifts one corner of her mouth. "How's that? You don't know what I'm talking about, do you, Dragon?"

He senses her vulnerability but does not understand it, and does not know how to answer.

"Dragon," she whispers, and when she says his name again he feels that she has taken him secretly onto her tongue. "An hour's walk from here, there's a mound of trash so big, as big as a building. It's just things that people used once, or maybe never used at all. People have so many things, they don't know what to do with them. Someday the things will take up the desert—will take up the whole world. There'll be no more room for people, for fire, for making love."

Her voice is so quiet he can barely hear it. He wonders if she will cry. Maybe she is lonely, after all. Isn't she? Doesn't she have to be? She's looking into the fire again. His mind grasps at this moment, searching for a way in.

"Did you have a lot of things?" he asks helplessly, not understanding.

She laughs. "No, but I knew how to get what I wanted. I could always get what I wanted. I'm good at that." Then she smiles at him, and he knows she's thinking of the way she stalked him in the sand while he slept, and he starts to lose himself—loses track of what she's saying. But she keeps talking now.

"Some other kids and me—we used to make bonfires in this abandoned lot, burn random shit just to watch it burn. Didn't matter what it was— trash, books, food, dead things, maybe even a few live things. It didn't matter because it was all the same to us. Nothing had any meaning. Could've been things I'd worked hard to steal, but they didn't matter to me once I had them. I'd sit there in front of that fire, like I'm sitting here now, only I'd have something in my hand to play with—anything, maybe just a stick or a piece of paper—that I could hold into the fire and watch it burn, watch it turn to ash, watch the flame creep up to my finger. We were so fucking bored. With each other. With everything." She pauses, slices her hand through his fire, leaves it hovering in the air for a moment. "Here in the desert, if I had something to burn, it would be so precious I would save it for when I really needed fire. That's what I mean by simple. In the City there are too many things. Even if you're poor and starving, you have too many things, all around you, and after a while none of them have any meaning. None of them can help you."

She looks up suddenly. "But I guess nothing is useful to you," she says, leaning her weight on one arm as she eases onto the ground, giving him that tantalizing little grin over her raised, bare shoulder, "because you're a god and you don't have any needs."

"Yes," says Dragon, his voice tangled in his breath. "I do." Pieces of her words crawl over his body. *Something in my hand to play with…*

But she ignores the lust in his voice. Now she is distant again, and now he wants her—wants her despite everything, despite the goddesses, despite his fear. He will forget everything, everything in that hot release….

"But not for things," she says.

Dragon cannot speak. He thinks he can smell the meat as she licks her fingers, oily and rich like her body. He wants to eat what she eats, to devour whatever it is that gives her life, to devour her.

But the fire is finally dying, slowly and without fanfare, almost without being noticed.

"I want you to leave," she says suddenly. To his horror, she stands up and wipes her hands on her jeans in a dismissive motion.

"Delilah," he manages. He can feel that horrible darkness filling him again, the darkness his mind disappeared inside the night he was cast out of the garden, and when Delilah overcame him that day, and when he took her in his arms again and ripped her clothes. He can feel it rolling over him, turning him inside out—his eyes blurring, his voice like hot water in his throat.

"What?" she says.

"You don't love me."

"*Love* you?" She wrinkles her brow as if he has just suggested a game she doesn't know. "I don't even know you."

He stares at her, his pain a weight that crushes his voice, his eyes dry and cracking inside his skull. He is crawling against the bottom of the earth in misery, unknown to himself, so crushed beneath his own feeling that he feels nothing....

"Don't sulk," she says. "I live here, and I want you gone. It's that simple. I don't want some pathetic needy little boy following me around."

Then fire shoots out of him. He doesn't even know where it comes from. His mouth, his hands, his heart, his penis—he doesn't know. He only knows that it catches the loose ends of her shirt in its blaze, and that—casually, without taking her eyes from him for more than a second —she wraps the cloth around it and smothers it.

"Look," she sighs. "I can't give you what you need. And you can't give me what I need. I just know that. I just know, okay?"

"No," Dragon shakes his head.

She laughs. And he wishes that she were afraid, but he can see that she is not afraid of anything. Maybe that's why he only lies there, ready, knowing she would take him instantly if he could only follow his urge forward, and yet unable to move. She is too easy. It frightens him.

Already she is walking away.

She is not at all what he knows or believes woman to be. Yet he knows this little oasis by the pink caves is where he will stay for a long time to come.

Inside her cave, Delilah spreads her legs and thrusts both hands down her shorts without bothering to pull them down. Her fantasy begins with Dragon's erection, growing longer while he tried to ignore it, demanding, as if it would break through the ridiculous disguise of the rainbow pants he wore. She would have taken him again, even though she had told herself she wouldn't, even though he stayed in her territory, and she needed him gone. The fear is so strong—of not knowing when she'll be touched again, when she'll feel someone inside her again. It is impossible for her to say no to something she wants, and she always, always wants this. Always.

But then his eyes kept speaking of that other hunger, and he kept crooning about how the fire was for her, and he kept talking about love—and he wanted to talk, like he wanted to be her friend. All of that makes her sick inside, and she wishes she hadn't said so much, and even now, it stops her hands, as the urgency drains out of her. His weakness irritates her. His confusion irritates her. She saw how badly he wanted her, and she saw how he didn't give in, and it was all because of some lofty ideal he has in his head. She can see that. She sighs, her fingers tired.

She wanted him that day he came striding across the sand with his body shining gold, his muscles swinging easy, unafraid and sure. He was a man that day. But she has not seen that man again since. And she doesn't want to deal with all the pain he brings, and that heavy, heavy male anger that has no expression, that she knows so well.

She hates him being out there. She hates that, when she goes out again, she will have to notice where he is and avoid him.

She hates that she let him see where she lives. She knew from the beginning that was a mistake.

Lonely and her horse pass another seven days through easy fields, keeping the sound of the river always close enough to hear. Lonely spends hours just gazing at the sky, rocking in the horse's rhythm and losing herself in dreams of her beloved. Birds fascinate her, though she does not understand them; they imply that this open land is only a step upward into the sky.

She doesn't know that the hawks, flying, are looking for something to eat down on the earth.

The sun is always shining, and the horse seems content being a horse, allowed by Lonely to tear casually at the grasses as he goes. She feels safe with her body connected to his. She finds it easier now to talk to him, to press him with her thighs or her hands to keep him going the way she wants to go. She sets her direction always toward the mountain now. At night, in her sleep, the rhythm of the horse's walk still throbs hot in the seat of her body, in tune with the rhythm of the cricket-song, and the wind flutters the slick cloth of her dress against her hips, and she turns restlessly in her sleep.

Many nights she doesn't sleep at all but lies awake, feeling the lowness of her own body against the ground. As long as she keeps her eyes open, she can see the space around her, not frightening but freeing, and when she looks up at the fountaining stars, she can imagine that she is lying again in her bed at the top of the tower, seeing the universe for the first time. More and more the fronds of the tall grasses shiver white over all the hills, as the moon blooms bigger and gathers them in its light. When she sees that youthful curve of moon cupped in space, she forgets the curse the old woman attached to it, and she lies surrendered beneath its light, feeling that some wild magic grows inside her—a great adventure of the heart that she has only begun.

How much further—how many days and nights—will the distances keep spinning out ahead of her? How big is the world?

But as soon as she closes her eyes, she can feel the darkness beneath her, and the horse and all other things tower above her, and the open space creeps over her and smothers her with its unknowns. The hills rise up, and she feels she will drown in their depths. She remembers the dark places from her father's dreams. She does not know where they are, but she fears that when she least expects it, they will suck her down. The face of the old hag lurks beneath the ground of her dreams.

You're crazy, the wind taunts her, *thinking the wind is talking to you.*

And when she finally sleeps, she dreams again and again of the darkness below the tower, whatever it is, and in her dreams she wanders that darkness alone, hearing the weak and tormented sound of her father's voice calling out to her—but unable to find his body, dead or alive.

Those nights that she cannot sleep, or wakes again and again from nightmares, are the longest nights. They are longer than the days. Sometimes they feel longer than the whole of her life in the tower, which she is already having trouble remembering.

One morning as she rises, her mind ragged from the long hours of fear, she tears the bottom of her skirt impatiently to free up her legs for riding. Something moves at her feet, and she sees an animal like a lost piece of river flowing away from her through the tall grass. When she searches for it, the snake pauses its waving motion and considers her with one eye. She can feel him watching her, though he does not turn his head. He has no arms, no legs; he is like an arrow toward some purpose, but an arrow that curves.

"How do you move?" she asks in desperate wonder. "How do you move with no legs?"

my movement is inside. my limbs are inside me, answers the snake, his answer coming warily through the earth as a vibration into her feet. He stays frozen there, waiting to see what she will do.

"But why?"

to be closer to the Earth. i caress the Earth. the Earth moves like this…. And he flows away like energy.

All that day she thinks of the snake—how he did not need a horse or even feet to carry him over the earth. She remembers his body like a single loose muscle, and wonders what it would feel like in her hand. She feels his movement, wriggling up and down her spine, and imagines his cool skin against her own. That night, when she lies down, she is not afraid to be close to the earth, for she feels the snake's ease against it and his body's loyalty to it. Inside the cold ground she remembers for the first time the nourishing warmth of that bed that cradled her all through her childhood, which seemed made of earth and was her only home. For the first time, she asks herself where it came from—and also where she came from. Her dreams are full of the earth, its deep heart not dense and hard but open and breathing. Her mind dissolves into it, the way the tower dissolved into nothing, into this new, vivid Life.

The moon rolls slowly around her dreams, and when she wakes she is staring right at it. It is not yet a complete circle but still an undefined whiteness. She watches it tuck into the horizon, into the other side of the world, and though she cannot yet picture the shape of the world, she feels it now in her body. She feels how the moon, like the sun, will come back. She feels the shape of returning. She feels how the moon, like she herself, loves the earth, is held fast to it, and will never leave it. And now she is touching herself, caressing parts of her body that have no name, and it feels to her that she is also touching the moon, and that the magic of her touch turns the hills to song. She closes her eyes at the crescendo and imagines her lover cascading over her like water.

She begins to wake every morning full of her own body, its weight poignant within her, heavy and echoing with song. When the horse goes to the river to drink, Lonely always finds herself thirsty and drinks too. She is humbled by this need, which makes her get down off the easy height of the horse and lower her body against the ground, and try clumsily to gather the water with her hands.

Each day, she listens to the wind, because she has no one else to listen to. She does not trust it, and she will not answer it back, but its voice is becoming familiar. And she envies the way it sings to the grasses, and the way the grasses murmur back.

Grow, First Life, the wind sings to them, in a voice of tenderness it never uses with Lonely. *Good, simple grasses, strong and faithful, make home for the kingdom of insects, make Place out of Nothingness....*

The grasses hold the earth together with the million tiny limbs of their roots—hold it in its springtime expansion, as with the coming warmth the whole planet takes a deep breath in. Their roots interlock like nerves beneath the skin of the earth. The wind plays them like an instrument, and they sing songs of those things the earth can feel: the footsteps of people and animals, and the scrape of human tools somewhere, where men dig deeper into the heart of the earth as if digging for their own hearts. The grasses grow up from the decay of wild things who died in peace, knowing they died in the service of other lives; and they grow up from the decay of human beings who died without knowing why, who lived without knowing why, who never did what they meant to do or spoke what they wanted to say.

The grasses bend easily for the passing of Lonely and the horse, and easily bend back again. They speak of their passing along the path of longing, a path that all living things know and travel. It is a path the grasses make easy, for it is the purpose of living things to seek after what they desire. The grasses rise up for the light, and they feel that Lonely rises in that direction too.

The wind sings to the grasses, and to the horse who does not yet recognize itself. And the crickets sing on, their song flowing beyond the girl and the horse (for the girl and the horse are too big for them to comprehend, too big to matter), with their song which is bigger than anything, which pulses in earth and air and in the sensation of all things, a song of desire which will and must be satisfied.

Soon Lonely begins riding at night as well as during the day, pressing the horse onward, anxious to be somewhere. She watches the moon grow, wondering what it is, wondering what it means. She is brand new to the world, and feels that perhaps it belongs to her alone. She hopes it is a sign of something coming. After all, she did not see it when she woke to herself in the tower. Only now that she is free has it begun to swell.

As they come closer to the serrated edge of the ridge that first separated them from the City, the hill on the other side of them soars into a high cliff, its side naked and dribbling dust, and hems them in close. They enter the passage between the two heights, and the river, which has become a tiny, rock-hidden creek, dives under the earth and disappears. The horse tarries, moodily eating what little grass he can still find, and twitches his ears at the wind.

"Come on," Lonely says, glancing around, unsure. She knows the horse is afraid to lose sight of water, but she wants to know what will happen on the other side of the passage. She slides off the horse's back and walks, looking back and beckoning him onward. But he rears his head and snorts, his eyes frozen.

"Fine," says Lonely, "stay there." For today her body is excited, her heart weary and panting from the hopeless infinity of the fields. Cool sand imprints itself against the curves of her feet as she rounds the bend and emerges into the light to overlook—the desert.

Is this where the wind comes from? It leaps off the ledge where she stands. It flies beyond her. Lonely can hear it roaring all the way into infinity. And looking into that vast canyon of strange shapes, murky with heat, the plants hard as coral and rampant with color, Lonely feels she is about to descend again to the bottom of the sea.

She drops to the ground, steadies herself on hands and knees. As the City tried to pull her in, so does the desert, but differently. It seems the wind is pulling her this time, calling her out into space. Her desire to let go of her body and fly, like the infinity she felt when she glimpsed the mountain from her tower for the first time, is so strong it terrifies her. She must hold to the ground. Her humanness seems to battle with the wind.

But she must go down. In all those mysteries of shadow, among such shapely and colorful living things, surely someone else must be out there? Though she imagines her prince on top of that far mountain, its white peaks only more unreachable the more she travels toward it, right now she hopes she will find someone nearer. She cannot wait for such a long distance. She is so lonely. The memory of Yora's body fills her with sweet exhaustion. She wants to feel finally, for sure, that her body is real to someone other than herself. Perhaps when she descends into this dry sea, a hand will grasp hers as Yora's did in the depths of the water, and pull her up into the salvation of flesh.

Forgetting the horse, she slides through the wind on her bottom in an avalanche of sand, down into the canyon of red and gold fire.

Deep in the green mountains to the east, a girl named Chelya wakes on the earth with a smile. Today is her birthday.

She is up fast; she grabs her blanket and stuffs it under one arm. The trees wave at her from the edge of the field. She hums as she walks, sending her song to the little beings in the grass. The earth sings back to her. She knows how it will be today—everything she touches awakening like magic. It is like this every year. She is so lucky to have been born in the springtime.

This year seems even more alive, even more wakeful than any that came before. Maybe it's because something is changing in the world. She knows her mother is afraid, and her grandmother dreams of anger in the City, but in her bones Chelya feels the coming of joy. She believes in it. People want to be happy. They want to love and remember their world.

Or maybe what she senses is something in herself, some intuition that a new fairy tale, like nothing she's ever known before, is about to enter her own life. Today she is sixteen.

Surrounded by mountains grander and older than all of human history, she pauses amid tiny details to pick flowers on the way to her house, talking to them as she pinches their stems in her fingertips. *For my birthday,* she tells them. She would never hurt them, normally. But she wants to bring her mother something pretty, something to say thank you for giving her life. She thinks about this, pausing for a moment—how in order to give a gift to someone, she has to first ask something to give a gift to her. *It's true,* she thinks. *We don't own anything.* What is giving, but some mysterious will that causes life to move from one being through another?

When she looks up, a man is coming from the forest, his hands out to touch the flowers with his fingertips as he passes. He is heading toward the house, but when he sees her, he turns toward her instead. She is so startled to see someone—it couldn't be her uncle, he just came, so would it be another farmer they don't know?—that she doesn't notice at first the way he is moving, as if his feet touch the earth only by chance. Then she realizes he is a god. Then the sun falls over his face, and he gives her his shy grin, and she sees that it is Moon.

She starts to drop the flowers, and then she grabs them up again, fumbling with them against the tangle of her nightgown. She is already shouting his name as she runs toward him. She flings her arms around his thin body, for she has already grown bigger than him. He's laughing his silent laugh, and his hair is shaggy around his innocent face, like her brother's, but unlike her brother he smells like cold dew or fresh puddles after a rain.

"I haven't seen you in forever!" she cries.

"I'm glad I found you here. I wanted to bring you all some salt, but I wasn't sure if I should go to the door. I might frighten your mother." He's serious as he says this, looking into her eyes.

"Oh," says Chelya quickly. "She loves you, really. We all love you, Moon. And she and all of us, we're so grateful for your gifts. She gets nervous around gods, that's all. My mother is very— But you know how she is."

"Earth people," says Moon, and smiles. "Your family is completely terrified of me. I know. They look at the City, and they see what a mess of things a god can make."

"No." Chelya shakes her head, embarrassed. "Only my mother. My father's much more open. And Kite, he isn't scared of you. He just doesn't—he doesn't believe you're a god, exactly. I mean he doesn't believe in gods at all."

"Yeah," sighs Moon. "I don't believe in gods either."

Chelya looks down and touches her flowers. "But Moon!" she says. "Thank you for the salt. I'm so happy. We have been *dying* for it, I'm telling you. We ran out a long time ago. The goats will be happy, too."

"I'm sorry I couldn't come sooner." He wrinkles his soft, girlish brow. "I didn't even go to the sea for so long."

"Oh, no! I didn't mean to make you feel—" Chelya begins.

But he waves her protests away and takes her by the shoulders, pressing her lightly between his sweet hands. "You look lovely, Chelya. I can't imagine you *dying* for anything. I mean, you always seem so happy with just what you have." He looks wistful.

"But I have so much. And I'm not *always* happy…" She thinks of her brother, how he sulks sometimes and won't talk to her, and of how her mother worries. These things make her unhappy. "But I'm so lucky, Moon." She looks at him, concerned.

"It's true, you're very lucky. You don't know what's out there in the world, how lonely people are, what kinds of things they do…" He trails off. "You're isolated here."

Chelya laughs. "Are you kidding? Isolated from *what?* This is the world, all around me. It doesn't end. There's no fence enclosing me. Everything I connect with connects with everything else. It's the people in the City that are isolated, from what you say."

Moon nods, but he's looking at the ground and doesn't seem to hear her. It suddenly seems to Chelya that he has grown too much older since she last saw him, that his clear kindness and love are confused by something, that he is forgetting who he is.

"Stay a while," she says. "Sleep out in the fields like me and Kite, and we'll talk about things. You never stay. I want to hear about the world! I want to hear about the sea and the desert, and my brother wants to hear, too. It would be good for him. Please."

But she has never known him to stay, never. Why won't he let anyone close to him? Why won't he let anyone know him? She's not surprised when he shakes his head, still not looking at her. "I've been avoiding someone. I have to go."

"Who? Why?" she asks, fascinated.

"Because I love her too much." He laughs and looks at Chelya, his eyes too bright. "You don't understand that, do you?"

Chelya shakes her head. "Not really."

"You're so good, Chelya. You have a good, clear heart. You love people and you act on that love, and it's that simple."

"Oh, I'm not that good," Chelya protests again, feeling awkward. "I mean, I tease my brother sometimes. And I go out on the full moon even though it makes my mother worry, and I don't tell her where I'm going. And sometimes I forget my chores because I'm distracted by… things."

"I'm sorry," says Moon, and she can hear the leaving in his voice. "I keep making you defend yourself. I didn't mean to." From seemingly nowhere, he produces a sack of sea salt, and she slings her blanket over her shoulder and takes it in her arms, still gripping the flowers in one fist. "Have you got it?" he asks.

"Yeah," says Chelya. The weight of it feels good, settling her into the warm reality of the day. She feels her feet sink slightly into the earth. She imagines a body of water so big that all this salt weighs nothing inside it. No one could ever cry enough tears, or run enough distance to sweat this much salt.

"Bye, Chelya," he says, grinning, and she feels happy again, loving him. "And happy birthday."

"Bye, Moon," she says. She stands still with the sack of salt until he begins floating away. Then she turns back toward the house. She feels like she's carrying a weight of tears. There is a secret message in that weight that she wishes she could decipher. She wishes she could take the real burden from his small, ethereal form, whatever it is, and toss it to the winds.

As she walks back, the sky covers her with grey musing, and she can smell rain coming. What a gift on her birthday, to have the sky make love to the earth for the first time since the melting of the snow.

That night the white horse hangs his head by the end of the river, unwilling to go after Lonely, and knowing he cannot go back.

Why don't you go with her? the wind asks him.

I'm just a horse, says the horse. *She doesn't belong to me.*

Go back then, says the wind, without feeling.

The horse is silent.

You are not just a horse, the wind adds. *And you know it. You are somebody's soul.*

The heat battles Lonely's flesh. She takes off her dress and carries it like a loose rag in her hand, its tattered edges dragging in the dust, and she follows the broken line of a winding ridge down to the bottom of the canyon.

It takes all day.

Sometimes the earth is hard, and sometimes helpless and soft as her own strangely smooth skin which mesmerizes her now in its nakedness. The sun swings recklessly across the sky, hurtling its rays at her, pressing her down so that she must stop to rest on random outcroppings and sleep beneath its weight. Being part goddess, she does not die, but each time she wakes, her mind is hazier. By the time she reaches the bottom of the canyon, she has forgotten the mountain. She has no direction.

Then the sun melts over the far cliff she came from, and a shadow swings over her, bringing instantaneous cold. Missing the warmth of the horse's body for the first time, she huddles in a cave, and cannot sleep. Now that the sun has ripped off its heavy blanket of heat, revealing the darkness, she is wide awake. The wind begins to sound like voices.

She doesn't know who the voices are or if they are speaking to her.

Yes, they say, and *No*, and *I'm sorry*, and *I love you*, and *Please*.

They go on into longer conversations that she cannot understand and cannot remember. She wraps her dress back around her and holds her knees against her chest, doubting everything, for it seems that no matter where she goes, her loneliness follows her. When she left the island, she had been so sure she would find her prince. She had thought all she would need to do was cross the sea to the mainland, where the empty loneliness of the tower would naturally find its opposite: color and warmth, life and love. Nothing existed on the island, so everything had to exist on the other shore. But how big this shore is, and how complicated by choices! Wasn't the City the most likely place to find love or at least another human being? That's where all the people lived, she knew that. It seems to her now that she passed it by not because of Yora or her dreams but out of pure fear. What if, in her fear, she avoided the one and only answer?

You trap yourself… The old woman seemed to say that Lonely herself was controlling everything that happened to her, making all the choices. If she makes the right choices, she will bring back her prince and win her freedom, and if she makes the wrong choices, or believes the wrong things, she will fail! She will be Lonely forever, as the old woman cursed her to be.

Listen, says the wind.

"What?" Lonely's voice bursts from her, rushed and trembling. "Are you talking to me?"

Nothing speaks to you. You speak to yourself. You hear what you want to hear. I am only an echo.

Lonely holds her breath, her eyes straining out into the darkness. Somehow she has taken herself far from the colorful live things she saw from high above, and around her now she sees only white earth, pockmarked with holes and scars—bulging with giant earth-flesh as if a great god long ago tossed the desert in his hands, mixed it, and then dumped it in piles of random shape.

She hears a scratching like fingernails and feels a tickle like cold water over her foot. The whites of her eyes glow as she jumps back and looks down. A lizard the size of her finger has scurried over her, and, despite his hurry, he seems to call out to her.

this way. where i am warm.

He is not an eerie voice in the wind, but closer and smaller, a voice with a beginning and an end that she can catch onto and hold, though tinny and distant with the chill of a reptile mind.

She crawls forward, following him into the open to a flat rock that still glows with the heat of the day. She lays her body against it, pressing tight, her face up close to the lizard as he flees to a far corner of the rock and watches her. The rock is low and protected from the wind by smooth pink sandstone that looks almost gentle in the evening light.

where i am warm, says the lizard's body, its stillness watching her. Lonely is comforted, and melts like the sun into a dream. In the dream she feels the lizard dreaming. Most of the lizard's life is stillness, and in that stillness there is room to understand the greater dream of the desert: its caverns the rooms of an ancient sea castle, its hills and turrets still guarded by stately cacti with hard spiked armor. But she feels the warmth fading now, and in her dreams she is running up and down the hills, searching for the lost sun.

"How can you bear the cold?" she asks the lizard.

i am cold.

"I am cold too!"

no, says the lizard. *you only feel cold. i am cold.*

And Lonely understands then that the desert decides the temperature of the lizard. When the desert is cold, the lizard's body becomes cold, and is still and stony like the cold. But Lonely's body is still warm, and the cold hurts it, and it shivers. It fights the cold.

And the voices rise up again in the space of her lone wakefulness, and she feels that the night has gone on forever and will not end.

"Who are you?" she whispers in real fear to the wind.

I am, I am! I am the one! I am strong, I can do it, I am worthy, I am unworthy, I want, I hate, I hurt, help me, I need, I love—

be careful, says the stone beneath her, and Lonely recognizes its still voice, and holds on with her mind and her body to a thin film of reality, as thin as the space beneath the body of the lizard. She listens to the depth of the stone which, though it offers no comfort, is sturdy. *do not trust the voices of the desert wind,* it tells her. *they are the voices of lost ghosts, fragments of things people were not brave enough to say, things they regretted. if you listen, you make them stronger. they are desperate.*

And the girl-goddess grips the rock with her human fingers, concentrating on the meditation of the lizard, trying to block out the voices of a loneliness even greater than her own.

Every time Delilah kills an animal, she cries. It's the only time she cries, and it's not the kind of crying that almost destroyed her when she walked into the desert for the first time, leaving behind the only world she knew, a world she hated. This crying is quiet, but still the tears bewilder her as they touch her face, and they still her inside. She never cried before she came to the desert. Nor did she ever have to ask for her life from anyone or anything that she respected. The tears hurt a little, as if her cheeks are made of some fine stone that dissolves at the touch of water, but she feels that she must bear them somehow. It is the least she can do.

It's okay, you don't have to feel guilty, Moon had told her. He would not kill anything himself because he was immortal; if he took life, he said, that life would be trapped forever in some nowhere place, unable to move on. But he told Delilah, *You're part of the cycle of life and death. For you, life is like water. It flows through you, in and out of you, and cycles around again like the rain, and someday the life in you will no longer be in you either. It will be in other forms, just as beautiful. You need to kill and eat to keep the cycle going.*

But it isn't that she feels bad about it. Maybe she cries because of the relief in it, because killing feels so natural to her. Natural and painful at the same time. When an animal falls from her arrow, she runs to it, kneels by it, and looks hard into its blazing eyes. It's the way those eyes look back at her that makes her cry, as if the animal recognizes who she really is, someone she herself does not wish to see. The animals know she is a killer. They know she is someone so driven by desire she will stop at nothing to fulfill it.

Moon once told her about a tradition long forgotten, where the hunter takes the warm heart from the animal after killing it, and eats it. But she could never do that. She buries it in the ground instead, wherever the animal falls. Surely the earth knows better than she does what to do with someone's heart. She barely knows what to do with her own, and is sometimes surprised that it knows how to keep beating, day after day, with no help from her.

For a long time she never killed anything big. She has seen the signs of bears in this forest, but would never dream of going after one. Too dangerous, and she'd end up wasting most of the meat. It took her so long to learn how to dry leftover meat without it spoiling, and even then there was the problem of bringing the animal's body home to her cave, and then removing the remains.

When she first went hunting for boar, she was so excited, so agitated, she didn't even think how she would get it home. She didn't think about what would happen after she'd gotten what she wanted. She knew only that she fell in love with those hefty, brutal swine, following and watching them downwind, knowing they could kill her as easily as she could kill them. It took her several nights to find them, crawling through the mud after their stampede of tracks, gathering the stiff spears of their hairs from the bark of trees. Moon had recently left her for the first time, and alone in the desert, she'd had a strange dream. It was not a dream of wings and animal movement, as she would have later on, but a dream of long ago, from some other lifetime. She saw a shield with the face of a boar painted upon it, the ancient symbol for warrior, and a knight stood behind it, stoic as a statue with his helmet's visor drawn down. As she approached him there was a ringing of metal and his sword shot out from behind the shield, and then the sword was the white tusk of a boar, its tip thrusting upward in defiance. She'd woken up sweating with desire, her body sizzling with the memory of the man who had betrayed nothing, not even his face, until she was close enough to see his weapon, clean and white and insistent. She had woken up alone, feeling that she could never sleep again.

She spent the night climbing the cliffside and roaming the pine forest, her body beating out the desire through movement. Without Moon's gentleness to temper her, she felt the old fighter in her awaken.

When she got close enough to the boars, she could follow their hot scent, a scent like sweating earth, like sex and death at once. She came to a part of the forest she didn't know, wetter and thicker with trees she did not recognize; breaking through underbrush caked with mud and hair, she came into a clearing that had been flattened completely by heavy bodies. She wanted to wait for them to return and then kill one as it slept, but the brush was too thick for her to see through unless she came very close, and then they would smell her. She feared them, and her fear excited her. Maybe it was her excitement that guided her; maybe hunger itself was her intuition. She kept on, pausing every now and then to listen.

When she found them, near dawn, she had to laugh at the strangeness of dreams, for these sows were the opposite of that stoic male knight in his faceless armor. As they plowed their snouts through the earth, they grunted with the joy of consumption, of *take-what-you-want*, of delicious, greedy, body-driven aliveness. Their short legs seemed only paddles for the forward motion of their mountainous shoulders; a proud mohawk of stiff hair ridged the back of each one, bristling with danger. Sometimes they raised their heads like great ships from the mud and looked right at her, but their tiny eyes could not differentiate her skinny form from the trees. They were not concerned with images; they were all about snorting and roaring and the scent of power, a scent they dredged up from the bottom of the earth. Their bare-skinned noses twisted and wrinkled, as flexible as fingers.

They were led by females: a group of sows with their children and their children's children. Delilah watched them all night from above, straddling the branch of an oak as they gobbled up its acorns in the dirt. All night they wallowed, occasionally rolling in the mud and shimmying their great shoulders into it, crying out from deep bellies. Whenever they moved they looked defiant, their shoulders weighing them forward as if perpetually charging. All night they swatted flies with the tassled ropes of their tails; all night they thrust their heads against each other as they dug in the dirt with their long snouts, their curved, magical tusks flashing in the moonlight.

A memory came to her then of her first day at boarding school, when she was twelve years old and had just lost her father, and the pretty pale-skinned girls had taunted her in their subtle ways. They did not surround her all at once but tossed sarcasm and barbed giggles as they passed her in the constricting halls. At the end of the day her roommate, who Delilah guessed was some semblance of a girl beneath the paste of her makeup, had two friends on her bed with her, doing their hair or something. Delilah was burning up like a caged animal.

Can we call you Lily? one of the girls had asked. *You're so much like a Lily—so fair and lovely.* The other girls laughed into their hands. The roommate said, under her breath, *More like something dragged up from underground.* Then they giggled openly, one of them leaning her face into the other's shoulder where she held the braid she was doing, and Delilah—who still cared then about being loved, whose heart was still raw from the scraping of a shovel over her father's grave—ached at that gesture, the way the girls' bodies could so easily tumble together like that, soft as the layered hems of their skirts.

Lilies grow out of the ground, you idiots, she growled. *There's nothing evil inside the ground. If there was, they wouldn't put dead people in there.*

They let these comments float by them, too complicated to warrant a response. She knew she was smarter than they were, but she envied them anyway.

Why is your skin so dark, Dee—lie—laah? Where'd they drag you in from? Why is your hair like that? Did you get electrocuted?

Her roommate got off the bed and sauntered toward Delilah, her skirt bouncing against her white knees, her curls dazzling in their perfection, as if chiseled out of sunlight. She looked down at Delilah's legs and said, *Why don't you shave your legs, Lily?* But her eyes held fear, and Delilah saw that, and she would always remember it. She punched the girl in the face, and then the face wasn't perfect any more.

Because I'm a warrior, she said. That came from nowhere, saying that, but she meant it. That night, after she got done with detention and the hour-long lecture from the headmaster about how they would give her one more chance, only because her mother loved her enough to advocate so strongly for her to stay in school (but Delilah knew her mother only wanted her and her crazy sister as far away from home as possible), she stood before the mirror in her new, single room, and chopped off her hair.

But the mockery only got worse. When she began fucking any man she wanted, not caring what anyone said, they said she was the dark hag from the sea—the ugly wife of Hanum, the one who dragged men to their deaths when they came seeking the princess. Delilah had never heard of such a person but she did not care to be associated with such a desperate deity. She wasn't desperate. She wasn't needy. She was a warrior. So when she left the City, she turned away from the sea, and headed to where water was sparse and the creatures tough and solitary.

When she first watched the boars, she remembered that question from another lifetime—*Why don't you shave your legs?*—and she laughed out loud, knowing those girls would have shit themselves in terror at the sight of these beasts. It was so hard for her to get how she and those girls could belong to the same gender, or even the same species. Who determined such things? It wouldn't have hurt so much if she had not believed, at the time, that those girls were the only example of womanhood. She hadn't known any better. Now she knew they would never grow up, never stop being girls. They would never come over and over again from the touch of their own hands. And these dark hairy monsters with their weight hurling them forward, the white horns rising from their faces poised to strike, their close sisterhood held tight by raw, primal sounds—these were Delilah's idea of womanhood.

She spent the rest of that night determining whom to kill, or rather, whom she could not kill. She would not kill the matriarchs, with the spiky silver along their backs like the spines of dragons, who held the herd together and made her heart shiver with a more fragile longing that had nothing to do with the hunt, nothing to do with hunger. She would not kill the babies, or their mothers, even though it was autumn and she thought the young ones might survive on their own now.

Around dawn the wind shifted, and one or two of them turned toward her, raising their snouts as if to howl at the moon, frankly questioning the air with their flaring nostrils. She had to act now. She chose a half-grown female who blended in with several others, still oblivious to her, ignoring her, drinking from a little pool. But as she shot the arrow, an old matriarch butted the younger one aside and stepped in front of her, sudden as the sword in Delilah's dream, and tilted her head toward Delilah to take the arrow in the center of her forehead. She fell quietly, and it was Delilah's cry of dismay that scattered the herd. They stampeded past her tree as she clung to it, and then she scrambled down, ripping her only pair of pants on a branch.

The old boar's eyes gripped her, swirling around pain in an attempt to focus, as if trying to tell her something. But Delilah could not—like Moon, like the gods—understand the languages of animals. She could only understand the pain.

"I'm sorry," she cried over and over. But it was herself she was sorry for. No one would stand between her and that pain. No one could make it stop. But the old boar had taken the arrow for the young one, and the young one was saved. There was a reason for that. A reason embedded deep in the communal soul of the boars, a sacred reason that all of them knew. A reason that Delilah could not understand, because no one would ever do that for her. Because she wasn't a part of anything, except her own solitude. Because she had no elders.

Back then, at least, there was no pain in Delilah's body, no exhaustion. She was young and fierce and could live in the desert forever.

She learned to survive. She learned to dry meat in the sun and the wind, and to store it in leather wrappings deep in one of the caves. She learned to clean the animal skins and soak them in the river to make leather—or at least something like it—and her body adjusted to eating almost nothing but meat. That first time she killed a boar, she had to leave most of it behind for the wolves and ravens. She didn't understand its body, didn't know how to take it apart, and she was covered with blood in the darkness, hungry and panicked and ashamed. But she learned. After that she brought sacks with her to carry the meat home. There was still a lot of the animal left behind. But she did the best she could, and she knew it did not go to waste, for there were others who would come after her to scavenge. If it was a boar, she had to take the meat in two or three trips, which might take hours. She was strong back then. Her back never hurt.

Recently, on the last full moon, she killed a male boar. It was spring, and she wanted to avoid the females altogether, in case some of them were pregnant. Besides, she knew the males would be more careless now, their minds blurred by desire. She hunted with confidence, following the dream of a man on his hands and knees with greedy eyes and a black, bloody face. It was the greed she saw in his eyes that reminded her of the boars. And she felt easy hunting a male, for she knew how to hunt men in heat—how helpless they were.

She found him eating, and his face was bloody because it was buried in the gut of a baby deer. Delilah came upon him in a clearing, having smelled him but not realizing how close she was, and they surprised each other. The boar reared his head up with a challenging snort. Delilah forgot herself for a moment, not realizing that boars ate such big meat, wondering if he had found the fawn already dead. She saw his dark shoulders tremble and bulk toward her like a gathering storm, and without thinking she pulled her knife from her belt and slung it at him. She had never been so close before. When it imbedded itself between his shoulder blades, he started to charge her anyway, but she did not run. She didn't move until he fell on his knees in front of her.

Not until he closed his eyes with a shudder and the tears broke her did she feel the ache in her own shoulders, and realize she'd been standing with them pulled up close to her face with her arms lifted halfway into the air, as if preparing to fly away.

For many days afterwards, a tension she could not relieve with her own hands lurked around her shoulder blades. When she let Dragon fuck her that night in the sand, the tension released, but only for a night.

She still eats from the body of that male boar—dried strips of meat that she sliced off in warm blood the night she killed him, hurrying while the ravens waited with restless cries from the tiered branches of the pines. She cooked her first meal of that meat right there in the pine forest.

Maybe it's the boar's spirit inside of her that makes her unafraid of Dragon, who is bigger than her but, she knows, softer. She clutches one of the boar's tusks in her fist while she sleeps, in case Dragon gets crazy in the night and comes after her. It's not his lust that is dangerous, she senses, but rather a desperation that comes from somewhere else, a belief he has that some woman, somewhere, owes him something. She doesn't want him to get her mixed up with that woman, whoever she is.

Not that he could find her anyway, deep in the belly of a cave beneath layers of animal skins and darkness—the mouth of the cave thin, only big enough for Delilah and the bats. She used to sleep so deeply during the day, dissolving into the skins like something that died with them, and loose herself fully to dreams. Back home in the City she slept during the day, too, sneaking back in the morning after her family was gone because she wanted nothing to do with them nor they with her. So the nocturnal life was already natural to her. But lately she has trouble sleeping. She lies awake during the day, while the heat of the sun creeps in, and she tosses to relieve herself of the weight of those animals, and then lies naked and restless. She holds the boar's tusk in her fist, watching it glow just barely in the ever-dark cave.

Maybe it was the fawn already part of the boar that got into her dreams somehow when she ate of his flesh: maybe that's why she still dreams of a deer, every day, and thinks of her while she lies awake. Sometimes she thinks the boar's spirit is whispering to her the story of that fawn, who lived briefly huddled in dappled shadow and died in a confusion of terror and infantile grace. But the memories of these dreams are vague and broken, not solid and lusty like dreams of boars. The story of the deer is some other kind of story that Delilah doesn't understand. Soft, glassy steps. A silence made of spider silk. Their movement as invisible as the coming of night. The fear they chew patiently in their neat, square teeth. The deep, turning cups of their velvet ears. Their modest yet shamefully honest gaze.

She's afraid the forest won't yield up anything else until she's found that deer and killed it. And she'll have to do it, or starve—a doom that has haunted her since she came here.

Maybe it was the tension between her shoulders from that moment when she waited, without wanting to, frozen with her arms in the air, for the boar to take her life as she had taken his with the knife between his shoulders. Maybe it was that tension that somehow spread into her body even after it seemed gone, and sent currents of pain up and down her spine, lodging first in her neck and then later in her tailbone, so that even her hips hurt. It only happens on certain days. On other days, she doesn't think about it.

But when she lies awake she wonders if the pain came as punishment, after all. What if Mira was right not to eat meat? What if that boar was meant to kill Delilah, before she killed him? How many times has she asked herself these questions, and dismissed them, because hunger rules her first and foremost? And how she misses Moon, in whose presence everything made sense.

When she closes her eyes, she sees the deer turning toward her, its eyes soft, but not as soft as forgiveness.

Today it hurts just to climb down the lip of the cave to the spring. Dragon is there, painting strange, white women and luscious, seductive flowers on the sandstone wall with damp pieces of colored stone. She slips a little, distracted by her pain and not anticipating his presence—his ready muscles, his hot innocent eyes turning toward her.

"Are you okay?" he asks. She hears the sweetness in his voice, and it makes her head spin. He's leaning toward her, and his breath sounds wet and clumsy. She can't believe she ever wanted him. She can't believe he is still here.

"Get the fuck away from my water," she says tightly. "This is my home. Get *out!*" She dips her head to the water and begins to drink so fast she almost chokes. Then she looks up and spits a mouthful in his face. "And don't fucking watch me!"

He doesn't look away, just licks the water that landed around his lips.

"Go away!" she screams. "Go away!" She knows now that she can't walk back up to the cave; she's in too much pain, and she'll have to crawl. She ignores the anger swinging in his arms as he rises and turns away. She closes her eyes and tries to breathe.

When she gets back to her cave she tries to find a position that doesn't hurt, where she can look out on the valley and watch the animals appear and disappear through doors of shadow. But her back chooses a position for her, locking her prone to the ground with one arm slung over her head. She tells herself she will feel fine by tonight, when she can hunt by an almost full moon. She feels the weight of the pine forest hanging over her, like death.

In the City, you wake in your bed surrounded by noise. Horns honking, dogs barking, sirens wailing, motors revving, brakes squeaking, people shouting. You wake surrounded by sounds of emergency, anger, and upset. But this is normal. This is what everyone wakes to in the City, and what everyone sleeps to, and what everyone hears all day long, as they attempt to work, think, and love.

The little earthquake is over. The flood waters have receded. Everything is okay now, isn't it?

You think of your upcoming day, a day like every day, laying asphalt for the long, straight road into the hills. What is beyond the City? Space, you have been told: wild, empty space. The City will expand, become greater. Some people say that the god who made this city, who ordered the road built, years ago, is dead. But you don't care. You do not listen to your wife when she goes on about some princess, who must be rescued in order for the magic of the City to survive, who is the City's soul. You know nothing about souls and care nothing for the fairy tales of women and children. What you care about is money to feed your family, because money *is* the magic of the City, the magic that keeps the City alive. Food is manufactured out of money. Houses are built out of money. It is an all-powerful substance that can turn into anything.

Long ago, your mother used to say, food came from the earth. But how could you understand what that means? How could food come from dirt?

Some people say, it was the god Hanum who created money. If Hanum is dead, then money no longer means anything. It's just pieces of paper, which can only mean something if everyone believes in it. But everyone does believe in it. People talk, but no one stops believing, not really. They cannot afford to. Not only because, as far as they know, everything they need to survive is gotten with money, but because money has become the life blood of the City. Money has become the breath, the energy that flows between people—the only thing that touches, uncleaned and unbleached, the sweat of everybody's hands, cycling through life after life like the life force itself. It is the only thing that truly connects you. Without it, you would be alone, floating away into that empty space beyond the City, that nothingness.

You find yourself in the kitchen now, not remembering how you got there. The kitchen is a place of shining surfaces and humming appliances, where food comes from but cannot be seen. You do not eat. You do not drink water. You drink something black to wake you up, to make the headache go away. Your body is a painful nuisance to you.

"If everything is made from money," your daughter asked you when she was a child, "then what is money made from?"

"It is made from trees," you told her distractedly, because that is what you had been told when you were a child.

"What are trees?"

"I don't know," you said.

"They must be great gods," she said, "because they are the ones the magic is made from."

"No," you said impatiently. "Hanum is our God, the one who made the City."

"But I think the trees are gods," she said again, pouting a little. "Because they make the money."

Your daughter never saw a tree. Now she is all grown up, and she seems cold and strange to you. And you wonder why she does not seem to know you, and sometimes you miss that trusting way she used to look at you, when she was a child.

The morning chill wakes Lonely from a thick, dreamless sleep. The air is fresh and empty, cleansed by the death of night's final, blank hour. The sun caresses her. The lizard is gone.

She walks out into the silence. The wind still blows, on and on. Lonely feels changed by it, as the stone has been changed by it over millions of years, her edges smooth and soft. Her skin darkens around the whites of her eyes and her frayed, paling hair. She still feels like a goddess. The fire of the sun does not burn her. She isn't hungry for food. She misses water but can do without it. Her mind feeds on color and light. She wakes herself with the sweet honey of yellow stone and sun, and quenches her thirst with the sight of green plants in the distance.

As she walks among the cacti and little skeleton trees, she begins to feel okay again, surrounded by birdsong. She can tell that what the birds are saying is simple and real; each call is meant for another to hear, and the others are listening and calling back. She doesn't hear any other animals talking, only the birds. They seem to love conversation. And their conversation comforts her with its busy-ness. Other animals whisper in silence and mystery, or cry out when they are afraid, but the birds actually talk around her, all the time. They ground her from the eerie confusion of realities that haunted her during the night; they drown out the memories of wailing, unheard human voices.

Yet even now, when she stops to look at them—for they do not hide themselves, but bounce ever-vigilant from tree to tree in ribbons of flight, arching low near her head and then snapping their wings with bright explosions of blue, red, and yellow—she is lonely. For they seem so much a community, and they spend all morning telling each other who they are and where they are, and what they want and who will answer. They have so much to say to one another, and she has no one to talk to, no one to call her name. The spaces behind the curved arms of cacti or the curtains of the leaves are whole rooms to them, within the mansions of little thickets and the mazes of stone. And she has no home, nowhere to return to, nowhere to keep her safe.

She must walk endlessly upon the ground, and the stony, thorny earth tears at her feet. She never thought about her feet before. She never saw them as having much meaning. Now she sees that they are her only connection to the earth. And they seem so fragile, their pads so thin, their balance nearly unbelievable. The idea of crossing so much space astounds her. Every time she looks up from her feet, the images around her are different, a miracle which both terrifies and excites her. She realizes how little she understands of her own direction, her own destiny. Yet, if she focuses all her mind on the contact of her soles against the earth, one and then the other, she can keep the fear manageable.

In the late afternoon, she comes upon three vultures huddled like old women in great black capes around the carcass of an animal she cannot identify—just an arrangement of flesh and bone. They look at her but do not seem to mind her. When they shift their weight to the side and heft themselves with a brief lift of wings to another part of the carcass, their waddling gait is awkward but huge somehow, and it chills her to see.

"Are you death?" she whispers to them.

not us, they say. *we are only guides.*

"But do you know about death? Do you know where my father went?"

who are you, that we should tell you?

"I loved my father."

then you know where he went.

But Lonely is angry at their riddles. "What do you know," she retorts. "You're ugly. Your heads are naked and wrinkled, like the old woman's." Then she feels afraid, expecting their anger.

our heads are naked, because when you look into the face of death, you must do so with honesty. you cannot try to cover yourself, or make yourself more than you are.

Lonely stares. They keep ripping at the flesh until it is no longer recognizable as flesh.

"How do I know I'm alive?" she whispers now, as a new fear occurs to her.

"How do I know I'm real?"

we know. we can smell you.

"What is smell?"

smell is taste before you can taste it. smell is longing. smell is something changing. smell is how animals talk, and how death calls for its release. They say all these things at once, at the same time, without any words.

Lonely sniffs the air where she stands, and the smell of the carcass says, *leave me alone. i am being undone. leave me alone to feel the pain of letting go.* And so she leaves, but as she does she keeps watching the sky where the vultures float and tilt on towers of heat, and they look beautiful, and she thinks wistfully, *How easy! How far away death is!* But she doesn't understand it, because she does not yet understand what life is.

Rounding a corner, she sees two men tying her horse to a tree.

She shrinks behind a rock, her heart shaking in its shadow. Instinctively, she pulls her dress down over her. Then from her crouched position, she tilts her head to see them, keeping the white of her face hidden from the sun. In her dizzy vision she tries to pull the pieces of information together. Wide solid backs and hairy cheeks like her father's, but eerily unknown faces, human yet unfamiliar. Their hands act instead of feeling; their movements are efficient and forceful and quickly over.

Lonely feels strangely still inside. Their bodies look fast and harsh, with no way in, and their scent speaks a language her own body does not seem to know. She does not remember now the way her body burned against the back of the horse, dissolving her like smoke up into the sky; she does not remember now how her body became the moon when she touched it, and turned the hills to song—or the fantasy of love washing over her. She does not remember the brush of the grasses against her toes, or the caress of the wind. These beings before her are nothing to do with any of that. Her body does not recognize them, and her heart beats fast, saying only, *danger.*

"We'll find some way to tie him to the truck on the way back," says the older one. "How do you like that? A treasure already, and we haven't even started digging. Someone'll buy 'im. Show horse, maybe. What's he doing out here in the fucking desert though? Didn't think horses lived in the desert."

"Shouldn't we leave him some water?" asks the younger one.

"Good point. Wouldn't do much good to us dead. Not that we can spare any." The man places a tray of water at the horse's feet. "Wish they'd finish that damned road so we wouldn't have to drive out over the sand. Takes so damned long, even without a horse to pull along with us."

Lonely was so shocked she did not even notice the vehicle, which they climb back into now as if climbing onto the back of a nervous, unwieldy creature. It is still until they touch it, and then it shakes and roars as if in agony. She feels for it, because it looks even lonelier than she is—its lines simple and stupid, not fitting with the reticent complexity of the landscape, not fitting with the silence. *How awkward it must feel*, she thinks.

Then it bumps and bumbles away, swinging around the rock formations, quickly out of sight but leaving a violent sound and a burnt stench in the air. Lonely is lost in these sensations until it disappears. Then she stands up trembling and goes to her horse, who has begun to drink the water.

"How did you let yourself get caught?" she asks him as she unties him. The horse doesn't answer but hangs his head and presses it to her knee—an intimate gesture that he has never made before. He lets Lonely climb on.

She rides holding tightly to his mane. She cannot stop thinking of the men, and her own relief at leaving them behind worries her. Wasn't *man* what she came looking for? But they terrified her. She remembers the nightmares in the tower now and wonders if her prince was not a man after all, but something different, something gentler.

"I'm sorry that I left you," she whispers to the horse, more to comfort herself than him. "But how will you find water?" she adds with sudden fear, remembering the thing the vultures surrounded—the thing that was once an animal. She remembers what the men said about leaving the horse without water.

the river is here, says the horse.

"What?" says Lonely. She is surprised somehow. The horse has never spoken to her before this. Did she imagine it? For the first time, she wonders how she knows when an animal is speaking to her. Was it the ripple of skin that twitched along his spine? Was it the gesture of his head toward the green life around them? Was it the smell of his aliveness, as if his blood was singing through him, calling to the water with its own full, wet life?

If he spoke before, he does not speak again, not that Lonely can perceive. But he begins to follow a trail of green through the desert. Flowers bloom from almost every cactus and from between the stones, their delicate colors saying over and over, *water is love.*

And Lonely knows that somewhere under the earth, the river must still run, and somehow they will meet it again.

Yora dissipates in the sky, a ghost of water, a dream of water—water forgotten. Water was not enough. Love was not enough. She could not love people into wholeness again. She did not have enough love to purify them. She has failed, and she cannot bear the weight of their suffering any longer.

So she dissolves. She loses herself in the sky of forgetting.

And yet the weight remains. She cannot remember herself, but the weight of their suffering remains, and she cannot forget that. She has no body with which to resist it. It gathers her together again, and her particles attach to the minute dust of their suffering which still rises out of their factories and into the sky. She darkens and contracts into a heavy, brooding cloud.

"You're going to break, Sister," Moon says, watching her from a mountaintop. "You can't drift like that forever. That pain is a birth that has to come, sooner or later." But he won't force her. Water doesn't use force, and it is not forced. Water simply follows itself, freed by heat today, following gravity like longing tomorrow. What can it do but flow?

She doesn't answer. Moon blows a breath out to her, a warm wind to carry her along, to soothe her for a while before she'll have to return to the earth. He would help her but that isn't his job any more. All he can do is pause here, arrested by her beauty, the mysterious fog of her silence. He could look at it all day: the white unattainable tears pouring into oblivion, inside that gray cloud. He could listen all day to the pale, wailing melody he hears inside its silence.

He closes his eyes and quietly covets that melody, tries to imagine what tears feel like—where they come from in the body.

For he must go now. He must rise and then descend into the rainless desert, with nothing to give, and Delilah will try to get him to live again. He will say he cannot—but maybe, really, he just doesn't want to. Dutifully, because she deserves it, he will submit to her love, but he won't be able to feel it. And even for Delilah, he doesn't know how many more times he can bear to go through that.

Every evening Delilah wakes from a dream in which the deer looks pleadingly into her eyes, and every evening she is angry. Angry like she hasn't felt since before she came to the desert, angry for no reason. She has an endless supply of anger, like a thick well of acid beneath her breast bone that seeps drop by drop into her day.

One day she wakes before sunset with tension gripping her shoulders, a ringing pain traveling the length of her neck up into her head, from a nerve caught and stretched to the limit. Impatient with it, she writhes on her back, hurls off the animal skins, and arches her neck.

When she opens her eyes, she is looking into the face of a rattlesnake.

They've come through here before, leaving their winter sleeping places in the stone and traveling through thin, secret passageways, through the wind-hewn cavern where Delilah makes her home and out into the desert to hunt for the summer. Generally, they seem to know her, and pass by her in peace. But this one has reared up as if to attack, its face stretched into a grimace like some ancient ritualistic mask, its startling, limbless torso swaying in space, its tail echoing against the cave walls. The snake's body is nothing but spine, and its rattle sends shivers of pain up Delilah's.

"Oh, come on," she whispers, pulling herself up on her elbows. The snake's face is inches from her own, but she tells herself she is not afraid. "I'm not bothering you."

But the rattle continues, a vibration in her mind that is no longer a sound but a trance that overtakes her, blurring her sense of self until the rattlesnake's eyes and flat gaping mouth are all she can see. Not fully awake yet, not fully in control of her mind, she feels the mirroring between the snake's tall body and her own spine. She feels the pain, not sickness but pure lightning, running upward from her tailbone to her skull, as the snake rocks ever so slightly back and forth.

Then the snake falls, melting into pure grace and—in the same motion— flowing away. While Delilah watches, it turns back to her once more, its body fat and long, its scales grating dryly against the stone. She thinks it is very old, bigger and longer than any snake she has ever seen, its tail still rattling beside her even as its head silhouettes against the cave entrance.

It goes, but in that strange way it turned back—a gesture so human, so unlike the tendency of a snake—Delilah, though feeling childish, feeling embarrassed, cannot help but see something like a call to follow.

She watches it go. She believes absolutely in the wisdom of animals. But she also believes it is a wisdom she does not have and cannot understand, because she is human. She sits up and shakes herself, rolling her shoulders. She crawls to the entrance and looks for the snake but it is gone. Instead, she sees Dragon on the sand below her, sitting cross-legged in the spot where she first seduced him. She can't stop looking at him because with his straight spine and his concentrated, wide-open eyes, he reminds her of the snake when it reared up before her. His erection stands up almost parallel to his body. And that irritates her, as if he's in league with the snake, as if he knows something she doesn't.

He doesn't look at her as she comes down and circles around him like a hyena, breathing her anger at him. "What are you doing?" she says finally.

Dragon opens his mouth and a flame shoots out, lands on the sand, and keeps burning. He turns to her.

"I'm learning to concentrate my desire and pull it upward."

Delilah stares at him. Her head is throbbing. "What for?" she snaps.

"So I can turn it into a different kind of power," he answers, and his voice takes on that quality of low, ridiculous serenity.

She keeps staring. She wants to ask what and why, but doesn't want to give him the satisfaction of her curiosity. She sees him more self-contained now, ringed neatly and confidently within a circle of concentration that she has not seen before.

He smiles at her. "So far, I've only got it up as far as my heart. But I think that's still important, don't you?"

"No," she says, but her voice comes out softer than she meant it. He feels so far away from her now, and that distance draws her, in spite of herself.

His little flame sizzles and dies. "You don't know. You don't want to know. Look at you. Look at the way you're hunching your shoulders. You've got them so tensed up, trying to hold in your heart. Why don't you let it out?"

Delilah laughs and saunters toward him. She doesn't know why she does it. Because he pisses her off, maybe, or just because she can. Or because she can't stop watching the way his erection nods toward her, how it speaks to her in secret, the way they always do, and she cannot help but answer. She walks slowly, watching his eyes get dizzy as she fills them, holding their gaze tightly in hers as she kneels simply before him and runs a finger up from the base of him, up along that hard vein.

Only when he leaps up at her touch and steps back does she realize the force of her own desire.

"You don't know shit about my heart," she snaps, just to say something back—to cover for this position she's in now, kneeling before him. She scrambles back to her feet, her hands ashamed.

"Sit with me, Delilah," he says, gently this time. "I'll show you a better way—"

She turns around fast and leaves.

At the water hole, she rinses her face, swallowing panic. She will ignore him from now on, and then eventually he will leave. She will not waste her time on him. Why did she—? How could she—? But she stops herself from thinking, to stop her own fury.

She has no dreams by which to hunt tonight, besides the one that is always there now. So she will go to the river and bathe, and wash the few clothes she has left. She will pick some of the cactus Moon taught her to harvest—another of the few plants she feels close to, hard and thorny like herself. She will look for more dry sticks, for whenever she does make her next kill, she will need more tinder for her fire. She can never have too much of it on hand.

Surely she will have another dream soon, a dream that tells her which animal to hunt next, so she'll have food when the boar's meat runs out. It is already running out. It will only last a couple more days. And what then?

What if the dreams she's come to count on abandon her, leaving her to starve? When she leans down to the pool to drink, she looks again into the deer's insistent eyes.

The next day, Delilah does not dream at all. Tomorrow is the full moon, and she must hunt, dream or no. She wakes up almost pain-free. But she's tired for no reason, her body shaky with weakness when she stands. She eats a little meat, but it doesn't help. It makes her nauseous. She ignores this. Walking will help, and breathing the night air.

She follows the moon out onto the playa, a dry field of mud where the invisible river opens up into an invisible lake, and she makes circles with the wind, thinking of the snake. She knows she has to listen to the animals. Besides Moon, they are her only true friends. She feels that the snake was telling her something, but whenever she tries to think of it, Dragon's image interrupts, and that infuriates her.

The playa's hardened mud whispers of water; the edges around its dry cracks are sharp on her feet. She misses Moon with a pain so strong that it, too, feels like anger. Where is he, and what is he doing to himself that makes him forget her, forget the desert? She knows he would be able to help her. Simply being with him would heal her.

But she cannot predict when he will come. Sometimes he is gone for over a year. It used to be he always came with the rains. Now the rains don't always come. Or they come without him. Like he doesn't remember, any more, who he is.

Suddenly the playa begins to vibrate like the dry skin of a rattler's tail, and she looks out toward the City, her whole body flushing. There's a truck coming, one that can travel over rough terrain. It stops some distance from her, just close enough to enter the realm of her vision.

In the moonlight, she can see two men dismount and begin to unload their things, laying out sleeping rolls for the night. She wants to laugh out loud.

She sees them first, as always. Of course, they are going to bed down right in the path of potential flash floods, knowing nothing of the land they've come to dig up and brutalize. It doesn't matter any more whether it's the rainy season or not: floods come at random. For a moment Delilah hates them, and hopes the river will wash them away.

Then she walks toward them.

She's aware of her body again, but in a different way. She is not self-conscious. She has no idea what she looks like any more, and she only keeps herself clean for her own sake, and to keep from being noticed by the animals. Her magic is a force that unfurls from inside. It is easy. It is simply her own desire, set free.

As she approaches them, the darkness becomes like water that she wades through, swinging her hips, trailing her fingertips across its invisible surface. She breathes into her chest, lifting her breasts, and begins to smile. She walks straight at them, both of them kneeling on the ground by now, and takes her time, watching their expressions of surprise. The older one, maybe in his mid-thirties, has a long, narrow, office-man's face, with a stern chin grown stubbly, and hard, skeptical eyes. He is obviously in charge. The younger one, hardly more than a teenager—a brother or a nephew but not a son, not the way the older man is ignoring him now—is slim and effeminate, with big eyelashes and long hair curling at the tips across his face and brushing his serious, open lips. He reminds her a little of Moon. He is looking lower than his older brother, his eyes unabashedly fixed on Delilah's body.

"Could I have a little of that?" she asks, sitting down on the sand across from them. The older one freezes with his fork in a can, but after a moment of tense silence, the boy rushes forward to hand her another can, unopened. She can smell his heat as he leans over on his knees, supporting his body with his other hand. She can smell boy loneliness in that heat, the uncleaned smell of a boy's bedroom with one poster on the wall and a single mattress on the floor floating like an island in cluttered space. She can imagine his whole life in a moment.

She holds the can in her hand, smiling, until the boy, still shocked, seems to remember himself and rushes forward again with a can-opener. He kneels beside Delilah with innocent yet nervous familiarity and opens it for her, his hands shaking. The man has not moved. Delilah opens her mouth to breathe in the nearness of the boy's body. He hands her a fork.

"Who the hell are you?" the man asks finally.

"Who the hell are you?" Delilah answers politely. "I live here."

The man pauses. Then, "You're that demon woman. The one they talk about." Of course. She watches his eyes widen and sighs. She stands and climbs up onto their vehicle so they can watch her, and she them. She stretches her legs wide with each movement across it, reaching down between them to steady herself, and then sits finally with knees open.

"That's right," she says.

The young one shoots a glance at her face, and she throws him a deep smile that makes him look down uncomfortably. Shy. She loves shy.

"But who are you really?" the boy presses, looking more concerned than afraid. "Are you lost? Are you okay?"

"Well," says Delilah, trying not to laugh, "I'm okay, but it's been so long since I've seen a man out here." She closes her legs, opens them again. Waits.

Now there is dead silence, uninterrupted. She eats while she waits for them to get used to her. She can hardly taste what she's eating; she can hardly even identify it as food.

"What are you guys doing out here?" she asks finally, counting on the boy's eagerness even if his older companion stays wary.

The boy glances at the other. "It's something my brother did, when he was my age. Went out and drilled the caves for dragon—for gold, I mean. It's mostly gone now, but we're going anyway, just to see what we can find, just to…" He trails off, shifting uncomfortably.

"Just to prove your manhood, brave the darkness and all that?"

The boy looks down, shrugs.

Delilah glances into the compartment beside her, sees the enormous lights and explosives, the heavy equipment. "Could be dangerous," she tells them. "There are sounds sometimes, down there. Maybe the dragons are still alive."

The older brother grins now, and she knows he's laughing at her, but the boy says, "Have you been in the caves?"

"I live in the caves," says Delilah.

"What are they like?"

"They're like this," she says, but she's looking at the older one as she slides onto the sand again, and pulls her shirt off fast. A few paces more, and she is kneeling. Not ready to look at him yet, she runs her fingertips over his thighs. She's missed the heavy feel of men's jeans. "Do you want to know what the caves feel like?" Again she has to keep herself from laughing from her own sheer power.

"You—" the man coughs, his voice seeming to come from far above her. "I'm a married man. Get away from me." His voice is dry and slow, caught between breaths, like someone dying of thirst.

"I thought you were brave. Why do you sound scared?" she asks. It's true. As if he is terrified now of what he's about to do, certain there is no way to stop himself.

"I'm not going to hurt you," she assures him. "I'm going to help you." He doesn't move as she reaches between his legs and cups the warmth there in one hand. She feels such tenderness for men's erections, constantly needing to be hidden away and subjugated to the reasoning mind, pressing endlessly against pant legs with their silent, instinctual plea.

Lying back, she looks finally up into his eyes, and finds him waiting there, behind his words.

He lasts a good long time, and she lets him take her in every position he can think of, listening to the younger one gasp beside them. When he's on top of her, she lets his eyes—so heavy with unspoken longings—fall into hers; she makes her own eyes into endless depths, knowing this desperate looking is part of his release. When she's on top of him, she tells him to touch her, and he touches her as if he's never touched a woman before, as if he can't believe his eyes. Then, after his eyes have poured out all their anguish, he flips her around and drives his anger into her, and she welcomes it because she knows its language, and she drives her anger back. Then he starts to cry, and then he comes, and while he comes he, too, laughs.

As usual, Delilah doesn't come. In high school she was known among girls and boys as the most sexual, not some easy bimbo who was too dumb to know better, but the most horny, the most seductive, the girl who craved sex and thrived on it. Girls assumed she came repeatedly with every lay, and she did not correct them. Guys didn't really care, or else they assumed they were making her come when she cried out in general ecstasy, and never bothered to ask. She didn't pretend for them though. And she tried not to care much. Even though she loved boys, she loved them in an obsessive, emotionless way, and it was her dance with herself against them that gave her pleasure. She could always count on herself to bring her own release after they had gone. It was a rule for her never to depend too much on anyone.

Delilah can tell when she is ovulating, and now that she lives in the desert with only the sun and the moon for light, that time coincides exactly with the cycles of the moon. This is something she figured out on her own to avoid pregnancy so she wouldn't have to slay her own baby (which she would have to do, and would not be afraid to, she tells herself). But so many times, like tonight, she's fucked a man even though she knows she's going to ovulate any day now, because she gets so few chances, and is so damned desperate. Maybe, she thinks, it's the bitterness inside her that makes her body uninhabitable by something so innocent as a baby, and that is why, so far, she's been lucky.

When the older one has spent himself, she caresses him mechanically like a child until he falls asleep, which doesn't take long. Then she turns to the boy, whose mouth hangs unabashedly open.

"Stand up," she commands, and he stands. She walks to him and presses her body against him, hugs him while he hardens against her belly and his heart moves like sporadic wingbeats against her breasts.

"Do you want me?" she whispers.

He takes a sharp breath.

"Promise me something," she says.

"Anything."

"Don't go digging in the caves for the gold. Don't send your drills and explosives down into the earth. This is my home. Understand?"

"Okay."

"Do you mean it?"

"Yes. I didn't want to do it anyway. He made me come with him. Said this is what men do."

He whimpers, and then cries out, as she falls to her knees and opens her mouth.

Later, while they're sleeping, she takes almost all of their food.

This way she'll eat for another half moon after her meat runs out, and the men will be forced to abandon their quest, with only enough food remaining to get them home. She also searches their pack and finds a pair of loose pants that must belong to the boy. She's stolen a good number of shirts, but no pants like this, light and easy for the summer. She can cinch them around the waist with twine.

When she gets back to her cave to inspect her loot, she feels sad to discover that nothing in the City has changed. What they call food still doesn't look like food. It is colorless and textureless, packed into boxes and cylinders that ring cold metal when she taps her finger on them. Not like anything that comes from animal, or was ever alive. She remembers how it was to buy food in the City. Narrow corridors of cans and boxes, shelves and shelves of their neat, artificial shapes, labeled with fancy advertisements. How could anyone sense, looking at those long rows of simple, odorless, symmetrical shapes, what the body needed?

She started stealing food long before she was too poor to buy it, probably because even then, she wanted to feel like a hunter. Even then, she knew that handful of paper at the cash register had nothing to do with the pain and beauty of taking a life.

The horse follows the scent of water under the desert, nibbling on leaves for traces of moisture and nourishment, and finding, after a day, and again after another day, muddy pools to drink from. He grows thinner and thinner, but his body remembers this from another lifetime, and it does not frighten him. He feels almost easier this way, lighter, except that he has a responsibility now, to carry Lonely. He feels sorry when she has to dismount and walk beside him because he is too weak.

"I wish I could carry *you*," she says, and he feels ashamed again. She doesn't understand that she does carry him, when he carries her. She carries him in the safety of her certainty, the direction she gives him, the sense of hope and longing which he does not understand and yet which soothes him. When Lonely rescued him, untying him from where the men had left him, calming his terror with her hands, he felt that he could trust her. Men were frightening and terrible and always had been. He was not surprised at being caught, but he was surprised when they did not catch her. He feels a little safer with her now.

When he bends to drink at the drying pools, he speaks with the pupfish who huddle together in slimy lumps at its bottom, trying to stay wet.

i'm sorry, he says, feeling helpless to his own thirst.

They say, *we'll just sink deeper. somewhere, deep in the earth, the water is safe from the sun.*

But after he drinks from the pool, the water level does not seem to go down. In fact, days after he leaves it, the pool remains, and it seems to the pupfish that the water rises higher. That it is easier to breathe, more rich in oxygen, more clear and pure. And they do not know the reason for this, but for them, reasons are unnecessary.

Rarely does Lonely stop and wonder, now, if she should turn back, or if she wants to go on. For the desert is always interesting, at each step offering new twists and mazing formations, leading her deeper into deeper design. As they follow the pathway of green, they leave behind the raw expanses where she spent her first night, where the earth looked gored and upturned. Now the desert becomes more intimate, and the jagged hills draw closer.

But sometimes, for hours, Lonely does not see where she is, but trains her listless eyes on an empty horizon that blurs before her. Sometimes her mind is somewhere else that only minds can go, far away from the body, where it wonders whether the old hag was right and there is no such thing as love. She wonders where she is headed, what she is really seeking, and why she thought she would find it on the top of that distant mountain that never gets any closer. Nothing feels certain. Even the rocks, feeling steady under her as she sleeps, are not certain: they, too, speak of fading with the wind, turning to dust, blowing away and traveling the world without direction or home.

Neither hunger nor thirst stop her, and so she finds no reason to take breaks, to focus her mind on any need. Sometimes she feels perhaps tired—not so much from riding but from the weight of the heat and her own sweat—and then she looks at the horse, and asks, "Should we rest?" For it seems that she could rest, or she could go on a little further, and it would not make much difference. She welcomes the horse's pauses at the occasional pools of water, for they give her a definite reason to stop. Sometimes she remembers to drink too, but then the soft water swells within her and reminds her so painfully of her deeper longing that she would rather stop drinking, and keep walking in dryness, her mind as barren and tuneless as the wind.

They pass the men, who are driving back home now. Lonely looks toward them and does not feel afraid now, with her horse carrying her again. She watches their heads turn to look at her and keep looking at her until her horse breaks into a sudden trot and turns her away from them, and their noise gradually fades behind her. She is even more confused by them than before. How will she know love when she finds it, or ever heal her own loneliness? These are men, but how is it that she does not want to go to them? Will she not recognize love when she sees it? Is she wrong to travel on? Is she wrong to disobey, after all, what her father told her? Will her prince come for her and find her gone? But the tower, too, is gone. There is nowhere for him to find her.

At night she dreams again of that formless place below the tower, where the old woman's aching voice awaits her, and those blinding eyes, and those hands which bind her wrists and test the very pulse of her heart as if Lonely did not own it. She dreams of swimming through that darkness as if the darkness were the sea, and she smells again the smell of death in the vultures' breath, and it is everywhere, so that she wakes fighting to breathe.

Then she wonders again at the moon, swinging lonely above her. It does not seem like something that lives solely for the giving of light, for the light it gives is murky and fickle. She thinks its purpose must have more to do with beauty—or perhaps it is only a piece of the sun that got left behind, or a memory to keep the hope of the sun alive. As she lies awake watching it, she is filled with longing, and wonders what it is that she truly longs for.

On the morning of the full moon, space spills open before her into a glorious expanse of open flight: the playa. Lonely looks up and cries, "Oh!" and feels a piece of the old thrill of meadows flare up in her chest. She feels hopeful again for the first time since then. The cool wind taps her face, relieving her of the heat they have slogged through for days.

I bring rain, says the wind. *Again and again, passing over the mountain, I forget. I let the rains fall in the mountains—I forget. I leave the rains behind, and the desert stays a desert, dry. But then sometimes, once in a great while, I remember. Today I remember. I have brought rain for the desert.*

Lonely doesn't know what the wind means, doesn't know what rain is. But she asks, *Why do you forget?*

You, too, will forget, answers the wind with its usual laughter, *when you pass over the mountains. Wait and see.*

"But why?"

Happiness. Love.

"Happiness and love make you forget?"

Happiness and love draw more happiness and love to them. That is why I cannot help but let the rain fall. But the desert is lonely, and loneliness brings more loneliness. So it stays dry. That's the way it is.

"But that's not fair," says Lonely, wondering if she will ever reach those mountains.

It isn't about justice. It's about what you name yourself. Anyway, loneliness, too, is important. It makes you pure.

As Lonely struggles with these words, wondering as always if she only imagined them, the wind becomes still, and in that long, silent moment, the clouds merge and thicken, losing their design.

The wind flickers one more time. *Look up, Lonely,* it says. *Those shapes are the dreams of your beloved.*

Lonely looks up at the great, looming fairy tale of the clouds: grey spires of glory to mirror the grand lost shapes of the desert.

Then the sky gushes down.

Lonely stands enclosed by water, barely understanding. The water is deafening. It touches her constantly, yet it cannot be touched. She cannot see any single drop, but only the confusing effect of many drops at once that only become real as they come together upon her skin, defining the slopes of her body. The water wakes her, and then she is too much awake. The water presses her tenderly, and then too hard. Clothed in water, she lifts her face as if to shake off its heavy cloak, but the rain slams into her eyes.

She can see nothing but the horse's head beside her, erect and alert, and though she is not riding him he is close enough to seem like part of her. She reaches out and touches his now glossy white fur, as if she has never felt it before. He shivers, and water pours from his sides. Then he turns back the way they came and runs.

Instinctively, Lonely follows him, screaming without knowing why. The horse has never run so fast. In the roar of the rain she does not hear the roar of the wave or the roaring of the earth shaking beneath it as it comes barreling across the playa, a great frothing bull of water colored with dusky mud. But after they reach the top of the slope and the horse turns around and around, snorting and trying to settle, she arrives in time to see the water's great mass seething up like an ocean storm right where they stood, and then receding.

A few moments later, the rain is gone. As the sun peels apart the clouds, she stands still, her pink skin as shiny as the sandstone cliffs. The playa is empty, covered as far as she can see with a thin film of water.

Then, with a gasp, she runs down into the scent of wet red clay, the scent of glowing minerals, the scent of live earth in love with the rain. The mud slips through her toes, drawing her body downward. It is so soft with the water, softer than anything should or could be, softer than clouds or sky or the wind through the meadow grasses—so soft she cannot get enough of it into her hands, her skin; she wants to absorb it, devour it, slide like an eel inside it. She sleds through it on her hands and knees, draws flowers on her thighs with the slick paint of it. She hears the horse whinny warningly from above, but nothing matters to her but this matter, this fluid solid, this joyful substance.

Skating on the callused soles of her feet, she crosses the whole playa in an ecstasy of mud. On the other side, the river is flowing rich and brown through smooth hills. Lonely wades into it, letting the mud fall from her skin, her whiteness turned pale gold with sun and earth. Her wet dress kisses her body, and she does not take it off because it feels so good to be touched by it. The water swirls up slow between her legs, and without realizing it she is dancing. From between her legs blooms a flower of heat that mushrooms into her hips, swirling her around, and the fingertips of one hand graze the bony V below her belly, and she touches her throat and her mouth, her lips clumsy against her hand. She rides her own motion, a motion that feels older than her life—the rhythm of the horse, the rhythm of waves under the surface of the sea, the rhythm of dreams recurring against the shores of waking. She rides it until she knows it so well that she is not afraid to see the god walking toward her: the very answer to her desire.

When she sees him—as if she knew all along that she would—she moves toward him with urgent, difficult strides surging through the heavy water. She hurries toward his deep dark smile, hurries toward his rescuing eyes, his capable, wide-hearted chest, his own easy stride, his bigness, his otherness, his heat.

She stumbles into his outstretched hands, and he grips her tight, holding her in front of his body with an expression of awed delight. He raises his eyebrows, as if waiting for one of them to speak, to explain what is happening. But his touch eclipses everything that went before.

"I'm afraid," she says suddenly, her body going blank.

Dragon is not concerned. He smiles easily. "Don't be afraid," he says, and cups one hand under her, hoisting her up against him. The press of his fingertips is so dramatic that she cannot feel it at all, but the musky smell of his shoulder makes her open her mouth against him, makes her turn to languid mud, and something inside her begins to weep. Water trickles down her legs, sticking her to him, turning immediately warm.

Dragon carries her up a hillside and lays her down in a little circle of grass surrounded by elaborate white pinnacles of stone. Lonely is dying, the story of her past replaying before her mind as the stories of her future used to play across the tower glass. For this, surely, is what her father never told her. This is what lurked behind his silences. This is what fell upon her from the midnight sky when the glass finally let reality in. This is what the wind is saying, and what she longed for, and the reason she first stood up from her bed. This is what the meadow was saying, what the City was saying, what the moon was saying, and what the vultures and the nightmares were saying, and what everything, everyone, was saying. This.

This simple touch, like a word.

You do not speak of sex. There is no particular place for it, no particular context, no particular time when it is okay. Everyone knows about it, and some people do it, but no one knows what it is. And that makes you nervous.

Still young, you run into sex like a black hole in space, not looking back. You are pulled in by something bigger than yourself, bigger than your lover, bigger than any rule or law or reason. It feels like the loving hand of a god you profess not to believe in, reaching through the darkness for your own hand, offering to save you from a world you cannot stand.

You reach back, but somehow miss, and end up with only a body. To your surprise, you are still alive after passing through that blackness. You are yourself all over again, only worse than before, and more alone.

Because nobody knows what sex is. Nobody can find the right word for it. You wake soft in the morning and you feel it. You choose your clothes, feeling it. You press the gas pedals of your car, and you feel it. Someone passes you in the hall, eyes turned elsewhere, and you feel it. You feel it all day long.

What, exactly?

You dream of Hanum, who is a god and cannot be touched. You dream of the princess, who may not exist. Your body itches. You are angry in your car. You rock against the others in the crowd, and you cannot feel each other's touch. In the City everything, everything is defined in straight, clear lines. But somewhere in the body that cannot be seen, there is a black hole opening into space. Somewhere in the body there is an opening into chaos, and everyone wants to go there.

You come home and duck your head against your mother's stare, stumbling to your room. Your mother says nothing. She is as terrified as her daughter is of the body's unpredictable ability to turn divine.

Something is wrong.

The horse is afraid again, with Lonely gone.

Since the day the men captured him, a fear as large as the world began to close in upon him, and only Lonely, like a ring of light, has held it at bay. Perhaps they would not be able to capture her, he thought.

But now she has been taken after all, and he walks in fear, breathes fear. Afraid of the heavy, sinking mud, he stumbles around the playa, over hills of crumbled stone, and he is careful with his big and tender hooves. His body is powerful but so fragile, so easily spooked by the ghosts that ride hungry on the wind. He is bigger than people are, but thin and strangely hidden; it is easy for him to hide himself among the forest of stone structures, or even to stand in the open and blend with the rock whose color melds with his whiteness in the direct sun. He sees where Lonely has gone, and he sees the man she has gone with, and he thinks he knows that man, and he will not go near there. Not ever.

Yet he cannot leave. For above them and far from the green and the river, he can see another woman watching them. He would not have noticed her, so far away and blending, in her darkness, with the black of the cave behind her. But he does because deep within him—where he is something else, not this body, not horse—he recognizes her.

Without meaning to, he moves closer to her, taking comfort in the fresh taste of the grass as he walks, smelling the constant breeze which orients him with its now familiar scents of water and dust—dust that still echoes with dryness in its wetness, giving its scent an intensity that keeps him alert. He is so hungry. He eats and eats. He cannot help it.

The dark woman stands in a tight, poised stance like a predator, each muscle aware and ready. He can see her clearly because something in him remembers her. He can see the pain in her face as she looks out toward Lonely. He can see the fire giving life to her body and eating it away at the same time. He remembers her courage, her determination; once, long ago, he thinks he remembers loving her. But he is not what he seems to be; he is not what loved. What he was, once—that other who knew her—could never say it, and was always sorry. He feels she is the one he should be carrying, though she would never let herself be carried, and anyway he cannot; he cannot go to her, not yet. It is too difficult. She is so strong, so bright. She would not have let it happen to her—what happened to that other.

But he wants to tell her that she shouldn't hate the pale, beautiful goddess he has brought here, because they are connected. He can sense the constellation of these three people who surround him now—the only human beings in this vast, red and yellow eye of lonely dust. He knows their importance to each other, and he knows they must see each other, and he knows—as if his very survival depends upon it—that something must be done or undone between them. But he does not know what, and the whole question—as if the desert itself is one great eye, watching, waiting to see what will happen—terrifies him.

He only knows that somehow, he remembers Delilah.

I am someone's soul. But whose, he isn't sure now. When he tries to remember, a white terror makes his mind go blank. He knows there was a perpetrator, and he knows there was a victim: one was male, and one was female. He does not remember which one he was, and he hopes that he was neither. But he knows that Delilah was the salvation they both longed for, the only one who could have stopped it.

And she didn't.

Every part of the girl is perfect. Her eyes are moist and clear as glass, their irises glowing with darkness, so dark that their color cannot be told. Her skin, though its glow has been dimmed by the sun, is such a fragile white, so tender that it is red at the edges of her eyes, and flushes in small hot circles under her high cheekbones. Her lips are a bubble of the softest pink, like swells of nectar that will melt upon contact. The line of her chin swoops back and upward beneath, like a caught breath, into the flesh of her bare neck. Her smooth skin collapses over her shoulder bones like fine thin cloth, and the graceful bones winging down from her shoulders are lifting and falling, stark and prominent in their delicacy. Below them her breasts lilt upwards, her nipples uplifted like an offering through her wet dress, and her arms fall to her sides like white rivers.

Dragon's desire pounds in his ears as he climbs on top of her, as he claws at her and for a moment she claws back, as he grabs her everywhere with his hands and drops his weight into her softness. It pounds so loudly that he can barely hear the girl as she gasps, "Wait—please."

But he does hear her, and he will make himself wait. He has learned waiting, and she is worth waiting for. He feels almost relieved by her rejection. He feels its familiarity, its holiness. And yet he knows that he will have her, for she wants him. He felt her wanting, in his hands, only a moment ago—something he never felt with the goddesses, something they would never let him feel. He has carried her here. He has laid her down, and she looks wonderfully up at him, at once willing and afraid.

"Are you the one?" she asks.

In answer, he leans over her again, intending the gentlest of kisses, his hand running down her body. Her mouth shivers under his, barely opening, but then she presses her hand to his face and pushes him away.

"No, stop," she says. "Please."

"Sorry," says Dragon. He lies down on his back and tries to breathe evenly.

After an awkward moment, he turns toward her and finds her facing him too, her eyes bright and earnest.

"Do you want me?" he asks, wanting to hear her say it.

"I don't know," she says.

"But," he fumbles, "why not?"

"I'm sorry. I don't know. I can't remember, what it was that I wanted."

Her face looks so childlike, so open. With such willingness she looks toward him, surrounding him with the beauty of her eyes, and he must forgive her, soften toward her.

"I'm sorry, too," he says. "But you're so beautiful. What were you doing in the river?"

"I don't know."

Dragon jumps up suddenly and takes one of her hands. He can't lie here and talk or he'll go mad.

"Let's walk together," he tells her. She stands up with him, letting her hand follow his, and her obedience melts him. This is the gift the river has given him. He knew she would come to him eventually—the woman who would finally receive him, the woman who would reward him for all his days of waiting, frustration, and patient meditation. *See, Coyote?* he wants to shout aloud. *See, Delilah? This is how it is.*

He doesn't know what to say to her. He doesn't care where she came from. He only wants to be inside of her, to be bathed at last in such purity.

"What is your name?" he asks quickly, automatically. When she doesn't answer, he looks at her and sees her brows furrowed in concentration. He thinks, suddenly, that she will lie to him. He pulls her hand sharply toward him, so that it brushes his thigh, and makes her face him. She gasps.

"Tell me," he demands.

"It's—Yora," the girl says. Dragon catches her hesitation and gives her a sudden look, trying to see into her eyes, which she keeps hidden. He has the anxious feeling that she is lying, after all, and immediately that idea hurts him, but he doesn't know what to say. They walk together for several moments, close to the river, their hands searing into each other. Out of the corner of his eye, Dragon sees Delilah watching them from the distance of her cave, even though she normally sleeps during the day. Out of nowhere, a fantasy arrests his mind of the two women, black and white, entwined together, laughing toward him. His body tenses as he walks.

The girl sighs and pauses, touches his waist with her other hand.

Without stopping his motion, Dragon lurches into her, pressing her against a wall of stone, searching under her dress with starving hands. His desire is like an unbearable weight that will crush him if he does not release it. She tilts her head back, starts to open her mouth. He kisses her violently, and catches one easy breast in his hand, and with the other he finds her opening under her dress, not as wet as Delilah's but moist and contracting around his finger—its fuzz softer and finer.

But then she begins to writhe beneath him, in a way that at first drives him wilder and then hurts him as she pokes him with the sharper points of her body, pushing him away again.

"No, no," she cries, "what are you doing to me?" He stands back, disbelieving, his eyes wild. But she curls up, presses her hands to her face, and begins to cry, and then again he softens. Again he can bear to wait a little longer. He kneels down and presses his face into her warm dress, feeling the burning that comes from her center, and this seems to make her cry even harder.

Dragon will always remember the bewilderment of that first moon in the desert, when he discovered his own fire, and it seemed completely beyond his control.

His body aches constantly and his heart is in constant pain. He tries to speak to the girl and his words come out as fire. He looks at her and his jaw comes unhinged with desire, his thighs shiver, and suddenly she is surrounded by fire. The more he wants her the further she moves away, because the more he wants her, the hotter the fire burns.

All he can make is fire: fire pleading, fire fury, fire lust. Flames come from out of him and make theatrics in the air, and they need nothing to live on, and they change shape like the clouds, and die leaving the air melted and deformed. The closer they get to the beautiful girl, the hotter they seem to burn, as if she were a wind that fans them. They never seem to burn her, but she turns away from him anyway, murmuring, "It's too hot. Stop, it hurts… "

"But I can't help it," he cries, his voice drowned out by the momentary roaring of the flames. "I want you. This is my love for you!"

"But how can it be love? I can't touch it," she says, standing sad and childish on the other side of it, her face cool and unmoved behind the seething flames, her eyes round.

"Enough with your stupid games," says Delilah suddenly, lifting a stick to the air and catching one of his flames on the end of it. "Fire is sacred."

He doesn't know where she came from, when she came, or which one of them she is talking to. In shock, he watches her walk away, and his own ethereal flames disintegrate, so that the flame on the end of her stick is now the only flame left in all the desert. He watches her crouch a shout's distance away, closer to her cave, and carefully light a tipi of sticks she has already arranged. Then he sees his little goddess floating toward her slowly, as if drawn, and he has to follow.

Delilah looks up at Yora, but not at him, and then turns back to her humbly burning, careful human fire and scowls. Its light unfolds its various arrays of color delicately, more subtle and introverted than the flames he just threw in his passion across the sand. These flames cackle deliciously over their meal of dead wood, whereas Dragon's were wordless, roaring palely over nothing.

"Are you jealous?" he asks Delilah, trying to regain some control, thinking he interprets the hint of pain in her darkened eyes as she turned away. He is wary and irritated by the interruption, even though the air between himself and Yora is calmer now, and Yora even reaches for his hand. He doesn't trust Delilah's influence on her.

"Jealous," says Delilah thoughtfully, looking up at Yora again as if she doesn't understand, but he sees the anger there. He sees it!

"Of this goddess," he explains shortly.

Delilah snorts. "She's at least half human, that one."

Dragon is hurt by her dismissal, the way she talks about the girl as if she were not there—as if she were not what she is. But to his surprise, the girl answers, her voice clear as night air on a cold day, with nothing but wonder in her tone: "How do you know?"

"I've seen your kind," says Delilah, but Dragon thinks she sounds uncertain now, and is perhaps as surprised he is.

"Have you?" says Yora innocently. "We're like each other, aren't we? You and me?"

"What are you talking about?"

"We look alike," his goddess says eagerly. Dragon knows what she means: both of them small and slim, with girlish breasts and pretty limbs, only Delilah is quick and muscular and mammalian, while the new girl is shining, glassy and bird-like. Delilah's hair is everywhere thorny and tangled, while the girl Yora's lies in an icy sheen down her back, never dry and never tangled, and lines her legs with the palest down. But they mirror each other in their stance, Delilah's eyes boring into Yora's in challenge, while Yora—crouching down now by the fire as if she were welcome there—faces her back just as directly, out of pure curiosity.

But Dragon doesn't think Delilah sees the similarity.

"Where did you come from?" she asks, her voice flat. "Women don't come to the desert."

"You're here."

"Where do you come from," repeats Delilah with impatience.

"A tower," says the girl, the quietness in her voice making Delilah's sound even harsher and more unkind. "In the middle of the sea. But it isn't there any more."

Dragon, who was watching the girl's lips as they carefully formed these words, and the beautiful newness of each gesture she makes, turns back toward Delilah when she does not reply. He catches the end of several strange expressions passing over her face.

"Oh, is that it," she says finally. "You're the Princess in the Tower. Of course. Right. I guess that's the best fantasy you could come up with for yourself. But it's completely meaningless, just so you know."

Dragon watches the girl's mouth open slightly and her eyes widen, and he turns to Delilah. "Don't speak to her that way," he growls.

"Don't speak to *me* about what you don't know, boy-god. You're only a child."

But Yora catches them both then with the sweetness of her sigh as she glances upward.

"Oh," she says, "look at the moon." They both look up, without thinking, and see the moon which has risen in secret and casts its looming beauty through silver clouds. They all stare at it for a long, long moment, as if they have never seen it before, and then he hears Yora's voice again, soft beside him.

"I'm on a journey," she says. "I am looking for love."

Delilah whirls back around and makes a grimace and a choked sound that Dragon thinks is a failed attempt at contemptuous laughter. She tosses her head toward Dragon.

"Dragon thinks he's looking for love," she says. "But he's really just looking for sex."

"Fuck you, Delilah," Dragon retorts, using her own ugly language which is so distasteful to him, for he can think of nothing worse to express his anger. "What do you know about love?"

"Nothing. But I'm not looking for it."

Then they are all silent again, and the silence is even more painful than before. After a while, Delilah says to Yora, without looking up, "What do you know about the City?" and Dragon can see that it costs her to ask this question, but there must be some reason she asks, something she wants to know.

"Nothing."

"Do you know anything about the Road? Have you seen it?"

"The what?"

"Forget it."

"What is it?"

Delilah sighs, rubs her hands over her face, and then looks away. Dragon hasn't seen that gesture before, but he can tell she is going to walk away soon, or tell them to leave. It doesn't matter. He has his goddess now. She is afraid, but she loves him; she will, she must.

"What is the Road?" Yora asks again.

"It's like another river," Delilah answers, her voice resigned. "A river of death. There are others. The people of the City build them, so they can turn the wilds into City, and find more places to build up their make-believe world and dump their trash. They'll destroy us all eventually, and then they'll destroy themselves. Fortunately, I'm purebred human, so I might be dead by then, of more natural causes."

"Where is your family?" asks Yora, which surprises Dragon, and seems to surprise Delilah, too. Didn't he ask Delilah that, too, when he met her?

"I don't have a fucking family." Delilah stands up. Maybe he's imagining it but she seems more and more edgy. Maybe it's his fault. Maybe he should leave. He'll take his little goddess and travel the world with her, searching for where the two of them belong.

"I don't have a family either," says Yora.

Delilah stares at her hard. Then she says, "Neither of you are welcome here. Don't you understand that? This is my home. I'll fight you for it if I have to, and I'll win. You take your little love games somewhere else."

But his goddess doesn't seem to hear her. She is holding her hand out now to the aura of the flames, as if she hadn't shied away from them in fear only moments before, when they belonged to him. He and Delilah both stare at her, as if from a terrible distance. Dragon's is the distance of longing, while Delilah's is the distance of hatred, though where this hatred comes from he does not understand.

She's looking at Delilah as she holds her hand against the heat of the flames, saying, "It's light, isn't it? Just light, moving and moving. Light with no body. Just light."

☾

For all the days of the waning moon, Dragon tries not to let his little goddess out of his sight. Sometimes he lets her sit and dream on her own, looking off at the mountains or back the way she came, but he watches her, haunting her with his desire. Somehow every night she hides herself, and he can never find her. But every morning she returns to him, her eyes open and hopeful.

She wants to sit and talk with him. She asks him about where he comes from, and pleads for stories about the goddesses there, and the things that bloomed there, and what it felt like. He doesn't tell her he did not always live in the Garden. He will not or cannot speak of his life with the dragons, though he doesn't know why. Perhaps those experiences were never described or recorded by any thoughts, and the memory of them is not something his mind holds in words. Anyway, he doesn't want to talk at all. Though she opens to him and listens to him the way he longed so badly for Delilah to do, he doesn't want that with Yora. He wants only to get inside her.

But he succumbs to her questions about the garden he came from, because explaining its shape is the only excuse he can find—after hours of frustrating conversation and walking separately in the sun—to touch her.

"Here," he tells her, "the heart of the garden. Here, its flowering breasts…." His fingers linger around her nipples, for which he cannot remember any symbol in the garden. Forgetting himself, he brings his lips to one of them. Her virginity is dazzling, so sweet he can smell it. He can feel her weaken—a single sharp breath out, as if she has slipped on a wet stone and begun to fall. He can feel her wanting him, and he lets loose before he can stop himself, grabbing her with his whole body.

But then the same thing again: her struggle, her pained cries.

He stops, furious. "Tell me when you really want me," he hisses.

"Okay," she whispers, pulling away from him in fear.

He swears he will not lose himself like that again. But one day in the river he sees her watching him, and he sees her eyes tracing the length of him with a look of awe and fear that makes him grasp himself—a sense of his own power pressing at him from inside until he wants to scream it. He wades over to her and bounces his erection in her face, watching her lips part in surprise.

"Touch it," he begs. "Just once."

She looks up at him, and he sits down beside her and gently takes hold of her hand.

"Touch it," he repeats. She looks down and nudges it with the back of her hand, then rubs its head uncertainly with her thumb. Her fingers are so light, like grasses in the wind, and he's so sensitive that her touch is like pain. She is laughing.

"It's like an animal," she says. She strokes it again so lightly he almost explodes, his whole body shaking. He grabs her, clamps her hand around it, and forces her to stroke it hard, up and down. She looks up at him, her eyes distant and surprised, but obeys. He leans in, breathing into her, giving in to the sensation. He doesn't mean to force her but he can't help it. He reaches for her breasts; she begins to pull away, but then remains. He feels her awkwardness, but just barely, for he is almost overcome.

"Harder," he whispers.

Then they are both looking down at the mess in her hand, and he feels his mind emptying out with exhaustion. They lower themselves into the river. When he looks at her, she is crying again, the redness around her eyes underlining their dark brilliance.

"Do you love me?" she asks.

"Yes," he answers without hesitation. "Don't you love me?"

"I don't know. I'm so confused now."

He stares at her.

"I think I want you," she says. "But I'm afraid. What do I do? How do I know if you're the one?"

And he doesn't know, because he doesn't understand what she is asking.

Whenever Delilah sleeps too deep into the evening, the bats wake her.

Their bedroom is just beyond hers, a little further into the cave, where it narrows and becomes impossible even to crawl through. Sometimes the wind of their mass exit awakens her, but even if she sleeps through that, their wild calls wake her once they begin returning to the cave to give their babies their first meal of the night. Then she crawls back and down to their doorway, and peers through the blackness to see the mass breathing of that living ceiling. She feels their little hot spirit-bodies maneuvering effortlessly around her head.

She chose this cave partly because of them. Also, the first cave she had chosen, about a day's walk from here, belonged to a mountain lion's home range. She'd found that out when the lion had appeared to her quite honestly in broad daylight, looming above her with a body chiseled from stone—in the perfect position for a pounce, but relaxed, with one paw dangling over the edge of the ledge and both eyes on Delilah, confident as suns in her lean face.

Delilah had backed away slowly. Only when the mountain lion was long out of her sight did she begin breathing again. She almost laughed with relief, but she wasn't stupid. She knew she had been warned, and she would not be warned again.

She stayed away after that. She knew the mountain lion had done her a great honor by showing herself, because she never saw her again, not

even her tracks. Sometimes, when she felt like the only person in the universe—and when that feeling made her wistful, and the desert space spun
around her, dizzying in its silence—she remembered the lion, and thought
she remembered all kinds of old, tough wisdom in that face. She thought
she remembered loneliness in those eyes. She wondered if the lion was the
last of its kind in these lands, or one of the last: she could feel her determination and strength, her tearless suffering, her undeterred loyalty to the
pathways of her ancestors. She felt a kinship with the lion, in her solitude.
She felt forever the way the lion had looked at her, as if that ancient predator recognized her.

The bats, too, were Delilah's kin. When she first met them, she was welcomed by a reckless young one who flung himself onto her arm on his way
out and gripped her with his tiny piercing fingers, his little body crumpled
like a lump of helpless black tissue on her sleeve, his eyes sad and intelligent,
his nostrils huge and flaring up at her. She liked his bold, nightmarish face
with its hairy muzzle.

"You're even uglier than I am," she laughed, because she'd always thought
she was ugly, with her wide nose like his and her big, intrusive eyes.

Her skin was black like his too, and when she slept that day along with his
tribe, she folded her body up tight like theirs, her mind swinging upside down
into her first animal dream.

She has never had to fight for this place before. The way it claimed her, the
way it became like her own body over the years, the way no one could ever
find her here—it was like she had always assumed that everyone in the world
knew she owned it. She's still reeling from the shock of Dragon's arrogance.
Maybe that's why she hasn't made him leave yet. That, and something else.

Tonight she sleeps in until almost midnight, waking slowly to the bats'
urgent conversation. She's been avoiding Dragon as much as usual, but it's
easier now, now that he's with the little white girl all the time. With that girl,
he is someone different than he has been with her. She sees in his eyes that
same reasonless, unstoppable lust that she saw the first night she seduced
him, when he fell on his knees before her cave. Now he feels it for this innocent other. She knows that's what does it for him: the other girl's innocence.
And fuck that. But still—watching him with her, watching him watch that
girl with his fists clenched in restrained desire, Delilah wants him almost as
badly as she did in the beginning.

Tonight she wakes up hurting again. Right in the center of her back, behind her heart, not a piercing, singing pain like the taut nerve in her neck
but a soft, humbling ache that goes on and on like the bite of a weasel on the
throat of its prey.

She crawls out of the cave and stands, arching her spine, trying to stretch the pain out of her. It stretches but does not go. What if she is slowly breaking? What if she gets sick out here all alone? But then she's ashamed of herself for even thinking like that. She can't remember the last time she felt sorry for herself.

Down below she sees Dragon with the girl, so she crouches down with a stolen can of beans to eat and watch them. She can tell they won't notice her, the way they're pressed so tightly together. Dragon is sitting on a stone and the girl is sitting sideways in his lap, her lips melded to his and her arms around his neck. Dragon's hand has disappeared up her skirt and the girl keeps lifting one leg and pressing it restlessly against the other, squeezing his hand and pressing her breasts into Dragon's naked chest. But every few seconds, she reaches down and pushes Dragon's hand away—pulls it out from under her dress. Dragon appears used to this, and he doesn't stop kissing her or trying to reach back in again. The game of it makes Delilah restless. *What, are you too good for this?* she thinks angrily at the girl, imagining herself on Dragon's lap instead and what she would do.

But then they stop. The girl is holding both of Dragon's wrists in her own, stopping him. They are speaking in tones Delilah cannot hear, both of them frozen in motion, and then Dragon simply wraps his arms around her, but she's still pulling back. Finally she jumps away from him, standing, and her voice is loud enough for Delilah to hear.

"Because I don't know if you love me. I don't know if I love you." Loud, like she isn't sure that Dragon will be able to hear her from a distance where they are no longer touching.

"How can you say that? How can you—"

Delilah freezes without knowing why, hearing the roar in his voice as he stands up after the girl, coming toward her with heavy hands, with anger, with a wound tearing up from his chest. The girl, clearly frightened and unwilling to argue more, turns and flees toward the river. Dragon stands and looks after her, and Delilah, with a sudden premonition that he will turn and see her watching, ducks back into her cave.

In the back of her mind, Delilah wants to search for Dragon, wants to caress that brutal longing with her own and meet it with the fury of her own desire. But she knows, too, that she is not the one he wants. And that makes her even more furious in her longing not to care.

Accidentally, she meets the girl instead. Her whiteness can't hide in the darkness, not that she's trying to. In fact she rises up from the spine of a stone giant as Delilah approaches, and then she hops lightly to the sand. Delilah keeps walking. She is tired. It's almost dawn, almost time for her to sleep. She's been wandering the pine forest fruitlessly all night, a nameless anxiety inside her causing the pheasants and hares to bolt from the bushes before she even saw them. But the girl falls into step beside her.

"Why do you sleep during the day?"

"Because I blend in better at night, don't you think?"

Silence. They keep walking, and Delilah is going to walk right up to her cave and go inside, without stopping. She owes this girl nothing.

"Why do you hate me?"

Delilah is mildly surprised but still does not stop. "You know? I don't know. I can't put my finger on it."

"But there's no reason for it."

Delilah turns to her again and is about to say something back—whatever, whatever comes out—but she stops. She's never been embarrassed by her own anger before. It's always comforted her, actually, to wield it around her; it is what she knows herself by. But something in this girl's eyes slips under her fury, cuts the thread that binds her to it, and leaves her words—before she even speaks them—hanging uselessly in the air.

"You and Dragon both," says the girl into her silence. "You don't really see me. You think I'm something else. I don't know what you think I am. I don't even know what I am."

It takes Delilah a few seconds to realize that she's stopped walking. The girl has stopped too, and they are staring at each other. She has to admit that this girl seems nothing like the girls she hated in high school—nothing, actually, like anyone she's ever met before. She is too bright, for one thing, like a soul without enough flesh to dim her light. She hurts Delilah's eyes.

"What does it matter?" she finds herself asking. "What does it matter, what I think?" Then she is surprised to see the girl struggling for an answer, as if the question is important—more important than Delilah intended. This, too, embarrasses Delilah.

"I'm so afraid," the girl says finally. "I thought, if I could talk to you, if you could help me understand things... Because you're—you're—"

"What?" says Delilah. "Do you know what *I* am? Do you?" But she knows what the girl was going to say: *because you're a woman*. She looks up abruptly, past the girl's shoulder. The strangest thing. She thought she saw a white horse pass beyond an arch in the distance.

She looks back into the open, pleading face, and shakes her head. "I can't—"
She tries to remember what the girl said. She can't do this. She feels like she is

falling into this face, beyond which lies some deep well she thought she'd long ago covered over, a place that no longer holds any water or any life, only a long dark fall and a long drawn-out death. It will hurt when she hits the bottom.

"I can't help you," she says, tearing her eyes away, and keeps walking.

This time the girl doesn't follow.

Dragon is blocking the entrance to Delilah's cave.

He doesn't speak, but that look is back in his eyes—a merciless, reptilian desire—and this time it's for her.

Delilah stops some distance from him, held back by something that she doesn't understand or recognize until it's too late: fear. Fear is so unfamiliar to her in the face of a man she desires that she ignores it and walks toward him, not knowing what she's intending to do. She's still confused by the words of the girl, confused by something she hasn't felt in a long time. Dragon is naked. She sees his desire. She sees his heaving chest, his fists.

"What are you—" she begins, but then his mouth is drowning her, and a sharp ledge of stone tears her back as he throws her against it. She can feel the animal of him fumbling between her thighs, and then his hand—more calculated, more deliberate—pushing her thighs apart to let it in. And that makes her realize, despite the flush of familiar heat that she knows is desire—pulsing through her throat, between her breasts, between her hips—that she is holding the muscles of her thighs tight. She is holding them closed. Realizing it, she opens them, confused, and feels him push on blindly, ripping the button on her jeans, sliding her down over the sharp stone onto the ground, lifting his hips. She feels the pain of the stone and cries out without meaning to.

"No." It's soft at first. "Don't." It isn't even that she doesn't want him. She always wants, always. And she wanted this, didn't she? No sickly sweetness, no professions of love, no holy intentions, just instinctual relief. Just the abyss.

But "No," she says.

And then she says it louder. Each time it becomes easier to say, though she has never said it like this before. She doesn't know why she's saying it, but she feels so amazed to hear herself say it, so overcome by the strange and surprising joy of saying something so completely unfamiliar to her, that she doesn't realize at first that he isn't listening, that he isn't sharing in that joy. That he does not feel its sudden freedom. That he is, in fact, trapping her inside his body, and that he is, in fact, already inside her.

Then something happens that Delilah does not understand, because she would never, ever imagine or believe such a thing. It's like something out of one of Mira's drawings of dramatic, magical lands when she was very young, before she went crazy.

A unicorn dances out from behind the stone and rears up over Dragon's head.

It's like everyone's dream of a unicorn, its body flowing like white syrup, its horn spiraling into the sky like the ascent of the spirit Dragon talked about. It has a wizard's goat beard and its eyes are made of the same stuff as dragon eyes, and it looks like it could kill him with the lightning of its legs, but it's as light as a deer. She can't see if it even touches him, or just swoops over him like a great bird, lowering its horn over them as it passes. But she can feel its heart singing right into her—as if it knows her, as if it knows her joy—and when it gallops away, it leaves Dragon sprawled on his back beside her, panting, staring after it with equal amazement.

Delilah watches his erection slowly subside, as he turns back and looks at her with an expression of terror that she has only ever seen a long time ago in the City, in the expressions of other children's faces when Mira had one of her attacks.

"Leave," she says quietly, and she knows it is the last time she will have to say it. She stands up, shaky, and climbs into her cave, which he is no longer blocking.

But she cannot fall asleep all day.

For the pale shining girl is gone for good. Delilah knows it.

She can tell, by the absence of a light, cooling wind that she realizes has blown every day and every night, constantly, since the girl arrived here, and which now, suddenly, has stopped.

2nd MOON

Lonely, says the wind, and she feels strangely relieved to have her name back.

She was not Yora, not that flowing, nourishing goddess of ocean and tears and refuge. She is as dry as the desert wind, a broken twig tumbling through this vast dream of emptiness. She hangs her head, and she walks beside her horse now. She doesn't know why but she never wants to ride him again. She wants him to be free.

Lonely, repeats the wind. *Why did you deny your name?*

"I can't say that name," Lonely whispers. "Or no one will love me."

Ah, sighs the wind, *but you must own your name in order to free yourself from it.*

"I can't," Lonely repeats. "I can't say it. I am ashamed." But inside, the wind has begun to worry her. What if Dragon didn't love her because she did not tell him her true name? What if he was, after all, her prince, her one true love, but he could not recognize her because she lied?

The horse hangs his head also, keeping his nose low to the ground, trying to stay in touch with the faraway smell of water. The river has fallen so deep below the ground that there is no sign of it, no green, no life. They travel for more than two days through a land of nothing but empty white sand, like the surface of the moon made soft and gentle, like the wing of a white bird folding over and over, its feathers the ripples of the wind's design. Lonely is too lost in thought to wonder how her horse survives without water for so long.

She didn't realize how lost she felt with Dragon, until she left him behind. A fog that dulled her mind for days now lifts, as if in the absence of his touch the wind can sing clearly through her mind again.

She wanted to believe he was the one. The way they found each other like that, in the river, at the peak of her longing, after the passionate rain—it was just the way it should have happened. He *had* to be the one. She wanted so much to believe she had found him before reaching that distant mountain. The mountain is so far. Seeing its distance now, she is overcome with darkness. She thinks of the way Delilah, too, turned away from her, and the way Dragon turned to Delilah then. When Lonely saw that she was still alone after all, she walked away from that place. She kept walking toward the mountain, her curse and her destiny, until her horse appeared from nowhere and walked alongside her. She was just Lonely again. It turned out she couldn't escape that name.

If he was the one, she thinks, then she must have ruined it somehow. She must have driven him to leave her. But why? Why did she keep refusing him? Why did she thrust away from her what she most desired? Did she ask too much? Did she have some ideal of love that was too big to come true, that would forever keep her from it?

You curse yourself. You push away what you most want, with your own fear. You will always be Lonely, she thinks she hears the wind say. But she isn't sure. Maybe it's the voice of the Witch, carried by the wind as their voices were first carried to each other the day Lonely leaned out from her tower.

But Dragon had said the same thing. *What do you want from me? I'd give you anything, and you push me away.*

For a whole day, the vultures circle above her, their V-shaped wingspans tilting slowly back and forth like scales in the heavens. The thought of her own choices makes her dizzy.

"I don't know how to do this!" she cries out. "I don't know what love is."

She thinks and thinks, and cannot think her way out of loneliness. The desert is just space, with no truth to hold onto. She remembers the vultures' ugly faces and thinks of the old woman's face on the island. Perhaps that woman is a vulture. Perhaps she is floating high above Lonely, following her along currents of invisible air, watching her wherever she goes, waiting for her to fail.

But the vultures do not waste time on such drama. They simply rise and fall, riding towers of heat, scanning the open heart of the desert for that which has already transformed. They sniff for the scent of bodies no longer held by the purpose and longing of the spirit, bodies that relax, finally, downward. No more work, no more carrying forward, no more fighting gravity upward and onward, no more trying. The vultures float down the long ladder of the sky and skid at once heavily and buoyantly to the ground, lifting the black tents of their wings, enfolding the trembling ghosts in the soft comfort of forgetting. *We are the ancestors,* they whisper. *We have come to take you home.*

At night Lonely is not tired, and she walks sleepless until the horse insists on resting. She cannot find the moon until long after dark, and then it is only a sliver the width of one hair, curling off into nothingness. She remembers the night by Delilah's fire, when it was still almost full, and her love—was it love?—for Dragon was new and hopeful and still believed in itself. But she doesn't remember looking at the moon since then. It has tricked her. When she wasn't looking, the pregnant moon lost its child, and all the beautiful light went out of the sky, and the darkness caught up to her, just like the Witch predicted. And still she cannot sleep all night, opening her eyes constantly in fear that the darkness will devour her, and that if she sleeps, she might wake to find herself beneath the tower in total blackness, her hands grasping at nothing, her body gone.

Each day at the first blink of sunlight, they begin walking again.

Gradually the white land begins to swell and change, into great ridges of sand piled without purpose by the wind, rising and falling and then rising again into stone that still holds its form, not yet disintegrated into sand. Lonely focuses on her feet as they walk over the crumbs of greater stone, into the foothills of mountains, where the river runs again and thorny shrubs make the barest of livings along its edge. Then the greenery thickens and begins to enfold them into the breasts of the lower, wetter mountains. Birdsong once again twirls in the air and a mist alights on Lonely's face, and she begins to cry again. *Why? Why couldn't they love me?* She remembers Dragon's fury and Delilah's cold silence. There is something wrong with her. Something about her that does not make sense. For a short time she had been able to fool them into thinking she was one of them and could speak their language. But the truth of it came out—that she came from somewhere else, somewhere apart from the world, somewhere with no explanation, that no longer even exists.

She remembers again the mist of heat rising from his chest as he leaned over her, his breath in her ear, his hand trying to break into the chambers of her deepest longing. She *did* want him. She did. But.

What is this desire, fleeing into so many hidden places inside her, and where does it begin? Why did her need for Dragon—and his need for her—hurt?

Crawling on her hands and knees within the endless maze of her own mind, she is not even aware for a long time that she has stopped, and that the horse has stopped, and that they are staring at a wall of water that blocks their way. Before her, water is falling and falling, losing itself in the speed of its falling, in the loss of stone or soil or anything to hold it in shape. It roars in this wild loss of shape, in this falling. Her horse stands still and they contemplate the waterfall together, this tower of falling. It rises up from the river, up a brown cliff, at the top of which the deep forest begins, that deep green ache of life. In its falling—pulling apart from itself, its molecules flying alone in the air—the water becomes white, like pure spirit.

But the cliffs on either side are so steep, they will never be able to climb them. They will have to wander along the edge of the desert, searching for a way up, to continue onward toward that white-tipped mountain that Lonely only half believes in now. And she does not want to leave the water, for again it reminds her of Yora, whose memory still comforts her like nothing else she has ever encountered. While her horse wanders carefully down the terraces of stone to find a drink in the pools below the falls, Lonely sits in the sun and pulls her knees up to her chest. She watches the water fall, watches it forget itself, giving itself up to the air. As if water could fly.

When Dragon first touched her, he spoke to something inside her that she had no words for. Something she could handle when it stayed inside her own body but that, once it reached out to his, terrified her. He drew it forth like magic. He told her she was beautiful and perfect, and he loved her for that beauty, as her father had. So why did it frighten her? Why had she felt so lost in the face of this love he professed; why had she seemed to watch her own body as if from a great distance as he touched it? Who was she then, and where? Wherever she was, confused and lost, was a foggy place where he could not find her. And yet his caresses trapped her there, in a cage of his own fascination, and she paced inside herself, crying out and afraid, like the days and nights she paced in the tower. She felt an agony of hunger that he could not answer. He brought it forth and then stopped it with his desperate hands. Maybe this boy, like her father, was a magician. But was he the one? Was he the one who could rescue her?

She watches the water, curving into a nearly straight line downward, and tries to follow the individual speeding droplets with her eyes, though they dissolve like powder. There is a meditation in watching the water fall, like watching fire. After sitting there for a long time, spilling her thoughts desperately into the river, she closes her eyes, and the roar of the falls encases her mind, and she begins to hear music inside that great white sound. She has never heard music before, and yet she seems to recognize it. Her tears fall over her knees, down her neck and legs, her body wet and crying, her body itself a waterfall backward into memory, whose untranslated story is so much longer and more complicated than birdsong.

Does she stand and walk toward the dark space behind the falls, or does he walk through the shining water to meet her? Later, she will not remember. He lowers his flute and smiles at her. His black hair hides his laughing eyes, shining as if with water, but he does not look wet.

"Hey," he says. "You look so sad."

Lonely touches her own face, speechless. The unknown boy's face is smooth and sweet, like a girl's, and his naked chest is soft. He is wearing a skirt made of colors that keep shifting and falling, and he does not frighten her at all.

"I was sitting there behind the falls," he continues, "feeling sorry for myself, feeling bad about myself. And then I saw that you were doing the same! But you, girl, have no need to feel bad. *You* have been following your heart, after all."

"But he might have been the one," says Lonely, as if the boy will know what she means, which he seems to.

"But do you love him?" he asks.

Lonely cocks her head, and the sound of the water is suddenly fresh and clear, each drop of water a separate, intimate stripe of sound.

"No," she says, and then she knows it is true. The thought is emerging already though she tries to stop it, tries not to expect anything: *Maybe all of that... was only leading to this...*

"My name is Moon," says the boy, and takes both of her hands in his. "I am a rain god." When he says that, his body seems to leap into fragments of light, the way the waterfall explodes into particles of brilliant white while still remaining itself, not becoming anything less wonderful than water.

"Oh!" she cries. "What does it mean, then, to be a god? You can tell me." Why did she never ask Dragon? She was afraid somehow. She was afraid he would not know. But this boy will know. "What does it mean? Are we not supposed to feel?"

But the boy turns away, and the motions of his face make her heart hurt. He looks to a place in the falling water that she cannot see. "No," he says quietly, "we must feel, or all the power we are given as gods goes to waste."

"What power?"

He looks back at her, tenderly. "We each have our own gift." He smiles, though the smile clearly hurts him. "Don't you know your gift? What are you the goddess of?"

She thinks maybe he is teasing her. But she is too full of wonder to answer. He steps toward her.

"You're beautiful," she says, hope making her blush.

The boy takes one of her hands and places it against his heart. "Thank you," he says seriously, and his eyes look into hers with gratitude, and she feels as if her heart is a gift she can give to another—providing comfort for another in a way she did not know she was capable of, the way Yora did for her.

Then Moon says, "Would you like to go with me up the rainbow? I can see you're headed upward."

Lonely sees the rainbow now, just revealed by the sun, a wash of transparent color over the falls. She cannot stop her own smile, cannot stop the relief. His kindness. His forgiveness. His sudden appearance out of the music. Wouldn't it make sense that love would find her here, in this great surrender of water, rather than out on the desert, harsh and bare?

"Hold onto me," says Moon. "It's not as gentle as it looks." Then he presses his body to hers and delicately wraps her in his arms.

Immediately they collapse like thin tinder into flames of red—a bold, spitting red that burns Lonely from the inside. She can feel the cruel and shameless reality of her own blood, a tributary of the blood that fills all the life of the world. At once surrendered and starving, comforted and torn to pieces, she boils with a passion that fountains from the very loins of the earth, where life began and begins at every moment. Its fury turns her body to raw energy, and she swirls madly against the body of this other that presses to her, trying with her whole being to devour him, to make them one.

Then they are gathered and focused into a pulsing womb of orange, where the fury cools to a simmering pleasure, and Lonely rolls against the boy's body, each of her cells coming loose in a frothing wave of touch. Her mouth licks and sucks; her hands grope and fondle. The orange focuses the red tighter and tighter until she cries out in an extreme of ecstasy—her body too much for itself—and then they are both released into a flood of yellow.

Yellow expands in fields around them, and they fly, and they are children, laughing like the sun. Love is joy, is hope everlasting, is everything sweet and palpitating with wonder. Lonely feels she can climb any mountain; the light opens her so that all things are clear and easy to her, and courage is only a clear shining of the self forward with no holding back, no hiding or denying. Lonely and the boy hold hands, pressing their hearts up into the sky, and the sky opens its light to them: waves and waves of unbelievable, heart-breaking light, so bright she cannot see.

Then they wake together, relaxed in their love, in cool folds of green. They nurse their life from the green and the green grows up around them, all of life opening for them and pouring forth its sustenance. They eat of the green and it turns their bodies silent and strong, and their bodies lift deep breaths from their roots. Slowly, Lonely turns to the boy, and her look is luscious and sure, irresistible in its doubtless love. That love is so rich that it animates every moment of her being and her life, until she is brought to her knees by the nostalgic weight of its abundance, dying into the earth.

Then she is crying again, and her crying is blue, and she will keep crying—again and again, throughout her life—and nothing will ever release her from this crying. The blue pours forth from her throat: a singing cry, a crying out for love and for her own life to begin. She is riding the wave of that blue singing, her feet sliding over it and under it like fish leaping from the sea, and she is singing forth her own journey, and all the creatures of the earth and sky are singing with her. Each of her movements is pure grace, like the reflection of a flame upon glass, and she is sad but the sorrow is the most beautiful thing she has even known. Finally she lies down upon that blue sorrow, and falls beneath the waves, and deeper, deeper below the blue, she sinks into indigo.

Indigo is more beautiful than beauty, more lyrical than song, and deeper than depth. Indigo holds up the blue and all the other colors, all the falling of the waterfall. Lonely sinks into it like earth, remembering something she had forgotten, something she will forget again when she wakes. Something bigger than her love loves her. Something wider than her life holds her. She sees the whole story of her journey, from the tower through the ocean through the fields, from the fields into the desert, from the desert up the waterfall and into the green mountains, and from the green mountains dreaming up to the high blue mountain of truth, and back down the river all the way back to the sea, under the tower, under the island, to where indigo traces the meaning of all life in a terrifying script of naked truth.

Inside the indigo, Lonely is nothing but a churning of raw spirit, her yearning deepening into the purer longing of her spirit to be devoured by its own original fire. There at the brink of violet, where indigo turns its face again toward red, Lonely brightens into her own body again, as if that earthly form is the most perfect form her spirit could take. She finds herself in a chamber of indescribable peace and low flickering colors—all the colors of the rainbow and every shade in between.

Her head rests in Moon's lap. Moon's fingers glide along her scalp like cool streams, stretching out the strands of yellow and spreading them behind her.

"Your hair is so bright," he says in his singing, laughing voice. "I can tell you are going up toward the sun."

"Are we at the end of the rainbow?" asks Lonely weakly.

"No," says Moon solemnly, for his expressions seem to flicker between any and every emotion without notice or reason, fickle as images upon water. She does not understand why he looks sad now when he says, "The rainbow has no end. It is a circle, and you can only see the part that rises above the earth. We're in the center of the rainbow now, where purple turns to light."

Lonely's eyes swim in that light, which seems to glow brighter all around them as he speaks, and she searches its infinity for her own voice. "I want to do it again," she breathes.

Moon laughs. "The path of colors? Girl, you *will* do it again. Again and again and again, until you can hardly bear it. That's what life is. Just try to remember it's a circle, and you are immortal, and you can always come here, to the center, to rest."

Then he bends down and kisses her on the lips, and his lips burn with softness, sweeter than the first rays of morning or the first caress of sleep, as different from Dragon's thick passion as the moon is from the sun. Lonely rises up after him, following his lips and opening her eyes, wanting. But he smiles down at her with an easy calm and will not kiss her again.

She feels an ache that is familiar somehow, as if she expected this. A cold stone in her heart. It will be this way again and again. She will keep finding the god, and he will keep leaving her, forever.

"You don't want me," she says to him. "You don't love me."

"No! It's *you* who doesn't want *me*. You must ask yourself what you want! Don't forget. Don't say it is someone else who made the choice you were afraid to make yourself. You know, if you keep giving your choices away to others—waiting for the ones you don't want to push you away first—someday you won't own your choices any more. Then, when you want to make a wish come true, you won't be able to."

Lonely looks at him, both sad and afraid. She knows that what he says is true—he isn't the one, and she knew it from the first—but this truth does not help her. She wants to stay inside his touch. She wants the simple assurance of Dragon's hungry eyes again, his hand moving up her thigh, making her forget. The colors are all fading, and she can hear the water falling.

"Don't worry," says Moon, "Keep on your journey. When we were sitting there at the river, both of us feeling bad about ourselves, both of us greedy with our sorrow, I looked at you and remembered someone I love who needs me. I realized how selfish we are when we deny ourselves like that. I mean, we can go on denying ourselves if we want to, but not if it keeps us from being there for the people who love us."

"But no one loves me," says Lonely.

"Your horse loves you," says Moon, "for example."

"My horse!" cries Lonely, though her feelings are still slowed by the strange, deep place she's in, her thoughts halted with wonder and the exhaustion of color. "I left him behind again."

"Don't worry," says Moon again, beginning to fade from her the way Yora did once, trailing away like tears. "I think *that* horse knows how to find her own way, anywhere you go."

But is the horse a girl? Lonely isn't sure now, and as she wonders, Moon disappears, and she wakes in a furry drapery of green moss under cool trees, with the sound of the water falling away below her.

It's not the time of year for rain, and the flash flood on the full moon moved Delilah with some feeling she wasn't expecting—something like sadness. The way the red clay smelled, that aching scent of lost wildness. She still thinks of it.

She's dreaming of rain the day Moon slips in, a rivulet of water through an invisible crack in the cave. He takes his human form and curls up beside her, shoving his body playfully inside the curve of hers, forcing her clenched fetal position open so that she is holding him in her arms before she even knows what's happening.

It's a testament to her love for him that she recognizes him even in her sleep, because she doesn't automatically reach for her knife or her boar tusk but only whines a little, nuzzling her face into his neck. When she wakes, he is laughing. She cries out and then gives him a shove. "You're late."

"Don't be angry, Lil," he pleads instantly, the love he felt for her momentarily shrinking back. Her anger is unbearable to him. If she is angry, he will leave.

But she softens right away, and wraps herself back around him. "I'm sorry," she says. "I was only afraid. I worry about you, all the time."

"Don't worry about me," he whispers. She sighs, and he knows she wants to ask him all those difficult questions. He pulls away from her just enough to see her face, and flashes her his best smile.

To his relief, she smiles back. Her eyes are feverish, as always, and they dazzle him; her smile is almost painful to look at in her raw face.

"Who's that handsome sun god I saw on my way?" he teases. "You must not have fucked him. He didn't have that blissed-out look they usually have."

"Oh," says Lil, looking inward, her brows clenching a little. "Was he leaving finally?" But something in her tone is unclear. He can't tell which answer she's hoping for.

"I don't know," says Moon. "Maybe. I think he was headed somewhere, back toward the mountains."

"Mm," says Lil. "Anyway, that was Dragon. He's sad over this little half-goddess girl who came through here. You know, they were both half-god so they had all that expectation of each other: the whole idealizing, be-my-god-to-raise-me-up-beyond-my-humanness thing." She smiles at him again. "I've had a lot of visitors lately."

"I met her," says Moon, the pain of that frail, childish beauty twisting him up inside for a moment, "on my way down the waterfall. She was sad too."

Lil twists a little in his arms, sucks in her breath.

"What's wrong?" he asks.

"New moon. Cramps. They last for days now." Her voice is tight.

Moon turns her over so that he can curl around her from behind, and places his hands over her belly. With the round spirit of water whirling from his hands, he smooths and caresses her womb, asking it to relax, to be at peace in the great flow of life and death. He feels her body slacken a little against him, her breathing relax.

"What else?" he whispers.

"Everything," Delilah whispers back. "Moon, I'm so scared. What's happening to me? Am I dying?"

"Shh," Moon says. "Tell me what hurts."

"My shoulders," she murmurs, as if still half-sleeping. "Back. Stomach sometimes. Get headaches sometimes. Tired all the time. Weak. Cramps in my legs. Can't eat sometimes. Feel sick."

"No," says Moon senselessly, "you'll be okay." He keeps wrapping his body around her, his legs and arms and hips all around her, unfurling his magic into her body, imagining the strength of light flowing through it.

"I'm okay now," she says. "But it will come back, when you leave. I don't know what's happening."

He lies still, barely breathing. She makes him afraid. He doesn't know what to do.

"Where have you been, Moon?" she says suddenly, turning toward him. "Were you in the mountains? Did you forget about the desert this year?"

Moon shrugs. "Maybe. Maybe I forgot."

"What makes you forget?"

Moon rolls onto his back, lifts his flute and begins to play. The music takes over the little space they occupy, spiraling it backward in time, and it keeps Lil silent until he is finished. She turns around again, and when he looks at her, she is staring at him, her eyes shocked with emotion. He wonders if his music hurts her more than it helps. But if so, he envies her even that pain. He wishes he could feel what she feels when he plays, but he can't feel the music, only play it.

Finally she says, "That's not what makes you forget, Moon."

"What?"

"You know what."

"Tell me," he says, though he doesn't want her to.

"I'll tell you what I think. And I'm not telling you because I'm angry. I'm telling you because I love you, because I'm scared for you. I think you go into the City again and again, as a human being. No one knows you're a god. No one respects you—just a little girlish boy. And you let anyone have their way with you. You let them fuck you any way they want to. You like the pain. You like forgetting. You don't do the drugs we did as kids, the ones whose spirits we knew, the plants who showed us the dreams of the earth. You do the drugs my father did, the ones that killed him, the mechanical ones made out of things we don't understand. You don't do them for wisdom any more. You do them to forget, like my father did. You do them because you don't think any better of yourself."

Darkness criss-crosses inside Moon's skull. The music stills within him. He tries to speak but his voice feels like a black hole; it won't come out as words but only as a pile of rubble. He spins his flute in his hands, staring at it, trying to remember what it is. This is why he didn't come back for so long, he remembers. This is why.

Lil pulls him close. His mind is blank. Her human heartbeat drums inside him, reminding him insistently of life, rapping against the closed door to his own heart. "You're destroying yourself," she whispers.

"Why do you think that?"

"Because every time you come back, you look older, but you're never any older inside. You're not any wiser. That's what those drugs do to you. They steal your life."

"But I can change my form however I like it—that doesn't matter. I don't get older. I'm immortal."

"Yes, you do get older. I love you, and I can see it. I know you think because I'm human my vision is simple, but being human means I see things as they are. I can see past your magic because I love you. And you're making yourself old. You're killing yourself. I watched my father do it, and now you're doing it, even though you're a god."

"Oh, Lil," says Moon, finding a smile and turning toward her as he senses a way out. "I'm not your father."

But she isn't distracted. "That's right," she says. "My father didn't give a shit about me. But you do. You're the only one who does. So don't leave me. It's much worse watching a god die, much uglier, because you're so beautiful." Her gaze mesmerizes him, more powerful than the desert in its love, its simple need. "Moon, without rain, everyone will die."

A hint of fury rises in him for barely a moment and then falls. He never has the energy for it. "There's nothing I can do, Lil," he says coldly, as if she doesn't know. "My father won't give me the rain. I am nothing to my father either. You know that."

Lil looks at him. "Is it because you love human beings?" she asks gently. "Or is it because you love men?"

Moon shakes his head, turns away. Maybe he doesn't truly love anyone. He hates the tension in his own voice when he speaks. Why does she make him speak of these things, again and again?

"Anyway," she continues. "That thing about your father—I think it doesn't matter. You're refusing something. Can't you feel the rain inside you?"

I can't feel anything, he thinks, but he doesn't want to hurt her.

"Something's wrong," she whispers. "It hasn't rained in the City for twenty-five years. All around it is desert—not this kind of desert, that's alive and full of color, but just an empty land of broken tree skeletons, land with no roots to hold it together, lost dust-storm land."

"It doesn't matter anyway," answers Moon, feeling settled now into a familiar dullness. "People pump their water in from far away, or from under the earth. They don't need the rains any more."

"They *do*. They need you. My mother told me about rain in the City. She said it used to happen when she was young. She said it would make children come out to play, and adults would watch them, and forget their important roles, and laugh. She said she'd come running into one of those cold City places, a bank, or a grocery store, or a department store, and she'd be all mussed up—her hair out of place and her face streaked with water like tears. Her clothes would stick to her body, and she'd be laughing because she'd feel silly, and because she was running. And everyone would look at each other, all dripping and sexy and humbled by these forces of nature that for once they couldn't escape—because they came from the sky—and they'd feel connected for a moment, and they'd really, you know, *see* each other, for once. And time would stop, and they'd forget about building that big stupid dream of destruction, they'd forget about money, they'd forget about the roles they were supposed to play in Hanum's plan, for a moment. That's how she and my father met, in the last rain that ever came. That's how they always remembered each other, and that's why they were drawn back to each other.

Because, I think, they missed the rain."

"Lil," Moon says, "you've told me this a million times." But it touches him a little, because it's the only time she ever speaks of her parents with anything other than contempt. It's the only time she ever speaks of anything with something like idealism.

"Well *do* something, Moon. Bring it back."

Moon is silent, but his whole awareness is filled with Lil beside him—and the knowledge that he hurts her, again and again, and never means to. It is her he cares for, not the City.

"I know," he says finally, though it is not easy, "that I forgot about you. I get lost sometimes. But I dreamed a bat came with a message from you. So I woke up and left the City, and I came back."

Lil looks at him, her eyebrows raised.

"Well, okay, I didn't come *right* back. I took a sort of roundabout route." She grins.

"Lil! Come on—I don't take straight lines to anywhere. I followed my music. It took me through the mountains."

"I followed my music,'" she imitates loftily, and they both laugh. Then she holds him, rocks against him.

"I'm glad you're here," she says.

Delilah and Moon play in the desert together that night, chasing each other through the darkness like rabbits. Coyote watches them, not hiding himself, smiling. Moon finally stops their game and holds out his hands, and Coyote comes warily over and sniffs them, his lips pulled back. Then Coyote stands on his hind feet and dances with Moon, while Delilah laughs and laughs.

The desert glitters in the remains of its own heat like an undiscovered jewel that as yet has no name, spinning its life in the darkness. To Delilah the starry sky is like the roof of a vast underground chamber, Moon's secret palace, in which he paints a paradise of drunken life. When he plays his flute, prairie dogs emerge from their burrows, sitting stupefied and silent on their beanbag haunches, because in all their repertoire of sounds for every predator and every need, they have no name for joy. The jackrabbit turns his complex, heavy-jowled face toward them, his eyes like tall dark windows; he is frozen by the music, and forgets the fear which is his essence. He forgets to be afraid of Coyote, who forgets to want him. A thirty-year-old tarantula makes love for the thirtieth time and is, for the first time, in such an ecstasy that she forgets to eat her mate. Tortoises emerge from their underground burrows, march over the land with heads raised like a herd of fast dinosaurs, and drink the music from the air. A green whipsnake coils around Moon's feet and then rises, swaying thinly, her tongue lapping up the music. Deep beneath the earth, the seventeen-year-cicadas, still in their youth, dream of the day that they, too, will rise up upon the breast of the world and give their lives away to song.

And Delilah watches. It is the only time she is happy being still, when she listens to Moon play his flute. Like the other animals, she forgets herself. She forgets what she has to be angry about, or afraid of, or sorry for.

She used to think sex was something she would never be able to deny herself. She thought it was something she had to have, because she got everything from it: beauty, magic, comfort, pleasure, satisfaction, peace, relief, confidence, everything. All the things that were impossible to find in the rest of human interaction, in the rest of the world she left behind. That was why it was the one thing she missed. Because there was ugliness and shame that she carried with her always, and sex could take that away. Nothing else could take it away, not even the desert.

Then the morning she said *no* to Dragon, she glimpsed something else—a possibility. The next day she barely slept. She lay on her back in the sun until it burned her, and then she walked all the way to the river and waded in, splashing like a child. That *no* turned out to be the key that unlocked a strange garden of forgotten life within her: things that had been locked up inside the need for sex—the only need she would allow herself in the City—and magic she had never believed in and never known she wanted to believe in, and games she had played with herself in the meadow as a little girl, before Mira was born—games she can't quite remember, but almost. She thought she remembered a time when she'd understood what animals were saying. The first animal that ever spoke to her: a crow. The way that crow made her laugh, and they had whole conversations then and understood one another. The way she was happy once. And the feel of Mira's baby skin. Her sweetness, in the beginning. The pictures she drew for Delilah, of unicorns. All of this, like a whole life she'd forgotten, Delilah remembered all at once that day, and the river passed over her body like some luxurious material she'd never thought she could afford.

But every day since then, the memory of all that has been a little less clear. She had glimpsed that other, remembered life in the river that day, but never fully entered into it. Sometimes the gate stands open still, and she stands at the door, but she doesn't know what to do. Most of the time she doesn't feel changed at all, and she doesn't know why she said "no," or what she was trying to prove. Listening to Moon's flute now, she's still just hungry and horny and sad, and if Moon weren't here, she'd even be lonely.

"How long are you going to stay?" she asks him when the music is over, and they lie together in the sand, staring at the stars as if they've just made love.

"How long do you need me?" he answers, and she smiles.

"That's a good answer. But you don't mean it."

The wind sweeps over them, dry, as if it doesn't remember ever bringing rain.

"If you love rain so much," asks Moon, "why do you live in the desert?" But she knows he's only teasing. He is the one who helped her make her home here. He knows the rain is more beautiful here than anywhere else in the world, because the desert's whole life is built on the longing for it. Delilah knows that, too, but she can't bring herself to explain it.

"Moon," she tells him, "things are happening to my body that I don't understand."

He is silent.

"My back. It hurts, in all different places, almost every day. My shoulders."

"Didn't you get hurt, a long time ago? Didn't they hurt you, when you were trying to save——"

"No," says Delilah sharply. "That's not it."

"But I think you hurt your shoulder then."

"But it never used to bother me."

Moon is silent again. She knows he's not buying it.

"A snake came to me," she says, to keep him from thinking about that. "He stood up—I mean he raised himself up. I think he was telling me something, something about my spine? Something—I don't know. It sounds stupid."

"Your spine is the pathway of your life, the pathway of your spirit upward."

"Why upward?"

Moon thinks. "It sounds like growing old to me."

"What?"

"I don't know. I've never grown old. It's just a feeling. Pain means something, though. Sometimes it's the only way your body can make itself heard. Maybe there's a way you have to travel inside yourself to get older, rising up toward your spirit. You can get older by accident or older on purpose, but you'll get older either way, you know."

"Are you sure you're immortal?"

"How would I know for sure? If I'm mortal, *that* I'll know for sure, eventually."

Delilah laughs. But she knows he isn't. Life isn't kind enough to make them both mortal, to let them both share the same story. Moon comes from somewhere so far away from this earth she doesn't understand it. His father is—what? She thinks maybe the sky itself. Whoever is in charge of rain.

Whoever makes it.

"I was thinking," she says, trying to sound casual. "This sickness. I don't feel well sometimes. I get cramps even at the wrong time of the moon, and—I mean, could it be some man gave me a sickness, when I fucked him?"

"Yeah. You can get diseases."

Delilah hesitates, frustrated and awkward with her own ignorance. "What are these exactly, then—these diseases?"

"They're all the angers and hurts people pass between their lovers, because they fuck each other without caring and they don't want to open their hearts. So they pass this pain and anger from lover to lover, unconsciously, not admitting it to each other or themselves. The kind of men you fuck—they're more likely than any to pass on this pain. It might have nothing to do with you, but you get it anyway: someone else's pain."

"I don't care," says Delilah, her voice low, "anyway."

"Yes you do," says Moon. "Don't try to act like me. Besides, you'll pass the pain on to others then, and that's not fair."

"Well it's too late now," says Delilah, bitterness grinding softly in her throat.

"Maybe I can make enough magic to heal you, if you promise to use some kind of protection from now on."

Delilah shakes her head. "Maybe I'll never have sex again," she says, letting herself feel the way the wind blows through her when she says it, terrifying and exhilarating at the same time—the idea of losing everything. Even though she doesn't mean it.

"Yeah, right," Moon laughs.

"You know"—she takes a deep breath—"I did say *No*. The other day. I said *No* to Dragon." She listens to the way the words sound.

"Oh yeah?" But she feels the distance in his voice, like he doesn't understand the importance of what she's saying. Like he doesn't want to, because it is something he hasn't ever had the courage to do himself. She shouldn't have said it aloud. She should have kept that *no* a secret within herself, a hidden power, fragile and potent, like a new virginity. She shouldn't have told him. But always before, she's told Moon everything.

"Let's talk about something else," she says now, frightened. "Please."

"Okay," says Moon, but she knows he won't talk about himself. That's why this conversation is so much easier for him than the one in the cave when he first arrived. Because it's about her. "Tell me about the animals," he says. "How are the boar people?"

"Oh, that's another thing. I keep having this dream. About a deer. The deer is the one I'm supposed to hunt next. And I'm running out of food. But

I'm not going to kill that deer."

"Why?"

"It'll sound crazy. I can't explain."

"Tell me. Please."

"The deer. She reminds me of Mira. Her eyes."

Moon waits a moment, knowing she's struggling with some emotion, but he doesn't wait so long that she'll feel ashamed.

"I think you have to do it, Lil. You know that. You're going to have to hunt it."

Delilah closes her eyes. It's so painful having someone to talk to who really cares, but she needs it—she needs to be broken like this. It's almost better than sex. But it hurts so much she would never do it with anyone else. One friendship this deep is enough. One heartbreak a year, for this comfort, this love she feels, is worth it, but no more.

"Maybe your sister's calling you," says Moon. "Maybe she needs you to connect with her in this way. It's like I was saying about your shoulder. I think it always comes back to her."

"But I'll feel so awful," says Delilah, her eyes still closed.

"Maybe this is why you hurt. Why you feel tense. You're holding something back."

"I'm holding back because I'm afraid of hurting her."

"No, you're holding back your love."

"But, Moon," says Delilah, feeling furious. She squeezes her eyes shut. The crying is like saliva in her mouth that she has to keep swallowing back. It makes her lips wet and too soft. In the City she was so unhappy, but at least she never had to feel things like this. She didn't have time and space, like she does now, just to think. For hours. For days. For moons. And something is happening to her. Something has changed, after all, and it's not magical like that morning in the river. She knows why she stands at the door and doesn't go in. There are other things in there, things she doesn't want to feel.

"I always loved Mira," she manages to say. "I always tried to love her and she wouldn't take my love. It couldn't help her."

"You tried to love her by holding back who you were, and that's not real love. Maybe she needs you to be yourself, be the hunter. Maybe she needs to be hunted. Maybe you're the only one, Lil, who can find her, wherever she is."

"Dammit, Moon, I already went through this. You know I already did. I looked. I looked fucking everywhere, I asked everyone, I went to every office—"

"Lil!" he cries. "Stop. I know you did. I'm just saying—"

"She's my sister," Delilah interrupts, turning her face away.

"I'm just saying maybe you need to hunt her in a different way. Not in that world. In another world."

In her world, wherever that is, Delilah can't help but think. She lies still for a long time, feeling in her belly that emptiness where hunger comes from, that emptiness that must be filled. As always, there is no way out of life and its needs. Or is there? Maybe Mira found a way out.

"Okay," she whispers finally, "I don't know why, but I'll do it. But I'm doing it for you, not for her. I won't try any more for her, do you understand? I made that promise to myself a long time ago, Moon. It's the only way I could survive."

Malachite was named for a stone, because his people are Earth people, but in his dreams he flies beyond this place, and that's why they call him Kite, for short.

While his parents are arguing he runs out the back of the house and into the field. His sister, Chelya, who is almost two years older than him, is crying. That's the worst part of their arguing—the only part he can't stand.

A swallow bursts from her nest under the eaves of the woodshed as he passes roughly by. "Sorry," he mumbles. His legs are strong, and he runs all the way over his grandmother's hill and into the woods beyond. He runs up the thorny hill that would suffocate anyone else in its tangle; he has a secret path. At the top of it, he climbs the tree that always remembers him, and roosts himself at the base of a branch that has thickened itself to support the weight of extending outward and upward above all the other trees around. Above him, it shakes its jubilation of leaves like a flag of freedom.

I won't let them destroy the life I've made with my family, his mother had said, her voice never raised but frightening in its fear. *It took my mother and me all that we had to make this life. And the people there—they only know how to destroy. That's all they know.*

And by holding on so damn tightly to what you love, his father had retorted, that voice big but helpless against his mother's shivering tightness, *you're going to destroy it yourself.*

From here, Kite can see the source of all the argument, or at least imagine that he sees it. It's too far away to see, actually, but he thinks something catches at his vision when he runs it over the white mirror of the far-off desert beyond his mountain home. Whoever lives in the City doesn't know about him and his family, doesn't know about the other families scattered throughout these mountains who once gave sustenance to everyone. But he knows about the City, because its power leaves no place in the world untouched. The river talks of it. The earth moans with it. The trees sigh in its dark breath. He tries to picture the houses taller than the tallest trees, the lights that burn all night, the speed at which things move. He doesn't assume anything about it. He will not listen to anything either of them says, good or bad. He just wants to find out for himself.

At night, he's sure he really can see the glow of it: a grey-white light, ethereal and sooty, like a halo, like an idea.

Lonely has changed, though she doesn't know it. Her legs are wiry and dirty; her dress, a ragged remnant, is torn from one sunburnt shoulder; her hair is bleached paler than ghost-wings. The flush of life stains her cheeks from within now, and four or five freckles, like stars, have landed near her nose. If someone could see her now who knew her before, they would see those changes. But there is no such person.

There is only me, whom she does not yet know.

She knows only her horse, still walking beside her for no reason either of them can name, and he has changed a little too.

They enter the forest as through a door, and as it closes behind them Lonely turns quickly, catching a last glimpse of open sky. She can feel the silence settle around her even before she can hear it—not the passionate windy silence of the desert, but the inward silence of dreams.

She walks in, and instantly, she is intimate with an enormous connected being, a being that is a whole world. It brushes her skin again and again. It leans close. It blots out the sky, so that she stumbles as if under the sea. It breathes. The horse's heavy footsteps press into layer upon layer of the forest's history. The top layer of leaves crunches with the recent ache of death; the layers below it hiss more softly with the mellow perspective of the very old; the deepest layers, the fertile black remains of forest hundreds of years before, compress without sound.

Around her head, the green leaves of this year's life hover expectantly.

Trees. She begins to differentiate them, like giant strands of an interconnected nervous system. Other green life climbs up the trees or crouches beneath them, or hangs from their tips like hair. She feels their presence like solemn kings and queens with their feet underground, their children tangled around them. They seem to ride their own growth effortlessly, being what they are without words, rising as if in worship of some great and gentle deity she does not know. The wind makes love to them, rolling in their arms, and they catch it and pass it one to the other.

Lonely keeps one hand wound tightly into the horse's mane as she walks close to him. She hears a great nation of beings scurrying with invisible tasks around her: hammering and swishing and crying out in the dark. Shadows move, holes gape in the earth like questions, and spider webs collapse over her like broken dreams. As she and the horse break through tight networks of branch and leaf, patterns long undisturbed, Lonely seeks hungrily ahead for some sign of the mountain. Now they seem to have left the main river. Now they follow a quieter stream. The birdsong, that endless conversation, comforts Lonely a little, though here it is different, less exuberant, more subtly crafted to ricochet through needle, leaf, and vine. She fights off the feeling that she has entered a maze with no destination, no purpose, no end.

The river forks and then dissipates into marshy thickets, impenetrable thorns, and murky, sullen silence. They stop. In front of them, a spider web remains fully intact, inches from Lonely's face. She doesn't see the spider, hiding at the corner, but she sees the design of the web like a far advanced language and knows someone mysterious must have written it. Following the light along its thin, icy wires, she sees other webs running innumerably across every space, and wonders suddenly if these webs hold the entire forest together in their careful silence.

Where will she go without running into them? All around her the forest weaves itself like a fate already spun, a mass of life she cannot push through or climb out of, only enter deeper into. She sinks down and takes her own feet in her hands to warm them, staring at the horse who seems unsure now as he nibbles around the trunks of the trees.

"Where do we go?" she whispers.

Where do we go? teases the wind back at her.

Without meaning to, she grabs onto the thought of Dragon. Not that many days ago, she was with someone; now she is alone again. Her mind begins to spin around the pain of it. How sorry she feels to have disappointed him! If only she could have surrendered, if only she could have answered that bright innocence inside his eyes, that trusted her to answer him! She could be with him still. But she denied him, until he was forced to turn away from her, turn to another. Her heart strains inside that final memory: the hurt in his howling yell as he stood up after her, the shaking in his body. Even then, he would have melted right into her if she had walked back to him. She knows he would have. But now it is too late.

The truth of it seems completely different now. She cannot remember why she left. What could be worse than this loneliness, after all? What is she seeking, that she left him for?

And why did her father leave her? Why?

She leans back against a tree, closing her eyes.

When she opens them, a dragonfly is hovering before her face, looking directly into her eyes. His head is nothing but eyes, like a thousand different ways to see.

follow me, he seems to say. *i'm as old as the ferns, as old as the moss, as old as water.*

"Show me," she says to him urgently, leaning forward. He must be a sign of something, he must be. "Show me the way home."

But then he is gone, gone so fast she can't track him. And she is left with only the word she just spoke, a word she has never spoken before: "home." It makes her cry.

So she stands up and keeps wandering, aimless in that shapeless stillness of marsh, where the trees are sad and heavy in their soggy roots, and the forest is so thick she has not the slightest sense of its bigness, nor of the curve of the earth's body beneath her, curving into greater and greater mountains. She wanders in a small dark circle, her mind lost inside her own questions and spun into the spirals of spiderwebs, until the sun shrinks within the trees, and the light turns cold, then drains away as if forever.

She stumbles through the brambles in search of dry land, thinking only of rest, pressing her body with senseless force through the tangle, crying continuously, her face dirty and wet.

She has forgotten her horse again, but when she lies down finally under a cloudy sky and a hidden half-moon, too confused to feel afraid, he is suddenly there, and she feels a twinge of gratitude. She rests her head upon his flank as he, for once, lies down beside her. But he remains alert.

She keeps her back pressed to the tree behind her, drawing comfort from it in her sleep as if to keep herself anchored within the drift of her own mind. Its simplicity is touching: she feels clearly its lack of question, its earnest life, its sincere growth upward, neither hopeful nor afraid. The wind sounds so much kinder as it passes through the tree's branches.

hush, says the tree to her mind. *i'll sing you the old lullabies, and you'll remember. you'll remember the Heart is greater than all of this. feel, now, how easy it is to love...*

Or maybe she is already asleep. Somewhere above her, she remembers, the tree has contact with a sky she can no longer see.

Yet she dreams the same old nightmare, the black hole of nothing beneath the tower, and this time she is crawling on her hands and knees through that putrid blackness, and something desperate is happening in her belly, a howling, painful kind of loneliness, and the very air she draws with her breath tastes so empty it vibrates. She knows for the first time, tasting that nothingness, that she will die. Her belly growls, and in that animal growling is the panicking knowledge of her own humanness.

When she wakes, she still feels it. She doesn't know that she is hungry, because she has never felt hunger before, but she has felt the hunger of her body for another, and this is worse than that. It isn't swollen and sweet but acid and angry, and it grates at her, this emptiness. She feels her mouth flush with wetness, and she looks wonderingly around her, wanting to take something inside her, wanting to bring something into her and make it part of her. The ripe fleshy scent of living wood assaults her, and the rich texture of earth-scent, and the sweetness of flowers, but none of these can fill her. She rises and thrusts on through the forest; she feels her body coming apart, her fluids dissolving her belly. She touches her tongue to each leaf, but they repel her with their bitterness.

On and on she walks, plowing on now without care for direction or spider webs, her hunger driving her like fury, and the emptiness sprawls inside her, until her spirit begins to hover around her starving body, leaving her legs weak and her head spinning. She is thirsty, too, her throat sticky and chest burning, but she's lost track of the river.

This is being human, this need. It is nothing but need, and the pain of need. It was not Dragon she needed, not another person but something more essential, something that must become part of her own self or she will be lost and cease to be anything. It is something of the earth that she needs, something that must die and be reborn inside her. Something so basic, something her very bones are made of, but she does not know what it is.

When her body collapses in the afternoon sunlight, she no longer feels the hunger wracking her belly like a nightmare, but only the slow, delirious song of death in each of her cells. The sky tumbles down in shards through the great loving canopy of the trees, their shapes warm and shifting and tender, their hugeness relieving her of her struggle.

I am mortal, after all, she thinks, and whereas immortality felt like the great open distance of her future stretching out before her to the mountain, mortality feels like this: the closed space of the forest, the going inward, the relief of giving up, the comfort of earth and trees. Mortality is the raw pain singing through all her body, singing it down into the earth. Mortality is the lift of her spirit into the treetops, separating in this way, watching as an earth-born, human man climbs down from his horse and scoops her into his arms. Mortality is his dense body calling her back into her own, and the smell of his heavy sweat, and her desire to press tighter against him as he holds her loosely over the body of his horse and rides with her, perfectly balanced, back to his home. But she is too weak to do so, and when she opens her eyes she cannot focus on his face, and so she closes them again, and sleeps.

You prefer, I know, the gods of Air. Hanum was one. His powers were those of idea, of fantasy, of the ever-expanding mind. There was no problem of life that could not be overcome by that mind. The entire City is still run by it, and the jobs that pay the most money are the jobs run by minds. And when you die, you think, if you have lived good lives, you will go up into the air, and finally escape all this. Perhaps you will even join Hanum there.

It is the lower races that belong to the other gods, you say. Everyone knows that the peoples who followed the gods of Fire were dangerous, vicious, bloodthirsty. Everyone knows that the gods of Water are weak. Or perhaps they are treacherous, seductive, or crazy. And everyone knows that the gods of the Earth are simple and stupid, the subject of comical tales. They think of nothing but food and sex. They are like animals.

The Princess daughter of Hanum is of course a goddess of air. And the Prince who will rescue her—he, too, must be of air. His identity is a cloudy mystery, as it should be. He is the Prince, you say, of some hidden kingdom. Some kingdom far away and up high, in a realm no human being can reach. It is a kingdom of golden light, of white billowing clouds, of song and wings and—and what, exactly? Something that cannot be defined, but that you long for.

When he rescues her, when they finally join! Then that magical kingdom will, perhaps, be revealed.

Nothing is wrong in the City. The City is everything and gives you every-thing you need.

And yet you believe in this story with a fierceness that not one of you speaks of. This story helps you to survive miseries you do not even realize you are surviving, such as boredom, self-loathing, and despair.

You do not believe in fairy tales. You do not think of such things. You do not dream, you say.

And yet, *when she finds her prince, when he rescues her, when true love uplifts you from the daily trials of this dull earth and you find perfection in each other's arms and "I love you forever" shall save you, finally, and none of this shall matter any more....*

You know this story, that lives up in the sky, where your dreams are. It is the only myth you still have to live on.

And I know it, too.

Everybody knows it.

Earth

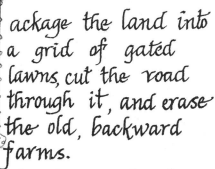

Package the land into a grid of gated lawns, cut the road through it, and erase the old, backward farms.

You cannot imagine needing farms — a relic of the past. Besides being unclean, the food they made could never be enough to feed the thousands of human beings that the City of everlasting life — with its advanced medicine and life prolongation and freedom from predators — produces.

But the City hardly needs food any more. You are almost gods. Often you forget to eat, and when you do eat you look for easy, quickly ingestible substances in small, magical packages. The tastiest, sweetest substances are the brightest colors—brighter than anything found in nature. They can be bought for small money in stores, and beyond that you do not know, or wonder, where they come from.

Will it hurt you if I tell you? They come from giant buildings, windowless and hidden in grey uniformity on the outskirts of the City. Inside the buildings, machines do all the work. A couple of plants, engineered to perfection, seem to meet all your needs. These plants are mass-produced in vast compartments, protected from insects and rain and drought and wind, their water measured, their soil stimulated chemically, their light made by artificial bulbs fueled by the decay of prehistoric creatures under the earth. You do not remember that these creatures died, or that the City still runs on the everlasting fire of their transforming remains. You do not believe that those remains will soon run out; in fact, if asked, you would say you do not even believe that those creatures ever existed.

What makes the meat, which is all you really want, is hard to name. They look almost like animals, in that they seem almost to be alive, but they have no feet or legs, and the birds have no beaks or wings, and the mammals are just giant, milk-producing breasts with tiny bodies attached. Each meat-producing lump of flesh is fattened and kept in a compartment until ready to be cut up and sold. A heart must beat somewhere inside each of these compartments, but there is no movement; there is no sound.

But no, it could not hurt you to know this. How could you sympathize? You sit still for most of your days, too, and hardly need legs either, though you still have them.

I will feel this for you, then, which you cannot feel. I will feel even this, which is yet too shameful for you to feel.

i'm afraid, says the deer.

That's how Delilah recognizes her: she can feel her fear, so strongly that she wonders if the deer has actually spoken. None of the other deer can see or smell Delilah—she's sure of it—but this little doe is standing still while the others browse the new buds from the trees, and she's looking right at the tangle of thorns where Delilah is hiding. She looks so young.

i'm afraid to die.

And Delilah realizes that she did speak.

This deer knows her.

This deer is waiting, waiting for her own death, with such trembling peace. It doesn't matter that Moon crouches lovingly in the trees just a little distance behind Delilah. Nothing matters but herself and the doe.

The moon is full, ripe for hunting. It highlights the introverted delicacy of the deer's body, her hard, poignant brows, her long face creased with gentleness beneath her obsidian eyes. Her fragile, innocently courageous stance in direct view of her killer reminds Delilah of the girl Dragon desired, that strange angelic human. And Delilah feels herself slain in that moment by her prey— by her eyes of pure night, her thin, beautiful feet, and her unearthly femininity.

I'm afraid, too, thinks Delilah, wanting to say it aloud, but not knowing how to speak back, and not wanting to hear the sound of her own voice. She wants to make herself as vulnerable as the deer, if such a thing is possible. Like every animal she kills, she owes it her life.

The deer keeps standing there, her people flowing around her. Delilah can feel how she wants to stay with her friends, like a frightened bride who feels safer staying with her fellow women, laughing with them from afar, but feels irresistibly drawn to that other who will ultimately claim her. Delilah remembers the girls from school again, so secure in their crowd, and she feels the familiar envy. She wants to feel the hard anger she felt for Dragon's white girl—for that prettiness, that perfection, that pretense at purity and goodness—but she only feels crippled, as she did throughout her life with Mira, by her own inadequacy. How ugly she is, compared with this animal's grace. How unworthy of living, when that living will cost this other her beautiful life.

Now Delilah has watched the deer for long enough to see that, unlike many of the others, she does not have a fawn. Not this year. She is still too young. How could she be so young? *Like Mira, who lost her life to madness before it began....*

what will happen when i die? asks the deer. And Delilah thinks that this was always going to happen, because it was what she expected of herself—to do something utterly wrong. It is wrong to kill this young doe. Yet she is being forced to do it anyway. It is her destiny, to fulfill her image of herself as bad. Maybe it was her father's image of her, when he used to say drunkenly, angrily, to her mother, *That one will never come to good. She has too much fire. She can only bring destruction.*

And she understands, too, that the deer will not comfort her, will not tell her it's okay. It is the least Delilah can do, to comfort the deer, whom she will kill. But she doesn't know the answer to the deer's question.

Carelessly, she shifts her weight backward, and last year's leaves snap under her heels.

what will happen when i die? the deer asks again, twitching once.

You will become part of me, answers Delilah, because that is all she knows.

why?

Because, answers Delilah, the passion she normally feels on the full moon rising into her womb and aching, echoing against the emptiness she keeps there, *I need you.*

they say when we die to become part of the coyote, or the mountain lion, continues the deer, her voice coming silently through her eyes, through her nostrils with her breath, *we continue in the ancient cycle. we remain animal. we keep who we are and are reborn again, safe in the circle of the earth. but what happens to us when we become part of the human? i am afraid. we do not understand you.*

I don't want to kill you, Delilah thinks helplessly.

i know, says the deer. *that is why i am afraid. tell me you will take good care of my spirit. tell me you will remember me always.*

I will, says Delilah, and she feels her own womb like a round circle of pain in which she and the deer face each other forever: desire and surrender, warrior strength and helpless fear. *But I don't even know you. I don't understand who you are.*

you know me, responds the deer, stepping toward her, and the herd parts as she takes a different direction from the rest. *we are both women. take me into you, and know me. stop denying me. i am afraid, and i need you too.*

The deer's silent voice, in the end, sounds like Mira's. In a blind rush of love that she barely recognizes as her own, Delilah aims her arrow and, perfectly and without thought, shoots.

It's like any other time she's shot an arrow. There is no effort, no force. She only straightens the three fingers that held the bow taut and, by doing so, lets go.

Up on the round mountain, the goddesses draw together beneath the cloud that hovers in the Garden's mind.

This cloud is heavier than stone. Its sigh as it settles into the sacred tree is audible. They can smell its stench: a burned, wasted, oily smell. They know it is water that holds all this wrongness together. But the water does not show itself; it is clear and selfless, showing only the color of that which colors it, smelling only of that which pollutes it. And the pollution, in turn, holds the water together—makes it a thing, a cloud, unable to dissipate.

"Yora," whispers the leader, "we know you. You are safe here. Be yourself again. Be beautiful."

"Yora," whisper the others, and they murmur words of love for her, this goddess of the earth's blood.

Yora holds forth her foul darkness helplessly. *This is all there is,* she seems to say. *Only this darkness. There is no Yora. Only this.* But something about the Garden draws her. She is not aware of making choices, but she remembers this place.

"You are water," says the leader more firmly now. "You are pure. This virgin water flowing here is also part of you. Though it seems long ago, it is happening now, too. Your youth, your age, your suffering, your death, your rebirth—it is all happening now. All of the river is happening at once. Return to yourself."

There is so much suffering, says Yora. *I was not enough. Never enough.*

The goddesses are silent, gazing up at her, their eyes tearing humanly from the toxins that evaporate from her.

"She cannot evolve in this form," says the leader. "She is stuck."

"But in this form," says another, "it is easier for her. She does not feel anything. Being in human form is so painful!"

"But how else can she transform this pain? This pain comes from human beings. She must feel it as a human being in order to let it go."

"Yes, otherwise it will return to the waters, causing only more suffering, more sickness."

"Who can help her, then? Who can help her to take human form after she rains down finally upon the earth?"

The goddesses sit in meditation. They know Yora more intimately than they know anything. They have seen her born and born again, eternally; every day they watch her fresh, unsullied youth laugh and gurgle through the Garden, flowing down from the spring at the top of the world. They know why she came back here, even if she does not. She still wants to heal the people with her song; she still wants to—she must—communicate the message of the river. There is no other choice. What would become of people's souls, if not for the river goddess who transforms the river's voice into a language they can understand? How would people ever be brought to listen to their hearts again; how would they ever remember?

Yet this dark weight, too, is part of the story. The leaves of the tree, shrouded in the cloud, begin to wilt. The cloud does not want to kill the tree, but she has no will of her own to stop it.

Every part of the deer is almost too elegant for the eyes to bear.

Supple hills of muscle, vulnerable ridges of bone dipping inward under the knee, beneath the quiet, child-like bristle of her yellow-brown fur. Her eyes still glowing, though the hallways of her body's house are dark now. The blood at Delilah's knife-tip bursting impossibly soft, like the skin of roses. The red of it reflecting black in the night, but with a black that ripples and shines.

The flesh undone from the skin, falling in slick handfuls of pure, tender life—absolute nourishment. The heart loose and nearly ungraspable in Delilah's small hands, bubbling its once precious rivers helplessly all over her wrists, her arms, the ground.

Moon cooks two portions of the meat over a magical, moon-white coal, while Delilah hangs the rest of it in strips with twine as best she can. She has never come up with a really good system. She will have to stay around every night for the next several nights until it dries, to shoo the other predators away when they come to steal it. She doesn't feel angry with them; she would do the same.

She and Moon do not speak while they eat. Delilah feels as if she will never again have anything worthwhile to say. The flesh of the doe surrenders to her mouth before her teeth even touch it, and kisses her throat as it goes down.

When they lie down in the afternoon, she's still thinking of the words this animal spoke to her. It seems a natural cruelty of her life, a natural conse- quence to her own greed, that the first animal that ever spoke to her was an animal she had to kill. She wishes she hadn't had to. She wishes she could still hear the deer's voice. And she remembers now the comfort in it, after all. She remembers Mira in it. She had been so close, through listening to the deer, so close to hearing that voice again—that voice when it was still wise, when Mira still saw her clearly as sister.

She can't sleep for so long. But Moon's embrace has been her only com- fort since childhood. When she finally does sleep, enclosed in his gentleness, she dreams of the deer again. This time she is not only a haunting abyss of eyes, but the whole form of herself, flowing like water through space, and one by one the faces of the other animals Delilah has killed and eaten emerge behind her. The mighty male boar with his bloody tusks and his grunt of ferocious confidence, the old female boar with her majestic sorrow, a pheasant whose wings lifted like a thousand whirring fans, a grouse who drummed her wings against the ground like the heartbeat of the earth itself, and a rabbit who appeared first in Delilah's dreams as a white wisp of fear. And the hundreds of others, pouring as if over a hillside toward Delilah, in herds and flocks.

Then behind them come the animals she ate in childhood, animals she never knew: the listless, shapeless animals whose meat her father brought home from the meat factory where he worked, the only food they could afford sometimes because he was given the unwanted parts for free. In each haunted, empty face she sees her father's eyes, and remembers what a hu- man being looks like when robbed of his spirit, his selfhood, his pride.

And still the deer stands before all these, sure of herself, unafraid now in death.

Was it hard? Delilah asks. *Was it painful?*

i can't tell you, answers the deer, *because my death is a different kind than yours will be. but you shouldn't fear it any longer.*

Are you coming to tell me of my own death? Somehow Delilah is not surprised.

no, we are coming to tell you of your life.

You are haunting me.

i'm in your body. this is an instrument of love, this body.

Delilah wants to laugh. *My body is sick, broken.*

reclaim it, says the deer, and as she speaks she becomes the Unicorn, who dashes across her vision as it did the night the white goddess girl ran away.

Only this time the creature turns right toward Delilah, pointing its spiral into Delilah's skull, and Delilah wakes in a flash of pain and light.

Moon is awake, his eyes sweet in the dark. "What did you dream, Lil?" he asks.

"Did I make a sound?"

"No. Your body jolted. Like it used to when we were kids. That's how I used to know you were a fire goddess. That energy jolting through you. You were so tiny, but it was like a fire came through you."

"I'm not a goddess," says Delilah, remembering the dream and suddenly sad. "I'm going to die someday."

"But maybe it's all relative," says Moon. "Maybe it's all what you believe. You're very powerful, Lil. I think maybe inside you are a goddess. In the City, they talk about you like you are."

Delilah turns on her back to stare at the comforting sand color of the smooth cave ceiling. For her, daylight signifies a time of sleep. As they lie awake now she can hear birds singing and feel the sunlight relaxing at the cave entrance, generously lending them its warmth. But it is like a dream to her, a world she has not been a part of for so long. She feels so much more comfortable at night. It seems more real to her, more honest.

"But death is death, no matter how you cut it," she says.

"Not necessarily," says Moon. "There are ghosts who don't fully die, and living people who aren't really alive. You've been away from the City for so long, maybe you've forgotten."

But Delilah has not forgotten. She remembers her father, her sister, the faceless people she passed in the street—so many variations of living death, people who could not or would not inhabit their own lives. Living is hard. Most people, as far as she can tell, don't fully manage it.

"I dreamed of a unicorn," she says.

Moon waits. Then, instead of telling him about what she saw, she says, "When Mira was a little girl, she used to draw pictures of unicorns. She had this fascination with them. I mean, I guess that's normal for a little girl, but we weren't a normal family. We didn't read fairy tales and fantasy stories like that. I think it must have been something my father taught her. Maybe unicorns were part of the mythology he remembered from his people. I don't know, he wouldn't have told me. But she kept drawing them, until our father died. They got to be really beautiful and elaborate. I didn't think much about it, honestly. She was so crazy. So much of what she did made no sense to me."

Moon thinks for a little while. She's afraid he's going to tell her she didn't respect her sister enough, didn't love her the right way, didn't understand her. But he says, "Unicorns have healing powers."

"Is that right?" She immediately regrets the sarcasm in her own voice, but Moon ignores it.

"I don't know, maybe. They're supposed to be able to cure any ailment, purify water, bring healing of any kind to a person or even to a whole kingdom."

"Well. That's useful," says Delilah She doesn't want to tell Moon that she doesn't believe in unicorns, although he ought to know as much. She believes in Moon, who is a god, and she believes in his magic, because she loves him. But what she saw that night—that miracle that rescued her from Dragon—couldn't have been real. Maybe she's going crazy like her sister, which wouldn't be all that surprising, after so many years alone in the desert she can't even be sure she's counting them right.

"I don't know why it saved me," she says, mostly to herself. "I don't know what happened."

There is no way Moon could know what she's talking about, but he says, "Sure you do."

Delilah lies silent, eyes open long after Moon falls asleep again. She is ashamed of how much she wishes she could believe. How she wishes that white horn would lean into her again with its healing light, and forgive her for giving up—so long ago she can't even remember it—her innocence.

"What are you doing?" says Kite, narrowing his eyes at his sister. *You know Ma doesn't want you doing that,* he's about to say, but stops himself. What does it matter? His mother worries about everything.

Chelya brushes the girl's hair away from her eyes and caresses her cheek, but the girl does not stir. The girl's skin looks inhumanly soft. She is wearing a material that Kite has never seen before, that seems to swim over her body. When Chelya looks at him, he looks away, scuffs the dirt with his toe.

"Shhh," she says.

"Whatever," grumbles Kite. "*You're* not being so quiet. I hear you in here talking to her, telling her little stories."

Chelya smiles at him—that smile that makes it impossible for him to be mad at her, that makes him ashamed of his own awkwardness. Why should it bother him that she sits with the girl? What is his mother so afraid of, locking her up out here in the barn?

"I don't want to leave her all alone out here," says Chelya. "I don't want her to get lonely."

"She's sleeping. You can't get lonely when you're sleeping."

His sister shrugs. The morning sun shifts into the doorway and stumbles over the scattered hay, lies down over the girl's face as if it has finally found its home. "She has nightmares," says Chelya. "I can tell."

The mother wakes on her bed of pine needles and hay, thinking first of her children. She already saw Chelya, her eldest, walking in from the fields—her hair still half webbed over her face, her blanket rolled clumsily under one arm. Malachite she has not seen yet. A flash of anxiety flips through her throat, but she swallows it out of habit. She doesn't like that they sleep out in the fields all summer, but they insist upon it. *What could happen to us?* they ask her, laughing.

Fawn is young to be the mother of two teenagers, but old enough to value peace above all else, breathing in the morning with deep lungs and unhurried vision. Maybe she has always been this old. Even as a child, her mother has told her, she never rushed, never took for granted a single moment of her day. She knit her life together piece by piece, and each thing she came upon she touched with solemn gentleness, as if immediately burdened with the weight of the world's wonder from the time she was born.

The pine needles crinkle under her as she rolls over and lays her hand on her husband's, which is resting on the rise and fall of his chest. They don't say anything as they watch the morning light creep over the eastern garden, kiss the fragile heads of the seedlings, and spark with cold freshness on the tall grasses that the deer and their children are nibbling with selfless grace. From their bed on the rooftop, the couple can see their whole world awakening: Fawn's mother's tent on the northern hillside, the horses grazing around it, the gardens to the east and the west, and the goats fenced in between the house and the eastern garden, already chasing each other and pushing each other off of boulders. The river runs through everything, through the gardens and the goat pen and even the front room of the house. The song of that moving water seems right for all times, all seasons: a lullaby when they are sleeping or sad, a hymn when they awaken or celebrate—even though in reality, it barely changes.

The wind touches their faces. Fawn lifts their wool blanket and shakes off the wet fuzz of dew, then lays it down next to their bed to dry. Rye stands with no sound except for deep breaths, raises his hands to the sky, and begins to stretch his body limb by limb. Fawn opens the cloth cover that holds their bedding and spreads apart the pine stuffing to air out in the sun. She spreads it slowly with her hands, feeling and looking through it for signs of mold or insects, and as she does so she blesses it with her touch, silently thanking the coming day.

Tough, flat feet pressing the cold earth of her rooftop garden, Fawn walks over the body of her house to the stairway, left open to the roof in summer. On her way, she collects a few herbs to add to the breakfast she will make. The innocent scent of cut wood welcomes her as she spirals down the stairs, reminding her to honor the trees that gave their lives for this house and these fields. Through her husband's hands, they reincarnated into forms of a different beauty—the stairs, the table, her rocking chair, the cradle the children slept in as infants, the walls that protect them—though never quite as beautiful or creative as the trees themselves, whose only function was pure life.

When she descends into the main room, she finds her son already lighting the fire, and she can breathe a small sigh of peace. She watches his bare back shining and lengthening, watches the way he balances himself, graceful as a beast but with a halting respect in his motions. It moves her, the way the child in him grapples with the weight of expectant adulthood, the frightening power of manhood wobbling precariously in his lean, sensitive body. But she knows he draws comfort from the power of his mind, a power he has known all his life and will always know, which holds him steady.

He stands up and wipes his hands on his pants, leaving small flames jumping behind the grate. For breakfast in the summer, they need only a few hot coals. He nods at her, his manner warm but his voice—a tremulous, changing thing which he keeps to himself more and more these days—silent.

"You're up early," she says to him.

"Couldn't sleep," he mumbles. Fawn thinks immediately, without meaning to, of the girl in the barn. She still makes Fawn uneasy. She is otherworldly in some way. She is too beautiful. There is some spell she casts over the house, perhaps, even asleep.

"Did you dream?" she asks anxiously. "Tell your dreams to your grandmother. She will know . . ."

"Ma," he says, striding around the firepit toward the back door, "I just woke up early, that's all."

"Malachite—"

But he is gone. Fawn sighs and comes close to the fire for a moment, drawing comfort from its warmth. The rest of the family call him Kite now, which she knows is what he wants, but she will not call him that. He is already flying too far from the earth, she thinks, at this age. He needs the name she gave him to anchor him, to remind him where he comes from.

Her daughter has already left seven fresh eggs on the counter, but Fawn goes through the south door into the front room, the greenhouse, to retrieve a few more from the glass box of meat and eggs they keep cold in the stream. She knows where her daughter is. She's in the barn, and she is not only tending to the goats but also watching that girl as she sleeps. No one knows if the girl will ever wake, though Chelya creeps in to watch her as often as she can, ever-hopeful. Each evening at dinner, Chelya makes her eager report.

"Today she cried for almost the whole day but didn't wake," she will say, or "She was talking in her sleep all day long. I didn't have time to stay and listen, but it was something about being cursed, I think, and she kept pleading for me to stay, though she didn't know who I was, and she said she needed to get to the high mountain, and something about love. But I think her fever has broken now! I think she is getting better."

Though these words frighten Fawn, she tries to present her daughter with a calm face. She tells her that if the girl is meant to wake, she will, and if she is not meant to be in this world, she won't. She can tell that her daughter is wild with the romantic fantasy she reaps from these fragments of sleep-talk, that she cannot wait for her beautiful princess to wake and tell her the dramatic story of her origins and her quest. And Fawn doesn't know what else to say. She has a bad feeling about the girl that she is afraid to speak aloud. She feels that something is going to happen, something she doesn't understand and can't control.

She doesn't understand what her mother, Eva, means, when after spending hours of her day at the girl's side, conversing with her spirit, she tells Fawn that the girl is not yet fully alive in this world, not yet fully human. Those words terrify Fawn. If not human, then what?

"She is afraid to wake up," Eva told her yesterday.

"But she can't stay here forever," said Fawn, ashamed of her own childish tone.

Now Chelya comes running into the house with some fresh garden vegetables for breakfast to go with the eggs. She grins, kisses Fawn on the cheek, and runs back out again. She's wearing a thin, shapeless nightgown that, nevertheless, wafts lovingly around her luxurious curves, a faded, patternless hand-me-down from what seems a far-gone era of Fawn's life. Fawn smiles at the way Chelya seems to move everywhere either running or dancing, her rainbow warmth catching the rest of the family carelessly in its wake. She is only sixteen, but as curvy and confident as a woman—far more confident, in fact, than Fawn has ever felt. Perhaps Eva, who is also outspoken, not shy like Fawn, was like this when she was young. Chelya's presence comforts Fawn. She feels its constant glow, even when her daughter is out in the fields. Most of the time her absence doesn't worry Fawn, the way Malachite's does.

Fawn brews tea for her mother from fir needles, which Eva says wake her and bring her down from the high of her dreams. She goes out the rear of the house, up over the mound of her mother's sacred hill, and to the other side where Eva has pitched their old tent for the summer. Eva has spread out a little altar in the sun, facing the great white-topped mountain in the east whose lofty height seems to inspire her. She takes the cup from Fawn's hand and then clasps that hand in her own, the worn palms as lyrically lined as the designs of bark beetles on old wood and always warm. Eva beams at her daughter, giving her love in a smile, and then turns back to her altar.

Fawn leaves her, knowing not to speak to her so early in the morning, when she's still on her way back from dreams, and her mind and spirit are busy in other worlds.

Fawn mixes green onions and sweet peas and summer squash in her one iron pan on the grate over the fire, which circles half the circumference of the round brick firepit. Through the cloth in her hand she feels the hot metal, that fiery, dark masculinity from under the earth. She is grateful for this magical material, which Rye's brother has hewn with fire into this round, useful thing. Such magic in life—such magic humans can create—yet its power frightens her, and she is happy with only a little of it, the barest essentials and no more.

It's still cold in the mornings, so they eat breakfast right there in the main room, with the windows open. Briefly, they bless what made their food.

"Thank you, chickens. Thank you, vegetable and herb plants. Thank you, ocean, for your salt. Thank you, animals, for your fat and oil. Thank you, river. Thank you, sun. Thank you, earth. Thank you, air."

"Thank you, Fawn," Rye adds. Fawn catches his eye.

Mostly, they eat in silence. They let the food travel slowly through their mouths and throats down to their bellies, taking pleasure in what the tastes tell them of the earth's growth.

Rye tells them of his greetings with the day.

"The clouds are thinking of raining again," he says. "Not yet, but maybe later, tonight. Some of the birds are still having trouble finding food, because the winter was so hard. I hear them still calling for mates, even now, because there are so few who survived to return in the spring, because they traveled over the City. Also, I found another nest on the ground. Eggs that died before they were born."

Chelya looks up, serious. Animals to her are like people. Unlike the rest of the family, she won't even kill or eat them. "I think it means something," she says. "Remember all the bees that died last year."

"I think the river has poison in it," Fawn says softly.

"Ma," says Malachite impatiently, "the City's downstream. How could there be poison in the river?"

"From the rains."

Malachite twists his mouth in that way he does, and shakes his head. Rye has rested his fork on the edge of his bowl, and is thinking.

"There is poison," Fawn repeats. "I can taste it in the rain."

"I think the water is still safe to drink, Fawn," Rye says gently. "It's so little poison, if there is any."

"But it might not always be safe," says Fawn, "and what then? Those people down there don't care if the river is poisoned. They get their water from somewhere else."

"Ma, you don't know—" Malachite begins.

"Kite," says Rye. But it is Fawn who looks down, ashamed of her fear.

"The two hawks who came to nest above the fields seem well though," Rye says, changing the subject. "Perhaps they will give us some perspective, seeing the whole land from above as we cannot."

Fawn nods. They finish their meal in silence, listening, as if even now the hawks are speaking to them from the sky, seeing a continuing pattern of wholeness that they cannot.

After breakfast, Fawn washes their dishes in water she heated over the fire. None of her motions are slower or faster than any of the others. She reaches into the water, rolls the rag in a circle in the deep, nurturing roundness of a wooden bowl, lifts the bowl and dries it with the same motion, and puts it in its place on the open shelves. When she has finished, she casts her eyes in a restful arc over the familiar textures: the varying grains and beans in their neat jars, black and red and yellow and green and white, the small stacks of wooden bowls and cups, the dried herbs hanging and the hand-carved wooden ladle with its swooping handle.

Rye has left for the morning, to check his traps in the woods and perhaps, if they yield nothing, to catch fish for dinner. Chelya is probably working with the bees, or maybe she and Eva are still conversing with the wasps who built a nest in one of the woodsheds, asking them to live peaceably with this family and to know that the people here mean them no harm. It's a long process, communing with such a big entity of beings, and it doesn't always work, but Eva can speak the language of almost any creature, and Chelya's loving presence is so convincing. Malachite, ever resourceful, is figuring out a way to fix one of the greenhouse windows that cracked when a branch hit it during a winter storm, since they have no way, for now, of obtaining more glass. She knows he is hurrying to get his work done so he can steal an hour sometime in the day to work on his plans and dreams for making energy out of sunlight or wind; he's heard there is a way to do it, and he keeps promising that someday they will learn to harness that power. To Fawn, this concept is unfathomable. They already have power: the work power of their own hands and bodies, the power of fire, the power of their spirits and their love. She doesn't understand the need for electricity, whose only purpose is to change the natural flow of things: redirect the water or make light when it is time for darkness.

The City is closer now than it ever was. To the northwest, near where Rye's brother Jay has his farm, a huge space of forest is gone. The roads reach their claws deeper and deeper in. Jay's family can hear the sounds of the machines even in their sleep. Little cities will rise up there, where the forest was, and the earth that the roots of the trees held together will slide down the mountainside and into the river. So close. Nothing can stop the roads. And according to Jay and Rye, it is more than just roads that are coming. Some mountains have been decapitated by gigantic machines. Where there was mountain, now there is a thick, leaking lava of poison, and then there will be only caverns of desert...But they will not tell her more than that. They shake their heads when she asks for explanations, as if they know this information will kill her. *There is a reason,* Rye says, *why they persuaded all the farmers in the north to leave their farms. There is something they want in there.*

In where? Fawn asked him. His eyes when she asked him were heavy and sorry and far away, almost as if he knew—as if there was some hunger within all men that even he, who was not one of these bad men after all, could recognize.

In the earth, he said, and looked away.

All Fawn can do to stop these realities from freezing her mind, freezing her body with terror, is what she has always done: dive her hands into the soil. She plants seeds, fertilizes with compost and chicken droppings, pulls weed, helps the climbing vegetables with small structures of sticks, and brings seedlings from the greenhouse to plant out in the sun for the summer crop. As she works around the plants, pressing and massaging the soil around them with nourishment, spilling water over them, she sings to them in a whispered voice only they can hear. They spread their hopeful leaves like wings in the breeze. How easy it is to convince them to live! She lay their simple seeds in the earth, and immediately they knew what to do.

She works all morning and into the hot afternoon, her knees in the soil, her body crouching low. She is sculpting the earth, day after day, year after year, and her hands always feel it, like a work of life she is molding forever.

She eats a small mid-day meal with her mother on the hillside, as she always does. It is the only time the two of them have alone to talk. Like the rest of the family in the middle of their long day, they eat whatever they don't have to cook: goat's milk, leftovers, meat jerky, fruit.

Today Eva tells her daughter, "I think the girl will wake soon."

"How do you know?"

"The fever has broken. And the moon is full tomorrow."

"Maybe she will die," suggests Fawn, her tone blank.

"Maybe," says Eva, "but I don't think so. She has something she needs to do."

They are sitting next to each other with their food in their hands, looking at the high white mountain which, from this distance, seems the only thing that never changes.

"I'm afraid of her," Fawn admits.

"Of course you are," says Eva. Her voice is deep and sure like stone striking stone, belying the dreamy realms that take up so much of her time. "You're afraid of anything that changes your routine."

Fawn bows her head. "I am just happy with the way things are," she says, though her heart tells her that this happiness is more shaky than it has ever been.

"I know. It is a gift you have, a talent that few people share: to be happy, to be stable and content like the earth. You are of the earth, even more than me, more than your children. But don't forget the river, Fawn, and the air and fire, which are always moving, always changing. Anyway, you know that change always brings us back home again, back to the beginning."

"Yes," says Fawn, but she is thinking. After a moment she adds, "We keep her horse with ours, and like ours he doesn't have to be tied. But he keeps his distance from our horses, and when I look at him, sometimes he seems to change, as if a light shines from him. And sometimes when I look at him from behind, suddenly I can't see his male parts any more, and he seems to be a mare! It is a strange, magical horse. Mother, what if it is not a horse at all, but a—a *spirit* of some kind?" She turns to her mother in horror as she speaks these words, but her mother, of course, does not respond in kind. Her mother is not afraid of spirits, nor even of gods. "What should I do with my fear?"

"Try to be open, Fawn. Learn from your daughter. She doesn't fear anyone."

"But what am I afraid of?"

Eva doesn't answer, but only places her hand on Fawn's back, behind her heart, and rubs softly.

On her way back to the house, Fawn enters the dim light of the barn, where the girl lies on a pile of clean hay in the shelter where the goat kids were fed in early spring. She remembers when Rye carried her into the house, his eyes surprised as if he didn't understand what he'd found, her body slung over his arms like a small, stilled waterfall. What did he think when he found her? Was he torn a little inside, as Fawn is, by her beauty so bright it seems unstable, by her childish lips, by the helpless grace of her arms? Did he desire her, so pale and smooth and delicate compared with Fawn?

There was this light in his face when he brought her in. Pine needles fell from her hair as if he had dug her up from the earth, but she was glowing. Fawn had not seen that expression on his face for a long time, the expression of a little boy the first time he watches something innocent die, or sees his father cry; the expression of a boy who promises, deep in his heart, that he will somehow save what could not be saved then, that he will grow up to make a better life for the ones he loves; the expression of a boy when he promises deep within himself, without telling anyone, to become a man. The promise she sees in her son's face every day now, which moves her and frightens her at the same time.

Fawn kneels beside the girl now, trying to be brave. Trembling, she touches her hand, and then strokes with her fingertips its fine, bird-like bones. When Rye brought her home, Fawn wouldn't speak to him for almost two days. She didn't mean to be stubborn, but she had never felt angry with him like that in the whole nineteen years they had been together. It was an unfamiliar feeling and she had no words to express it. She simply could not believe he would bring a stranger into their home when things were so unstable around them, the City creeping closer every day—and not only a stranger but someone who seemed not quite human, who came from who knew where and for who knew what purpose.

"I couldn't just leave her out there," Rye had told her. "Could I?" But he laid her down in the barn like an awkward package he didn't know what to do with either and left her there. Only Eva and Chelya tended to her. She has been sleeping for twelve days now, without need of waking, without need of food or water. Impossible for a human being.

The girl moans softly in her delirium and curls her body toward Fawn. Something in Fawn's heart leans forward, as if in suspense. The girl reaches for Fawn like a hungry ghost, her eyelids still closed but fluttering, her fingertips brushing Fawn's hip and breast while Fawn freezes in shock, then jumps backward in a movement completely alien to her. She sits still for a long time, keeping her distance, watching the girl sleep again with limbs piled in her direction, trying to slow her own breathing.

A couple of brief hours in the afternoon are Fawn's favorite time of the day, her time alone in the forest.

Sometimes she goes to the river to bathe. Other days, like today, she gathers herbs for Eva, though there is nothing her mother especially needs right now. She picks up a few feathers she thinks Chelya might like to use in one of her necklaces. More than anything, this careful searching with her hands and mind over the forest floor is an excuse to caress the body of the mountain. With all her senses she touches that body, and breathes its breath, and learns about its health: what pains it, what is growing and what is dying. She knows all of the deer and rabbit paths, and how and when they change with the seasons. In the winter she always knows who has died in the night. In summer, she knows what trees have fallen in the storms, and sometimes she goes to them the next day to say goodbye. In her dreams she feels the earth ever in her hands, and she can feel the textures of the plants against her palms as she passes her hands over the shape of the mountain, and it seems as if the earth blooms and opens under her touch, and closes its wounds against her skin. When she wakes she is sorry that she is just one human woman after all, and cannot hold the earth to her breast, and cannot protect it from whatever is coming.

Before returning to the house, she always goes to the river, for it comforts her. Whatever changes have happened that day or that year—whatever bird flock is missing from the sky in the spring migrations, whatever groves of trees have been destroyed by some new blight—the sound of the river makes it all rest a little easier inside Fawn, at least for the moments she sits by it.

Yet even the river, whose voice she can usually understand, tells her of changes that have come and are coming. She thinks its rhythm and its pitch are somehow different now, perhaps heavier with the poison it carries, or interrupted by the vibrations of drilling near one of its tributaries up the mountain, where Jay's wife's childhood home was taken from her.

Today when she returns, she finds that Rye has brought home a wood-chuck for dinner, and she spends the evening skinning and cleaning its different parts, unraveling its life piece by piece and thanking it as she does so. Before he goes out to the eastern garden, Rye wraps an arm around her from behind, rubbing his chin against the top of her head and brushing her nipple with his thumb. She feels lonely for him suddenly, her earthen body turning inky and soft; it seems a long time since they have really looked at each other. They have been so caught up in the height of the planting season, and before that, the winter was so hard. She wants to turn around now and open her mouth to him, the man of her heart, the man who first discovered the fire in her shy body so many years ago. But her hands are bloody, and she is tired now. And something is making her anxious nearly all the time—not a terrible anxiety, but something disturbing her familiar peace. Maybe it's that girl. That girl in the barn.

She keeps working with the animal, pressing back against Rye a little, trying to let him know she hasn't forgotten him, that she isn't angry with him any more. He was only being good and kind when he brought the girl home, like he always is. She hears Chelya's laughter outside, and finds herself wondering if the children will remember to go carefully around the wasp nest outside the door. Why do there seem to be fewer and fewer honey bees, those messengers of sweetness, and more and more angry, aggressive insects like those wasps? She thinks it must be a reflection of something changing in the human world, though she doesn't know.

By the time she comes back to herself, Rye has walked away.

Then Chelya and Kite are breezing through, sweeping the main room and bringing in vegetables for dinner. Outside the rain is beginning to surround them, hushing them inside its husk of sound. They will eat indoors again, but this time with words pouring more freely, excited to be in contact with each other again and sharing the experiences of their day. Chelya will talk about the bees and the wasps and the antics of the goats, and Fawn will report with a few, soft words the progress of the garden, and Rye will listen, his big elbows on the table, tired and smiling. Eva's voice will be rare but opinionated, and will often come with laughter. Unless he is excited by some new discovery he's made, Kite's face will brood as he devours his meal, and he will shift with an irritable restlessness in his seat, and ask his father if he can go with him on his trip to Jay's farm tomorrow. Rye will say yes, as always, even though he knows Kite is more needed here, because he worries that the children don't have enough connection with others, and he knows Kite hopes for some adventure along the way—any adventure at all. Every winter, Rye talks of a trip they will take in the summer: just him and Kite. It will be an adventure to see who else is still out there, he says, and find what other farms are still left. They'll meet other people and hear their stories, and they'll bring things to trade, and come back with all the things they have needed for so long: glass, dried fruits, seeds that have been lost here. But come summer, Kite no longer reminds his father of that promise, no longer asks when it will happen. He knows it never does. They don't have time. It is an impossible dream, now that the City has swallowed up so many of their people, now that they live all alone out here and must work so hard to survive.

After dinner, while Rye helps Fawn clean up, Chelya—because it is raining too hard to go out tonight—will sit by the dying fire and make jewelry out of small bones or stones or feathers. This is a relief to Fawn, who never knows where Chelya goes at night or if it is safe. Eva will talk with Chelya about the old legends of the forest spirits and the tree people, answer her questions about whatever she dreamed last night, and laugh and whisper with her as easily as if the two of them were sisters.

When the dishes are done, the compost turned, and the kitchen cleaned, and Fawn can finally rest, she will lean her head against the back of her rocking chair, close her eyes, and listen to Rye's voice as he picks thoughtfully at his guitar. She will try not to worry about mold growing inside the house from the excessive rains, parts of it weakening and sagging, because she knows her family takes care of those things. She will remember she forgot to ask Kite if he was able to fix the window. The sound of the hard, insistent rain will make her restless, and she will find that her eyes are open now with sudden, nameless worry. But then she will close them again, and Rye's voice will come deep and swinging, like black earth turning over in the hands of the seasons, and it will rock her into herself, keeping her safe.

And the girl in the barn, Fawn hopes, for now, will still be sleeping.

"You're leaving," says Delilah. She's been sleeping fitfully for hours, in and out of dreams that she forgot repeatedly because of the discomfort they caused her. Now she realizes that Moon has gradually been pulling away from her. She sees him sitting in the entranceway to her cave, haloed in sunlight, his face tilted upward but with no joy upon it. He looks back at her and smiles with sad tenderness, and she wants to take that tenderness in, she wants not to be cruel, but she can't seem to help herself.

"Fuck you," she says. "Coward. You weren't even going to wake me."

She knows it's hard for him, too. And it isn't as if he had to pack any things; he could have stolen off in an instant if he had wanted to, if he had wanted to sneak out without her knowing. But that doesn't matter. She hates being the one left. In the City, she always fucked the boys in their rooms or apartments; they never came to her. How could they, anyway? But she'd liked it that way, because then she was always the one to leave, and she never had to see that look on their faces, which—whether it was contempt or fondness or even long-ing—might contain some trace of pity too. Every time Moon leaves her, she is reminded again that she is the one with a home now. Home is vulnerable. When you have a home, it means people can find you and people can leave you. They can learn what is precious to you and they can destroy it.

He's still not saying anything. She throws a pebble at him. "Just GO then." She turns around, faces the wall.

She feels his soft mind behind her, coming toward her hesitantly and turn-ing back, coming toward her again, unsure. His heart struggling to stand.

"Come on, Lil," he says. "I always leave. Why does it have to be like this?" She doesn't hear footsteps but she feels his hand, as unknown to itself as a child's, on her shoulder, pulling her hair back from her face, and then his breath, the palest kiss on her cheek.

"That's not an excuse. '*I always do it.*' How is that an excuse? How does that make it okay? You go on about how I have to face my fears, face death, kill the deer, save Mira, blah blah blah—and what do you do? What are you going back into the City to do? To lose yourself. To forget. You're a fucking coward."

She feels him freeze, and she freezes too. She had to say those things, because this was love too, this need, but she didn't mean for him to stop coming closer. Now that she's said the words, she wants him back. Doesn't he get that? Doesn't he know what she wants, after all this time? Doesn't he know she doesn't mean to hurt him? Why does he have to be so fragile?

But, "Maybe so," he says. "Maybe I am a coward."

That's all, and he is gone. And maybe she will always regret that she did not simply take his hand, and hold it against her heart, and beg him to stay.

But she had no words for that, then. She has no room in the little survival kit of her heart for regret. Anyway, she will tell herself later, it wouldn't have changed anything.

Lonely's eyes open to a dark roof, like a cave—like being underground, though she has never been underground—and for a moment she is sure she's back in that terrible place beneath the island, where she will find out that all her brief passions, the waterfalls, waving fields, and birdsong of the world, were a dream. But light drifts in from somewhere. The ceiling arches protectively over her like an upside-down nest. She closes her eyes again. Then the girl's voice calls a second time, soft but startling,

"Hey!"

Lonely turns toward the voice. The girl grins at her, her sunny face hung all around by ivy-like red hair, her round freckled shoulders rising magnificent and warm.

"You're *awake,*" she whispers, and giggles, as if she and Lonely are carrying out a mischievous, secret plan. Lonely can't help but smile, too, though she doesn't know what the secret is. She feels relieved somehow, as if she has finally arrived at a place she's been avoiding, and it's turned out to be sweet after all, sweet as this eager, heart-shaped face.

The girl is studying her. "Your eyes are so dark," she observes, "even darker than ours! I never saw anyone like you. I thought your eyes would be light, like the rest of you."

So did I, thinks Lonely, who is not yet sure that she can speak.

"What's your name?"

Lonely looks away, back at the ceiling. Certainly it seems an important question in this world, the question everyone asks first. It seems she will not be able to come close to anyone without first having a name.

"Can't you tell me?"

Lonely looks at her. "Yora," she says, but it comes out like a question.

"No, that's not your name."

"How do you know?"

The girl grins again, as if enjoying the game. "Because I heard you call *that* name in your sleep. And I don't think you'd call your own name. Anyway, Yora is the name of the river."

"But—" says Lonely, and she wants to explain that Yora is not a river but a woman who can disappear into the ocean at will, but that feels too difficult, so she only asks in return, "What is your name?"

"Chelya."

"What does that mean?"

"I don't know. It just means me. It's something my mother made up."

"Oh," says Lonely, wondering what a mother is, and wishing she'd had one to name her, instead of the wind. "Do I have to have a name?"

"I think so," says Chelya. "Or else no one could call you, if they need you."

If they need me, thinks Lonely. Does anyone need her? It's something she has never thought about before. No one could call her if they needed her. Is that why she was lost? Is that why her prince could never find her?

"You think a lot," observes Chelya.

Lonely turns, and tears blur her image of the girl, making her look like a reflection or a loving spirit rising from underwater. She struggles up onto her elbows, then her hands, wondering if she will be able to stand. "My name is Lonely," she says.

"Oh!" says Chelya, her brow furrowing urgently. "That's so sad. How can that be your name?"

"I don't like it. I don't like my name."

Chelya hesitates, her eyebrows still drawn together in a stormy sort of way, but even the storm looks gentle and sweet. "It's okay," she decides finally. "Maybe someday you can change it."

Lonely looks at her, her own life pounding over her in waves.

Then animal faces are leaning in behind Chelya's, long like the face of Lonely's horse, but more sculptured, more face-like, with square eyes that make Lonely shiver. One of the animals cries out, and she recognizes the cry from her dreams: half-animal, half-human.

"The goats live here," explains Chelya. "You're in their bedroom."

"Goats," says Lonely, trying out that name. Everything has a name. She sits up, which seems to cause Chelya even more excitement. She throws out her hand, and Lonely reaches for it.

"Come on!"

But standing up makes Lonely dizzy. Her feet feel heavy, as if filled with sand. Her hips and waist start to buckle, and she reaches out and grabs hold of splintered wood. Chelya's arm wraps around her like earth.

Outside Chelya tells her, "Your horse sleeps in there," and points to another shed. All the goats bound out with their kids, the older goats trotting with uplifted, questioning faces and the younger ones bucking and kicking with each bound, a sassy challenge in their eyes. Their eyes look right at Lonely, smart and present, and seem to demand honesty. One of the big ones sniffs at her hand as she holds it out to him.

who are you, girl? the goat says. *don't you know how to laugh?*

"That's their man," says Chelya. "One man to all these women, isn't he lucky?"

And Lonely remembers, suddenly, the hot male body that secured her, carrying her away from her loneliness. It smelled faintly animal like these goats, only quieter, like the earth under the leaves in the forest.

"Chelya," she says, while the girl moves quickly among them, her body bent, her deft hands at once caressing and herding them, gathering the ones she needs. "Who was the man who rescued me?"

"Oh, that was my father!"

Father. The word echoes in Lonely's body, and her own father's sad eyes flash inside her mind, then turn away. "Where is he now?" she asks.

"He and my brother went to my uncle's," says Chelya, innocent of Lonely's longing. "They'll be back tomorrow night, I guess."

Lonely aches to see him, to see that face more clearly, and to breathe his scent again, even from a distance. She feels dizzy again. She follows Chelya back into the shed and sees her squatting close to a goat's body, pulling thick white liquid down from its belly. The dim room is heady with the smell of bodies, the smell of Chelya and the goats, the hay and the damp wood. The shadows hold them close. Lonely sinks down in a pile of hay, her body weak with so many hungers she cannot identify where they come from.

"Here," says Chelya, "I know what you need." She hands Lonely a cup. "Drink." Lonely slips the edge of the cup between her lips, her tongue burning with the bitter taste of the metal. The milk flows into her body, comforting and musky and smooth, almost perversely physical, like the hot blood of the moon. It quenches her thirst and fills her hunger at the same time, and her stomach opens, full of glory and desire.

"What is this?" she mumbles.

"It's life," says Chelya. "When you're born, your mother can feed you from her own body. Isn't that amazing? That's what *mother* tastes like. That's what love tastes like."

Mother, repeats Lonely again in her mind, and it's a word she has never known. But when she hears it, she begins to cry. It's like the word *home.* She knows this girl Chelya has something she doesn't have, as she comes over now to lay her arms around Lonely—something that softens her body, that creases her mouth with ease and smiling, that cushions her. Something that the angry woman Delilah did not have either, looking down hard on Lonely from her cave, her body like a tough, dry net she'd patched together over and over so as not to let the knives of her own hunger pierce her. Delilah had no mother, and neither did Dragon. Lonely knows this suddenly, the way she knows it about herself.

"I don't know who my mother is," she says, knowing it, feeling the sorrow of a whole lifetime in which she never even asked herself the question, never even knew what was wrong.

"Come on," says Chelya. "I have something else to give you, and then we'll go inside." Lonely rubs her hand across her face, stumbling dutifully behind Chelya, and when she has wiped all the tears away, Chelya is coming back from a wooden box with insects vibrating the air around it, her hand outstretched.

Lonely smears the honey off Chelya's fingers, onto her own fingers, and then she licks them clean. The sweetness is a burning ecstasy. "That's what love tastes like, too," says Chelya, licking her own fingers. "Only that's the love between the flowers, like the love between lovers." She says this with her eyes shining boldly into Lonely's, and Lonely wonders if Chelya, who seems so young, already has a lover—if love is as easy for her as she makes it sound.

"The bees all have one mother," the girl adds. "And we do too, really. We all have one mother, you know?"

Lonely doesn't.

Then there is a house. It's like nothing Lonely has ever experienced. She goes inside it, and all the sounds of the outside go quiet. It's like going inside her own mind. But it is nothing like the tower. There are all kinds of shapes around her, but they are still, not like the shapes outside. They have a carefulness to them, an intelligence in their placement. They all mean something, something Lonely does not have time to figure out, because now another woman stands here before her.

Behind the woman is a fire. Not like Dragon's fire, but enclosed in`earth and metal. The woman is not like anyone Lonely has seen before. She has much more body than Lonely—rich slopes of it, both soft and solid. She looks comfortable, snug inside her own flesh, and Lonely's first thought, though she will forget it in an instant and not allow herself to think it again, is that she wants to be enfolded in those arms.

"Her name's Lonely," Chelya tells the woman, taking Lonely's hand again and looking up into her face. Lonely is taller than either of them. Chelya's warmth in her hand brings Lonely rushing headlong back into her own flesh, her life of a thousand hungers. Emptiness spills messily inside her. The woman keeps staring at her, her face full but reticent, her simple brown hair falling straight around it. Lonely feels drawn to the mystery of that face, a face she cannot know by looking at it only once. It takes her a moment to focus in on the woman's eyes, and when she does she has to take a step backward at the look she finds there. She remembers the old woman on the island, and her heart clenches and shrinks small. There is something wrong with her: *Lonely*. Some reason she is not wanted anywhere she goes.

But Chelya says, "Please, Ma, she needs food. We have to feed her before she goes, at least."

Then she is outside again, with Chelya's hand the only thing real, and then later the woman is there too, but despite her painful gaze she says nothing unkind. Everything is a sunny blur now, the heat and the sweetness dazzling. They eat breakfast in the grass, with the clover and the violets and the pollen and the ants. The food anchors Lonely to the ground. Eating is like an actual place she discovers, a nest of earth, as if all those days she wandered free but lost, confused and yearning, in the open fields coming from the sea, she had kept missing the heart of life right beneath her feet. She had had nothing to make her stop, nothing to bring her to stillness. But this is what the hunger was for. To take her own life in her hands, and bring it into her. To take of the earth, and become it. And everything—the body of man, the body of woman—is made only of this. The tastes of other bodies, other lives, surge upon her tongue like answers.

Her own body sucks her inward, and the stubborn spunk of humanness centers itself in her belly where the food is welcomed and warmed and transformed. All her days after, long after she has come to love these people, long after her love has become too much and she must leave them, and later when she wanders alone in the high dream of a mountain, through empty fields and emptier skies, she will remember this breakfast in the grass, on the

earth, with the two women of sun-worn skin and curvy weight. This breakfast seems a place that happens eternally into the past and into the future, a
place that seems always right here, right now—if she can only center herself,
only bring herself down.

"Where did you come from?" asks Chelya. "Tell us, please! Who are you?
Where are you going?"

But Fawn murmurs, "Not now, Chelya."

Maybe, she will think later, it was Fawn—though she did not love Lonely
then, and would barely look at her—who provided that sense of eternal
home, that sense of a stable moment in time at the center of the earth, where
nothing ever changes, and life is given and received over and over again.

Today Fawn doesn't ask Lonely any questions, but she gives her fresh eggs
and bread, and slices of sweet tomato, and leaves of herbs.

Moon has traveled every part of the Earth's body, and he knows that the
City is built on Her heart. Maybe Hanum made the City here because he,
like everyone, loved the Earth. But maybe Hanum, like almost everyone, did
not actually know how to love someone other than himself.

Moon doesn't mean to keep coming back to the City, but he has to.
He doesn't mean to come into these dark, blurred places, windowless and
hidden beneath concrete, where the tuneless sound from the speakers is
so loud it numbs him to all memory of the earth and the wind, cocooning
him in thick blank space, laying waste to his mind and making him weak
as a human being. But he has to. He has to have something to stop up
the emptiness, if only for a little while. Not the dreaming plants that Lil
and he used to eat to make themselves wiser and clearer, to become more
intimately aware of each droplet of thought and feeling and how each
connected to the other. No, he needs the opposite. Something to make it all
stop. Something to clear him out like the death he will never get to have. A
drug that makes a god out of a human being and a human being out of a
god, that blurs the distinctions, makes him irrelevant, without responsibility or purpose.

Moon comes to the City after days of walking through the fields, ignoring
the kisses of the grass stems and the beckoning of the breeze, hating himself
for leaving Lil again, hating himself for fulfilling her fears and doing what
he promised he wouldn't, knowing he let down not only himself but the only
one who truly loves him. His father's hatred roars in his ears—his father, a
god of sky, whom he let down long, long ago, merely by being what he is.

There is nothing he can do about any of this. He can feel the City like some awfulness walking beside him, like a shadow that walks forever with him, copying his every step in a chilling, clownish mockery.

Maybe Lil is right about rain. Maybe it would melt people's hearts, soften them, call up their longing and their memory of music. Maybe the City needs rain. Maybe that's all it would take. But the shadow walks ever beside him, steely and cold, and he has no faith. The City is bigger than he, and stronger. It overpowers him every time.

The first glimpse he gets of the City, as he enters it, is of loss. The debris of it sifts out to its edges: unwanted things, unwanted people, unwanted animals. Empty cans make metallic ghost music, plastic bags dawdle in the wind, homeless people huddle, the same color as the trash, and stray dogs trot tirelessly among them, noses to the ground, until they drop dead. Their vacant eyes show that they have long ago given up hope of ever being satisfied, but only keep searching out of habit, out of compulsion. Surely someone has forgotten something here? Surely someone's long-ago lost love, their dream denied, their childhood treasure abandoned, is here now waiting; surely they will soon come wandering through, a surge of color and hope, seeking it in the rubble? But then, maybe no one remembers where to find what they have lost. Maybe they don't even know they have lost it.

Moon wants to stay here. It is quieter here, and when he crawls through the empty streets he can press his ear against the concrete and try to listen to what cries far beneath it. There seems to be someone calling him, someone always alive but endlessly dying, someone to whom he belongs and to whom he owes his life. Someone trapped, who needs his help. But the voice sounds so far down, and for all his godness, Moon cannot do anything important, cannot lift the concrete, cannot blast through it, cannot melt it away. What powers do gods really have? Magic tricks fit for children. Moon takes his flute from the inner fold of his cloak and tosses it behind him, not looking where it lands but hearing it echo—a dry, clumsy, hurting sound, nothing like music—against the unforgiving pavement. He will lose it here, where everyone loses something, where everyone loses. If he ever actually needs it, he thinks, he will find it. If not, it doesn't matter.

Beyond this outer realm of the City, where the grass is brown at the boundary between civilization and wildness, there is a graveyard. Moon used to spend days there, listening to an earth filled with death, trying to understand what it meant to be human. There were no spirits there; ghosts who refused to pass on to the next life had other places to haunt, places that had meant something to them in their lives. But Moon used to lie between the graves and try to understand death. Was it something about this ending that made humans afraid, that made them turn to evil? The place felt peaceful and the tombstones held no malice. But today he passed that place by with his head turned away. Lil's talk of pain and sickness reminded him of what he always tries to forget, that she is mortal. He cannot look there without thinking of Lil someday dying, though he knows of course that she would never end up caged in some grave-yard. She'd rather be thrown to the vultures. He wishes he could hold onto her forever, for when she is gone, what else will hold him to his sanity? He wishes he could make her immortal, but that would be selfish.

She doesn't know how lucky she is to be mortal, to be able to own her own pain, to be able to feel it, so certainly, so constantly. Moon would give anything for that.

In the outer ghetto of loss, Moon curls up around a heap of rags, human-ness sick on itself, folded in on itself, and the heap turns out to be a man— barely. If he pushes Moon away, or beats at him or sticks him with a knife, Moon doesn't care. He wishes something could kill him, but it can't.

The man doesn't do anything, just shivers, and keeps shivering, as if Moon is cold rain. He mumbles in his sleep. Deliriously, he takes hold of Moon's hand, but Moon feels like the man is holding his heart, and he has trouble breathing. A dog comes and stands before them, sensing Moon's aliveness, his mouth hanging open. Moon can feel the dog's hunger and the man's hunger, and he has nothing for them. Through the body of the man he can feel the anguish of the silent earth far beneath them, and when the wind comes, it carries the loneliness of all the people of the City, who do their jobs without knowing why, who never feel quite loved enough.

He feels the soft flatness against his heart where the flute should have been. He feels a little sorry, suddenly, for leaving it, because Lil will be sad. Ever since they were children, he's played it for her. He's played it just to watch the different expressions cross her face: that special human mix of passion, nostalgia, hope, and all the others. When they were little, he used to wander the City collecting all the beautiful sounds he could find inside his flute, so he could play them back to her: laughter, birdsong, a lover's whisper, the turning of dry leaves over empty streets. He believed in beauty back then, or at least he believed in what beauty did for Lil: the way it softened her face, the way it made a girl out of her. He loved to watch that. But now he would not know where to find such things. Though he still plays his flute for her every now and then, he doesn't feel that sense of wonder for the world any more, even when he tries.

When the pain of the sick man becomes too heavy against Moon's dull heart, Moon drags himself through the streets, seeking the throbbing depths of it, seeking to lose himself in that great cauldron where the pain is made.

But even in those screaming caverns beneath the streets, where music is only violent sound and people are only flailing bodies, and his mind collapses beneath the lusty demon of the drug, still the emptiness is bigger. Then all he can do is offer himself to them, for if he cannot die, if he can do nothing for them, the least he can do is take their pain. He wants to feel that pain inside him. He wants to feel that he deserves it—that he at least deserves this. This man he drinks with now can do whatever he likes to him, can hurt him any way he likes, if it will make him feel better. It makes Moon feel better. It makes him feel justified in his helplessness.

Somewhere out there in the dark, the river is always running, but in the City, it is too polluted to sustain any life. It pours forth its suffering into the sea. What would rain be anyway but the same poison falling down again? It seems to Moon sometimes that people don't even want water. They pump it in with their machines from lakes far away, and then pour it over their cars, letting it disappear into drains while they stand talking, and they distill their urine in it and then flush it underground into chambers of filth. It is an overabundant substance that they take for granted, always pouring forth when they need it and conveniently disappearing after they've sullied it. It tastes dull, too subtle for their strung-out senses, and they dose it up with chemicals and sweeteners until drinking it gives them the high they've become accustomed to.

But in a room somewhere, this water god Moon lies in the arms of the man who chained him and fucked him until he bled, and the man is crying. And still Moon feels nothing.

All around, the deep forest hovers in its own shadow. In the center of the field sits the strange wooden square of the house, high in the middle and low in the front, with windows of glass. Paths of stone wind out from it, and wind into bushes and flowers, and the flowers twine into vines, and the vines erupt now into birds as Lonely watches.

She didn't think of following the mother and daughter back into the house when the food was gone. They carried the bowls and wooden utensils back with them, and she didn't know what they would do with them. She didn't know what would happen next or what to do. She found herself walking across the field to where she saw her horse grazing, lifting his head in greeting. She cried again when she touched him, when he brushed his warm head against hers. But then the house called her gaze back. She didn't realize how hard she was gripping the horse's mane in her fist until he shook his neck fiercely and pulled away.

Now Chelya is running out to her, and now standing next to her, her presence full of breathing and laughter. She follows Lonely's gaze.

"Who made your home?" asks Lonely.

"My father. He built it for my mother, when she was pregnant with me. I guess to prove to her and my grandma that he was serious."

She takes Lonely's hand and looks into her eyes with longing. "Please, will you stay a little longer? Come see inside. Ma won't mind."

So they go back into the house.

"This is the greenhouse," says Chelya, leading Lonely over the small footbridge that crosses the stream just inside the entrance, "which keeps the baby plants warm all winter." She stops and sits with Lonely on a swinging hammock shaded by young fruit trees, still holding her hand, and they listen to the stream echo intimately in the round, glassed room, a comforting tapestry of small, manageable sounds that relieves Lonely a little from the weight of her journey.

"This is the basement," says Chelya, now leading her down the stairs outside the main room. "It's the belly of the house, where we keep all of the food cool. Deep down in that hole, it's always cold, and that's where we keep meat and things that have to be preserved." Lonely stands for a moment in this secret cavern of nourishment, and something that seems like a memory tumbles through her mind, but she can't catch hold of it, because it is not a memory of the past but of the future. She follows Chelya back up and they pass the mother, who is leaning over a bucket, washing something. Chelya squeezes Lonely's hand.

"Ma," she starts, and the woman stands up. Lonely sees her wide brown hands draw together over her belly and then drop to her sides again, unsure. The gesture reminds Lonely of herself somehow, and she wants to smile but stops herself. This woman doesn't want her here. She feels sure of it.

"Ma," says Chelya softly, "can't she stay, just a little longer? Let Kite meet her. It's fun to have a visitor, don't you think?"

The woman looks down at her hands, then brushes them against her hips and looks away. "Wait until they come home," she answers, her voice betraying nothing. "Wait until your grandmother sees her. We'll see, then."

Chelya nods and pulls Lonely away, while Lonely trails her thoughts behind her, still tangled in the woman's expression and the question of the word "grandmother." *We all have one mother....*

"It isn't that she doesn't like you," Chelya is saying, leading her back out into the sun. "It's only that she's afraid of—" She seems to stop herself and her eyes toss an unreadable question at Lonely. "She's afraid of what she doesn't know. We never see other people. We don't trust strangers. So much has been taken from us."

"But *you* trust me?" Lonely isn't sure what it means to be trusted, but it sounds like a good thing, somehow akin to being loved.

Chelya looks at her a long while, and Lonely, who until now had seen Chelya as younger than herself, now thinks about age for the first time and wonders for some reason if this is true. "I trust you," says Chelya.

"Why?"

Chelya looks off into the forest as they wade through the field. "When my father brought you home, a white horse followed him. The white horse stays here in the fields, knowing you are here, and—"

"And what?"

Chelya shakes her head. "There's something magic about him, right? About that horse? I feel like it's a good magic. But I don't know what it is."

"Neither do I," says Lonely.

That night, Lonely sleeps in Chelya's bed, while Chelya sleeps outside somewhere. Chelya asked her to join her but Lonely prefers, for once, to sleep indoors. She wants to feel the comfort of indoors, that arch cradling her, pretending that for the first time she has a home. Over the years Chelya has stuffed her bed painstakingly with feathers, one by one collected from the chickens and other birds who dropped theirs from the sky, like pieces of a dream, mythical remnants of flight. Lonely seems to sleep on a cloud, the dream of a young girl awakening to fantasies of womanhood. In the morning she stands and walks slowly around the chimney that rises through the loft, that great channel for the spirit of fire to grow like a tree into the sky.

Indoors there is shadow and stillness, close people and the bright substance of words. Outdoors there is the familiar freedom, where voices get lost in the wind. Lonely climbs down the ladder and walks out to the fields. She goes first to her horse, who does not rest like the other two horses they keep there, but always stands by himself between the house and the high mountain, holding private conference with the grasses and sky. She walks out to him, and she thanks him again for staying with her, and then she walks back to the house.

She discovers the great gift of hunger. Over and over that day, and for countless days afterward, she will experience hunger, and thereby will get to experience over and over again the pleasure of being filled. The pleasure is not even in the satisfaction itself, perhaps, for that is only an ending, but in the full-body experience where hunger and food mingle, where each part of her body awakens with the fire of eating, like each part of her has something unique to say about spiciness, grains, juicy meats, cream, the crunchiness of green things full of sweet water. Her taste buds, like a rainbow. Her throat like the long precious moment between desire and fulfillment, powerfully swallowing and releasing. The space inside her stomach collapses into substance, warm and real and rich with process.

Now she understands the day. Now the day—which was once a ghost, a spirit with no skeleton—has a structure with beginning, middle, and ending, and that structure is built of meals and the spaces between them. Hunger is a clear, grounding entity that breaks up her day, a reason to stop or to continue. Food fills her in, brighter and brighter. Her own womanhood overcomes her. It splashes her hips from side to side as she walks, as if she is fleshy like Chelya and Fawn, and her body seems to change, rounding a little more over her bones, as if she changes from bird to mammal. Her own lips taste sweet to her, soft under her tongue.

Everything is delicious. And here is Chelya's buoyant touch, drawing her here and there through the stations of life: the animals, the gardens, the river, the house. Lonely has so many questions. She wants to know where everything comes from and what makes it what it is. The clay of the round plates and the colors painted on them. The smooth floor of the house. The cloth bow that ties back Chelya's hair. But when Chelya asks her questions back, she avoids them.

"I come from nowhere," Lonely tells her, for she remembers Delilah's reaction to the story of the tower, and she senses that the words to describe her past in the lonely sea will not be made from the language of this land, where buildings are made of trees and straw and a little mud, crouching low to the earth. And Chelya, who is wild with joy at the realization that all of being human is new to Lonely, is so busy showing her the world that she doesn't press too hard yet for answers.

Lonely meets the grandmother on the first evening at dinnertime. Now there is a fourth woman at the table, and all three besides Lonely are connected by this important word: *mother.* No one introduces Eva to Lonely, but her presence is everywhere as soon as she sits at the table, and the soft but silent reverence that seems to surround her calls Lonely's attention as strictly as if she had been ordered to do so. At first, Lonely cannot look her in the eye. She doesn't know who she is, but she remembers the first old one she knew, who still waits for her on the island of her childhood, ready to greet her in every nightmare with that long-suffering face.

Then, when Eva doesn't speak to her, Lonely at last looks up, steeling her eyes. Eva is sitting directly across from her, and she nods. Lonely's heart relaxes and Eva smiles. No one speaks that night, except for Chelya making nervous comments about what she's shown to Lonely, and what the plants and animals are doing.

On the second day, the rains have begun again and do not stop. The old woman is nowhere to be seen, which is a relief to Lonely, for she still frightens her. Chelya and her mother spend all day in rows of plants with strange, lively characters, plants whose hands and heads and feet become the food they will eat for dinner. Both women's faces are tight and focused today; they say nothing as they dig deeper trenches around the rows to let the water flow in rivers away, and as they mound up the muddy soil, and as they cover long rows of earth with what looks to Lonely like blankets. Lonely, accustomed to being outdoors in any weather, lets the rain run over her face like she is part of the field. She watches them helplessly for a while, then tries to follow what they do. Distractedly, Chelya hands her some tool, which Lonely tries and fails to use as they do. She waits for Chelya to help her, but even the girl is so urgent now, so intent on her task as the rain washes the soil from the roots of these precious, speaking, nearly human plants, that she has no time to notice Lonely standing there, waiting. Chelya's hands are muddy and smart and quick.

Lonely sits on a stone and watches the women, and thinks idly, habitually, of longing.

At dinner that night, she is ravenous. She dives into the joy of hunger and fulfillment, not minding the silence at the table, unable to imagine the conversation that is usually there. Even Chelya seems too tired to talk. But out of the corner of her eye, Lonely sees Eva's hand stroke Fawn's hair once, and hears Fawn sigh, and hears herself sigh, too, though she did not mean to. Suddenly the food is no longer quite enough. What is wrong?

"We'll be all right," Eva nods softly to her daughter.

Fawn shakes her head ever so slightly. "Last year the drought—now this."

"We always make it, Ma," says Chelya. "Don't worry." Her voice sounds smaller and sadder than Lonely has ever heard it, and yet in these few spoken words which she doesn't understand, Lonely hears the deep assumption of teamwork, of mutual knowing, that holds a family together. Like the network of trees in the forest. Like the birds that know each other through song.

"The boys will be home," says Eva now, "by the time we finish cleaning up. I can feel them coming." Lonely feels almost surprised that she gave this information to Fawn, so great is her own longing and expectation—so clear is her own body's memory of the man's arms.

True to Eva's prediction, she sees Rye for the first time a little later that night with his son at his side. The two men enter the house soaked with the rain, bringing a gentle thrust of dark, weary masculinity into the round stillness. Eva has now retired for the night, and Lonely still feels the weight of the old woman's gaze, which followed her all evening and seems to know something that Lonely does not. After Eva was gone, Lonely watched Fawn put down her mending and rest her eyes on the door. Love and hope changed her face so slightly that Lonely could barely detect them—her mouth still set in its wide, full line, but her jaw relaxing a little, her cheeks falling, her chest rising. The yellow light of the candle played a dramatic theater of shadows over her modest profile, like a piece of the sun's great soul had come to sit intimately among humans, shrinking itself into a small but powerful glow that made a circle of wonder in the room. Chelya and Lonely are sitting on the floor when the man and the boy walk in; Chelya has lain out her jewelry for Lonely to see, asking if she would like a necklace or a bracelet for her own.

Now Lonely's whole body vibrates, and if she were a cricket the very friction of her trembling would make a song, as Fawn goes to her husband and son and kisses them both. As if she were standing before him herself, Lonely feels Rye's helpless bigness, his tender, naked aliveness falling with relief into Fawn's breast, and how their bodies complete each other with a quiet, delirious sizzle, even from across the room. The boy—not a man at all yet but a poignant approximation of one—stands gaping at Lonely, his hair light and messy around his ears, his T-shirt so old it's as soft as skin, his pants hanging loose, his feet smooth and finely contoured in their frayed sandals. He is slimmer and paler than anyone in the family, and tall like his father and like Lonely.

"Dad," Chelya starts. "The girl you brought home—"

"My name is Lonely," says Lonely, rising suddenly, full of shame but wanting the men to know her, wanting them to look at her and keep looking, feeding her with their deep brown eyes.

Rye turns to her, and she sees his bearded, weather-darkened face tense with a kind of perceptive thoughtfulness that he seems accustomed to keeping silent. He nods his head, raindrops falling from his hair, unconscious of his sturdy grace. When he looks at her, her whole body changes. All that it has learned in the past two days of eating and drinking and being led by a small eager hand—all that it has learned of humanness—rises in her throat, her body waking again as if looking at itself, replicating again and again inside itself. The blood emerges beneath her skin, coloring her in. Her own beauty dizzies her. She can feel it. She needs him to help her carry the weight of it. She needs to pour it over his dense, muscular form, to make it real.

You saved me. You made me real. She stands there boldly, willing Rye to look at her, and he complies, his gaze smooth and contained.

"Hello, Lonely," he says, the two words separated stiffly from each other, but firm. Lonely realizes that both Chelya and Fawn have avoided speaking her name since she arrived. She breathes out, and her breath sounds loud in the quiet. Rye's face barely changes but she imagines a hint of a smile there, and to her that smile holds a sad, knowing weight and an infinite capacity for goodness. She realizes it again: he is the first person to speak her name. That must mean something. It must.

But he goes with Fawn then, almost right away, without eating, and Kite, after a mumble that serves as his hurried introduction, talks with Chelya briefly, drinks a cup of milk, and rolls himself up into a blanket in the corner. And there is no answer that night, about whether or not she—Lonely—will stay.

Instead there is only another question for Lonely: what secret space— what paradise, what dream—do Rye and Fawn rush off to, when they so quickly leave together, when they so quickly mount the ladder into the attic where Lonely last night slept? She does not sleep there tonight. Tonight the rain continues, and Chelya and Lonely sleep on the floor below, Lonely pretending to sleep as soon as Chelya lies down beside her, to avoid Chelya's questions and her dauntless joy that Lonely cannot share.

There is no answer. Yet the next day, Lonely is given breakfast again, and is not asked to leave. And the next, and the next. Every day there is hunger and eating. Every day there is this love to witness all around her, painful to watch and yet impossible not to. Every day there is work, and at times this work is given to her also, and Lonely discovers the happiness of feeling necessary in small, occasional ways.

There is the fleeting passage of the men, their thrilling presence in and out of her day as they pass from field to forest, from house to horses, from kitchen to shed. At the table she waits, with the luxury of food turning in her mouth, for Rye to speak, so that she can rest with relief in the slow, deep nest of his voice. When she walks through the fields with Chelya or finds only Fawn at the house when she returns, she tries not to show her disappointment or to mention Rye's name.

"Why can I still stay?" she whispers to Chelya one evening as they wash dishes together. "Is it all right?"

Chelya shrugs. "Why not? More of the crop survived the rains than we expected, so we have plenty of food. You can help out."

But Lonely wants something more. She wants to hear that she is wanted by at least one person in the family—and not just by Chelya, who, she fears, would rejoice in any companionship, and who looks at her with questions that Lonely cannot answer. Chelya's kindness is so frequent and warm, and the luxuries of food and soft bedding and the circle of family at the table in the embrace of the house are so wonderful. Yet Fawn still avoids her eyes, and Kite acts like she isn't there, unless they find themselves alone together, and then he bolts so fast that Lonely looks around her, wondering what could have frightened him. Sometimes she convinces herself that Rye feels something for her, for his glances remake her body every time, the knowing in them so penetrating and tenderly confident that one of them can claim her for an entire day, but those glances are few. Eva watches her but says nothing. Lonely realizes that though everyone seems to allow her, though she feels no malice from anyone, with the exception of Chelya no one is speaking to her more than a word here or there. And maybe, Lonely thinks in confusion, there is nothing strange about that at all. Perhaps it is she who is strange. She thinks of the birds as they called to each other in the desert brush. She thinks of the sound of her name. She tries to remember the few brief conversations of her life. What is it that people talk about? Sometimes these people talk, but she doesn't understand them. They speak of leaks in the barn, and of too much rain. They speak of people whose names she does not know. They speak of the way the house is made and the way things grow, but she does not know these things. And she has her own questions but is afraid to ask them, because she doesn't know the rules.

What is that wetness in my body and in your eyes, deep down, when you look at me? she would ask Rye.

What does it feel like, to make love to him? she would ask Fawn. *And what do you think of me? What are you thinking about, when your face changes like that?*

Where are the secret places you go in the afternoon, and why? she would ask Kite.

Am I doing something wrong? Do you curse me too? What do you see, and what does it mean? she would ask Eva desperately, when Eva follows her with her eyes and does not mind that Lonely knows it.

But these do not seem to be the kinds of questions that people ask each other. So she stays quiet for now.

3rd MOON

Delilah isn't skilled with sorrow, which feels to her sneakier and more deadly than anger. When it comes—which happens whenever Moon goes— she does her best to sleep through it. Besides, she is always careful with herself on the dark moon. It's a quiet, murky time, with no light to focus the darkness, no syrupy white orb to guide one's dreams. The sky abandons itself to a chaos of blackness.

Tonight, walking makes the new-moon cramps less acute. So she walks, feeling that her body is held together by strings of pain. She allows a fantasy, sometimes, of the strings breaking—all her joints disconnecting from her limbs, her vertebrate floating apart, relaxing and scattering over the desert floor and dissolving into dust and sunlight.

She walks toward the mountains, and wonders fleetingly if Dragon's girl left by this route. For a moment, she tries to imagine that leaving. What it would feel like to walk away and start all over—again. Maybe she feels a little wistful at the thought, which has not crossed her mind in years.

The air is fresh and cold, and her breath energizes her. She walks with a determined stride, as if she knows where she's going. It's surprising how much light the desert, with its face as ugly and pockmarked as the moon itself, can reflect. The stars, and an hour's worth of walking and adjusting to the darkness, are enough for Delilah to see her way by. Following the lighter glow of the cliff beside her, she begins, for no particular reason, to run.

She stops when she sees smoke rising from around the next bend, from one of the caves where old legends say that dragons once lived. Instinctively, she crouches into a corner of stone. Already the thought of men quickens her body, but she is bleeding, and besides she doesn't like to be caught off guard. She is a hunter and will not be hunted. But when she scans the darkness, she sees no movement, no sign of a vehicle, no sign of disturbance. She presses against the rock wall and climbs, following a shadow path up and over, and peers down to the place where the smoke rises.

It isn't smoke. It's steam.

She has never seen such a thing—not in the desert, not anywhere. Thick, luscious balloons of steam rise from what seems to be a pit of boiling water in caverns of earth at the base of a cave. She can't see anything below the white puffs, but she can hear the writhing water like magic in a cauldron. The vapor melts open her pores, unpeels tension from her face that she didn't even know was there. The sound is delicious, the stench—like something fermented and rotten—somehow intoxicating. She feels that tearful, child-like joy that she never used to believe could be hers, the joy that she felt during her first days in the desert, to know that for the first time in her life the universe had given her a gift—her alone, as if she deserved it. She feels the joy of realizing that there is still something more to be discovered.

But before she can slide down the rock, before she can lose herself in this luxurious secret of earth, the shape of a man materializes in the haze below her. As he looks up, she knows it is Dragon, though his face never comes entirely clear. She is crouched like an insect on a thin ridge of stone, damp and exposed, and cannot move. She feels something in the blackness of her own stomach that should be fury or disappointment but is neither.

"Dragon," she says, without meaning to, simply because he rises here from this place of dragons, and it is his name, and there is nothing else to say.

She can see the rusty darkness of one human shoulder rounding out of the steam into the invisible light of the desert night, and if it were not for that, she wouldn't know for sure that he is real. In his shroud of mist, he seems to lurch drunkenly toward her, the posture of his body so familiar to her now: a pillar of desire and will. She thinks, absurdly: *He really is a god. He is the god of something. I just don't know what.*

The dark moon is such a dangerous time: it makes everything shift, so subtly you don't realize it until it has already happened. Suddenly Delilah feels as if, in all her years of fucking men, maybe there are ways one body can meet another that she has never known or even imagined.

He stands as if waiting, and she can feel his gaze upon her, though she cannot see it. The moment stretches on indefinitely, with a dream's irreverent sense of time. What was that "no" a moon ago, and who was the person who spoke it? Now the pride of it freezes her, and makes him more a stranger than ever. Dragon stands like a statue in the white mist, white like the disappearing tail of a unicorn over desert stone, and in spite of herself she thinks of the girl again and is confused. Desire is so familiar. The "no" was not. She feels vulnerable in her bleeding now, and the vulnerability feels so unnatural to her that she shrinks against the stone. She knows with a painful, conscious knowing that she wants Dragon. But in the clarity of that wanting, she knows this is not the time. This isn't like the wanting she has felt in the past, in which nothing really mattered.

She can hear the moist brush of her own quick breath as she draws it in; she is aware of the shapes of the stone not fitting her palms as she scrambles back down the way she came. She watches the motions of her own seemingly determined body with wonder, as if it belongs to somebody else. The way it jumps with confidence to the firm sand below, the way it runs. But the memory of Dragon's gaze is all too real, and the emotion in that gaze is more familiar to her than it should be. She can feel his eyes on her back—she's sure of it—on the back of her heart, all the way home.

When she finally tires and slows to a walk, she tries not to think because her thoughts don't feel like her own. She can't stop thinking, not of Dragon, but of the girl. *I'm on a journey,* she had said. *I'm looking for love.* Who spoke like that? Who could be so ridiculously simple? Who goes looking for love? As far as Delilah is concerned, love is something you get or you don't get, through no fault of your own, and whoever goes looking for it is certain not to find it, because when you reach for it, it disappears. But that girl had a different kind of certainty in her eyes. Maybe she was blessed somehow. Delilah realizes that, of all the things she spoke to Moon about, it was that girl she really wanted to speak of. That was the most important thing she needed to tell him: what that girl had said, about love. No, not what she'd said, which was simple and childish after all, but something else. What was it?

Whatever it was, she couldn't have told him. What that girl said, what she sought—it wasn't something that would have made sense to either Delilah or Moon. Even in an unconditional friendship, the one that can always save you, there are limits. The more closely you understand each other, the greater stretch the expanses—beyond that intimate circle—where neither of you have ever been. There are whole worlds that neither of you knows. And even when one person glimpses them, there is no language with which to tell the other.

In the mountains a wind is coming like a fall breath in the middle of summer, bringing weather that no one can yet predict. Lonely watches it through the window of the house: a watching that began with waiting for Rye, trying to conjure up his broad-shouldered figure on the horizon. She does not like to be so obvious, but sometimes she feels so useless that she doesn't care. She'd rather turn invisible against the window, losing herself in her watching, and her watching losing itself in the wind. The women are cooking behind her, murmuring to one another, and no one has any need of her. No one speaks to her.

The more she watches, the more Lonely can actually see the wind. She would tell them but they don't know her; they don't understand her. She couldn't tell them how more and more, she can see the actual body of the wind—the whip of its muscle, the gape of its mouth, the metallic blue of its skin, the flecks of red around its hollow eyes.

The sound of it, wordless now, is so lonely. Loneliness seems all that it is, moaning terribly against the earth and the walls, nagging hungrily at the trees. It calls like the way it called to her when she paced between her round tower walls, and she did not know what it was saying. Yet she remembers, also, when the wind has not been loneliness but freedom. She remembers when she rode through the meadow sea of it, when she lifted her face to it, and it seems to her now that in those moments she breathed the power of it, as if that power belonged to her.

She touches the glass. She can see the wind now, and she wants to go outside. Something is there for her, out in the mad universe of the wailing wind—some answer, some promised thing. Something that belongs to her. Silvery blue, blood red glitter, yellow leaves, and the wind slings its body apart, explodes open again, hurling itself faster now against the house, slamming into her ears, her eyes—

"Lonely!"

Lonely turns, breathless. It is Eva who spoke her name, and as the indoor sounds catch up with her, Lonely feels that she may, in fact, have spoken it several times. Eva has lain down the knife with which she was cutting the garlic. Her eyes are calm, but the eyes of Fawn, who stands just behind her, are not. Lonely looks anxiously back at the window. Did she do something? Did she call the wind to her? It seems to pale a little now, but not before she becomes suddenly aware of the rattling window. Trying to calm her own breathing, which she had not noticed rising, she presses her palm to the glass.

"What is this?" she asks, trying to keep her voice steady. She looks at Chelya, knowing it is she who will answer.

"It's glass," says Chelya, who is accustomed now to Lonely's childish newness to all the ordinary things of the world. Eva is still staring at Lonely with a stare that Lonely cannot meet, and she doesn't say why she called Lonely's name.

Lonely looks back at the window and thinks she can see hints of her own face inside it. Suddenly she remembers that face, which she has not seen for so long but which once she saw every day.

Her own face. She remembers its stillness, and then the way it teared and flushed and opened, like summer, when she saw the mountain.

"But what is glass made of?" she asks.

She looks back at Chelya, but it is Fawn who says, her voice small and cold, "Sand." When Lonely looks at her, Fawn is looking back down at her work. She is cleaning one of the three large fish that Rye caught today, while Chelya dusts the table and clears out the insects. They will eat inside again tonight, the night of the dark moon, by the light of little candles held in ornate, animal-shaped holders that Chelya made out of river clay. Eva is working with the herbs and vegetables; in her old age, she neither handles nor eats meat, saying that it brings too much heaviness into her body, which is worth little to her now, and muddies her conversations with the spirit realm.

Lonely stares at Fawn, but Fawn still doesn't look up. "It is made of sand," she elaborates softly. "Sand shaped by fire."

"But how is sand made?"

Fawn hesitates, and Lonely can hear her breath. "By water."

"That's beautiful," says Chelya, laying a cloth over the table and arranging the candles. "I wish we knew how to make glass, here in the mountains."

"So glass is melted by fire, too," says Lonely. "Like ice." She says it to the window, forgetting them again, but Eva's voice calls her back.

"Girl," she says abruptly. "Where do you come from?"

Lonely keeps staring at the glass, and cannot see her reflection now—only the wind. She cannot see the mountain or the tender face of her prince. She feels a terrible need to see her own face again, to know the comfort of its familiarity, the comfort of that high distant room where there was no longing, no fear—nothing other than herself, safe within herself.

"Lonely," says Eva sternly.

Then the wind begins to circle into stillness, and at its center Lonely can see the coming of a great rain. She can see the inevitability of that rain in the stillness the wind draws for her in the sky.

"I come from a tower made of glass," she says without feeling.

"Oh!" cries Chelya behind her. "How beautiful! Where is it?"

"In the middle of the sea. But now it's gone."

After a long, long silence, a silence in which Lonely turns again to see joyful fascination in Chelya's eyes and a sudden, icy tension in Fawn's, Eva speaks again.

"Lonely," she says, gently this time, "come speak with me tonight. When dinner is over. Will you do that?"

"Okay," says Lonely, and she looks back at the window, hoping the wind, and only the wind, can see her tentative tears, and hoping the wind will know why the tears have come, because she does not.

But the wind closes its eyes now, and the sky slackens, and the water comes down. And Lonely remembers Dragon and that day she stood in the river, full of hope.

She doesn't think once of Eva's request during dinner, because she is seated next to Rye, and that hot, embracing scent of earth and skin and subtle, unconscious sweat overwhelms her.

The family is talking quietly about the rain, and how it has come too soon since the last rains. Many of Fawn's new plants are dying in waterlogged soil, and mold creeps into their wooden house and rots the supports under the sheds. The front room is raised high enough to give room for the river to rise, but only so much. Outside now the rains shroud the house in sound, and every now and then the wind thrusts through it again—the wind, who doesn't take sides, only accentuates what is.

Then Rye says to Fawn, "Is something wrong?"

She is sitting next to her mother across the table. She shakes her head. The older women, Lonely notices, seem unusually silent. And she knows it has something to do with her, and the wind.

"Dad," says Chelya, "you can take a couple of the goat kids when you go to Jay's next. They're old enough now."

Rye nods, glancing again at Fawn.

"I was thinking," continues Chelya, her voice overeager, and Lonely can tell how the silence unnerves her too, "if we ever find any other families, I was thinking I could trade my jewelry someday."

Then Lonely looks at Kite, for no reason she knows. Maybe it's the scent and presence of Rye beside her that causes her, more than usual, to notice the mysterious quiet of the men. Suddenly it seems clear to her that the silence isn't coming from Fawn or Eva. It is coming from Kite. That's where the silence of the whole family lies—inside his mind, where no one can see. Something there is making everyone uneasy. Or maybe it's only Fawn who is uneasy. But that uneasiness spreads. Lonely tries to trace it, the way she tried to trace the wind. Kite to Fawn. Fawn to Rye. Then to Chelya, when she sees the tension between Fawn and Rye.

"Start thinking about what we need," says Rye now, smiling at Chelya, "when I do go. Maybe I'll make a trip before the harvest, when the planting's done. Maybe further south. I think that's where the other farms will be, if any are left." He looks at Fawn again and Lonely remembers a conversation when she first arrived, the morning after Rye and Kite returned. About how the farm he'd visited to the north was gone. Just gone. Nothing but bare, torn earth, and the house empty, the people gone. Even the crows had seemed solemn as they pecked their way through the emptiness, said Rye. Lonely, caught up in the newness of her own experience then, mesmerized by the movement of Rye's mouth as he spoke, had not understood Fawn's bowed head or Chelya's soundless tears.

Now Fawn says simply, without lifting her face, "Wool. And flour of course."

Chelya puts her fork down. "Maybe someone is growing fruit?"

Rye shakes his head. "I don't know. Fruit trees aren't doing well. The weather has been so strange. The late freeze we had this spring—all the trees are confused."

"I don't know why you're talking about this," says Kite, reaching over Chelya's plate for the little bowl of dill and lavender. "You won't go anyway. You never do."

Rye looks at him, his jaw tense, but Kite won't look back.

There is silence, and now it seems to stretch from Kite to his mother. Lonely has stopped eating, and is unabashedly watching, following the pathway of glances and unspoken feelings from one person to another.

"Fawn," Rye says across the table. "Why won't you look at me." Lonely catches herself staring at him, and looks away.

Reluctantly, Fawn looks, but only for a moment. "I don't want to talk about this again."

"Talk about what?"

"The two of you going to the City. I know you're thinking about it. There's no need for you to go there."

"Nobody said—"

"But it's here. That idea is here at the table. I can feel it. Kite." She turns to her son. "I know you want to visit the City. I know you think about it all the time—"

"Ma," Kite raises his voice a little. The unexpected power in it makes Lonely shiver. She pictures him walking in from the fields this afternoon, an image she didn't know she had stored. "They have things we can use there. We could fix what we have, make things run better. They know how to—"

"Come on, you just want to meet girls," Chelya teases.

"That's not true!"

"If you go there, Kite, you could bring some of my jewelry to give away, and the girls would like you."

"Shut up."

"Stop," says Fawn, not raising her voice, but they stop, and Chelya remembers herself and looks sorry. "We have everything we need. The way we live is fine. We have so much. When I was growing up, I didn't even have a house."

"So what," says Kite under his breath.

Rye sighs. "We do have enough," he says, directing his words at Fawn. "But to just turn our backs on the whole rest of the world, to say it's purely evil—"

"They have turned their backs on us."

"Because they don't know. They don't understand. They don't remember where their food comes from. We understand these things. We could teach them."

"How?"

"I don't know," he answers, but then he continues, and this momentary pause of not knowing—this willingness to admit not knowing, but continuing on anyway—makes Lonely love him. "I know you're afraid, Fawn. I'm afraid, too. I'm afraid that our world is dying around us while we sit here and do nothing. I'm afraid that one of us will get sick beyond Eva's ability to help—or Eva herself, who is growing older, will grow sick one day—and we don't know any other healers. I worry about our children, who are restless, who have no social connections, who are growing up isolated."

"I'm not restless," Chelya interrupts hopefully, looking back and forth between her parents' faces. Lonely sees the warmth reddening Fawn's face, knows she wishes she had not spoken of all this in front of everyone—or, really, in front of Lonely. Then Fawn looks up into Rye's eyes, and her voice is small but even. "They're afraid of *us* there, Rye. They think anything that comes from wild places is evil."

Rye sighs, his voice weakening, as if he knows his words will not reach her. "It doesn't matter, Fawn. They need us."

After another moment of silence, in which nobody takes a bite, Chelya turns tenderly to her mother and offers, "Just think, Ma. Not everyone there is bad. There are children growing up in that world who have never tasted real food. There are so many animals living in the streets. Aren't there?" She turns to Eva.

Eva says nothing, but Lonely notices her sad smile.

"I don't understand what you want to do," Fawn says to Rye, her voice tight.

"I don't know exactly either," Rye says again. "I just wish you'd think about this with me."

With me. Lonely imagines the two of them, lying together in bed or walking in the woods, sharing a space together that no one else can ever enter. How can Fawn refuse such an invitation? How can she not come to him right now, and think about anything—feel anything, do anything—with this beautiful man, so earnest, who loves her?

Fawn looks right at him. "Something bad is going to happen there, Rye," she says quietly. "I know somehow. Something is going to happen there soon. I can feel it all around me, in the world, in this wind even. I can feel it. Things are changing somehow."

Eva looks at her daughter, and Lonely thinks she wants to say something, but she doesn't. Instead she looks down at her plate and sighs.

Then they are all silent again, this time for so long that Lonely loses herself in the taste of food in her mouth and the faint brush of Rye's leg against hers. She notices that Chelya is looking down at her plate, not eating, her normally lively features drawn together and dulled.

After a long time, Rye says in a new tone, "How was your day, Lonely?" using her name as if it were common and easy, as if it made sense and were nothing to be feared.

"Oh," says Lonely, surprised, pressing her fingers to her mouth as she chews, drinking in his gaze through her skin but afraid to look at him. "It was windy," she murmurs.

He laughs, and his laugh is like music through a deep wind instrument, that at once soothes and makes her tremble. "Yes," he says. "It was. Do you like the wind?"

Lonely presses her leg against his, and he doesn't pull away. But out of the corner of her eye she sees his smile fade, and he doesn't press back. Still, his muscle, both huge and humble, against her, stirs her with such heat that she begins to panic, trying to remember what he asked her. She wonders suddenly if the animal between his legs that makes him a man would rise for her the way Dragon's always rose whenever she was near him. The thought makes her face hot. She tries to remember what he asked her. *The wind, the wind*....

"Yes," she breathes. "I like it." She wants to feel his hand there, where the wetness comes from. She would let him do anything to her. Anything. She needs him to find that secret well within her—that well from which she draws her life, and yet which she herself cannot see. She looks sideways at Fawn, terrified that her own longing might be visible on her face. But Fawn is looking out the window at the wind.

"There is something strange about this weather," Fawn murmurs, as if to herself. "The winds blow differently, or they speak differently, and the weather they bring is always wrong."

No one responds to this.

Across from Lonely, Malachite finishes his meal hastily and doesn't take seconds. "There's a leak I need to check on," he mumbles, and leaves the table.

The companions of Dragon's earliest childhood came in every color. There was an indigo dragon, an old male with gnarled muscles and a grizzled face but eyes like flowers. There was a pink dragon, small and catlike, who used to leap from spire to spire in the blackest depths of the caves, his body snapping like elastic in the light of the ever-shooting flames.

There was a jade green dragon who could make fire in the shapes of animals, and a hot yellow dragon who used to wrestle with the boy and feed him flames from her mouth.

The more Dragon remembers, the more he remembers more. Their spirits lap and hiss at the inside of his mind in his dreams, boil around his body as he rises to greet the day. As if they are still here, in the caves where they raised him.

There were so many dragons, and sometimes their fire was terrible to behold, and sometimes it was like laughter. Some dragons woke by day and others woke by night, but once they stopped coming out onto the land, it didn't matter, for they lived always in darkness. They had always been misunderstood. They were passionate, sentimental, and restless. Sometimes they howled like wolves, and other times they sang sweet songs like the lullabies of angels. They were unpredictable. When they made love, they stayed locked together like snakes for days and days, even moons.

Once, they told him, they lived all over the world. They peopled this world. The remains of their magical flesh, chemically reacting and transforming into a slick chocolate oil—richer than the most nutritious earth—lie beneath all the landscapes of the world, and most especially within the mountains. It is this rich substance, once the bodies of dragons, that human beings pull out of the earth to fuel their great City. But they do not know what it is. Already they have used it up so fast—as fast as their forgetting—and already it is almost gone.

In those final years when Dragon lived among them, the dragons moved deeper into the earth every year, and eventually they never saw the sun. Once they had lived all over the world. They had lived in all shapes and sizes, adapted to every climate. In the Heart of the World, the mother of all dragons had once luxuriated beneath a deep green swamp, haunting the original people there, who worshipped her. But the people who built the City, though so much smaller than the dragons, had found the power somehow to destroy almost all of them. Hanum made heroes of men who would slay them. Even now, men came seeking them with weapons, projecting all the ugliness in their own hearts upon them. Now they came with machines that were even greater monsters, that could tear apart the earth with their rusty iron teeth. They sought the precious stones under the earth which were the scales and the eyes and the teeth of the dragons themselves. They sought to kill the dragons, whose blood, when released, hardened into gold.

Now people said they did not believe in dragons, and at the same time they hated them for still being alive, and their young men sought them secretly. Dragon could feel that hatred echoing, even deep down in the earth that housed him, even as a young child.

When, in his sixth year, the dragons held their council and decided to move deeper into the earth than any man could ever go—so deep that the stone swelled and rolled into liquid fire, so deep that they no longer knew what they would become, and the lives they knew would end forever—they had to leave the boy behind. For even with his fire-loving young body he would not survive it, and they knew that one day in his humanness he would need the light of that greatest of all fires, the sun, and all the wonders that the lit world could offer him.

So the leader of that last remaining clan, a woman dragon, risked her life to carry him from the caves across the desert, into the forest and up into the mountains. He remembers the terror of that journey. They were never safe. Finally, she left him at the gates of that Garden, a place ruled by women, where she thought he would be cared for. As she wrapped him in a shroud of mild blue flame to warm him through the night, and as he watched his second mother leave him, he felt the danger recede with her. He realized for the first time that it was the dragons who were hated, not him. And that as long as no one knew that he had once belonged to them, he would be safe.

The goddesses loved him. But they called him Dragon. Why did they call him that? He was proud of his name, always, and yet he felt they did it to remind him that he wasn't one of them. That one day he would be cast away from them, too, as he had been cast away before.

Still he is part dragon, after all. He can feel it. It makes him feel powerful and it makes him ashamed, but what is it that makes him afraid? Why were the dragons hated? He tries so hard to remember, but maybe he never knew.

When Yora left him and Delilah cast him out, he walked back over the desert to these caves. He knew exactly where he was going. There was no question. It was the sight of the Unicorn that made him go, that made him end up here. That creature inspired in him a terror more primal than anything he had ever known he could feel.

Now, living beneath the earth again, Dragon is safe, and he feels the presence of the dragons, though they are not here. The fire is gone now, and instead the caves are filled with water. The water boils as if with fire inside it, and the water makes him soft with longing. He can remember, almost, what it felt like to live among such creatures. How easy it was to be touched, how they lived in nothing but body and spirit, roaring together, a constant friction of hot being. Sometimes now, he thinks they are speaking to him again. In his dreams they tell him stories, and sometimes when he wakes, he can remember them.

The dragons were selective about their food. In the old days, when they walked upon the land, they sometimes ate fruit if they could find it—but only the sweetest, most unblemished fruit, at the exact moment of ripeness. Occasionally, they ate each other, but this was done only under certain circumstances in certain, ritualistic conditions which the boy Dragon neither knew nor remembered. Most often they ate virgins.

No one understood what this was about. Everyone feared the dragons. They did not understand that the way a dragon took a virgin into his body was like the way Dragon now takes women into his boiling lair, into the belly of the desert. She comes of her own accord. Something moves in her, a gentle sea of heat lapping at the inner shores of her body, and her feet are naked against the bare, tossing sands. Dragon doesn't know where they come from, these women who have come to him ever since he returned to the caves. Some of them are goddesses, perhaps, and some of them are women that the treasure hunters bring with them, or the dream selves of women in the City who leave their bodies in desperation, seeking some answer to the forbidden questions within them. He doesn't even know if they are real. But it seems to him that they are. It seems to him that more and more, what the men who explore the desert and even Delilah do not know is that the women are seeking the dragons too. And what they seek is the same, and yet it is also different, for the women do not hate them.

They pause in the onslaught of steam, touching their own skin, their small moans lost in the roar of the water.

When the cavern devours them, they might feel pain, but only to the extent that they fear their own desires. The warm, pulsing water wins against their resistance immediately. Drawn slowly downward as if by the pull of Dragon's own need—the pull of that Other who remains as yet unknown, terrifying and necessary—they are not burned. The pain is the pain of a sore muscle that is pressed to relax, the pain of tears that sting dry eyes, the pain of pleasure splitting open the seams of their bodies. The water leaves no part of them uncaressed. When they reach the center where Dragon awaits them with his worshipful hands, his slow tongue, his tireless longing, and his increasingly practiced, patient body, their melted bodies shudder with relief. Their bones are made of fire. Their mouths have come unhinged, like the mouths of snakes. They shake their hair like manes and growl. They start coming at the mere touch of his breath.

It was like that for the virgin who was devoured by a dragon. Inside the timeless paradise of his colorful body, she lived a life of bliss. Sometimes she would remain there for years, though it seemed only days. And then the dragon, finally restless, would cough her back up in a belch of fire, back onto the earth, and be hungry again for another. The woman, infected with that same restlessness, would wander the earth in a state of eternal agitation. But she would be confident and glorious, and she would walk in a voluptuous manner, and dance like a snake. Other women would tremble in her presence, feeling things they did not understand, and no man would ever be able to tame her.

It was for this reason that men slew dragons.

The indigo dragon has told him this, and the jade dragon too now, in dream after dream. This is the reason why dragons are hated.

But what about the Unicorn? he asks them. *Why did I recognize that terrible creature? Why do I know its name, as if from a story long ago?*

Days and nights are the same now, all darkness. Dragon dreams again. A story the red dragon is blowing out in bubbles of fire. Or perhaps not a story exactly, but images repeated again and again, throughout history.

Two figures stand on opposite cliffs in the misty dawn of some primeval forest that no longer exists, a river running between them. They have been there forever. Dragon and Unicorn.

The Dragon, who does not fear hunger because he always feels it, laughs, and the Unicorn, who does not fear hunger because she has overcome it, looks noble. In every way they seem to be opposites. Dragons are communal, whereas Unicorns live alone; in fact, some say that there is only one Unicorn that ever lived, a Unicorn both male and female, or neither, or that changes sexes every hundred years. The Dragon is musical and lively, whereas the Unicorn moves silently and has no voice. The Dragon is passionate, of expressive face, while the Unicorn's face is ever still, its eyes deep wells of impassable peace. The Dragon enjoys the taste of blood, while the Unicorn eats nothing. The Dragon is born of fire, while the Unicorn loves cool water, and can make water pure with a touch of her horn. The colorful Dragon rises up from darkness, while the Unicorn is sometimes blinding in her white light. But inside the Unicorn lies the darkness of the whole world's sorrow, whereas inside the Dragon burns an everlasting fire of joy.

The Unicorn fell in love with the virgin, so the stories say, but it was a chaste love, and the Dragon, by contrast, always wished to devour her. So they fought. But why did the Unicorn always win? What magic in that horn could be any match for fire, teeth, and claws?

Dragon doesn't know, and when he wakes, longing snakes up his body, and gets caught in his heart because there is too much pain there. One day, he thinks, he will meet that Unicorn again. That Unicorn who judged him. That icy cold light that stood between him and the object of his desire, white as loneliness. That which has always stopped him. That which made him feel he did not deserve—would never deserve—to be loved back. The Unicorn seems male to Dragon. Its sword of white light harder than Dragon's body-sword, and everlasting. Like some stoic god that holds Woman away from him, forever.

Sometimes, in his dreams, he still sees Coyote far out in the desert hills. Coyote laughs at him from a distance. "Kill the Unicorn," Coyote says simply. Or seems to.

But then sometimes, he wants to hate the Unicorn and cannot. It makes him anxious. The memory of its beauty hurts him. Maybe he wants to meditate in the shade of that beauty like a holy man under a sad willow whose leaves are white feathers, and wake up better than he is—wake up calm and clear and never lonely again. Sometimes he dreams the Unicorn stood between him and that pure girl Yora—not Delilah—because that girl was too beautiful for him. Because he wasn't evolved enough yet. And then he thinks, maybe the Unicorn was female.

The more he remembers the dragons, the more he thinks of the Unicorn, though he does not want to. He cannot help it. The idea of the Unicorn is embedded in the idea of dragons; it is intrinsic in their consciousness, their closeness, the whole possibility of ever knowing them again.

For days and days, Dragon does not see the sun. For nights and nights, the water spirals around him, round and round, and does not burn him. He dreams and wakes, wakes and dreams, and prays for the women to come.

Walking to the hill of the old woman, Lonely feels her own body so strongly it pains her. The rain fills her hands, coats her skin, covers her back. Her nipples rub inside the pinched wet folds of her dress as she walks—this dress she has always worn, that holds her together, that separates her from touch.

Now her fingertips fly against herself through the cloth, just lightly, because no one is looking, and the nub of her desire stiffens until it stings, and her flesh cannot hold itself together, like water overflowing. She wants to lie down for just a moment in the tall grass, just to feel the press of something against her body, just to be held by something.

When the grass touches her back, it's so cold in its wetness that she starts to shake all over, but then the rain keeps coming and blurs her skin, coating her in a water-shroud of her own heat. Rye did not press her leg back, did not look at her, and yet she feels certain that if she found him right now, he would take her, and they would hide behind these curtains of rain, enfolded in its drunken, blameless passion. Because Dragon wasn't the one, and Moon wasn't the one, but he is. He has to be. Because of the easy strength of his hands pressing her to his body as he carried her. The hands that made her real. The hands that made her human. The hands of earth that separated her—the only hands that can keep her safe—from the nightmare abyss beneath the tower.

His kind goodness, unlike Dragon. His comforting sturdiness, unlike Moon. Maybe the dream of the mountain was only a dream, to lead her onward, to guide her up into these hills where Rye, in the truth of his love—oh, the way he looked at her that night he first came home—could find her.

But he is in the kitchen now with Fawn, and anyway Lonely does not know what she would say, so she reaches down into her own mystery instead, bewildered by its urgency, and from the first time she touches it she cannot stop. Her hips, beyond her control, begin to spiral around her fingers, and a whirlpool sucks them inward, and deep within that whirlpool is a prayer—a prayer she needs to speak to someone but doesn't know how. She knows only the sound of her own voice, coming in waves of windy crying, lost in the rain, and her own death billowing up from her insides in deep purple waves, and her mind overtaken by an urgency of sensation—the whole world over-taken by it, the meadows blurring and the sky rushing down upon her. In that sky she sees her own face, as if in the ceiling of the tower—her face over and over in a universe of the same face. She sees her own mouth open wide, her nostrils flare, her forehead crease, her cheeks redden and stream with water. She can hear her own gasps, like secrets released, and she rubs around and around, harder and harder, and with each circle layers of her are coming off, coming away, and when she gets down to nothing she closes her eyes, as her body seizes up like a twisted rope and then falls slack.

She lays her hand on the cold ground and opens her mouth to that lonely water from so far away in the sky, and cries.

"Lonely," calls Eva, the soft voice beneath it all. "Come down."

Lonely can feel her everywhere, calling her inward, into the earth. She sits up, afraid. She cannot see past a wall of falling water. She stands and stum-bles to the tent, but the tent is empty.

"Lonely."

She turns and sees a small round door in the hillside. Nothing else—no windows, no structure of any kind—just a door. She opens it and steps in.

Behind the door lies dry darkness like an animal's burrow. Lonely has to crouch to get through, but once inside, she can stand on the earthen stairs, and light simmers up from below. The air is mellow and still.

She closes the door behind her, and silence settles over her like when she first entered the forest. She comes down step by step, shivering uncontrolla-bly. She has the strange thought that she is entering the inside of the moon. By the time she reaches the bottom, though only a moment has passed, she is surprised to see Eva's face turned expectantly toward her from within a circle of candlelight; she had almost forgotten whom she came to see.

But suddenly she wants to leave.

"Sit there," says Eva quickly, as if she knows, and motions to a rocking chair. "It might help."

Lonely sits. But she doesn't rock. She is frozen now in the shame of what she has just done—something she cannot name that she did to her own body, something that has changed her. She fears what Eva will see in her. She fears Eva's gaze the way she feared the gaze of the old woman by the sea, and she has only come here tonight because to disobey that gaze was more than she could endure. She had no choice but to come here. But she cannot imagine what will happen, and she is afraid.

On the small round table between them, three candles are lit. The walls, which expand around them into surprising depths of shadow—the room bigger than she expected—are lined with shelves and piles of what seem to be vaguely colored blocks, most of which reach higher than their heads. Above them hang dried herbs that speak to Lonely's senses of subtler, more mysterious things than her single-minded longing at this moment has patience for. She is still thinking of Rye. The thought of him falls endlessly through her.

Eva sighs and hands her a blanket, and Lonely moves into the darkness and peels off her dripping dress, goosebumps making her skin feel less romantic than before. Then she wraps the blanket around her body and sits back down in the rocking chair across from those eyes.

"Lonely," says the old woman. "I want you to tell me about where you come from."

The eyes meet Lonely's, and they wait, at once firm and trusting. This old woman is different from the one Lonely remembers. Eva's skin is a maze of lines just like that of the old Witch by the sea. But Eva's lines don't stretch her skin painfully over her bones, or stretch her mouth into a thin line, or pull down the corners of her eyes. They seem woven by a different hand, the same one perhaps that wove the spider webs of the forest. As with the spider webs, the more Lonely looks into them that night, the more they seem to weave the world together. Just as she begins to lose herself in the maze of them, they break, curling around Eva's eyes and mouth in a design that seems more familiar to them than any other: a smile.

"I'm sorry," Eva says. "Sometimes I'm so single-minded in what I'm looking for. My daughter says I can be too controlling. One of the flaws of an earth person, and not one borne easily by an air person, which is mostly what you are."

Lonely stares at her, surprised at the accent of her words, which she notices now is different than anyone else's in the family—and by how many words she uses, after all the silence that Lonely has lived in for so many days. Eva rises, her body graceful and lean in a simple, faded robe, and hands Lonely a cup of tea which has been sitting on the table.

"Please drink this. It will calm you and ground you. It's a little cool now, because I have been waiting for you."

Lonely doesn't drink, though she is embarrassed now of her own stubbornness. Eva sits with her hands folded in her lap and waits.

"I told you," says Lonely, "I come from a tower, on an island, in the sea."

"Yes. How did you come there?"

"I don't know. I was always there. For as long as I could remember."

Eva nods. "Go on."

Lonely looks away.

"Girl," says Eva, her voice harder and more certain now, "you owe us an explanation of who you are. We have taken you in, we trust you. I know that you have no wrong intentions. But you do not know yourself, and you are not paying attention. That can make you dangerous. We want to be kind to a lost stranger, but I will allow nothing—*nothing*—to threaten the integrity of this family. Do you understand?"

Lonely, who looked down while Eva spoke, now looks sharply up. She doesn't ask what Eva means. She cannot speak.

"It's all right," says Eva, her voice softening again. "You know so little, poor girl. Don't be afraid of me. What do you remember in the tower?"

"My father," Lonely says, swallowing tears. "He lived there with me."

Eva nods encouragingly.

"He used to come to me every day. Then he stopped coming."

"He stopped coming?" asks Eva, leaning forward.

"Yes, that's what I said." But the tower is behind her, gone. It doesn't matter now. Without meaning to, despite her fear of Eva, she thinks again of Rye. It is so much easier to think of him than of this.

"Where is it that you would rather be right now?" says Eva.

Lonely doesn't answer, but her body flushes.

Eva leans back in her chair and considers Lonely. "Girl, you cannot seek your future until you know your past. If you don't know your past, you will fall into a future that you do not understand and will have no control over. Please drink some tea. Take these plants into your body. They are wiser than you are, and you must begin somewhere."

Lonely takes a sip of the tea and leans back in the chair, her body feeling sore, and the chair begins to rock her, guided by her weight. Once she begins rocking she can't seem to stop, for the rocking is that familiar rhythm that soothes her—the rhythm of the horse between her thighs, the rhythm of the sea waves carrying her and finally birthing her onto the earth. The rain drums into the hill, quieter than it sounds inside the house, but with a deeper tone.

"Please tell me what you remember, Lonely."

Lonely opens her eyes. "My father stopped coming," she says, throwing her words out quickly, to get them over with. "I thought I was trapped in the tower. The Witch guarded it. I—I was lonely. I needed to get out. One day I saw the mountain through the glass. And I saw—I knew, I felt that someone was calling me. That the mountain was calling me." Lonely stops, remembering this, remembering the face—one she has never yet seen on this earth. "I made a hole in the ice. The glass was ice. Then I had a dream, and the tower disappeared."

"And then?"

Lonely stops rocking, startled by Eva's lack of surprise or reaction. "Then I spoke with the Witch. She was—" But Lonely finds she cannot describe her, or that place, or that time. The horrible face looms in her mind, and the eyes hold her frozen and stop her voice.

"What did she say to you?" asks Eva.

"That I had to find my true love within thirteen moons," answers Lonely dully, finally, feeling defeated, as if she is admitting to her worst flaw. "Or else she would bring me back there." She lowers her face into her free hand to catch the tears that she feels rising and then finally falling from her. She can't help it. All the fear, all the longing never answered, building and building inside her through dinner, through the day, through every day before this, since before Rye took her in his arms, since forever—the tears come, shaking her body with the same release she just felt from the touch of her own hands. "I don't ever want to go back there. I will always be alone there, forever," she cries.

Eva's voice is soft and steady. "This woman holds you back and pushes you forward at the same time," she observes.

"What?" says Lonely, her face still hidden, confused by Eva's easy description of the Witch as "this woman," as if she were no more than that, not a witch, not all-powerful at all.

But instead of answering, Eva asks a different question. "So you are journeying to fulfill this woman's demand?"

Lonely lifts her head. "No, I am journeying to find love, because I am lonely."

"Are you sure?" asks Eva. "Going toward love takes no effort. It is as easy as a river flowing naturally to its source. It is not painful and desperate."

Lonely looks at Eva. Her hands are shaking, so she puts down the tea. *What do I want?* she thinks for the first time. *What is this constant longing, tormenting me?*

"Who was your father?"

"I don't know," answers Lonely. "He was…my father."

"Was he a magician?"

"Yes. He made my tower for me, that's what the witch said. And she said that he died."

"Ah," says Eva, and she closes her eyes.

Lonely leans forward, stopping the rocking of the chair. "Do you know something about me?" she asks. She doesn't know what it is that she needs to know—just something that would still the anxiety deep within her, that fear she felt from the moment the tower disappeared and she clung to the dark rocks, that swirling emptiness of not knowing. Suddenly it seems that all the desire she has felt has been only a distraction from this emptiness, from its inevitability.

"I know less than what you will find by looking into yourself, child. But I can tell you a story that I think will be important to you. You must be brave, because this story will hurt. But I can see that you are ready to hear it, and that means you will survive it, and it will help you, I think, in the end."

Lonely has never heard a story before. The things her father told her were not stories; they were only fragments of lost places and lives she would never live. She doesn't know that a story is like music, the way it takes control over your heart. She doesn't understand how a story can hurt, or how it can hurt even more when left untold.

"Are you listening?" asks Eva.

"Yes."

"Are you sure?" asks Eva again, after a moment of silence, leaning forward.

"Yes," says Lonely, surprised again. "I am listening." She doesn't feel impatient any more. Thoughts of Rye have been swallowed temporarily by the dark cave of this room, which more and more, the longer she has sat here, has begun to feel eerily alive.

"Then I'll tell you. This is a story that everyone in the world knows, except for you, because you are at the center of it.

"Everyone knows a different version of the story, or sometimes only pieces of it, distorted over time. I believe that my version is truer than many, because it was passed to me by the spirits of my ancestors, whose intention is understanding, rather than by those whose intention is fear or manipulation. You will know if this story is true by how it feels inside you. A story that is true for you feels like nourishment, even when it hurts."

Lonely swallows, opens and closes her hands. She tastes garlic on her own breath, and the sweetness of berries on her tongue. She stares at the earth floor, which she cannot see.

"Once there was a great magician, who was mostly god, with a little bit of humanness mixed in. No one knows where he came from. Some say he came from the air—a sky god. Some say he came from the other side of the world, the other side of the great mountain, where everything had already been destroyed and the earth was all used up.

"When the power of a god comes through a human being, it frightens him. He doesn't know what to do with it. He doesn't know how to surrender to it. And someone who is part-god, part-human can be dangerous, because he wields the power of a god with the small-mindedness and greed of a human being. Being part human, he also understands people—their longings and fears—which means he can control them if he wishes to."

Eva looks away to think, then back at Lonely with a testing glance. "This magician, whose name was Hanum, was able to gather many of the earth's people together and put their human skills to work to create a great masterpiece of his design. At that time, people lived very differently than they do now. They lived more like we do, close to the earth, only they also had a sense of community and connection which we have lost now. They knew and trusted one another.

"But then Hanum gave them special powers. He gave them the power to make and run machines, which are like people without souls. He gave them the power to create a virtual world on top of this world, separate from it, and he told them they could live in a world of their choosing, where they would never have to suffer from drought, disease, hunger, or loss, and that this world could be self-sustaining. In this new world, they would not be dependent on the earth, which sometimes yielded sustenance and sometimes did not, and which made them dependent. Maybe the people were not unhappy before, but Hanum convinced them that they were, that they needed more. Actually, he wanted them to depend on him, instead of on the Earth. So he gave them these incredible powers, to transform reality at their command, but he did not give them the humility, patience, or insight with which to use these powers wisely.

"This magical world that Hanum created is called the City. I have spent many years dreaming into this story, trying to understand his motivations. It could have been that he was a god of pure Air, whose dreams were not grounded in reality. It could have been insecurity, which translates into lust for power. Or it could have been real artistic inspiration, which, as often happens with the influence of the divine in a human being, overwhelmed him to the point where he became drunk with it—terrified of his own flawed humanness in the face of such beautiful dreams, and ever trying to escape from that humanness by building the dreams bigger and bigger. I do not know. It is terrible when something is set in motion that you cannot trace to its roots. It is very difficult to stop.

"There was a time when people worshipped the Earth, and the gods they saw moving through it, and they had advanced ways of communion between their spirits and the spirits of the elements. We no longer know many of those ways, since so many of our people have been lost, absorbed into the City. We who still live here in the mountains do our best to be grateful for all that the Earth gives us. To us, eating, bathing, drinking, and everything we do in connection with Earth is a sacred act. We grow in our spirits through understanding its cycles, and when we feel suffering, we listen the best we can to the wisdom of the elements and creatures and plants. That is the best we can do.

Most of us who are left in the mountains do not trust in gods, since we saw what Hanum did. We trust only in what we can feel and work with our hands."

Eva takes a deep breath. "I myself once lived in the City," she says. "I was raised there, and grew up there, and Fawn was born there.

"I know you have not been there. If you had been, I do not think you would have survived it, because of how you are made. In the City, spirit is a relic of the past, something now laughed at. Instead of Earth, they have technology: that is their god.

"It is so hard to describe what the City is. It is made of Things. In the City whoever has the most Things has the most power. When a person feels a longing in her heart, she seeks a Thing to answer that longing. The Things take her further from what she wants, but she does not understand this, so she seeks more Things. Here in the forest, it is hard to understand how a Thing can have power over a person. Here we know what things are, and where they come from, and what beings made them. But in the City, people do not understand what Things are made from, because they are so complicated and were made by secret, destructive means, and they do not know what hands have made them or what hands they have passed through. And so these Things wield power over them—and even more so because a person calls a Thing 'mine', and whenever you claim to own anything, it also owns you.

"The City is a vast web of illusion. Truly it is the greatest magical feat of any god or man. In this illusion, food seems to appear spontaneously and ready-made from nowhere. Waste seems to disappear without a trace. The people travel in vehicles more huge and dangerous than any wild beast, yet they enter them daily without a thought, and they feel completely safe. Hanum had them believe that everything could be done by machines and computers—*everything*. That youth can be extended forever, and should be. That pain and winter and disease and death are all evil and can eventually be stopped. That every want can and must be satisfied, and that only constant noise and bright lights will bring us peace. Most importantly, he wanted them to believe that humans have *total* control, that they can do absolutely anything."

Lonely is frozen, still leaning forward toward Eva, her hands curled awkwardly like helpless baby animals in her lap. She remembers her father's words: *You and I are gods, and our bodies need neither food nor touch to survive. We are beyond all that....*

"Of course none of these things is true," continues Eva. "The truth is that the people in the City are terrified. It terrifies them to think that they can do anything, because to have such power is awful and incomprehensible. It feels to them as if nothing they do really matters, as if there is no god who cares about them enough to stop them when they do wrong. No predators hunt them. They cannot remember what it felt like to be humbled by something larger than themselves, or by a web of life greater than their own lives. The only thing which can hurt them now must be of their own making. Sometimes they do hurt themselves. They hurt themselves and each other, because they long so much to feel anything at all. In the world Hanum created, they have nothing to fight against but themselves."

"Stop it!" interrupts Lonely. "Who are you? You're not making any sense. This—" she stands up. "I know what you're trying to say. This is not my father. It's not."

Eva looks at her, her expression unchanging.

Lonely feels hot—and too big for herself suddenly. She wants to throw off the blanket but is ashamed of her nakedness. She needs to kick something or throw something. She whirls away from Eva and paces around the rocking chair and back. "My father wouldn't create that terrible place," she cries, furious at Eva's calm wordlessness. "My father was good and gentle. You're crazy. You don't know him. You don't know—" She stops because she's crying again. *You don't know what it's like to have only one person in the whole world who ever loved you,* is what she means to say. *Don't take that away from me.*

"I didn't say he wasn't good," says Eva. "And I didn't say he didn't love you. How could I know that?"

"But you're saying—you're saying—" Lonely fumbles, her mind out of control, her heart bleary and wild as if melted by the endless rain. "Why wouldn't he have told me? Why didn't he tell me *any* of this? Ever."

Eva's eyes seem to shrink a little, and they look more human suddenly, the eyes of a tired old woman. "I don't know," she says softly. "Please, try to breathe." It's the compassion in the "please" that makes Lonely sit down again.

"Do you want me to continue?"

Lonely nods. *No,* she's thinking, and the *No* keeps ringing through her brain, but Eva's voice carries through it, like the voices of the animals when they speak—gently and without force, but with absolute certainty—into her mind.

Eva takes a deep breath. "Hanum had a daughter. No one knows for sure who bore her. But when Hanum first held this child in his arms, something changed in him. He remembered something pure and innocent, something sweet in his heart from long ago that was his first sensation of magic, before his dreams got out of his control."

Eva stops and looks silently at Lonely. When Lonely won't look at her, she continues. "I think when Hanum saw you, he felt frightened of the great illusion he had created, and he saw the evil in it, because of the lies it was built on and the violence that was beginning to take hold of it as people acted out the emptiness inside them. Quite suddenly, he abandoned the City. Through technology, he fed his voice into it still, his voice echoing the lies that kept it going, but he no longer appeared there to inspire the people to keep building, seeking Things, and making themselves greater. He had a government of rulers who could carry on his work for him now, a quiet fortress in the heart of the City that no one thought about or questioned. The last command he gave, before he disappeared, was to build a great road out into the wilderness. For he perceived that the earth around the City was running dry: they had sucked all the life out of it and would need more. He did not tell them that. He only told them that their power must ever expand. And, I suspect, he no longer wanted to be responsible for it.

"Then he disappeared with you onto a distant island, separated from the City and the mainland by the vast, moody sea which all men feared. I believe he saw in you something pure and good, something he wanted to reclaim, but he didn't know how to stop the evil he had begun, and being an artist at heart—a romantic, as all gods are—this saddened him almost beyond bearing. His one aim was to keep you separate from all of that, to keep you pure and holy. So he locked himself away with you in a tower, far from the earth and the people, where he could spin for you the dreams that comforted him, dreams he hadn't been able to stay true to.

"Perhaps he should have let himself be redeemed by you, Lonely. Perhaps with you he could have remembered a better part of himself, a tender and innocent part, and perhaps he did. But though he'd abandoned his City, he couldn't let go of the dream. Though he kept you separate from the City, he also used you to rule it. You became, to him, more than just his child: you became a symbol of eternal youth, perfection, and that ethereal, immortal separation from the earth. You reminded him of the good intentions he had begun with, but he didn't know how to use those intentions for good, for he was afraid to let go of his power. So as you grew older, he used the idea of you to keep the people loyal to the illusion he had created. He spread stories of your great beauty, without ever letting them see you. The idea of you became something for the people to worship, an ideal to make them believe they had something to strive for.

"Now part of this story as it was told to me is that Hanum also had a wife or a lover. How much of her was human, and how much was goddess, I do not know. Only that in the beginning, in her youth, she fell in love with him for his big dreams, inspired by his passion and his power. Like so many, she was easily swept up by the persuasiveness of his belief in himself. But later she felt, long before he did, the pain that was swelling inside this grand illusion. She spent time in the City and she saw people who did not have everything, people who in fact had nothing, who were cast aside like the trash and conveniently forgotten. She saw animals abused. She saw that people denied their hearts and no longer knew how to communicate, except through money. I cannot sum up all that she saw. Someday you may understand. Layers and layers of silence and pain. Women, especially, were silent.

"She grew bitter at Hanum when she saw all this, for he had disappointed her own ideal of him. She fought with him and criticized him, hating him for not being what she had believed him to be, until he retreated from her, because like an insecure little boy he could not bear to be faced with his mistakes. He pushed her away and would no longer love her, especially as she began to age—faster than normal because of the anger and pain she felt. Over time, she came to hate him. When he turned to you as his new ideal, perhaps she hated you even more—not only because you took him away from her, but also because you represented his denial of the truth."

Lonely begins to speak again but Eva holds up her hand, and she falls silent. "Now you say that Hanum is dead," Eva continues, holding Lonely with her eyes. "My dreams tell me this is true. I dreamed something shifted in the web of the world; something broke. It does not matter to the people. They will continue on as if he is alive, for it is too terrifying for them to imagine that he who made them believe in their own immortality has died. But I think that soon, the structure of magic they have built, which is so great but so fragile, which has no soul or guiding light, is going to fall. Before it falls they will feel it tremble. And when it trembles, they will be so afraid, deep inside, that they will do even more terrible things. So, in a way, my daughter is right. It is a dangerous place to be now, even more dangerous than before.

"There is one more part to this story, but this part is not clear. It is said that another reason Hanum built the tower, and placed you in it, was to distract the people—and himself—from what he hid beneath the island. I'm not sure what is beneath this island, but I have felt it in dreams. I believe it is something that people fear because it speaks what has been denied. That is all I know.

"You say the tower is gone, but this place under the island remains. Hanum's wife still remains, older than we can imagine and more timeless than he turned out to be. We don't know where she really comes from, or who she is. But it is this place down below that she guards now, not the tower."

Eva stops speaking and silence overcomes the underground room, folding around it like the wings of a bat. The darkness pulses against the walls. Lonely stares at the candle flame, its light meaningless, and struggles to release her voice from under the weight of her heart.

It seems to her that there is a whole world built around her that she never saw before. It's as if she's been walking in a landscape that was invisible to her until now: a land where people idolize her and hate her, where she is beauty and truth and innocence and lies and betrayal all at once, and all of it has been decided by other people, beyond her knowledge, beyond her control. As if what she is, whatever she is, has never been her own to decide. No wonder she has felt so confused, so lost. How could she ever find what is real, inside all those layers of other people's dreams? How could she ever know her real name?

And what did her father mean? That she was invincible? That she would never hunger? That her body would never ache for the touch of another? Is this what the people of the City believe of themselves, as if they, too, are gods?

When she speaks to Eva her own voice sounds low, and very old. "That woman," she says. "She is not my mother."

Eva considers her. "I don't know that."

"But you said she was his wife. He never called her his wife. He never said she was my mother. She can't be. She hates me." Lonely finds some comfort in the strange slow weight of her own voice. No more tears now. She doesn't know what she feels—not sorrow, not anger, not fear—though it is all of those things, too, and heavier than all of them together. Black and heavy and peaceful. Like truth, maybe, if truth were a feeling. Like earth.

"I did not say she was your mother because I do not know," says Eva. "All I know is that your father took you for his own, took you away into that tower and kept you for himself, away from the world and away from your mother, whoever she is. I think he thought of you, Lonely, as another of his accomplishments; you made him believe in himself enough to forget the great wrongs he had done. It would not be the first time that a man has denied a woman's role in what he accomplishes. I think he denied that woman in every way that he could, because she failed his ideal of womanhood, just as he failed her ideal of manhood."

Lonely cannot speak. She cannot explain the sense of loss that she feels. She cannot explain the strange sympathy she feels now with this terrible woman who could be her mother and yet cannot be, as if she expressed some part of Lonely that Lonely never knew about—things she needed to say to her father but never said because she didn't know the whole story. There was something wrong. There was something about the tower that frightened Lonely, always, but she didn't know anything different, so she couldn't have put it into words.

And the way she felt with Dragon. Why she couldn't bear to give herself to him. It was because she couldn't bear to lose herself again in someone else's ideal of her, when she had just barely begun to find herself.

Then again she remembers how her father called her *Princess*. Again she feels that *No*—no, he cannot be that man, not that man that Eva describes! The full weight of losing him falls over her for the first time, completely and all at once, bowing her down until her face almost touches her knees. She needs to know if he really did love her, but Eva doesn't know, and no one knows—and she needs to know, now, immediately. She will die if she cannot know.

If only she could lie down on the cool floor and never get up, anchored to the earth by her heart heavier than buildings, heavier than all the world's machines, heavier than that tallest mountain in the far east that once she longed toward. If only she could stay in this room forever, where the darkness dissolves her just a little bit. She doesn't want to live and breathe and walk among people—every one of whom has heard of her, every one of whom knows where she comes from and expects something of her that she doesn't understand. No wonder Delilah hated her. No wonder Fawn fears her.

Thoughts like this flicker uselessly through her heavy mind, their meaninglessness making her nauseous.

"Breathe," Eva reminds her.

Lonely feels the woman's warmth in the darkness, and when she looks up Eva is standing there before her, her hands outstretched. Lonely stands, trembling, and sinks into her arms. Eva smells like smoke and flowers, and her hands against Lonely's spine are very strong. Lonely cries, soundlessly, without tears, her shoulders shaking. Not because of the story, which is just a great murky weight above her, but because this is what her mother, whoever she is, ought to feel like. Because these are not the arms that reached out to her like claws before the raging sea and pinched her wrists as if to test her life. These are the arms that forgive, and comfort, and release.

"I'm not that," Lonely murmurs.

"Not what?"

"Not anything. Not—whatever he thought I was." She thinks of all that is bad in her. Her desire for Rye, the way she abandoned Dragon, her weakness before the old woman of the sea, her fear, her selfish need.

"Of course not," says Eva. "No one could be."

"I don't know who I am," sobs Lonely, but it isn't what she means to say; it's the sorrow that's killing her, the sorrow of her father falling away from her into the abyss of some distant story, a man she did not know, who loved someone who was not her. *Lost*, he used to say, over and over. *Lost*. She did not know then what it meant, but she knows now.

"But you have some piece of that light he saw in you," says Eva, as if she understands again what Lonely is thinking, holding her away from her body now and looking into the face that Lonely tries to hide from her. "I think you have a gift for the world: some piece of innocence, something he took from them when he locked you away and made them worship you from a distance. You were right to come into the world in search of your heart's longing. It is through this world, walking upon this earth, that you will redeem yourself, and maybe them too."

Then Lonely feels angry. "I don't know what 'redeem' is, but if he's made this mess I don't want to fix it. It's not up to me. Why should I be cursed—" She stops, swallowing the emotion that erupts inside her from this single word.

"You are not cursed, child. Nobody's making you do anything."

"But *she* is!" cries Lonely. "That woman. Why did she send me to find love? Does she even want me to find it?"

She wishes Eva would say *Yes. And you will find it. You deserve it. It will come to you.* But instead she says, "All I know is that up until now, you have done what you are told. You have tried to be the good girl for your father. You have obeyed his wife's demand, allowing your heart to obey the fear she instilled in it. You are obeying a dream you don't understand. But now you have a piece of your own story, and you will continue to grow into it, to understand it, and even to change it. Stories grow and live with us; they are alive. I did not tell you this story to hurt you. I told it to free you. Knowledge allows you to make your own choices."

"I don't feel free."

"You will."

Lonely spends the night with Eva, who is so unaccustomed to sharing her space that she cannot sleep the whole night. She stays up with one candle, which, on this night of the new moon in a cloud-covered sky, seems the only light in all the world. She isn't surprised when, as she lifts Lonely's wet dress to hang it up, it disintegrates in her hands. She gathers up the pieces in a pile, thinking that perhaps she can use them to stuff her old pillow a little thicker. Who knows what that material was, but it certainly wasn't made to last in this world.

Then she watches Lonely's beauty as she sleeps, clear and firm in the flickering light. Lonely's face doesn't move; her sharp cheekbones forever make their serious, dramatic arches behind it as if insisting upon a story of rise and fall, tragedy and redemption, that must be played out until the end. She's still wrapped in the blanket, with her mouth open like a child's. She breathes deeply and never stirs. The rain doesn't stop until morning.

Rye spends the night in Fawn's arms, resting his head against her full breasts, his arm thrown across her waist. Before they fall asleep, he tickles her belly with his tongue. She smiles but lifts his chin away. She's too distracted to feel desire.

"Rye," she tells him, dropping her voice to a whisper. "Something happened today. We learned something. We learned that Lonely is the princess from the tower."

Rye makes zigzags with his tongue up to her breastbone.

"Rye, did you hear me?"

"Yeah," he answers. "Sure."

"Don't you believe me?"

"Of course. So what?"

Fawn sighs, her fingers combing his beard. "I'm afraid."

"Of what?"

"She comes from something evil."

"Love, what does your gut tell you? Does she seem evil?"

"No."

"I'm going to know her for who she is, then, not based on some story about her," says Rye. "I can feel that she is good, that she can love. She's so young, Fawn. She's afraid too."

"I know. But she has something secret inside her. Something unpredictable, something wild."

Rye leans over her. "So do you," he whispers, and presses his lips to hers. She wraps her other arm around him but doesn't kiss back. Her eyes are looking past him, into thoughts he cannot see.

In the morning Fawn sits with Eva while she drinks her morning tea.

"Where is Lonely?" she asks.

"I don't know," answers Eva. "I dozed off at dawn, and when I woke she had gone. I hope she doesn't leave us."

"Why not?"

"Because I think she needs us right now."

Fawn is silent, breathing in the memory of rain from the soggy earth.

"Why is she called Lonely?" she asks. "I don't understand this name."

"Don't be afraid, Fawn," says Eva. "She needs you."

"I'm afraid of where she comes from."

"No one knows where she comes from, daughter, because no one knows who her mother is. No one knows in whose womb she spent the first, most important moons of her life."

Fawn thinks on that, and holds her mother's hand.

"There are other versions of the story that I didn't tell her," says Eva after a time, as if to herself. "Some of the ancestors say that Lonely is the daughter of the Earth. That what made Hanum crazy was that the goddess of the Earth Herself chose him, as a young man, for Her lover. They made love as the earth and the sky make love. But Hanum was also human, and he became drunk with the proud idea that he had conquered Her, and he thought himself the greatest man in the world. He thought that he could rule this world. So he abandoned Her to pursue his own greatness." She pauses to think, and Fawn sees that familiar mixture of remembering, intuiting, and imagining in her bright eyes. "Then many years later when the City began to disappoint him, when he feared that his magic would fail him, he remembered the sweet love of that goddess and searched everywhere for Her. But that goddess had fled from him, as he built the City on top of the Earth and denied Her, keeping Her from the rains and from life. All he could find was the daughter She had borne by him—a half-immortal child who slept in a bed of leaves and clouds, and when he saw her beauty, he took her away with him to remind him of the love he'd lost."

Fawn shakes her head, almost angrily. "I don't want to hear this talk of goddesses."

But Eva ignores this. "Others say," she continues, "that her mother was a woman of the Dream People. Or those that call themselves the Dream People now: the First People, the ones who disappeared into the sky above the east mountain when the City was built on top of their land. They say that Hanum loved her but could not win her, and so he kidnapped her, or he destroyed her people out of anger—I don't know. Both of those stories are muddy and confused. And overly romantic, if you ask me."

"But you said you didn't tell her all this?" asks Fawn.

"No, I didn't, because I did not want her to make the same mistake as her father. Already, she feels the overwhelming drama of her history. Already the importance of her role in the world is burdening her too greatly. She needs to feel less important. She needs to be humbled by daily life. It will soothe her." Eva turns to her daughter. "Be kind to her, Fawn. She won't be with us forever. Give her work to do, make her feel useful, teach her gratitude. It is the best we can do."

Fawn is silent for a long time. "But what if Hanum's wife *was* her mother?" she says finally, in a whisper.

"What if she is?" says Eva.

"But I mean," says Fawn, "then Lonely has that inside of her."

"Has what?"

"You know. She's the Dark Goddess. You told me. Remember, Ma? Was it just a story? You told me once, before we even left the City. You think I was too young, maybe, but I remember. You told me about the secret garden in the mountains, the garden only women know, where the Bright Goddesses keep women safe with their prayers. Safe from the Dark Goddess, across the sea. *That* was Hanum's wife, you told me. Not some beautiful earth goddess."

Eva shakes her head. "Ah, daughter, I was so young then. Women in the City—we grow up being taught to fear not men, not the powers that oppress us, but our own selves. They teach us to fear the darkness in ourselves, and that way we enslave our very selves, without them having to do it for us. It saves them work."

"But there is something inside of Lonely that frightens me," Fawn insists. "Something unpredictable and desperate, something so intense and—"

"And unafraid?" says Eva, turning to Fawn. "And free?"

)

Lonely walks, bent over, around the edges of the forest, the blanket still enshrouding her. She will not put that dress on again, nor will she reveal her nakedness. She thinks of Rye—how could he want her, the daughter of such evil? How could she take him from Fawn, who is so good and kind, humble and graceful?

Her horse whinnies at her from across the field and comes trotting lightly toward her, his big body a windy river, fringed by the long fin of hair along his neck. He seems somehow different than before. When he stops, she stands and holds him, her arms around his neck. This is what she has, she remembers: this good animal, simple and hungry but white as the clouds, and her own body, her heart, and desire.

She talks to the horse for a long time. First she tells him that her father was evil. That everything he created, everything he did, everything he seemed to feel for her was illusion. He was a master of illusion. He made an illusion of her life. It will take her whole life, again, to find out who she really is, and to find out what real life and real love feel like.

But saying all that makes her cry so hard she can't breathe.

So then she begins to say other things, about how her father was not who she thought he was, but that still, maybe, she will try to love him. She tells the horse she is going to be strong, and not cry so much any more.

She tells the horse how really, she is angry with Eva for the story she doesn't want to believe.

No, really she is angry at her father. But he isn't evil, necessarily, is he? Is she? There must have been something beautiful in her, to take him away from all that powerful magic he'd created, which was so convincing and en-tangling.

For a while the horse stands still, nibbling at the grass, listening.

Still her heart is so heavy. Nothing she can say or think will make it lighter.

Did her father know about the prince she would see later, his face shin-ing through the glass from the mountain? Is that who he meant, when he promised someone would come, and how did he know? And what did that prince have to do with the story? Should she have waited for him? Was the old woman right to hate her? But how could she hate her, when it wasn't Lonely's fault?

That woman could not be her mother. Her mother would love her the way Fawn loves Chelya, and Eva loves Fawn.

The thinking weighs her down so much, and she leans, heavier and heavier, against the horse, until the horse grows restless under her careless, unfocused weight, and bolts forward a few steps, shaking his head. Startled, Lonely lifts her own head and steps back, then looks up at the sky.

The sky swells like the sea, and shakes its white foam. The clouds reach so wildly over half the sky that they break apart and fluff happily into oblivion, whiffs of them bumping without impact against each other, against the sun.

Then Lonely's heart lightens—just enough—because it has to. It lightens because she is not a heavy sort of person. It is unnatural to her, to be held under such a weight. Like air she floats upward, and cannot be held down.

Come on, says the wind, with compassion. *I love you.*

Lonely smiles a little and begins to walk back toward the house. She feels unsteady on her feet, as if nothing she thought was real can now be counted on, almost as if the very earth cannot be trusted. In her childhood of mist and dreams, her father was the only thing real. Now he is not real, or at least not what she thought he was. So what is real? She is walking toward this little house without knowing why, except that the way it sits there nestled in the crest of two green swells makes it look as if it belongs. That belonging makes it real.

Then someone is running toward her who cares about her, who likes her. Lonely tries to focus her eyes. It is Chelya, who woke her with milk and honey, who helped her start again.

"Lonely! I've been looking for you."

Lonely stops, and Chelya keeps running toward her. In a moment, she feels Chelya's warm hands in her own.

"I want to know about the tower you grew up in," the girl is saying, as if she doesn't know, and maybe she doesn't. "Was it beautiful? How did you—? But what happened to your dress?"

"I'm sorry," Lonely says slowly. How can she explain? "I—Chelya, I can't talk about it right now. But something happened, and I can't wear that dress any more. It's not—it isn't real."

Chelya nods, as if this makes perfect sense. "It's all right. You can borrow something of mine. I'll make you a new dress. A dress just for you."

Rye's and Fawn's horses avoid Lonely's horse for a long time.

This is not hard to do, since Lonely's horse avoids everyone, except for Lonely. He does not sleep in the stable, even when it rains.

There are two horses who live here. The stallion is a work horse, with a rough tail and thick feet and dirty fur the color of seeding grass. He seems peaceful and uncaring, but he makes Lonely's horse nervous: Lonely's horse doesn't want the resident stallion to think he is challenging his authority in any way. The mare they use for riding, at once jumpy and innocent, makes him uneasy, too, though that uneasiness has more to do with himself and the question of his own power.

But one day the mare grazes near him. That is how she questions him, not by approaching him directly, as the stallion might, sniffing his flanks or even nipping him a little in challenge, but simply by passing near him. Neither horse looks at the other, but each is aware of the other, and that awareness is just slightly heavier than the awareness of anything else.

Lonely's horse is gathering clover from between the tall grasses with his lips, unpacking the gentle pleasure of their taste with his teeth. The gathering of the clover—lips and teeth, reaching and chewing—is a rhythm in his skull that keeps him anchored. But his eyes focus elsewhere, not down into the grass, but from the sides of his head outward, to where the mountains hold their darkness on one side and the mare grazes near him on the other.

It is uncomfortable for him to watch her. She is quick with her hunger, stepping constantly forward, moving from one patch to another without finishing. With her shoulders thrusting toward him and her tail swishing, she is saying *i know you're there. these are our fields, and we know everything. we know you're here.*

i'm not really here, says the body of Lonely's horse, shifting away from her slightly. But that isn't quite what he means. Something changed in him since he rescued Delilah in the desert. He did not know himself when he lept over Dragon and lowered his forehead and…he did not know what happened, but he knew he must stop that man from what he was going to do. He did not know he was capable of such a thing. A light shines in him all the time now, and he can't turn it off, and it frightens him. It is the hope of it that frightens him.

The mare doesn't look at him directly but sends a shiver from her head all the way down to her flanks. *you are here,* she is saying. *but you're not like us. you are something else. you make me nervous. please declare yourself.*

Lonely's horse doesn't answer. He immerses himself in the grass. This is all he has to do, all day long: move slowly forward, and gather grass with his lips, and pay attention to the wind. This is safe—almost.

But the mare raises her head again, and this time she prances a few steps in place. This startles Lonely's horse, who cannot help but raise his head, too, and trot a few paces away.

i love to run, the mare is saying suddenly, prancing in place.

Lonely's horse says nothing, his head held stiffly in the air, his eyes at once frozen and flaming.

don't you love to run? she tempts him. She seems so brave. She trots a tight circle around him, her mane slipping through the careless hand of the breeze. Over the next hillside, the stallion is hidden from view and has not yet noticed their conversation. *don't you love...?* She begins again.

The horse who is not a horse feels his muscles shiver. He has swallowed his last mouthful of grass. The wind holds its breath in anticipation. He knows why Lonely has been pushing him on toward the mountain. Of course he knows. He knows what it's like. The grass is not enough. Food and water are not enough. Even the sun in the grass and the scents on the wind are not enough.

Now he finds himself running across the field, his body unfolding into a gallop without knowing what motions began it. The mare is running beside him. He lifts his face to the wind. His heavy feet reach out to embrace the ground and then pull together, a round circle of legs in the air, and then out again to stretch over the earth. The motion is lighter than his feet, something beyond his feet that makes him fly. The earth is so deep it does not shake and does not hurt upon impact; the wind burrows into his fur, burning with cold against his skin until he feels his skin will peel away, his flesh peeling back to reveal a spirit whose running is a crying out into space.

His hooves pounding the earth like fists. The wind of his running knocking open the doors of his heart, the wind running through it, the pain flooding out...And as he runs he is crying, for running is crying, the only way to express a passion he could not bear to speak in his former life.

The spaces he's been occupying for days fall away, as great distances open under him, opening him to the unknown before he has time to be afraid. When the house and the stables are far out of sight, and the thickening grass begins to catch them with its tangles and thorns, and the forest looms before them, they slow.

The mare trots around him, laughing with her tail and shaking her neck like a snake. He is standing still now, his belly heaving in and out, his body weeping with choked-back joy.

Slowly, they walk back. They eat along the way, saying nothing directly. Her question to him continues to move in the shape of the space between them.

who are you?

Up in the loft, Lonely waits on Chelya's dreamy bed while the girl digs through her trunk of clothing. The summer heat sits stuffily around them. Chelya comes toward her with a handful of pale turquoise cloth. But then she stops.

"Lonely." She laughs. "You smell."

Lonely looks at her, not understanding. "Like what?"

Chelya laughs again. "Like *you*. You need a bath!"

Lonely is amazed. She remembers the way Rye's smell weakened her, and the way Eva's wild, ancient scent comforted her. It never occurred to her that she could have her own smell. "But what do I smell like?" she asks again, wondering why she can't smell herself. Why could she see herself in the glass but not smell her own body?

Chelya stops giggling and considers, trying as always to be helpful in answering Lonely's many questions. "I don't know," she says. "But honestly, when people haven't bathed in too long, they all start to smell the same. They just smell like *humans.*"

Lonely looks down at her hands, then lifts them up and sniffs them. "Then I guess I'm human now," she says quietly, remembering Yora suddenly, and feeling afraid but not knowing why. Somewhere far away, she can imagine the empty chill of the sea wind. Somewhere far away, her father's wife waits for her always, where the only scent is the salty waves. Lonely wants this smell that belongs to her. Already she feels more real.

But Chelya's face has grown quiet. "What do you mean?" she says.

Lonely looks up, scared, realizing what she said. But Chelya's face changes again, just as quickly. "Oh," she says, and thinks a moment. "I knew you were something more than human. It's okay. I won't tell."

Lonely stares at her. Chelya's smile is so easy. As if maybe the story she remembers Eva telling her last night was nothing but a bad dream, something she could never make sense of and doesn't have to.

"Anyway," says Chelya. "Now you are human and you smell. I'll ask Ma to take you to the river with her today. You have to be clean before I let you wear my dress."

That is how Lonely ends up crossing the southern field and entering the forest again, wrapped in a length of old, torn sheet, following Fawn.

Fawn says nothing but her awareness seems to trail behind her, catching each sound that Lonely makes. She never gets too far ahead of Lonely. She never forgets to hold a branch back after she's passed under it, allowing Lonely to pass through behind her. But Lonely's steps sound nervous and loud behind Fawn's comfortable, quiet ones, and Lonely keeps worrying that she is doing something wrong, like breaking a sensitive spiderweb. Curtain after curtain of arched boughs fall behind them as they enter deeper into that world that swallowed Lonely up only a moon ago. Fawn travels with a sense of direction that Lonely did not have, and the trees seem to fit easily around Fawn's passage, as if they know her. She ducks and swings her hips aside to avoid tangles, but she never has to push anything out of her way, or struggle to get through.

Then, abruptly, Lonely emerges behind Fawn into open space where the stream has opened into river. Here it is like an old woman, slow and brooding, running deep and brown with earth.

An old fallen tree descends into the hidden depths, and dragonflies whirl there, and across from where the two women stand, a single branch of blossoms bows over the water, smearing a hot pink flame through the reflections below.

Fawn turns to Lonely, then turns away before Lonely can catch her eyes. Lonely watches Fawn gather her soft green dress about her hips, bend forward slightly, and then roll it up over the arch of her shoulders and over her head. She drops it onto the log and descends into the water, fingertips sliding along the log for support she doesn't need, so practiced is her grace. Lonely is startled again by the fullness of Fawn's body, which seems to belie her shy silence. Fawn pauses with the water rippling around her waist, eyes closed. Her pleasure at being immersed in the water is so obvious to Lonely, though her expression hardly changes, that Lonely can almost see colors—the pink of those flowers, deepening into purple—misting around her.

Fawn doesn't look back, and so Lonely drops her sheet and walks into the water beside her, staring at the lush swells of Fawn's subtle, browned body, her full breasts twice the size of Lonely's—breasts that have nursed life. Such luxury of flesh she bears so modestly, without thought. That is what amazes

Lonely: the way other people carry their own beauty without even noticing it, taking it for granted.

"I'm sorry," she says, as Fawn meets her gaze and then lowers herself into the water up to her neck. "I've never seen another woman before—without clothes."

Fawn ducks her head under and comes up, pressing the water out of her eyes with the heels of her hands. Water slopes over her child-like cheeks, and her eyes widen carefully behind them. Her face is like Chelya's, but less obvious in its beauty, smaller, her nose straighter and more serious, her eyes more deeply and closely set. Her chin is round and tough, and freckles spill over her cheeks, making her look vulnerable, and easier to know than she is. She begins to rub water against her body with the palms of her hands, rising a little from the water again so that Lonely can see the tops of her breasts. Lonely envies her ease. The simple, clear life she has; the simple womanhood of her body. There are people who love her, whose relations to her are natural and easy, who can always be counted on. Lonely has learned all of the words for them now: daughter, son, mother, husband.

Lonely turns away and copies Fawn's motions—rubbing the smell away, whatever smell is. But secretly, she clings to the knowledge that this smell belongs to her. She remembers what the vultures told her. Her smell proves she is alive.

"Fawn," she says, not looking at her. She feels heavy again with Fawn's silence, and it is a weight the water will not wash away. "Are you angry with me for being here?" Then she catches her breath, afraid of her own daring.

When Lonely looks at her, Fawn has stopped her bathing, and is standing still in the water, looking startled. "No," she answers, and her voice tilts a little higher at the end of the word, giving Lonely hope, leaving an opening.

"Then why don't you speak to me?" Lonely's ears are burning, and she can feel her heartbeat in the bones just under her throat, and she dips down lower in the water to steady herself while she waits for the answer.

Fawn looks down at her reflection. "It's only been me and my family all my life."

Lonely feels sorry for herself again, at that word, *family.* That secret belonging, to which Lonely will never be admitted. But Fawn's voice is sweet, like a hidden flower cupped around a tuft of pollen beneath the grass of some wide field. Lonely pats the water with one hand, splashing it from side to side. She tries to think of a simple question to ask, to make a conversation before her opportunity is lost.

"How long have you lived?"

"Thirty-four years." Fawn hesitates. "And you?"

"I don't know. What is a year?"

"Oh," says Fawn, looking at her, confused. "You know."

"No. I don't. Please tell me."

"It is…summer, fall, winter, spring." But Fawn looks truly frightened now. "There are no seasons, where you come from?" she almost whispers.

Lonely shrugs. "I don't remember. Which season were you born in?"

"Winter." Fawn pauses to think, despite her fear. And this small consideration, this kindness, moves Lonely. "It's the opposite of now, of summer."

"Where is it?"

"Oh. No, it's—it's everywhere. But not now. Later." She looks at Lonely. "All places have winter," she adds. "In the desert, it's a different kind of winter. The City had a winter, too, but now every day is the same there. At least that's what Mother says. She knows because of her dreams."

"Weren't you born there, in the City?" Lonely asks quietly.

Fawn lowers herself into the water up to the middle of her chin. "I was."

"What happened?"

"My mother ran away when I was a baby. It was hard. We were always hungry, always afraid. But now I know the Earth, and now I am home." Her eyebrows tense into little arches then, and she looks like she will ask Lonely a question. Lonely waits, but nothing more comes.

"Did Rye come from the City?" Lonely can't help but ask.

Fawn starts to rise from the water and wade cautiously back. Lonely can feel her wary attention, though she will not look at Lonely again. "No. Rye's family are farmers. They are of the few who did not leave." Then she looks suddenly past Lonely, to something Lonely neither heard nor saw. Lonely spins around.

An otter stands on her hind legs on the opposite bank, watching them with frank curiosity. Her forehead slants low and sly, and her eyes are big and communicative. She rests her paws on her white belly and gazes at them for an instant, and then, with a voluptuous wriggle, drops to the ground and slips like an eel into the water. She reminds Lonely of Chelya, playful and womanly. The otter rolls on her back and curls her rear end into the air, then flips with abandon into the water.

Lonely laughs.

And she notices laughter for the first time—the wonder of it, the humanness in it, and the way she never did it when she lived in the tower. It feels as if the reality she was stuck in cracked open for a moment, and the cracks spread through it in zigzags, and now she falls through them into something ridiculous which feels good. *why so careful?* the otter seemed to say. *you can do this life any way you want!* When Lonely turns around, Fawn is smiling, and Lonely can tell by her soft face that the laughter has gotten her, too. It feels sensual, this secret pleasure they share together.

"I guess I've never seen another woman naked before either," Fawn says now. "I mean, except my mother and daughter."

But the laughter has opened Lonely's whole body, and now some memory pulls her gaze from Fawn's face. She watches the water shift and tremble, feels it pool around her in a cool sweep, with movement hidden inside it no matter how still it seems. The last time she stood in a river, Dragon's hands gripped her hips, his hot chest leaned into her, and the animal of his desire pulsed against her belly. She remembers his smell, spicy in the sun. It seems so long ago, so amazing that such a beautiful, naked man could have pressed himself to her body with such desire, and she refuse him. She slouches helplessly into the water. She lowers her head and then her face into the depths. All the way under, she opens her eyes. And sees Yora's face.

She bursts out again, gasping.

"What happened?" asks Fawn, her expression all open now, her own fear gone.

"I don't know."

Fawn smiles. "It's okay," she says. "We're made of water. Don't be afraid."

Lonely tries to grasp this new gentleness, but Fawn walks out of the water now and sits down on a stone in the sun to dry. When Lonely comes to sit next to her, Fawn gets up and walks away. Body pulsing, Lonely watches her wander nearby, gathering little plants in her deft, wide-palmed hands. Then Lonely lies down under the sun, helpless to thought and desire. Deep in her belly she feels a longing for the arms of the only lover she's ever had. It was everything to be dissolved in such warmth. To touch another body—that was everything. To be held those few times, wrapped in the oblivion of Dragon's heat, not having to understand who she was or where she was going, but only giving in to that darkness…

"Come, Lonely. You can help me make dinner." Lonely sits up, hearing her name. As she follows Fawn back to the house, the image she just saw in the water comes back to her. *Yora.* Who was she? The woman who first rescued her, who brought her into this world. Without her Lonely would still be lost, perhaps, at the bottom of the sea.

The dress, which Chelya made for her own curvy body, falls loosely around Lonely's, but it has strings sewn into it that Lonely can use to gather the cloth around her, tying it under her breasts and around her waist. Her arms and knees remain bare. The cloth is thin and light, but compared to the dress she always wore, made of some silken god stuff, it rubs like an animal against her skin. It makes her shiver uncontrollably as she climbs down the ladder and then stands before Fawn. At the same time, the turquoise color soothes her like clear water, brightens her senses, eases her breath. When she moves she is swimming.

"You are beautiful," says Fawn with a concentrated gaze, as if assessing a difficult situation.

"But where does the dress come from?" asks Lonely. She must know where each thing comes from, for this is what she is learning here, that everything comes from somewhere. That everything has a story, an origin. Maybe if she understands where everything else comes from, she will eventually figure out her own origin.

"The dress?" says Fawn, who speaks to Lonely more easily now, but still seems a little surprised by her own voice. "My daughter made it."

"But what did she make it from?"

"From an old sheet, I think."

"And where does a sheet come from?"

Fawn looks at her, finally understanding. "That was made from cotton, and cotton is a plant that grows in the ground. But no one around here grows that plant any more. They make it in the City, some other way. We use animal hair now, animal skins, and some plants. Only a few people know how to make these things. We don't know anyone near here who knows. So we use what we have, again and again."

Lonely looks down at the dress and strokes it gingerly, until Fawn beckons her to the wooden counter. Then they stand beside each other and cut vegetables while beans simmer on the stove. "Rye didn't catch any meat in his traps today," says Fawn. Lonely starts at the sound of his name.

"Is that okay?" she asks, not knowing what else to say, and wondering where Rye is now.

"Of course," answers Fawn. "You feel different when you eat only plants. Plants eat light. They talk right to the sun. So the light comes through you better then, when you eat them. You can know things easier, I think, on a day that you eat only plants."

"So why do we eat meat?"

"Oh, not everyone eats it. Chelya won't. She feels too close to the animals. But some people need it. You need it, I think, because you're so—" She looks embarrassed. "You know, like air. You need that heavy flesh to bring you down to the earth like us, right?" She laughs. Lonely bows her head because she thinks it is true. They are tougher than her—all of them. She likes Fawn's laugh, a low, one or two-syllable sound, like a quick dip into dark water and back up again.

"I don't understand what people mean when they talk about air people and earth people," she tells Fawn, remembering the words of the Witch about her ancestry.

Fawn slices into a beet, and its blood spills onto the old, already stained wood. The color surprises Lonely, and so does Fawn's attention. There was something there, under the belly of that closed silence, all along, that Lonely did not see. Something warm. Something dizzyingly alive. Fawn's hands keep flowing in their familiar, efficient grace. Lonely waits for her answer, distracted by the freckles she is noticing for the first time at the fleshy curve between Fawn's neck and shoulder, and the way they sink into that brown skin like seeds into the earth.

"Well, you know," says Fawn, though Lonely does not know. "We are earth people, mostly. Only Chelya is lots of water, too, but she can be happy anyway because she has earth. Kite is air and earth at once. And my mother," Fawn smiles. "She is everything."

"What do you mean about Chelya? A water person can't be happy?" She thinks of Yora.

"I don't know. Water is feelings. Maybe sorrow is the heaviest one."

"What about fire people? What are they like?"

"Fire," Fawn sighs, and stops cutting. She is listening to Lonely and thinking up her own words, but she is still cautious. There is something else happening that Lonely cannot define. Something else she is managing, inside herself. "I don't know. They frighten me. Fire is what gives us life—it's pure spirit! But most people don't know what to do with that. It burns them up. It burns everyone." She seems to think about this, as she stares into the fire that is burning now in the grate.

As the memory of Dragon burns Lonely's skin, even now.

"I think I met a couple of fire people, or gods, in the desert," she tells Fawn.

"Maybe." Fawn nods.

"A man," says Lonely, "and a woman, too, but the woman hated me. The man—he was very passionate. He wanted— But it was too much for me."

"I think it must be very strange to be a fire person" Fawn says. "Scary. They feel, I think, that if they cannot satisfy their desires, they might die. Fire is the only one that has to eat to live."

Lonely looks at Fawn. "I think I am part fire, too," she says. "And part earth, and part water."

Fawn nods, but does not reply. Her face looks wary and closed again, and she does not look back at Lonely as they gather the pieces of vegetables in their hands and bring them to the pot, to heat and change and soften.

That night, lying alone in Chelya's bed, Lonely can hear the sound of Rye's guitar on the rooftop above her, as he sings Fawn a lullaby. She touches herself, fantasies of Rye's intense gaze and sure, deep-reaching fingers making her bite her lip to keep from crying out. Her orgasm shocks through her so powerfully that her body stretches and turns all the way over in the bed against her will, and in the moment of its peak, a flash of Fawn's shy, careful nakedness, her modest fullness rising up from the water, crosses her memory. Turning all the way around to lie on her back again, Lonely rests, breathing fast and then gradually slower. She lets the clear, comfortable pleasure of her day with Fawn sink through her. She remembers Fawn's gaze in the pool after they saw the otter, and when she came downstairs in Chelya's dress. She remembers Fawn's presence beside her and the vulnerable aura of Fawn's familiar motions when Lonely stood with her inside the space that belonged to her. She can't sort anything out in her mind, but in her body—in her chest and in the fluid muscles of her arms and in her lips and in her belly—she can feel that Fawn is attracted to her. She can feel that attraction peering from the shadows of Fawn's silence, dreaming deep under the brown waters of Fawn's presence—something Fawn would never, ever express. But Lonely can feel it. It fills her with wonder, like the sky.

In the City, you put your hopes and fears on a screen, then sit in the dark and watch them play back. People more beautiful than you are act out your lives. People braver than you are doing what you ought to do.

But most of the time, on this screen that you watch in the darkness—too dark for you to see each other's faces, the screen too mesmerizing to allow you to turn and look at the real person sitting close by—people do things that you would never do.

People on the screen drive their cars off of cliffs, smash them into each other at top speed, and explode into flame. They shoot, they punch, they slice their enemies into pieces; their machine guns vibrate with deafening white light and smoke, and blood fountains like freedom from chests, heads, throats, bellies. There is screaming and cursing and more fire. Buildings collapse in an instant, and calm herds of people and animals are slain in a single chain of blasts—a few flicks of a finger.

You sit in the dark room watching the screen, and you do not move, except occasionally to put something in your mouths: something to grind your teeth against, or something that tastes strong enough to sting. Your bodies are saggy and malformed inside rectangular clothing. Everything in the room is covered with a fine grey dust of skin cells and lint.

You keep chewing, wanting more. More guns, more fire, more blood in higher fountains. It still isn't loud enough to drown out the din you hear inside; it still isn't violent enough to express your own silent anger. Your heads shift forward in a slow, bleary eagerness; your necks crane unnaturally, leaving your bodies behind in your seats.

After the movie you stumble out into the day. The sunlight makes you dizzy; you cannot remember what it is. You do not remember where your clothing comes from, but it feels too tight. You herd your children irritably, reprimanding their unruly chaos.

All around you, everything is known. All around you, you have nothing to fear from a world you control perfectly. Your bodies sag hopelessly toward the ground, unnecessary to you, longing for the earth. Inside your chests, your hearts trip over themselves. Your breath comes fast, as if you will fight or flee, but there is no longer any reason. All the other animals are gone.

People are saying now that there is no Princess in the Tower. That it was just a lie Hanum made up. Some people are even saying that there is no such thing as love, no such thing as destiny, no such thing as one other person who can understand you.

You look out into the parking lot at the neat rows of cars extending over the flat pavement, and are nauseated by the lust and fury inside you that you do not even realize are there.

For a long time, Fawn does not speak as much to Lonely as she did that day. But now she invites Lonely to work in the garden with her. Sometimes the two of them glance at each other with puffs of silent laughter, at the sound of Chelya's excited voice in the distance followed by a carelessly slammed door, or the passion of a squirrel as it tells off a rival.

Fawn chooses Lonely's company in a different way than Chelya did. Her words of friendship are not spoken, but seem rather made from the gestures of her hands over her work, and her way of caring for Lonely is to teach her to do that same work which is sacred to her. She shows Lonely the way to water and weed the plants, the way to dig in and lay out the different seeds, the way to harvest the greens, the way to knead dough, the way to clean and cut a fish, the way to build a fire. Lonely learns how these miracles are achieved, and she learns the pride of helping. Sometimes the feeling of being necessary, for the first time in her life, is enough to still all her longings, all her doubt.

Sometimes as they walk into the fields in the morning, Lonely feels a thrilling mystery like a new sea lapping at her heart, and when she turns to Fawn, Fawn ducks her head and hides a smile.

They do speak occasionally, and over the course of many days, the whole family seems to relax around Lonely, as if Fawn's acceptance was the door through which they could finally trust her, and the conversations at mealtimes grow more interesting. Lonely learns the basic stories that make the family what it is. She learns, for example, that Fawn has brothers, who live in the City still, if they live at all—sons that Eva had to leave behind and will not speak of. She learns that Fawn worries over Kite because of his strange fascination with the inventions of the City, his curiosity, the longing she senses in his restlessness. She learns that when Chelya is out in the evenings, she is most likely spending time with forest spirits she has befriended, and taking part in magical events of which Fawn has only vague and fearful suspicions. Ever since she was small, Chelya has been able to relate with perfect ease to everyone—whether human or animal, real or ethereal. It is a talent that has been encouraged and nourished by her grandmother.

For a long time, Lonely does not find herself alone again with Eva, which is both a relief and a disappointment to her. In the old woman's presence she feels uneasy, for though surely the others also know of her history, only Eva has spoken of it directly. At the same time Lonely knows that somehow, for Eva, everything about her is all right—her father and the tower, her longing and her imperfections. She yearns sometimes to fall once more into those forgiving arms, that loving grace like milk, in which everything made sense. But she can only glance at Eva, anxious questions in her eyes, and occasionally take in the reward of Eva's slow, reassuring smile. It is as if they share a secret—a dangerous secret with which Eva has entrusted her—but Lonely does not understand yet what to do with it, and she is not even convinced that it belongs to her.

She only knows she does not want to leave this place now, because to leave it would mean thinking once again of where she is going, with no one to stand between her and the painful question of her destiny.

Sometimes at night, Lonely sleeps in the fields with Chelya and listens to her whisper sleepily about the creatures and beings that are her friends. Chelya knows the otter that Lonely saw with Fawn, and all the otter's family for three generations. She knows the love affairs of the birds—their daily rivalries and flirtations and who loves whom. She knows the most important trees, and the fairy families that live in their branches, and the work that they do for the forest.

"It's different talking to you, though," says Chelya. "I've never had a human friend before."

"How is it different?" Lonely wants to know, still doubtful of this assurance that she is human.

Chelya thinks. "I don't know. It just is. It's sweet, talking to you." She turns to Lonely—cold grass shivering between their faces, moonlight in their breath. "Tell me about the sea," she whispers, her voice barely carrying above the song of the crickets.

"What do you want to know?" Lonely asks warily.

"I don't know. Is it scary, so much water? But you saw it all your life, so you couldn't have been scared."

"No," says Lonely, "I didn't see it all my life. And yes, I was scared."

"Is it like a river where you can't see the other side?"

"No. It doesn't have one direction like that, or one voice. It's more like the wind or the sky."

"Did you have to cross it to come here?"

"Yes."

"Did you take a boat?"

"No."

Chelya stares at her, eyes glowing in the dark. "Can you swim that far?"

"No. I can't."

"Did you use *magic* to get across?"

"I guess I did. But I didn't mean to. Suddenly I was in the sea, traveling under there, at the bottom. I felt very far away from everything."

"What did you see under there?"

Lonely rolls onto her back and looks at the stars. She imagines the sky is the surface of the sea, with the pins of light struggling to pierce through from far above. "I saw things," she said, "without voices, things that were very close to me, touching me, and then suddenly gone. I saw things that were only half there, and then darkness. They were creatures, I guess, and plants like the trees, but they seemed to be from another time or place, where I could not reach them even though I was there."

"Was it very beautiful?"

"Maybe," says Lonely, feeling sad. "I was too lost to know. I did not know anything then. But Yora took my hand—"

"Yora?"

"Yes, she was a woman, and she pulled me up from the bottom of the sea, and brought me to the shore, and saved me. She gave me my horse."

"Oh," breathes Chelya, in a kind of ecstasy. "She is the goddess of the river you bathed in with my mother—the great river of the world, that connects us with the sea. I've never seen her! What does she look like?"

"I don't know. Like you, only grayer and sadder, and like the river, with old, old eyes—older than Eva's."

In the morning, Lonely will not be able to believe she spoke of these things. Yet she will feel relieved, to realize that she could name them.

On other nights, when her longing is too much for her, and she must be alone with her own body and imagination, she sleeps in the fields far away from Chelya and Kite. The fields are big, with room for everyone's solitude and everyone's secrets.

One night, she sleeps again in the loft, wanting the embrace of home around her. She wakes at dawn to the sound of Fawn's gentle footsteps down the ladder from the rooftop garden where she and Rye sleep, continuing downward to the ground floor. Then, to her hungry surprise, the hatch opens again, and Rye's smiling face peers down in greeting.

"Sleep well?" he asks.

She nods, smelling her own sweat under the sheets, and stares at him, unaware that she has not answered. She watches his smile widen, watches the flex of his naked shoulders as he supports himself against the rim of the square hole above her. The hair on his chest comes almost to his neck.

"Have you ever been up here?" he asks her.

"N-no," she says, finding her breath and her voice, and sitting up sharply with the sheet clutched to her breasts.

"Come on up, if you want, and take a look." His face disappears. She rises bare from the bed and throws on a dress that Chelya dyed yellow with the heartwood of a mulberry tree. She splashes water on her face from the drinking cup by the bed. She climbs the ladder.

When she reaches the top, Rye's body jerks a little toward her as if inclined to give her a hand, but she scrambles quickly over the edge and stands. She fears his touch as much as she wants it, though she doesn't know why. Now they stand beside each other in the morning breeze. Lonely sees the fields in their entirety, the wheat and the gardens, the goats and the chickens, the stream going happily homeward into the forest, the soft mountains and the great, hard, impossible mountain in the distance. She sees Rye's gentle, patient body out of the corner of her eye, aware of her and waiting for her to see. She sees the silent, tumbled blankets where he and Fawn slept together, the still-warm pockets of their careless folds as distant and unattainable to her as that mountain. She turns her head toward Rye a little more, but he does not look at her.

"You built this house?" she says.

He nods.

She looks out again. The land is still grey with the dawn, but the sun begins to creep across it, with tendrils of hot light that look new and unfiltered as if they will burn upon contact. The work of the day is laid out before them, beautiful but lonely. What does Fawn think, when she stands here beside him? *Don't go,* thinks Lonely. *Don't leave yet.*

"I'm going fishing," says Rye. "You want to come with me?"

Lonely cannot get any sound to come. She nods, choking quietly on her breath.

"Only if you want to," says Rye. "It's quiet out there, peaceful. I just thought— I mean you might— Well, if you want to come, I'm leaving in a moment. I'll be downstairs."

He leaves her standing there like a leaf, shivering in the sun, smiling with tearful joy at his awkwardness and the reciprocal hunger it might imply.

After a series of breathless moments and a breakfast that Lonely cannot remember, they are walking into the forest.

Rye names the birds that are singing. "Song sparrows," he says, after a song that bounces and twinkles in the high air. And "robin," after a pretty lilt upward and downward, feminine and full-breasted. "Titmouse," after a high piercing squeak.

Lonely thinks of music, of the songs that Rye sings—their patterns familiar the way the wind is familiar, the way her bed of earthen things was familiar in the tower though she'd never felt the earth. *There are songs everyone knows,* she thinks. *There are ways we know each other, languages we recognize.* For the birdsong does not make her lonely today.

 Her hands brush the yellow dress as she walks, sometimes trotting behind Rye to keep up. He points out the mourning dove with her bobbing, owlish coos. He tells her of the nuthatch with his cynical rasp, who can walk vertically down trees and speak the language of chickadees, who are tiny, brave, and curious, and whose mating cries are a faint off-key echo of lazy summer. The cardinal, a sacred bird made of fire, sends up high explosive notes that afterward come peeling downward like shooting stars.

At the river, Lonely sits on a mossy stone and watches the reflection of Rye's bare torso in the sun. She imagines touching the solid vessel of his chest, smelling the scent caught in the web of brown animal hair over his heart—hair in places where Dragon was smooth and shiny. His muscle rolls beneath his clay-earth skin as he leans back and winds his arm, and the line soars over the water and falls. He's wearing loose pants rolled up to his thighs. His dark hair is curly and damp, his beard heavy, his face a magical animal. Lonely sees his shoulders drop back and relax, sees his hips settle, as the bait falls into the water.

She has been watching him for so long. She has learned to watch him even without looking at him. She watches him at the dinner table without turning her head. She pauses where she can just see him through the cracks in his workshop behind the house, pretending to listen to Chelya's talk, as carefully and roughly, forcefully and exactly, he hammers pieces of trees into shapes. She watches him in the fields, the twisting sling of his body with the scythe through the grass. She watches him kiss Fawn goodbye and hello.

"Kite used to come with me," Rye says thoughtfully. "Fishing," he clarifies, clearing his throat. "But he doesn't often, any more."

Lonely tears through her mind in search of some answer to continue the conversation. There is sadness and a sense of importance in Rye's voice. But she doesn't know what to do with that. "I don't think Kite likes me," she blurts, because it is the only thought that comes.

She cannot see Rye's face, but she can hear the smile in his answer. "He's only a little shy," he says with a gentleness that makes Lonely ashamed of her rude words. "He's never had a pretty girl come live with us before. He's hardly ever met anyone outside our family."

These words take all of Lonely's voice away for several moments. But while she struggles, Rye continues, his words quicker now. "My daughter feels a connection with you, though. And Fawn, too—and that is something."

Again, Lonely tries to think of what to say. She bows her head and succumbs in frustration to her own wordlessness.

"You traveled a long way to come here, didn't you?" says Rye, casting the line again.

Lonely nods, though he cannot see her. "It felt like a long way."

"Did you meet any other people in the mountains?"

"No," says Lonely. "Not in the mountains."

"What is the land like, between the mountains and the sea?"

"There is desert where nothing grows, and then desert with giant stones in different shapes, and caves, and then desert with a river, full of green. Then there are fields." But that doesn't describe it at all. Lonely wants to talk about the people she met, and her loneliness and her longing, and the painful beauty, but she doesn't see a way in.

"What animals did you see out there?"

"Vultures and a dog. A lizard and a snake. Butterflies, hawks. Birds like here, that talked to each other all day long. I wish I knew what they were saying, but I couldn't understand them like other animals. I guess they were calling to each other, not to me," she says helplessly.

Rye thinks a moment. "Sometimes they are calling to each other," he says. "But sometimes more than that. I think when they sing—just sit in a tree and sing so beautifully!—they're talking about themselves. They're describing themselves to the world, you know? Saying this place is mine, and this is me, beautiful and strong, powerful enough to have all that I want and to defend what is mine! That's how they attract those they want to them and keep the ones they don't want away. Listen, and you'll hear it. You can't translate it into our kind of words, or it wouldn't say the same thing."

He sounds so certain about this, even proud. Lonely has never heard this boyish joy in his voice before. Unconsciously she leans forward, her whole body smiling, wanting to taste it. She imagines that her own being could be so definite, so easily expressed as the birds—that just by saying with clarity who she was, she could have all that she desired.

But there is Rye, standing still in the water, and here is she, folded small around a stone, and he does not look at her.

Then there are no more words for a long time. Lonely listens to Rye's silence, and the way the birdsong fits inside it. She listens to the wind, and it seems to her now that the wind knows the water where Rye casts his line more intimately than it knows her, and that it winds around Rye with tenderness, protecting him from Lonely's desire.

"What bird is that?" she asks once, listening to a few watery trills from some deep shadows far off, haunting, like riffs out of the flute music Moon played from beneath the waterfall.

"Thrush," says Rye in a soft voice that does not interrupt it, and the word is sensual; Lonely can hear his tongue slipping between his teeth as he says it. "That's one of my favorite calls. I hear them in the dark forest at dusk or when the sky clouds over before a rain. They're like calls to another world, don't you think?"

Lonely nods, though he cannot see her, and clutches the moss in her fists.

Rye laughs a little. "I almost forgot you were there. Being out here, my mind gets to be like the fish, swimming around down there in a dream." Then he turns to her, and she remembers his face all over again.

"You can go," he says, "whenever you like. I mean, you don't have to stay. I'll be here a long time."

Lonely shrugs, trembling. "I don't know the way," she says in a small voice, hoping this is reason enough.

Rye, who was preparing to fling out his line again, puts it down on the shore and comes toward her. So easily he comes and stands beside her, then crouches beside her, then—before she can even take it in, before she can even steady herself to survive it—leans his face very close to hers and points, looking into the forest.

"There," he says, and she can feel his breath. "You see that? It isn't a cleared path, but if you rest your eyes on it for a bit, you'll see how there's a path there, that we made. You'll see how the leaves are all turned where we passed, and how the light concentrates, and there's a broken branch—see?

It's not far that way, if you follow the path we came by."

But Lonely's eyes are closed. She is holding her breath and doesn't care if he knows it. She can smell the hearts of trees, the sweat-hunger, and her father, and smoke and skin and sun all at once. "But—" she says.

He starts to look at her, seems to notice the closeness of her face as if for the first time, and stands abruptly.

"Can I stay?" she says, looking up at him, scared. "Is it all right? Do you mind?"

Rye smiles and ducks his head, and he starts to walk away, but in his face she sees something sweet that she will not be able to forget. "Nah," he says, and there is irony in his voice. "I don't mind."

Then he walks back out, throws his line, and becomes silent and far away.

Lonely cannot sit still. It is all she can do not to cry out. She moves toward the water. "Can I go in?" she asks, thinking it might disturb the fish.

"I don't mind," says Rye again.

She wades into the soft river. Every motion feels heavy. She knows that Rye is watching her, and knowing that burns her secretly from the inside out. She thinks of Yora and closes her eyes. *I want to be beautiful, like the river. I want him to search inside of me, the way he searches in the river for his food.* The water is so cool, and the day so hot, that she keeps walking in, the yellow dress shining around her and then swallowed whole into the darkness. She dips herself in with a splash and turns around, rising a little with laughter, the cloth clutching her breasts.

Rye does not laugh and does not look at her, but she knows that he sees her. She is right here, in front of him, not far from the rippled path of the line.

I want you, she could say, and rise up with the wetness all over her. She could lift the dress away from her body, and she would be the river, and she would sweep him in. She sees the clenched determination in his face, the weak kindness in his stance. She feels the hard tower in her own spirit, the ice of it and the silver song of it, and her father's power running cold and greedy in her blood. She feels her own beauty. She could do anything.

"Thank you for taking me home with you, Rye" she says, feeling the courage to speak his name for the first time. "Thank you for saving me."

Rye looks at her then, his eyes just turning, without moving his head, and she is shocked by the sadness she sees there. She feels instant remorse, though she doesn't know why.

"I'm sorry," she says, rushing her words. "I was so lonely. I was going to die if you hadn't found me." Tears bubble out from beneath her eyes, unplanned, and all her power is gone. She wants to drop into the water, cover her head beneath it, but she is ashamed to move. She feels her body freeze beneath the wet dress. His eyes remain focused on hers. But they are heavy with some sorrow she does not understand, and they want to fall upon her, and she would do anything to lie down under the weight of that gaze and let it press her into the water and the deep earth beneath…

"Why do you call yourself Lonely?" he asks her very quietly, not moving a muscle in his face. "Why do you call yourself that?"

Lonely doesn't answer, only stands still and lets the tears spill over. They are the only part of her that moves, and the water moves around her, deep and slow, and she sees the forbidden tenderness in his eyes as he watches her, and she drinks it and drinks it as if she could never be filled.

"Would you believe that I am a goddess?" she murmurs finally.

He nods. "I would believe it."

"Did you know, when you saw me?"

"When I saw you, I saw——" He looks away, shakes his head. "I could not stop myself," he says so softly that she almost doesn't hear.

"You thought I was beautiful," she says. For the first time, she feels this beauty, not as Dragon saw it, nor as her father saw it, nor as the world, perhaps, saw it. She feels it living in someone's heart, growing there, something given.

"Yes," he says.

She thinks the look on his face will break her, and yet she, too, cannot stop herself. "Are you ever lonely?" she says.

He looks back at her for one more moment, his eyes sharpening. "Yes, sometimes."

"Isn't it…hard to be lonely?"

She waits for his answer. She waits a long, long time, hovering in nothingness over the abyss between their voices, terrified but unable to turn back. *Don't you want me?* she is asking over and over in her mind, and she knows that he hears her. She knows.

"Some things in life are hard," he answers finally, but his voice is hard now, too, and rough, and he has turned his face away. "It's hard when we don't have enough rains, or too many rains, and we go hungry. It's hard when we don't get to see the family we love in far places. It's hard when our children grow away from us. It's hard to see other human beings tear apart the land all around us, tear up the mountains. Some things are hard. But because something is hard, or painful, doesn't mean it needs to be fixed. Sometimes it can't be changed, and doesn't need to be. It just makes us what we are."

She stares at him.

"No, I am not lonely," he says now, shaking his head again, as if speaking to himself. "I love my family more than my life. I have everything."

"But I am," says Lonely. "And I—" But she cannot say it. She knows it is wrong to say it. "I am lonely," she finishes quietly again, hanging her head.

Rye nods, pulling in his line. "There is a time for that, too," is all he says. Then he begins to wind the line and put the bait away, and she knows there will be no more of this conversation.

"Fish aren't biting today," he says, and his voice is tired now, the feeling drained from it. "I love to be here—I could stay all day. But we have to eat." He looks up at her, his face blank. "I hope you don't mind taking a longer route home. I have a couple of traps I can check."

Wordless, Lonely pushes forward with her thighs against the water, her body cold now, and arrives at the shore. She wrings her dress dry around her legs, not looking at him. She follows him back into the forest, shivering.

She ducks in and out of the leaves, watching his movement fit the spaces of the trees. She stands aside and watches the patient compassion in his hands as he unwinds the dead body of a rabbit from his trap. She watches him kneel at a second trap where a rabbit is still barely alive. She watches the confident caress of his grip as he steadies its head, and the swift and intimate certainty of his arm as he slits its throat. She offers to carry his fishing gear, and he goes ahead, one pair of furred feet gripped in each sad, knowing hand.

And it seems to her that he is the god, who can save and kill, who can survive all this, who can give life with his eyes, and who, finally, can stop himself, when she cannot.

On the morning of the full moon, the young goats chase each other in bold arcs around their pen, and then the grown-up goats join in. The boy goats rear back, tensing their square bodies in the air, and then swing their heads together with a dull and gleeful thunk, knocking each other off the stumps and an old broken cradle that has been turned upside down for them to play on. The boy goats chase the girl goats, and shove-climb over their bodies, and the girl goats bleat and run. Then the girl goats start to hump each other, and then they chase and hump the boy goats too. All the goats gallop and bleat and groan, their little hooves like falling rocks, and climb against each other's bodies and bump hard, and they are laughing. Sometimes they are playing and sometimes they are for real. There are no rules. In their passion they pay no attention to the quiet girl outside the fence, who watches them in a pale and shivering way, her knuckles white around the handle of her bucket.

Chelya, their favorite human, touches the girl on the shoulder and startles her from her reverie. She leans close and murmurs excitedly into the pale girl's ear. If the goats were listening, they would catch the words "come" and "full moon," and "night" and "friends." These are all words the goats know, and they know more or less what the giggles mean too.

The two girls walk away together, and a few of the goats pause in their antics to gaze after them, as if only now realizing that having an audience was part of what made their fun.

Later, Lonely will try to remember the exact texture of her mood, the thoughts in her mind, everything about who she was that night, in that moment when she stood in the heart of the forest facing Chelya and could not imagine what would happen next.

The lights of the house are long gone. When Lonely looks up, she can barely see the sky, its sunset colors ripe and golden, shining like a fruit that will fall into her hand at the instant of darkness. Chelya has stopped them in a place that feels like nowhere to Lonely, somewhere between the familiar lights and distant drumbeats, which are a sound Lonely has never heard before, like a heart turned inside out. Chelya herself holds a slim, womanly-shaped drum under one arm, though Lonely as yet makes no connection between it and the sound from the distance. Her own innocence will fascinate her later, when she remembers it.

"On the night of the full moon," Chelya explains slowly, looking at Lonely and searching for words she has never had to find before, "everything can change. People can become animals, and animals can become people. The spirits of things come alive, and can dance on their own, and are real enough to touch. It's hard to explain. You'll see. It's easier if you don't try to figure it out. Just know that these are my friends—all of them. I know everyone in this forest, in all of their forms. Some beings are tricky. They may not even mean to be, but they're just different from us. You have to know what you want. Do you know what you want?"

Lonely stares at her. The drumbeats in the distance seem to grow louder. She remembers the men's boots as they stomped toward her in her old nightmares. Chelya stands perfectly still, waiting for her answer. But Lonely can't possibly tell her what she wants.

"Just be careful," says Chelya. "You can have a lot of fun. You might get kissed or worse. But be careful. Listen to your heart, okay?"

"Okay," answers Lonely, feeling like she is the child, and Chelya the mothering voice she never had. She can see the mother in Chelya: the abundant fullness of her love, the generosity in her breasts, the ease in her hips, and the way she will guide and gather her children someday with a playful voice and a confident hand.

"Oh, and one more thing," says Chelya. "You can't tell my mother *any-thing* about this. I love her, and I tell her lots of things, but not this, okay? It would upset her."

"But I thought she knew you went to the forest to be with—the spirits?"

"No, not like this. The full moon is different from any other night. She doesn't know. She's afraid of these things. Really, she can't handle it. Promise me!"

"Okay," says Lonely. They continue on toward the drumbeats, moonlight unwinding their long hair in white ribbons, wind taking form in their wake through the leaves behind them, as they walk on bare virgin feet, and then they run.

The trees blur around them, everything moving, and when they stop before a fire higher and wilder than anything Dragon ever spit out onto the empty desert floor, everything continues to move. The flames are moving, their light convulsing across moving faces, and the wind is moving, swaying the trees among dancing, living bodies. Someone's eyes across the fire—narrow, with pupils bigger than a human's can ever get—flash at Lonely. Hands slap the bodies of drums. And between the shouting, howling, and laughter, still there is also silence—loud and insistent between the drumbeats—and each beat is like a black hole in space. Lonely is glad for Chelya's hand in hers.

"Our ancestors are here," Chelya whispers close to Lonely's ear, "and spirits of plants and animals, meadows and streams. Fairy people are here. Anyone can come here."

Afraid to look further into such a multitude of faces, Lonely draws close to the fire, losing her vision for a moment in its depths of spirit and motion, its white and orange, its impossible brilliance in the night. But the heat is so powerful that she has to step back. Little people the size of her hand are springing around and through the flames like grasshoppers, contorting their bodies into fantastic positions. Sometimes two of them merge in the air to become one person, and then separate again into three.

"Fire fairies," says Chelya, and she holds out her hand. Two of the min-iature people, a man and a woman, land in her palm, and entwine their hot, elastic bodies around each other—the man immediately penetrating the woman. Their bodies shine like melting glass as they thrust for a moment back and forth in that ancient rhythm, and Lonely sees the man's penis rise into a flame within the woman, reaching all the way up to her throat and out her mouth, where it becomes a fiery tongue that wraps around the man. Then the woman overcomes him like a wild-eyed demon, and he opens his mouth wider until it opens his whole head like the hinged head of a snake.

And then they are both snakes, devouring each other and spinning into a circle of flame, from which they fall in spiraling acrobatics onto the ground, where the man chases the woman around the fire, spiraling into it and out of sight.

Lonely gasps as Chelya drops her hand and spins around. Everything happens so fast. Chelya is laughing amidst a flickering multi-colored presence that flutters all around them—brushing Lonely's neck and ears, wriggling like a gently lecherous breeze under her hair, her arms, her skirt. Lonely clasps her hands to her body, but her dress is falling from her, dripping from her shoulders as a young man in a flurry of color and wings hovers before them both.

"This is my friend the butterfly man," Chelya says warmly, and opens her mouth to accept his greeting. The butterfly man unfurls his spiraled tongue and flicks it into Chelya's mouth.

Sweet as ever, says Butterfly, his voice like clanging shards of wind. *And who is this? A bright yellow flower…*And before Lonely can even wish for it, he is encircling her own tongue, and his is gripping and mobile, a boyish fire, well-experienced in desire. She feels the spiral in her mouth, whipping the energy of her breath round and round, sending a warm line of bliss straight downward, where it keeps spinning. When she opens her eyes, his face is so close to hers she cannot see it, and she cannot remember if it was human or animal, and all she can see is the slow folding and unfolding of his glorious, ecstatic wings as he concentrates on her sweetness. She is amazed at his delight in her, and his delight fills her even as he drinks her, and it seems for a moment that she is floating in the air, the center of her body thrust upward in offering to him. *What is this place, this dream?*

Then suddenly he is gone, flown off to another flower. She hears Chelya's voice, though she doesn't know where it is coming from, or where she herself is.

"Remember what you want, Lonely."

She lifts her heavy body from the ground, too heavy for a butterfly to carry. The light touch of his wings all over her skin has left her stinging with her own aliveness. She forces her hands to rest on her heart.

What do I want? What do I want?

Surrender, says her heart. *Adventure*. Somewhere a flute begins to wail and sing, and then the deep leaping music of pipes joins in. A goat man with a goat's beard and smooth boy's chest hops up to her on hooves that make the earth beneath her bounce. She hardly has time to see his red lips grinning before he takes one of her breasts in his giant mouth, and she hears herself growl like a dog. What has she become?

Here, toss her here, says another, and the goat boy takes her hand and whirls her on. Another grabs her from behind and presses something between her legs. Only the thin layer of her dress protects her. Between them she is squeezed and rubbed, until she feels she will melt in the heat of their bodies so close and willful, playing her against one another. When they drop her, she collapses, and one of them inserts his head between her legs, and butts her with his hard curved horns. Then he trots off, and they chase each other, whooping and grabbing hands around the fire. Lonely lies hot and beaten on the ground.

Water, says her heart weakly.

She opens her eyes, breathing in, breathing out, but there is no water anywhere here—only fire enclosed and haloed by the dancing shadows of half-human trees. But a woman slides up beside her.

I'm Chelya's friend, she says. Lonely recognizes her instantly: otter spirit, with her open, smiling face and sleek, voluptuous curves. Without thinking, Lonely wraps her arms around the woman, and Otter nuzzles her hair. Her body softens Lonely's. Their hands play over the hills of each other, at first without intention, without differentiating one body from the other. Then Lonely's desire is everywhere, slow and big and sensuous—a more serious desire now within the play, her lips round against the otter woman's roundness. She moves with the otter's waves, and without knowing it she she rises; she flows now over the earth.

She flows like water over the body of someone sturdy, whose breath echoes within his stony frame. Her head swims in birdsong. A chest thick with vines expands and rises, and she is pressed into its comforting heat by slow, muscular arms. She winds her legs around him, and slowly they rub the perfect forms of their bodies back and forth. His eyes hold her like old rock formations, and his hands around her hips are earth that her body takes root in. He is a mountain rolling its strength beneath her, its hard, sad silence filling her, soothing and anchoring her passions. In his arms she becomes a lake, deepening into her own depths, her heart pooling in his eyes which are wells of seeping tenderness that remind her of Rye's. His beard encircles her with ivy; his shoulders are breezy mountain peaks that she collapses upon like a bird resting tattered wings, exhausted by her own frenzy. The stone of his erection supports her, and like a deep undersea current she churns against it, not letting it enter her, not thinking, not trying. Her virginity opens inside her like a great infinity of possibility.

As they roll together, other water women are rolling with them, making love to the mountain man in all the different moods of water. One is dew, each molecule of her body a frail, sweet kiss. One is a waterfall gushing down him, wild with release, splashing down to his hard center and foaming there; her thighs rise up beneath Lonely's, charging her with their thrill like galloping horses. One is rain, sighing against him, covering both of them with hungry needles of touch, so that Lonely begins to shiver even deeper against the man's hardness, whose friction finally overcomes her, and her flesh melts into waves that peel over him and then gradually subside into the simple lullaby of her own breath. She keeps rocking against him gently—the drumbeats carrying her life, the water women everywhere, moaning and singing and brushing their delicate, flowering bodies over her—and she feels his continued hardness as if it will always be there, neither urgent nor desiring, but simply masculine. She can feel his voice humming deep in his belly. When the continued friction begins to pain her, she flows away from him, her passage eased by the comforting arms of the women, through whom she drifts away into the darkness and into herself again.

The great fire draws her in, and her heart says *Love.* And because her love is not here, because she has not yet found him, she begins to move her body around his absence, her heart giving her body rhythm. The first joy of her life was the joy of the body, the joy of her hips that now rollick and swing, making loops over the bare, stampeded earth. The first longing was the longing of her body, her shoulders rolling around the longing in her heart now, her arms fluttering, her eyes closed, her face resting in the air, head swaying. Her waist twists and twirls, a vulnerable stretch between hips and heart. Her belly swells in and out, finding its inner weight. Her feet clap against the ground. What is desire but the need to move her own body in its special dance, to be seen, to be held and caressed by the elements into something beautiful? The fire sees her. The black sky sees her. The wild loving animals see her. The trees—who seem still yet are the only ones who know how to release their bodies to the wind, who in their rootedness have learned how to sway and swing in motions of pure whim, who among all the beings of earth are the only ones besides humans who know how to dance without structure, without purpose, without form—dance with her.

Now she is dancing with the spirit of an aspen tree. The girl-like form is lithe and giggling, slim and silver, shaking against Lonely with winds of pure energy. Spirit of a maple joins them, and spirit of a hemlock. Hemlock takes her hand, her touch light and forgiving. When she brushes Lonely, Lonely shakes and tears come suddenly to her eyes. Her body slows. Maple is warm on the other side of her, at once big-boned and strong, and fluid as melted syrup. Her eyes, her hair, the energy dancing around her, all dazzle with an aura of pure magic. Lonely feels dizzy.

Hemlock presses a feathery hand to Lonely's heart and says, *What do you need, dancing heart?*

But it is her body, not her heart, who cries out this need every day, every night—this longing to merge with another. Lonely understands that suddenly, that she has been confusing the two. What, then, does her heart want?

The trees close around her and she hears the song of the wind in their hearts—that song so true and yet so treacherous, so lovely and yet so sad. The heart wants so many things it does not yet understand. The heart wants something so complicated, so much more difficult to seek than the simple hungers of the body. She hears the wind in her mind, neither friend nor enemy but always with her.

You only want Rye because you cannot have him. You only want someone you cannot have because it is safer that way. What your heart wants is neither safe nor easy. What your heart wants will bring pain.

Lonely is still now and the trees are dancing around her. The desire of her body is so simple. She needs touch: warm, satisfying touch that meets her body in every secret, tingling place, that meets her pleasure at every moment of its expansion.

Away from the fire, safe in a shadow, Maple introduces Lonely to two stag-men, painfully perfect, their skin brown and smooth over young bones, their bodies graceful and poised and strangely feminine, their faces kind but distant, their erections straight and handsome and polite. Their hands are full of soft longing like the hands of women, submissive and questioning, sensitive to each small convulsion of her desire yet firmer where she needs them to be firmer, their brown fingers angled and confident. The aspen, who is now not one but many women connected, a ghostly and trembling chorus, rings them around and around as they play together on the earth. The stag men smile at her, their antlers curving in spires of twisted bone from their chiseled foreheads. One of them kisses her deep on the mouth, his tongue like a beast that rises from watery depths and shakes its glory in the sun. The other one kneels between her legs, licking her and the other stag at the same time, his tongue flicking playfully with hot youth against their desire. Lonely can no longer remember her promise to her heart. She wants the feeling of man inside her, and the drumbeats convulse with the sucking of that emptiness. In the confusion of tongue and bone, she lifts her hips and cries out. The second one slides up beside her and the two embrace her and roll together against her, so that she is surrounded by their heat and their tender, woody scents. They roll her over and pull her buttocks into the air, holding her in an animal position as if to be mounted. But suddenly she is afraid.

"No!" she cries, shame tensing her face, and flips back over to look at them. But they have scattered. In their place is the snarling face of a coyote. In a single drumbeat he has pinned her to the ground, his face against hers, his teeth hanging over her. She can feel a human hardness against her wetness, human thighs enclosing her.

Isn't this what you want? says Coyote.

No, thinks Lonely. *It is sacred, what I want.* She knows this. She has felt it, all this night, in the arms of the many creatures, in their beautiful motions.

But Coyote laughs. *Are you sure?* he seems to say. *Perhaps this is what you mean.* And his face turns human. Lonely gasps because it is the face from her vision long ago, when her prince appeared in the ice wall of her tower. His innocent lips, his long lashes, his high sweet forehead, his shadowy-gold skin—but still with coyote's flashing eyes. The eyes close and the beautiful man mouths, *You are mine.*

Lonely closes her eyes, too, as he twirls his tongue slyly around hers, and now around her ear. Is it really him? She tries to breathe.

And she smells death on Coyote's breath. No, it cannot be her prince, for he would not speak like this. There is something about sex, she realizes suddenly, that is like dying, and you have to die in the arms of someone you trust, because in that moment of death you can remember nothing; you are a disembodied spirit in blackness, a soul that could be stolen forever.

It's all an illusion, Coyote whispers into her ear, and she feels his lips at her neck, the way her body bucks against him uncontrollably, the way the door between her legs opens. *We seem human, but we're not. It doesn't matter. Nothing matters.*

Lonely thinks she hears Chelya calling her. The sound of her own name echoing in the chambers of her heart.

"Chelya," she says out loud, and Coyote disappears like a nightmare. She sits up, dirty and sticky, delirious but relieved. She hurries to stand, and brushes herself off as best she can.

"I'm sorry," she says shakily to Chelya, who has arrived suddenly from somewhere. "I…I lost your dress." She's too confused to feel ashamed.

"It's okay," says Chelya, her voice as bright as daylight. "It didn't fit me any more. That's why I gave it to you. Are you okay?"

"I think so."

She offers Chelya her hand, for she can barely stand on her own, and Chelya guides her away from the fire and dancing. The night is cool and peaceful, its silence swallowing the memory of the drums as they move further and further away. The trees are still, their boughs softening to the side to let them pass.

Lonely cannot catch her breath for a long time. *What just happened??* she wants to ask Chelya, but at the same time she can't admit it. Was it like that for Chelya too? She is embarrassed to ask.

Together they wash their bodies in the river, cold with darkness and milky with moonlight. Chelya doesn't explain why, and Lonely doesn't think to question it. It seems exactly what she needs.

"Where were you?" asks Lonely, shivering afterward.

"I was there. Playing my drum, mostly. You have to be careful with Coyote. He plays tricks. He knows what people want, sometimes better than they do."

Lonely turns away, not knowing how much Chelya knows. She looks at the little drum. She hadn't thought about the people who created that rhythm she danced to, that rhythm beneath her that carried her through the night. She tries to imagine Chelya among them, peaceful and sure, her face radiating the simple joy of her music. She longs for that solid tree-strength inside the girl, that holds her so steady. "What are you wearing tonight?" she asks as Chelya puts her dress back on, a thing that Lonely has only seen in darkness, that accentuates her curves with ruffles of deep, blood-thick color.

"It's a dress the fairies made for me," says Chelya. "It's made of flowers that never die."

"Oh," Lonely breathes, wrapping her arms around her own chilled nakedness.

"They're going to help me make one for you," says Chelya quickly, "only different. One that's meant for who you are."

"What is it for?"

"What?"

"Clothing. I don't understand. It only separates us from touch, hides us from each other."

"No, but sometimes we need protection. We need warmth, too, and something to speak our spirits, like a shield that says who we are, what we want and what we don't want. That's what clothing is, for me anyway. It's like art, you know?" And there is something in her hesitant inflection that reminds Lonely of Fawn.

They begin hopping along the stones, following the river back home. The sound of the water is comforting. It knows exactly where it's going.

"People are the only naked ones," Chelya continues a little later. "Trees have their leaves, and animals have their fur. I think people come naked so they can decide for themselves what they want to wear. That's what's so special about being human—being able to create and make choices about who we are. Don't you think?"

"Yes," answers Lonely, remembering the abyss of Coyote's breath, holding her virginity—all the creative potential of her body's love—safe inside her now. She feels relieved to walk in the pleasant, easy aura of Chelya's presence. "I do."

After Chelya says goodnight, Lonely lies down alone next to the river near the house, and masturbates right away. The orgasm feels small and silly but necessary. Then she sleeps instantly in the warm night, curling her body close to the sound of the water, whose sound reminds her of the first innocent days of her journey. She dreams wildly for what seems like all night, but when she wakes she only remembers the last dream: a steady, single-frame dream in which she is sitting in a field across from her prince, the two of them lightly holding hands.

"That wasn't you," she says to him. "Was it?"

He smiles, his face open like a boy's. She remembers him from so long ago, longer than she's been alive. "I am the only man," he says, "and you are the only woman. Nothing else is real."

Then he draws her inward with his spiraling eyes, and she knows that he is everything, everywhere; she knows that every time she makes love with her body, whether by touching another or by taking food and water into her mouth, she is making love to him. Everything else is only another expression of him, and her longing for it only another expression of her love for him, and one day she will cleave against him in his original form, and know what it feels like to fit perfectly.

She begins to cry. "There's so much I have to tell you," she says. "I've journeyed so far, and I have a new story now, about being the daughter of a magician who is destroying the earth. They changed my name to 'Lonely', and it hurts."

He squeezes her hands. "I know," he says, his voice stretching out to her, reaching for her. "I miss you. When will you come?"

She wakes up crying. She has known him since the beginning of time, since before any of this happened. She must go to him, immediately. And she remembers, she has another name. Lonely is not her real name; it is something else, a name she always had, more real than this one, in a life more real than this one, that started long ago. She would recognize it the way she recognized the drumbeats and the birdsong, if she heard it. She knew the name in her dream. She remembers knowing it—that deep confidence within her, that certainty in who she was and her place in the world and her connection with everything, as she held her true love's hands.

But she can't remember it now.

Delilah doesn't know what happened to her after she walked away from Dragon's boiling lair that night, and she doesn't want to think about it.

But what happened is that she hardened up inside—hardened until she is even harder than she was before. Whatever bloomed inside her with the wonder of the white goddess girl who so briefly passed through—Delilah didn't know what to do with that, and so it shriveled, and around it thickened a layer of shame that she refused to acknowledge. And around that hardened the belief that she could never be like that girl, could never be anything but what she was. That belief was all she had to cover her shame with. And around that belief hardened forgetting.

She forgets Dragon. She never thinks of him. She goes on living her life as she always has. It's such a relief.

And yet that isn't entirely true.

She cannot forget him, not really. Moon's visit made her forget for a little while, but now that Moon is gone, she cannot ignore the fact that her world is undeniably changed. She no longer has the desert all to herself. Somewhere out there, in this wide and blessedly empty universe of soft blown sand, another person is existing every day. Every day living. Every day walking this dust, every night breathing this cold starry air.

She can feel him out there. He made his home there, in the dragon caves where before only strange men came, pillaging. Dragon.

"No," she whispers to herself in the morning, washing her face in the pool, accidentally thinking of him. What the hell is he doing? It never occurred to her that he could live here, too. That anyone, besides she, could make a home here.

Sometimes she imagines herself walking back there, throwing stones into the water until he rises from it, and then demanding an explanation. But of what? All she knows is that it's not okay. This is not okay.

She finds herself having cruel fantasies. She lures him out of his lair, wet and steaming, and she's wearing just the little brown skirt of leather he first saw her in, and his jaw hangs open, and he is hard already, of course. She tells him she will teach him to be a lover. She'll teach him how to go slow. She'll teach him what that girl wanted. She teases him. She makes him touch her in all the ways she wants to be touched, and she doesn't let him get inside her, and she doesn't even let him touch himself, not until he's satisfied her. Only then will she let him satisfy himself. She will teach him….

She catches herself smiling as she stares out, unseeing, at the horizon. Then she realizes what she's thinking, realizes that her fantasy is no longer cruel, but hungry, and her own horrified fury at herself makes her curse out loud.

She keeps thinking he's going to come back, and she plots how she will refuse him. Because he's going to get desperate again, eventually, knowing him. But the nights pass, and worst of all the days, and the moon is waning again. And he doesn't come.

The hope of the high blue mountain, which seemed a perfect promise from the top of a tower long ago, is no longer simple to Lonely. Untold mazes of rugged dark forest stand between here and there, and she fears the loneliness in between. The nightmare of that inevitable, humming blackness below the island has returned, and she does not dream of her prince again. In a subterranean cavern within her own self, she doubts for the first time that he is real.

It seemed so clear to her at first, what she was looking for. Those days in the fields coming from the cold sea, she didn't have to think. She moved toward the light like a tree. She moved with the grasses. The wind, though it teased her, felt good. But then she met other humans, other loves, none of whom rest easy in her heart. What if he can only be reached in dreams— that face on the mountaintop?

Two things haunt her, and she cannot reconcile them. First, there is the memory of fire and drums under the moon, ecstasy in the arms of spirits, where her body fell like a river from butterfly wings into the arms of a mountain god, where she passed through the songs of tree goddesses to the face of her prince shining as if the moon looked back at her and made her divine.

Then there is the memory of her wet dress slapping ugly against her legs, and Rye's cold dry back moving before her, and the dead animals—forever dead—in his bloodstained hand.

He did not turn around that afternoon; he did not look back again. They returned to the house, and they ate the animals, and Lonely—even throughout that night of passionate spirits—was still human. For the first time, she had seen that killing. She had seen what it took for her to live.

It has taken her a while to recover that other memory, from underneath the memory of fire and drums and body-joy. It has taken her this long to realize that this memory—of the dead rabbits in Rye's hand, the hand that would never touch her—is the reason she can no longer fully believe in her dreams. She watched those hands, all the way home. Those hands, and Fawn's, made the life she lived. Those hands asked her, *What more do you want, than these things I have killed for you?* There is a sorrow in each day now. As eating once made the structure of the days, now sorrow also makes their substance, and there is a sense of obligation, too, crushing and impossible to understand.

Now it rains for many days—more days, says Fawn, than it should ever rain in the middle of summer. Almost every day from morning until evening, the whole family is out in the gardens, trying to rescue drowning crops. Plants that Lonely spent days carefully sowing and tending with Fawn are broken from their stems by the deluge, or washed away in the mud. Watching it happen makes Lonely feel a kind of despair, but Fawn and her family do the best they can. They bale out the puddles. They cover the new rows. They build up the soil and start again. Sometimes they can't do anything, and they sit inside and keep busy, trying not to think about the loss that is happening right now, constantly. When they enter through the front room of the house, their feet are underwater.

Sometimes Lonely goes out to the fields alone and sits in the rain, feeling lonely, hating herself for feeling sorry for herself, imagining she will wash away and never have to feel anything again. She stares out at the mountain until she can't think any more, until Chelya finds her and, without asking questions, offers her hand.

The day the sky finally clears, Chelya is wild with joy. "Come on!" she says to Lonely, when she finally finds her. "My uncle's family has come!"

Lonely stands for as long as possible in the shadowy kitchen near the back door, waiting for her eyes and emotions to adjust to the explosion of so many people into this small space. Several moments pass before she can differentiate and count them, amidst the blur of their surprising noise and laughter and all that touching.

The touch between Rye and Jay is firm and quick, their hands sounding hard against each other's backs, as if at once both testing and admiring the sturdy structure of each other's manhood. The hug between Fawn and Jay's wife, Willow, is so softly complete, at once full and whispered, that Lonely wonders if she might not need the love she thought she was searching for—if only she had that. The hug between Willow and Chelya is tight and fast and laughing, and Jay hugs Fawn and Chelya both at the same time, at the same time that Willow is hugging Kite, and Kite is standing awkwardly in her arms and looking away. Chelya is the first to bend down and open her arms to two little boys, smaller than any human Lonely has ever seen. The smaller one throws his arms around Chelya, while the taller one leans shyly into the edge of her embrace.

"…Lonely." Someone is saying her name. She hears it more by the silence afterward than by the word itself, which she has become used to now. All of their faces turn toward her at once. For some reason it is Willow's that catches Lonely's eye first, quiet and appraising. Willow is beautiful in a different way than Fawn. There is no innocence, nothing childish in that face. Her skin is rough, her hair rough, her eyebrows thick and rough, but the contour of her face is smooth. Instead of fear or confusion in that face, Lonely sees a knowing but suspicious curiosity, as if perhaps Willow does not believe that *Lonely* is her name at all.

But it is the littlest boy who breaks the silence. "Are you a goddess?" Lonely can feel the familiar tension clenching the bodies behind him when he says the word, and she is aware of fourteen eyes watching her. But she is comforted by the trust of the boy, who walks to her now with his belly leading him. She thinks suddenly of Delilah, the way her head and shoulders led her, and even Kite, the way he hunches over his own chest, pressing it slightly behind him as he walks. This is the first she understands of children: adults lead with their heads, children with their bellies.

"What's your name?" she asks the boy instead of answering him.

"Morgan," he answers readily. "And my brother is Blue. And I'm going to have a little brother soon, and then I won't be the littlest any more."

"Oh, well," says Willow. "There goes our surprise." And then again there is so much laughter and touch and crying out that Lonely is forgotten. But she will remember later that it was the child who broke down the wall between her and them. If it hadn't been for Morgan, with his happy belly leading him, they might have stood there forever in the doorway, staring coldly at her, shocked by her presence—and explanations would have been required, right then and there, and those explanations would never have been sufficient.

She goes out to draw water from the stream, and takes her time, knowing no one will come into the greenhouse to talk—it's too hot. Then she gathers wood for cooking, even though Rye has already brought some in. For the first time she wishes she could be old and left to her own space like Eva, hidden away in her home in the hillside, not expected by anyone until she decides to come out. How she longs now for that cool darkness.

By the time she returns, Chelya is outside chasing the boys and jumping out at them from the tall grass, and Rye, Kite, and Jay are examining the tools and blades that Jay brought. Fawn and Willow are sitting on the floor of the main room giggling. Lonely has never seen Fawn smile so constantly, her hand circling over Willow's belly.

"Can I start dinner?" Lonely asks. She's hungry and suddenly irritable. She wants to be doing something, so she doesn't have to wonder how to interact and with whom.

Willow looks at her again with that strange and distant curiosity, and Fawn looks surprised. Too late, Lonely realizes it wasn't her place. Fawn will decide when the cooking begins. It is Fawn's home, Fawn's gift to give. Lonely has nothing to give. She remembers again that she is an intruder here, an outsider. She looks down, away from the fleeting shadow that passes over Fawn's face, wishing herself gone.

"Come sit with us," comes Willow's deep voice.

Lonely sits, feeling much younger than they are, envious of Willow's easy, brash grace. She looks down at Willow's belly. She knows what pregnancy is. She has seen it in the goats, and Chelya has explained it to her. But she can't believe it when she sees it in a human being, and doesn't know whether or not she herself came in such a way. Who was her mother? The question makes her own belly ache. That glowing ball. That peaceful ruminating, the beginning of a world inside. Lonely stares at it.

"So you are a traveler?" asks Willow, and Lonely can feel the real questions, unasked, and they hurt. She glances up at Willow and looks away. She can tell, from the way others look at her, that eye contact is expected, and yet it overwhelms her. When she looks into someone's eyes, she sees the whole world at once, and cannot remember anything specific enough to say. Only Fawn avoids her eyes too, which makes it easier for Lonely to know her.

"Yes," she answers Willow shortly. Then she adds, "They took me in. They are letting me stay—I don't know how long." She glances at Fawn. "I am very grateful." But she feels she will cry, especially when she sees something like pity—though distant and pensive—in Fawn's eyes looking back at her. She feels how desperately she needs them, how in every way they have rescued and filled her, at least in every way but that one.

"There are so few of us left in these mountains," Willow says, nodding. "So much has been taken from us that it can be difficult, sometimes, to let others in." It seems to Lonely that she says this more for Fawn's benefit than for hers. "But Fawn is very generous. And long ago, we took *her* in." At this Willow takes Fawn's hand, and Fawn looks right back at her and smiles.

"What do you mean?" asks Lonely, feeling thin and empty, looking at the comfortable abundance that is Fawn and trying to imagine her, one day long ago, feeling the same as she does now.

At this moment, Blue comes wandering in through the greenhouse and comes to sit beside his mother. He is silent, but once he leans his head against his mother's body, he has the courage to look up into Lonely's eyes, and after that he keeps staring. His eyes are simple and pale like crystal, neither kind nor unkind, interested nor distant. They settle down on Lonely and rest there, watching her, and do not leave her. They remind Lonely of his mother's eyes, and it is those connections —between mother and child, father and mother—that both fascinate and pain her to see.

"When my mother and I came into the mountains," Fawn explains to Lonely, "they took us in."

"We all grew up together," Willow adds, shifting her weight. She seems to relax a little, as if sensing the ease that Fawn and Blue feel with Lonely. "I lived with my family on a farm very close to Jay and Rye's farm, and I was over there playing with them all the time. Neither of our families gave up their farms or surrendered to the City life, when so many others did. And Jay, Fawn, and I were all the same age. We spent our whole childhood together."

"But what about Rye?" Lonely asks.

"He's older," says Willow. "When we were children, he was already a young man, and even as a teenager he had this wanderlust. He'd disappear for months at a time, traveling to other parts of the mountains to see what farms were left, trying to convince the other farmers to stay, even venturing near the City though I don't think he ever went in."

"But I didn't want to go anywhere, ever again, once I got here," says Fawn quietly. "I felt like I was finally safe."

"When he was twenty-one years old," continues Willow, "he came back to us after having been gone for a couple of years." She turns and strokes Blue's head thoughtfully, and Lonely learns something else about children: their presence is pure love, and can comfort an adult in moments of sadness. "His family had thought he might be gone forever," she says slowly, still looking down at Blue's head, "and his mother had died never knowing that he was still alive."

Then they are all silent, and Blue looks up anxiously at his mother's face, which is a little damp around the eyes. "I'm sorry," she says to Fawn. "I'm so emotional lately. It's the pregnancy." Fawn shakes her head forgivingly and takes Blue's hand, as if he is an extension of Willow. Willow continues. "He came back to tell us that he was going to the City, to try to make some change there, to try to bring the farmers back to their true lives. But when he found his mother had died, he fell into such grief."

"He understood, finally," says Fawn firmly. "He couldn't keep leaving." Lonely listens. They seem to be telling a story they have not told themselves for a long time, and they are telling it more for themselves than for her. They are telling their own explanation of how the world is, what is right and what is wrong.

"But actually," says Willow, "what made him stay this time after all, and change his plan to go off to the City, was that he fell in love with Fawn. She was fifteen then, and he saw that beauty she'd tried to keep hidden for so long, finally blooming."

Fawn blushes; Willow smiles.

"So then he courted her for a few years. He didn't rush her, because she was so young. But when she was eighteen, she got pregnant with Chelya, and Rye said he would make a home for her and Eva and their child. Then they started this place here." She looks back at Lonely. "So you see. We took Fawn and Eva in once, and both Rye and Fawn can feel, I think, how much it means to take someone in when they have nowhere else to go. How you can save a life that way."

But Lonely is thinking of Rye, and the romance of this story. There is no way she can come in between them—ever. This story is as firm as earth. What is it within her that wants to break it all apart? What evil would make her long for this?

"I worry that Kite is like Rye in this way," Fawn says. "He has this longing to wander, to see new worlds. To see the City. Even Rye still has this longing, though he keeps it hidden for my sake, for our family's sake. You cannot be a farmer and also a traveler. But Kite—he's at that age now. I worry," she sighs. "I worry so much, Willow."

"You always worry," says Willow, stroking her back. "Have you told him the story of what happened when Rye left?"

"Yes, but it doesn't matter to him. He is young. He thinks none of that has to do with him. Young people think the actions of their parents and their ancestors have nothing to do with them."

"That's not true," cries Lonely, too suddenly. "I mean sometimes they feel those actions but they—they just don't know what to do with that. It's so much pressure, so much responsibility. Maybe he needs a little freedom to work things out for himself."

"How do I not give him freedom?" Fawn turns to her sharply, and though she never expresses anger openly, Lonely feels sorry. "He can be whoever he wants to be."

Lonely turns awkwardly away from Fawn's stare, and is rescued by the loud, bumpy entrance of the men and boys.

"Isn't anyone around here hungry?" asks Rye.

There are times, living here, when Lonely thinks the end of all loneliness is somewhere in the circle a family makes around food in the evening. Would she have ever begun to feel lonely, if she and her father had known what it was to hunger, and had come together each night to join themselves with the bodies of other beings in this way? She had not even known day and night. She had not been a part of anything. Earth and sky had not joined in her. There was only her father and his sorrow.

Around the blanket on the grass where the food is laid out today, Lonely tries to understand all the different kinds of love. She sees the way the little boys, more than anyone else at the table, love their food. She sees the way Eva teases the boys, and the almost clumsy, happy way that youth stumbles out of her in their presence. She is telling them about invisible colors that surround them; Morgan easily believes, and Blue doesn't want to but looks tempted. Morgan is continually boasting about his baby brother who isn't born yet, certain that it's a boy, because that's what he wants, and Lonely also sees this kind of love: the love of a child that arises from desire, that decides what it loves before it even meets the object of that love. Though Lonely has never met a child before, that kind of love feels familiar. It makes her twist a little inside. Anxious, she wants to tell Morgan that the baby might be a girl.

She sees the love of the boys for Kite, who loves them because they admire him—because they make him feel like a man whenever he can lift something they can't lift or explain something to them like how he and Rye placed the traps for the rabbits they're eating tonight. She sees the tenderness of Willow for Kite as she watches him talk to her sons, and the laughter that relaxes Fawn when Morgan takes down her hair while she eats because it is prettier that way, and the way Blue always wants to sit next to Chelya, and the way Chelya and Willow whisper together, and all the serious, interested questions Jay asks Kite about the projects he's working on. She also sees hints of loves not expressed at all—like the way Jay looks at Fawn, every now and then, with a glance so brief that no one but Lonely, who is quieter than the rest, would notice. She sees Rye's hunger to be near his brother, the subtle surrender of his gratitude in being among their larger family again, and the hint of a loneliness, or a restlessness, that Lonely never noticed in him before but which makes her want him all the more. She thinks of him wandering all those years, before he fell in love with Fawn. She wonders what he was searching for, and if he knew he needed love. She wonders if his body and heart hungered the way hers do now, or if he searched for something else—something she will never know.

She assesses Jay, this new example of manhood, for she can stare openly at both him and Rye now in a way she cannot do normally, so distracted are they by their conversation, so oblivious to her. Jay is shorter than Rye, and shorter than Willow, but the muscles in his arms are bigger than Lonely could reach around with the fingers of both her hands. His palms are black, his face is darker and more rugged than Rye's, and he hardly smiles at all. But when he finally does, that smile is so innocent, so boyish, so incongruous with his heavy face, that she realizes it is only shyness that keeps him serious. He was more animated before when he showed Rye the tools than in the midst of conversation and discussion, not like he's unhappy now, but like he doesn't have that many words inside of him. Once, when he glances toward Lonely, as if feeling her gaze, he gives her a simple, polite nod and turns back to his food.

The children are the center of life at the table. Lonely smiles in wonder as she watches them. She hopes they will not turn their dazzling, knowing eyes her way, and at the same time she wishes they would. She sees the most primal hues of each emotion in their bodies and faces: joy and fascination, hurt and anger, hope and wariness, played out in quick succession as fluidly as their soft limbs turn. Morgan, five years old, makes exaggerated faces for each feeling—one moment tightening all his features together in mock rage when Kite pretends to steal his bowl of strawberries, and the next moment beaming up at Fawn in love-struck joy as he throws himself down on his back in her lap. Lonely thinks that perhaps he is trying out each emotion for size, and she watches the experiment with wonder. In that tiny body his spirit seems so big, so much to contain. In Blue it is his wisdom that seems bigger than his body—or something like wisdom that Lonely imagines in his silent attention to everything, his skepticism, his curious staring every time she speaks, as if, like Willow, he knows she is hiding.

At first she listens with interest to everything they have to say. She learns about an animal Jay's family raises called sheep, which provide wool, from which Willow makes much of the clothing for the whole family. She learns that fire also shapes metal, and that Jay works with that fire to make cooking pots and knives and Rye's tools out of those hardest of substances, copper and iron; this skill, Lonely thinks, explains the hard, quiet intensity in his eyes. She learns, as they plan for the birth and talk of Eva's healing skills, that they worry what will happen when Eva is gone and they know no other healers. Willow had an older brother and a younger sister, who both died when she was a child. Lonely learns, through the family's discussion of the river, that they suspect those children died from a sickness that was carried in the water—a sickness from the rains, which held the poison of the City. She learns the fear that they live with, that this could happen again.

"I know some things," murmurs Fawn, "that my mother has taught me, but I do not know much." She bows her head, and Eva lays a hand upon hers.

"You know very much, Fawn."

Fawn shakes her head. "There is no need to reassure me." She looks up suddenly at the others. "I have not lived here as long as the rest of you. I wish sometimes that I had something to give, the way Rye works with wood, and Jay with metal, and Willow with wool."

Willow laughs. "Fawn," she says, not looking at her, "you give so much. It's funny what you say, like asking what the mountain gives."

There is a pocket of silence then, in which Lonely hears the wind turning over thoughtfully.

Rye nods. "It feels sometimes as you've been here longer than the rest of us, Fawn. When you came here, the mountains took you right into them, as if they knew you."

Jay nods, too, staring at Fawn, and his jaw tightens a little. Fawn refuses to look up. "Please," she says.

Chelya laughs. "Let's talk about something else," she says. "Ma's embarrassed."

At first Lonely is grateful to find how little attention they all pay to her. The food is so important. Their joy with each other is important. They see each other so rarely that the excitement of being together outweighs the interest of a new person, or so she supposes.

But she also feels that, despite Willow's warm conversation in the house, which never was for Lonely anyway, but more a story she enjoyed with Fawn, they're afraid of her, like Fawn was in the beginning. And Lonely is thinking about other things too, things that make her sad. She listens to them update each other on which crops got ruined, and discuss how hard it will be to stay fed all winter. She hears in those quiet, determined calculations that she, Lonely, must go. She, who is not even human. She, who never knew what it was to eat before she came here.

She discovers jealousy for the first time. Until she came to this place, she'd never in her life been with another person without being the sole object of that person's attention. Now she watches Fawn and sees how little she means to her in comparison with her family. She sees how Rye never glances at her now, with curiosity or kindness or hidden desire, like he did before. She sits open-mouthed with this new feeling—a crude, painful feeling that makes her throat sore, a feeling that, unlike hunger, cannot be soothed—and forgets her food for moments at a time. She tries to distract herself by looking around at the sunset hills, watching her horse graze peacefully in the distance, as if he doesn't need anyone.

"They've started building on Willow's land," Jay is saying now.

Fawn puts her fork down and stares. "Oh, Willow. You didn't say—"

"What are they building?" asks Rye.

"Homes," says Willow, looking down as she eats, the shine gone out of her face. "The kind where people live in boxes and never see each other, and they have to clear all the trees, not for growing crops but so they can see places far away and feel like kings. Like lonely kings."

"That's why they wanted that land," growls Jay. "Because it was up high. They probably don't care about the springs that start there. The whole river will be polluted with their waste."

"Or maybe it will be one of those enormous homes, just for one family. These people have to live indoors, you know? They're forever expanding their houses, trying to build enough rooms to hold the whole world without ever having to go outside. Why don't they come outside? The whole world is right here." Willow's attempted smile is broken by an old, rueful anger.

The children are silent now, Morgan frowning and Blue sitting very still. Chelya leans across the table to Lonely and tells her in a low voice, "Willow and Jay used to live with Willow's parents on the farm Willow grew up on. But a few years ago the people from the City made them leave, took it over, and destroyed it. Now they all live where Dad and Jay grew up—they fixed up the old place where Dad's parents used to live."

Lonely nods. She tries to understand what Chelya is describing, but she's still stuck on this idea of family, stuck on the word "parents," trying to imagine another family connected with this one, and another, and webs of connected people expanding ever outward.

"We can hear it from our house," says Willow, her voice flat. "The machines."

"Oh, Willow," says Fawn again.

Willow looks up as if surprised, and smiles. Then she puts her hands in her lap, then lifts them up again, touches the corners of her eyes, and glances away.

"Oh, well," she says. "It's not like I had to move far. I'm still home in the mountains that love me. I'm with my family. I'm more at home than those people in their big boxes will probably ever feel."

"Do you ever go back there to see?" says Chelya.

Willow nods. "But I haven't been for a while," she says.

"I go," grumbles Jay. "They won't keep me off." Lonely sees Blue imitate his expression, jabbing his greens with his fork, and turn inward to mysterious child thoughts. His silence reminds her of Kite now.

"What if we go try to talk to them?" asks Rye.

"Rye—" Fawn begins.

"Why not?"

Jay looks up, eyes darkened, and waits for Rye to continue.

"I think we need to make connections. Remember we're all human. We all need homes, we all have families we need to protect. Why can't we understand each other?"

"Good question," grumbles Jay.

Morgan, restless, has crawled around the blanket to sit next to Lonely. Folding his limbs in a little pile in front of him, he pushes himself softly up against her, falling halfway into her lap and leaning his head against her breasts. Lonely begins to cry.

She's not making any sound and she's looking down so they won't see, but

Eva, the only person who can be aware of everything at once, and who is sitting next to her anyway, places her hand firmly on Lonely's back. Lonely doesn't know why she is crying, when none of this is about her, and Willow is the one who ought to be comforted, and she doesn't know why Eva is holding her, but, at the touch of Eva's hand, she begins to cry so hard she can no longer keep it silent. She sounds as if she is choking. Everyone stops and looks at her. Only Morgan doesn't seem bothered at all. He just snuggles in deeper as if this yielding to emotion is the deepest, most comfortable place for him to be. But Eva, with a gesture so subtle that Lonely doesn't really see it, lifts Lonely's arm and leads her away.

They go around to the side of the house and sit in the last rays of sunlight on a couple of stumps by the woodshed. Lonely cries and cries, relieved to be with the one person who she knows doesn't need an explanation. In fact, maybe she can give Lonely one.

"Why am I crying?" she asks finally, between hiccuping breaths.

"Oh, I don't know," says Eva with a deep sigh. "Because you feel alone. Because you have no family. Because everyone is ignoring you."

"But that sounds so selfish."

"Well. That's what needs are. They're selfish. That's okay."

They keep sitting together, Lonely resting in the hopeless bliss of release. The wind pounces in sudden bursts through the grass, nudging at her heart, and she realizes how long it's been since she's listened to it.

"The wind talks to me," she says to Eva suddenly, "when I have no one else."

Eva nods. "That makes sense. Spirit of air."

Lonely wants her to say more, to explain the wind and what it means, and why it makes her lonely even while it takes the loneliness away, but she doesn't know how to ask.

"I had this dream," she tells Eva, "about my prince."

She looks at Eva, and when Eva doesn't answer, she adds, "He's the one I'm searching for. He's the one I have to find. He's waiting for me. I don't know where he is, except that I think—I feel I need to go to that mountain, that high mountain in the east. But I don't understand why he doesn't come for me." She shakes her head, her heart pounding now that she's finally spoken it aloud. "Maybe he's not even real," she adds, but that makes the tears start to flow again.

"Maybe he doesn't know yet that he needs you," says Eva.

Lonely looks up fast, breathless. "But he said, in the dream, that he missed me, that he needed me."

A light smile twirls the corners of Eva's lips, and she looks at Lonely. She seems in no hurry to answer. Sparrows converse over their heads, and the breeze makes a hollow sound in Lonely's ears. The weight of Eva's thoughtful stare keeps her anchored to the ground, holding her restlessness at bay as she waits for a response. For a moment she can see this other way of looking at life—the way you look at it, maybe, if you are very old—as if life were simply a fascinating story, even in its pains and sorrows, that you are ever delighting in figuring out and piecing together, playfully wondering what comes next.

"When a person comes to you in a dream," says Eva finally, "he doesn't always realize that he has come to you. His waking self may not even know. What came to you in the dream might be a message his soul wants to send to you, of which he himself is not aware. We have dream selves that act separately, sometimes, from our waking selves."

When Lonely doesn't answer, she adds, "Maybe his spirit is speaking on behalf of his real self, asking you to come rescue *him*."

"From what?" asks Lonely, frightened.

Eva smiles and says nothing. They sit for what seems a long time to Lonely, whose heart is tightening again with urgency.

"I need to find him," she says.

"Yes," says Eva, still smiling. "But you *are* loved here, too, just not in the way that you want." She pauses. "I wasn't sure if you knew that."

Lonely looks down, trying to take nourishment from those words. She feels selfish for keeping Eva away from the meal, but she needs her so badly. Eva looks to the side, off toward the high mountain; its snowy peak looks impossible in the heat of the day.

"There is a legend of a certain people still living on those high peaks," she says thoughtfully. "Or perhaps not people exactly. Perhaps spirits, or gods, or ghosts."

Lonely reaches out without thinking and grasps Eva's hand. It is soft and hard at once, the veins warm and ropy against her fingers. Real, just as the old woman by the sea said that Lonely's hand felt real, when she reached out and grasped it. Without surprise, Eva turns back to her, her hand steady, not pulling away.

"Tell me," says Lonely.

"They were the first people," says Eva. "They were the original people, the ones who remembered, who lived at the heart of the world. Who understood what life is and what it is for. Who understood the Earth and our part in its cycle." She pauses. "They didn't die, exactly. But they would not be ruled. They transformed themselves into animals, spirits, or some kind of—others. We call them the Dream People, who became like dreams instead of real people, hiding in a world close to the sky, where they could never be captured or destroyed. Some say they are behind those most powerful, life-changing dreams that call us back to our deepest selves, that they still dream for us and keep our dreams alive."

"But are they real?" *If he isn't real, then I am not real. Nothing is real, if the dream that keeps me alive is not real.*

"No one knows. No one has ever found them, of course. They are not in a form that can be found. Besides, no one has been able to climb that mountain, the highest one. It is difficult even to get close to it. And when you get close, there is no way up."

Yet something in Eva's face keeps Lonely from despair. Eva is looking toward the mountain again. "But you've been there," Lonely whispers.

Eva is silent for a moment. "I have been close," she answers. "When I first came into the wilderness, from the City, I was afraid. I had Fawn with me and I did not know how we would survive. I came to the base of that mountain and prayed and prayed. I was young, so when I prayed I was only begging—begging to be saved somehow by these Dream People I had heard of, to be taken to some magical land where we wouldn't have to struggle with hunger and fear and cold. I was so passionate, so romantic, like Chelya— only with less sense than she has, because I had no one to guide me.

"I was delirious, and Fawn cried with hunger day and night. But I started dreaming. Animals came to me in my dreams, teaching me things: plants I could eat, how to catch fish with my hands like the bears. I knew how to make a fire. Still, it wasn't easy to survive. We lived for a long time barely making it, in the little tent I'd brought with us in the lower, warmer mountains, before we eventually met Rye's family, who took us in and taught us how to live off the land.

"Through those dreams and those first moons of hard survival, I understood that the Earth was calling me back to Herself. That my place was here, a human being in a physical, tangible world, and that the learning of my soul had to come through my body's trials of survival. It wouldn't come by escaping to some dreamworld. Instead, the dreams came to me, helping me to live better in reality.

"So Lonely, I don't know why that mountain calls to you, or what your prince has to do with it. Perhaps there is a way for you to go there that I could not find, that was not right for me. Or perhaps there is something for you to discover in the journey itself—simply in *trying* to go there—as there was for me. All you can do is follow where your heart leads you, and sometimes there is no point in asking questions. Certainly I am not the one who knows the answers." She meets Lonely's gaze pointedly, as if recognizing the demand in Lonely's eyes. Almost everyone's eyes in this family are shades between green and brown. But like Blue's eyes, Eva's eyes are a painful shade of blue. They burn like ice. They seem to look right through Lonely, and they make her feel naked inside, as if she herself is made of glass.

Lonely sighs. The wind starts up, roiling around her. Is that a sign? Is it saying she's headed in the right direction? She glances back toward the table, where the others sit talking and forgetting her. How easy their life seems to her, with everything they need right here.

Eva clasps her hand, which was drifting away, and pulls her attention back. "No one else knows your path, Lonely," she repeats, as if she can read Lonely's thoughts. "Only you. When you ask the same question over and over, it is only to avoid what you already know you must do."

4th MOON

She tells herself she's just out walking. She always goes walking on the new moon, to stretch away the pain in her womb. And this is where she's often walked before, past the dragon caves, and she's not going to stop doing it because of Dragon.

When she stops at the edge of the billowing steam, hidden behind the stone, she tells herself it's because she needs to know what's going on in her territory. She lives all alone out here. She needs to know who's around and what they're doing, in order to survive.

But her body aches, and she has to crouch down for a moment. Tendrils of the steam reach her unbidden and soften the skin of her face. From a safe distance, she watches the bubbles arise from themselves in sleepy meditation. She watches until she is sure—she can feel it—that he is no longer here.

And in the moment when she knows that, when she ought to feel utter relief, instead the pain gets worse than ever before. It gets so bad she can't think. She can't remember where she is. All she wants is to be home in the safe darkness of her cave, wrapped in her blankets, her familiar old animal scents, but she is doubled over and cannot even raise herself up. It's never been like this before. Usually the pain of new moon bleeding makes her hot and restless. Now for the first time, she is cold and afraid, like a child, and she cannot move.

She barely notices when Dragon lifts her up and carries her in his arms, down into the soft water. She tells herself she's dreaming, so she won't have to hate herself for not fighting it.

When she opens her eyes in a cavern of dim, warm air—some magical chamber inside the water, shifty with the echoes of water's reflections like the flickering memory of fire, like the inside of an organ surrounded by hot swirling blood—the muscles in every part of her body seem to have relaxed.

"Where are we?" There seems to be more space inside her body than there was before. She's too curious and too weak to feel angry yet, though she can feel that her head rests in his lap, and she's not sure how it got there. Her hips and legs are supported by a smooth floor like limestone or hardened lava. Dragon's fingers grace the edges of her face, the sides of her neck, her shoulder bones. He feels different somehow than she remembers him; there is something wise and protective about the frame of his body around her. He feels more like a man than a boy. But he is behind her. She can't actually see his face, and she doesn't want to.

"This is where I was first raised," he answers her finally, his voice still distant and unsmiling. "For the first six years of my life."

"In this boiling water?"

"No. There was no water then. Back then, there were only dark caves of fire. That's where the dragons lived, until they had to descend into the earth, and leave me behind. I've come here since then, but the caves were empty. Then one day, while I was wandering the desert, after Yora left me, I came here again. And there was water. Just like this. Water bubbling up from fire. I don't understand it. But I feel like it's a message from the dragons. I feel like they're sending me a message of love, because water—do you know, Delilah?—water is love. I realize that now. They're telling me this is my home. Even though they're not here, they still love me, and this is my home."

His voice grows more animated as he speaks, and for a moment Delilah wonders if he is insane, because the possibility doesn't seem incongruent with her general sense of him. But he is a god, after all, or at least partly one, so maybe he really was raised by dragons.

"I know what you mean," she says, "about home." She's surprised at how relaxed she feels, maybe from sheer helplessness after days of pain. Or maybe it's this place, which doesn't make any sense—like a dry womb inside the water—but she's too tired to care. She'll only rest here for a moment. Only for a moment, before she leaves …

"Delilah, why did you come to the desert? Where did you come from?"

Delilah starts. Apparently she fell asleep, and his voice woke her.

"Please tell me," says Dragon.

"Why."

"Because I love you."

Delilah is silent. *Here we go again.* She wants to tell him off and get up, but she doesn't do either. She feels so tired.

"I do love you," he repeats. "You're like a hummingbird."

"Are you kidding me?"

"Have you ever met a hummingbird?"

"Yeah, there's hummingbirds in the desert."

"But have you ever hung out with one?"

"Not really."

"You are like them," Dragon insists. "I used to see them all the time in the Garden where I grew up. I used to watch them. They're really tough, like you—even though they're tiny. They take lots of lovers. They love to make love and they're messengers of love between the flowers, too. They're always hungry, like you, because they're always moving—lots of energy, like fire. See?"

"Dragon, you're a romantic. You don't get me. I'm not loving. I eat nothing but meat, and I'm always angry."

"But you are like that, like a hummingbird, in your spirit. That's how you are inside. That's how you would be if you didn't have so much pain. That's how you were when I first saw you, touching yourself outside your cave and laughing at me. Shimmering and bright like a hummingbird."

Delilah is silent. She notices that she's been playing with one of his hands, rubbing his fingers between her own. She lets it go, embarrassed. All she can feel is her own blood flowing out of her. Though in reality it is only a few drops, it feels to her like a river that will never stop. How can Dragon not feel it? Isn't it everywhere, flooding the cave? The death of possible life flows out of her, as senseless as the death of each creature she kills to sustain her one, meaningless life. There is something wrong with her that she lives alone out here in the desert forever. There is something wrong with her that no man can make her come. There is something wrong with her that she doesn't want a child, that she wants to be fed again and again by the bodies of men but never give up her own life up for anyone else. There is something wrong with this desire that can never, ever be filled.

"Tell me who you really are. Tell me where you come from."

"My past is *not* who I am," snaps Delilah.

"Maybe it's what's keeping you from who you are then. Tell me anyway."

He's peaceful and calm now because I'm helpless, she thinks. *Because I've let him carry me here, and that makes him feel manly or something. Because I'm being vulnerable. If I fought him again, tried to run from him, he wouldn't seem so mature and wise any more. When I'm ready to leave, he'd better fucking let me out.*

"Why did I come here," she repeats after him bitterly. "Because there was nothing left for me in the City, nothing holding me there. That's why." She doesn't say, *They had taken my sister away. That was the last person I cared about. Nothing mattered any more.*

"What was your home like, in the City?"

She sighs. "I was at this boarding school. My mother sent us—my mother sent me there after my father died. My father died of a drug overdose, and my mother didn't want me any more." *There*, she thinks. *That's about it.*

"Tell me about him."

"Why?"

"Please. What are you afraid of?"

"I'm not afraid of anything. He was really unhappy. He didn't love me. I made him even more unhappy."

"How?"

"I don't know. I worried him. Upset him. He used to say I'd come to no good. Too much fire in me. Always getting into trouble. My dark skin, I think—" She sighs again. "It was weird. Even though he was dark, even though I got it from him, I think he wanted me to turn out more like my mother, who was pale." *And more like Mira,* she thinks, *whom he loved. Whom he taught all his secrets to. Maybe even his magic.* "He was probably afraid because he knew what happens to dark people. Their lives don't end up well. Bad things happen to them, in the City at least. They're feared. That's what sucks about the City. It makes a man like my father, who was once a respected shaman among his own people, fear that part of himself that the pale people hate— want to erase it, in himself and in his children."

"Why do people hate the darkness?"

"Fear. Everyone's afraid of the dark."

"Are you afraid of it, too?"

"Are you fucking kidding me?"

"No."

There is an awkward silence. Delilah holds her own hands in front of her face, and turns them around as if she's interested in them, as if she's looking for something.

"What about your mother?" Dragon asks now. "What was she like?"

"Not much to her. I didn't respect her; I still don't. All she cared about was my father. Her whole life was wrapped around trying to save him from self-destruction, trying to make him happy, trying to ease his pain. My father was a very intense person. Before the City sucked up everything, he was part of a certain people, who, I think, lived out in the desert. But I'm not sure, even. He knew lots of magic, but he didn't use it any more after he lost touch with his people and was forced to work in this meat factory in the City. Then he was just a regular guy. Only he had so much power locked up inside him, it didn't have anywhere to go. So he started to drink and lose himself in drugs. Eventually he destroyed himself that way. And then my mom was a mess. She couldn't even function. It was pathetic. And she didn't want to deal with—me. So she sent me away."

She doesn't know why she's denying Mira's existence like this. She doesn't mean to. It's just too complicated to explain. But no, that isn't it. She's trying to protect Mira somehow, like she always tried to. But she doesn't know why or from what.

"Were you sad when your father died?" asks Dragon, and she can tell he's sad for her, which embarrasses her.

"I don't know," she answers, shrugging into his belly. "I didn't want to be like my mother, wailing and carrying on like an idiot, not caring about anything else but him, like the whole world had ended." She's relieved to find that none of the things she's talking about seem to hurt much any more. She can do this. *Bring it on, Dragon,* she thinks. *See if you can move me. I'm like stone.*

"What's boarding school?"

"It's where they lock you up, and try to make you forget about your body. All they care about is numbers and words. Shows you how much my mother knew about me."

"Right," says Dragon, and she can feel his little laugh. "No one can tell Delilah what to do."

"Right," says Delilah, smiling a little in spite of herself. "There were these bitchy girls there. I was the only dark one, they hated me, etcetera. It's kind of boring to talk about."

"Didn't you have friends? Those kids you made fires and burned things with?"

"Yeah," says Delilah, surprised that he actually paid so much attention to what she said, that night he made the fire for her. "A few kids of other colors, from other peoples that got lost somewhere, like my father's. And other kids, not from the school—whoever was on the outside of things, I guess. But we didn't share anything. We had no loyalty to each other; we just got together to burn things and steal stuff and help each other feel *something.* I was never able to spend a lot of time with them, though, because they did so many drugs, and I didn't do that because I didn't want to end up like my father. So I spent a lot of my time fucking, honestly. That was the only thing that got me through. Boys didn't have a problem with my dark skin when they wanted to get laid. In fact, they liked it then. And I liked sex. Made me feel powerful and alive, you know?" *Helped me block out my sister's empty stare,* is what she doesn't say.

"It made you feel wanted," says Dragon. "Made you feel loved."

That's your trip, Dragon, not mine, she thinks, but she doesn't want to hear about his issues so she only snaps, "Don't psychoanalyze me."

"What?"

"Nevermind."

"So then what happened?"

"Then, like I said, I got fed up. I ran away. I was failing school anyway. I was smart, but I hated my teachers. They didn't understand me. I hated everyone. I don't know how I didn't lose my voice from all the yelling I did in those two years there. I didn't want to be there so I didn't care how much trouble I got into. It made me crazy that nothing I did could get me sent away, maybe because I had nowhere to get sent away to. I never beat anyone up or did something that would put me in jail, though. Anyway, I hadn't heard from my mother in over a year, since she got evicted from our apartment because she couldn't pay the rent anymore. She probably ended up wandering the streets somewhere, or dead, but I didn't want to find her. She never cared about me. My father, at least, disliked me or was afraid of me or something. My mother didn't care at all. So anyway I lived in the streets for a little bit, too, and one day I found myself back on my home street, which was out at the west edge of the City. Of course, I had no home to go back to at this point. But I climbed up the little hill to a meadow overlooking the City, above my street, where we—where I used to play. I looked out, and I saw the desert. I remembered that there was this whole world out there, so much bigger than this reality which I hated. And the desert just looked like the answer. So I decided to go there. And I went."

"That's it? You just went? I'd think any other human would die out here."

Delilah sighs. Whatever. No need to keep everything secret. "Moon helped me."

"That's your lover. The boy who stayed with you a while ago."

Delilah tenses. Was he watching her all that time? Is that jealousy in his voice? "He's not my lover. Moon and I don't have sex."

"Why not?"

"Because he's different. He's my only true friend." She feels a little more interested suddenly. She wants to talk about Moon. She misses him so much, all the time. Now that she's recovering from the pure agony of his initial absence, thinking of him can bring her closer to happiness than almost anything. "I knew Moon since I was little. Like my earliest memories are of him—playing with him up in those same fields, dancing around while he played his flute for me. He was a rain god. By the time I was born there was no more rain in the City, but sometimes rain clouds would still pass over, and we'd hear thunder, and I would always go up into the fields and stand in the wind, hoping that the rains would finally come. Because I'd heard my mother talking to my father about them. They never did come, but Moon came, first by chance, I think, drifting by with the clouds, and then later to see me and play with me, because he could tell I wasn't like other humans. I was way more fun than other kids. He was sweet, and he loved me for who I was and understood me, from the beginning and always. He kept me alive. He made my life worth living when everything else was ugly."

Dragon lets out a gushing breath, something like an "Ooh," but softer. It weirds her out a little, the way he seems to feel viscerally everything she's saying. Maybe more than she herself does. She wants to pull away from him now, but then he asks, "But what happened to him while you were at boarding school? Wasn't he your best friend?"

"No," says Delilah, her voice still even. "I lost him for a long time. It was my fault. I started to get sexual when I was really young. Something about the feeling of touching and being touched like that made me feel—I don't know, anchored to something, and okay somehow. When I wasn't being touched I felt out of control, disconnected from everything and at the same time burning up. When I was still pretty young, eight or nine, Moon and I started touching and pleasuring each other. It was beautiful, and we had fun just exploring each other's bodies. I felt safe and alive with his hands on me, and his body was like the only thing real in my life. Then one day, when I was about twelve, I caught Moon making love to another boy. I found him in an alley, not in the fields, and he was kneeling down and sucking that boy off while some other boys stood around and watched. I felt so betrayed, I couldn't bear it. I never went to the fields again, and I hid from him until he finally stopped looking for me. He probably could have found me if he'd really tried—the neighborhood wasn't that big, and he's a god after all—but I think he felt hurt, and Moon isn't the type to go chasing after love. If he's hurt, he just runs away.

"Anyway, that same year my father died, and I got sent away, and it seemed like nothing from my former life was real. Then two years later when I left the boarding school and returned to that field for the first time, Moon found me there. He said he came there sometimes because he still missed me—" Delilah has to stop. This is ridiculous. This all happened so long ago, but it must be saying it out loud that's fucking with her. She never talks to anyone any more, except for Moon.

"Why would you abandon the one person who loved you?" asks Dragon.

"I thought he'd abandoned me," Delilah tries to snap, but her voice comes out low and shaky. "Anyway," she continues, "he told me I had been his best friend, that he loved me more than anyone." She talks fast, to get it over with. "That his father, who was some god of the sky, hated him now, and that he couldn't bear for me to hate him, too. I told him I didn't hate him, that I thought he wanted boys instead of me. But he said it wasn't an either/or thing. That he didn't want to be sexual with me any more, but not because he didn't love me. It was because he loved me so much that he didn't want to get sex mixed up in that love. Which didn't really make sense to me but I got it, at least, that he loved me. He was the only guy who ever wanted to be with me for something other than sex, so I guess that meant something to me, too. It's weird, but I don't want that from him any more. I never think of it when I'm sleeping with him. He's like my brother. No, like more than that. Like a better part of myself. Anyway, he came into the desert with me. He taught me how to hunt for food and gave me a magical bow. He's the reason I survived. And he still comes back to visit me, sometimes."

Dragon is silent then, which is a relief to Delilah. There is a sound around that silence, the faint roar of the water boiling somewhere near, but it's impossible to pinpoint.

The more she lies there, the more vividly she feels the shame of the position she's in. Lying in his arms, with her back to him, she thinks she can feel the sticky substance of his pity, and she hates it, but now she's trapped. If she gets up suddenly and tries to leave, he'll think she's frightened. Her body begins to tense as she tries to plot a way out.

"See," says Dragon. "Now we're friends."

For a moment Delilah's face freezes, and then she snorts derisively.

"Aren't we?" says Dragon.

"Dragon, the animals are my friends, and Moon is my friend. That's it."

"You can trust me more than Moon. He only shows up once a year, and you never know when." Delilah can hear what he doesn't say—that Moon might, at some point, stop coming back at all—and she hates him for reminding her. *It's true*, she thinks. *I don't love Moon because I can trust him to stay with me. I love him because I got sucked into it when I was too young to know better, and now there's no way out.*

"I think you have these rules you make about who you are and what is possible for you. You're the only one who's holding yourself to those rules," says Dragon.

"Those rules are why I'm still alive."

"That's only another rule. Something you made up."

"Fuck you. Who the hell are you to think you know me? *Fuck you.*" She spins around, hands curled against the earth, ready. She expects his pleading, his longing, and she hardens herself against it. She feels like herself again.

She feels fine.

But he says, "Fuck you, too. You think you're tough. I'm tough, too. I was raised by dragons. I'm as tough as you."

Delilah laughs.

"I am," he roars, his words booming suddenly through the strange, still space like two explosions as he rises up faster than she can see and pins her to stone as smooth as skin. His eyes seize her. He holds her wrists above her head.

Delilah bends her knees and presses her feet into his chest, too many emotions—of memories, of vulnerability, of the surprise of Dragon's fury—making her careless. With her feet she presses her own power against his, willing him to break her. She no longer feels any pain, and she is wide awake.

They wrestle. They bend with the force of their hands against each other, twisting and shaking with the effort of each body trying to hold the other down. Delilah becomes knees and elbows and bones, banging herself into Dragon's beauty like metal, her body a broken toy some child forgot—that doesn't fit with anything, whose edges are all sharpness and danger. Dragon flames over her, his heart roaring. And Delilah feels her own fire, her muscles as powerful as a man's, her passion as furious as a god's, but her power doesn't make her feel good. It just makes her angry. It makes her beat Dragon's chest with her fists and scrape his belly and his soft groin with her sharp toes and her bony knees. She can't throw him off so she concentrates on keeping his body away from hers. But when he manages to free a hand enough to reach down and touch her exactly where she wants it, she falters a little.

"Stop," she breathes. "I'm bleeding."

"I don't care," says Dragon, rubbing harder. But she keeps fighting. She drags his hand away, growling, because she hates him for making her do this. She hates him for making her fight him when all she wants—all she has ever wanted—is to give in. To receive pleasure. To be touched. And she can't. She's not that girl full of light, that other. She's only herself, broken and empty.

So they keep wrestling, their bodies embracing each other in their fury, making a ball of writhing muscle that whirls like a galaxy in space, while the water boils somewhere beyond them, all around them—and there is stillness in the center of their whirling, and beyond the wild water, the great whirling space of the desert is screaming. But gradually Delilah is tiring, though she keeps pushing just to have another body to push against, to make her feel alive. She wants to lose herself in exhaustion, until she has no more will to control herself or to care if she loses control, no more energy to think about the shame of all she has revealed. Gradually Dragon is winning, and as he wins he surrounds her with his body, clamping her tight against the ground with his weight while fingering her deepest desire at the same time. She concentrates on fighting, trying to ignore the rising pleasure. She keeps fighting as Dragon embraces her with one arm, his grip holding her absolutely but now with gentle ease, his lips skewed against her neck, his breath hitting her, his hand determined and slow while her body beats faster against him. He's not trying to get inside her this time.

She keeps fighting because it is the only way she can stop thinking about coming. Because the coming is the release of something, and she thinks that something could be love.

But if she stopped to think about that, she would never allow it to happen. And it does happen. It explodes through the fighting, through the memories, through her body itself—and it is not her body, and it has nothing to do with sex. It has nothing, even, to do with her—this orgasm. Which is why when it happens, she feels completely lost, like a child reborn into a life she doesn't remember.

Fawn's mare finds the new horse even further from the stable this time, but this time she trots up to him with her head held high. She stops soon enough to keep from frightening him, swinging her head in a low, humble arch. Then nervously, making soft little jumps toward him, she traverses the length of his body, sniffing toward his tail.

you're a woman, she says finally, her nostrils flaring.

Lonely's horse doesn't move.

i don't understand. you were pretending to be male. how? why?

i'm afraid.

of what? The mare stands still as Lonely's horse looks toward the mountain. Lonely's horse is male but her soul is female. Or she is someone's soul, and the someone is a woman, whose body is lost somewhere. She isn't sure any more. She feels the joyful beauty of Fawn's mare behind her, her confident wonder as she stands still and watches. Lonely's horse doesn't know how to feel that.

i'm afraid to be female. we're so vulnerable.

But Fawn's mare sees grace before her now. *no,* she says, following Lonely's horse comfortably, grazing with her. *you were afraid before. you were afraid to be male. now you are easy to be with.*

Lonely's horse keeps moving. As long as the stallion doesn't appear, she is safe. If he appears, she will run, or become male again.

i know you're a woman, the mare continues. *and i know you're a Unicorn.* She says this by casting a sideways glance at the other horse's invisible horn.

The white horse raises her head slowly, like a moving boulder made of dusty quartz. She stands still in the wind. *how do you know?* she whispers.

everyone knows, the mare snorts into the grass, butterflies emerging around her face. *the humans don't know, but their lives will be different this summer, with you here. no one will go hungry. the water is purer than it has ever been, and it cannot sicken us, no matter what it carries from faraway places. miracles will happen. the hunters will never go hungry, and the prey will never be caught. all of us are riding on light.*

The white horse keeps standing still. Only the wind is moving. *it's not true,* she says. *can those things happen?*

it is true, says the mare. *the way i am speaking now. not like a horse. the way the flowers are listening, not like flowers. the way the grass is reborn again and again under our mouths.*

Slow and unconcerned, the stallion is coming up over the hillside. Dizzy with fear, the white horse wheels and runs into endless distance. She is not the female, no, nor the male who overcomes her; she is not a body who can feel, not a soul with a purpose or a past, but only running, disappearing into a blur of motion that blends white and grey, white and grey, into the air.

Delilah returns to her cave. She lies on the cool dry floor and breathes deep into the comfort of home. The space around her is like a being that welcomes her, relieved at her presence. She touches each thing that she owns: the things that have become her life, that have kept her alive for seven years in her solitude. Her hunting knife. The smaller, cutting knife, a little rusted. The old plastic water jug. The bundle of clothing which now includes several men's shirts, a pair of men's pants, and a man's coat. The sweatshirt her mother bought her when she sent her away to school is still mostly in one piece. It was the only thing her mother ever gave her. It was her mother's small attempt, she supposes, at making up for giving her away forever.

A bat huffs a breeze of wingbeats past her face—a straggler. The others have already come home for the day.

She cannot close her eyes. It was a mistake to talk about the past. She'd known it was a mistake, but somehow she let Dragon talk her into it. It was a mistake because the past never fades. Not her past, anyway.

She's overcome a lot of trials out here in the nothingness. The terror of hunger before she began to trust the dreams of animals. Climbing up and down the cliff to the pine forest, even when her body pained her, and dragging the bodies back home. Thirst, the years when the rains never came, and especially the year of her first drought, when she didn't know enough yet to prepare, when she didn't recognize the signs and later had to follow the

empty path of the dead river up toward the mountains until she nearly collapsed. She got sick sometimes in the beginning, before she learned how to
store the meat properly, but to her surprise she survived, though at the time
she was too exhausted and dehydrated from vomiting to feel relieved. Also
there had been loneliness. A little.

But none of these triumphs—the obstacles she's overcome—really matter.
Because when she lets herself think about the past, she knows that it has
never stopped hovering on the brink of her consciousness, surrounding her,
just as clear as the day she walked away from it. The pain of her loneliness
among people, and the pain of losing the people she lost, and the droning
emptiness in the apartment where she grew up are all more real to her still
than anything she's suffered in the desert.

The animals she's killed and that have saved her. The rains and the floods,
the river and the drought, the heat and the winter, the snake and the fox,
Moon coming and going. All of these things flow together and have become
part of her.

But she remembers that silence in the apartment when she used to
come home in the middle of the night: a silence that was not real silence,
but a fake silence stretched taut over fear and fury that, when released,
would be too loud for a home. Her mother hissed that Delilah must not
bother her father, for he was struggling again and must have his space,
and she didn't care where Delilah had been. It didn't matter how many
days she'd been gone. It didn't matter that her father was only drunk
or high and completely delusional; it didn't matter that their supposed
respect for him was really fear. Mira must go to him, because she understood that magic he worked with. Delilah must make herself gone. She'd
only come back for a change of clothes anyway, and maybe a little food,
if the kitchen seemed safe.

She remembers the sadness in Mira's voice when she spoke to her for the
first time in months—and for the last time ever, though Delilah didn't know
that then. Delilah had just seen Moon in the alley. She stumbled into their
bedroom and found Mira, as usual, on the floor in a corner, curled up in a
ball and gazing up at the dim light from the window. Delilah didn't even
know why she'd come home. Maybe she needed to see Mira. Maybe she
believed then, somehow, desperately, that her sister was the one other person
in this world who could potentially love her.

Mira turned to her and said, "Go back to him."

Delilah put her hands on her hips. Mira was only nine years old, but somehow she knew things she shouldn't be able to know. "You don't know what
you're talking about," Delilah said, more confused than angry.

But Mira said, her voice calm and sane, "Lilah, go back. You need him."
And Delilah didn't go.

She remembers after their father's death, how Mira started screaming.
How Delilah thought she was possessed, even though she didn't believe in
such things. After that, Mira never spoke again.

She remembers every girl she beat up at school, who called her sister
names. But her sister wouldn't look at her any more. She wouldn't eat the
food Delilah brought her from the dining hall. When Delilah shook her,
sometimes, she was like an empty sack.

Delilah remembers that. That feeling of hopeless flesh. She couldn't bear
it. She had to go out and fuck some boy. She had to feel someone's life force
inside her, driving inside her, to the point of pain.

When they took Mira away, Mira was eleven years old. She didn't fight at
all. Delilah thought she seemed relieved. But Delilah fought. She fought until
they had to restrain her, until they tied her arms behind her back so hard her
shoulder came out of place and wouldn't work quite right ever again.

Delilah remembers all these things and more—each one in detail, each
one with edges sharp and colors blinding. The color of the blonde girl's
hair, the color of her lipstick. The color of blood on Mira's arms. The color
of her father's eyes, green on fire. The color of her mother's flushed cheeks
as she prepared dinner in a frenzy and tried to soothe him at the same time.
The colors of the fire where Delilah burned all of Mira's few things, once
she decided she was done trying to find her; there was nowhere else to try,
and she was going to walk away from this and never look back. The color
of the brick building that was the school and that absence of color inside
it; and the rainbow colors beneath her own black skin as she stared at her
own hands to keep herself sane—to keep herself from scratching her eyes
hungrily over the stiff shirts of the boys at the desks in front of her, wanting
to tear off their clothing, wanting to make them scream, wanting to drown
them in her own trapped fury.

All of these memories still clear to her, their details sharper than her
own knives. As if, when she left the City behind, she'd frozen them all in
little packages along the hidden vertebrate of her spine, and they remained
there—and because they were frozen, they were never able to decay. They
were perfectly preserved. Possibly, they are even still alive.

She lies on the stone floor of her cave, trying to be still inside. Remembering Dragon, and not understanding this longing she suddenly feels to be
held, though not necessarily by him.

She tries to understand why she feels so confused. Maybe it's the absence
of pain in this moment—pain that has, for so long, reminded her constantly

of her body. Is it possible that she misses it? It doesn't matter, for she knows it will come back. It must. She can remember that tension behind her shoulder blades like the tension of a bow before she releases the arrow. When Dragon made her come, the arrow had shot, and she'd killed something, but she doesn't know what it was. She knows only that she understands desire now. It is not a need to be filled but a need to release something—a need to express something held inside.

Perhaps because of her night with Dragon in a place surrounded by water, Delilah's dreams that day are filled with desert fish, the kind that live in the river and stay alive during the mud of the dry season when only tiny pools remain. In the dream, Mira is one of them, her eyes shining cold. At the same time those eyes are the eyes of the oldest woman in the world.

Mira talks to her more in this one dream than she spoke in the entire last few years that Delilah spent with her. "The desert fish are the keepers of time," she says, her voice coming without sound into Delilah's mind. "They keep the water until someday the desert becomes ocean again. Someday everything will be ocean again."

"I'll be dead by then," says Delilah, as if Mira will not also die, as if Mira is no longer part of this category of the living.

"You don't know anything about age," replies Mira. "You don't know why you came to the desert. You came because you were seeking your elders. We have no elders where we come from. We have no wisdom. But I was taken where the wise are taken. I was taken to where they keep them, under the sea."

Then—because it's a dream, you understand—Mira becomes me, the Unicorn.

Foaming in the waves, my white hair is the white hair of age, of death, of the truth you forbid yourselves because you know you are not ready.

And Delilah wakes, her sister's name a silent word forever caught in her mouth, and her own life feels meaningless.

Her sister would be eighteen years old now.

And the desert wasn't the answer after all.

Fawn and Lonely still speak very little, and Lonely never speaks of her past. But in the quiet work of each day, in the peace of Fawn's nearness, Lonely holds conversations with herself. She understands things she didn't understand before. Like about Dragon. How his body moved so fast and hard, reaching for her most secret places from the moment they first touched, and how she simply wasn't ready for that. How she had to tell him to stop.

How she had to leave. How she did not love him, after all. He wasn't the one. It seems very simple now.

The stories Eva has given her, however, are not simple, nor is the meaning of Lonely's dreams or her longing for the mountain. Even the story of the Dream People only confuses her further. For even if they are real, even if she could find them, it was her own father who destroyed them. What if it is this terrible secret that keeps her separated, forever, from true love?

In the mornings, Chelya's laughter as they feed the animals is a relief from such questions. Lonely's hands in the earth of the gardens are real to her, and meals in the grass and at the heavy oak table are real, and the warm closeness at dinnertime is real. The family seems easier and easier in her presence. She could almost pretend she is one of them. It is less often now that she goes to her horse in the fields, but when she glimpses him sometimes, he seems happy. And though she tries not to think of it, she begins to catch Rye watching her again, turning her body every time to wet gold fire.

One evening it's still hot by the time Fawn starts to make dinner, and Lonely is alone in the fields, finishing the weeding of two last rows of vegetables. It hasn't rained in some time, and the saucy sun-dry scent of new tomato plants fills her pores. She takes off the shirt she was wearing and ties it around her waist, leaving her breasts bare, because no one is around and the sun is making her dizzy. She's wearing an old pair of Kite's shorts. Kite and Chelya have gone into the woods to gather some herbs that Eva requested, and Rye is either not back from the woods yet or he is helping Fawn with the fire or the water or the cleaning of the meat for dinner.

For once she isn't thinking. The heavy sunlight flattens out her thoughts. The focus of discerning the weeds from the new sprouts and working the tougher ones up from the soil with a shovel, and the tenderness she feels for them as she tosses them into the sun to shrivel and die, takes all her concentration. It feels good to her, this knowing exactly what to do, not having to wonder, knowing that what she's doing is necessary and useful. This is what it must be like for a family, moon after moon, year after year, living inside this rhythm. Lonely is too restless for such an endless routine, but in this moment she doesn't know it. Only the ideal of it sits happily in her mind, as she fantasizes about staying forever.

When she stands up to stretch her knees, Rye is standing beside her, holding out a jug of water. Her surprise makes her laugh, but he doesn't laugh back.

"You have to remember to drink water," he tells her, still holding out the jug until she takes it. She remembers her bare breasts when she sees the reflection of her nakedness in his eyes, though he does not look down.

"You're always rescuing me," she says softly, to cover the embarrassment of her own excitement.

This time he smiles back, and she feels a little easier. She tilts the jug to her mouth and drinks, aware of his unwavering gaze and the openness of her own moving throat. Carefully, she places the jug on the ground and brings her hands to her mouth, wiping her lips with her thumbs.

"Can I help?" he asks.

"Don't you have to help Fawn?"

"I will. But you have a lot left here." He steps over the row and begins weeding opposite her, and so she kneels again and keeps working—their heads bent toward each other close. She wonders if she should put her shirt back on, but that would only draw attention to her nakedness, and also she's too hot. And also—

"I haven't talked with you for a long time," he says. "I wanted to ask you, why were you so quiet when my brother's family was here?"

He doesn't say, *Why were you crying?* and she can't decide if she is grateful for that or not.

"I've never been around so many people."

"Yeah," he says, and there is a dense pause between his words. "We aren't either, any more. Hardly ever, I mean."

She hungers after the hint of dissatisfaction in his voice. Though only a moment ago she fantasized about being a part of this family, living on this land forever, now she must stop herself from imagining that Rye will leave everything behind, and travel with her into—

"Where are you headed, Lonely?" he asks, as if he can read her thoughts.

"To that high mountain," she says, choked, unable now to say the reason. "Because I have to."

"And what would you do if you didn't have to? What would you do if you had no obligations to anyone, if you could do anything?"

Lonely looks up, surprised. She had thought he would ask more about where she was going and why, and she would have to explain. Instead he just jumped right over all of that, into a place she's never been, never even looked at, never even known was there.

"I—I don't know," she stammers. She sits still in order to think. Rye doesn't say anything. She watches his dark, bent head, his dutiful attention to the earth and his invisible attention to her voice, and loves him. "I never thought about it before. Maybe I'd wander around the world, and see every place there is to see, all the different landscapes, all the different animals, and hear all their stories."

He smiles, not looking up.

"Where have you—" she begins.

"Can you talk to animals?" he interrupts. "Can you understand what they're saying?"

"Yes. Can't you?"

"Not the way you can, I imagine."

Lonely likes his words: *I imagine.* It excites her to imagine his imagination. She senses that originally he asked her a question that he was really asking himself, and she wants to know his own answer. At the same time it moves her that someone should ask questions just about her, not about where she came from.

"Are you happy here?" Rye asks.

"Are you?" answers Lonely.

Rye smiles a different smile now, one that makes Lonely ache. Still he does not look up, nor does he answer. The look on his face makes her sad, as if there are things he will never tell her, no matter how long he knows her. That look is the separation between family and not family, that can never be crossed.

Then out of nowhere, as if explaining something that everyone's been wondering about, he says, "Fawn used to be different, you know. She was more free when we first fell in love. She wasn't so afraid of things. But the City's been creeping up on us, little by little, and it's too much for her. It's like pure evil to her, like the end of all things. Her fear is so big that even when she doesn't speak it, the whole family feels it. When you first came here, we all felt her fear of you. She's afraid of anything otherworldly, strangers, the unknown, or anything magical—because it was magic that created the City. She didn't used to be like this. Part of her has been, I don't know, shutting down inside. Putting itself away somewhere, where it's safe. Somewhere even I can't go."

"But she loves you," says Lonely, who tastes tears in her mouth, and wants to wrap Rye in her arms. She feels afraid of her own heartbeat and the way even her skin seems to listen, when bare.

"Of course," he says. "I'm not saying we don't love each other as much as ever. But I remember she used to be more open to me. In her whole being, not just her heart but her thoughts, her spirit, her *body*. You know?" He looks up at Lonely, and Lonely's mouth waters, and she swallows but it doesn't help. She nods, her body frozen like the day she stood in the river and waited and waited for him to look at her. Now he is looking. And she looks away.

"Am I embarrassing you?" he asks.

"No." She can feel his desire like an avalanche he's holding back, so much heavier than she is, making him sad, making him angry. Like Dragon's desire, like her father's sorrow—these feelings men have, so heavy, too much for them to bear. Maybe he holds it back because he knows that, after all, it will be too much for her—to have what she thought she longed for. Because she feels afraid now, and she changes the subject.

"Why does Jay look at Fawn like that?" she asks.

"Like what?"

"You know."

He breathes out, a little laugh, or something like it, and goes back to his weeding. "Jay was in love with Fawn once," he says casually. "Maybe he still is."

Lonely stares.

"Funny, isn't it," Rye says, "the way love criss-crosses around like that, never respecting the boundaries we've drawn, the decisions we've made?"

"But—"

"I didn't steal her away from him. I just came back one year, and she had become a woman, and we fell in love. All that time Jay lived right there with her. He could have told her how he felt. But he never did. And he regretted that for a long time. He regretted it for years, before he and Willow finally became lovers. He didn't want anyone else. He didn't tell me for a long time either, so I didn't know why he hardly ever visited, why he turned cold. I thought he was angry with me for not being there when our mother died, for leaving him alone with the farm and our father, who was also dying. When he finally told me, we had a good long talk about it. I think that's what finally freed him, to move on."

In his words Lonely hears his younger self, someone headstrong and more powerful, more confident than his brother, someone who did what he wanted and took what he wanted, and didn't feel sorry. Because that confidence is tempered by his tenderness, it doesn't seem cruel to her. Instead it excites her. Instead it makes her lean back and stare, wishing he would look at her again, until finally he does.

"What?" he says.

"Nothing."

He smiles. She thinks he's breathing a little harder, though the sun is sinking now and it isn't that hot any more. "So how was it—how was Jay looking at Fawn? I didn't notice, actually."

"Like this," Lonely answers, knowing her words won't surprise him. "Like the way you're looking at me."

This time she can't look away. Rye is leaning forward over the plants, on his hands and knees. He takes her jaw in his hand and kisses her.

In his mouth she dives down into a dark forest, and they walk for days through silent pines, where ravens croak an ancient language above their heads and moss sinks juicy and cold beneath their feet. She feels his hand grip her hip, slide up, and stroke with one finger the underside of one breast. She feels his holding back and also his certainty, his hand—with its intention, its clear ability, its rough heat—a hundred times more certain upon her body than she has ever felt of herself.

Then he pulls away, leaving her desire to course down her legs, leaving the memory of his hand in every place on her body where it did not go. He stands up fast and wipes his hands on his shorts, dirt dribbling down to where they're cut above his knees. Then he runs them hard across his head, dirt in his hair, not caring. "This never happened, Lonely," he says. "This never happened." And then he's walking away fast.

Lonely pauses for only a moment and then keeps weeding. She has to. The movement of it, and the feel of life and earth in her hands, are the only things she can hold onto. She listens to her own fast breath. She feels the pathway his hand traveled, more vivid than anything else real, so lit by the friction of that touch it is like a different color, a different temperature, a different material, even, from the rest of her body. The fire in her devours the memory of his tongue, turning her body so ravenous it frightens her. The earth in her awakens and is comforted by the firm reality of his hand, the desire of this other that makes her real. The air in her already draws her mind away into the dream of love, the person who belongs to her, who will one day caress her all over, only her—only for the love of her. The water in her rolls in stormy waves all through her, pained by the impossibility of Rye's love, furious at her own loneliness.

The fire and the air pull her skyward toward hope. The water draws her downward, and backward toward her past. The earth cradles her, rocking her with her own motion, until she finally feels safe to stand up, and walk back to the house as if nothing has happened.

"Where were you on the full moon?"

The oldest goddess sits down on the stone balcony, level with the highest branches of the great tree where birds no longer alight. Only the cloud of Yora hangs there darkly, pretending to sleep. Yora cannot hear the question the goddess asks her companion, because pain cannot hear.

The younger goddess who sits before her is different from the others. She is the one who has always wanted to go down and enter the City, to work her magic among people—not stay cloistered up here in the garden forever. A few nights ago, she returned from somewhere. Her eyes in human form are suffused with clear light. She hangs those eyes boldly on the leader's gaze, like treasures she's taken from some grand, distant land.

"I found Dragon," she admits without hesitation.

The older goddess's attention flows toward her. She is not angry, only attending.

"I needed to feel what it meant to be human," the younger goddess continues. "Ever since Dragon left, I could not stop thinking of his desire, the boldness of his body." She breathes in deeply. Her tongue still burns from human kisses. The thrill of her adventure sends her gliding forward into what she will say. She has no fear. "I wanted to know what it would feel like to be touched by such intensity. We take human form and we speak of humans and we try to help humanity, but it is all a lie if we do not experience these fundamental passions, these desires and urges and needs that make human beings what they are. That is what I believe."

The leader stares back at her with equal boldness. "So?"

"I wanted him to touch me. I wanted him to show me what it felt like to be a woman. I wanted to know this pleasure that could be so great, so great that he would beg and plead for it, that he would shame himself for it, that he could not bear to be without it." She pauses, as if expecting protest, but she receives none.

"I found Dragon in the desert. I spoke to those who had witnessed his passing: Coyote, the vultures, a scorpion, cacti. Even the river knows him by now. They are wary of him but had nothing ill to say of him. They had not seen him for some time. So I went to the caves where we know the dragons lived long ago. But they were changed."

She stops again to catch her breath. What will it be like now, to continue on in the Garden? Will the passion she has known infuse her prayers, making them more powerful? Or will it tear her apart, drawing her ever backward toward humanness, impossible to resist? But she is not human. It was only an experiment, the briefest meeting with what could have been, in some other, mortal life.

"The caves were seething, writhing with water like the hot inside of a woman's desire. I could not resist them. As I stepped toward the water, the steam enveloped me, opening the pores in my skin, opening all the openings of my body, undressing me and peeling me apart. I lost control over my form. For the first time I felt the luxury of my own breasts, the pressure of my own sex, the crying mouth between my thighs. The water roared from below, like the mouth of a dragon. I kept moving deeper into its heat. I do not know when my body became wet, or if the wetness came from inside of me or out. The water came like hands around me, swirling against my most sensitive places. I could not stand. The movement of the water was driving me mad, my body overflowing, falling apart—"

She stops and takes a short, deep breath through her mouth. The older goddess watches her and smiles softly at her beauty.

"When I landed, deep down in that place, I was helpless. I was afraid but I could not move, my body convulsing and soft as clay. I was all body, I was nothing but body. I did not know flesh could be so mutable, like water, changing from solid to liquid, and then, when Dragon touched me, into a vapor of pure joy."

"Dragon was there?" the old goddess interrupts.

"Dragon was everywhere. His hands were the caress of the water, his breath was the steam, his body was the roar of the dragons and the answer to all the desire that had built in me as I traveled downward through the water. The days I'd traveled in the desert, whole fields of desire opened inside me that I did not know were there. The form of his body was everywhere to me—in the stones and the upright cacti and the dunes and the hot animals running. I remembered his hard smooth skin, the desire in his eyes, his broad chest, his strong penis—these things so wonderful, like nothing we have here, nothing I'd ever known. I could think of nothing else. My body became wholly a body, itching with these memories, itching with the absence he had left behind.

"So when he began to touch me— I cannot describe it. I will never be able to describe it. Like a castle built of pleasure. But more than that, he taught me about beauty. He traced my form and made me, and I saw the light that I am and that I have to give. I felt this in the touch of his hands, and how they loved me, how they gloried in my womanhood.

"I am not the only woman—or goddess—who has come to him. There are others who come to him. He has a human friend, a woman, who came to him on the new moon. There were others, too. It is a gift he gives them, this loving."

The older goddess is silent. The still air of the mountaintop is grey and cool today, heavy in the room of the heart below them. "The body's form reflects the spirit, but it is not the same thing," she says slowly. "If we become too focused on the body, we lose touch with the spirit."

"But sometimes we must begin there," argues the young woman. "Sometimes we must begin with the body. I've returned here to tell you: I think Yora must be reborn in human form. I think it is Dragon's purpose to heal her—to remind her of herself, to remind her of her own beauty and power. To make her feel the way he made me feel. That *is* how she will return to being a goddess, and then the river will awaken."

The elder raises her eyes again to those of the younger, and is silent in thought. She herself is only half-formed into a human state at this moment, the lower half of her body fading into mist. She remembers Dragon's presence before her the day they said goodbye, the way it made her retreat inside herself like a child in the face of thunder. The truth is, this young goddess has entered a realm she could never enter, would never want to. This young one's spirit is made of flame, easy to excite, its passion sinking or soaring with circumstances, naturally adjusting to change. By contrast, the elder's sense of peace in this life—the quiet cradle of imperturbable understanding with which she unifies the Garden and the spirits who occupy it—is a delicately strung structure like spider silk, whose perfect balance could survive very little of the rough passions beyond this small world.

"Dragon needs Yora, too," adds the younger goddess. "He needs water, the cool water of the river. It will soothe him, for even now, I know, he suffers."

The two goddesses look toward Yora, a cloud hanging like a deep bruise in the now brittle tree. Yora doesn't mean to, but she brings death. She will continue to bring death, until she releases her own death, and agrees to be reborn.

The air is still and sultry, the day of Lonely's second full moon in the mountains. In the twenty days or so since the last big rain, everything has dried up. Layers of soil sift into the wind, as if giving up their attachment to the earth. Dead grasses turn brittle and creak in the sun, waiting for relief. The idea of rain sits tense in the air but so far the sky is clear.

Heat clutches Lonely's body as she escapes through the back door into the darkened main room. Fawn has covered the skylight to cool the room, but it still feels stuffy to Lonely. She longs for the cold touch of the river but is still uneasy about entering the forest alone, afraid to lose herself again in that in-between world where she is neither human nor god. She thinks of Eva's cool underground chamber beneath the hill, but knows better than to bother her in the middle of the day. Fawn and Chelya are still out in the gardens planting seeds for the fall crop, but Lonely, her body formed in the high-pitched delicacy of cold ocean air, cannot stand up to such heat the way their sturdy earth bodies can. Seeing her swaying under the weight of it, they sent her home.

Rye is gone. He went alone to Jay's farm, and said that maybe he'd return tonight, or maybe tomorrow morning. No one went with him. While Lonely was still in bed, she could hear him arguing with Fawn above her. She could not understand what they were saying, because both of their voices were so soft and controlled. But she knew he was going, and she had not spoken to him since what happened happened. All morning she watched him, watched his bare muscles in the sun—hard in their motion but obedient to the tasks his mind gave them—his body innocent of her watching, his face shaded by his hat. All morning she remembered the words he had spoken to her in the fields, and understood the hunger between them, and all morning her body belonged to him, but he never once looked up.

Now she stands inside the main room, out of breath, feeling the resting stillness of the family's absence. She hears the echo of Chelya's laughter in the rafters, sees Rye's other boots sitting in a pool of dried mud by the door to the greenhouse, feels the slow prayerful motions of Fawn's hands weaving the whole space together even in her absence—caressing the space over the wooden table, and nestling among the jars and herbs. Fawn says that the house itself has a soul.

Then she remembers that the house, too, has an underground room, like Eva's under the hill. At the southeastern corner of the room, a spiral stairway connects all three levels of the house: the rooftop garden, the main room, and the basement. Though in her earliest memories, height was a cold, windy place, she has learned that here in the house, deep in the lands of earth, heat rises, and cooler places are hidden below. So she opens the hatch in the floor, and descends.

It smells like Eva's chamber, at once dusty and clean—free from the live, animal scents of ordinary life in the family. The same coolness meets her feet on the black earthen stairs. Spiders move at the faint stir of her passing. And as in Eva's chamber, a light meets her arrival.

No sunlight can enter here to reveal the arrangement of crates and jars of stored food, only the palest light streaming behind her from the room above. Little is stored here in the summer, and the family find their way by candles when they have to search for something—all except Fawn, who knows the placement of things so well she can find what she's looking for in almost pitch blackness. But across the long cavernous room, past shelves of preserves and lines of dried meat and fruit, Malachite jumps at the sound of her step and looks up from a circle of candlelight.

"Oh!" cries Lonely. "I didn't mean to—" She stops. What didn't she mean to do, exactly? She knows only that Malachite's nervousness makes her afraid of herself, whenever she's around him.

"It's okay," he mumbles, closing something and standing back. He looks at the ground and stands there, as if waiting for her next move. Everything outside the ring of candlelight is grey, but in the shadow she can see the finely contoured fists at the ends of his lanky arms, the sharp bulge of his throat as he swallows. He is thinner than the rest of his family but with the same rich hue to his skin, like the desert when it turned to silk mud in the rain. He reminds her of the stag gods with their cool, handsome faces.

"What are you doing?" she asks, seeing his hand drop from the table.

"Oh I was—" Kite looks up at her, then quickly away again, as if remembering a taboo. "I was reading."

"What is reading?"

"Oh," He looks up at her again, and this time he doesn't look away. She sees him stand a little straighter. "Something that Grandmother knows how to do. She taught me. In the City, the people use symbols on paper to talk to each other. They say the same things on paper that they do with their mouths, only it's—different." He falters as Lonely crosses the room toward him, and runs one hand through his hair just like Rye did after he kissed her. He turns his body away from her, toward the thing he was looking into before, but she can feel his heat rising, as from a stone in the sun. He opens the thing and she sees it is not a container at all, but a beautiful bound packet of crisp square sheets as thin as birch bark.

"This is a book," says Malachite. "Each of these is a word."

"Each of what?" says Lonely.

"This," he says, framing tiny black marks between the tip of his thumb and forefinger, but she still doesn't understand. When she leans closer, he backs away as if stung—his hand suddenly clumsy, wobbling the candle so that it almost falls over.

"I never knew about this," Lonely says.

"I'm the only one in the family besides Grandmother who knows how to read," Kite mumbles beside her, and even though she's not looking at him, she can feel his eyes on her breasts, coming back to them again and again. "My mother never wanted to learn. She doesn't understand the point. No one else in my family understands why writing is important."

"Why is it important?" She looks up at him, more interested in his passion for the thing than in the thing itself.

"Because," he says quickly, his voice tense as if he expects her not to understand either, "it's different from speaking. When people say things or make promises, they change their minds later, and then they don't remember what they said. But books keep information forever. Someone wrote it down, and it's still here, so you know it's real."

What if it wasn't real in the first place? Lonely wonders. Then she asks, because she knows Kite wants her to, "What does it say?"

"A lot of things. About the City, and the way they operate there. The way they make machines do things, the way they make light. My mother doesn't believe in all that, but she doesn't know how to read either. The City is a magic that is made possible by writing. Writing can explain things that we can't."

Lonely looks at him, and he avoids her gaze, but she's got him trapped in the space between her and the wall. Remembering something, she asks, "Why didn't you go with your father today? To Jay's."

Kite shrugs. "We just saw them. I want to go somewhere new. I want to meet new people."

"Like who?" Lonely teases him, remembering Chelya's jest. "Girls?"

Kite's mouth twists. He's holding himself as far from her as possible. He is exactly her height. "No," he says sternly. Then suddenly he looks right up at her, and his words come out fast. "Someday I'm going to go to the City. I don't care what they say. I know there's evil there, but there's also great wisdom. They don't understand that, but I do, because I've read these books."

Finally, certain images from Eva's underground room fall together in Lonely's mind, so clearly that she can't help but smile a little. That's what all those colored blocks were, piled to the ceilings around her walls! What stories, what truths could be inside them! No wonder Eva knows so much. "Where do they come from—all these books?"

"My grandmother brought them all, from the City. It took her years. After she and my mother came to the mountains, she kept making trips back to get them. She missed them." His voice is quiet with awe.

"And you want to go there, even though they don't respect farmers?"

Kite shrugs again. "I'm going to bring back their wisdom, and it will change our lives. It will make everything easier. My mother thinks any change you make to nature is evil. But it's not that way. We make changes whatever we do, even when we build our homes. There are other animals who make changes, too, like beavers and ants. If you do it respectfully, without harming anything, I think there's a way."

Lonely stares at him because she doesn't know what to say. Her destiny and her past are tied intimately together with this mythical place of evil and power that she knows nothing about. When she looks into his eyes, she knows suddenly, with a sharp, emotionless knowing like a blue light flashing in space, that one day she will go there too. To the City.

The darkness is so still, so quiet, like the bottom of a lake. Their aloneness surrounds them, wrapping them in the kiss of secrecy. She sees Kite shift from one foot to the other, twisting his shoulders as if irritated, as if trying to harness something that itches inside him. She wants to name that something, wants to tell him that what they feel is the same.

"How old are you?" she asks him, imagining him crossing the desert by himself, sleeping under rocks—hungry, hot and then cold, haunted by the voices that haunted her.

"I'll be fifteen this winter," he says. "How old —?"

"I don't know," Lonely interrupts. She feels every age—eager and young when she's with Chelya, passionate and innocent when she's with Rye, old and pensive when she's with Eva—but maybe she feels most like Fawn's age, which is also unclear, for though Fawn is young, she is also old. Fawn is a woman, and yet she is also the earth around that woman, older than time. Lonely still feels some knowledge lying dormant between herself and Fawn, something that could rise like the moon between them and turn the whole world breathless and inside-out with its wild, dark-light glow.

"You don't know how old you are?" Kite looks at her suspiciously.

"No," says Lonely. Her chest burns. She is so tired of the questions she can't answer. "What does it matter?" She leans on the table with one hand and rolls her shoulder toward him, shifting her hips. She's so close to his body she can feel their sweat evaporating into a mingled cloud between them.

"Lonely," he says, trying out the word for the first time, and his voice drops soft and saggy like something with the bones taken out of it, and she can feel that he's never noticed the feel of his own lips before the way he notices them now when he says her name.

But then in an instant he is bouldering past her, angry or scared and striding fast toward the door, toward the light. The candle huffs out in the wake of his leaving, and Lonely is left in the darkness of the space she stole from him, holding her own body rigid with confusion and shame.

By evening, the heat shows no sign of releasing them from its fists. Lonely takes a bucket of water from the river and carries it behind the house, dunks and rinses the faded sundress she was wearing, wipes her body down with a rag, then dumps the rest of the water over her hair. As she wrings out the dress and pulls it back on, still wet but drying fast, she shakes her hair and imagines that Kite is watching her. She can still feel his hungry eyes exploring her, as droplets of water travel from her hair down the easiest pathways of her body. She walks carefully into the house to help Fawn with dinner.

It's too hot to cook, so they cut salad vegetables and boil eggs. No one will feel like eating much. The quick fire they make to boil water for the eggs turns the cool water on Lonely's neck to sweat, and even Fawn's face is flushed and damp. The windows are still covered, so the women work in shadow. When Kite returns, he will remind them that if they had electricity, fans could be cooling them. But this idea is so foreign to both Fawn and Lonely that neither of them think of it; they only move slowly and try to breathe deeply, every now and then splashing cold water on their faces from the water tank by the stone counter.

In silence, they wash and shake dry the lacy, violet-green leaves of the lettuce. Lonely snips the ends of the little pregnant boats of the peas with her fingernails, and slices them in half. The juicy stiffness of the peppers falls easily into strips under Fawn's knife, and then she chops fennel to add its strange, leathery taste to the salad, too. Lonely scoops the sweet wet lumps of chopped tomato into her palms, lifts them dripping over the bowl, and drops their redness in. Then she dips her hands full of bean sprouts into the rinsing bowl, and accidentally sprays a few drops of water on Fawn's face as she brings them up and shakes her fists to dry them. Fawn raises one eyebrow, something Lonely didn't know she could do, and then, a moment later when Lonely has forgotten, comes around the other side of her and splashes her on purpose from the same bowl.

They both laugh then, and their laughter is happy and grateful in the hot darkness. Lonely turns to Fawn and watches her face for a moment, a face she has earned the right to gaze at occasionally. Fawn's teasing thrills her a little—the surprise of it bursting out of her shyness, yet without disturbing her placid grace. Her face is beautiful to watch, even when its expression doesn't shift, like a mountain forever the same yet forever changing in each moment of the day's light. Her slick brown hair, pulled tightly back, leaves her neck open and elegant in its simple strength. Her eyes, focused on the cucumber she is slicing, are restful; her lips fit perfectly together but are ever so slightly uneven.

"Lonely," says Fawn, for she says that name more easily now, without looking up. "My mother says you are searching for something, someone."

Surprised, Lonely nods, and looks back to her work.

"Where are you going when you leave here?" Fawn asks, pronouncing the words carefully as if they are foreign to her. Lonely is surprised to be asked a question.

"I have to go to the high mountain, the one that's white at the top," she answers, wondering now if what she says is true. Does she *have* to go there?

Then it is Fawn's turn to nod and say nothing. She begins moving again, shelling the eggs in a bowl of cold water that will quickly turn warm. Lonely can't tell what she is thinking.

"Fawn," she says on impulse. "Did you long for someone, before you found Rye? Did you search for someone? Did you feel alone?"

The slightest quaver interrupts the seamless grace of Fawn's motions. She shakes her head. "I did not search for love. I didn't know I needed it. My mother and I were trying to survive. I just *lived*, here in the mountains with the earth, and I loved things, I always loved but—I don't know. I don't know how to explain."

Lonely turns to her. "You weren't waiting for him," she says.

"I was, I think. But I didn't know it. Something inside me was making a web of my own life, a web that included all the beings of my world, and included him, before he ever arrived. I didn't know it, but he knew it. It was like he recognized me and said: 'Here you are, you are *Fawn*.' He made me see myself for the first time."

"Didn't you long for touch?" asks Lonely. Fawn blushes.

"I didn't know what it could be like," she fumbles, pausing as if surprised at the memory. "I lived in touch already. The touch of the water when I bathed, the touch of the leaves and grass as I walked through them, the feel of food in my mouth."

She has stopped her work, her body frozen. Lonely nods. She knows those touches, and how they feed her body's glory in itself, but with the glory comes desire. Always. Just as Yora predicted, she realizes, she constantly wants more.

Something else haunts her tonight, too: Kite's fantasies of the City, and her sense that someday she, too, will find herself there. She feels certain that some part of herself—some dark part she doesn't want to know—comes from there and is alive there. Perhaps neither her past nor her longing will ever make sense to her until she sees that place with her own eyes.

When they sit down outside, an icy breeze flies almost imperceptibly through the fat layers of heat, and the sky begins to cloud.

"Storm coming," cries Chelya. "Finally!"

Kite arrives last minute and falls on his knees in front of the blanket, helping himself to the salad without looking up. When he avoids Lonely's gaze, she can tell he is nervous, and then she feels sorry.

"You got more tomatoes than me," he accuses Chelya, grabbing one with his fingers from her plate.

"I deserve more tomatoes than you," Chelya teases, mouth full.

"Mmff," says Kite, chewing with what seems to Lonely an exaggerated passion.

"Lonely," says Chelya, "are you coming out with me again tonight? It's the full moon. It's going to rain, so it could be wild." She winks at Lonely, lowering her voice a little, and Fawn looks sharply over.

Lonely smiles at Chelya, not trusting her voice.

"Can I come?" says Kite.

Chelya looks at him, surprised.

"You never take me to meet your friends," he adds.

"I didn't think you were interested. Anyway, you wouldn't like it."

"How do you know?" says Kite, flaring up.

"Neither of you should go out tonight," Fawn interrupts, and Lonely starts at the tension in her voice. "It's not safe, going out in the storm. It's going to storm."

"Oh, Ma," Kite says. Eva looks from one to the other, her expression curious but uninvolved.

"You're not coming, Kite," Chelya says. "Girls only." She shoots a furtive glance at her mother. Lonely watches Kite scowl and feels sorry for him, but she doesn't want him to go either. She doesn't want him to see the way she will surrender to those animal embraces. Or will she? Will she go again, after dreaming that dream?

Something bigger than a god growls in the distance, from the direction of the high mountain. Lonely looks up, her eyes wide.

Chelya laughs at her expression. "Thunder," Fawn explains.

Lonely doesn't know what thunder is. It sounds like an avalanche. "From the mountain?" she asks, confused.

"No," answers Fawn, smiling a little. "From the sky."

It happens again and Lonely doesn't understand how the sky could make such hard sounds, or what form it could take and what surface it could grate against to create such chaos in her belly. The sound swells like anger, growing louder. She remembers the voice of the wind, suddenly, telling her the clouds were the dreams of her lover. She remembers his face in the dream, and the face of Coyote, and fear.

She sees Fawn's smile fade, her brow darkening like the sky.

"Lonely," she says softly. "Will you stay here tonight, with me?"

Lonely hears the helplessness in her voice and understands, for the first time, Chelya's true power. There is nothing Fawn can do to stop her daughter from going. For whatever reason, it makes Fawn afraid, and she will have to live in that fear all night long.

But Lonely doesn't know what she wants. She looks away from Fawn's questioning gaze. She doesn't answer. She sits still, looking down, as Fawn stands abruptly, perhaps embarrassed by her own request, and begins to bring the dishes inside. Chelya, hurried and eager, and Kite, restless and already finished with two helpings, jump up and follow her.

In the silence and distant birdsong that remain, Lonely looks up into Eva's eyes, without meaning to, and finds them waiting for her. She starts in sudden fear, like prey that realizes it's been discovered—that it's been watched for a long time, in fact, so that by the time it becomes aware, it is too late.

"What are you waiting for, Lonely, in staying here?" says Eva quietly. And Lonely knows she doesn't mean staying at the table.

She shakes her head. "I don't know."

"I think you do," says Eva sternly. "It's time for you to begin owning your own desires, taking responsibility for them, and deciding what to do with them. It's time for you to take control, instead of letting them control you. It's time for you to make choices consciously, because whether you are conscious of them or not, you are making choices anyway. And they're affecting other people."

Lonely just stares, horrified. How much does Eva know? How does she know?

"It's not that I want you to leave," Eva continues. "You're becoming part of our family. And I believe that you help Fawn, even if you shake the structure of her life a little and shift things around. I think maybe that's good for her. Though don't tell her I said so." She smiles, but Lonely can't smile back. Then Eva says, without changing her tone, "But I also think you're dangerous, Lonely. Because you're not paying attention."

Lonely is so shocked that she can't speak until after Eva has closed her eyes, rested a moment longer, listened to the birds, and then stood up and turned to go. Then she calls, "Eva," but her voice sounds cramped and scared.

Eva turns, and her eyes are tender, and Lonely wants that tenderness so badly that she's overcome with all the things she could say, and can think of nothing to say. But how she longs to tell someone who would understand, who would be able to explain to her the confusion of her longing, how it reaches out its tentacles to anyone near, how it grasps and pulls. She needs to know if that is some evil in her, some evil that comes from her father. If she could only find her true love, it would all go away. Eva's story would melt away behind her, forgotten…

"I don't want to be like my father," she blurts. "I mean, I don't—I don't want to go to the City."

"Then don't go," says Eva.

"But I feel like I have to. Like I belong to it, or it belongs to me. We're connected somehow, aren't we? I know I'm supposed to do something about what my father has done."

But Eva doesn't answer, and Lonely knows why. Eva doesn't have all the answers, no matter how much Lonely wishes that she did. The thunder roars again, like judgment that will come down upon her. But right now the air is fresh and cool and young, and this little valley is raised up to the heavens on the hand of a single moment.

"I want to know what's real," she says helplessly. "If the things I feel are real. If the things I want are real. My father lived in illusion. Everything, everything was an illusion."

Eva nods. "It's hard to avoid the mistakes our parents made," she says. "But at least if you know what they are, you can try." Her eyes face Lonely's but she isn't looking at her. She is looking inward, as if talking with herself, about some other story that Lonely doesn't know. "It helps," she adds, "if you're not guided by fear. Fear will draw you right back to the same mistakes, over and over. Focus on your choices instead."

But it isn't fear, thinks Lonely. *It's need. It's desperate, raw need. How can you understand that?* "What am I afraid of?" she asks, feeling tired.

Eva raises her eyebrows, as if surprised that Lonely doesn't know. "Of your name," she says. "Of loneliness."

By the time Lonely comes back inside, Chelya is ready in her magical flower dress, and Kite has disappeared somewhere. Lonely tells Chelya she isn't going. She is going to stay here with Fawn. Because Fawn said her name. Because of what Chelya once told her: that you have a name so that someone can call you when they need you. And because she doesn't know the answer to the question Eva asked her, and she needs to know.

Fawn meets her in the kitchen after bringing the food scraps to the chickens and locking them up for the night. She's opened the shades to catch the last of the light as the storm encloses them. She lights a candle on the table and another on a shelf above the counter.

"This dinner won't take long to clean up," Fawn says. "I can do it. Sit there, by the fire, if you want."

Lonely can hear the unusual energy in Fawn's voice that comes from gratitude and relief. She sits on a hay-stuffed cushion in front of the fire, feeling dazed, while Fawn boils water again for washing the dishes. There is something serious about her now. Her soft lines seem harder, her fluid motions caged by some inner fear that Lonely can see behind her eyes.

"Rye might be very late," she tells Lonely, suddenly talkative. "He'll probably stop somewhere to keep out of the storm, unless he is very close to home already."

Lonely doesn't answer. She wonders what it would be like, to know that love is coming home to you, to know that it's on its way to your door and all you have to do is wait.

"Rye and I were arguing this morning," Fawn adds, and Lonely looks at her, startled.

"Why?" she asks.

"He wanted to take you with him, to Jay and Willow's."

"What—me? He wanted to take me?" Lonely stammers, unable to control her voice. Fawn doesn't seem surprised and doesn't look at her. Could it be she already knows how Lonely feels? "But—" Lonely begins, and stops. *But why didn't you let him?* her desperation wants to ask, imagining a whole day alone with Rye, perhaps riding behind him on the horse, her legs around him. Instead she only asks, "But why?"

Fawn shrugs. "Company, I guess. I never go with him any more. I don't like to travel."

"But why not?"

Fawn looks at her now. She doesn't seem angry. There's something pained and confused in her face, something lost beneath its surface as if trapped beneath ice—looking for a way out, and drowning. Lonely can't understand why Fawn is telling her this. It's so strange for Fawn to start a conversation about something personal. But her voice is steady. "You would have gone," she says, ignoring Lonely's question. "Wouldn't you?"

Lonely doesn't know how to answer. Is it wrong to say yes? But Fawn will know anyway. Like Eva, in her own way she seems to know everything.

The sky explodes above them, shaking the house with the impact of pure sound. Lonely jumps up, too surprised to notice Fawn's reaction. Then she looks back at Fawn, and Fawn smiles with shame, her shoulders shaking a little. She turns back to the dishes, and Lonely sits down again.

"I'm so worried," Fawn murmurs.

"About Rye?"

"Yes, and Chelya and Malachite."

"Where is Ki—Malachite?"

"He said he was going for a walk. He has this place he goes, up high. I've seen him there before. But I wish he wouldn't go there in the storm."

Lonely looks out the window and sees the wind slinging a single hemlock side to side against the chicken shed. She wonders what will happen in the forest tonight, in the storm. Will there be a bonfire? Will everyone make love in the rain? Her body is so full with desire, like an overfull bucket of water that will brim over at a single touch. She holds herself uncomfortably, her hands in her lap. The wind thrashes against the house, reminding her of the tower, reminding her of the primal, wordless place inside her where longing first began.

"But what are you afraid will happen to them?" she asks. "Is the storm dangerous?"

"I don't know. Yes, it can be." Lonely hears dishes bang together, and the sound startles her almost more than the thunder. She has never heard Fawn's voice like this—broken and uneven, as if splashing over stones. She doesn't know what to say. She wants to go to Fawn and comfort her, but she knows that Fawn will feel embarrassed by her touch.

And she feels a sense of helplessness, seeing Fawn's fear. There is some memory of her father here, huddled like this, with his back to her. Lonely had gone to him, placed her small hand on his shoulder, told him it would be okay. But she didn't understand what was wrong. He did not turn to her, did not even seem to know she was there. Like her father, Fawn seemed so strong. Fawn, she realizes, has saved her. Is saving her. It was Fawn all along, not Rye, who rescued her from that lost, unearthly state, where she traveled forever in a circular abyss unconnected with anyone or anything. It was Fawn who made her human. It was Fawn that she needed.

"Fear is so heavy," Fawn says, as if talking to herself. "If Chelya knew, going out like this—how heavy fear is—" She closes her eyes, and Lonely watches her clumsy hands, terrified herself to see the weight of that fear dragging her friend down. "After this," Fawn adds, "I just want to lie down, not think. But it never works. I can't stop thinking about them until they're home."

Lonely looks down at her hands, feeling guilty for knowing where Chelya goes—and having shared in the joy of it.

"Tell me about something," Fawn says. "Talk to me."

"About what?"

"Tell me about the tower. Tell me about where you came from."

Lonely looks at her. "What do you want to know?" she asks dubiously.

Fawn's face is rigid. "I don't know. Was it …cold?" Her voice is a whisper again, like when she talked to Lonely for the first time, and asked her didn't they have seasons where she comes from.

"No," says Lonely, after thinking for a moment. "It wasn't cold."

"Was it warm?"

"No, it wasn't warm either."

"Did you see birds?"

"No. I mean I don't remember." What had it been then? A space of nothingness, a now blank expanse in her memory.

"Were you afraid?" Fawn whispers.

"I don't know. Sometimes. Not really though. I didn't feel much of anything." It makes her shiver now, that nothingness. *That's what loneliness is,* she thinks. She feels frustrated with the questions, stupid for not having the answers. She watches Fawn's comfortable body lean over the fire and the water, watches her hands move—an assumption in them about what life is made of that Lonely's hands have never taken for granted, and have had to search out and discover. She can't remember any more what happened in the tower. She can't remember feeling anything. She knows only that sometime tonight, in the middle of the night, in the middle of the storm, Rye will enter Fawn's bed. Perhaps he will run his hands over her body, meeting and understanding every detail of her being. Perhaps he will enter her with that strange instrument, and make melodies inside her that Lonely can only imagine.

"I guess I was only dreaming," she tells Fawn dully. "I wasn't really alive yet."

"What made you leave? Your prince—you wanted to find him?"

"No," answers Lonely, surprising herself. "It was really the old woman who made me leave." It's true. If it hadn't been for the old woman's face swirling before her in a dream, she wouldn't have screamed that hole in the ice. If she hadn't looked through and seen the old woman facing out to sea, ignoring her cries, she wouldn't have felt so determined to get out. Then it was the old woman who pushed her into the sea, who challenged her to seek out that which she kept saying she wanted. Maybe if it weren't for her, Lonely would still be dreaming up in her make-believe tower, dreaming up love and never going in search of it. Is it possible the old woman didn't hate her so much, after all? But she hated Lonely's father….

Fawn is staring at her, hard. "What's wrong?" Lonely asks, alarmed.

But then the thunder crashes upon them again, and the weight of rain collapses fast over the house—the sound of release.

"Let's go out," says Lonely, standing.

Fawn doesn't respond but watches Lonely as she tears past, around the fire and the wide chimney, to the back door that opens toward Eva's hill and the high mountain. When Lonely opens the door the rain comes in to meet her, stinging her body and flinging itself past her into the shadows of the house. She steps forward, emerging into the wind which seems to know her more intimately than anyone, though its grey fury slashes the rain across her face. She can feel Fawn's presence behind her, fading behind the magnitude of the storm. How amazing, that the air is everywhere, blowing and formless; how amazing, that the rain falls evenly through the whole world as far as she can see, filling space without form or intention, free-falling into her skin. Thunder breaks through her, shattering the idea of her human bones, shattering—for a moment—her memory of where she has come from and where she is going. She presses her chest toward the sky, where desire is not emptiness but a living, breathing flower that must unfold or die.

Out in the rain-hazed fields, through water-heavy eyelashes, through a confused rainbow, she sees a white blaze of fire burst up under white light and noise, a tree transforming, flailing its arms of flame. She sees the spirit of the tree rise up in smoke as the rain falls over the fire and extinguishes it, and she sees the earth as the water sets it free, flowing downward and onward where once—in the dry heat—it blew upward into the air.

Then she sees a Unicorn rearing up in the storm, her voice—neither horse nor human—sending tremors through her magnificent body. Or maybe it's a flash of lightning.

At the same instant, she hears her own name—*"Lonely!"*—cried out as if from all sides, but when she turns, she sees that it is Fawn who has called her, though Fawn is standing silent in the doorway, the name only a whisper on her lips. She looks so small, her cheeks round and childlike around the tightness of her mouth, and her eyes, beneath the shadow of her hair fallen shaggy around her face, are as dark as the room waiting behind her. And Lonely, feeling suddenly her power over all the world, emboldened by the storm which speaks her own name—whatever it is, and it is not *Lonely*, but that other name that she cannot remember—must go to Fawn, must go to her friend and wrap her arms around her feverish, shaking body.

Fawn's arms hang loose at her sides, but Lonely feels the other woman's breath rise up hard and sudden against her.

"Lonely," Fawn whispers into her neck, and Lonely's hips shudder ever so slightly against Fawn's. "What is it?" she asks Fawn to cover her confusion, thinking her voice will be lost in the storm, not understanding how a woman so strong could lean into her like this, as if with need. The pressure of their bodies against each other is subtle but as loud as the rain.

She can hear Fawn's answer as clearly as if they stood in perfect quiet, though they have not moved from the wild doorway, and the rain still coats Lonely's back with its cold paint of water.

"I'm afraid of so many things, Lonely."

"Why?" Lonely asks, but there is no meaning in the question. The looseness in her own throat tells her what will happen, as Fawn reaches for Lonely's lips with her own, her breath young in its quick urgency, her body old in its confidence as she pulls Lonely closer. Her lips are ten times softer than a man's, slippery as the thin green leaves of the corn plants that wave in the wind of the eastern garden, almost ready to bear fruit. When the kiss ends, Lonely is dizzy with the emotion she can see contorting Fawn's face. She wants to know where it has hidden all this time.

"But you've never been lonely," she gasps before she can stop herself. "Have you?"

Fawn opens her eyes. "I don't know, Lonely. I don't know why, but what you have, what you are—I want it. I don't know what it is. It terrifies me, too." Her voice is so soft. She lays her hands on Lonely's shoulders and then runs them along her arms in a way that melts Lonely, a delicacy so delicious that Lonely cannot believe how easily it is traversed—this pathway of pleasure that Dragon never knew. Fawn takes both of Lonely's hands in hers.

"Come lie with me," she whispers. "Come lie down with me, for a moment. The storm frightens me."

Lonely, amazed, lets herself be led inside, up into the loft where Lonely has slept so many nights of the summer alone in Chelya's bed. Following Fawn up the ladder, Lonely sees her motion more than her form itself, the skeleton bones of the ladder meeting her hands like extensions of her own body—and yet tonight Fawn's hands are hesitant, as if this once-familiar terrain feels suddenly new. She leads Lonely to the wide bed where she and Rye sleep together in the winter, and the two women kneel before each other, neither one knowing what to do. Fawn's courage, apparently, brought her only this far. She looks across at Lonely, her eyes flickering in and out of emotion like candles.

Downstairs they hear Kite's light footsteps, the closing of the door so quiet it cannot be heard above the sound of the rain. Kite always moves quietly, and never seems hurried, even when he's running. His footsteps fade as he descends to the basement, and Fawn sighs and closes her eyes. He is safe.

"I know where Chelya goes on the full moons," Lonely says clumsily. "I don't think you should worry." She pauses, not knowing how to say that Chelya is wiser than both of them together, that she'll never get herself in trouble, that she alone seems to own herself entirely and know exactly what she's doing. "She has so many friends, so many—spirits protecting her, when she's out there."

Fawn stares back at her, and says nothing. Lonely wonders if she should feel guilty somehow, as if she has stolen something from Fawn by loving her family in ways that Fawn cannot—sharing things with them, in that love, that Fawn cannot or will not share.

The thunder, which no longer surprises Lonely, bursts again around the walls, and she sees Fawn stiffen. The loft is so dark, Fawn's body merges into it, a shape of lush warmth shaking in its bonds of shyness. Once again she seems the quiet, contained woman that Lonely knows and admires, except for the shaking.

"I'm going to take my dress off," says Lonely. "It's wet."

Fawn seems unable to answer, her eyes trapped and wild—as if it is Lonely who has brought them here, Lonely who has initiated this ceremony, whose rites Fawn does not know. Lonely pulls her dress over her head, keeping her own eyes trained on Fawn's face. She lies back on the bed and takes Fawn's hand, waiting to see what will happen.

"Who are you?" breathes Fawn.

Lonely shakes her head sadly. "I don't know." She remembers Yora, long ago, who remembered only her own name. At least she had that much. But she couldn't stay with Lonely. *You can't be with anyone else until you remember who you are,* thinks Lonely. *That's why.* But it's so strange, because she, Lonely, could see the beauty in Yora, even if Yora could not see it herself. Just like

Fawn seems to see something in Lonely that Lonely cannot see. *Is that how you find yourself, after all? Through other people's eyes?*

"I think you're very beautiful," says Fawn. Lonely watches her lips, the way they fold carefully together again after she speaks, and how a ripple passes over her chin and down her throat as she swallows.

Then with a quick intake of breath, Fawn slides down beside her, her eyes bright and close in the dark. Lonely holds herself still and lets the storm inside herself bleed quietly into Fawn's warmth. All the longing, all the need— she tries to just let it ease over Fawn like water, without moving, without grasping. It floods over the bed, pools over the floor.

"I miss Rye," Fawn whispers. Lonely can feel puffs of breath on her cheek, dark and hot. "I should have gone with him—there's a little more time now, before the fall planting begins, and it's the first time he's asked me to travel with him for a long time. He wanted me to go with him. He was angry with me when I wouldn't. He said, 'I'll take Lonely then.' And I cried, because I wanted—I don't know. I wanted—I wished I could be like you. Brave. Hungry for things, like you are."

Lonely says nothing. She's still holding Fawn's hand, and the back of her hand brushes Fawn's breast every time Fawn breathes. The cloth that covers it is faintly rough, and so thin, like the inner lining of an eggshell. Warmth comes through it fast. *How could someone so warm be afraid?* she wonders senselessly.

Fawn closes her eyes and presses her face to Lonely's neck. Lonely stiffens, afraid of her own longing, and closes her eyes, too. She listens. Listening is easy, and so sweet in the safe darkness, with the thunder fading outside and the rain going on forever.

"I know loneliness like yours must be hard," says Fawn. "But it's hard to have love too, because the more you have, the more you're scared to lose. Every day I love my children, and my husband, more and more. Every day I'm so grateful, and every day I'm terrified I will lose them! Whenever I'm not with them, whenever they're not *right* beside me, Lonely, I'm afraid."

Lonely squeezes Fawn's hand; she kisses her cheek. The thunder comes again, but Fawn doesn't tremble this time.

"When I was a child, when we first came into the forest, we could never make a shelter strong enough to stand up against a big storm. My mother tried to take care of me—and she did. We both survived because of her. But it was so hard, Lonely. She was scared. I could tell she was scared, though she tried not to let it show. She would tell me we'd be okay. But the thunder was coming louder and louder, and I did not believe her. Things came crashing down around us, and once a tree caught on fire, and there were floods. The earth was crazy to me then. I was so scared. But the worst thing was knowing she was scared, too."

"I know," says Lonely. "It was the same with my father. He tried to take care of me, but he couldn't. He didn't know how to save me."

Fawn holds very still. "I was always afraid," she whispers. And Lonely listens to the rain and the wind behind her voice.

"I didn't stop being afraid until Rye's family took us in," Fawn continues after a long silence. "Until I finally had a home with them, and things started to make sense. Finally I understood, then, what the world was, and who I was inside of it. The seasons, the growing and dying of things, and what I had to do every day to help all that happen. They loved me so easily, and we played and laughed, and when Rye found me again later—when he came to me—I was so alive then. My world was clear to me then, every part of it known to me, and beautiful. I recognized his touch then, Lonely. But it is harder for me to recognize it now. I don't recognize the scents on the wind sometimes—and the sounds Willow hears from where her home used to be—and the things Kite talks about, and the way the seasons are all mixed up, and the way the spring came too early and the trees flowered and then it froze again and everything died—"

Her voice softer and softer, the words running together like rain, her eyes closed. Lonely looks at her in the dark, her own eyes wide open, trying to get inside her dream. Trying to imagine the comfort of childhood in easy meadows with other children laughing, the sunlight on her face when she turned and saw Rye riding home for the first time in two years, the way she stood and her dress tumbled around her, the way her hands opened in surprise.

"Please touch me," says Lonely.

There is no sound, no resistance. With the fingers of her free hand, which Lonely feels suddenly from somewhere beneath them, Fawn traces Lonely's throat, the nubs of her collar bone, the valley between her small breasts—and so slowly, as if stroking the feathers of a bird from some distant, fragile other-world, she circles her nipples. Their bodies are close enough that, without using their hands, they can move into each other—their legs sliding between each other's secretly, as if against their will. Lonely can feel Fawn's desire—sweet and so much lighter than Dragon's or Rye's—misting out from the helpless folds of Fawn's fleshier body, and the innocence in the recesses of her deep softness, the darkness between her thighs, the hungry weight inside her breasts. Lonely can feel these unseen places speaking to her from Fawn's body, whispering to her from behind the walls of her fear.

"You're so beautiful," she says to Lonely again. "Like nothing in this world. I think it's safe being human, knowing what is possible and what is not, knowing how just to live. Then you come here and you're something else—not part of this world. You make me feel something different, and I don't know, any more, what I am."

Lonely strains to see her in the dark, because she sounds like she's crying. But tonight it is Fawn who can speak easily, and Lonely whose voice is trapped.

"But I'm human, too," she manages. "Like you."

"No," says Fawn, pressing her face close to Lonely's. "You're a goddess. I know. Everyone knows, and they try not to tell me, but I know it. You're not bound by what binds us. But it's true," she adds thoughtfully. "I used to go out in the rain too, and when I first met Rye, he danced with me once in the storm...."

She sounds like she's dreaming again. Lonely can feel her fingertips against her hips, like Rye's that time, not holding on, beginning to float up her waist but hesitating. Breathing harder, Lonely locks one leg around Fawn's and rubs up against her, feeling Fawn's heartbeat inside her own chest. Somewhere amidst the herbal sweetness of Fawn's scent, she thinks she can smell Rye—the confidence of his masculinity breathing from deep within the sheets. She tries to imagine the sound of Fawn's voice when Rye makes love to her—if she makes any sound. She imagines Rye's brown, gentle hands flowing over Fawn's body. She wraps her arms around Fawn and begins to sob.

Fawn seems to relax a little, then, the curves of her body spilling out more freely over the sheets. She breathes into Lonely's ear, "What is it?"

"I can't go back out there," Lonely cries. "I can't go back out into the cold and the forest. I'm scared. I'm scared, too."

"No, you're not," says Fawn, and she flicks her tongue against Lonely's ear. With her arms around Lonely, she brushes the edge of her hand against the backs of Lonely's thighs. In her mind, Lonely feels Rye's tongue rolling around her ear and down her neck, and feels Fawn's body rising beneath his, and feels their hunger for each other, and feels Fawn's uncertain, feminine version of his breath—delicate and windy—against her skin, feels Fawn's hunger for her, and Rye's hunger for her through the body of Fawn.

Now Fawn's palm curves over her hip bone, and Lonely rolls onto her back again to give Fawn room. And she opens her legs, waiting in tearful expectancy as Fawn's hand brushes the insides of her thighs, up and down, up and down, like wings. She's still crying as Fawn cups her hand over the raw, round heat of her, and just holds it there, while Lonely's whole being froths and pounds against it.

The rain is steady and the thunder has stopped. The night is complete around them, and Lonely can see Fawn's eyes in the dark.

"You're going to find your love someday," whispers Fawn. "You're going to forget this."

Lonely closes her eyes again. She feels only one thing, and her whole being is that feeling, and her whole being is here. She feels utterly at home.

Then there is a creak on the ladder and a light.

Fawn sits up fast, and Lonely rubs her own face, grabbing at her tears, confused.

Rye doesn't speak. He doesn't tremble as he steps onto the floor of the loft. He's unbuttoning his wet shirt as he walks toward them in bare feet, and Fawn gazes up at him. Lonely looks at her as if for the first time. She is beautiful. The low arched collar of her dress hangs askew across her neck, and her legs are bare to the tops of her thighs where the cloth bunches around them.

There is a moment of silence where all decisions are made and done. Rye's jaw clenches as his gaze wavers over Lonely's body, and then finds its way to Fawn. Fawn smiles up at him with the innocence of a child. Lonely looks into Rye's eyes, and sees what he realized after stealing that kiss out in the fields, and then riding all this day alone in the forest. And it isn't that he wants to be with Lonely.

Fawn reaches for him, pulls him down into the softness of her body. Lonely is so close she can feel the wind of him falling.

She rolls over and stands up. Her body feels cool and quiet for the first time. She watches Fawn and Rye forget her, even as they must know she is there—so comfortable with her that they do not mind her watching. She watches the heartbreaking story of Fawn's flesh: her long bulbous breasts, the lined swoop of her belly that carried his children, the hair below as dark and wild as the night forest Chelya travels through on the way to her full-moon orgy. She watches Rye re-tell that story that he knows so well, with his hands, with his mouth. And she knows it is a good story—a story that she, Lonely, has been grateful to briefly witness.

Everything is clear to her. Rye rises above Fawn, kneeling between her legs and helping her pull the loose dress over her head. Lonely watches them and understands how she herself was a vehicle for their love to express itself, a spark to rekindle the flame between them, and she sees how they ride on, on their own now. She sees how their mouths fill up with each others' mouths, and how in a moment their pelvises will lock and rock, diving into each other as if their lives depend on it, each one pushing forward and forward as if to get somewhere, but the only place they get is into each other.

And they love each other. Even though they argue. Even though Fawn is afraid. Even though the world is changing all around them, and the fruit trees and the honey bees are dying, and the crops are flooding and the City has turned its back on them, still they love each other. And Rye will never betray Fawn. Even if he touched Lonely, and kept touching her, he would still love Fawn. And Lonely wants that kind of love.

So she leaves the bed while they cry out, and she pulls on the dress she was wearing—an old one that Fawn no longer wants—even though it's damp.

She climbs down the ladder that Rye climbed up, and she dips a cup into the water basin near the fire and takes a long drink.

Then she goes out of the house and breathes the wet air. The rain is falling only lightly now, and she can see the stars in some places. Fawn's whispers, her listening, her breath still linger around Lonely's throat. She can still feel the cup of Fawn's palm against that tortured, magical core of her own body, like a blessing. She breathes in and out, in and out, in and out.

Then she starts walking over the hill toward her horse, and tries not to think about how much she wishes she could see Eva one more time.

Because she can't. She can't wait here any longer.

☾

It is the memory of Lonely that finally brings Yora down from the sky.

She crosses the heavens, borne by her goddess sisters who, for her, have become mighty winds. The winds cradle the heavy spirit of this most sorrowful river, rocking her gently as they lift her over the desert. In only a day, she travels from the mountain tops to the valley—a journey that will take Lonely, traveling in the opposite direction, an entire moon. Yora blows at high speed, but from the ground she seems to move at the rate of a dream, too slow to be noticed, inching across a distant sky that never looks real except when the rains touch the earth with their fingers of water.

Over the spires and turrets of the desert, Yora hovers for a day and a night, like a long-ago queen haunting her abandoned castle. Through the oblivion of the dark moon, her sisters, the winds, nudge her. But she will not go yet. She will not rain. She will not be reborn to flow among people.

The desert is far from the City, they tell her. *No pain here, only a fresh expanse in which to start anew. The desert needs you. The desert needs water more than anywhere else in the world.* But Yora does not wish to be needed again. And she knows the desert is not far from the City at all. It is a part of the City, as intimately as the sea is a part of the earth, and the earth a part of the sea. The river runs everywhere, from the top of the world to the bottom.

All night they wing about her, whispering encouragement into her dark, eyeless mass, trailing the mist of her cloud body into streams of starlight.

You have chosen a form that is distant and vague, without substance, without identity, they tell her. *But the nature of such formlessness is change. You cannot hold on. You have nothing to hold to.*

In the night sky, other water droplets join the cloud that is Yora, huddling together in the high cold air, as if pieces of her, numerous as the stars, were scattered across the sky long before she can remember, and from everywhere return to join her now, weighing her down. So much self. And yet what is this self, after all? All rivers are one. There is only one water.

There was a time when Yora willingly took in the pain of the people. That was the identity of the river: something that purified, that washed clean, that soothed. But she had a body too, just as humans do, and that body had limits. When that body of pain became too much, she thought she could wash it away in the sea. But even under the sea someone called to her, needed her. She traveled as Lonely walked, as if forever under the waves, but in the other direction—toward that black hole of unspoken need at the center. When she arrived, it drew her in—the same pain, only deeper—and she stayed there for a long, long time, in human form beneath the island.

What was it that made her leave? She is only water, surely with no will of her own. What turned her briefly human, swimming back then under the waves, then rising from the sea into mist, into cloud, and now floating over the Garden in the mountains, and now revolving slowly over the desert? The sun! The sun is what made her rise into the sky.

And oh, when it did, when that light, that god of gods, lifted her into heaven, evaporating her water body into mist, how joy dissolved her! She was nothing but light, with no memory and no past, leaving the tear-salt of the sea and all the impurities of the earth far below. She transcended all that had weighed her down for years upon years, all the impossibility of suffering, and was rescued in the warm arms of the sun. She was the purest form of water, and then she was not even water but only misty air.

Why ever leave such brilliant love? Birds drifted below her, and even that layer of atmosphere where they flew seemed too low for her now, too heavy.

But in actuality, she never reached the sun itself. The sun lifted those pieces of water up only so high, so Yora hovered in between that light and the earth, where the air was very still and cold. She wanted to stay up there, as close as she could be to that warmth. But a sitting cloud collects things—smoke and dust, ash and pain—just as a pool upon the earth collects debris and clay and sometimes life. Those little particles of the suffering she gathered—for even in the sky, somehow, they reached her—began to weigh her down. Still, still she resisted falling. Why would she ever return to such ugliness?

Because the longer you stay up here, grey cloud, the more you block that light from the earth. And the earth needs it more than you do.

Yora hovers in the black night. Above her, other clouds hang in even colder space, a space so high they will not fall—made of pure ice. But Yora is low enough to feel the body of the earth lying still below her, waiting for morning. She doesn't mean to steal the light from anyone else. She only wants to dissolve in it, and disappear.

But you can't. Don't be afraid: you will find the sun again on the earth. You will find it in a human being, half god, who walks and breathes and whose love will wake you with fire.

Then Yora remembers Lonely. She remembers a young woman who looked back at her with eyes like her own but filled with light. Someone she rescued from the bottom of the sea—one more person who suffered, one more person who needed her, when she thought she could do no more and had nothing left of herself to give. But this person was different. This one weighed nothing. This one went down toward gravity and up toward light, and nothing interrupted her. She was like the way water was once, before it got clouded. She fell down from the tower, she fell upon the earth, and there was the fierce earnestness of a child in her eyes. She was so easy to help, and like rain she would help the world without even trying. Simply lift her above the waves; simply set her face toward the mountain, and she would go forth instinctively toward her dream.

Yora seems to cover the whole sky now, she is so big. She is so heavy that her mist already bleeds downward toward the earth, so that the people of the earth can see the rain coming.

But it is the memory of such light, walking on human feet upon the earth, that finally allows her to relax. She remembers the way it was in the beginning, when loving was natural, joyful, and effortless. She is so much water that finally the water must separate, hurtling through space at terrifying speed, faster than a waterfall, faster than a look passes from one pair of eyes to another.

When the sun rises in the morning, it radiates through the clear blue eyes of the sky, all memory of darkness gone from it.

Yora lies upon the thirsty earth and falls in.

Air

ever in Delilah's memory have the late-summer rains felt the way they feel this year. She will remember one rain in particular, when everything begins to change. It is a female rain, a sad rain, slow and delicate, and yet each drop falls as heavy as a broken heart. It's not a passionate rain, not the kind of rain the desert has come to expect. It is the kind of rain that should fall on a damp autumn day in the mountains. A rain steady and resigned, like something foretold.

Delilah stands still when it begins to fall in the middle of the night. She's been watching the cloud, but she didn't believe anything would actually come of it. As it folds around her, she thinks not of Moon but of Mira. The gentleness of the deer passes between the drops; she can almost feel its animal heat against her skin, but it is only the intensity of her own body's warmth in contrast with the cold water.

She knows now that the deer asked her to take it into her body so that it could tell her something. Something that can only be said in the language of the body. Something she has forgotten. But she still doesn't feel ready to remember.

She looks up, squinting, and watches the grey mass disintegrate into the atmosphere. Right before it reaches her, she can remember the exact weight of Dragon's hands on her hips.

Raindrops kiss her skin, and her skin, unbidden by her, kisses them back.

5ᵗʰ MOON

At the beginning of her fifth moon in the world, the last of the food Lonely carried with her becomes part of her and is subsequently lost. But she's still made no progress toward the mountain, and the forest still feels unknown.

The river has many arms, spreading out to nourish all the mountainsides, and there is no straight path to the source. Every time she leads the horse up a hill for a view of the high mountain again, they are somewhere different than where she thought they were, and seemingly no closer than they were when they started.

This morning they came upon another farm. Though the horse lingered in the trees like a frightened deer, Lonely quickened her pace when she saw that house, especially when she saw two figures, a man and a woman, bending over their garden. This house was made of logs and surrounded by crumbling walls of stone. Flowering ivy grew over it. Lonely hoped for food, but more than that she hoped for another brief respite from loneliness. She thought she would tell them about Fawn's family; she would tell them there were other farmers out here who wanted to know about them and who were lonely too. Then someday Chelya and Rye would thank her for the new friends they had found, and Lonely would have found one small way to repay them.

But her fantasies dissolved when the woman hurried into the house at the sight of her, and the man walked fast at her with tensed and swollen chest, wielding his hoe like a weapon.

"Who are you?" he shouted. "What are you doing here?"

Without thinking, following an older instinct than the friendlier one she'd learned at Fawn's home, Lonely ran.

She remembered what Chelya had told her when Lonely first came to her home. That the mountain people didn't trust anyone. It was something new—something different—for them to take her in.

Tonight as she lies in dead, forgotten leaves, crying for the ache of the woman's cold back and the man's angry mouth after so many days of separation from all contact, she thinks seriously of turning back. But she does not know the way. Her instincts are like wind, with no obvious sense of direction. And she cries because, in all this vast miracle of forest, she could not possibly find Fawn's home again by chance. She cries because she was so busy longing, when she stayed there, for that one love she could not have, that she did not appreciate enough the love that surrounded and comforted her all the time, that comfort of friendly human companionship.

Then, without realizing it, she grows still, and her eyes run dry as she stares unblinking at the black windows of sky and remembers that final night. No, she cannot go back anyway. She could hardly look at them again, after what happened in the loft that night. It was shame enough when Chelya came running, just returning from her full-moon revelry while Lonely attempted to slip off unseen.

Chelya was laughing, her hair falling out of the band that held it back, in dizzying spirals that stuck to her damp, flushed face. She looked beautiful, with a trace of elegance beneath the childish fullness of her face, her white teeth flashing when she smiled.

"Lonely," she said, taking both of Lonely's hands, and her smile trembled. "I'm in love!"

Lonely stiffened.

Immediately, with something that Lonely could only remember now as pure grace—a grace far beyond her years—Chelya forgot herself and became all concern, grasping Lonely's forearms and rubbing them as if Lonely were cold. "What's wrong?" she asked, her eyes searching into Lonely's, but Lonely looked away. Like so many times before, she contracted into a cage of awkward pain in the face of Chelya's easy warmth. She wanted to be so free.

But those hands did soothe her, with their unthinking, confident warmth, as comforting as food. Lonely relaxed a little. "I don't know," she said, feeling that she might cry.

Chelya looked at her, her expression as perplexed as it had been that morning Lonely first awoke to this new world, and Lonely remembered that Chelya was only a child, after all. She pulled herself together and said, "I'm sorry, Chelya. But it's time for me to go. I have to leave here."

Still it sounded so abrupt, almost cruel. It hurts Lonely now, to think of saying it. Chelya swallowed hard and stared at her for a long moment. Lonely had never noticed how lovely her eyebrows were, perfectly arched and even, like the wings of a bird whose body was invisible at the center of her forehead, its heart beating between her eyes. For a moment, in the moonlight, the girl seemed to see right into her, but her smile faltered and she answered only, "How mysterious you are, Princess from the Tower. I guess you won't tell us where you're going?"

Lonely looked at her, her voice caught, and did not know what to answer. What she left behind seemed more real than where she was headed. Chelya interrupted her confusion. "Never mind. But will you wait a minute, please?"

And Lonely turned away as she ran back to the house, wondering if she had hurt Chelya, wondering if she was being selfish with her own life. What had she ever given these people, who had given her so much?

After several long moments, in which Lonely hovered in the dark, backing further into the shadows and glancing around for her horse, Chelya returned with three things.

The first was a sack of food—dried fruit, dried meat, bread, honey—with a strap made of horse hair to sling over her shoulder and across her chest, where it pressed between her breasts and scratched against her heart.

The second was the dress Chelya had made for Lonely, with the help of the forest spirits.

"Wear it when you go to meet your prince," said Chelya with a grin, "because it brings out who you are, and it will light you up." The dress was wrapped in rags and tied with yarn. Lonely attempted to speak, but Chelya hurried on. "I was going to tell you about each part of it, and what it means, but now you'll just have to figure it out on your own. I'll tell you one thing, though. It's made of silk. You'll understand silk when you touch it—it's like you. It takes a thousand years to make. It's the most beautiful material, like from another world, but it's made by worms. Remember that."

Then Chelya handed her the third thing. It was a wreath of white flowers such as Lonely had never seen before—like the hands of the moon, if the moon were a sorceress that walked upon the earth.

"This isn't for you, exactly," Chelya said. "It's for your horse."

"For my horse?"

Chelya laid it in her hands and the petals melted against her skin like a thicket of slick tongues.

"It's a crown," Chelya said, looking down at it, her voice a little hushed. "The animal spirits gave it to me. They said that your animal, the animal that carries you, is known throughout the forest. She is like a queen among the animal spirits, but she does not remember herself. They want you to help her remember herself, because they need her." She finished, looking up at Lonely's face.

Lonely shook her head. "I don't understand."

"They said to place it on your horse's head, over her forehead like a crown, and she will remember herself," Chelya answered, though this did not make things any more clear to Lonely.

Then Chelya leaned forward hastily and kissed Lonely on the cheek. Her lips looked raw and human, and Lonely wondered who had kissed them tonight. "I'll miss you," she said to Lonely, and then she turned and ran.

"Chelya!" Lonely called, not understanding the abundance in her arms, not knowing what to do with such kindness. A thousand years? Had someone been making her something for a thousand years? The idea of such a past, like the story of her own past, was something she had to swallow back, to dredge out of her heart much later on. "Thank you," she whispered.

That night, somewhere in the woods when she was too tired to go on, Lonely stood before her horse with the crown in her hand. She wondered what it meant, and if something would happen when she placed it on the horse's head, and if she should say something special as she did it. She looked at the horse to see if it might give her a sign, but the horse hung its neck low, and seemed unaware that she was holding anything.

So she laid it around the horse's ears, and then tied the bundle of the dress to the horse's back, and slung the food over her own shoulder. Her heart was heavy, but the heaviness made her feel calm, less wondrous than on her first journey from the sea through the meadows and less dazed than on her first journey through the forest which had landed her in Rye's arms. Every day that she traveled after that, she ate of the food that Chelya had given her, and every day she tasted the memory of love. She tried to understand again what love was, and how it was given.

How had she loved, or had she loved at all? Had she loved Rye, or Chelya, or Eva, or Fawn—or only needed them to ease the terror of her nightmares and the ache of her past and the emptiness of her future?

Fawn. Who had loved her despite her own shyness, despite her fear. Who had taken Lonely in, trusted her, shared with her, touched her, and given of the warm, gracious planet of herself, perfectly, in every moment that Lonely had been near her. Had Lonely ever loved her back, or only taken what was given, all the while betraying every gift with that secret lust for Rye—for which she knew she ought to feel shame and yet never did? These are the things she wondered as she walked, and then climbed.

Tonight as she lies among deep-breathing trees, her horse wandering awake near the river, she wishes she'd asked Chelya about her love—whoever she met that night. She feels sorry for envying her. Chelya deserved love because she gave it so freely. And Lonely sees that love is, after all, something that is given. Which is maybe why she still feels lonely now, even after all the love she took.

How else can she go forth, in pursuit of love, if not in a loving manner? Surely she must somehow walk in love, the way Chelya does, so that when her prince sees her, he will recognize that love. But how? She glances at the bundle she untied from the horse's back and lay by her side—the demure bundle of rags that holds the magical dress made just for her. She has been afraid to open it. She has been afraid to see who Chelya and the spirits think she is.

After the rain, Dragon emerges from his cave. He rubs his eyes in the sunlight, not knowing why he has risen. For a long time, there has seemed no reason to.

On the full moon after Delilah left, one woman came to him: a goddess. He thought he recognized her. She reminded him of one of his mothers and sisters from the Garden. But when he began to touch her, when his fire rose for her, the resemblance faded. He could not allow himself to believe she was one of them. They were purely goddesses in his memory: always noble, always more holy than he could ever be or touch, and he needed them to stay that way.

After the goddess was gone, he could not remember her clearly.

But he kept remembering Delilah. He remembered vividly the small weight of her head against his belly, and the childish pride in her voice when she struggled to find words for her past, and her pain which was killing her but which she could not see. The memories repeated mechanically, without thoughts attached to them. There was some emotion they triggered inside him that he could not get enough of, and yet he could not fully feel it.

He isn't sure how long it has been that he has lain on the floor of his lair with the boiling water roaring in his ears, remembering her and watching the dreams of dragon ghosts play over a ceiling of fire. Sometimes, he suddenly wondered if he would stay here forever after all or if there were other worlds out there for him. Where did all those women come from? What was his purpose, in this land?

After Delilah had lain still—after it had happened—he felt strangely numb. They lay still for a long time. He no longer had an erection. Perhaps he slept. Then she said, "Take me out of here, please." He was able to follow this easy, clear instruction. When they reached the sand, it was dawn, and she turned quietly out of his arms and walked back the way she had come without looking back. Still feeling nothing—or almost nothing—he, too, turned and went under again.

This morning he goes to the river and sits beside its song. He feels a little less dazed now. The fresh air excites him. But something nags at him too. When he remembers the feel of Delilah's wetness on his fingers, he feels a compassion so hot it sickens him. And he felt spent, then, though he had not come. He felt happy, but for the first time he wanted to be alone. How complicated it was! Yet now he thinks of her and wonders if he should go to her. He wonders what she is doing, what she is thinking right now, if she is thinking of him. He wonders, in a way he never wondered with all the dream women who came to him on fire, what she felt when that was happening to her. When she came. For the first time since that moment, it explodes upon him: the memory of her explosion, how he was right all along about the beauty that lay dormant inside her and the veils that only he could see through.

But then he doesn't think of Delilah again. Because as he stands up and fills his chest with a mighty breath, he looks downstream.

And he sees Her.

Lonely must have fallen asleep at last, because she wakes now to a shining light above her face. It's not sunlight but a spear like a castle spire, spiraling from the center of her horse's forehead. It is glowing like a beacon, with the new moon darkness still complete around it. The horse is lowering its horn over her head, so that its tip almost touches her own forehead.

In that moment, Lonely feels a sense of absolute certainty. She knows she will keep going. She knows she will reach the high mountain and not turn around. She knows that what she seeks is real.

Then she must have been sleeping again, or perhaps she never really woke, because now she it is morning. Her horse is sleeping by her side, standing with one front ankle tilted against the other. Lonely scrutinizes the horse's lean, weary form and can find no sign of that other: no horn, no brilliant light. But she feels that light anyway, shining through the horse, pointing a direction. She feels the pathway unrolling in her own heart.

"It's this river," she says aloud. "This is the river we follow." The horse opens her eyes, lowers her head, and takes a long drink, her lips whispering against the silk that flows under them. Then she looks right at Lonely, and Lonely knows the vision she had was not a dream.

from now on, says the horse, as if they have always spoken together, *i will carry you. i know the way.*

Dragon wants to kiss her—this beautiful woman whom he has never seen, lying by the river in the desert—but he doesn't. The moment he sees her, he wants to do everything right from now on. And that includes not kissing her until, someday, she asks him to. He lifts her easily, wades back through the river flooding heavily against his thighs, and carries her all the way back to his lair. He carries her down inward, into the hot belly of the earth. There is no resistance.

Softly, as if she might break, he lays her head in his lap. Because it is the only thing he can think to do, he begins to caress her silver hair with his right hand. His fingers slip through it as through the limbs of a jellyfish, and it runs cold over his thigh. She opens her eyes in flickers, and does not seem to see him. Tears pour soundlessly and continually from those eyes—tears he will see again and again, never with any words, and never with a single tremor of her face.

He has no idea what to do with his other hand, and finally when it draws attention to itself by tiring, he notices he is holding it in midair, where it hovers above her belly in tremulous awe. He lowers it, and touches her fingertips where they lie against her hip. She murmurs and turns her head into his thigh, and opens her eyes again. Their electrifying darkness, at the center, gives way to light.

"Who are you?" he whispers, daring now to trace the long white outline of her face, her skin like milk spooned over waves of ocean.

She clutches convulsively at his fingers and then drops them, so that his hand sinks through the dress made of water and touches the warm flesh beneath. The shock of how easily her body can be reached tears his breath from him in gasps. But something magical has happened to him. He is able to ignore his desire—an insignificant thing that he tosses aside. He wants only to help her.

"Shh," he says, though she makes no sound, and he leans over her. "Look at me," he says, willing his voice to wake her into this reality. He hears its animal solidity in the darkness and she looks back at him, her eyes contracting around the picture of his face. She smiles with her slow, naked mouth. "It's all right," he says, "I'll take care of you." Without noticing his own motions, he opens his left palm over the contours of her body, lets it fall like the water over her curves as if in prayer. Simply to feel her luxury in his hands intoxicates him. With a swift passion he clutches her endless hair in his fist and lifts her head toward him. "*Who are you?*" he asks again.

"I don't know." Those are her first words. Her voice is like the last memory of rain before it dries in the hot sun—at once clear and hazed by rainbows. Its sorrow stops his words.

So he just hums to her a wild cascade of notes with no melody, that it seems the dragons sang to him long ago.

For days and nights in that timeless space without sun, among the formless shadows of fire and water, he holds the sleeping goddess in his lap, never taking his gaze from her face or his touch from her skin. His body aches so badly with desire and stillness that he begins to shake, but he keeps singing. Then the aching closes up, and the passion swarms back inside, shooting into his chest, into his throat, consuming him in fire. It fountains up through the top of his head and pours down his body, and he collapses hunched over himself. When she opens her eyes again, he knows only that she owns him. That he will do anything for her. That he is here in this world to love this woman and nothing more.

Like him she needs no food, and there is nothing he can give her. So for days and nights he sings to her, and he speaks to her, and he tells her the stories the dragons told him. For though she gives no sign of understanding, her mouth remembers a slight curve like a smile whenever she hears his voice, and often she closes her eyes and nestles into his chest, as if resting in the cradle of it, and sighs deeply. Softly, experimentally, he touches her with his fire. He wants her all the time, with a rage that ignites every particle of him. When he touches her so lightly with that fire, caressing the faraway hills and valleys of her as he did the first morning, flaming his hands around her waist and raising her up, he thinks he sees a divine delight pass over her ageless features, and she tosses her head back in slow motion, and her hair swirls around her face as if alive.

He longs to pump his fire into her, over and over, and let it all be cooled and relieved and gone—and yet he cannot reach her. Never does she welcome him with desire, and it seems impossible to him that he could force her, even if he wanted to. There is something about the fluid, everywhere map of her that yields no specific entrance. She is unattainable and yet at the same time she surrounds him and drowns him, and he fears he might die in her embrace.

All this feels so terribly familiar that one night, in a state of confusion, he collapses his face against the cold pillow of her hair and weeps, and the name—the memory—that comes unconsciously to his lips is to him the sound of sorrow, the sound of loneliness beyond bearing. "*Yora,*" he whimpers, not knowing or caring any more whether or not he speaks aloud. "*Please.*"

She pushes warm against him, then turns with a suddenness he has not felt from her before. "Yora," she repeats after him. "That is my name."

Dragon starts, waking abruptly from his bleary sorrow. How can this be? He had thought Yora was a different girl, a young virgin, whom a Unicorn stole away from him two and a half moons ago. And yet he murmured her name to this goddess, as if they have some connection, for one reminds him of the other. "Have you come through the desert before," he asks, "in another form?"

"Maybe," she says. "I've been here in many forms."

Dragon pulls back and grips her. There is a furious suspicion in his heart that he does not understand. "Another Yora came to me once," he hisses. "Who are you? Tell me the truth."

"The truth," she repeats, and her eyes turn back on him with an otherworldly tenderness that makes his mouth contort with longing. "I don't know the truth," she says gently, without fear.

"Yora," he chokes. He pulls her whole body onto his lap so that he can feel her smooth coolness against him. Sick with the heat of his own body, he leans into her, brushing her cheek with his.

"Ask me to kiss you," he begs in a whisper.

But she doesn't answer, only caresses his face with her hand. It is the first time she has ever deliberately touched him. He shakes as if a monster rattles him from inside, and she holds him, not tightly but completely.

"The goddesses sent me here," she says then.

"What goddesses?"

"The Garden," she says.

And Dragon's gratitude shakes him even harder, whether with tears or laughter he does not know or even care.

There is a change in the horse as it walks beneath her, as it fills her again with that familiar comfort of flesh: a soft knowing that extends beyond Lonely, and at the same time guides her forward. She calls the horse female now.

"I'll keep your secret," she tells her, smooth arms wrapped around the hairy neck. She caresses the horse as they walk. She looks into one nervous eye, that looks back at her from beneath a bony brow. The flower crown that dangles above it never dies. Lonely remembers the men in the desert, how they tried to capture this beauty. And she knows that at least, if she loves no one else, she loves this animal—this animal that has carried her for as long as she can remember, and has both followed and led her, everywhere she goes. Even at the times when Lonely walks beside her, still the horse seems to carry her.

The river guides them for two days more through trailing thickets, and little meadows offered up like sunlit gifts between patches of forest. The mountains seem to pull her in, into that mysterious magnetism that keeps all life from floating into the sky. At the same time they rise to meet her, lifting her.

Everywhere—in the slow turning of the earth from hill to valley, in the humble blinking of tiny blue flowers from the depths of the grass, in the tremble of rabbits as they freeze to let her pass, and in reflective interludes of shadow—Lonely still feels Fawn's presence, Fawn's confident feet upon the earth. Those feet seem to echo Lonely's when she walks, as if the earth is a frozen pool beneath which her counterpart lives reflected, as if Fawn and the others are all parts of her—other lives she could have lived.

She is lonely. But she lets it hurt, day after day, and does not fight it. She knows where she is going.

She is hungry for a day before remembering she is a goddess; then she decides she can eat anything. As in her earliest days in the desert, she reaches for colors that seem to fulfill her. She eats the meadow grass, and the pieces of sunlight caught inside it melt on her tongue, turning her hair an even brighter yellow like the yolks of eggs. She eats flowers that make her eyes bluer, with rainbow flecks inside them. She eats the earth in its many textures—eats the death and the life in it, the wetness and the dryness, the dust and the clay. And it makes her calm.

She eats feathers she finds on the ground or caught in the branches of trees, and they pull her gaze upward toward the mountain, shivering in her belly with restless hope.

Then the forest thickens, and the meadows end. Sometimes, when the trees grow too thickly to pass through, Lonely and her horse must step from stone to stone in the middle of the river, all of their concentration focused on making one step and then the next, their minds stilled by the rushing of the river. Soon the river slows and deepens, leaving no rocks bare, and its color turns a rosy brown like the flushed cloth of Fawn's skin. Lonely and the horse must bend their bodies in and out of the underbrush along the river's edge, so that if one could see their motions in empty space—with all the dense life of the forest removed from around them—they would seem to be engaged in some strange, bobbing dance.

Sometimes they cannot see the river right beside them, and sometimes it makes no sound. But they keep track of it by a cool breath, a feminine softness, a relieving openness which all things around it lean toward for reassurance. Sound is again made up of birdsong, but the bird calls are all new, wild and hot-blooded in the night, laughter and screams. Trees bend and tangle any way they wish, not only upward but also sideways and even downward, angling and curving so that it is impossible to tell which limbs began at which trees, all of them clothed in vines and connected like one being that sweats and pants in the late summer heat.

It is hard going, but the going itself makes Lonely feel strong, and her heart proud in its determination. Most days, the old woman's curses seem more distant, and that island in the sea so many moons behind her. She does not imagine that anything could ever stop the simple power of her legs to carry her forward, the power of her desire, the loyalty of her horse who walks beside or beneath her. The story that haunted her—the father who built that terrible dream, the people oppressed beneath the illusion of it, the woman he forgot, the secret buried beneath the island—all these seem pieces of a life not really hers now, not part of who she will become. She is all her own, a soul he never saw clearly, on a journey of her own making which no one understands but she and the one whom she seeks.

This is what she believes on the days she believes, when she sees her prince's face in the river, his smile in the sky. Then she knows there is some-one else out there who knows her, who will love her, and her glimpses of him in the patterns of life around her tell her which way to go.

But sometimes, at night, the forest seems endless in all directions, even upward. The sounds frighten her, and none of them sound like her name. There is no wind here, only stillness and heat and the invisible pull of the river's depth. Sometimes when she drinks from that darkness, something changes inside her, and she wastes hours crying by the river's edge, overcome by a sense of loss and hopelessness that she cannot define. She thinks of the love between Fawn's and Rye's bodies, and knows that no one has ever felt that way for her. Then her own body begins to weigh her down.

She thinks of the empty sea and the homelessness of her life, and when she tries to remember the mountain—its cool, idyllic shape—she feels only a chill deep inside, as if the word "lonely" echoed like a stone through ev-ery layer of what she is, bouncing pointlessly from wall to wall into a black, waterless abyss. She both misses her father and hates him, and she wishes he would come back to her somehow and tell her if she is doing the right thing, or if she should have stayed in the tower, as he told her to, until her prince came to rescue her.

As she lies awake on those nights, she feels the curse of what her father has done, and in her sleep she tosses as if to free herself from the bonds of it. Sometimes she sees the horse awake, too, pacing under the trees.

But in the morning she shakes it all off. Whatever she was to Dragon, that was not real. Whatever she was to her father, that was not real. This, only, is real. This climbing the mountain in material sewn by Fawn's hands, and the tender face in her dreams, and the strengthening ache in her legs.

She still eats whatever she finds, which now includes nuts and fruits of all shapes and sizes, and leaves both hard and soft, crispy and wafer-thin, juicy and bitter. But her horse, she notices, eats less and less, and begins to shine.

It is hard to notice that they are traveling gradually upward, since this tangled nest of jungle dips them up and down, up and down, the land as complex as the shapes of the trees. But after five or six days of this, the river thins again, and ahead of them they can hear the sound of water falling. The trees finally open a breathing space above them, where murky clouds brood and swirl in a silver sky. Massive boulders meditate between trees, sparkling with flecks of mica and whispering about the great mountain they fell from long ago. The hope of rising spurs Lonely onward and makes it easy for her to scramble up a rock face, her body thrusting opposite the rush of the falling river beside her. Several times she must stop and wait for her horse, who often hesitates. She feels they are closer—much closer. Perhaps they are almost there.

Yet by the time night falls, still she cannot see the mountain! Though the bird songs are sweet and easy again, low, muscular trees with flowers in colors of the heart lean low all around them, hemming them in. The flowers are heady with sweetness, but Lonely feels claustrophobic as she lies down to sleep, wondering if they are going the right way after all. The ground has leveled out a little. She lies awake for what seem like hours, intermittently talking to the horse. Since the vision of the horn, the horse has not spoken to her again, but Lonely asks her questions anyway, to comfort herself.

"What's *your* purpose?" she murmurs. "Why are you coming with me all this way? Why did you come with me at all? Why would you want to climb such a mountain?" She remembers what Chelya said about the horse, and what Moon said, long before that—how that horse could always find her way back to her.

"Other people know something about you that I don't," she muses. "Something strange about you, but I don't know, I trust you. I think you're like me, somehow, aren't you?"

The river tumbles through her sleep. She dreams she is back in the tower, pounding her fists against a wall stronger than ice, stronger than glass, while the sickly face of the old woman laughs outside, as if she's already won. Lonely wakes furious and afraid, and falls asleep only to dream the same thing again.

By morning she is shaken and exhausted, but grateful simply for the light of the sun. She walks another day through the endless forest. The river, only a stream now, tiptoes through. Moss softens their step.

In the last gold handfuls of day, thunder breaks through the distance, and the horse lifts her head and bends her ears sharply. At first it is only a rough powder of noise tossed far away and high above, but soon it asserts itself more grimly in the closer distance, as if bearing down on the swaying roof of the woods. The wind grows grey and hurried, and the trees, just faintly, begin to wail.

"Come on," cries Lonely to the horse, bending forward in the first raindrops, which are far icier here than in the meadows she came from. She does not feel now as she felt in the house, with Fawn standing sturdy behind her in the kitchen—as if she knew that despite Fawn's fear, nothing terrible could possibly happen in her presence. Now there is no Fawn; there is no kitchen;

there is no house, no bed, nothing warm but the horse, whose mane Lonely grips as she searches frantically for cover.

She hopes for some cave—some leaning bank at least, some cozy darkness. But the rain is coming on so hard now that they cannot continue further, and must settle for a dense thicket, into which she tumbles and rolls herself into a shivering ball. How was it that she felt so wild, so frenzied by passion, that night with Fawn when she stood in the lightning and rain and seemed to hear the thunder shout her name? She thought she must break away from Fawn then. She thought at the time that Fawn's fear held her back from the full moon ecstasy, and yet now it seems that the soft safety of Fawn allowed her that courage and freedom to feel, without which she would never have run out into the rain.

The horse stands over her, only partly covered by the brush, her hard legs and caged chest far sturdier than her ethereal grace so often makes her seem. She seems bigger than she is, her body somehow covering Lonely completely, so that Lonely does not feel the rain. But the thunder comes loud as if it will break the earth, as if it is the ending of all stories. Like a child, Lonely grips her own knees against her chest and stares wide-eyed out at the thrashing nothingness. She remembers how it was, that night with Fawn. How the sky darkened before the sunset and closed in the world. How the trees became a nightmare. How Fawn trembled and cried against her, and how this life seemed to have utterly changed—the sunny fields and the laughing dinner further away than a dream—as if nothing could ever again be the way it was. Yet in the morning, when Lonely found herself alone in the forest again, the birds were singing and the world went on, the storm forgotten as if imagined. And in that darkest center of darkness, inside the room within the house, inside the rain and the obliterating thunder, inside that roaring night, she—Lonely—had felt and lost the most intimate closeness of her life.

She remembers that now, as the sky seems to crash to pieces around her, and the world seems to end again, and though Fawn was so quiet, so meek, so small in her voice, now the walls of rain around the horse fall like the whole world is Fawn's body, Fawn's tears.

Lonely does not remember the end of the storm, nor falling asleep. But she dreams of Delilah standing on the lip of cliff outside her cave, her tiny, warrior's body silhouetted in the ruthless desert sun. She dreams of the City spread out before her, and the dog's friendly face beckons her downward, but then turns snarling and fierce when she takes a step toward it. She dreams of Yora's face under the water where she bathed with Fawn, the sadness of those eyes holding her there until she can no longer breathe.

She wakes up gasping, feeling that someone has grabbed hold of her hand and torn her upward from the mire of her sleep. *Come on*, he seems to say, *I need you*, and she's sure it is her prince calling to her, but when she wakes, it is only a squirrel, his miniature hands scrambling in the dirt near her to collect a nut that's fallen there in the night. When she lifts her head, he darts away instantly, then sits on his haunches at a safe distance to survey her while eating his meal with hyperspeed motions. The rain is gone, the sun clear and everywhere. She leans forward and stares at the squirrel, certain there is something familiar about him. But at this he leaps off, running in quick grey puffs, and like a fountain of weightless fur leaps onto a tree trunk and spirals up it. From the lowest branch he shouts down at her, bright and happily incensed.

get on with it. move on, you! we're busy, everyone is busy with their life's work, and no time for lazy dream and sorrow. this is my place, where i find what is mine, and you—you get on, get going, go find what is yours. do you think life lasts forever?

The squirrel's chatter is a relief, almost like a human voice. She stands and brushes the golden needles from the dress she took from Fawn—now threadbare. One day soon, she'll have no choice but to open the bundle Chelya gave her, and wear whatever is inside.

As she stands, the wind passes over, and Lonely remembers its voice in the storm last night—the first time she'd heard that voice in so long. The heads of the trees swirl together in a chorus of expectancy, like the swish of two realities passing each other by, where one scene is exchanged for the next.

Missed me? The wind asks.

Secretly, Lonely feels a rush of gratitude, but she lifts her chin. "I know I can't depend on you," she says carelessly.

You can't depend on anything.

Even my prince? Lonely thinks, but she doesn't say it aloud, because she's afraid to hear the answer. "Anyway," she tells the wind, "You are only air. You can't carry me to where I'm going."

I've carried you all the way here, says the wind, and in the silence afterward, Lonely is tempted to believe it.

"Am I going the right way?" she asks, suddenly vulnerable.

You're going the only way you can go.

And Lonely, relieved for those few moments until she begins to doubt again, mounts her horse and continues on.

Yora walks to the river on the full moon. It is the first time she's walked so far on these legs. She goes because the moon's face is familiar, and because she remembers her own name.

There are so few things she remembers. Like the sound of the river, which must mean something. It has so many layers—the outer roar, the many folds of music, and the twisting secret passage at the center—just as her body has many layers, layers she keeps uncovering, deeper and deeper in. At the core is something she remembers, and it has to do with the direction of the river and freedom. It has to do with the moon's white face in the center of the black sky. She turns her head from where she kneels, fists in her lap, and blinks as she gazes down the river's path, which squeezes between stones in the distance and disappears.

She cannot remember where the river is going. It is somewhere bigger than this human form she's in can comprehend. She closes her eyes and weeps, though she feels nothing. She takes the tears on her fingertips and places them in the water. The river will know. The river will know what to do with these.

She came here tonight because she remembers her name and because of Dragon's sweet eyes, and the beauty she sees reflected when he looks at her, and the beauty she feels when he touches her. His eyes tell her she is someone who has so much to give, but she can't imagine what. The thought of it tires her. At the same time, those hands and kisses awaken something within her that frightens her, and so she takes that feeling to the river, to wash it away. The sound soothes her. It drowns out the voices in her head, which are familiar and anguished and full of a need she cannot fill.

She came here because he calls her *Yora*. She doesn't know, or can't remember, what that means.

But when she speaks it in her mind—*Yora Yora Yora*—it sounds like the river.

She watches it. Sometimes she thinks the stones are moving, surging backward through time, while the river is still—just shivering and pulsing in the light. Sometimes the rocks look so sharp, slicing through the smooth flesh of the water, that she must close her eyes to stop the pain, though of course water cannot feel pain. Sometimes the music of the river becomes a wail, like the din of so many screams they are no longer recognizable except as a haunting blur of sound.

They are almost there, Lonely can feel it. In the trees, and in the rain that falls grey and steady for half the next day, she still can't see the mountain. But she draws hope from the cold clarity of the air, the blue tinge to the evening, and the angelic quality of the birdsong.

She can feel the stillness, a stillness even within the breeze—more still than the desert, a stillness like the bottom of the sea. She can feel the mountain as if it is coming toward her.

Walking becomes easy, and the wind is thin and lightens her. She no longer needs to eat anything. She only drinks occasionally from the stream, which is barely moving now, and whose taste is primal and windy.

They pass through a forest of aspen whose roots are all one, who are all one tree and who sing a clattering chorus of wind. Their white trunks shock against dazzling beds of green moss. Lonely can glimpse the sky, leaning down through the treetops, so close she can see its dreams written across it in clouds of such intricate and varied architecture they would take a whole other story to describe. Sometimes their mist swings low into the very branches of the trees, and even the wind hushes itself in awe.

The last trees before the sky are a stately mass of solemn spruce. Lonely walks more slowly now, winding between them. They are very straight and tall and quiet. There is a loneliness in their dark spaces, in which Lonely must fight the fear that her lover is nothing but a ghost, after all.

That night she dreams of her father's touch. His hairy arms encircling her, pillowing her small head. His big hand in hers. When she wakes she knows, for a moment, that that was all that ever mattered. Not his godness, not his dreams, not his mistakes or his illusions or his power over the world, but only his humanness. Only his touch. Without that she would never have thought to search for love. She would never have left the tower.

She walks on, her body weak with emotion and yearning, and there is light ahead. Abruptly, the spruce trees end. There are no more trees. Lonely steps into a yellow field that ends at the sky.

Beyond it, what was one mountain is many mountains, or a mountain with infinite sides. It is made entirely of beauty, some material that human beings have never invented. From a distance it had been a simple silhouetted pattern that formed a story Lonely couldn't read, like the spider webs in the forest or the black marks in Malachite's book. But now, as if she is already inside that story, the mountain is no longer a simple outline but countless crooked angles turning in and out of her view, into the nests of far valleys and the shoulders of other mountains around it. In mysterious spaces high above her, she can see meadows with smears of color languishing inside them, swaths of white snow, and a series of peaks that disappear into ringlets of clouds.

I've done it, she thinks slowly. *This is the mountain I saw from my tower, on the other end of the world.* What chills her is that it looks just like the tower. Cold, icy, remote. As if she's come all the way around the world and come right back. As if maybe all this time, her prince has been trapped in a tower of his own.

The air is so still. No birdsong. No old woman cursing her, no one stopping her. Nervous for no reason, Lonely turns around and looks back, for the first time, on the distance she came. All the mountains she never explored, with all their hidden recesses and tempting peaks, their steep rocky outcroppings untouched by human hands and their hidden valleys with hidden houses and families—they sheathe themselves now in a smooth painting of green, hiding the tumult and decadence of the jungle and the darkest lengths of the deep river. Through fields and valleys she has never walked, she can see the river winding and winding away.

She cannot see the valley that was her home for two and a half moons, and the desert is only a distant white mass dissolving into the horizon. But the expanse of all she has crossed shocks her with a kind of staggering exhilaration. *Why does being above something make me feel powerful? Why do trees spend their whole lives reaching up?* For when she traveled among them for so many days, they had told her as much. *We are going where you are going,* they had said. *We, too, seek the sky.* Whatever the reason, it must be why her father built the tower.

Lonely gazes for a long time upon the expanse of her past, which from this angle looks as mysterious as her future—the earth such a complicated reflection of a sky so clear and open. She misses Rye and Fawn, Chelya and Eva. She would have liked to see them again. She would have liked, too, to see Yora's face again, and ask her about that sorrow lost in her eyes.

And she would have liked to know—she wishes she had known, as she traveled through each scene of her journey—that everything was okay after all. That she would make it, in the end. Because then maybe she could have seen that nothing she did along the way was wrong or a mistake, but merely one of the steps she had to take to get here. Maybe she would have seen, as she thinks she sees now, that every love she felt—for Yora, for Dragon, for Moon, for Fawn, for Rye—had in fact been real, had in fact been love, and was not worth less than the love she would feel for her prince, the one she was destined for. Each was only a different kind of love. Some loves more of the body and some more of the heart; some loves frightening and some peaceful; some loves waking and some soothing. Each one was important, each one real.

Now she will go up into the sky, and everything will change. She will find the one, and that will be enough. For he is her one purpose; he is the answer to the long, passionate question of her life. Even though the question, too, was beautiful.

But when she turns back around, she must stand still in a sudden, seeping despair that pools around her feet and sucks her heart downward. That mountain, as intimate as its beauty may seem, rises from a fog with the same unyielding finality that she could see from all the way across the earth and the ocean. She cannot see its peaks in the clouds, and the sides sweeping up to those peaks are swift as flight. There is no way up.

Her second cause for anxiety is the openness all around her, whose sudden eeriness she cannot explain to herself until she realizes that the horse is gone. She stumbles forward over the jagged crystal of the stones. The wind begins to pour over her, like a river whose current travels against her.

Lonely, it says. *Lonely, Lonely, Lonely.* An emptiness seems to open beneath her feet, as deep as the mountain is tall, and as white, as silent, as familiar. *Lonely shall be your name.*

"No," Lonely whispers, closing her eyes, the old woman's curse rushing in upon her. She tries to sense the horse's presence, certain that she must be near. She needs the warm anchor of that body beneath her hand, to keep her from the abyss that keeps opening and opening, and has always been opening.

I would rather have no name than be called Lonely, she thinks in a panic, struggling for balance. *I would rather have no name at all.*

When she opens her eyes she sees a bundle in a thicket of bulbous leaves that trail close to the rock as if they could draw life from it. It's something that has fallen from where she tied it to her horse's back. It is the dress that Chelya gave her.

Quickly, she bends and tears it open. She barely looks at the dress as she rips the old one from her body and puts the new one on. She catches a whiff of feathers and grass, blood and stones. Whatever it is, this is the dress that Chelya, little goddess of love—goddess of milk and honey, laughter and fulfillment—told her she would meet her prince in. It clings to her body, affirming her form, and at the same time it sails beyond and behind her, as if opening spaces for her legs to stride. This is not a body whose name is *Lonely.* She feels its heat, its determination.

There is no way up. But it's okay. I, who am more than a horse after all, will save her now.

A butterfly with miniature yellow wings draws her attention to the flowers that bloom from that strange vine over the rock, and with her eyes, and then with her feet, Lonely follows it. It flies around a corner, around a scrubby, tough little evergreen tree whose needles hold the wind at bay, as if giving her space to pass. It flies down to the smooth, glassy stream, whose flow is slow and prayerful now, and thinner than Lonely's body. It flies across the stream and up alongside it, and around a silver boulder covered with a stubble of lichen like the stiff fuzz of maleness on Rye's face.

The butterfly skips upward against her vision. *once i crawled upon the earth,* it says. Then it is gone, leaving a waterfall behind it, and me.

In her vision I am white, but I feel blue, and the clear color of the water feels blue to me, too. And that blue that I am feels like light, not color at all. The waterfall is thin and wispy, as if more air than water, and neither of us is aware of its making any sound. Lonely looks at me, and her body turns all to grace. At this moment in the story, I can say who I am. At this moment, in Lonely's eyes, I am safe.

She sees my horn and she knows it means something—that somehow the form of the horse she knew now has meaning—but she doesn't know what it is. She remembers the white horse from the fairy tale, and wonders again, *Why?*

Her dark eyes surge toward me, but she is falling, but falling and rising at the same time, and the earth is rising toward her, and the sky lowering to meet her.

She must crawl on her hands and knees to reach me, dizzy. I wish I could help her but I am too shocked by this realization I am having, again, of who I am, and cannot move. Both of us are dizzy, remembering now, suddenly, the divinity that we are.

She collapses against my belly, and gazes up, and she sees through my head, up the tower that spires round and round from my forehead. She remembers that the place where she herself comes from is high at the top—the top of that tower, where she was born of dreams, born of the clouds and the freedom of possibility. And so her eyes spiral up and up and up, and we keep going, higher than she could ever see, and still she spirals upward until she is so dizzy from spiraling, she forgets everything but her own soul.

White clouds open above her, revealing light behind light behind light. Lonely is in the tower again, and the white bird is there, his wings constantly waving—never lowering him fully to the ground—and his feet are careful and spider-like as they lift her heart. His eyes are blue like Eva's, but they glint with the reflection of her own. And she thinks, *Oh yes, I forgot about you. I forgot there was no tower after all—only love.*

Where she is going now, she will forget me: the one that carried her. I know why. The lips that wake her draw fire into her mouth. They are wet like ice that is melting. They feel like the slick clay at the bottom of a river she has never yet entered into, only walked beside all her days, full of a longing that began before she can remember. The tower is gone again, and fear folds around her like the universe, and she knows why she waited so long to arrive.

For in all her father's fairy tales of love, this was always the end of the story. There was nothing that came after.

Lonely, I call, because I am afraid.

But she is gone.

Dear Moon,

I'm so lonely. I had no idea.

This is the letter I would write you, if I could write a letter.

If I had paper and a pen. If I could still form words with these hunting, killing hands, which I'm not sure that I can.

If I knew where you were.

If I thought you would understand.

I have a lot of questions. Dragon made me come. What does that mean? I don't want to be owned by anyone. I don't want to see him any more. I avoid him. But sometimes (I don't know why), I watch him. When he finally emerged again, he brought a woman with him. I don't know where she came from. I tell myself I don't care.

She's definitely a goddess, not like anyone I've ever seen. She's like some terrible grey cloud, but she moves like the inside of her is made of glass. Like she's afraid that if she steps too heavy, she'll break, and be pierced by her own shards. She holds Dragon, but when he touches her she looks back at him in a strange, empty way, like she's really somewhere else.

I can tell that drives him crazy. I know, because Mira used to look at me like that. I want to know, how can someone love you but be somewhere else at the same time?

Moon, when I saw the Unicorn, I saw that there is something else to life, something more that we haven't realized. Something so beautiful it's worth following, and not giving up your body to whoever and whatever wants it along the way. Like you do. Yes, okay, like I do.

I thought that girl who came to Dragon in the spring—the bright white girl—was pathetic. But what pisses me off is that she wasn't. If I know anything for certain, I know that girl owns herself. When she speaks the word "love", she knows what she's talking about. When she looks at you, she's all there, you know what I mean? I don't even know how to be looked at like that. It scared the hell out of me when she did it.

That's the way the deer looked at me, too, though. That's the way the animals look at me right before I kill them.

Moon, I thought wanting was the only thing I could be sure of, but I don't know what I want any more. I try to do what the snake told me, to follow the pain upward. From my vagina, which is always frustrated and hurt and angry, through my stomach, always hungry, through my heart, which is—I don't know. I try to follow the pain upward but it's so—well, you know, painful.

You told me to follow the pain, to go inside myself, but you don't know what's in there either. You won't look inside your own self. You can't bear it, can you? Why do we hate ourselves, Moon?

I ran away to the desert, but it swallowed me up, swallowed me up inside my past. You know how your past follows you—not just the things that happened to you, but the things that didn't happen. Not just the things you did, but the things you didn't do. I think about death all the time, and you'd think I wouldn't care about death, but I'm so afraid of it. I don't know what it means to be old. But that Unicorn was old, I think. Older than I will ever be.

I hate to admit it, Moon, but sometimes I want someone wise. Someone who knows more than me. Someone who can explain to me what it's all meant, how it all fits together, what I'm supposed to do. I'm not okay any more in this mortal life, hunting animals, hunting men. The hunger never ever goes away, and I'm tired of it. It scares me that if I stop feeding it, I'll die.

Sometimes I wish I could find that Unicorn. I know it won't love me. I know it won't want to look at someone as ugly inside as I am. But I long for it anyway. Should I try to find it—somehow?

You would tell me yes. You would tell me to do whatever I want, you would say something wise. But you're not wise. You try to get me to love myself but you don't love yourself either. So you don't really understand.

I have to tell you something, Moon. I hate you for leaving me. Every time you come here, you leave again. Couldn't you be the one person who doesn't? Don't you get it that I'm going to die someday? You'll have eternity to fly around the world, wasting your powers and denying yourself. Why can't you stay with me while I'm alive?

I tried to be the one to leave once. I came here to leave everything and everyone behind. But it didn't work. Because they left me first, a long time before that. They won.
—*Lil*

"Open your eyes. I need to know if you're real."

But I can't, thinks Lonely. *I've died.*

"Please."

"I can't," she says, surprised at her own voice. "I'm afraid."

"Of what?"

"I'm afraid to find out *you're* not real, not really there."

"Of course I am." But the voice is soft—caught and hushed, as if it will at any moment flee with the wind, leaving her in silence again. "I've always been here," he whispers. "Every part of the way. Don't you remember the squirrel, the dog, the snake, the dragonfly, the thrush?"

She can feel his breath with each word against her cheek, and her lips buzz where his mouth a moment before weighed them down. His hand cradling hers is cool and tight, with slim, confident bones—his thumb hooked in hers. The pleasure of it hurts. But still she cannot look.

"Lonely is my name," she says, not knowing for sure any more if she's speaking aloud. "What if I don't know how to love? What if I mess it up?"

"But you're already here. Haven't we already loved each other this whole time, journeying toward each other? Hasn't love always been happening, and loneliness, too? Nothing is ever gained, and nothing is ever lost. So you don't have to be afraid. Lonely, we are the only ones in the world."

She's not sure, later, if any of it was spoken aloud. But when she opens her eyes, no one is there.

Sometimes you get a glimpse of the absurdity of it all.

Information leaks—in the form of a smell, or the mumblings of a homeless person, or accidentally taking the wrong route home one day and finding yourself in an unknown neighborhood. And you have the faintest realization that something is wrong. Where *does* all the trash go, anyway? And the fumes from the cars *do* make people double over in tears and cough, if they get too close. And was this food something that was once alive? Where does anything come from, and what is sacrificed in the making of it?

Maybe, for a few of you, the questions grow. Maybe you cannot stop thinking about them, for a while anyway. Though you never speak of them, they obsess you. *Are cars destroying the sky? The very air I breathe?* You notice your own breath for the first time. Yet without your cars, you could not get to work, and you could not make money, and you would starve. Without your cars, you could not see your loved ones. Without your cars, you could never leave this little lot you call home, which does not actually produce anything you need to live or be happy.

When your shoes are worn out, should you try to repair them instead of throwing them away? But no one knows how to repair shoes any more, least of all you. No one knows how to make shoes. Isn't there some natural way to make things waterproof, or to stick things together, or to store food, or to sterilize things, or to clean, or to heal a wound? But no one remembers, or knows where to begin. Maybe a few of you—I know it sounds crazy—miss nature. You wish, almost, that it would come for you. Come find you, come take you, even if—*oh god, Hanum*—it tears your lives apart. Because you cannot find your way back to it.

You have good intentions, after all. Do not be angry with yourself. You are trapped in the world you grew up in, where the knowledge you were trained in and the mechanical body of the life you were given is not made for those intentions. With every move, you destroy—without even meaning to, without even always knowing it—as if your limbs are the limbs of a giant and merciless machine even while your soul still thinks itself human. Deep down—how can you help it?—you are living your lives in shame.

Maybe some manufacturer takes advantage of this secret shame and begins to sell "natural" things. Their origins and making are just as confusing and complex—and more expensive. *You cannot do it yourself,* say the advertisements. And you can't. You wouldn't know where to begin, and there is no one left to teach you. Deep down, you are living your lives knowing those lives are wrong, and yet you close your eyes and ears and noses now to the signs, because there is nothing you can do. You close up your senses, and cease to trust them, and live your lives outside of your bodies.

It's as if one day you decided to be happy from now on. But you've never been happy, that you can remember, and all the neural pathways in your body are rigged for sorrow. The entire architecture of your being was built that way, so long ago that you don't remember how it was built, or how to take it down, or how to begin again.

Lonely sits up fast beneath a copper sky. *I am somewhere different,* she thinks, *so it can't have been a dream.* But fear moves in her belly. She remembers the image of her prince in her glass tower, how she cried and cried for it to return, and how it never did.

Her first impression of this sweep of earth before her, rising into a last, humble bluff of dead grass, is of finality. Bare rock painted thickly with close sun, only the tiniest of scattered trees, and a giant lake with no disturbance upon its surface, reflecting only clouds. There is no sound but for a very slight wind. Like the end of all things.

Then a flock of soft white birds explodes around her body from behind, from nowhere, so close she can feel them. Now already they are a great distance ahead of her, spiraling like scattered pages over the still lake and coming down. With a kind of angry determination, Lonely rises to her feet and follows them. She recognizes them. They are like a hundred copies of the bird that held her heart in the tower.

It seems that in an instant she has arrived at the edge of the lake, though it seemed far away before. She can see every bird clearly, as it floats there in ripples—as if she were close up to them, though the lake is large. It is like this, she will discover, here at the top of the world. Distance—the time between a thought and a word, the separation between two beings—is so thin as to be hardly noticed and is crossed instantaneously.

Someone in that white mass is saying her name—that name she has forgotten, that is truly hers.

She searches among the birds, and then she sees him: a stranger in their midst. A stranger to her, his face turned away. His body blurred by their beating wings, but unable to hide among them, for his skin shines and the shadows between his limbs are dark. The birds begin to fall apart from him, as if willing her to see him. Still, he does not face her, but she knows that he can see her. Water drips from his black hair; his bare shoulders twitch beneath the cold drops. The birds puff along the water like clouds, heedless and free.

The moment they leave him, he turns and wades fast, almost running, through the water—away from her. She has no doubt that she will follow, but she moves more slowly than he, afraid of his coldness and the hidden expression on his face. Quickly at the shore again, he walks upward, but his walk is oddly smooth, as if he moves by more than walking—to the top of a bluff that seems the highest point of this lost peak among the clouds. At the very top of the world, he stops between two leaning outcroppings of stone: eerie, ancient stacks of grey fragment that Lonely will remember for the rest of her life. Though he is far away, he looks at her now; he gazes at her solemnly as, catching his gaze, she begins to run.

Then there is a point when she feels she must stop running, for his gaze casts some invisible separation between them—not close enough for their hands to touch if they reached out, but close enough for her to see every detail of his face, a face it will take her a long time to take in. A prince stands before her, someone she has seen as if she knew him forever, in her dreams, utterly familiar and yet utterly strange to her. That face will seem to change each time she looks again. This first time, her mind grasps at details that surprise her, like his bright teeth and the way his cheeks slope in tight to the point of his narrow mouth, and the tangle of lines at the edges of his eyes. He wears nothing but a skirt of black and white feathers, and a pale crown of lichen. But what startles her most is the strangling sorrow in his expression, a sorrow that she feels she would never be able to reach, were she to stay here with him for a hundred years.

She stares at him and doesn't know what to do. She can hear songbirds in the grass now, and their calls seem to happen within her, a ringing in her skull. Then she notices also the sound of water, and sees that a spring bubbles up from near his feet, and flows downward toward the lake, as if water itself begins here at the top of the world. The man gazes at her and betrays nothing; he could be a statue, except that as she looks deeper into him, she notices a tension that is pulling his shoulders inward, freezing his arms and hands at his sides. She sees that he is, almost imperceptibly, vibrating with that tension, that he is halfway between coming toward her and bolting, and that this point in the middle is not peace but a wild, fragile, temporary pause.

As soon as she realizes this, she feels desperate. It is not even a desperation that comes from longing, but rather a sense that the world will collapse if they separate, and that, more importantly, he needs her. So she calls out clearly, because she can think of nothing else to do, "What is your name?" *At least if you leave me,* she thinks, *I'll know how to call you back.*

For a moment, she thinks he will not answer. Then he lifts his right hand and gestures hopelessly toward the infinity beyond him. "Sky," he says.

Then he is gone.

She scrambles up to stand where he stood. She looks beyond it.

It seemed to her that he simply turned his back and jumped, though it happened so fast she could not be sure. She looks to where he disappeared. Beyond the stone outcroppings is purely nothing. She stands at the edge of a cliff, whose gashed side—nearly vertical—falls beneath the clouds that stand in a dense bank below her.

"Sky," she tries, tasting his name in her mouth, feeling an incongruent joy to finally know it. "Sky!" It seems impossible to her that he will not answer. "Sky!" she calls at the top of her lungs now, because it doesn't matter, there is no shame—there is only the actual sky, vacant before her, endless, like a joke.

Now the man she saw seems as absent as he ever was before. "Come back!" she shouts, her voice hoarse. "I came all the way here for you! You told me to come! You told me! I came across the world for you! For you! Sky! Sky!"

She stops, breathless with her own fury, but in the echo that comes back to her she thinks she hears him listening. It seems to her now that he *is* the sky, and that the whole sky becomes suddenly textured and close, like a living thing that is afraid or cannot move, and it is him. "Sky!" She stands up tall on the stone; she leans out over the edge. It doesn't matter. Nothing matters but that she is with him, and wherever he goes, she will follow.

It has always been this way, and always will be.

She lets herself fall. It doesn't feel like falling, but rather like the wind sucking her in—as if finally welcoming her into its secret center, the face behind the voice—and then it stops, and she tumbles over and comes to rest face down against feathers so thick she cannot feel any warmth beneath them. But she knows a white bird is carrying her, and that it is one of the birds who revealed that human form in the lake, except there is a wide slender freedom to this one—something even lighter than they were, with their fluffy masses. As she raises her head, panting, to look at it, it disappears beneath her, leaving her lying alone upon a cloud.

It is nearly impossible to stand. Though something must support her, for she does not fall through, nothing presses against her hands or her feet as she tries to push up from it; the cloud is air against her flesh, helpless and unhelpful. By the time she makes it to her knees, clawing at the white wisps, she is nearly crying with frustration. "Sky," she says, "please. Where are you? Sky!"

"Shh, it's all right."

She turns in the bleary mist to see his face even closer to hers than before, and he holds out his hand from where he kneels on the cloud just above her. "Come here," he says gently. She reaches for his hand, and struggles in the stuff of nothingness, unable to get there. "Oh where are we? I can't—"

"Shh," he says again, still holding out his hand. His voice is very quiet, as if he doesn't trust it. "Don't fight. Come toward me."

The kindness in his voice makes Lonely feel her heart so acutely, it seems to press out from her ribs. She lifts her chest, and her body follows, and it seems that as soon as she makes this movement forward, the air carries her forward a little more. She moves her hips and her legs, not trying to walk but simply moving toward him, and each movement she makes is increased and carried further by the air she moves in, so that quite suddenly she can grasp his hand. It comes like a waterfall into hers. He squeezes it, and in the same motion turns and pulls her.

They rise up into the palace of the sky, on tiers of clouds. Somewhere, in her wonder, she loses his hand—or he loses hers—but he is still close beside her when they stop. For as far as she can see in one direction, there is only a flat field of clouds, thick and white and lumpy. In other directions: sudden towers of cloud, spiraling like the Unicorn's horn into a broken ceiling of clouds above, split through in places by sunlight so bright she fears she would disintegrate under its rays.

There is absolutely no sound. There is only Sky's breath, and hers, brushing lightly past the insides of their throats and their mouths. His hand seems a universe away now, and he no longer looks at her, though his not looking, and the tilt of his face a fraction toward her, feels more utterly attentive to her presence than when he looked directly at her down below.

"Where are we?" she asks as quietly as possible. Again she isn't sure if she's speaking aloud or only inside her own mind. The mass beneath her does not feel solid, and yet they do not fall.

Her question makes him turn a little away, gazing beyond the mysterious question of their two bodies in space.

"We're in the clouds," he says. "The clouds are dreams. They are part of the circle of water that started at the beginning of time. They are the dream of water before it is reborn. Ideas of what life will be, before it is begun."

"Whose ideas?"

Sky hesitates. "Everyone's. Everyone that breathes."

Lonely stares at him, watching his face from this new angle, its bony cheeks and sharp jaw and the way his hair swings against his lips when he turns. His slim chest is bare, his casual posture belying the tension of his muscles. She wills him to look at her, but it seems the one thing—with all his magic—that he cannot do. Yet she does not feel angry any more. She is beginning to feel the vaguest shadow of that sorrow that overwhelmed his face down on the mountaintop, and that still covers him now, silently all over him, like clothing.

"Are you all alone up here?" she whispers.

He doesn't answer. She can feel the heat between their two bodies, and that great question and emergency that hums there in that space: a live heat of longing and terror, an animal quality that perhaps the sky has never felt before. She feels that heat. She feels him feel it. She feels him want to bolt from the nearness of it, but hold himself still.

"I have not spoken to anyone for a long time," he says finally. "I have never spoken in your language before."

His words are food to Lonely.

"Are you one of the Dream People?" she asks.

He nods.

"Where are the others?"

"Down below there. You saw them. The birds." His voice is neither cold nor distant, and yet it is far away. She keeps looking at him, unwilling to stop looking. His body is shaking.

"I didn't think it would be like this," she says.

He looks down. "What?"

"The land you lived in. I thought it would be like—what my father dreamed of. He told me you would rescue me. He told me you would come from a place—not like this. A green place, shadowed by giant trees. A place where the limbs of the trees were so big that a grown-up man could walk and run across them. I saw it in his dreams. There were bridges, and everything was bigger. Birds as big as you. Animals whose chests were taller than my father. And white birds rose up from the water—"

She stops. She thinks he is shaking harder than before. She wanted to wake him with her knowing, wanted to see if he would admit, like she does, that they have seen each other before in dreams. But now she feels that her words hurt him, and she cannot bear it.

"I can't show you that place now," he says, and his mouth twitches as he speaks. "Someday, perhaps, I will show you."

For a moment, Lonely is wild with the joy of that *someday*. The great expanse of that word, which stretches out their future together for so much longer than just this moment, so much longer than she dared hope for, though she knew it must be so.

She allows herself to turn her gaze back to the cloud castles around them then. They begin to turn color, colors that don't exist in the real world. Pink like the inside of a body, but fluorescent. The color of the kiss that woke her below—the kiss that must have been his, though it seems forgotten now and forbidden—shot through with a long blue cry of longing.

The turrets seem to sink below them, or perhaps she and Sky rise above, through raining layers and wet pink tufts, and finally into a high universe of deep blue cold. Lonely is not afraid. It is a relief, finally, to see the color of her own loneliness, to see in clear darkness a mirror of her own emptiness—that emptiness she always knew about that lay beneath all the shifting realities of her life, beneath her hopes and dreams, beneath her pathways through col-ored fields. Only maybe it wasn't really beneath her after all but above her. She feels relief to be sitting here finally before it, with the person she wants to love here beside her, the only real person in the world. *That emptiness didn't belong to me*, she thinks. *It was the world's emptiness. It is a part of everyone.*

The moon is so big here—far bigger than they are—that she can tell it is a sphere, not a circle. She can see its blemishes, its bruises, its face.

"It's not a light after all," she says out loud, feeling somehow that he will know what she means. "It's a thing. It's a world."

Her voice is not loud. This isn't the kind of silence that feels empty, that a sound can fill up.

"When the Earth was born," says Sky softly, "she had a twin. While the Earth was rich and fertile—" He pauses and swallows, as if the words are too wet in his mouth. Long silences lie between his words, but Lonely doesn't mind. Time is no longer important to her, and she can tell that each of his words is given as a gift, meant only for her. "The Earth was rich and physical, giving birth over and over to color and laughter and the million lives, but her twin was barren and cold, tossed to pieces by the brutal nothingness of the universe. That twin, too, had a soul, and though her body was broken and barren, her soul was rich with dreams, and she carried the longing and wisdom from the beginning of time. The Moon is what remains of that twin, and they gaze at each other—the Earth and the Moon. They are sisters."

Each of his words comes nakedly intent, as if with an ecstatic and aching wonder at its own sound. She has never heard such a voice before, that calls her attention as vividly as if these words are the last she will ever hear. For no reason, she thinks suddenly of the Unicorn, and her moon-soft glow. What became of her?

"The Moon is like another world beside this one," Sky says. "When she shines full like this, people get tempted by other worlds, memories and dreams they have forgotten. She pulls at them. She pulls at the ocean, and she pulls at the water inside the people and the animals. They remember things. But it can be dangerous, too. They might want to leave the Earth behind. They forget their bodies. They forget what they have and what loves them."

But other people's lives don't matter to Lonely any more. There is a tiny, downy feather caught by his ear, and she reaches out and catches it between her fingers. As she pulls it out, feeling the damp threads of his sleek, warm hair, he turns suddenly toward her, as if that simple gesture was something his soul recognized and was waiting for. As if, in their hearts, seeds waited thousands of years for the right signal—the exact expression or gesture remembered from hundreds of lifetimes before—as a seed in the forest waits for a rain or a fire or the long days of spring to begin growing.

She shines her eyes into his, and something wakes there, something new beneath the sorrow.

"It was you," she says. "You were the bird who carried me just now. And you were the bird who lifted my heart when I could not see the door. You did rescue me from the tower, after all." She feels it as she says it, her heart lifting again, as if he holds it aloft to the moon, and beyond the moon to the sun that lights it.

He says nothing, but with fast hands grasps her and pulls her to him. He melts hot into her chest, and smells like the first scent of wind she ever breathed off the sea. She can feel his breath by her face, delicate, like air woven into fine lace. The texture of it against her skin is like no other air she has ever breathed. She can feel the design of the body it passed through, the shape of his depths. He has no idea of his own beauty. He is gripping her with the power of a god and trembling. No one has looked upon him for countless years. She has only now found him, and he has only just now spoken for the first time, and she must save him.

So they kiss, and they taste tears in their kissing—a long winding rainbow, a wet luxurious pathway of kissing, of soft bottomless lip and tongue, of one mouth. Their minds are eclipsed inside each other's hot throats. Lonely reaches up his thighs with her hands, and he bucks toward her with clumsy animality, driving his tongue deeper. His hands mirror hers.

But this single kiss exhausts them, and they collapse against one another. As the night completes itself around them, they rock together like infants, never speaking another word, for a long span of time into the night, until finally his body seems to trust hers, and in response she relaxes and falls asleep.

In her dream, he touches each part of her dress and names it.

"Moonstone," he says with a singing tenderness, tapping the beetle-sized, fog-white stone in the hollow below her throat, which hangs on a thread of silver between her shoulders. "For the moon that guides you inside."

Then his fingers trace a string of glass beads that hangs from the stone and falls between her breasts. "Glass," he says, and smiles for the first time. But she can't see the smile clearly, because it is a dream. "Glass because you are innocent, because you see through—because you can see me, and no one else can."

"It was really ice," she murmurs.

Hummingbird feathers fan a circle in the center of her chest, tied with spider silk, at the point where the V of the dress dips down between her breasts. "For the joy that hums there," he whispers against her ear. "For the language your heart speaks. Oh Lonely, dreams are so big. How can I ever tell you all that is written here? You are so young."

"But aren't you young, like me? Aren't we like each other?"

"No." But he smiles at her still, and his fingers float lighter than snow, which she has never felt, over her breasts. There is a band above her waist, and one below, of snakeskin. He kisses her as if her mouth is a well of desire which somehow feeds his own. The joy of him flowers in bursts within her skull.

"Butterfly wings. The transformation from hunger to spirit. Dragonfly wings. For passing between worlds." His hand trails down over them, over the very center of her desire. He does not stop. His words make her restless now.

"Eagle and gull feathers," he points to the designs over her legs. "For illumination. For the ocean where you come from. And this," he pauses at the deep magenta designs, formless and aimlessly swirled, like something simply spilled over the grey-blue silk. "This is blood."

"Blood? But why? Whose blood?"

"I don't know. Maybe your own." He pulls away his hand, and Lonely is afraid.

"I don't understand. I didn't bleed," she protests.

"But in dreams, things happen differently. There is no time, no past or future." She sees the wrinkle on his brow deepen. It's the thinker in him that she does not yet know, which forgets her for a moment and goes within himself, and through himself as through a portal into another world.

"But am I dreaming?" she asks urgently, shaking him.

Sky sighs. "Lonely," he says with a passion that changes him, makes him suddenly like a boy. "Let's try to find each other. It will be confusing sometimes. It might be difficult, seeing each other through all the different realities. But let's try. Will you stay in this world for a little while, do you think?"

"I'll stay always," cries Lonely, feeling lost and shocked at the distance from which he seems to speak. "I have nowhere else to go. Don't you know that? I came here for you. I've known you forever."

"I know. That's what makes it so dangerous."

"But I don't know what you mean," Lonely says, her eyes filling with tears, and he pulls her back close and holds her.

"I love you," he says. "I have always loved you." Now she thinks this must be real and not a dream, for it seems that all those moons of wandering, in between the tower and here, were only a moment—between the time he woke her, and the time she truly opened her eyes.

"How did you find me?" she asks.

"If someone has loved you once," he answers, "there is a path laid out for love to follow. Your father loved you once. So I followed that path he made to your heart. In the dreamworld, these things are very clear. You can see love with your eyes."

And she falls deep into his eyes, so deep that she can no longer see, and maybe it was a dream after all.

For when she wakes, she is alone again.

Never has she felt so afraid. When she woke to her father's absence every day in the tower, she did not yet know enough to feel anything. At least she knew the place she woke to, even if it was only an illusion, for it was the only place she had ever known. Everywhere she has woken since then, she has known at least where she was, and nothing surprised her. But on this night—the night after finding her prince, the one who rescued her, the one who would take her loneliness away forever—she wakes up knowing she should not be alone but is. She is lying on a cloud, in the middle of the universe, with no way back to the earth.

The clouds are so thick she cannot see their shapes; they hide the light of the moon.

"Sky!" she cries blankly. "Sky!" But her voice dies into nothingness, muffled by infinity as if she screamed into a cushion.

That night lasts forever. She curls up and sobs interminably into her knees, and her thoughts, not knowing if they wake or sleep, trip downward into the nightmares below the island, where the Witch and her father's death await her, where she is already imprisoned and has always been imprisoned in her own loneliness. What the Witch said is true: all that she found in the great world was a trick and a dream. All that seems real now is that cold tower, that cold island, which stands hard and stubborn and terrifying at the center of her soul wherever she goes and whatever she does. It feels that way. Though yesterday it seemed gone forever, now it feels like the only thing real.

This feeling goes on and on.

Yet when the dawn comes, and flocks of swallows come swinging through the air and alight on taller trees below her that she did not know were there, she sees that she is much closer to the mountaintop than she knew, and she dries her eyes. Though her heart is still scared and angry and bloated with sorrow, she feels a little foolish, too. She sees that something has kept her alive through the night, and that is the insistant hope that he will return, after all. Won't he?

An eagle is soaring steadily beside her, and she does not know for how long it has been there. The eagle is absolutely supported by the air, and it seems to Lonely as if neither of them is moving. Its wingspan stretches almost as long as her body, and the feathers on its regal head shine as glossy as fish scales.

we've been waiting for you, says the eagle, *for a long time.* Lonely is surprised to recognize, somehow, that it is female.

"Where is Sky?" Lonely asks, ignoring the eagle's statement, which she does not understand.

he doesn't know, says the eagle.

Lonely puzzles on this answer, trying not to panic. The eagle continues to float calmly near her, as if she knows that Lonely has more to ask.

"I mean," says Lonely, "when will he come back to me?"

call him, says the eagle. *maybe he is right here.*

"But I did! And what is this place, where the river begins and the world ends? Where is *here*?"

it's the dream of a Unicorn, says the eagle. *don't you know that?*

"Then you mean it isn't real?"

i didn't say so. what is "real?" Then she lifts higher, and Lonely drifts lower, and backwards, and can no longer see her. It seems the cloud is no longer beneath her, but all around her, and she feels the spongy earth now soaking through her boots, and that which was the cloud is the morning mist rising off the water and slowly dissipating.

Other birds have joined the white birds on the water, coming from all different directions. They slide onto its surface, rooting their feet in its depths, folding their wings, resting from the weary glory of flight. They float there, their heads bowed, letting their reflections do all the work of carrying them, and each one—the gull and the tern, the swan and the heron, the duck and the pelican—moves with seamless peace among the others.

Lonely closes her eyes and tries to remain calm. The lake feels gentle before her.

Sky, she whispers, pleading with her whole heart. She holds out her hand, because it feels right to do so. When she opens her eyes again, it is because she feels the whisper of tiny feet against her fingertips. It is a dragonfly, and the dragonfly is him.

She knows by the rainbow of his eyes, and his slim body, and his quickness, the way he will dart off at any moment into nothing. She falls to her knees, though the ground is wet.

"Stay."

i can't. come with me.

So she follows the dragonfly through the mists, as he skips from the tip of one reed to the tip of another. Colors come and go through his wings, whose motion she cannot see. At first she doesn't wonder where they're going, only focuses her sight on his tiny form so as not to lose track of him. Space by space, his wandering path curls around the edge of the lake, following its contour, never leaving the water but never moving out over its depths.

When he finally pauses on a stone and fans his wings slowly in one of the first morning sunbeams, she crouches before him.

"Why won't you be human with me again?"

He doesn't answer, but the wind blows softly. She feels a familiar sorrow pass like a shadow over her heart with that gust, and then it fades.

did you know, Lonely, that we are made of air—you and me?

The earnest plea of his voice in her mind overcomes her. She wraps her arms around her knees. She would stay here with him forever, even if he is only a tiny fleeting creature, no longer than her finger.

"What do you mean?"

you know what I mean. this is our element. this is why you found me here. this is why the wind talks to you, too. doesn't it?

"Yes! But what does it mean?"

air is the element of dreams, of imagination. when we open our minds that way, the wind can blow right in. we can understand what it's saying. it lifts open our hearts for us. we can understand anything, everything! we can start again in every moment, Lonely. i can become anything. there is no past to weigh us down, and no future. we are free!

"But what does the wind tell you? Sometimes it mocks me. Sometimes it is kind, and sometimes not." Lonely's knees begin to ache.

Sky laughs then. *it's like that. it's a trickster. it's trying to help you let go.*

Lonely notices he didn't answer her question. But now he is gone, and so is the sunbeam, so she stands, to find him in feathery grasses a short distance away. She goes after him and he flies away again, following his flight as if a straight thin thread spanned the air wherever he wanted to go. Now she is impatient, for she felt as they paused together before that they were coming closer to each other, and that he was nearly human again. An emptiness begins to yawn inside her.

They come to a forest of spruce on the far side of the lake, that Lonely does not remember being there. Perhaps she could not see it before through the mist. Into it Sky flies, and into it he disappears again.

"Sky." She breaks into a short run, but the dragonfly is gone. She stands still inside a lonely moment, and dark tunnels open before her into the woods, broken painfully by occasional sun. Something aches in that path; the spruce boughs dip low but curl hopefully at the ends, and the shadows seem to shiver in their nakedness. There is something of him there, she feels, something of his heart. So she steps forward and enters into it, feeling that strange sadness again. A shadow in a dead log becomes alive, and flits with a motion similar to the dragonfly's between trees. She starts after it. It appears again, on the other side of the thin trail.

follow me, says Sky. *i'll take you somewhere beautiful.*

She looks fast and glimpses the movement again: it's a fox.

She follows the fox, or sometimes only the echo of his image slipping between shadows, so deep into the forest she feels she could never find her way out. But nothing matters to her except reaching him. Traveling is so easy, almost as if distance did not exist. She is simply here, and then there, as in a dream.

here, he says finally, though she can't see him. She stands in a little valley where red, blue, and yellow flowers sprout thickly around a tiny spring. She is exhausted. She sits down in the soft needles.

"Come to me," she whispers. In the silence around her she feels a kind of tense yearning like she felt in the sky where he jumped—a cautious, hesitant expectancy. She knows he is there somewhere. She curls up in the bed of spruce needles, and closes her eyes.

She wakes vaguely, soon after, to the feel of his small fox body curling against her back, lighter than grass. But before she can wake fully, the dream that held her reclaims her, and she is lost in a nightmare, where the old witch grasps both her wrists and won't let go, her face close and laughing hideously, whining *You're human after all, and you're alone,* and she is dragging Lonely down into the space below the tower . . .

"Shhh," Sky is saying. "Wake up."

She wakes to his arms, his human face leaning over her.

"Sky!" He has saved her, from a dream she thought she could never escape.

He holds her away from him. "What happened? What was chasing you?"

Now she shakes her head. She feels ashamed to tell him. She feels that, if she tells him, the whole structure of the life she has created up until this final, destined meeting—as if she has built the very mountain with her own dreams, her journey a living structure of hope—will collapse.

"Something is haunting you," says Sky, his forehead tense. He sighs and lies down beside her. "I know."

Lonely rolls toward him, props herself up on her elbows and kisses his forehead experimentally. He smiles, and the smile is clumsy and new, bigger on one side than on the other. Lonely wonders if he knows he is smiling, and if it would frighten him if he knew. He takes her hand.

"You know so much about me," Lonely says. "But I don't know about you."

He looks back at her. "I haven't spoken to anyone in a long time," he says again.

A long time has passed while she slept. The sun has almost left the clearing, and the parts of her body that he isn't touching feel cold. The vulnerability of his prone position beneath her, his eyes calmly resting in hers, and his wordless patience as he watches thoughts pass over her face all belie the power she knows he has—to change into something else or leave her at any instant. And that surrender is sweet to her. She wonders how long he has been alone here, without human companionship—how many years or even lifetimes. She wonders if he has ever touched anyone else the way he touches her now, the way he strokes her hair in wonder.

"Sky," she asks, "we have known each other before, in dreams?"

"Yes."

"Do you know about my father?"

"Yes," he says again, after only a moment's hesitation.

"I can't believe that's my story."

"Don't be afraid of your story."

Hearing the acceptance in his voice, she drops down beside him, and rests her cheek on his chest. She wishes she could tell him everything—or maybe he already knows?

"Did you know," she asks cautiously, "that my father had a wife?"

"Yes," he says again, but this time his voice sounds a little tighter, or maybe she's imagining it.

"She's not my mother," she adds quickly.

"No," Sky says. "She couldn't be."

"Why not?"

"Because you are bright inside, and loving. And she is not."

Lonely relaxes a little. "But she cursed me," she says. "She said—" She struggles with how to say it, but she wants to say it now.

"It doesn't matter," he interrupts. "Whatever it is, it's not a real curse. Because she's not your mother, and she has no power over you. She was jealous of your beauty. She was jealous because she knew you'd find the love she couldn't have."

He turns his face toward her then, and she feels his warmth blend tenderly with hers, and she believes him. But what does he know of that old woman?

Why does he speak of her that way? She has to leave those questions behind, for the sake of other questions which are more pressing now.

"But don't you hate me, that my father was evil?"

"No. It's not your fault. And your father wasn't evil. He was only doing his part."

"His part of what?"

"Of what had to happen."

"Why did it have to happen?"

"We don't know yet. Maybe someday we will know."

"But you sound sad."

"Yes."

"Who are you sad for?"

"I don't know. Everyone."

Lonely thinks. "Do you go into everyone's dreams, everyone in the world? Do you make their dreams?"

"I don't make them. I only appear inside their dreams, in the forms of different animals, and try to guide them."

"Do you know the people I met on my journey here? I met a man named Dragon, and a woman my age, who was dark—Delilah."

"She's your other half, your shadow, and you are hers."

"What does that mean?"

"It means she is going to complete the circle for you, somehow. It means until you recognize each other, both of you will be lost. You have to come to each other in a dream."

"Do you come to her dreams?"

"No. She's different from other people. The animals come into her dreams on their own. They trust her."

"Why?"

"Because she loves and understands them. Even though she doesn't know that. She doesn't think her love is good enough for anyone. If you ever see her in a dream, make sure to accept the love she offers. She needs you to do that."

"Okay. What about the man—Dragon? He frightened me." Lonely feels so relieved to finally have someone who understands everything, who sees every part of her life with her, so that it no longer weighs anything. The more they talk, the lighter she feels.

"He frightens himself," says Sky of Dragon. "It's far worse for him than for you."

"I wish I had loved them more. Both of them. They seemed so alone."

"Maybe you will one day."

But she doesn't like, now, the lofty tone in his voice. "But I want to stay with you."

"But Lonely—we can't hold onto this."

"Why? You told me—you said, let's try. Didn't you?" Or was that a dream?

"But it's hard to keep seeing each other clearly, especially when we dreamed each other so many times," he answers, insistence in his voice. "There are other realities, or illusions, that get in our way. There are stories we are part of, that started before we were born, that can take over. I know, Lonely."

"But I do see you for who you are. You have the dreams of all the world in your eyes."

"But you want something from me."

Startled, Lonely props herself up on one arm. "Don't you want something from me?"

Sky is silent. For a moment, he seems like a boy again, younger than she thought he was.

"Don't you?" she asks again.

"Yes."

"Do you want me?"

"Yes."

"So it's all right then."

But he is quiet. She wants to ask him if he belongs to her as she belongs to him, if this thing between them is certain, whatever it is.

"Will we live up here forever together?" she asks.

He closes his eyes, shakes his head.

"What?" she asks.

"I don't know yet. I can't imagine all that—yet."

"Why not?"

He looks up at her, takes her chin in his fingertips, and smiles a little. And despite all her fear, she thinks for that moment *Yes, he does love me.*

"I have to speak with my grandfathers," he says. "Those white birds you see, those are my elders. They are wiser than I. They will know if you can stay."

Lonely narrows her eyes. She doesn't like this answer, nor does she understand it. But there is nothing else she can say. So at last she asks what she has been most afraid to ask—for fear the very question will drive him away.

"Where did you go last night?" She feels embarrassed of her own fear, the way she cried and felt so helpless.

"I had to Dream. That's what I do."

"Every night?"

"Yes."

"Forever?"

He shrugs.

"Will you come back to me in the morning?" The light is so dim. They did not see the sunset, yet already the shadows enshroud them.

He lifts up his body and looks at her. He strokes her face. "Are you afraid?"

She doesn't answer, but her tears answer his touch.

"Come," he says. He takes her hand again, and they stand up together, brushing the spruce needles from their bodies. They begin to walk through the forest back the way they came, two humans this time, and their silence together is the sweet silence of two human lovers who recognize each other's hearts. They seem to weigh nothing. Up here in this high world, their steps are almost silent and barely touch the earth.

When they come to the edge of the forest, they look out over the lake. The flock of white birds is there at the center again, glowing and moving in the grand twilit space of the grey mountaintop, spiraling around and around as if stirring some unseen power.

"Those are my grandfathers," Sky repeats. "They are what keeps this place alive. You are safe here, always. They will protect you."

But to Lonely, they look so far away. She squeezes his hand, feeling sound-less tears spill over her face. Already she feels alone, yet he holds her now, and now he kisses the tears with his rich, warm lips.

"Sleep and be at peace," he tells her. "I will find you."

When she opens her eyes, he is gone, and the whole flock lifts together off the lake. It spins upward into the darkening clouds, and then it spins down again, landing without a ripple.

She wakes curled like a fox in the shadow of a fallen tree, in the early morning. She remembers waking beside him the day before, and the shape of his body. His belly dipped in restrained surrender between his narrow hip bones. His slim chest lined thinly with muscle swelled outward—not with flesh but as if his breastbone itself were huge with heart.

She cannot bear to be still and wait. She stands up, trying not to feel afraid this time, and walks aimlessly across the broken field around the lake. Even if she did not love him, there is a way in which this land would force her to need him—would lead her every thought and feeling toward him, as if he were the endpoint of all things. For there is nothing else here. There is no barrier—no interpreter—between the land and the sky. Nothing moves but the wind. She remembers something incongruent, and therefore desperate, in the warmth of his body. For here there is nothing but low winter grass, transparent shadows, and thoughtless handfuls of tumbled stone.

Snowflakes crawl softly down the hills of the air and melt upon touching the ground, but Lonely doesn't know what they are. A creek spills from the lower end of the lake, and widens into a small river, leading her through scattered boulders and the tiny fuzz of hardy tundra blossoms. All around her, the land wings out into nothingness; nothing and no one but herself stands higher than a flower. Cloud shadows murmur continually over the expanse, like the shadows of whales on the bottom of the sea. There are no mountains visible beyond the land she stands upon. There is nothing but sky. *Sky…*

good morning, says a small gold songbird, and then, to his mate, *i love you, i love you.* They fly together to their nest in the stones.

Lonely stretches her mind toward any life around her, yearning for some connection. The miniature white and yellow blossoms have the still, preserved quietness of those who must endure over hundreds of years. They are too low for the wind to touch, but Lonely can touch them.

"Do you know about love?" she asks them.

After a long time, they seem to answer, or perhaps the answer was there from the first, but took her some time to understand. *everything knows about love*, they say.

"It doesn't feel like I thought it would," Lonely says, sitting still. "It felt easy in my dreams. I never thought I would feel lonely again."

The whole tundra seems to sigh. *what is 'thought'? what is 'lonely'?* Yet it doesn't seem to her that anyone but she even wants to know. The tundra offers these questions up to the day, turning them in the light, to be considered at leisure by the clouds.

"Don't you want anything?" Lonely asks the flowers sadly. "Don't you long for anything, the sun or the water?"

we do not long for anything, they say. *we only express the Earth. we only say what is. that is for the animals, to want and fear.*

"I am an animal then," says Lonely, remembering how each person in her life has named her—by her smell or by her beauty or by whatever they longed for—as human or goddess. She walks to the river and sits down beside it, comforted by its continuous sound. She rests her chin on her knees. *I will lay this heaviness in the river*, she thinks. *I will lay down this heaviness that is in my heart, and it will float away, because I don't need it, and he doesn't need it. He is so light! He doesn't miss me. He doesn't worry.*

But the longer she sits there, her mind immersed in the low strange sound of water—like ongoing breath and soft tumbling stones at once—the more she wonders why he hasn't come back to her yet, and the more she feels afraid, and the heavier her heart feels, in contrast with the lightness of the airy mountaintop and the way that yesterday—when she walked with him— her feet sometimes left the ground.

"Why won't he tell me again that he loves me?" she murmurs. "Was it a dream? There is some distance, some mystery—Why won't he be human, and stay with me, now that I've finally arrived?"

all you can do, sighs the river, *is open your heart more. open and open and open. it is all you can do.*

maybe he doesn't trust you yet, says another voice near her, and she turns to see a little rodent with round haunches huddled among the rocks. *we don't know what you are. to be human, he has to leave us. everything will change.*

"But what is this place? Aren't you real?"

what do you mean? The little creature looks startled and slips away, as if her voice has become too much for him.

Lonely walks back up the river toward the lake. She walks all the way around the lake, searching for the spruce forest she slept in with Sky, but she cannot find it. She begins to panic. How could an entire forest disappear? The fog is closing in. She begins to run, stumbling through marshy ground, searching for the spring or the forms of the two stone outcroppings where she first stood before him—or anything she can recognize.

Without warning she hits the warm body of Sky, and his arms come around her.

She pants into his shoulder and falls into the open bowl of his chest, curved to let her in. She feels such a lifetime of joy in that moment that everything she thought or felt before seems foolish and unreal.

When he pulls away, she is unable to speak. She watches his smile spread like a miracle over his face, and devotes herself to him over and over again without even being aware of it.

"I'll stay human with you today," he says, and when she sees the happy determination in his face, she feels sorry for all her doubt. "I will."

He kisses her, then takes her hand and leads her back toward the two stones where the spring begins. As always, they move very quickly, and are there before she can even imagine arriving. They climb into the midst of the waving grasses at the top of the world, and they are not tired. A cloud floats around and around that highest peak, as if in worship, and they step from the rock right onto it.

"See," says Sky, as if this is the answer to all her questions, snuggling into the mist with her. "This is how light we are. We don't weigh anything."

They lie still, and Lonely feels utterly at peace, and nothing seems to matter but now. She thinks about where he has been in the night, but without pain now, for she has him back again.

"Tell me about the Dreaming," she says. "Can you? Tell me about the dreams."

"I can't. Each person's dreams are a secret, that only they can know."

"But it's your life too. You enter those dreams, and I want to know you. Please, tell me what you did last night." Bravely, she wraps her legs around him, feels his body pulse there, feels his mouth brush her neck and holds back her desire like a mouthful of water. She presses her breast into his hand. His thigh slips upward between her legs, where she is bare beneath the dress, and together they gasp. Then he is still, holding her tightly but steadying his breath.

"I was a bear," he whispers, "last night."

Lonely listens, breathing in with his words as if she can feel the beast he speaks of rising inside her.

"I came in the dark forest, I opened my jaws." His lips move against her ear, and she shudders repeatedly toward him like waves bursting upon the shore. "She ran away. But I come again. I come again and again, night," he breathes in, "after night. Inside my great belly—the great blackness of my lungs where voice rises— She needs to know that instinct is the only knowledge of right and wrong. She needs to rumble and mountain her way through those people without fear, and know that her hunger—" he breathes out, and Lonely cries out softly as his hand grasps her, "—has meaning. I will protect her. I will devour her, and then she will be safe, and she will know what it feels like, inside me."

Lonely pulls back and looks into his eyes. The wind blows strong, and the cloud that holds them drifts far from the peak. *I love you,* she thinks, but cannot say it.

"Tell me another one," she says.

He closes his eyes. She watches him this time and sees the tremble at his throat, sees the struggle he undergoes to remember, to bridge the distance between the Dreamworld and now. Perhaps the fire they made between their bodies, when they held each other close, melted him as it did her, and made it easier. Now his voice strains a little, and he doesn't breathe quite enough.

"I was a kitten. The kitten was dying. I cried, so that the dreamer would rescue me. At least if he would only *think* of rescuing me! Then he would no longer mock the other children, he would no longer force them to give up their innocence and swear their allegiance, if only he could hear my cry, and remember—"

He opens his eyes and shakes his head. "See, I can't tell it without telling about the person too. I am all intertwined with them. I am part of them, when they dream me."

Lonely draws her fingertips up his thigh, aware suddenly of her power.

"Please," she whispers.

Sky grasps her hand, stops it. But he goes on.

"There is a man," he says, this time looking into her eyes, his voice seizing her, "who can no longer feel his body—whose whole life is a connection between his mind and a computer. This man has no time to feed himself real food, or to remember what real food is. He does not remember that he has a body. Nor does he have a spirit, for even his work does not nourish him, does not inspire him." Sky sighs again. "I was a dog in this man's dream. I licked the man's hand, licked his body. I ran with the man, tried to show him the pleasure of scent—the scent of bodies, the scent of closeness. I sniffed at a turtle in the road, trying to show him life. I sniffed at some food in the garbage, food that the man had forgotten he needed. Soon this man will become ill, but he doesn't know it yet! I sniffed at the place where the cancer will begin, and I growled."

"When a dog comes in a dream, it means we must connect with our bodies?" asks Lonely, who feels a little lost now, who does not understand what kind of "work" this is, or what computers are.

"Sometimes," answers Sky. "Dogs have many things to say. They have clear things to say that everyone knows because everyone knows dogs—they live closely among people."

"A dog came to me once, outside the City," Lonely says, "but that was real, not a dream."

"It is the same thing," says Sky. "And if it is real, as you say—more real than a dream—then it is even more important! Why would dreams have meaning, if real life meant nothing?"

Lonely smiles. "I like the dreams though. They're different somehow. Tell me another."

"No," says Sky. "It's too tempting for me. It feels too good to have someone to tell, to share—" He stops, but she can hear the rest of his thought.

"Is it a burden? The Dreaming?"

But he is silent for a long time.

"For one woman," he says softly, "I was the color blue."

"What do you mean?"

"Blue. Blue for breath. Blue for peace. Blue for forgotten romance. An elegant, graceful blue, like the feminine softness she's lost inside herself. I filled the whole dream. The whole dream was blue, nothing else! A beautiful blue."

"But I thought you were always an animal?"

"Not always," says Sky.

Lonely kisses him. "Why won't you come into my dreams?" she asks.

"This is my life," answers Sky with a sharpness that surprises her, and hurts. "It isn't for fun. It's my work. As long as I can find people who still have hope living in their hearts, and give them a dream to awaken it, then dreams survive. We—my people—survive. The future survives, and the wisdom that we took with us is not lost. This is my calling, my purpose."

"Then what is mine?"

"I don't know. You were born of the man who created the City—"

"Stop." Lonely doesn't want to hear that story. She is tired of the curses that hang over her, tired of the voices of all her elders—even Eva's—which laid upon her this weight. "It's not my fault what my father did. I don't want to be part of that. I will never go to the City and I will never save the people from what he did. What if my purpose is only to—" She stops, afraid again to say the word *love*. "To know you. You're the one I've looked for, Sky, forever."

"But that can't be your purpose in the world. It doesn't help the world just to care about one person. You have to do something for the larger world."

"Why? Because you're not important?"

Sky shrugs, looks away. It's so easy for him to turn away from her, with the whole sky, for which he is named, there before him.

"You don't have to do anything," he amends quietly.

But Lonely doesn't want this. She doesn't want for him not to care. And she knows that he needs her love. *Maybe he needs you to rescue him,* Eva had said. *But he doesn't know it.*

So she kisses his neck, teasing his skin. She feels him soften, his lashes falling against his cheeks as his warmth leans back into her. He pulls her close with both arms, hooking her mouth in his. For a moment they swim like fish in an embrace bigger than the sea. Then he pulls back and gazes at her— she who is a garden blooming in the rain, who is the only woman, and only woman, over and over again for him.

"What will we do today?" she asks, feeling her own desire. But again she looks into his eyes, and again she sees that he is afraid. What will happen to this god-animal of Dream, if he allows himself to become more human?

"Let's just stay on this cloud, and see where it takes us," he answers. And this is enough for her, because the mystery of him—the mere mystery of his distance, what he keeps hidden, and what little by little he reveals to her alone—is, to her, like flying.

Sky wrestles her foot playfully with his. The cloud smokes around them in a noncommittal way, an unkempt nest of water and air—deep feeling diluted by dreamy, abstract space.

"I can't remember my real name," Lonely says, trailing her arm down into space, and brooding a little still on their conversation about her destiny.

"I can't remember mine either," admits Sky to her surprise. "Maybe no one can."

"So what do we do?"

"We live," he says. "We befriend the names we have. We learn to understand them, and maybe they will help us. Didn't your feeling about your name change as you journeyed? Didn't your loneliness change?"

"Yes," says Lonely. "At first it was scary, and then it was pretty and hopeful. And then I was ashamed of it. Then I was proud of it and determined to find my love. Then, in the end, I let it guide me."

"See," says Sky thoughtfully.

"What about you?" Lonely says. "What about your name? What does it mean to you?"

"Oh—how can I explain?" He makes his silent laugh, and she can feel it—the crumpled, vulnerable gracelessness of it. "How can I explain the sky?"

She smiles at him. "You have to. For me."

He looks at her. Their faces are so close, their noses almost touch. "I know I had another name," he says, and his smile fades, and he looks down toward the earth below. "Once, when I was a little boy. I was someone else then, perhaps." She waits a long time for him to continue, holding her breath, trying to picture what he is remembering in his mind, or not remembering. "Maybe when we came up here, and began living in the clouds, my name changed to Sky so that I would remember my connection to the universe. So that I would no longer be one, helpless human being suffering from the loss of personal connection to other humans, but would identify instead with—everything. Possibility. Dreams. Freedom." Without knowing it, perhaps, he breathes in and then sighs a great sigh. "This is my life now."

Lonely keeps staring at him. There is something wrong with what he's saying. There is something about it that makes her afraid, deep in her belly, but she can't identify it. Something she doesn't believe.

But when he looks back at her again, she relaxes. "I know," he says to her, as if he can read her thoughts. "I'm afraid, too."

"What? Of what?"

"Of love."

"But—"

"I'm just telling you. What we feel—it feels like the universe, like the sky, like me, but I'm afraid too. Because I don't . . ." He trails off.

"Did you ask them yet?" she whispers, terrified of the answer. "Did you ask them if I can stay?"

He shakes his head.

"But don't you want me to stay? Why couldn't I?"

"Because everything is different with you here," he says, and that sudden sharpness is there again, and it shocks her so much, she doesn't dare ask anything more, so she tries to forget.

"I'm sorry," he murmurs after a little while. Lonely says nothing.

They drift on a while, looking down. The earth twists and turns below them like an old wrinkled body.

"Look down there." Lonely says, trying to be easy again. The cloud is moving, over the course of the day, across the whole landscape she has travelled. "I think that's the valley where my friend Fawn lives. You see the field? Like a little eye in the forest. And there are the fields I traveled through. There are so few fields—the forest is so vast!"

"One day it might not be."

"What do you mean?"

"One day it might be completely gone. Can you imagine? When trees are just a legend—giant plants that once ruled the earth. No one will remember any more."

"No. I couldn't bear that."

"No. Nor could I."

Lonely can see where the desert begins. She can see its whole formation now: the cliff running along the south where Dragon and Delilah live, rising up into seemingly endless forest, and the ridge running all the way along the north edge, between the desert and the City. The river is forced to fork on either side of that ridge—one branch running secretly under the desert and the other running through the City and into the sea.

"Sky," she asks, thinking suddenly of something she has never thought of before, "do you know what's on the other side of the mountain where you live? How far does the land go? And where does it end? And where does that dark forest above the cliffs end?"

"It doesn't end," says Sky. "The earth is round."

"What do you mean, round?"

"You know. Like a seed, or a fetus. Like a baby's head. Like the way cats curl up to sleep."

"But it's not round when you walk on it."

"It is round, but you can't feel it, because it is so much bigger than you. That's how life is. No one knows. If people could be aware of that big roundness all the time, how big it is, and how it completes itself over and over— Well, things would be different."

"Do the animals know?"

"The animals know."

"And the plants?"

"The plants know. They know it and they live it. They live that way, in a round way."

"But still, what is on the other side of the mountain?"

"I don't know. Maybe the same. Another world like this one, where people and gods make magic and love and hate, where they forget themselves and destroy what gives them life."

"Is there another City?"

"There are many cities."

Lonely is silent, aghast. Could there be more than one Hanum, and more than one Lonely? It dizzies her to think of, and at the same time feels like such a relief—if she could only understand it.

"There are so many possibilities," Sky continues. "Life is infinite. But the people in the different cities don't know about each other. They are afraid to know each other. If they did, they would not see each other as reflections of themselves—reflections to teach them about themselves, the way dreams do. They would hate each other. They would fight."

"But why?"

He pauses for a moment, his face caught in a net of sorrow. "I don't know," he answers finally. Lonely aches for him, that there are sorrows too great for him to understand, that she can feel his light being struggling to soar beyond, and failing. She nestles closer.

"Do you have a mother and father?" she asks him, surprised that she never thought of it before.

"My parents died. They were killed, when Han—when the City took over."

"But I thought your people all escaped…." She hesitates, aware that she is drawing on Eva's story, not sure how much she is allowed to know.

"No. Not all of them."

Lonely looks at him: this random form in space, the only human left after all others are gone, the only one she wants.

"Did all your people have eyes like yours?" she asks. "So blue?"

"No," he says. "Most of them had dark eyes, like yours."

She tries to smile. It is good, she feels, that she should remind him in one small way of his people. For she sees now that what keeps him from her, when he seems far away, is this mystery of a lost people—this other world she has still never known, from which he draws his meaning and his life.

Yet they lie together here, two orphans in space. They turn their faces toward each other, choosing the infinity of each other's eyes over the whole expanse of the universe. Birds fly in formation far below them. The sun throbs inside the fog of ice clouds above them. Lonely ensconces herself inside his eyes, inside the protection of their warmth which saves her from the chill of space. Lonely and Sky are so far from the earth. They might keep drifting, higher and higher into forever. She must hold him close, and stay beside him, to survive.

But still the old woman by the sea will not leave her. Not even after what Sky told her, not even when he holds her in his arms. That nightmare face waits for her at the end of thirteen moons, and what then? Lonely will not go back. She will hold onto Sky with all her being, and nothing will tear her away. She will die before she returns to that place. The woman's demand echoes in her mind—the question that must be answered: *What is the proof of love?* And she will have to ask. She rushes in before doubt has time to stop her.

"Sky, do you love me?"

To her surprise, he answers easily. "Yes. I have loved you ever since I saw you in a dream, in the tower."

Almost, she feels easier then. Yet the doubt does not completely vanish. His voice feels cloudy somehow. Is he talking about the same kind of love that she is? What kind of love did the witch mean, anyway, and what is the proof of it?

"What do you mean," she says, "by love?"

He looks at her, his eyes a little distant, but still warm. "Don't you know?"

"I don't know. How do I know? How do I know you love me?"

But it's a strange question now. It feels different—inside her mouth, inside her ears, inside even the air around them—from anything she has ever said to him before. It scrapes the sensitive skin inside her throat. It must feel different to Sky, too, for he pulls away from her in a way he has never done before—lifting himself up on one elbow and looking down at her with eyes cold and scrutinizing. They are still open, yet they seem closed. Deep inside her, so deep she can't even locate it in her body, Lonely feels again the subtle beginnings of fear.

"What do you mean?" he asks. "Why don't you believe me?"

"I just want to know," she stumbles, not understanding the hurt in his face, not understanding how this question she asks could hurt—though it hurts her, too—and not understanding (though she will, a long, long time from now) that the hurt, itself, is her answer. "I mean, you don't know if you want to be with me. Forever," she says, though she wishes she would stop, and wants already to take it back.

"Love isn't defined by forever," he says. "Love is—love. Here. Now. I love you. That's all. What do you want forever for?"

"Because—how do I know if you love me enough?" she asks helplessly, knowing it doesn't make sense.

"Enough for what?"

To still the fear inside me. To make the old Witch let me go. Lonely is silent. She cannot explain. He seems to know everything, as if he has always been with her ever since that first moment when he lifted her heart from her chest. But that wasn't her first dream. Before that dream that saved her, there was the nightmare of the Witch chasing her round and round. And does he know that? Could he understand what haunts her? She remembers again those words: *It'll be as if you'd never left, and all that happiness you found in the great big world was just a dream.*

She strokes his back. "I'm sorry," she pleads. She wants him to turn to her, take her in his arms again. But he lies down on his stomach and rests his chin on his folded hands, gazing out at nothing. She is alone in the sky without his eyes to hold hers in their depths, without his gaze to make meaning out of thoughts. She lies beside him, looking out as he does, trying to be still and at peace, but her heart is running so fast it could travel around the whole world and back before he turns toward her again.

He will turn toward her again. The conversation will lie as if forgotten. But it is not. The dead, silent interruption of it in the otherwise shining path of their history together—like a break in time, like a hole in space—will become part of her, as every moment of her life has become part of her, as if her body is a written story of herself. Each sensation, each cell, corresponds with an emotion she once felt, something she could not name at the time. And someday she will have to go back over each moment of her life and fill in all the spaces that were left blank.

6th MOON

The moon falls away, then begins its hopeful return. These days with Sky pass so quickly, and yet much later, they will seem in her memory like a whole lifetime.

At first, she will remember everything. She will remember several layers of each word he spoke to her and the shape of each kiss. She will remember the way he sat beside her and traced the bones of her hand, or lay on his side and traced her spine—full of wonder, as if he had never before touched another person. She will remember where his hands reached and where his hands stopped, the fit of his hips against hers and the way he held them back.

She will remember how he came to her once as a stag and once as a frog, once as a hawk and once as a cricket. How it became a game to find who he was, to chase him, to wonder when he would surprise her finally, as coming around a bend in pursuit she would find not the animal but the warm arms of the man. She will remember how, more and more, he forgot to be an animal first—how he began to trust her. How he took her hand and led her over fields of rainbow lichen, and onto and off of the clouds, and through expanses of stubby, needly trees and bare stone, and into a cave of ice, where they made simple sculptures by carving with stone. She will remember how she thought of sculpting with her tongue, and the look on his face when he saw that—how the smile got lost in desire, how he came and wound his tongue around the icicle to reach hers. How he pressed himself against her there in that cold place, gasping with the thrill of it—but would go no further, and she did not know why. She did not know why she, too, was afraid.

She will remember the dreams he told her. How he was a butterfly in the dream of an old woman, locked away in a sad grey building in which people store elders until they die. How he lightened that woman with the innocence of childhood. How he showed her that as an elder, she is transforming into pure spirit, more beautiful than she has ever been. How she will see that elders have purpose and beauty in the world, as butterflies are useful in a way that caterpillars are not.

She will remember—as if she were inside it—the dream of a teenage boy who took himself so seriously. That boy isolated himself, and his body grew pale and withered. He wrote dark, empty poetry that brought him nowhere. In his dream, the boy was underwater, drowning. Sky smiled beneath him, a dolphin, and carried him up above the waves.

She will remember the dream where Sky was a flock of ravens, surrounding an arrogant man who pushed other people aside like things. Sky formed a black mass around the man and called his eerie call. He let the man turn round and round, gazing with panic into that winged blackness, knowing for the first time that he will return from whence he came.

She will remember the way Sky's voice cradled the stories of these people, which he could not help telling after all. She will remember the tenderness in his voice, and how she knew that each dream was an act of love.

She will remember how this prince of dreams introduced her, Lonely, to all the different birds of the air. How they joked with the squirrel, and shivered at the ancient, haunting tales the wolverine told them one morning during the first blizzard, when Sky used magic to keep them warm. She will remember the first snow she saw lying upon the earth, and how Sky translated the footprints of the animals for her, and turned them into songs that he sang in a sweet voice she had never heard before, shyly, under his breath.

She will also remember how on many days, he did not come until the afternoon. How if she got angry and asked questions, he would turn cold. How it seemed that the days he came latest were the days after the most intimate evenings, when he had revealed to her some feeling, or when he had felt to her, in his easy laughter or the surrender of his body against hers, more human than ever before.

But all those memories will fade, and eventually, some of them will disappear altogether. One day all that will remain are pieces: a single expression, a single touch, a feeling of longing and joy and loneliness all at once, as she gazed with him at a snowflake on his finger whose pattern she will remember forever.

One of the memories that takes the longest to fade is the first day he doesn't come to her at all.

On that morning, she has been thinking only of making love to him. She feels that they are coming closer. Last night, they played a game. She touched him in a way she wanted to be touched, and then he had to touch her back in the same way. Then it was his turn to touch her in a way she had to mirror back upon him. She liked his turn the best. She liked watching him grow serious, afraid of his own longing, and feeling his suddenly shy fingertips reach beneath her dress and play around the hair below her belly, again and again, until on his final turn he slipped his fingers inside her and she was so slippery she felt she would slide into nothingness and bliss. And then she copied what he had done, by caressing that silent limb of desire that had already risen and revealed itself through his skirt of feathers. Last night, for the first time, there was no place on each others' bodies that they did not touch. Yet still they did not remove their clothes. Still he had to leave her as the night grew darker.

This morning, she imagines that finally the snakeskins around her hips are loosened; finally the silver strings that bind her throat are torn. The dragonfly wings will lift their veils as she opens the truth of her body to him, and spirals him down to her center. It is for him she has waited. It is for him she has resisted the temptation to be broken by anyone else before this.

And yet as she lies awake in the mossy bed where he left her, she hears for an instant the thunder of the men with their knives, their inevitable stomping of boots. For an instant she wishes for the comfort of her simple bed in the tower, which she never thought to question, and where she never wished for anything. What is inside her? What will he find there? What will she feel like, to herself, when he enters her? She tries to imagine the striking instrument of his maleness. Instead she imagines Dragon, whose fiery hands hurt her.

She remembers Rye's desire as it hovered tensely above Fawn's. How she longed for it then, but now in her memory there seems something cold and unforgiving about it—something unyielding in his urgency, the way that lust consumed his eyes, the way his face changed from the one she knew.

She rises and begins to wander, as she does every morning while she waits for him. Somehow he always finds her, so she doesn't think to stay in one place. For the first time in her life, on these mornings, she travels with no reason, no endpoint. The wind offers her the scent of the spruce trees: an old, oceanic smell. Rather than overtaking the earth with her steps, as if swallowing up the land in her passage toward a goal, now she allows the land to emerge into her. She surrenders to it.

The fields twist and turn, as fascinating in their contours as the desert. She feels as she did in those days before the mountains, when she did not yet know hunger or thirst, and there was nothing to mark her hours or tell her when to stop. She begins to feel lonely when the sun passes the midpoint in the sky, and then the hours pass more slowly. And then as the sun shrinks and brightens toward the western mountains, she begins to feel heavy with the fear that shocked her that first night in the cloud, when he left her for the first time.

When he still hasn't come by the end of the day, she sees again the vastness of these mountain ridges, and how far she is from any knowledge of real place. She is not even sure in which direction the lake lies. Though she has come to know that the spruce forest and the rocks she explores with him do not actually disappear when he is gone, still there is something elusive and fickle about this place. Even now, after all the time she has spent on this nowhere mountain, she seems to find the same places again only by chance.

She stops. She realizes her absolute helplessness. He must find her, for she can never find him.

To calm herself now, she stoops down before a plain of snow, and examines it. *This is the light I saw from across the world,* she tells herself, *from the tower.*

She presses one bare foot into the powder of it, just thicker than a cloud. It bites her with cold like the ice of her father's tower. She kneels in it, ignoring the chill in her knees, and lifts a handful to her face to taste and smell. *This is water.* This is water in some other form, some other lifetime. *Is this what happens to water when it dies?* She thinks of Yora, the faraway look in her eyes. She thinks of the ice of the tower, how it melted into the sea and then she was born. This is water stilled, turned inward and dreaming. She licks it and it reincarnates on her tongue, reborn into a trickle of life that pours with neither urgency nor resistance down her throat.

When she stands up again, the force of her own panic makes her stagger.

What will happen to her if Sky never returns?

She walks to a bare rock that still holds a window of sun, and curls upon its warmth like an animal. *Where are the animals today?* No one has spoken to her, as if all of them are keeping themselves secret—all of them a part of him, absent when he is absent. Quietly, she cries herself to sleep, hoping that when she wakes she will find him beside her.

She sleeps in little bursts, sinking into cushions of yellow warmth that seem to press over her eyes, and then tripping into nightmares of endless loneliness, in which she is trapped in this cold crystal world forever, never able to find him, never able to return.

But in her final bout of sleep, she dreams something wonderful that she cannot quite hold onto when she wakes. Refusing to open her eyes afterward, she keeps her body perfectly still, trying to remember it. Something she'd forgotten, at the beginning of her life. Something that did happen inside the tower after all, or something that the tower was made for. There were stars all around her—she could feel them speaking to her. There was a free communication in all the universe, in languages she cannot remember, and the tower caught it and channeled it into her mind. She and her father used to stare together up through the glass ceiling into space—long before she was grown, long before he was gone—and watch galaxies form and undo themselves, spinning fabulous designs and singing songs made of light. Didn't they? Didn't it seem so clear then, how the two of them were only a tiny part of a galaxy among galaxies, how their tiny lives and struggles were not the point at all—but rather the designs that all the galaxies together wove in the sky in their harmonized union of motion? Only the beauty: that was all that mattered. It seems as if long ago, she and her father were friends. For he understood something so big, something bigger than pain and bigger than fear—something he'd been trying to live up to, and had failed. But he didn't completely fail. Because he had her, his daughter. Because she understood his soul, and the beauty in it that no one else had ever seen. She, in her small, child's heart, understood what no one else did.

The dream felt so good that she tries to fall back into it, but it's like a magical space that, once she rises out of it, shrinks and will no longer fit her. All she is left with is a terrible thought: *But you could not save him. You could not save your father, even though you loved him. The love wasn't enough.*

She opens her eyes and two elk are standing before her. She is relieved to see someone—anyone—and yet these two seem more reticent than the other animals she's met with Sky. The female's head rests lightly upon the male's shoulder, the two of them facing opposite directions, their bodies just crossed.

Now the female tilts her head toward Lonely and puffs a white cloud of breath into the air, and Lonely wonders if every cloud in the world might be only someone's breath. Their eyes are so gentle, as if capable of nothing but peace. They have only been together for a moment, and in a moment they will walk away from each other, to rejoin the herd that stands beyond them. But Lonely feels as if they have been standing this way forever, their two bodies perfectly aligned.

"Do you know where he is?" she whispers. "Please, I'm so afraid."

The female elk's answer comes in those same small clouds, one after the other. *don't be afraid. we're all trying to remember where we are. it's the fear that makes us lost, and tears us apart.*

poor Sky, says the male. *he lives in a world that no longer exists.*

and he doesn't realize it, adds the female.

"What do you mean?" cries Lonely. "Do you mean that he doesn't exist, or that I can't find him, or—?"

hush, says the female. *everything loves you. everything loves him. there is nothing to fear.*

But the effort of communicating seems to have broken their peaceful connection. They curve away restlessly into the wind, and begin to move—fluidly and with a hidden swiftness—across the field.

"Wait," Lonely cries, tears suddenly and easily springing from her eyes. She stands up and begins to run. The elk herd scatters and is immediately gone. But she keeps running, then slows to a fast walk when she tires. She walks as hard and fast as she can, crying out his name, her fear turning to fury—and the harder she walks, and the more desperately she searches, the less she sees.

After sunset, she finds herself back at the lake again, and feels some relief in knowing where she is, though he isn't here. She sees the white birds on the far side of it, scattered and floating as if at rest, and she wonders if he might be one of them. But she doesn't think she is allowed to speak to them, even if she could swim out to them, which she has never imagined doing. She never touches the lake, because he doesn't—at least not as a human—and she feels that he has some fear of it.

She climbs the peak where the spring begins, and steps onto a cloud. She watches the birds for a long time, wondering about his secrets, remembering that, after all her shared moments with him, she still doesn't understand who he is or where he comes from. Still he has not spoken to these elders about her, or asked if she can stay. She has avoided asking herself what that means, until now, because it hurts so much.

As the waxing moon rises over her, Lonely lies on her back and tries to figure out what the fear is, what the pain is. Maybe if she can understand it, it will go away. As soon as she focuses on it, it wails like water in her ears. She fights to stay afloat, and reaches with her eyes for anything solid—an image to hold onto, to steady herself. But there is nothing in the sky to hold onto, except for the moon, and she remembers the story Sky told her about the moon, and it only makes her sad. Then she thinks of the old woman's curse about the moon losing its child, and she doesn't understand what she meant, but it all begins to terrify her again, and she closes her eyes.

But she cannot sleep, and so she gets up and walks on the clouds. They make an unbroken carpet, tonight, over the world. They hang so low over the mountains that the mountain peaks strike right through them, and Lonely can walk onto and off of these islands of stone into unsolid fields of grey mist. These fields extend forever, and the sun is somewhere else, on the other side of the world. She walks with an eerie steadiness over an expanse of silver wisp, evenly illuminated white. Everything is white in a solid container of silver. It is the loneliest, most beautiful thing she has ever seen. If she spoke a single word out loud, that word would become the whole universe and she would die. She hums a little, under her breath. She isn't even aware that she is walking.

After a while, she doesn't feel afraid any more, only terribly sad. She walks across the meadow of white soft nothing, feeling the essential loneliness of being alive, feeling that it will be like this forever, wondering if he feels it too and if that is what drives him into dreams.

It will amaze her later to remember that somewhere in that infinity, he was able to find her. He comes to her in the early dawn of the next day, and she is so grateful, for a moment, that she collapses in a smile and runs to his arms.

But she will remember how his hug wasn't quite long enough to make up for how long he had left her.

She will remember how he gave no explanation of why.

You sit up high, in the office cubicle, high up in the City, high up in the air.

Between your feet and the earth there are: hundreds of square rooms, fifty-one floors made out of something you know the name for but would not be able to explain if you were asked (you won't be asked), and the distracted bodies, frustrated exhalations, and confused emotions of more people than you know. You are unaware of your hands on the desk, or of the ache in your eyes, or of the strain in your shoulders as you crane your neck forward. If asked (though it will not be), your soul would not be able to say where it is.

"Our job is to fill the emptiness," your boss said in the interview before hiring you. "It's as simple as that. The emptiness is getting bigger and bigger all the time. People feel it, and they don't want to feel it, and we don't want them to feel it. So we're all working together, you see, toward a common goal. People have an endless need for things to do and things to get. That's what we provide. That's what advertisement is. Really, we are offering solutions. Endless solutions."

High up in the air, you stare at the computer screen. You need a new gimmick for these women's shoes. Something about sex and love—always sex and love. What do shoes have to do with love? No one you know can find it. Your mind drifts. You are unaware of the corners at each angle of the room, or the difference between the shape of your body and the shape of the cubicle. You are distracted by the bustle and gossip of the employees next door—but please forgive yourself, for they are the only life around you. You are unaware of your own tiredness, unaware that you forgot to eat today. You know that you have a headache, and you take a pill, and drop your head in your hands. You are thinking about a lunch date you had yesterday, with a coworker, in a shopping mall. You miss the shopping mall, your only sense of community. You repeat over and over in your mind the conversation you had over lunch, and your irritation with your coworker, just because it is something to feel.

Now you play with the image of the Princess in the Tower on your computer. You cannot figure out how to connect it with shoes, and anyway that image is becoming so old and overused. It is getting to be a joke. Why can't you think up anything new? Why can't you be *creative*?

But you were once, weren't you? You used to climb up to the sky without elevators, and it was a different sky than this one. When you were a child, very young, your parents and teachers told you how "creative" you were. You could play by yourself for hours and were never bored. You never wondered what to draw or paint. You never wondered what toy to play with next, or what to pretend, or what to imagine. There was a time when you lived in joy. You were always moving. You were always following your ideas and making something wonderful just for the wonder of it.

Of course, that was a long time ago. You feel pretty old now. Years of school and heartbreak stand between then and now. Of your body, you know only what it looks like in the mirror, and you do not like it. Of your imagination, you know only that your paycheck depends upon it, and that it is so elusive these days—no longer your friend.

So you check your computer for messages. You check all your machines. You pick up each communication device and listen, for the fourth time this morning, for an automated announcement that someone has tried to contact you. You should be working, and yet you cannot stop doing this.

Please forgive yourself. It is only that you want so much to hear someone say your name again—and know what it means.

One day Lonely is so angry at Sky's absence that when she finally sees him at the edge of the lake, she turns and walks fast in the other direction. She hears him call to her, and she keeps walking, up onto the higher rocks. She hears him running.

"Lonely," he says, and touches her shoulder. The hesitation in his touch irritates her. She shakes it off and keeps walking.

"What?" she says.

"What are you doing? Turn around."

"No." But she turns around in spite of herself. Where would she go? Where would she keep walking to? She hates this place, which goes on forever and goes nowhere—which, according to the animals, is maybe nothing but a dream, and not her dream either.

"What's wrong?" he asks, and her first reaction at seeing him is sadness—that pain and anger should contort his sweet face, and that she should be the one to cause it.

"When were you going to come to me? Why do you take so long?" she says tearfully.

"I'm doing my work, Lonely."

"Why can't you come to me sooner?"

"Because." He looks away and shakes his head in frustration. "I just can't. You can't depend on me so much."

"Why not?"

The way he looks at her now, she's scared he is never going to touch her again. "Lonely, I haven't been with any other people since—I don't know if I'm ready for this. I'm used to being alone, or being with the animals, the birds. I feel more at home that way."

"You want me to leave?"

"No, but I don't want you to be so attached to me. You'll never understand yourself that way. You'll never stop being lonely."

Lonely is shocked. *I thought it was so hard,* she thinks, *climbing through the wilderness. I could hardly believe I would ever find him, or that he would be real. But finding him wasn't the hard part at all, and it wasn't even the answer.*

"Don't you want to stop feeling lonely?"

Embarrassed, she looks away. "Don't talk to me like that," she snaps. "Like you know everything."

He sighs, then begins to walk away.

She hurries after him. "Okay, but what am I supposed to do? I left the world behind to find you. You hide up here in the clouds. You refuse to come down. I have nothing up here but you!"

"So get to know the animals. Get to know the mountain." His voice is cold, and he keeps walking.

"I *do*. But—"

He turns on her, his eyes hot. "What do you want from me? What? Proof of my love? I can't give it. Either you believe in it or you don't. I can't make you any promises. I can't put you before my people. I don't want you to hold onto me or think you own me."

Lonely looks at him, her dress in handfulls at her sides, trying to be brave. She remembers what Eva said about her father's wife. How she criticized him. How he pulled away.

"Sky," she says, hoping that saying his name will wake them both from the memories and fears they cast upon each other, hazing their clear sight of each other's hearts.

He looks at her and his shoulders fall. "I'm sorry I didn't come back sooner," he says. He looks tired, tired like she's never seen him before. But she stares at him, waiting.

"What?" he repeats sadly. "What do you want?"

"I want to know you. I want to see where you really come from. This place isn't even real. I know it isn't."

A look in his eyes tells her to stop, but she keeps going. "Where is that place? The place with the still water, so still the shadows of the trees look solid, and they're green everywhere, dripping with green. It's warm there. It's not like this. I know. I *remember*." She feels she will cry—longing for this place she saw in her father's dreams, this place she and her love were supposed to spend forever together. She feels her father's heartache for this place. Something was lost there. Her name is there, not "Lonely." Everything is there.

"You want to see that place?" he asks, his eyes narrowing. "Is that what you want?"

She nods, frightened.

He nods back. "Then we'll go."

Lonely takes the hand he offers, and he leads her to the top of the rock bluff.

"You'll have to learn how to fly," he says abruptly. "There are no clouds to carry us where we're going today."

She stares at him. His eyes soften, but there is still a hint of impatience in his voice.

"Here," he says, "Let's not stand in the snow. The cold is distracting when you're first trying to lift off the ground—it's too powerful."

He takes both her hands in his. Closes his eyes. Takes a few careful, serious breaths. She has no idea what he's doing.

"You have to imagine it first," he says. "What it would feel like to have air under your feet. You know, you jump, and you don't come down."

Lonely closes her eyes. She imagines jumping. But the rhythm of the jump includes coming down. "But without the down, there's no up," she says, confused, feeling his unhappiness and afraid to anger him.

"Don't push away from the ground. First feel that you have the ground there, under your feet, and then feel that you have the air there, in the same way as if it were the ground. See? Imagine the ground is gone."

Lonely tries again, to please him, but what he's saying seems impossible to her. She starts to panic. The more she tries to imagine air, the more she feels the ground, hard and pressing into her feet.

She opens her eyes. Sky drops his hands to his sides and looks at her sternly. "Focus all your energy into yourself. All of your being inside you, not connected to anything else. Pull your feet inside themselves, so they're not connected to anything." He rises a little way into the air, his bare feet resting in a casual tilt against nothing.

Lonely concentrates but she can't pull herself all the way inside. She's connected with him, wanting him, wanting to be up there with him even though he is no longer touching her. They stare at each other, not knowing what to do. Sky looks discouraged and a little scared. Lonely wants to apologize for her failure. She's afraid she's not right for him, after all. Maybe she doesn't even want to fly. She feels the safety of the earth, which saved her from the distance of her tower—saved her from the memory of the lonely sea. She feels the security of the earth's power to hold her close, forever: its pull toward its center. *I will never leave you*, it said to her, when she first walked through the fields beside her horse. She remembers the way the snake taught her to surrender to its depth. All through her journey, she slept against the earth, and belonged to it over and over again. It is the earth that lifted her, step by step, up to the sky.

The earth loves her. She knows this. She doesn't want to let go. But he, her love, is standing there waiting, in the air. And he will leave her. He will lift into the sky.

Then suddenly the wind comes between them, and she remembers she is also made of this. This air. So much less safe—so much trickier—that she often tries to forget.

Touching is not the only way to love, it tells her. *Sometimes you can love better when you let go.*

It's the first time the wind has spoken to her since she came here. The voice is so powerful that for an instant she forgets Sky, forgets the earth, forgets everything but a sense of wonder that makes her lift her face to meet its caress.

Her feet part from the earth.

"Yes!" cries Sky, sounding momentarily happy, and before she can think he grabs her hand and pulls her. They slide along the air, a little above the ground, the wind waving between the grasses and their bellies. Then they sail higher, freedom opening like a great white breath under her chest. They are so much faster, not dependent on the movement of their bodies. The sky doesn't feel like anything. Clouds and blueness tumble beneath her. They watch the earth sail below, and the whole purpose of flying is to travel over the earth—to see its beauty from another angle, to love it even more.

Love separates her from the earth, and love holds her close to it, and love is her hand holding Sky's, and they have both forgotten their fear, their irritation, or their hurt, and they no longer even remember what those feelings were for. They are laughing, and it is the first time in Lonely's life that she understands how love is everything that breathes and how it is everywhere.

They fly as vultures fly, or mosquitoes—their bodies still and quivering, as if balanced upon precarious peaks of air. They soar over the green mountains, over the falls, over the river that succumbs to the desert and then splits into two—two choices but it did not make a choice, only gave in to both. One of those paths leads into the valley of the lights, which during the day is only a grey fog.

The cloud they land upon is small, and very high. It seems flimsy to Lonely, but is the only cloud for as far as they can see today.

"There it is," says Sky, and everything has changed. He's let go of her hand. He sounds like somebody else. "There is the land I come from."

"But that's the— Isn't that the City?"

Sky nods.

"But—"

He looks at her.

"It was there," she says quietly. "That's where it was."

She sees the pride in his eyes, the pride of his own suffering, and she is so sad, to realize that she can never go there with him. His green haven—he could have taken her there, she could have shared it with him. But the suffering that remains after it is gone—that, she can never share.

"I don't want to get any closer," he says. "I can't stand the smell. I can't breathe when I get too close."

"But don't you come here every night?"

"That's different. That's when I'm a dream."

"I thought you said it was the same thing."

He looks at her, his eyes like fists now. "Is it, Lonely? Is this still life, what we live up here? Or are we only ghosts of what we were? Dreams can't fight. Dreams can't make love."

Can't you? she worries. But the anguish in his voice is so powerful it stills her. She just looks back until he turns away, and looks down again at the grey place below.

"Why is there no color?" she whispers, following his gaze.

"Because that is a lifeless place. That is a place without dreams, without spirit, without feeling." The tone of his voice echoes the same colorlessness.

"You see the shapes there," he continues. "How they hurt your eyes, how cruel and sudden those lines are. That is how they seem to us, because they are written in a different language than the forest and fields are written in. The natural places we know are written in curves and subtleties so minute that when a person of the City looks at them, they seem all a blur. They seem either boring or frightening, depending on the person, and how that person chooses to defend himself against them."

"But why?" Lonely asks, remembering the tiny, fairy-curl marks on the paper Kite showed her, wondering how those marks could be easier to read for some people than the free hand of the universe.

"Because they are afraid of mystery. The lines of the City tell one thing, and they tell it clearly. They do not have other meanings, designs within designs, hidden patterns that change with the light. All the angles are the same. That way people don't have to think, or enter into something which their minds cannot control."

They sit for a long time, and Lonely looks down at the tight, clumped angles of the City. She imagines the deafening noise of it, too far for them to hear. The City doesn't look that big from here. She wonders about the dog she met, and if he still lives, and where he runs, and if he is succeeding in loving. She wishes she had asked him to tell her more about loving. He was so easy, happy, and warm. Nervously, she inches closer to Sky, and to her giant relief he takes her in his arms, and settles in against her warmth.

"Sky," she whispers, feeling encouraged by this gesture. "Tell me about it. The green water place."

Though he holds her, she can just barely feel his presence.

"It was there in the center of the City," he says. "There where they built their Center, where the greatest power lies." He swallows against her. "The Swamp, they called it."

"What is a swamp?"

"A swamp is a place..." he begins, then hesitates. Lonely waits.

Maybe the City isn't a place, she thinks. *Maybe it is a terrible idea, that—even though it seems small now—has already taken over places. Maybe it is an idea that destroys places.*

"A swamp is a place where water and earth sit together," he says finally. "Where water and earth understand each other. It is the place in between the earth and the sea. Without it, the sea and the land forget each other. The sea will soon flood over the earth, without the swamp to draw it down and bring it peace. Once, the swamp purified the waters; once the waters were reborn there. Now they are filled with despair. The swamp was the love between the sea and the land. The Heart of the World. Now it is gone."

But this isn't enough for Lonely. "And you lived there..." she begins for him, encouragingly.

"I lived there. With my family and my people. Also the most ancient of creatures and plants lived there, who will never again be found on this earth."

"Not anywhere?" asks Lonely. "Not even on the other sides of the world, where other possibilities are?" She thinks she understands what he said about the world being round. Perhaps nothing is truly lost, and no thing is the only one of its kind.

But he doesn't answer her. And she thinks that the heart, perhaps, sometimes forgets this truth. In Sky's heart, he has lost everything. Nothing can replace it. A chill passes through her like the ghost voices in the desert, like the bottom of the sea.

"What was it like?" she insists.

"The water was protected by a sheet of silent green life. A boundary between worlds. You could see the eyes of ancient creatures just breaking through the surface from the deep. The trees were hung over with curtains of moss, and these, too, hid worlds within worlds, and were like the beards of Unicorns. There was a constant mist, revealing and hiding and revealing again all the faces of the gods in the trees and the water. You could spend a whole lifetime seeking the nests of the white birds. Like that white bird I was, when I came to you. I appeared to you as an animal that doesn't exist any more."

"How did you live? Did you live in a house?"

"We lived in houses, built of sticks on poles above the water. We traveled on bridges above the water, or we swung. The elders spoke with the birds, who were the guardians of the place. They learned to shapeshift . . ."

"Go on," she tells him, when he stops.

"Lonely," he says. "If words were all we needed to bring a thing back, to bring a life back to reality—" He doesn't finish but Lonely thinks again of the written language in Kite's book. Those were words. Those little marks—

they did not stand for lives or things or feelings, but for words. And the words stood for things. But that was so hard to understand. So far from the thing itself. Was there something the people of the City were trying to remember with their words? Something they were trying to bring back to life with their books full of tiny, colorless lines?

"After we changed form," says Sky, "to escape the destruction, I was the only one who could still turn back into human form at will. I don't know why that is. Why I kept this ability to be human, and no one else did. The elders say the future is in me. The chance for us to be reborn as a people. Or that I will carry out the work we still have to do in human form. It is up to me to keep us alive, by keeping the dreams of the people alive; it is up to me never to sleep, to stay conscious, because they say my mind is the eternal flame which, if I keep it burning, will keep our wisdom alive, our spirit alive—*I must keep us alive*—"

His words come faster and faster, and then he stops. Lonely squeezes him. He remains perfectly still, but his tears burn the skin of her neck.

Later she will know: it was in this moment that he finally owned her, this moment when he was weakest. Ever since she left her tower she has been searching for him, and when she first saw him she loved him because she had dreamed him, and he had dreamed her, and they recognized each other as if from forever ago. But now he cries, now she feels his tears on her skin, and now she knows she loves him as if she never knew it before. She loves the person living inside this body, whom—she realizes now—she barely knows at all.

How long has the City stood? A hundred years or more? Sky must be older even than that, if he was alive when it covered all his people's land. But he still feels like a little boy in her arms—whatever age he was when everything was taken from him. When he traded his own life for the responsibility of an entire people.

Now he seems to gather himself and pulls away from her to hunch reluctantly over himself, as if his own body is a kind of exhausting punishment. He turns his sleepless face upward toward infinity. She watches that face, a landscape more complex than her whole journey here, and forms her heart into the shape of its pain. She smooths back his hair. He doesn't seem to notice.

"How old were you" she asks, "when you lost your family?"

"I was thirteen. My little sister—was four."

His little sister. Inside her chest, Lonely feels such strange silent tears for these words. He never mentioned a sister. He never mentioned that she, too, was killed. And Lonely doesn't know what it feels like to have others made of the same stuff as oneself. But she feels, intuitively, the sense of tenderness Sky might have for a female relation who was at once very young and very vulnerable. She imagines a love so beautiful—a blood-sure, unshakably devoted love that he can never give to Lonely. This sister was innocent. This sister was always good. This sister did not doubt Sky's love or make any demands of him.

"The birds in the lake—those are my elders, my grandfathers," says Sky. "They are the most important, because they hold all the knowledge of the ancestors. More than I could ever learn. When we first came here, after the swamp was destroyed, they helped my soul to survive. They explained to me that even the things which are most sacred to us, even the very fundamental reality of all that we know to be true—the earth, beauty, harmony, family—is illusion, and can be destroyed and reborn whenever it needs to be, and that the truth of it does not die. They told me I had work to do still, but that someday I would see my family again. They taught me that Hanum's people were not evil, and that things are more complicated than they seem."

Lonely tries to imagine them: a council of white birds that soothed his horror, his red-hot grief, his bewildered pain, with their fanning wings. She tries to imagine their holy logic, their wisdom, their calm.

"Sometimes I think they are weakening," says Sky now, with a kind of abstract thoughtfulness that sounds eerie to Lonely. "They rest in the lake nearly all the time, and do not fly far. Sometimes I am afraid they will die. I don't know if they can die. Many have already disappeared, one by one, as if they were ghosts who could only last in this form for so long, and the elders who remain will not tell me where they have gone. They say I am not ready, that I will not understand. But I wonder if maybe the only reason we've been able to exist in this form is because people still dreamed. Because we were able to stay alive in their dreams. Maybe our whole lives are dreams—even my love for you, my time with you, maybe all of that is a dream."

That's not fair, thinks Lonely, wanting to stop him. *I'm real. Don't drag me into this. Don't deny my love.* But she wants to let him speak. She wants the trust he is giving her, so she stays silent.

"Now people don't believe in dreams. They remember their dreams less and less. They deny them. They say they do not remember. And I'm not talking about remembering images they saw in their sleep. I'm talking about that part of us that dreams, that part of us that keeps the soul alive. They are forgetting that. And when they do—when they do, maybe, we die."

She feels it again—the loss, the deadly weight of grief—and his fear that it is not yet over, that the loss will continue happening again and again. He is not feeling it now, as he speaks; she can see that, as he stares upward, his body squeezing itself shut to resist the wave that roars over it when he speaks these words. She feels it for him. For years, she thinks, this pain has been washing over him, daily, but he has been squeezing himself shut, trying to keep it out, trying to stay dry.

For the first time, she understands how far away he is. She was so mesmerized by the gift he gave her with his tears, the way he offered himself to her like that and let her hold him. But what he is saying—it isn't about their love. It isn't about Lonely. She doesn't own him. His people own him. And when they die, maybe he will die, too.

"When will I meet them, the white birds?" she asks, her voice broken and harsh and careless.

"I don't know. I'm afraid."

"Of what?"

"I don't know. I fought for my people, for the land. I was one of the few who fought. The elders told us not to. At the time I was angry that they would not join us, but now I see that the fighting only made it worse, only brought the inevitable on more strongly. My people respect me, but they are all my elders, and so I respect them far more."

He pauses, and in the seriousness of his silence, she feels all that he doesn't say. That he belongs to them utterly. That he would do anything for them. That he will never quite measure up to his own respect for them, and that whatever they ask of him, he will do. That he lives to serve something that was lost—more than to love her, more than for anything.

But then to her surprise, he turns to her and kisses her. He kisses her harder and harder, and then he is coming down on top of her, kissing her. Not like the sweet rainbow kisses they shared in the clouds. Not like the cheerful waking kiss at sunrise. Not like the blissful interlude of kissing between words. This time he is made of metal and fire, his hands clawing down her body with a desperation that shocks her. It belies all his words. It belies all his distance and the lightness of the great sky itself—this hot black dive he takes into her flesh, the careless determination of his tongue cracking her open. She hears her own hard breath as she clings to him, trying to open herself wide enough to take him—like a parched desert wanderer who is suddenly showered with waterfalls of rain but is washed away in the flood before having a chance to drink.

Under her dress he is already pressing to get in, and she feels it there, and it is beautiful. But she wants to touch it and look at it first, and it just wants to get in. His head now bent over her chest, his breaths furious, his body rocking against her as if he were weeping, pressing to get in—and she feels his fear.

She cries out as that thing that is his begins to crack her open where she's not ready—still dry, still new. Her cry has anger in it, because something is not right. He stops.

"I'm sorry!" he cries back in anguish, dropping his head into her chest, not looking at her.

"No, I want—" Lonely pauses, bewildered. Didn't she want this?

"I'm sorry," he says again, more softly, and the lonely resignation in his voice is even worse. He rolls off of her, rubs his hands over his face in a gesture she has never seen, and then lets his arms fall to his sides and stares up at the sky.

"How can such a personal, selfish love not take me away from my duty to the world?" he says after a long time, his breath still coming hard. "It distracts me, to think of my own need for you. How can I be with you, and be joyful, and make love to you, when my people are dying? When all people are dying—inside?"

"Sky—"

"Lonely," he interrupts, and she hears the bitterness in her own name, for the first time. "I could not save my parents or my sister. I could not save—I could not save anyone, yet. I have not yet proven myself. I don't know if I'm ready to love."

"But," says Lonely, willing herself to be strong, not to let the fear take her as it has taken him, "you already saved someone, remember? You saved me."

And even though you don't know it, she thinks, *you called me here, so I could save you. Now look at me.*

He does. His eyes are so hopelessly blue, unlike those of his people—and she thinks she sees the secret hunger inside them, the only gift he has to give her.

But he doesn't return the next day.

Or the next.

On the first day, she doesn't go anywhere. She sits by the edge of the lake and watches the white birds and the other birds that mingle among them. The ones that are Sky's elders are like swans, only slimmer, and when they come to shallower water they stand up on thin spider legs and wade. They do nothing quickly. They never come near her.

She is sitting close to where the little spring enters the body of the water and loses itself. As the day grows old and quiet, she tries to draw comfort from its sound, to understand its language. But when she closes her eyes, she feels only the weight of the water in her heart. She feels its darkness, moving slowly beneath the rushing patterns of light on the surface.

She begins to feel the cold in a new way. She begins to understand that this place of white and brilliant stone and painful sunshine is not only magical but also the coldest land in the world. Everything is cold. The raw, barren peaks, the steely grass, the faceless snow. It feels cold and it looks cold and its silence, glorious and endless, is cold.

Today she feels too heavy to walk or to wander.

I can't believe that after last night, you wouldn't come to me. Last night you trusted me. Last night you were almost mine, after all.

Sitting by the lake, she is able to watch, for the first time, animals coming one by one to drink. After all her days wandering the barren slopes that emptied into sky, filling up her vision with windy stillness, she had never imagined there could be so many animals here. Where do they come from?

The mice and the songbirds come in the morning. The elk come at midday. The raccoon comes in the late afternoon. The weasel and the fox come at twilight.

Each has his or her own way of drinking. Some lap with their tongues and others scoop with their lips. Some press their mouths to the water and do not seem to move them; others lift their heads with every swallow and glance around. Many come quite close to where Lonely is holding still, as if they do not know she is there. She wants to ask them questions about Sky, about this place, but she is silenced by a sense of sacred order, a sense of ritual around their meeting with this water that she does not understand. Something happens to the animals when their mouths touch the lake, and a fervent, deliberate peace falls over them.

Once, in the warmest part of the day, she watches a beetle walk to the water, close to her foot, and lift his mandibles as he bows down to drink. But then a gust of wind arises and sweeps the edge of the water a fraction further over the stones, and the beetle is caught up and swept out struggling into the abyss. Lonely finds it strange, for up until now the day has been perfectly still. Without thinking, she leans forward, her back stiff from a long time spent hunched over her knees, and lifts the beetle with her finger, placing him back on the stones.

Carefully, he steps forward again to drink. But the wind strikes up again, lifts the water higher, and pulls him back out.

"Oh!" says Lonely, and lifts him onto her finger again. "Stop that," she mutters to the wind. Whether or not it heard her, it does not blow again. But the beetle is nervous now. He crawls around the stones, looking for a safer place to catch a small drop of water that would quench his thirst. Lonely watches him. Long ago she knew what it was like to thirst and hunger, though she never feels it now. With her fingertips, she sculpts a little depression in the pebbles near the edge of the water, so that it catches a tiny pool that is separate from the lake itself.

"Come," she tells the beetle, and nudges him toward it, and watches him finally drink. As he walks away, stopping occasionally to wipe his antennae dry, she feels soothed.

That evening, after the darkness has already gathered, a doe slips thoughtfully down to the water and takes a sip. Lonely envies her graceful humility—something she wishes she could feel.

don't you wonder, asks the deer suddenly, *why all the animals came so close to you to drink?*

Startled, Lonely looks at her and doesn't know what to say. The doe looks back. *it is because they want to be near you,* she says.

"Why?" asks Lonely.

But the doe disappears into the darkness.

On the second day, all Lonely does is cry. She feels almost sure, sometimes, that Sky is never coming back. She follows the river down from the lake. She glimpses one of the birds and, thinking it is him, splashes across, the water clamping its icy jaws around her calves. But if it was him, he is gone now. She follows the river back to the lake. The sun weighs her hair heavy against her back. Sometimes her mind rests for a while, but then she thinks of him again, and the tears come. She walks through the forest, then along a jagged ridge like a broken castle wall. In the distance a herd of elk are moving over it like muscular spirits, following their noses as they nuzzle the grass. For the first time she longs for the silent presence of the horse beside her, her friend, like a comforting truth she held close to her all through her journey without ever understanding what it was.

All the world is soft and silent, the wind puffing through it and ringing, higher up, against space. The tears are still falling when she comes to a meadow, arrayed with rooms made of clustered spruce trees. Passing through one of these shadowy rooms, breathing deeply, she finds that suddenly the doe she saw yesterday is walking beside her without sound.

i was wondering if you might help me with something, says the doe, as they step out into the sunlight again.

"What? Me?"

yes. will you follow me a little way?

"Okay," says Lonely, who has nothing else to do, and can't help but feel gratitude at being needed by someone. They cross the meadow. Most of it is still covered in snow.

The doe says suddenly, *do you love him?*

Lonely, in her surprise, stops. The doe looks around warily, tilting her ears. "Sky?" The doe looks back at her. "Yes," breathes Lonely. "Why doesn't he come to me?"

The doe keeps walking. *oh well,* she says. *there's a time for that, i'm sure. the stags never come for me unless it's the right time of year—and that'll be soon enough now, come autumn. they don't come all the time, you know. at other times, it's better to be alone.*

Lonely says nothing.

i'm asking about love, though, the doe continues. *what is it like—this love?*

"It feels," says Lonely, starting to cry softly again, "like every part of every-thing that I feel about him—even the suffering, even the pain of not knowing and missing him and being hurt by him—is beautiful. So beautiful that I would always choose it, over any other feeling that wasn't connected to him."

Now it is the doe's turn to stop suddenly, and she doesn't even look around her, or bother that they're still standing in the open. *ah yes,* she sighs. *i can almost remember that.* She lifts her head a little as if she will look toward the sky, which a deer would never do.

"Did you love like that once?" asks Lonely, though she's not sure if it is possible for an animal to feel such a thing.

The deer does not answer immediately but leads her down into a valley where Lonely has never been. In this valley, the field bends into a softer, more mountainous distance, peopled with occasional small spruces; at the end of it, further valleys lead on to the other side of the world in a fading tunnel of successive V's. Lonely never imagined before what might lie on the other side of this mountain—the mountain where all her dreams pointed her. Yet here it seems almost visible. There is some perfect curve, some pattern of indefinite beauty, that catches together all the images of this place—the shape of the meadow, the neat and distant triangles of the trees, the V's of the valleys—so that it all has a kind of meaning, like an arrow that draws her vision toward some important beyond. Lonely stands still and stares quietly. For the first time since she arrived here, she feels mountains rising around her, holding her.

once, the doe says, *a long time ago, there was held in this place where Sky lives a great Council of Beings. the Unicorn made it happen. she called all of us together. she asked us to be at peace with one another, and she gave us a language with which to understand each other. certain things were understood then, like the kind of love you just described, but i have forgotten them now.*

Lonely fills up with questions, but the doe stops now before a gnarly bush with withered leaves and faces Lonely in a way that seems surprising for an animal normally so reticent.

my daughter is dying, says the deer. *the winter has gone on so long—for as long as any of us can remember. but the flowers of this bush have magic in them that i know will help her to last a little longer. they may even heal her. please will you pick a few with your hands, and bring them to her? i have only my mouth, and hands work so much better. hands can create and change things, not only devour them, like a mouth does.*

"But there are no flowers," says Lonely.

oh, says the doe, as if it is only a detail she has forgotten to mention. *just breathe there, on the bush. i am sure it will bloom again.*

Bewildered, but wanting to be kind, Lonely leans forward and breathes on the little branches of the bush. The warmth of her breath gets lost in the cold, and nothing more happens.

no, of course not like that, says the doe, though her voice is still patient and gentle. *with your heart open. i mean, if you are able to love us, as you are able to love him.*

And what Lonely thinks first is, *Of course I can't love you—or anyone—the way I love him,* but then she feels so sorry for the doe, her heart bleeding with compassion for this sweet animal-woman with the silent voice and the earnest plea. For the first time in her life she sees that others suffer as she does, and she sees that everyone needs love. What the doe asks undoes her. She had no idea how tightly and fearfully she had held the doors inside her closed, or even that there were any doors at all.

Her eyes sting with tears and her breath is more of a gasp that struggles through, but as it touches the bush, the bush bursts into flower. The flowers are pink, and the color tastes good to her eyes, after so long living in this white wasteland with only the enduring grey-green of the trees. She gathers a few of them into her hands, feeling the doe's gaze upon her and unable to look her in the eye.

we've never had a woman here before, the doe says.

Then Lonely follows her deeper into the valley, and through another meadow she could not see from where they stood before, and into a thicket where a little deer lies, her legs splayed thinly around her and her breath difficult. Lonely kneels and feeds the flowers to the fawn, one by one, and as she does so she strokes her hard, bony head. And without sound or words, but in some language that Lonely can feel, the fawn cries as Lonely cried when the doe asked her to open her heart. Then the fawn stands and walks to her mother.

thank you, says the doe to Lonely. *it has been so long since magic was made here. we Animals were called here once, but now we are like ghosts, passing lost from field to field with no reason. you could bring us all together again, if you wished. together, you and Sky make One. you, together, are the Unicorn.*

Lonely can only look at her.

She and the fawn lead her back out of the valley, to where the doe first found her. Then, discreetly, and without glancing back, the two deer pass into the trees and are gone.

On the third day that Sky doesn't come for her, Lonely enters the lake.

Her own desperation carries her forward until the water almost reaches her breasts, before she even notices that it's as cold as the sea. The day is warmer than most, but it doesn't matter. She begins to shake, but keeps walking. The earth under the lake alternates between a slick caress and a slime-coated stubble that eagerly encloses her bare feet. She tries not to think about it. She tries not to think about the darkness around her body as the water rises up to her neck. She tries not to think about the deeper abyss before her or the unknown that swirls against her legs, her hips, her belly. The white birds, still circling upon the surface, do not look any closer, nor do they seem to notice her.

When the water reaches her chin, she leans forward and tries to swim, but at the same time she calls out, involuntarily, "Help!" because she doesn't know how to. As she splashes about, she feels suddenly her wrongness in this place, the gruesome commotion she is causing in this eternally placid calm— this sacred center from which, yesterday, she watched each animal draw its life. Though she waded into it desperate to speak to those birds, now she is terrified that they will notice her.

They do. As she struggles back the way she came, trying to get a foothold again in the fickle softness beneath her, she turns in a panic and sees them coming.

They float in wavering lines, like a handful of lost prayers from the distance, sliding over the water and leaving delicate threads of darkness in their wakes. Lonely is gasping, shivering so hard that her teeth knock against each other and her shoulders clench around her spine. She wraps her arms around herself and watches them come, feeling nothing but fear.

When they are close enough, she can see the beauty in their feathers and the pale sorrow in their eyes, and they stretch their necks out long and tilt their heads toward the water in a gesture that seems to Lonely full of emotion. They surround her. Then she is submerged in quivering softness, blinded by hovering white light, and their feathers seem to cloak her in comfort so that the water no longer feels cold, but rather warm and kind. She can see nothing but white light, and yet it is not a bright light, and now it is easy to close her eyes and rest on the deep down that seems to lift her up and support her.

Are you afraid? they ask her.

I was, thinks Lonely. *I was, because he is. Isn't he?*

He is, say the birds. And to her surprise, the voices are female. Maybe she isn't remembering right now, but she thought he had always called them his Grandfathers. She thought they were all male.

For him we are, they say, hearing her thoughts. She can feel the softness of feathers all over her body, melting her muscles. It seems that as she spreads her arms and opens herself wide, it is she who has wings, and that inside this lake is the true sky—in which she glides now, with no effort at all.

Why is he afraid? she asks.

Because where he comes from—where all of us come from—something frightening lived in the water.

But you're not afraid, says Lonely. *You're here all the time.*

Because we surrendered. He hasn't yet. He hasn't learned. You are the one who will teach him.

Lonely turns her body into the light, surprised. *But how?*

You already asked one question, they answer. *We will give you two more. Is this one of your questions?*

Lonely hesitates. *No.*

Then speak.

She decides she will save the question she came with for last. It seems less important now, somehow, in the slow comfort of this feathered dream, and she wants to make sure it is really what she wants to know. Before that, she asks the question that comes to her right now, spontaneously out of this moment.

What is the Council of Beings?

It is Love.

Lonely holds her breath without meaning to. She wants to know what kind of love, and if it is the same kind of love she feels for Sky—and now she wishes she had asked about love to begin with, and whether or not Sky loves her the way she wants to be loved or the way the Witch demanded. Now she is overcome with all the questions she could have asked, about why she is here and where she has come from and all that she hasn't told Sky because she was afraid, but she only has one more question left to ask, and she begins to cry.

The powerful wings embrace her, and she feels their compassion pour into her, entering all of her empty places the way water immediately finds all the spaces between stones. She feels the warmth of their bodies and hears the soft and sorrowful clacking of their beaks like rain around her.

There is only one Love, they say. *Yours for Sky, and Sky's for you, and the Unicorn's for the world—it is all the same. It only appears sometimes in different colors.*

What is your last question? What did you come here to ask?

Lonely opens her eyes. She feels the earth, rising beneath her, and the water lapping against her skin with the reverberations of her passage. They've been floating her back all this time, and she is almost at the shore now.

"Can I stay here, with Sky, forever?" she asks, and then adds timidly, "He said that he would ask you."

No, they say. *That is not up to us. Only he can decide that.*

Then without sound or ripple, they rise on outstretched wings and float away from her across the water.

Lonely sits at the edge of the lake for a long time, still naked, before she begins to feel cold again. During that time, she thinks only of Sky. She thinks of his fear. She thinks of where he comes from, which she has never seen, and what haunts him, which she doesn't know. She thinks of the smiles he gives her, the adventures he shows her, and the way he found her that day with his heart open and not understanding why she walked angrily away. She thinks how rarely he gives words to the sadness in his eyes, and she thinks of the gift he gave her with his tears the other day.

When she is cold enough, she steps out of the water and clothes herself again in her dress, something that lives and breathes with his words, his voice, his naming. She looks around at the snow-covered rock, the grey shrubs, and the still pines, and sees the loneliness he lives with. She sees the eternity of his life here—never changing, never touched by anyone until she arrived.

She walks out into the field of snow and drops down to her hands and knees. She breathes against the ground, the way she breathed upon the bush for the doe.

I offer this love to you, she prays. *I offer you to this love.*

First, the snow becomes clear, and then it becomes water, and then the soil softens and drinks it in. Then the soil begins to fuzz over with a light green haze, and then the swords of the grass press through.

Laughing with amazement, she crawls forward, careful not to crush them, and breathes again. For the first time in a long, long time, she remembers she is part goddess.

She crawls and breathes over that meadow, until the paths she has melted begin to connect with each other on their own, and the grass begins to spread. Then she stands and goes to the bushes each in turn, and to the earth between the evergreens all around the meadow, and lilies sprout from her breath.

To every living thing that she breathes upon, as the doe taught her to breathe, she says the same thing:

I offer you up to this Love.

She falls asleep that night in the center of a field of flowers, surrounded by birds that call to her from the surrounding trees in joyous songs of goodnight and gratitude—for the insects have woken, and seeds are ripe that have not been ripe in many years. She doesn't know what will happen next. But she feels happy.

When she wakes in the morning, he is lying by her side. He isn't sleeping, of course; she has never seen him sleep. He is looking at her, his eyes serious and his face very still. A butterfly shivers around him, and then spins off deliriously into the summery air. Lonely leans close to him and touches her nose to his. She takes his hand between their two bodies. Without moving, hardly breathing, he grips hers tight.

"I love you," she tells him, and tastes his tears with her lips.

This day is like no other. They hardly touch, and yet they are closer than ever. They wander their world together, scarcely speaking, and they gaze at each other constantly as if they have never seen each other before. They speak to each other without their voices, as the animals and plants speak, and use their mouths only for kissing.

Everywhere they go, they make the summer come. Lonely makes the plants bloom, and Sky calls out the animals, and many of the animals follow them for a while at a little distance, as if caught up in their wonder. For the first time, they feel their power together. They feel as if they could remake the world and make it real.

At the end of the day, Sky kisses her long and slow by the edge of the lake. Then he looks out toward the white birds, and she imagines she sees his shoulders droop a little, and a heaviness come over him. She tries to keep her mind from the question of how long he will be gone.

"Sky," she says out loud for the first time. All that has passed unspoken between their minds and hearts today has passed easily because they seemed to be one in all their thoughts. But now she asks a question to which she does not know the answer. "Who are the animals in this place? They are not like animals down on the earth below. They are like spirits."

Sky nods. "They are spirits. They came here long ago when the Unicorn called a great Council. They are the representative soul of every kind of animal and every kind of plant. Like each being in a dream of itself, in which it knows itself—knows beyond its own life."

"What was the Council of Beings?" She has not told him that she spoke with the white birds, and she doesn't know if she ever will.

"The Unicorn brought together the souls of different animals that were bewildered, whose homes were destroyed by humans," answers Sky. "She told them that all the animals of the world would have to come together in order to understand what was happening, even the predators of these animals, even the ones they feared. Then when all the animals came together, she said they had to invite the spirits of the trees and plants, too. Finally, she said they had to invite the humans, and so they invited us, the Dream People. The animals were afraid of us, and when we came they demanded answers. But we had no answers, because our homes had been destroyed, too. Then they understood: human beings were not only destroying other life but also themselves."

He looks at her. "The Unicorn did that for us. She brought all the world into communication, and helped us to understand how we suffer together, how we are all connected in a greater Love. She taught us the language we speak in dreams, through which any being can understand another. That is how you and I can speak to each other, even though our peoples speak different languages. The Unicorn taught me how to speak to you, because she knew that you would come."

The wind flutters against them, touches their ears, rolls by their sides in the grass like a happy dog. "So that's how," murmurs Lonely.

Sky touches his lips to her face and closes his eyes. "I told you," he whispers. "We have always been coming to each other. I am the only man, and you are the only woman. But sometimes we forget. Everyone is forgetting what the Unicorn taught us."

"What happened to the Unicorn?" Lonely asks, clinging to him as the day darkens.

"I don't know."

"Is the Unicorn female?"

"It is both male and female, and neither."

"Where does it come from?"

"It is immortal, but our people were the ones who performed the ritual of its rebirth. It was born and born again from our waters. Now those waters are gone, and it is lost somewhere."

Why are you afraid, then? Lonely wonders. *Why did the birds say something terrible lived in the water?* But her intuition tells her not to ask, not now. She wants to hold onto the feeling of this moment, which seems to circle back eternally into itself, into its own perfection, in which she and Sky are together and that togetherness is meant to be.

"It seemed to me," she whispers, "that I followed a Unicorn's horn into the sky, and that's how I came to be here. When I first arrived at this mountain, I couldn't see the way up and I almost lost hope. But then I saw the Unicorn, and after that I didn't have to think anymore."

Sky squeezes her ever so slightly. "They say a Unicorn appears to a person when he or she has lost hope—or when a miracle is needed." His voice is very quiet, because they are so close and because their hearts are so connected that speech feels hardly necessary.

They continue to hold each other for a long time, and when it comes to her, Lonely is not afraid to speak her next thought out loud. It doesn't sound crazy to her. "A doe told me," she says, "that you and I could call this Council of Beings again. She said that we—together—were like the Unicorn somehow. Do you know what she meant?"

Sky pulls away then, in a thoughtful way, and looks out at the water. Lonely turns to him and tries to read his mood but cannot. "The union of masculine and feminine," he says, as if speaking to himself. When he looks back at her, she is surprised by the watery uncertainty in his eyes. "The Feminine was lost to us for so long," he says, "after our world was destroyed."

She takes a deep breath. The mood has shifted and the moment has changed, but it is suddenly clear to her that this must be said, and she is the one who must say it. "Let's call the Council again."

Sky sighs.

"What?"

"I don't know."

"Why not?" She is surprised by her own impatience. Somehow she senses that if they can do this successfully, he will let her in. He will let her stay forever. And maybe it's a selfish longing. But she tells herself that their love—this love she shares with Sky—will begin to heal the whole world and all the sorrow her father created. She's sure that deep down, Sky can feel that, too.

"How is it done?" she asks now, as if it's already been decided. "How is the Council called?"

"The original Council," says Sky, "was held inside the lake. Because the top of the world mirrors the bottom of the world, where I come from, where the water was sacred. The animals still know it. That's why they come here to drink. The Unicorn blessed this water, and within it, everyone can understand one another again."

Then why are you afraid? Lonely wonders again, but now she thinks she understands his hesitation to hold the Council: he doesn't want to enter the lake. She squeezes his hand.

"It's okay," is all she can think to say. "I'll be with you."

It happens on the full moon.

They gather around the lake at dawn—all the animals—and then one by one, they descend.

Lonely and Sky sit between the two outcroppings and watch. Sky wants to make sure that everyone is there. Animals come from all directions, including from behind and around them, and everyone is silent. The weasel passes near the rabbit, and the fox near the squirrel, but nobody pays any mind, and no one seems afraid. Soon the doe that Lonely knows passes close by her, and Lonely calls out a soft greeting, but Sky pulls at her hand.

"Hush," he says. "Don't speak now."

This irritates her a little, for her secret journey with the doe feels like her own proof of belonging, and it is something she claimed on her own. But she swallows the irritation back. She wants to be holy today. She wants to be the goddess who stands with her god, and allows this great thing to happen.

They watch the animals wade into the water, and it's so strange, to watch them go down. They do not hesitate, and they do not swim, and they do not flail about as Lonely did. They pass smoothly, directly in, and are gone. The squirrel takes only a few short bounds. The rodents come en masse, and the ravens and wild turkeys wade like the four-legged animals all beside each other, their beauty incongruous and exposed, shifting at different paces into darkness, in the eerie magic of the rising sun.

When the last turtle is submerged, Lonely looks at Sky. "Will we go now?" she asks.

But Sky's brow is clenched. "Where are the spirits of the trees and the plants?" he asks. "Do they not know they are invited?" He jumps up. "I will go and speak with the Spruce."

"I'll come with you," says Lonely.

"No. I'll go alone." Apologetically, she thinks, he turns and gives her a cursory kiss on the cheek, then bounds away.

She waits alone by the lake, trying not to feel left out, trying not to think. She wonders what the animals are doing down there, waiting in confusion, but she sees the white flock turning over the surface as if guarding them, so everything must be all right.

The sun has lit the field evenly and sits comfortably in a nest of clouds by the time Sky returns. He stops before Lonely, looking lost.

"They won't come," he says. "None of the plants will come."

"Why not?"

"The tree spirits say we have decided too hastily for them. They don't feel that we are ready. They say they do not feel that things are stable enough, rooted enough, to hold this Council now."

"What things?"

"I don't know. I think…things between you and me."

Lonely turns cold inside. She looks away. "Did they say we shouldn't hold the Council?"

"No, they didn't say that. But they said they won't come."

She looks back at him and waits, her gaze hard. He shakes his head. "It doesn't feel right," he says. "The Council is for all beings. It isn't complete without them."

"But they're already down there," she pleads. "All the animals are already down there."

She sees him hesitate, and she knows that he, too, longs for this. She sees the childishness of that longing—that child part of him that is like her—wrestling with his more serious sense of responsibility. "It'll just be a beginning," she says. "We can hold another Council later, when the trees are ready."

Sky takes a deep breath, and she can tell it's against his better judgment that he says, "Okay. Let's go."

Heart rushing forward, Lonely takes his hand again, and in a moment they are at the water's edge. Sky walks in fast without pausing, as if to prove that he has nothing to fear, and when she looks at him she sees his jaw set rigid. But then the white birds surround them, and everything feels easier, and Lonely leans toward him and wraps him in her arms. She feels the thick beingness of the water, so much heavier than she is. The birds rise into the air around them in a stir of quiet wings, tickling their faces. Lonely looks at Sky, and he laughs, and she laughs, too. Then she sees the sadness in his eyes, and she sees the pain of his humanity: raw, hot skin all alone among the feathers, rich colored body alone and barren in a long-forgotten world. She remembers his face from her vision in the tower, the strength and the struggle she saw there, and understands again that she is the first human he has touched in physical form since the City was made.

Then the white wings turn to darkness, and Sky and Lonely are underwater, as Lonely once walked underwater long, long ago, traveling from nowhere to nowhere beneath the sea. This time her lover's hand holds hers tightly. And there is a light at the center of a circle, though she can't yet see what forms the circle or what makes the light. She notices now that she is breathing the water. It fills her with that strange weight she remembers from the sea, slows her thoughts, and changes her, and she doesn't need to suck breath in or let it out. The water flows through her, is part of her. Because she has no air to push out, she cannot speak, at least not with her voice.

The more she breathes the water, the more she is able to see who makes up the circle. Their images waver in and out of her vision: some of them made more of color, some made more of movement, and some made more of light. They are all the animals she has ever known, and more. Animals she has never seen on this mountain, from all over the world. So many animals—so many they should make a circle bigger than this lake, bigger than the mountain—and yet every way she turns, magically, the face of each animal appears near her, as if the circle is close enough to touch. Whiskers. Dark, flaring nostrils. A canine gleam of tooth. Antennae. A hundred, thousand eyes. A hooked beak. Her own body surges inside itself. Out of a deep sea of memory, she remembers drum beats, a spiraling tongue, the press of bony horns. But under the lake in the silence, even her own feelings are slow to form. They linger slowly, and they move slowly.

Sky squeezes her hand. She turns to look at him and sees again the painful, naked form of the human being. The shame of it. His fine, vulnerable face, its detailed language of shape, shadowy with secret pockets and twists of age and the small liquid softness of the mouth. His neat, hidden row of teeth. His eyes full of lonely, unspeakable mind. His elegant throat. His body reaching upward toward the sky, like trees. The helpless, dead curtain of his hair.

In his sad eyes she sees that it is a punishment for him, in his mind, to have remained human. To be the only one. To stumble about alone in a form that no longer has any meaning in the world he has chosen, high up in the sky. No wonder he won't surrender to that form and make love to her. How can she ever convince him of its beauty?

She squeezes his hand back. She feels the animals looking at her, but she doesn't feel afraid. She feels the water welcoming her, all of her—her body, her heart, her mind. It makes her insides warm, though perhaps the water itself is cold. Later, she won't be able to remember.

They sit down in the silken earth, and at once seem to float just above it. Lonely takes in the silence that is like no silence she has ever heard, with no air moving inside it.

"Is she human?" asks the cat finally.

A spider crawls over Lonely's knee. She pauses at the highest point, as if resting at the top of a mountain. "I can't tell," she says.

Lonely hears panting in her ear. A dog worries his nose against her chest, and she offers him her hand. This one is grey and graceful, his nose polite and powerful. She doesn't understand how he breathes like that under the water. She doesn't understand how he can smell her.

"I think so," says the dog. "I think she's human."

"I'm still deciding," says Lonely, though she doesn't say it with her voice. In fact throughout the Council, everyone speaks and understands, including Lonely, and yet later she will not remember how. The first time she speaks, the faces and their thousand gazes seem all to come into focus, for an instant, as if the whole world's eyes are upon her.

"In this Council, she is the embodiment of the Goddess," says Sky. "Since the City was made, the Feminine has been lost to us. Now we appear before you, God and Goddess united, to hold space for this Council as the Unicorn held it long ago. We hold space for you to speak again of your wisdom, your memories, your experience of the human world—the suffering it creates and what we can do to alleviate that suffering among all beings. You are safe here to speak what you will, as you will, in this Circle."

Nothing is said for some time. Lonely feels the sorrow that sits around her, filling the lake. And she doesn't know why Sky's words do not make her happy. Something in him still sounds far away to her, as if it hasn't caught up with his words.

"Why be human?" asks a snail after a long, silent moment, her lip-shaped body recoiling into her shell. It seems to Lonely that the question is directed at her. "It seems very difficult. Very complicated."

"There are too many humans," murmurs the fox. "But each one acts like the only one, and uses up the whole world. I want my fields back. I want my running."

"They are everywhere," says the eagle, his eyes hard, his head turning to sweep the circle as if he recognizes the touch of humanity in every animal here.

"Their poison in the sea," says the starfish, lifting one arm.

"Their noise, shaking us, under the earth," says the lizard.

The deer begins to cry. Lonely knows that she is crying because she herself is crying, though the tears are meaningless within the water. "I can't stand the noise," the deer says. "I can't stand it." And the whale, whose bigness runs deeper than all of them, deep into the lake and perhaps into the very earth beneath it—whose voice is bigger than the lake—says nothing, but her tiny eyes are wracked with sorrow, and she rolls her white belly away.

"Why do they make so much noise, all of the time?" cries the rabbit. "It frightens me. It hurts me. I can hardly think any more."

"It's because they cannot be happy," says Coyote. "They want to change wherever they are. They cannot stand to be inside themselves. They want to be somewhere else, wherever they are." At the sight of him, Lonely stifles a desire to flee, while shame and fear drizzle down her spine. But his seriousness surprises her. There is no mockery in his voice now. He looks at the rabbit not even with hunger, and not with cunning, but with something like tenderness.

"Why would you want to be human?" the fish asks Lonely, and when Lonely looks at her, the fish's body is like a mirror, silver and wordless.

"For love," says Lonely. "And maybe, for laughter." That last part surprises her. Laughter. She thinks of Fawn, in a warm valley of cut wood and vegetables and summer sun, so far from here.

"What is laughter?" asks the cat. "I have heard it, and I do not like it."

Lonely looks at Coyote; he looks back at her and grins, and Lonely feels herself blushing. But the subject is not mentioned again. None of the other animals understands laughter.

"But we know about love," whirrs the hummingbird, her body tiny and royal on a throne of colored motion.

"Human beings can love with a love bigger than any animal's," says the dog with quiet awe, standing up and quickly sitting down again. "And they can hate just as big, and destroy. It is so powerful, what humans feel. It takes you over. You don't know why it affects you—you just feel it. It's terrible and exhilarating and—and—" He stops, panting, wordless.

"It's true," says the spider. "You never know what's going to happen when you come in contact with a human being. Some animals go their whole lives without ever encountering one, and they never have to question anything. But maybe, once in your life, a human finds you. I don't know how it happens. There isn't a certain place or a certain time. It can't be predicted, not at all. But one day you are lifted into the sky as if a bird caught you, or you are trapped inside something you don't understand. Maybe you die instantly, as you expect to. Or maybe you are tortured first. It has nothing to do with hunger: they don't really want you, and you don't feel their souls in the killing, and you can't understand. But maybe, if you're lucky, something else happens that doesn't make any sense. I can hardly describe it. The human carries you, and then you are somewhere else. Or it keeps you for a long time, and then, for no reason, it lets you go."

There is silence all around the circle.

"It's like meeting a god," the spider says. "Or like fate itself. You never know what's going to happen. You can never understand. But maybe it makes you question, in a way you might not otherwise think of until after you've died, what it all means. If life could be different than you thought. If *reality* could be different."

More silence, and then, "A human child once picked up my beloved," says a phoebe, "when he was wounded by the cat. And I thought she would eat him. But then, a while later, she brought him back. He was whole again, and he flew to meet me!"

"Yes," says the cat. "Sometimes the humans stop me, when I'm killing something. They make me drop it. They carry me away. But they don't want it for themselves. I don't understand!"

"They picked me up," sings the snake in a long, hushed breath. "They picked me up and held me there, and made noises, louder and louder, and then they let me go."

"But you can't trust them," interrupts the mountain lion in a voice that stills the others. She settles down with her heavy paws stretched out before her. Her eyes are beautiful, like rain falling over the moon. "I don't, anyway."

"It's true, they are very clever," says the squirrel nervously, chewing on something in his hands. "Cleverer than even you, Coyote." Coyote just smiles.

"No, what I mean is," says the mountain lion, "they are clumsy. They don't know what they're doing. They don't see you and they don't know where they are. That can be dangerous."

"Exactly," says a glossy, diamond-shaped beetle with a complex purple design on his back. "They can crush you."

Lonely looks over at Sky, who has dropped her hand and sits very still, his eyes closed.

"They have to do with the killing river, don't they?" asks the deer suddenly.

"What's that?" asks the otter. Lonely remembers her, and is touched by her warm, feminine curiosity. She lounges on her side, voluptuous and easy, her quick eyes concerned and loving as she looks at the gentle deer.

"I mean—the other river," stammers the deer. She is so pretty and shy. "The one with the bright lights at night, out of nowhere, and the rushing that grows and fades, all the time, but without any rhythm—without any meaning."

"That's the road," says the raven. "We get a lot of our meat there."

"It's so sudden," says the opossum, "when you die there. Like getting taken by an owl, only there's a noise first, absolute and terrible. You feel the world has ended."

"But owls are taken there, too," says the owl.

"Even cats and dogs," says the cat. "Those animals don't care. They'll kill anything. They are vicious."

"They're not animals," says the dog. "They're cars. You can get inside them, with the humans. It's fun."

The cat looks at him. "What?"

"Never mind," says the turtle. "It's best to stay away from that Other River. The things that come are faster than anything you can imagine. They don't make sense. There is no escaping them."

A seal sighs. "There are so many things connected with humans that we don't understand," she says. "I don't know about this other river, but there are things changing everywhere that we can't explain. Sometimes you eat a fish and it isn't a fish. Or some dead-like thing catches you under the sea, and it traps you, though you cannot see it, and it follows you forever until you drown."

"Or you smell them near," says the wolf, "and then a noise—always the earthquake, horrible noise with the humans, that's how you know they are around—and then you are dead, or pain and blood stream from your body. You don't know how it happened. Your brothers lick your wounds and ask where is the enemy. You don't know how to answer. And soon they, too, are dead."

"I know you are dying," the deer says suddenly to the wolf. "Your people are dying." Lonely looks into the wolf's eyes, old and moonlit, and sees that he has loved the deer since the beginning of time. Always, always he has desired her. This, she thinks, is the kind of love the deer spoke of, the kind of love the animals remembered when the Unicorn created this space for it to happen. "I know you have always chased me," says the deer. "And I always run from you, and that is the way. But I don't want to see your people die. Without you, my people are lost and afraid. They don't make sense, any-more, to themselves. They outnumber themselves, and die slow deaths. And in our souls we feel lonely. I mean, not lonely like when you're missing from the herd and you're afraid and vulnerable. Lonely in some other, deeper way. I don't know if *lonely* is the right word."

It is, thinks Lonely.

"The humans feel like that, too," says the dog eagerly. "They feel that kind of loneliness."

"You love the humans," says the chicken to the dog.

"I do," says the dog. "I was born to love them. They need me."

"I don't understand that."

"They love you, but they hate me," says the wolf. "I can't understand that."

Lonely can. It's like the way her father loved her but hated his own wife, even though they were both women, even though—maybe—they shared the same blood. *You can love half of something and hate the other half, but unless you love the whole thing,* she thinks, with the strange knowing that comes in dreams, *it is not real love.*

"They've forgotten you," says the dog. Lonely thinks she can hear his heart beating inside his chest, big and proud and longing to be good. "They've for-gotten that I am connected to you and so are they. They have forgotten their wildness."

"Remind them," says the wolf.

"I try," whines the dog. "But they don't always listen to me."

"And for this you love them?"

"No. I mean, I don't love them for a reason. I just love them. You love them, too," he charges the cat.

The cat looks aside. "I do," she murmurs. "When they're good."

"Maybe you can help us understand, then," says the eagle. "Why they do what they do, and how we can protect ourselves. Myself, I oversee a long, long food chain. Through what I eat, I keep track of the health of many, many fishes. There was a sickness being passed to me, through them. The water is sick, and I don't know why. But that whole system of life lived inside me through what I ate, and then my children died. I know there is something wrong."

"We die from it," adds the salamander. "We breathe it into our skin. We die by the millions, and the water is poor without us."

"The trees tell me," says a woodpecker, "that it's in the air, too."

"I don't know," says the dog. "I think the humans are sick. I think it leaks into the world."

"Also," says the loon, "we can't always make it to our summer homes, where we love and make children. Where we used to rest on the way, now the lakes are gone. They are filled in with hard earth; they are full of noise and people. What is this?"

"The humans," sighs the dog, after shifting on his front feet, turning in place, and settling down again—anxious with the attention that is placed upon him and longing for approval—"are always making new places, to go on top of the old ones. They don't want the old places. They want new ones."

Lonely feels something happen in Sky, beside her. It is very subtle. Not a movement or any tangible tension, but like something falling inside him, as through a long tunnel.

"But why?" asks the dragonfly.

"Because—because of Entertainment," says the dog desperately.

"What is that?"

"Something to do. Something to play. You know…play?"

Most of the animals do not. The fox says, "Our children play, when they are young, so they can learn to hunt. Does this have something to do with learning? What are the humans trying to learn? How to hunt?"

"I don't know. I think, yes—they want to get something. But not food. I don't know," the dog whimpers. "I think they are trying to feel alive. They don't feel alive."

"Can anyone else here speak for the humans?" breaks in Lonely. "Who else knows them? Who else besides the cat and the dog has lived with a human intimately, and knows a human's longings?" She feels Sky turn toward her, but out of the corner of her eye she cannot read his expression.

"What about the cow?" someone suggests.

"I don't want to talk," says the cow sullenly.

"The cow was created by humans," explains the horse. "It is hard for her to speak with the other animals. I'll tell you what I know about humans: they want to be in control. They have incredible power. What the dog says, that they don't feel alive—well, maybe they are not exactly alive. Maybe they are gods. Maybe gods are not really alive. I mean, they're not always down here, in their bodies."

"What does that mean?" asks Lonely. "Where are they?"

"I don't know," says the goat. "But it's true. It's a funny thing. I like to tease them, check them out. They take themselves very seriously. They forget themselves. They are thinking all kinds of things up in their heads. I wonder what?"

"We must help them," says the dog. "It's the only way. They are suffering, and they don't understand, and they don't know how to love. Men need to learn how to cry."

"And women," says the cat, settling down companionably beside the mountain lion, "need to learn confidence. They need to remember themselves, trust themselves, like we do."

"Humans are angry," says a yellow jacket, his voice a hot, painful hum.

"They have no elders. They fear death," says the vulture.

"Yes," says the bat. "And darkness. They keep the night lit up. They are afraid of it. But you can't live without darkness."

"They need to remember silence," says the cat. "They need to sit still and remember their souls. Whatever this Entertainment is, it makes them nervous, and crazy like fools."

"They have forgotten their community," says the bee. "Their great Mother."

"Maybe," says Lonely, and everyone turns toward her again, "they long for themselves. They feel lost from themselves, from their own flesh. They feel lost from themselves because they don't remember the earth—the earth which carries them. The earth which Sky remembers." Lonely looks at him and sees him stiffen further, as if she has spoken a forbidden word. Why doesn't he speak?

"And," adds Coyote, looking pointedly at Sky, "they have nightmares. So they refuse to remember their dreams. What are you going to do, Sky? What are you going to do about the nightmares?"

Sky shakes his head. "I fight the nightmares. They were not created by me."

"Do any of you live in the City?" asks Lonely.

"What is that?" says the snake. Lonely remembers that most animals cannot travel as far as she can. They have no sense of the big picture. She looks at the eagle, but he looks away now.

"My people live there," says the pigeon, stepping forward. "We can live there because we can eat whatever they leave behind. Because we're ugly, and they don't care about us."

"What is ugly?" asks the butterfly.

"The City is ugly," says the loon. "It's when something doesn't fit right with the rest of the world. You are not ugly," she tells the pigeon.

"But I think there is something beautiful about the City," says the pigeon. "Something I can't explain."

"Yes," agrees the rat. "Some kind of magic."

"It's like a community there," says the ant, and when Lonely looks at him, she sees not one ant but hundreds, holding together like one body. "A higher mind, like ours, that guides them all together. But it doesn't help them. They are not conscious of it or of us. It lives beyond them."

"Whatever it is," says the bear, gazing steadily at Sky, "we feel that the world is falling apart. We feel that not only are lives being lost but also souls. There are animals who are not present today. Who will never be present again."

Sky nods. "I know," he says.

"But what are people for?" asks Lonely passionately, standing up. "You said there was beauty in the City. There has to be some reason why we exist. There has to be something good that human beings can do."

There is a dark, low murmur of voices now, like a river bending close to where she stands. Sky feels far away. But she hears his voice right behind her.

"The purpose of human beings," he says, and she feels the coldness in his words, the absence of her name in them, "is to hold the sacred rituals that keep the world in harmony and the cycles turning as they should. Humans mediate between the animal and the sacred. They are meant to assist in the spiritual evolution of life, and they must do that by honoring each being, and keeping the sacred order of all things."

Lonely listens carefully.

"All of that has been lost now," Sky concludes. "The City knows none of that."

Lonely turns to look at him, and all of the sudden she recognizes the emotion in his stiffness. All this time she thought it was fear, but it isn't. It is anger.

She says it anyway. "There must be something good in the City. There must be something beautiful in all that."

"Haven't you been listening?" says Sky. "You weren't there. You haven't seen how it crushes everything beneath it, how it rules out all life, how things are not even seen before they are killed, how everything, everything—is lost." She knows that he stops because he can't go on. He is shaking so hard that she wants to drop down and wrap him in her arms. And she wants to cry because she knows he will not let her.

Go on, she thinks. *Say it. My father killed your people.*

"I don't believe it," she says, not even knowing what she means. She can feel—whether from Sky or the other creatures she does not know—that she isn't supposed to be standing, but she doesn't sit down. She can feel that she isn't supposed to break the circle, but she walks right through it now, underwater, and kneels down before the dog. She knows that he, at least, will not reject her. "You spoke about a kind of love," she says, "that only humans can give."

The dog licks her hand. He is calm and solemn now. "They have compassion," he says. "When the cat wounds a bird and leaves it to die because she doesn't want it, they might save it. When a deer abandons her child because the winter is too hard and she cannot feed it, they might save it. Just because they want to, for no other reason. Even a person in the City can do that. Compassion happens all the time, when you don't even expect it. It can happen to anyone."

Lonely turns to the cat. "What do you think?" she says. She can feel the whole circle listening.

The cat sniffs her hand and turns thoughtfully away. Lonely can tell she won't be rushed, and that to pressure her would only cause her to refuse. So she waits.

"The humans can certainly do a lot of strange things," the cat says at last. "I've watched them all my life, and I don't understand a single one of the machines or the magic that they make. I will not judge if it is good or bad. But it is very powerful, what they can do. It seems to me that such power can be put to good use or bad, depending."

"They can put it to good use," comes a new, turquoise voice from the other side of the circle, and Lonely turns to see two dolphins floating beside each other, their bodies comfortably touching. "Humans have great intelligence, beyond what we can even imagine. They are here to make meaning out of the Universe. They are here to make it matter. See?"

Lonely looks around the circle, and she does not think that the other animals can understand, exactly, but she can feel them listening hard, as if something like wonder opens their senses. She is close to the center of the circle now, and she can finally see what lights it. It is a Unicorn's horn.

"Yes," murmurs the spider, as if to herself. "I remember now. They make art. They write."

"What is that?" asks a firefly.

"I don't know," says the spider, walking around and around in her spiraled web, weaving lines into shapes. "I know but I don't know…I know but I don't know…No, I do not remember. But all of this began long ago, and it has some reason…."

"Who remembers?" cries Lonely. "Who knows what the City is for?"

She cannot see Sky now, so she walks around the whole circle, past every pair of eyes, until she finds him. It seems to her that he is fading from her, that she can no longer clearly see his face, and this terrifies her. She kneels and clasps his hands in hers. "It's us, Sky," she says. "We are the humans in this circle. It must begin with us somehow. The love between us—this love is the beginning. This human love."

But Sky shakes his head. "It doesn't work that way," he says. "Personal love like that feels good, but it does not change the world. In fact it can tear the world apart. It can separate us from the world completely—from our community and from what is right."

Lonely drops his hands. "What are you talking about?"

"I'm saying we called this Council to unite our wisdom and our powers, to understand the suffering that humans cause and how to fight it together—as one."

Coyote rises on his haunches and cocks his head. The whole circle is silent, and Lonely can tell that the word "fight" surprises them, as it does her. She realizes how much, through holding this Council, she has longed to understand Sky—and how irretrievably he seems to travel, moment by moment, away from her understanding.

"I mean," says Sky, "that I want to understand, from what all of you have to say, what we can teach the humans that will change the course of this suffering they cause. I go into their dreams. What can I teach them?"

"What about what they can teach *you?*" says Lonely, frustrated and hurt because it seems to her that he would rather she not speak at all.

"You don't know what it's like in the City," he tells her again. "You don't know what's happened there."

"But I know that I'm human. And so are you. So you should stop being afraid of it, because we're good humans. We don't have to hate ourselves so much." Lonely feels tears bleeding from her eyes into the lake. She covers her face in her hands. Her heart feels sore and strained, and she almost forgets the presence of the animals.

"It's not that simple," Sky grumbles. "We can call ourselves good, but we have as much selfishness as the rest of them."

I'm not selfish, cries Lonely alone inside her mind, thinking she hears what he doesn't say. *I'm not selfish for loving you. And it's not selfish if you love me.*

Suddenly the wolf throws back his head and howls. It's a long, round, wailing howl, arched like the waning moon. For it will wane again, after tonight. Lonely knows now. The moon will lose her child, again and again, and it will never stop. Now the coyote joins in, his voice leaping and hysterical, at once exaggerating and seeming to mock the sad call of the wolf.

Lonely wants to be silent with the others and listen to those dark sounds and the truth they call up within. But she cannot. She says, "Sky, you have to look at yourself. You have to look inside and see what's frightening you, before you can expect humans to understand the dreams you give them. Otherwise they will only be nightmares."

"Stop," he hisses, speaking only to her. "You're ruining this. It's not about me."

"I won't stop!" she cries. "If you know so much, why aren't the dreams working? Why does nobody hear you?"

He doesn't answer her, but everything turns wrong. The animals begin to move and twist around her, and then slowly fade. They are breaking the circle. They are rising up above the water. Sky looks at her as he has never looked at her before.

"Look what you've done," he says.

"No," Lonely whispers, her tears meaningless inside the huge water of the lake. "Not me."

They are alone now in the eerie darkness, and then Sky turns and rises toward the sun. She, too, turns and chases after him, waving her arms and kicking her legs. She doesn't see the white birds anywhere. She follows him to the shore, where he stands shaking himself like an animal.

"Sky, it wasn't my fault," she says.

"Yes," he says, turning on her. "It was! You burst in with your questions and tried to make it all about you, and me, and what you want from me. You made a chaos of the Circle."

"Only because you had some idea of how it had to go, that you never talked to me about! You think you're the only one who knows. It was supposed to be both of us. I was supposed to be part of this. What did you want from me? What did you want to come of this?"

"Not that." Sky storms up onto the land, and then he turns back to her one more time.

"You were the one who insisted we do this," he says, "even though the trees said we weren't ready. And we weren't. Now we've brought only more confusion."

"What are you talking about? You're the one who's not ready. You won't look within yourself. You won't surrender to this."

"To what? What do you think this is about, Lonely? This isn't about your loneliness. The whole world is at stake. Don't you get that?"

Yes, thinks Lonely, as she stops herself from reaching out to him—and then watches him go.

She turns and sits down on the earth. Every single animal is gone, for as far as she can see. She curls up. "I'm sorry," she whispers. But inside she thinks, *You said everyone in the circle was safe to speak as they would, to say what they had to say. But you didn't mean me. I could not say what I had to say in the space you made. I was not safe.*

All that remains here is the humble quietude of the Earth. It is so deep and sure beneath her bones, and yet it took so long to become what it is. Under the water, in that magical confluence of realities, the animals and humans could all understand each other—could, for a short time, speak the same language. But how could that ever happen in the real, complex world, where each being lives its long-ago predetermined existence, only gradually changing over millions of years? She thinks of Fawn. Of her fear.

The night comes over her and grows cold. Lonely thinks, *What if the old hag on the island is my mother after all? What if loneliness is in my blood? What if there is a darkness inside me that Sky can't see, but that little by little is pushing him away forever....*

Then the Earth speaks to her, and it says to her body, *I forgive you.* And in this moment, the Earth is Lonely's mother, soothing and rocking her in a rhythm she never embraced until now. Lonely never noticed before that the Earth was even moving. It is carrying her, like a mother whose softness is endless, and yet at the same time tired. Who is sometimes warm and rich, and sometimes cold and dry, but who has never left her. Who rises beneath and around her, singing in the wind and the sun.

Maybe you are my only mother, she says to the Earth, and in answer it seems to take her in, and she loses herself for one moment inside that womb where everything began. For one blessed moment, she allows herself to forget that she is human. She leaves her consciousness behind in a molten, loamy paradise in which ferns and dragonflies, eagles and mammals, crabs and horses and trees all dream their futures and remember their pasts and surge upward again and again into the hope and futility of life.

Then she lifts her head as the moon rises, and she tries not to remember who she is.

☾

The moon is waning.

Lonely has learned to watch it happen. She wants to understand the curse the old woman made: how the moon loses its child, and where it goes. At night when she can't sleep, she stares at the darkness where a piece of the moon was, trying to see behind it.

I'm still here, the moon seems to whisper. And Lonely knows now that it will keep coming back.

But Sky doesn't come back.

The days and nights pass in a haze of misery. She doesn't know where she goes or what she does. She wants to run away, wants to leave this place, leave this life, leave everything. Yet where would she go? This pain will follow her everywhere. She can never escape it.

In seven more of those dark moons, she will have to answer the old woman's question. *What is the proof of love?*

But the voice of her father, even in memory, is stronger.

Lost, he used to say into his helpless hands. *Lost.*

7ᵗʰ MOON

What happened to the animals when the Council broke apart? Lonely doesn't know, and in the days of Sky's absence that follow it, she speaks to none of them. When there is pain and distance between her and Sky, it seems that the world, too, must be broken apart from itself, and whether from guilt or from anguish, she cannot bear to engage with it.

Yet as time passes, the animals begin to come near her again. Ravens converse over her head, but she cannot understand them. A butterfly alights on her arm and travels with her for half of one morning as she walks over river stones, though if he is speaking, she cannot hear him. Sometimes when she lies for a long time in a thicket or a field, unable to move, rabbits feed close to her, or songbirds peck near her feet. Their presence comforts her, and yet she no longer seems able to remember how to communicate with them.

She spends one whole day yelling at the sky.

Other days she only wanders.

She decides that pain, though it feels at first like a live beast moving animatedly within the soul, is actually—when she focuses in on it—an absence of something. Like her very first feeling of absence, after her father stopped coming to the tower, only more acute. There is a nothingness inside her that over time has taken on its own energy, has begun to open wide, has begun to burn.

She loses track of the days. The meadow that she turned to summer begins to show signs of dying, and then another snow falls and covers the flowers. But on the day after that snow, she finds the footprints of his bare god feet, which cannot be harmed by the cold. They spiral slowly toward the center of the field, where he and Lonely lay that morning, and kissed each other in wonder. There in the center, she can see where he sat down, and then lay, in the snow. She follows the spiral back out to where he left it, and to where his human prints become the four thin lines of bird prints, and to where those prints end at the bare peaks of stone where he took off and flew.

But it gives her hope. She comes to the meadow often, hoping he will come again. Once, on a warmer day that melts the earth, she also finds his footprints at the edge of the lake, in the mud. She never saw his footprints before these two occasions, and she wonders what they mean. Perhaps he never wandered about in human form before, unless he was with her. And she even has the strange thought that somehow he is trying to find her again, but is lost in some other reality and doesn't remember how to get back to her.

At sunset on the new moon, she arrives at the edge of the lake and considers going in. She hasn't, all this time, because she cannot imagine that she belongs there. The more she has thought on what happened, the more she has felt that the ending of the Council was her fault after all, that she was selfish with her questions and the things she wanted to know. Yet she feels, still, that the lake is where the only answers lie.

The white birds have not spoken to her, nor acknowledged her in any way that she can tell. Now they float in different directions around the lake, without any apparent purpose, restful and quiet. She sits at the edge where once she watched the animals drink, and thinks back on the story of her love. How she crossed the sea and the fields and the desert, and climbed the mountains in search of him. *What was I searching for all that time?* she asks herself. *I still don't even know who he is.*

She tries to think where they went wrong. She remembers the way he trembled beside her, and then pulled her so sweetly and so violently to him on that first evening alone together in the sky. She remembers how he carried her into clouds, how he spoke of the moon—the first words he had spoken in perhaps a hundred years. She remembers how he kissed her each time he returned from dreams; she remembers how each time his face betrayed a longing—a need and a fear of needing, equal to hers—that in the midst of all her own fear she discounted, not trusting that it was enough.

"Sky!" she calls into the abyss over the lake, and it is the first time since he left her that she has actually called his name again. She was afraid of the pain of it. "Come back," she says more quietly. "I'm sorry. Can we start again?"

"Sky!" But the very word mocks her: not the name of a real man or boy, but the name of the whole universe, untouchable and vague. She stands up, shaking in that echo, and she can feel the weight of her own skin.

She throws a little stone into the water, to make something happen. And she stands there until the ripples have completely disappeared. In that time, the water calms her a little. It is old, and held perfectly still within the confident confines of the ancient stone. The water reflects each cloud, one by one as they pass over, and it reflects Lonely's face, and in the end the water is innocent; it only shows what is, without decision or judgment. This innocence touches Lonely. She feels the sincerity of her beloved inside it. She sees that he is only the mirror of her dream—someone trying to be more perfect than is human or possible, who loves her but is always just a little further than she can reach. Whatever he is, he only reflects her own loneliness; he reflects her question; he reflects her fear.

Now she lifts her face, and all the way out across the lake, all the way on the other side of the water, she can see Sky, standing there looking back at her. She wonders at first if it's a dream, for though he has told her there is no difference, there is a difference to her. She needs him to be real. But when he steps into the water and begins walking toward her, she knows that he is.

She does the same. She doesn't know what will happen, or how long it will take them to reach each other, or if they will be able to survive going down into it the way they did the day of the Council. The water pumps like a heart against her legs. The earth beneath the water sinks under her feet like fur. The white birds that she passes part away from her, like curtains opening. Sometimes he looks down as he walks, and sometimes he looks right at her. Sometimes he slows his pace, and sometimes he seems to hurry. Of her own pace, Lonely knows nothing. She can hardly feel her own body.

It seems to take forever. As they come closer, Lonely imagines every emotion he might be feeling—anger, loneliness, longing, joy—and feels sick with the anxiety of not knowing and of wanting. When she can see his face, he gives her his sad little smile, and she can't breathe.

They reach the center of the lake, but still the water reaches only to their ribs. Not looking at her, Sky reaches for her hand; when she takes his, she feels a jolt as if she touched the sun.

"It isn't deep now," is all she can think to say.

"It is deep, though," says Sky. "Deeper than we know."

Something about the word "we" moves her. She can see the emotion in his body—in the tension of his jaw, his shoulders curving in toward her— emotion like muscles rippling beneath smooth skin. Later she will remember this moment and wish she'd had time to trace every ripple with her fingers, exploring and coaxing into passion each fragile expression of his heart. She sees at once his strength and his helplessness. She sees the light of what he knows and the shadow of what he does not know.

She gives him her other hand.

"I came here looking for you," he says.

She nods, still not quite able to take a full breath.

"It took me a long time to come back here," he says, "because I was afraid."

"But you could have met me somewhere else. I am not always here."

"No," he shakes his head. "What I fear here, it is the same thing I fear in you. It's the same. I had to come here to the water, to face it. I can't explain."

She smiles now. "But you always explain everything to me."

He smiles too, but his look is stark and unsteady. "What do you want, Lonely?"

"I want to know you."

"Why?"

"How can you ask?"

"Because there is more to me that you don't see. When the City destroyed my home, I fought— So much happened. I still have strange feelings in me, feelings I don't want you to see."

"You don't want me to know you."

"No, it's only that I'm afraid to be needed. I can't trust myself."

"Or maybe," says Lonely, "you're afraid of needing me."

"Yes. That's true, too."

She holds her breath. But she can't hold it forever. She can't hold it for him. "Why?"

He looks down. "I fought for love once before, Lonely," he whispers. "I fought for it, and I failed. I was foolish. I didn't know."

"Didn't know what?" she whispers back, touching his face with her hand. "What happened?"

He turns his face, not toward her eyes, but into her hand, brushing it with his lips, and he keeps his eyes closed.

"I've lost so much, Lonely. I'm afraid to love! And if I'm afraid of that, how can I help anyone?"

She thinks suddenly, *That is why my name is Lonely. Not for suffering, and not to separate me—but so that someone else can look at me to find a mirror for his own loneliness and see it for the first time. Because only I can reach him. Only I can touch him.*

She won't remember later who first reached for whom, or how their bodies became once again entwined, their arms making a circle that surrounded them. She thinks that later, later, they will have time for all her questions to finally be answered. For now they only hold each other forever. And yes, there is such a thing as forever: the happy ending that stops the pain of the story and fills up the rest of eternity with its even peace. Even though the story will continue to unfold, as if unrolling down the other side of the mountain, where everything is different now, and loneliness lives again in new and different forms, and the humble details of life continue their slow excruciating march into nothingness—even so, in that godlike place where humanity can hold infinity (call it dreams, call it memory, call it soul), that happy ending extends on another plane crossing this one into forever. She will always know that this moment was forever, just like every other moment when everything changed. A moment between worlds, between eras, a moment of no-time. A moment when she lost herself, when she died, when a greater hand than her own dipped her for a moment into a nothingness that was not loneliness but pure bliss.

"I missed you," he whispers into her shoulder. "I love you."

She believes him.

The lake calls all the light out of the sky, bit by bit, and swallows it into darkness. The new moon rises unseen. Still, Sky does not leave.

They keep holding each other, and sometimes she feels her own body, and sometimes she feels his, and sometimes she is thinking and other times only feeling. She feels the water pulse against her skin, amazing. She feels their hands—the hands that reach and grasp and mold—forget themselves in the larger embrace of arms, of hearts blurring together. She feels the moonlight in their lips as they lean away, making space for love to glow, and kiss. From the moment his tongue first begins its exploration of her own, she knows he will stay with her all night.

He slides his hands under the water, up her thighs and under her dress, which slops wetly over his wrists, and his palms are smooth and sure and innocent of their perfection. She parts her thighs as his thumbs draw near, her body moaning open to the water as he traces its contour ever so slowly and with the same motion raises the dress over her head.

Like something that is no longer needed. Like something she needed to draw him to her, but now she has him, and will never need to cover herself again.

With a sigh, as if something in him that he cannot hold suddenly broke—like he knew it would, like he feared it would—he falls as if through some inevitable darkness into her arms again, dropping the dress into the water behind her and enfolding himself in her nakedness. Her flesh unwinds, and his body is an extension of her own heat, an extension into the universe, as if through his body her body enters the universe—a direct link. Before, there was a line between herself and the universe, thin as a thought but unbreakable, and now his body has blurred that line into nothing, like the lake dissolving the earth beneath it.

The tower of her prince's being—the young, firm tree of it, the fountain of it, the earnest cry of it—at once encloses her and sprouts up inside her. Her mouth falls open and his mouth falls open on top of it, so that they become an openness together, widening and widening, wet with the tight wetness of rain—where there is no separation between the wetness and the skin. He seems to swirl all around her—his hands, his lightning, his soul, his mouth—until pleasure makes her lose control of her face, makes her bump blindly against the softness and hardness of him, her body weeping against him, aching to let go.

He begins to walk her backward toward the shore, his thighs sweeping between hers. She can feel their wiry fuzz on her tenderest skin—their rough thrust, with each step, communing already with the depths of her. When the water reaches only just above their knees, he falls on his, and, to her wild bewilderment, hooks that tiny spike of need between her legs with his tongue, pushing at it with his own wetness. He grips her thighs so hard that she stumbles against him, holding his head like a magic ball, doubling over and sick with ecstasy. She feels the peak of pleasure she experienced with her own touch speed past her like an old landmark that no longer matters on the way to her true home, and then the feeling loops upward into a spiral that is neither pleasure nor pain, only purest, absolute intensity—something she could never name but which seems the endpoint of all need.

The untraveled road opens. Her body is a luxurious passageway, laid out in the jewels of her wetness for his coming. Desire is, she realizes, when pleasure is too much, too much for one body to bear on its own. The spirit of her body is bigger than her body itself—big enough to encompass two beings who smear their flesh together in a ridiculous chaos, two beings which in their twoness are the complete universe, as if two is the biggest number there is.

Now he lays her gently on the stone, and she looks up into the shifting, arched canopy of a willow she never noticed was there. The water still laps up their calves and their bent knees, as if they are creatures only partly evolved from the sea. She can feel, in the falling thrusts of his legs between hers and his body into hers and his tongue into her, the urgency he has held back, and his unspoken reverence for the goddess in her that can be touched by human hands. That longs for the touch of human hands.

What is that other, that live humanness that wants to come inside and be reborn into god? It wants to come inside her. It seems a part of him and not a part of him at the same time. It is like someone else who has been present but ignored, or maybe it only now makes its presence known. This simple, earnest being between Sky's thighs that presses teasingly against her openness—it is almost funny somehow, with a humor that brings her relief and pleasure at once. It is so simple, really. She wants to laugh because she feels so helpless in this incredible desire, and he too is helpless with it, panting, gripped by its emergency, when really it is so easy. She pulls apart the feathers that hide it. It seems so obvious to her that this presence should enter her, when it obviously fits perfectly, when obviously that is what it is made for. Like a piece of her that was taken out for just a brief time, for no reason, that now she will pull back in. *Come in,* she calls with the cradle of her hands, gripping his hips with the muscles that once gripped the horse, *come in.* There is no glass, no ice, and the tower will melt inside her. It seems so easy.

"Lonely," he says.

It is not quite easy. First there is pain. Pain like the earth. Pain like climbing the mountain, when she climbed hard and impatiently, and pain pumped through her tired joints. Pain like pain is simply part of her, part of the road into her life. She has been feeling the pain of his absence, for so long, and the pain of love's brokenness. This is only the pain of the body, which now she can bear.

That is why first you have to love, the wind might have explained, when she fought to refuse Coyote, when she knew inside herself that though love was more complicated than the needs of the body, she needed to be held safely inside it before she satisfied those needs. She needs him to hold her and hear that she cries out, feel the tenderness of his self-restraint as he pulls back and goes more gently, less deep, and then deep again, slowly, breathing out his relief. They do not fit as perfectly as she expected. At every point of contact there is at once the shock of agreement and the clash of disagreement. She pushes more desperately against him and at once scrambles at a thousand tiny nerve endings to escape. The need to get closer and the need to escape feed each other until she is crying out in a frenzy of desire for nothing that could ever fill her. But sometimes he does fill her. The deep clouds of flesh that line her, inside, do not feel touch like the skin of the outer body. Inside, sensation is a formless wave, at once full-bodied and ghostly, flushing her whole inner pathway with indefinable, needful goodness all the way up through her chest and her throat and her mind.

Sometimes she is thinking. She wonders what will happen when it ends. She wonders what will happen tomorrow. She wonders what he is thinking. She wonders if this is enough.

They roll over the earth. She sits on him, her breasts lifted proudly in the free-riding air, and rolls her hips in circles, pressing her own erection against the bone above his—and the creature of his desire struggles inside her, nudging her inner walls, wanting the quick rhythm of linear friction. But in his face he loves her, watches her in awe, rides the wonder of his own need with patience. She wants him to reach that peak. She wants everything for him. She wants him to allow himself the purest of joy. She kisses him slowly, and he kisses her back, filling her and filling her as if the pleasure of eating could continue without stopping, without ever being hungry or ever being full. Now he rises up, pushes back against the earth with one hand and encircles her waist with the other. He closes his eyes, his mouth against her breasts, his thrusts serious and intent, and she presses and slides in an arching thrust at once forward and down, pressing every part of herself against every part of him. He feels longer and longer, slaying her with pleasure, sucking her inside out, until that single point that was the center of all desire is tossed up into the vast galaxy of her body—vaster than she ever knew—and scatters into stars, and she doesn't know who is inside whom, or who makes the rhythm that rocks them. But for a single instant she is higher than this highest mountain, riding her own, immortal unicorn through crazy fields of forever, and she can feel the joy shocking upward through the pound of her hooves, and the joy flying through the sunlight of her hair into the wind. Then she looks down as her beloved shouts his hot breath between her damp breasts, and then drops his forehead heavily against her shoulder, his face shadowed and handsome and etched in a design she has never seen, his cries quick and as fragile as the baby fish that are tickling their feet in the darkness. And she understands why he feared to let his body speak its truth, why he feared to release himself into the hands of such merciless love.

Then they fall in a tangle of limbs that could never be undone, and let the high mountain water, still rocking faintly with the reverberation of their passion, wash them with its cool hands into sleep.

She wakes once during the night. She sees the humanness in his collapsed form, as if his bones became soft; she feels his surrendered weight against her and sees his eyelashes long against his face, flickering with the torment of consciousness lost beneath them. She cradles him against her. She strokes his back, that part of him he cannot see. *I will stay awake for you,* she thinks. *You who have stayed awake for a hundred years—I will keep the flame burning tonight, so that you, finally, can rest. Rest inside me. Let go, finally, beloved.*

Then she looks up at the stars: the night sky that knew her before anyone knew her, when she first saw through the image of herself into the universe. She watches that sky for a long time, and she knows that sky, and that sky knows her. She feels the wind touch her cheek—very slightly, just barely, only a whisper in the stillness—and that wind knows her name.

In the unconscious clinging of Sky's sleeping body, her own body dreams, and her mind tiptoes off into memories of long yellow fields that stretched unhindered from dawn to dusk. The infinity of the sea behind her; the promise of the world before her. The beat of the horse's rhythm against the humming earth. The sun melting into tomorrow. The sight of the desert from the high cliffs, and the things the wind told her, as if she were its secret and only friend.

Standing on the edge of the cliff overlooking the desert, she was dizzy with the fear of falling, but even then she'd known that what she truly feared was her own desire to fly.

All those days riding her horse through the meadows, walking upon desert, climbing the hills, pressing through forests—all those days she'd ached with such a pain of longing, yet those days had been hers alone. They had belonged to her and to no one else. Even her longing had been pure somehow: somehow whole in itself, somehow holy.

What if just as Sky fears his own need, she fears equally her own longing for freedom?

Because she now finally holds in her arms the man she so longed for, she allows herself for one instant—an instant she will forget later—to ask herself this question. She wonders what her life could have been like without this destiny laid upon her. She remembers what Rye asked her out in the simple, peaceful fields, when she held fresh soil in her hands: *What would you do, if you didn't have to go to that mountain?*

It isn't a painful question, or a question that must now be answered. It is only a question, as passing as the breeze.

The dead cold night chills the water tight against her skin. "Sky," she murmurs gently, and tries to roll them together out of the water onto dry land. He murmurs back, grasps after her with his arms as she shuffles awkwardly onto the ground without rising, scraping her hips on stone. He reaches for her, clutches at her and then relaxes again into sleep. She sees him anew, a boy who has lost everything—who tries in his proud, earnest, childish way to be the prince that was left for him to be, and to stand tall and godlike in the place of an entire people who are gone. Now he is clinging to her as if somewhere in her body, somewhere in her womanness and her loneliness and herself, she knows something that he, in all his knowing, has forgotten—something he needs to survive.

She wants to be good, to do everything right. When he opens his eyes in the morning, she is waiting. She holds his gaze tight in hers.

Love is the first thing that wakes there. Love wakes like a revelation in his eyes; she can see the memory of the night there, and the inspiration of another life he could live, a life all his own where he is free to love again.

The fear wakes second. She sees the nightmare of it begin to dawn. That he—the dream god, the one whose wakefulness would keep his people alive—has slept. That he surrendered. That he let down his guard. She feels the echo of that fear inside her. She reaches, quickly, for his lips with her own, but his mouth is slow and cool, distracted by something.

"It's okay," she whispers to him, because she knows it is. How could it not be? How could love ever be wrong?

He keeps looking at her, and she can feel the fear creeping up inside him, filling him, making his throat run dry. He's still waking; he's still recalling the consciousness of who he is and all that he must be. He is still dizzy with the love they spent with each other last night. But she needs him to say something about it, before he separates from her again. She needs him to name it. Why is it so important, what her name should be, when this event of love that passed between them has no name? Why does no one name this—this love that they became when they were two, when they were not themselves but an action, a gift, a ceremony of embrace? What was that?

He comes closer, grips her in his hands. But she thinks his small, lonely smile looks strained, as if while he holds her tight, something is pulling him inexorably backward and away.

For this instant he gives her his smile—so soft, like a ripple around the memory of their great plunge, last night. "When I was inside you," he murmurs, "I felt like I was home again. I felt the softness, the depth, the sturdiness of those earth-waters where I was born. I saw those creatures again. I felt that magic, inside you."

Then stay, she wants to say. But she doesn't, because to plead with him would be to admit the awful feeling she has—that this is the end. A feeling she cannot justify or explain.

"I want you to meet my grandfathers, Lonely," he tells her, his voice slow. "Really meet them." But he is so afraid. She can see it all over his face. He wants to love her, she knows. He wants to be with her. He wants to believe that it doesn't matter that he fell asleep. But he is afraid, and his voice is cold.

"Sky—" she begins anxiously. "Promise me, before you go to them— Promise me—" She tries to hold his eyes with hers, but they leave her.

He seems calm as he rises. Calm as he sits and pulls his knees to his chest, staring out at the empty lake.

For a moment she thinks he will be okay. There is no panic in his motions. He stands up, his human feet lapped by the ghostly water. Then he throws back his head and makes a long, eerie call that reminds her of twilight falling over uninhabited hills. Then he stills himself and listens, and keeps his head tilted back as he watches the sky.

Then comes the long white flow of silence over the sky above him, and the stillness that rises from the too-smooth lake, over and over and over. The birds are gone. Before either of them can react or feel anything, she already knows that nothing she can say, nothing she can do, will ever convince him that it isn't his fault, for surrendering one night to personal, human love.

He stands up fast.

They are gone like the dream that they were. He has slept and now he has woken, and they are gone. He is alone now, like she was, in the beginning. Without people. Without place.

Lonely watches, behind him, as he makes the call again, and again. Now he doesn't stop between calls to listen. To Lonely he sounds more than ever like a wild thing, as if the human form she knew him in was only an illusion she created with her longing—as if he never belonged to her, as if love was only a distraction from this haunted call of emptiness, of incompleteness, of the loneliness which is truly life. She scrambles to her feet and grabs ahold of his arm; she tries to turn him back toward her, needing to see his face. But when she touches him, he bolts. She runs after him, her legs tripping against the heave of the water that bears its weight against her, stumbling and splashing, while he—in the grace of his grief, in the release of falling into that fear which has always haunted him and now finally claimed him—flows as easily as a spirit toward the center. And still the water will not let him in, though he turns and turns, though he kneels inside it, though he calls and calls—the skin of his arms needling into wings, his form slimming and shrinking into the distance, into desperate, splashing flight.

Through black, heavy fear she runs after him, runs and sinks, terror bleeding through her body—and his face is hidden from her as he lifts from the water. The center of the lake sucks her deeper, and then the sun burns its surface pure white, and then the surface is gone. Then again she is moving as if under the sea, only this time she is trying to run. The water fills her lungs, leaving no room for voice, no air with which to expel the cry of his name, only water which speaks the silence of all the things they will never say.

It is she who sinks, and she sinks alone. For Sky is a bird now, small and black with muscular, angled wings. He flies above the lake, high and away into the airy sorrow of forever, while Lonely—as if she *is* whatever he feared down inside the water—falls deeper and deeper into darkness, until she breaks through into a paler, warmer sky, and keeps falling, back to this earth far below.

When Mira was small, she used to hide in the fields above her neighborhood, a hidden stillness contained within her. The details of the grasses made a net of safety that held her, a kingdom so minute that the great shouting world could never reach it. Masses of ants swirled like the cosmos. An inchworm—arching into a miniscule mountain and then flattening out again—was eager and hungry, but its urgency was manageable for Mira, its path fitting neatly into her span of vision without her having to turn her head.

She listened for footsteps or noises in the alley below, feeling delicious in her secrecy. She closed her eyes to feel her invisibility swallow her like a warm cup. When the rude sounds had passed, she might open her eyes and see, in the little haven of her immediate and close-up vision, a brown spider riding low on its bent legs—running out from under her hair, blurring under her nose. It paused on the arch of a bent grass blade, slowly lifted two legs on each side, and balanced on its remaining six legs like a dancer.

Sometimes Mira still remembers these moments, when she cannot remember anything else.

How she loved being small! If only she could have stayed small forever. To the earth she would always be small, because it was so much bigger than she—her growth so insignificant.

She loved seeing the people pass by and knowing they could not see her. It wasn't that she wanted to watch them. The only people who came to the fields were the older boys who frightened her, their whoops of laughter hurting her ears, the smell of beer turning her stomach. But she loved sensing this danger all around her and being able to save herself again and again with her invisibility. It was the only thing she could control: this stillness, this ability to make nothingness out of her own body.

It's okay, she would whisper to the spiders and the ants. She felt that she lived here, in the fields—that this was where she belonged. The boys who came were intruders, invaders at a disadvantage because they did not know the secrets of the land. They did not know about the insects that crawled beneath their feet, slipping easily away unseen. They did not know the languages Mira knew, of the birds who cried in their nests. They had no patience, and they could not hear the silence, and she knew that eventually they would go.

Only Mira could hear the silence, even amidst the noise. It was older than noise. Even though, as Mira grew older, the noises increased—so that not one moment of the day or night passed without the sounds of trucks, people, construction and destruction, dogs, and stereos indenting or breaking its peace—she could still hear the silence. There were sounds, far more subtle sounds, that referred to that silence. The gasp of the wind awakening the grasses, and the songs of wrens or doves, held the silence in between them. These sounds existed solely to dress that silence in beauty, so that at the instant of their ending one's attention was so alert, seized by rapture, that the silence afterward shone that much more brightly. By focusing on the language of nature beneath the language of the City, hidden there in the pattern of the meadow, Mira could always find the silence. It was a living entity that breathed even while the noise persisted.

She stayed safe there, in that silence. And one day she would learn to speak it herself, and when that day came, it was the only language she would ever speak again.

Lilah used to come there, too, long ago when Mira was too small to think yet of hiding herself. Lilah did not know the language of the spiders, but the wild spirit of the meadow itself knew and loved her, and Lilah ran with it, and Lilah used to run also with a young god—a boy who was gentle and girlish and did not frighten Mira, though still she preferred to play alone. She was happy to know that Lilah and Moon played near her. In those days, she would walk out in the open, or crawl through the grass with her ear to the earth, knowing that the tough fire of her sister, wherever she was, would keep her safe. Moon knew the language of silence, too, and he could play it on his flute, and he never asked Mira any difficult questions.

But the time came when Lilah no longer came to the meadow, and Moon, sad and lonely, dissolved. Lilah stayed now in the alleys with the other boys. Mira did not understand what passed between them as well as she understood the languages of the spiders and the flowers, but for some reason she found herself hiding from her sister now, just as she hid from everyone else.

Except for her father, of course. He was the only one who could always find her.

Mira's father was a holy man from another place long ago—a place ruled by tall shadowy gods and tusked goddesses that the City men later razed to the ground. Alone without his people or his land, he had only Mira to confide in. He taught her everything she knew. He taught her the languages of the animals and how to speak to them with respect. He taught her about the Earth trapped beneath the City and how it longed for the rains of the sky, its lost lover. He told her about shape-shifting, though he no longer knew how to do it himself. He knew all about hiding, because everything beautiful and good in the world was hiding—hiding in these pieces of meadow marked for development, hiding in people's breath as they slept, hiding in the unmarked graveyards of dustlands that once were forest, and hiding sometimes—perhaps—in the body of a girl.

He told her about the Unicorns, and he told no one else.

Once, he said, there might have been thousands of them, flowing through the night, and every ancient culture had a story about them. Maybe Unicorns came from the sea, or maybe from the sky. But he could not remember, any more, what they looked like, or how to find them.

She was his last hope, he said.

Her father could always find her. And why would she want to hide from him? He was her father and knew everything. He understood her, and she understood him. He loved her, and he needed her as he needed no one else.

He loved her more than Lilah. He taught her his secrets. Why would she hide from him? For she could tell that he was dying inside. That this world could not sustain him—that his day, whatever it contained out in the grey haze of the City, flattened his spirit, flattened his eyes, made him come home wild and possessed by other spirits that were not his own. She knew about the medicine spirits, contained in sacred plants, that could connect him with the other worlds. But there were other spirits that turned his eyes to fiery spirals and his words to curses and her mother's expression to fear. Only Mira could save him at those times. She was the goddess for him, the goddess his people used to honor, who had been taken from him. He took her into his arms—he would save himself in her.

Why would she hide from him? She needed him. And yet she trembled now, when he came.

She who became so skilled at watching, so skilled at silence, watched the women in her family carefully. There was something she did not understand, something that frightened her, but how could she be frightened of her own father, who loved her as no one else did?

She watched her mother, who never touched her father, and who was never touched. She watched her mother, bewildered, as if from a great distance, for the sound of her father's entrance was a roaring in her ears that made it difficult for her to concentrate. He always knew where Mira was. His spirit sought hers before he even entered the room. And her mother's eyes were always upon him. Sometimes she said to Mira, *Go and comfort your father. He's always calmer when you're around.* So Mira went to him, and after a while her eyes burned whenever she looked at her mother, and what she felt toward her mother—a fire that could kill her if Mira let it out—had no name and frightened her.

She watched her sister. She watched the things her sister did with the boys in the alley. She thought her sister was happy doing those things. She did not feel the burning toward Lilah; instead she felt cold whenever she looked at her sister. She knew that Lilah was stronger than she was. She knew that Lilah had found some way to survive, some way that Mira could never know, and she knew that Lilah would not teach her.

Mira did not want to grow bigger, but she did. She couldn't stop the growing, except by eating less and less—and even then, she grew. Then they began to mow the meadows every year, and the grass no longer hid her. So she stopped speaking, but even then she could still be seen.

Only after her father died did Mira realize the hatred she felt inside her. When it came, stinging her throat with its acid tide, making her scream and wail sometimes beyond her control, she felt such terror—to know that she had hated her father so much, perhaps it was this very hatred that had killed him. She could tell no one. She only wanted not to exist. Every part of her existence was painful. The spirits that her father had spoken with haunted her, babbling accusations in her ears until she could not hear her own thoughts. Even the earth seemed to hate her now, stabbing her feet like broken glass with every step, for she had betrayed him. She feared the creatures that once had trusted her, and she feared herself—her own rage and her ever-growing body, her breasts that men would look at. There was the guilt of knowing she had not fulfilled the one role that made her worthy of her own life: to save her father. And she hated herself, for she missed her father—without whom the world was alien and cruel—and it was her fault that he was dead.

The strange thing is that now she is hidden again, after all. She is more hidden than she could ever be in the open meadow or the corners of the apartment. She is hidden in a place where no one in the world can ever find her. Not even the animals. Not even the soft voices of the wind. She knows that she deserves to be here, that she is safe here. She knows that she is crazy.

But underneath all that craziness, hidden even deeper than this most hidden place, deep inside herself, she understands everything.

She understands the way her mother lost herself. She understands why Delilah will never forgive herself. She understands what her father truly wanted. *Mira, Mia, my own….*

Sometimes on days when she felt brave, she used to creep to the edge of the meadow, to the edge of the world—not where it overlooked the City, but where it overlooked the River Yora that ran out of the City, away to the sea. Mira never went down there, never touched that hurried water with her hands. But she liked to dream her way along its currents from up above, for from there its passage looked slow and silver. She knew somehow that the river was the way out—the way out of everything, and the way home.

Later, after she was locked away here, she met the goddess of the river Yora in human form. But by then, such beauty only hurt her. She no longer wanted to be rescued. So she gave the river her soul, so that she wouldn't have to keep it. Mira gave her soul away in the form of a fairy tale, something that would stay safe in the realm of imagination and dreams, something she didn't believe in any more and that she would never have to feel inside her again. It would pass on forever in the river, she thought, always moving, always escaping away.

She did not understand then that the river would return in the end, as all water does, to the place where it was born.

"Delilah!" Dragon calls. It's him, again. But she doesn't move.

The desert is no longer safe.

She stares fiercely into the darkness of her cave, her body rigid, and into that darkness she follows the spiral dance of the grouse, and deeper into the depths of herself—still awake, still not dreaming, no—she can feel the deer, her sister, the one who recognized her.

You thought you knew darkness, the deer's eyes say, *but you were wrong. It lies even deeper.*

"Delilah, I know you're in there. I came out for you. Come out for me."

She holds the boar tusk tightly in her fist, but in that gripping there is pain.

For seven years the desert's silent winds have wrapped Delilah in forgetting. The animals have distracted her with their ever-present lives, waking, hunting, and dying with no memory or question. The desert has daily opened before her, season after season, pages of infinity. Every day is blank. Every day there has been only hunger and solitude, and the purity of these two states of existence has kept her safe from pain. Almost.

But now the men are coming, in the distance, paving a road before them. On clear days Delilah can see their black insect forms shimmering in the heat waves on the horizon. On still days she can hear the low hum of machines, almost an octave lower than the hum of the river.

On the last full moon, when her body's old lust for the violence of men overcame its various pains one more time, she walked out toward them, richly glowing in that honeyed light of the moon's ripeness. The cold night air ached, and she did not know what she would do.

But when she came within sight of them she stopped and could not go on. The men—working at night because, like her, they could not survive the heat of the day—moved with a cold finality. They didn't have that innocent brightness like they'd had when they came wandering across the desert in search of things. Even then, she realized, when they'd come to loot the jewels of the land she loved, they'd at least brought with them a sense of wonder—a yearning for mystery, even if that yearning was misplaced. Now they only wanted the road: a way to cross space, a way to get through it and past it—destroying it as they went—and get to another place where a new City would be built on top.

That was what Moon meant, she realized, when he spoke of disconnected places, the way cars sped people from one place to another, with no sense of what lay in between. This was what lay in between. Delilah's home, and the whole universe around it. But the road would erase it. For the people, it would only be an empty space between one City and the next.

That night Delilah watched the men lay explosives in a part of the ridge that stood in their way, and that formation she'd known for years—that certain pattern of reality, of earth that softened and pinkened in the sunset—disappeared in a puff of moonlit dust. Delilah felt that explosion in her own spine, as if the bones of the Earth were the bones of her body; she felt it at the roots of her, where she had, only moments before, longed for the sword of that male body to slide in and fill her. The explosion filled her instead, sending a ripple of pain up her spine that dropped her to her knees, where she sat for hours with her chin tilted forward toward that gruesome wreckage as they kept working, silent tears stroking her face in mockery.

She'd been fooling herself all those years. She was so lonely, she'd convinced herself she was a goddess, that she had the power to turn men's hearts away from destruction with the touch of her little black hands. But she didn't have that power. The truth was, she'd done it for herself. She'd done it because her own need was so great. She still felt that need, pulsing and pulsing from that soft, ridiculously vulnerable nest between her thighs, and she cried because nothing could fill that need but more pain—and she could not accept any more pain. She'd had enough.

"*Delilah,*" he whispers now just below the opening, as if whispering into her breast, and she shivers. "I need you. I'm so alone."

These days she can't remember her dreams because when she wakes the first thing she thinks of—eclipsing all memory of sleep—is the men coming slowly toward her, dragging the road like a great blindness behind them. As soon as she wakes she strains to hear the hum of it, wondering how long it will be until they lay an explosive right outside her cave.

She doesn't go to the pine forest. She learns to catch fish in the river. She digs for them under the mud. It takes most of every night, and sometimes into the morning, but it's easier now in the dry time of autumn, when fish get caught in shallow pools or wriggle panicked in small channels where the water barely still clothes them. She's not very good at catching them, especially when the delirium and irritability of constant hunger make her clumsy. But there is a carelessness about her now, as if this won't go on much longer. There is some decision forming within her before she is fully conscious of what it is. She sees the helplessness of the fish who are stranded, and thinks it is not so bad after all, to put them out of their misery.

Whatever Dragon thinks he loves in her, he is making it up. He is only desperate, because his goddess leaves him day after day, and he cannot find her (Delilah knows this, for she has watched him). He thinks now that, because Delilah spoke to him once in an unguarded moment, because he made her come, he has some kind of power. Or maybe he feels sorry for her. Maybe he has some ideal about his love, how it's going to heal her, how it's going to turn her into a sweet and colorful winged thing. But she doesn't want his pity.

Days before the moon forgot itself in darkness again, she could already feel the blood that would flow from her, a song of loss waiting to be sung. A body thin and angry and starving cannot support a child, and it knows no love will come to it now.

Her bones hurt when she crouches so long in the water waiting angrily for the fish, and her wrists hurt when she supports her weight as she leans over her little pool to drink. The pain that began in her spine has spread through her body. Maybe she is growing old, like Moon said. Maybe she has lost track of the years, or maybe time passes differently in the desert.

But when she lies awake in her cave during the day, she can still feel the animals move inside her. The ones she's killed. She feels bigger then, with a whole universe of creatures possessing her. The great boar slashes pain through her body with his tusks, but there is no malice in his gesture—only a sense of inevitable opening. The gentleness of the rabbit, too, at once nervous and steady, one blade of grass at a time, brings her inward, making her want to hide in her cave all through the time of bleeding, wrapping herself in the black moon of solitude.

yours will be the hunter's death, the deer had told her. But if the hunter's death is starvation, she won't accept it. She won't accept that humiliation, that emptiness—so much worse than the quick surrender of the prey to its killer's jaws. There is at least romance in such surrender, and some satisfaction in the union of two bodies, whereas starvation will be long and painful, full of weakness—days and days of helplessness to the needs and agonies of the body. One cannot even control when the ending will come. There will only be nights and nights of failure, of disappointment, of loneliness when she knows that the great web of life itself has abandoned her.

She is trapped. The road will keep coming, and there is nowhere else to go. Every night she wakes hungry and dreamless, with the taste of fear in her mouth, and knows this: the desert is no longer safe. The desert is no longer home. Her dreams have abandoned her, the animals have abandoned her. Because the road is coming now, and she can no longer deny her own humanness. She can no longer deny that she is no better than those men, who do nothing but destroy, and for whom she has lusted and lusted again.

But still, she refuses to die this way. She refuses.

Each day the ravens pick at the fish heads and bones that she scatters on the sand. They are loud and excited, talking about the treasures they found in the trash heap on the edge of Delilah's horizon—a heap that grows almost as quickly as the road. To them there seems no distinction between human and animal, bad and good magic. They can take their nourishment from the debris of the City or a kill in the road just as easily as from the leavings of an ancient predator. It doesn't matter to them. It all comes from and returns to the same darkness.

"Delilah," says Dragon one more time, and she wishes that wasn't her name. "I'm not leaving until you come out."

She throws a stone out the opening and hears him swear.

What a ridiculous thing to say, she thinks. *Of course you will leave. Everyone leaves.*

And she is right. By the time she has finally made up her mind about what she will do, and she cautiously peers into the light, he is gone.

What you might not know, what you might forget, is how strong you are.

You are stronger than any other creature. Even though you live the myth of the City—the myth of ease and pleasure—your lives are harder than anyone or anything else's. The hardest part is that you can never admit to it.

Teenagers who enter the streets at a certain age and never leave them again: you have the strength to make your own rights of passage, where none are provided to you and you have not one elder you can respect. Office men and women who have no time for lunch or headaches: you are strong enough to live completely independent of your bodies. Rich people who turn your heads away from the beggars and clutch your money tight to pay for the new addition to your house: you are strong enough to completely deny your hearts. Beggars: you are strong enough to throw away all of your pride.

Wives who are never touched, and never touch yourselves: you are strong enough to keep smiling, even when everyone knows those smiles aren't real and no one cares. Children who are beaten for being who you are: you are strong enough to become someone else—to completely shapeshift, in order to live. Husbands who have nothing to believe in: you are strong enough to stoop low during the day, and stand tall and stern when you come home at night.

Everyone survives. Later—when you see the waves coming, when you feel the wind tearing you apart, when you smell the smoke, when you feel the touch of a dead hand, when you recognize someone you loved in the dark crowd that will rise out of the sea—you will shake and cry, you will think yourselves lost.

But you are so strong. You can survive anything. *Anything.* If only you could see yourselves, as I do.

Yora kneels by the river, listening. It has not rained again since she came, and so the river has shrunk thinner and thinner, starving. But this, too, is familiar. The river will shrink to almost nothing, but the space of it will remain. As it grows thinner it becomes more detailed, no longer a single roar but a complicated web of individual pathways; its sound becomes more like language, more like words. She recognizes this language, faintly, but she cannot understand what it is saying.

Yora, he calls her. He will be angry. She feels his anger reverberating in her stomach. But what can she do? The sound of the river washes away her path. She can hardly remember how she got here, or how to return.

She did not mean to come to the river again, but something drew her back. She cannot remember now what, exactly. Her breasts are hot and sore with the pressure of his hands. Her mind feels warm and liquid with his eyes sharp inside it. Her thoughts form around their need. The air she breathes is misty with his sweat. She cannot see clearly. She feels slow and soggy, dragging her body like a grey weight whose end she cannot perceive.

Maybe she falls asleep. Bird cries flash in the air. The breeze riding through the trees follows the water. She can hear the heartbeat of a lizard. She can hear even the sand—the tiny grains nestling between each other toward gravity, settling toward the center of the earth, and then lifting at random with the wind. Falling and rising. She remembers this. She remembers, somehow, that to understand the language of the river, one must listen to everything at once.

But now—what?—she hears a sudden sound, disrupting the flow. She is momentarily erased. All of her being flips back into the safe haven of forgetting. She opens her eyes.

The sound was only the subtlest turning in the path of the river—like a single hair turned backward. A tiny trip in that seamless flow, whose rhythm she is beginning to know in her body. She looks up and sees, far away, hands reaching in, interrupting the river. This was why she came, she remembers now.

The dark girl's hands enter the river, her motions surprising the motion of the water and changing it. No, not surprising—for the water has no expectation. It is Yora who is surprised. Why? Why does the girl surprise her? Yora has seen her before, but she is surprising every time. Unconsciously, Yora brings her own hands together in the air, hovering in front of her belly, one hand cupped inside the other.

The dark girl disappears behind a tree of green tears. Then she emerges on the other side, squatting down again with her hands in the river. Yora can see the way her body closes in on what it wants, fitting around the shape of its desire. In a few moments, the girl's clapped hands rise up with a fish. The fish is twirling, still alive, but the dark girl does not hesitate in her grasp. She pulls the fish between her knees, and holds on tight.

Yora envies the girl's simple wanting, the plain hunger that drives her hands into the water and brings them back up again full of something clear and alive.

The dark girl, Yora thinks, would know what to do with Dragon's desire, which only confuses Yora. She does not mean to anger him. She does not mean to make him cry. She always gives in to him, in the end. She lies down under him and lets him move over her and into her, and it does not hurt her. But still he cries.

She wishes she could want him back. She loves him. She loves the deep cradle of his voice, which finally allows her to rest. She loves the warmth in his eyes and his heart—the way it dissolves her. But sometimes when she looks into his eyes, the beauty she sees reflected there hurts so much, she has to look away. She doesn't understand what he sees inside her. She cannot see it. She sits by the river and listens, listens for the sound of her name.

The dark girl stands up with the dead fish inside her hands, clasped to her belly, where Yora knows it will go inside. Humans eat other life. They take it inside. Yora wishes she could get that close to something. But she does not know the feel of hunger.

Now the girl is looking across the curve of the river between them, through the shadow of the blowing, crying tree, through the hot dry air. She is looking at Yora. Yora can see her eyes from here—can see the fire, which she wishes she could feel, and beneath that the pain, which she can feel, so deeply that she must look down, close her eyes again, and wait until the girl turns away.

No, she does not want hunger. She does not want need. Not Dragon's need, not this girl's need. Yora remembers need, now, from long ago—the abyss of it, the abyss of eyes that would not let go, and the begging voices. Even the merest taste of this memory exhausts her.

Need was never a simple question, something nameable in a clear waking dawn: "I want love." Turning from the sea toward a high mountain, riding a Unicorn toward the horizon. No, it was never like that.

It was anger. A face aged far beyond its years, contorted by demons of rage, leaning close up to Yora's face because if you have no sense of yourself, how can you recognize the space that someone else needs around her? *I hate you. I can hate you if I want to. You don't know me. You can never understand us. You're too beautiful, too perfect. Fucking goddess. You don't have any idea who we are.* Yora would cry later, not because the words hurt her, but because she could not answer the need she felt inside them.

Need was a smell. The cramped, doubled and redoubled stench of bodies unwashed because the spirits who lived in them did not love themselves— had no reason to be clean, no one to be clean for, no one to love.

Need was in the blood that ran from slashed wrists, and in the hands that clung to her in the night and would not let go, and in the stiff, death-like stillness of bodies once Hanum had drugged them into sleep.

Yora does not remember why she came there in human form, but she knows she was there to help. To fill that need. And she did fill it—every day with kind words and listening and even, sometimes, touch—but every day it was there again, bigger and wider and deeper. Until she realized she could never fill it.

She was ashamed of the way she took comfort from the little girl. That was not her role—to take comfort from one of them. She could not allow herself to rest that way. But the little girl understood her, and asked for nothing. Even when the girl screamed sometimes and tore her fingernails against her face, she was not asking for anything. Yora held the small body in her arms, held it still, and when the screams were over, the girl neither thanked nor blamed her. Her body did not yield into Yora's touch—only bent over into itself, cracked and brittle as dry winter grass. But her huge black eyes understood Yora. *You come from some place beautiful,* they said. *Why are you here?*

Yora leans over the river, breathing in the fresh air that rushes over it. Why is she afraid to reach in, the way the dark one did? Why is she so afraid of what she will find?

Come back, I say, and I don't know if I am speaking aloud. I don't know what it feels like to speak, and I don't know the difference between voices that sound and voices that do not. I hear them all.

But I say to her, *Come back. Please.* I tell her about the yellow fields we used to walk in. I tell her about the deep home of the forest. I tell her about the river, how it filled her and filled her! Doesn't she remember the valley, and the bees in the summer?

I can feel her sad little head on my belly. I think she is the only person I have ever trusted in this lifetime, though still it has taken me this long to speak. A red leaf and a yellow leaf spiral down together, and brush her cheek before coming to their final rest upon the quartz of the mountain. She opens her eyes and freezes. I can tell now that I have spoken aloud. I lower my head, expand my spirit, and make room for the sorrow that is about to overcome her.

There are no more flowers around my forehead. The sky is thin and grey, and already looking forward to winter. She has heard voices before from those certain sounds of nature that are infinite—the wind, the river, the fire—and she doesn't trust my voice now, or the sound of the thin waterfall behind me. She is still waking.

Her first motion is to lift the edge of the dress before her with one hand, slowly, her eyes not turning. That dress is lying across her now where once another person lay, and it's all open and torn. The patterns of wings half-lost and asymmetrical, the snakeskins gone, the red swirls at the hem blurred and cloudy. Blood. Still she does not understand what it is for, what it means. Is this the proof then? These tatters and frays? The things lost? *Is this the proof of love?* she is thinking.

"No no no," she whispers, closing her eyes again. For she knows now. Where she is, what just happened, what is gone.

Yes, I say, because it is urgent that she stay awake. *We have only just begun. You thought the journey was going up the mountain. But the real journey, for both of us, is going back down.*

"No," she sobs again. "No." That last *no* is so pained, it sounds like a question.

I touch her with my horn.

I am going to save her.

Water

"Why are we here?" I ask.

Lonely's face and body are stiff and pale, as if she is covered with snow.

"I don't know," she says. And I cannot remember, either, how I came here. I cannot at first remember how it is that I am this, or why being this frightens me. I can only remember Lonely and the need to return her to where she came from.

Lonely stares at the sky. She is searching the sky for him. *Sky*.

I know everything she is thinking, the way I know what everyone is thinking—everyone in this story—because it is my horn their thoughts are spiraling, trying to reach the sun. It is not that I am wise. Only that I know all of the stories; I was born knowing them.

Lonely wants me to take her back up there into that dream, but I can't now. It wasn't me that did it. I was only a ladder that she climbed.

"He's gone." She sits up suddenly and faces me, wide awake. "But is that true? How could it be? I know he loves me. He *does*."

"Love," I repeat back to her. My voice comes from somewhere in me, not my throat. Perhaps from my spine. Or from my eyes. The word sounds dangerous to me. Something impossible to pinpoint or trust, like the moon. "What is love?"

She drops her head in her hands and begins to cry. I can't bear it.

"Come," I say. "I will carry you."

"I'm not going anywhere," she cries, but she shuffles over to my body and wraps her arms around my neck. I can feel the melting of it. *Ah,* I think, and remember: this is love. I wish I could take her into me, with all her love, but I cannot. I cannot yet quite stand the pain again.

"He's gone," she repeats, and I feel her listening to herself, trying to understand the words. "Why?"

And I am silent. Perhaps I am only an animal, after all. What can I know? Our bodies are warm, that is all.

"Let me carry you," I say again. "I am asking you. I have never spoken to anyone before now, that I can remember."

"Where will you take me? Can you take me to him? Do you know where he went?"

But her questions confuse me. "I will carry you," I say. "I will bring you home."

Lonely begins to cry again. She doesn't know what I mean. *Sky is the only home I have,* she is thinking. *Sky was always where I was going.*

And I don't know what I am, exactly. I am an animal, but I am spirit at the same time. I know exactly how she feels and why, and yet her words hold no meaning for me. I don't know why I am afraid of what I am, or why her innocence frightens me. But I did come back to this form, finally, for her. Because she needed me to get her up there and back again. Because her longing—though it makes her suffer, though it is mistaken and misplaced—is like the center of the world to me. Like the only feeling that means anything, if I could remember what it means.

Delilah doesn't know exactly where the mountain lion lives. She's never seen it since she followed those tracks seven years ago. But she did find tracks two other times, in other places, and had the sense to leave them alone. The mountain lion's range covers such a great expanse of earth, including desert and forest, valley, hill and mountain. Delilah has never seen her, but she is the greatest hunter that Delilah knows; there is no one more purely solitary, more absolutely certain of her power. Delilah has often thought of her.

During that special pain of her dark moon bleeding, Delilah turns the tables on life. Instead of stalking her prey, she stalks her predator. She stalks her own death. Because she is not going to watch herself slowly weaken beneath it. She is going to track it down and demand it.

How bad could it be, after all: the pain of the lion's teeth at the back of her neck? Could it be so much worse than the fire of the pinched nerves in her neck and spine, the throbbing of her womb, the terror of slow death, the agony of hunger? Could it be worse than the unknown of aging? Who would she become if she allowed herself to grow old? Her mother, wailing in grief over a selfish man who probably never even loved her?

But she feels stupid when she finds no sign of the lion in any of the places she's seen tracks before. Why would she? The lion is surely more interesting than that. Delilah is determined she'll do anything to find it, and yet she has no idea now where to begin.

When the bleeding makes her weak, she lies down under a hot, dry tree to rest and quietly whispers her plea into the sky. She lets the blood run out between her legs; she dips her fingers into it and paints her throat and belly and heart for the lion to scent out: *take me here, open me, kill me. I have nothing. I have no one. My life is pain and hunger, and is worth nothing to me. Take it. I give it to you, great hunter, great queen of loneliness. You know what to do with it better than I, and you are worth it. You are worth the lives that surrender to you.*

The shade of the tree swings slowly over her, and the afternoon sun melts her without mercy into the stone. Above her, winged shadows spin under clouds as brightly chiseled as Dragon's body. Without noticing, she rolls into a dream.

In the dream the mountain lion stands over her, straddling her body like a man, her face small and fierce and elegant compared with the huge grace of her body.

you insult me, growls the mountain lion, her jowls curling back, her white teeth like little prisms of violence inside her mouth. *i am a hunter. i don't eat what's already dead. leave that to the vultures.*

Delilah aches. *already dead?*

your life is worth nothing to me if it's worth nothing to you. you call this courage?

Then fight me! Delilah swings her fist at the lion's head, determined to meet her death head on, as she promised. The lion catches her wrist in her jaws, lightly, barely closing down, but the teeth are so sharp they cut almost to the bone. Delilah screams. She screams and screams until the lion's roar drowns her out. When the lion opens her mouth, Delilah's arm falls out, landing on her belly where her hand dangles in a widening pool of blood.

are you afraid of me? the lion asks, while the ridge that separates them from the City still reverberates with that keening howl.

No, Delilah says.

then you are not facing what you truly fear. and until you do, you are a coward.

When Delilah wakes, she sees for the first time that the tree above her is covered with velvet pink blossoms. A hummingbird hangs in the air, its mouth deep in a flower, its wings a lullaby hum of blurred sound. It is so small, so fragile, so perfect.

Then she passes out from the pain.

When she wakes again, she will find herself in Yora's arms.

Autumn is crows. Their calls like gravel in our stomachs, like fists.

The trees seem lit from within, glowing and blowing, holding in their branches wild lanterns of color. Lonely doesn't notice the colors at first; her eyes are closed. Even once she opens them, maybe she wouldn't have seen them if she'd walked on her own, eyes downcast to the ground. But because I carry her up high, she cannot ignore this fire all around her.

We are going back down the mountain, and everything else is going down with us. The leaves are falling. Animals are burrowing into the ground. She is thinking now that the dream of reaching upward—the dream of the sky that the trees spoke of when she climbed this mountain—was a lie. But it wasn't. It is only that *up* wasn't everything. She has followed the river before, but now it is time to follow it forwards.

Once, a leaf falls into her hand. I see its shape in her mind: the shape of a tree, with lines striating it in spiderweb patterns, and not green any more, but the color of dried blood. There are holes in the leaf, and places where the webbing shows through. But its shape is wavy and sure, as perfect as a human hand, like a page of something written long ago and tossed away. She is wondering about it. What the message was. She lifts her eyes, asking what she will live for now. She sees the opposite of the green land she knew: the opposite of smooth, easy love, of refreshment, of growth and lush hope. Instead, raw, ruinous fire. Passion burned to brown dust.

"Wait!" she cries once in her delirium. "Where are you taking me? I have to stay—I have to stay up there, where I left him. He might come back. There is nowhere else for me to go."

I don't know how to answer. I feel her tears. I don't know how to tell her that the mountain that mattered so much once does not matter now. That's not where he is.

Yellow: more than flowers, more than bees. Red: deeper than roses, deeper than the sky at the end of the day. A festival of fire and light. But she thinks it terrible, how the wind tears the leaves down one by one. How it cannot let such beauty be. How it draws its breath and blows again, and there is more falling, and she thinks there is no mercy in the world. She hates the wind, who bore her love away from her.

I know. It's true, there is a cold objectivity to the wind. It does not brush her face or seem to speak to her now; it sings as if far away—in the treetops, or a field somewhere that she cannot see. But the wind is not her mother or her father, or her sister or her brother. It never promised anything.

This will be a difficult time.

She doesn't know that autumn happens every year. She doesn't know it has nothing to do with her. When she stood on the mountaintop in midsummer in her new dress, gazing up at the mountain like she knew just what would happen, it never occurred to her that the world wouldn't always be green. But I know. If I know anything, I know I've done this so many times.

Despair dulls her senses. She doesn't see the way the leaves play together as they fall, or the laughter in their dying. Or the strength of the evergreens, whose green is rich and tight and preserved perfectly in shadow. She doesn't breathe deeply enough to smell the rotting ripeness of the earth, and she doesn't hear how the crows are calling all of life to attention.

She doesn't see how the baby firs finally get their fill of light now, now that the branches above them are bare.

She doesn't see the squirrels nesting, or how prepared they are for what is to come. She doesn't know about the seeds inside the pinecones. She doesn't know that some of the acorns the squirrels bury will be lost and forgotten in the earth, and that in that forgetting will bloom new life.

She is only colder and colder. The old dress Chelya's fairies made for her does not keep her warm. It seems a child's plaything now, with no use. Now, too late, she knows what clothes are for: to protect from the pain of the air when the wind no longer loves her and her body begins to shudder deep inside.

So she huddles close to me, and I do what I can, just by walking, just by living. Sometimes we can't remember any more who we are or where we are going, or what we are leaving behind. Every now and then, for a moment, the glory around us tricks her into letting go of her tense heart, and she feels an incongruent flush of joy. But then it goes, leaving her confused.

I walk and walk, and it begins to rain. It rains for days over her body, the dress hanging from it, as we slip between the trees, and it beats open her senses.

She begins to bleed. From between her legs, where blood originally came from. Now she must surrender to a womanhood far bigger than herself. This pain, this blood—it is something she never had any control over, something she was born into, something she will die of with every darkness of the moon and be reborn to. It is the sadness in the witch's eyes and the deep red swirls at the bottom of the dress that Chelya—a girl becoming woman—made for her. It stains me red, and it warms me. It is something that I, in my last human life, knew too well. It is the thing that killed me.

Now you are finally human, says the rain, bleeding all around her. *Now, some day, you will die.*

"Who are you?" she says to me once.

And I just nod inside myself, feeling understood, because that is the question I ask myself with every step. Only later do I realize it was a question she wanted me to answer.

$$\text{☾}$$

It hurts. Delilah's right arm.

The arm that held back the string of the bow. The arm that reached for the fish. The arm that hurled the knife. The arm that has reached and grasped and held, over and over. But it has no strength now. There is no strength in all her body. Only pain, more powerful than life, flying faster than light from her wrist up her arm and into her shoulder, shattering her bones, erasing her mind.

After the initial shock of it fades, the pain flickers around her hand, tugging at the nerves behind her fingers, making them curl inward. The pain there remembers pain elsewhere, so that her entire body is a network of fleeting pain messages, shooting back and forth to each other like arrows, communicating a pathway of suffering she knows so well and yet never wants to follow.

Delilah wants only to sleep. But something from the outside hurts even more, waking her again and again.

"It is not the wound that hurts so much," says the cool, cloudy voice. "It is the healing that hurts. I think."

Delilah opens her eyes. "What are you doing to me?" she croaks. She feels like things are breaking inside her. She doesn't know what they are. Not bones.

The woman, Dragon's woman, with the long, serious face, and those eyes and those lips, is bending over her. No, she is surrounding her, her body or her dress or the form of her made somehow of water, floating Delilah above the hard packed sand. This is the slow, silent flood she felt coming in that rain. It was always coming. It was inevitable.

"I'm not doing anything to you," the goddess says.

She *is* a goddess, Delilah remembers, tensing. Only she looks like a human woman—or like a poem about womanhood, not the real thing. Like an image painted by someone who has never lived it—who romanticizes it, who sees it from a distance. *If Dragon imagined a woman*, Delilah thinks, *he would imagine this.* These languid, comforting breasts. These cradling eyes. The taut, expressive throat; the dramatic, arched brows. Her cheeks curved inward around her mouth, making her bones look stark and her lips lonely. Or would he? This woman looks old, too. Not old like an old woman, but old like a grown-up. As if all of this time, they've only been children playing at life, forgetting they had a real mother after all, far older and wiser than they—

I'm delirious. Delilah breaks away from the loose, peaceful arms and sits up, growling as she does so because it's so hard. Her arm lies in her lap, wrapped in a blood-soaked cloth.

"But it was a dream—" she starts, remembering the mountain lion. "It was a dream!" But what is a dream, anyway? She's been living half in and half out of dreams for so long. The longer you're alone, the harder it is to tell the difference.

"Here," says the goddess, and hands her cooked fish, folded inside a nest of crisp, burnt leaves. Delilah, starving, eats it like a monster, never taking her eyes from the goddess's face. She tries to connect the nourishment in her mouth with the soft hands that held it. She doesn't remember, in her whole life, anyone ever doing such a thing for her, for no reason. Her mother fed her, but she had to, didn't she? And Moon is her friend, and Dragon wants her. But who else has ever handed her sustenance—who has ever held her in their arms out of sheer kindness? No one she can remember. Certainly never a woman.

"Why are you helping me?" she asks, but the words come out flat. It's not a question as much as a warning.

The goddess looks at her, her smile thin and tired. Her eyes are lit caves. *There is another life in there*, Delilah thinks, startled. *Somewhere else she could be.*

"You don't want my help?"

"No," says Delilah. "I mean, thank you. You don't have to. I'll be fine."

"Can you stand?"

Delilah tries. No. Maybe she lost a lot of blood.

"I don't understand," says the goddess thoughtfully. "I don't understand why people won't be loved."

"What?" says Delilah, beginning to panic a little.

"They cry out for love. They scream and they cry, but when I try to give them what they need, they push it away. They keep crying. Why is this? Can you explain this to me?"

"I'm not crying," Delilah manages, her voice constricted. If she could only stand, she'd be gone. Where is she? How far from her cave? She looks around, sees the steam rising in the distance. Dragon's lair—a day's walk away from her home. She'd never make it. She looks back at the goddess reluctantly. The goddess is looking at her.

"Yes you are," she says.

Then she turns toward the river, looks into it with her liquid dress pouring down its banks, and speaks to it as if continuing a conversation she's been having for a long time.

"I can love them," she murmurs. "I have love to give. But they don't want love. They want something else. Something I don't have."

Fuck, thinks Delilah. Whatever this is, she doesn't want to get involved. Having finished the fish, she sits up dizzily. With difficulty, she maneuvers herself between stones to lay the lower half of her body in the riverbed, where she is barely shaded by two small trees. In some places the river is completely dry now, but here there is a little stream that's enough to cool her feet. She rests her bandaged arm, burning hot in the cloth, on the stone beside her, and accepts the discomfort of bumpy earth against her spine. At least she can relax, now that she isn't lying awkwardly in someone's arms.

"Who are you?" she says.

"Yora."

"That sounds familiar."

"Yes. It sounds familiar to me, too."

Delilah tries to look over at her, but the movement hurts her neck.

Neither of them seems to know what to say next, so they don't say anything. They remain there in silence, because neither of them is able to leave.

Delilah rolls in and out of sleep. There are no dreams. Maybe it's only the wind, but she thinks she can hear the sound of the river, as if its ghost flows audibly even when it's gone. The song vibrates through her, reminding her of the loneliness in her hips, and quieting it at the same time. Her feet soften. Her belly relaxes.

She opens her eyes. The sun is sinking, blinding, behind Yora's head. The goddess, sitting next to Delilah upstream, is still gazing into that motion, as if she sees something Delilah cannot. There is nothing difficult in her presence. Delilah almost forgot she was there. Yet still, she would rather be alone. This kind of silence frightens her. She doesn't understand what is expected.

With men, it is easy. She can offer her body. She knows what she wants from them. And she can get it. But she has never had anything to offer a woman. Not Mira. Not her mother. Not the girls at school.

Drawing up her knees, she tries to push herself backward, out of the riverbed. She doesn't want to be in this position now, with Yora behind her where she can't turn her neck to see. But it's so difficult to move herself. This is what's been happening to her for the last year: her body has become more and more difficult to move. That is what the pain is doing. It is trapping her. Realizing this makes her struggle harder.

"It's okay," says Yora, and Delilah feels hands on her shoulders.

"Stop!" she yells, so suddenly that her own voice knocks her forward. "Don't touch me."

"Why not?" cries Yora, and Delilah can see her face, looking down from above, upside-down.

"I don't know," she answers, and she is crying now, after all.

"It's okay," murmurs Yora again, floating her with those soft hands deeper into the riverbed against her will, where suddenly the water seems deeper than she knew, so that her whole lower body lies still in the rushing water, and the water rushes in the direction of her body, from her hips down to her feet and away. Yora enters the water with her and cradles her head in her lap.

"No—" says Delilah, still struggling. She would fight this woman with teeth and claws. With everything she has, if she had anything—if she weren't so weak. She feels like she's being killed.

"It's okay. Just let go. The river holds you. It doesn't hurt."

"But it does," sobs Delilah, who wonders if she is going mad. What hurts? Unraveling? Compassion?

The river holds her and flows away from her at the same time. Her tears flow by and are gone. Her own blood carries her, floats her endlessly through herself. She lies in the arms of the river and the goddess, squeezing her eyes tight shut and then gradually relaxing, because she doesn't have the strength not to. Time passes more and more easily. The sun shrinks, losing its intensity.

Perhaps moments later—or perhaps much longer—there is a time when Delilah is aware that all the points of pain in her spine were only points where she could not let go. She begins to feel that her spine is not a solid chain of rocks but a river of liquid fire, carrying messages from one end of her body to another, and that the river is the spine of the Earth.

There is a time when the anger disappears, at least for a moment. At least long enough for her to understand how terrified she is of what lies beneath it.

"I don't need your help," she murmurs half-heartedly. "Really."

"I know," says Yora. "You have everything you need. Far more than I have."

"What?" Delilah closes her good hand around an assortment of tiny pebbles beneath her, loose and bouncing in the water. Her left hand. The one that's connected with her heart, and still works.

"You have your body. I do not have a body—not a body that lives and dies and feels pain, like yours does."

"You have no idea."

"But I feel pain. I have felt the pain of so many, many people. And I have had nowhere to put it, no way to express it. You have your body to do that for you. Something real! Something that aches and cries. Your body takes all that passion and suffering and makes it into something beautiful—something that can make love and play and run toward what it desires."

"You don't know what you're talking about."

"Perhaps not. But I think you do."

Delilah is silent. She squeezes the pebbles, because it helps with the pain.

"Your body is a map of the Earth," Yora continues. "Through it, you could understand the whole world. But because you are part of that world, it is hard for you to see that."

"What are you, then?"

"I am not a part of this world."

"Yes you are. You're the goddess of this river." She's surprised to hear herself say it, and she doesn't know where the knowledge comes from, but then she knows it must be true by the silence she feels behind her in response.

Something awful flickers in that silence, and Delilah wonders if there is such a difference between gods and humans after all. Everyone is afraid of themselves. Everyone dies and is reborn, not once but many times, and no one can stop it.

"You're the goddess of this river," she repeats, irritated by the silence, by the possibility that Yora will deny it.

"Is that true?" asks Yora in a small voice. "Yes. Yes, maybe that is true."

"Did you forget?"

"I do not know. Maybe I did."

"I can tell. I can tell you're a water goddess, because my best friend is a water god."

"Yes," says Yora, as if she knows. "You know all about water."

"But I don't," Delilah whispers to herself. She pictures Moon hopping like raindrops over the desert floor in the night, all the creatures and plants awakening to his music because in his soul he is rain itself. She loves him from a deeper place in herself than she even knows, and deep down she understands him—or does she? In her heart she has been dry for so long. Her anger has been a fire that nothing could put out. Has she ever truly understood water? Has she ever understood what Moon is made of? She has surrendered to his embrace, but what has she learned from it? Only to tighten and constrict and dry up again, the moment he leaves her.

The truth is she is afraid of water, afraid of that surrender. She is always encouraging Moon to be himself, to let it out, but maybe she never meant it. She, the one person who professed to honestly love him.

Delilah can barely feel Yora's presence now. Instead she feels something like sorrow darkening and slowing the water around her.

"Are you okay?"

"I have been sitting by the river for many days," Yora answers. "But not until today did I go inside it. With you."

"But why not? You *are* the river. Aren't you? I mean, what is the purpose of a god anyway?" She's starting to feel angry, hearing this vague voice, reminded of Moon and the way he runs away. "Why are you all so afraid to claim who you are?"

Silence again. Delilah looks at the sky, a dusty rose. There are so many, many moons before the rains will come again. The water is beginning to chill her, as the desert opens its empty palm to the beginnings of night.

"Sometimes," says Yora, "you want to be anywhere but inside yourself. Do you know what I mean?"

"Yes." Delilah can feel Yora fading. Then all of the sudden she herself feels strong and clear. She sits up, pulls her body together, rolls onto her knees. She looks back at Yora's face again—she'd forgotten what she looked like. She takes Yora's arm with her good hand, and pulls her up. Yora yields as easily as water.

"Come on," Delilah says, pulling her. "You're not leaving." Maybe she's being selfish. Maybe she only wants to keep her close for another little while.

Yora sits down on the bank with her, and then folds over, her face on her knees. The dress is flowing everywhere, clear and useless, and her body looks naked in the twilight. Delilah guesses she is crying, though she can't hear anything and can't see her face.

"Tell me," Delilah says, "what's in the river that you're afraid of?" Even though, in a way, she does not want to know. Even though nothing has ever frightened humans more, throughout time, than black depths of water.

"Suffering," says Yora in a muffled voice. "Suffering so thick that the fish cannot breathe. It chokes off all the life. It takes and takes and takes."

Delilah waits. She feels like she is walking into pure mystery. But she's done that before, hasn't she? The desert, the pine forest, a life of solitude. If there is one thing that can be said for fire, it is certainly brave.

"The river only has so much to give," Yora says. "The river is a body, with a beginning and an end, like a person's. Like yours."

"But why? Why does it suffer so much?"

"It does not suffer. It is filled with people's suffering. Suffering that does not belong to it."

Delilah thinks about this for a long time, her mind gentled, trying earnestly to put into words what this un-human creature cannot. "You must mean pollution," she says finally.

But maybe Yora doesn't hear her. "When the river became too heavy with this suffering, I went deeper," she says. "That is what water does. It flows deeper and downward. So I went down, down into the center of the sea, inside of the island where the heart of all the suffering lay. It was calling me there—this place. This center of darkness, where all the pain was held. You know. Like the place in your body that always hurts. The place that holds all the pain, so that the rest of you will be okay. So you can go on about your day and not have to feel it."

Once again Delilah wants to stand up and walk away. The impulse has never been stronger. *Run,* it says. But then the deer moves inside her. *Listen,* says the deer. *Be still.*

"They wanted me to take the pain away. They wanted the river to wash it all away. They wanted to be cleansed, and they wanted to be loved. The suffering was filling the space where the love was supposed to be."

"Who are you talking about?" demands Delilah, but her voice comes out a whisper.

"The people there," says Yora, looking up now, her eyes murky like the eyes of a human being. "The people He keeps under the island."

"The people *who* keeps?"

"The god. The one who made the City. The one who took the people away from the Earth."

"Hanum?"

"He had all those people taken away. The ones who held the suffering for everyone else. The ones who spoke it aloud. The ones who said the world he had created was not real."

Delilah is silent, gripping the stones. *No,* she thinks. But when she closes her eyes, the deer's eyes are looking back at her, as if they are her own, as if the inside of her mind is a dark pool that reflects her own eyes back to her, over and over.

"But I could not help them," Yora says with finality. "So many years I lived down there in the darkness, trying to love, trying to wash all the pain away. But where would it go? The rivers of the world go round and round, and nothing can ever be lost. It just comes back around again. The pain has to transform somehow. Become something else. But I could not transform it. It is not in the nature of water to transform. Only a human being can do something like that."

Or fire, thinks Delilah, against her will.

"It did not matter how much I loved them. Still they suffered. Still the world was not right, and they knew. Still they were trapped there, and there was nothing I could do to free them. Still they clawed at me, reached for me, drank from me and were never, ever filled. And even as they drank my love, endlessly, they could not feel it. Because they would not let their suffering go."

She looks suddenly at Delilah, her voice pleading. "Why wouldn't they let it go?"

Delilah's face feels frozen, her eyes very still. She can barely move her lips. "Because it was all they had," she says. "They were afraid of the emptiness, if they lost it."

Yora nods. "Now you tell me your secret," she says.

"What?"

"You know. Why you hate yourself. Why you won't let yourself be loved."

"Oh," says Delilah, as if she's just remembered, and then she feels foolish. "Oh, well …Whatever. Fear of abandonment, I guess." She tries to smile.

"No," says Yora. "I mean, why you don't think you deserve love."

Delilah looks at her. It is too much effort to pretend she doesn't understand.

"I had a sister," she says sharply. "I couldn't save her. I couldn't protect her. She went crazy. They took her away."

And my father, she thinks. And my mother. And the meadow.

Yora nods. "She wouldn't accept your love."

Delilah looks away. "I don't know. I don't know if I know how to love." But she can feel Yora's eyes on her. She knows they are talking about the same thing.

"I know where your sister is," the goddess says.

"Stop," Delilah whispers. "She's gone."

Yora doesn't answer. Delilah knows it is not in the nature of water to argue. She is having difficulty breathing. "Sometimes it doesn't matter how much you love someone, okay? They're still crazy. You can't fix them. You can't love them into sanity again."

She didn't even mean to say that much. It doesn't matter, because they took Mira away, and Delilah searched and searched for her, and pounded her fists on the desks of the officials, and yelled until they dragged her away. And none of it mattered; none of it had any effect. She closed that door a long time ago. The deer is a dream. A memory, an association. That's all.

But when Yora does not respond, Delilah turns to her again. Her face has that quiet, knowing look that Mira's always had. That look so full of wisdom that she wasn't going to force on anyone—wasn't ever going to speak aloud. A look without judgment, but merciless in its knowing. Mira was beautiful. She had eyes like a female deer and long, slippery brown limbs and virgin-black hair. Delilah wonders if she would have grown up to look like Yora. More beautiful than anything real. She will never be able to say aloud how much she wishes that Mira could have gotten a chance to grow up beautiful, to emerge gracefully into womanhood. To make men long for her, and walk with pride, and live the life that Delilah never could.

"You remind me of someone," Yora says.

Delilah keeps looking at her, but Yora is looking into the river.

"Someone much older than you. Someone who closed up her heart from bitterness. She lives on that island still, and perhaps she will live there forever. But you have not gone that far yet. You are still open."

Delilah hears her. She does. But she doesn't think she wants to talk about where Yora comes from any more. "How did you end up here?" she asks, feeling tired again. Both of their voices are very quiet now, as if each is so aware of the other's listening that there is no need to put any effort into communicating. As if they are one being, speaking within itself.

"I do not remember exactly. I was in the sky for a long time, lost. But water always has to come back down. And then there was Dragon."

"Dragon." Delilah doesn't know what to say.

"Dragon," Yora says again, and the corner of her mouth lifts.

Delilah smiles before she realizes it, and Yora lets out a little explosion of breath. Delilah did not know that a goddess could laugh. Then quite suddenly, from nowhere, she is laughing, too. It's such a relief, to let it roll through her, breaking up all the tension with a pain that isn't painful—just ironic and ridiculous.

Yora reaches for her hand, and her dancer's face is stretched by her smiling in an eerie, poignant way. She clasps Delilah's left hand. "He takes himself so seriously!" She laughs, shaking as if she, too, feels relief.

Delilah's smile fades a little with the shock of Yora's hand in hers. "He does, doesn't he?"

"Oh," says Yora, and now she looks a little sad along with her smile. "I should not laugh. It is so painful for him, to be so important to himself. To need so much reassurance."

Delilah's laugh is drier now. "He's full of himself is all."

"Yes," nods Yora seriously, as if Dragon's ego is an affliction that merits compassion. Then they are both laughing again, and Delilah has to laugh at herself, too, for still feeling desire when she thinks of him.

"I think," says Yora sadly, "like everyone else he wants something I cannot give."

Delilah says nothing, so the two of them stare at the river again, with the darkness softening their forms. Winter in the desert is so much more subtle than in other places. No ice, no snow. Just a bigger emptiness.

"I envy you," says Yora. "I wish I could feel the fire you feel, and then I could give Dragon what he needs."

"Dragon doesn't need more fire. He needs love, like everyone else."

Yora doesn't answer. Maybe she already knows she is good at loving but is too humble to say it. *Because that's what really loving people are,* thinks Delilah. *Humble. Not like me.*

"What is your name?" asks Yora.

"You can call me Lil," she surprises herself by saying.

"Lil, what are you thinking about?"

"About envy," Delilah says. "I envy the river. It always knows exactly where it's going. All it has to do is flow downward, wherever downward goes. It never has to make any decisions, and it can't make any mistakes. There is only one thing it can do: flow down. It doesn't matter what happens to it—a great fall over a cliff or getting bashed against the stones—because nothing can hurt it. So it doesn't ever have to be afraid of what's coming or figure out what it wants. It doesn't have to want anything. *That's* how I wish I could be."

Yora squeezes her hand, and Delilah doesn't pull away, even though it terrifies her—because that hand doesn't want anything from her, not sex or love or anything at all. The mountain lion challenged her to be brave.

"You will be like that," says Yora. "I promise. There will come that time when you know. When there is only one thing you can do. When you cannot help it. You can only go."

In an apartment building in the City, a pipe breaks somewhere, and there is no water today.

How angry you are! You call the landlord. *Where is the water? Bring back the water.*

The landlord is angry, too. He doesn't want to be bothered. *Who are these people?* he thinks. What connection do you have to him? You do not live on any land—you live in a nowhere lot, marked by numbers. He does not know your names.

He calls a plumber. *Where is the water? Bring back the water.*

You are fuming. How will you go about your day? It's so inconvenient for you. The water must come out of the faucet, like it always does. That is where water comes from. But now your dishes sit in the sink. Your toilets are stinking. Your hands and teeth are dirty. You never realized, before, how many times a day you turn that knob—how many things depend on—what is it? *Water.* What is it? You never thought about it.

But now, without it, everything sits in filth. Stagnant.

Of course, you do not need water for drinking. You have other things in your refrigerators for that.

Still, you sit furiously, stewing in your little, dirty rooms, looking outside and thinking how beautiful it is out, but you cannot go out because you cannot possibly go anywhere without your daily shower. But what a beautiful day. Is that a cloud up there? You hope it doesn't rain. It hasn't rained for many, many years, but still how hateful it would be if it did. The rain is so dreary, and today is so beautiful. But you can't go out without your shower.

You are having such a bad day, and have been having such bad days for so long, that—alone in your room—you begin to shed tears. Feeling so angry, you begin to sweat.

Oh, you know there is water everywhere. You learned it in science class. Water comes out of your bodies, flows in the river, falls from the sky. But once water has touched a body—once water has come anywhere near a life—it is dirty. Life dirties water. Life is dirty.

Only water with the right chemicals in it—chemicals that *purify* water—is clean. Call the landlord again. *How long?* How long will you have to wait for the water—*does he have no respect for our rights?* You are so angry. You are so angry about the water that has abandoned you. You are so angry to be forced, finally, to do what water has always asked you to do: to surrender.

But water does not come from the landlord. Nor has it abandoned you.

You are made almost entirely of water. There you are—the gush of you: your water arm reaching, your water head turning, your water legs stretching, your water mouth opening and closing. How amazing, that water can be made into such meaningful shapes! You can do anything with water.

Yet how stiff, the way you shape it; how unwillingly you seem to carry it. How carelessly you sully it, with your colored drinks and your angry thoughts, while you glower at that faucet, and demand what you cannot control.

How murky and sad it becomes: that beautiful water which is you.

The next day, when we lie down to sleep, she asks again, "Who are you?"

I look at her, and then I remember—at least part of the answer. "I am somebody's soul," I say.

"Whose soul?"

"A little girl's." I look away and try to think. *No, perhaps she is a woman now, or an infant. I don't know. I don't understand aging. I always forget which direction it goes in….*

"But—why are you here with me? Doesn't she need you?"

I shake my head, making eddies of white light in the air. "It is not safe there."

"Not safe where?"

"There. Inside the girl. A girl's body—it's not safe. Nothing to protect it. It grows and grows, and people can see it." *Isn't that obvious?*

"I don't understand."

"I don't want to talk any more. I haven't talked in a long, long time." My body is crying, all the silver falling from it, glossing the red leaves. That night I have to stand away from her on my own to sleep. I cannot bear to be touched. I go silent again.

Is my voice confusing? It confuses me, too. I am the Unicorn, who speaks all languages and makes all voices one. Yet also I am the safekeeping of a single soul. I am, somewhere inside, the soul of a single voiceless girl, who forgot she was the universe and knew only pain. Though it was her pain that brought me forth into the world again, it is also her pain that holds me back. It is this pain that draws me apart from Lonely. It is this fear....

"Unicorn," she says the next day, startling me, "I'm starving."

Her body, her body, after all this time—bringing her back, drawing her away from the dream she left behind.

In the middle of the day, I stop to rest, and Lonely slumps against my back, not bothering to climb off. Ladybugs land on us, one by one, their tiny legs shivering against us, harmless and intent. They roll over and stand up again. They slam into our bodies and then begin walking, gently, over Lonely's skin. More and more of them come, in careless abundance. She begins to cry.

All she has left is her tired body and hunger. Now she is hungry all the time. Her beloved was not human, but she is. Now she can't eat the colors, or the air, or the light. She can't eat the leaves or the earth. Soon the memories blur, and the sound of the river haunts her.

I'm going as fast as I can, knowing she will not last much longer.

Delilah enters the pine forest for the last time.

But she doesn't know it is the last time until she meets the old boar.

He is older than anyone Delilah has ever seen. Except maybe Yora. The boar is blind, but his glassy eyes look right at Delilah. The spiny ridge of hairs on his back, like the spine of a dinosaur, is pure silver, and the silver spills over his shoulders and dusts the course hairs around his chin and mouth. His snout is wrinkled and dry and cracked as the desert winter, and his body arches with thinness—a thinness unnatural to a boar. When he moves, Delilah can see the pain in his joints; she can see the way he rides it, sighing as he goes.

His tusks, made of the same stuff as Unicorn horns, arch toward the ground from the sides of his mouth.

He doesn't say anything to Delilah, but Delilah knows he wants her to walk with him. Cradling her bandaged shooting arm in her left hand, she stands from where she has been sitting—for hours and hours, being still with the pain, waiting for some sign because she had to come back here, finally—and follows.

They walk for a long time. Delilah can feel the heat of his body and the gruff mortality of his hoarse breaths, keeping her anchored in the continual immediacy of her own legs thrusting one after another, like a thousand legs, across the earth. Sometimes, when the brush grows dense, she holds the low branches out of the way for the boar to pass, out of respect, even though she knows that, if the old one has lived this long, he surely knows how to move past these things on his own. She feels the boar's tired sorrow, the peace inside the sorrow, and the strength inside the peace. The boar, blind, knows exactly where he is going. His shoulders reach almost to Delilah's breasts. He never trips or stumbles. He never shows any sign of weakness, and yet the peace within him is humble. Delilah feels utterly at home, walking beside him. They are like two warriors who have always known each other, treading the land they have conquered through sheer endurance.

The light of the half-moon pours through the forest, and the forest floods around them, the wind above them remembering the sea. As they walk, all the animals of the forest that Delilah knows—the hare, the grouse, the deer, the squirrel, the weasel, the porcupine, the owl—appear in colorless flashes of eye and tail and wing, each one watching expressionlessly as the oldest creature of the forest passes by for the last time. Delilah knows that it was this, too, that caused her such suffering in her life before the desert: that in her whole life, there were no elders. There was no one she could respect. No one to give her any hope that something better lay ahead.

What would she have done without the desert to save her? What would she have done without these animals who, quietly and without shame or question, offered themselves to her, over and over again, so that she might live?

Yet the pine forest is a dream. It has been the dream that saved her, her very own dream, and yet a dream that came from beyond her—dreamed by someone or something she cannot understand but is grateful to. Now, walking through these realms of moonlight, she doesn't know why she has never before seen that it isn't real.

by hunting here, you have kept it alive, says the boar, whose body is so real Delilah can feel the connection between his pain and her own—the two bodies aching beside each other, walking the path of pain back to its source, where they will finally let it go. *now it is time for you to pass the dream on to someone else—the one who truly carries the responsibility.*

"Am I going to die now?" asks Delilah, who does not feel afraid.

no. you have already died, and been reborn. now it is my turn, and you will help me, as She helped you. everything is connected.

Delilah doesn't have to ask who he means. It must be true. Yora's cool, restful arms must have slain her with that love she couldn't fight. That's why everything feels easier now. That's why she came to the forest and knelt inside it, even without her dreams to guide her, and told herself she would accept the pain for a little while, and just listen, and try to trust it.

They come to a river, which Delilah has never seen in this forest, and which flows so slowly here it is almost still.

The boar looks at Delilah. *I am your father,* he says.

Delilah stares at him, unable to take a step further.

I am your father, he repeats.

She knows it is true, because she sees a shame in his eyes that she did not see before.

She looks down. Maybe if she stops looking at those eyes, she won't have to hear what he has to say. Already there is a trembling in her heart that she hates, a shrinking in her body that dizzies her. She grits her teeth.

She can hear him anyway. *After I die,* he says, *and you give my body away, I want you to burn this forest down.*

Delilah looks up, bewildered. The trees rock softly in an icy fall wind.

It's only a dream, remember? he says. *But when you burn it down, it will have a chance to be reborn again, for real.*

She has never heard such gentleness from her father—not directed at her, anyway. And yet she recognizes it. There is some memory from long before all the others, from before Mira was born. Before Mira took up all the world with her suffering, and her father's suffering, and there wasn't room for anyone else.

There is some memory of her father cradling her, Delilah, in his arms. He was singing a song, and he said it was the song of the wind through the pines. From the place where he came from, long ago.

So this is where his people came from.

He still smiled then. His eyes were clear.

My daughter of fire, he says now, *I am telling you to burn this forest down. You are the only one who can do it. You are the only one who can release us from our mistakes. You are the only one who can set Mira free from what I've done.*

"What did you do?" Delilah says out loud, her voice hard. Something shifts inside her, something vaguely in the shape of fury. But she feels unsure and cannot quite muster it.

The boar only nods his head, as if she's just answered what he needed to know with her very defiance. He turns and walks a little way along the river, and Delilah follows, her body suddenly full of pain again. Even her feet hurt from the rawness of the ground.

The boar lies down in a thicket of flowers.

Hold me, he says, *if you're willing.*

Delilah finds herself kneeling down, and then leaning her head on the great shoulders, like a child, wrapping her arms around the hugely breathing body.

Sometimes, after she hunted an animal and the arrow went in, she was able to come quickly enough to the animal's side to feel the spark of life just before it went out. This time, she is given many moments to rest on the simple rise and fall of life, before the breath stops.

"But this is the forest of your people," she whispers.

But it's already been destroyed. They already destroyed us. And we kept passing on that destruction to our children, ashamed of ourselves for what they had done to us, powerless to stop it. Now we must take the power of destruction back into our own hands, and make it a rebirth. We must let go of the dream of what was lost, and reclaim ourselves. You, daughter, will do this.

They feel like echoes of words he once spoke, in real life, long ago when he was her father. As if he warned her, long before she was old enough to understand. As if he spoke to her as he rocked her to sleep, knowing that one day he would forget, knowing that one day he would no longer be able to trust his own flawed, human self to remember.

The deep rise and fall of the boar's body feels so good. Like it doesn't matter if she never eats again, or makes love to another man.

I was always afraid of you, whispers her father. *I was always afraid you would look into me with those eyes of fire, and know the truth.*

Delilah dreams of a spiral winding round and round, each circle passing the same points of time in the same places, winding deeper into its own story, deeper and deeper into the relief of darkness. She is following the spiral of a pinecone. And in each hidden pocket of truth, in each point of the spiral, passing itself again and again, drawing on its own history for sustenance, is a seed. That seed needs fire to germinate. Everything else must be destroyed. The parent tree. The cone. The past. Even the spiral itself.

Now please, kill me, says her father.

Delilah takes up her knife, and slips it into the boar's heart. She can feel it going in—the tough skin, the brittle bone, and then, inside, the wild softness of the heart, which opens instantaneously, as if it had been waiting its whole life to give in.

Delilah looks up as the boar dies, and there is the girl, sitting quietly across the river. It is the girl who fled from Dragon with the Unicorn, only there is no Unicorn now. The girl is naked and skinny, her bony knees drawn up to her chest. Her eyes are hollow and she doesn't seem to see Delilah, though she is looking right at her. Delilah stands up and walks toward her, her legs shaking. She crosses the river. The water is colder than the river in the desert.

She emerges into a forest she does not know. A forest thick and confusing, where the moonlight gives in to blackness. The leaves are moist and tender around her as she stands over that white mirror of herself, the bloody knife still clutched in her left fist. She looks down at the pale, fragile head of this princess—so helpless, and yet so beloved by Dragon and by every man in the world—and for a moment she feels hatred shine through her like a familiar dawn. Then it goes, and she kneels down before the girl, whose eyes struggle now to meet hers. Delilah sees the hunger there, the desperation. And she knows suddenly that the path ahead of this girl is far more difficult than her own. She herself has already battled her greatest demons. That's why she feels so old now.

"I'm trying to find my beloved," the girl tells Delilah, her eyes tearing up. "But I'm too human. I'm going to die."

"Not yet," says Delilah. "I've killed a boar for you. It's going to feed you until you get where you are going."

Delilah isn't sure the girl understands. She keeps staring at Delilah, her paleness strange in the darkness. "Where do you come from?" she asks finally.

"From the other side of the river," says Delilah. "This river is a dream we share. Yora. Remember?"

"Yes. I remember…."

"We're always across the river from each other, whether we like it or not. And for the next seven nights, I'm going to be here with this animal that I've killed, helping its spirit pass into the next world. Each of those nights I will cross the river to you, in your dreams, and share its meat with you. Okay?"

"But why?"

"Because once—" She hesitates. "Because once, your Unicorn saved me."

The girl shakes her head. "She's not my Unicorn," she says.

"Well this isn't my meat," says Delilah. "So this has nothing to do with either of us, then. Nobody owes anybody anything."

Maybe it is easier to come down than it was to go up. Easier to fail, and to finally give in to what one feared.

I can hear her thoughts. They are inside me. The whole world is inside me, and the whole world is Lonely.

All around her a beautiful kingdom goes up in flames of color, but she feels like it was made for someone else. It doesn't seem to have anything to do with her. She finds herself longing for it faintly, as if she gazes at it through a window, as if she does not have what it takes to experience it. Her senses are sleeping.

Something in me knows what that's like.

As the way gets easier, and the slope downward less steep, she begins to speak out loud.

"Maybe he never really loved me," she murmurs first. "Maybe that witch knew it, that whatever might seem like love is just a dream and has no proof."

But she can't bear the silence after that.

So then she says, "Maybe he loved me, but I pushed too hard to get him to promise. But why wasn't I enough for him? Why wasn't I as real to him as the birds? Why couldn't he have spoken to me in the end, or even said goodbye? I came to rescue him. I was supposed to rescue him."

I carry her, and I carry her words as she speaks them. Her words fall into my listening like snow. The words are not important, but when they fall into my heart, I remember my heart, and they become something else. It comforts her, to speak them. This time of grief: this is the most sacred time.

"Maybe I'm being selfish. Maybe I've always been selfish, like the Witch said. Maybe…." I know what she doesn't say. *Maybe that old Witch is inside me after all.* It is what she fears more than anything: that she is not that image of sweet innocence her father made of her, not that bright goddess of unconditional love that Sky needed her to be. Rather there is a desperation inside of her, a need so terrible in its own ugly fear—

And yes, I know what that's like, too.

The sunlight in the cold is thin, though sometimes it murmurs in patches of mellow warmth and looks like summer again. Lonely looks down at the leaf-strewn ground, her sadness so soft, her eyes welling up with the mystery of a love so beautiful—even in its pain—that she thinks she could have spent a lifetime following it, and would never have tired of exploring his depths. She wants to tell him how all the leaves are falling from the trees, and ask him why.

It's so cold now. Sometimes, when we stop to rest, she buries herself under dead leaves to keep warm.

I don't know why I began this journey, carrying Lonely. When I began it, at the edge of the sea, I was not aware of myself. Now, as we ride together back down, and I translate her feelings into words, I remember more and more. I remember again the wholeness of love, and the sacredness of what I am made for. I remember again the darkness that made me.

"I wish I could tell you what loving you feels like," she whispers, as if he is here. "So big! How could it come to nothing?"

Sometimes the force of the question makes her look so sharply at the world around her. And then the world turns on its axis of reality, and catches the light of that close, sad, curious autumn sun which leans low over the treetops now, concentrated in a little ball like a swollen heart. Yellow leaves somersault in that light, and the world is silent, moist, and intimate, and she feels that mystery all around her that used to thrill her mind with hope before she met him—and she almost believes that he is here somewhere, close by, if only she could recognize what form he has taken. She feels the sun's closeness, and feels that closeness within herself, that question of who and what she is in this empty universe, and why, and what for. The universe is so vast but the question is close!

She is riding on my back but her face is all around me, and her sorrow is so precious to me—that helpless, good, earnest sorrow—and I want to explain to her what has happened, but I cannot.

Then we walk beneath a cloud, and she is alone again—estranged even from herself, even from me. And I am only an animal, and yet I am more than animal. Where I come from, I must return to, to be reborn into a new life. But where I come from is paved over and gone now. Sky flies in search of it, endlessly, in the wrong direction. The child that dreamed me—she, too, was lost. Somehow, it is only Lonely's journey that can take me back home.

I alone see how everything—the whole world—is personal. A simple love, a simple desire, a simple pain. One little girl was torn open, and because I am her soul now, I cannot shine, and because I cannot shine, the whole world suffers. One man built a whole kingdom out of his simple human lust, his grief, his wounded pride. And now this one girl who rides me will mend the world back together if she can only mend the inner fabric of her own self. I alone see her courage. I need that courage—that courage she has to keep loving, even when hurt. That's the only way the world can become whole again.

Lonely feels the world through her love for Sky. Her love is big and complex, like an ecosystem of life. She knows, in her soul, that Sky was afraid. She wants to comfort him, to hold him close, to relieve him of the fear of her own love. She wants to help him. She wants to follow him in his search for his people. She would do anything for him—she would go with him anywhere.

Yet she feels the grief of her father again. The way he just stopped coming, and she never knew why. The way she lay on her bed night and day, with nothing to keep her company but dreams, tied to the bed with a sorrow as strong as ropes—a sorrow she did not recognize because he had told her she was not human, and could not feel. A pain she did not know about, until the nightmares came.

I understand that, too—the kind of love that can trap you. It becomes your fate, and you feel you never got to decide, and then it betrays you.

At night she lies down under the leaves, exhausted by her thoughts. She doesn't know where she is. She looks into the black starry sky between bare trees and wonders if he is still traveling into other people's dreams. Desperately, she wills herself to fall asleep and dream of him. Her desperation keeps her awake for hours, during which she cries continuously, knowing with total honesty that she has no way of reaching him. That she might never see him again. That there is nothing she can do—nothing. No way to speak with him, to call to him. Only the weight of that despair is heavy enough to drag her finally into the relief of sleep.

She dreams only of Delilah.

Those arms are slippery and tough, and they will not comfort Lonely, but they give her what she needs to survive. The hair around those burning eyes is wild and thorny, but in those eyes there is peace now. In that food, Lonely feels the dark blood of her own need pump through her: instinctual, mammalian, and determined—so strong she cannot doubt its validity, or wonder at its purpose. In that food she swallows the shock of her own self, and the freedom in it—her own stubborn path onward, her own will to survive. In that food she tastes the sweet weakness of sorrow, and in the hours she sleeps she gives in to it, and in the morning she wakes slowed and centered, her mind cold but clear.

Delilah gives her the skin of the boar to keep her warm, and the meat warms her inside. Every night in this dream which is real, Delilah makes a fire, and Lonely watches her as she twists the little pieces of the trees between her fast, hot hands.

They talk a little. Delilah explains to her the mystery of bleeding. It's normal, she says. It happens every moon. It doesn't matter, really.

"Is there anyone you love?" asks Lonely once.

"Yes," says Delilah, without elaborating. Her eyebrows are black and rich, shadowing her eyes.

"You live with Dragon, in the desert?"

"No. I live alone."

"But—"

"Dragon can stay or go. I don't care. I've lived where I live for seven years, alone."

"Are you happy?"

Delilah blows on the newborn flame, making it disappear for a moment, and then appear again like magic, this time bigger. "Happy," she mutters, and seems to think.

Lonely admires the serious lines of her face, the certainty in her muscles. Every motion she makes seems independent of the things around it, and yet intensely comfortable among them.

"But whom do you love?" she presses.

Delilah looks up, as if she'd forgotten Lonely was there. "I don't know," she says. "What's love, anyway? People throw that word around like they know what they're talking about."

"I think maybe my love is selfish," says Lonely.

Delilah shrugs, spears a slab of meat with a stick. "So be selfish," she says. "Selfishness is the only way I've survived. If you don't take care of your own needs, no one else will." And she feeds Lonely with neither warmth nor coldness, neither compassion nor resentment—at least not that Lonely can see. But once Sky said, *If you ever see her in a dream, make sure to accept the love she offers. She needs you to do that.*

She is feeding Lonely. She is so different from the way Lonely remembers her when they first met in the desert. But maybe Lonely is, too.

"When I was younger," Delilah says once, looking down at her hands, "these other girls used to say I was like the Dark Goddess, that old hag in the sea, who drags men to their deaths. Just because I wanted men, wanted sex, or because I was tough, or because my skin was dark— I don't even know. Because I was something different, I guess, than what they thought girls were supposed to be. Even now, people say the same things about me that they used to say about her. That I eat men, or something. Because they're afraid."

Lonely just listens.

"I used to fear you that way," Delilah continues. "That's why I hated you. But I don't any more. It's so hard to look at someone and really see them. But I think as long as we don't, we just keep following the same roads that were carved out for us and feeling the same things over and over again, and we're always alone."

After that, Delilah doesn't look at her again, and Lonely knows to stay silent, so that Delilah won't feel ashamed of those words it cost her so much to say.

Every night Lonely eats of that boar—that boar who died in that forest which isn't really there, which is also a dream now, because her own father Hanum destroyed it. His men destroyed it long ago, clearing it for lumber.

When Lonely gets to where she's going, maybe she won't ever see Delilah again. But when she wakes from these dreams she feels the boar running inside her, beneath her, with its white horns curling not from its forehead but from its hot, roaring mouth. The dark unicorn.

And that nourishment she takes—I take it too! That goddess of the dark unicorn, sister of the pain—I know her. All these moons, all these years, rising hidden and trembling up the mountain, waiting alone and white and invisible at the peak, coming down broken, I have needed her strength. That constricted soul has waited for her, unable to breathe fully again until she returned. How I have needed her, to protect me!

The more Lonely drinks of that blood—the more she takes from Delilah's hands—the more easily I can carry her, and the more closely Lonely and I entwine. I feel what Lonely feels. Yes, whenever Lonely bleeds, it is that black unicorn that tears her open, and Lonely will think of Delilah, lighting her fire in the darkness. Sometimes when she is lonely, she will remember Delilah's aloneness. Sometimes when she tries to deny her own need, she will remember Delilah devouring her portion of the meat across the fire, the juices dripping shamelessly down her face. And whenever she eats she will thank Delilah—for her humanness, for her life.

○

Dragon finds her awake at sunset, leaning over some object, pieces of meat hanging in the wind around her. When she looks at him, he remembers again what humanness looks like. The way life makes a story on her face. Her skin lined a little like the desert earth, its darkness full of depth like a windless night sky, her hair longer now, dreaded, and coated with dust. Not like Yora, whose face could quench the thirst of the desert with a single gaze, and controls his mind and his body and his very breath with its beauty. But when Delilah looks at him, her eyes dive straight into his, quick as falcons.

It's been so long since they've stood face to face. Dragon sees her tremble under his gaze, ever so slightly. He's caught her off-guard, and the power of it makes him happy. He draws his breath, and lets it shiver down through him, containing himself.

She turns back to the thing in her lap now, wrapping her psyche up neatly again, a step removed from the nakedness her eyes revealed. "This backpack," she says, not looking at him. "I carried this backpack into the desert so many years ago and it's only got a couple of holes. That's the glory of man-made things, Dragon." She laughs with that laugh he can't understand—the one that holds no joy, but sounds like a bird shot out of the air, dying. "They never return to the earth. People wanted to make themselves immortal but all they could make was immortal junk."

"What's it for?" asks Dragon. But she doesn't answer. She stands up and turns her back to him, taking up an animal's skin that was lying on the stone and stretching it in her wiry hands, this way and that way. There is a bandage around one of her wrists, but she uses both hands as if they are strong. He can see she won't honor his presence there unless he makes her, and that angers him, but he tries to ignore the anger. He isn't here about her.

"Delilah," he says, and tries to make the word a command, thrusting himself into the weight of his own voice. She turns and eyes him curiously. "I want to talk to you about Yora."

He sees the secrets flickering in her face. He sees he was right to come. But he doesn't know how to stand. He wants to sit down with her and talk, but he doesn't know how to ask. It's so confusing now—this landscape that lies between them. It's like a place once lush and green that's gone without rain for too long, and lies abandoned and still. The ground between them is sharp, covered with fallen spines and bones.

"I know you talk with her," he begins sternly. "I want to know what she's keeping from me. I want to know where she goes when she leaves me. I need you to tell me."

Delilah draws her eyebrows together, apparently pretending not to understand, although he draws some satisfaction from the frozen posture of her body—the intentness of her listening as she holds the backpack loose in her hand. "Keeping from you?"

"Don't pretend you don't know."

"Well I don't," she snaps.

"Where does she go?" he breaks out, and then hisses at himself inside for giving away his desperation.

"I don't know what you're talking about. I've only ever seen her by the river."

"No," he says, gritting his teeth. "Not by the river. I've been everywhere, up and down the river, across the valley, everywhere. I can't find her. Every day she leaves me—where does she go?"

"Does she come back?"

"Yes. Eventually. But—"

"Then what does it matter?"

Dragon holds himself still, trying to slow his breath, and searches her eyes. Women are so subtle, so deceptive. They have ways of interpreting and expressing things that he doesn't understand. He wishes he knew that language. How to trick Delilah into revealing her secrets. How to stalk her from the side, instead of just coming out with it like this. But he doesn't know how else to express his thoughts except by saying them.

"I want her with me," he says helplessly. "Why doesn't she stay with me? Where does she go? Who is she with?"

Delilah laughs. "*Who?* What, you think she's having an affair? What, with Coyote? Trust me, if there were another man out here, I'd have him before she even saw him coming." But something about her usual bawdy confidence seems fake this time, and he doesn't know why.

He clenches his fists. "Don't mess with me, Delilah."

Delilah shakes her head now and bends over her work again, but he can see the tension of her anger, which means something—he's just not sure what. "Yes, well," she says. "You're dealing with a goddess, Dragon. You don't own her, you know."

"So you do know where she goes."

She looks at him, but just when he thinks she's about to give in, she says, "You're crazy, Dragon."

He can't stand it. He is so sick of all the denials—every woman he's ever known pushing him away. Anger closes the distance between them: it is only a few steps to where she stands, and he's there in an instant—his body on top of hers, pressing her into the sharp stones, his hands squeezing her wrists. His erection between her thighs is a knife he will use to tear her open—force her to reveal everything, force her to her knees.

"*What the hell do you think you're doing?*"

Instantly, he lets go. The image of the Unicorn flashes before his eyes, as if it's happening all over again. He remembers the evil inside him. "I'm sorry," he mumbles, covering his face with his hands. When he opens them, he can see her still looking at him, and the fact that she hasn't moved from beneath him—that she's not afraid, only outraged and, perhaps, a little curious—breaks his heart with gratitude. He wants to fall into her arms, but he knows she won't hold him. And he won't betray Yora, even if she betrays him.

"What's wrong with you?" Delilah whispers.

Dragon closes his eyes again. It's so difficult. He's so tired of trying, so tired of fighting himself. What is that endless, cruel secret they all keep from him, that secret of womanhood? Even when Yora's with him, she's not with him. She is somewhere else, always.

"She's not with anyone else, okay?" Delilah is saying, her voice steady and slow, as if he's stupid. "She's trying to find herself. She's lost herself and she's trying to find herself again. *Herself.* Not anyone else. Don't you understand?"

But why won't Delilah hold him? Why won't she love him? Why won't she care for him?

He doesn't realize he is clenching his hands into fists until he feels Delilah's small palms pressed to his knuckles, drawing them with the slightest pressure of her fingertips downward, away from his eyes. Her hands are hot and dry, and slippery like thick desert leaves in the sun. She pulls them away almost before he can draw any nourishment from the tenderness of that gesture, and says sharply,

"Step *back*."

He does, his arms like dead things at his sides.

"Sit down, please. You're scaring me." But she doesn't look scared. Her black eyes follow him as he lowers himself. Then she sits halfway down on the stone across from him. Her legs splay on either side of it like a boy's, and her chest curls inward as the top of her spine rests on the rise of the rock behind her. She's wearing that little brown cloth around her hips like she did the day they met, and its open edge falls between her thighs. Autumn in the desert is hot as ever.

"Okay," she says. "So we're friends, right? Didn't you say that? So tell me." Her eyes don't leave his face, but she looks doubtful, like she's not sure she's going to be able to understand whatever he says.

"I love her," he says dully. "The only time I can feel my heart is when she's with me. When she's gone, I can't feel it, Delilah. It doesn't belong to me."

"And you think that's romantic?" says Delilah. "You think it's beautiful, don't you, that you let your heart belong to someone else. Well Dragon, if you don't own yourself, you own nothing."

"I don't," he says sullenly, that darkness rolling over him again, like it does whenever Delilah challenges him. He doesn't know how to be angry, he realizes suddenly. He doesn't know how to feel anything. "I don't think it's beautiful."

"You're idealizing her. I can tell. She's not——"

"No, no, I idealized the first Yora, the young one, the one who came in the spring. I idealized her because she was made of air, and she made me burn hotter and hotter. She just fueled me, she made me so hot I couldn't bear it, I was going crazy. But this Yora, the real Yora—I feel I have known her forever, Delilah. She's made of water, and that's why I long for her, that's why I need her—because I need her to soothe me. I can't stand that fire in me any more, Delilah, I can't stand it. I look at her, I feel her: she's so peaceful, without desire. She doesn't suffer with herself, she only *is*. She only loves. Oh, Delilah, it's something you and I could never feel, that peace inside her. But I want to feel it, I want to feel it even a little, because I can't stand it any more, this fire——"

He loses himself here because he's crying, and it horrifies him with shame, so that he must muffle his face in his hand, stop his mouth, stop his own breath. He can feel Delilah like a shifty flicker of energy, moving where she sits on the rock, hesitating, and then moving toward him, but in a zigzag, halting way. He remembers the hummingbird in her—her whole being so light, so essentially good. He can feel her nervous love as she kneels before him. When he opens his eyes, her hands are balled tightly in her lap, tense and unsure, and she's leaning a little toward him, her eyes wide and urgent and without a trace of the mockery he saw there before.

"Dragon," she says, in a way that no one has ever said his name before. She says it like it's a precious stone she has kept for a long time without knowing what to do with it, smoothing and polishing it every day, exploring its form with her fingertips, as if she knows it is sacred and someday she'll know what it's for.

He looks at her silently and lets the tears continue down his face, under his chin, over his neck.

"We have to learn to trust this fire, Dragon," she says softly. "Maybe someone told us that we couldn't be loved, that we weren't lovable, because of this fire. But we have to love ourselves. We have to give in to this fire and let it teach us."

Dragon hears her, but he wants to touch the gentleness in her face—and her small breasts, the way they swing, full of love and yet unaware of themselves as she leans toward him….

"But I need—" he begins.

"I know," says Delilah, smiling. "It's what we need, but it's also what we are."

He stares at her, not understanding.

She bows her head. "When I was a kid," she says, "my father was broken. He used to be powerful, but his manhood got taken from him somehow." She laughs a little—a laugh without sound, that same, mirthless laugh. Dragon watches her carefully, looking for the wings inside her, the wings he knows are there. "It's the same with those men who come through the desert," she says. "They're weak, they're desperate, even though they think they're strong. I make them give me what I want, but I hate them all the same. And I hate Moon, too, for being—I mean when he lets himself be weak, when he—" But she can't seem to explain it, and her breath catches.

"I love you," he says.

But she doesn't seem to hear him. He watches her work her jaw against her own tears, her hands open now in her lap. "Remember when you made that fire," she says, "that burned all on its own? That first night?" She's looking at him now. "I was so turned on by that. That fire that didn't need anything."

He remembers the way in his cave she rolled under him like a summer flood. He's hard again, now, with a flame that roars up from the bottom of him as if right up through the earth. For a moment the fear of not being loved is gone, and when the fear goes a barrier dissolves between his pelvis and his heart, and the fire shoots right up there and fills it up like the sun, and the desert shouts its rainbow all around him, and the sky blinds him with joy. He shuts his eyes and lets go, and the fire pours right upward into his skull, into that halo of humble, hopeful prayer above him that he never knew was there, and his whole being opens wide to the heavens. And he laughs with gratitude—that he has so much life inside him, that the desert is so wide and beautiful, and that this strange, amazing woman sits before him, trying to understand him.

He holds out his hands. Delilah laughs, shakes her head, and crawls onto his lap. She nestles her pelvis into his, so that he slides right into her. He hears her let out a breath of relief, and he hears the pain in that breath—a gentle, naked pain. He slides his hands up her thin spine, feels its strength and its barren hunger, feels its tightness and its crying out.

"It's okay," he whispers, caressing her. But what he means is, *I am a god, and I can feel that, finally.* He is rocking her body against his. He realizes why he suffers so much for Yora. It's because there is nothing he can give her. Nothing that she needs. Not food, not pleasure, not listening, not touch, not even love. But it's so plain what Delilah needs, even if she doesn't always ask, or admit to it.

Delilah leans back and kisses him—her lips swift and impulsive. Then it just feels right, so he lets go. He sees his own fire go shooting right up through her, an upward cascade of light through her dark body, releasing every string of pain, healing every part of her.

It happens very quickly. Afterward, they rest that way, against each other, as the morning gets hotter, sweat slinking lazily down each other's backs.

When Dragon opens his eyes, he sees her backpack, discarded on the ground, its dark pocket open and foreboding.

"You're leaving," he says, suddenly understanding. "You're going away."

She pulls back and looks at him, and he sees her eyes reflect inward for a moment as if checking on that place inside herself that he can never see.

"Yes," she says simply. "I have to."

"When?"

"I don't know. Soon."

"Where are you going?"

She hesitates, again. It's so new, to see this uncertainty in her. It attracts him and frustrates him at the same time.

"Tell me," he says, trying to be gentle.

"I'm going—" she begins. He watches her. "I'm going to find the Unicorn."

He can feel his own face stiffening. "What Unicorn?" he growls.

She stares back. He can see her trust fading. He can see her remembering her walls. He can see the shame creeping over her, for letting herself open to him again.

"Delilah—"

She releases him from the grasp of her body and stands, shaking herself out.

"I'm coming with you," he says desperately.

"No. You're not."

They face each other for what seems to Dragon an interminable time. Then Delilah says, "Dragon, I'm sorry. I have to go." She begins to climb up toward her secret caves.

And that's how it ends. Just like that. Cold and sudden as that white shining horn. Dragon turns away, hulking off into the brittle morning, ready to search again for Yora.

Someday, he swears, he will hunt down that Unicorn, whatever it is, and kill it.

Then there will be no more walls between them. Then they will both be free.

What makes the motion of the river? Not the passion of the water itself but only its reaction to the land that shapes it. The water only outlines the contour of the land; it is a song about that shape, a song about the land, or the empty spaces in the land….

Sometimes Yora hears new voices now—not the voices in her head or of people, so heavy, but voices from the river itself. She hears the minnows that remain, pretty and quick, and now holding completely still even as the stream glides past them. She hears the dragonfly nymph, gripping the loose soil at the bottom with crooked legs, and the algae sunning itself on the stone. *Yora*, they say. *Yora, come home.* How do they know her name?

She can look at the river in different ways. She can watch the image of its form, for it has a form, though the form is glossy and blurred and made of pure motion. Every drop of water that passes follows the same looping roll over the same stones, and that continuity gives the impression of permanent shape. Yet she can also follow the motion of the river—each drop passing so swiftly she can barely understand it. It is here and then gone. She could never run that fast.

The river is like a person, like a human being. Like Lil. The way she seems to be the same person, day after day—every time Yora sees her, she's in the same form, the same image, with the same gestures and ways of speaking.

Yet the cells that make up a human body die and are reborn constantly, just as the river's water is replaced by other water, coming and coming, instant by instant. So it is not the same river, and not the same Lil. Maybe that's the secret to magic. Maybe that's the secret to the river's freedom.

Still, the illusion holds.

Except that Yora has sat here long enough to see that even the illusory sameness of the river will change very gradually over time. The water flowing again and again over the same spot will begin to wear it down, or at some moment that cannot be predicted or explained, a pebble will finally come loose. Then the pathway will change just a little, and the shape of the water will change—but only enough to be seen by someone who has watched it for a very long time.

This happens because of the conversation between the river and the stones. Things change because of conversation. Yora knows this.

Also she knows the relationship between the river and the sun. She knows why the drops of the river move not only onward but upward, why they lift into the air by the thousands without ever being seen, why one day in early winter there will be nothing left but a channel of dust where the river once was.

Sometimes Dragon comes near. Yora can hear him calling her name, or she can feel him pulling at her heart. But more and more, the river pulls stronger. She cannot go to him yet, because she is figuring something out, and it excites her, though it pains her too. She wants to call out to him, to reassure him, to comfort him in some way, but when she speaks, her voice sounds like the voice of the river. And Dragon isn't listening to the river, because he doesn't know that's who she is.

But Lil knows. Maybe that's why only Lil can see Yora, when Yora is here with the river. Or maybe it's because Lil is a woman.

It was Mira's father who first told her about the Unicorn. All the original peoples, he said, know about these things.

The Unicorn is descended from the moon, he said. The Unicorn brought the people written language, and stood by the people, right beside their souls, throughout all the centuries of their mistakes and arrogance and hope and failure. It is the only immortal animal. One day, when we see it walk among us, we will know that we can feel hope again.

But where is the Unicorn now? asked Mira.

Ask the animals and the plants—they are the only ones who know.

So she asked them. She knelt in the grass, pressed her lips to the cold earth, and whispered. She called to the Unicorn, whom she had begun to dream of at night, whose smooth face was cold and pure, and whose eyes were her mother's eyes before her father had changed. She knew she could never be like that princess from the stories who tempted the Unicorn to lie down beside her, and who was rewarded for her beauty by the unicorn's white, magical fields of comfort. She was too ugly inside, too hateful and frightened, too guilty.

haven't you ever felt the Unicorn? said the grass. *when it comes, you feel the air snap and spark, like when the sky holds its breath before a thunder storm.*

there are many Unicorns, said the ants, their voice a wave that made her close her eyes.

no, there is only One, said the praying mantis, his arms flexing, his green face more human than Mira felt her own to be.

the Unicorn is very proud, said the caterpillar, hurrying away. *he won't speak to you.*

But the butterfly said, *the Unicorn is the humblest animal alive. she travels round and round the world, but will spend all day hearing out the sorrows and longings of a single flower in a single meadow.*

Mira crawled on. In those days, she'd taken to moving about the meadow almost entirely on her hands and knees. It felt too dangerous to stand up. And also lonely.

everyone loves the Unicorn, explained the dandelion, who trembled because it was not in his nature to speak. *but we can't understand our love. we can't say what moves us, what happens to us. when the Unicorn is near, we know, suddenly, what we are. we can even perceive our own beauty, or understand suddenly what beauty is, and that we are a part of it—something larger than us—and the colors, when one looks upon us… but what is color? it isn't something i understand, but when the Unicorn comes, i know it is in me!*

Mira stroked the dandelion with her finger.

the Unicorn is masculine, said the dragonfly. He seized the body of his mate with thin brutal legs, curling his body to touch its tip to hers, and Mira began to weep. *when He comes, the flowers overflow with pollen and all females are immediately fulfilled.*

no, whispered the mosquito, hiding in the grass so the dragonfly wouldn't see her, *the Unicorn is infinitely female.*

But where is She? begged Mira. *How can I find Her?*

i have seen Her, said the ladybug.

no you haven't, said the mole. *no one sees the Unicorn and lives.*

what do you know? countered the ladybug. *you're blind.*

exactly, said the mole cryptically.

But how can I find Her? asked Mira again.

oh, answered the ladybug, *you can't find Her.*

the Unicorn has a secret, hissed the deadly nightshade.

What secret? asked Mira.

the only secret. the secret that holds the world together.

you must tame the Unicorn, said the blackberry vine, pushing its way mercilessly through the field and over the heads of the less assertive plants. *if only you could tame the Unicorn, we would all be free. no one would ever again be afraid.*

Me? asked Mira.

whatever you are, the vine said carelessly, clutching her in its thorns as she tried to back out of the thicket. *a human, or whatever.*

I don't want any blackberries, said Mira. *Why are you tearing at me?*

She had to crouch low to the ground, lay flat against it, and slither her way out.

the Unicorn smells like saltwater, the snake told her. *Like tears.*

Everyone said something different.

One rabbit, peaceful and still as he spoke about it—in a way that rabbits never are, not in their whole lives—said, *the Unicorn is the gentlest of beings. when He comes near me, i finally feel safe.*

But another twitched all over at the mention of the name. *the Unicorn is terrifying!* she said.

it draws you irresistibly, said the luna moth. *you become obsessed. you lose yourself. it's terrible. you must be careful.*

it is only this, said the spider, when Mira finally returned to her—the one whose web spanned eighteen grass blades at the very center of the meadow, and who, if she was in the right mood, would always tell Mira the truth about what the other animals said, or what was really going on. But often she was mysterious in her statements. Mira admired her but was a little afraid, too. The spider was giant and black and yellow. *the Unicorn is the holiest aspect of every creature,* she said today. *your reaction to it depends on your relationship to your own divinity.*

I don't understand.

The spider tapped each central string of her web, as if testing for echoes.

don't listen to what the other animals say. how will you *react, when you come face to face with what you seek?*

But it was a bee who spoke plainly to her, finally, one day when Mira had given up searching, and lay in the field with her spirit floating above her, trying to understand what her body was—what it was for, why it felt so awful. The bee bounced in the air, touching her skin, brushing it with his tiny feet, here and there, here and there, kissing and waking each sensation. To Mira it hurt more terribly than if he had stung her.

Stop, she cried. *What are you doing to me?*

the Unicorn is inside you, Mirr, said the bee. The animals did not call her *Mira*; they called her *Mirr,* the name she called herself by—the name that, even then, sounded like a murmur at the bottom of the sea.

What do you mean?

the way the color is inside a flower, but the flower can't see it. the Unicorn is inside you. that's why your father wants to get in. he wants the Unicorn.

Mirr remembers that time still, when all the animals surrounded her, when they knew her name, when they answered her. Each of the parts of her body was an animal. And over time, isolated here beneath the earth, beneath the sea, those animals have been dying one by one. Look now, if she holds out her arms, she can hardly see her hands. Look now, at her belly—it is pooling into hips that don't belong to her, that belong to someone else. She cannot feel her feet. She cannot feel her ears. One by one, these animals that make her up are dying. No one can see her. No one knows her. Soon, there will be nothing left here in this corner of darkness under the sea but a space, and the smell that animals leave behind.

Her father overdosed the same night that he finally entered the girl he called *Mia* all the way. After that, Mira couldn't feel her body any more, and she didn't speak any more, not even to the smallest blade of grass. Because she believed he had found that Unicorn inside her, and taken it with him into the Other World. She had never seen it, never understood it for herself, but she thought she could tell that he had taken it away, the way a flower would be able to tell if it no longer had a color, but just stood bewildered, lightless and grey, in the sun.

On the last day of our journey, it rains nonstop. Lonely shivers all the time, her eyes bulging out of her head like the eyes of the dead. Water beads on the boar's hairs and drips silver to the ground. But I keep my pace steady. I do not think about what will happen once we get there.

She doesn't recognize the field when we arrive after nightfall. Her eyes are not registering things the way they used to, and anyway she has never faced it from this direction before.

She doesn't recognize the waving grass because it is pink and brown, its tassels full of empty seed husks. The wind hurries a mass of chill mist across the hills and empties the rain like ice chips against her face. But there is something familiar about the shape of the darkness.

Then she sees the smoke rising and thinks of Delilah. What she learned about fire—its mystery, and the hope in that mystery. I carry her over the brink of a hill and she sees the little wooden house with the tiny yellow lights flickering inside. And she knows that fire is the spirit of the house, and that where fire is lit within a house, it means someone is alive inside. She feels something burning inside her, too, after all. She feels both relief and anger. Because she realizes now: she realizes how much she hoped that I was, all this time, taking her to him.

She realizes I wasn't.

She sees she is back again, with nothing. Just as she will arrive one day soon at the feet of the old woman, trapped in the middle of the sea, with nothing to show for the love only she believes in. But I had to come here. I think she will be safe here, and that they will show her what to do next.

We hear Rye's and Fawn's horses locked in their stable, stamping, whinnying, aware of our arrival. I remember when the mare called me to run with her. Life was easier then. I did not yet admit to who I was, and I had no responsibility. I was just an animal. Almost, I want to stop and speak with them, but I have no time. I have work to do.

I stop at the crest of the hill. Lonely thinks she sees movement inside the house. Her mouth waters suddenly at the thought of food.

"This is where I leave you," I say.

Lonely looks down at a Unicorn's wet mane. I am that Unicorn. I kneel.

She stumbles off, too surprised to resist. But as I stand again, she wraps her arms around my neck.

"You can't," she says. "Where are you going? You're all I have. You said you would take me home."

"This is as far as I can take you. You have to go the rest of the way yourself. So do I."

"What do you mean?"

"I'm so sorry," I say. "But once before, long ago, someone owned me. And it destroyed me. I don't want to be owned again."

"But I won't own you. I won't ride you any more, not ever. Just be my friend. Please."

"I am. I am going to help you," I say desperately.

"How are you going to help me? Do you know where he is?"

I can see the stars behind her head, framing her face as if they are not billions of distances away, so much sharper in the cold. We speak more easily to each other now. "I think," I say, "when a man feels unsure about his own power, he will always hurt the woman he loves. In one way or another."

I know she isn't fully listening, but to me this is what I've been meaning to say all along. This is the wound that must be healed. Now. I have to go and find him.

"But where is he?"

"The where does not matter," I tell her.

"Of course it matters! I would do anything to have him here with me again, anything just to trace his face with my eyes—" She tries to see through her tears into my eyes.

I do not know what that feels like—the kind of need she speaks of. It is another language for me. But we both think of Sky and his fear.

"What do I do?" she whispers.

"You know things," I say, suddenly angry. "You must realize the things you know, so that you will not get hurt this way, over and over again!"

We are both startled by my passion.

"Here," I say, feeling sorry, "take this. I don't need it." I bow my head and rest my horn in her hands. When I lift my head, the horn remains in her hands, loosely glowing. I feel relief. For a moment, I glimpse again the easy, simple suffering of mortal life—and I think I will spend all my days running with the mare, and all my nights sleeping in hay, and I will never fear men, and I will have no body but this one, and when I die, any earth, anywhere, can claim me.

"But you do need this," she says, frightened. "You're somebody's soul."

I hang my head. In a way I don't even know what the horn was for. But I know it was heavy.

"I know," says Lonely suddenly. "I understand. I want to deny the darkness in me. It terrifies me. And you—you want to deny your light! That's why we're together."

But I am moving now, because I can't bear it any longer—I am a wind of fading light, flashing across the field faster than any animal can run, and gone into the darkness.

I don't want to talk about myself any more. Not now.

Back in the field, Lonely looks down at the horn. Then she closes her eyes and remembers her lover's face when she first looked up at him, his eyes illuminated beneath the wings of his brows, his jaw loose, his lips heavy, unconscious of their own hunger. She remembers the firmness of his hand in the clouds, and the way that certainty gave way to trembling.

She wraps the horn in a fold of the boar skin and tucks it against her body. She's not sure what it means, but surely it means something. Surely it will help her somehow. She will keep it until she knows. *Maybe it will help me to find him.* But at the thought of losing the Unicorn, she begins to cry again, feeling she has lost the one and only thing she could depend on.

Cold and hunger make her walk onward toward the house. She doesn't know what she will say when she comes to the door. She holds her humbled heart still, in its quiet womb of sorrow. She carries her heart carefully, like a jug of sacred light, and she wears the skin of that dark animal that feeds her in dreams—that dark animal that keeps her alive.

When she arrives at the door, knocks, and stands under the woodshed to keep out of the rain, she is holding her heart in her hands, as her beloved once held it in his, so she can use it to see by.

Delilah eats fruit only in the fall, when the pomegranates are ripe.

She picks one from the grove she knows, by the sandy cliffside at the river's edge. It's the last of the season, but still white like an old man's head most of the way around, and it'll be sour. She doesn't mind. She likes them sour. Smiling to herself, she sits down by the waterless river and slices it open on a stone with her little meat-carving knife. Its bloody juice drips into the mud.

She sees the shimmer of Yora's body where the water once was—like heat waves, like ice—but at the same time that human form is fading more and more into the movement of the river. At first Delilah was surprised that Dragon couldn't see her, but now she knows why.

But I don't get it," she tells Yora. "The river was always here, right? But I didn't really feel it before. I don't understand how you're a person but also the river. I don't understand what a god is. I don't understand how you're here with me, in one place, but you can't be, because the river stretches all the way from the mountains to the sea, and isn't your spirit everywhere?"

"Yes."

Delilah laughs. She peels pomegranate seeds into her mouth with her front teeth, feeling them drop like gel jewels onto her tongue and then burst.

Yet still. Still the silence aches lately, in a way it has never done before. And today—the night stretches so long before her.

I'm going to find the Unicorn, she hears herself saying to Dragon. So certain, as if she would go right now, as if she had no fear. But where will she go? She doesn't even know what she herself means by it.

"What do you feel now?" asks Yora.

"Angry," says Delilah, though she didn't know it before she spoke the word.

"At whom?"

Delilah closes her eyes. She can't see Yora at all now, only the river. Maybe she's imagining this conversation inside her mind. But it doesn't feel that way. She can feel the river listening, and that listening makes her mind clear and softens the sharp edges of her feelings.

"At Mira," she says.

The water sounds like thousands of people all talking at once, like people flooding from a subway station or conversing in a giant room before the leader calls the crowd to order.

"For leaving me," she adds.

"When they took her away."

"No. When she left me. When she stopped answering me. When she stopped looking at me. Wouldn't eat the food I brought her, wouldn't even know me any more."

The wind slips through the trees like a casual passer-by and is gone.

"When we got sent away, to school—" It always seems such a funny word to use out here. School. Meaningless to the desert, meaningless to the river. "When we got sent away, she was all I had, you know? I wasn't ashamed of her, I didn't care if she was crazy, I stood up for her no matter what. But I wanted her to love me, to talk to me, like—you know, like a *sister*."

"There was something wrong."

"Of course there was something wrong! But that's what I mean. Why couldn't she tell me?"

Delilah holds the remains of the fruit loosely in her hands, suddenly uninterested in it. It drips over the river like a bleeding heart.

"Why are you still here, Delilah?" asks Yora. "When you ran away to the desert you were only a child, and you were not thinking about the future. You only wanted to escape. Are you still the same girl you were then? Are you still so helpless, so alone?"

Delilah holds her face in her hands, tugs at the roots of her hair, sighs. "There's something holding me here," she says, and her words feel cottony and useless in her mouth. "My father asked me to burn down the pine forest. But I can't."

"Why?"

"Because I can't let it go. Because it's kept me alive for so long, and even though I know now it's a dream, maybe I still believe in it, because I have to. I can't bear to destroy it. I can't bear to be that person, Yora."

But Yora is silent, and the silence is gentle and sweet.

"I don't know," Delilah says. "I don't know why. I just can't. My father died there. It's his place. I can't be the person—" She stops. She takes a tear out of her eye and looks at it, surprised. "I can't be the person who destroys it."

Yora waits, like an eddy between stones. Then she says, "You want to be someone who rescues, for once. Not someone who destroys."

Delilah nods, not trusting her voice.

"Why do you *not* want to believe, then," Yora whispers, "that she still exists somewhere—that you can find her?"

"What do you mean?" cries Delilah. "Don't you think I tried to find her? Don't you think I tried? How could I not wish—?" But she stops. Maybe it's true. She doesn't want to know. She doesn't want that obligation any more. Why not? *Because I'm selfish, after all.*

"That is not why," says Yora.

"Fine. I suppose you know how to find her?" Delilah hisses.

She waits, but the sound of the water is her answer. The water knows everything. It is always flowing home. And Delilah sees her sister everywhere. She saw her in the deer's eyes. She saw her like a light over the white girl's shoulder, as they ate across from each other at the dream fire—like she was there all the time, but Delilah was afraid to look. She sees her when she closes her own eyes; she sees her inside herself. She sees her in dreams, where once she saw wings and fur.

"I know where her body is, not her spirit," says Yora.

Delilah hangs her head again. "That's not enough. Trust me. I know."

"But the body is the only place you can begin. It is the only place she can ever come back to, whether she knows it or not."

Delilah stretches her legs, immerses her feet in the river. Her shoulders ache. Her toes turn white in the cold water, like small eroding stones. She places a pomegranate seed on her tongue.

She knows that Yora, the river, won't always talk to her like this. She knows it is a gift, for her to use while she can before she's left alone again.

Secrets lie under last year's dead leaves, whispering. The leaves beneath them are only skeletons of leaves, making a network, a cage of fibrous darkness, and the leaves beneath those are earth, black and luscious and ready to start again. Yesterday's rain damps it all together, so that my feet make hardly any sound. But I know what is happening under the leaves. I know the way the silence unfolds. I know so much, so much that I used to think was forever closed to me, once my father died.

But *me.* What do I mean by that? I am a Unicorn now. Of course I know everything. But also—it makes me afraid, all this knowing.

I travel. I run now, nearly flying.

I run over burned hills like the moon. I run through deep brown grasses, the white of my back breaking through their surface, scared. I run over bright green moss shining with the cold. I run over mountaintops covered with tumbled boulders like shattered castles. I run through sunlight, so real and tangible in the autumn, like a live being. I skirt around the desert, where that desperate Dragon still hunts for the soul of Woman, as if to devour Her. I run far from the City. I am not ready yet. I run up into the sky, and run down, and walk wearily up again, too afraid to be still.

When I was a horse, without meaning to, I came to know the land again. What I had loved once—the grass, the wind—came to know me again. My body, my animal's body—at least in that form—was my own again. It was safe to speak with spiders again. It was safe to listen to bees, and even without him there, I understood them. And Lonely! What a miracle, to know that I could love that way, and survive.

But this horn, still here between my eyes! I am still Unicorn, like a nightmare I keep waking up to. I keep giving it away. I gave it to Lonely, so that she could learn and heal from it. I give it to the river, so it can breathe again. I give it to the moon, because she's never had anything of her own. I give it to the earth in a forest that's been torn down, so that the new seeds will grow strong. Again and again I give away that light, but it keeps coming back, stronger than ever.

I want it to be gone. I stand under the waterfall and cry, silver tears that fall like fish into the river, and I wish it could wash the horn away. The fish come alive and wriggle their bodies downstream, finding their way to slower currents where they can hunt water striders in the shadows. No one will ever know those fish were once tears.

The idea of the horn terrifies me. I don't want anyone to see. The horn—its very power—makes me vulnerable. It is not free, such power. Someone will hurt me for it: that is what always happens. The horror of it fixes me in this shadow behind the waterfall, hidden from the sun, hidden by the water's deafening roar.

True, the water loves me again; the earth loves me. I do want to help Lonely, because when I was with her I remembered my holiness—where I come from, and where I must return to. And I understand something about her. The girl is carrying someone else's pain, and the girl wants to fix that pain, even though it is not her own. She feels it as if it were her own. She can no longer separate herself from it.

It makes me feel bitter; it makes me angry. It isn't right! This desperation she feels. This suffering. I want to find the person who makes the girl suffer. I want to stop him. The fury of it tastes like blood in my mouth. But I'm afraid.

The water keeps falling before me, forever. I dip my horn into it and let it burn there, like a wound. I can't feel it. It doesn't feel like anything. It's like a naked bone, with no nerves to feel, no muscles to move it, no flesh to hide it, sticking straight out into space.

Listen. I am the only character in this story who knows for certain where I come from, and what is going to happen to me. The identity of the Unicorn is very simple. Unicorn is for One, for Only, for I. I am. I am born in the Heart of the World, and I go back there to die, and be reborn again.

But sometimes I forget that.

Because in this life things became complicated. I was not born this time in the usual way. Something happened to stop the ceremony, and it was never completed. Instead I emerged somewhere else, through someone else, in a painful way. I became someone's soul, when that soul got chased out of its body by violence. And he was always chasing me, that man who thought he loved me. Still I run from him. And the only salvation is to return home and be reborn again, start over—but how can I return to that paved-over place, where the Heart of the World once was?

It is not safe in this world for a Unicorn. It is not safe for anything sacred, not now. I will hide, as I have always hidden. I will hide inside this story, and the confusion of its people, who do not yet remember themselves.

Fawn flings open the door, her face white. Her hair loops in tangles about her cheeks. Lonely has never seen her so messy, as if her seams have been cut open. She's holding several shawls tight over a soft brown dress, and the tight protrusion of her shoulders, thinner now, makes her look fragile like someone very young or very old. Her eyes skim Lonely's face without under-standing, and then, in the split second that they do, they slam shut—the light inside them blinking out as certainly as if her eyelids had actually closed. She leaves the door flung open and turns away.

Lonely is still standing in the doorway in shock as she hears Fawn's unshod footsteps hissing against the rungs of the wooden ladder, ascending to the loft where Lonely last saw her, long ago, in Rye's arms. Then Eva appears before her.

She doesn't know what to say so when Eva holds out her hand, she just takes it, and lets the old woman lead her into the house with the same calm, tired shuffle, as if she knew all along that Lonely was coming. Of course she did. She knows everything. Why couldn't she have told Lonely before, what would happen?

They sit down on the cushions close to the wood stove. Beneath the cush-ions, the floor is covered with wool and animal skins, scattered and layered like the cloths around Eva's shoulders. The dim, windless silence of indoors is comforting. The deep nest of heat that fogs around them from the wood stove feels like love.

Eva sits down across from her, slowly, cringing a little. "So you're back," she says.

At the sound of Eva's voice, Lonely begins to cry. She doesn't stop crying for a long, long time. Eva sits there, watching her.

"What's going on?" Lonely asks finally, trying to find her way back. "Why did Fawn——?"

But she stops in the face of Eva's silence, and then slowly she takes in the mood of the house—this house she so remembers, whose wooden body sheltered her and gave her family for the first time, whose soul she came to recognize in the fire that burned at its center and the water that sang through it and the mingled breath of its people and the shapes and spaces they left behind. There is something wrong. She feels the presences of the people in the house, but there is a dark space hanging open somewhere, like a gaping wound. She turns back to Eva's face and sees, for a heartbeat in the tricky light, a scar of fear running across it, as if Eva is still struggling to survive in a cold stormy forest from years ago, fearing at every moment that she might not be able to keep her daughter alive another day.

But then the shadowed planes of Eva's face come together again into their familiar picture of webbed, level peace—almost. The light of the living, present moment moves in her eyes.

"Kite is gone," she says.

Lonely stares.

"He left seven days ago. He left a note."

Lonely imagines Fawn finding the note, perhaps left on the table, or on Kite's bed, and handing it with trembling fingers to Eva, the only one who could read it. She imagines Eva looking up at her daughter with heartbreak in her eyes, not able to find words to speak it aloud.

"To the City," Lonely whispers.

"Yes."

Lonely feels something falling inside her, the downward spill of that same sadness—all the men turning away, going off somewhere with other worlds in their eyes and sad silence in their hearts, searching for something they can't define, cold at the touch of women's fingers, unreachable.

"Rye's gone to look for him," Eva sighs. "He left days ago. When Fawn heard the knock, she thought maybe...."

Lonely nods, though obviously Rye would not knock, nor would Kite.

"Why are you here?" asks Eva. Lonely feels her heart constrict. She cannot determine the emotion behind the question. Maybe there is no room for her here now. Maybe this family is like a wounded animal, wary and defensive, with no energy for anyone or anything but its own survival. And what then? Where will she go? The desperation of it brings bitterness to her voice—more than she intended.

"I failed," she says.

"In what?"

"In love."

"You weren't able to love?"

"No. I wasn't able to …keep it."

"Hm," says Eva, and nods. Then she keeps still, her eyes still holding Lonely with neither judgment nor compassion, as if waiting. Lonely remembers that she is starving. That she hasn't eaten since last night, in a dream. But she doesn't want to ask for anything. Maybe she shouldn't even be here. But the thought of carrying her hunger with her back out into the cold, and being alone without the Unicorn, without a future, makes her cry again.

When she is able to stop crying for a second time, Eva is sitting closer to her, offering a small plate in her hands, and on the plate there is bread. Lonely pushes it into her mouth, barely chewing, and it rolls like fists into her stomach. Then Eva hands her a glass of milk, and she drinks it fast. She's still so hungry, it's hard to focus her eyes on Eva; it's hard to keep her hands still.

"We don't have much," says Eva more gently. "It's winter now. But as far as I'm concerned you can stay a little while. Maybe there is something you still have to learn here, that you didn't learn last time." She stands up, and Lonely feels ashamed of her helplessness, always asking of others.

"I'm going to bed now," says Eva, "because this time of year, my bones hurt, and if I stay up with you longer I will be irritable and say things I don't mean. My dreams await me. I sleep here by the fire, and tonight you can sleep here too. We'll talk tomorrow about where you will sleep, if it's okay for you to stay. It is crowded in here in the winter. Everyone sleeps in the loft, except for me."

Lonely nods. She watches Eva as she ever so slowly, as if bending the limbs of an old, old tree, rises, walks the few paces to her mat, and lowers herself length by thin length back down to the floor. She tosses Lonely a blanket, and then curls up under her own.

It's like a different house. A completely different house than the one Lonely remembered. Everything has changed.

"Thank you," Lonely remembers to say to Eva's small back. But she's too hungry, and too frightened by the look she remembers in Fawn's eyes, to go to sleep. The full moon is keeping her awake too, though she doesn't know it, for she did not notice it rising, and the passion of such a thing seems alien to her now. She watches the firelight flickering from behind the grate, one hand under her cloak and clasped around the Unicorn's horn.

As she watches the fire, she climbs up into the distant attic of her own mind, to get away from the endless, redundant pain of her heart's turning and the anxious rumble in her belly. Her mind, airy, spiders around the changing shape of the flames, considering, looking for thoughts to hold onto. She tries to decide what color the fire actually is. It seems orange, or maybe yellow, but then when she really looks at it, it's not. Maybe white, but not exactly. The more she looks, the more there is no color—and the more there is every color. Then she remembers Moon, for the first time in what feels like a hundred years. She remembers the rainbow, and his soft kiss at its center.

The path of colors? Girl, you will *do it again. Again and again and again, until you can hardly bear it. That's what life is. Try to remember it's a circle, and you're immortal, and you can always come here, to the center, to rest.*

Lonely closes her eyes. But she doesn't sleep. *Lonely,* she thinks. *Lonely.* Her mind is a language, like Kite's black marks on the page. If she could only follow it to the center. If she could just get through that depth of indigo, and back to that center, where that single kiss stilled her—no more than that one kiss, and no less.

But she's not immortal any more. She's here at the place where she first became mortal, where she first tasted food, where she first began to survive. At the center of her mortal body is her heart, and it hurts.

Lonely, she thinks. Because somewhere in that word is comfort. Something familiar, like the only home she has. *That's what the Unicorn meant,* she thinks, falling into sleep. *I have to get back to the center of the rainbow, and then I'll know what to do....*

But when she wakes, someone is yelling, and she does not remember her dreams.

8ᵗʰ MOON

●

Coyote keeps calling him a coward.

Or that's the way it seems to Dragon, when Coyote follows him snickering, leering when Dragon turns around, and then bolts before Dragon can make a move. Coyote is laughing: Dragon is sure of it. *Coward. Not enough man to hold onto a goddess....*

Is her intangible grace, her foggy peace, too awesome for him ever to grasp or enter? Does she leave him because he isn't powerful enough to keep her? He looks for her every day but has not seen her now for a quarter of a moon. The loss of her terrifies him. He never sleeps.

The rains come: winter rains, sudden and long but noncommittal, just as suddenly gone again. There is no compassion in them. Dragon stalks along the riverbed, glowering into the water that has returned there, searching its deepest places. He sees Coyote drinking from the other side. The subtle sensuality of Coyote's lips over the water makes him angry. He can see the muscle of Coyote's throat pumping up and down. A dry breeze passes upriver between them. Coyote's eyeballs roll up to meet Dragon's, but he keeps drinking.

Delicious, says Coyote.

"Raawww!" yells Dragon, hurling a stone, hating Coyote for his ability to satisfy a simple need. Dragon has no human needs, no purpose, except for the one need which is never satisfied.

Drink then, says Coyote and walks away.

Dragon kneels, seething.

He bends low, his face close enough to the water to feel the icy aura of its passage. He glances up, to make sure that Coyote is gone. A bird cries out, and he freezes. Is it talking about him? He's so lonely out here that sometimes he thinks everything is speaking to him, in a language he can't understand.

Now he looks at the water, and the water changes, as if by magic, and seems to still. Maybe Coyote left some magic behind. Now the water shivers to a pause, in a way impossible for it to do, the rushing around it blurring on the edges of Dragon's vision, and now he sees a face emerging in that stillness—and he's panting like Coyote himself in his eagerness, because he's sure that Yora is finally appearing to him again.

But it is only his own face, which he has never before seen.

A beast there, unbearable to behold. Not a god, not a man, but a mad demon of desperation, hairy and red, his eyes rimmed with black, the whites of his eyes blinding.

He stares in horror yet cannot look away. Who is that other that overtook him, when he plunged into Delilah for the first time? Who is that other who drives him furiously onward after Yora, wanting her so badly that the wanting is murderous, merciless, unfeeling? Who is that other who has no heart, who eats his heart into darkness whenever he starts to feel it?

Without meaning to, he is leaning so close now that he feels the water on his lips, and then his tongue. It doesn't feel the way it feels against his hands or his legs. It moves again, the moment he touches it, and it pours upward against his inner mouth.

Something is coming at him in that water—something that could devour him, erase him. He pulls back swiftly and stands, then glances around once more. His reflection is gone, and he doesn't want to see it again. He doesn't want to remain here, on the outside, looking in. He strips off his magical pants, his hands trembling unaccountably. Clenching his fists, he enters the river, and stands with feet wide apart, as if straddling it. For the first time in his life, he feels vulnerable in his nakedness. He kneels again, this time inside the water. It reaches his belly. He has to hold onto the stones to keep from being swept backward by the current. He bends down and tries again to drink.

The water enters his mouth faster than he can decide it, and he swallows without even trying. Something wakes inside his rib cage; something dawns.

She's inside the river, he thinks.

But where? How? How to get inside? He buries his head in the layers of cold. He can feel the water battling him; it closes his ears. He breathes it in and breathes out fire, and the water boils momentarily and keeps going, bubbling past him. He screams her name, but underwater it comes out in a language he doesn't know. He can't see.

His determined fury makes him crawl against the stones, dragging himself forward.

But this cannot be Yora—not this roaring, fighting thing, not this wildness. How can she be so angry, so violent in the face of his need? He begins to cry, the tears of an orphan abandoned in a den of dragons—his tears the first tears that come from drinking real water—but his tears, too, are swallowed up in the river that bore them. *Please,* he cries soundlessly. *Come back to me. Come back and hold me. Mother.*

Then he has to let go, and the water rushes him backward so fast he can hardly remember himself, or the story of where he came from, or why he is here in the desert, all alone. It tumbles him over and over, crashing him against the stones until his blood reddens the rapids, and he's aware of pain but moving too fast to know where it comes from or where on his body it strikes, or even that he has a body, with any form at all. Then the water drops him into a pool that deepens and deepens, or maybe he is only deeper beneath the rapids, in the depths she has always hidden from him, that he never knew were there.

He opens his eyes in the blackness and sees, alone in an open space, the single, small body of a girl, wrapped up tight like a pebble. Her skin reflects an opaque light, from nowhere. She seems so far away, but when he reaches out, she raises her head and opens her eyes. Then she unrolls herself and crawls toward him, swims toward him and over him, and she is at once human and fish, and now bigger than the moon.

"Yora!" He calls her name to save himself. She will engulf him. He will die inside her. Yet this is what he has always wanted. She comes over him—is everywhere, but untouchable, unseeable, like the goddesses of his childhood. She comes over him, a grey mist of confusion, not knowing him, her eyes as cold as the eyes of snakes, and also everywhere.

He waves his limbs with the unfocused randomness of fear, like an infant.

Yora chills against him. Liquid flesh, she rubs his warmth, spills around him, seeking him. Something like rage moves her. Something like rage makes her so cold she might freeze, so lost she must cling to him, so determined that she will not let him go.

He has something that belongs to her.

What is it? She cannot even remember. She circles him, as if water could be a predator.

Something inside him.

Like a human being, she sings the song of her body against his chest, leans back, lets her hair stroke his neck. Breasts, nipples, she brushes him. She will feel something. She will remember. In the touch of him she will find it.

He sits perfectly still now, trembling, a fetus in its original waters. "What do you want?" he whispers.

But Yora has no hands, no feet, no words. She wraps her tongue around him. She slithers her body against his—each crevice cupping him, pinching tight his flesh—and a movement that belongs to neither one of them is opening her in circles. What is it? A motion, a rhythm they are trying to remember, to which their lives were once aligned....

Be still, she tells him, when he reaches for her. She will use him if she has to. She will use the longing in his eyes, the tension in his muscles as she touches him, to remember herself. She moves against him until she is lost inside that motion, until she cries out inside it, until it—not he, not her memories, not her fear—owns her, and then he is moving too, desperately, and in that movement she does remember, after all.

She feels it now, as she whips her endless tail: she is the river. *She* is the mystery. *She* is the bottomless source.

Long after he is exhausted, long after he has forgotten, long after he has crawled like a tattered impression of himself to cling to that shore which is precious to him—that world which is all he needs, though he never knew it—that movement will continue inside her, and will carry her on.

For she, the river, cannot linger. She remembers now. She has gotten her self back. She takes it in her mouth and runs.

Moon meets the Unicorn in a dream. He has never seen a Unicorn before.

Nor does he see her now; instead she comes to him as music. Music as delicate as silence, and then coiling forth in a rich thicket of bells.

Then it is thunderous, and then waves, then notes as close together as raindrops but with the spiral of a single, deadly melody vining its way up from the center.

"You sound sad," says Moon.

"Because I remember you," answers the Unicorn, in words made of glass, "and you don't remember me."

No, thinks Moon. *I have never heard anything so beautiful. No wonder Delilah was afraid to search for you after she dreamed you. She doesn't believe she can face up to such beauty.*

"Never mind," says the Unicorn. "I came because I am looking for someone."

"Where am I?" asks Moon suddenly. He isn't aware of having a body. Only consciousness, thrusting urgently into the white music of the Unicorn.

"I don't know. You are dreaming. You left your body somewhere. Be careful. I know where I left my body, a long time ago—and it isn't going anywhere. But your body—do you still want it? Do you know where it is?"

"I don't know," answers Moon, though far away he can feel the weight of it, the pain of it, the muck of it. "Do I need it? Does a god need a body?"

"I wouldn't know," answers the Unicorn.

Moon considers. "I keep breaking it," he says softly. "It doesn't matter. It's still alive. Why? What does it want from me?"

"Perhaps it loves you," says the Unicorn.

Moon has a glimpse of fur—a flank, a soft spine. He wants to touch something, but he can't because he has no fingers with which to touch. "My body?" he repeats, not understanding.

"I do not know," continues the Unicorn. "I left mine long ago. But lately I have been like someone else's body. I have carried her. I have felt her hunger and her thirst when she could not feel it. I have made her come alive. As her body, I have come to love her."

Moon follows the spire of the Unicorn's horn with his listening, round and round and into the blue and lavender ethers. He is fascinated by her words. He wants, with his soul, to move in the direction she is going, whatever that is.

"Who did you say you were looking for?" he asks.

"I am looking for my father," she answers. "And I am looking for you. I am looking for the man who desires the River, and wants to conquer her. I am looking for every man who denies himself, who fears his own heart, who destroys what he loves because he is lost from himself. I am looking for him, as he looks for himself—as once he looked inside me, to find himself."

Moon nods. He understands, more or less.

"Do you know a boy named Sky?" she asks.

Moon shakes his head.

"I thought you might know him," says the Unicorn, and he can see her eyes, which remind him of Delilah's, "because you are a rain god. You come from the sky."

"But I haven't seen the sky for so long," answers Moon, and as he says it he feels that it is true. He no longer lives there. Maybe he left to escape his father's fury. Or maybe his own hopelessness pursued him, after his father denied him and refused to give him the rains. Maybe he left to escape himself, or the role he was supposed to play, a role he didn't believe in any more—even if his father would let him—because no one on the earth believed in it, and it no longer seemed like his gift to give. But for whatever reason, he left the sky behind long ago.

"If you see him," says the Unicorn, ignoring his denial, "tell him a Unicorn is looking for him. Tell him I request his presence in a dream."

Then the Unicorn, from wherever she is in that music, bends into him, pours her horn into his heart. He feels it pouring into every molecule of his soul, as if that soul stood there in the wind with her in the same form as his body—that same perfect, star-shaped human form, with its wild legs and its waving arms and its shining head. He feels parts of his body that he didn't remember were there, as the numbness of forgetting sifts out of them like dust. He is filled with joy, as if joy is nothing more than that pure hope of the flesh: that hope he was born with, that each person's body emerges into the world with, when it still believes it can do anything.

"In you there is rain," says the Unicorn. "It is like new life inside you, untainted by anything on the earth. It is a fresh start. And if you can get up into the sky, you can send it down. Start giving people love instead of trying to take away their pain. That's the job of rain. It's the part of the water cycle that gives. Don't you remember?"

Moon stands there on nothing, his soul smiling foolishly.

"Go and find your body," the Unicorn says in a fading voice, "and tell it what I told you, before you forget."

Moon wakes instantly. His limbs rush inside themselves and his toes are tingling and his penis stands erect and happy. He had no idea he and his body were so closely connected. He lifts his fingers before his eyes and stares at them. He misses his flute. Where did he leave it?

"I love you," he tells his body. That seems like the main point of what the Unicorn was saying. When he says it he remembers something: another time when he felt like this, when he felt alive again—really alive, like the whole universe manifested through his being. It was when he traveled with that girl through the rainbow.

He remembers how she stood to meet him at the waterfall, how she took his music inside her. How she stood and came toward him, her heart like a sky. How his little kiss transformed her. How such little love as he could offer filled her with hope. It was she who carried him through the rainbow, on the lightness of her wings, though she thought it was the other way around.

He needs to be that light again now. He needs to be up in the sky, if he is ever to let the rain down—which right now, for the first time, feels possible again. How water shimmers in the air, how gifted and excited it is to carry every color in the world in its prism! And what music—what music it makes. He can almost remember what that's like.

But how does water reach the sky? This he cannot remember. *How does it rise?*

A flame lights the darkness. For a split second it is the original flame—the flame in the Unicorn's eyes, the flame he remembers from too long ago to remember, the first flame that humans ever invented, and the surprise of that new world exploding into being in the once-eternal blackness of some deep, lost cave.

Then he remembers where he is. A room somewhere. The dull mask of a passionless face leers toward him in the dim light, and smoke makes him cough. He smells chemicals, old clothes, rotting food. A human hand reaches toward him in the dark. But he sees Delilah's eyes, from somewhere far away, and her sadness for him. Why has he never allowed her to truly reach him? Why has he kept himself away from the scorching truth of her love?

"Fire," he says out loud. That's how water gets into the sky.

He stands, shaking himself like a dog in the cold room, and makes his aching way to the door. He has to get back to her. Back to his own dear sun, Lil, who will finally dissolve him back into the heavens.

A fire burns constantly behind the grate, and Lonely stays by it as much as she can. She doesn't go outside if she can help it. The sorrow of her long journey down the mountain endlessly chills her, and it seems that all she wants, all the time, is to be warm. Hunger, too, makes her cold, for though there is food, there is never quite enough of it.

It seems clear that Kite's bed will remain empty—not to be used by her—as if its very emptiness might bring him back. Lonely doesn't mind sleeping downstairs, though. Most of the time she only wants to be alone. Eva's presence is so light, so clean, that it barely disturbs her. She has to concentrate to hear the old woman's breathing, as she herself sits awake through most of the night, mesmerized by the flames.

During the day Lonely tucks herself away wherever Fawn is not. If Fawn is working outdoors or in the greenhouse, Lonely huddles by the fire, imagining herself invisible in the shadows. If Fawn is working in the kitchen, Lonely curls up in the greenhouse swing, closing her eyes and listening to the sweet talk of plants in sunlight who think it's still summer, until she falls asleep.

Indoors is different in the winter. In summer, the inside of the house was a brief space of repose, where the ongoing thrills of the outdoors were concentrated and savored within the live circle of family. But in winter, most of life happens within this single room. The house breathes slowly, hibernating but conscious. Upstairs in the morning, the secret family—the family whose deepest intimacy is hidden from Lonely, and which she envies above all else, even in its sorrow, even with its wound, even with the hole that Kite left because even that hole implies with its pain how much love holds them together—all wake beside each other. The scent of their bodies is thick in the air. Lonely is always awake already, though she doesn't want to be, while Eva keeps breathing deeply and Chelya tiptoes down the stairs. Sometimes she can hear Rye and Fawn, still up above in what she imagines to be the coziest of winter beds—the bed on which Fawn once made love to her. But their voices are always tense.

"Of course," Rye told Lonely right away when he came home that first day, "you can stay as long as you need." But he sounded tired, and that morning Lonely had woken to the sounds of him and Fawn arguing—she'd never heard them yell before—and Chelya had stood crying at the edge of the room, her hands over her mouth. Lonely had gone to her and put her arm around the girl, moved out of her own self-pity by tenderness. But though Chelya did not move away from Lonely's touch, she did not seem to feel it either. Her body kept shaking with heartbroken cries, and Lonely knew again that she herself was not a part of this family—and that the ties of family hold stronger than any ties of friendship, or any laughter spent together in times long past.

Rye had found Kite. There was little doubt that he would; he was such an experienced tracker that he knew the pathways, kinships, and life stories of over half the animals in the forest. The forest didn't need to speak to him to tell him who had traveled where, and when. But before he came upon Kite, Kite had turned back and confronted him.

"Stop following me," he'd said softly, emerging from the pines.

And whatever Rye had said in the long night after that, sitting across a fire in the black forest with his only son, had not mattered. Kite had gone on anyway, and Rye had returned with his arms limp at his sides, immobile as Fawn shook him with her small hands.

"He's almost as skilled a hunter as I am," Rye told Fawn. "He'll survive."

"You don't care," Fawn growled. "You don't care what happens to him. He's only fifteen."

"Fawn," Rye said. "I'm only trying to comfort you."

"I don't need to be comforted!" she cried. "I need my son." Then her body seemed to break, as if all her bones, all this time, had been made only of this one love. "I need him," she sobbed, her face in her hands, doubled over at the waist, rocking forward and back. "I need him."

Eva came to her and took her in her arms, guided her like a child to the fire, and sat her down. Fawn buried her head in her mother's thin chest and Rye stood there, looking more alone than Lonely had ever seen him.

There is loneliness in this family, too, she thought, and she saw that it had been there even before Kite left.

"You could have gone with him," Fawn whimpered.

"And leave you?" Rye said.

She didn't answer, and after a moment Rye shouted, the pain in his voice shocking Lonely. "Do you want me to, then? Do you want me to leave you here alone for the winter? Shall I go now, and find him again, though he doesn't want me, and follow him? Should I?" Silence. "*Should I, Fawn?*" He was yelling, but Fawn only cried harder, shaking her head, her body bouncing heavily with her sighs, as if a brutal horse rode heavy and hard beneath her, without caring for the safety of its rider.

These conversations continued, indoors and outdoors, for days. Fawn saying, "Why couldn't you make him come home? You're his father!" And Rye yelling. Rye saying, "If you didn't make it so forbidden, he wouldn't be so desperate for it, Fawn. If you didn't try to rule him with your fear, if you didn't tell him he could never go——" And Fawn yelling again. Even Fawn.

Then there was silence all over the house, in which love floundered and struggled, alone and afraid, and anger paced restlessly, and pain was the only thing that anybody heard.

On that first day, Eva explained winter to Lonely. How life hides in darkness. How the surface parts of life die, and the deep inner heart of life becomes still. How night rules. How the body sleeps, and the mind wanders curious and alone in the darkness in search of the soul.

Lonely wants only to rest. She knows she should help out more and earn her keep. Part of her wants to help. And sometimes Chelya gives her tasks. But most things she could think of to do in the house would place her in the way of Fawn. Whatever is happening inside Fawn in Kite's absence is terrifying to Lonely. Whenever she looks at Fawn's face, she feels like she can't breathe. Fawn does not speak to her. It's like in the beginning, when Lonely first came here from the tower.

The place that once rescued Lonely—her only home in the world—does not feel like a home now. Fawn acts as if she doesn't exist. Rye is out all the time, staying away from Fawn. Eva speaks to Lonely sometimes at night, after the others have gone to bed, but often she falls asleep early, cranky with the pain in her bones. She's different in winter from how Lonely knew her in summer. Suddenly being old seems to Lonely not like wisdom and power after all, but like a constant, defeated falling.

And Chelya is often away from home, with her new love.

"Who is he?" Lonely asks her one afternoon, when Chelya is cooking dinner to make up to her mother for being gone so much. "Why doesn't he come here?" She is desperately curious in spite of the pain it brings her, or perhaps because of it, as if the pain knows something she doesn't, and yearns to bring her deeper into itself. How much can she bear to hear of Chelya's love and its happiness—a love that began in the flesh before her own did, and continues long after?

"He's a tree spirit," says Chelya. "An oak." Her voice sounds older now, less jubilant, more even. *Why is it,* thinks Lonely, *that being older means expanding to contain more sorrow? Why is that wiser? Why is that better?*

There is fish tonight, and kale. The grains are all gone. So many crops were ruined last summer by the heavy rains. Lonely doesn't understand the significance of the world's changes in weather. She doesn't have any sense of the pattern that came before, for however many thousands or millions of years. To her the weather is the moods of the earth, like her own. Unpredictable.

Chelya opens a mixture of onions and fruit that they canned in the summer. "He can't come," she adds. "He can't leave the grove where he lives, though he can move within it.

"But—" Lonely begins, confused. "What will you do, then?"

Chelya smiles at her. "I can visit him there. We're happy there together, and it's better because we can be there in secret without my mother knowing. It's the most magical place in the world. We dance in the moonlight. We pray in the morning. We talk about the world, and we dream together. You know."

"What do you talk about?" asks Lonely. She wonders if they can kiss, if they can make love. She remembers the spirits of the trees who danced with her at the great fire last summer, how she could feel their breath and the brush of their leafy arms—how that touch tickled and tantalized her, how gentle it felt. She supposes this spirit of Chelya's can love her with a purer love than a human being can ever know. She imagines his devotion, his eager awaiting for Chelya's arrival. Rooted to his one sacred place in the earth, never to leave it, never to yearn for anywhere else, never to fly away, he will always be there waiting for Chelya—and she will never have to wonder where he is.

"We talk about—I don't know, everything. The earth, and how it's changing. The other creatures and plants of the forest, and all the stories he knows and learns from the wind and the water that runs through him. He's very wise. We talk about my mother and father. And the things Grandmother says. And Kite—"

"Do you think he's going to be okay?" Lonely interrupts. She's been wanting to ask. She thinks of Kite often, if only because it is impossible not to, in this house. The agonized question of his absence hangs inside every interaction, lurks in every familiar place and behind each person's eyes. Yet Lonely has felt that she could never mention him, or something or someone will explode.

"Yes," says Chelya without hesitating. "I think he'll be okay."

"Why?"

Chelya shrugs. "Because he knows what he's doing. He's smart and he doesn't get carried away by things like me or my mother. He thinks everything out. I know he's been thinking this out for a long time."

"He told you?"

"No. He wouldn't have told me because he wouldn't want me to get in trouble, after he was gone. He thinks of everything and he wouldn't want anyone to get hurt more than they have to. My brother has a really good, big heart. He just doesn't always say what he's feeling. Anyway, he talks to me in my dreams sometimes. I know he's okay. And I think when he gets to the desert...."

"What?"

Chelya shrugs again. "I don't know. I think someone will help him. That's the feeling I get."

Lonely had never thought about the love between a brother and a sister. She had only seen Chelya tease Kite, and Kite scowl and bite back. But now Chelya talks of love. She talks of her brother's heart—a heart Lonely never dared imagine, he kept it so secret—as if knowing it is as easy for Chelya as knowing the timbers that frame the house's walls. *How sweet*, thinks Lonely, *to have a brother. To love a boy so easily and to be so easily loved, to belong always to each other even without words, even when you are far away, because you are family.* Not knowing what else to say, she stands up to help Chelya. She places the biggest pot on the fire and begins to fill it with water from the basin to boil for washing dishes. She feels Chelya's easy, human movement near her, and remembers the kitchen again as the space of Fawn's movements, Fawn's quiet, careful expression. Then the longing for that modest, self-contained peace beside her, for the dark silhouette of that head bent attentively near her own, for that flicker of curious hunger that linked them through a mystery of untraversed wilderness between their bodies—Lonely feels that longing suddenly with such force it turns her stomach over. That was friendship. It came once, and never again. More innocent than romantic love, and easier, it slept beside her loyally every night while she dreamed and dreamed of a love who was already leaving her, completely taking that comfort for granted.

"What happened to you?" asks Chelya, her voice uneasy with its own knowing, like the way she looked at Lonely the night Lonely wouldn't tell her where she was going but left as if she would leave forever. "You came back."

Lonely shakes her head. She wants to tell Chelya everything, but she doesn't know how to explain her return. The thought of it only emphasizes her failure.

"You didn't find your love?"

"No," Lonely says, her voice tight. "I did. I did find him." Her words feel too big for her throat. She shuts her eyes for a moment.

"Then what happened?"

"I don't know if I can explain." But that's not it. She feels that Chelya is the only one who might understand. Maybe she doesn't want to know what Chelya will say. Maybe she's too proud to find out that this young girl knows more about love than she does. Because Chelya is loved. Because she has always been loved. Because she breathes love every day, without ever having to think about it.

Chelya is silent for a moment, and Lonely is afraid she has angered her. She never wants to be in Chelya's disfavor. It would be the last thing she could bear—like losing the love of the sun, which should belong to everyone, and which no one has to earn.

"What happened to the dress?" Chelya asks more gently.

Lonely looks down "I can't wear it any more."

"Why not? Aren't you still you?"

Lonely wants to laugh at the innocence of the question. She wants to throw her arms around Chelya. She wants Chelya to grab her hand and gallop off with her into summer fields, but those fields are frozen over now, and Chelya's free spirit is linked now to another. Instead she says, "Chelya, why is your mother angry with me? What do I have to do with Kite's leaving?"

She expects Chelya to tell her it isn't that—that Fawn acts crazy lately, crazed by grief, unpredictable. She expects her to dismiss the question. She wants her to. But Chelya shakes her head and says, "I don't know. You know more than I do, I think. Something happened between you the night you left. I could tell by her mood the next morning. She never spoke your name again."

Lonely shivers. For a long time, the contemplative grumble and crackle of the fire is the only sound. She feels the canyon of Fawn's loss for the first time, as if a trap door opened beneath her feet. It seems only another expression of the same loneliness: the absence of Sky, the absence of Fawn all part of the same, their sorrow like water that flows through her the same way over and over, carving a channel that began with her father's death, and is carved ever deeper by every successive loss.

$$\mathbb{)}$$

When Yora calls to Delilah in a dream, she wakes immediately, slings her backpack over one shoulder, and walks across the glowing sand in her broken sneakers toward the sound of water. It's already dark.

She hasn't seen the sun for more days than she can count. But there is no one to tell her that her face looks gaunt and pale.

I wanted to say goodbye, says Yora, who is nothing but the river now.

Delilah nods. She feels calm inside. She takes a handful of water and splashes her face, even though she is shivering with the cold. A little sunshine wouldn't hurt, perhaps. She's wearing most of the clothing she has, layered on top of each other, and sometimes, in moments of weakness, she wants to call out to Dragon to come make her a fire she doesn't have to work for. But she doesn't know where he is these days, and she doesn't want to think about him. The thought of him fills her with something like shame.

"Back to the ocean?" she asks Yora.

I have to.

"It was so painful for you there."

No. No pain—I just let go.

Delilah says nothing. But she knows. She, too, has lost much of the pain she used to carry. Her neck doesn't hurt. Her spine is like a waterfall, sometimes, when she wakes up. It almost frightens her, how easily she moves. There is something empty about that movement.

I cannot be a ghost any more, hovering outside myself, Yora continues. *This is my story. I go to the Sea. I come out of the Sea and I return home. It is better than being homeless, being no one. It is better than being lost from myself. If I do not remember the story of the water, no one ever will.*

Delilah traces the patterns of the moving water with her fingers, feeling them break and change with her touch.

The Unicorn came to me, adds Yora. *She helped me. I am stronger now.*

Delilah lifts her head and looks around. "The Unicorn was here?"

She is returning, too. But I do not think she realizes it.

"I'm coming with you," says Delilah, dreamily, as if she is only comment-ing on some small, sweet wonder, a desert flower she's noticed in passing.

She doesn't hear anything from the river, so she adds, "You don't have to take care of me. I've been planning this for a while."

I cannot carry you. I am still sick.

"No. I'm going to carry you. I already carry you, Yora. I carry you in my blood, in my body, like I carry every creature I've ever taken into me, and every man who's ever entered me. That's the power of being human, remember? We carry the river inside us. We carry all of life inside us. You taught me that."

Yes, but I will not speak to you any more, like this, Yora warns. *I am only the river.*

"I know. But I still hear you. I listen to you day and night. I listen to my own body. I listen to you inside my own body, Yora. Do you hear me?" She's never spoken such things before. She would never say such things to anyone else.

The river just roars and whispers, continuing.

Delilah begins walking beside it, not looking back.

"Lonely," says Eva from the doorway, over the dry winter sound of the stream. Lonely doesn't turn her head. The greenhouse has a chill in it, and is already dark in the late afternoon, but she hasn't moved for hours. She is watching the sky. She could watch it forever. Every mood, every way it changes—the shifting kingdoms of its clouds, the fur and feathers of them, the ridged golden edges—reminds her of her lover.

Chelya said it might snow. Lonely keeps wondering about that, watching the grey hardening of the clouds now and their intimate, untouchable join-ing. She is hungry for snow, remembering that cold joy on her skin that told her she lived in his world, and that he might be near—somewhere—and every animal, every tree, knew him. But she hasn't gone outside since she arrived. She can't bear to look at that white peak that takes up the whole eastern distance—that was once her whole future, her whole hope. She can hardly believe it's still there, just as distant as it used to be, as if her whole journey meant nothing.

She feels lost, even while contained inside the tiny house. She misses her horse—the Unicorn—that, outside in the fields every day, once anchored her to the reality of her life. The Unicorn knew where they were headed, and why, even when Lonely forgot.

"Enough feeling sorry for yourself," says Eva to her now. "Enough waiting to be rescued. We need your help around here."

Lonely feels a vague fury rising in her throat, a sure rebellion—*you don't understand!*—but it gets tired by the time it reaches her lips. Weary with herself, she stands somehow and turns, walks obediently toward Eva and past her into the house. She knows Eva is right. Somewhere inside herself that she can't fully feel, she is aware of the burden she adds to the household. Fawn is so emptied by despair that she spends almost all her time somewhere out in the forest, and even when she's in the house, she is not really present. She sits in her chair and rocks, staring out the window, or she lies in her bed. Lonely feels guilty when she sees this, as if it's her own fault. She feels guilty for being here, for being useless, and the heaviness of her own sense of failure makes it even more difficult for her to be useful.

But as she brings in an armful of wood and begins placing the logs, with a natural intuition for air and space, on the fire, Eva's voice softens.

"All right, child, tell me. I know you came here seeking wisdom. What is it you want to know? Or do you have a story you need to tell first?"

Lonely, struck dumb, sits back and considers the flames.

"But only if you help," says Eva. "Pour the water from that pot into the basin. If you wash the sheets, I can start dinner." Chelya is out cutting ivy branches to bring to the goats, and repairing a hole in their fencing. Rye is out listening to the trees, asking for a message—for news of his son's safe passage. When Lonely first arrived, there was a tightness to the family in the wake of Kite's loss: everyone keeping close to the kitchen fire, Chelya nervously looking for ways to help her mother. Now it seems like everyone disperses in the morning as quickly as they can. The house is too small for five people anyway, Lonely feels, and with the added presence of such pain and anxiety, there is barely any room for the people at all. Still, the house smells of them even in their absence. In winter, they bathe more rarely. It takes hours to boil enough water to heat a tub, and they take turns in the same water. Sometimes Lonely can even smell herself. It frightens her almost, this smell, like something calling to her that she'd rather not remember.

She lifts the pot and pours the water.

"I found him," she says simply.

Eva nods. "And then you lost him."

"Yes."

Then she tells Eva everything. The journey up the mountain. The dress Chelya made, the Unicorn at the waterfall, the dream she woke in. The lake at the top of the world, the nights in the clouds, the dreams he left her for, the white birds. Flying. Crying together. The meadow she made bloom for him, the Council of Beings and the loneliness of a single perfect human being who would never return to the earth. Making love, and the long fall, and the Unicorn again, and the heartless colors of autumn. Every word she speaks frustrates her. Every word spoken belies the hugeness of her emotion, the shadowy romance of her memory, with its music-less simplicity. Eva's reaction, calm and unsurprised, doesn't help.

"And now I've failed, after all," Lonely says finally. "She's going to bring me back to the island. And I'll be a prisoner there forever." She bites her lip to keep from crying.

"Don't be ridiculous," says Eva, and Lonely looks up from the wet sheets she's squeezing furiously in her fists, shocked. "It's still your life, after all."

"Maybe I don't want it," Lonely says dully, looking down.

Eva snorts and shakes her head. "Lonely, we are earth people. We know and believe in our lives right here, right now. This house, this earth, this family is everything to me. This is what is real to me, and all I can give you—"

"You don't believe me!" Lonely cries. "You think it was all a dream."

Eva shakes her head again. "You're only naming your own fear. I'm saying that you must begin where you are, right now. Where are you? You don't even know."

Lonely punches the sheet into the water, balls it up, presses it back in and punches it again. Her hands are red.

"I'm sorry," says Eva, but her voice—again—sounds more irritable and cold than the voice of comfort and wisdom Lonely remembers from her journey up the mountain long ago. "I know you want answers, and I can't give them to you. But you're hiding out in your sorrow. You're taking the easy way out."

"It is *not* easy."

"Lonely, you haven't even begun. Actually drink from that bitter stuff inside your heart and you'll see. Follow that sorrow and you'll see. Go out into the winter and see what it feels like! See if you can love him even after you've lost him—love him here and now, in this life. What does it mean to love, Lonely? Forget this old woman who has told you to bring back proof of some illusory thing. I tell you, she is leading you astray with her own mistakes. The point is to prove if *you* can love. That's all that matters. That's what makes you real."

Lonely stares at her. She remembers the doe in the fields of winter, and her gentle endurance. She feels held by some familiar warmth that floats around her, something she's always felt, perhaps, when she's paid attention: something she felt in the first meadows of her journey, and in the tower and in the sea and on the earth and in the sky—everywhere. Yet it is so vague . . .

She keeps staring at Eva, but Eva keeps chopping vegetables, not bothering to look up.

Dragon can see Delilah's lover haunting her empty cave. Or the boy she said was not her lover, but he doesn't know if he should believe her.

Dragon has never seen another man, and he's suspicious. He watches Moon's arms, his legs, his swift torso, his silence. He doesn't trust the boy's brooding face. He doesn't trust the careless darkness that swings in those muscles. He doesn't trust the emotions of the boy which, unlike Delilah's, remain unseen.

For days, Dragon hides and watches from among the pink-gold archways of stone, those same archways under which he once fell to his knees before the mystery of Delilah. He doesn't want Moon to see him until he is strong again. For he can see that this boy is a god.

Sometimes, lately, Dragon thinks that he has never really known himself. Rising up in the Garden, tearing down the mountainside, stumbling through the desert, clinging to Yora, crying out in boiling caves—he never knew what he was. Now he has been consumed. He has been devoured by the very woman he trusted, the very woman to whom he sought to give his soul. She has emptied him out; she has almost destroyed him. He feels weak, his bones clanking inside his human body, his flesh wasting away as if with hunger. He has stayed near the river, a slave to it now, always thirsty since he took that first, fateful drink.

At first Yora was a relief to him. He braved her turmoil and she drew him in, and finally she swept over him and took him, welcomed and laid to rest his fire just as he had always wished her to do. There was such peace then. Or was there? Was it peace, or only a dry desert inside, which began as emptiness but ended in terror—his fire spent and sucked out of him, his selfhood lost? He could not feel himself. He woke alone, and the fire rushed upon him all over again, filling that vacuum of space, and he was more desperate for her than he'd ever been.

He wants to kill the Unicorn that he saw thrusting its brazen horn inside the river—blinding him with its light as if whatever passed there was not meant for him to see. Ever since the Unicorn walked out of the absence of moonlight, out of the winter darkness—while in that stricken silence Dragon lay on the sand, too weak to move—and stepped past him, ignoring him, unafraid of him, and sunk its horn into the river, he can no longer feel Yora's presence. He seeks her in the river. He seeks her everywhere. But she is gone.

Only when he sees Moon, the boy god, shimmering in and out of his consciousness like a rainbow around the immobile, wordless blackness of Delilah's cave, does Dragon remember Delilah again, and realize that she, too, is gone. They are all gone. The first Yora and the second, and Delilah, his first love. Just as the three mothers—human, beast, and goddess—abandoned him, one by one.

The landscape inside him feels so dry now that the fire catches on nothing, and burns hotter the longer he focuses upon it. The boy called Moon hovers in the air outside Delilah's cave, going in, going out, and then holding still like the morning fog in the deep thickets of Dragon's youth, untouched by the sun.

Dragon steps into the light. He tries to feel the way the sun makes him glow, makes him mighty. But it makes him nauseous. He coughs a flame at Moon, steps forward, curls his fists in and out—but each time he closes them, they close on emptiness.

"I know who you are," he tells the boy, and he makes his voice blank and hard.

Moon turns slowly, his form solidifying a little. He floats down to the ground to face Dragon, and this gesture of politeness irritates Dragon terribly, like pity. He feels the grey peace inside the boy. He feels the subtle apathy of his thoughts, impossible to know, and the strength of his secret patience. He hates him for these things.

"I know you," he growls again, unsure of himself, impatient for a response.

"I don't think so," says Moon, and his words betray only a cool, thoughtful consideration, but Dragon can hear the unspoken challenge. Dragon is nearly jubilant in his fury now, the fire tumbling out of him in fast-peeling petals of flame. This boy is a water god. Dragon realizes this and is stunned. He is drawn to the boy as if his very life longs for its own death.

"*Where is Yora?*" he roars. And that name includes all of them. It is all the same loss and the same deception.

"*Where is she??*" He flames toward Moon. "*You are only a little boy, you are a girl, you are nothing. You are nothing. I will destroy you.*"

He cannot see the boy's face. In his fury he is already crushing the watery form of him in his own skull, and the waves of his own heat blur Moon's image. But he expects the boy to deny his accusations. He expects him to say he doesn't know where the woman is—that he has not taken her, that he is not keeping her secret. Just like Delilah denied it. He expects this and waits for it with an inexplicable anxiety. When he receives no answer, he keeps yelling, just to drown out the frantic suspicion that what stands before him is nothing but a mirage.

"Don't tell me you don't know where she is, you coward. You—don't tell me you only love boys. I don't believe it. I don't believe it!"

Then he feels the first blow. The glory, the relief, the instant redemption of that first hard fist against his madman's faceless face! He had no idea that it was possible. He had no idea that this little water god could hit him. But now all faces, all words, all thoughts fall away and there is only the tumult of flesh and pain over his body, and his own body reacting, transforming with the boy's punches and punching him back. The boy's skull in his hands, the boy's knuckles in his ribs, the boy's bones meeting his bones as if the flesh around them were inconsequential and always had been.

All the lovemaking—the surrender of falling into Delilah, the sweet friction of the first Yora's virgin skin, the luscious pleasure of the goddesses who came down to his cave, and the melting relief of the second Yora's ancient wave—was all so precious, so needed, so wildly good. Yet nothing in his whole life has ever made him feel more alive and more real than the simple, unfeeling violence of his body interlocked with the body of another man. He throws his fist into that body and it does not get devoured, does not surrender, does not lose itself in the mystery, but rather bounces right back off the hardness of resistance—the other man just as angry, just as sure.

Now, for the first time, anger is real. He knows what it is. He knows its language and the taste of that language in his mouth, metallic and red and striped with gritty darkness.

They fight all day, and all night, and all through the next day.

Finally, Dragon, in a roar of frustration at seeing his flames die and die again in Moon's cold embrace, opens his mouth and bites down. He feels the flesh of Moon's shoulder come apart in his teeth. He hears Moon's uncensored, un-silent scream—like the most primal pain of manhood, like the first question, the first injustice, that high, gut-risen cry. He lets go.

Moon stands and gushes blood. Dragon did not know a god could be wounded in this way, and he feels at once proud and envious. He wants something he cannot name. He wants to say something to the boy but has no words for it. The feeling pulls up his chest, beautiful and broken. He wants to give the boy something.

For the first time in his life, he wonders who his father was. And as soon as he thinks it, he wants to know so badly it makes his knees shake.

"You win," says Moon simply, and then he begins to dissolve into vapor, and then he is gone.

But in that last moment before he disappears, Dragon sees Moon's face clearly. He sees the anger, still there, still fully alive. He sees the red fire born within Moon's watery depths: that very first rebellion, that very first *No.*

Dragon remembers it from his own birth: he remembers, even before the scream he screamed in the cave of the dragons, his first scream upon exiting the womb, his very first fury against life.

No, say Moon's eyes, with an anger so hot it is cold, an anger so deep it dissolves him before Dragon's eyes. And when Dragon, suddenly silent and exhausted again, reaches into the place where it seemed Moon stood, he finds only the faintest impression of coolness there in the sand under his hands, as if the circumference of a person standing—not much bigger than a heart—was shadowed for just long enough to lower its temperature by one, maybe two degrees. But in the time it takes him to realize for sure that Moon is gone, the sand is hot again.

He understands that Moon wanted him to wound him. He came here for that. He needed to feel that—he needed so badly to feel something, to know he was real.

Dragon understands, because he needed that, too.

Kite has always loved the winter.

He loves the cold. He loves the quiet elegance of it, its tactful calm, its thoughtful steadiness. He loves even the clench of cold around his skull, like a helmet, and the way it crawls over the skin of his head, pressing at the pressure points of his mind.

He is happy to be walking through the mountains when the first snow falls, because he knows he'll miss that in the desert and in the City where no rain or snow ever touches. When the flakes begin to fall, he lifts his face into the silence and lets each one imprint his face with the careful importance of its design. He closes his eyes and sees visions of things he's never seen—creatures that haven't evolved yet and the vague thrust of human minds toward the future for the sake of the future itself, whatever it is. In winter, the world dreams up what it will be, or what it could be, or what it never was, or what it could have been. Kite loves the possibility inside this silence. He feels the trees ache with its poignant weight. He feels the wise thoughts of the earth and loves the mystery of them—that bigness too big to understand. That freedom of the unknown.

He turns back to the rabbit runs, searching for where they converge. It takes a long time to travel when he has to stop so often to hunt for food. He crouches with his slingshot and decides to wait. As the snow thickens, the rabbits will begin to move toward their burrows. He's not far from where he left his pack, where he plans to make a fire and camp for the night. It might be the coldest night yet, and it scares him a little, but he planned on being scared sometimes, so he figures he can handle it.

Kite has been planning this journey for so long that he can't remember when he started. He was planning it long before he finally decided to do it—long before he felt himself old enough, strong enough, ready enough to do it. The City has fascinated him for as long as he can remember. There is knowledge there that will make their lives easier. There is knowledge there that will bring light and security and warmth, and it will make that nameless, floating anxiety that his mother feels—that she makes everybody feel—go away.

He left at the end of autumn. It was that summer when he finally decided for sure. It was, in fact, that night he stood close to Lonely in the basement. She had leaned toward him, her body smelling of the sun. She was the mystery of all that he had yet to discover: all the excitement of other people, other powers, other lives out there that he'd been forbidden. His mother was afraid of her. Kite was afraid of her, too, but something about her eyes that night, and her questions, and her hesitant hand on the pages of his book, and the quickened, fervent smell of her nearness, made it so that the life he knew could never fully satisfy him again. He felt that he had to act on his dreams immediately.

So he decided then, but he waited until his family didn't need him as much. He waited through all the summer and fall harvesting. He was trembling on that last day they gathered the hay, as they closed up the barn, as they brought in the horses, trembling at the nearness of his journey and at the guilt of not telling them. But he never doubted his decision.

While he's waiting for the rabbits now, he tries to stay focused on the sounds of the night and the presence of things coming and going. But he thinks, too, of where he is going, and the great mystery of what he hopes to find. He shrugs his shoulders, which ache a little from the weight of his pack. He couldn't resist bringing one book with him—the one about solar and wind energy. He is fascinated with the idea of energy. What is it? What part of him can feel it? Sometimes he searches the air with his own aliveness, trying to sense its presence. He knows that the life of the animal passes into him and gives his own life when he eats it, but what is that? It is not the animal's spirit, which leaves it before he takes its body into his own. It is something contained within the cells of life itself, even after it seems dead. And how is it that the wind, too, can be made into life, and the light of the sun can be eaten by the trees? How is it that these things, too, can make a house alive, can make it live and breathe and light up like an animal?

Nothing excites Kite more than this: this raw, absolute power which cannot be seen or sensed in any way, yet is more real than spirit, more lasting than life.

The night shrinks colder, and he sees no sign of the rabbits, but he smiles to himself in the twilight.

Back on the mountaintop where Lonely first recognized her, the Unicorn studies the shapes of the clouds for many days. Every shape of cloud is new and random, completely unrelated to any shape that came before it. The clouds have no system, no theory, no future. Watching them is the easiest way she knows to forget the past.

Everything on the mountaintop is frozen now. The grasses are frozen so the wind cannot turn them. The stream is frozen in mid-thought. The highest mountain, above her, where she sent Lonely once in a dream, is as frozen as it ever was. The ring of wetness around the waterfall is frozen, like a gleaming mouth. The broken chrysalis of the butterfly is frozen, and the butterfly is dead.

The Unicorn doesn't sleep or eat. Her only need is to watch the clouds, her body hidden, waiting. Finally, one day when the clouds have lost their design and amassed into a pregnant grey ceiling, and the snow begins to fall with lacy, anticlimactic slowness, a crow lands on her back.

She turns her head so that she can see him, because she can barely feel his weight. There is pride in his upright stance, his full chest, his glass eyes. But his claws on her bare back are gentle. She senses his respect. When she shivers, he doesn't let go; he rides her shiver like water, and remains standing firm when she settles.

She turns away from the clouds and walks. She walks fast—and then she trots—and then she runs. Then she slows, circling the waterfall, her white hooves sure like little picks in the ice. The crow remains.

He stays all day and all night. The Unicorn doesn't look at him again but she feels his presence, his spirit bursting with air, his body intensely calm, his mind as patient as the desert. He frightens her. He haunts her like a shadow that rides above her body instead of below. His darkness, his undeterred stare, imply to her some curse she has tried to forget, some inevitable distress.

"What do you want?" she asks finally, in the morning as the sun advances behind them. It seems ridiculous to her that this bird should ride her. He, a creature whom the sky itself can carry, sits down here on the back of someone who stumbles over the earth on four legs. He must want something then. Everyone does. But she cannot imagine what she could give him.

"You asked me to come," says the crow, bowing. "Don't you remember? I came, and now I ask a favor of you." It is apparent to her from the readiness of his answer that all this time he was only waiting, out of respect, for her to speak first. In her heart, she trusts him. But it is not in her nature to come out of hiding. She would like to help him, but cannot imagine how to do this without risk to herself.

Yet it is true what he says. She did call him.

She turns in place, as if she could come closer to him by turning, but of course she cannot, because he is attached to her. It occurs to her that he, like herself, does not wish to be looked upon directly.

"I want you to take me to the other side of the world," says the crow. "If you will do this for me, I will do anything you ask. I will give you anything. I will give you my soul if you ask it."

"What would I do with your soul?" asks the Unicorn.

The crow bows again, as if it is nothing. "Whatever you see fit."

The Unicorn looks toward the white mountain. It's still there. It didn't crumble or fade into memory when the people who thought it existed for them lost their dream of what it was. It is there—right there—for anyone. "Just go," she whispers. "Why can't you just go? You can fly. What do you need me for?"

"I cannot get there on my own. If I could, I would have gone long ago. But I am too much of this earth. I am too much attached, after all, to what I love, what I want, what I am. My—my memories."

The Unicorn shakes her mane. She can hear the breathlessness in his voice, the human mind rushing faster than wings into hope. Already, she is crying with pity for him. She turns away so he won't see. This is how they claim her. This is the way they always claim her. It isn't fair.

"I would have gone a long time ago," he repeats, "but I've never seen a Unicorn before. Only a Unicorn can see beyond the realities we believe in. Only a Unicorn can cross between worlds. Not only between the sea and the land, or the earth and the sky—but to the Other World. Did you not know this?"

"I knew," says the Unicorn bleakly. His words are so familiar. *Only you, Mia; only you can comfort me.* She stares at the mountain which hides the Other World from this one—obliterates all thought or idea of another world with the dazzling dream of itself. One sees only the mountain, and is so desperate with the idea of reaching the top, one never wonders at the possibility of anything beyond it.

"But you don't want to go," the crow observes.

No. It does not matter which world. They are all the same. One sees only what he wants to see, no matter where he goes. "You told her it was the same world," she says, angry now, "on the other side of the mountain. The same, you said, over and over again."

"I lied," says the crow.

Suddenly she knows why he has taken the form of a crow. It is only the most appropriate and safest clothing for the journey he wishes to make, and for the place that they will find there.

She considers. She made a promise, after all, to a woman. A woman who still knew how to love, without being destroyed. She wants to believe in that woman: in Lonely.

"If I take you there," she says, "however far into that world you wish to go, I want you to make me a promise."

"Anything."

"When you get there, you will know what you have to do. You will know where your heart calls you. And I want you to go there, where your heart is."

The crow is silent.

"I know who you are," she adds, by way of explanation.

When the crow finally responds, it is the only time the Unicorn will ever hear his human voice. It has nothing to do with the pride and politeness of the bird. It is weary and desolate, as brittle as autumn leaves crushed on pavement. It is so frightened, like the bewildered calls of the boy Moon to his friend Lilah in the meadow after Lilah left and never came back. It is so small inside its bigness, like the barely contained sobs of the ruined medicine man the night he raped his own daughter, when he sat beside her lifeless form on the bed and hid his face in his hands as if he could hide it forever.

"Okay," says Sky. "I will."

So the Unicorn sets off, toward the path that leads under the mountain.

Delilah knows the river will lead her to Mira. She knows because of what Yora said, and she knows because Mira is everything you have to return to in the end. Chaos. Madness. Home.

Besides, she knows the animals didn't give her their lives for nothing. They didn't give her their lives so she could live her own life as if dead, and be responsible for nothing but herself.

The blissful silence of the desert did not make her feel alive after all. Relief from humanity did not make her feel alive. Even the suffering of deprivation and loneliness did not make her feel alive.

Once sex made her feel alive. But now it is pain that makes her feel alive. Not the pain that used to hold her tight, cringing and growling along her spine, but a different kind of pain, as if something new lives inside her. It shifts uncomfortably at the base of her, and pushes for more room. Sometimes while she walks along the river, she has to stop and fall on all fours, and throw up.

She tries not to think of what lies ahead, or of where she will actually end up, or of whether or not she will actually find her sister, or of which outcome frightens her more, or of what she will do, what she will say—and what Mira will say back, or not.

She hasn't had to think of such things for seven years. She tries not to think of them now but she thinks of them constantly. Only the pain brings her back to her body. She is grateful for it. In its own way, it feels like home.

When she lies down on the earth to sleep, and lays her mind down inside the river to dream, she feels the same networks of pain within the earth that she feels within her body. The underground system of the prairie dogs' escape burrows are like a network of pain where the earth was dynamited. She feels the terror of the lizards as the earth shakes. She feels the massacre of desert tortoises, their helpless falling only a few inches to the ground. She has always felt this pain in her body. Maybe it was only a premonition of what was to come.

She tries to avoid the noise, and keep herself hidden from the men. But the river can't help where it flows. She pulls her layers tightly around herself and walks in darkness, lest they see her, though once she would have walked straight up to them and hungrily opened herself. One day, sleeping fitfully too close to the noise, she dreams of the Great Road, completed and with cars speeding down it—covering in less than a day the distance it will take her a whole moon or more to walk, disappearing in puffs of deadly smoke into the mountains. In the dream, the sound of the river is the sound of the cars, and she is inside that river somehow, as if trapped inside the pavement, and she knows Mira is inside one of those cars, but she doesn't know which one. Delilah screams until the road cracks open around her body, her scream louder than dynamite and completely unexpected, and she is there, shattered and heaving, as the car doors open and naked men stumble out, their bodies vulnerable and soft without that steel speed to surround them. They are so lost. They open their hands and look around. They look at Delilah, but they don't recognize what she is. No one has heard of women any more.

She opens her eyes into the bitter sun. She remembers the fire in her body in high school, how she squirmed with it in her little square seat at her little square desk: her nipples, her hands, her tongue, her throat, the hunched shoulders of the boy in the seat in front of her, how beautiful it was, and how she had no idea—no idea of what it meant, or what she should do with it.

The idea of not having sex again, which always terrified her in theory, now that she has committed to it, astounds her with relief.

In the absence of that desire's determination, she feels things she thought she had lost a long time ago. What it felt like to love. What it felt like to see Moon cry. What it felt like to hold Mira in her arms. The magic of knowing she had been born, and believing that life was a fairy tale in which she had an important, central part, and believing the story had an ending, and a point. Maybe sex hadn't been a release after all but a black hole, into which she had stuffed every part of her life that had ever felt like anything. Because for some reason the feeling of sex had become the only feeling she believed in.

She thinks of Dragon sometimes. She thinks of him fleetingly, like the shadow of a desert fox over the sand at dusk. She is surprised that the memory of him weighs so little, and yet tastes so sweet. She realizes she does love him, and that surprises her a little. She wishes she could have helped him, but she has never really been good at loving and wouldn't have known how.

And she thinks of death. Her only fear of the strange sickness inside her is that somehow she won't live long enough to reach her sister, now that she has determined it must be done.

Wouldn't that be the universe's best and final joke?

The snow has come, confident and complete, in the night. Lonely breathes in, and the cold air brightens her mind. For a moment she remembers the unknown that exists beyond her thoughts, the possibility of a future.

Chelya takes her hand in the morning, like she used to, and Lonely's eyes are wide, like they used to be. Full moon tonight, though they'll return before it rises, because it's so cold now. Lonely wonders if Chelya's tree spirit can hold her like a human, can keep her warm.

"I'm so happy you're going to meet him," says Chelya. The sun focuses like a narrow eye above them, piercing the edge of Lonely's vision, and the snow reflects its light like metal. The air is absolutely open. The trees shut off their colors and surrender to whiteness. Lonely doesn't look at the mountain behind her.

Winter is a place, Lonely decides, connected by only the thinnest of threads to summer. Is it possible for that thread to break, or has it already broken, inside her alone? Will winter end, as summer did? She never thought about summer. She took it for granted—that soft easy tide of color and song that buoyed her whether she was happy or afraid, peaceful or longing, loving or lonely. Beneath everything she felt, there was that thoughtless richness: there was life, free and without obligation. Now silence grips her by the shoulders, and the cold glares hard into her heart, and the stillness all around will not allow her to forget her pain. Everything, as if holding its breath, says *Pay attention.*

The red cardinal. The blue space between clouds. The yellow stain of the fox who left his mark in the snow. The twilit summer green of Chelya's eyes. Each color bewilders Lonely, impressing itself urgently upon her mind like an image from a dream she's forgotten—a dream that still contains the seed of her life, and the memory of why she should live, if only she could remember it.

They walk through white fields, their feet laced in fur and deer hide. Lonely is already shivering, and Chelya puts an arm around her. Lonely feels the full, uncontrollable joy of the girl's body.

"We have to be careful in winter," says Chelya. "I mean, we can't stay out here too long, because it's cold, but indoors—You can't stay in there too long either, can you?" She laughs, but it's a strained, confused laugh, like the ease of her nature has begun to question itself over time. "I feel like I'm going to suffocate in there if I stay too long, you know?" she says, a little too fast, and then rushes forward down the hill.

Lonely stands frozen for a moment.

"Come on!" cries Chelya, snow puffing around her boots like smoke. Lonely comes slowly, imagining Kite out there in the snow, wondering if he made it down to the warmer desert before the deep cold set in. If she wonders it now, Fawn must wonder it every day, every moment.

She follows Chelya into the silver shadows, into the heavy mind of the forest, and she feels Chelya's urgency now, her hurry toward the one she loves.

They walk a long time, and then it happens without warning. The silence when the two come together takes Lonely's breath away. There are no words of greeting, no calls or even preliminary smiles. Chelya's hurried step, nearly a run now, simply ends in his arms, which are open for her, waiting, for she knew exactly where he stood, and he knew so much more than Lonely can know: exactly how Chelya was feeling, exactly what she needed. Chelya collapses into him with such relief that Lonely sees the weight of sorrow and desperation that had driven her forward to this place—feelings Lonely wasn't even aware of, so well did Chelya keep them hidden beneath the habits of her laughter and kindness.

He is looking over Chelya's shoulder at Lonely, and for a moment he has a face, but then that face is gone. Lonely cannot remember the features, only the surprising, slow passion of the eyes—passion like every emotion pulsing as one, as if emotion were life, no more and no less. The face shines by her and turns to shadow again, like one of a thousand faces of a world that keeps turning and turning, and for whom one moment is nothing. Yet it is personal, too, that look—as personal as the world can be when it seems to freeze around you in time, bringing your attention swiftly into yourself with a sudden, echoing boom.

Suddenly Lonely, who never knew her own age, feels that she is so much older than Chelya. She is very, very old.

The tree is a tree: its limbs the arms of the earth itself, its heart innocent and ever-growing, its tears invisible. Yet the tree is also a man, who bends, from love, out of his given form and embraces Chelya, and as her body is swallowed into his, she, too, becomes like a tree: lush and rooted and ever-green. Lonely sees this. How each becomes the other.

Introductions are made. Lonely is allowed to hug the tree. She leans into him. Chelya doesn't mind that he presses Lonely's heart to his for a moment, but Lonely does. She breathes in his fresh green peace, but his love is so warm that he feels like a man. She can feel the excitement of his youthful growth. She can feel the aching sincerity of his deep ancestry. He reminds her of Sky, only with more hope and more joy. She pulls away.

"Welcome," says the tree spirit. "Welcome to my Community."

"How big is it?" Lonely asks, looking around.

"It doesn't end."

Chelya laughs. "He's young still," she says. "But he'll be taller than anyone else one day. It's a lot of responsibility. That's why he's so serious."

"I'm not serious," says the tree, brushing Chelya's cheek.

"I have to go," says Lonely, in a panic, but they don't seem to hear her. She can see the man's face again, bearded and wide, his cheeks gentle hills. Broader and more yielding than Rye's face. Sturdier and more masculine than Kite's. He smiles and raises his eyebrows.

"How does he become a man?" Lonely whispers.

"For me," says Chelya simply, with no trace of pride, but perhaps a drop or two of sorrow. "For me, he can become that."

Lonely nods, remembering the night she said goodbye to Chelya—how fast she turned from Chelya, how she always felt sorry, how she promised herself she wouldn't resent Chelya again for the love she received and deserved. But maybe her own sorrow will always make her selfish.

"I'm sorry," she says. "I have to go. I wish I didn't, but I do."

She turns.

"Lonely!" cries Chelya, as Lonely pushes aimlessly through the trees and away, aware of each one's potential spirit, wondering if she's being rough with Chelya's lover's friends. But she doesn't respond to the calls. Who would respond to such a name? Who would turn around and come, to the call of such a word? If she turns and comes back to that name, it will claim her again.

Nameless, she drowns herself in the sound of her footsteps in the snow. Nameless, she places distance at once intently and thoughtlessly between herself and the lovers. Not that life for her any more. What is left? White silence, still space. Nameless, she finds herself somewhere familiar. Nameless in a place of spirits….

A coyote howls at the moment she enters, unexpectedly, the fire circle.

Or maybe it's a wolf. It sounds far away and she doesn't know one call from the other. But she hears the moon in that voice. She hears the great sorrow of the predator, who cannot live without killing, who cannot survive without taking something else's life.

The emptiness of the fire circle astounds her. She almost doesn't recognize it. But even pressing against those dancing bodies, even surrounded by heat and sound, she had felt that emptiness. It was that emptiness that had driven her dancing, and her desperate, futile joy.

Silence, and the beaten ground where the dancers danced is white. There is a chill where the fire once was, and clumps of ash make the snow cover lumpy. The trees lean in. No one is there. Lonely stands opposite the point where she first emerged with Chelya, so many full moons ago. She looks to where she stood. She looks at the hunger she came with then, a hunger she could not fill because she herself did not understand yet what it was.

It seems impossible that she could be alone here. Why her, among all the lives and spirits who were there that night, and every full moon night in summer? She has no importance, she realizes suddenly. All that gave her importance was this name: Lonely. That's what made her stand out. That, perhaps, was the name's only purpose. She shivers, and closes her eyes. The clearing seems to shiver around her. Somehow the heart of the drums still beats, even without the drums, even without the sound. The movement of the dance still moves, even without dancers. She can feel something talking, low and wild, the way rivers talk, beneath the silence. She can feel the touch of spirits who are passing between each other on another layer of reality. Is it actually happening all around her after all, but she can't feel it, because she came here alone without Chelya's magic? Or is it just the memory she feels, of a time long forgotten by winter, the way night is forgotten by day?

It's just me, says the wind. *Don't you remember me?*

Lonely closes her eyes, shakes her head. It seems like a hundred years ago that the wind last spoke to her, when she was young and hopeful, flying with Sky, and the world was made of light. Now it rocks cold around her and she feels its inevitability, how its loneliness owns the world.

Stop, she says. *I don't believe in you any more. You lied.*

Don't believe in me? But what did you think I was, to believe or not believe?

She looks up. The sun draws its warmth in tight, in preparation for evening, as if in winter it has only so much energy to give, and must conserve its life force like everyone else. The Unicorn's horn, which she keeps always against her body, begins to burn. Then it begins to hum. She reaches for it, and then he is there.

Sky.

He clasps her against his chest, his eyes quick and desperate, his mouth so close she can taste his breath. He whirls her halfway around, as if beginning a dance, and then he is gone.

Then agony, even before the bliss has faded. She screams his name, clutching at the horn though she doesn't know why. She screams his name, and then cries it, as she turns and turns in place, looking all around, for *he is here, he is here*—he must be, for she felt him in her arms.

"Where?" she calls out to the trees, to the invisible animals. "Where is he?" Underwater in her own tears. *They know, they know.* "Please."

When she finally finds herself again in stillness, her face in her hands, and even her mind exhausted from crying out, the wind speaks to her again. This time it whispers warm in her ear, like a childhood friend she never had.

Stop. You can't find him now. It's not time.

"But I saw him," she cries. "I felt him."

No. You were only passing by the same place, at the same time, on opposite sides of the world.

Lonely opens her eyes, sees her own breath. She feels absolutely hopeless. She wants to lie down and let the winter take her forever.

At the edge of the clearing, a great tree has fallen. She doesn't remember it from the summer, but then again it was night then, and everything distorted by fire. Its black roots web the air, and where those roots still hook the earth, a black cave sucks at her vision. She feels the horn in her hands, feels the Unicorn nodding, the way the horse nodded to her one day long ago in the desert, saying *There is water. The water is here.* She is so cold, and the cold makes her tired. She trudges to the tree and lies down under the dark roots. She curls up her body against the frozen dirt, nestles close to the wood, lets soil collapse into her hair. She closes her eyes.

Please, she prays to Sky for the hundredth time, with all the tenderness in her heart. *Dream me.*

On the first day, Dragon lies still in the dry absence where Moon's vaporous presence once stood, and dreams delirious dreams. He dreams Delilah comes down to him in her animal-skin cloth, and passes her naked breasts over his body the way she did the first day he came here, her mouth moving toward his hunger and her legs opening above his eyes into bottomless blackness. He dreams of Coyote, laughing. He dreams of the Unicorn, slipping its horn silently into the waters where Yora lived, and it must be drawing her soul out of those waters; it must be stealing her away, taking her from him forever in its wind of light. He dreams of Moon with erection in hand—twice the size of Dragon's, reaching up to his chest—and when Moon comes, he comes blood. He dreams of fire coming at him from behind, but he cannot turn and face his great dragon mother, for he has wronged her somehow. He dreams of the goddesses in their cold white robes, and they open their robes and there is no woman's body there, only the Unicorn. *The Unicorn.* And Coyote's laughter.

He feels thirsty for the river. He crawls to it. Yora is gone, but there is still water here, and it still quenches his thirst, at least for a while.

"What now?" laughs Coyote. "What if you never find her, little boy? Can't you survive on your own?"

But when Dragon looks up with his mouth dripping, no one is there. He stands and begins walking home. No one loves him. He is completely alone. He has never before really allowed himself to admit this.

On the second day, he just walks. He wanders like he did in the beginning, when he was waiting for Delilah to return each day, only now he's not waiting for anyone, and he's not looking for anything, and he's not fighting or trying. All the desert is silent, listening to his footsteps. When he looks up, he can see his own face in the sky. When he looks down, he doesn't recognize his feet.

When he feels like it, he masturbates. He does it lazily, sometimes out of need, sometimes for no reason at all. He watches that part of his body in his hand, watches it grow tall, stretches its skin and toys with it, then does exactly what it wants him to do. He closes his eyes and indulges in fantasies of the bodies of all the women he's ever desired, as well as women he's never seen. He wallows especially deeply in images of the women who would not have him—the women in the white robes and the first, virgin Yora, forever unattainable—and in his fantasies they all fall under him weakly, and all the power is his.

When he's spent himself he lies still and stares up at the sky. He wonders vaguely about where he came from, why his mother threw him away, why he doesn't remember his father, where the dragons went when they disappeared. But he has no feelings about any of these things. The thoughts come apart and drift away with the clouds.

He walks on without intention, numb to the landscape, and sometimes, to feel something, he takes a bite of some piece of the land—the dust, the cactus—to feel the grit of it, but then he spits it out. Sometimes as he walks, he stretches his arms in imaginary punches, reliving his fight with Moon or imagining how he will kill the Unicorn. Will he strangle it? Break its horn? Spear it with a knife in the heart? Does the Unicorn have a heart? But his fighting stances fizzle out vaguely as he walks, because how will he find the Unicorn anyway? And anyway. *Anyway*...He can't seem to hold onto a thought any more. He stops again and masturbates.

On the third day, he's still walking. The earth is flat; the sky is flat. The sand is hot; the sand is cold. Day, night, day.

He realizes again that he isn't even human. He doesn't need anything. The only thing he needs is love. Is woman. He has enslaved himself to this one need. He has enslaved himself to Woman. And that must be why Coyote laughs.

Then Dragon, half-mad with loneliness, laughs, too. He can't stop. He has never laughed before in his life, and he feels like it might destroy him, but that's what laughter is. It's not caring. It's realizing that what you thought was most important is not important at all—is, in fact, ridiculous. When he laughs, he seems to see his own face before him, and it is laughing, too.

"That's the only gift I ever wished to give you, bleeding lonely boy," says Coyote, suddenly walking beside him. "The ability to laugh at yourself."

Dragon realizes that, all this time, ever since the first day he walked into the desert as a man, he has only wanted to win Coyote's approval. He feels that he wants it even more than he wants a mother or a lover or an end to his own pain.

He keeps walking, alone again, and without meaning to, he walks home. But when he arrives at his lair, the dragons' boiling cauldron, all the water is gone. There is nothing but a black hole where the water once swirled, and coiled at the edge of the hole is a rattlesnake.

What do you want? says the rattlesnake, his whole body moving at once, and Dragon freezes, unable to tell where the movement begins.

"I want to meet my father," says Dragon, without thinking.

Faster than he can see, the snake rears up, flies into the air, and bites him on his shoulder—a wound to mirror the wound that Dragon gave Moon with his own teeth. It's his left shoulder, the one that protected his heart. Dragon sinks to his knees, his eyes flashing colors, his penis convulsing up and down like the body of the snake itself, as if the head of the snake had been severed and the body continued to convulse on its own—a mindless, spiritless, mechanical body. Then pain engulfs him and knocks him flat.

He is dying. He knows he is dying by the way his body is carrying on like that without him, and he cannot feel it and has no control over it. He knows he is dying by the way all the longing of his life suddenly crowds up at once into his throat, so intense it will explode, and once it explodes—once it blows past that wall of resistance that is the reality of his life—there will be nothing on the other side but empty space.

He thinks that never before in his life has he ever truly felt afraid. It had never occurred to him that he could die.

He is inside his own lair but there is nothing there, no water and no earth, only that nothing blackness that doesn't touch him, all around him. "Please," he whispers. It isn't the roar of his infancy, when dragons surrounded him and he should have been afraid, for he wasn't afraid then. There was *something* then. And it isn't the rage of his fire, or the rage that lurks beneath his silence with no way to express itself, when women keep their secrets from him. It is the voice of a childhood he never knew about, the childhood that existed in shadow behind the childhood he remembers where he was blessed and cherished and surrounded by flowers—the secret, unconscious childhood, in which all along he was terrified of being left again, and of what he was and of what he would become, the only creature in the garden with this strange, uncontrollable, extra limb.

It is the voice of this child now, this silently terrified child. "Please. I don't want to die."

"Give me a reason," says Coyote, whose voice is the voice of the darkness, the voice he knew before he knew anything—before he knew the fire of sunshine, before he even knew his very first mother's breast. "Give me a reason you should live."

"I don't know," says Dragon, astounded, and he doesn't. He just wants to live. Isn't that enough?

"Oh well," Coyote says dryly. "Make something up."

"Because I have to kill the Unicorn."

"You want to live so you can kill something!" cries Coyote and laughs. "That's exactly right. That's how we all live."

"Will I live, then?" trembles Dragon, who doesn't understand the joke.

"Oh, don't be stupid," says Coyote. "It isn't up to me. Are you, or are you not, afraid?"

The question makes Dragon even more afraid. He is trapped in the nothingness now, with no control over anything—his senses useless, his body touching nothing. Quickly, he fights down a vomit of panic. Should he admit it, or not? If he gives in to it, will the poison overtake him?

"Coward," says Coyote. "You aren't brave enough to be afraid."

"I am. I am afraid!" When he says it, he feels the power of it. "I am afraid!" he cries out into the dark. "I'm afraid!" He hears his own voice, booming back to him: not the scream of his infant self, the scream of helpless baby limbs, but the roar of manhood, with voice steeled into words, with certainty, with decision. "I am afraid." He finds himself standing on two firm feet now, and the inner recesses of the cave wink at him from their corners.

"How do you know you're afraid?" whispers Coyote.

Dragon opens his eyes wide. "My heart," he says. His heart punching so hard at his insides, it lights up the darkness with the friction of its weight against his ribs.

"Your heart is beating?"

"Yes. So hard it hurts."

"Then you're not dying, are you?" Coyote snarls.

Then Dragon laughs again. He laughs and laughs, and his laughter sounds strange to him, like a wild dog barking its loneliness on a moonless night. The more he laughs, the more he feels alive, and the more he feels alive, the more the snake wound in his shoulder hurts, and he falls to his knees again.

Coyote is on top of him. Coyote's teeth are at his throat, Coyote's claws in his shoulders. Dragon fights back with everything he has. He uses his teeth, too, and his claws, and he protects himself, like Coyote does, with a shield of shaggy hair. He snarls like Coyote, and when Coyote turns into a dragon, he breathes fire back at him. And when the dragon turns into a Unicorn, Dragon fights that Unicorn's spear of light with his own hot spear of darkness.

Then Coyote turns back into Coyote and then into Moon and then into his goddess mother and then into the father Dragon realizes he's pictured over and over in his mind—someone who looks just like him, only cruel and distant and infinitely stronger—and then back into the Unicorn.

"What is the Unicorn?" demands Coyote. "What does it look like?"

"White," pants Dragon. "It's white." But then he closes his eyes and knows what he means. *White like the robes of the goddesses that I could never touch. White like the virgin's skin, that I wanted to be worthy of but which forever shamed me.*

"What else?" demands Coyote.

*Beauty. Grace. Sad eyes, disappointed in me. Cold eyes…*Dragon hangs his head now. The shame eats him up, both within and without, hotter than his own fire.

"What about the horn?"

Unbreakable. Unbendable. Holy.

"And you want to kill it?"

"No."

"What, then?"

"I want—" But Dragon doesn't know. *I'm so tired of this shame,* he thinks. "I want to be a man."

"A what?"

"A man."

Dragon opens his eyes and there is Coyote, sitting coolly, his paws crossed neatly before him, smaller than Dragon but entirely confident. They sit there together, underneath the world. Dragon feels something spinning behind his heart, like fire and water at once, and he thinks it might be his soul.

"Then you must no longer seek all your nourishment from women," says Coyote.

In the dream, Lonely is walking over white frozen fields. She has been walking forever, searching, following the fleeting shadow of someone who is afraid to be loved, and does not want to be seen.

But she is tired. Her body is tired, and it is also hungry, thirsty, and weak. She falls to her knees on the ground. That's when she sees the tree, the one she's sleeping under in real life, but in her dream it's less than one year old, long ago at the beginning of its life, and only beginning to grow.

"What are you looking for?" asks the tree, in a voice full of wonder.

Lonely brushes the snow from its tiny, leafless body, and sees the red wounds at its tips where the new life will sprout again in spring. She thought she was looking for a boy called Sky. But instead she says, "I'm looking for my name."

"What is a name?" asks the tree.

"It's what someone calls you by," says Lonely, "when they need you."

"Ah," says the baby tree. "But everyone calls you differently. It depends on the caller, doesn't it?"

"What do you mean?"

"When the water calls me, it feels different from when the earth calls me," says the tree.

"But the water doesn't need you, does it?" asks Lonely, distracted a little by her confusion, and also by her concern for something so fragile in such a brutal cold. "It's you that needs the water."

But the tree sounds very sure. "No, the water needs me also. We call to each other."

Lonely looks at the tree and says nothing.

"A moment ago," continues the tree, "you could say I called you. I called you through the earth, and the earth called you through your body, and your body called you with its tiredness and hunger. But are tiredness and hunger your name? Maybe there is no call, but only a connection that connects us."

"How do you know all of this?" cries Lonely. It is only a little tree, only a simple life, with no brain.

"How do you not know this?" asks the tree, without judgment.

Lonely is silent again. *Because I didn't come from this world,* she thinks. *Because I don't understand where I come from.*

"Anyway," says the tree. "I don't know what a name is. You have to figure out what it is, and what you want it for. Is it something you truly need?"

"Yes. It is."

"Why?"

"I don't know."

They sit for a little while. Lonely hasn't moved. She is thinking. The wind is quiet. This is a dream, so she doesn't feel as cold.

"Do you remember how you began?" asks the tree after a time.

"No."

"That might help. If you could remember how you began."

"How did you begin?" asks Lonely.

"In a squirrel's forgetting."

"In a what?"

"A squirrel. He buries the seeds in the earth. He does it for himself, because he thinks he owns the earth, and he thinks when he puts them inside the earth, he will have them all whenever he wants them. But the earth takes us back. He can't remember us all. And the forgotten ones—we are the ones who become something else. We become trees."

"You are the lucky ones, then. The forgotten ones."

"No. The ones who are eaten become Squirrel. We all become something."

"So it doesn't matter what happens," says Lonely slowly.

"Of course it matters. Everything matters."

Lonely smiles. She spreads her legs and then crosses them, repositioning herself so that her knees surround the little tree and her warm body leans over it. She bends down and gently breathes over its tender form.

"Does that feel good?" she asks.

"Yes," says the tree. "Does that feel good?"

"What?"

"*My* breath."

"Oh," says Lonely, surprised. "I hadn't noticed!"

The tree is silent then, and Lonely feels sorry. "Thank you," she says quietly. She breathes out, and breathes in. She does one and then the other, and then the first again, in endless alternation. But the tree does both at the same time.

"Your breath comes from trees," the tree explains. Then, as if the two ideas were connected, it says, "I know Sky, too, of course."

Lonely pulls back sharply. "You do?" she cries.

"Why are you surprised? You know him too."

"But I—But, how do you know him?"

"The way I know everything."

"What way?"

"The way everything knows everything."

Lonely closes her eyes. The tree breathes out, and she breathes in, and her body shifts. Beneath her, that tiny vibration runs through the surface of the earth. It makes a hibernating insect turn over in the cradle of its cocoon. That friction melts a drop of water, and that drop of water is drunk up by the roots of the nearby grass. Then the drop of water travels up the blade of grass and evaporates into the air. The wind, in a force of randomness, tosses it back and forth between its billowy hands and then slings it off toward the forest beyond. It joins with other droplets, and the droplets make the air heavy, make it drop. The wet air sinks and gets colder in a black hollow under a stump where a weasel is crouching, and the weasel twitches once, to warm itself. The moonlight catches on its fur, and the movement catches the eye of the owl who was watching, trying to determine if what it saw was alive. The owl pounces and kills the weasel with a quick squeeze. It carries the weasel back to its nest and calls to its mate to come eat. The call of the owl wakes a woman in an isolated farmhouse in a valley nearby. She lies awake and thinks of her daughter, who went to work in the City and never came back. She has no phone, but she thinks so hard about her daughter that the daughter catches that thought—in a way that sometimes happens between human beings who are connected through blood or deep emotion—and her daughter, working late in an office far away, looks up, looks out the window. She stands up, sees the moon, and tries to remember something. The motion of standing sends invisible waves of dust—skin and hair and particles of her life's path—swirling into the air. Some of them contain the scent of salt from the sweat of the people who sat in the same seats she sat on in the subway that day. The salt smells like the sea, and she remembers suddenly a day she spent with a lover once by the sea, and she wants that moment back, suddenly, now, so she picks up the phone and calls him. He isn't home, but as she leaves a message on his machine, her voice travels through the telephone line under the feet of the shivering starlings, and they clasp their feet tighter around the vibrating wire, but a few of them fly away. They fly over the moon for a moment, casting a shadow over the path of a moth, who shifts its direction to get back into the light. And the moth, veering in its path over the marsh where it lives, is seen by a fish lurking under the water, and the fish leaps up and catches the moth in its silver jaws. As it leaps, the splashing water catches the light of the moon, and the woman rocking her baby on the open porch of her little hut looks up and smiles. Then she looks back down, and gives her little boy a name—something beautiful that this single, soon-to-be-lost-forever moment inspired in her mind.

Lonely can't remember that name, because it is only a dream.

But she knows the baby is Sky, and maybe the past and present and future are all connected as easily as places are—though they seem unreachable. "But why is he only a baby?" she asks, crying.

"For the same reason that I am only less than a year old," says the tree. "In the other world, I am over a hundred years old, and I am dead, and you are sleeping under my roots which once held the earth together. But you are dreaming into the past, because you are searching for how things began. You are searching for your name."

"I love him," Lonely says, remembering the baby's face, which was very serious, but not sad. "I have to find him again. I will."

"Yes," says the tree. "Everything is connected. Everything knows everything else."

"But how do I know where to go? I don't know what world he's in, or what form he's in, and even if I did, I don't know how I would get to him."

"It's not so complicated," says the tree. "I, for example, love the light. Right now, the light is easy. It's all around me. But even when I'm older, and other trees grow up faster around me (because I'm the sort that takes my time, but I live longer than the others), and I can't see the light any more—or only in glimpses—I'll never have to wonder where it is. I'll simply keep moving toward it. I'll change my direction, I'll wind and turn. I'll grow any way I have to just to reach it. I never have to think what to do or where to go. I have only to keep growing. And when it's time to grow leaves, I grow them, and when it's winter, I drop them, go silent, and wait."

"But you have an instinct in your body," says Lonely. "You know to grow upward."

"You have an instinct in your body too," says the tree. "And I'm not just growing upward. I'm growing downward. For every branch I send up, I have to send a root down, or I'll fall."

"That's why I came back down the mountain. Because you can't go up without going down."

"That's right. Now you and Sky are part of the same tree—part of the same growing. One of you is the roots and one of you is the branches, and you're growing at the same time—that's how you keep each other alive, on opposite sides of the world."

"But then we're growing in opposite directions!" Lonely cries.

"Don't worry," says the tree. "Life is a circle. There are no opposite directions. Please, don't think so much."

Then Lonely wakes up.

She wakes up through layers and layers of earth, as if rising from the clay into the richest soil, into the leaves still decaying from ten years ago, five years ago, and one year ago, until she opens her eyes with her head cradled in the noisy youth of the still whole, dry leaves who died only two moons ago. But she can feel the richness of centuries pillowing her head.

And oh! The moonlight in the snow all around her looks so curvy and sexy and wild, she wants to laugh. "It's beautiful!" she cries out, but her cry makes no sound. For a split second, she feels every tree and being in the forest connected in joyful anticipation, leaning in as if with love, holding tight together as if with hands.

Rye is lifting her up. "How many times do I have to rescue you?" he smiles at her, but she sees a tense concern in his eyes, and that longer hallway of sadness behind it, deep into the rooms of his hidden mind. She can see everything. But she can't speak. Nor can she feel the ends of her body—the tips of her own branches, where the leaves would sprout in spring.

As he carries her home, again, his body gradually warms her, and the first sensation she feels of her own human flesh is excruciating pain.

Dragon listens to the dragons whispering, as they do sometimes. Since he came here, their ghosts have not given him wisdom, nor answered his questions, nor taught him what to do with that great fire within. But they have kept him company, and he is grateful for that. They have understood him. How he longs to be deeply among them, to live carefree among the wild and the lustful, to live unjudged by other creatures who live so naturally in their fire that they never question it, never fight it.

But he cannot live among them. He is all alone and human. So he tries to be brave, takes a deep breath, and says to Coyote, "I must learn to conquer this need. I must no longer need this. Do you hear me?"

"Then do not be afraid of sitting with desire, not knowing when it will be satisfied. Why are you afraid? What will happen to you, lonely boy?"

Dragon closes his eyes. *It feels like a force that will overtake me.*

"But what can it do to you?"

Dragon breathes. He sits with it. He stands up and walks around with it. This is his home, and he knows this hardness against his feet. Held in, the fire feels different. He doesn't masturbate. He doesn't try to raise it up into his spirit. He sits and he walks around and he sits again. He feels like he is holding a breath in his throat. He feels calm in his decision, but he doesn't know if the calm is real. Maybe there is anger behind it, that he still cannot feel.

He feels heavy. His face feels heavy. His arm muscles, his belly. He feels joyless and calm. He tries to breathe into that area of his body, but his mind turns hazy, resisting contact.

"It's your thoughts that make you desperate," says Coyote, without moving his face. "The thoughts make it worse."

Dragon thinks about his thoughts. There are other ways to look at the situation, surely—other than to think that the women torture him, to think that he is under their control, to think how unfair it is. But he doesn't know what those other ways are.

"Aaaaaaaaaaaaargh," he roars. Coyote says nothing.

To truly be in control, he must not think of revenge. He must not imagine them coming back to him and begging him, and himself holding back and keeping distant in order that they suffer what he has suffered. Because if there is anger in it, it won't work. He can see that. If she never comes back, he can't let that frustrate him. If it frustrates him, that shows she is in control—not him.

The thought comes, as it always does: but *why* must he control it at all? Why can he not have what he wants? *Isn't it natural, what I want—and not evil, after all?* This is the thought that has always stopped him before.

"But it isn't fair," says Dragon.

Coyote laughs out loud. "I know nothing about fairness," he says. "I couldn't care less about fairness. What is fair?"

"Then what is the point?" yells Dragon.

"You tell me. I know nothing about points."

Dragon sighs. The point is that he doesn't want to suffer any more, and so he must learn to feel these feelings without suffering.

He is strong, isn't he? He can live with anything. He can live through anything. He survived dragons and solitude and abandonment. He can survive this. *Nothing can hurt me,* he tells himself. *Desire cannot kill me. Frustration cannot kill me. These things just happen.*

"Shut up," says Coyote.

"I'm not talking."

"You're talking in your mind. Shut up and listen."

"To what?"

"To yourself," says Coyote. "I'm bored." And he disappears.

Alone alone alone. Dragon tries to listen. He tries to watch desire rise up, tries to understand it. No, not understand it—not think. Just watch. Just listen.

But eventually he has to listen to himself out loud.

"What is this? This that I feel? What is desire?"

"It wants to express itself. It has something it wants to say."

"What? What does it want to say?"

"It wants to be heard. I want to be heard."

Dragon swallows. This seems like something. But the desire remains.

"I want to put myself out there and I want you to receive me," he tries again. "You, Woman. That's it. *I want you to hear me. I want you to see me!*"

Silence.

"Because I'm alone. Because I have only myself here. That's why."

It's nice, talking to himself. He finds he can trust himself more than he realized.

"But I feel lonely. I always feel lonely. Why does everyone leave me? Why?"

"What is this. What is this desire. WHAT IS IT."

"Why does it make me suffer so much?"

"Because I feel bad about it. That's why."

Dragon sighs.

"Maybe I have to love myself more."

"But I still feel lonely. Why?"

"Enough with the why," says Coyote loudly, and Dragon opens his eyes and finds him there again. "Try this, boy-man. What would you be *without* this desire?"

Dragon looks up. He hadn't realized he was looking down. When he raises his head, energy flows up his spine, connecting him head to foot.

"I would be nothing," he says, shocked. "This is my only purpose in life. Without this desire, I have no purpose. I don't know why I'm alive. I don't know what it means to be a man, besides this."

The realization falls into his stomach as if from a great height, like a boulder that had wavered precariously over his head for his whole life, and he hadn't even been aware.

"Okay," he says quietly, after a long time.

Coyote is silent.

"What is my purpose then, if not this?" His erection aches terribly. It cries out. He wants to touch it, comfort it.

"You're a god," says Coyote. "You don't have to condemn the human part of yourself to be a god. But you *are* a god. So get it together."

Dragon closes his eyes.

"Okay," he says again. He will surrender because he has to. He did it once for Yora, and he can do it again for himself.

Dragon meditates for another day, and another night. He doesn't move.

When he thinks he is finally at peace, Coyote appears to him once more. "What do you feel now?" Coyote asks.

"Grief," says Dragon, and then he puts his hands over his face, and out of nowhere, his body begins to shake.

"Good," says Coyote, and he is gone again.

Dragon shakes so hard he thinks his limbs will fly from his joints, and his skin will crack like stone. The tears don't even seem to come from his eyes, but rather like sweat from his face—his face twisting so hard inside his hands that his jaw and forehead cramp up and his hands are dripping. Then he begins to sob out loud, croaking and rocking into the darkness, and he can't stop.

He sobs so hard that rocks crumble in the mountains above him and loose themselves in helpless avalanches over the desert. He sobs so hard that the dragons, far below near the center of the earth, clutch at each other, and the women of the City turn in their beds, moaning and spreading their hands over their forgotten bodies, dreaming of the princes they glimpsed in their husbands' eyes when they first met them. He sobs the sob of a warrior who has watched fellow young men slain at the most earnest peak of their manhood. He sobs until the sun bends low in the sky to see, peeking with its most vulnerable rays into the forbidden caverns of his home, quivering with primal fear. He sobs until, for the first time since the dragons of his childhood gave him up, he owns his own heart again.

On the last day, he has a vision. He sees the form of a boy lying face down in the sand, on rolling dunes far from the river, where he himself first crossed over from the mountains. The boy's hair is long and wild, like his own. And he realizes that so many moons ago, when he left the Garden behind, he also left some part of himself behind on the way, because it shamed him. The goddesses had abandoned him. But he made it worse by abandoning himself.

Dragon stands up and climbs through the boiling water to the light of day. He feels calm and thoughtful, with the past and the future swirling around him, as if he's standing in the eye of a storm. *I am a man*, he thinks. He thinks fleetingly of Delilah, and he knows that she knew this about him, and he knows again that he loves her, and this thought is happy and completely without need. But he puts that thought aside for another day.

I'm a man. He closes his eyes and laughs.

Then he sees, behind his closed eyes, the boy again. He sees the boy lying in the sand. He realizes suddenly that the boy is not only a symbol of himself.

There *is* a boy, half unconscious, lying somewhere out there in the water-less expanse of the higher desert.

The boy is human, and the boy is real. And Dragon must rescue him. This is his first task, as a man.

Because of what happened to her, Lonely gets the bathtub to herself. She is the first one to enter the hot water, when it's still clean, and no one makes her get out so that someone else can get a turn.

The winter almost claimed her. She almost entered into it forever, so that if she'd lain under that tree a little longer, all her body's feeling would have left her, and for her it would never have been summer again. *Winter is not a season to be fooled with, child,* Eva had scolded her as she wrapped her in blankets while Rye heated the water. *This is not the kind of courage I was speaking of—throwing yourself out into the cold with no intelligence, no intention, no respect, lost in your own selfish melancholy. This is not a responsible way to dream.* But in her scolding, Lonely felt her love. She felt, too, the love of Chelya, who had left her beloved in order to search for Lonely, and who had come running home to tell her father that her friend was unconscious and would need to be carried. She felt the love of Rye, who carried her, and who gently poured the water, bucket by bucket, into the tub without looking at her or Eva. Even Fawn had watched solemnly from the doorway as Rye carried her in, and she didn't look angry—only scared.

Because of what happened to her, Lonely gets to relax all alone in the luxury of warm, loving water, the heat of the stove just reaching her through the curtain from the main room, and she gets to stay there as long as she likes. The warmth snuggles up to her muscles, curls up like a lover inside her limbs, makes her fingers and toes ache with life, and melts tension from her shoulders, her neck, and her face that she didn't realize was there. But alone in the tub she feels sorry, for all the love she has been given and not returned.

How much this family has done for her! And for no other reason than kindness. Despite all their fears, despite all their sorrows. She resolves, from now on, to be a better friend, to be the kind of person who is worthy of the love she wants. To find Sky, she must begin all over again with love. She must learn to love, starting here, starting now.

She hears Rye's voice on the other side of the curtain. "Lonely?"

A feeling too fleeting to name rustles through her. Her stomach turns over gently. "Yes?"

"Do you need any more hot water?"

"That's okay."

"But is it getting cold?"

She hesitates. She wants to ask nothing more—nothing.

"It's okay," says Rye. "I'll heat one more pot."

Lonely is truly starting to shiver a little by the time he returns. He hands her the pot through the curtain, and she doesn't see his face. She pours the water in, hands back the pot. She doesn't hear any footsteps.

"Lonely?"

She doesn't answer. She traces random pathways on her body with her fingertips, in and out of the water, feeling the way the line between water and air slips over her skin like a kiss. She doesn't remember, any more, the exact pattern his hands traveled that day. She doesn't remember the look in his eyes. She can only remember Sky now.

"I wanted to tell you something." She hears a deep breath. Where is Fawn? Upstairs, maybe. Already in bed. The house is very quiet, and she realizes he is the only one left awake besides her. His voice is so sad now, it seems, all the time. Since she came, she has not heard laughter. Not once. Suddenly she is amazed by his endurance.

"I wanted to say I'm sorry for what happened that day, a long time ago, out in the field. For when I kissed you. It was wrong of me."

"It's okay," says Lonely, surprise making her breathless.

"I was just starting to enjoy talking to you. I wish we had kept talking. I think I needed a friend, more than I needed—more than I needed anything else. I wish I had realized that then."

"I'm still your friend," she says, and feels tears balancing on the lower edges of her eyelids, like dancers.

"I know."

"And I didn't leave because of that," she says. Even though, in a way, she did. "I just had to. I had somewhere to go."

"I know," says Rye. "Did you find what you were looking for?"

Lonely closes her eyes. "I don't know." She feels too tired to say more.

But after a moment of silence, Rye answers, "I know. It's so hard to make sense of things sometimes, isn't it?" And she feels that he understands exactly, without her having to explain. For maybe his sorrow, though it is different, knows the language of hers.

"You know how sometimes," she says impulsively, "you call out to—I don't know to whom—but you cry out, as if to the universe, begging for what you long for, asking why you can't have it? Do you ever do that, Rye? Do you ever cry out and cry out, and not get an answer?"

She feels his slow thinking on the other side of the curtain. She feels him weighing the question, turning it over, wanting to be sure, wanting to say his words right.

"A long time ago," he says finally, "I stopped praying to any god. I stopped praying to whoever and whatever I could feel around me, as if I could ask anything of everything, as if I could carelessly throw my wishes out into the world and expect them to be answered. I'm not saying it's wrong to do that. But it just made me lonely."

"So what do you do? You accept whatever comes? You don't wonder?"

"No. I do. But I think now I only believe in praying to other people—and to other lives that I'm connected to. I pray to the crops to rise and thrive every year, and I pray to the clouds to rain when we need rain, and I thank the earth for what it gives us, and I thank our food. Sometimes, now, I pray to my son, or to the spirit of my son, to stay safe and come back to us when he's ready. I pray to my wife, and to both our spirits, to understand each other better. I pray to the love that moves between us. I imagine it like a river that carries my prayers back and forth. I don't pray to any god, or anything else. I pray directly to the person I'm praying about. Because I think our souls can speak to each other, and I think we're in charge of our own lives. When we pray like that, we give as well as take."

Lonely is silent, because she knows she doesn't need to say anything back, and there is nothing to say. When she hears Rye finally rise, she says quietly,

"Thank you."

She hears him pause, then walk away. And she thinks, *In that summer long ago, I did not yet know what intimacy was. It doesn't have to have anything to do with touch. It just has to do with where you sit inside yourself, and where you listen from, and whether or not your heart is open to the prayers of another.*

The boy turns his head fitfully while Dragon tries to hold it still, dripping water into his mouth and over his body. But he does not murmur; he does not cry out. His skin is lighter than Dragon's, but dark enough to accept the sun's fire without burning too badly. It's only lack of water that brought him down.

The boy is younger and smaller than any other person Dragon has known, and has a backpack like Delilah's, with an empty bottle tied to it with rope. Dragon looks through the pack while the boy sleeps. He finds dried meat wrapped in leather, objects he doesn't recognize but with strong smells that tell him they must also be food, a shirt, a coat, a coiled rope, a knife. Dragon saw the same things lying by Delilah's pack when she planned to leave. Perhaps they are the objects humans always carry with them: something to put inside themselves, something to cover the outside of themselves, something with which to tie things together, and something with which to tear things apart. But there is something else here that he has never seen before. Something square that opens like a flower—hundreds of thin white petals on the inside, detailed elaborately with black designs like the footprints of spiders. After Dragon goes out to the river to fill the boy's bottle for him, he stares at this thing for a long time, holding it in his lap and fanning through the petals. The detail of the marks, the thinness of each white sheet, amazes him. He feels the sacredness of it, the effort of it, the reticent meaning of it, like a dream he doesn't understand.

"Can you read?" says the boy, his voice a little cracked. Dragon looks up, startled, but then he puts the thing down carefully and goes to the boy. He doesn't bother with the question, which he doesn't understand. He smiles. He likes the lack of fear in the boy's eyes, and the willing presence there. He was afraid the boy might speak some other language or want to fight. Not that he would be difficult to fight, but Dragon would rather not hurt him.

"Where are we?" asks the boy now.

This also seems a difficult question, so Dragon says simply, "I'm Dragon."

"I'm Malachite," says the boy. "Or Kite." He turns his head, and pulls himself up weakly to sitting. Dragon hands him the bottle and the boy drinks all the water.

"We'll have to go out if you want more water," Dragon explains. He's a little dazed by the way the idea of water has suddenly changed, from something mysterious and holy and containing the secret of his beloved, to something easy and immediate for the boy—something a human being can and must take in constantly, an everyday encounter. He struggles with his envy. He doesn't want to hate this boy. He senses he was given the task of caring for him for a reason.

"Thank you for saving my life," the boy says seriously, and Dragon nods back as seriously. He likes the boy's simplicity of speaking and his honor for what's important.

"Where are we?" comes the question again.

"This is where I live," says Dragon.

"Where?" The boy struggles forward, but he's still a little weak for standing. "It's some cave. Are we under the desert?"

"Yes," says Dragon proudly. "Once there was water all around, boiling with the fire of the dragons."

The boy looks at him sharply, studies him. Dragon meets his stare. "Who are you? You live here?"

"I'm a god," states Dragon proudly. "A fire god."

The boy shakes his shaggy head, then continues to gaze around. Dragon can see him figuring, waiting for his own mind to clear.

"My mother is afraid of fire gods," he murmurs, as if to himself.

Dragon nods. His mother was afraid of them, too.

"What happened to you?" asks Dragon.

Malachite shakes his head again. "I don't know what happened. I had a good map. I got it from a book, and my dad made some corrections in it from what he knew by traveling when he was younger, so I thought it was pretty up to date. I brought it so that I would know where the water sources were, in the desert. But things must have changed. My grandmother has said that before. That the City has changed the sky, so the rains fall differently, and the 'river goddess' is missing, and the rivers are confused. But I didn't totally believe in all that. I didn't think it would make that much of a difference."

"It's hard to predict the water, where it goes," says Dragon sadly.

"So what is it that you can do with fire?"

"I can make it. You know, without—without anything. From nothing."

"Can you show me?"

"Uh—it has to be at the right time. When I feel it."

"Feel what?"

Dragon shifts awkwardly. "The fire."

"You can't always do it?"

"I don't know." Dragon is surprised by this thought. It has never occurred to him to try to create the fire when he didn't already feel it. Usually, he is so concerned with trying to hold it back or calm it. He never thought of it as something someone might need and ask him to call up on purpose. But then, isn't that what the goddesses were always telling him? Wasn't that the purpose of the meditation after all—to turn that energy into some kind of power? But for what?

Dragon looks back at the boy. He likes him even more. There is no hiding in him, no teasing, no laughter unexplained. He feels that they understand each other.

"Where were you going?"

"To the City," says Malachite.

"Why?"

"Because they have Knowledge there. They know how to harness the energy of the elements. And because I want to know what it really is. Not anyone else's ideas about it. People all have different ideas and emotions about things, and they get muddled. I want to know the truth."

Dragon nods again. It fascinates him more than he can say—what the boy is saying. He wants to grab onto those words and the light in them, but he doesn't know even what questions to ask. *Truth.* He works the word around in his mouth, wanting to say it aloud.

"I'm still thirsty," says the boy.

"Come." Dragon stands and offers his hand, feeling strong and proud. "We'll go back out. I'll take you to the river."

Dragon helps the boy to stand. Leaning with his thin arm across Dragon's shoulders, he walks with Dragon up a winding dirt path, as pale and dusty as if there had never been water anywhere. Dragon helps him climb over the stones and into the sun.

Dragon looks at him. Malachite stares straight ahead without seeming to see for a moment. "It was weird in there," he states finally. "I couldn't think clearly."

They walk together in silence—the boy thinking, Dragon wondering. The river is lower again since the last rain, its shallowness making it sound youthful as it twists through the sunlight. Malachite kneels, fills the bottle, drinks, and fills the bottle again.

"What do you mean," asks Dragon, "about 'energy'?"

Malachite stands. "Energy can be made from any element," he says. "From water, from this river. Or from the air, the wind. Or from fire, the sun. My family knows how to draw energy from the earth. We have always known that. But there are other kinds of energy besides the kind that keeps you alive, the kind that keeps your body moving. People can make magic with those other elements. They can make lights. They can make hot and cold—they can make all kinds of things happen!"

"But what if there are too many things?" asks Dragon.

"What?"

"I don't know. Someone from the City once told me there are too many things there." He doesn't know what Delilah meant, but he knows it made her sad. Thinking of her now makes him miss her. He misses those first words she spoke to him—and her vulnerability then. All of her hesitation, he realizes suddenly, was out of fear for herself, her own heart. It was never because she didn't like him. In fact she was the only one who seemed to understand and accept him right from the beginning, without ever questioning, without ever being afraid of him.

Malachite is nodding. "My grandmother says that too," he says, after a moment's careful thought. "I don't understand how the making of things can get out of the control of the people who are making them. That doesn't make sense, does it? But that's what I want to find out. I want to find out the truth."

"I would like to go with you," says Dragon, deepening his voice, trying to bring forth the gravity that he feels. "I want to find out the Truth, too. I want to go where knowledge is. There are things I need to know."

Malachite looks at him with that same studious, unabashed gaze. Dragon's heart is racing. Everything is different now. The constellation of his world has shifted. The patterns—the familiar thoughts, the familiar longings, the connections that bind him—have all shifted. There is nothing left for him here. The boy's face is gentle, but with a hard sure profile, like a clear line of manhood running down the center. "Are you ready right now?" he says.

Moon, where are you when I need you?

When Delilah first came across the desert from the City, she didn't follow the river and she didn't follow a road. She followed Moon. And she's not going back the way she came now, because she's not going back to the City. She planned to follow the river however it goes, figuring it was the most direct route to the sea. She brought her two empty water jugs, tied to her backpack, mostly so she wouldn't leave any trace of herself behind. She didn't think she would actually need them, as long as she stayed by the river.

But tonight, the river disappears.

It's about midnight when she comes to the place where it dives into a mouth of white, blocky stones, and the desert continues on above it, pale and graceful and almost completely barren. When she looks ahead, she sees no sign of the river all the way to the horizon. Maybe it's because she's so hungry right now, having not eaten since the morning, but standing at the edge of the end of water, she finds herself screaming into its passionate sound.

"No! You don't get to fucking leave me! No!" She sits down and flings her backpack at the ground, bending her head and pulling at her own hair because she knows she's being ridiculous, that Yora has nothing to do with her, that the river has nothing to do with her, and that she's let herself be tricked again into depending on the love of someone who cannot be depended upon. Yora doesn't love her. Yora is a spirit, a goddess, belonging to another world completely alien to Delilah's need.

Of course it would come to this, eventually.

She sits there for a long time, her mind spinning into its own despair, until her stomach begins to tug irritably again at the strings of her thoughts. Out of habit as much as necessity, she gathers her mind to find a rational solution, at least to the problem of food. As the river has gotten faster, she's found fewer and fewer fish. Two days ago she broke her own rule about hunting in the desert and killed a jack rabbit. Tonight, it appears, she'll do it again.

She's luckier tonight and finds three roadrunner eggs in a hollow in the sand. No dreams guide her: she simply knows where to look, and frightens the bird off her nest. She feels sorry, though. It takes so much energy to create life, she can hardly imagine. The roadrunner will return to the nest, find everything gone, and have to start again. Animals do this over and over.

Delilah swallows the eggs raw and returns to the river's end. For a moment she feels she will be sick again, but she concentrates hard on keeping the food down. *I'm not going to waste all the effort and grief of that poor bird by hacking it back up on the ground again,* she thinks furiously.

She fills her two water jugs and sits down again to think. It's almost dawn now, and she's exhausted, but she can't sleep until she figures something out. She has to get across this desert. This is the only thing left of any importance in her life. Just to get to Mira.

It never occurred to her, coming into the desert with Moon in her heady escape, in her relief, in her driven determination, that she would one day be equally desperate to get back out. Or that the desert—her home, her salvation, the place that finally accepted her—might one day become her prison.

She rests her chin on her knees and listens to the river, stronger now after another rain. She misses her little cave so much. She misses the fox and the bats, the snakes and the owls; she misses the shadows of the pines waving over her head; she misses her dark sanctuary and the power of knowing how to keep herself alive forever, without needing anyone. She misses the only place she ever honestly called home. And she feels this so much now, vividly, all the time: homesickness.

Water is love, Dragon said once. She remembers those words suddenly. She listens to the water disappearing into the stone, disappearing over and over, drop after drop, like a scene of loss re-enacted eternally before her.

The journey beneath the mountain seemed to continue for days.

The earth lay cold both below and above; there was no sky, no light but the Unicorn. Sky held onto that light in the pitch blackness, curling his wings over her back like arms, holding on with all the strength of his life. He felt so sick inside, he could not think. He could tell that the Unicorn was not afraid at all, that her light could never go out, that she knew exactly where she was going. He concentrated all his mind on her, so that he wouldn't give in to that fear—because the fear would make him fly, and if he flew he would be lost in the directionless blackness of the mountain's insides, forever.

Neither of them spoke. But he trusted her sure, delicate footsteps. He recognized and trusted her heart. Some things were very simple, and had always been known to him.

The first light ahead does not welcome them. It's all noise and motion—motion so fast it rips holes in reality. But he recognizes that light, though it makes him even sicker inside. He recognizes the cars shining smoother than water and speeding fast to nowhere, and the tight locked spaces, and the doors separating worlds, and the concrete walkways where feet leave no tracks, and the violent bodies, and the homeless hearts. It all comes fast on him at once: the nightmare he has always avoided, all his life until now.

But it means he was right, and there is hope in the center of all this.

They emerge into that garish light, and he tells himself not to look back. He never wants to know how the mountain appears from this side. Perhaps it's a monstrous hill of eroding dust, or perhaps it's a heap of trash.

But of course, he looks back anyway. There is nothing there. He cannot see from whence they came—only the City all around them.

For in the City, people cannot even see the mountain. They do not even know that the dream is there.

The truth is that on the other side of the mountain, everything is opposite. So if here in this Other World, the City covers all the lands that were still wilderness in the world Sky has come from, then what was City in that world will be wilderness in this one.

Therefore in the heart of this world, his people's home will still be wild.

9th MOON

●

Lil,

If I had words to give you. If I could say, somehow, that I love you.

The best I could give you was always enough for you. A fleeting visit you could never expect. Showing up empty, and only when I wanted to—not when you most needed it, not when you were most alone. A protected love—that's what I gave you. A conditional love, only when I felt safe.

You deserve better. But because my love was the best love you ever got, you figured you'd take it.

Lil, I couldn't love you all the way because I wasn't all the way myself. I guess you knew that. Now I'm going to try to be myself, but it means I can't be with you that way ever again. It doesn't make any sense.

Lil. I tried to find you so your fire could dissolve me up into the sky. But you weren't there for me when I needed you, like I have never been there for you when you most needed me. It was my own anger that dissolved me, instead.

You know what that anger feels like. You feel it all the time. It always frightened me, so that I turned away from you when you felt it. But down in the desert I fought your lover, and he caused me pain, and it was the first pain that I ever got to feel, and it was the anger that made me feel it. That burning. You know.

My own fire. If I'm rain, and I have fire inside me, then you, little fire goddess, must have water inside you too. I wish I could tell you that. Maybe it would help you.

Do you know what tears feel like when you can't find a way to cry them, what anger feels like when you think you have no right? It seemed so easy for you. I envied you, Lil.

But I can't be with you any more. I can't talk to you ever again, in that form.

Lil, the days we chased each other, hot legs pounding, stomachs clenched, in the meadow. The nights we spread our arms and turned in the desert, feeling the wind spiral into us. The noise of our heartbeats in the still forest when we hunted, the ache of my breath leaving my lungs as I played my flute, fur against my palm, skin against my bare chest, the breath of your whisper around the labyrinth of my ear. The touch of your child's hands, as if I were human, as if I were yours and you, mine.

Lil, I took my body for granted. I let other people use it. I thought pleasure was meaningless. I knew taking human form was only an excuse to avoid what I'm here for. I knew it was an escape. And I felt guilty about it. I tried to punish myself; I tried to make that body hurt. But I couldn't feel anything because I wanted so desperately not even to exist.

But now that I've lost my body, I long for the tears to cry for it. I long for a heart to ache for its loss. I miss it so much. It wasn't a hungry body, but now I see that it could still experience joy. And your memory was stored inside the habits of its motions, its synapses, its pains, its impulses. Because through that body, I got to love, and I didn't realize that that was part of the story, too. That was part of why I'm here. I wasn't wasting all that time while the world went thirsty and the heart of the City dried up and forgot the rain. I was learning how to love.

I'm up here now in the sky, Lil, where you can never, ever be, and I know how Yora felt. I know how the easiest thing is to hang up here forever. It's so easy to be nothing. Forgetting calls to me and pulls at me and tempts me, the way sleep tempts a human being when he is lost on a cold winter night that will kill him. You'd think it would be easy to rain. To let go. But I must have turned human all those years with you, because I'm afraid. I wish you could be here with me.

Yora had to face up to returning in human form. But me, I have to face up to never being human again. To being, instead, what I was meant to be.

Lil, if I had words to speak. But I don't. Because I have no mouth, no tongue, no throat, and no lungs. Not any more. I am rain, only rain. Or I am an idea of rain, something I hardly remember now.

What is the purpose of a god? I can't remember. The water exists and flows. It needs no god to oversee it. Being a god is not about controlling anything—I've known that for a long time. What, then? Why am I here?

I feel like you would know. I feel like you've been trying to tell me, but I haven't been listening.

—Moon

Ever since she talked with the tree in her dream, Lonely feels something she could almost call faith. If she thinks about it too much, she feels afraid again, but when she's not thinking she moves with grace, as if she knows what she's doing. In the mornings she does everything she can to help the family. She tries to rise before they wake. She lights the fire and heats the water. She asks Eva what medicines she needs for the pain in her bones, and gathers them for her the best she can. She helps Chelya and Rye make breakfast when Fawn can't get herself out of bed. She learns to chop wood.

In some quiet moment when the others are busy outside, she, too, leaves the house, and then she enters the forest. She doesn't want to ask too much of the family, so she takes no food with her—only water. She explores each tree, and the shapes between it and each other tree, with her eyes and her fingers and her sense of smell, until she can recognize a certain path for herself to find her way out there and back again.

Every day she comes to the fire circle, and greets the fallen tree, and sits on the feet-stamped ground where in the summer the fairies danced. She tries to be patient. She sits all day with the birch, the chestnut, the dead log, the mushroom, the empty hole of the weasel or a bird she hears cheeping, unseen, in the snow-shrouded bush. Sky could be anywhere.

What do you know about him? she asks each one.

She asks again and again. She lies back on the snow, which feels warm through the layers of her clothing, and opens herself up, opens the question up to the world.

he is afraid of you, say a cluster of branches that become the limbs of a deer, and then, when she starts up and looks after them, are gone—*but he needs you.*

he doesn't even know if he is real, says the snake who hibernates now beneath the frozen mud, who takes all afternoon to form the words that Lonely dreams, *but your love makes him real.*

maybe he looks for you, chatters the squirrel, heedless of winter's somber silence, *but he's looking backwards.* He leaps and laughs, circles the tree, up and up.

Their voices comfort her, even while they worry her, and even when she doesn't understand. She is not so alone any more. In her heart, she feels that truly it is the elders of his people who speak to her now; and this does not seem incredible to her, for though Sky saw them as only those white birds, she feels they have always been everywhere.

We are always with him, they seem to say. *But he does not know. Nor does he admit to himself that he has lost us forever. That we are gone. That we died long ago. That he is living in a land of ghosts.*

"Did I break him apart from you," asks Lonely, with pain, "when I made love to him, and caused him to sleep?"

You did not cause him to sleep, they say, speaking through eddies of snow and the invisible moon. *You woke him. You woke him from that dream of the past, in which he did not yet have to feel.*

"But how can I find him now?" Lonely is crying as she lies open in the snow, her heart breaking with compassion for the idea of him wandering alone, awake to all his own sorrow—sorrow so painful that he created an entire dream of a life up on that mountain so that he wouldn't have to feel it. She watches the colors of the sky twist and turn, watches it swallow and spit back the light, watches it pulse silently with the sun and foam up the clouds. "How can I help him?"

only love, say a flock of starlings rising, the last dead leaves falling. *only love and love and love. you are no bigger than this.*

And all she really wants to know is, *How can I be with him again?* And all she really knows is the memory of his helpless animal breath in her hair, when she touched his body as he spoke of dreams. All she has is the memory of his light voice and his unconscious arms as they held her that last night, and the thousand memories of those eyes and that kiss in that snow and that ice—and that smile, that childishly brave smile like a lasso of hope tossed out to her over a frozen past. All she has is the sequence of each moment they spent together, which she replays in her mind every day, as if it will tell her the end of the story.

At the end of the day, she prays to him. Though all she can hear in response is a wordless, heartless wind, she whispers his name. *Sky. I know you are here. I am your roots. Come down.* She prays, though she does not understand her own prayer. She prays to make herself believe. She remembers how she stood on the cliff overlooking that nothingness into which he had flown, and how—without thinking, because there was no other choice—she jumped. How he caught her then, because he had to—he had to admit that he loved her.

For she would leap again now. *I'll do anything,* she tells him. *Tell me what to do. Tell me how to find you. Tell me how to save you.*

Still, only the wind replies. But sometimes, like the day she stood on that cliff and shouted his name, she thinks she can feel his silent, fragile listening somewhere in the ethers like a wild animal unsure if it can trust her—holding his breath, listening for the guidance of her voice. As if he had flown to pieces and his spirit, his heart, his eyes and his ears, all rest in frozen waiting in the trees and stars around her, waiting for her to find him and wake him and put him back together again. Waiting for her to breathe into him and say, *You are human. Be human again.*

In the evening, light and dreamy from hunger, she whispers against each tree trunk to find her way home, and walks up the moonlit field to the house, with its warm lonely eyes of firelight and its blue shadow in the snow. In the winter, darkness closes in on either side of day like two cradling hands, stretching its arms around from the black body of the night's center—the abyss of midnight—when she will wake starkly in the silent room, the fire gone out, the stars hissing at her from all the way in the sky in a language too far away to hear.

At dinner, she sits by Chelya, puts her arm around her if she seems sad, strokes her hair. Sometimes Rye will talk to Lonely in the evening, while Fawn is silently working or tucked away in the womb of her own fear, and Lonely will help him lay out his sorrows in the blanket of her listening—for they do not weigh much—and understand for the first time that loneliness does not belong to her alone.

For Rye tells Lonely things he has never spoken of before. He tells her how beneath his own anxiety for Kite's absence, there has also risen up this intense longing which he has not felt since before he fell in love with Fawn— which he has not allowed himself to feel. How he lies awake at night, imagining Kite's journey, and then imagining his own, as if it were he who could walk away without thought for his family, and go wherever he chose, and live by adventure and chance, and be utterly free. How maybe what Kite seeks is something that's missing in this family—something Rye has felt for a long time and denied to himself. They honor the seasons and the giving earth and the food they eat, Eva and Fawn did an initiation ceremony for Chelya when she came of age, and Rye tried to do one for Kite too, but still something is missing: that which is dangerous and brings unforeseen change, that which is masculine, that which blazes out into the world, whatever the world is—that which must prove its own life, and prove it by being brave.

Rye talks, and Lonely listens and tries to understand through him the fight that rose up in Sky, what he longed for, and why he could not stay inside her arms and be at peace. For sometimes she thinks that maybe Rye's words are—at least for now—the only answer to her prayer.

She feels a sense of certainty sometimes, and in that certainty a surprising nostalgia, as if this time is almost over and soon she will know what to do. When that time comes, she will be gone from here, for a long time or perhaps forever. But the time has not come yet, so she lies awake after the others fall asleep, and battles with the fears that come creeping back in.

What did you learn today? they mock, in the voice of the wind. *Nothing.*

The moons continue, and you'll be back on the island trapped in the old woman's stare. As far as you know, he only drifts further away—and you here, locked against the earth, locked in your own human ignorance.

She clutches the Unicorn's horn always at her side, wrapped in her cloaks against her heart. But never again does she feel its singing sting, as she did on the night Sky reached out to her so briefly through the skin between worlds, and held her once more.

"You can call me Kite," Malachite reminds him.

Dragon says nothing. He feels awkward, somehow, dropping the formality of the boy's full name. He feels that there is honor in calling each other by their whole names, like men.

"My mother still insists on calling me Malachite. It bothers me. Like she doesn't get that I'm choosing who I am—that I want to fly, that I'm freer than she is, tied so hard to the earth and so afraid. She keeps saying, 'That's the name I gave to you. That's your name.' It drives me crazy. She doesn't own me, just because she's my mother."

Dragon is thinking that Malachite is lucky, to have a mother who loves him. But he tries to focus on what the boy is saying, as they climb together—Malachite's feet in sandals and Dragon's feet bare—over red rock formations, the clouds above so thick and white they look solid as they skid fast into the horizon. He loves the way being with Malachite makes him use his mind—makes him have to figure things out that he never tried to figure out before. It pulls him away, a little, from the obsessions of his body and the sickness in his heart.

"What is owning?" he asks, though he thinks he knows. "What does it mean?"

"It's like, you think you control something. When people create things, they think they own them. My mother created me, so she thinks she owns me. People in the City create things, so they think they own them. But they don't own them. That's why things get out of their control, my grandmother says. Because they don't give them proper respect."

Something about what he's saying is tugging at Dragon. "So no one owns anything?"

Malachite thinks. "No. I guess not. It's a made-up word, I think. A word the City made, but everyone uses it now. It doesn't make sense, when you think about it."

"But what about when you love someone? And you want to—to give yourself to her." Because it doesn't seem wrong, suddenly, despite what Delilah said. It's true, he must own himself. But there is more to it than that. Something Delilah didn't understand. Something she feared.

Malachite twists his forehead a little. "I don't feel that way about anyone."

"Haven't you ever known a woman? A woman who owned you from the first moment you saw her, because she was so beautiful?"

Yes. Dragon sees the boy's face soften, sees him turn away. But Malachite avoids the question. "It's like fire," he says instead.

"What?"

"You don't own the fire, right? You make it, but it's not yours. No." He stops to think. "Maybe that's not the same thing…."

They see a jack rabbit freeze in the near distance, and they both freeze, too. Malachite pulls out his slingshot, and waits a moment, letting their stillness make a quiet space around all three of them. Then he whirls it, his wrist turning faster than Dragon can see, but not too fast for the rabbit, who becomes a blur before the rock has left the cloth, shooting like a star across the sand and gone.

Dragon feels sorry. He knows the boy, who hasn't eaten yet today, must be hungry. This is the second animal he's missed.

"I wish I had that kind of magic," he says. "So I could help you."

Malachite shrugs. "I don't believe in magic."

Dragon stares at him, as they keep walking.

"I mean," adds Malachite quickly, as if afraid to hurt Dragon's feelings, "I know you can do things. I know you can go without food and make fire and—I don't know yet how you do it. But you can't make things happen like that. You can't make an animal come to you or die for you. That's what I mean about owning."

Dragon thinks he understands now. But he doesn't want to. "I think I want to own something," he says.

"Why?" Malachite stops.

"Because if I can't control anything, then nothing responds to me, nothing answers me, nothing—there's just nothing! I'm alone." He thinks of Yora's nothingness. Of her absence everywhere, all the time, how it haunted him. How it still haunts him, despite all that Coyote taught him. Yet at the same time, he's surprised by the calm with which he can think of these things now.

"But you don't need to own something for it to respond to you," says Malachite. "If everything responded just how I wanted it to—if everything fell down and died right when I wanted it for my food—then things would be boring. You know?"

"Are you happy?" Dragon asks.

Malachite looks up at the sky and keeps walking. "I think so. Yeah. I like finding out new things. Things were too predictable back at home. I'm excited to see the City."

Dragon knows the general direction of "the City," but it is Malachite—Kite, that is—who leads the way, who has planned their route exactly once he found the river again on the map. Dragon is amazed by the map: a tiny symbol of how everything in life is connected, like a window into the mind that dreamed this world, whatever it is. His dragons' lair did not exist on the map, but Kite, with a god-like ease that unsettled Dragon, made a mark that showed him where it is. The river extends past his lair, past Delilah's abandoned cave, and then stops. But east of his lair, back toward the mountains, the river forks off toward the City, and this fork continues almost to the ridgeline. Following this branch, they pass the development in the distance that Dragon once came close to, from the other side, on his journey down from the Garden. But Kite keeps walking. The people he's seeking are at the heart of the City, where knowledge is kept.

"I thought it was some god who created the City," says Dragon now.

Kite shrugs again. "I don't know. I think that's all stories. I mean I know my grandmother believes all that, and she knows a lot, but my dad says we're all just people, you know? We have to be responsible for ourselves, not blame things on...." He trails off. "There's Coyote," he says suddenly. "Let's follow him."

Shocked by this suggestion, Dragon turns in time to see Coyote running away into the brush, and Kite is already ahead of Dragon, starting after him. Dragon says nothing, but follows. It's easy for him to make his footsteps as silent as Kite's. He crouches when Kite crouches, steps when Kite steps, and then finds his own quiet route through the shadows. Never before has he tried like this to stay hidden, and it makes him feel strange and humble and lonely, but then after that a silent laughter starts jumbling in his belly, because he feels that they are playing some trick on Coyote, though he doesn't know what it is. Without Kite, he never could have imagined such magic. The silence between him and the boy as they creep along—the silent understanding between them—feels good, like nothing he's ever felt before. There is a sense of companionship with someone who is like him, in some way that doesn't require words, doesn't require anything of him. It isn't the loving, devouring embrace he both needs and fears from woman, but it is a closeness just the same, a kind of gut-level agreement: to be men together, to be bold, to travel onward and onward, no matter what, into an unknown but deliberate adventure.

Now he sees that Coyote is trailing a running bird. Kite has already seen this. Kite is circling around. Dragon stops and crouches. He watches Kite's lean, focused arm unwind. He feels such a tenderness for his friend—for the instinctual confidence in his body, for the glorious manhood in him held out like an offering to life in the hands of the still-innocent boy. This is the first love Dragon has ever felt that doesn't involve desire.

The rock whirls. Coyote spins in mid-stride, then sits back and looks casual as Kite walks to the bird's body to claim it. But his ears are pinned back, the romantic grace of his hunt deflated by his awkward snarl, his slinking backward. Kite is smiling.

"Sorry, friend," he says, looking kindly at Coyote but without regret. "You'd have done the same to me, if you could."

He and Dragon begin walking again, Kite swinging the bird by its feet. They are walking toward a hillside to get out of the wind, so that Dragon can make a fire for him to cook with. They both know this without saying anything. Dragon feels Coyote watching them go, and he makes himself look back so he won't feel like a coward. Coyote is only sitting and watching, but Dragon thinks he sees him smile.

"Sometimes," says Kite, "it's good to play a trick on the Trickster. Keeps things in balance, you know?"

They sit in the lee of the hill, and Dragon sits cross-legged and focuses. He's already made a fire on purpose for Kite once, but he's still nervous. He's so unused to *trying.* What if he can't do it this time? But when he closes his eyes and breathes, it's all still in there, closer than he realized, as if the act of leaving this place behind has brought it right to the surface: all the longing, the fury, the unspoken love. He cries out. When he opens his eyes to the flames, he can barely remember at first who Kite is.

Afterward, he feels for the first time how his fire is a blessing, a gift he has, something special he can awaken at will. And at the same time he feels, for the first time, how it doesn't belong to him at all.

The colors on the signs are too bright—a uniform kind of brightness that leaves no room for wonder. You know how it is: those shapes are so hard, they knock a hole in your stomach, and that hole remains, aching and aching and nothing can fill it but more of the same, so that eventually you can't see anything but those colors, those shapes. You keep needing more of them to fill you.

For the Unicorn, Sky knows, beauty is food. Yet for him she steps resolutely, head hanging, over gutters, through the blasts of machines turning over and over the earth, between the alien rectangles and the swells of the land cut to patternless pieces by random metal, concrete, and plastic lines. The people—what are they fed on? Not food, not the lives of real animals or plants, but some artificial mockery of these, so that their bodies no longer take the shapes of real life—their limbs malformed, not shaped for movement, their graceless bodies bulging in the wrong places, their clothing rectangular. Lost hips, sagging bellies, concave chests, weeping breasts, flapping arms. The angular lines of their shirts and shorts cut them into pieces.

In their dreams Sky had seen the most beautiful part of them. He had seen the truest part of them that remained. He cannot see it any longer.

But the Unicorn carries him onward, though Sky is sure she will die of such ugliness. She has already taken him under the mountain. She could leave him now, and return to the world they came from, where most of the earth is still beautiful. But though she has not spoken of it, he knows that she, too, comes from where he is going. He could lift into the air on his own wings, and soar above this place, searching from a more distant height for the center he seeks. Yet—whether for her own sake or his, he does not know—he cannot leave her.

She walks on, day and night, never stopping or changing her pace. In her stride Sky feels at once the ease of rivers and the broken, rhythmic seesaw of the land-bound mammal's humble step: back and forth, right and left, an endless prayer knocking against the earth, whether with hopelessness or ceaseless faith Sky cannot tell.

At night she says to him, "It doesn't matter. I have nowhere else to go but where you are going."

He sees the people who sleep in the streets and the lonely people in their beds behind the windows. He sees the people who stay awake all night, seeking and fighting, pause to watch her pass—even if they don't actually see her—and lift up their chests without realizing it, something like hope beginning there. Something they haven't felt since they were born.

"Who's there?" cries one man, unfolding himself from rags and standing on shaky legs. Sky can see the lost ghost of who he could have been standing in front of him, the hero's destiny his heart once planned for him but long ago gave up on. "Who's there?" he cries out again, tears making acid paths across his cheeks.

The Unicorn bows her head to him, and though still he cannot seem to see her, he lifts his hands to her horn, and seems to feel the light that lies in his palms. He smiles. As she turns away he clenches his fists as if determined, and his muscles seem to glow. He walks away down the street, standing tall, his stride purposeful.

"But if you heal them," Sky whispers, "the ones on the other side—the world we come from—will only suffer more. Because everything is opposite there. Don't you see?"

The Unicorn keeps walking. "No," she answers calmly. "I do not believe that everything is opposite, Dream God. That is not why I exist."

"But here you see it," cries Sky, unable to stop himself, though he knows—he thought he knew—the meaning of the Unicorn. "There is City and there is Wild, and they are not the same! They cannot understand each other."

"Of course they can," says the Unicorn. "They are the same. Aren't they dreams of each other? Is the mind opposite the body? Don't they only need to know each other, and love? Doesn't the City always yearn to be wilder, and the things of the wild always yearn to grow stronger, live longer, do all the things that the City has done?"

Sky enfolds his own face in his black wings. He doesn't want to hear about love, or to care any more about the world. He is so tired. "When we get there," he says to her, "you can stay there with me. You'll be safe there, forever."

But he knows he only speaks his own longing, and he knows she doesn't believe him. "Remember your promise," is all she says.

The closest Fawn ever comes to yelling now are swift hisses in private, always out of Lonely's sight. Now she and Rye are arguing outside, and Lonely can hear them from where she picks greens in the greenhouse. Outside, twilight is already pinching closed the day, but Jay's horse has just carried him off running back to their farm, and in a moment Fawn will have to follow him. Willow is giving birth.

"Chelya is never here!" cries Fawn now. "She's always with *him*. When is she going to learn that no one is more important than her family—no one!"

"Fawn, you're not making sense," Rye sighs, not bothering to raise his voice. "Chelya didn't know this would happen today. You know she would want nothing more than to go with you."

"But I never know where she goes. She's always gone. She thinks she's in love—but it's nothing, it's nothing, when it's all we can do to keep our family together." Lonely hears the familiar tightening in her voice that is tears fought back. "And it's so late. She knows better than to stay out so late on a winter night! How can she—? It's so dangerous—and now Willow—"

Then there is silence, and Lonely wonders if Rye is holding her, comforting her, or if they are only standing several hands apart from each other, staring awkwardly, each full of emotion they have no place to unload. She wants to shake Fawn, to break her open and unloose that tension that clutches her own heart just as tightly when she's forced to listen like this.

"Mother can't go," she's murmuring. "She's in too much pain to travel by horseback in the cold."

"You don't need anyone's help," Rye says gently. "You can do it without her."

"I don't want to travel alone," hisses Fawn. "How can you ask me to—?"

"Take Lonely," Rye interrupts, impatient again. "I'll go find Chelya. I'm sure she's fine. I'll go and find her. You go with Lonely. That's what we'll do."

Lonely hears a whimper that sounds like "no." She straightens up, her heart panicking against the inside of her chest, and stares at the door. Then without waiting to hear more of Fawn's response, she goes into the main room for her cloak and boots. She wraps her head in a shawl. She slips the Unicorn's horn into the inner folds. She is shaking from the fear of Fawn's quiet anger, from wanting to do what is asked of her and fearing she'll mess it up—and now Fawn is waiting at the door, her eyes raw, her face soft. Lonely doesn't know why Fawn should be so angry with her, but the way she ignores her, and has ignored her for so long, makes it seem that she must be.

They stare at each other for a long moment. Fawn knows that Lonely was listening. "We'll take Rye's horse," she says finally, and that's all she says to Lonely until they arrive at Jay and Willow's house deep in the night a long time later.

Rye's horse, being a work horse, is slower, but strong enough to carry them both. Lonely feels awkward in her tallness, towering slightly over Fawn's head from behind. She doesn't want to put her arms around Fawn's waist, she doesn't want to intrude on the space of someone who has kept her at a distance for so long, but once the horse starts moving, she has to. Fawn gives no indication of noticing.

Fawn's silence is all Lonely hears, all she feels, all she knows, for a long, long time. She doesn't think of where they are or where they are going; she doesn't even think of Sky. She is so afraid of that silence, and it surrounds her, bigger than winter.

She tries to focus on her own body, and on fighting the onslaught of the cold.

But finally, eventually, she becomes aware of the peace inside Fawn. That peace, settling into the rhythm of their riding, settling into the night, sits at the very core of Fawn through everything that happens. Still, at the heart of her, Fawn is gentle. Lonely feels the warmth of Fawn's deep body as if it, not the horse, is carrying her, and she remembers the first food she ever tasted, and waking up for the first time to humanness inside Chelya's smile. She closes her eyes.

Then subtly, inside the warmth of Fawn, she feels Fawn feeling her. She feels Fawn's nervous, surrendering awareness of her own flesh, and in turn she remembers her own body, and also how once it danced with Fawn's. Once their bodies called up each other's joy. Once their hands lingered at each others' secret doors. Almost, she feels Fawn shiver. She feels the tears wash quietly over her own cheeks, and she does not know what they are for and does not want to know. Now she is grateful for that silence. Together with Fawn, she wraps her own soul in it, to keep her soul warm. She looks up and watches the stars she can glimpse through the treetops—that were long ago her first vision of the world—and no matter how far into the night she and Fawn travel, and how long, those lights never seem to move. She loses herself in that stillness above them, under which the horse's movement seems void, under which she and Fawn seem to pace in place forever, trying to get somewhere but always right here. Only the ache in her neck finally rouses her from her meditation, so that she has to bring her face down again, and smell Fawn's river-scented hair, and see the shapes of the trees shifting soft before her in the darkness as if they were made of flesh.

Something like a path seems to carry them, but not one that Lonely could ever have found on her own, even with the waxing moon to guide her. When they've traveled so long that Lonely is no longer aware if she's awake or asleep, or which side of midnight they are on, an owl calls out to her left— first a single hoot like a bottomless hole in the blackness, and then a windy trumpet of open notes like some eerie announcement of either beginning or end.

"We're close," murmurs Fawn, and says nothing more, leaving Lonely to imagine what relationship must exist between this owl and Willow's family: perhaps he has always lived here on the outskirts of their home, and always calls when Fawn passes, perhaps he is the voice of some ancestor of that family, or perhaps he is a harbinger of births. But most of all Lonely wonders at Fawn's brief words, which could only be for her benefit, and whether or not the effort of Fawn's speech signifies some forgiveness for whatever she has done wrong.

This is where Rye grew up, thinks Lonely as they enter the open field. *This is where Fawn played with her friends, never imagining the love that would come to her, living in day-to-day harmony and companionship and touch, needing nothing, not even knowing her own beauty.* And Lonely's idea of this friendship, this laughter in the grass, this sharing of play with animals and this whispering together in earthy beds, is so real to her it is like her own memory, for which she feels the most vivid nostalgia.

The hills are deeper here, and Lonely still can't tell where she is as Fawn ties the horse and, without rushing, unties her bag from the horse's body with perfectly efficient motions. She turns without looking at Lonely, and Lonely slides down and follows, remembering again suddenly that they are here for a reason, with no time to waste on dreams. What will Fawn ask of her? They pass between two cold white hills, and what must be sheep bleat nervously from somewhere near. A shed or two hide between trees. They are beginning to enter the forest again when Lonely sees—or perhaps she feels it first, like a quiet deity—the house, which is built into the side of a hill, with trees emerging out of it. She can see one lit window, and then they are through the door, into deep warmth and the scent of blood and a cascade of soft, watery moans.

Jay explodes upon them almost before Lonely can take in the room. "Did Eva send you with medicines?" he asks, hugging Fawn. Fawn nods, hushing him, stroking his head for a moment like a child's, and only then does Lonely see his trembling. "Something to stop the blood?" he whispers. "I don't know why it's so hard—it wasn't like this with Blue or Morgan."

Lonely can hear Willow crying out now—tired, hollow screams with no finish—from behind a curtain where the edge of a bathtub peeks out. Someone bent and feminine, maybe Willow's mother, is crouched down there, speaking softly. Lonely watches as Jay and Fawn move toward that place. She is given no instructions. She walks slowly toward the curtain, but it seems that her feet will never get her there, she's suddenly so afraid—as if that is not Willow behind it but some other creature, some demon of pain, some lost soul in the darkness like the voices that chased her in the desert long ago. Will Fawn want her help, or will she only be in the way? Why is she here? She tries to remember that she is taking the place of Chelya. She tries to think what Chelya, in her eager love, would do. But Lonely is frozen, without knowing why. She can't feel anything. The word *mother* repeats over and over in her mind, like panic, and she doesn't know what it means.

Then, as she stands helpless on the wrong side of the curtain, she sees Blue and Morgan standing in a corner of the kitchen, their heads barely reaching the counter where dirty dishes are piled in a dirty clay sink. They look more frightened than she is, and this helps. She walks to them, and swoops down to them, grateful for their need.

"Do you remember me? My name is Lonely. I'm—a friend of your aunt's. Remember?" Morgan nods, his lower lip stuffed out and cushioning the upper one.

"Are you afraid?" This time they both nod. Now she doesn't know what to say. How can she comfort them? "Do you remember when Morgan was born?" she asks Blue.

He looks at the stone floor. "I don't remember."

"Do you remember?" she teases Morgan, trying to smile. He shakes his head.

"I think it must be very hard work," she says to them, "giving birth. That's why your mother is making so much noise—because she has to work so hard. She has to make a person! Think how hard it must be." Lonely, herself, thinks about this. Her father did not make her. No, not her father....

"We were in there with her," says Blue anxiously. "We saw the hole where the baby will come out, and mama was sweaty and red and crying, and daddy was talking to her, and grandma, and then—then there was blood. She's crying so much. Morgan got scared." He glances anxiously at Morgan, to cover his own fear.

Lonely wants to take them somewhere else, somewhere where she can think clearly, away from those screams.

"Are there are other rooms in the house? Where do you sleep?"

Morgan points.

Now Jay comes out from behind the curtain, his face limp with emotion, and he kneels down beside them. "Boys, your mother and I want you to go and say a prayer for her and the baby, to help them. Can you do that?"

He turns to Lonely. "Will you go with them? See if they can sleep?"

Lonely nods wildly, as speechless as the boys. She stands up and offers her hands, and faster than she expected each one is clasped tight by a tiny warm one, soft and fleshy as the udders of Chelya's goats when she milks them. Even Blue has taken her hand with urgent immediacy, despite the caution and reticence in his face, and in this she understands even more deeply their fear, their smallness. She has given Blue too much credit for his emotional distance—seen him as older than he was, because his gentle silence reminded her of Sky.

Now she feels ashamed of her own shyness, and wishes she had taken their hands sooner.

"Show me your room," she whispers, "and we'll make a quiet place to pray." As they lead her, she tries to gather together quickly some idea of what prayer is. She thinks of Rye on the other side of the curtain as she lay in the bath. She thinks of the wind, whose voice she can never imagine when it's not speaking to her. She thinks of how far away the sky is.

The children lead her into a low clay hallway, pale white in the dark, which twists and winds deeper into the earth, then emerges into a round room with a big window facing upward toward the moon. There is one big bed on the floor which they apparently share, miniature animals of wood and cloth who stand together in conference, a big stick twined around with feathers and beads, a bow and arrows, a flute, and small clothing strewn about the floor. Nothing seems placed with any sense of order. *So this is childhood*, thinks Lonely.

They need only the moonlight to see by, the walls are so light.

"Okay," says Lonely, and then on impulse turns to the children for help. "How do we make a prayer?"

The boys both glance around obediently, and she sees their relief in their own knowledge. "The talking stick," says Morgan.

"No Morgan," says Blue impatiently, "the talking stick is for *Council.*"

Morgan holds onto it stubbornly. "I want to use it anyway." Blue glares back and then turns away muttering, "stupid." Quietly he gathers a bowl, a candle, a stone, and a feather.

"Go get some water," he commands Morgan. Morgan looks sullen but turns and runs out of the room with the bowl.

"You should be nice to your brother," says Lonely. Blue glares at her.

"It's not enough to know what you're doing," she says. "Isn't a prayer supposed to be a loving thing? If you're going to make a loving thing, you should do every part of it with love. Including how you interact with the people who are doing it with you. They're part of it. Morgan and I are part of the prayer." She doesn't know where that comes from, but she needs people to be kind to each other. It's too much for her, this unnecessary meanness, after her long night of cruel silence with the woman who used to be her best friend. "You were only snapping at him because you're feeling scared," she adds, trying to make her voice more gentle. "But we have to act out of love, not out of fear."

"I'm not scared," says Blue, but his eyes are downcast and he places the things he has gathered very carefully on a blue cloth on the floor, in a circle. And then Lonely realizes it's Sky she's talking to, again.

"Well then, be nice to Morgan," she says. "Because he's scared. And so am I."

Morgan comes back into the room and crouches to place his bowl of water in the circle. Blue lights the candle, and they sit. The boys close their eyes and Lonely copies them. Is this how you pray? She has never made a place for prayer. She has only prayed to Sky wherever she was, and argued with the wind, and called out to nothing, when she felt like it, without stopping first to be silent. Eva's face appears briefly in her mind, calm and knowing, nodding. Then her father's. And then she knows why she doesn't know how to pray.

Because I don't know where you are. Because I don't know what happened to your body after you died, or if you even had a real body, or if you—though you were my father—were only a dream. Because the only place I ever knew you no longer exists. If I cannot find you, how can I find God? How can I find myself?

"Ancestors," comes Blue's small, clear voice, "we invite you to pray with us. Helping animal spirits, helping plant spirits, we invite you. Earth, we invite you; sky, we invite you. Wind, we invite you. Rivers, we invite you."

He's quiet then and they all open their eyes, as if by signal. "We are praying for our mother and for her new baby," he says. "To make them be okay. To make the baby be born okay now, and for mama to be well."

Morgan takes the bowl of water in his hands and looks up at Lonely. "We have to ask each of the elements to help," he says, but there's a question in his eyes.

"Okay," says Lonely. "Water, we ask—we ask for your grace, for easy flow, for Willow's baby to easily flow out of her."

"There's water inside a womb," adds Blue.

"How do you know that?"

Blue shrugs. "Everybody knows that."

Morgan puts the bowl down and picks up the feather, looks at Blue and Lonely again.

"Air," says Blue, "we honor your breath. Breath for the new baby." He takes a deep breath in and out, fast, his eyes closed again. "Breath is life." And Lonely remembers that first breath on the shore in Yora's arms, how she was born into this world, and how that element carried her, in the arms of the wind, all along her journey.

So serious now, Blue continues to the stone, taking it in his hands. Lonely sees Sky again, deep in concentration, deep in the seriousness of his spiritual task, from which nothing could distract him. She sees Sky, only a child after all, pretending to be older than the sky itself, holding onto the idea of his necessary role as Dreamer because it was all he had. When she closes her eyes she sees Coyote's awful, yet knowing grin—*What are you going to do about the nightmares, Sky?*

"Earth," says Blue, but he can't seem to find words.

"Cradle us," says Lonely without thinking. "Keep us safe." Because it's all of them, isn't it, whose foundation becomes unstable, when the mother suffers? Lonely knows because she has no mother, and all her life this hopeless abyss has lurked beneath every hope and journey, beneath every love and joy, and behind every connection—this fear of falling, this fear of earthlessness beneath her feet.

"Keep us anchored," she says, thinking of Fawn. "Keep us strong." *Give us something, in our pain, to hold onto.*

Morgan picks up the candle. "Fire is my favorite," he says.

"You can't have a favorite," says Blue, and then, at a look from Lonely, adds, "Sorry."

"Go ahead," says Lonely.

"Fire," he says, "give Mama energy. And—?"

"The fire that makes the pain," says Lonely, "also will make new life."

Although she's not sure about that one.

"Now we make an image in our heads," says Morgan.

"Like what?"

"Something good."

"Okay," says Lonely. "Like your mama happy and holding your new baby brother or sister in her arms?"

"Yeah," they say together.

"And all of you together and happy?"

"Yeah."

So they close their eyes together, and imagine that. When Lonely opens her eyes again, she is crying, but she's not surprised this time.

Afterwards they thank all the spirits they invited and then put the sacred things back where they were—for they are the only things in the room that seem to have special places.

"Let's get in bed," says Lonely, and she sits on the edge of their mattress while they crawl under the covers, their eyes still wide. They can all hear another of Willow's wails through the walls, and though it is terrifying it also tells them that she's still alive, still trying.

"Can you tell us a story?" says Blue doubtfully.

"A story?"

"Mama tells us stories," explains Morgan.

"Oh," says Lonely. "What kind of stories?" She only knows one story. She has only ever been told one story in her life, and she doesn't like that one.

"Like about animals," says Morgan. "Or about us. Or about a warrior, or a magician."

"It doesn't have to be real," says Blue, and Lonely sees the grown-up man in his eyes again, and it moves her somehow, to know that he knows this— that stories are not always real. Whether it makes him seem older or younger than her, she cannot tell.

"Okay," she says and closes her eyes. "I have to close my eyes to tell it."

"That's okay," says Blue. "Mama does that too."

Lonely, surprised and grateful for this tiny, unintentional connection between herself and Willow, begins.

It is the story she knows, and yet it is not that story—it's a story she has never heard before in her life. She doesn't know where it comes from. She only knows that the children need a story to survive this night, and she will have to tell one.

So she begins with Morgan's suggestion: *magician.* "Once there was a great magician." She hears Morgan turn toward her under the blankets, snuggling into anticipation. *Why are stories comforting, even if they're sad?* she wonders, grateful to Eva for the first time. *Just because they have a beginning, a middle, and an end?*

"Once there was a great magician," she says again, "who was lonely. When he was a little boy, everything in his world was destroyed, and he didn't know why. He lost everyone and everything. He was an orphan."

"Why?" asks Morgan.

Lonely thinks. "He didn't know why. Maybe another people, or someone bad, destroyed his people. Or maybe his own people had a bad relationship with the earth—they took more than they gave, and in the end they used everything up."

"Like the City," says Morgan.

"Yes. Like the City. So this magician's land was all destroyed, and there was nothing left for him, so he traveled to the other side of the world, where everything was still green and beautiful, and the rivers were still clean, and the rains were still fresh and happy. And he said, I am a magician, and I will make a better world than the one I came from—one where people live forever, and no one is ever unhappy, and everything is always beautiful.

"But he was lonely, because he didn't know anyone in this new world. There were lots of different peoples: people who lived in the desert, people who lived in forests, people who lived on the seashore, and people who lived in the swamps. There were people who lived on mountaintops and people who lived in valleys, people who lived on red soils and people who lived on light soils. Everywhere he went, the people looked at him with suspicion, and he always felt like a stranger. He never felt like he belonged with any of these peoples, and they didn't understand his magic or his language. And though he wanted to make a new world, still he was also so sad, because of all he'd lost, that it was hard to start over.

"But in the world he'd left behind, he had always been told that there was a special place, at the center of everything, where life was still thriving and sacred. There was a secret swamp near the edge of the sea that the City in his world had never touched. But he had never seen it. Now he was very curious to know if the same center existed on this side of the world and what power lay in that place. He was fascinated by the mystery of it and felt that perhaps the secret of all the world's magic lay there. So he asked every people about it until, eventually, he found it: a misty, quiet, watery place where the most magical people of all were living—just like the place on the side of the world he had come from, which he had never seen."

Lonely takes a deep breath. If she opens her eyes she will remember where she is, and she will not know the next words to the story. If she thinks at all, she will realize that this is not her story, not a story she knows, but a story that is coming through her from someone else. It's familiar, but it is also different. If she were to open her eyes, that which she does not understand would frighten her. So she keeps her eyes closed, and doesn't let herself wonder where the words come from, any more than she wonders where the world comes from, or where the screams out there in the darkness come from.

"In this secret marshland, where everything was damp and silent and vivid green all year round, people lived for a long time. Time moved very, very slowly. Love always lasted forever. A couple might only make love once a year, but when it happened the entire village shone and shivered with bliss, and everyone's existence was elevated to a new threshold of understanding and connection. Every day, people meditated on each aspect of their simple existence. They spent long hours gazing into each other's eyes. They prayed to the fish that they caught with their silver rods and marveled over their taste as they ate them. They touched each other, and touched the hanging moss and the giant, deep pink flowers, with reverence and with wonder. And once every so many years, about as often as a person died, a new child was born.

"The strangest thing the magician discovered about these people was that they lived their entire lives up in the air. There was something ethereal about them, and perhaps that is why they lived so long, and why they were so fascinated by the simple earthly pleasures of mortal existence. They lived in thatch huts built on giant stilts high above the water, or sat in woven swings—modeled after birds' nests—which they hung from the trees around the edge of the swamp. Swinging footbridges connected their houses, and the most athletic among them learned to be great acrobats, swinging and flipping from strong vines. But they had to be very brave to do that. Because the reason the people lived all their lives up high was that there was something terrible under the water that would devour them if they fell."

Now she stops. She has to. She is not aware of being afraid—she's so deep in some other place that she feels nothing, only the story—and yet she finds she cannot go on yet.

"What?" comes a small anxious whisper by her side. It's Blue, in his soft voice like Sky's—that heavy-wondering, that dark-light call. "What was under the water?"

"Wait," she says. And she, herself, waits. She feels that it will come to her. "The Dark Goddess," she says finally.

"What's that?"

"Something like a dragon, with a long giant mouth and teeth as long as tusks. And a creeping body like an insect, and shimmering scales, and a whip-like tail. She has eyes on the top of her head that peek above the water, blending in like little nubs of moss so that no one ever sees them, and that's how she watches you."

She feels Morgan snuggling closer to her, feels the innocent softness of his flesh, feels all the vulnerability of a human being—no outer shell, no scales, not even any fur.

"She was the most ancient of creatures, the Dark Goddess. She was the goddess of destruction, of chaos, of death, of darkness, of every fear and sorrow and loss. And they could never come near the water, because they saw what happened sometimes to the long-legged white birds and the marsh rabbits and the few other animals who had no choice but to walk among the reeds in search of food: like an explosion she rose up, and then she pulled them down forever.

"The magician learned all this by watching, in secret, from a magical, invisible, floating glass ball in which he hovered for a long time over that place. He could not explain his fascination with this people, except that they seemed perhaps to be closer than any other people to achieving what he longed for—eternal life and happiness, without loss or pain or regret. He thought that perhaps the one thing holding them back from immortality was this darkness that lurked beneath them, haunting them, keeping them forever in fear. He could not understand why they worshipped it.

"For they did worship it. He saw them singing the most beautiful, eerie songs to it in the middle of the night, and once when a baby was born, he saw them throwing all of the fish that any of them had caught back into the waters, to be gobbled up by this monster—like an offering. And then the most horrible thing happened.

"There was among them a beautiful girl, more beautiful than any woman he had ever seen or imagined in all of his journeys around both sides of the world, and among all the peoples with all their different bodies and colors of skin that he had ever known. This girl—who was nearly a woman, but still very young—had long black hair, but it was so black that sometimes it turned as blue as dusk, and sometimes every color of the rainbow could be seen in it. It was straight, so straight and smooth that it shone, but sometimes it seemed to ripple like fire. Her skin was dark and changing, sometimes golden and sometimes tinted like the metallic flame of desert sands. The tilted swoop of her shoulders from the base of her graceful neck made him feel like he was flying, and the slow river glide of her body's curves around and around and downward made him shudder with longing. When she walked, her hands seemed to finger the air, and her spine seemed to tremble. Her eyes were huge and sad and wise, and seemed to hold the whole of both worlds inside them, and once when she stopped in the middle of a bridge and looked out across the water and then up into the sky in contemplation, she seemed to see him though he knew he was invisible. In her eyes, he thought he saw the deepest understanding he had ever known—the compassion he had always longed for, and the love he had always needed but never found.

"Shortly after he arrived, he began to see this girl more and more, and often there were other women gathered around her, touching her and ringing her round with flowers as if worshipping her—and then the men gathered around her too, and the magician was so jealous at their closeness to her that his whole body hurt all the way down to his toes. He had already decided he would convince her to run away with him somehow, when the terrible thing happened.

"It was dawn. They all gathered on the central bridge. The girl was crying—beautiful tears that seemed to call the tears out of the sky, for right then it began to rain. All the people surrounded her, so that they covered the bridge and spilled out onto the decks and bridges around, and some of them hung from the trees, and the children sat on the branches. The women were singing a song that chilled him to his heart, and weaving round and round her with garlands of white feathers, and the feathers had come from birds who had been devoured by the Dark Goddess. The magician knew this because he had seen an old woman gathering them after a bird had been taken just yesterday, lowering herself deftly down on a rope to pluck the floating feathers right out of the water.

"Then the girl he adored climbed over the rope railing and stood on the other side, just barely holding herself to it with trembling fists, and all the people went silent. And the magician understood, suddenly, that they were going to sacrifice her to the monster.

"He had heard about human sacrifice, it seemed, long long ago. It was something he'd thought no one in the world did any more. But in that moment the understanding came rearing up into his mind as sudden and real as the monster herself, as if sacrifice were an intimate piece of his body's unconscious memory of human history—as if the horrible idea of it had always lurked inside him, waiting to become real.

"The magician was young then, and at the peak of his powers. The anguish and the loneliness he had held in for so long, and the magic he had hidden from people who feared it, and the passion he had struggled to hold down in these long days of watching this beautiful girl he desired—all this exploded forth in him now as incredible, unstoppable energy. He strode forth from his invisible glass ball, and walked right across the air toward that swinging bridge, and sliced his sword through the air and cried, 'No!' His voice was so powerful that the rains stopped at the sound of it.

"Of course the people all turned in shock. As he continued to stride toward them, many of them bent down in fear and the women covered their heads, for they were a peaceful people, though acrobatic and strong, and they had neither weapons with which to fight nor any knowledge of fighting in their bodies. Some of the elders stood their ground, too old to be afraid, and just watched him come with a sad, silent resignation in their eyes, as if they had expected this all along. But the girl herself did not even turn around. She was still holding onto the rope railing and leaning out over the water, facing away from him. The magician thought it impossible that she could not hear him, could not feel the commotion all around her, and so—remembering the look she'd given him once when she'd stood on the bridge alone—he could only surmise that she had known all along that he was coming. She had known all along that he would rescue her.

"As much as he longed for a world of eternal life and happiness, this magician was so full of pain that without thinking too much about it he sliced his sword in a circle all around her to clear the way, wounding several people. For now he hated them and thought them all murderers. He gathered the girl up easily in one arm, and to his joy she wrapped her arms around him and pressed her face into his shoulder as he leapt off the bridge and back into the air again. The feel of her body surrendering against him made him feel he could do anything.

"But as he reached the tops of the trees and was about to fly off with her somewhere he did not know, something clamped around his neck and began to choke him, pulling him backwards, downwards, toward the water. For a horrifying moment he thought that somehow the Dark Goddess herself had risen up to take what belonged to her. He thought he had violated some ancient magical law—for though he had faith in the invincibility of his own magic, something about the mysterious songs and prayers that supported this people's magic had always made him uneasy. But as he twisted and struggled in that grasp, grabbing hold of tree limbs with one arm and still clutching the girl close with the other, he became aware that what bound his throat was only small human arms, and that what pulled him back was only a human boy. Then that nameless fear which had weakened him for a moment dissolved, and he was able to throw the boy off, and in the branches of the treetops he faced him.

"The boy was unarmed, but he was wild. His eyes filled with a deadly fury that seemed foreign to this peaceful people, and which the magician had not seen in any other pair of eyes here. The magician was vaguely aware of the wailing and crying behind him. Because he was a magician, he could dance in the air, but the boy could step and leap nimbly over the branches of the trees the way other people can move on solid ground—so nimbly that sometimes it seemed to the magician that the boy stepped on nothing but leaf and shadow. The boy did everything in his power to make the magician let go of that girl. He bit the magician's wrists with his teeth. He leapt in his face, screaming. He poked his eyes and his throat and punched him in his vulnerable places. At first the magician was so startled by such mad, sense-less courage—a kind of violent determination that he had never witnessed before in anyone but himself—that his magic faltered. Even though he was a grown man with a weapon, it was difficult for him to fight without his other arm for balance and with the boy ducking and dashing so expertly beneath each blow of his sword.

"But then something happened that changed everything. The girl spoke to the boy. The magician did not know what she said, of course, for it was spoken in their language. Her voice was gentle, and what she said seemed only a few words long—made at once of animal hisses and angelic song—but when she said it the boy's face fell, and he stood still and his arms dropped listlessly to his sides. Then he took a step back, and the magician saw shame in his eyes, and pain, and loss, and all the emotions he himself felt which he never wanted to feel again.

"It took another moment for the magician to recover from his shock and realize that the boy was no longer fighting him, and that the girl he longed for still clung to his side. And then, with a cry of victory, he rose into the air and disappeared."

Lonely pauses and takes a deep breath. The children, her only anchor now to this reality, say nothing, but she can hear their soft breathing, and how light they are—not heavy enough yet to fully occupy a space on this earth, still half in that other world from which they came, not yet grown big enough to encompass all of their spirits with their bodies. And so their spirits hover around them, big and wide, watchful and listening.

Tell the truth, those spirits say. *Tell the truth.*

"Hanum," she says, her throat closing for only a moment, and then relaxing. "Hanum and his bride traveled aimlessly, then, through deep jungle, the deepest darkest jungle which surrounded that marshland. Sometimes Hanum thought that they would never find their way out. But he was in ecstasy for he was no longer alone in the world. He had his bride, and he made love to her day and night, and she gave her deep eyes to him and held him, and though he could not understand her words, he imagined that she loved him back. The more intensely he felt the thrill of that love, the more he began to believe that the magical secret of that place—and indeed the secret that powered the magic of all the world—lived in this young woman, and now belonged to him.

"But by the time they emerged suddenly from the tangled depths to a bright day on a desolate beach by the sea, something had begun to shift. He could feel the girl drifting away from him. She no longer responded when he touched her, and her beautiful eyes were often elsewhere, and sometimes she would not eat the beautiful fruits he brought to her or wear the beautiful flowers he picked for her. On this beach, ever encroached upon by the sea, covered with the sun-bleached, twisted corpses of giant oak trees and the hard delicate blossoms of a billion tiny snails, he followed her round and round for days, helplessly watching her weep. Finally she sat down at the edge of the waves and looked out into the infinity of the sea, and would not rise again. He had talked and pleaded with her for so long, without receiving any answer because they spoke different languages. But now, without looking at him, she spoke one word in his language:

"'Home.'

"Hanum froze. 'But they were going to sacrifice you,' he said quietly. 'They were going to *kill* you!'

"'Home,' she said again. She would not move, and she would not follow him any more.

"But still he believed that she belonged to him. Still he made love to her, and still he felt himself the owner of that secret magic that he had stolen from the hidden depths of the swamp. That's when Hanum, in his desperate fear of losing this woman's love, began to remake the world. It was easy for him, once he set his energy to it, to gather people into the thrill of his dream. He would make a world without darkness, without solitude, without death or loss. A world where people would eventually live forever, and could have anything they wanted, at any time—any food, any thing, any reality. A world where people were always surrounded by other people, and always showered with the thrill of new things, new wonders, new discoveries, new pleasures. A world of magic where no one was ever lonely.

"He gathered a crew—an army—of builders, transformers, developers, initiators. The first place they destroyed was the swamp. Hanum did not go with them. Never again did he wish to come near that darkness, or hear those eerie songs, or meet with that strange, disturbingly vulnerable people who worshipped monsters and fought with teeth and fists. In their submission to that monster they both disgusted and terrified him, but more than anything else he wanted to forget that boy, and the hatred in his eyes. It was easy for his army to lay flat that place, fill in the waters and disintegrate that more primitive magic. They had weapons and machines now, and a magical, thick grey lava that filled watery and empty places and turned solid as stone. He never knew what happened to those people or their monster. But he turned that place—whose magic still seemed to emanate up from the very core of the earth—into the Center of the City, where all Things were invented and created, and from which the City was controlled and ruled.

"It was true that many lands had to be destroyed, in order to create this new world, but Hanum believed his world was better. His memories of the swamp convinced him to do away with all that was unpredictable and mysterious, to do away with ancient rites, to do away with tangled jungles and watery depths. In his world, people would not move about in that strange, slow wonder. Instead everything moved fast, things happened fast, and there was too much going on to think on the past or to remember what was lost. To make sure that he would never again have to think of the Dark Goddess, he encouraged the men of his people to go out and destroy all the monsters of the world; he made heroes of men who slew dragons, to make sure that not one remained to haunt him or steal his beloved away.

"With each new creation, Hanum returned to his bride on that lonely beach, and said to her, 'Look! Come see what I have created for you! A world without darkness, even at night—a world without frightening mystery, a world where nothing will ever harm you. Come see this wonderful place, because I've done it all for you, my love. It is better than that place from which you came.'"

Lonely barely pauses, but she notices the eerie coldness of her own voice, and how far away it sounds.

"For a long time the woman never spoke. She did not even turn her head to look at him. She would only look out upon the sea forever, as if she saw something in that nothingness that he could not see, and rock and hum to herself, and wrap her arms around her belly. One day, after searching for her and not finding her and then finally dragging her out from a cave far down the beach, while she cried and tore at him, he forced her to come with him. He made her walk those streets with him. And everywhere, he stretched out his hand to show her the glory of what he'd made.

"But she did not seem to see what he saw. She looked around and her dark eyes darkened and brewed with storm, and she pointed to things he had never noticed before—mistakes that he couldn't explain and didn't realize had happened. Children in rags, people with haunted lonely faces at windows, women crouched in alleyways bleeding, mass graves where peoples who had resisted the encroachment of the City had been buried, and animals in cages.

"He could not bear her criticism—her noticing only the flaws in what he'd done. He was furious. So in a final explosion of pent-up frustration and pain at her rejection, he cast her off and left her to find her own way out of the City.

"He returned to the beach. In his anguish and sorrow, he believed that she must be keeping some secret from him, and he was determined to find it out once and for all. Something had made her turn away from him. Something had made her turn against him—perhaps there was some other that she loved, some secret lover in the waves! But he went to the cave where he had found her, and inside it he found a baby.

"That baby was his daughter. He had been so occupied with his creation of the City, so desperate in his pleadings with his bride and his violent, lonely attempts to make love to her, that he had never even noticed when she became pregnant—never noticed that her belly grew, or that she hid from him more and more, until this day, when she had actually given birth all alone. He found that baby on the brink of death, and he realized that she was going to keep it from him; she was going to hide it from him in this cave and never tell him that he had a daughter. When he looked at this baby, he saw all the beauty he had first seen when he looked upon the woman in the marsh, for that baby looked back at him with that same wordless innocence, untainted yet by the knowledge of the monster he now saw that he truly was.

"And he wanted to be better. He wanted, at all costs, to keep his daughter safe, to keep her innocent, to keep her from ever being touched by that terrible world he'd created or even knowing that it existed.

"So he fed his daughter on magic instead of milk, told her she was a goddess, and took her out into the sea. He made an island in the sea. With his magic, he removed all of the unsightly, suffering, rebellious people that his wife had pointed out to him that day in the City—all those who made the City seem less than perfect. He would continue to remove them, and he would charge others to help him remove them, as the suffering in the City increased over the years and the mad ones became more numerous. He trapped those mad ones under the island where they could never be found or heard, and put them to sleep. And on top of the island he built a magical glass tower to hide the darkness beneath it, and there he kept his beautiful princess daughter safe from everything: the emptiness he'd left behind in his first world, the longing he'd had to suffer, and the great creation that he himself had made to fill that emptiness—which had ultimately brought the same destruction all over again.

"It took his wife years to find her way out of the City. When she did, she was much wiser and stronger, and she knew the suffering of the people there, and she had learned the language that they and Hanum spoke. There were many who secretly remembered her after she was gone, and for a long time after called her name in their dreams to comfort themselves in that bright, harsh world. She came back to the beach and looked first for her child. When she could not find her, she swam across the sea, riding dolphins and whales, until she came to the island, and she pounded on the door to that tower. But his magic kept her out. In her years in the City she had become old beyond her years, wearied and bitter and ugly, and when he saw her, he no longer loved her. And so she haunted the island forever, circling around that tower, and the hatred between her and Hanum grew, until the woman's bitterness encompassed even her own daughter—whose beauty seemed now like her own youth stolen from her, and who distracted Hanum from the truth. Over the years, that old woman came to be called a witch, and maybe the Dark Goddess claimed her somehow after all, because in the City, sometimes, they called her that—though they did not remember what the words meant. They said she *was* the Dark Goddess: that old, angry, broken woman, who had once been a virgin of the light.

"But Hanum, too, suffered in that tower. He saw that he had not created a perfect world after all. He saw that his loneliness was greater than ever, and that no one in this world had ever truly loved him except for his daughter. So he hid who he really was, and all that he had done, from his daughter, so that she would never stop loving him—but then he had no one to confide in, and that brought him such pain. Worst of all, he felt that he was dying from the inside out, and he was afraid, for whenever he thought of death, he thought of that watery depth where the monster lived, and it still lived on in his dreams with its long glistening jaws, even though all the dragons of the world had been destroyed.

"'He will come for you,' he began to tell his daughter, as he grew old and his mind began to confuse things. 'He will rescue you.' He said it with a finality, a sense of inevitability that he could not help, because in his nightmares that boy with the hateful, anguished eyes was always fighting him, fighting him into forever for the right to possess that sacred feminine beauty. How those eyes haunted him! Those eyes—unlike the eyes of the woman or the rest of that people—were a brilliant blue, just like his own. Those eyes seemed to know him. And in his nightmares, those eyes knew the worst of him.

"Now Hanum felt that, after all, the boy would win. Because he knew something Hanum didn't or had some power in that community of love that Hanum had never known—some purpose, some sense of order in that ancient ritual that Hanum had not understood. Now, in his failure and despair, Hanum almost wished that the boy *would* win after all, and take the woman back from him, and that none of this would ever have happened.

"'He will rescue you,' he said to his daughter, for in his delirium of old age he hardly knew the difference between his beautiful daughter and the beautiful maiden on the bridge whom he had once loved. He knew only that he wanted that boy to win: to save both himself and her. He wanted that boy to take the girl back, and complete that ritual which he, Hanum, had never understood. Because more than anything else in the world—more than immortality, more than power, more than all the brilliance and excitement and dazzling magic of all the great, ever-expanding kingdom that he had created—he wanted that sense of unquestioning loyalty and rightness that the boy must have felt when he risked his life for his simple, peaceful village. He wanted the quiet understanding that those people seemed to feel when they walked and swung through the misty moss together, hardly ever speaking, frequently touching, frequently looking into each others' eyes. He wanted what he'd never had in his whole life: to be loved like that, to belong.

"Only his daughter loved him, at least more than anyone ever had before. And when he died—"

The children are breathing quietly. "When he died," Lonely whispers again, and then she opens her eyes, horrified that she could tell such a story to children, and she doesn't know the end.

He just wanted so much to belong, is her final, stunned thought. The boys are asleep. Their faces are peaceful, carefree; they have forgotten their crying mother, forgotten pain and fear, forgotten the frightening story, forgotten everything—in a way that Sky never once allowed himself to forget.

They are asleep, and so they do not see her crying. They do not hear her sudden breaths as she holds her shaking head. She doesn't know where she is, or remember who they are. But she knows that her father is dead, and her mother—? She can still hear Willow's screams in the distance, quieter now. The moon has turned away from the window as it moves to set, and the room darkens.

As if still in a dream, she bends low and kisses each of the smooth, still foreheads, though she doesn't know why. As if still in a dream, she stands, wipes the heels of her hands against her eyes to dry them, and creeps back through the winding hallway like a dark birth canal into the main room. As if in a dream, she walks to the curtain—a short distance, but longer than the distance from wall to wall in the tower she lived in for all the years of her childhood. As if in a dream, she sees the familiar silhouettes of kind, warm-bodied people bending over the tub, and hears an old woman's voice crying,

"She's coming now, she's coming—just a little more now, it's almost over."

And a man's voice, "You can do it, love— I love you. I love you."

And the woman's cries, so weak.

As if waking from a dream, Lonely sees the woman, squatting in the bathtub with one arm around her husband's shoulders and the other arm around her mother's, and the hands of Fawn—the friend she has loved since childhood—reaching strong and sure beneath her, covered in blood, the warm water red, the head of a human being emerging into them. When the baby comes out of the water crying, the mother is lifted, astounded and weeping, out of the bloody water, and dried and wrapped in blankets, and laid in a soft bed by a crackling fire. And Lonely sees her mother in that cave all alone, and hears her hopeless cries, as she watches the baby girl lifted up into layers of eager loving hands, and then pressed against the mother's breast, the mother's face collapsing in exhausted, disbelieving joy, the pink helpless skin of each being folding into the other—and Fawn turns to Lonely kindly and says, "Come, Lonely. Do you want to see her?"

But as Lonely moves between the warm loving bodies to kneel beside Willow, obligingly touches the baby's tiny wrinkled shoulder with one finger, and looks at Willow's face, she seems to remember screaming helplessly into that blackness—she, a newborn human creature, as small as this, screaming until she lost her voice—for the lost mother whom, so many years later on a bitter, deserted island, she would not even recognize.

"Friend," says Dragon solemnly, "I want to ask your advice."

Malachite doesn't say anything, but Dragon can tell he is listening. It's dawn and though neither of them would admit it, they're walking slower now, now that they can see the City in the distance. A shroud of murky fog seems to hang around it, graying the already gray shapes, and nothing in those shapes welcomes them.

Dragon takes a deep breath, and the breath is heavy, something he has to lift up from the bottom of his chest. "There is another being somewhere with whom I have a destiny." How to explain? "Once when I tried to unite with a woman I loved, this creature stood between us. I used to hate it. I used to want to kill it. This creature has battled my people, the dragons, since the beginning of time. But then recently, before I found you, I—I was initiated. I became a man. Since then, I no longer believe that creature can stand against me. Sometimes I don't even know if I am supposed to kill it after all. But we have a destiny together, that I am certain of. I think now that this creature is female, but I'm not sure."

Dragon glances at Malachite, and Malachite's brow is furrowed in concentration. He doesn't change his pace or look at Dragon. For a terrible moment, Dragon imagines that the boy will have no idea what he's talking about.

"So what is it?" Malachite asks at last, abruptly. "What is the creature?" He sounds irritated, but Dragon hopes he will take him more seriously when he hears Dragon's answer.

"The Unicorn."

Dragon waits. The boy says nothing.

"I am seeking the Unicorn," Dragon says importantly. "That's what I wanted to ask you about. If you have heard about it, in all your studies, and if you know where I can find it. You say that truth and knowledge lie in the City, so I will begin there. Perhaps there I will find a clue."

Still no answer. The comfortable silence that they have shared for days now begins to make Dragon a little angry. Why does his friend not respond to this important confession? Why does he not recognize the respect and honor Dragon gives him by asking his advice about this quest so close to his heart?

"Kite," he says, remembering to use the boy's preferred name. "Why don't you answer me?"

Malachite sighs, shakes his head. "Sorry, Dragon," he says. "I really don't know. I don't know about things like that."

Dragon is still staring at him, even as they walk. He raises his eyebrows. "No?"

"No. To tell you the truth, I don't believe in things like unicorns. I don't believe in magic. I don't believe in gods."

Dragon stops, forcing the boy to stop, too, and look back at him. "*I* am a god," he says.

Malachite's eyes are distant. He shrugs.

Dragon turns and plows on again, his body leaning over his stride, his eyes boring into the ground, too furious for words. Malachite falls into pace beside him, and neither of them looks at the other.

"You were my friend," growls Dragon. "I trusted you!"

"So why don't you trust me now?"

"Because you deny me! You say I am not—you say I am not real!"

"No, I'm not saying you're not real. I'm only saying—"

"What? That I am not a god? Where do you think that fire comes from that I make you, you ungrateful—"

"I think it's great!" Malachite shouts back at him, stopping just as suddenly as Dragon did only moments before, and Dragon stops ahead of him and turns back. "I think it's amazing. I want to understand how you do it. I want to understand everything, because I think we can all do whatever we want to do. Why do you have to believe that the things you do, I can't do, too? I can make fire, just differently than you can. Why do you have to think you're so special? Why do you have to believe you have this special destiny with this special creature? Why can't we just be two people, two friends?"

Dragon draws himself up sternly. "There's something you don't know," he says. "I come from dragons. And the dragons—they are the energy—" He struggles to remember now, for he's never spoken it aloud. "That's where the energy of the City comes from," he says with relief, finally, feeling certain now that Malachite will be interested. "The City's energy comes from the bodies of dragons, who died long ago and melted into the earth!"

Kite shakes his head, drops his gaze.

"Don't you believe—?" Dragon's voice is choked. "Don't you believe me?"

"What makes you believe it?" asks Kite quietly, not looking up.

"They told me. In a dream."

"Who?"

"The *dragons.*"

Kite looks at him now. He doesn't look angry, which unnerves Dragon. "Look. Dragon, I need to figure things out for myself. I need to see and understand things, or I don't know if I can believe them. I can't—I can't trust something that just comes from anger, or fear, or passion—"

"But it doesn't—"

"I can't trust it."

Dragon is strong. He is a man now, and he is also a god. But he feels a little shiver go through him, and though it's so minute that perhaps the boy would not even notice, he is ashamed of it. It is the same shiver he felt in the presence of Yora the first time he beheld her, and needed her from then on to survive. It's the same shiver he felt when the Unicorn passed over him. At the end of that shiver, he has to turn away, and something closes inside him.

"You cannot be my friend, denying who I am," he says in a low voice chiseled cleanly from the stone he feels inside. "You don't believe in gods. You say you don't need the power of a god to help you. So I'll leave you. Good luck in the City. Don't follow me."

He turns and starts walking, carried hot inside his own anger, feeling the cold, quiet respect in the silence behind him—the absence of Kite's footsteps, as he stands still and waits for Dragon to traverse the next hill and be gone.

All through the waxing moon, Delilah is barely hanging on. It's not only the disappearance of the river that stops her, or the too-soon frustration of this ending after the exhilaration of finally traveling again—the fire inside her for so long needing to move. It's not only the fear that she really is trapped, after all.

It's that she's so sick. It takes all of her energy to keep herself alive: to gather up enough strength after nights of vomiting to fish or hunt for food again. Then, when the food is in her belly, it won't stay there. It's as if her body has turned into something she doesn't recognize, a creature no longer human, no longer able to digest human food. Her stomach turns upside down into her chest, and her heart thumps scared in her belly. She cannot even surmount the basic challenge of survival each day enough to think clearly about what will happen next, or where to go from here.

"Is this it?" she cries to Yora one grey dawn, still hating her own weakness. "All that I had to change in myself, all that I had to realize, all that I had to let go, all the courage it took to finally decide to make this journey, to leave everything behind, to find Mira, and this is it? It ends here?" She hates the sickness, she hates the stuckness, and she hates having to sit with herself again, understanding nothing but her own fury. The river, of course, gives no answer, except its own surrender.

Yet something sustains her. She feels safe under the damp rock overhangs where the river goes galloping into the earth, for inside the noise of it no one— if anyone were around—can hear her cries, and she cannot hear the noise of the machines in the distance. No matter how much fire moved her, Delilah— like Mira—has always loved the power of keeping a secret hidden space for her very own. Some tiny flame within her keeps her going now. She doesn't know what it is. Maybe Mira's spirit, after all. But it's like something is still alive in there, something tough and wild, even after she's coughed up everything inside her—a spinning light at the base of her spine, whirring below her belly.

The strangest thing of all is that plants begin to speak to her. This has never happened before. Animals spoke, in dreams and when she was a child, but never plants. They don't speak in words, or into her mind, but sometimes she'll wake from a pained, nauseated sleep with a certain scent in her nostrils, and she'll have to search half the day to find some small winter flower that makes it, and then the leaves of a tree overhead will suddenly seem to shine, so that she cannot refuse them. She touches these things to her tongue. She takes a bite, wary but with a rising desperation she did not even know was in her. Like maybe there was this other hunger she never knew about, beneath all the familiar desires, and that's why her body has twisted so uncomfortably inside itself all these years—because her diet lacked the purity, the innocent transmutation of light, the rainbow of nutrients that would come to her in the bodies of the plants. Deep inside her belly, even now, where the mystery turns and digests, the deer seems to sigh.

I don't know anything, she thinks to herself quietly sometimes, without realizing it and without speaking it aloud. *Each time I think I've let go of everything, I have to let go again of what I thought I was.*

Dawn now, and they have not slept, but Fawn wants to be home again as soon as possible. Lonely tries to guess why. Did the birth make her long to be closer to her own family? Did it make her remember the birthing of her own children; did it make her need Chelya all the more, and feel that being at her own house was the closest she could come to being with Kite again? Willow and Jay urge them to stay: they have plenty of room, and she and Lonely should get some rest. But Fawn kisses Willow and her baby and says she will be back to visit soon enough, with the whole family. "The whole family," she says meaningfully.

Fawn's silence on the way home doesn't feel the way it did on the way. The fog of light beginning under the forest's boughs feels to Lonely like her own exhausted mind; at once bright and clouded. She is fitfully, drunkenly wakeful. Her thoughts move fast and impatiently. She doesn't know where the story she told the boys came from but she knows it is true, and it belongs to her father. It bewilders her. She feels the hollowness of her mother's loss, stretching long between her hips and her heart, and she has always felt that hollowness—not an abyss beneath or above her after all, but within her—and only not fully recognized it until now.

The secrets that are kept from her in this life! What her mother never told her. What her father never told her. What Sky never told her. The gifts they could have given her—the truths they could have given her to fill in those hollow places inside! She is angry at all of them; yes, anger is what she feels. That is why Fawn's silence, now, finally, is intolerable.

"Talk to me," she says. "*Fawn.*"

"What do you want me to talk about?" comes the soft answer.

Lonely is surprised to get any response at all, and it makes her hesitate. "I don't know—anything. I don't understand why you never talk to me. Why you're angry with me."

"I'm not angry with you."

"So why don't you talk to me?"

"I don't know."

The 'I don't know' surprises Lonely too, because it admits to that silence. At least Lonely knows she's not going crazy, to imagine that once this woman was her friend, and now is no longer. She closes her eyes and leans her head on the back of Fawn's shoulder. The owl calls again, and now they ride on into the cold expanse of forever between here and home. Lonely feels that forever clinging about her: the dawn so cold, starving in its empty light, and every vestige of warmth from the previous day's sun, so long gone. It's cold like the dawn when she woke in a cloud and waited and waited for Sky, who never came. Cold like the dawn she woke on the beach, and Yora left her with nothing but longing and a horse. For the first time in so long she feels a physical desperation, feels the horse's rough rhythm rubbing between her legs, feels the full reality of Fawn pressing into the empty spaces of her body, and she needs someone warm to hold onto in this nothingness; she needs that touch that will make her body more real than the whole senseless universe around her.

A light wind sings some song now, and Lonely knows it is a song only she can hear, and she thinks suddenly that she doesn't belong to anyone, that she is utterly free, and that even if she comes from evil, it doesn't matter. Nothing matters.

She wraps her arms more tightly around Fawn. She leans forward, pressing friction and hungry sensation into the body of the horse, and whispers a kiss against Fawn's neck. She doesn't care about the silence Fawn is trying to keep; she doesn't care about the rules she doesn't understand and has been trying for so long to follow. Sleeplessness, loss, and the heartbreak of a story she could only tell to children who fell asleep before the end make her careless. She feels Fawn tremble, and she loses herself in the rub of the horse, sighing into Fawn's hair—how can she not feel it too?—and falling into a dream of sad, never-satiated pleasure that goes on and on into the morning. Lonely's eyes are closed. Slowly, slowly, she lets her fingertips tell stories over Fawn's belly, under her breasts, over her throat. The winter layers are thick, but she imagines she can feel Fawn's body responding all the way through them, and at the very least Fawn does not resist. Lonely can feel that heat. She can feel the way Fawn's legs tighten ever so slightly around the horse. She can feel the tension between the rise and fall of Fawn's breath, pulling tighter and tighter together, until the rise and fall are like one quick, tripping cry.

He wanted so much to belong, she finds herself thinking again. She understands it now, not with compassion but with a kind of sinking horror: that loneliness which was his, and which has ruled her whole life. That willingness to do anything—*anything*—just to feel connected to any people, or even to any one person, in this world.

When Fawn finally takes Lonely's hands gently in her own and pulls them away from her body, Lonely doesn't resist, because those hands keep holding, and because she can feel that Fawn is crying.

"I am empty, Lonely," she whispers. Words made of nothing but breath. "Without my son, I am empty. Empty."

Lonely is silent, weak with exhaustion and emotion, listening helplessly with face still pressed against Fawn's back.

"All my life, the City has been coming. Haunting me, like it's coming to take me back, coming to destroy the happiness we made. It has taken Willow's old home. It has changed the seasons little by little, twisting the weather so that our crops fail and we fear one day to starve. Now it has taken my son. It is all I can do to hold on, Lonely. I have no place in my life for—that kind of passion. It only makes me afraid. Do you understand? It only makes things seem more—unstable."

Lonely tries to think of an argument. She wants to say something back. How can she argue with a feeling? But the horse keeps moving, moving, between her thighs, and she thinks, *But how can you stop it?*

"I keep accusing Rye," Fawn says. "I keep accusing Rye of wanting to go to the City, wanting to go there to look for Malachite. I keep saying that's what he secretly longs for, an excuse to go there. He's always longed for that. That's why Malachite learned to long for it, too. I know that. But maybe it's I who long for it, too, Lonely. When you've been afraid of something for so long, run from it for so long, sometimes finally you want to turn and face it—fall into it and let it take you! I mean, so you won't have to be afraid any more. Sometimes I think that deep down, I just want to find out what it really is, now that I'm grown up. Because the truth is, I can hardly remember."

Lonely didn't expect this. She expected talking about Malachite. She didn't expect Fawn to speak about the City. Yet the City is always present, it seems. Everywhere. As if it's already taken over the world.

"What *do* you remember?" she whispers into Fawn's hair. It's a question she asked Fawn long ago, when they lay in the loft together, but that first time she received no answer.

"Faces," says Fawn after a moment of silence, "appearing for a moment in the light, and then dark. Light and then dark, light and then dark. There was a train that ran under the earth: this roaring no-place, an underworld with no color, no voices, only this roaring in my ears and the faces—hundreds of faces I didn't know, appearing suddenly out of the darkness in bright light, and then blackness again. I thought they were the faces of ancestors appearing to us from death, but my mother said no, they were only other people, like us, trapped in this place that was forever moving but never going anywhere.

"But we were going somewhere. That was the day we left. It seems like all I can remember now is that leaving. That long train through the earth, and then another, and then we were walking through fences and broken fields, and always I felt that my father was coming—always coming behind us— and I was so afraid of what would happen if he caught up to us, if he found us. But I can't remember why.

"I remember hunger, storms, and the cold. I remember this feeling of freedom, too. I remember I found—I don't know, something greater than myself, something almost safe, inside those first storms. I can't remember what it was now. I can't remember."

Silence. The yearning in Lonely's body never reached its peak, only turned to pain. She aches now all over; she aches against Fawn. Fawn says, "But I knew that my mother was leaving the City for my sake. I knew that she would do anything for me. I knew she gave up everything for me—her life, her friends, her love—and that nothing was stronger than the bond between us. Nothing is stronger than the bond between a mother and her child, Lonely. Nothing."

Now both of them are crying, each for her own reasons, but the reasons are the same.

When they arrive home, it isn't with the joy of having witnessed a new healthy birth into the world, Fawn's own niece. Fawn runs—Lonely has never before seen her running—into Eva's arms.

It's a strange, confused moment. No one says anything at first; no one asks about Willow or the child. The others are standing there, their lips slack and soft, and then Fawn gathers Chelya against her too. Only after many moments have passed does she turn to Rye. And then finally, very briefly, to Lonely.

Lonely....

The Unicorn carries the crow so deep, between buildings so tall, it is as if they walk inside the buildings, though they never pass through a door. Nothing grows here. The only things alive are people, insects, pigeons, and rats. The people swarm loud and hungry. The insects are quieter, but more successful in their pursuits. The pigeons stalk thoughtlessly along rooftops, everywhere and loved by no one; they have turned grey like the concrete, their grace lost in numbers and trash. The rats hold meetings and wage wars beneath the streets (the Unicorn can feel them whispering, even shouting), and they live like people—a greedy mockery of people—and the people hate the rats, because the rats are happier.

The Unicorn carries the crow through strange, cold shapes, their surfaces—whether flesh or metal, concrete or glass—all alien and colorless like the surface of the moon. Every touch makes noise against this hardness. Nothing can be done silently. They walk and walk, and the noise never stops, and they never see the stars.

The Unicorn carries the crow past the backs of buildings, where nothing grows either, and people are dying—sometimes quickly and sometimes slowly, sometimes violently and sometimes imperceptibly. In these places, the stubbled asphalt shingles seem to whimper in their own ugliness, because though they can crumble and weather and fade and mold, they can never become anything else. These walls can never truly decay, or be reborn into anything better, because they were never alive to begin with.

The Unicorn carries the crow through the few vacant spaces left between the City spaces—spaces not yet developed—where some things grow, but not the community of things that once was. The row of shrubs they pass through cannot be called a forest. Even the few trees standing, though the Unicorn bows and acknowledges them in passing, are disoriented and sickly, and the dialects once spoken in working ecosystems have all been lost. These spaces have been chopped too small, and separated by too wide a span of noise and car and street, to survive intact. Only certain animals, the hardiest and meanest, can live here. The Unicorn carries the crow through rectangular meadows, over which birds fly calling, searching for the shapes they remember. She carries him through fields made of only one grass or grown over with plants who long ago lost their place in the greater community, who now plunge along raging, unchecked, not knowing the rules—as confused and frightened by their own power as the people buying endlessly more Things in the giant indoor planet of the shopping mall.

The Unicorn carries the crow through the outlying edges of the City, where voices die away and trash twirls ominously across empty lots, and the only buildings remaining are dark inside and half-fallen. It is some old part of the City, vacated for some human or natural disaster, that was never recovered. It has a difficult, sour smell. Then finally the lots peel away into stubbly brown fields overgrown with thorns, and the Unicorn pushes through them, threads of blood appearing on her white hide. Then they pass from thorns into thickets, and from thickets into trees, and they walk through the trees for days, but the trees are young and thin, with broken branches dangling. Wide, mossy stumps are all that remain of the older trees, and the sky now is scrambled with the impatient, thoughtless overgrowth of those kinds of trees that grow straight and easy after human disturbance. A few birds make feeble, echoing cries, but they are only the most basic calls they must use to locate each other; they never sing.

As the Unicorn and the crow come closer to the center of the world, there are barbed fences and signs. A Unicorn can read any language, but Sky cannot, so the Unicorn reads the signs to him:

<u>Nature Preserve</u>
Do Not Enter.
This is the last remaining example of undisturbed Nature.

Sky doesn't understand what is meant by "nature," but the words make his stomach sink, because "preserved" is exactly what he has been wishing for, in the depths of his heart. And the moment he hears the word, he knows it isn't possible. Nothing alive is ever preserved or stays the same. Either they're lying, or what's inside must be dead.

While he's still puzzling over the word "nature," the Unicorn walks right through the fences, as if they are made of smoke.

Eva's room inside the hillside has no stove, so in the wintertime she cannot live there. But in the winter, to respect her need for solitude and space—because she is their only elder, and because she is a Dreamer, a woman of medicine—the family leaves her alone in the warm loft all day, where Rye carries up to her as many books as she needs to last her through those cold, dark, indoor months. At night she sleeps alone downstairs by the fire, except for this year, when Lonely sleeps near her.

Normally, she is still busy working with the dreams from last night by the time Fawn brings her morning tea. Dreaming during the night is hard work, and working through those dreams in waking life is even harder. Her grandchildren imagine her, perhaps, peacefully sitting over a stream of incense smoke or a bowl of water, divining in her mind as if dreams were spider silk to be woven with misty thoughts and then gazed upon in stillness as the light shifts over them. It is true she doesn't often have the kind of nightmares—those sweaty, confused, repeating dreams—that younger people have, who have not yet come to recognize their dreams. But dreaming is still work, and it's still a process of the body. It is work to enter back into the dreams with her waking mind, facing and uncovering the masks of the characters, changing them if need be. It is work to become those characters in her body, moving with the shapes of the dreams—both her own and the ones her family members tell her—so that she can feel in their dance what they are saying, what they want. It is work to dream out the suffering and yearning of the greater world, to feel all that inside sometimes, in her aging human limbs. It is work to go out into the fields and the trees, summer and winter, and focus her dreams into the shapes of leaves and wind, in order to translate those seemingly random patterns into meaning.

Often by the afternoon she is exhausted, so she spends the hours until dinner soothing her body in the rhythm of her rocking chair, soothing her mind by skillfully turning it off. Once, when he was six or seven, Malachite caught her in the midst of this, and his eyes widened as he backed away—for surely he thought that was what dreaming looked like, that blank stare. But that was only Eva thinking nothing; that was Eva resting, so that by dinner she could emerge into the world again for that brief lovely evening-time, absorbing the innocent laughter and longing and love of her real-world, earth-flesh children and grandchildren, before it was time to return to the night and dream again.

It's solitary work, but Eva doesn't get lonely. She dedicated herself to this long ago, when her daughter and her daughter's husband finally began to take over the even harder work of living, and whatever spirits she had spoken to when she prayed to that distant mountain finally answered her prayers and initiated her into Dreaming after all. Those dream spirits, whether they be the "Dream People" or some others whose name she does not know, have kept her company now for a long time. They are there for her when the answers are too difficult, dowsing the flame of her mind in their deep pool that is at once the top and the very bottom of the world, bringing her back to stillness and reminding her that everything is sacred. Even when Eva was a little girl, something in her knew she was destined for this. She was an earth child, but she had stars inside of her.

So she doesn't need her family to know what Dreaming entails. She doesn't need them to know how she spends her time up in the loft, or under the hillside, or how hard the work is, or how unwise she sometimes still feels. She doesn't need them to know that sometimes, in the last few years, when they think she is up here Dreaming, she is actually rocking fitfully with the ache in her bones—an ache that comes from too many dreams of too many people suffering, that will never go away.

Neither does she need them to know that more and more, when they think she's up here Dreaming, she is actually lost—for the first time in so many, many years—in memory. That for some reason the memories flood back now, haunting her. Not the memories of her husband beating her, which she long ago overcame, or the memories of the City itself beating her—with all its harsh sounds and hard surfaces and callous faces, every day, even worse than her husband. She got over all that long ago, and knows better than to dwell on her own suffering, lest it become a choice she makes again and again, without meaning to. No, she chooses this life now: this earth, this family, this love. And yet the memories come back now of the other things she tried even harder to forget. Things Fawn never knew about. Memories even older, even more deeply denied than the faces of her two sons, the way they turned away from her, the way they toughened in imitation of their father, the way they learned to mock her as he did.

No, the memories that come now are worse, because they are memories of pleasure. She doesn't ever need her family to know the kind of magic the City held. The way she and her girlfriends could turn themselves into goddesses with clothing that shone and dazzled and squeezed up the most voluptuous parts of their bodies into fists of overflowing passion—and with glitter around their eyes and flower color on their lips. The way a car filled up with music could become the whole world, and the way laughter could bind you to your friends like the most precious secret, make your hips spin, make your lips so confident, make you bigger than the world. The way it felt to grope in that rhythmic, make-believe darkness, letting someone whose face you could never see slide his leg between your own and pulse there, like a god.

She doesn't need Fawn to know that she gave up everyone she loved for her, so that she and Fawn could have a life together, a better life, a life where they valued what was important and returned to the cycle of the seasons, a cycle they could always trust even when the supposedly sorrow-proof world Hanum created collapsed. She doesn't need Fawn to know what it was like to leave her friends behind, leave her sons behind, leave them to the fiery thrill of that too-fast, too-hot life that would one day burn them out, that would one day betray them. She doesn't need Fawn to know what it was like to give up touch forever, never again to feel the wonder and relief of another life pumping inside her, never again to feel the slick weeping of her skin when rough fingers softened against her thigh. She doesn't need Fawn to know how for years she cried not only for the loss of her sons and their trusting arms, which she'd lost long before she left the City, but also for the loss of dancing in a dizzy crowd, for the loss of eager, thoughtless kisses, for the loss of a friend's lipstick grin in the mirror beside her own. How in the middle of a thunder storm she would remember a lover's breath. How alone in the most beautiful grove of aspen trees on a full moon, she would wish for cigarette smoke and the feel of thong underwear cutting between her legs, merely for the sake of seeing other human faces leaning out to her from the darkness and recognizing her as one of that reckless tribe of youth.

But Fawn does know. She knows what her mother gave up for her. She knows the way all daughters know the rules their mothers make for living, not in their minds but in the very rhythms of their bodies. The things unspoken. The things assumed. The losses that are never mentioned, the truths that are not questioned, the innate, ingrained, physical understanding of what sacrifices have become necessary in this life in order for a woman to survive. Fawn knows. And Eva knows that she knows.

But there are things Fawn does not know. And that is why, on the day after Fawn returns from the birth of Willow's daughter, Eva does not dream but goes to find her.

The maple trees have always been closest to Fawn. Their sweetness—their deep, strong, quiet woman magic—knows her. They are happy to tell Eva where Fawn is. She is sitting up high, in the branches of that old oak tree, on the top of that hill.

Eva lifts her skirts and breathes hard, one step at a time, carefully up the icy slope. When she gets to the top, she stands at the base of the tree. "Fawn," she calls gently but firmly, in the manner of an elder who is accustomed to being obeyed. "Come down. I need to speak to you."

But Fawn doesn't budge. She has always been stubborn, but it's rare that she won't listen to her mother, won't even look toward the sound of her voice. She looks nervous up there, clinging with all her limbs to the branches, and she isn't very high. It isn't like Fawn to climb trees. But she won't come down.

"Daughter," says Eva. "What are you doing?" The winter air is very still, and Fawn isn't far enough up for Eva to need to raise her voice. She waits for Fawn to answer. If Eva stands here long enough, she will answer. Eva is just as stubborn as she is, and Fawn knows that.

"This is where Kite used to sit," Fawn says finally, in a voice so small it seems strange to Eva. No, it's not the smallness of her voice; it's the fact that she called him "Kite." Now Fawn says it again, even more softly, as if to herself. "Kite."

Eva waits.

"The tree told me," Fawn adds. "It wouldn't tell me until I called him by that name. As if the tree knew him better than I did. As if the tree knew his real name, and I didn't."

Everybody knew him by that name, thinks Eva. *Except you. Because you refused to.* But she doesn't say so.

"Daughter. What are you doing up there? You look ridiculous. You're afraid of heights. Come down!"

Fawn doesn't smile. "I'm trying to see what he saw. I'm trying to imagine what he wanted, when he looked out there. Why he left."

For the first time since the loss of Kite, Eva feels a little angry with Fawn. But she knows it's not Fawn's fault that she is angry. It's the fault of these memories that have been haunting her, these other emotions from long ago, that don't belong to this life.

"Fawn," she says, as calmly as she can. "I have come here to find you. I have something to say to you. But if you will not come down, then I will speak to you from here." Fawn tilts her head slightly to listen, and that is enough for Eva. But suddenly she feels nervous. Nervous! Nervous in front of her own daughter—nervous like she felt when she was fifteen years old and her husband-to-be came to her door for the first time and looked up and down her body, from her breasts to her knees, and back up.

What is it, exactly, that she will say, that makes her so afraid?

"I want to tell you," she begins. "I want to tell you, daughter, that it isn't your fault. It isn't your fault that Kite left. You have not failed as a mother. You have not failed in protecting him. He left because he had to go. Being a good mother to your child does not always mean keeping him with you."

Already she can see that Fawn is crying, but she knows she has not yet said what she means to say. She knows because she herself is shaking now.

"You kept me safe," Fawn sniffs, barely louder than the ghosts of leaves touching each other in the sudden breeze, but Eva can hear her. "All by yourself, you kept me alive, you rescued me from the City."

"Yes," nods Eva. "That's the story you learned. And it's true in a way, but the City is not all evil. Your brothers are there, and others who are related to you." Eva's whole attention is focused on her daughter in the tree, and she's not aware of her own face, her own tight throat. "Others who loved you. People like us, living the best they can. And there is magic, and there is knowledge. There is music, beauty, and joy."

She can see Fawn listening, and she can feel that still she has not told anything that Fawn does not know deep down. She still has not said it. She takes a deep breath. "It's not your fault that I left."

Fawn takes a breath, too, and turns away, looks out over the still untouched forest, over the beautiful womanly mountains, to the haze of that hungry mystery where Kite has gone to find the truths that no one told him. "I know," she whispers.

"No, you don't," says Eva. "You feel guilty. You feel that you are bound to me forever. And I made you feel that way. Because I used to—I used to resent you. When we came out here, and I found out how hard it was, and how much I had lost, sometimes I regretted it. And I blamed you, because you were so delicate, so sensitive, and in so much danger from your father, that it *was* because of you that I finally left. But you weren't the only reason. You were only the final reason. I blamed you then because it was easy. I never expressed that to you, or I never meant to. But you felt it anyway. I could tell by the silence you kept, and by how hard you tried not to cry when you were afraid. And later, when finally I was grateful to you—so grateful to you, Daughter, for bringing me back to what was deepest, what was most true, what was most vulnerable and sensitive and alive within me, and for inspiring me with your precious gentleness to leave that place behind, return to the earth, and become stronger than I'd ever been, it wasn't enough to take that first guilt away from you. You still felt it. You still feel it.

"I think it isn't only the City you're afraid of. It's failing. You're afraid of failing to keep me happy, failing to keep your family safe, failing to hold everything together, the way you think I held it all together for you. But it was you, Daughter, who kept me strong. *You* were my earth, my center. *You* were my gentle, steady rock, all through those storms, all through the hunger, all through the fear. Do you understand?"

Fawn nods, still not looking at her, her face clenched in tears.

"Tell me, do you understand?" Eva repeats.

"I don't know," says Fawn.

Eva sighs and tries to keep the earth beneath her feet.

"I wish I could know that he's safe," whispers Fawn, leaning over the tree now, the big branch she's straddling pressed into her stomach as if it could keep her guts from overflowing in grief. Eva knows that feeling.

Not since Fawn was a child, cowering beneath the form of her father, has Eva felt such a powerful urge to wrap her in her arms. The feeling punches her breath right out of her, makes her double over, makes her eyes swim. But she straightens up and says, "You never know if your child is safe, Fawn. You don't know if Chelya is safe right now. I don't know if my sons are okay. I don't even know if you are okay. But I do know that you have to stop living as if he has died, and you don't deserve to live. You have to know that it is okay to feel joy. It is okay to let Rye hold you, it is okay to let him touch you, it is okay to feel that pleasure again. It is okay to live again. You don't have to blame him, or yourself, or anyone, and you don't have to choose between loving him and loving Kite. You don't have to choose like I chose. That isn't a choice I ever wanted to pass on to you."

Then she makes herself turn away, and she walks back down the hill to the house.

Lonely says goodbye to each member of the family in turn, on the day of the full moon.

Rye is the easiest, not because she cares for him least, but because everything in their friendship feels easier now, including letting go. Before dawn, she watches him through half-closed eyes as he pulls on his boots to go out and check the traps. By the time she wakes enough to speak, he is out the door, so she pulls as many clothes around her as fast as she can and runs after him. The cold feels dry and shiny on her face, and makes her breath come fast. He turns to watch her coming with a small, complicated smile on his face. The moon is sinking behind the trees and the shadows hover behind him in expectation. His beard looks solid and old, like granite.

"I'm leaving today," says Lonely, out of breath.

He nods, and looks down at his boots like a boy. Neither of them knows what to say, until they both think to put their arms around each other, and then they rock back and forth like that for a moment, their bodies gradually relaxing. In his embrace, Lonely feels the thrill of that first rescue, his arms lifting her up out of a dream into warm, luscious humanness; she feels that first taste of tenderness; she feels the romance of such longing, and the innocence of the summer sun in the field where he knelt before her and tore from her body one of the sweetest kisses she ever knew.

He stands back and looks at her. "You seem stronger, more confident, these days." He pauses. "And you also seem heavier, and sadder than ever."

Lonely doesn't know what to say, so she says, "Thank you. For being my friend, I mean." Then she feels bold, because she's leaving, so she adds, "For being my brother. For loving me."

Rye smiles. "Will you be back?"

"I don't know."

He looks at her and takes this in. She wishes she could say more, but her mind feels strangely empty. Her heart is elsewhere, and the thought of how long the journey will be to find it exhausts her.

"This winter," she says finally. "It does end, right?"

He laughs, and she laughs, too, though not quite as sincerely.

"If you look carefully," he says, "you can already see signs of spring. Even now."

Lonely looks past him at trees that look dead to her, and cannot imagine what he means.

"I wish you all the blessings of nature on your journey, Lonely. And I wish for you that you discover your true name, because that one does not suit you. If you ask me, that is. It is not how I will remember you."

"How will you remember me, then? By what name?"

She is joking now, after all, for these things that once tormented her seem laughable at this moment, though perhaps the laughter is bitter—perhaps she only laughs because she has come to accept some things as unchangeable. But, of course, he is taking her question seriously. He is looking out toward the fields where once her Unicorn waited for her. She thinks now, suddenly, that the reason she waited so long to leave here again—the reason she waited so long to continue on that search which she once believed to be her whole purpose in life—was not because she didn't know where to look for Sky or because she was afraid or because she felt hopeless, but because of the loneliness that overcame her when she imagined continuing on without that magical body to carry her. That gentlest of beings loved her utterly and unconditionally just by moving eternally beneath her, bringing her forever home to herself, and forever onward. The Unicorn had left her here, and so, obediently, she had stayed. But now she knows that the Unicorn is not coming back.

"Meadow," Rye says, and it takes Lonely a moment to remember that he is telling her the name he will remember her by. "That's how I think of you. Like meadows. That kind of freedom, like childhood, like the wind. I'll call you Meadow. I wish I'd thought of it before."

"I wish you had, too," says Lonely.

"Goodbye, Meadow." He kisses her on the forehead, and turns away.

Chelya is digging up roots in the greenhouse. It has taken Lonely all day to make herself begin these last conversations. The house feels so safe, so warm.

"Where's your mother?" she asks Chelya.

Chelya shrugs. "I guess she needs a lot of time alone these days."

Lonely looks around, as if she might suddenly see her. She hasn't had a real conversation with Fawn since the morning they came home from the birth, but at least Fawn shows a sad kindness toward her now, and no longer avoids her. "I've—Chelya, I've come to say goodbye again."

Chelya looks up, but doesn't seem surprised. "But you can't leave now," she says. "It's getting dark soon. Leave in the morning?"

"It doesn't matter. Where I'm going, it doesn't matter."

Chelya nods slowly and puts down her spade. She hugs Lonely, but her body feels tired. "At least you're really saying goodbye this time," she says, and smiles. But it's the same smile that Lonely sees on everyone's face. It's the smile that says, "Kite is gone, and this smile is all I have to spare."

"Is food going to matter, then, where you're going?" Chelya asks.

Lonely looks down. "I don't know."

"Why don't you take some, just in case?"

They go down to the basement together and gather dried meat and fruit. In the back corner, Kite's books are still piled exactly as he left them. Lonely can't see them in the dark, but she feels their presence, as if in that tiny, whispering language of intimate black lines, they contain the secret of who he was, why he left, and whether or not he is ever coming home. As they walk back up the stairs, Chelya says,

"I'm sorry I don't have anything else to give you this time."

And Lonely realizes with a little shock of shame that she was almost expecting that, some gift of magic from Chelya, some mystery that would later make sense and bring her closer to what she longed for. It isn't that she needs anything. But she misses that time in life when so much was possible, when so much was still left to be discovered. Why does she no longer feel like that? Maybe because nothing—no mystery, no gift—could compare with that dress, what it meant, what it led to, and what was lost.

"It's okay," she says, recovering herself. "I feel like you're always giving to me, always helping me. I wish I could give you something."

"Oh," says Chelya, shrugging. "But I don't need anything."

They're back in the main room now, and Chelya lays their bundles out on the counter and begins wrapping and packing them into a bundle Lonely can carry on her shoulders. Lonely thinks again of her lost Unicorn, and is overcome with the memory of what gifts she's been given in this life. The horse, from Yora. Her very life, from Rye, and from Delilah, who saved her with the body of the boar. Whatever she needed, whenever she needed it.

"I want you to be happy again," she cries impulsively. "I want you all to be happy."

Chelya turns to her and smiles bigger than before. "Thank you. I want you to be happy again, too."

"What will it take? Give me your wisdom, Chelya. That is your greatest gift to me."

Chelya shrugs, as if embarrassed. "Gratitude probably. Trust. Loving each other."

Then it hits Lonely again: why Chelya is the way she is, and why Lonely is not. "You come from love, Chelya. All around you is love. You were born of love. And so life feels right to you, doesn't it? It makes sense. But I didn't come from that. Chelya, I was born of…I was born of misunderstanding, and violence. I don't know how to live. I don't know where I belong—*if* I belong. That's what's wrong with me."

Chelya doesn't look up or stop her motions. She ties the bag tight. "There's nothing wrong with you, Lonely," she says evenly, almost casually.

"I have nothing to give."

"But you have given something, Lonely. I mean, you've given my mother something, and in that way you've given me something."

"What? What have I given her?"

Chelya shrugs again. "I don't know exactly, but it's true."

Lonely stares at her.

"Are your parents dead?" Chelya asks. Lonely feels surprised, and then sorry, to realize that she never told Chelya anything—when Chelya was so eager, especially last summer when she still seemed like a young girl, for the stories Lonely could give her. It was the very first thing she had asked, as Lonely ate her first meal of this world with them: *Where do you come from? Where are you going?* Maybe Chelya hasn't changed so much. Maybe she has only changed with Lonely, because she finally accepted that Lonely would not open to her in the way she opened to Lonely. So now she is closed. But why? Why has Lonely kept herself a secret? What has been so important, so frightening, so special, that it could not have been told to these loving ears? The thought of such betrayal is terrible to Lonely now.

"Oh, no," she stammers. "No, they—My father is dead. But my mother. My mother is still alive." It's the first time she's said it. "But she hates me," she adds. "She cursed me."

"Oh." Chelya looks at her in a way that embarrasses her, with a kind of compassion that Lonely finds painful. "But," she says, "people only make curses when they feel hurt and helpless, and they don't know what else to do."

Lonely looks away. This is why she didn't want to say these things aloud.

"You should love her. That's what I have to say to you, Lonely. You should give your mother your love. I think she needs it."

"But you don't know who—I mean, you don't know her. It's too late for that."

"It's never too late."

Then before Lonely can think any more, Chelya's arms are around her, and Chelya's tears bless her cheeks, and Lonely, strangely dry-eyed, wraps her own arms slowly around Chelya, feeling that she is embracing a star.

Chelya climbs to the loft ahead of Lonely and whispers to her grand-mother. Then she climbs back down and gestures to Lonely, and Lonely begins to ascend. After this, she will only have to say goodbye to Fawn.

It came to her, only last night, that the full moon is what she's been waiting for. For it was on a full moon that she dreamed of her beloved before she ever knew him—both times. It was on the last full moon that she saw him again, felt him again, for an instant. Even the wind has not been able to explain that miracle to her, but she knows: it is the full moon that opens a door between worlds. It is on the full moon that she will enter the forest for the last time, return to the fire circle, and not come back. Either that world that holds him will open for her or…Whatever happens, she will not come back.

"I'm sorry to bother you, Eva. I wanted to say goodbye to you alone."

Eva is lying in Kite's bed.

"Sometimes I lie here," she explains, "to see if Kite might open his dreams to me."

"Has he?"

"I don't know," Eva says, sitting up and patting the bed next to her. "Sometimes, lately, I get confused. I don't know if I'm seeing his dreams, or the dreams of my sons, or the dreams of other men I left long ago."

Lonely sits down, disturbed as always at being forced to remember Eva's age—and at having to imagine that Eva might one day not be so wise, that she might one day look around her in confusion, not seeing, and then finally forget everything, and be gone. She knows that this can happen because Eva herself has said so, though when Eva says it, she is always laughing.

Lonely looks around at the room she has not visited since that wild night long ago, when she watched Fawn and Rye become one tangled cry of body and soul together. That time is gone like another lifetime. *No wonder,* she thinks now, *that Eva gets confused. Why doesn't everyone? How can we make sense of all these separate pieces of a life, a life that changes form so quickly, so completely, that we cannot even be sure it is still our own?*

They both stretch their feet toward the warmth of the chimney where it rises through the center of the loft.

"I have something for you," says Lonely, and she takes the Unicorn's horn from out of her cloak.

Eva looks up at her sharply. Eva's eyes are more like Sky's than anyone's, Lonely thinks, not for the first time.

"Do you know what it is?" Lonely asks, uncomfortable in Eva's questioning gaze.

"Yes, child. I know what it is. Why are you giving this to me?" She still has not taken it.

Lonely plays her fingers over its smooth, spiraled slopes, runs them along the grooves. If white had a texture, it would be this. "Because I don't know what to do with it. Because once it gave me a window into another world where I thought I could feel my lover's touch, but it was not real—only a dream. I don't want to feel that ever again. It's too painful. I only want to feel it for real, if I ever feel it. But mostly," she adds, looking up again and meeting Eva's eyes, "I want to give you something. I want to give all of you something, but this seems like it was meant for you. Maybe it will help you with your Dreaming, because you would know better than me what to do with visions like that. I don't know. But maybe the reason it was given to me was so that I could give it to someone else. Maybe the gift was teaching me how to give."

Eva takes the horn in her palms. "Thank you," she says. And in that *thank you,* Lonely knows, is the acknowledgement of all the love that Lonely has given and tried to give, all the strength she has tried to grow, all the dreams she has tried to live up to, and all that she fought to do that—the pain of her past, the confusion of it, the loss of it. Eva knows all of this, of course. It was Eva who told her her own story. And the understanding and forgiveness in that *thank you* brings to Lonely's eyes the tears that moments before she could neither find nor feel.

"I don't need help with Dreaming," says Eva. "But Unicorn horns can purify any body, any water, anything. Like fire, they heal by transforming, turning the heavy build-up of the past into ashes and smoke. Dissolving suffering with light." Then she smiles at Lonely's expression. She laughs to herself and looks down at the spire of beauty she holds in her hands. "So maybe I can heal these old aching bones after all. That *will* help everyone, because they won't have to hear me complain any more." She laughs again, and Lonely knows Eva means more than what she is saying, but she doesn't understand exactly what. She just knows that giving Eva the horn was the right thing to do.

"Eva…" she begins now.

"Ah, yes. Here come the questions. I knew she wouldn't leave without questions." But the old woman is still smiling—a good, real smile. If only Lonely could take that smile with her, and carry it with her to that dark island of pain—where there is no love, no love at all. Only barren rocks, and merciless wind, and an angry face that waits and waits forever, expecting nothing but failure.

"Go ahead," says Eva. "I'm only teasing you."

"My beloved—"

"Yes."

"My beloved is a shapeshifter."

"Ah."

"So, in order to find him, I need to learn how to shapeshift too."

"I see."

Silence. What was she expecting? That Eva would give her a list of simple instructions? That Eva would even know? Lonely comes now to the truth within herself. She knows that she is leaving. She has known ever since the night she told her father's story to the two boys, then left it behind to sweeten and transform into the lost, innocent dreams of children. She has known it is time to go on again in pursuit of her destiny. But she does not know, even now, where she is going. Or if, where she is going, it will be day or night, winter or summer, or who she will be—or if she will survive.

"I'm scared," she whispers.

"Well, that's the first thing," says Eva, and her voice is firmer now. "You've got to let go of that fear."

"What do I do?"

Eva shakes her head, tightens her hands around the Unicorn's horn. "Girl, I couldn't begin to tell you. Shapeshifting is the most complicated, ancient art. It is absolute surrender and absolute control."

"What do you mean, control?"

"I mean, where everything you feel, every part of who you are, becomes a magical substance that you can mold at will."

"Dreaming is like shapeshifting, isn't it?"

"I suppose so. Perhaps that is how your lover does it. But I do not enter dreams. I only see them."

"But you must know something, Eva. You always do. I'll do anything. There is no other choice for me."

Eva sighs, leans forward and takes Lonely's face in her hand. Lonely lets her gaze into her eyes; she does not turn away, even when it hurts. "Yes, there is a dream I had," Eva says finally, "that I didn't fully understand until now. You must go to the river."

"But I was going to go to the—"

"Go to the river," says Eva more sharply, sitting up, her eyes turned suddenly inward. "I don't know why, but go now."

"But I haven't said goodbye to Fawn."

"Just go."

Startled, Lonely stands up and hurries to the ladder.

"Don't be afraid, granddaughter. You are goddess as well as human," calls Eva after her. Then Lonely hears her mutter, as if to herself, her last words to Lonely:

"Don't keep forgetting."

On the night of the full moon, Delilah's body feels clear and strong for the first time in many days. Restless, she climbs to the top of that tumble of stones under which the river disappears, and watches the moon rise. She can see the men dragging their slow machines across the cold sand in the distance.

There is no way to cross the desert without water. She will have to ask for their help.

This obvious realization has been creeping up on her ever since she came to the end of the river, only she didn't admit to it until today. And she didn't really think about it until tonight, on this night of pregnant moon, when her mind is so intent on going onward toward Mira—so intent on figuring out a way—that it seems to vibrate inside her skull. There is no other choice. What else can she do? Turn back like a coward and retreat to her cave forever? It seems she has never, until this moment, truly thought about that "forever"— never actually imagined if she would spend her whole life there, or if she would have to. She was only living each day, one day at a time, because she thought she had made that choice, and would continue to make that choice each day that she wished it: to stay. Now she sees that once she made that first choice, she was always trapped. There was never a way back out.

No way, that is, except to surrender control to the very people she hates, the very men who are destroying all that she loves. She will have to go to them. She will have to ask them for a ride. Is this her punishment, then, for depending on them for so long to meet that darker need?

Earlier today, she wandered experimentally out toward them. She wanted a closer look. Or maybe she wanted to gaze out at their mechanical, stubborn bodies and hurl her hatred out at them for what she was being forced to do. She had manipulated men for what she wanted in the past. But she had never believed that she needed them for anything she couldn't survive without. She had never believed she couldn't make it on her own. Never.

When she got close enough, careless in her own self-righteous resentment, she forgot that they could see her, too, and several men stopped what they were doing and turned toward her. She wasn't yet quite within shouting distance, but she thought she could see their grins. She thought she could see the leer of their bodies, and the way one of them laid a hand on his machine and leaned back in relaxed anticipation, looking at her. Their surprise, their muscles rippling in their hands, their tongues moving in their mouths.

Then one of them whistled, and then two of them started to walk her way.

She didn't want them. Not at all. She felt a strange protectiveness in her belly, and crossed her arms over her chest. Careful not to run (for any predator knows that a running animal is prey), she turned around and walked fast, and she made sure to zigzag and duck where she needed to, so they would not see where she had come from or where she was returning to.

Now as she sits up awake, watching their tiny silhouettes in the distance, she has to admit that what keeps her up watching is not only the fury or the plans she is forced to make, but also the barest hint of fear. She will get what she wants from them, if she has to. But for the first time, she doesn't want to give what they will want in return. She suspects now that all those years she thought she was making that choice, she wasn't. All that time she thought she was manipulating and seducing to get what she wanted, contemptuous of these men who could give her whatever she needed, she wasn't in control at all. Because she was the one giving, and whether she wanted to give it or not, they would have taken it anyway.

Water is love. They will not give her a ride for free, and they will not give her that water she needs to live for free. Just like love has never been free.

Basically, she thinks, *now that I don't want to stay in the desert, I will be forced to die here. Now that I don't want anything to do with these idiots, I will be raped by them.*

"Fuck," she says, standing. *"Fuck!"* She hurls her empty water jug across the sand. It's the chill of the word "rape," which she doesn't remember ever thinking before, that makes her angry. Later, she will wonder why she thought it—why she assumed that it had to happen. But right now she can do nothing but stomp out across that same expanse, kicking sand with every step until she reaches the jug, and then she swoops it up, and then she stomps back again to the unhelpful river.

"Fine. I'll go." She kneels by the raging water, and dips the jug in. "I'll go, I'll go, I'll go. What does it matter? What do I matter, right? It's Mira that matters. It's for Mira." But the plastic jug hangs there in her hand, battered against the stones by the rushing water, and she is sobbing, holding her belly with her other arm—and it's like that day she walked into the desert with Moon, only that time her tears were like being born, and this time they are like dying.

Come, says Yora. Or was it only her mind?

Come in.

Delilah lifts her head, lays the jug on the ground in the moonlight.

Come in with me.

"What?"

Come in with me, Lil, says Yora. *Tonight, for one night, become a goddess and enter the river with me. So that you can learn better how to be a human being. And so that I can finally let your pain go.*

The river crosses all through the forest in that direction, so that it would be impossible for Lonely not to arrive at it eventually, but where she arrives it is only a little stream. The water slips by as silent as owl wings, and all she can see of it is the moonlight twitching on the arched contours of each ripple, fogged by the ice above it, so that the water does not seem to be flowing either way but only shivering in place.

She kneels and touches her fingertips to a place where the cold water gushes through, hoping to feel something, hoping that something will suddenly make sense. But she can barely feel the water. Her mind tries to fit around the sensation, and cannot. Her body sits alone in the dark, as empty as air.

There were times when Sky seemed to be everywhere, alive in each living being, and everything beautiful would remind her of him—and she knew that he *was* everywhere, and could be anything. But tonight all she can feel is his absence.

In the night there is the flicker of a question—the question of fear—as she remembers that story which is always in her consciousness now, and tries to imagine, again, what that *Dark Goddess* looked like, and what her hunger looked like, and in what way she would emerge from dark water, and in what way a person might die.

Lonely tries to imagine Sky as a young boy, fighting her father as if he would give up his own life. For of course that was Sky—Sky with the blue raging eyes, who had another name then, a name she never knew.

What was it he fought for? The woman? The ceremony? Some sacred promise? His people? The Dark Goddess Herself? The water curling smoothly under Lonely's fingers is like a heart, beating and surging and falling, overwhelming her with tenderness for the mystery of that man she loves. How child-like, how frightened, how delicate that heart he held inside him, shielded by his eternal wakefulness, his hard declarations of duty. She remembers how each time she begged him to come closer, each time she spoke harshly to him for abandoning her, he wrapped that secret heart in one more layer of protection, until she could barely come near it at all. Until that final night when she forced him, perhaps, to surrender too quickly all that had made him feel safe for so many years. She wishes she could start over now, coaxing that heart out slowly, not so overcome by her own need, her own fear. What had he lost that day in the marsh? How had his spirit been broken by his failure, and by her father's triumph? How ashamed he must have felt. And how she must have shamed him again, to tell him over and over that his love was not good enough.

But who was that woman? She almost forgot, but now she remembers. *I am part of you, Sky! I am descended from a woman of your people. Don't you realize? Why didn't you tell me? Why did you deny me my past, my mother?*

Lonely looks up, clenching her fists around the water as the water runs right through, and is forever running through, and forever lost. *Mother,* she thinks suddenly. *Why did everyone deny you?*

Then a movement before her catches all her senses by surprise, and there is Fawn. Fawn walking toward her.

When Lonely sees her, she can tell that Fawn has been approaching her long before now and is not at all surprised to see Lonely. Her gaze is serious and hidden in the shadows, taking Lonely in without emotion, as she steps carefully on the river stones and doesn't stop.

"Do you want to come with me?" she says softly as she passes.

Lonely stands so fast she almost falls over, freezes, and then begins to follow. "You have to be careful," says Fawn.

It's true. Some of the stones are damp, and some are icy. Some of them tremble, and even begin to fall under the weight of their feet. This water that runs so sweetly, so much like a beating heart through the living forest, could kill them with its cold if they were to dip their bodies in it. After slipping once, Lonely decides to follow Fawn's path exactly, stepping on the same stones, which Fawn has obviously chosen with more knowing than Lonely.

Gradually, the river runs wider and a little deeper, and it takes all of Lonely's being—all the concentration of her mind and body—to place her feet exactly on each tiny island, to balance her weight, and to keep Fawn's moving shape in her vision at the same time as the stones. All thoughts are crowded out of her mind; all feelings go unconscious. She has no time to wonder at Fawn's courage, or where they are going, or why. She is the muscles in her legs, careful and tensed. She is the rhythm of her steps. She is the tilt of each stone beneath the soles of her boots. She is the loudening *shhhh* of the water, an eternity of sound surrounding her.

Around a large rock where the river pools deeply, the trees open to the moon above them; Fawn kneels. There is no space for Lonely there, so she stands where their path left her, balanced. Fawn removes her mittens and dips her hands deep into the black water, where white light threads between them.

"This is the river Yora," she says. "When I was a child, I knew something about this river. Something...." She trails off.

Lonely steps carefully to a place on the shore where there is room for her to crouch down. She faces Fawn and puts her hands in the river too. She is so lonely. *My name is Lonely,* she thinks. *It is my only name. I accept it. It is my name.* Longing stirs between her and Fawn, turning slowly in the moonlight, moving in the water. Lonely watches it, not knowing who it belongs to or what it is for.

Fawn looks up at her, and the surprise of it almost knocks Lonely off balance, like seeing a ghost.

"You're a goddess, aren't you?" Fawn whispers.

Lonely says nothing. It doesn't seem like a question that looks for an answer.

"I was jealous sometimes," Fawn says, still whispering, still staring at her, her body eerily frozen. "I was jealous of you and Rye. It seemed that you were so alike. It seemed that you understood each other—"

Lonely shakes her head. "He became a friend to me. That's all."

"I know."

Lonely hangs her head and trails her hands in the water. They are both silent for a long time, and Lonely feels sorry. Once, long ago, she had thought nothing of stealing Rye from the woman who truly loved him.

Now it seems to her that sadness is all she is, and each moment can be translated into one more drop of sadness, until there is so much she could lie down in the deep sea of it and go to sleep forever.

The forest is absolutely silent. So silent that the moon, who Sky once told her was the Earth's sister—the lost earth, the shadow earth—very quietly seems to creep a little closer.

Then Lonely looks up and sees Fawn lifting her hands from the water, one at a time. She lifts one hand and the water spills off of it, a slow waterfall back into that pool of moonlight, and as she dips it back down into the water, she lifts the other one. Back and forth, back and forth—and both she and Lonely gaze at the water as it curves over the flesh of her palms and falls, its sound a caress.

"Thank you, Lonely," says Fawn. "Thank you for all that you've made me feel. Even the pain. Everything."

But Lonely says nothing because as she watches, the water seems to change, so that it becomes smoother and slower and thicker, and now churns with faint rainbows, like saliva from the mouth of some dragon. Blue and violet it stretches between Fawn's hands and the pool, and they both watch fascinated, until finally Fawn lifts both hands so that what seemed like water now swirls around her fingers in the air—some magical substance Lonely has never seen but which is at once familiar and terrifying and heartbreakingly beautiful.

"What is that?" she whispers.

Fawn stands, removes her cloaks one by one, and steps into the water. As Lonely watches in amazement, she steps forward, and sinks up to her waist. The rainbows swirl up her body. "Come in," she says, gazing up at Lonely, her face suffused suddenly with a feeling like joy—and Lonely tries to remember what that feeling is, because it's something she recognizes from long, long ago, when she herself was still a child and she did not know her age because childhood is eternal, and she remembers now: *wonder*.

"It isn't cold," says Fawn.

Lonely tears herself out of her clothes and half-crawls, half-tumbles in— not careful at all, hardly aware of which limbs move first or of what carries her—giddy with surrender, as if falling finally into her lover's arms.

They have stood here for days and days, nights and nights, and the Unicorn cannot bring herself to go on.

The fences have ended, broken off into nothing. Like everything else in the City, they were an illusion, built to hide the heart. That boundary between the City and its heart is marked by a fog so thick it seems to pulse—so heavy it drenches her fur on contact, pressing it against her skin, making her feel more than ever like nothing but a body.

She is unaware of Sky now, who also waits silently as if he could wait forever, upon her back. She is unaware that his fear is as great as her own. She would rather stand here forever, seeing nothing, hearing nothing, than go forward or back. But tonight, on the full moon, this painful weightiness of her own damp skin is all that she can feel. The feeling of herself fills up the whole universe—the dry inside of her mouth, the raw insides of her ears, the cold bones of her ankles and knees, the pull of her belly, the wail of her spine—nothing but herself inside herself inside herself, and it is the most terrible thing to feel this, and she is screaming, but the scream of a Unicorn cannot be heard. It comes in another language, not made of sound.

But Sky, who has become a boy again, about thirteen years old—his strong, nervous young hands clasped around her shoulder blades, his back leaning over her—hears. He doesn't throw his arms around her neck or tell her to hush. Instead, he bends his head down and presses his forehead to that place where her neck connects her head to her body, and prays. Very gradually, his calm calms her, and his respect releases her into the safety of her own true nature, and the feeling of actually being heard makes her stop screaming.

"I'm sorry," she says.

"It's okay," says Sky, speaking for the first time since they arrived. "I'm scared, too." He feels tenderness for her like he has never felt before for anything.

"But what are *you* afraid of?" she asks him. "Isn't this where you wanted to be? Isn't this your home?"

"But what will it be now? Who knows what remains. The only one who lasts forever—"

"I know," says the Unicorn. Then they are both silent again.

"I couldn't believe it when I found you," Sky says. "I couldn't believe there was a Unicorn after all. How could it be true?"

She doesn't answer him. "What is She that remains?" she whispers. "Why can't I bear to come closer?"

Sky holds tighter to the Unicorn's mane. The mists begin to take form before him, swaying and sighing, and he has to close his eyes to still his pounding heart. "She is the Nothing from which we come. She is the Goddess we thanked at each birth, and surrendered to at each death. She is the mystery behind the reflection. She is the truth that each of us is afraid will kill us if we face it."

The Unicorn trembles and cannot stop trembling.

"But you don't need to be afraid," says Sky. "Because you come from there."

"No," whispers the Unicorn—the horse who is not a horse, but someone's soul. "Not me." For she is remembering now: the chemical smell that surrounded the infant Mira's birth, the white masks, and the place of shouting and dirty shadow where she sat in her crib and watched, for hours and hours trapped, and the desperation—even then, already—in her father's eyes, and the sorrowful, unseeing envy in Lilah's.

"Every year," continues Sky, his voice turning cold and distant, "a woman of our people is chosen, through a dream, to meet with the Dark Goddess. We perform the rituals. We prepare her. Then we send her down. There, beneath the water where we can never see and never know, the light and the dark meet and become one, and from that union rises the Unicorn—the most sacred being, the bringer of Transformation. It is this meeting that makes death turn to birth, keeps the cycles of the seasons turning, keeps the people falling in love over and over forever, keeps hearts open. It is this meeting that holds the paradox of the world together."

Then his voice softens, and turns a little more real again. "But now I think that maybe the Unicorn must be born even if the ritual is not held. Nothing can stop the Light, any more than the Darkness. If we do not consciously facilitate this sacred meeting, if the meeting is for some reason thwarted, the Unicorn will still be born, and life will still go on.

"Only that birth will be much, much more painful. That is why you've had to spend your whole life, Unicorn, trying to remember what you are."

The Unicorn shakes her mane. "Enough," she says. She begins to walk. For the stillness, she feels now—for the first time in this life—is no longer safe.

Later, though Fawn will tell Chelya all about it—of course she will tell Chelya everything, and Eva, too—and though she will tell Willow and Jay about it, and one day she will tell Chelya's children about it, and Willow's daughter Thea, and Thea's children, the first person she wants to tell—whose arms she cannot wait to come home to, finally—is Rye.

He wraps her up in blankets in the middle of the night, the way he wrapped her in his cloak one night when she was sixteen, and came running in from a thunder storm with the flush of gods still hot on her face. That day, the way she remembers it, was the very beginning of their love.

"It wasn't a dream," she mutters wildly now, "because she's gone, she's gone now."

"Who's gone?" says Rye.

"Lonely."

She feels like a child, held out from him at arms' length, watching his serious, searching expression as if from far away. Not until this moment has she really seen the distance between them. It is alive and solid, as real as what she's experienced in the river. She doesn't know how or when that distance got so big. But she comforts herself thinking, *it is only the length of his arms.* Absurdly, deliriously, she thinks, *That's as far as anyone can push you away—only the length of their arms.*

"Fawn," Rye says, and he looks into her eyes. "What happened? What dream?"

"It was like a dream," murmurs Fawn, turning into her mind, afraid of forgetting.

"Should I get Eva then?"

Fawn looks up suddenly and sees him, sees him really there, because his hands are no longer touching her and he is turning away. And in that passionless willingness to get her what she needs, that resigned assumption of his turning body—the assumption that what she needs, he does not have to give her—she sees for the first time how she has hurt him. She sees for the first time the wounds she has made, so long after the fact that those wounds are already scarring over, perhaps irreparably changing him. How, she wonders, could she not see it before? How could she feel revulsion at the violence of the dream she just ran from, when she herself has been inflicting this real violence on the one she loves all this time? She did not even know she was angry. *This* has been a dream. This strange living, ever since Kite left.

"No, not my mother," she manages to tell Rye now. "I want you. I want to tell *you.*"

He turns back and faces her. He looks at her face, and she can tell he wants to do something about the tears in her eyes, but the steps they once knew so well, between them, have been blurred. It's like he doesn't remember the way back.

"I'm sorry," she says. "I'm so sorry how I've been. I'm sorry." Then she is unable to speak, but he comes and holds her the best he can, and she feels his helplessness. How could she never have seen this, that he felt just as helpless as she? And what will she do now, as he steps away again, still not understanding what she wants from him, still afraid of not being able to give it, still afraid of being blamed?

She takes his hand, and the earth floor carries their feet toward the fire, where they sink down. Always, the earth reminds her, things happen slowly. Slowly, the seasons will come around again. Here is her love, her first and only love—the adventurer, the restless boy, the stronger of the two brothers, but always so gentle, so gentle in his heart! Oh, the person she has been in the last few moons—she did not know she could be that person!

"I want to tell you—" Fawn begins. "The dream I just had, that was real. A nightmare, but I think, maybe, it was good. Can I tell you?" The formality of her own voice breaks her heart, but he takes her hand and nods, like a little boy. Like her own son, the only time she ever yelled at him—the way he stood there afterward, the need in his eyes. All men are like this—only boys. They don't know what she has now learned. They have not surrendered to the swirling waters. How could she forget her duty as a woman to give them that deep compassion, that deep sea?

"Lonely and I went into the water together," she begins carefully. "Into the river."

She looks at him, to see if he will be confused. But his eyes say, *I will take anything. Your love in any form, except anger.* Will she be able to explain that part too, when it comes?

"The whole time, we were under the water," she continues. "But we could breathe, and it wasn't cold," she says. "It wasn't cold because—" She takes a deep breath. "Because it became something magical. It became emotion."

She looks at him. "Did you know that emotion is magic?" she asks, hesitantly.

He shakes his head, and smiles a little, but sadly.

"I didn't know either. We have to remember how to work with this magic. We have to become sorcerers of our own emotions. That's what Yora said."

"Yora?"

"Yes. Yora. She was there. Yora, the goddess of that river."

Rye raises his eyebrows.

"There is a goddess," Fawn whispers, leaning forward, "of that river. I knew it, when I was a little girl. Everything has a spirit, everything has a keeper. I remember now. They are trying to speak to us."

She looks up at Rye, as if for confirmation. He nods, but she can't read the expression in his eyes.

"Lonely and I held hands, and we went under together." She speaks slowly, choosing her words carefully. "We didn't have to think about it; it just happened. Something was pulling us down, and we weren't afraid. Under the water I saw many women's faces, as if there were hundreds of women swimming around me, and then it was as if we stood in the river again, only it wasn't the same river. It was like the river beneath the river, in another world. The water was warm, and swirling slowly around us, and I don't remember seeing the banks of it. There was nothing but water. And me and three other women standing there."

Again, she looks carefully into Rye's eyes. He is simply there, listening, waiting.

"The three women were Lonely and Yora—and this other woman I had never seen. She was called Delilah. I could never tell whether she was human or goddess. She was very small and dark, and always moving, always climbing out of the water onto stones, like a creature who couldn't bear to be in the water too long. But I could see by the way she moved, restless—I could see by the meanness in her eyes, and the anger there, and the way her body sliced into the water—that she was made of fire. She scared me, and I didn't understand why she was there, or who she was.

"I think we were all naked. Yora was so beautiful, the way you'd dream the river would be, if the river were a woman. So graceful, and she was constantly changing into the river itself, as if the way she moved was the way the river moved. It's hard to explain." Fawn looks at Rye and feels the impossibility of this story, how difficult it will be to put into words. She sighs. "Oh, Rye, I wish you could understand what I'm telling you. I wish you could see how it was." *Don't you feel anything?* she thinks with sudden desperation. *Am I the only one who feels so much? What happens inside you, all these days since we lost our son, and why won't you ever show me?* She feels the tears rise up in her eyes again.

"I'm sorry," he says stiffly, dropping his hand from hers. "Lately I don't seem to be able to do anything you ask of me. I can't bring Kite back. I can't tell you what's going to happen to him. I can't feel exactly how you feel or do anything to fix it. But I do know—"

Fawn shakes her head. "That isn't what I meant, Rye!"

"I was going to say," he continues, "that I do know who you are, and the strength inside you. If you remembered your own strength, Fawn, you would not feel so helpless."

Fawn looks carefully into his gaze and sees the kindness there. "I know," she says, ashamed.

"Go on," he says.

"In the river, Yora said, 'This woman (she meant Lonely, but she never called her by that name)—this woman is going on a journey. She wants to journey to where someone else's heart is, and to do that she must learn to shapeshift. She must learn to change the very elements inside herself. Each of us here has a gift to give her, to help her do that.'

"Then this girl Delilah, whose name I knew somehow in the dream, spoke up. She jumped up on the rock like a little girl and turned around and around, avoiding everyone's eyes, and she said, 'I've already given to this girl. Enough. I have my own journey now.'

"And Yora's voice was strong the way anger is strong, but not angry. She said, 'Delilah, you think that giving always means sacrificing. You think it will always leave you empty. You think it is you losing, and the other person winning. I am not talking about that kind of giving.'

"Then Delilah was silent, and she actually sat down on the stone and rolled herself up into a ball and was still, but listening, I think, though she didn't want to show it. Then Yora looked right at me, and she spoke to me first, though I don't know why. Her eyes were tender, and I believed she remembered me from my childhood, when she used to comfort me in the wilderness before I had a home. I remembered her from even before that, from the womb itself. She said, 'We all bring the gift of the emotion that most haunts us. Fawn, what emotion do you bring?'"

Fawn takes Rye's hand again. "Rye, you understand, of course I said, 'Fear.' It was fear that had made me forget her, fear that had made me forget even myself all these years that I've felt the City coming closer, coming to take me back.

"I could feel the others looking at me, and I felt ashamed. This girl Delilah looked as if she felt contempt for Fear. And for me.

"But Lonely walked to me through the water, and she put her arms around me. Something about her embrace felt so forgiving and also so like a child's. I realized she'd always seemed like a child to me. I realized how much I'd both loved and almost hated her because she lives her whole life with that innocence that I was forced to give up when I was very, very young, because life was so—because it demanded so much of me.

"She said, 'Teach me about Fear.'

"And Rye, I could only stare past her into the fire of Delilah's eyes. I don't know who that girl was, but everything she was made me afraid. She was staring right at me now. It was so frightening. I felt like if I spoke out loud, I might die.

"Then finally *Lonely* spoke again, and she said, '*I'm* afraid of being alone forever.' I remember the stillness of the moon behind her head, like it was holding its breath. She went on—it's amazing how I can remember every word. She said, 'I'm afraid of an old woman on an island, and the curse she placed on me, and I'm afraid to realize that she is my own mother. I'm afraid that no one in this whole world really loves me. I'm afraid I'll never see the Unicorn again, and I won't be able to find my way. I'm afraid I'll never see my beloved again, and I'm afraid it will be my fault.'

"That gave me courage, somehow, when Lonely said all that. I knew she'd said it for me. I knew she was my friend, and I guess I've always known that. It's only been hard, sometimes, to know it, because of what she asks of me. So I said, 'I'm afraid to speak right now.'

"I know my voice was really small, and I know that fire girl was still looking at me that same way, but once I said that, I found I could keep going, and it got easier.

"I said, 'I'm afraid that something terrible will happen to my son, or has already happened. I'm afraid I'll never see him again. I'm afraid to lose everything I have, I'm afraid of the world coming undone, I'm afraid of the seasons changing their course and the very cycle of life we depend on coming unraveled, and I'm afraid of my home being taken away from under my feet the way Willow's was.'

"Then Yora lifted the water up in her hands like a magical thing, thick like glue—like the glue that holds the world together—and it sparkled in the moonlight. She said, 'This is Fear.'

"And I could see that it was! The way it sparkled like that, the way Fear starts to tingle all sharp and bright at the base of your spine. And that's only the beginning. But she said, 'We cannot hide from ourselves any more. The world is falling apart. We are all dying, all lost, all lonely. Women, this is all we have. We cannot be selfish any more with our emotions. Fawn, this is Fear. This is *your* power. So lead.'

"Then it was like— Oh, how can I explain? She seemed to open the river to me. The spiraling water we stood in—she opened the center of that spiral, and there was this dark abyss between us. I could tell that was where I was supposed to go, because it was so terrifying. Like something saying to me, here it is, what you've always feared: do you want to see it? Well here it is.

"I don't know how I did this. Except that I found out, in that moment, that inside of Fear is courage. As if because I was the keeper of this emotion, Fear, I was also the only one brave enough to enter. I felt that for the sake of the others, I had to lead the way. I stepped forward, and felt the water pulling me down.

"I'm glad I didn't know what would happen or I would never have gone. In a second I had completely lost the ground, I couldn't tell which way was up, I was spinning and the spiral overcame me. Everything was dark and the water became icy cold, so cold I was afraid I would disappear. I was reaching and clawing at nothing, feeling all alone. I thought I was drowning. It seemed to go on and on like that—pure terror—until I realized that I wasn't drowning, that I could breathe down there in that blackness, and that the others were in there, too, except we were all spinning with no control over our bodies and could not reach each other. Then finally there was a stillness; we were floating there as if lost together in the night sky. It was so quiet, and in that blackness, Rye, I saw the most terrible things. It was so still, but these images came at me, slow and horrifying, and it made me feel like we were floating in the eye of some storm, and that at any moment the Fear would come blowing in again so intensely it would kill me.

"I can't remember everything I saw. There was Kite lying dead, of course. But there were other images, too, that were not mine. There was a baby all alone and starving, screaming in a dark cave, and then there were footsteps coming, but whoever came wasn't its mother and was angry. There was this feeling of falling, endlessly. There was this little girl with madness in her eyes—like her soul had left her—tearing out her hair and rocking and claw-ing her face. There was a man with that same madness in his eyes, throwing glass bottles against a wall next to a woman's face and yelling. There was a monster leaping out of black water and devouring a woman in an explosion of blood. Throngs of people wailing and reaching. And there were things I didn't understand, too, because they didn't seem like they should be frighten-ing. The sound of someone quietly crying or an image of someone reaching out her hand—whether to plead or to offer love, I could not tell. Everything felt eerie and awful. And I knew somehow that these images were all the fears of the women around me.

"But instead of something horrible happening, nothing ever happened to us. Only these frightening images and ideas floated by, and then nothing. Amidst them, I could hear Yora's voice: 'What is this, Fawn? What is Fear?' At some point she was there with me, passing the magic substance of this emotion back and forth between our hands. I thought it would be cold but now it was hot. When it touched my hands, it seemed to change form.

"I was surprised to find that I could speak again. I said 'Fear is when you stand on the edge of change, on the edge of the unknown. It's how you know you are moving.'

"I looked at Delilah and I saw that Fear is fire—unpredictable, destructive, and changing everything it touches—but also it is that spark of life itself. It is what makes us go forward, what makes us know we are alive. I looked at Lonely and saw that Fear is air—that abyss, that nothingness—but it is also freedom. I looked at Yora and saw that Fear is water, that terror of fast surrender, that fast falling into the unknown. But also how good it felt, to let go. I remembered those first thunderstorms in the wilderness—when all the elements came together—and how my body felt free and alive for the first time, and how for the first time I knew what God was and what I was. I re-membered the first time you touched me.

"I don't even know if I said all this aloud. But then Lonely cried out to me, 'What can we do, when we're afraid? Eva said I must not be afraid. But I'm afraid!' And I said to her—and this is how it was like a dream, Rye, the way I said things I wouldn't have said in real life, wouldn't have known to say, and

I don't know why I said them, but they seemed right—I said, 'Before you can let go of Fear, you have to learn *how* to fear. You have to learn the power of Fear. That is the gift I have to give you.'

"She said, 'What do you mean?' and I could see her now again, wherever we were, and touch her. I said, 'Have you ever been lost in a world you didn't understand, not knowing what to do or where to go, but letting your instincts guide you the best you could?' And she said, breathing a little more calmly now, 'Yes, that has been my whole journey.' I said, 'That was the power of Fear. It made you stop thinking. It forced you to act on your instincts, and your instincts were always right. Did your fear ever stop you from doing something that wasn't right for you?' And she said 'Yes, with Dragon. Yes, at the fire circle, with Coyote.' We were standing again now, our heads clear above the river, the water down around our bellies. She said, 'But sometimes Fear haunts me. Sometimes it keeps me from someone I love; sometimes it keeps me from trusting him and makes me lose him.' Then she started to cry. I said, 'Fear is also courage. Look for it there. Inside the Fear is courage. That same whirring, dizzy churning that makes you afraid can rise up inside you and make you leap. If you face your fear, it will make you powerful. Didn't you ever face your fear?' She looked at me with wonder, and in her eyes I saw an old woman with a terrible face, and then the black sea rising up, and she said slowly, 'Yes. I did. Or I would never have left the island.'

"Then I took her in my arms, and I held her close, and I could feel my own warmth, my own depth holding her deep. I said, 'When you don't understand Fear, when you cannot find the answers inside it because it has tricked you into thinking it is bigger than you are, then come home to the Earth. Come home to the Earth.' Now we could feel the firm stones beneath the river again, holding our feet and carrying the river forever.

"I said, 'The Earth reminds us to go slow, one step at a time.' Then I looked at Delilah, and she was still now, staring at me. It wasn't contempt I saw there after all, but Fear itself.

"Then Lonely and I stepped apart, and I saw the new determination in Lonely's eyes, like she'd already started on that journey, wherever she was going."

Fawn looks at Rye now, almost afraid to continue, and yet feeling the thrill of her own fear. "Rye, it's true. Emotions are like this magic we are given, that can give us so much power if we understand it and know how to use it, but that can destroy us—and everyone we love—if we don't."

Rye nods again, his eyes wide. "What happened to Lonely?" he says.

"That's the part that seems really terrible, but I think maybe now I understand." She looks at the anxiety in his face and feels a little of the old envy, but mostly she feels sorry, that what she has to tell now might frighten him.

"Yora turned to this girl of fire. The moon lit Delilah up, and I saw how really powerful she was, only her power was too much for her, and it hurt her somehow. Yora said, 'What emotion do you bring, Lil?'

"Delilah looked back at her, and she was flicking little stones hard into the river, and she said stubbornly, 'You already know.'

"Yora said, 'But I do not know. I do not understand it. I feel it—everyone gives it to me—but I do not understand what it is. What is it for? Where does it come from?'

"We waited a long time and Delilah wouldn't answer. Then finally she said quietly, 'I won't talk about where it comes from. It's what keeps me safe, so I don't have to talk about it.'

"'Then all you have is Fear,' said Yora.

"Then Delilah exploded, and I realized I'd seen it coming all along, and that's why I was so afraid of her. She threw her words in red fire across the water, and they burned all of us. I don't remember the details of all she said—about how we didn't understand her, how she didn't ask to be here, how she didn't need us and didn't need Yora, how she didn't need anything. She used words I'd never heard before—hard, hate words that were meant to hurt. Then she turned the fire on Lonely, and she told her she was selfish, that she thought she was a princess, that her father had taken everything from Delilah's people and ruined Delilah's father, and many other things. Only she didn't say them like that; she said them in ways I can't repeat. Cruel ways, although when I think of it now, I feel more sorry for her than for Lonely. She seemed in so much pain.

"As she yelled, the water swirled up around her, harder and harder, and swirled around all of us like a great storm, so that I had to hold onto myself to keep from being washed away—I had to hold onto the Earth, and close my eyes to keep the Fear from killing me, and try to remind myself that this was fire, which I needed to live.

"Yora said, in the stillness inside all this whirling, so that somehow we could hear her, 'So Anger is need. Only need.' She sighed and sounded very sad. I looked at Lonely and, to my surprise, she didn't look hurt by Delilah's words. She looked like I had felt when I saw the swirling water which was Fear itself in front of me—as if relieved that something she'd always feared was finally being revealed to her.

"But now Delilah was sitting down on a little stone and holding her face in her hands. She shook her head, not looking up, and murmured, 'No, no, it's more than that. It's what makes us strong. It's what helps us survive.'

"Yora said gently, 'Who is *us*?'

"Delilah didn't answer that, but she shook her head again and said, 'Anger is all I have.'

"Yora said, 'These other women here—we have other emotions, besides Anger. If you will teach us the power of Anger, we will give you these gifts in return. Then you will have other powers and other tools to use as you wish, not only Anger.'

"Delilah looked up at her. Yora held out her hands to her, as if asking for this gift. So finally Delilah closed her eyes and screamed, louder than you've ever heard anyone scream—not even human, but like the way a wolf howls to call its people home. As she screamed, the waters rose up and engulfed us all, but before I had time to feel afraid, the Fear turned into—"

She pauses here, smiling to herself, pressing her face into one hand.

"The Fear turned into—I guess you'd call it passion. Like when you know exactly what you want and you'll do anything to get it, and the power of your own desire and certainty is so big, you have absolutely no fear that anything will stop you. And nothing will hurt you—nothing will ever hurt you. I was so afraid of her fire as that water came rolling toward me, but once it was inside of me, I felt safe for the first time since I can remember. I felt safe because I understood my own anger. I understood my own fury at having to live in fear, and at what is done to my life that is not in my control, and I felt like a mountain lion—I felt like the strongest, wildest *beast*, Rye, knowing that nothing would stop me from trying to keep my children safe and keep the home I love safe. I knew what I wanted, too. I wanted the beauty of these mountains to embrace me forever, and I wanted to see Kite and Chelya grow up happy, and I wanted you inside of me."

She lowers her eyes, courage burning her face, her body tensed as if to spring. She feels, from across the space between them, the curious, animal hardening of Rye's body—cold, almost calculating in its rising, though tentative, desire. But neither of them, right now, can move. How long ago, she wonders, did they lose track of each other like this? How long since they've made love? What was it about Kite's loss that made her forget who her husband was—or did it only make her realize that she never really knew?

"But when the scream was over," she continues, her story like a lifeline now, the only real thing to carry them both forward through the pain of that question, "Delilah was still and calm, like she had not been all this time. She came forward to Lonely and she pulled out a sword. I don't know where it came from. It was like this was her dream now, and I was only watching from some strange other place. Her voice was eerily calm, like something that did not belong to her, though her eyes were still blazing. She said to Lonely, 'Do you know what Anger feels like, my white mirror?'

That's what she called her. It was like this ritual they both knew, somehow.

"Lonely answered, her whole body tensed now, her teeth clenched, her face unlike I'd ever seen it: 'Yes! I am angry for all the ways they try to define me and use me that are NOT ME. At my mother who hates me for the pain and loss I represent to her, at my father who locked me up for the ideal he wanted to make me, at the people who left me lonely there because I was only a dream to them, and at Sky who left me because of how I reminded him of something he lost long ago that he wasn't brave enough to try for again. I'm angry at this curse that was placed on me, that DOES NOT BE-LONG TO ME, and at this name which IS NOT MY NAME and for never ever being able to reach the love I long for! And I'm angry at YOU, for hating me, for all your resentment, for all your blindness to who I really am.'

"Delilah heard all this, not moving, her expression unchanging, and then she spoke back. She stood straight and tall for the first time.

"'Anger is your self trying to become better than what you were,' she said.

"'Anger is your own true power longing to grow, longing to stand up inside you. I tell you this now, and if you don't hear me now, you will never hear me. Don't use it against anyone else, and don't use it against yourself. Use it to blaze a path, and use it to blaze a space around you that protects you. If it ever gets so hot it burns you, look inside yourself, be still, and find that flame that burns in you. When you see that, there is no need to feel angry, because you won't feel helpless any more. You will see that flame, and feel only—amazement.' Then Delilah said to her, though maybe she said it for herself, 'Use it to free yourself of what you were. Use it to cut away all those expectations, all those ideals, all those fakes that people placed over who you really were. When you're free, you can shapeshift into *anything*.'

"This is the terrible part. I want to say it was a dream, but it was not. Delilah lifted up her sword and sliced right through Lonely's body. I mean, all the way through. Lonely broke apart like she was made of clay, and then she broke again, and again. Into pieces—but it wasn't like you would think. That's why it *was* like a dream, in a way. There wasn't any blood that I can remember, and it didn't hurt me to watch. It only frightened me when I came out of the river later, and tried to remember it. Yes, I remember now, it seemed completely *right* at the time. Because that wasn't the real Lonely. There were pieces of her scattered now, but they weren't like bloody pieces of a body, they were like—like shattered shards of glass. And then they be-came, I don't know, like things of nature. Branches, feathers, old dry bones, tears. But they were still Lonely. Her spirit was still in those things or rising out of those things, somewhere, and could speak, though I don't know where the voice came from. Delilah sat down on the stone and laid her head on her arms. The whole time we were there, I don't know if she ever lifted her eyes again. I felt so sorry for her, for what she had had to do. I thought she was so brave, and I wanted to tell her so, but I couldn't seem to move."

Fawn looks at Rye and his eyes are closed now, but she can tell he is listening, though he is barely breathing. She used to see him sit like this sometimes, long ago when he came home and found that his mother had died, and he was slowly deciding within himself not to travel ever again. She used to watch him shyly sometimes, from behind the trees, her heart filling with wonder for the mystery of this man she had chosen to love.

"Yora's gift was Sorrow," she says now. "Yora was the river, flowing over Lonely, healing her, turning those pieces into liquid so that they bled together and were one again—but still without form, something we could not really see now but only sense around us. Yora said to her, 'You already know Sorrow. But do you trust it yet? Let it carry you. When it comes, all you can do is give in.'

"And there was Delilah crying on the rock with her head in her arms, and me looking on silent, not knowing why I was there. Lonely was a rainbow, or a school of silver fish, or a shadow of something passing over or under—something in the water that kept coming and coming, going and going. I really did understand, then, how sometimes we are helpless after all, and we have to accept that. Sometimes we have to let go, not understanding what the pain is for or why we're alive, and simply wait. In the images of that water, shifting in the moonlight, I felt I could see all of Lonely's journey. I didn't see her; instead I saw her reflected in the lands she'd passed through. Landscapes of sorrow. The black silence under the sea and the silver quiet of the waves on the surface, with nothing to break against. Long, slow rain in a field. Even the shapes of these mountains, as they fall into shadow. The lonely sky, with a single bird flying through it, lost in grey clouds. You know how every landscape, every shape, holds a different emotion—makes you feel different things. You know how it is. I remember, too, the places we traveled through to come here, when I was a child. It's been so long I'd almost forgotten.

"Lonely had traveled so far. To me it seemed as if that broken list of memories was in itself creating her sorrow. Just having so much past, so much she'd walked through and would never see again—so much to make sense of, and none of it making any sense.

"But Lonely's voice came through the dream of that river and said, 'I thank the land, for carrying my emotions for me before I ever knew what they were. I thank the sea for carrying my grief when I could not yet feel it. I thank the desert for carrying my passion when I did not yet know what to do with it. I thank the forests for keeping my secret fears before I was ready to face them, and the mountains for holding my love before I knew how to express it, and the sky for holding my dreams even when I did not always believe in them.'

"Inside myself I suddenly felt all my love for Lonely, all the feelings she had brought me—that were brought to life in me since I met her—and I thought to myself, 'But you are made of air, so free! Air and fire, they have no trouble shape-shifting at all. Become whatever you want. Why let sorrow pull you down?'

"And as if she could hear my thoughts, Yora said, 'What *is* the gift of Sorrow?'

"Lonely said, 'It is Sorrow that brings me home. So I don't get lost. So I don't float away forever. It gets so lonely up there in the sky. The first time I felt sorrow was when my father died. I am grateful for that, because it brought me down out of that tower, down to the earth, and through the sea, and to the place where I first felt the fire and knew I was real.'

"Yora said, 'Sorrow brings you home. Let the water flow you back together. It will feel, Princess, as if we have given you nothing. It will feel as if you have nothing, for a time. But that is a good darkness you are in. In that darkness, if you stay awake, you will begin again and become who you truly are.

"'For all of the gifts we give you are Love. Sorrow is Love. Anger is Love. Fear is Love. When you realize this, you will use those emotions as powers, to do whatever you want with—make whatever magic you wish. Each of you will become sorcerers of emotion. But remember'—and she looked at all of us — 'that you love each other. Remember that the Wind blows the Water, and the Water shapes the Earth, and the Earth smothers the Fire, but the Fire changes the Earth, and the Air feeds the Fire, and the Fire heats the Water, and the Water puts out the Fire, and the Air blows the dry Earth, and the Earth pulls the Water down into its deepest valleys, the Seas.'"

Fawn pauses and takes a deep breath. "Then we could feel Lonely leaving us. We could feel her in the river passing on. We could feel the way she swirled around each of our bodies, thanked us, and said goodbye. When she came around me, in the form of the river, she was warm. My body went weak. I felt my body alive, desperate to be touched, the way I haven't felt in so long. That was always her gift to me—one of her many gifts to me.

"She didn't feel like Sorrow now. She felt like laughter—the laughter of falling apart, of letting go. I even thought I heard her whisper to me, *It is for the laughter we once shared that I will return one day. It is for this laughter that I am human.* Then she was gone.

"But the three of us remained. I was shaking. I felt like I had just been born. I wasn't even thinking about Kite. The pleasure of my own life—the soil under my palms, the sugar of food, the flow of the hills, the first flowers of spring—was almost too much for me to bear. I wanted to be with you again, with this completely selfish desire that I didn't know I had in me. But Yora was beckoning me, and I came toward her, and in coming toward her I came closer to Delilah, who was still curled over on the stone, unseeing. The two of us came around her, making a tight circle with our arms. I wasn't afraid any more. This pleasure within me was so abundant, so overflowingly warm, it was as if I had too much to give to draw back from anything in fear. I had to give it. I had to. I don't know who began it or how I knew, but somehow we both began to caress Delilah. Her fast, quiet sobs immediately stilled, and she tensed her whole body for a long time under our touch. I touched her the way I wanted to be touched. I touched her the way I once touched Lonely, as if I had never seen such beauty. Soon she began to relax, but at the same time she twisted under our hands as if in pain. I don't think she knew where she was or what she was doing, but she began to clutch at herself, and she began to cry out—breathless, shocked little screams—and then between our hands she became a whirlwind of fire that rose into the air and was gone.

"Yora and I stood then alone, and the empty air between us felt very serious and very still. She said, 'Poor Lil, she is so lonely, and doesn't even know. She will wake from this dream forever changed, but she will forget the dream itself. Tonight she saw the darkest part of herself emerge, and surrendered in a way she never meant to surrender. In her waking life, it will be too much for her to remember, and so she will not.'

"I said, 'Will I remember?'

"And Yora said, 'You alone, Fawn, will remember every moment and every word. It is you, keeper of Earth, who will keep the Story, and you will always remember it, and you will pass it on, and you will learn to understand it in your waking mind and heart. You have no choice in this.'

"'What about you?' I said.

"She said, 'I *am* the Story. I just go on.'

"And then she was the river again, simply flowing on, and then there I was, at the river's edge. I was no longer inside it but now watching it flow by, while I stayed there, the same, in the same place. I was back at the edge where I had first knelt with Lonely, and I was still in my dry clothes, as if I had never gone in."

She stops now. Never, perhaps, in her whole life, has she spoken so many words at once, and so easily, and with such certainty. She knows it is Rye who allowed her to speak them. It is only him she feels this safe with, this unconditionally held.

Yet she doesn't know if he truly wanted to hear or if he understood. She wonders if he is worrying about Lonely, wondering where she has gone. She tries to see his reaction inside his eyes, and cannot. "You are the one I wanted to tell first," she repeats urgently. "You are the first person to hear this story." Then she adds, in a whisper, "You, always, have helped me to remember myself. You were the first person who ever saw me, before I even saw myself."

Rye smiles. "Now I am seeing you all over again," he says.

Fawn nods, letting the tears fall, for she is seeing herself again, too, and now she is looking back at Rye. Who is he? Suddenly it seems clear to her what the distance between them was made of. It was made of the whole landscape of *his* emotions. What Kite's loss feels like to him. What he wakes to every day, the only man in a house he once shared with his son. What he hides inside that calm silence she so envied. What he felt walking back through the forest after saying goodbye to Kite, knowing Kite was grown now, knowing he could not carry him home. All these feelings she does not know and has never even asked.

Like an injured animal, clumsy and soft, she inches toward him, her knees and buttocks scraping the hearth made of stone that he once laid by hand to prove his love for her. She wraps her arms and legs around him, and he bows his head into her warmth.

"How are you?" she whispers, and feels his shaking response.

And she hopes that someday Lonely, if she doesn't already, will understand—in the chords of her own body—how inside Fear is courage, and inside Sorrow is the joy that comes from simple release, the muscles finally relaxing.

How Anger is only the longing to connect more deeply, to hold fast with claws of fire, and how, through that ugly, painful, mortal merging—in which we are split open, in which so much that we knew of ourselves is lost—comes the only true empathy that allows us to finally forgive.

"Miri," says Delilah, before she even wakes.

She comes to consciousness slowly through aching memories of love: Dragon's listening body, Dragon cradling her, Dragon asking her to tell her story when she had so many emotions she didn't know how to feel that the only way she could let them out was by coming in his arms. A light, cold rain is falling, and she can feel Moon inside it, silently desperate, like the pleading inside someone's eyes when they have no words to tell you what they need.

"Miri." That's what she used to call her sister, and *Lilah* is what her sister said back. Those were their names when they knew each other, when they were truly kin.

Delilah is lying in the river, and it's still the middle of the night. She feels her fear of the men, who know now that she is out here. For an instant, she feels the sorrow of her loneliness. She crawls out of the water, takes off her wet clothes, puts on her mother's sweatshirt and then a tattered man's jacket. Her body is so tired.

"Miri," she whispers. The barest fragments of a dream make her tremble, and she feels a calling she hasn't felt for some time now, from deep within her body, like the way she used to feel when a man touched her. It's like that now: that first, most tender yearning, her body softening into colors, deliciously sexy, and yet it is not a man that she wants. She misses again the cave she lived in for so long, and feels the strength of earth that she breathed in from that cave for years and years. She feels the quickness of air, and the longing in its uneven stretch around her. She feels the elements that make her the warrior she is—not only fire. But she can't remember the dream.

All she is left with in this moment is her sister's name. When she closes her eyes, she sees her sister screaming, back when screaming was the only sound she had left. From the moment they took Mira away, Delilah had taken over that rage. She had said, in her heart, *I will take this now, for you. I will carry it. I will continue the fight for you.* But for what? She doesn't even know what Mira was angry at, or why she was screaming.

Maybe that rage wasn't what Mira needed her to carry after all. Maybe what Mira needed her to carry was this tiny light that's been glowing in her belly now, that has seemed to sustain her for longer than she thought possible. Maybe it was a kind of unspeakable tenderness that the world had no room for, like the look the deer held in her eyes, that Delilah never admitted to because she never thought she was the kind of person who could be the guardian of such a thing. But maybe that's what Mira's rage, all that time, was trying to protect, somehow.

"*Miri,*" she says out loud now. "What do you want me to do?"

The wind blows a little, fresh with the night right around her but bringing scents of things far away. Salt water. Fields. Smoke.

You have to follow the other river.

Delilah looks up. The stars squint at her doubtfully. She felt like she heard something, from somewhere, though no one is there.

Lilah.

"What?" Delilah cries in a rush, standing up as if that will help, as if straightening her aching spine will help the voice to flow into her more easily. She steadies herself, closes her eyes again. "Miri." She tries to breathe slowly, tries to stay calm. It wasn't the voice she remembers. But then again, Miri is an adult now, if she's still alive. Delilah always forgets that. She would sound different, if she spoke.

Follow the other river. The voice—is it inside Delilah's head?—isn't kind or suffering or crazy or loving. It's barely even alive. But it has to be Mira's.

"Not the road," says Delilah, and she knows she means it, suddenly. She will not ask the men for help. Not for anything. Not even for her sister.

Not the road. The real river. Under the desert, it forks. One way, straight from here to the sea, you'll die. The other way, through the City, it will come up again.

Delilah's heart beats so hard it hurts her chest—clumsy and fast, as if it's forgotten its own rhythm. She did not truly realize, until this moment, how much the idea of returning to the City repulses her. She would rather turn around. Is it fear? Hatred? What is it?

"No," she says without thinking. She squeezes her eyes tight shut, tenses her throat. Why couldn't her sister ever talk to her before? Delilah knew that wisdom was in there. She felt it in Mira's gaze. She knew Mira knew so much more—that could help her, that could make everything make sense—if only she would speak.

You're braver than me, is what Mira's voice seems to say now.

Delilah waits, hungrier than she's ever been. She wants the voice to say *Please. Please rescue me.* But it doesn't. It doesn't speak again. Why should she go on? Does her sister even want to be rescued? Will she even know who Delilah is?

But she spoke, and who knew what effort it cost her, to reach across worlds into Delilah's mind. She is alive. There is so much Delilah isn't sure of, any more, but in the strange clarity that came to her when she woke from this dream that she doesn't remember, she feels sure that she didn't make this up.

She stares across the expanse of nothing between herself and the lit haze of the City. She'd tried to avoid ever looking in that direction until now. The sight of it makes her nauseous again, as if the world is turning upside down. She hates its power—the way its lights beckon to her across the desert from over a day's walk away, as if knowing they will win in the end.

She lies back down and, tucking her backpack under her head, tries to sleep again. She doesn't want to figure anything out, not now. But her mind keeps spinning, long into the morning hours, until the air is so warm she has to take off all her layers except her T-shirt and jeans, and then she finally loses consciousness under the weight of its heat. A tiny lizard crawls into her open hand and sits there in the light, and in her sleep she feels the love coming down through its body from the sun.

It isn't until the next evening, when she forces herself to walk in thoughtless, delirious faith across the empty sand with the river's comforting roar receding behind her, and the lights of the place she hates the only hope to guide her, that she hears Miri's voice one more time. And this time she isn't at all sure that it is real.

What if I can't love you, Lilah? it says.

Delilah keeps walking, looking down so she doesn't have to look up.

Will you still rescue me, even if I can't give you anything, even if I can't love you back?

Maybe it isn't Miri's voice, but only Delilah's own mind, that speaks this fear—for she knows that to do this, she is going to have to let go of even that last, final hope: that hope she's been cradling so gingerly against her heart, without admitting it to herself, that somehow Miri will be different now. That she will look back at Delilah from behind her own eyes, that she will answer in human words, that they will hear each other's stories and finally make sense to each other and to themselves, that Miri will recognize her and call her *Lilah* in her real human voice, and that Miri will laugh and smile and be her friend, her sister, her companion.

Yet whether or not the words are real, Delilah still feels the empathy they bring. Because she knows what that feels like, to wish hopelessly but defiantly against all odds that someone will take you just as you are, for no reason.

Sky clutches the Unicorn's mane in one fist. He isn't aware that he is only thirteen years old now. He isn't aware that the Unicorn can feel his sorrow, though she cannot see him, as moments before he could feel her scream, though he could not hear it.

The marsh is as he remembers it, only without people.

The water is a perfect mystery of patterned green, as unreadable as a snowflake, just as he remembers it. The trees' roots enter the water like mossy hooves and cast long, lichen-bearded shadows over the water as clear as solid forms. A council of dragonflies wings a web of air among the giant, saucer-shaped leaves that float their ruffled edges like flying lily pads. Birds that seemed to be branches suddenly and slowly stretch their long, long necks out over the glimmer of a fish. Herons pant and fan their wings in solemn puffs, in a day-long ritual of heat and stillness. Giant spiders meditate in their giant webs. A kind breeze turns up the faces of the flowers—all as he remembers it. But there are no voices. There are no houses.

The Unicorn walks, and he knows she walks because she is afraid. For all of their magic, Unicorns cannot climb trees. She is almost up to her shoulders in the green water, almost swimming, and the water creeps up to his thighs now, and then to his groin. Every muscle in his body tells him to flee, to leap up into the trees, to climb and swing up to safety. But he doesn't want to leave the Unicorn.

"Unicorn," he whispers. "I think it's better if you keep still."

But she doesn't seem to hear. She carries him away from where the people used to sing and fish, and into the thicker vines, and deeper, where almost no light penetrates. She plunges faster, stumbling, with no direction. Sky hears a familiar bird, a bird that warns of crossing a boundary. Its call is musical but off-key, ending on a note unbalanced, like an interrupted cry.

He tells himself he isn't afraid—here in his homeland.

But maybe he is.

Where are all the people?

The idea of fear begins to nag at him. What if he was always afraid? What if it was his very fear that made him fight so hard, as if to deny to himself that he wanted the very thing he fought—that he wanted the maiden to get rescued; he wanted someone to stop that terrible process that he could not, because he was part of it, though he never understood it?

Now as he looks around him, he seems to see things differently. A tree drapes its vines close to his hair and sways there softly. A mouse pauses on a branch and looks directly at him. The wind blows, and for a moment all the lilies seem to turn in unison. It isn't like when he lived at the top of the world, and all the animals were spirits, and he spoke their language as if it were his own. These beings seem mysterious to him, and far away. And yet he suddenly sees them differently.

Don't you recognize us? the wind asks him.

A strange idea of reality comes tumbling through his mind like a stray autumn leaf with something written on it—nothing but an idea, and yet it comes through him whole, as if he'd thought about it for a long time. It seems almost as if his people were never destroyed after all. As if none of what happened really happened. As if Hanum's coming, and the stealing of the maiden, and the breaking of the ritual, and the destruction of their world, had all happened to Sky alone—as if in some foolish dream from which he never remembered to wake—while his people went on living without him in the real world which could never be destroyed. Over hundreds of years they lived on without him, continuing to evolve into the light, their lives stretching longer and longer, slower and ever more sweetly, until they evolved beyond themselves and no longer needed their human forms, and surrendered themselves fully, finally to…to what?

The Unicorn is trying to keep moving, but she's sunk up to her neck. Sky is up to his waist, and the water is colder than he ever knew—because he never knew how cold it was, because he never touched it, not once—and it smells of salt and death. Now the Unicorn's horn is tangled in the vines, and she is thrashing about in a panic beneath him, and he wants to tell her again to be still, but by the time she stops he knows it is too late. All they can hear is the sound of her wild, rasping breath as she pants into the stillness, the swell and fall of her belly between his calves gradually quieting.

On the other side of the world, the people will wake. They will wake as their Dream God is waking, though they do not know him, and they will feel the deep water against their thighs that has always been rising, as he does now. They will see the illusion they've been holding onto—and they will see that it is not real and cannot nourish them. The same realization that Sky is coming to now.

The boy and the Unicorn wait. Sky's last thought is of Lonely. It catches him completely by surprise. She is waking beneath his kiss on the mountaintop, and her eyes are so frightened and at once so trusting. Her hands are like young birds in his. *Come in*, those eyes say: *I can fit all of you inside me.* Why could he not let himself go?

He hears the Unicorn's last breath in, and then the great mouth opens beneath them, and they are gone.

☾

It is inside the City that Kite first feels the need to write.

He has never written before and does not know how to; until now, he has only read. He has only absorbed information that was written by others. But surrounded by the constant hurricane of the City's sights and sounds, he feels for the first time the necessity of putting down words himself—careful, still words that will contain it all in quiet permanence, that will capture and hold information of such complexity and overabundance that he no longer trusts his mind to do so.

He'd thought he was the one among his family who would be able see things clearly, his judgment unclouded by preconception. He'd expected, at least, that he *would* be able to see and understand, that the closer he got to the City, the more its truth would be revealed to him.

But he can barely register his surroundings, because it all happens so fast and never stops.

How to explain or record the substance that makes the floor and walls of the City, the way it sits and the way it stands, the way it smells and the voicelessness of it, and the shapes which are no shape he has ever known?

His feet ache from walking all night on this unyielding ground. Nobody will look at him. He is not even sure if anyone can see him, so opaque are their eyes. He cannot tell his direction or which way is home. It is impossible for him to memorize these shapes, all of which look the same, are the same color, and do not move or communicate in any way. There is no life but the people, and the people don't stay still. He is surrounded to the point of near panic by motion and noise, and he knows all of it is cars—cars which he's read about and wants to understand, but it's impossible in this moment to do so. He is too disoriented. He avoids the cars because he doesn't know if the people inside them can see him—they are going so fast—or even if there are people inside them at all. He had no idea they would go so fast. He simply had no idea.

Dodging racing cars and racing people, he lurches into a dark corner. Hunger makes him weak. The door stoop he sits in is damp and cold, and he doesn't know what lies behind the door or if he is safe. He can barely escape the all-dominating light, and people walk by him shouting, their breath at once sweet and sickly. He holds his ears between his hands and tries to piece together what happened and where to go from here. *I'm here,* he reminds himself. *I'm finally here. I can do this.*

At first, he was still happy simply to be on this journey. The thrill of his adventure still carried him: knowing that he was brave, that he was utterly free of limits and other people's worries and moods. He still felt the confidence of his own knowledge, the pride of his own accomplishment in traveling so far from home, and the joy of seeing the City ahead of him and knowing he was doing exactly what he'd set out to do.

The argument with Dragon had thrown him a little, and being so suddenly on his own again. He hadn't meant for the fight to happen and he wasn't even sure how it did. Dragon had been the first real friend he'd ever had. After the fight he felt the fleeting nip of insecurity, and then he felt frustrated, and then he couldn't stop thinking how stupid the whole thing was, and then he just needed not to think about it any more. He kept walking into the City, telling himself he hadn't needed Dragon before and didn't need him now.

First there came rows of white, rectangular houses in flat rectangles of green grass—greener than any grass he'd ever seen, yet nothing else grew there. Kite will never forget it: that strange nowhere land between the desert and the City. The City, at least, is wild in its own way, but that place in between—he could never describe it to anyone. The houses were not like any home he had ever seen, and yet he knew this was where people lived. Cars sped by, and occasionally someone got out of a car and went into a house.

Otherwise he didn't see anyone. The windows were lit as the evening came on, and the houses kept their mouths shut. The lights inside were like fire, and he knew they were electric. There were lights in the streets, too—everything blazing as if for some celebration or emergency, but there was nothing like that. There was absolutely no one out, and no life—only dogs crying out from unseen places, the loneliest sound he'd ever heard. Nothing was happening in the streets, and he didn't know what the lamps were lit for. But he was astounded by the abundance of that light, and he imagined the people inside their houses in wonderlands of light, where everything was clear and confident and known. He thought if he were braver, he would go up to one of them and knock on the door, but he was too shy.

Then there were flashing lights across the streets, and the streets got closer and closer together, and the lights became colored and the buildings dirtier, and the words more crowded. The pathways were all hard, and all angled in strange, organized patterns, like a grid, and they reminded him of the order and organization of words. How he longed to understand what it all meant! There were so many people that, at first, he could not believe his eyes. He thought there must be some trick, some illusion which made them mirror themselves and seem to multiply. So many of them looked the same, wore the same expression, and were headed in exactly the same direction, without looking around them. For a long time he stood still and tried to take in all of their faces. But they overwhelmed him.

He could never explain it all, never sort it all out in his head. It's impossible. He still feels the same as when he first arrived here: the onslaught of shapes, lights, and words makes him want to weep for all he has to learn.

How had he met the other boys? How had he arrived in their dark, stinking apartment? He cannot remember now. His own fear was making him careless—his own realization at the mistake he'd made in thinking everything would be clear to him, that he'd know where to go and what to do as soon as he arrived.

Maybe he asked directions. Yes, that was it. *I'm looking for the City's Center, where the knowledge is kept.* Why did they laugh? He was shocked by them. They wore clean, bright costumes of varied designs, and their faces were grinning and bright, but there was something unhealthy in their gauntness, in their skin—as if they were dying. As if they'd been dying all their lives, just barely surviving. He stared at them. They were like wounded predators, dangerous. They frightened him.

We've got something better than knowledge, they said. Why did he go with them? He had no idea how desperately he needed human conversation. He needed someone to explain *something* to him. Anything.

Without realizing it, he imagines telling someone from home about what he saw inside that place. Telling Chelya. But he pictures her sweet face, and she could never understand this. He could never explain it. He could never explain the "apartment"—that's what it was called, like "compartment," a tiny box. Things were scattered around as if they had no relationship to the people. The walls smelled poisonous, and were not made of wood or stone, earth or straw. The boys threw themselves into elaborate, structured cushions and opened glass bottles, and there were girls there, too. The girls were so beautiful that the whole night he couldn't speak one word to them without losing his breath. Their clothing stuck to their bodies, and their breasts overflowed from them, and they sidled up right next to him like it was nothing, and they glittered. They were like nothing he'd ever seen. They were like the river in the morning in springtime, and they had no idea. They talked like the boys, except with more questions.

Where did you come from? they wanted to know.

How can you live out there? What do you do?

Are there animals?

Do you live in a house?

Whatever he answered to these simple, ridiculous questions seemed to fascinate them. They ogled him.

And such wonders the boys showed him!

There were small, shining, rectangular creatures which looked at first like containers of crystals or ice, but whose faces then showed words and lights, and whose minds were more advanced than any human being's, and who could speak and understand and do anything at all, except for feel, hunger, or thirst. Like gods.

These were called computers. There was a computer for every function. You could make words appear and send them away, and you could talk to people who lived on the other side of the City, and you could keep things cold or hot or make pictures or catch an image and keep it like a memory you could see forever, and you could do anything. At first Kite asked questions, and then his questions became too many, and he could not ask them any more. The boys did not know who had created these things, or where they would go when they died, or what gave them their power, or where that power came from. And the strangest thing was that they did not seem to care. Kite became more and more desperate, the more things they showed him and the less they were able to answer his questions about those things—or to know *who* knew the answers, who held the key to it all.

He felt increasingly uncomfortable because he knew they were all playing with him, laughing at him. He knew he was so deep in a sea of unknown that he could never climb out, and this sea was dangerous to be in. Repeatedly, he swallowed panic. No one paid any attention to each other; they all talked into their computers, talked through them to people who for Kite seemed imaginary, as if their real friends were not right there in the room. Kite didn't know what he should do. He walked around the place, trying to understand the things he saw. There were no windows. He desperately needed a drink of water, but he no longer felt able to speak. He had water in his pack but he didn't know where he had put his pack. For some reason all he could think of was water. It was the only evidence he could imagine that the life he'd once known was still real.

Now they were bending over, sniffing powder into their noses, sneezing and coughing. He saw that it was medicine, something they needed. He hoped that it would help them, for their sickness made him sick, made his stomach turn over. Now a girl was handing him a glass pipe, and he saw that he should put it to his lips as they were doing. He wanted to, because he'd seen the girl touch it to her lips, and he wanted to touch those lips—those lips were like a drink of water. But the smell of it gave him a headache, and he didn't trust it.

Then they became insane, as if they were other, nightmare creatures. Their words deteriorated into garble. They tripped around and broke things. In the deep shadows, he saw the girls climb on top of the boys and ride them in slow waves; he saw the flash of their skin and stared at them without knowing he was staring, without knowing what he was feeling until someone reached fast inside his pants and grabbed his erection.

The girl's face was up against his: her lips looked sticky, her eyes looked dusty, and she smelled like something dead and was no longer beautiful. And yet he felt that he would come instantly at her touch, though he hadn't even been aware of his hardness. Not knowing what he was doing or why, he hurled her against the cushions with both hands and stood up—a disgust bordering on hatred closing his throat.

Then he knew he had to get out. He went to the other side of the room and crouched down, like he's doing now—and tried to breathe, tried to think. It was very hard to breathe in that room. The first thing he noticed was that he was starving. He couldn't remember the last time he had eaten, and he had no idea where to find food. He didn't bother asking the other kids. He knew they could not help him, and he felt afraid of them now.

Then he remembered where the door was, and he went toward it. His pack lay next to it, and he thought he would cry, he was so happy. But everything was all torn out of it, spewed all around it, and he didn't know why. Had he done this? Carefully, he retrieved each of his things and replaced them. Then he slipped out the door, hearing someone behind him vomit.

He's so exhausted now that even more than food, he's thinking only of sleep. It's not an exhaustion like anything he has ever felt before. Not like coming in from the fields after making hay from morning until dusk; not like riding all night with his father coming home from Jay's. It's a tiredness in his mind, in his very core, that frightens him. But walking completely lost through the streets, he cannot find even a moment of stillness, let alone a safe place to rest. The constant noise weakens him, as if his senses have been running all night without stopping and are dying of sheer bewilderment.

Finally, at dawn, he finds a stand of a few trees in a small field. It's not actually a field, only a square of grass like the ones around the houses, but it's the first green he's seen for a long time. The grass in the field is cut shorter than his thumb, making it look tight and surreal. The trees probably can't hear each other speak amidst all the noise, but the wind still moves a little through them. A squirrel talks importantly to the people on the benches, but they ignore him, and a few grey doves walk with strange confidence between their feet, pecking at crumbs. They would be an easy target for Kite's sling-shot, but he feels so disoriented, and senses that it might not be acceptable to hunt here, though he doesn't understand why. Here people only sit, and they look strangely peaceful. Kite feels as if he is entering the mere relic of a forest, someone's symbolic representation of what the world once looked like—a crudely sketched drawing without the soul.

Still, the breath of trees dilutes the poisonous smell of the air a little, and he can take a deep breath of his own for the first time. People slow down a little more here, at least most of them, though some still tear across the green, shouting into the computers they hold against their heads. Kite is glad to see children, bounding and chasing each other in apparent happiness. The comfort of soil under his feet makes him so weak with relief that he thinks with new hope of asking for help. His heart flushing hot inside his chest, he moves toward a couple of mothers who sit together talking. But when they see him, they stand up fast and walk away. Kite looks down at his dirty body, his ragged clothing, and sees why.

So he curls up at the base of one of the trees, as far from the others as possible, and falls headlong into sleep.

He wakes with an urgent feeling in his rib cage, as if something bad is going to happen. A large man, dressed in metal and black, is making a straight line toward him, and his eyes are cold. Kite is on his feet before he knows it. He hears the man shout. He starts running.

In a moment, the small oasis of green is far behind him, and he is lost in the crowd again. But he determines in this moment that he will not give up.

He will not turn back. He has come this far. He only needs to understand how to survive in this place for a short while, until he can learn what he wants to. He is surrounded by more people than he ever dreamed could be in the world: surely one of them is kind enough to give him food or point him in the right direction.

But maybe he's not asking the right questions.

"Please," he begins with an older man. "I am a traveler. I need to find food. Can you tell me——"

But the old man looks at him the way his mother would look at a god, swerves around him, and is gone. He tries to think what he said wrong, what frightened the man. He stops and looks at his reflection in a window. Is something wrong with his face? Has something happened to him? Is it only the dirt on his clothes that makes them turn away?

He drinks the last drops of water from his bottle. How can the most basic aspects of survival be so hidden here? Don't these people hunger or thirst?

Kite had his whole journey planned out. He had all the supplies he needed, and the skills to survive. He just didn't think about what he would do when he got here. It was as if he thought the City would be one big answer waiting for him, as if once he arrived the everyday needs of life wouldn't matter any more. All that would matter was truth. And in a flash he sees now that this is exactly the same illusion that created the City in the first place, the illusion his grandmother always meant when she said the people of the City forgot their bodies, forgot their humanness, and stopped believing in gods because they thought they were gods themselves.

Kite leans against a building, trying to think. Gradually, now, the noise is beginning to settle inside him. That must be what happens to people here. The noise becomes like silence: it is all you know.

To get to the Center, he thinks, he will simply have to follow the sun and head south, finding paths around the walls. How could people have transformed the world so utterly? It must have taken so much energy—more than he can imagine. Where did they ever obtain so much?

It takes a long time for him to realize that the people coming out of this building are carrying food. At first he's simply mesmerized by the doors, which slide open magically to allow their passage. What they carry is wrapped tightly, and has no smell. But then he sees a leaf peaking out of a bag, and it is the leaf of a carrot! He can hardly believe it. He begins to look more carefully.

He approaches the doors cautiously, not knowing what gives them their life, or if he will know how to make them open. But before he can figure it out, the doors open on their own. It's almost too easy. Everything in the City is made easy by the magic of the City's knowledge, isn't it? Wasn't that the promise of their god? Perhaps finding food was so easy, he didn't realize it was right under his nose all along.

The inside of the building is warm though there is no fire, and so big he cannot see the other end of it. There are piles of vegetables which don't exist in the winter—more than all of these people together could eat all winter—and he doesn't understand where they could possibly come from, or how they are being kept cold in this warm room.

"Where does all this come from?" he asks a woman standing near him. She is strangely misshapen, her hair an unnatural color, her face pasty and cracked as if part of it might flake off, her body fat in some places and wasted away in others. She is picking carefully through a pile of apples as if they do not all look perfect—so perfect they look unreal. She seems unfazed by the abundance around her.

She looks him up and down. "What do you mean?" she snaps.

"Who grew this food?"

The woman shrugs irritably. "How should I know?" she says and moves away. Maybe it's because her body is so unwell that she is unhappy. But Kite cannot imagine how she could be unwell, with so much variety of good food around her.

Something feels wrong to him—all these foods at the wrong time of the year, and so much of them, and not a single blemished one. But there is so much, whoever grew them could not possibly need them all, and he's so hungry. Though he would never steal, he sees so many other people taking the fruits and vegetables that he thinks perhaps there is enough for everyone.

He eats an apple as he wanders around the building, fascinated. The apple looks like a real apple, but it tastes terrible, like an apple with the soul of it sucked out. He can't imagine what happened to it. It isn't rotten, and yet it doesn't taste fresh.

He is so dazed by the lights and colors and all the people that he doesn't realize for a long time that inside some of the unidentifiable shapes on the tall shelves are actually more foods. A loaf of bread. Meat. Kite begins to read the words on the things, and discovers that they are actually almost all food. In fact, according to the words on the labels, they are foods with magical qualities, foods better than food.

"Where's the regular food?" he grumbles to himself, but he takes what he can carry.

A man comes around the corner as he slips a box into his pack, and starts yelling.

"Hey! I saw that! Put that back!"

Kite stands still. He doesn't run. He didn't mean to steal, and if he wasn't supposed to take this, he's prepared to give it back.

"What do you think you're doing?" the man shouts, though he's standing right in front of Kite now with his hands on his hips. Kite stares at his face, trying to figure out what's wrong with it, what feels untrue about it.

"I—" begins Kite. "I thought— Can I take this? Whose is it?"

The man's expression changes. Kite barely has time to try to read it, before suddenly Dragon has appeared beside him, from nowhere.

"You leave him alone," Dragon growls, and out of his mouth comes fire.

Then before Kite knows what's happening, he and Dragon are both running, and the man is running too, as if *they* are chasing *him*. But they are not. They are looking for the door.

Outside Dragon puts his arm around Kite and laughs easily, as they walk fast into the lost streets again, as if they were still out in the desert and everything made sense.

"Hey, friend!" he cries. "It's good to see you again. I've been looking for you ever since I got here. I knew you'd need me. I realized I'm not a god so you can worship me or admire me; I'm a god so I can use my powers for good! To protect the people I care about. Right? That's the purpose of a god." His voice is hearty, weighted with some deep joy that Kite cannot right now imagine. These have been the hardest two days of his life.

But feeling Dragon's presence beside him again makes him weak with gratitude. He doesn't care about gods or not gods—he is only grateful to have a friend.

"We should stop so you can eat," Dragon says, and Kite can tell his kind concern is bolstered by his pride in being the reason why Kite can, in fact, eat at all.

"It's okay," murmurs Kite. "Not yet." He wants to keep moving until maybe they find another space of green. He can barely speak. He has no room for hunger any more. He thinks of the place where he got this food, and he doesn't understand anything about it. He doesn't recognize the feeling inside his belly, something he's never felt before: a cold, reasonless numbness, like terror.

Inside the swamp, the man who forgot himself in being a god and the woman who forgot herself in being a Unicorn dream the same dream.

Each of them remembers what they wished never to remember.

For Mira, falling into those great jaws is not like being devoured, but rather like falling into the pain of some great, wet, pulsing wound. That wound has been lurking, not only beneath her but inside her, ever since she sent her soul away in the form of a Unicorn, and for as long as she can remember. Nothing will ever heal it. Nothing will ever close it. Nothing will ever protect it. It horrifies her, that this is life. That this is simply the way things are.

Here inside this vulnerable place, the earth is made of water.

The Dark Goddess sucks her in, and now she is inside that place, inside that fear. She can hear the Goddess's enormous breath, expanding and contracting the great belly that contains her. She can hear the shuddering pain of it, a pain so big it nearly crushes her.

"Shhh," whispers Mira desperately. "Someone will hear!"

The Goddess roars—a crazy dragon roar that makes Mira's body collapse against Her soft inner walls. "IT'S ABOUT TIME THAT SOMEBODY HEARD."

Then the Goddess laughs, and Mira recognizes that laugh, that voice, and she stands up inside the body of the Goddess, not realizing yet that her form has changed, that she is no longer the Unicorn. "Who are you?"

"Don't you remember me?" the old Witch says, her voice creaking through her veins.

Mira begins to cry. "It hurt so much."

"Ah, Mirr," says the Goddess, using the name that Mira gave herself and that only she knows. "Don't cry. You were the first person I loved after so many, many years. Do you understand now, what I asked of you?"

"Sacrifice."

"But not the kind your father asked of you. That's stealing. They took everything from us, Mirr. Our bodies, our souls, our beauty, our youth, our tenderness, our lusciousness, our will, our knowing, our intuition, our ability to choose. I did not ask you to sacrifice yourself for me or for anyone. I asked you to sacrifice the pain you'd gotten so used to, you'd learned how not to feel it. I asked you to sacrifice your hiding place, your numbness, your belief that you were dead—that nothing would ever wake you again. I asked you to sacrifice what your father left you with, in exchange for your own self back again."

Mira remembers now. How the old Witch came to her in that room with walls of stone darkness and a ceiling of glass. How she asked if Mira would be willing to leave behind her fear and pain in order to serve another—another woman, who needed her. *The river will carry you to the shore. You will be safe.* How the old hag embraced her, and in that instant Mira felt her whole lifetime of pain at once—the fear in the meadow, the fear in the house, her father's touch, her father entering her, her father's death, the loss of her sister, the brutality of the world enclosing her—all at once, and she wanted to cry no, that she could not, but then in an instant everything had changed, and she was the Unicorn after all. She was riding the seas in the arms of the beautiful Yora to a lonely beach where a fragile, vulnerable girl she did not know stood waiting.

"You are braver than me, Mirr," says the Witch, who seems also to be the Dark Goddess—or is she? "I resisted my own sacrifice. And it only brought me a lifetime of pain. Was it truly a sacrifice after all, that you accepted? Did you not learn anything, in that long journey, about love?"

"Yes," says Mira. "I learned to feel—something. But I'm still afraid."

"Where are we, Mirr?"

And Mira knows. She shakes her head and curls up into herself, her head still shaking back and forth: "No no no no no no no…"

"Where are we?"

That great wound, never closed, with no protection. Where the Unicorn comes from. Mira cannot hide it—no, not even in the meadow, not even in the deepest shadows of the grasses, not even if she keeps it perfectly, perfectly frozen and still.

"He's coming," she sobs.

"No," says the Goddess softly. "He isn't. This is the place of women. Only women enter here. Only women know these secrets."

"But he is here! He is everywhere."

"Look," says the Goddess, and she spits Mira out into the darkness. Mira puts her hand on the strong, scaled spine of the Goddess, and grips it tight. "Look at him."

Then Mira sees Sky, flailing tiny in the distance, spinning in the underwater abyss. So alone, so afraid. Like she is.

"Man isn't all-powerful. See?"

But Mira—*Mia, Mia*—feels the old tugging, the guilt, the pain in her father's eyes drawing her irresistibly toward him, the ugly relief when he laid himself over her. "But what can we do? How can we help him?" Her voice choked.

"Nothing," says the old one. "It's not your problem."

"But what will happen to him?"

"What will happen to *you?*"

Mira is silent. She cannot get her mind around that question.

"Do you want to see where the swamp ends? He could only ever enter so far. He never went all the way inside you, Mirr, where your deepest womanhood is kept. Do you want to know the secret?"

Mira can't see herself; she doesn't feel solid, and she doesn't know what this word "woman" means. She still feels like she is nine years old, which is how old she was when her father died and she gave up her body forever.

She holds on tight to the Dark Goddess's rough shoulder, because she has nothing else to hold onto. If such strength, such sure feminine power, had been offered to her when she was a little girl—if some old wise woman like this had come to her and had offered, in the middle of her father's turmoil, to tell her the secret that he could never, ever claim, and keep her safe forever—how desperately, with what claws and superhuman grip, she would have clung to that person and asked to be taken away. But now she cannot even manage an answer.

"Come back to the Island with me, Mirr."

"But why?"

"Because you left part of you behind there."

My body, she remembers, confused. *What is it? What is it for?*

But now the Dark Goddess is that old woman she remembers, who takes her hand and leads her through the murky marsh, still underwater, into the silkier, hidden inlets, and out into the great salt sea. Then they swim together, under the waves, where brilliant green forests sway and dance, and colored creatures fly among their fronds, and everything is fluid and free, and the world is like the world was long ago, before Man made it over into what he wanted it to be.

Mira wavers, upright under the sea, like a little seahorse holding to a particle in the current before being swept away.

"This, Mirr," says the Dark Goddess, "is what He doesn't know."

The swamp is the vagina of the world.

This is the first thing Sky understands, once he is finally inside it. The marsh is that opening, and the sea is the womb. For in the body of the earth, the vagina and the heart are the same place: the same entrance.

Why did he never understand that before, when he lived above it all his life, and thought he had learned all the secrets, thought he understood what the elders meant, thought he understood the reason for the sacrifice?

For now the blackness under the water shows him as clear as light what he never wanted to see: that he was always alone up on that mountaintop. That the people he dedicated eternity to were only ghosts, only memories. Because when Hanum's army came, his people had already forgiven. They had already spoken to the Dark Goddess and made peace. They had already understood love. They did not fight. Sky remembers now: after the maiden was taken from them, they took her place. All of them. They went down to the Dark Goddess in her place: every man, woman, and child. By the time the army came, they were already gone. But not Sky. He had stayed behind to fight the fight he hadn't been allowed to fight before—the fight she had stopped him from fighting. He'd thought he had something to prove. Maybe he'd thought, somehow, that he could win her after all. Maybe he'd thought, like Hanum, that she belonged to him.

But really, he had only been afraid to go down into that darkness. Really, he was the only one who hung on.

It all looks very simple, once he's inside. All this time he's remained human because he was still afraid of surrender.

He remembers a dream he dreamed the night he and Lonely made love, as he lay on the shore of the lake in her arms. He didn't remember until now that he had it.

In the dream, he sat in Council with all the animals, all the trees, all the plants, even the stones and the mushrooms, and the smallest, most original life in the depths of the sea.

"We are here to discuss the fate of the world," he said, in a great booming voice that even to him sounded clumsy and foolish.

Then a delicate white bird came forward, a bird that looked like himself in the form he'd taken to rescue Lonely from the tower long ago. All the other creatures were looking at him, and he could tell that the bird spoke for them all.

"No, Sky," the bird said gently. "We are here to discuss the fate of your own heart."

Then Sky broke down before the whole world and wept. He said, "I don't want to keep this place any longer. I want to be down there with her. I want to run through those fields with her and lie down under the trees with her in the ferns." He said it sobbing, full of shame, without being able to stop himself.

And the bird said just as gently, without any judgment, "Then go."

The river forgives Lonely everything.

Her past, her longing, her mistakes, her ignorance, her doubt, her fear and her sorrow, her anger and her selfishness, even her own name. Shapeshifting wasn't so much about becoming something else, after all, as much as letting go of what she thought she was.

Perhaps she is a snake: a pure motion of eyes and spine, threading into the current. Or perhaps she is a only a ripple, a ribbon of shade, a thin passage. She can no longer tell if she is moving or being moved. Everything is released. She is no longer human. She is no longer female. Then she is no longer moving.

Perhaps she is only an invisible atom, invisible to an eyeless universe, blinking in space before the world ever was.

This seems to go on forever.

Then there is Something in the Nothing.

It isn't wanting, exactly. Or is it? There is no reaching, no hunger, nor any satisfaction. But she is pulled toward another. Or rather, she and another meet, for no reason, and yet they do not meet randomly. In fact, they come together so hard that they fuse; they merge; they devour one another; then they explode into flame. The very heat of their union pushes them apart again—exploding back out into space, in which there are no opposites, and there are no sides.

A billion years go by. The two atoms come together again. Pretend they are the same two atoms. They believe they are. They press tight, and their center burns hot, but they hold. They hold so strong that they become one being, so strong that they develop their own gravity—and that gravity, like hunger, pulls other masses toward it, and those merge, too, and get hungrier and keep pulling.

Maybe they will always be nothing more than those first two atoms, but they will be reborn over and over again, just trying to remember that first time, and why. *Lonely...Sky....*

Now Sky is stone, recently cooled. Black, the color of dead fire. The world is fluid and broken, constantly restless, a newborn screaming into space. He pops and crackles. He feels his own heat rising within him. Lonely is lava and flame, fountaining up from his own depths, at once destroying him and freeing him, and the sound of the explosion which no one is around to hear is the sound of his own name.

Now she cools over him. There are so many elements now. Elements that do not yet have names. Elements that can change form by the second, elements that transcend realms, elements that follow no rules. Now he is the rain, and she receives him. He rains for thousands of years, without stopping. She forgets the sun. She forgets her own restless fury, and her heat drums softly within. She rolls over, relaxes, receives him in bowls of earth that are wider than the moon. She sighs under him, deepens, yawns him in. He splashes and subsides. Through thunder and wind, the earth and the water keep pressing their bodies together. They are the only life. Fear does not yet exist.

But in his next life, Sky is only the moon, watching the lovemaking of earth and rain from a distance. Like the earth, he is nothing but a rubble of stone. Like the earth, he is mountained and pockmarked by the smaller stones that flew at him when the world was young. But unlike the earth, he will stay naked forever. No wind will touch him. No water will feed him.

No warmth will grace his flanks. Nothing will ever grow. Nothing will ever change. He will remain like this forever, spinning grey and cold around her: a stillborn planet, a lifeless memory of the beginning of time. And she, in the lush and painful miracle of her transformation, will forget him.

How could they have been water, but also stone; sky, but also fire? There was a time when things were not so delineated. When male was also female, and female was also male. Then the elements came together—the lightning and the clay, the salt-sea and the nameless spirit inside the stone, the heat of volcanoes and the mixing of the winds—and made life.

Sky and Lonely, two chemicals that no one will remember. Coming together for no reason, yet desperately. Each one a single heartbeat of magic, a universe of layered wisdom, like a word.

The first word. The first story. Life is that which passes itself on, told and retold. Life is that which carries a message, where the message is carried on. It happens in the sea, where the fluid of that original love-making still swirls. Sky and Lonely float in that dream. How easy it is! There are no questions, no needs. Yet he wants her. Why? Why does he bump against her; why does he change his shape around her; why does he engulf her smaller form inside his larger one now?

She settles in there, inside him. Now they are a single cell. He is the being, living and dying. She is the knowing inside the being, the nucleus, the brain—who remembers him and why they are here. Who remembers where they come from, and the story that must be passed on.

We'll live in the mud, he says. And they live there, in the black bliss of the deepest earth at the bottom of the deepest sea, and their descendants will live there forever—exact replicas of themselves—until the world ends.

In their next life, they recognize each other. They are two different cells, and yet they remember: once they were the same. They want to be one again. They merge their bodies, but in the process they become something else—something that does not remember who they were, and can feel no satisfaction in the union, and does not know that it itself is love.

Now all the cells are merging, each to each, and each one comes out different. The more they come together, the more new different ones are born. So the more they join, the more they become endlessly diverse; the more they try to become one, the more differentness arises, until they are millions upon millions, and none of them the same.

The cells form a community, and Sky is a cell in the brain. Then he is the brain, and he forgets that he is also the cells in the brain. He forgets that Lonely is a cell in the stomach, and that both of them function to create a life greater than their individual selves. He thinks he is the brain, and he thinks he is the identity of that thing, who decides, who moves, who wants and takes. He forgets what makes up his kingdom, what makes him what he is.

And this is only the beginning of that forgetting.

Now they are both whole creatures, not knowing what makes them up, not knowing what they are. Lonely is round like a flying saucer. Sky is a leaf, long before there are any trees, living unattached to anything in the debris of the ocean floor. Both of them are busy changing the energy of the elements into life. They are doing the new work of the universe: transformation. They flicker at each other in passing. They have no relation to each other. But don't they? They seem to remember something. A time when they were the same, when they were part of the same, when they were one. A vague yearning pulls them closer.

Or maybe it is just the ocean current, which is moved by the shifting of the earth, and the winds, and the moon.

The first hunger is not beautiful. The first predator is neither stealthy nor clever. Lonely is nothing but a giant mouth, and the mouth has no jaw, and can never close. She scoops in the worms from the ocean floor, and Sky is one of them, but she is never full: she wants him again and again and again.

In her next life she is only hungrier. She is a giant mouth full of teeth. He has legs now, and a hard shell, and he is starting to dig.

Desire and fear. Reaching toward and pulling away. Three hundred and fifty billion years, and what else is there?

She is pretty this time, a soft cup with waving pink arms. He is invisible, climbing the tides.

She has claws now, and her claws are bigger than her body. She has a shell, because now there is something that she fears, too. He digs down deeper, and in digging, finds there is food to be found in the soft black water-earth to feed his own hunger.

In his next life, he stalks her. But she can no longer be found. She is a fish climbing the underbelly of the shore, wondering at the light on the surface with her new eyes and her new brain. Or she is everywhere, a city of coral. Or she is the water itself, just for the sake of holding him.

He is a shark and she is a lobster; she is a horseshoe crab, and he is a tiny fish. In each life they devour each other without love, only need. They do not recognize each other; they only recognize the hunger.

Now they are two land masses, two worlds, drifting together so slowly that the ocean cannot feel it, yet unstoppably. When they collide, the whole world shakes. The sea falls apart around them, leaving shallow pools.

Life out of the womb is hard. In a land of barren white stone and barely living soil, the first creature, tiny and creeping low on six legs, must grow its walls thicker to withstand the sun. It's food will not flow into it without work; it must climb. Lonely is a tree with scales like a lizard, green from top to bottom and perfectly vertical with two furred arms. She knows only the sun, the rain, and the earth.

She does not know about Sky, who is a herd of insects that gallops almost accidentally onto the sandy shore, leaving the first footprints ever made.

Or Lonely is the sea, who sighs without him, whose children one by one are leaving her to colonize the new world.

Each soul is on its own now.

Two amphibians: their heads in the air, their tails in the sea.

They are like snakes, their heads shaped like arrows. Sky wants to get close to her, but the only way it can be done is by creating something together. She lays her eggs; he blesses them with his magic. They swim over the eggs together, not touching. Their children hatch, swim until they are older, and then trek out onto the land to seek their sustenance. Their children and their children's children will continue to re-enact this transformation—childhood to adulthood, water to land—over and over, long after all the other creatures of the earth have chosen one element or the other. And they will never touch.

But they keep reaching for each other, reborn and born again. Now the earth, too, is changing. Here are the first trees with needles like rain. Here is the first thicket of green ferns, but with no lovers to lie down inside it—except for the insects, who own the world because they are the toughest, with their skeletons on the outside.

Lonely and Sky are becoming reptiles. Sky wants to reach the eggs while they are still inside her. He wants to feel in there, what it's like at the very beginning—where he comes from. He can no longer remember the sea, and the dryness of the world hurts him. He climbs over her as she slinks away. He reaches in. He places himself inside her, inside the ocean in there—and he leaves himself there. *You will remember me now,* he says harshly. *Not just the egg, but you. You will remember me.*

Now Sky is a tree, living older than trees have ever lived before. After he forks once, he forks again, each fork forking. Each choice leads to more choices; each pathway leads to more answers. Life is becoming more complicated, and the older you get, the more things cannot be simply one way or the other. Now he has a hundred tiny branches. He and the other trees make a new world up there, a new landscape under the sky, and under them a new world of darkness is born.

But the earth is still restless and young, and nothing lasts. The rains have no seasons, and the earth itself often moves. Lonely is sudden fire, and she loves him. She wants him, and she destroys him—and everything in her path—in the taking. He grew so old, so complicated; but her hunger is so brief and so simple.

One day no one will remember the insects. People will crush them under their feet and hate them. But the insects are the only ones who survive everything. They are too small to be destroyed. Lonely is a dragonfly, the first animal to take to the element of air. She doesn't know her wings are made of rainbows. She doesn't know that Sky is the wind, and that when she leaps, it is he who catches her.

In their next life, they are two dragon friends, both female, who raise their children together in a small community in the jungle, on the edge of a pond. They stand on two legs like people and have graceful, armored heads. Every evening they watch the sunset together, and talk about how it feels as if things are changing—their time is coming to an end—and one day, no one will remember who they were. People will think they were stupid, that their blood ran cold, that they were ugly and slow. When the mammals take over the world, no one will remember that dragons had culture and highly developed intuitions, that they sat in council together and talked about how to keep peace in the world, that they respected their elders, passed down songs, and ran races through complicated mazes of trees. People will say that they were vicious.

In his next life Sky is a salamander, and Lonely is a turtle who sees him, once in her life, beneath her reflection in a pool. When he moves, she is so startled that she snaps shut into her shell. She is still haunted by memories of dragons, and they have made her jumpy. When she peers out again, many moments later, he is gone.

The mammals are still living in secret. They live small and silent under the leaves, invisible to the big reptiles, and their secret is this: blood whose temperature they can keep constant, regardless of the world around them. Even at night, when the reptiles are sleeping, their bodies are warm enough to move: to scurry, to climb, to attack and escape. So they live in the night, laughing slyly with the moon their only witness, about their secret autonomy. *The world does not affect me*, thinks Lonely, running warm in her fur. She is a primeval mouse. And she has another secret. She is going to make her own baby inside her body, and she doesn't need to lay an egg on the ground—she doesn't need the earth to hold it, no: she will hold it herself. She will carry it wherever she goes, and it will belong to her, and it will be safe until it hatches inside her, and even then she will keep carrying it. She is smarter than the reptiles—her warm blood allowing her brain to grow bigger—and she chews her food with teeth, so it can feed her faster. She smiles in the darkness as she receives her child in a quick rush of blood. He looks exactly like her. He is

Sky, and he is the same as her. They are the same flesh. She can even make her own food for him, from her own body! She does not need the earth. She owns herself. She owns her child. Delirious with her own power, she devours him before he is a day old.

Lonely is a flower. The first flower! The animals all make love now; why cannot the plants? She opens herself to that longing: all color, all softness, all sweetness. She knows the secret—why all the animals long for each other, long to place themselves each inside the other. It is so that they can give each other the message of who they are. And she has a message from her own tree; she wants to give that message to another.

Sky is an insect, crawling along her lips. *Come*, she says, for she is so open, so full of love to give, that she'd welcome anyone. He slips in. He is hungry. He is searching for something that has no name. He drinks from her but it doesn't hurt her; her love is boundless, and cannot be diminished. When he leaves her, he feels her love all over his body. He carries it to another. And so love is carried, without even trying. Both Lonely and Sky, the flower and the insect, serve each other without meaning to, simply by following the truth of their own longing.

The sea is almost unrecognizable now. Sharks and dangerous fish prowl in its shadows. Fish form societies inside giant clams. Sea turtles feel as if they are flying. The wisest creatures in the sea are quiet, shelled creatures with elaborate scripture on their coiled spirals, each one different than the other. Sky is one of these, and Lonely is the sea, who is always sad, and finally has someone to talk to. She teaches him nostalgia and tells him of all the eras she has seen pass, all the creatures who have left her, forgetting the smooth swells that once carried them. He listens, and he loves her. But she knows that one day soon, all of his people, too, will die out, and only their fragile imprints will remain under layers of dry stone. This conversation will be forgotten, buried under layers of history.

Everything is different now. The mammals are growing large on the land. Plants are so lush that the earth steams and darkens. There are cats now, and hooves and feathers, and animals with eyes on the fronts of their heads, so that their left and right brains can converse. The whole earth is warm. But the land masses have split apart again, and animals who once knew each other by name are separated—never to see each other again, never to remember that time when the world was one and dragons kept the peace.

Some animals, finally, return to the sea for good. It happens gradually. They let their hearts lead them. Lonely and Sky are both whales, and it is the first time they've seen each other in a hundred and fifty lifetimes. Sky still has at least one set of feet, and is afraid to let go. *We can't breathe underwater,* he says. *It's okay,* says Lonely. *Our chests are huge now—we can carry the sky down with us. We have lost our fur, we have lost our thin bony running, we have lost our greedy nocturnal eyes. Now we live by song. Can't you hear it?* He can. The song of the sea, which no one in the world will ever be able to put into words—now it issues forth to him, from the great lungs of his beloved. The sea sighs. Sky remembers, and goes in.

Back on the land, the earth is drying up in places. Forests are opening, so that large animals can lumber peacefully between the trees. Bears and beavers, elephants and horses, and the first dogs. Some form clans. Some climb trees.

Sky is the first monkey and Lonely is the tree he lives in with his family. He travels between many trees, never touching the ground, but she is the tree where he makes his nest. She is everything to him. She is his home, his food, his protection, his bed, his freedom. It is for her that his people have developed hands that grip, with thumbs that hook around the opposite way. It is for her that they have gotten so smart, so coordinated, their vision so deep and clever to judge the distances they must jump between the branches. It is to live in this height that they birth babies who cling to them, and it is to live among this complex canopy that they have developed a language of many tones and variations, and it is by being held in the joy of these arms that they have created community, and love, and family.

But one day his people will come down from the trees, and forget the trees, and destroy them.

Now the earth has a rhythm of seasons. It isn't always warm, nor always wet, nor always dry. Ice forms. Cold sweeps through channels of ocean and whips up the winds. Entire forests fall away where the rains stop falling between mountains. The first meadows, the first grasslands, the first deserts— gradually the earth is moving, in its old age, toward spirit. Opening to the sky.

Now animals who lurked in the forest, glimpsing other faces only a few times in a lifetime, can see each other for the first time. When Sky and Lonely, two deer, see each other, they are amazed. And it isn't only the two of them. How many of them there are! They come together; they run in a great wind of many; they flow together like an ocean over the plains.

Everything is mixing up. Anything can happen now. Mammals take to the sea; birds take to the land; primates come down from the trees, because they want to stand tall and reach for the sky on their own.

Sky and Lonely are brother and sister. Sometimes they walk on four legs, and sometimes on two. They prefer to walk on two, because it makes them feel bigger, but it's easier to walk on four. Their toes can still curl around the tree limbs, like their fingers.

They swing down from the tree on the full moon, while their parents are sleeping. They stalk through the grass on two legs, pretending they are huge, laughing and waving their arms around. Now that their arms are free, they can do anything with them. They can walk on the air. They can make shapes with their hands. Sky grabs Lonely's fur as she walks ahead of him. She whips around and grabs him around his waist. They fall on the ground, whooping in wonder and joy and terror. She tries to stand, and Sky pushes her back clumsily with the side of his arm because he sees a pack of hyenas snarling at them: they've come too close to their kill. But Lonely says *No, I'm big!* She stands and waves her arms like they were doing before. And Sky, not to be shown up by his sister, does the same. *It's working!* The hyenas back down.

Afterwards they stand in amazement. They are the most powerful creatures in the world, because they can be anything they want to be. *I'm a hyena now,* Sky laughs, and crawls to the abandoned carcass, and takes a sip of blood. They have never eaten meat before. But they can do whatever they want to now.

So they learn that to be human is to pretend, to become, to change. To be human is to shapeshift.

Human beings live everywhere now, and now there is no other history but theirs. Everywhere they go, they create the world. Where the world does not suit them, they change it, or they change their ways to survive. They make tools. They make homes.

One day Sky, a hunter, gets lost on his way back to camp. He sees a woman who looks like him, only more beautiful than anyone he has ever seen. She is slim and tiny, her forehead slopes low like an animal's, and her hands curve like long paws. She says to him, *This is the last you will see of my people. We are going under the earth now, where we will live only in myth.* Then she drops to all fours and runs into a burrow.

Sky walks on, a member of the only human species that will survive, and he notices for the first time that his people no longer know how to walk on all fours, even if they tried. How lonely it is, with his heart no longer facing the earth but shining all by itself into the air! He begins to run, because he remembers the way home now, and he wants to wrap his arms around his woman, Lonely, and press his heart to hers, because now they are each other's only earth.

But when he gets home, he sees her kneeling on the ground, digging in the earth for roots. He throws down his kill, and sees how different they are. He does not know how to approach her. He does not know what to say to her. His own frustration makes him hate her: the way she moves so gracefully, so quietly over her work, and the way the earth seems to know her still, the way it yields up its fruits to her hands.

The humans move north and build shelters to withstand the cold. Sky is only ten years old, in love with Lonely, a girl who has never looked into his eyes. After a forest fire across the river, while the forest is still smoldering, he braves the smoke and the heat to creep up to the edges and steal a still-smol-dering branch. He only wants her to notice him, how brave he is, how he will do anything for her. And she does. When he returns, holding that branch in the air, the whole village stares, and some of the women start screaming in fear. But the girl smiles and takes it from him. *It's warm,* she says, and, shiver-ing, some of the others creep closer. *I give this to you,* shouts Sky. *I give you fire!*

So it becomes a tradition. Whenever a boy wants to win a girl, he must steal a branch of fire for her. But what if the fire goes out before he gets home? What if there are no forest fires, no lightning storms, and the only fire lives inside his own body, as he waits for many moons, itching with longing?

They must learn to control the fire. They must learn to make the fire themselves, and channel it for their uses. They must learn to harness this energy for good.

Another life, and another. The lives happen closer together in time now, for the years pass more quickly as the earth grows old. Now Lonely is a girl who sits quietly with her elders around a campfire. She has done something wrong. Sky, her grandfather, stands up and tells a story, to teach her the right way. Lonely looks into the flame—that dazzling, feathering, blue-hot dream where imagination lives, where all stories begin—and lives out in her mind what her grandfather is teaching her. For this teaching is a matter of survival.

In her next life she is a mother, and times are hard. Animals are dying out, and the weather is changing again. Sky is her infant son, who dies of star-vation before he is one year old—his life shorter than the life of a butterfly.

Thousands of years later, they live in a land of ice, in a world where ev-eryone takes for granted that life is hard. This time Lonely is a man and Sky is a woman, and they have just fallen in love. Life has been cold for as long as they can remember. No colors; only ice, and the red blood of their prey. There is fire, and there is making love, and these are the only warmths. One morning, the man wakes in his new lover's arms, and spring is coming—the first spring in three hundred generations. They hold the first flower in their fingertips and gasp, *It is our love that made it! Our love made the spring come! We make the world, and re-make it again!*

But the man will live the rest of his brief life in that memory, because later that day the ice begins to thin and crack, and homes begin to melt, and many people—including his lover—are suddenly drowned.

You ask how to shapeshift, says the river, *but you have been doing it forever. You cannot stop changing.*

I'm afraid of never finding him again, cries Lonely, *and that is why I keep changing. And I'm afraid I will lose myself inside him, and that is why, when I do find him, I have to change once more.*

And she is a rabbit, and he is the fox; she is a chickadee, and he is the seed.

She is a heart, and he is the eye it shines through; she is the moon, and he is the lake she shines upon; she is a rainbow, and he is the nothingness beyond.

She is a fish, and he is an eagle; she is moss, and he is stone; she is a flower, and he is a girl's long hair; she is a path, and he is a bridge that carries it over the water; she is a geyser, and he is the still, measured moments in between; she is laughter, and he is shame; she is an ant, and he is the dirt she drags over a grave.

How many lives pass does not matter; there is no time. Now she is a tree, and he is one of her thousand leaves—finally, finally part of her—but she does not know it. It is winter and he hung on desperately, though brown and cracked, for no reason he could remember, through wind and snow. When the spring comes, the new leaves will bud through, and he will fall. He will become part of the earth which nourishes her, and part of her again, forever lost and forever gained.

Again and again they will reach for each other, the way the river stretches forever toward the center of the earth.

And what are their names, the names they can no longer remember? Their names are what they call to each other, when they need.

Their names are the answer to a prayer.

Within

This room is white. Not holy white, not white you can see through, not white that illuminates, but rather a suffocating white. The nurses in the City hospital are tired; they have been awake for too many hours and miss their families. But yet another woman is giving birth.

Where this baby is born, faces are masked. The hands that receive him are coated with a smooth, stickless material designed to keep life out. He is lifted and passed, checked like a product, turned and prodded in the sterile air. The room smells like chemicals meant to kill and destroy the most basic elements of life.

Why is everything covered, and so carefully white? Because birth is dirty. Because touch is dirty. Because babies are dirty, and more than anything else, mothers are dirty. The black hole of woman opened in this white room, and the red gush of blood poured out, and keeps pouring.

How strange it seems to another mother, in the adjoining room, when the doctors tell her that her body is not designed correctly to give birth. It will be easier if they cut her open, and remove him by force. There is no cause for alarm; this is now common procedure, the way most babies are born these days. It keeps the hospital running more efficiently. After they cut her open, they will lean on her chest to force him out, and for a moment she will not be able to breathe.

The most important choice in this human being's life is taken from him: his birth. White hands lift him, and white faces carry him away. The only place that should ever be absolutely safe—the mother's womb—is unsafe now. It was broken into. It could not protect him after all. It was not up to him, after all, when to enter this world.

The baby feels powerless. What can he ever control, if not this? The mother feels powerless. What can she be sure of, if not the ability of her own body to perform its most ancient rite? The nurses, tired, swarm around her, snapping commands. She is not holding him correctly. She is not nursing him right. They grab at him with their synthetic hands. The mother begins to cry. The baby holds tight to her breast. He can still remember only seven moons before, when he breathed through gills, and swirled his primitive, knowing tail in that darkness that no one but the unborn should ever be allowed to see.

He can remember when he was a fish. He can remember when he was an amphibian, and why he wanted to emerge. He can remember the entire evolution of life. But he cannot understand where he is right now, or how all of life could so suddenly have been wiped clean.

And in the shock of that confusion, he begins to forget.

10th MOON

They say the outskirts of the City are dangerous, but Delilah has never felt afraid. It was easier for her to learn the rules here than in school or in her own household. Behaviors are more or less predictable among people who are only trying to survive. By contrast, the home she grew up in was chaos: reality changed constantly, and people shape-shifted without warning. Different kinds of pain happened that came from no definable cause or enemy. In school, the rules made even less sense, and other people played games she was forbidden to play but which involved her in ways she could not control.

Here in the outer City, life functions like wilderness. You are careful lest the shadows in the alleys stalk and eat you. You search for sustenance, and you fight for it once you find it. Compared with hunting, stealing is easy. Compared with starvation in the desert, the shadows are hardly frightening at all. Delilah walks with confidence. She needs nothing now from anyone, and there is not much they can take from her.

As she crept back into that maze she had once sworn never to return to, she remembered she was a predator. She remembered that a single straight line always connected her to what she wanted, and that she always got it. All her life she had tried to hide her own fire from Mira and her family. But now Delilah hunts her own sister, and she will find her, and there is no shame.

"I have food to share," she tells a group that huddles around a fire at twilight, in the courtyard of an abandoned temple that long ago burned halfway to the ground. "Food in return for a safe place to sleep. I'm only staying for one night, and if anyone tries to rape me I'll stick you in the balls with one of these two knives." She presents them both.

"Humans have advanced beyond knives in recent years, cave girl," someone mutters. She can't see their faces in the dark. "You'd better put those away."

"Maybe we have and maybe we haven't." But Delilah obeys and stands respectfully, waiting.

"What have you got?" asks a woman finally.

Delilah unloads her pack. As they lean in, she catches glimpses. The men have haunted faces with eye sockets like deep closets, bright lit from within as if their eyes are all they have left. The couple of women in the group won't look at her directly. She can see one child, who does nothing but look, reach, and cry.

For sleeping purposes, she judges it safer to pair up with someone. She chooses an old man who has kept quiet all night, not eating. He doesn't smell too badly.

It would have been easier to keep sleeping during the day, like she's used to. She could keep to herself, she'd be safer, and there would be none of these games to play. But during the day in the City, there are other dangers. There are those who enforce the rules, and the rules of the City are that people sleep at night. There are those with uniforms and clubs for whom the breaking of rules is so terrifying it drives them to madness.

When she crouches down before the old man, she is startled by the intent, animal honesty in his eyes. She thinks of Moon.

"Would you share your blanket with me for one night?" she asks, her voice gentled unexpectedly.

Without answering, without seeming even to twitch any other muscle in his body, he raises one arm and opens the blanket for her. The resemblance to Moon disappears. She sees cooled lava in those muscles.

She slips under the wool blanket and tenses, but nothing bad happens. The man turns his face back up to the hazy, starless sky, so Delilah does too. In the silent moments that follow, she begins to relax, and yet she knows now that she won't sleep tonight. Not only because of the closeness of another human being, but because the noise doesn't stop at night, and she's come to take silence for granted. She feels so closed in. How do people survive here? She tries to remember. They learn to make their homes between these battering shards of noise in the same way that she made her home between dry and jagged stones that some people would find forbidding, that some people would find inhospitable to life.

Dry leaves flip and turn through the winds along the temple walls. Winter is no longer truly cold in the City. Whether on purpose or by accident she doesn't know, but somehow those who created this world have altered even the sky, so that it traps the heat against the earth, keeping everyone comfortable and dull and sleepy.

Delilah has not slept beside anyone other than Moon for more years than she can remember. But of course she can remember, if she tries. Before Moon, there was Mira, like a tiny kitten curled tight beside her, her body seeming to hum in her sleep. Delilah didn't think about her own love then. She was too young to feel any sense of separation, or responsibility. She held Mira against her like her own heart—something she took for granted, something she needed so much she never thought of losing it.

She can feel the old man's body close to hers, giving off very little heat but surprisingly solid. For one strange and inexplicable moment, she can feel his body as if it were her own. She can feel his bones touching at the joints. She can feel his shoulder muscles flexing against the earth. She can taste the dry air in his mouth as he opens it, about to speak.

"I know you," he says.

Delilah is silent. This could mean anything.

"She carried your picture," he murmurs, each word whispered as if it were heavy, like a hoof dragging in soft dust. "Showed it to me all the time. You look like her. Even though she was white."

Delilah wracks her brain. Does she know this man? Impossible, in a city of millions of people.

"She died though," continues the man. "Died a couple years ago. We had a flu here, came through—killed thousands of us." He clears his throat. She can hear the stuff in there, like there's not much room left for a voice. She wants to turn and look at his face, but she can't seem to move.

"She always wondered where you were."

No, thinks Delilah. *No, she didn't.* She wants him to stop now. She wants it to stop.

"Stop," she says.

She can hear him breathe. After what feels a long time, she thinks he may have fallen asleep. And then she needs to hear him again, desperately.

"Who—?" she starts.

"Oh, I'm no one," he says. "Just someone who loved her. I loved her, that's all."

"But—" Delilah presses her hands to her sides—tries to stay anchored to this reality, whatever it is. *But that's impossible*, she wants to say. *Impossible for another man to love my mother. Impossible for her to be anywhere other than where she was in my memory, always at my father's side. She was the woman who lived for my father. That's all she was. She had no self of her own.*

"Delilah," he says. "That's it. Right?"

Delilah swallows, all the moisture gone from her throat. Her voice like a little girl's. "That's it."

Then, like it makes sense, he says, "Do you pray, Delilah?"

"No." *Why?* she's thinking. *Why is it I can never lose myself, never get out of this dark, dark hole? Why is it everywhere I go, I step in this muck of my past?* "Do *you* pray?" she asks back, so he won't think she's feeling anything.

"I'm a warrior. Of course I pray."

"Well I'm a warrior, too," says Delilah. "And I don't."

"I can see that. What are you fighting for?"

Delilah shakes her head. It's a damned good question. "Maybe just for myself."

"And who are you fighting?" he says quietly.

Delilah kind of laughs then, and it comforts her. "Maybe also myself."

He grunts.

She wants to ask all the questions now. Did her mother live here, in the ghetto, in the old temple? How did he know her, what happened—? But she doesn't trust her voice.

"What do *you* fight for?" she asks instead, because it's easier.

"I fight for the ones they call mad—which is all of us—to keep them from taking us away, locking us up where we lose our voices."

Delilah turns toward him in the dark. She admires his sturdy self-sufficiency—his body at once relaxed and focused, restful and awake, completely uninterested in her woman's body beside him, watching the sky as if the enemy might cast its shadow there when it arrives. How did her mother awaken the love of this hard, quiet man? How could her mother love again, after existing as nothing but the shadow of her father for so many years?

She doesn't ask if he knows of Mira. Did her mother carry that picture, too, or did she disown Mira once Mira no longer served the purpose of "comforting" their father, once she failed him and went crazy? Her mother wanted everything normal—that's what Delilah remembers.

"Where do they take the mad ones, when they take them?"

"To an island in the sea. Under the tower."

"How can I get there?"

He turns to look at her now. She fights to keep from averting her eyes. She senses that she must prove her courage or he will not answer.

"No one can get there," he says.

"I have to get there."

He turns back to the sky. "Then you will, won't you?" After a moment he adds, "Your mother, she was like that, too. Determined. A warrior, like you."

"My *mother*?"

"She wanted to get there, too. Thought your sister would know something—some magic. Some magic to make your father come back or communicate with him or something."

The fury hits Delilah hard from inside, behind her face, but it feels good—familiar. That's the mother she remembers. Of course she didn't give a shit about Miri. "So why didn't she go?" she asks from between her teeth.

"She couldn't. Couldn't think straight any more. She wasn't herself. She was weak, sick."

"What did you love her for?" cries Delilah. She can't help herself.

"I don't know. She loved someone. She believed in something. Almost nobody believes in anything, any more."

Delilah looks up. She thinks she can see one star, struggling to make itself real in the haze. "I've never been to the sea," she murmurs. "Is it far?"

"No. But people are scared of it."

"Why?"

"Same reason people are afraid of what's under the earth. Dump their trash there. Then they're scared of their own trash, scared of what they stuffed away, what they denied—their own lies rotting out there, feeding on themselves..." His voice disintegrates into a growl and he clears his throat again.

"But some people live out there," he adds.

"By the sea?"

He grunts. "Some live there. Worship that goddess who once came to us, saw our suffering, and cradled our heads in her arms."

"Who?"

But he doesn't answer, just grunts again. Maybe he regrets having said so much to a stranger. The wind sings above their heads but the earthen courtyard holds them close. Little moans and whispers escape from the bodies near them. Somewhere within earshot, two people are quietly making love. Delilah feels a wave of sorrow pass over her, so heavy and fast that it feels for a moment as if it will kill her. Then it is gone.

Did her mother love other men besides her father? In her mind, Delilah looks suddenly out a window at a landscape she never knew. She has never thought about her mother—who she was, what she wanted, what more to her there could have been besides her father.

"What's the matter with you, girl?"

And Delilah realizes she's breathing hard; she is gasping because she's so angry at this man who claims to have known this whole other woman, this other woman who should have belonged to Delilah but whom Delilah never knew, and now never can know.

"So my mother is dead," she whispers, stupidly, and now, truly, she feels nothing. Her breathing steadies, and her stomach tenses—the stomach of a warrior.

The man grunts again, and she supposes that is his best attempt at sympathy. Which is a relief, because the last thing she wants is that.

The City. Day 12.

Library. I got paper here so I can learn to write now. I'm keeping a journal so I will know later what was real.

The library is the only place you don't need money for. I can read here all day, many books with every kind of information, also stories. I forget about food. At the end of each day Dragon finds me. I want to stay. But we can't sleep here.

There are people here who don't have homes and one of them showed me the library. It is a place you can stay warm, he said. He didn't even care about the books.

It takes so long to write and I don't have time to describe everything. There are beautiful buildings in the City. There are parts that were built a long time ago. They look like icicles or carved stone. Not like our houses. Not like anything my parents have ever seen. They are huge. Also most of the doors in the City do not lead to homes. They are places where magical Things are sold. Sold means you need money to buy it. You need money for everything here. It takes me a whole day to look at the Things in one store until they make me leave because I am dirty.

I can't remember everything now. One thing that Dragon stole for me is this pen.

It is good that Dragon keeps taking me out of the stores and keeps us moving. If he didn't I would stay all day in one place, and we would never find the Center. Dragon is more interested in the people than the Things they make or how they make them. He wants to make friends.

Kite wakes without knowing why. He's on the floor, facing the bed, and the room is brighter than any place in the forest could ever be at night, even though the moon is not quite half full. At least, he doesn't think it is. He's started to lose track here. He rarely sees the moon rise, and the light in the City never changes.

He props himself up on one elbow, hearing something. But maybe it was only Dragon and the woman, moving against each other in the bed again. Silently, he stands up and walks to the window. He looks out at nothing. He can see only another wall, empty light reflecting against it, distant screams bouncing off of it. A couple of moons ago, homesickness was not a feeling that Kite had ever even heard of, let alone imagined. Now sometimes at night it makes his belly hot, as if he will be sick. He longs to be outside, anywhere, but in the City it isn't safe to sleep outside.

In the beginning they did, because they had no choice. One night they were attacked in their sleep by four large men, who began to beat them when they were found to have no money. Kite did his best, but he's slim and only fifteen years old, and Dragon—though ultimately victorious—received a knife wound to his shoulder that took many days to heal.

Kite hates living by stealing. He hates living by deceit, when he is used to working for his own sustenance, but he doesn't understand the rules of this place. He understands that everyone wants money and will kill to get it, but he doesn't understand what it is, where it comes from, why it is important, or if there is any way to get it besides violence. There is so much he doesn't understand, still, and so much he has to learn.

At first, the effort of keeping Dragon calm was enough to keep his mind focused, and keep his own terrors at bay. For many days, Dragon was constantly raging. The pain of his wound made him angry. His lust for the thousands of women parading around him in their strange, body-accentuating costumes, and the pain he felt when they responded to his approaches with fear and coldness, made him angry. The rude silence of unhelpful people and his loyalty to Kite when anyone tried to stop him from getting what he needed made him angry. Again and again, Kite had to talk him through his anger. *They don't understand us,* he would say, *any more than we understand them.* Or, *They're afraid, just like we're afraid. Can't you see? We should try to understand them. They don't mean to hurt us.* For whatever reason, Dragon—who was older than him, after all—seemed to respect him. He listened to Kite as if he'd never thought of these perspectives on his own. Kite decided that Dragon must have been so alone for so long, it had never occurred to him to try to think inside the mind of another person.

Kite has learned that one of the fastest ways to soothe Dragon's rage is through praise and reassurance. He doesn't give it untruthfully. He simply looks for Dragon's power and tells him about it. *When you use your fire,* he might say, *you light up. A light appears around your body.* This seems to make Dragon very happy. Or Kite thanks him for saving them, over and over again. It isn't hard to think of these things. There is a lot to praise about Dragon, and Kite is truly grateful to him. Yet it is amazing to Kite that someone so powerful could have so much fear. Kite has never met a person like that before, though horses are like that.

No one will tell them where the Center of the City is, where knowledge and fuel are kept. Kite can't decide if the people of the City are keeping it a secret, or if he has been mistaken in his belief that it exists at all. There are books about the City in which he's read of it, but he didn't bring those books with him. Still, he knows that the food, the computers, and the power that powers the lights, the heat, the Things, and the cars must come from some-where. Dragon continues to insist that it all comes from dragons, or from the bodies of dragons, but what does that mean?

They make slow progress through the City, for Kite is so quickly exhausted by the noise, the fumes, and the constant stimulus of discovery that he re-treats as often as possible into quieter alleys or any space of green they can find. While they rest, they practice managing Dragon's fire. Kite sits by him and asks him questions, fascinated even though Dragon cannot answer any of them. Dragon doesn't know how he creates his fire, or else the explana-tions he gives are incomprehensible and senseless to Kite. Yet it is wonderful to Kite—this mystery. What power there is in the world and in people, and how much to be discovered!

The more Dragon works with his fire, the more he is able to create it at will, so that now they have it whenever they need it. Kite has learned a strange thing, which is that Dragon associates fire with women, or with his desire for women. Kite saw the way flames sometimes leaked around Dragon when he saw women he wanted, and the way his whole body began to glow. At first, the women he met were frightened by this, but the more Dragon has learned to control his fire and use it as he wishes, the more often he seems to meet women who are drawn to his glowing and his heat. And when Dragon and the women come together, the women's bodies seem to glow that way, too.

Every night now, for the past four nights, Dragon has seduced a woman who then invited them back to her home for the night. Kite watched him do it each time, keeping quiet while he studied his map or worked on his writing. He watched Dragon sit down next to a woman on a bench, or call out to her as she passed, or lean beside her at the corner of a building. He watched the woman light up like a firefly and then move imperceptibly toward him. He watched Dragon's easy, joyful motions, his newfound delight in his own power.

Kite had never seen so many women in so many different shapes or in so many strange costumes. There were women whose skin glowed rosy and moist as if just born, their lips bursting from their faces and their breasts splitting apart like fat mouths from the dip of their tight shirts. There were graceful women whose eyelashes left shadows on their cheeks, whose skirts played like sunlight around their thighs and whose long legs were smooth as melting ice. There were earthy women like his sister, with swinging hips and childlike shoulders, but wearing dresses that fit their bodies so tightly and smoothly, like a mere splash of color painted over them. Sometimes Dragon gestured toward Kite, after he and the woman had been kissing for a while, their hands squeezing the material at each other's thighs, and sometimes the woman would glance Kite's way—but Kite would look quickly down at his book, or at his hands, or at anything but their eyes.

Tonight's woman is small and fairy-like, with little breasts that dip downward and then point up, her nipples big and round through her tight shirt and her belly bare with a silver ring smiling from the middle. She reminds Kite of Lonely—her smallness, and the innocent, eager mist of her skin—except that she has curly hair, short, with a couple of ringlets falling around her face. Now, facing away from the bed, Kite hears her sigh—a sigh deeper and wilder than he would have expected from her or from anyone in the City. He hears the blankets twisting against themselves, and wetness touching wetness. Maybe they stopped when Kite woke up, and were waiting until he turned around again, and now could wait no longer. Embarrassed, Kite slips back under his own covers on the floor and turns away. He wants to drag himself further from the bed but he's afraid they will notice.

There are still so many things Kite doesn't understand, about the energy of life which so fascinates him. One of them is why every day and every night, the same City which seems to energize Dragon—seems to awaken his senses, his pride, his lust, and his simple joy in living—utterly exhausts Kite, to the point where when they reach a woman's apartment he usually falls asleep instantaneously, even if Dragon and the woman are engaged in such throes of passion that they're tearing each others' clothes off right in front of him, crying out as if they will kill each other.

Another mystery is his own fire. For it is there, too, of course. Doesn't everyone have fire? Yes, he has always known this: each person must have all of the elements inside him. The fire rises in him, too, and in its own way glows in the dark. It rose in the middle of the night when he was just a boy. It rose when he watched the goats making love. It rose for no reason when he was out in the forest, when a thunder storm was coming or after he bathed and lay on a stone in the sun, or when he slept alone in the forest for the first time—he had woken up then to that rising, a rising that kept rising until it overflowed, and in his innocence and amazement then he had wondered foolishly if there were gods after all, and if he were one of them. The fire rose again when Lonely leaned toward him in the basement, and it rose every night after that for a long time, when he couldn't stop remembering her breath against his lips and her breasts eyeing him and her hips—the way they trembled, and the smell that came from them. Kite's sense of smell has always been better than anyone's. He can smell the rains a day before they come. And right now he can smell the passion of the woman who rocks against Dragon in the bed, and he can't help but turn his face slowly into the pillow and then to the other side again to watch her. The blankets are all tossed away.

Never in his life, in any other context, does he feel such a concentration of pure life energy in his own body. It feels so powerful, so real, and it fills him with wonder. He would like to save it for whatever it is meant for—something as beautiful as this woman's arching spine, something sacred. But it doesn't want to wait. As he touches it, as he guides it forth with his hand and presses his face into the pillow, he knows that this energy—though it is a gift, though he wants to use it wisely—is something that wants to express itself, wants to come through, wants to be given.

He thinks he cannot yet begin to understand the connection between fire and the love of a woman, between energy and desire, between the body and the spirit. But as he lies there still now, hearing the woman's soft cries crescendo and then break into tearful whimpers of secret exultation, he has the strange thought that the whole City, instead of trying to power itself with money, or with Things, or with sunlight or with earth, or even with knowledge, could power itself with this fire.

Whatever it is.

They cut the tree down.

Lonely knew they were coming for a long time. She felt the earth shaking with their passage: not the rhythm of something walking but the continuous unrest of a machine. Other trees fell around her, and then the sunlight embraced her for the last time, filling her more utterly than it had ever been able to do before. She felt every leaf: its perfect green reception, its perfect gift.

Then she felt the soil came loose around her roots, and the very truth and direction of her life felt unsteady for the first and only time. She felt them coming. She felt the absence of their souls in her slow, golden blood.

Lonely has been a tree for a hundred years. Her parents and children are somewhere near her. They have already fallen.

In her community, there were slow trees and fast trees, abundant trees, shy trees, and aggressive trees. Some trees were born in deep loam and others started in the merest dust of the topsoil and worked their roots down. Some passed from their parents into their own beginning through the transformative passageway of an animal's body, and others dreamed as seeds along the motion of streams, and others nestled in hot fur, and others—like Lonely—rode the currents of the wind. Each tree, with its different beginning, its different original understanding of life, has a different personality. Some trees grow in opposite pairs, each to each, and some grow in spirals. Some remain forever in the pyramid shape of their youth, and others flip inside out and reach upward like open cups. Some peel constantly, like snakes, and others grow patiently and long, cell upon cell, coating themselves in rugged walls.

Lonely grew up carefully, slower than the eager aspens but faster than the ancient oaks. She has always remembered the wind that carried her, and her yearning for the sky is light and sweet. She began in the earth and the water, down below, and from these she drew enough strength to rise up into the wind again, and catch the elements from above—air and light—in a flag of green. From these four she made life, from the beginning and forever, every bright day of the spring and summer and fall.

She grew in twos. Each branch forked into two more. She knew the sacredness of twos: how wherever there is one direction, there is also its opposite. Also, for every branch she sent upward, she sent a root downward: as above, so below.

She knew that life is a journey—many journeys. She traveled in different directions at once, and learned to adapt to each new pathway. Here in this part of the earth, there was a lot to eat, so she grew fast and further. Here in this part, there was too much water, so she turned away. Here in this part of the sky, she was shaded, so she bent backwards and sideways to get back to the light. Here in this branch, she had grown too far, and was too heavy, and had to stop. Here in this branch, she was exposed, and the wind that once carried her now fought her, so she had to thicken. Life was an adventure. When she was injured by insects or storms, she could replace what was lost, though the new growth would never be the same as the old; it had lost that innocence. The wind and the snow had come, pulling downward, and the squirrels built their nests, and the antlers tore her bark. She was tough, and she worked hard. But she housed a symphony of birdsong in her branches, and she was happy. The twisting curves of her body—their maze and their tangle—were the story of her life, and at once the story of the forest that made it, and the years that changed and guided it.

Water was her intuition, her connection to herself. Through the movement and tension of water, her roots talked to her branches, and the branches talked back. Through Lonely, water rose into the sky and fed the rains. Through Lonely, minerals became food. Through Lonely, light became color. Through Lonely, wind developed language.

She was several years old, tall enough among her elders to take her first draught of unfiltered sunlight, when she bloomed for the first time. What wonder it was, to bring the elements together into flowers this time, instead of leaves! They were not for obtaining food, not for survival. They were for something poetic, something beyond herself, something that called out and was beautiful. The bees came, and they knew, and she let them know for her. Her flowers turned to fruits, and then to seeds, and she gave them to the wind. She felt how it was then: to give something back to what had brought her here, what had brought her home from her own parents to this earth that had raised her.

Years passed, and she came into her own; she made a shape in the sky, a round domed top, and now her leaf body lived in the sky and was a circle. Her leaves are a whole country now, talking to one another about the sun, helping one another, bending to let the light pass to the lower ones or to reflect the light back and forth.

When the machines come, Lonely is only one hundred years old, but her roots already have 50 million different pathways, and span the distance of nine men. Her children are growing up all over the forest. She is looking forward to the spring.

She has a mind, but it is all through her, not concentrated in one place. She knows in every part of her body what to do: whether to grow or not, which way to grow, what nutrients are needed, and what to keep out. When they start cutting, the youngest, most innocent parts of Lonely—the most recent years of her life, up in the sky, waving their jubilant hungry leaves— do not know yet. They feel a shaking but cannot understand that what has always held them will not continue to hold. Down below, in the thickest, darkest part of the tree, the blades are whirring. First, they cut through the newest layer: the growth she worked so hard to make this past year, even though the rains were late and few. Before she can respond to this loss, they keep cutting, through all the experience, growth, travel and loss, all the long, wind-talking days and nights of animal feet running, all the changes in the sunlight recorded in her, all the songs the water had to sing of far-off lands— all that she learned in that year, last year, cut through and now gone.

And now the year before, the year before that, and the year before that. The whole story.

They cut all the way through all the years to the oldest part of her being. They cut through to the dead wood that has been there since her childhood; they cut through to her heart, the place that no longer lives. This place no longer carries food or water, no longer talks. In this place, all that is discarded from past years comes to rest. But this place is the very structure of her being. This place holds the wisdom of memory, of history, the strength of age itself. Death is not nothing. Death is when the singular focus of living fades, so that the true meaning and complexity of life can emerge—like when the green of her summer leaves faded, and all their true colors multiplied and revealed themselves.

But this dead center is what humans lost, when they threw their trash in the sea and forgot their past. Because for them age is only loss, memory only refuse, and the past only waste—because, for them, nothing lasts, and history has no value—they cut right through the center of this tree, its heart.

So Lonely falls.

The earth begins to embrace her, but she cannot return to it. They are chaining her; they are dragging her away. Her body kills as it passes.

She knew so much in her life as a tree. But now she knows nothing. Now the different parts of her body are ground and mixed into pulp. Now she is pounded and bleached. Now she is paper. Now she is stamped with the faces and symbols of a dead ruler named Hanum, and his princess daughter, and now she becomes the instrument through which their empty memory rules.

Now she is money.

And through all those lifetimes in which Lonely changed form, she thought it was enough to shape-shift, not knowing what she would become. She thought it was enough to surrender, because whatever change happened, it always brought her back again to her love. When carried by nature, because nature is love, surrender makes sense. But the shape-shifting of men has other motives. She will not find Sky again in these hands, these pockets, these hurried streets. Love is not the purpose here.

Now she enters cold, closing hands, in a pile of other bills that look just like her. Now she folds into darkness, and soaks in the nervous sweat of a forgotten hip. Now she unfolds into the hands of another.

Now she lies under a mattress for a year, as it shakes and groans over her, not feeling the emotions and dreams that bend it. Now hands fight around her; now she whirls into dead air and falls, and is caught again. She is never let go, never free. She is always held, or placed between surfaces that hold her. Now she is piled in metal. Now she is balled up in a fist. Now she is torn and smoothed and kissed and thrust angrily; now she is sat on and torn and stained with blood, saliva, and sweat again.

But nothing transforms her. She does not remember herself. She does not provide nourishment, or give anything, or ever become anything else.

Something is changing in the City, in the world. The people can feel it. So many people are whispering about Hanum's death that the whispers have gotten too loud to be called whispers. They are like voices that the City hears inside its head, voices it strains to ignore for fear of being diagnosed with madness. People forget their work and stare out their office windows, fearful and distracted.

Money changes hands faster and faster, and people die for it, but Lonely never knows.

Unwillingly, Delilah stays at the temple for days, once again too sick to continue on. The old warrior cares for her, brings her food, and wraps her in blankets when she is too weak to rise. His silence and his respectful distance are a relief to her, and she is grateful. But it makes her uneasy the way he looks at her sometimes when she's sickest, like he knows something she doesn't—something she ought to know. She wonders if he cared for her mother this way, when she was dying. Then she realizes she can't imagine anyone taking care of her mother. That wasn't her mother's role, to be taken care of by someone else.

The other people who sleep here call the old man "Chief," though he doesn't act like chief of anything, and rarely talks to anyone. "He seems harmless," a woman tells Delilah once, "but he's killed men before. He used to fight for the rulers when they took over this land, but now he protects us. And he's got a sixth sense. He knows when they're coming for us."

Any day now, the people say, the temple is going to be overtaken. The City is going to turn it into a museum, and the people will have to find another place to sleep. But no one comes. Something strange is happening in the City. Plans are on hold. Order is gradually, with clumsy secrecy, falling apart.

Across the street from the temple is a gas station. This is where humans feed their cars instead of their bodies. One day the people gather to watch an argument happening between two men at the pump, soon joined by another man, and then a woman, and then a crowd. Everyone is yelling, so that it is difficult to understand at first what the problem is. Some of these people at the gas station have wads of money in their hands, and are thrusting them toward one man, the one who works there. They are thrusting their money angrily, like a weapon, trying to get him to take it—but he won't take it, which is a very strange sight to see.

The old warrior chuckles to himself. Delilah turns to him, unnerved. She's never heard him laugh before.

"What?" she says. "What's going on?"

"They've run out of fuel," he says.

"Well obviously," she says, irritable and nauseous and in no mood for enigma. "That's why they're at a gas station."

"No," says Chief. "I mean everyone. The City has run out of fuel. There is no fuel left. Now all of the cars—" He begins to chuckle harder, and Delilah can't help but smile a little. His face changes, and his whole body shakes with his now silent laughter. "All the cars," he cries, "will just stop!"

Delilah shakes her head. "But how could they not know?" she says, staring at the angry crowd. "How could they not see this coming? Who do they think they're angry at?"

"This is the first lie that will come undone now," the old man says sternly, all trace of humor leaving his face as suddenly as it came. He says no more.

And though what he said, in some way, gives her a sense of thrilling, disbelieving satisfaction, it also makes Delilah uneasy. She understands the panic of the people at the gas station. She understands the eerie silence beneath their screaming, as they realize. It is what she always feared too, in the City, and what the City makes everyone fear, and why she never wanted to come back here: that feeling of being stuck, like she was stuck for eighteen years, and like she's stuck now. These people, now, will have to sit with that feeling, and they will have to sit alone with themselves in the isolation boxes of their cars, in the middle of the maze, and realize that there has never been anywhere to go. They will have to realize that the eternal life and happiness that Hanum promised will never come—and that with all this getting they are not getting anywhere. They are still right here, where each street looks like the next, and each one leads right back to where they started. They have no past and no future, but only grief, anger, and deadly fear.

A couple of cars speed past now. They don't know yet. Delilah tries to imagine the stations posting their "Closed" signs one by one, and all the cars coming to a stop, right where they are. At intersections, on highways, at the exits of parking lots, on neighborhood streets two blocks from home, the lights will turn green, but no one will go. Everything will simply stop.

It won't happen instantaneously, but it will feel like that. Even once they know there is no fuel left to be bought, people will keep driving anyway, because they won't remember how not to. It is, after all, a funny image, Delilah thinks later, that the old man must have had in his mind. Maybe when their cars stop, these people will keep staring out their windshields in shock. Maybe they will honk their horns, as if it's the cars ahead of them that are to blame.

Then they will step out of their cars and look down at their legs, and then they will look at the people around them who have stepped out, too, and wonder where they came from.

Sky knows the world is about to radically change, because suddenly everyone is having the same nightmare, though of course they don't know it.

Everyone is dreaming that they are going down into the basements of their homes, even if their homes don't have basements. In the back corner of those basements full of junk—all the stuff they thought they threw away over the course of their lives, but which has remained right here beneath their feet all along—they find an animal in a cage. For some people it's a cat, and for some it's a dog. For some it is a bird, a mouse, a horse, an opossum, a rabbit, a wolf, or a raccoon. Everyone has their own animal. And this animal, living in the filth down there, is starving and on the verge of death. They have forgotten to feed it. In fact, they have forgotten they ever owned it. They have forgotten that when they were children, they captured it because it was so beautiful and wild and mysterious that all the delight of their souls desired it.

In their dreams they feel horror, because they realize that if they weren't going to care for it, they could have set it free long ago to fend for itself in its natural way. But they kept it in this cage, dependent on them, and now it is dying. In their dreams they are panicking, because they don't know what to feed it, and they are searching their houses, flinging open cupboards as it cries and cries now from down below, not knowing what it eats. Now it is eating its own body. It is eating all the things in the basement, and it is eating the house, and it is eating their children.

People are waking up from these dreams, their bodies exuding water from their eyes and from every pore, and trying to remember why.

This isn't a dream Sky is part of. Sky doesn't enter dreams any more. He no longer has that responsibility. But he knows about it anyway.

He sits on a cloud, with a white bird perched on his shoulder. *I've come to tell you that we're not really gone,* the bird told him when it came.

"How long will you stay with me?" Sky asked desperately.

Until you no longer need me.

But the bird has not spoken since, and it does not comfort him as once his elders did. Sky sits on the cloud, unable to move, watching Lonely play out a karma that has nothing to do with her—a cycle of greed and suffering that began long before she was born. As a thing, she has no choices. Even when he and Lonely were alive, he thinks, they were still like things, tossed about by an ancient destiny that they did not design, torn apart by forces beyond their control and yet blaming each other for their pain.

"Unicorn," he says into the nothingness, laying his human face in his hands, "I am a coward."

The Unicorn is not there and the white bird says nothing, but beneath him, he feels the cloud move. He's not sure of it at first, because it seems impossible. The cloud seems to roll, pressing up against him ever so subtlely, as if there's a body in there. But he waves his hands through the mist below him, and there is no body.

He rises up on his knees, wary. His muscles twitch restlessly, and his feet tingle. Loneliness lies over his skin like a thin cover of new snow.

The cloud begins to curl around him. Tentacles of mist nuzzle his thighs and creep up the back of his spine. In one move he leaps to standing, spreading his hands as if to fight something unseen. For a hundred years he has ridden the drift of clouds, walked and lain upon them and even, for those few precious moons, wrapped his beloved in them, without ever feeling them to be alive. Without ever thinking about them. Now he feels the kiss of the cloud's cold water rising to meet him, rising up around him, enfolding him in fog. He feels the weight of it, the weight of rain unfallen—like the weight of his own sorrow, which he thought unbearable, and yet here the empty sky alone seems to carry it. Without meaning to, he closes his eyes, and the cloud strokes his arms, his legs—

The cloud, like the physical body of a dream—passion of water mixed with holiness of air—feels familiar somehow and unmistakably masculine.

"Who are you?" he whispers.

"I'm the rain," says Moon, caressing his ear with a tongue of dust and vapors.

"Show yourself, Rain."

"I can't," says Moon.

Sky doesn't ask why. "We have to," he whispers, his breath caught inside some furry place in his throat. "We have to become ourselves. We can't be afraid any longer. It's not right that we should hold back our love from the ones who need it."

When the cloud doesn't answer, Sky begins to shake. His eyes feel hot. The cloud holds him, supporting his emptiness—that empty husk of a life, so far up in the distant sky, so lost from anything of this world. *Sky Sky Sky*…. "It's not right," he says again, though he can barely understand his own words. "I can't feel anything. I can't feel my own heart. I can't feel it." Shaking so hard now, his words breathless, as if someone is fighting him.

"But you're crying," says Moon.

And Sky, still crying and not knowing that he is crying, feeling nothing, says, "Please. Enter me." Because he can feel that the cloud wants this, and he wants it too. He wants to feel the pain of water inside himself, between the walls of his own body.

So Moon, first tentatively, and then in a wave, harder and stronger than a cloud and harder and stronger than the rain, flows into him from the bottom up. Sky's body is ripped in half and yet it stays together, and his high, mortal cries crack open the heavens in jagged zigzags that fill instantaneously with light, and then close up again in darkness and thunder. He tries to catch his breath, and then stops trying. He feels his heart trying to break through his chest and be free. But it can't get out. So he clutches his hands against it, trying to hold it, trying to offer it some kind of comfort.

The sky buckles and explodes, surrounding him. Sky isn't aware of anything for what seems like a long time, and yet he is aware of himself. He is aware of the hard pain inside, and the incalculable relief.

Slowly, he tries a long breath in. He can feel the cold aliveness of the cloud filling his chest. He can feel the waters of the marsh itself filling him in—and all the beauty of its love, the love of the Dark Goddess herself devouring him from the inside out, all the world inside him weeping and weeping—and then he breathes out. And Moon releases himself into the air again, and faces him.

"It feels good," Moon says softly, "to be felt."

"It feels good," says Sky, "to cry." And he bows, with the tears still on him. Moon bows back, almost a man, but also a ghost in a haze of indigo.

"Be brave, brother," says Sky, smiling. "We are gods. There is no shame."

"Can I carry you somewhere?" says Moon. "Is there somewhere you need to go?"

Sky shakes his head. "Down. Only down." He turns to his right, and then to his left, and sees that the white bird is gone.

The City. Day 20.
Apartment Buildings
- hallways: straight narrow passages lined with doors.
- hundreds of people who are not related and not friends, each
* with their own apartment.*
- televisions: images of people that are not really there, and the
* people living there do not know them.*
Food Markets

- *Where does the power come from to light, heat, and cool buildings?*
- *Where does all the food come from?*
- *People look lost and confused here, not sure what they want.*

Shopping Malls

- *What are the walls, floors, and ceilings made of?*
- *Many kinds of computers, but they are not for everyone, only if you have money to buy them. Like the food.*
- *There are places you can buy food that someone you don't know has cooked for you. It is cooked in different ways and given different names.*
- *People are laughing here, and are in a hurry, and don't look at me.*

Office Buildings

- *People wear uniforms here.*
- *People are serious here, and in a hurry. They don't look at me.*
- *Inside each room, someone sits all day behind a long counter, and waits for someone to come in. Sometimes there are lines of people waiting to get in. The people in the lines do not wear the uniforms.*

The City. Day 21.

Dragon has found where he wants to be. With the Artists. They live in the streets or in small messy apartments. They forget to eat. But they have a special purpose, to explain what is real in some beautiful way. They paint pictures on walls, under bridges, or on paper. They make shapes out of trash. Sometimes the pictures are of animals or the mountains, sometimes of the City. The pictures do not look like those things, not really, and yet they look right. They look like the truth of those things. Very difficult to explain. Chelya would understand. She would love it. And Grandmother would understand too, because it is like dreams. I think it is good what these people are doing. I would like to see them paint pictures like this of the place where I live, or of something beautiful I know, like the old oak tree or the first snowfall or Lonely.

Dragon says he is an Artist, too, and says that is a kind of god. I think it is true he is supposed to be an Artist because, since he started painting, he is calmer and not angry any more. He focuses on what he is doing. He does not think of women so much when he is painting. His paintings look like fire, full of color, and also lots of white and black mixed together, and they are pictures of dragons, unicorns, and goddesses. They are frightening, but they make you want to stand and look at them for a long time.

There are so many kinds of people in the City, who have learned to do so many different things that we do not do, like the Art. But the hardest part is understanding how to survive here.

No one will answer my questions about what makes everything run, and where the energy comes from. They all walk around as if they know everything, but they will not tell me. It takes so much of their lives just to see all the sights and do all the things, perhaps there is no time for them to care why.

I still have not found the Center.

"Why is he so quiet?" one of Dragon's girlfriends asks Dragon one eve-ning, and Kite looks up from studying the letters on his pen. She and Dragon are smoking what Kite calls, in his journal, "the stupid medicine." He calls it that because he can tell they need it like medicine, but it makes them stu-pid, and he doesn't get it. He doesn't like when Dragon smokes it, because Dragon becomes unable to answer simple questions or make simple plans, and, worst of all, he forgets how to make fire when they need it. But Kite keeps his opinions to himself, telling himself he is lucky to have the protec-tion of Dragon at all.

He scowls now as Dragon answers the girl as if he isn't there, though Dragon's voice is respectful. "Kite is very serious about things," says Dragon.

"Like what?" says the girl, whose voice annoys Kite. He doesn't find this one attractive, but Dragon has slept with her more than once.

"He's looking for the Center where Truth is," says Dragon. "Truth," he repeats, with philosophical emphasis.

The girl turns and blows rings of smoke at Kite. "What are you talking about?" she says, as if Kite is the one who said it.

"Where *knowledge* is," says Dragon. "Where people know what it's all about."

"You mean like school?" asks the girl.

"What's school?" asks Kite, who has heard of this but not quite understood it.

Much to his annoyance, the girl begins to giggle uncontrollably. Kite waits awhile, but when she shows no signs of stopping, he repeats his question loudly. "Hey!" he adds.

"Over there!" she says finally, and starts to giggle again, and this incites Dragon to smile and start groping her, so Kite gives up on them. But he stands and looks to where she pointed. The three of them are on the top level of an abandoned parking garage, and across the street from them, and a little further off, a cluster of lights shines from a green space that they passed earlier today. Judging by how things are going, he figures Dragon and the girl will sleep until halfway through the day tomorrow, so he resolves to go to sleep now, and get up early.

The next morning, he takes the stairs down from the parking garage, and walks to what is called a college. It's prettier than a lot of places he's seen in the City. The buildings have interesting shapes and ornate, detailed edges, and are made of something like red clay. The windows make pleasing patterns, and it makes sense to Kite that wisdom should shine out of the faces of these houses, unlike the blank stares of so many of the blocky buildings that line the busier streets. Great old trees stand quiet and proud around these buildings, and he can hear more birdsong than he's heard in all the rest of the City. He begins to feel excited, for there is some real conversation happening here, he feels—some real, elegant contemplation.

He finds the quiet buildings a little intimidating. He doesn't dare to enter any of them. He sits on a bench by a little dirt path, and takes up his comfortable pattern of watching, determined to figure this out on his own. He doesn't think this is the Center. But it seems important, nonetheless.

The first thing he notices is that all the people walking here are young. They walk with a relaxed, intent kind of grace, and they all carry books! They laugh together and seem happy. Before he knows what's happening, a tall boy has sat down beside him. The boy smiles and nods at him, then takes a book out of his backpack and opens it.

"I've got to stop doing my reading ten minutes before class." He laughs.

Kite stares at him, astounded. No one else in the City has greeted him with this kind of friendliness, as if he has a right to be here, as if they are all simply human beings in a common place.

Perhaps aware of being stared at, the boy looks up again. "What happened to you?" he asks nonchalantly, glancing down at Kite's bedraggled clothing.

Kite shakes his head, still a little awed. "Nothing," he manages.

But the other boy can't stop staring now either. Later, Kite will be unable to describe in his journal exactly what the boy looked like. His well-structured, pale face, his light brown or dirty blonde hair, his neat clothing— nothing stands out that Kite will be able to remember. "Do you go to school here?" asks the boy.

"No," says Kite. Then, to get it over with, he adds, "I'm from the mountains. We don't have school there."

With that, the boy slaps his book closed and turns to face Kite with a big smile. "No kidding? This is great. Are you really?"

"Yeah, why?"

The boy shrugs. "I've never met a kid from the mountains before. I didn't know anyone really lived out there." He holds out his hand. "I'm Mark."

"Kite," says Kite. He takes the boy's hand, confused, and lets go. Then he decides to do something brave; he decides he wants to get the information *he* needs right now, before the boy can start hammering him with questions about where he comes from. He doesn't even care if the boy laughs at him.

"Please explain to me," he says, "what school is."

Mark does laugh, but the laughter doesn't sound unkind. Kite can't understand how he acts so easy, when the rest of the people in the City seem so closed and suspicious. Maybe it's because he is young like Kite. Or maybe this place is different somehow.

"It's where we learn," says Mark. "Things we need to know, you know, to get jobs."

Kite fumbles around this answer, not understanding it enough to formulate a good follow-up. "What kinds of things?" he tries.

"It depends. Me, I haven't chosen a major yet. I don't know what I want to do. It's a pretty hard choice, if you ask me."

Kite shakes his head. Maybe this isn't going to work. "What do you mean?"

Mark sighs and sits back. "Okay. Look, everyone has, like, a specialty. Everyone chooses one thing they want to study, so they can go be that thing. Like a doctor or a lawyer or a teacher or a social worker. Right?"

"Right," says Kite, hoping he'll continue. But he doesn't. "What's a social worker?"

"It's someone who helps messed-up people, or homeless people."

"That's a job?"

"Yep."

"So you can only study one thing?"

"Pretty much," says Mark.

"So if you're a doctor, you can't also help—homeless people?"

"Well, I guess you can, but you can't make money at it. You have to have a special license."

Kite thinks on this. "I want to study energy," he says finally. "Is that a job?"

"Yeah. An engineer maybe."

On an impulse, Kite rifles quickly through his bag. "See," he says, pulling out his book. "Like this." He holds it out to Mark.

Mark takes it carefully. "Whoa," he says. "This thing is old."

"It's not," says Kite. "It was written only thirty-three years ago."

Mark looks at him and smiles a funny smile. The expression reminds Kite of the kids in the apartment, and he wishes now that he'd kept the book to himself. "Uh, yeah," says Mark. "That's old." The book jacket is gone, so he opens to the title page. "Alternative Power Sources," he reads. "Solar, Wind, and Water." He flips a few pages. "Yeah, I've heard of this stuff. But it's not up-to-date. That's not what people study now."

"Why not?" says Kite, who has been watching him anxiously.

Mark shrugs. "I don't know. We have better, more efficient, simpler ways, using the fuel we use. And it's cheaper."

"What do you mean?"

"The technology for this stuff—solar, wind—it's too expensive, too complicated. It's not realistic."

"But who owns the technology? Who makes it expensive?" Kite asks helplessly, frustrated.

Mark shrugs again. "The people in charge, I guess. The rulers."

Kite looks away. Money is a whole other subject he doesn't want to even broach. He is ashamed by how much it baffles him.

"Here you go," says Mark, handing the book carelessly back to Kite as if it were a pair of old socks he had borrowed. He picks up his own book and opens it. The book is called *Hanum's Great Design: A Practical History of the City.* The chapter heading reads, "The Uncivilized Territories: Methods of Expansion."

"How do you get into a school?" Kite asks quietly.

"Oh, you have to go to school all your life, and then you have to take a lot of tests and prove that you're smart enough and know enough to get into a college."

Kite looks at his lap, trying to hide the emotion he feels. At first it feels like frustration, and then he even feels something like rage—a feeling that, like the terror when he first arrived in the City, is completely new to him. He doesn't think of himself as an emotional person. But he can't believe he never knew about all of this. He can't believe his parents deprived him of even knowing that this opportunity existed, and now he's wasted his whole life not knowing it.

"Does everyone in the City get to go to school?" he asks, still not looking up.

"Most people," says Mark. "Most adults have been to school."

"You will get to learn whatever you want to," says Kite.

Mark shrugs and looks away. "I guess so."

Kite looks away, too, and watches a group of girls pass by on another path behind them, murmuring to each other sweetly. He thinks of the grey masses that part around him out on the busy sidewalks. How is it that all those people possess the key to all the knowledge he has yearned for his whole life, and yet they look so unhappy, so lost?

"Do you know where the Center is?" he asks Mark. "I mean, the heart of the City where they make the power the City runs on, where they know how it all works. Do you know what I'm talking about?"

Mark looks at him for a long time, and Kite can't tell what he's feeling or thinking. "Yeah, I think I know what you're talking about," he says slowly. "Although I don't know that it's all that. What about it?"

"I want to go there."

"Why?"

"Why—why not?" Kite stammers, shocked by the question.

Mark laughs again. "I'll tell you how to get there, if you want. Although you'll have to walk. Apparently there's a fuel shortage or something, but I'm sure they'll fix it soon enough."

"But where does the fuel come from?" asks Kite, seizing his opportunity. "Who will fix it?" Surely this boy, a person of learning, will know.

Mark shrugs. "It comes from underground, I guess. I think from prehistoric animals of some kind, when they decayed."

"What is 'prehistoric'?"

"Before history."

"Before history?"

"Before the City began."

"But—"

"Look," says Mark, sounding a little irritated for the first time. "That's not my department. I'm not a biology major or whatever. You'd have to ask an expert. I'm not really into that kind of thing. Nature and all that."

Kite is silent, understanding that the conversation is over. Mark takes out a piece of paper and starts to write. Then he stops. "Can you read?" he asks uncertainly.

The question makes Kite want to cry, though he doesn't know why. "Yes," he mumbles, looking down.

Mark writes out the directions, and adds, "Here's my number. Let me know if you—if you ever need anything."

Kite nods and takes the paper, though he doesn't understand. What does it mean for a person to have a number? But now he feels a great heaviness inside, and he only wants to be gone from this beautiful place.

"Thank you," he says.

"No problem," says the boy, watching as Kite turns and walks away across the grass in soft shoes that make no sound. Then he shakes his head and looks down at his book. He can't seem to focus on the words. How he wishes he could walk away like that, with no weight of expectations or books on his back, and be free.

○

For the last time, Delilah washes her body with paper towels in the gas station bathroom. She thinks there is nowhere more claustrophobic than this tiny, toxic room, that has never breathed fresh air since it was made. In this room people have not only eliminated their sickliest wastes, but vomited out their ugliest fears and hopelessness, sat on the toilet with their heads in their hands, smoked cigarettes and flushed down secrets and cried and torn at their faces in the mirror. Delilah tries to breathe as little as possible, and leave as quickly as she can, but what else can she do? This is the only free water. It was easier to get water in the desert.

For the last two days, she's felt better again, and she will not wait any longer. Chief told her, if she wanted to get to the sea, she could follow the river: the brown river of refuse, sewage, and sorrow.

When she comes back out onto the street, the quiet is eerie. No revving engines, no idling, screeching, honking traffic. She can hear the pigeons cooing. She can hear a door slam, and someone talking on a television. She can hear the strange fallings, like uneven heartbeats, of everyone's footsteps: some bewildered, some panicked, some tripping and tired, some running as if they will never stop.

Someday, if they survive, people will realize what cars meant to them. How that time of sitting quietly, closed off from other people and the world, gave them the only peace they ever knew in their frantic lives. How cars became not vehicles but enclosed capsules of music, where they could lose themselves in the romance of their own unspoken feelings, the dreams of what they wished they could say or who they wished they could be. How safe they were inside their cars—how contained, how relaxed, no matter how fast they were going!

But for now, the stopping of cars means thinking about survival, which no one has thought about for a long time. Without their cars, people don't have that look any more, even walking—that look like they know where they are going, and have no time to acknowledge anyone else. Now they stare blankly, questioningly, wordlessly into each other's faces, if they go out at all. There are so many stares from so many windows, all with the same expression of terror.

In the temple, Delilah has been feeding her temporary friends with rats and pigeons she kills with her magic bow. She tells them it was given to her by a god and they barely blink. She tells them she dreams her animals before she kills them, and they nod blankly. They'll believe in anything, but they are hopeless. Even out here on the outskirts, they depend on the City, like anyone else. Sooner or later, they will die like everyone else. Delilah wants to get out, immediately. She feels the hopelessness swarming around her like flies, clutching at her throat in the night.

Soon there will be no more food in the stores, because the food was driven from somewhere else, and no one knows where that is. Soon people will run out of money, because they can't drive to their jobs, and there are no more jobs. Soon money won't matter, because there will be nothing to trade it for. Factories have stopped breathing smoke. Cars have stopped breathing, too, and some of the lights have burnt out, and no one is fixing them. So the sky has cleared, and at night a few more stars can be seen. The very atmosphere is changing, and it's getting colder, as if, after fifty years or more, winter is returning to claim the City back.

In the courtyard Chief tells her, "I have something for you, Delilah, before you go."

Delilah kneels down and takes his dry, warm hands in her own. She thinks he may be the first older man she has ever respected. If only she could have felt like this about her own father. His hands remind her of desert stones, and the comfort of them comes over her so fast, she has to close her eyes. For a moment, she is lying in the sun like a lizard in the grand empty silence, and the tortoises and bats and scorpions are singing their songs of silence all around her, and she knows she is safe.

"Why do you live here, Chief?" she whispers, opening her eyes. "You don't belong here. Where I lived, you could be free. You wouldn't have to steal anything, you wouldn't have to fight."

"I told you," he grumbles. "I'm a warrior. I go where I'm needed."

Then he hands her Moon's flute.

Delilah's face doesn't move. She doesn't let it. But her eyes open up and swallow the sight of that instrument, that magical creature—the only beauty beyond this world that she has ever believed in, that music. The only love that transported her beyond herself, ever. And she knows Moon must be dead, just like she always knew he would die, despite his godness, despite what he told her.

She doesn't cry. She doesn't feel anything. She doesn't understand why the old man is smiling.

"I found it," he says gently, as if speaking to a child. "Look how lonely it is. It wants to be played. But I can't play it. An old, hardened warrior like me has no music left in him."

"Neither do I," says Delilah, her voice cold.

"Take it," he says, suddenly hard and stern. "I am telling you, this flute knows you. I'm not an idiot. I know."

Mutely, Delilah takes it, and then she stands, and her body is made of concrete, with no more life in it than the City walls.

"Goodbye, grandfather," she says. "Thank you."

He nods. "Play that thing, Delilah. You only refuse to play it because of what it will make you feel. That's selfish."

She stares at him.

"Go!" he says, and she starts, but then she sees the emotion there. He looks up at her and nods again, more kindly. "Go, friend."

She walks down the empty street toward the river, the flute swinging in her left hand. No one else is going this way. The river makes no sound. It doesn't even look like a river, this crowded chaos of froth and refuse, its own weight pushing it ever onward. If Yora is anywhere here, Delilah cannot feel her.

The air has turned very cold. It has drawn itself tight together, holding its breath, parting its lips dryly, unable to make a sound. Delilah pulls one layer after another out of her pack, until her pack weighs almost nothing, and her body weighs too much. In her very bones, she misses the plants she ate in the desert while she was traveling. Maybe that's why she's been so sick. In her belly, in her hollow chest, in her throat, in her mouth, she craves those certain colors and smells. She ought to steal some vegetables, before everything is gone.

But now it is hard to tear herself away from the river. Walking beside its pain, she feels at home. When she walks beside the inevitable falling of it, her own pain feels more comfortable, and at once so much, so overwhelmingly much, that she can't hold it inside any longer. The pain of losing Moon, the pain of the river, the pain of missing Yora, the desert, and even the old man who became her friend—losing everyone. Without thinking about it too much, she raises the flute to her lips.

The first sounds are terrible, like crows at a trash heap. The next sounds are like baby birds, songless, crying for food. The sounds never get good. Delilah herself would not call them music. But through them she is able to say something of what she needs to say. And she can tell that the river is listening, and that it comforts the river a little.

When the first snowflakes kiss her cheeks, she doesn't even notice, they feel so natural. When she does notice, it happens so gradually, so gently that—though she has never seen snow in her life—she is not afraid, and she knows she has to keep playing. Slowly, the air fills with them: flecks of white bliss, like sparkles on the edges of some great, invisible god's arms, as he reaches around to embrace her. The air turns blurry with them, like eyes tearing up, like mist. When it touches her skin, Delilah can tell that it is rain, after all, but rain in some other form—like rain's memory, or the idea of rain before it dares to fully let go.

Now the river, though heavy and slow as if with terrible age, feels like Yora after all. Delilah can hear her voice. She is not speaking to Delilah. She is whispering, *Little Brother, let it go. Cry, Little Brother….*

No rain god would send the rain like this—no rain god but the most sensitive, the most tender, the most sweetly sorrowful rain god that ever lived. What's crazy is that when she thought Moon was gone, Delilah didn't feel anything, because in a way the experience wasn't new to her. Throughout their friendship, he had always been leaving; he had always been dying; he had always been gone. It's realizing that he is still alive, after all, that makes Delilah finally feel something—that makes her finally able to feel him, and herself, and all that they never allowed themselves to feel but tried to call up in each other anyway, out of love and longing.

It snows for hours and hours, and by the time Delilah has almost reached the other side of the still, lost City at sunset, hungry and exhausted and cramping in her belly but still happy—feeling that she and Moon are talking to each other honestly, at last—it is still snowing, slow as a dream. All the grey is covered with white, the hard corners curved over with white. And the trash, the rooftops, and the ugly signs are all covered with white—a white that falls roundly, that undulates like primeval hills of wilderness over the contours of the City, insisting that once we lived like this; once we were shaped like this; once we dreamed like this. People have come out of their apartments, and are standing in the streets, looking more dazed than ever. They hold out their hands and even their tongues. Some of the children, knowing only this moment, begin to play.

Down by the river, a tall young man in a suit, with sunken eyes and open mouth, holds out a shaking hand to Delilah. She lowers the flute and sees a dollar bill, limp and damp, half falling from his hand. Anger—habitually, obediently—begins to stumble up to standing inside her, its legs shaky but determined, but then she looks into his eyes and stops when she sees the longing there.

She will never know what this man was asking for. At first she thinks he wants to give her charity, or money for playing, as if he thought her some desperate, badly-playing street performer, whose music was not much better than begging. Then, when she sees the longing there, she almost wonders if he wants to pay her for sex—even though she can't delude herself into thinking, with her pale, sick face, her unwashed smell, and her tattered men's clothing, that she could look in any way seductive—simply because she can't imagine what else she has to give someone other than her body. Then she wonders if he thinks her some kind of goddess, walking apart from the rest, unafraid, playing an eerie flute along the river, calling the snows. Maybe he thinks she has the answers. Because it seems clear that everyone needs *someone* to have the answers; everyone seems so bewildered by what has happened, and everyone seems to understand that Hanum is dead.

"What do you want?" she asks the man sharply.

His lips tremble. He looks down at the dollar, then back up at Delilah, and he steps forward, and Delilah—though she doesn't mean to—steps back in disgust.

But the man keeps holding out the dollar bill as if he doesn't know what to do with it. It's as if this thing which used to be everything to him—used to be the very energy, the very sustenance, the very meaning and drive and reason for his life—has now become nothing, and he can't understand that. He holds it out to her like something sick or broken, this machine that once ran his life. As if he hands her this broken dollar bill, thinking she is some goddess, and wants her to fix it.

Delilah shakes her head. "I…" She's been playing the flute all day, and now her own silence surprises her. Everyone else seems to notice that silence too. Behind the man, other people are coming toward her, men and women and a few children. They are all looking at her with that same terrible expression on their faces.

"No," she shakes her head harder. "No." She doesn't know what she is saying No to. Maybe it's that same *No* she said to Dragon long ago, when he tried to—yes, she can admit it now—he tried to rape her. *No, you misunderstand me. No, you are not listening.* Her exhaustion begins to make her shiver.

"Look," she says. She takes the dollar bill roughly from his hand and tears it in half. He looks down at it quickly, and then back up at her, and his face crumples. Later, she won't be able to imagine why she did it, but she steps forward and takes him in her arms.

As they stand there holding each other, small whimpers can be heard up and down the street, like waking birds, and other arms are wrapping around other bodies as people fall into each other.

The two halves of the dollar bill float apart between the delicate universes of the snowflakes—each flake a microscopic, webbed pattern that will never be seen, a new language that will never be learned—and Lonely's spirit is finally set free into the wind.

"Listen, Father," says Moon. "This is what I remember.

"The City was not always surrounded by desert. The Earth, my mother, was not always silent.

"But then they covered her with concrete. They covered her breasts, her arms, her face. They covered her sex, her heart, her eyes. They covered her mouth, her ears, her skin and her hair. They covered her until she could no longer call to you, and no longer receive you. Your fertile waters ran in wasted rivers through gutters, and pooled in lifeless places, and fermented.

"You were so sad, Father, that you turned the rains away. You thought she did not want you any more, like I thought the world didn't want me. It made you bitter. It made you cold. When you found out I loved men, you denied me. You could only remember the love you lost, from the woman who once loved you, the Earth.

"But Father, this is what I know. Everything must be turned upside down now, for the world to be right again. The world must be flipped over, and the concrete shaken loose. The Earth must rain into the Sky. You, Father, must also be the Mother, and Earth shall also be the Father. Women will love women, and men will love men. Because women, now, must learn how to love and believe in themselves, and men must learn how to weep. Everyone must be braver than they have ever been before.

"Father, I am the love between you and the Earth. It is my job to call the rains. I used to dream of standing before you, challenging you, offering to fight you for the rains. But I am not a fighter, and today I understand: I do not need to fight. The rains are already in me. You will make love to the Earth again, and I will make that happen, in my own way."

Moon opens his eyes but there is no one there. He is still floating out here in the endless universe, clouds and sky, feathers and light. But between the snowflakes, he can feel the whole universe listening.

"Mother," he whispers. "I am so tired of being nowhere. I am so tired of being alone."

He bows his head to catch the tears that fall into his palms, and in all his body—whatever and wherever his body is—and in all his spirit, he can feel the opening and surrender of Sky's flesh, Sky's heart, Sky's manhood. He cries until he can no longer see, until his hands fill up and overflow, and then he can no longer catch all the tears, and they fall.

On this, the full moon, Kite and Dragon reach the Center of the City at last.

The concrete cluster of rectangles from which the rulers rule is so big, it covers several blocks. Kite cannot believe they never found it before. But when they arrive, they find it ringed around by iron gates, armed guards, and electrical alarms.

Kite looks up, and the wonder of snowflakes touches his eyelids, his hair, his lips. He realizes that this knowledge which makes the City run is not for the people of the City to access.

He realizes that they have not told him all this time, not because they wouldn't, but because they did not know.

☾

Delilah arrives at the seashore at night, crawls into a cave, and collapses. She hasn't eaten since that morning, but all she cares about is sleep. She doesn't even care what happens after this or how she will reach the mysterious island. She hears the ocean nearby, a wall of giant sound like the calling of Death, and that is enough for now.

But she cannot sleep. Voices seem to croon and cry in the squeeze of the wind through the passageways of stone. They sound like Mira screaming, Mira humming to herself and deaf to the world, Mira moaning, Mira whimpering that time their mother beat her for screaming like that at their father's funeral. Mira whispering her name. *Lilah.* Hadn't Delilah tried her best to take care of her: hadn't she fought off the other kids, hadn't she defended her despite her own shame when Mira sat and rocked, and the others snickered and whispered? But that was after their father died, when suddenly Delilah needed Mira like she'd never needed anyone, when they were sent away to school alone and had no one else. Before that, at least the kids in the outer City respected her. Maybe she didn't have friends, but she had lovers and people who let her be herself. And before that, there was Moon.

She can't shake the feeling that all that time, when their father was still alive, Mira was calling out to her, and Delilah wasn't listening because she was too scared to hear what Mira would say. Then by the time Delilah wanted to listen—by the time she was so desperate for the companionship of her sister that she shook her by the shoulders once in the middle of the cafeteria with everyone watching, and cried, and begged her to speak—Mira wouldn't say a word. It was too late.

All night Delilah cannot sleep, and she turns and turns, missing the mound of animal skins she used to sleep on that's rotting away in her desert cave still, so far away and cold. All night she tries to remember a dream she had by the river before she heard Mira's voice and set off for the City. But more and more, the fearful reality of the ocean—its tumultuous nothing—is rising up inside her, and the best she can do is try to turn off her mind.

In the morning, the stone around her is black and salty and cold as a reptile's insides. The base of her spine aches, like it does all the time now, and her belly bloats out hard like when she menstruates, only she hasn't menstruated in almost three moons. Maybe she caught some sickness from one of the men, after all. She hasn't exactly said it to herself, but the idea has begun to settle in, in the back of her mind, that rescuing Mira will be her final task—the one good deed for which she has remained alive this long—and that once she does rescue her, she will have faced all that she fears, and can therefore be justified in finally giving up this life. How tired she is of the fight.

When she sits up in her shallow hollow, she sees with a shock of uneasiness that someone has left food for her. A fish. Did she sleep, after all? Wary, but too delirious from hunger to hold back, she stumbles around the tiny beach between the cliffs, gathering driftwood, and then she lights a fire with some matches she took from the City. She didn't have to buy or steal them. The stores were a free-for-all now, and the only thing people fought for at this point was food. They hadn't gotten beyond step one of survival yet; they hadn't thought about needing warmth. They no longer remembered what survival was made of. They still took their whole lives for granted and were still getting over the loss of their cars.

She cooks her fish and tries not to pay attention to the sea, because its presence overwhelms her. But she can't help but wonder at it, out of the corner of her mind. Its sound reminds her of the song the desert sang, beneath its silence. As if the desert—all those long, lonely years—was only a veil covering this deep, luxurious abundance of living water. As if all those long hours she spent listening to the talking of the wind and the silent voices of the desert animals, and thought they were talking of hunger and thirst and fear, escape and hunting and sex, they were actually talking about the sea.

She was too lazy to build a cooking platform over the fire, so she balances the fish draped over two sticks, which she holds in her fists and props up on each knee, her arms trembling with hunger. When pieces of it begin to crumble into the fire, she reaches right into it and pulls them out, shoving them into her mouth without feeling the burn.

Around her are black caves, and above and beyond them, the black forest she just came through. She's staring into that blackness, and then she realizes she has finished eating. The fish was huge after all, and it filled her, even if it wasn't fully cooked. Almost instantly, she falls asleep. She dreams Yora is kneeling by her, in human form, laying fish upon fish on a fancy golden platter. She realizes it is Yora who is bringing her the fish.

"Stop," she murmurs. "I don't need all that. I'm dying anyway."

"But it is a good dying," says Yora.

"Whatever."

"Why do you not come? The sea is right here, waiting."

"I don't like it."

"You are afraid. You think it will not accept you. You are wrong."

When she wakes, the sun is already setting. She tries to work out the time. She's lost track of day and night. She wanted so badly to get as far from the City as possible, as fast as possible, forever. Yet she survived it again, after all. It wasn't such a big deal. No family, no boarding school. It was only the memories that scared her, after all. Now there is only loneliness to deal with, and that got easy a long time ago.

Gulls pass over her like jeering ghosts, or they sit with other slim, crooked birds cloaked in black on bleached white driftwood trees. What will she do now? There are too many things in the wind she'd rather not hear. Something sounds like a woman crying, wailing. Or a baby. Or both.

She cooks the next fish that was left for her, and then it's nearly dark, and she stands up and paces the shoreline with one hand clutching the knife at her hip. She lets the water creep up to her toes. She has never seen water like this: water that comes toward her and then draws back, hungry and then afraid, threatening and then fading. It extends too far out to understand, then becomes one with the blackening sky. She remembers the stories she heard in childhood, the stories everyone knew, about how the Dark Goddess held the Princess captive on a magical island, and how her league of mad souls beneath the sea would howl and rock the waves when any ship came close, confusing its men, always sending them astray. Little boys Delilah knew would wave sticks like swords, crying that one day they would ride into the sea and save the Princess.

But when they grew up, they forgot all of that. They believed in Hanum and the City he made, but they didn't believe in the rest. Delilah has to admit she's not sure if she does either.

I am the wind, thinks Lonely, tossing here and there, roughing up the trees, spiraling the trash, and not knowing why.

"Are you?" says the wind.

She cannot see or hear or touch, and yet she touches everything: the animal's fur, a girl's ragged dress, the grass, the dust, a boy's long hair, the lizard's impermeable skin. She connects everything. Then just as suddenly, she is gone from it.

"Don't you know yet," asks the wind, "who you are?"

And Lonely remembers everything. She remembers the distances that loneliness has spanned. The hunger between predator and prey, the journey from water to land, the pathway of a river from mountaintop to sea, the open meadow and the labyrinthine desert, and most of all the tower, so far out to sea and so far up in the air. She remembers the distance between herself and her past, constantly changing, and the distance she once felt between herself and her future, and how once that distance closed, she had everything and lost everything in the same moment. She says to the wind, *But who are you? You never tell me.*

"Maybe I'm only yourself. A voice in your mind."

Tell the truth. You come from somewhere else. Where do you come from?

"I come from where the earth is uneven, from empty spaces, from the very restlessness of your soul."

But why won't you face me?

"I have no face."

But isn't there anything that matters? Lonely cries desperately with whatever part of herself remains herself, through every life. *Isn't anything real? Isn't there one true love, one true destiny, one name that is mine? Isn't there one God above all other gods?*

In the distance now, she can feel the sea.

"There is no above. Over and over, the people will try to build themselves higher, above all the rest. But the world is round, not flat. There is no above and no below. There is only further out and closer in."

In the City now there comes a breeze that never falters, never dies. It brings dust from the wastelands around you. It brings the smells you paid good money to live away from. It bolsters itself; it grows; it begins to howl.

That night and all the next day, and the next, it is a dry, desperate windstorm, its gusts like curling tubes of light. It knocks you against the walls. It shatters windows and rips off clothing, blinds your eyes with dust and makes holes in rooftops. Neat potted flowers that were only kept alive by water pumped from far away or underground fall easily off balconies; abandoned cars tip against each other. Asphalt shingles sling sharp through the air like weapons. The houses of the poorest people are half gone, their furniture tumbling down the street. They run to your houses, and some of you open your doors. They rush in raving, like madmen, and you pity them, but increasingly your pity turns to fear. Outside your windows, you can see the neighbors' trash come smashing against your walls. Later, you will never be able to sort out whose trash was whose.

Caught in the street, you circle up and gather your children into the center to protect them, like a herd of bison—only you face inward instead of out. With your faces tilted into the warm security of other bodies, into dark anonymity, your backs are open wide to the wind, and all the stored angers, resentments, and swallowed longings you rolled up tight all your lives in your spines are released now, given voice. Terrified, you clutch each other tight, as you hear the hinges break from doors and the screams of people wounded, and yet at the same time you are holding your own breaths in the hope of some barely admissible relief, ecstatically biting your own lips in the expectation of that final orgasm of chaos.

Some of you want it so badly, you are running loose and alone, making it come. You are torching houses, bashing windows, shooting guns, stealing whatever you can and then destroying it—as Delilah once did. Violence pants beneath the very concrete of the streets like a lustful monster too long chained up.

Oh, that everything might come undone! That you might let go of everything you thought you wanted! For though you wanted it so much, it was difficult to clench your teeth constantly in failure, to try so hard, to feel undeserving, and to be so afraid of losing it. Oh, that you might give up what you thought was most important! That you might be able to survive after all without it! Or that you might not, and it would not matter.

In the dark hollow of your collected center, where the children move restless and frightened and look up at you with dazzling new eyes, questions you never allowed yourselves before begin to move and talk. What if Hanum's world can break after all? What if what has always been known is not so? In that cave of possibility surrounded by the round white erasure of the wind's roar, Imagination begins to wake again.

See, children, I am stirring it there in your center: round and round and round.

11ᵗʰ MOON

On the night of the new moon, Delilah finds the sand castles. She lets go of the knife, forgets to close her mouth, and drops to her knees. She hasn't cut her hair for a long time and it lolls around her face; she has to keep tucking it behind her ears. She can barely see in the darkness, and at first she doesn't believe it, but the sea is a mirror, and gives her all the light it can.

She bends over the tower and the walls around it, the hidden hollow inside, the moat and the gate—all made of sand. Then she sees a man and a woman with a baby in her arms, each of them about half the size of her littlest finger, walking wearily up to the bridge and beginning to cross.

"I don't think anyone else is here," the woman is saying. Then the bridge begins to collapse beneath her feet, and the man, rather deftly, wraps his arms around both her and the baby and manages to pull them after him. He takes the baby and they run the rest of the way across, the bridge collapsing behind them.

"They never build them right," says the man bitterly, as they turn to look back. "They're not made for real people."

"Now what will we do?"

"It doesn't matter."

Solemnly, they turn and walk around the castle. They seem unaware of Delilah's face hanging over them. They are searching for a real opening, a real room inside the pretend structure, to lay down and rest for the night. At the top of the castle, they find a little turret with a clumsy window big enough to make a small cave. They sit down, and the woman takes out her tiny breast and nurses her whimpering baby.

Delilah stares in horrified wonder. She wants to pick up the little people and hold them in her hands, see if they feel warm, take off their little clothes and see if they're real underneath. Now they are staring out listlessly at the sea. There is something wrong with them. The woman says,

"How long do you think we have?"

"Not long, this one," says the man, and then neither of them say anything. The waves are soaking Delilah's calves and knees, already wiping away all trace of the moat and the bridge, smoothing out the west castle wall. She looks beyond them—why do they stay?—and yet now she sees many more sandcastles, dotting the shore along the edge of the waves. She sees the lights of hundreds of tiny lanterns, some of them in ones or twos and others in clusters of many, moving toward the various castles, finding ways inside despite the waves that are even now destroying them.

"But why?" she cries helplessly, unconsciously holding her belly in one hand.

"They want so much to have a home," whispers Yora, and Delilah looks up to find her human-sized, human-shaped, beautiful friend at her side. "Every day, every night, the castles are destroyed by the tides, and then they are rebuilt, and every night the people come again, but nothing ever lasts."

"But who makes them? Who makes the castles?"

"The children."

"What children?"

"The children who live here."

Delilah glances swiftly around her. She seems to see shadows crossing the path she just made. She seems to see small, stubborn eyes looking back at her and then disappearing. She remembers the voices she's been hearing for days now. She thought she was going mad.

"The children do not realize," Yora says, her voice slippery like a black fish in moonlight. "They think it is a game. They are only children."

"But who are these tiny people who never get to stay anywhere?" says Delilah, feeling sick again.

"What do you mean?" asks Yora, who was smoothing the falling sand with her hand but now looks up at Delilah. "Do you not know them? Are they not familiar? Have you never felt this?"

Delilah looks away. The man and the woman are holding each other now, with the baby in between them—standing up and holding each other as the water collapses the levels below them—and they are crying.

"Come, friend," says Yora and takes her hand in her own. It's cold, but dry. "Do not stay here at the edge forever. There is only suffering here. It is time to decide."

"I have decided," says Delilah.

"Have you?"

Yora turns and wades into the sea, keeping her human form all the way, as if to show Delilah what it will look like when she follows. Delilah shivers and can't stop shivering. Yora wends her way, like a river through rivers, in a curved pathway between the bones of dead trees and the looping, leering, hole-riddled remains of giant stones that once were part of the shore. Beyond all these, when all that's left to be seen is the goddess' white head floating in the misty drift of her dress, Yora calls softly into the wind,

"If you are ready, come after me. When you are too tired to keep going, I will carry you."

Then she is gone.

"I don't know how to swim!" calls Delilah. But there is no answer now, not even the screaming of the gulls. There are no nocturnal animals at the seashore, at least not above the waves. She looks around, ashamed of herself.

"Fuck," she says. After all, courage is all she has. She walks in fast, though the waves, rather than reaching to devour her, seem to resist her now, as if she's walking upriver. By the time the water is up to her thighs, they almost knock her down. But when the water reaches her waist, it just shakes her, and when it reaches her chest, it doesn't move her at all, only tugs at her legs down below. Delilah is so scared she thinks she might be peeing, though she can't tell. She has never entered into water so deep, so endless, and something about it engulfs her with familiarity, memory, and premonition at the same time. Just before she goes under, she realizes she isn't breathing. Then with a start, she remembers that all this held-breath, dizzying tension of courage she's clenched inside herself isn't so that she can drown herself, but so that she can survive. That's what courage was always for.

She knows what swimming looks like—she's seen dogs swimming in the filthy river—and so she does that now. It doesn't keep her from mouthful after mouthful of terrifying, choking darkness, but it does keep her afloat, at least for a moment. She can't tell if she is moving forward, but there is no going back now, so she tries not to think about what will happen when she tires. Then she does think about it, and the fear, finally, is too big for her. The dream she couldn't remember flashes in her mind for an instant and then is gone. Flailing, she spins around, finds that her feet can't touch bottom, and finds that the shore is so far away she can barely see it, undulating faintly white in black space. And then she is no longer Delilah; she is no longer anyone she ever knew or wanted to be; she is only fear in the blackness, the cold water speaking inevitability all over her forgotten body, screaming, "Help! Help! Help!"

Then the entire earth, warm and slippery as the inside of a woman, seems to rise up beneath her.

"Hel–Hoa—" she gasps, gripping it, riding it, dropping her forehead against it in relief before she can even breathe enough to wonder.

A fountain of air bursts up with a great squeaking sigh in front of her, as if to celebrate the miracle of breath. She cannot grab hold of any part of the smooth roundness that supports her, and yet it carries her sturdily, her hands flat pressed upon it, her legs spread wide and helpless around it like a child's. It disappears back under the water but remains near the surface, so that Delilah's head and shoulders stay above water as she looks all around in shock at an emptiness bigger than the desert.

They speed forward.

Then the whales begin to sing. Deep in the earth-black water, they sing an ancient song about the fire-charred sky, the broken-open universe. They sing about where they've been and where they are going, and how it is the same. They sing about the sad human heart who rides the great aching body and still does not believe. They sing the answers to all the questions that will ever be asked. They sing their love for each other, their family memory of each precious, long life, each child born and each death. There is no unrequited love among whales. There is no warfare, no forgetting, no jealousy, no doubt.

And Delilah, though she cannot understand, closes her eyes in laughter, because she understands for the first time the freedom in surrender. She understands what she wanted, when she wanted death. She laughs to keep from crying, because the whales, more than any human society she knows, understand true community. Through their song she understands that—though she, Delilah, does not know how to do it—it is possible to live among others, even among those you love, without this constant, constant pain.

Back home, Kite used to study each element, trying to understand its secret. He lay in the sun, stood inside the push of the river, closed his eyes in the wind, thinking with his mind and his body. He learned a lot about motion, heat, and force, simply by feeling them.

But these people in the steel tower, whoever they are, whatever they are doing, cannot feel the wind or the sun, or watch the movement of water. How, then, can they understand energy?

For two days, he has watched this scene from the rooftop of a vacant building, living on nothing but pigeon meat. The guards have gradually disappeared, slinking off into the shadows like lofty statues shape-shifting back into degraded human form. People arrive in growing hordes, banging on the closed steel doors, and demand answers: lights for their homes, food, water. The City is breaking down.

Yesterday Dragon said to him, "You want knowledge. You think that's what you came for. But what is this knowledge? You have love. All these people that you left behind love you. I would do anything for such love. For a family."

"Then go and give it," Kite said, a little too sharply. "If you want love, you have to give it. Stop complaining."

They both shut up then, Kite with his arms around his knees, Dragon stiff and frowning in an upright lotus. Kite felt sorry but he was irritable from constant hunger, malnourished and homesick and disappointed in his own foolishness, frustrated to know he had endured all of this for nothing. His sense of himself and the peace he'd always taken for granted erode more and more quickly in the violent cacophony of City existence. But he can't turn around and go home, not yet. Not after everything he's gone through to get here.

He and Dragon did not say anything to each other all day. Then that night Dragon said quietly, "You're right." He stood up and climbed down the metal stairway, and Kite, too surprised to move, watched his proud, vulnerable figure make its way down the street to be lost in the crowd. By the time the terror of aloneness hit him, it was too late.

Then he knew why he'd left home. It was this same nameless anxiety—this hovering, seeping, everywhere mist of anxiety that floods the senses of all the people in the City, that moves them, stops them, and makes them lost. It made them drive their cars incessantly until their cars stopped, made them yell at their children, made them smoke up their apartments and take off their clothes for anyone who asked, and it makes them pound now on the steel doors in fury and terror. This same anxiety haunted his family, even though they knew how to survive, even though they had everything they needed—even then. It was different at home perhaps, more subtle and tucked away, but he could hear it in his mother's questions, in the nervous conversations about the future when Jay's family came to visit, and in the way they all avoided strangers and would not travel beyond each other's homes. What was this awful, nameless fear that human beings lived with, that could never be outrun? It was to quell that fear that he had come looking for knowledge, for light, for answers.

Now he stands up and stretches his cold limbs. He wants to yell down to the people, "Stop pounding at the door! Food, energy—it doesn't come from there! They don't own it. No one owns it. It doesn't come from them!" But they wouldn't listen.

At the bottom of the metal stairway, he kills a rat with his slingshot. But Dragon isn't there to make him a fire. So he carries the thing through several blocks of wreckage—still within sight and hearing of the mob—until he finds a fallen tree in the rubble of what was once a park, and he breaks off the sticks he needs, makes his bow drill, and starts twisting it fast between his palms. It works faster than he expected, because everything is so dry. He skins the rat while the fire is building, spears it with a stick, and roasts it. He's already wondering where he's going to get water, because he's been out of it for a while, and clean water is hard to come by since the City stopped working. Faucets don't work, and all of the bottled water has been stolen and used already. The more he thinks about it, the thirstier he feels. He's feeling so frustrated and sorry for himself that not until the rat is almost done cooking does he notice he is being watched on all sides. First it's the children, some huddled in groups and some alone, with arms hanging at their sides, mouths open, eyes hungry but also curious. Kite makes himself look them in the eye.

"What are you looking at?" he asks gruffly, but he's scared, because the adults are coming, too, now. Why are they staring at him like that?

When he starts to eat, he hears a little girl cry, "Ew!"

He jumps up, the meat in his hand. "What are you looking at?"

The people shuffle back slightly, but then regroup and come closer. They move with the mad, fearless tension of the desperate.

"Are you a god?" asks an older man, staring into his eyes.

"Of course not!"

But he hears them whispering to each other as others join them: *I saw him kill that animal, and then he made a fire without matches, out of nothing, and then he cooked it and ate it. I saw it!*

"Here!" Kite cries, stepping toward a young boy who's staring open-mouthed at the meat, "take it! Do you want it? Take it! Eat!" But the boy stumbles backward into the bodies of the adults, his eyes panicked.

"He's a god!" come a new chorus of voices. "He makes fire from nothing. He makes food from rats!"

There is a great swell of voices then, like aspen leaves clattering in the winds before a thunder storm. Kite stands there, bewildered. Once someone came to these people and offered to build a life where they would never hunger and never thirst, where everything was made for them—and they thought that person was a god. Now they look at Kite, who does what they once knew how to do, simply making his own food, making his own life—and they think he is a god.

"Hey," someone says, "if he's a god, maybe they'll let him in! Maybe they'll listen to him."

"Yeah, send him in!"

"Make them open the doors! Make them open the doors!"

Kite's protests don't matter now, as the tide of human hands swells around him, lifting and carrying him, touching him everywhere, thrusting him forward toward their singular purpose: the great steel door. Kite turns and faces the crowd, his back against the cold metal, crying, "Listen to me!" and it's a nightmare, because no one is listening. He closes his eyes, waiting to wake up. He can feel fists reverberating against the steel around him: *Let him in! He's a god!*

Flattening himself against the door, he walls himself off from the sound of them; he makes the sound of them like the river in his mind, far away, flowing through the meadow of his home. Through his half-opened eyelashes, far away, he thinks he can see Dragon moving through the outskirts of the mob, where quieter people are standing—mothers and children swaying against each other hopeless, and people who stand alone as if they have always been alone, as if their aloneness is slowly killing them. Behind him, through the crack of the steel door, he thinks he can hear someone breathing.

Kite sinks down, turning his face, pressing his ear to the crack, pushing the noise of the crowd further away. And now he can hear it distinctly: quick, strained intakes of breath, the breathing of someone who cannot imagine that someone is listening to him.

"It's okay," murmurs Kite, without thinking. And then, louder, "Can you hear me in there? I don't want anything." *This is it*, he thinks. *This is my only chance to know the truth.* "I—I want to help," he says.

Faster than he expected it, like the fire from dry tinder, with the same fierce speed of desperation that sent him flying through a thousand hands from the fallen tree to this door, the door opens a crack more and he is sucked inside.

Delilah wades ashore, only human again, with no magic to keep all her fingers and toes—and then her feet and ankles—from going numb. No pack, no knife, nothing in her hands. She manages to throw off her sweatshirt, which was weighing her down, and keep moving. She is unaware that she's crawling by the time she hits the rocks, or that she is moving toward the presence of some other before her, someone she can sense more than see.

"Take your clothes off," says a low, croaking voice, and she realizes she is out of the water, nearly face down on the wet stone. It sounds like the voice of a raven, if ravens had human voices. Maybe they do. Delilah is prepared for anything, and she has also decided that she wants to live.

"Take your clothes off. Now." Something deeper than fear tells her this makes sense, and so she puts all of her energy into doing it. The icy things seem to wrestle with her for hours. The whole idea of clothing seems impossible to her now—how could she ever have gotten herself into anything so complicated? Panting, she lets the other person, who now appears to be an old woman, wrap an old wool blanket around her. Then she looks up, and then she bows her head.

"Thank you," she says.

"Hmph," says the old woman, who trembles now in the cold.

Delilah looks up again. She beholds the elder's features, uneven, the eyes shiny in the gnarled face. The darkness blows around the two of them, and there is nothing else here but a faint, aching smell of seaweed and salt. Delilah doesn't know who the woman is. She is quite sure she herself is delirious. But suddenly, what she can feel most clearly is her own mother's death. It is not a feeling she could name. It is the first feeling she has remembered ever feeling about her own mother, and she does not recognize it. It has no tears. It is just a wide, empty knowing. She has no mother. This is what she knows. This is what is wrong with her, and there is nothing she can do about it; this is what has always been true. It is what makes her sick, what makes her desperate, what makes her utterly, unfixably broken. And yet it helps, suddenly, just to know this.

"Do I know you?" says the old woman, and Delilah can see that she is blind.

"No. I'm Delilah."

"What do you want, Delilah?"

"I want my sister." Words she spoke a hundred times over so long ago, with such fury and such passion, but now they sound calm and strangely certain.

"Hmph," says the old woman again. Then she is silent for a moment, her own head bowed, and Delilah watches her. She reaches down to Delilah's hands, which are splayed out on the ground on either side of her, as if she knew exactly where Delilah would leave them, and touches them gingerly with her own fingers. Then she pulls herself back up.

"I thought you were that other girl," she says. "My daughter."

Delilah knows, then, without her even saying it. She always knew—that the girl Dragon longed for, the girl she found starving and helpless in the forest, was the princess from the tower after all. Of course she wasn't lying. That girl could not lie.

"My spoiled daughter," the old woman says, her voice twisting harshly. "So spoiled she names herself 'Lonely', as if she is the only lonely person in the world. So selfish she steals the name of the river goddess, 'Yora', when she cannot even own up to that—"

"No," Delilah interrupts, shaking her head hard, surprising herself. "She isn't like that. You've got it wrong."

The old woman says nothing. She looks down at her own hands, which she cannot see.

Delilah feels angry now, and she hates feeling angry at this person, because it's all backwards: why are the elders not wise? Why must it seem that she is the elder, after all—the only one who can see things clearly? Yet she cannot put it into words, this sudden pain she feels at this mother's denial of her daughter. She cannot put into words what Lonely is. "Don't you know?" she mutters hopelessly. "She's your own daughter—don't you know her?"

The old woman shakes her head. "No," she says. And sighs.

They are silent then, for a long time. Long enough for Delilah almost to forget why she is here. Long enough for her to forget that she *is* here. It seems to her that she is fourteen years old, climbing in the window—her face unwashed, her hair uncombed, her arms scratched by barbed wire and her fingers burned. Her mother is standing in the doorway of her bedroom, silhouetted by the hallway light. Delilah freezes, one foot touching the floor. It is the only time her mother has ever caught her entering at dawn. But her mother doesn't say anything. She looks at Delilah for one moment only before she turns away and shuts off the light. Was that sorrow in her eyes, after all? A hopelessly tender question, that she despaired of ever being answered—*Who are you?* Or was it only the usual condemning coldness, the denial of hope for one who is not worth hoping for? Delilah will never know. But she lay awake all that morning, wondering.

She comes back to attention now, back to the dark wind and the smell of salt, because something is happening to the old woman. She is shaking. She has not moved—her body hunches tight over her hands, unchanged, and her eyes stare emptily—but she is shaking so hard that Delilah stands up quickly and clasps her body between her hands.

"Are you all right?"

The woman stops shaking. She is breathing heavily. "Don't touch me," she moans, but she seems to crumble somehow inside Delilah's hands, and Delilah can feel the tears in there, and for some reason she cannot let go. She crouches next to the woman and holds her. The woman is making sounds that Delilah does not understand, like words in some other language mixed with hisses and hums. But then she begins to shake again, shuddering as if with brutal, soundless sobs, and if Delilah knows anything, she knows to keep holding onto her.

The old woman's bones shake against Delilah's heart, her body shuddering down into itself, deeper and deeper into an ancient, wind-wailing sorrow— as if all the world were torn to pieces, and all that is left is this one moment, and this one moment is a tiny, black pebble, bouncing, echoing step by step down an endless flight of stairs into the cavern at the center of the universe.

"Where is she?" the old woman cries finally, softly to herself, her head in her hands, her breath loud. "Oh, Hanum, where is she?"

When she is still again, Delilah releases her and stands up. She takes a good look around for the first time at the windy stone, its damp knife edges lit by starlight. Emptiness circles itself, like the vast territory of the old woman's loneliness consuming the world. Delilah's throat clenches.

"Please," she whispers to the darkness, "tell me Mira isn't here." For she feels now that she'd rather search her whole life, and never find her, than know that her sister has spent the last ten years of her life in this place.

But at these words, the old woman raises her head. "Mira," she says.

Delilah looks at her.

"Mira," the old woman repeats, staring past Delilah's shoulder, her eyes wide and milky white behind the dark moons of their pupils. "You come— you come for Mira?"

Delilah falls to her knees and grabs the old woman's arm, all pity gone from her. The old woman cringes and Delilah knows she must be hurting her, but she doesn't care. She feels now that she will kill her if she has to. "Where is she?" she demands.

The old woman's mouth hangs open, and she is trembling again. "Are you—" she begins, and she licks beads of saliva off the edges of her lips. "Are you—the Dark Goddess?"

Startled, Delilah loosens her grip and rears back. "Of course not," she snaps.

"But then, who are you?"

"I told you," says Delilah. "I'm her sister. I am the only one who could ever rescue her, I am all that she has, I—" Delilah covers her face in her hands, stopping herself. "Please." She forces herself to be calm. "If she is here, please tell me where she is."

"A woman rescuer," the old woman murmurs, her voice soft and quiet now. "No one has ever come before. No one has ever come for any of them."

But to the surprise of Delilah, to whom it seemed that the old woman was part of that bony chair and could never uncleave herself from it, she rises now, as if easily. "Come now," she says firmly and holds out her hand.

In a moment, the two women are walking hand in hand to a flight of dark stairs, there between the stones of the island.

They stop on the top step. Below them, a black hole opens into the center of the earth.

"The people think I guard them," the old woman says, her voice steady, creaky, and knowing now, like an elder's ought to be. "But I do not guard them. I do not keep them sleeping. It was Hanum who put them to sleep, and I don't know how to wake them."

"What happened to Hanum?" Delilah asks, stalling now despite her desperation, still shivering with cold as she stares down into that blackness. "Was he your lover?"

The woman beside her nods. "I think so." But she doesn't answer the other question.

"What happened to him?" Delilah repeats, a fascination creeping over her, though she can't bring herself to look at the old woman's face again.

"I killed him."

"Why?"

"I didn't mean to."

"Didn't you?"

"I don't know." They are standing there, staring down into this ridiculous black hole—absolute nothingness around them, the universe holding its breath. "I just wanted to be— I wanted her to be free," whispers the old woman. So fragile, so vulnerable this woman seems beside Delilah, that Delilah wonders how she could possibly have survived here for so long.

"What did you do?" she whispers.

"I put him to sleep. With the same magic he uses to put them to sleep." She pants the words tightly now, as if each breath is only long enough to contain a few of them. "I used that. Used his own magic. But it killed him. Or they killed him. I don't know! I don't know."

Delilah turns and stares at her now.

"I came from behind him. And I hid there behind him, where he could not see me, when he went down to them. When he made his web of magic, I took it in my hands, and I wrapped it around him, around and around, so that he would sleep with them. And when I came back later—" She stops, panting. "When I came back later, he was dead."

Then she nods to Delilah, and she seems the raven again—seems, for a moment, the Witch everyone accused her of being, with her eerie smile. "Now we will go down. You and me. See what we find, eh?"

Delilah looks down, feeling the old woman's hand still in her own, and thinks of Mira, and steps over her own fear. Down. In a moment, she can no longer see anything.

Two more steps. Ten. Delilah closes her eyes and doesn't see any less, and it is comforting to keep them closed, as if this is only a dream. She tries not to think about anything. Not about the darkness. Not about the fragile, frightening hand that guides her. Not about how terrified she is of finding Mira in this place.

"I gave his body to the sea," says the voice beside her. "I did not care what happened to him. I do not come down here any more. Not any more…" Delilah thinks she hears fear in that voice now.

They keep stepping down. Delilah forgets how to count. She has no images, no sensations, no smells, no sounds, nothing at all from which to make a reality, except for this steady downward motion and the hand of death in her own.

But when they reach the bottom, there is a light glowing in the distance. It's a moonish light, hazy, that throws just the barest hints of reality upon the fallen, contorted bodies, large and small, that rise and fall with unconscious breath. Delilah looks to her right and sees the beak of the old woman's nose, the white of two teeth.

"The Unicorn is the only one awake," comes her raven's voice. "When she was gone, we had no light here at all."

Delilah's mind, spinning, has no room to wonder about the relationship between the blind woman and light. Forgetting her, she creeps one step at a time, slowly, toward that pale, heaving glow. How she has wanted, always, to move toward it! How she used to stare at it hungrily, inside Mira's eyes—believing it could never be for her, believing it something shared between her father and her sister that she could never, ever touch. But now she moves toward it. She dares to move toward it because she remembers—she remembers the light arching over her as Dragon's body trapped hers in the unforgiving desert, and how she knew for the first time that she could stop it, and how Mira the Unicorn saved *her.*

She doesn't mean to look at them—she is not even interested—but she has to step around them: the others. These sleeping bodies, heavy from within, twitching and snorting, eyelids fluttering, fists contracting. There is no particular reason why anyone should fear them. There is no reason why she should pause to stare at their soft, bewildered faces, their safely closed eyes, and feel such recurrent shock and recognition. She turns once around, suddenly and without knowing why, and cannot see in the darkness whether or not the old woman is still there. She turns back to the Unicorn, ashamed of her own fear.

"Miri?" she asks.

She thinks she can feel Mira there, maybe, in the nothing, holding her breath in a small, girlish suspense, not knowing if touch will hurt. But Delilah does not see her; only the Unicorn.

"She's sick," croaks the old raven voice behind her, closer than Delilah expected. "She's all come apart." The voice sounds hideous to Delilah now. She kneels. She touches the Unicorn's hair.

"Miri, it's me."

Only the horn is glowing strong. The Unicorn's body—a neatly folded, suffering thing of thin, elegant bones—huffs tortured breaths, and is barely white, and does not turn toward her. Its body is so small, smaller than Delilah's own. In a way, Delilah does not believe at all, any more than she ever did. But what else is there but to try? Why come all this way, if not at least to try? There is nothing stranger about this creature than anything else Mira has ever done.

Delilah lifts the Unicorn's head in one arm and strokes her hesitantly with the other hand: her shoulders, her back, her long neck. The best she can, she wraps her arms around the Unicorn, and bends her head into that dry, feverish fur.

"Miri," she whispers. And what she means to say is, *I've come to take you away from here,* or *I love you—just tell me what you need,* or *I'm here now, I'm so sorry I ever left you,* but what she says instead is, "Oh Miri, the meadow is gone."

And she wants to be the strong one; she wants to be wiser, for once, so she doesn't cry, but all she can do is hold the Unicorn in her arms and rock back and forth, and whisper it over and over, until again she cannot remember where she is or how long she has been here. "Gone, Miri, gone."

Until finally Mira says, "I know." Delilah looks up fast, but still she sees only the Unicorn in her arms and the darkness around it.

"Mira," she cries loud, not caring if the old woman hears. "Come back to me. If you love me, come back to me." That's what she says. Because what does she have after all—what weapon, what strength, what motivation, what tool with which to rescue—but her own need? It is all she has ever owned.

"But you didn't keep me safe."

Delilah turns all around, at the sound of this cruelly eerie voice—a voice like a woman's twisted into the ghost of a little girl's, a mockery of the voice that once was Mira's. But still, there is only the Unicorn. Mira's voice comes as if from far away, as disembodied as it sounded way out in the desert at the river's end. But maybe Mira is not talking to Delilah; maybe she is still talking to her own soul. Or her soul is talking to her body. And each one blames the other, for what happened, and each one is afraid to return.

"*I* will keep you safe, Miri," says Delilah. But even as she says it she feels Mira's fear, like the Unicorn's own sickness—an ugly bile beneath that smooth white—rising up in the back of her throat, because she knows. She doesn't know how long she has known what happened to Mira and not admitted it to herself, but she does know. She knows the great network of pain within her own body and how it mirrors that same vast network of pain in the Earth itself. She knows the paths men make in the earth, realigning the rivers, changing the very course of the winds. She knows that every time she gave her body to a man without even thinking, she was only letting what happened to Mira happen again. With every heartless, spiritless lover, she was betraying Mira again, because she could not admit to herself that it was happening—and even worse, because in some sick, unconscious, impossible way, she envied Mira for being, in Delilah's mind, the only daughter who was wanted.

Delilah doesn't know where to begin when she realizes this. She lowers her head into the Unicorn's body.

"Lilah," Mira says, and her voice is softer, and seems to come from the Unicorn this time. "Where will we go?"

It's another question that Delilah never thought about. All she could think of, once she finally surrendered to it, was the goal of finding Mira and rescuing her. But what is a rescue, if there is no place to take the rescued *to*, once she is rescued *from*? There is no meadow. The pine forest must be destroyed. She can't take her to the City or even, for some reason she can't define right now, the desert. It must be somewhere they can truly *live*—not on the brink of survival, not in endless self-denial and escape, and not that half-life they were taught to live.

Then she remembers something, after all, from that dream she had by the river. She couldn't put it into words if she had to. The memory comes like someone she knew once, and cannot put a face to. But she thinks suddenly, *Return to the Earth.* She feels that place calling, wherever it is, though she has never been there—worlds and worlds away, beyond the desert, where the land embraces valleys of green. And for a moment, her fear is gone.

"I know where we'll go," she says, suddenly smiling with the thrill of her own wild leap of faith. "Trust me. I'm with you now. I'll never leave you."

She does have the strength, after all, to carry Mira, to save her, to love her no matter what, because somewhere out there, there are people—whether human or god—who love her, too. And they have people who love them. It is this connected chain she never admitted to before, which makes everything possible.

Now she stands up, and the Unicorn is safe in her arms, and Mira—she feels sure—is somewhere inside the magical illusion of that light. Now she turns around, and, with all her strength—not thinking of their father, not thinking of anything—begins to walk back around the sleeping bodies, trying to sense her direction in the dark. She tries not to feel fear at the sight of the nothingness before her and all around her, so that she has no front and no behind, only blackness circling and circling. With relief she stumbles over a body, seeing the old woman ahead of her. There she is after all, small and firm and waiting, her black swirling dress reflecting the Unicorn's horn.

The old woman's eyes are not unkind. They are only older and sadder than any silence Delilah has ever known, as Delilah stops before her and cannot go on. Only this elder, this guardian, can navigate through such blackness back to the surface of the world.

"No," she says to Delilah now. "You cannot take her. The others are still sleeping." Delilah whips around in surprise, takes in the sleeping darknesses, turns back.

"But I don't care about the others," she says, her own desperation making her honest.

"You have to," says the old woman, "because she does not exist without them, nor they without her."

Delilah stares, her heart breaking through her body.

"I'll take you out," continues the old woman, "if you wish it. But you cannot take the Unicorn with you, as long as the others still sleep here. She is their only light. She is all that keeps them."

Go and find your flute, Sky said, *in the place where it lives. It will have found its way back, to that place where you first used it to bring someone joy.*

Go and stand in the wind, and breathe in deep. You will be breathing someone's soul into you. Then face the sea, and breathe it out, and make of that breath the music that only you can make. The music that brings the rains.

There is a parking lot here now. Abandoned cars, their doors hanging open in shock, stand still with the wind whistling through them. A stray cat, without surprise, watches what looks like a rain cloud lower itself until it almost touches the pavement, and then it becomes a boy. The boy wavers for a moment, and then walks in the direction of the cat, where she sits tight beneath a dead bush in a corner of the dark building. The cat is not surprised because she can feel that underneath the pavement is a meadow, or the memory of one. She can tell that the boy is looking for the thing the girl left for him, and that they have some shared memory of this place—as if together they make a single ghost, who once lived here when it was alive. The cat cries softly and runs away, leaving the boy to find the beautiful thing which lay beside her.

No one sees him pick it up. No one sees him fly to the top of the building with a few modest, careful steps through the air, and stand there, feeling the direction of the wind. No one sees his delicate chest swell, or sees him close his eyes as he opens his mouth.

He remembers when Lil saw him once, so long ago, closing his eyes and opening his lips like this, taking the hardness on his tongue. How she turned away, scared. And he wanted to tell her that he did it just to make the other boy weep. To make him break down with longing and ecstasy. It had nothing to do with power. He only wanted to be able to see the sweetness, the vulnerability inside a boy that no boy would let him see. He wanted the impossible. He didn't think Lil would have understood, but of course she would have; she wanted the same thing.

Please, Sky said, taking his hands. *Do me this favor. I cannot go into the City again. Send my love to where the Unicorn lies, and I'll find her there.*

Remembering the love he felt for that man with the lonely chest and the feathers at his thighs, now Moon blows, and the song takes form, as if it is something that already existed in the air and was only waiting for his breath to make it move. And as the song flows through that sacred instrument—that song that is the sound of the rains before they come—he realizes it isn't his breath, and it isn't his song. Rather it is something else that comes through him, and all this time it hasn't had anything to do with him. All this time, he hasn't had any responsibility, or anything to fight, or anything to do differently, other than just to stand here, and breathe. Just stand here, and not be ashamed to be.

The rains do not answer right away. But the clouds are gathering; the clouds are thinking. In the City around him, the hearts of men lurch for-ward, and women look up. The Earth, hearing his song, remembers, and begins to shake with longing. She shakes so hard that the walls of banks and jails, offices and convenience stores, begin to crack and even crumble. The pavement heaves up and splits, and water bursts through in fountains. Harrowed and starving, you scream as fissures open up into black mystery. You lean in, clutching at each other to keep from jumping. Something calls to you in there. Something misses you. And you didn't know! All these years, you did not even realize that you were walking upon the Earth. You see Her bare Her dry teeth, raw and bitter and dusty in the cracks, and a few of you remember: *this is where food came from once, and this was how we survived, long ago, when we owned our own survival.*

Soon the rain you did not know you were waiting for will come shattering down like glass.

And Lonely, no longer the wind but now a breath, no longer a breath but now a song, begins to fly—even though it isn't even time yet, even though she doesn't have to, but because she chooses it, because she knows somehow that the love she seeks is right there, at the very center of her loneliness, where the longing itself began—back to the island.

Inside there is only blackness and a deep, tense cold. Kite blinks, steps back and fumbles for a door handle, but the door has slammed behind him and he cannot find it.

Then he hears the breathing again, a little quieter now, but close.

"Show yourself!" he says, not out of courage but out of terror, though he does not know how someone could, since there is no light. But it feels hauntingly familiar, all of this. The cold nowhere room in the center of the unconscious City. The faceless breathing in the darkness.

When no answer comes, he turns and fumbles wildly at the knobs of cold metal. "Let me out!" But instantly he stops himself. *Panic won't help,* says a very clear voice inside him. He freezes, wondering which way to face, which way to hide his back, and it seems he hears the breathing all around him now, like raw space ripping apart.

"Who are you?" comes a voice finally from the darkness, and the voice is calmer than Kite expected, and it sounds tired or maybe just very old. It's a man is all he can tell for sure.

He turns toward it.

"Are you a god?" The voice sounds neither curious nor hopeful, and yet

Kite is afraid to answer, because he doesn't know yet what the voice wants or even what he wants. He's not even sure if it's the same voice that spoke before.

"Why is it so dark?" he asks.

"They're saying you are a god," someone says, and it's definitely a different voice this time, though it sounds the same, because it's coming from another part of the room.

"Why is it dark?" Kite repeats stubbornly, his voice unintentionally cramping into a near whisper. "Why are you so afraid to open a window?"

"There are no windows," says one of the voices.

"Why not?"

Silence. Then, "He's not a god. Just a boy."

"Throw him out."

"No." Gruffly, and from a greater distance. "He'll tell."

"Tell what?" says Kite. "I can't see anything!"

"But now you've heard our voices, and you know."

"Know what?!"

"That this is all there is."

More silence then, while Kite feels his courage rising, and hears the echo of fear in those words, whatever they mean. When he can't stand the nothingness breathing any more, he steps forward carefully and reaches out, trying to stay oriented to the door behind him.

"Where are you?" he whispers, stretching his fingers out in front of him. Closer than he expected, things crash together and clatter to some hard metallic floor, as the person nearest to him stumbles backwards to get away. They are afraid for him to touch them. Why? Suddenly he hears the fear again, which he heard so clearly when first he heard the breath through the door, and he can feel it and smell it and taste it too—acidic and tingling on his tongue, pulsing in sweaty waves against his body. How many of them are there, sitting in the darkness in silent panic?

"Who are you?" he says, trying to keep his voice calm, trying not to catch the contagion of that feeling. "You've just been living in here, in the dark?"

"There were lights," says one, after a pause. "But they went out. Don't you know?"

Of course. The City has no power. In the City, light does not come from the sun, but from something else he does not understand—something, it turns out, that even the people of the City do not understand. "Even here?"

He hears a long sigh, a sigh that spans from the top of the room to the bottom. "Even here, boy."

"So why do you stay here? Why don't you come out?"

"They'll kill us."

"But just tell them you don't have any power either."

A sound like laughter then, but not quite. "We can't tell them that."

And with more hissing laughter—"No, no," echo the other voices, and now Kite knows for sure he wasn't imagining their numbers.

"But…" Kite can feel the danger in what they're saying—the danger for himself—and he knows he should be quietly working his way back to the door, working his fingers around the knobs, trying to work out the lock. But he's too curious. He has too many questions. He is finally here, inside the Center of the City's knowledge. He wants to understand everything. Systematically, his mind begins to organize his questions, and the organization calms him and excites him at the same time. When he begins to ask those questions, he finds that the objectivity and the logical order of them seem also to calm the people in the room, for they answer readily, their voices perfectly even.

"How many of you are there?" he begins.

"Ten."

"Are you all men?"

"Of course."

"And you make—You brought the energy to the City? You made the food? You made everything?"

"Yes. This machine. This machine made everything."

"What machine?"

"This machine you're in."

"And it doesn't work any more?"

"We have no more fuel."

"Why not?"

"We've run out."

"But what was the fuel?"

A pause then, but only briefly. "It comes from inside the earth, from things that died long before humans existed."

"What things?"

"It doesn't matter."

"It does matter!" says Kite, frustrated. "It matters where we come from. Those are our ancestors, the ones who came before us. We need them. That's what you've been living on. History. That *is* the wisdom."

Silence.

"Is it—is it all gone?"

"Gone."

"And you didn't know it would run out?"

A shuffling now: discomfort in the dark. Bodies slide against themselves, fidgeting. Kite wonders what they are wearing, what they look like, how old they are. "We had no choice," someone mumbles.

"But we can get energy from other places. I know. I've read about it and I thought you knew about it here. The sun—"

The laughter-like sound again, at once uneasy and patronizing, like a nervous hand patting the head of a vicious beast. "No, that's mythology, boy."

Mythology. Kite tries to remember this word, what it's about. Isn't it a kind of story? An explanation of things? The basis for meaning in existence?

"But," he starts again, wanting to continue the thread but unable to see it. "But I read about it," he repeats.

"We don't allow those writings here," speaks a clearer, firmer voice, a little closer.

"But why not?"

"We don't allow them."

Kite can hear the quickening tension in that voice, so he stops. No one speaks for some time. He feels hopeless, suddenly. He has learned nothing, after all. These people at the Center of the world's knowledge—they don't know anything.

"Do you have food here?" he asks quietly. "How will you survive?"

A long, long pause. "We have a little food," comes the wary answer.

"But what happens when it runs out?"

"We can't open the door," explains one voice, with the first hint of emotion Kite has heard. "They would take what we have left! They would kill us!"

"But you need them!" cries Kite, for it's suddenly so clear to him. "This is the answer, I'm telling you. You need other people. You need to work together. Human beings can do anything! We can figure this out. Just go out there. Tell the truth."

But the silence that greets his words is empty. The men don't understand him. It seems as if he is speaking another language, and they cannot do what he asks. Why? Why not?

"Is it—" He tries to understand what is holding them here. "Is it Hanum? Your god?"

"Hanum?"

"Don't you believe that Hanum, the man who began the City, was a god? Don't you serve him, or something?"

"No. We run the City. Hanum—that was a long time ago. It is this machine that runs the City."

"But not any more," says Kite.

A silence, and in that silence is breath again, and in that breath, in that very hopelessness—almost—there is something like the opening of wings.

"No." Quietly. "Not any more."

Kite senses his chance. "Come on, then. Let's go," he says gently. "Let's go outside."

"But what's out there?" someone whispers.

Kite hesitates. "When was the last time you went outside?"

No answer.

"The world," Kite says, impatient now. "The world is out there."

But then the things go knocking together again, because someone is lunging forward, and not at Kite, but at someone else. Some filthy, rotting anger has been broiling in the darkness, unseen and unheard, and now there are strangled cries, and now there are shouts—sounds foreign to this closed metal room, and the layers of metal rooms above it, and the mindless limbs of the machine.

"How dare you!" comes the first choked voice. "How dare you speak of Hanum that way! He will return. He will return and take this City back. Then we will see—we will see who survives!"

Then all the men are arguing, things are toppling, and the bodies who feared Kite's touch are slamming together in violence. The building itself begins to shake, rattling its insides to pieces and hurling the bodies like refuse into piles, and Kite falls down, scrambles up, and falls again. But that solitary, calm part of him takes over—the part of him that turned his face stony toward the distant horizon when his parents argued, the part of him that walked comfortably alone through the wilderness, the part of him that walked away, as if easily, when Dragon got mad. Quietly, he gropes his way backward, shutting his mind to their panic and his own.

Maybe this whole great building is a machine, and maybe every part of this machine is operated by a tangle of complex wires and triggers and codes and electrical stimuli, like a body, if a body had no soul. But the power has gone out, and it is dead. This door that let Kite in had not let anybody in or out for how long? When was the City created? No one has ever used it. No one even remembered it was there. So there is no complicated, coded system for keeping it locked. There is only a rusty iron bar that scrapes like the latch on an old barn as Kite lifts it, and then the light blinding him.

He steps out, forgetting himself, looking up in wonder. The first tremor of the first earthquake has just passed. No one has died yet. The crowd cannot foresee what is to come. They only help each other shakily to their feet and look toward Kite, who emerged as the earth came back to stillness. Then they follow his gaze—as if he himself made the miracle—up toward the sky. The rain is coming for the first time in twenty-five years.

Later on, he will already be far away from this place. Later on, someone will tell him what happened here: the men refused to leave, and eventually the people broke in and murdered them all out of sheer fury at the nothingness they found. But Kite will never forget that darkness, as if those faceless men still shuffle forever in their own self-made jail, as if he can never escape their confused humanness or the sickening stench of their stubborn helplessness. He will never forget his disappointment, or how much he longed, inside that cold immortal place, for the warm dinner his mother would serve him in a bowl made of river clay, and the easy curl of Chelya's cheeks into laughter. He will never forget his own selfishness, when he stepped outside and was so dizzyingly grateful for the light of day that he forgot to turn around and hold the door open—forgot to call out to either the people or the men, or to hold that door with all his strength against the force of their fear, so that they wouldn't rush forward and slam it shut again behind him. Because maybe if the door had stood open then, what happened later wouldn't have happened. Maybe that was the only moment, when Kite stepped out again into that churning web of humanity, when humanity would have actually forgiven.

Because in that moment all the colors were so much brighter and at once running together in rainbows. Kite took his jug out of his pack and held it under a stream of water pouring from a gutter, and a few people saw what he was doing, and instead of shouting at him that he was a god, they did the same. People were looking up at the sky instead of at the building, and holding each other, and weeping and dancing, and you could see their wet, beautiful bodies through their clothes.

How can I describe the song that is Lonely, now that Lonely is a song? She is a song everyone knows. She is a song you remember when you close your eyes, listen, and remember that the wind knows your name.

This is the end. There is nowhere else to go but back again. Knowing that makes the longing so bright, so big, so loud inside her—Sky's memory in her mouth, in the formation of her body, in the shape of her spirit, in the very color of her eyes changed by the beauty of him—and her longing is her song; her longing is all that she is. It is a longing whose history began before the world was the world, before life knew itself and lost itself again. Before anything had a name. For the first time in her life, she feels herself a goddess, and she knows what it means to make magic—not the magic of her father who wrestled and changed things into his own image, but the magic of surrendering to a humble human need so deep and universal that its fire rips the rains right out of the sky.

Her longing—bigger than she, bigger than Sky—calls forth the rains, and they come. The rains are soothing, and she is not afraid now of returning. For she misses the sea. She misses the waters that rocked around her all through her childhood, that kept her safe, that blurred all boundaries so that everything felt possible, and that she didn't realize saved her over and over in that empty place, dowsing her soul in its depths and tossing her up reborn.

She misses the sky, which she enters into again now, as if all she ever wanted was that feeling again, of flying.

And she isn't angry or desperate, but really quiet now, in the center of her long, flying song over the sea, as she asks the wind, "But why? Why couldn't I have what I really longed for?"

"Beloved," says the wind, "you can have anything you want."

"But why did you say that time, in the meadow, when I was so alone, *Love is right here, all around you?* It wasn't enough for me, the love of grasses and flowers. It wasn't enough!"

"I was only telling the truth. You are love—all the time."

"But I needed the love of another. You mocked me. You would never help me."

"You never asked."

And Lonely! *Lonely.* She feels very soft then.

What once was Lonely flies and flies, through all the colors of the sunset, as the wheel of the rainbow winds back into darkness.

"Do you know yet, Princess, what you truly longed for? Do you know yet what longing is for?"

And she feels the purity of it, the virginity of it: that longing. Inside that longing, she is absolutely whole.

She remembers that first awakening on the sand, that first breath, the drops of water on Yora's throat. She remembers the horse endlessly rocking beneath her and the meadow spinning her in dazzling light. The song of crickets, the nights dissolving in open earth, the animals talking, the wind making her laugh. The story of the desert on the soles of her feet, the miracle of water, the hooded mystery of the vultures, the rising of Dragon in the river, his touch and the untouchable fire. The black hole of the rainbow, the journey of the waterfall, Moon's single, tender, forever kiss, and the forest's silent, wet surrender. The weightless embrace of trees, the firm arms of Rye, the first breakfast with Fawn and Chelya, the goats who knew her, the drumbeats, the forbidden kiss, and her own story in Eva's old, complex face. The muscle in her own legs, climbing and climbing, and the dream of the river beside her, and the determination of the Unicorn, and the kiss of waking. And every moment she spent with him—in the clouds, in the meadow that bloomed, in the lake, in the snow—whether with him in flesh or searching for him in dreams, finding him in every animal, every person, every living thing. Always that longing was what made her alive and what made life worth living. That bright tension, holding her to the divine.

It's okay, she whispers to the people—to the children abandoned in the streets, to the teenagers who left their families long ago, to the old people locked in rotting buildings, to the husbands and wives who cannot remember what desire felt like, to each and every woman and man who thinks no one will ever understand. *It's okay*, whispers the wind, who is Lonely. *Everyone is lonely. Everyone.*

Rain, rain, rain. And what is her name? It is this song, played through a flute by a boy on a rooftop—a song of risk and longing and forgiveness. But the song is too long and complicated to remember or repeat, and so she, like everyone, ended up with some strange, misleading abbreviation.

Like everyone else, she could only remember that word. *Lonely.*

The old woman never had a name. Because she was chosen from infancy to meet with the goddess, because she was never meant to live that kind of personal, human life in which one loves and is loved for one's differentness, and feels that one's personality is one's soul, she was never given a name. She was meant, from the first, to embody something greater than herself. From the time she was born, the divine was channeled through her, so that she became a vehicle for beauty, a receptacle for light, with no name but the breathlessly uttered, the reverently whispered, "She."

It was dangerous to be given such power. But her people had done this over and over, for as long as they had existed. Every thirteen years, a woman was given to the Goddess. And they knew she would be safe from the unwieldy egotism that such power could bring, as well as from the fear of death, as long as they never gave her a name.

When Hanum took her, he called her "my love". That was his name for her. But later, when he no longer loved her, he stopped calling her by that name. He called her other names, always changing and never kind. So she knew that wasn't her real name. The Bright Goddesses across the sea, at the other end of the river, call her Dark Goddess—but she is not She. Once she was a child, once a girl, once a virgin, once a lover, once "woman" with reverence, once "woman" with scorn, and now an old woman, now a "witch". Yet she knows herself. She recognizes herself, in a way she did not when she was young—if not by a name, then by something else: perhaps by pain itself, or by the very things she has lost.

Things were lost because she did not take the path that was destined for her. She turned away and lived another life—a life she chose but which she could never understand, a life lived in the shadow of the life she should have lived.

She used to think that the real Dark Goddess would never speak with her again, once she had turned her back, once she ran away with Hanum for this other life. But when she came to the island, and Hanum turned away from her forever, she found the Dark Goddess here waiting for her after all, speaking to her in the voice of the sea, and this is the only real conversation she has ever had since.

Perhaps she is immortal now, like the gods. For some reason, she has not needed food for a very long time. She belongs to water and also to earth, while Hanum was made of air and fire, neither of which she has ever since trusted. Yet it was fire—a falling star fizzling out above the ocean's horizon— that told her of Delilah's coming. And now it is the wind, always present and yet never before speaking to her, which tells her of her daughter's return.

Above her, the moon is losing her invisible child, bit by bit, like she always does. Nothing is ever kept. Nothing is ever safe. The moon, now, is almost gone, but the old woman's daughter is returning, and for what?

She always told herself she would feel nothing. Yet when Delilah held her before—the first time anyone had touched her in many, many years—she realized the tension she had kept in her spine and her hands and her face, the tension that had held her for eleven moons in expectation of her daughter's return. She also realized, to her surprise, that she wanted to know that her daughter had succeeded, after all. She wanted to know that she had found him. She wanted to know what he looked like now, what he felt like, what he sounded like, and if that fire still lit his eyes.

Now, sitting again at the edge of the sea, she feels Lonely's body near her. Once, the old woman was also a mother. Once, this girl's body was part of her—aching inside her, stretching her insides wide, yawning her open. Once, she nearly died for this body, and was reborn again in the hope its tiny fingers and big eyes brought her. Now she feels nothing. Or almost nothing.

"You're not as frightening as I remember you," says the girl. The old woman can feel her youth—those young, stubbornly fervent thighs near her own crooked knees, that quickly beating heart leaning over her own head. She remembers how ashamed she felt on that night so many moons ago, of her own daughter's desperate loneliness and determination to seek out one man. Yet she admired it too, didn't she? Now there is something changed about this girl. No anger now, demanding and selfish. No fear, that fear that made her stupid—made her think she couldn't get off the island on her own.

No sorrow—that sorrow that blurred her, that she didn't understand she was carrying. No, now there is only some deep peace. Some strange, deep peace that the old woman, who has sat here for more years than she can count, has never felt.

"Why didn't you tell me?" comes the inevitable question. "Why didn't you tell me who you were? Why didn't you tell me you knew him?" But her daughter's voice still holds no anger.

The old woman shrugs, not raising her head. "I am no story-teller." Her voice hurts. She had hardly spoken to anyone in years, and today she has already had to explain things to two people. And there is so much more for her to explain. Too much.

"Who will tell me then?" asks the girl. "My father would not tell me. Sky would not tell me."

"Ah," she closes her eyes and nods almost involuntarily. "Sky. Is that his name?"

"No. That wasn't his real name. But you know his real name, the name he had before. Don't you?"

"No, I do not. I never knew anyone's name."

The girl is silent then, and the old woman is, too, except that she seems to hear someone screaming. It could be she herself who is screaming, but she isn't sure. She remembers, eleven moons ago, that scream she heard from the tower, how it knocked her and dragged her down to the stones on her knees, how it took her breath away with grief, how almost—almost—she wanted to go to her daughter, finally, at last, but even then she could not reach the top of the tower, even once Hanum was dead. Even then, it was closed to her.

Now, gradually, she becomes aware that someone is shaking her. Her daughter's thin hands, bony-strong, around her shoulders. But no, it is she who is shaking, and her daughter is holding her still. Like before, only before it was that girl Delilah. Life repeats itself, a spiral passing the same point over and over again as it turns ever inward, each time more painful than the last.

Gradually, the island becomes quiet again, and the old woman becomes so still that only her heart is moving. Water runs down her face, and she doesn't understand where it comes from.

"Mother," says the girl, and the old woman strains forward, wanting to hear it again to be sure, wanting to hear it again and again and again. "There is no proof. I have brought no proof for you, of the love I feel, and the love that he gave me. But it is everywhere. If you cannot feel it, then I am truly sorry for you."

The old woman shakes her head. "Neither of us," she says. And she means to say, "Neither of us have names." She means to say, "No one has a name.

We are only what others call us. We have nothing of our own." But she's not sure if she finished the sentence.

The girl says, "Please. I want to know the truth. I want to know who I am."

The old woman takes a deep breath. One more answer, and then truly, she will rest, and never speak again. "The truth is within," she whispers. "Deep within. You wander this island. You wander in the dark; you come to the place where you are most afraid. You come to the place where the tower once stood. There is nothing there but a black hole in the stone. You go in there. You go inside."

She waits, but the girl has not gone. Stupid girl. Why does she stay? The old woman begins to rock, trying to pick up the rhythm of the waves again, trying to forget that the girl is there. Finally, the girl is holding her hands in her own. Now these hands feel different: soft, luscious, and deep.

"Mother," she says. "I forgive you."

Then she is gone.

The woman tries to call out—because she knows now: she knows what she wanted to say, and it wasn't about truth, and it wasn't about names, and it wasn't about Sky—but she has no voice.

So she sits. These past eleven moons, she has felt, in the sea's conversation—sometimes passionate, sometimes calm—when exactly the moon grew full and emptied out; she has felt, on purpose, the exact passage of time. But now her daughter has returned, and for what? Nothing has changed. So she returns to the kind of time she always knew before that, time that does not pass but swirls around her, nebulous and meaningless. What has time ever given her? Here on the island there is no summer, no winter; here in her blindness there is no day, no night. Despair makes time irrelevant.

So maybe years pass, or maybe only moments. The rocks murmur the same old tunes. The sea cuddles into them, then whisks dramatically away, then comes tiptoeing back, delighting in its own ridiculous drama. Once, the old woman thinks she feels two spiders alight on her left shoulder. Then she thinks they are not spiders after all but feet—the feet of some delicate bird. The bird is silent, but when she listens to that silence, she notices a sense of peace in a deep cavern just beneath her heart—a peace she had forgotten was there. Inside that peace, inside that silence, she hears her daughter's words again: *I forgive you.* When the bird lets go, she thinks she feels its wings blow by her face, brushing through her hair like the fingertips of a lover who touched her so long ago and yet whose touch her body remembers like it was yesterday.

This grief is going to kill her when she lets it in. She has always known this. But would it be so bad, to finally let go?

When will they come, then? She imagines she can feel them coming, already. The ones who haunt her now, like they haunted Hanum. She imagines them like hungry, angry crows, flapping up from the shadows between the stones. She imagines their silent footsteps, their little cries as their bare feet—so long unused, so long pressed to nothingness—tear and wobble over the uneven stones, and the hiss of their breathing.

In every whimper of the sea and the wind, she thinks she hears them coming. *The Mad Ones*. The ones he kept in darkness all these years. For they must come, they must wake, if the girl who calls herself *sister* insists on bringing Mira away with her—they must come, too. She could tell that the sister, Delilah, will have her way. She will not leave Mira behind, no; nothing will stop her.

But oh, when the Mad Ones wake, how they will hate her! How terribly they will wail in her ears, saying if she had never called Hanum's attention to their brokenness, their poverty, their violence, their suffering, their madness—if she had never pointed her angry finger, not knowing his language but pointing as if to say, *How can you tell me this City is perfect? How can you tell me it is good, when there is this, when people suffer like this?*—then he would never have gotten angry, and he would never have sent his men to take them, one by one, away to a forgotten island, so that no one else would see. The Mad Ones always spoke the truth. That's why he took them away, locked them in the darkness, and drugged them to sleep. She is a traitor, though she did not mean to be. She betrayed them, like she betrayed her own people when she went with Hanum. No wonder the Dark Goddess claimed her after all. Not one good thing has she ever done.

She waits for them to come, waits for them—oh, terrible. She tenses her face with the waiting, rocking and rocking.

But someone is speaking to her, and it is not the Mad Ones. Someone has been trying to get her attention. The old woman focuses on the voice, which is coming not from behind her, where she expected them to come, but from right in front of her.

"Queen," Delilah is saying. "Queen of this Island."

"What?" she hisses irritably. "What did you call me?"

"Queen," repeats the warrior girl, with some kind of incongruent joy in her voice. "If your daughter is a princess, then you are the queen."

The old woman has to laugh at that. She respects this girl, who has a sense of humor, even though she herself does not.

Delilah's voice comes from down lower than Lonely's did; she is kneeling again. She has the Unicorn with her. The old woman can see that light—the only light she has ever been able to see since she lost her sight.

"Your daughter has offered to sleep down there in place of my—in place of the Unicorn," Delilah is saying. "She said to the Unicorn, 'I will sleep here in your place, to redeem the mistakes of my father.' So the other people are still down there with her. Do you understand me?"

The old woman nods, and yet she does not understand. *My daughter,* she thinks, remembering the young woman who came to her only a moment— or was it a year?—ago. Is she still here? Didn't she go? *But how could I be a mother?* The old woman thinks suddenly, confused. *I am so young—only thirteen, fourteen years old! Like little Mira. My life ended on that beach of dead trees, long ago, when I found out I could never go home.* However old she is supposed to be now, she does not feel wise.

"So we're going back through the sea," the warrior girl is saying now. "Yora will carry us. Goodbye, Queen."

The old woman with no name nods. She feels something wet on her knuckles, and doesn't understand, and only long after she is alone again, does she realize that Delilah kissed her hands in farewell.

She stands up now. She opens her hands, lets go of an imaginary string, and imagines the waves pulling it out. "I am done now," she says to the bright beings in the distance across the world, whose sweet voices once called *her* the Dark Goddess, and comforted her from a mystical garden of love on a mountain far away that she would never see. A place she could never get to, a place opposite of all that she had become. "Release me. I am gone."

She turns around. She feels for the chair, and moves past it. Then she walks deftly, without stumbling, to the place where she knows the entrance is. She feels shaky with relief, and the relief bleeds into a kind of escalating urgency. The steps feel watery beneath her. Her hands stretch out, pressing against each cold wall. Her knees weaken with each step. It's as if she is returning to that same cave, that cave where once she hid her agony, her terrifying transformation into motherhood—and where once she thought she was finally safe, and where her daughter was torn from her arms for the first and last time.

She has reached the bottom. She knows the exact number of the steps without counting. Maybe gravity is stronger down here, closer to the center, or maybe it's because she is so old and has already taken two long walks today—down and up and down again. But she finds herself sinking to her hands and knees now, grasping at the cold hard ground, her body touching other bodies, recoiling faintly.

"Oh," she says sadly, in this darkness which is no more dark to her than the light, feeling forward with her fingers, feeling the bony rib cage of some- one sleeping who turns and groans under her touch. They are so old now, old like her. When Hanum was alive she used to sleep down here among them, curling around their unconscious bodies—bodies that were only memories of the lives that once lived in them, that had not needed food for years and years—and she would mumble her memories into their unhearing ears, in her own language. But after Hanum died, she stopped coming. She sat out on the rocks, haunted by her own guilt, and sometimes they tossed in nightmares below her and began to scream, and she did not know how long it would be before they were silent again.

"I did not mean to," she moans softly now, touching the thin hair on a bony, sleeping head. The touch of it horrifies her, like a corpse, but she cannot stop. "I did not mean to betray you. I did not mean for you to end up here."

"It's okay, Mother," comes a light, clear voice. "None of us mean to do what we do, not really."

"Daughter," the old woman cries, hurrying forward on her hands and knees. The voice sounds close, and yet far. How wide this room is—if it is even a room, or if it even has walls and doesn't expand endlessly into space, for she has never known. "My daughter, where are you?" She hears herself—her horrible, choked-monster voice—and what is she? What has she become? A bitter, twisted creature, without light, without love, barely human, without one good thought to redeem her, crawling below the earth. She crawls over the bodies, not caring. She drags herself.

But her daughter's voice is simple and clear. "Here I am," she says. As if they two are standing together in a lit green place, the sun filtering between the trees, looking across into each other's eyes. As if they could walk right to each other, and take each other's hands, and go carefree together through a bright forest, where there are no dangers from below and no magicians from above. Just the two of them.

The old woman crawls forward. "Right here," says her daughter again, softly, and the old woman recollects herself—she is, after all, the elder—and gets up on her knees and takes her daughter's hand, where her daughter is lying on the floor.

"You have no bed to lie on!" the old woman cries.

"It's all right," says her daughter. "Soon I will be asleep, and it won't matter."

The old woman begins to sob. She knows it. She can feel it now. It is she herself who is sobbing. "Oh, but you will never wake," she cries.

"No, no," says the girl, caressing her hand. "Don't cry, Mother. I will wake. We will all wake, me and the others. For he is coming back to me, and he will see what this place is. He will see in the dark, as we cannot, because he is a Dream God, Mother."

The old woman shakes her head. "Who?" she mutters. "Who will come? No one will come."

"Yes," says her daughter gently, patting her hand. "You never believed, but he will come. Perhaps that will be the proof you always wanted! You will see. He has to come, because the world is round, and love is round, and so he will end up back here with me, because there is nowhere else to go."

"Aren't you afraid?" asks the old woman suddenly, drying her eyes, taking her daughter's head into her lap. For what the girl says frightens her, though she does not know why. She does not believe it.

There is a moment of silence then, and the old woman wonders in a panic if her daughter is already sleeping. But then, "No," comes the slow answer. "It's strange, but I'm not afraid. You said that I would come back here, and it's not so bad as I thought. I've been in underground places before. One time I was with an older woman like you. Her name is Eva. She has a peaceful, candlelit room under the earth, in a hillside, and that's where she dreams her dreams. She brought me down there to tell me the story of my father, and where I come from, for the first time. Also, underneath her daughter's house, there was a dark place like this too, where they kept all the food. It was a place of nourishment and safety. You'd go down there, and know that you had everything you needed. Once there was a boy down there—so young, so innocent, looking into the dark places where no one else looks, for the roots of things—and we shared a secret moment, that no one will ever know."

The old woman is holding her daughter's hand so tightly that she doesn't even realize it until the girl moves her fingers a little, trying to loosen the grip. Who is this beautiful, beautiful girl, and what has she done, and what has she lived? The old woman tries to remember the word again: *daughter.* How could it be that she has a daughter? For it seems that this woman lying in her lap knows so much of the world. She seems so wise. And she herself, the old woman, is so young—only thirteen years old—and she does not know anything but this island and the sea. She does not know anything except that this grief has been lurking around her forever, like an unshrinking fog hanging over the island, like a destiny of brutal ending, and it is beginning to creep closer. Yes, it is beginning to close in around her.

"Mother," the young woman says now, "did you make that bed for me?"

The old woman leans closer. "What bed?"

"The bed I lay in, in the tower. The bed I always slept in. Made of feathers and clouds, grasses and earth. My father could never make a bed like that."

No, the mother thinks. *I never saw you again. I never did anything for you.* But she doesn't want to tell her daughter that. And now as she traces her daughter's face with her fingertips, she does seem to remember, in her mind and in her hands, a bed that she wove together out of whatever she could find on the beach—a place she prepared for herself and her infant, in advance, knowing what would happen. It is possible that Hanum took that bed, just as he took away everything else that belonged to her. "Maybe I did make it," she whispers.

"I thought so," says her daughter, and sighs a sigh that makes the old woman sigh, too. The grief is coming. Oh, it is coming down, it is coming in, like the ocean. But in a way it feels soft, and so good, more precious than the touch of a lover—more real, even, than the voice of the Goddess.

"I want to know your story," says Lonely.

"But I want to know yours," says the old woman. "And we don't have much time."

"Please," begs Lonely. "Because you are my mother, and I need you to. Please."

I am the mother, the old woman thinks again, and she remembers the cave. She has never been able to give her daughter anything, but for one meal from her own breast, before she was taken away. At the very least, she can give her this much—one sad story, all that she has to give.

"But first tell me," she says to her daughter, "why did you give yourself? Why did you sacrifice yourself to set Mira and her sister free?"

"Because I feel responsible. I mean not guilty, but the way I feel responsible to everyone who has done so much for me in this life. Like my father, who was only trying to love me. And Yora, Dragon, Moon, Fawn, Rye, Chelya, and Eva, and Sky, and the animals and the trees—everyone who gave me so much, helped me so much on my journey. And Delilah, who was my mirror and who saved my life, who helped me even though she didn't understand me, even though it cost her to do so. But especially, especially the Unicorn, who carried me to my dream, without whom I may never even have left the shore and never known where to go, and to whom I never gave anything in return. I wanted to set her free. Doesn't that make sense?"

"Yes," says the old woman.

"And who knows," continues the young voice with urgency, "but that these people sleeping are not my brothers and sisters. Who knows—they could be all the forgotten children of my father, that he made in that City, children of all the peoples he—he raped and—that he denied. For you know, Mother, you know that he was terrible."

Then she begins to cry.

"Don't cry," says the mother. For she cannot bear it, and yet she cannot think of a single word of comfort. "You are braver than me," she says finally. "I refused to give of myself and have paid ever since."

"Please," murmurs the girl. "Tell me."

"What do you want to know?"

"Were they going to sacrifice you to the Dark Goddess, in the swamp?"

The old woman hesitates. She did not expect this to be the first question. She expected questions about Hanum, about Sky, about the men. This part of the story, for her, came before the story even began, and she never questioned it.

"I was chosen from birth," she says slowly, "to meet with the Dark Goddess. The Dark Goddess spoke to me always. My whole life. From our union—the union of me and her—the Unicorn would be reborn. That was my destiny."

"Do you mean you would become the Unicorn, or that the Unicorn would be born of…? What does it mean, mother?"

"I don't know. I was not really *I*—I was not an individual person the way other people were. I was raised differently, kept by myself. I cannot explain it."

"But what was the Unicorn for? What would the Unicorn do, once it rose again?"

"What would it do?"

"Yes. What was its purpose?"

"I don't know. It was just the Unicorn. It was pure beauty. It was everything we long for, without understanding what we long for, when we think we long for other things. Haven't you seen the Unicorn, child? Haven't you ever seen something so beautiful that it was simply enough?"

"Yes," whispers Lonely.

"Well, then." Hearing silence again, the old woman continues. "It was not seen as a sacrifice. There was nothing to give up, because I had always been destined for this. At least—I did not think there was anything to give up, until I saw Hanum."

"You saw him? When did you see him?"

"When he was waiting for me there, in the sky. I saw him."

"Then what? What happened?"

The old woman sighs. "I know I was chosen for this rite, I know. But sometimes I wonder, was I not the right one after all? Because I was willful and romantic, though I did not always know it. I had been taught to *be* all the light parts of being, so that I could meet the Dark Goddess as her opposite, and the light and the dark could join. So up until then, all sense of those dark things—lust, greed, selfishness, betrayal, rebellion, anger, dark passion, grief—had been connected only with Her, while I was only the light, the gentler love, compassion, wisdom, spirit. But when I saw Hanum, I felt those dark things rise up in me. I felt that they were in me, after all. I also saw, for the first time, my own beauty—reflected in his eyes. I thought, why should

I be sacrificed? For it seemed like a sacrifice then. I thought, why should I be forced to this suffering, when this powerful, magical man comes to rescue me? I saw him coming. I knew he would come. I began to feel things I never knew I could feel." She sighs. "And so."

She had never known the relief that could come with telling one's story. She had never even known she had a story. All this time….

"Was it Sky, who tried to stop you?"

"Yes, but I did not know him. I did not know—intimately, by name—anyone in the village."

"What did you say to him, to make him stop fighting?"

"I told him to stop. I told him I *wanted* to go. I know that shamed him. But I could not bear the guilt of seeing him fight so hard for me, when I knew, somehow, that this was my fault. I had longed for it. I was betraying my people, and I knew it, and I did not want this boy to get hurt or killed for me."

"How old were you then?"

"Thirteen."

She can feel her daughter thinking. "How old were you when you had me?"

"Fourteen, I think."

"Then I must be very old, because you are so old, and you were young when you had me."

She shrugs. "Who knows. I do not understand time that way. I know, when I lived in the City, I aged perhaps a hundred years. And when you lived in the tower, you did not age at all."

"What happened? Did you ever love my father?"

"I don't know. I thought that I did. I loved the idea of this new life, this adventure, this whole new possibility I had never dreamed of, of what my life could be and who I could be. He treated me like a princess. He made me know something of myself for the first time, with all the good and the bad that such knowing brings. But then I began to feel homesick—for the safety, the safe ancient wisdom of my people cradling me, and for the place and the sense of belonging and even the Dark Goddess who had loved me—and he became angry. He did not love me any more. Then I felt so lonely, because we could not even speak each other's language, and I felt so guilty for betraying my people, and I thought all the time of that boy who had tried to stop me. I wondered who all those people were who had loved and worshipped me, that I had never even known. I wished, sometimes, that this boy would come after me, and rescue me back from the man I *thought* had rescued me—but who had actually ruined me."

"What happened in the City?" Her daughter's voice sounds a little drowsy now. The old woman notices the part of the story she skips, but says nothing.

She knows they will come around to it again. She knows intuitively that the girl is saving it for last, a final treasure before she falls asleep.

"Hanum cursed and blinded me, as punishment for showing him all that he did not want to see. And also, I think, so that I would not follow him. It was because of my blindness that I could not find my way out of the City and never returned to you to try to claim you." But then she knows that is not the whole truth. "Also," she admits, "I was afraid."

"Then how did you come back to the island?"

The old woman's answers are brief now. She feels her daughter fading, and is ready for her own death—which she feels so clearly now—to come more quickly and make the final blow. How nice it would be, if she could die before her daughter goes silent forever. "Hanum made his men remove the Mad Ones—the ones who suffered openly in the streets, the ones who spoke the truth about the City's illusion. He had them removed to this island, and above it he built your tower, to hide them. One day, they removed me, too. I had become one of them."

"And what did he say, when you came to the island with the Mad Ones?"

"Nothing. I had learned his language by this time—your language, the language everyone speaks in the City and almost everywhere—but it did not matter. He denied me. He said he did not know me. I had one brief moment of happiness again, the last I have ever known, when they told me you were up there in the tower. But then I found out I would never see you again." The grief is crushing her now, very gradually, taking her breath away bit by bit....

"Why didn't he lock you up with the others?"

"Because he needed me. I was willing to care for them. I could soothe them, help keep them quiet. Because of where I came from, I could speak to the spirits of things, and for a while I was able to convince the River Goddess, Yora, to come here and give them the love I did not have to give. I could catch fish from the sea, and harvest the seaweed and the snails, and keep us fed so that he did not have to do it. Until we all began to change into something else. Until somehow, we no longer seemed to need food."

"But what have you done all these years? How have you survived?" The old woman hears the tears in her daughter's voice.

"The ocean talked to me," she says. "The Dark Goddess spoke to me again, through the ocean. And then through the ocean and through the thread of the river, the Bright Goddesses on a faraway mountain began to talk to me, too. We talked about the cycles of the world, and I understood that what was happening would not always be happening, that though I might die in misery, someday beyond me the world would turn again, and things would be right again. As I did in the beginning, I denied everything human in myself. I denied that I had ever loved. I denied that I had ever been a lover, or a mother."

"Don't they call *you* the Dark Goddess? Why do they call you that?"

"Because I understand Her. Though I ran from Her, it was that very darkness that made me do so, and I know who she is, and I know her power. I came back to her in the end, without even trying. We always come back to our fates anyway, daughter. Hanum, running away from destruction, only created it again on this side of the world. You, running away from this island, came back. And I, fleeing the Dark Goddess, became Her."

"And the Unicorn was born of it after all."

"Maybe so. But this Unicorn was born of pain and suffering, a sacrifice forced upon her—ah, something you should never have to know."

"But Mother, listen. What if you didn't do anything wrong? What if you did exactly what you were supposed to do? What if everything you did was your way of meeting with, living with, experiencing that darkness within yourself? What if you were sacrificed to the Dark Goddess after all, but in a different way? Haven't you suffered enough, Mother? What if all you have to do is forgive yourself, and it will be all right?"

The old woman bows her head. *Maybe, maybe.* But soon her daughter will be lost to her forever, again. What else matters? And she has not told her daughter that she killed Hanum herself. It is too much for a child to bear.

Now they are silent, and the old woman feels desperate, knowing her daughter will soon be asleep and all will be lost, wanting something sweeter than all this darkness, wanting to lift herself out of it but overpowered by her own grief, as if she lies prone at the bottom of the sea.

Lonely says, "I wonder who he really was."

"Who?"

"Sky. He did rescue me, after all. He was that white bird that opened my heart so I could see beyond the tower. But I still had to make my own journey, and I had to come back here, and go deeper, and understand the truth of things. Sometimes I think of him now, and it seems so long ago, what we shared, that I wonder if I still remember him right or if I ever really knew him. The longing, sometimes, feels more real than he does. But then, sometimes I remember little moments—looking into each other's eyes in a cloud, holding hands while we flew, hearing his stories of dreams, seeing his tears in the meadow I made bloom for him one perfect morning, touching and forgiving each other in the lake—and I think, that was so much! I had everything then! Why wasn't that enough? Why did I always want more?"

"There is no such thing as love." The old woman says it again, because it is the only advice she knows to give. "At least not the kind that people imagine."

"But there is. There is, Mother. It's just so hard to let it in. It takes courage. It takes the bravest kind of person to be happy."

The old woman sighs. "Perhaps. I never was brave."

"But now I know where I got my courage from," cries her daughter with renewed passion. "I got it from you. I jumped into the unknown like you did. And I had the greatest adventure. Nothing could stop me—I traveled so far!"

The old woman strokes her daughter's fluid, milkweed hair. "It is foolish to go running after love, child. That is what I tried to tell you. We think we see love, but we do not know what love is. We see only a silly fantasy, a mocking mirror of ourselves. Hanum and I, we never saw each other, never knew who we were."

"Then why did you push me off the island," insists Lonely, "and challenge me to go after my dreams?"

The old woman is silent. She does not know.

"Come down here," says her daughter quietly, "and hold me."

So the mother wraps her body around the daughter, crying as she does so because she realizes that this is all she ever wanted, but she was afraid to do it without being asked, afraid her daughter would no longer want her.

"Did you have a name for me?" is the girl's final question, the question the old woman has been expecting.

"Of course. What mother does not name her child?"

She feels the girl take a wild, surprised breath, suddenly more awake again. "But why didn't you tell me?"

The old woman sighs. *Because I thought I had no more love to give. Because I thought my motherhood had been taken away from me. Because I could not bear to love you. I could not bear to hope again.* "Because it is in another language," she says. "My language, from where I come from."

"Is that Sky's language, too?"

"Yes." She feels the sadness of this, for her daughter—that Sky kept his own language secret from her—but she doesn't know what to say.

"Tell me my name," whispers her daughter. "Tell me my name, as I fall asleep."

"Our language is different than yours," begins the old woman. "It is made of different sounds. We did not use our voices as much as you—as much as the people of the City do. The breath that makes voice was sacred to us and saved for sacred purposes. When we talked with each other, intimately, person to person, our language was made instead of sounds that we formed with our mouths and hands, without voice." She says a couple of things for Lonely, to show her. *I love you,* she says. *You are so beautiful I can almost see you,* she says. She says these things with soft sweeps and clicks of her tongue, her lips, her teeth, her fingers tapping on the ground. There are some words that cannot even be said without the earth or the elements to make sound against with one's body. And all of these kinds of words are awkward for her, because this personal human language was not one she ever used in the holy life that was given to her.

"Our voices we only used for sacred communication," she continues, "like prayer, or to speak of sacred things. Usually, a person's name is a little bit of both. A little bit of voice-sound, for the god in them, and a little bit of human-body-mouth sound, for the human in them and all the other people's love for them that makes them what they are."

She takes a deep breath, hears only silence from Lonely, and continues quickly.

"I don't know much about naming, because I only ever heard a few names in my whole life. But I named you the best I could. Your name—it's like this." Then she says it. It starts with a light kissing sound, and flows into a long wailing "aaaaiiiii," and ends on a low, contented hum. Then she has to struggle harder to explain, because saying the name aloud has made her begin to lose her control over Hanum's language, the language she learned more recently. "It means—It means something like hope. Where hope begins, where it takes you...."

But her daughter is silent, her breaths deep and even, and the space between each breath is as dark and final as the sea.

So the old woman says her daughter's name, over and over again, and the sound of that name is the sound the waves have always made against this bony shore on stormy nights, over and over, though she never admitted to it until now.

And she herself does not sleep, and she does not die yet after all, and when—a long while later—she hears footsteps coming lightly, slowly, down the stairs, she knows why.

The water rains down. Finally, like a god that is no longer a cloudy dream in the sky but closer in—closer to the center, here among the people—it slicks you down, pressing you to the earth.

Who was he? you ask yourselves, as reality falls away beneath you and bares your hearts to fear. As the quakes begin again, most of you run; a few of you stand still.

Who was he? you ask as you hold each other in streets you once recognized by name, and as reality transforms, solids breaking apart and crumbling while the wind rolls into liquid form.

The rain has stopped now. But not the wind. The rain did not rain long enough to dampen the sparks that ignite from the wires, that fall when the ground shakes itself loose from the concrete.

Who was he, whom we trusted without question, and for whom we gave up the life of our ancestors—a life we can no longer remember?

Husbands and wives are buried beneath this wreckage—they have been calling out for days. Computers, which had no programs for survival, freeze like prehistoric jewels, and then fade and pile up in the rubble. You must return to recognizing your friends by their faces alone. What happened to the elders in the old people's home? No one can get into that building. The teachers who tried to keep the schools running now gather their weeping flocks in the broken classrooms and try to remember their first aid lessons.

Who was he, that he could cage the imagination of an entire people?

In the hospitals that still stand, and even in the ones that do not, there are those of you who are staying alive to help other people, to save each other. You are not trying to be heroes; it is just what you do.

Who was he? Did he truly love us?

Was he a man or a god?

What did he want?

Do you wonder it with hatred, with bitterness, or with tears, like children betrayed? Those few of you who never fit in, who were strange and sensitive, who could never quite manage in this world—though you will be the first to die—wonder it with a tenderness you can neither explain nor defend.

In his lifetime, he had everything: ultimate loss, courageous adventure, romantic bliss, ecstatic love, bitter disappointment, the dizzying power of success, despair, nostalgia, desire, the touch of his own sweet child, the beauty of his own dreams. He got to feel everything, and yet nobody knows him at all, and he died alone, and he died weeping.

Hanum. You know only his name.

At first the old woman will not look up. Stubborn with shame, she follows the lines of his feet, the bent grace of the bones that crease a knife's edge between his ankles and his elegant, golden toes. She waits for him to speak, but when he doesn't, pride she did not even know she still had fountains up her spine, and before she knows it she is looking into his eyes. Then she realizes she *is* looking. She can see him, all lit up and pure, as if the room were full of light.

She drinks in his face, his whole body. She recognizes the vulnerable stretch of skin over his thin breast bone—a design she held in her memory since that first and only moment she ever saw him, without realizing that she remembered it, without realizing that she even saw it. She sees the swell of his breast and remembers his young shoulders stretching apart, his body thrust forward in challenge, his murderous eyes. But now his hands are soft at his sides, and beneath that boyish breastbone she can see his heart trying to hold still. She can see right into him.

She can see the surprise in his eyes when she lifts her head, the recognition, and then the door that shuts over it. And as soon as he shuts that door in his eyes, she is herself again: a blind old woman in a black cave in the middle of a nowhere sea. She cannot see him any more. But she knows he is there.

"Prince," she says in their language, "will you help an old woman?" She holds out her hand. Stiffly, he takes it in his, and she feels the force of his body in the pull. But she cannot stand like this. "Aaagh," she cries out, her spine cracking.

"Sorry," he whispers hurriedly, apparently coming to his senses, and kneels to help her up bit by bit, her body slung over his shoulders in a tangle of veins and skin and hollow bones and wrinkled-up heart. By the time he has finally brought her to standing, they are holding each other as intimately as lovers. She feels his gentle, respectful lifting and turning, his polite hands, the hidden heat in his chest and pelvis, and she nearly falls again with the weight of this new, hopeless longing. *Ah, it could have been like this. This could have been mine. Or could it?* Then she remembers. He would only have rescued her for death. He would only have carried her into the waiting jaws of the Dark Goddess.

Now he stands back awkwardly again. "You're still young," she says dryly. "You haven't been living down here, on the earth, like me."

"Grandmother," he begins, using the respectful term for an elder, as if he does not know her.

"Oh, stop," she tells him irritably. "Don't pretend you don't recognize me."

She feels him shift his weight. She focuses her blind eyes on the spot where she thinks his heart is. She waits. But he doesn't respond.

"What? You are angry with me. I turned you away, yes? Tell me."

Silent.

"Sky," she says softly. She hears him draw in his breath, feels the anger in that breath, anger at the threat of his own feelings, perhaps. "That is your name?"

"Yes."

"What is your real name?"

"Sky," he says again, his voice hard.

"Sky," she shakes her head, "you torture yourself over nothing. I did not reject you. I was only afraid. I was young and stupid. You came to claim me for my own death, did you not? I was only afraid. Can't you understand that?"

Silence. And then: "Yes."

"Why did you try to stop me?"

Silence.

"Why?" she repeats.

She hears him take a deep breath. "Because it wasn't right. Because if the rite wasn't completed, the world— Everything would come undone. I had to fight—"

"Oh!" she cries out, lifting her arms. "*If the rite wasn't completed.* Be serious! You stand there, hurt. Tell me the truth. Be brave, boy! Tell the truth."

She feels his tears coming, feels them wash over him. "Because I wanted you for mine," he whispers. "Because I was jealous."

"There," she says gently, taking him in her arms. "There now, it's not so bad, is it? We were only silly and young. It's not important now." But in her heart she is so tired. He is just like Hanum. Another childish boy who thought he knew what was best for her, who, terrified of his own feelings, hid them behind grand statements of righteousness and worldly purpose. Another boy who wanted to decide her future for her. Well, she decided her own future, in the end. Even if it gave her nothing, even if it yielded nothing but years and years of empty sea, still she had chosen.

"Now," she says, standing him back again, feeling him square his shoulders between her hands and obligingly letting him go, "what did you come here to fight for this time?"

"For love," he says.

The old woman feels her daughter's breathing, that warm sleep behind her in the blackness where he cannot see. She knows she can feel her own daughter's presence in a way that Sky never can. But she nods. "Good. It's foolish what she is doing. It is too long that women have had to pay for the sins of their fathers and lovers."

They stand there silent now, and in only a moment they are both young again, neither one of them understanding what will happen now, both full of passion and without wisdom. Or so it seems to the old woman. Fear begins to close around her again, that familiar damp cloak. She stares sadly into the beautiful boy, feeling the darkness of her own eyes.

Finally, she says, "I suppose you will have to do something with all of that." She gestures behind her to the mess of bodies there—her own mess, she feels now, a mess that she made and is unable to fix. "I suppose you will know what to do, warrior prince. But first—" She swallows. "What will you do with me?"

For now she wants to go back; she wants to give up that choice after all. She wants to be, for the first time, in a way she never allowed herself to be since the day she first saw Hanum, humble. She wants to believe in Sky. She wants something, at last, to surrender to.

"I will rescue you," he says. Then he lifts her, easy as a handful of flowers, into his arms.

Then that chosen one, who once was light, who once was pure, who once was virgin and unafraid, leans her head into his shoulder. *Now he will return me to that destiny I ran from long ago,* she thinks. *Now at last I will have to meet that darkness; now at last I will be swallowed into it. But at least for these few moments, I can feel the pleasure of his warm, living heart. What pleasure is greater than this!* And she almost forgets her daughter, Hanum, the City, the island, and her whole story, for the sake of absolutely melting into those sweet earnest arms.

In a moment, she feels the familiar steely cold of the winter sea around her and hears the sound of the waves circling and doubling back on themselves, reinventing themselves again and again. She hears the cries of the gulls, flashing white in her body. Perhaps he will toss her into the sea, as she did to her own daughter. Where, finally, does that Dark One await her?

But he is holding her aloft, as if she weighs nothing. Indeed, her bones now to her seem to weigh less than flames. The heat of his arms and his hands consumes her. She no longer feels the cold.

"What are you waiting for," he whispers in their language. "What are you waiting for, my love?"

She opens her lips. They are the lips of a young girl. They are lips which want to taste what the eyes could once see, lips which press eagerly against the call of death, lips which cry out and refuse. But she says, "I am waiting for Her to take me."

"Ah, Grandmother," he says. "You have already been taken. You have been taken and devoured, broken and washed clean. You have surrendered, and you have come through, and here you are—just born, and finally knowing how to love. Isn't it true? Hasn't the Unicorn been born, after all?"

The old woman begins to laugh, and she laughs and laughs, knowing it is true—knowing that what she always feared has already happened. With each laugh she is bounced higher and higher, like a laughing baby in his arms, and he laughs with her, until, with one final laugh, she flies out of his arms like a bird of smoke into the impossible air, into the impossible sky. Forgetting him, forgetting everything, she flies finally upward on her wings of fire, into the light of her own new eyes.

☽

Yora is a river, and Yora is also of the sea: for all rivers circle around and meet in the sea, meet in the sky, rain down, and meet again in the sea.

The moon, growing, pulls her in. She groans—too big, and heavy with too much pain, to remember the names of the women she once humanly loved: Delilah, Mira, Lonely, Fawn. She is full to bursting with that old pain, and she can no longer resist the insatiable demand, the agonized desperation, of that man who is all men—that man who first called her back to earth with her own name. On the shore, she can still feel Dragon's longing, pulling at her, pulling her in with the impossible strength of a child's arms. She can feel the suffering that calls to her, the thirst and the hunger of the tiny creatures that crawl among the rocks of the shore. She loves them, and she will give them everything, over and over again, without regret.

But when the moon wanes, she will feel the deep comfort of the bodies of whales, who sing her home again to herself, her center. She will retreat. Back inside that center, she will feel the deep darkness that refreshes her—opposite of the moon—and she will close in upon herself, water within water. She will feel the whole history of the world—how it rose up from her—and the black hole from which it rose, rich with forgotten silence.

Back and forth she will swing forever—with no decision, only rhythm— between the call of the earth, her children crying out for her, and the call of her own self, within. With that swing she will bring life and death, at the same time. Never one without the other.

Mirr. Mirr. Mirr.

She misses the sound of it: the way it sounded in the dark, in the safe silence, and the way the Mad Ones sounded humming it in their dreams. She misses their dreaming, which kept her anchored as it wove around her. True, they were broken. True, their dreams were pockmarked, bruised, emaciated with longing or sluggish with the fat of self-loathing; those dreams dragged under the island with ugly sounds, and never woke up. But they were familiar. Most of all, those people accepted each other, and were safe in that sad, comfortable fellowship of suffering. Where are they now?

For now Mira is carried in an older embrace, an embrace she loved and longed for but which before was never sturdy, never certain, and which, in fact, was connected, in its very blood, to everything that she feared.

"Miri," Lilah whispers, through the sea, on the soft backs of whales, emerging with her through wet sand into the sun. *"Miri."*

But Mira is still afraid to speak, because if she tries to speak, she might begin to scream again, like in the old days, and Lilah doesn't realize that the screaming terrified Mira more than it terrified anyone else. She doesn't want to see that fear emerge from behind Lilah's face. That face is a good, old face, as if each face of her sister's life—woman, teenager, girl, and every phase in between—is layered under the other. If Mira looks deep enough, she can see the child Lilah, the one who ran with Moon—the one who, like Mira, mistakenly thought that the meadow was eternal. And beneath that face, she can see the face of the old woman Lilah, the wise one that Lilah doesn't know she is becoming.

"Miri, Miri," she is saying. "Come back to me this time. I'll keep you safe this time. Come with me."

Why is she calling, calling? Mira is sitting in a ball, knees against the soft protrusions of her unfamiliar breasts, at the edge of the sea. She can only look at the sea. If she looks anywhere else—at the beach, at the dead trees, at her sister's face, at the world beyond—the screams begin to rise up in her throat. But as long as she looks at the sea, Yora can hold everything. The Dark Goddess....

"Miri," But poor Lilah, who is lonely, needs her.

Now Lilah touches her, hesitantly. Sand on her fingers, in Mira's hair. The water so heavy still, on the blanket Lilah wrapped around her strange, naked body, and the sunlight so light.   •

"My beautiful sister," says Lilah, but Mira can hear the fear in her voice, and knows that it is she—Mira, Miri, Mirr—whom Lilah fears. "It's just us now, see? We're free."

Mira closes her eyes. The sand sparkles underneath her body and says her name, and she remembers what she knows now: that she is also the Unicorn, and that the Dark Goddess told her no one can steal that from her. Her father didn't take it away after all. In fact, it was the Unicorn who kept her safe. Knowing this makes her feel a little calmer inside. Something walks white and fluid inside her, its hooves kissing the earth. It feels so good to fold inward into that light that she has to use all of her energy to stay present to her sister, to stay here in her human body. This body is wounded in ways that will never heal, and she doesn't think she will be able to stay inside it much longer.

"Miri, I'm sorry," Lilah is crying, and Mira turns to her and touches the tears with her fingers, wondering if her own tears feel like this. The touch seems to make Lilah cry harder. "I thought I was so alone, I thought you had left me, I thought he loved you more than me and that you shared something I could never have. I was nothing to him, and you were everything."

"No," says Mira, but she can see by Lilah's continual tears that she didn't say it aloud. *You were the stronger one,* she wants to say. *That's why he left you alone. He knew your power. How I wished I could be powerful like you!* But instead she says something else. She doesn't know what it is until Lilah repeats it back to her:

"Fire?"

"Fire," croaks Mira, unable to remember the girl she once was, who formed all those words, as if they made sense. "Fire fire fire."

"Where? What...?"

"Everywhere. Fire." And it's true. She can't feel it, but she knows that inside herself—inside the Unicorn, inside the center of the earth itself—she is so angry that the whole world is on fire. That fire killed her father, and it almost killed her. In her head she can see the whole City on fire, and she knows it is true; she knows that right now half the City is burning to the ground, and the people are crawling in smoke. And she is sorry but there is nothing she can do about it. There never was. The fire does not belong to her, any more than her body belonged to her when her father took it.

"Yes, I think that's why," Lilah says pensively. "Because of the fire in me, he couldn't love me."

"No," chokes Mira. "I fire. I am fire...Mia. Mia." And she closes her fists over her face, because she is afraid she will scream.

"It's okay," says Lilah. "I know. You can scream. No one can hear us here. We're safe. Scream if you have to."

With that, all the scream comes pouring out of Mira, but it doesn't come out as a scream—because, once Lilah says that, she is all of the sudden okay. She doesn't have to scream after all. Instead there is a long easy silence, a breath that falls out of her, a tree falling inside her and coming to rest finally on the earth that has given it life. She reaches out her hands and Lilah takes them, and then Lilah comes close and wraps her up to keep her warm.

"Oh Miri," she whispers. "What happened?"

But Mira knows she doesn't want to know. Anyway, she cannot imagine the words for it. The words to tell it are lost under so many other words— words that were not shameful to say but that were also lost.

But she loves her sister (she remembers now), and so she says to Lilah, "You are going to have a baby."

This time she knows she spoke out loud, because she feels Lilah stiffen.

"There's a baby," she says again, to make sure Lilah understands, "in your body." She touches Lilah's belly and Lilah doesn't move. "There," she says. She's pretty sure she is saying it right this time. That the words are coming out in order.

"No," whispers Lilah.

"I know why you're scared," says Mira. "Because it's a girl."

"How do you know?"

"The same way you know." Mira looks into her sister's eyes, tries to see in there, wondering if she is mistaken. "Don't you?"

Lilah nods slowly, her eyes flashing white. She knows. Mira watches her look down at her belly, at her own body, like it belongs to someone else. Mira knows that feeling. She watches Lilah touch her fingertips—just the tips of three fingers—to the swell of her belly, as if afraid to break a fragile glass ball.

"I didn't think—" Lilah says. They are facing each other now. Mira places her fingertips in the edges of the waves; she is wet, and most of all she is cold. It is the first clear physical feeling she can remember feeling in years. The cold opens the doors of her body from all sides, accentuating the solid separateness, the freedom, the untouchable aliveness of her flesh. Something like a scream sears through her, almost like joy. *Cold!* she thinks. *I feel cold!*

"I didn't think," Lilah says again, "that I was that sort of woman." And Mira has a sudden memory of holding a magic pebble in her hand—she'd found it in the dry streambed at the edge of the meadow, black with white rings—and as her father came toward her, accidentally she dropped it behind the bed, and she reached frantically with her hand as he came closer, feeling that if only she could keep it with her she would be safe, but she was so frightened that she could not find it, and even later after he left her, she could never find it again, and she always thought that pebble was magic; she always thought *if only.*

That's what Lilah's voice sounds like right now, so small and lost. Like that pebble.

"What—sort of woman?" asks Mira, feeling the word "woman" grow big and achy in her mouth, like something that swells when it gets wet.

Lilah waits a long time, while Mira sees the answer already in the determined glow of her skin, the new center in her weight, as she sits there surrounding her own belly.

"A mother," Lilah says finally.

Mira presses closer. She wants to. She wants to feel that beginning of a body in there, brand new, newer than she can remember herself ever being. She presses her own belly—empty, inhumanly empty—against that brilliant swell, and wraps her legs around her sister, and her sister wraps her legs around her back. Then they lean into each other, without saying a word, and make circles on each others' backs, very small, with their hands. And she knows that Lilah wants to ask a hundred questions, and say a hundred things. She knows that Lilah wants to tell her how sorry she is for leaving her to be with those boys, and how for Lilah, being with those boys was beautiful—not at all like what happened to Mira herself. She knows Lilah wants to ask her what has happened to both of them between then and now, and wants to tell her she loves her, and wants to say how good it feels to make circles like this with their hands, and how those circles protect each other. Or maybe it is Mira who wants to say those things to Lilah. But either way, neither of them say anything—Lilah because, though she doesn't even know it, she is still angry, still hoarding her own words out of hurt and bitterness, and Mira because it still costs her too much to speak, because she only has a little bit of this life left in her and she wants to use it right.

But between them the fetus murmurs an old song, not knowing yet what it will mean to be a girl or a woman—only recognizing the taut, tentative stretch of their love.

They stay together like this for many days, on the beach where in the past, things were only lost and never found. Mira cannot bear to leave the sea, the only place that ever kept her safe. So they stay, not knowing what to do or where to go. The sea comes and goes and is always there, and Yora cares for them.

It begins with lightning, like the beginning of the world. It begins with the falling of live wires in a dry wind. It begins with the mixing of chemicals together in factories whose walls melted and fell, and which became houses of destruction instead of creation.

Now fire embraces the houses, fast and easy as instinct. Like a lustful spirit, it climbs the highest, loneliest towers and licks the cloudy fields of heaven.

Through flame-framed doorways, you must run now from a hunger too powerful to bear. Fire leans forward in an eager cursive slant, in waves and jagged moving tiers. Collapsing beams fall through it, as through the arms of ghosts.

If only you could see how beautiful the City is, as it goes down! How beautiful the buildings with their beating wings of flame! How the Things laugh as they come undone! But you cannot look now. For you are all of you running for your lives, howling as if the fire were already inside of you.

As for the mad people in the island, they sleep with the Princess, and they will wake with her, as the darkness wakes with the light. Then they will want to go home. They will want to be where you are. They will want to look into the eyes of the living, and they will claw at the cloth of your forgetting, twisting their faces in its dewy depths. They will call out your names.

The sea pulses, nauseous with their suffering, and pumps larger and longer waves onto the shore.

They want you. They want to come home.

Over the mountaintops there is the faintest mist of red: not the red dying of fall, but the red beginnings of maples in spring. Yet it is not quite spring yet. The buds are too small to be noticed down on the ground. They can only be seen en masse, by certain birds, from the air.

Chelya comes out the back door, tying her skirt up around her knees, muddy pajama bottoms flapping beneath it and over her boots. Rye stops chopping and straightens up, watching the falling snowflakes perch in the red, buoyant hills of her hair. Not all women wear skirts. In fact most that he's met do not. Willow wears pants when she works. But there seems to be some unspoken rule in his family that women must always have that undulating roundness moving over their legs, hiding them. It's a secret he doesn't know. "Helps me flow better," Chelya told him once. "Brings the earth up into us," Eva said.

Now Chelya, smiling a little to herself, picks up the other axe, drags out a log, and swings. She's as strong and certain as Kite was, and the two pieces tip neatly apart, their white insides shining smooth. But for some reason this was something Rye almost always did with Kite, not with Chelya.

And though doing it alone, up until this moment, he was okay, now that Chelya has come and lifted that other axe herself, he has to turn away and pretend to be checking the woodpile for mold. He can't remember the last time he cried. Maybe when his mother died. His eyes blur and it dizzies him, as if they are dissolving into rivers and falling away, and he will never be able to see again. He holds onto the wood and tries to steady himself. He feels Chelya's small hand on his back. She doesn't rub it or say anything; she just stands perfectly still behind him, her hand firm and calm, like truth.

Gently, he shrugs her off and begins stacking the cut wood. Chelya begins chopping again, and neither of them speak of it.

"Dad," Chelya says, "why do the women always do certain things and the men always do others?"

"What do you mean?"

"Like you and Kite used to chop wood most of the time. And Ma and I usually cook, and prepare the meat, but you are the one who kills it."

He stops. "I don't know. That's how it's always been. But I don't mind, if you want to come set the traps with me." He looks at her.

"No—I just wondered. Eva says in the City it's different. It's important to the women now for them to do the same things men do. They want to, and also, if they don't, the men won't respect them."

Rye thinks about this. "That doesn't make sense," he says finally. "Why would I respect someone more for doing the same things I do? I mean, I respect women because of their differentness. Because of their mystery." He thinks a little more. Is that it?

"In the City," Chelya says, pausing in her work and thinking, too, "I guess when the women spend their time raising children and making food—they call it home-making—they aren't respected."

Rye is still staring at her. "But why not?" he asks, bewildered. "What's more important than that? What's more important than making a home?"

Chelya shrugs. "I don't know. I've never been there. They don't have real homes there or real food. Maybe that's why."

Rye shakes his head and goes back to his work. "Well," he says, relieved by this intellectual discussion, relieved to sound once again like the confident father who knows. "Like I always say, it's not all bad in the City. There's a lot of creativity there, a lot of new ideas. It's good, maybe, to change roles sometimes. Human beings can do almost anything, if they try."

"You sound like Kite." Chelya laughs, and Rye doesn't know what to say to that. He is always surprised by how easily she can say his name.

They start chopping again, their faces intent, their voices silent, and the memories of trees release themselves with quick, explosive cracks. Chelya is sweating but she doesn't look tired. They're about half through, already, what he wanted to get done today, and the snow is still falling tenderly and respectfully, the air absolutely still. It's the kind of snowfall Kite would like. He'd be out all day in it, and no one would know where.

"We don't see you around much lately, Chel," he says quietly, when they both stop to rest.

She lowers her head. "I know," she says, and nothing more. But Rye hasn't been Fawn's husband all this time not to learn how to interpret what's going on beneath the surface. It must be all the tension in the house that's keeping her away. It's the fights between him and Fawn. Lately, he and Fawn are doing better, but maybe Chelya hasn't been around enough to know that. Or maybe it's more than that? Maybe it's the strain of being the only child now. That feeling that all her mother's worry and fear is focused on her.

He says, "How are things? I mean, with your tree god."

His daughter sighs and looks off toward the higher mountains. He is surprised to see her hesitate. Then she says, in a calm, clear tone that saddens him, "It has to end soon, I think."

"Why?" He wants to go to her and comfort her, but already she is stronger than he, so much older in some ways, and he knows she doesn't need that. He misses her laughter. He misses her at eight years old, like it was yesterday— the way she'd run to him.

She takes up another log and swings. Crack. She stands back and looks at the two pieces. In the beginning, when he and Fawn first started fighting, she would cry all the time. Now she never cries. Now her face is closed to him. "Because it *can't* last," she says finally. "I mean, he's a god. We're not the same. We love each other, but we can't— You know. We can't go anywhere together, we can't have children together, we can't live the same life together. I want my own home, my own family someday."

"Do you?" he says, smiling.

She looks at him. "Of course." Then, when she sees him at a loss for words, she adds quickly, "It's okay. I just need to end it soon, before it gets even harder. Before the spring, you know? But he was such a comfort to me. I needed him, during all this."

Rye nods. He starts stacking up the wood they've cut. All the trees they've taken since Chelya met her lover have been approved for the taking by that same god. The forest is healthier when thinned in the right way.

"We'll have to find you a human husband," he says then.

"How?"

He stops and looks up, to find her staring at him earnestly, not angry or desperate the way Kite sometimes seemed, but asking him, seriously, to consider the question. It's true. He knows why Kite left. He keeps telling Fawn, and he was telling her even before it happened. They are too isolated here. But what are they doing about it? Nothing.

He sighs, tries to think of the answer she deserves. "We'll travel around, you and me. We'll go to each farm, and say we're looking for a husband for you." He grins.

"But there's no time. There's always so much work to do. That's the whole thing, right? If I had a family, and I made my own farm between here and Jay's— See it's like we'd start to form a chain, and someday everyone would be linked up again, a community. But because we're so isolated, we can't even begin. We have too much to do here on our own, to make it through each year."

Rye's face falls. "I don't know, Chel. I don't know. But we'll make it work somehow. I promise."

Chelya keeps chopping. He knows she doesn't quite believe him, but she isn't the type to press, and that makes him sad. He almost wishes she would challenge him, fight the answers out of him—wherever they are inside him.

"It's okay," she says again, instead. "The last cold moons of winter aren't the time to be thinking of answers."

"It's so much harder with Kite gone," Rye says suddenly, helplessly, dropping his hands. "There'll be even more work to do in the growing season.

You'll have to work harder. We all will."

But she surprises him by saying, with certainty, "He's coming back."

"How do you know?"

"I just do. I mean, he went out there for us. To bring us back knowledge. Don't you know that? Do you think he went only for himself, that he would abandon us forever?"

Rye shakes his head. He doesn't need to name all the fears, the endless possible calamities that could cause Kite to no longer have a choice about whether he comes back or not. "You always want to see the best in people, Chel. But I know what it's like to be a young man, out for adventure. It's not bad. It's not selfish. It's just where he is in life."

Then he can see Chelya thinking, deliberating over whether or not to say something. "Do you ever wish it was you?" she asks finally. "Do you wish it was you out on that adventure?"

"No." He shakes his head, and at the same time feels relieved to find that he means it. "I mean, it *was* me, once. But what I realized is, I stopped traveling when I met your mother because my adventure continued with her. I never knew how hard it would be, just to love—to love right. It's harder than any of the traveling I did." He sighs and laughs a little to hear himself say it. "But Kite will continue the journey I started. Because, Chel, I was looking for something a long time ago, when I was wandering on my own, only I didn't exactly know what. Maybe Kite knows. Maybe he picked up that thread I left behind—maybe it wasn't me who was supposed to carry it on."

Chelya nods, and he can see her pondering this. She starts to stack the wood and he starts chopping again. He feels lighter suddenly. How light the snowflakes fall; how light his arms feel, swinging in this rhythm they know so well! Winter is almost over. Already they hear the owls calling for their mates, and in less than a moon the tips of the branches will grow pregnant with the dreams of new buds. Already they are planting seeds for tomatoes and herbs and greens in the greenhouse, to transplant when the earth melts again. And every year there is this lovely longing, this delicious anticipation, for what it will feel like to eat the sweet fresh vegetables they've gone so long without, and even—every winter they almost forget what it's like—the taste of fresh fruit.

It is true what Fawn fears, that the world is changing. The seasons are shaky, spring starting too soon or too late, warm days in winter and cold storms in summer, things confused. It is true that the very atmosphere is changing; it is true that the river and the rains carry so much pollution sometimes that they kill the very things they have always given life. Yet the earth always adjusts. No matter how much is lost, something, somewhere—even if it's not him, even if it's not his family—will adapt. The crows, the insects, even the deer—or some creature hiding on the brink of existence, something no one has ever seen—will be ready to emerge and re-create the world. Someone will always continue this story that is life, and that comforts him.

He pauses to rest and watches Chelya as she stacks the last logs, her brow slightly furrowed, her limbs intent and unselfconscious, her hands so capable and ready. He imagines how it would be to ride around the countryside with her, exploring all the lands he's visited only in memory for so long, stopping at each farm to find out who's left and to see if there is any young man worthy of her. How beautiful she is! He wouldn't want to give her up, but he knows he's never had to worry about her. Of course she would choose seriously and right: someone who values the right things, who is kind and hardworking, who respects her. But she'll be forgiving, too. She won't have to have the handsomest, the wisest, the strongest, the most romantic, the one who lives up to some ideal in her mind; she won't have to travel forever to find perfection. She'll be willing to love whoever's heart is simply good enough to deserve her. Rye senses that she already knows what it's taken him a lifetime to learn: that it isn't the decision you make that matters, but what you make of it, and how deeply you commit to it. It's up to her to love well, and she will.

"I'm going in to help Ma with dinner," she says to him now, turning.

He nods and watches her go. He watches the snowflakes close around her as soft as eyelashes, like ceremonial weeping.

Far from the flames, far from sound, far from hunger and violence and the pounding of feet against pavement and the crash of buildings, cushioned by the long, long landscape of the sea, the woman who was once named Lonely dissolves in the deep cave of sleep.

How delightful it feels, finally to rest! There was something she wanted once, something she wanted so much that this wanting was her whole life, and yet she can no longer remember it. Someone was whispering something sweet to her, and that something was sort of a name—as much as the calls of the gulls over the black water are names for each other, or the barking of dogs in the night is the naming of love, or the hollow cry of the wind through the grasses is the name of time—and yet it is not exactly a name. It is more like a sweet, blessed gateway into a high, golden room that feels familiar. Someone is waiting for her there, in the light, and she wants to go in.

But she is distracted by someone else, someone whose tears wet her face. He cannot stop crying. "I'm sorry," he is saying. "I'm so sorry, beautiful girl.

I only wanted to keep you safe. I wanted to keep you safe from this terrible mess I made...."

She can see her father, back there in the fog, and she wants to tell him it's okay. That she is okay, that she forgives him, and that, though he is rocking her in his arms, though his tears fall all over her, he can let go now, because something else is already rocking her, already keeping her safe. Something else that is not her father, and not her mother, is rocking her deeper than the earth, deeper than the sea, deeper than the sky....

Fire—mindlessly brutal, soullessly hungry, wordlessly roaring—runs faster than Kite does. It singes his hair. It makes a dance that does not include him except as fuel, like the universe's great masterpiece made at the expense of hundreds of individual lives, for the sake of which nothing but merciless, inhuman beauty matters.

But as he stumbles, his timed-out lungs expiring, the sea comes cold and oblivious from the opposite direction. It comes at the fire and does not see him, and he collapses backward in its wake, and emerges sputtering to deep breaths of smoke. Blackened water swirls around him, mechanically responding to the desperate thrashing of his arms, his heart. Then it falls over him.

And it is not the life energy that beams out graciously from the cozy stove; it is not the peaceful crackling that makes its comforting, steady light in the winter. It is not the sweet melody that quenches thirst; it is not the cool summer relief; it is not the lusty relaxation of a warm bath. It is not the romantic dream in the evening to which music is softly played and stories are told; it is not the fresh awakening in the morning. It is fire, water, and air in a pure, loveless chaos, in that most banal, universal form. In this universe, he does not matter at all. He does not even exist.

Why, when he thought of energy, did he think of magic? Why, when he thought of harnessing the elements, did he think of warmth and light, when the elements unleashed are nothing but those very things which return us to darkness?

He wanted to quell his mother's fear.

He wanted, finally, to prove to her that these things could be controlled, and that they—their family—could be safe forever. Anything to stop that worry in her eyes and her voice, that tension in her coldness to his father, that tearful look on her face when he went out; anything to stop the fear that clamped their lives so tight together, so that he could never breathe out all the way, or breathe in with certainty. He wanted to go to the City and bring home light, and warmth, and control, so that she would finally relax, finally let him go.

But now in this racing tide of the elements released, he knows that this is impossible. Willingly, he stumbles; willingly, he lifts his face; willingly, he falls into that bed of wild darkness. Because all he wants is not to be afraid any more.

The sea finally recedes, and the fire is only a memory of black and dusty things, but even the wind slashes cold in his wet ears and ignores him as it steals away the last of his strength. He does not recognize the earth beneath him. His last thoughts before he loses consciousness are of Chelya's laughter, Dragon's heavy loving hand on his shoulder, and the sweet, throaty cries of a bright girl in Dragon's bed as he, Kite, lay awake in a foreign, unknown city, in the darkness.

The fires in the City rage for days.

Mira sees herself a white Unicorn, cool and peaceful as ice, walking sad and slow through the crowd of flames and people, through the burning rooms, through the foggy smoke in its circles and curls, through the falling, nameless pieces of unidentifiable things. She cannot feel the flames. They mesmerize her like calligraphy against her skin.

Then she realizes she is not the Unicorn after all but a girl screaming in her sister's arms. She knows she is screaming by the tears in Lilah's eyes, tears she can feel pouring down her own neck. She feels the tears and then she feels the heat of the scream, inside. The scream starts at the base of her body, where the wound is, and heads upward. She cannot seem to stop screaming, but she knows suddenly that Lilah's tears will slay the fire. So she keeps holding on, waiting.

Inside the scream—which does not even belong to her, which surrounds them like a red cocoon—she says to Delilah, strong and clear, "We have to find him. We have to tell him he has to let Her go."

At first Dragon feels completely free for the first time in his life. There is no question, no self-doubt, no loneliness. Everywhere, everywhere, he sees his own passions and furies mirrored back to him in flame. The City becomes flame—and becomes one with him. He feels the wild, rising heat of their mass bodies, and he feels their fear like the very serpent of life itself lifting them up, tickling his skin as they brush by him, infusing him with ecstasy as they press him close, pushing and pushing and ever-exploding forward. For days and nights before this, he has made love; for days and nights he has healed the lonely, the lost, and the desperate with his magic, sensual touch; for days and nights he has dug the people out of their own ruins, lifted concrete chunks that were light to him, tossed aside the debris easily and carried people in his arms without need of food or water or rest, because he is a god. Because he needs nothing but their love, their heat, their aliveness all around him. He would do anything to keep that fire of life itself burning inside them.

Finally he, Dragon, who has always needed them so badly, has become the one who is needed! Finally, they started coming to him for help and for love, as they came to him in the desert cave—only more of them, women and men alike—and that ancient life force he had tried his whole life to hold back came rushing finally through him, inexhaustible and endlessly useful. And so he runs with the fire now, on fire with his own self, bigger than life, raising his arms and roaring with the craze of its drunken, joyous hunger.

But eventually the human being in him tires, his running slows, and he begins to look around him. No one is sharing his joy. In a gradually awakening horror, he begins to see the twist of the people's faces as they run by him, and to recognize that twist not as passion but as agony. He sees that the things the fire devours are the things that once housed the people or that are beloved to them, and some of those things are alive. He sees them running from the fire. Then all his old sorrow returns—the sorrow he himself has run from all these years—as he understands again why the women avoided his gaze in the streets, why the first Yora wouldn't let him touch her, why the mothers of his youth cast him out. Because this fire could hurt them so much. But it isn't what he meant to happen. He knows now, what it feels like to help other people. *I am the god of this,* he thinks. *It is my job both to give it and to take it back, when it is too much for them.*

So it is that Dragon begins running again, only this time not making the flames or feeling the flames or rejoicing in them, but rather devouring them. This time he is taking them back.

In the burning bedrooms, he eats the flames. In the abandoned buses, in the long hair blowing, in the falling tangles of wires, in the City Center itself, he eats the flames even as they eat the things. He takes them back inside and swallows. He feels them hotter and hotter inside, until they burn so hot he can't tell his insides apart, and then he can't feel the fire at all any more, because he himself is that heat. He is the dragon, who, when it dies, when it transforms itself finally into the next life, becomes a star.

That pure fire follows its pure hunger toward that which has called him all his life, and which he has never understood, but which he has tried so hard to name.

He flames over empty pavement, and abandoned lots which cannot burn.

He flames out toward that something, that something he desires, until he feels that it, too, is coming for him.

Have you ever seen the sea? Kite whispered to him once on a cold desert night, when they lay awake and listened to the wind. *I have always wanted to see it.*

At first the people do not run away. For at first it seems to leave them, receding from the beaches, contracting inward into the great bowl of the world as it has never done before. Young lovers, laughing—still thinking they are above all this and will survive it through brash will alone—actually follow it out as it returns to the center of the earth. All their lives, the world has been a show. The world has been made to entertain them—a great glamour of thrill and pleasure and everlasting life that Hanum made for them alone, the everlasting youth. They run toward it. Daring each other, they go chasing after the sea.

But the birds rise crying from their hidden ground nests, and never see their children again. They know that glossy body is coming, and nothing will make them stay. They grew up with its sound in their ears, and they knew from the first that it never struck any deal with them; it owes them nothing. They knew from the first what they were up against, choosing to nest at the edge of the abyss.

The wave rises, and the lovers begin to scream.

But before it can get to Dragon, he is running toward it. He is running from the warm joyful flames into that cold empty coming, forgetting all his godliness, forgetting the salvation of giving, knowing only that She is all he has ever needed to survive, and that She will destroy him if he doesn't take Her first.

She is the water he learned to thirst for, whom he rises for at the merest thought of nourishing breast and pungent female sex, who lured him and sang to him and tormented him in the dry, abandoned desert. She is the mother whose love was his only hope of life, and who cast him into flames to destroy him. She is Yora who brought him to his knees with longing and nearly ended him. Now as he comes running upward into the last empty fields beyond the City, She is what he knew She would be: that one perfect, magical white creature who will elude him forever, who will deny him forever, who will mock his darkest, deepest needs and his wildest, beastliest outrage forever if he does not overcome Her now. If he does not destroy Her.

He sees Her in the crotch of the wave, Her horn lowered, the wave radiating out and above her like a great roaring shell that encloses her. The wave will destroy the City—will destroy all those people who have saved him from loneliness. He feels only rage, and that rage is lust, and that lust is fear, and that fear is need. He is only fire, taller and taller now, and this time fire will win. He is taller than the wave, taller than the sea, as tall as his own erect and endless need, leaning over her and spearing her with the whole weight of his soul.

Then he is a dragon, his teeth at the throat of the Unicorn, his breath turning her white skin black.

Then she roars, and he realizes it is She who is the dragon—She whose dark longings bruised him and weakened him and kept him from that sweet virgin, that first Yora, whom he loved more than anyone. Yes he—it was he all along!—*he* is the Unicorn, with his pure thrusting sword, when the fire of his lust finally rises up through his body and erupts through his skull into his great father the sky! Yes, She is the dragon, as if the Dark Goddess herself was a dragon all along, who tortured him and fed on his lust, who taught him to love, who—in the form of Delilah—was fire and loved the fire in him right back.

And then, his hands still clutching at the warm flesh of something—Unicorn, dragon, or woman he does not know—still needing it, still holding it tight to keep it from destroying him, he actually sees Delilah rushing toward him, and she is calling out to him, just before the wave falls over him.

She is crying, "Don't! Don't hurt her."

Blue. Grey. Black. Flashes of red in silver space. Dragon falls to his knees, and the sea draws out; the wave draws back, sucking him down in its retreat. But he is a god, and he rises again. He rises and stumbles toward her, as obedient as any god to a human being. He is cradling something in his arms, and whatever happens, he feels that he has to keep it safe.

He meets Delilah on a sandy shore. She is kneeling, doubled over in pain, her belly swollen and dropping between her legs into the earth. He kneels before her and holds out this sacred thing for her, and only then does he see what it is. It is the Unicorn, which is not really a Unicorn after all.

It's a little girl.

Then he meets Delilah's eyes, and remembers again that she, too, is afraid, vulnerable, and alone.

And that he is all grown up now, and can no longer be rescued by anyone but himself.

☾

"Let Her go," she had said, and he had.

It was that easy.

When she saw him coming, she knew he was coming for her. She had known it from within her mind, which still lived in the depths of the sea, long before he even knew his own purpose, long before he saw or even imagined her. She felt his coming the way she'd felt her father's coming in the whispering grasses that were always safe until suddenly they were not. She knew how his soul worked. She knew that whatever he loved, he needed to own, and whatever he owned he would destroy through that owning. She grew four legs in the formless sea. She struck out her horn and stood staunchly in the cave of a wave. Before it fell she would kill him. Whether she survived did not matter, only that she never again allow herself to be taken.

But when she saw him rise up in towers of flame, she shivered in her cold shell. For what was she, really? Never before had she truly tried to claim this body, in all its power. What power did it have? Fear drained her breath, her own horn like an icicle in her skull. Only when he touched her—only when his hands closed around her tense, breathless throat with their magnetic fury—did the rage come back to save her. A holocaust of flame, big enough to consume a city, thrust against her ribs from inside, and she knew again that she would kill him and that nothing would stop her. Too late, she realized that to take hold of her own power meant to give in to that mystery within her own soul that she had never wanted to face—that very mystery that her father had sought, the mystery he scented her out by with his magical mind when she hid from him, the mystery that kept her silent every year after he died. It wasn't the pain, it wasn't the anger, and it wasn't the fear. It was knowing she was human, too. It was what she recognized in the dragon that came for her—the dragon within herself. It was her own desire.

So that now *he* became the Unicorn, and *she* became the monster, battered and torn into inhuman shapes, her face a bleeding vagina, her hands missing, her body gutted. Then all that pain and fire was her only power, so that her strange, fantastical body flashed its wonderful tail, and her wound was her fury, and her voice was flame, and she knew that the secret to the Unicorn's magic—the secret her father, who banished Lilah from his love, never knew—is that within the Unicorn roars the passion of the dragon.

He did not hurt her—this boy-man who had come for her. She knew he wouldn't, finally, when she felt Lilah coming, and felt Lilah cry out the way she'd never cried out all those years of their childhood—when she felt how at last she would be rescued the way she'd always longed to be rescued, those long lonely years, by someone who loved her. So she didn't kill him, after all.

When she felt Lilah near her again, she was able to open her eyes, and then she felt no rage, but only tenderness, for that tortured, square-jawed face above her—that smooth human skin with the sharp animal hair bursting through, those wild, womanless eyes—because she knew that he would listen to her, and she knew that all he needed to be at peace were those three words that only she could give him.

"Let Her go."

Now the sea, exhaling, has receded to its own center as easily as it advanced, arching downward and inward in liquid tiers of bounty and death. Yora, released from Dragon's hold, lets the people go.

And a girl who calls herself Mirr sits on those bare wet rocks now, hidden from the sun, watching the sea go.

"Don't leave me," she whispers, though she knows she is supposed to be strong now, she knows her sister will stay with her, and she knows this man will not hurt her. Almost, she knows these things. Perhaps she is still afraid of the dragon man, after all. She waits to see what Lilah will do with him.

Mirr won't tell the secret of the Unicorn. How the Unicorn carried upon her back once a girl of perfect innocence—a girl whose heart was fearlessly open, who believed in love and nothing else. How beautiful that girl was! As if from a dream, as if from another life, Mira remembers that girl—the lonely fields and desert water they shared—but she will not tell. It is not safe to tell. First, she must watch Lilah and the dragon man to see what will happen.

Back on the beach, Lilah and the man are moving near each other, not knowing what to say. At first they held each other for a long time, as the waters swept past them, and Mira watched the sturdiness of their holding, despite the entire ocean sweeping by them, and knew that this man was the baby's father. But neither of them said that. In fact, neither of them said anything at all. Now Lilah sits alone with her big belly, and the dragon man walks around with a twisted face, jabbing restlessly in the sand with a long piece of driftwood. It is familiar to Mirr—this cold, awkward speechlessness, this denial of what is most real. No one in their family ever had words for real love. But the silence frightens her, because she knows it is from that kind of silence that hatred is born, and those dark urges that no one admits to will play out unseen.

"Don't leave me," she whispers again to the receding waves, lowering her head to her knees, not knowing what she is now.

You have a choice now, Mirr. You can be a girl, safe in the harmless innocence of girlness, sweet and loved, but vulnerable in that way that only a girl can be.

Or you can be a Unicorn, with all the power and magic of that untouchable creature, but living always with the fear of being hunted by those who envy your power, those who want it for their own.

You can be safe in being small, or safe in being big, and yet neither one is safe.

"But that was always my choice!" Mirr cries. "Nothing has changed." She feels like the Dark Goddess is giving her a riddle. That what She says is not exactly what She means, but Mirr doesn't know what the truth is.

What's changed is that you cannot be nothing any longer. That is no longer one of your choices.

Mirr looks up and sees the sea finally, for now, at peace, rocking in the deep bowl of the underworld. She feels raw, exhausted, and alone, but at least she feels something. She also feels her sister's love reaching for her like fast and hungry paws. But still Lilah does not know Mira's deepest shame, and Mira does not want to be human, for fear that the shame will show.

Yet for Lilah, she will at least begin. For Lilah she will leave the sea and begin that painful journey outward again, onto the land. When she sees Lilah's wary, hopeful eyes glinting at her from that childish, ancient face, she says inside herself, *No, I will not choose. I want both.*

Then inside the wound, for the first time, the Dark Goddess seems to smile.

For a long time, there had been no thought for Fawn. She had lost the ability or the need to think. When she fell into the blackness that was Malachite's absence, when she found out that he was gone, it seemed as if she returned to that state of being that she existed in before he was born, when he was growing in his ancient, unconscious way inside her. When he had lived inside her womb, she had lived there with him, not thinking, not caring for complex questions, not even speaking when she did not need to. She had moved fluidly through dark, instinctual patterns, and known nothing but the sensations of her body. Pain, heat, weight, hunger. While pregnant there had been times when, though she remembered who Rye was, she could not remember exactly what he had to do with her, and she wouldn't try.

After her son disappeared, she went back to that place, where words could not reach her. Again she was only a body, aching with emotions too big to have names, and now sometimes with terror gouging holes along her spine and leaving empty spaces in her skull. Though her womb was cold now, instead of warm, in a way she felt as close to her son in his absence as she had felt when he lived inside her. She felt that close to him simply because she could think of nothing but him all day long, and all through her sleep, and in everything she did. When people spoke to her about something else, she did not understand why.

Inside her womb, she saw the tracks his salamander body had made; she felt the shape of him in the curved shape of her own arms. She saw his hungry face at the table, saw the color of his eyes, saw the intensity of a little boy leaning close over the movements of insects in the grass. She saw him beside his father, quick with his hands, the two of them working and not looking at each other. She heard his questions, first in sounds and then in words. She saw the shape of his back over the fire he built in the morning. She heard his voice in the evening, "Watch me, Ma, I can hit that tree with my slingshot, eyes closed." She was confused because all of these were real, all of these her body recorded, and yet everyone wanted her to believe this was not real any more. That Malachite could be gone from her life, now and maybe forever.

It was easier, in a way, to live in that dark terror without words, without thought—close to him in that darkness—than to endure the pain of hope. Grief and despair did not require thinking. Hope did. Hope made her realize all over again that he was gone.

But how long could she go on chewing the emptiness? Eventually she had to sigh, open her eyes, and hear Yora's questions, feel Delilah's and Lonely's pain, and then, finally, Rye's. That night after her dream, she and Rye had switched off telling stories about Malachite—Kite—both past and future, real and imaginary. Each story was a step she used to climb out of her own womb, until it was light enough to begin thinking again, and then she had to start asking questions and couldn't stop.

How did this loss manage to toss her so easily, so effortlessly, from the rooted center of her life, as if she weighed nothing? How was it possible so suddenly to lose the quiet peace she and Rye had spent nineteen years lovingly, tenderly, trustingly building? What was that peace built on after all? Only the circumstance of good fortune? Only a beautiful piece of this earth that, as Willow's experience showed, they could so easily lose at any time?

She went down into the basement of their home, the foundation on which this home was built. With her fingertips she traced her way between the rough mounds of old canvas bags, sacks of potatoes, turnips, onions and beets, the strung heads of garlic, the light, thin brittle of hanging herbs, the last sack of flour and the two last sacks of rice that Willow and Jay had given them at the end of last summer, before Thea was born and before Kite was gone, when they were all still laughing over watermelons and climbing to reach the first apples. She brushes the shiny globes of jars in the darkness: tomatoes, pickled green beans, apples, blueberry jam. She knew the placement of each one. A barrel of dry beans, and another of dry corn. Muskrat jerky wrapped in leather. A wooden door beneath her feet, echoing from the little space below full of aging goat cheese. All of this abundance, so precious to her, so comforting, but which was not enough for her son—who must cast off the beginning of his name, and fly.

She came, still in darkness, her hands on her belly, to the dusted-over table where he used to do his secret work. She lit his candle. In all the time he had been gone, she had tried to forget this one place—asking Chelya or Rye or Lonely to go down and gather the food they needed for supper, so she would not have to come near it, or remember the absence he left there. She had climbed his secret tree and looked out to the distant City, and she had sat by his bed for hours until some duty called her urgently enough to drag her away, her fingers pressed to his cold pillow, staring dully into the form he left behind as if she could find him there. But she had avoided this one place, down here below the life they lived, where he used to plot and dream of running away.

She opened the books whose little spider footprints were meaningless to her. How could the secret contained in those tiny marks be so convincing? She rubbed at the page with her fingers, leaning closer, as if she could rub open the truth—as if she could find in those lines where Kite was, if he was safe, why he left, and if he would come home. What could it all mean? How could there be so many words? Kite, with his dreams, lived in the sky some of the time—a sky she did not know, beyond what she could see—but he also lived down here, trying to understand the roots of things. It was something he was born with, this questioning: needing to know why we believe the things we do, why we live how we do, and how life itself becomes. *How does the sun burn? What makes the water run? What did the fish lose when we took it from the water, that made it stop moving?* He had wanted to know these things from the time he was old enough to speak.

Was he trying to get closer to things, that way? Because now she asks the same kinds of questions, trying to get closer to him. *Why did you leave? What were you seeking? Who are you that I, your own mother, did not understand?*

That night in the basement, she knew that to understand him she would have to open to something she had never opened to before. She did not know exactly what that was, but standing there, her world illuminated only by the small, fragile light of that single candle, she felt panic skitter again down the back of her neck like a cold insect. Those meaningless marks, those imageless words, made her stomach turn, make her bend over and close her eyes. She caught the familiar desperation in her fists. *I can't bear to lose him. I can't bear it.* And yet, if only she could be still inside, if only she could calm her frantic heart for one moment, she might know something. She might know—the way she always knew, when he was out in the fields for the night, or coming home through the forest, or anywhere—if he was okay. Before he left home, she had always been able to sense that. She could always feel when he was on his way back. She could feel his mood even when he was out in the garden, and she was in the house. Of course she could! But since he left, she had felt nothing but her own fear.

If only she could be still inside, she thought, then she might know. Yet how could she bear to ask herself the question: *Is he okay? Is he coming back?* What if, inside, she did know? What if this darkness, this emptiness, this endless bleeding inside *was* her knowing—the answer she had always feared?

It was like when Willow's family lost their land. Over and over, Fawn went to the river and told it of that loss, and the river—which was Yora, though she would not, for a long time, remember—said, *Let go, Fawn. Surrender.* Fawn knows she cannot control the rains, the pace of the seasons, the storms, or the marching of the City over the land. She has let go of whole crops that failed; she has let go of seeing Willow's family and children more than a couple of times per year; she has let go of the longing she used to feel to have a real father. She has let go of so much that she knew she had to let go of. True, it was that very surrender that gave her a sense of peace in life—that let her feel that, despite everything hard, the river always carried her, like a pillow of soft motion beneath the mysterious journey of her life. But certain things she could not let go. No one knows how she has denied everything she has been given, how she has refused the song of the river, the songs of the birds, the hum of the insects and the wind in the leaves—everything, everything that made up the life she knew and loved, crying inside herself "No, I will not surrender this!" *I will not surrender my son. I will not surrender the earth itself into the hands of evil men.* There are some things one should never, ever have to give up. It is too much to ask. It is not part of the sacred flow, to lose such things. There is nothing left, in the absence of such things.

How is it possible, Yora, to surrender to such losses?

But on this night, all night curled up on the basement floor, her body rocking ("Don't—please leave me," she cried out to Rye when she saw the light coming from the open door above), she knew the answer. First, surrender to the emotion. *Let the emotion carry you.*

Yora's face, a faceless face, like the contours of a waterfall. Fawn falls and falls through herself, down beneath the basement, beneath the earth itself, down into the deep liquid of the earth, down to the center of the world. In a sea of tears she rises up, feels the surface of the earth like her own skin, feels it boil under the hard floors of the City, feels it tingle with the growth of trees. Like the Earth feeling the footsteps of her children, she feels her own son's footsteps walking his long, faraway path over the land, over the pavement, over the land again—each footstep burning her, wounding her, cutting her as the actions of people cut the earth, and yet she cannot bear to live without this pain: this pain brings her joy. Simply to feel the light, innocent manliness of those perfect young footsteps. Simply to feel his path over her body wherever he goes, even knowing that he does not think of her, knowing that he travels beyond her and forgets her, knowing that he does not—has never—belonged to her.

When she comes upstairs in the morning—the sun beginning to rise earlier again—she makes the fire without thinking and milks the goats before Chelya gets up. When her daughter finds her in the kitchen, she touches Fawn's hand, tentatively, as if that hand might burn. "Ma?" It almost makes Fawn start crying again. She draws her daughter into her, and silently holds her. She feels her daughter's proud, strong breasts against her own, feels her sturdy frame, taller than her own, and feels the knowing womanness inside her. What a miracle, that she, Fawn—knowing nothing, still afraid of thunder—could have nurtured the growth of such a beautiful, capable, wise young woman! She kisses her daughter's face.

"I love you, Ma," says Chelya nervously.

"I love you, too," are the first words that Fawn speaks on this morning. The reality of the morning strikes at her with its cords of light through the windows, and she is unsure now how real her determination is. "Chelya," she says with all the firmness she can muster, "Willow asked me to visit her old farm with her. She has asked me more than once now. I should go. I feel it is time now, today. Come with me?"

Chelya nods. She doesn't ask why Willow wants to go, or why she asked Fawn to go with her, and not Jay.

Before they leave, Fawn goes to her mother and asks her to tell Rye, asks her to be with him today, to keep him company, and to help him understand why they had to go without him.

They take both horses. As they ride, Fawn tries not to think. She tries to focus on the new red buds, the new spring angle of the morning sun—its newborn joy, as if this year were the first year ever made. But she can't keep out the memories of the last time she stood in the place where they are going. Blue, only five and a half years old, came riding on a galloping horse all the way to Fawn's home, his dark face tense and frightened. "My mother says to come. They're taking our home." Then, realizing it, he began to cry. But when they arrived, Fawn did nothing. What could she do? She stood rooted to the earth, holding Blue's tight hand, Willow's mother crying on her shoulder, while Rye and Jay, Willow and Willow's father spoke first gently and respectfully, then angrily, with the men there. While Jay threw his first punch, while the strange men took out their guns, while Willow wept, while the strange men turned from her, and while Willow and Rye carried Blue's wounded father away, Fawn stood there rooted, as if she could be rooted, as if her roots were strong enough to hold that land to her body—but they were not strong enough. Not even the roots of the trees were strong enough. And there is a road cutting through now, all the way up the mountainside. The big machines are still coming.

To calm herself, she remembers Chelya, riding in respectful, wondering silence in front of her on the thin deer path. She tries to concentrate; between the blinding drowning of all the losses, she tries to concentrate on remembering her own daughter, and who she is. What is happening in Chelya's life? Does she miss her brother? Fawn thinks of all the evenings that Chelya has sat whispering with Eva, or stayed hidden away with Eva in the loft, while Rye finished doing the dishes and Fawn sat alone, staring into nothing. She thinks how, behind her grief, she envied her own mother for the closeness she shared with Chelya, a closeness Fawn had lost.

"How are you, Chelya?" she says now.

"I'm okay, Ma."

"Are you?"

Her daughter's profile before her does not change, but Fawn sees something: a little shake of her head, a tightening between her shoulders.

"Are you lonely?" Fawn tries again. Because she remembers now that Chelya has broken with her love, the one she used to go to in the forest. Though at first Fawn was relieved, she has seen the sadness this brought, though Chelya never spoke of it. She wants her daughter to talk to her about it, but she doesn't even know how to ask. What does she know of that kind of romance? Rye was her first and only love, and he continues to stand by her to this day.

"Sometimes," says Chelya.

Fawn tries to think what to say. "I miss you. I'm sorry."

"It's okay.'"

Fawn bites her lip. Sometime soon, when they are home, both facing each other before the fire, she will ask the right questions somehow. She will say, *Please tell me this story. I want to hear your story. I want to hear all the parts I've missed. Please.* Will Chelya refuse her? Is it too late?

"Chelya," she says.

"Yes." Not angry, not cold.

"Do you long for it, too? Do you long for what Kite longed for, to see the City, to see the world?"

She sees Chelya shake her head. "No. Not like that. Don't worry, Ma. I won't leave."

"No," says Fawn, embarrassed at the implication of her own fear. "I only want to know, do you long for it?"

"Well, I'm curious, I guess. I will like to hear Kite's story when he comes home. But I want to be here. Everyone, everything I love is here."

But at the mention of Kite coming home—upon hearing this amazing statement of simple faith—Fawn begins to cry, hard enough that it takes all her effort to keep silent. This goes on for a long time, and she keeps it silent, though she feels that Chelya knows, because she can see the stiffness in Chelya's shoulders, and the girl says nothing. Finally, when she can speak again, Fawn says, "But what *do* you long for, Chelya?"

Chelya has to think about this. "I don't know. For us all to be happy and together again, I guess."

"But don't you long for, I don't know, something more? Your own husband maybe, your own family?"

"But that will come," Chelya says. "It will come when I'm ready."

"How do you have such faith? Where did you learn such faith?" Fawn thinks of the world through Chelya's eyes: the butterflies in summer, the otters laughing over the banks, the goats galloping up to her, fruit falling into her hands in ecstasy. It's a kind of beauty she used to be able to imagine, in flashes, particularly when Chelya was a little girl.

But Chelya says, "I learned it from you."

And while Fawn is still reeling from this information, Chelya continues: "You were always calm, always sure. When I hurt myself, when I feared the spring would never come, when I couldn't bear to live another day hungry and the winters lasted so long, or when the rains came flooding and we missed the sun so much, still you were always peaceful—you made me feel like everything would be okay. You never panicked. You never grabbed at the future."

Fawn shakes her head. Chelya seems already a grown woman, able to articulate all this about her past, able to look back on her childhood and make sense of it, as if she can take care of herself now and doesn't need Fawn to do it any more. How strong she is! Like Eva. "But now it's you," Fawn says, sighing, "who has been there for me. I have not been there for you in this way since Kite left. It is you who have been there for me," she emphasizes.

Ahead of her, Chelya shrugs. "We're family," she says. "It's the same thing."

When they arrive, Willow is turning the spring earth with Jay, hilling up the half-frozen garden beds with sharp shovels. When Fawn tells Willow why she has come, Willow stares at her for a long time, and then, finally, almost smiles.

"I'll go and get Thea's pouch."

"But is it safe to bring her?" asks Fawn.

"I don't know." Willow shrugs. "But I can't leave her that long without nursing." Then, in response to Fawn's frightened eyes, "You and Chelya can go ahead of us and make sure no one is around."

They tie the horses at the house and walk.

Chelya walks on the other side of Willow, making faces at Thea, whose mouth hangs open—a tiny sweet darkness—and who talks occasionally and loudly without words. Blue and Morgan love to watch over her and tease her; they didn't want Willow to take her away. "Ma, leave her here! We'll take care of her." Fawn couldn't bear to look at them. She saw their eager faces and thought of nothing but Malachite.

"Jay says they dug up the earth and put in walls of concrete, plastic tubing, cleared a bunch more trees," Willow tells Fawn and Chelya. "They put in the foundation. He'd always see some big machine there—one of the yellow ones, resting its claws against the ground. But then something changed. They stopped building. In fact they tore down part of what they'd started. And then something else began that I think is much worse, but I don't know what it is."

"What do you mean?"

"Aaah yaaahaaa!" cries Thea, her eyes focused vaguely ahead through Willow's blowing hair, her arms and legs waving from her pouch. "La la la," says Chelya back, softly but distractedly, her eyes on Willow's face.

"They're drilling into the earth," says Willow. "I mean with a drill bigger than that tree, and deeper—much, much deeper than a foundation or a water 'system' would ever go. And I don't know why. I guess they're looking for something, the same thing they were looking for inside all those other mountains that they tore apart. They thought it wasn't here in these mountains, but now they think it is, or they're desperate. Jay says it's far more valuable to them than a home, whatever it is."

"What's more valuable than home?" asks Fawn, but she says it to her feet, to herself, knowing that Willow has no answer. "Something so strange is happening in the world."

"I know," Willow surprises her by responding. "My parents say their grandparents told them about a time like this one a long time ago, when all the weather got strange, and the seasons came early and late, and the river had a funny sound in it. They said there were great storms then, in the heart of the world. But they didn't hurt anyone then, because the City wasn't there. It was only those other people, the first people who lived there then. They knew what to do to survive it."

Fawn is thinking hard. She can hear the dry leaves rattling, harsh and insistent. "I have felt something." She nods quietly. "I have felt it. I knew that something was coming."

"But," Chelya breaks in, "what are you saying? That these storms are coming again? What kind of storms? And why in the heart of the world?"

Willow shakes her head. "Why was the City built in the world's heart?" she asks back. "I don't know, Chelya. But I think your mother is right. Some big changes are coming soon. Doesn't Eva speak of it, too? A time when their structures will begin to fall, and there will be so much destruction and chaos—" She sighs.

"But why are you so calm about this?" Chelya interrupts again. "Kite might be there!"

At the mention of his name, Fawn looks sharply at her daughter. It seems like the first time that someone in the family besides herself has truly broached a fear for him. She takes Chelya's hand.

"He's going to be okay," she shocks herself by saying, giving Chelya's hand a squeeze. And she is even more surprised when Chelya allows her hand to be squeezed and does not pull away. Chelya bows her head without saying more, as if Fawn's simple, meaningless words are comfort enough.

They walk for another hour in silence. Fawn is afraid now. Willow, too, is bracing herself; Fawn can see it in her body. Chelya's eyes can hold more sorrow than Fawn ever knew. Thea, sensing their feelings, says nothing more, only chews on Willow's hair and looks around, her face burning against the cold. Old, hardened snow still clutches everything. The hardiest maples try out their new buds, but everything else continues to hold still. The ravens are the only animals awake who have anything to say, and they speak only to each other.

"I haven't gone for so long," says Willow finally. "I was afraid to see it alone."

When they arrive, it's nearly sunset. Fawn and Chelya forget to go first.

Where Willow's family home used to stand, where the apple orchard grew, where the horses and sheep used to graze, the earth is turned inside out. It is like a desert, not even recognizable. Fawn looks around in a dim panic, unable to understand where the land she knew has gone. The tree where Willow's older brother Morgan, who died when Willow was ten, built his treehouse—and where Willow used to spend days and nights when she missed him so much she couldn't bear it—is gone. In its place, there is not even a stump, though the powdery, turned earth is still sticky with sap. The far hillside has been blown away, tunnels pouring open from its side.

The silence tenses, unsure of itself. All Fawn can hear is her own gasping breath. She turns to Willow in astonishment at what she must be feeling, wanting to take her hand but feeling a distance she has never felt before between them, as if the horrid transformation of this place has made them unrecognizable even to each other and themselves.

Willow stands still, absent-mindedly curling a finger into the hand that Thea holds out to touch her cheek. She shifts the pack on her back and leans forward, her face like ice.

"I'll take her," says Fawn impulsively.

Without speaking, Willow swings Thea off her back and around to her front, kneels down, and works her little legs out of the pouch. Fawn knows intuitively that Willow doesn't trust her own voice at this moment, but Thea cries out again: a general cry, neither angry nor afraid. Fawn holds out her arms and Willow hands Thea to her. Fawn bounces Thea and strokes her back, as if Thea is the frightened child inside her, though Thea herself wiggles restlessly and turns her head with lively curiosity from one face to the other. Finally she rests her eyes on Chelya, her tiny brows tensing. She reaches a hand toward Chelya, but Chelya is not looking at her.

"Someone's here," says Chelya. "I heard something."

A gunshot rings out—a sudden, incomprehensible sound, like when a tree hits the earth.

Without thinking, Fawn begins to run, not away from the sound but toward it. She runs over the embankment with the baby suddenly crying in her arms—and the first thing she thinks, absurdly, is *It's Kite. They've shot Kite. He is dead.* Her breath stabs her as she stumbles over the hillside, and then she sees the men who must have killed him, struggling together in a chaos of muscle and dirt, and then hurtling away from each other.

In the noise of their scuffle, they must not have heard her, and they do not seem to see her now. They stand bruised and tensed in the twilight, their heads shrunken into their shoulders.

Fawn stops behind the big machine and catches her breath. At the same time that she remembers the weight of Thea in her arms, and becomes aware of the whimpers that warn of renewed crying, she sees where she is, and knows that Kite is not here. Now Willow is beside her, and Fawn hands Thea back to her quickly, hoping the comfort of her mother will stop the cry. This is no time for a baby to cry.

Five men Fawn does not know stand apart now, their bodies bent forward and their fists hanging useless but dangerous below their hips. The sixth man, who faces them, holds a gun.

"Go on," the sixth man growls. "Try again. I'll kill ya this time. I will."

"Put it down," grumbles one of the other men.

Silence.

"We've got rights to this place," growls another, more loudly. "We've been diggin' here weeks now. Who's your boss?"

"Don't have a boss. Don't have lights in our house—no heat, no stove, nothing. Don't have a job. Government says what's under this land will get us our dinner."

"Who cares. You think it's any different for us?"

"You got others with you?" says another.

"No, but I got a gun," says the sixth man.

Fawn steps out from behind the machine.

"Ma!" comes Chelya's terrified whisper behind her.

Fawn walks toward the men, but she is behind them still, and only the man with the gun sees her. Startled, he nearly drops it. He gapes at her.

"What are you men doing here?" Fawn asks quietly. Her hands go numb, and then her knees, and then her face. Her body wants to run, and then it wants to crouch down on the ground and fling her arms over her head. "What are you fighting for?" she asks.

"Who're you?" barks the man with the gun, looking strangely terrified. The others turn around, and some of them begin to glance quickly back and forth between her and the sixth man, as if trying to keep track of both.

Fawn puts her hands on her hips, to steady herself. She grips the cloth of her dress.

"Ma'am," says one of the other men politely. "I don't know who you are, but this is no place for a woman."

"There are three women here," Fawn hears Willow say, coming up behind her. "And a baby." She watches the men's faces, which, despite her terror, break her heart. They look so helpless. *They don't know what to do with this land,* she thinks with ridiculous compassion. *They've got it, and they don't even know what it's for.*

"We live here," says Fawn, "in the mountains. Please—what are you doing here?"

Some of the men look down now and shuffle their feet. They seem to have forgotten all about the man with the gun, and he, too, seems to have momentarily forgotten himself. He's letting it hang in front of him, and his jaw hangs down too.

"Well, ma'am," says the same polite, eerily gentle one. "What's inside this mountain makes the whole City run. We're all out of it, see?"

"How do you know it's in here?" says Willow.

The man shrugs. "Don't know for sure. But we got no other options now. Can't bring the road further, because we're all out of fuel. That's the problem, see."

"Yes, I see the problem," says Willow, and Fawn, who does not look at her, can imagine the lightning in her eyes. "You raped all the other land around, and you used up everything you had. And you'll destroy all this, and then what? You're a bunch of stupid boys who can't see past your noses is what you are. You don't know what the hell you're doing."

Panicking, Fawn reaches back and grabs Willow's hand. "Shh," she whispers fiercely, because she is afraid of what these men will do—afraid for the baby. But the man who spoke only shrugs, and his careless response makes Fawn a little angry, too.

"I think you should all go home," she says.

"You're the ones who should go home, Ma'am," says one.

"I am home," snarls Willow.

"Don't you have families?" asks Fawn. "Don't you have wives, children?"

Most of the men nod ever so slightly.

"You should go home and care for them," says Fawn. "How is what you dig up here going to make you happy? It will only last for a little while. Then what will you do?"

They shrug. One of them looks back at the man with the gun, and that man has balled his fists up tight around the gun, but he isn't holding it like a gun any more. He's holding it the way a child holds the only toy that belongs to him when a stranger frightens him.

"How long will this—whatever it is here that you want—how long will it make the City run?" And when they don't answer, she keeps going. "Why are you going to kill each other over something like this?"

More silence, and then one man blurts out desperately, "We need it. We need it. We have to eat!"

"Then," says Fawn, "you learn how to grow your food in the earth, instead of destroying it." And though she doesn't want to, she adds, "You come home with me if you want. I'll give you something to eat, and I'll show you what to do." It sounds ridiculous, childish, but she means it. She can't think what else to do, how else to save these people. She's more sorry for them now, almost, than she is for Willow's land.

The man with the gun looks up at her. With every moment that goes by, he seems to Fawn another year younger, another year further back into childhood. She wonders if he even remembers how to speak. Far off, for the first time, she notices the sound of the river, like a memory that nearly brings her to tears.

They all wait there—the men and the women—not knowing what will happen next. Then, unable to bear her own fear any longer, Fawn walks straight toward that man. Instead of pointing the gun at her, he pulls it up toward his chest, holding it tight. The other men scatter backward, with a fear equal to hers that astounds her—and that she will never be able to explain.

"Give that to me," she says to the man, and she holds out both hands.

The man keeps looking at her face, not at her hands. His face, she sees now, has many years in it after all, maybe as many years as Rye—the face of someone who has watched children grow up, and maybe grow up hungry. Its lines are complicated and beautiful.

"Come on," Fawn says, quietly now, and nods at the gun. She doesn't have a strategy. She only feels absolutely certain that this thing cannot be trusted in his hands, or in anyone's hands.

The man hands her the gun. It's warm and heavier than she thought it would be.

"Do you want to come home with us? Do you need something to eat?" says Fawn gently.

The man looks down, shakes his head.

"You go home then," she says, because it seems to her that the man needs some direction. She holds the gun clumsily in front of her. "Some bad things are going to happen in the City very soon. There will be storms, and many things will be destroyed. People will die. You should all go home and stay with your families. Keep them safe."

The man freezes for a moment longer, then turns and sprints across the clearing and into the woods. The trees crash in his wake, and then he is gone. Fawn turns back to the other men, and knows it was for fear of them that he ran. But they, too, turn their faces away from her.

Nobody says anything for a long moment. Fawn doesn't think they are going to go home. But she doesn't want to stay around to watch what they will do to this place. She turns to Willow and sees her face for the first time. She was still picturing Willow's angry eyes burning into the men, imagining having to drag her away. But Willow's body is standing soft, and she's looking at Fawn with an expression Fawn has never seen before and cannot read.

"Do you want to go?" she asks Willow. For it is, after all, Willow's land.

Then she notices that Chelya, standing near the machine, is crying. With her face in her hands, barely able to stand, she is shaking with sobs.

"They don't know where they are," she cries, her voice low and water-logged. "They have no idea. They can't see." Though she is the one with her hands over her face, tears clouding her eyes.

"Hush," says Fawn, coming to her and taking her arm with gentle firm-ness. "Maybe they will see," she says, loud enough for the men to hear, and as Willow turns to go, she glances back at them one more time. They are looking at the ground. They are looking at the earth, not realizing how the sight of it comforts them—how throughout time, people have always looked down toward the ground whenever they have felt uncomfortable or sad or afraid. Whenever they have wanted to turn back inside themselves for the truth but not known the way. "Maybe they will see."

On the walk home, the women are silent for a long, long time. Chelya has not stopped crying. Fawn walks with her arm around her, and they walk slowly.

When they do begin to speak, they speak with a strange, quiet confidence, as if they knew all along what needed to be said, as if the events of life are connected, after all, with some sense of meaning. They talk about the number of people living in the City now, where Hanum has tried to do away with death through artificial medicine—a number none of them can conceptualize. They talk about the meadows where their farms nestle and how few of these meadows are left, formed by fire thousands of years ago and maintained by the tillers and the grazing of animals. If everyone lived like they did, if food were needed for all those people, wouldn't whole forests have to be taken down? Would it be wrong to take them down? And would it be wrong, then, for those trees to be used for building? Certain trees were cut for the building of their houses and the making of their fires, but those trees were chosen carefully from within an ancient community of trees. Fawn cannot imagine clearing away a whole meadow. She has always left such things to the elements.

They talk about everything but what happened, and what the men are going to do—or not do.

"What are we going to do with that?" says Willow, and Fawn knows she means the gun.

She thinks for a moment. "Give it to Jay. Maybe he can take it apart, use the pieces for something."

Willow nods, and Fawn looks at her. Will she do it? Or will they keep the gun, not telling Fawn, and secretly store it in case of "need?" She shakes her head and looks away. She doesn't want to think such thoughts.

Right before they reach Willow's house, Willow stops. Fawn and Chelya stop with her, and then suddenly the silence is filled with the memories their words were avoiding and with the wonder of what Fawn has done. Chelya smiles and takes her mother's hand, looks at her, and gives her a kiss on the cheek.

"Sister," says Willow softly. "You don't have to be afraid any more."

Fawn looks back at her and sees in those eyes the familial, intimate understanding of all the fear that Fawn has ever carried, that has haunted her family all their lives. She sees the reflection of her own courage. It is not advice that Willow is giving her; it is acknowledgement.

Then she thinks of Kite in the middle of that sad, messy place far away from her, and for an instant feels so proud of him—because he always knew what was right, he always knew who he was and what he wanted, and surely he is being smart and doing what he should do. Maybe he is even helping those people somehow, or teaching them something with all that he knows, with all that her family has taught him. For the first time, she thinks back to the words in his note that Eva read to her, words she memorized and repeated back to herself in her mind a thousand times but which she never truly heard until now: "I love you all. I have to go and discover the truth about the City. I'll be safe. I'll be back soon. Don't worry about me."

Why did she take those words as the end? Why did she take them as hopeless? Only because she had forbade it, only because she had always believed it so unsafe, did she assume those words to be meaningless. And that's why he could never tell her. Because she wouldn't have believed him.

"I know," she says to Willow.

Willow smiles, her eyes jeweled at the edges with tears.

They walk on toward the house. The boys are crouched on the step, leaning over some little contraption, Blue directing Morgan's hands. Jay comes to greet the women.

"Where did you get that?" he says at once, reaching for the gun.

Willow looks steadily at him for a moment. He's looking back and forth between her and Fawn, his eyes shocked and then gradually darkening, swirling. Setting his jaw, he looks past them with a violent eagerness, as if ready to attack some hidden assailant.

"We just found it," Willow says quietly. "We found it on the old land."

Later, asleep in her own bed, Fawn dreams that the man with the gun shoots it, and somebody dies. It is her own son, her own Malachite. Her own boy is crying out those words, "I need it! I need it!" as if it is the lack of something that is killing him, and she shakes him, sobbing, "What? What do you need?" She would give him anything! What did he have to go so far away from her to find?

But somewhere behind her, she hears the river, and she knows in the dream that the river is coming, and will one day cover all of this. And she knows it doesn't matter, that this land doesn't belong to the City or to Willow; it belongs to no one. Then she feels a tap on her shoulder, and she turns around, and Kite is there, alive and well after all, so much younger than the man with the gun, and she remembers it isn't his time yet to die.

"It's okay, Ma," he says. "I know what these things are for." He moves the giant machines as if they are toys, moves their giant limbs, arranging them, examining them. And she sees now that they are magnificent, that they are wondrous ancient creatures—only she couldn't tell before because they were in disguise. "They're just in the wrong place," says Kite. "We just have to remember what they're for." And they crowd around him like a herd of beasts with their groaning metal shoulders and their heavy rolling feet and the tinted windows of their eyes, looking toward him for guidance, and she knows that he will lead them. He will know what to do with such power. She knows that he will help them return to their true selves. He will do what a man ought to do.

She looks back to where she thought Kite lay, and Lonely is standing there, and her brilliant eyes are urgent.

"They're coming," says Lonely. "They're coming up the mountain. The people of the City."

Fawn knows it is not a warning, but a plea. Those people are lost and afraid, with a fear that she understands. Those people need her.

She reaches up, and Lonely grabs her hand, pulls her up fast into waking.

Kite wakes to the stench of sewage and the face of a woman he has never seen. The clothes were ripped from his body by the wave, but he is wrapped in something warm and dry now, with concrete bracing his spine and head. The woman's eyes are too big for her face, which is like a child's except for the fiery eyebrows and sharp, determined bones. A strand of her shaggy hair tickles the edge of her half-smiling, sensuous mouth. Kite can't read the expression in her eyes.

"Shhh," she says, reaching out to him, though he didn't know he was speaking, and she touches his cheek. No sooner does he feel that touch than tears are burning his face. He swallows. Her little girl face moves him to pity, but at the same time he reads motherhood in her eyes and sex in the mischievous twist of her lips. He would do anything for her to hold him in her arms.

"Don't worry," she says. "Dragon is coming back with food."

"From where?" he starts to say, but it's too much for him, and before he knows it, he is sleeping again.

Now there is fire again, and water, but in those forms more familiar to him: Dragon's gentle, warming flames in the center of their circle, and water in some kind of container being tilted to his lips. He struggles to sit up, ready to be strong again. Outside the half-room they're enclosed in, it is raining again—that steady kind of rain that is not going to stop for a long time. He leans forward, trying to understand where they are. He sees that the room is not half a room after all, but rather a room with half the building missing from it, and the building is lying on its side—though once it nearly touched the sky—and they are sitting in what once was the twentieth or thirtieth floor, but is now just a step above the ground.

"Mm, pigeon," says the woman sarcastically, taking the meat on a stick that Dragon holds out to her. "My favorite."

"Mine, too," says Kite, smiling. He sees now that the woman, though beautiful, is not well. She's got that pallor in her face that everyone in the City has, only it's less obvious in her than in many because her skin is dark like Dragon's, and she is already so small that her extra thinness is painful to look at. Still, he can't stop looking at her. He sees that she is pregnant.

"What are you staring at?" she says flatly, not looking at him, and he looks away fast and blushes. Out of the corner of his eye he can see her smile.

"This is Delilah," Dragon says, "my—" He stops.

"His ex-lover," says Delilah, but there is no love in her voice.

Kite sees the familiar storm shifting behind Dragon's darkened face and looks nervously back and forth between them. "This is Mira," Dragon adds, motioning. Kite sees suddenly, behind Dragon, standing outside by herself in the rain—but clean and shining as if no storm or ash or sea has ever touched her—Lonely's horse.

He recognizes it instantly, by the strange, circular black mark on its fore-head—like some eerie birthmark. Yes, he remembers that horse. He used to catch that horse watching him sometimes out in their fields, the way no animal watches a person. He thought he remembered it being male, but he must have been wrong. He's still dizzy from waking and surviving. But there is something about the horse, like Delilah, that keeps him from looking away. It's like she's electric. It's like there is something plugging her in, a cord that runs from her forehead into the sky. But why did he think that? He narrows his eyes, trying to focus. She bows her head.

"Never seen a Unicorn before?" Dragon mumbles.

Kite pulls his gaze away. *Unicorn?* His mind goes blank. Dragon is poking at the fire, staring furtively from under lowered brows at Delilah. Delilah is engrossed in tearing up the meat with her predator teeth. Kite has never seen anyone so hungry. Watching her fascinates him so much that he forgets the horse and even his own hunger, though the grease of his meal runs down his shaking hands. But as she starts to turn toward him again, he turns to his food and looks away. Before he can even taste it, he has eaten it all.

"We have to get Delilah out of here," Dragon informs them when they've finished eating. "We have to get her out of the City."

Some emotion falls fast as water through Kite's chest and down into the cold hardness that holds him. He tries to focus on what's around him. The City seems strangely silent. He sees that what he thought was the pavement just below their broken shell of a room is actually a channel of floodwater, still and colorful with the combined refuse of animal bodies, trash, and slicks of fuel—what is it, after all?—and other unidentifiable substances. As he watches, an old man floats past on a piece of roof, trying to row himself with a broom. He nods to Kite with eyes like coffins, and turns away. It may be the first time any stranger outside the buildings of the City has acknowledged Kite in passing.

Kite tries to pull together the pieces of his strange journey: the constant hum of automobiles, the dizzying towers, the angry wake of people, the great warehouses of too much food, the locked gates, the wailing crowds, the rains, and the loneliness unlike anything he'd ever known when Dragon left him on the rooftop. He tries to remember setting out on this journey—that innocent excitement that propelled him forward, the first snowfall in the mountains beyond his home.

He looks out at the giant mass of ruin beyond him, where everything, in rubble, looks the same now, and shapes are meaningless, and everything is trash, a scrambled and ruined language which to Kite is no more decipherable than the City was before it fell.

He realizes that the emotion falling through him at the sound of Dragon's words is relief.

"She needs real food, she needs nourishment," Dragon is saying. "She needs medicines, or whatever women need when they're—" Again the pause.

"Pregnant," finishes Delilah, and Kite can see the tightness in her face.

"My mother would know," Kite finds himself saying. "My grandmother, too. They know all about those things. In the mountains there is everything you need, if you know where to find it. And plenty of food there, too—not just pigeons."

Delilah looks at him. To his delight, he sees her face open to him a little more, her eyes softening, and he sees the weakness there, and again he wants terribly to hold her. "Green things," she murmurs.

"Yes," he nods, though his lips feel full of water. "Green things."

But he can feel Dragon looking at him, and the look makes him turn away from her again.

Delilah sighs. "It'll take us years to get there," she says.

"But we have to," says Dragon, determined. "It'll only take a moon or two."

Kite sees Lonely's horse step forward, her toes impossibly light, and bend her head toward Delilah's body, and again he seems to see that cord of electric light, now between her forehead and Delilah's heart and belly. Delilah closes her eyes. Again Kite's mind goes blank. He tries to figure it out, but he can't remember what it is he is trying to figure.

"Mira will keep you alive," says Dragon. When Kite looks at the white horse, something happens to him, like a revelation he continually forgets, and continually re-remembers. There is a connection between her and Dragon. As if Dragon could not be here without her, nor she without him. But like every thought in connection with this animal, the origin of this thought cannot be explained.

"Let's make some headway before sunset," suggests Dragon, an easy leader.

Kite stands on shaky legs and tries to find, behind the rain clouds, the sun in its late afternoon stance. Time has ceased to hold real meaning since he came to the City. Back at home, the course of the day was marked by real events that could only happen at the times they happened: the light creaming over certain mountainsides in its regular golden order, the crowing of the rooster, the opening of flowers, the warming of the day, feeding times and mealtimes, the times the deer came out to graze and the times he felt stronger or more peaceful. Also the seasons could easily be seen and felt. Here, where it's light at night and grey during the day, where concrete never changes, he is not even sure if spring has already begun, or if it ever will.

He stands now, and does not feel tired. He stands with a sudden hunger for home so powerful it stills his heart—to know again where he is, and when it is, and what is real.

12th MOON

For a whole moon, the waters do not fully recede, and the rains keep coming. The fire is out, but now you slog bewildered through fields of water, through curtains of water—veil after veil of falling water into caverns of desolation. You emerge from the pieces that buried you, or from the libraries or parking garages—those few sturdy buildings whose basements sheltered you—to find nothing of the world you once knew. No trace of your loved ones. Naked bodies, anonymous, piled by wind and wave beneath a bridge. The objects you held most dear in life swirl around your thighs and hips, together with the things you threw away, and they cannot be told apart. Your homes have been torn limb from limb, and what remains of them mingles with trash unbuckled from the depths of the earth in the quake, freed from dumps in the windstorm, and turned toxic in the fire. Dead people float with dead dogs. A dish set, a clock, a wedding gift, a fancy tire rim, a plastic sand-wich holder, a broken phone, are all meaningless now and make sharp edges under lost, bare feet. But suddenly last year's fashions are useful, like a skirt thrown away in the garbage that, floating to the surface, you grab up eagerly to tie as a bandage around the arm of a child cut open by falling glass.

Out in the desert, Coyote chases his tail around a dried-up pool, then lies back and sings a song up into the black hole where the new moon is not. If hu-man beings are all destroyed, the Earth will gradually heal. The skies will clear, the rains will run pure again, and the river will no longer cry. Salamanders and frogs will breathe easily again in fresh running water, birds will reclaim their migration stops, and tortoises will be able to hear each other again in the quiet that is left behind. Trees will get to grow, once again, many hundreds of years, and when they fall the earth will drink them in, and fairies will rise in joy from the mushrooms that bloom in otherworldly colors where they rot. Ecosystems will make sense again, and every creature will recognize every other creature, and be able to find its way home. Rabbits and prairie dogs will once again have noble names for their fears—Eagle, Coyote, Weasel—instead of terrible, nameless fears that come without purpose, tearing up the land with machine and poison. The Earth will be young and new again: the sweet, proud virgin that Coyote remembers from when the world was born.

But as Coyote watches his own weird and lonely song play out across the dark canopy of night, he sees the City, as if in reflection, in the silver clouds. He sees those people wading there, pressing urgently through water as if water were air, cold and missing the fire now though only days ago they screamed for it to stop. He sees a starving man, who didn't get to tell his wife that he loved her before she disappeared, rescuing a puppy and carrying it with him everywhere. He sees people standing inside the wreckage of houses, staring as blankly at a floating sofa cushion as at the body of a beloved pet. He sees a woman who gave birth in the burnt-out kitchen of someone's house—a kitchen with only two and a half walls now and no ceiling—her head cradled in the arms of two other women she does not know. At her side: one iron pot and an old can filled halfway with dirty water. He sees people clutching things to their chests, crying, not even remembering what those things are. In the whole expanse of this make-believe, ridiculous place, he hears things that have always been heard since humans began—things you wouldn't think could still be heard, like whistling, drums, and even laugh-ter. Inside people's minds, those strange, incredible human miracles are still happening—miracles like forgiveness, realization, mischief, self-questioning, nostalgia, and wonder.

And he knows that if humans disappear forever, if they don't survive their own stupidity and the elements come back to reclaim them, all the other animals and plants and even the mountains and the rivers and the clouds will probably be terribly, terribly relieved.

But Coyote alone, for no reason he can name, will miss them.

The group decides to walk around the south side of the City; maybe, once they reach the purple ridge, they can walk that straight up into the mountains.

"I came this way," says Delilah.

"So did we," says Dragon.

Up here in the meadows, it feels at first as if nothing has changed. The sparrows and wrens sing as if they've never heard of the City, and the grass tilts lazily to and fro in the sun. But where people have never bothered to come before except as children or in drunken teenage frenzies, dirty starving forms now lurk, and half-naked families huddle around the first fires they have ever built. Delilah and Kite work together to find food, their eyes quiet with unspoken admiration for each other's skills. Delilah, who stashed and later recollected her pack from a desolate beach somewhere, still has the basic tools of survival as well as a change of clothes—which she lets Kite wear, since they're men's anyway.

Though Dragon seems to lead them, and though they all need that strength and determination to uphold them, Kite sees that really it is the horse they all look to for guidance. It is she who senses where danger is hiding with a gun or a knife, and leads them around it. It is she who knows where fresh water lies. It is she who, when the light begins to fade, keeps circling around them, forcing them close together despite their shyness of each other, scanning the fields for hungry eyes. She is their intuition.

Who is she? And who is Delilah? To Kite, Delilah is the whole mystery of womanhood, both beautiful and ugly, abundant and frail, loving and wicked. He can tell that her angry, fast jokes are aimed at denying her own weakness, and holding at bay the pity they keep holding out to her. *I am one of you,* the jaunty fierceness of her walk says, and yet there is a grace in it—a falling back in her shoulders, a softness in her hair that she cannot hide, a hidden womanness all the more powerful to Kite because he feels he is seeing it on the sly.

"I think I've become a new man on this journey, Kite," Dragon is telling him eagerly today. "When I left the desert, I was so desperate for Yora, I couldn't think. I didn't know how to survive without her. But now I can take care of myself, see? I don't need her any more. I was able to let her go. And it feels so much better, for both of us! Because you see, I am the lover of the world. Although in a way, she will always be my one woman—even though I can't have her like that, she is still my true love in spirit, my Goddess. By being dedicated to her, I will always stay on a good path, and do right by women and the people I love. Because I do it for her. Everything. Even though I'll never see her or touch her again. Do you see what I mean, Kite?"

"Sure," says Kite. It sounds a romantic to him, Dragon getting carried away as usual on some dream of what he should be. But he has to agree that something has changed in Dragon, that he seems lighter.

"Then I realized," Dragon continues, "that I kept meeting women like Yora in my life, because that's the only way I could understand love, the kind of love that made me lonely by abandoning me over and over. That's what my mother did, see. But now I've gotten beyond all that."

"That's good," says Kite, tired and already hungry again. He imagines how tired and hungry Delilah must be, pregnant, and is amazed by how uncomplaining she is. Why doesn't she ride the horse? He wonders what it is that Dragon obviously intends her to overhear in his words, and he wonders if she is hearing it and how it affects her. There is a certain concentration in her, and he doesn't know if it's about what Dragon is saying or just about her own survival, the baby inside her, or something to do with the horse and the silent bond that runs between them. *What happened to Lonely?* He keeps wondering. He's thought of asking Delilah if she knows the original owner of that horse, and yet he senses somehow that the question would be offensive. Delilah's bond with the horse is so deep and obvious, Kite begins to question whether it is in fact the same horse Lonely once rode. Yet how could he be mistaken? He remembers that mark on its head. How many horses could have that same mark?

By nightfall they've reached some of the higher, newer developments that escaped the flood and even the fires. But they are abandoned, or else the people in them, with no electricity and no food, are hiding.

"I'm not staying here tonight," Delilah says, as she and Kite share a small meal of a quail he killed with his slingshot, and its eggs. Kite gives her all the eggs and half the quail, feeling proud.

"Let's go up to the ridge tonight, then," says Dragon, but he glances at the horse uncertainly. She doesn't seem to object.

"I wonder what's happening in the City," says Kite.

Neither of the others says anything at first, and he wonders if he's brought up a subject that can no longer be mentioned.

Then Dragon says, "They got into that building. The one at the Center, where all the knowledge was supposed to be."

Kite looks up fast. "They did? What happened?" He feels Delilah looking at him curiously, her gaze mocking, tired, and gentle all at once.

"Nothing," says Dragon. "There was nothing there. Those powerful people in there weren't powerful after all. They'd run out of fuel for all their operations, they had nothing, they were hiding out in there eating all the food that was left because they didn't want to share it. I think the mob ended up killing them."

Kite shudders, but he notices that Delilah does not. He decides never to tell them what happened to him in there, or that he was in there at all. He still doesn't know what he himself feels about it, and he doesn't want their feelings and reactions to confuse him even further. If he told them, wouldn't they think he should have done something more than what he did?

"What will happen to them?" he murmurs.

"What, their bodies? No one—"

"No," says Kite, "I mean everyone. The people of the City. What will happen to them? They have no food, no homes. They're turning into the wilderness, shooting whatever moves, desperate. Right?"

"Right," says Delilah.

"Then what? Where are all those people going to go?" But he already knows. They'll go into the mountains. They'll have to find food. They'll have to find materials and fuel to make new homes. Little by little, everything will be destroyed. Because they don't know how to live without destroying. Anyway, there isn't room for them all, is there? He doesn't even know how much world is out there.

Delilah is staring at him, smiling her wicked smile. "We could say it's not our problem, but it is our problem, isn't it?"

Kite shakes his head. "I don't even know who they are," he says, "after all this. I didn't find what I came for. I don't even know what I came for. Sometimes I think I could help them more than they could help me, if I knew how."

"Come here," says Delilah suddenly. Startled, Kite obeys, ducking his head as he sidles up next to her and lets her arm encircle him, lets her lean her small head against his and stroke his back like a mother, sighing. Her body feels like a hot snake beside him. He's glad of the darkness, but he can feel Dragon watching him.

That night, Dragon sleeps spooning Delilah with his arms around her belly. Delilah encourages Kite to stay close, and gives him their one blanket to take with him when she sees that he won't. He wants to be by himself and think. He finds a spot on the hillside where the horse lies still in the grass, hiding her whiteness as if she knows she might be stolen, but with head upright and alert. He doesn't know why, but he feels safer being near her.

He lies down in the grass and feels for the first time as if he could almost be home again. He's glad at least that he will be back in time to help his family with the spring planting. He misses having something useful to do with his muscles and hands. He misses being needed.

He lies awake for a long time, thinking. He thinks about the boy he met at the college, who had been learning so much all his life, and wonders if that knowledge will help him now. He thinks about the expressions on the children's faces as he, Kite, cooked an animal over a fire. He thinks about the panicked voices in the dark inside a tower of steel, and how terribly sad that was, to find out that they were the only answer—the only conclusion to his long journey in search of the City's truth. He thinks about his own wonder when he first used the computers in the library, which were free for anyone to use, and how those computers could connect him, with a tap of his finger, to anyone in the City. That's why he believed there was no such thing as a god, or if there was, then human beings were gods, because anyone could create and use this kind of magic. With this magic, he could type in any word, and find all the information in the world about that thing. But there was so much information, he needed a lifetime to learn and understand it all, and a lot of it he could not understand because he hadn't been learning all his life like the boy in the college. He couldn't print out the information on the machines that printed words, because he had no money, and he couldn't stay in the library all day because he needed food, and he still hadn't learned—he never learned—how to survive in the City.

He remembers the cars, which he'd longed all his life to see, and which he has still never been inside. But he has walked close to them, when they were parked, and looked inside them, and felt their eerie magnetic presences still cooling from the whir of the machines inside them, like great animals without souls.

He tries to piece all of these memories together into something that makes sense. He still believes what he believed before he came here: that human beings have so much power, and that energy is magic, and that he and his family and everyone in the City could do anything with it if they wanted to.

He's not sleepy at all now. He rolls over and takes from his pocket a tiny flashlight that Dragon found as they were leaving the City. It doesn't work any more, of course, and the plastic of it is dented and worn, but Kite insisted on keeping it. Now, carefully, he takes it apart by starlight and holds the battery and the tiny bulb in his hand, and reads the poetic words on them—"ever-ready, everlasting". He's seen lights like this before. He knows they can light up a whole page of a book, or a whole person. And yet this one has died, and cannot be re-lit. What gave the light? What changed about that substance that makes it unable to give light now? Did it really come from the bodies of prehistoric creatures, and could those creatures have been dragons, after all, as Dragon once begged him to believe? He never found out.

He's lost his book, of course. The sea took it. Or maybe it's layered under the rubble somewhere like a fossil, and someone years from now will find it, and wonder at it, and be inspired to look again at what was once forbidden and forgotten. Surely those people in the City are more desperately in need of such knowledge than Kite is. But when he rolls onto his back again and closes his eyes, he can still turn the pages of it in his mind. He's read it so many times, he can even recite some of the words. And in his imagination now, he reads about how the light of the sun can make the electrons inside an atom spin faster, and how that is energy, and how a building can drink in that energy to make every part of it function without the work of human hands, like a tree turning the sunlight into life. He reads about how energy can be made from the rising and falling of waves, and from the falling of water, and from the decomposing of dead things—how from the heat of death itself, new life can be created. Just as nature does this on its own all the time, people can make it happen too, and they can control it and make it faster.

But something that Kite always noticed in those explanations was that they did not seem to have a way of creating this energy without also destroying. The technology would make noise under the sea or pollution in the air, or it would stop up the rivers and flood the land, and millions of animals and people would have to leave their homes or die. Everything changes when people take nature into their own hands. And this, he knows, is why his mother is afraid.

Kite thinks how the people of the City—though someone in the City, somewhere, sometime, did write that book—do not seem to know about all of this. How in a way, he knew more about these things than they did, before he even left home. Maybe he came here because he wanted to know more than this. He wanted to know more than where energy comes from, more than how all the parts fit together in the long path between the simple sunlight or the decay of ancient creatures and the computer in the library. He wanted to know why. He wanted to know the root of this magic. He wanted to know what makes the world run. And he wanted to know if it is truly wrong for humans to change the face of the world.

He opens his eyes again, feeling suddenly alone. To comfort himself, he thinks of Delilah and Dragon nearby and mentally thanks them for their kindness, feeling shyly gratified to know that they want to see his home, that they believe it must be good for them and want to follow him there. He feels proud of his home for the first time. He imagines his mother meeting them, and it almost makes him laugh out loud.

The moon is thin, recently reborn, but the stars are ecstatically bright. Their brilliance seems to babble happily about the world a billion years before, from that world they lived in a billion light years away, in a language this world no longer speaks or understands. Kite watches them, thinking he is too cold to sleep, until sleep takes over after all. But before it does, he has the funny thought that before he came on this journey, he never would have liked a girl like Delilah. He would have been wary of her, turned off by her sarcasm and crude toughness. Now she dazzles him.

In his dream, the elements speak to him one by one, each one a god. Now they are no longer the soulless forces that overtook and nearly killed him. Or maybe they are, but there is a stillness within them, too, from whence they gaze at him, and speak to him, and there is once again a sense of meaning in the universe, even if it turns out that there isn't any mercy. He won't be able to remember, later, exactly what they said. The water goddess, her voice echoey and her dress flowing clear over her breasts, seems to say something like "it *does* mean love," but he can't remember the context of what she is saying, for that context has no beginning or end, like the story of a mountain stream. The fire god, young and dauntless and lusty like Dragon, makes a flaming frame around the wickedly smiling Delilah. The air goddess is Lonely, swinging her bare legs in the sun off the edge of a cliff, and while Kite waits breathlessly for her to leap, she looks thoughtfully upward and slowly asks questions of the wind. "What do people use energy for anyway? It's so beautiful, but used for such boring things! Computers, refrigerators, lawn mowers? What are these things? What is money for? Why do they leave the lights on all day and all night long?"

The questions make Kite nauseous. He wants to touch her, and he knows he will never reach her, that she is only a dream. Then he hears the earth goddess, and he does not know who she is, but her voice is the voice of his mother, and it makes him weep.

"We're all here," she says. "The earth, the wind, the water, the sun. We have so much to give. But the people are not ready yet. They do not have respect, they do not have gratitude. Whatever they are given, they waste and forget. If they learned to use the power of the sun, they would clear all the trees to get it. If they learned to use the power of water, they would dam all the rivers and turn the world to desert. Whatever they use, they use selfishly, and without wisdom. It is their hearts that must change, Kite. The knowledge itself is not so important, for it comes easily to them. They have the knowledge to do whatever they wish to do, but they have nothing to guide their choices but desire, and even they know that desire is not enough."

The dream seems to carry on forever, and Kite's mind is frustrated with its whirling attempt to understand, his hands lost and numb in his thin blanket, and only his heart at peace. Finally the dream Delilah reaches her hand through the fire, her eyes watery and vulnerable, her breath hot, and grips his painful erection with her small, knowing hand. "I'm scared," she whispers.

He wakes coming inside his pants, inside the blanket, and now he has nothing else to change into. But before he can worry about that, he wonders if he is truly awake after all, and then decides he must not be, because there is a beautiful girl he has never seen kneeling beside him.

She is like Delilah, and at the same time not like her at all—more like another form of Delilah, a gentler shade of Delilah in the dark. As if Delilah were the earth, fiery and alive and pregnant and tormented, and this girl were the moon—a ghost version of a girl, a girl immortalized in time.

She gives him a sad smile, her lips so slippery they don't seem able to hold solid form. Her eyes are the eyes of a deer, if a deer could truly love, if a deer could feel compassion for the predator that hunts it. Her brows, black and full like Delilah's, are at once more delicate, like porcelain, and her hair, black and thick like Delilah's rich mane, falls straight and sleek as an underground river. Her mouth and the curve of her lashes at the outside of her eyes are a girl's—but her eyes are an old woman's, and he doesn't feel ashamed as she gazes down at him where he woke from his passionate sleep. Nor does he feel tormented by the need to touch her, though he desires her more than anything he has ever desired.

For what seems like many moments, she sits still and gazes down at him, her long fingers pale in her quiet lap, her whole body cloaked in something dark, so that her face—though only a little lighter than Delilah's—above that darkness glows. He tries to understand what he sees there. Longing, curiosity? Is she telling him something? It's a warm feeling, and yet fragile, so that he dares not move a muscle in his face or his body. She is a dream, perhaps, of all the elements merged into one. The delicious weakness, the soft falling caress of water. The intensity of fire in that gaze he could never turn away from if he tried. The far-off wisdom of air. The silence of earth. Remembering the dream, he does not reach for her; he does not ask for anything. This gift has come to him, on her own, and he simply gazes back, not even trying to understand but only to love this moment with all the love he has, letting her presence change him in whatever way he must change.

He doesn't remember falling asleep again. He doesn't remember her leaving. Yet suddenly he is waking in the morning, and Delilah is already standing and stretching her arms in the sun, and his pants, as if by magic, are dry and clean.

The next night, the moon girl comes to Kite again.

It's the same as before. Delilah appears first, and this time with a mere brush of her downy hips makes him come. Then again he wakes and lies still in the moonlight of the young woman's eyes, and again he finds himself waking again in the morning with his pants strangely and conveniently dry.

Then the next night, the whole thing happens again.

He is distracted during the day, even as they travel further from the barren roads, and the silence of the hills settles around his mind. He begins to wonder, though he cannot understand it, if the real Delilah is coming to him in his dreams on purpose, making sure that he comes before waking to the sight of this beautiful girl—making sure he has already spent himself before he sees her. But why would that be? The mystery of it obsesses him, and he considers asking Delilah even casually, "Have you been having any dreams?" Because maybe she knows something about this sweet silent girl who comes to look sadly at him every night, whom he longs for but in whose presence he is afraid to move or breathe, lest he frighten her away.

But even the word "dreams" embarrasses him, and he cannot.

After Sky let go of the first woman he ever loved, after he felt her float away from him for the second time into the ethers, he walked out onto the island alone. He took the fragile, driftwood chair in his hands, broke it into pieces, and scattered the bones into the sea. Then he sat down on the cold stones and tried to remember why he was there, how old he was, and why he was lonely.

At first he felt simply relieved. *I have done it,* he thought. *Finally, I have fulfilled my duty, my promise. I can call myself a warrior again, without shame.*

He had come out of the dark hole and smiled, and the sea was nothing to him, and the wind was nothing; there was only this great empty relief. *I am no longer afraid,* he had thought.

And yet...

And yet what?

Yet there was another promise to be kept. *A promise you made to the Unicorn,* said the wind.

Time passed imperceptibly. The sea, pacing a cold rhythm against the shore of endless night, was no help. A fog curled in and wrapped itself around the island, then around his shoulders and around his ankles, like a stubbornly loyal dog.

It is I, he thought finally. *It is I who must go down to the Dark Goddess.*

The thought did not startle him. He thought of the Unicorn and the darkness below. He knew he must go. Yet for a long time—in fact for a whole moon, growing and dying again—he has felt no urgency in this knowing. He has sat here on the surface of the island, or at times he has stood and walked, but he has needed nothing and has felt no sense of past or future. He feels beyond sorrow now and beyond hope. He knows he must go, and yet what will make him go?

Perhaps, in the end, it is a kind of curiosity. Something nags at him. Someone is down there, below him, deep down within, and she has something to do with him—something important.

So he stands and walks, the stones sharper this time against his airy feet, and comes again to that hole between the stones with nothing to mark it but a simple blackness, a mirror of the dark moon, and he tries to remember. He tries to remember who she is, down there.

There is something else beneath the stubborn memory of his distant past in the swamp that he has lived with for so long, something more real and more painful. For so long, he feels now, he has been avoiding what is down there, and he cannot remember why. He squats and looks into that sad, black hole, like a wound, and feels tenderness like new spring grass begin to break its way through him, but of course the breaking through causes pain.

To calm himself, he tries to count the stairs as he goes down. But it is impossible. He loses track.

Though he came here before, without the old woman standing before him the darkness is different, bigger. When he arrives, he thinks at first that he is inside the lake. For there is *that* kind of darkness, the kind that listens, with a listening both comforting and terrifying. There is that impossible light too, though he cannot quite look at it yet, for he cannot tell where it comes from—the way sometimes one cannot tell the source of a sound, though one turns and turns.

He blows a breath, speaking to the wind in his own language, and listens. But there is no answer. The wind is not here.

He steps. His footsteps make no sound.

He sniffs. He smells a green vine growing, somewhere near, and wet earth.

The first thing he can see clearly is rainbows. Here and there he sees them: frames of rainbow as from a crystal, bouncing and shaking, appearing to his right and then to his left, and then gone, and then there again, and there. Yet, for there to be rainbows, there must be light and water. For rainbows to dance, there must be wind blowing the thing that made them. For rainbows to be visible, there must be light behind them too, or a thing they shine against—and yet there seem to be no walls. There seem to be none of these things. Only the rainbows.

He reaches toward one of them, and it flits away. But his hand brushes leaves.

He is hardly aware of taking a direction, until he realizes he is moving toward the light. For there is a light, though when he tries to focus upon it, still he cannot exactly find it. He only knows that it guides him, this physical, moon-like light. It is not really like light at all but like milk that pours over things.

Just barely, it illuminates a garden.

Now he is walking through reeds, that whisper as if they have almost forgotten their song, and over a wooden bridge, and into a great breathing place, encircled not by walls but by interlacing ivy, whose sharp-edged leaves cut into the soft light. And in the light he can see another room beyond, and his eyes, following the rainbows, glimpse even a room beyond that, silken and rose, and beyond that a door.

If this were a dream, he would say that he could hear, even fainter than the voice of the wind which is not here, the voices of women singing, soaring high, as if in prayer. If this were a dream he would say, *I am inside the body of a woman. This garden is the body of a woman.*

But he cannot go further, into the deeper rooms—not yet. For the light is here. Right here, in the chamber of the heart. The only sound now is the sound of this fountain, from which the light bubbles forth: not a leaping geiser of spray, but a smooth, lava-like churning of water and light, water and light, rolling forth in an endless froth of rainbows.

All around the fountain are the bodies of sleeping people. But they are so quiet, so still, so utterly peaceful, that they seem like stones. They look and even feel—for he kneels and touches one now, with tenderness, for he can tell they were forgotten here—like the kind of gnarled and ancient stones that have come tumbling through every cavern and storm and quake of the world, to land finally in some still place at the very bottom, even lower than the sea.

There in the center of them, in the center of that circle of stone people like a silent council, is that light, so familiar to him. Yet it is not a Unicorn's horn after all, that makes the light, as in the Council of Beings beneath the lake.

It is a woman who makes the light.

He feels foolish now, seeing her there, as if all the animals—and all the beings of the world—knew this obvious truth that it has taken him all this time to learn. It is she who makes the light. It is she who waits at the center of the darkness.

He stands again and walks cautiously to the pool of the fountain, which bubbles slowly in the center of itself and hardly disturbs the surface. He looks in.

There he sees her: the woman who loved him is floating there, like the thing they all spoke about for all those years without ever saying its name, without ever really looking at it. Now she is all he can look at—literally the only light. She floats curled on her side with one arm under her head, tangled in her strange yellow hair, and the other arm drifting, her fingers curled as if she reached for something sleepily before she closed her eyes. She is naked, though the moving water above her blurs her form. In sleep her eyes are hidden, but her body is alive and moves as if with breath, though she breathes underwater. And he sees her. He sees her like he saw her when she slept brand new and innocent in the tower, and when she slept, sweetly calling him, by the waterfall on the mountaintop, and when he came to her each morning in the places where the animals told him he would find her.

How accustomed he is, after all, to approaching the soul when it is sleeping. How much easier it is to come in the dark like this and not be seen!

Without noticing what he's doing, he leans forward, trying to see where the light in her comes from. He curls his hands over the stone ridge of the fountain's edge, clumsily, like paws.

He misses her. It's true! He breathes out suddenly and smiles, wanting to call out to her. But something stops him. What is it? He leans forward, so close now that he can smell the water, and it smells like her, and he closes his eyes. The silence of the garden around him is so gentle, the flickering of the ivy so secretly alive, it seems to cradle his thoughts like sacred embers, blowing on them faintly with its own mysterious breath. He remembers unwrapping such beauty, such fresh joy, from a cloud in the morning when he returned from sad dreams, and feeling her hot, damp arms curve around him, her fingers on his spine. He remembers that surprising warmth in a cold so familiar he had ceased to wonder at it. He remembers the trusting grip of her smooth hand, the openness of her eyes when he spoke, the love in her voice when he cried, and, most of all, the luxury of that oblivion, that terrifying melting, that wild deliverance, when he brought her body down into his arms on the shore of the lake that final night.

But something stops him, for there was something wrong. For the first time, he tries to remember what it was.

Why did you leave her? the silence seems to ask.

He always felt there was some reason. Perhaps she had done something he could not forgive or had proven that she could never truly understand him, or perhaps she had betrayed him in some way? They had woken that morning, and there was something wrong. Yes: he had slept, and the lake was silent. His people were gone, and she could never understand. She could never save him from that loss.

But that isn't it.

The silence is so loud now, he is forced to open his eyes again and look at her. His heart jumps. No, he realizes, it was because *he* would disappoint *her.* Because he could not give her what she wanted!

She kept asking something of him, over and over again, which he could not give, and she was angry with him, and it hurt him so much that he could not even bear to be near her. He remembers. When he woke that morning, he saw it would only be worse. When she opened her arms to him, he felt empty. He saw only his own failure.

So he had to run away into the past, into the loss he knew so well, into the familiar grief. He could not give her what she asked for: his whole heart. He had not even looked at his own heart for so long, and he did not know what was there, and he did not want to know. Not then.

Is that all? he thinks now.

He folds his arms upon the rim of the fountain, rests his head upon them, and gazes in. He lived in this death-like stillness for a hundred years. He could rest here for a hundred more, only gazing at her, and what would it matter? What if he still cannot rescue her? What if he cannot give her what she needs? The truth is she is braver than he. The truth is that he fears the things she will feel, the things she will ask of him, if she wakes.

Yet how lonely it is—how lonely it has always been—to be the only one thinking, the only one awake!

He tries to see her. He tries to see her as if he has never seen her before, as if each detail of her body and each moment of her being were a gift made innocently and earnestly by a pure-hearted child. He tries to see her as if he were truly a god, and she were truly nothing more than what is.

He sees the woman who loved, though she, too, was afraid. He sees the helplessness of her hair and her flesh to gravity, the helplessness of her mind to sleep. He sees the good intention that led her here, the tender foolishness of her humanity, and the way her eyes move beneath her eyelids in search of the light and ever forgetting. He sees the shape of her: the hips that spread and circle to welcome and nourish love, the shoulders that hold and protect her, the breasts that offer life to him who would take it. He sees the lips that do not know themselves when they speak, the cheeks that fall sadly, the heroic and hardy feet turned together in rest.

The more he watches her—the more he watches that moonlight that comes from her and tries to understand where it is and how it arises—the more he wants to touch her. The urge lurches, breathless and heavy, through his stalled mind. He feels his own hand, like an undiscovered creature, crawl of its own volition toward the surface of the water, toward the place where hers is drifting. As it draws closer, he hears the ocean screaming in his ears;

he feels his heart panting in his mouth; his ankles burn; his earlobes vibrate.

He stops when his fingers touch the water, for the water is so warm it is nearly hot. Then he moves quickly, suddenly knowing that he must rescue her again, that it is for this he is here, to wake her from this dream. He reaches through the warm water for her smooth waist and cups his hand beneath her shoulder. But he cannot touch her. She is right there, but he cannot reach her. Something is happening to her body. Rainbows flash on her skin as the light turns back on itself, playing tricks with his eyes. The more he tries to catch those rainbows in his vision—here at her throat, here in the crook of her elbow, here under her eyes, here burning between her breasts—the more they draw him in and the more they thicken. Like the fog out on the shore, colors surround her and hide her face—indigo, blood red, midnight blue, ecstatic yellow, lucid green, flaming orange, violet. Then he is spinning among them, and before he even knew he would go in, he is in—he is underwater. He is spinning lost in a whirlpool of color, and she is spinning, too, and still he cannot reach her.

"I love you," he says. "I love you! I love you! I love you!" The words, underwater, bubble from his mouth. He paws at the rainbows, pulling them aside. He reaches for her body.

The colors merge into light. He sees her eyes. They are open. They are dark, like her mother's—nearly purple in their darkness, but so bright.

She smiles. Lonely, the woman he loves.

He is kissing her. This time, he knows what he is doing. This time he means it, not because he has a dream of what will happen, but in spite of his fear of what could happen and all that happened before. How easily she touches him now! How easy he feels in the water, how much more real than he ever knew. She draws him in with her hands, her warm everywhere-ness, so fast it overwhelms him. How he missed her! How could he never know how much he missed her? With a giant need he did not even know was there, he is already inside her, so recklessly does the hot dark cave of the goddess engulf him. All his thinking gone, all his dreams—he is something else now. He is so deep inside her that he cannot see himself, and there is nothing to hold onto, and he rises above his own self and then falls inside the fingernail grip of her small hands on his shoulders, exploding before he even knows what is happening. He falls asleep inside her arms, inside the ocean, inside the world, before he has time to feel afraid.

Maybe she hasn't rescued Mira after all. Because what is this silent creature, like an unsolved mystery, walking beside her?

They are following the purple ridge now, which is not purple up close but many colors in the changing light, bushy in all its crevices with gnarled ever-green shrubs and waxy serrated leaves. A stream runs between the ridge and the City, from which they draw water into a leather bag every morning. But it narrows more and more until they reach the place where several moons ago—though it seems many lifetimes ago now—Delilah watched the ridge blasted through to make way for the road. The road is black and shining with nothing on it. They cross it and continue upward, through ever-young, scratchy forest that has been cleared again and again, and through newly cleared wastelands of stumps and crows. Using Kite's map, they find a new stream that is one of many forks connecting to the one Kite says runs right through his house, still a long way away.

In order not to let the sight of these forest wounds, these deep emptinesses, weaken her further, in order not to go mad with the silence of the Unicorn and the feeling of despair that sweeps through her every time she looks at it, in order not to weep with the frustration of her constant, ravenous hunger, in order not to think of all the things she craves, in order not to let her despairing bones collapse beneath her, Delilah tries to focus on love.

She knows that Dragon loves her. She knows that all she would have to do is ask, and he would support her physically with his strong body, even carry her, perhaps, every step of the way. It is too much for her to imagine such a thing, but she tries, little by little, drop by drop, to let herself acknowledge his love, even if she doesn't show it, even if she avoids his eyes.

At first she hated to need their help; she hated for them to come quickly to take her arm whenever she stumbled. But maybe that is only something she has gotten used to telling herself. Maybe she doesn't hate it at all. Maybe she only wants to hate it, because not to hate it feels selfish. These are the strange, delirious thoughts that come to her as they walk, when she is so tired she can barely register her surroundings.

Now she is listening to Dragon as he listens to Kite, as they talk behind her. She listens to Dragon's earnest, serious response, and she can imagine his brows drawing importantly together, his head bent to concentrate on the words of this new friend he holds so dear. It almost makes her smile. Kite is talking about some girl he likes.

"…more beautiful than any woman I have ever seen," he's saying, "and I don't know…" But she can't catch the rest of it because he is whispering in a choked, embarrassed sort of way.

Dragon's voice is a little louder. "What do you think she wants?"

"I don't know," Kite says. "I never thought of that. Maybe she wants something from me. But how can I know what it is?"

"Maybe she needs some opening from you, some offering."

Delilah doesn't know who the girl is, but she feels a silly little twinge of sadness, like she's never felt before, that no one has ever spoken of her that way. With that kind of reverence and wonder for what is innocent and pure, that boyish desire which the boy holds back because he respects so much what is desired.

It must be the pregnancy that makes her so unpredictably emotional. Suddenly she loves both of them. But most of all she feels for Dragon, who has loved her, from the beginning, with an innocence she could not accept until now. She has wanted to tell him the child is his—she has wanted to and yet cannot. She does not want the burden of his pity, his sense of obligation to her, or whatever he might feel about it. She doesn't want how vulnerable it makes her feel, as if somehow telling him would mean admitting to that last time they made love—as if somehow he would know, by her pregnancy, how deep he really got inside her that time, how deeply he claimed her, how vividly she always remembered the world inside his arms that day, and how vividly she always will.

What is the love of this life she carries within her, something her body acknowledged long ago even though her mind is still catching up—a different kind of love, a love no one has ever felt for her? The love of something that needs her, that would die without her, that is part of her, that decided, against her will, that she was good enough, whole enough, to grow up inside. She tries to be grateful for that, though it terrifies her.

But Mira—is this really her? Is this strange white being who walks beside them any more or less her sister than the empty shell of a girl that Delilah shook by the shoulders so long ago, who could no longer form human words? That blessed moment on the beach where two sisters held each other and felt the skin over each others' spines, where they spoke to and understood one another—that time, like a dream fulfilled, is gone now. Mira has not been human since, nor has she spoken, nor has she given any indication of recognizing Delilah, except by traveling with them now. Sometimes Delilah tiptoes to the Unicorn in the night, thinking she will stroke its back and whisper Mira's name. But the Unicorn stands untouchable and does not look toward her as she approaches. Delilah always stops, her heart falling through her rib cage in sorrow, and cannot go on. She stops the way she stopped as a child before the sight of Mira sitting in their father's lap, in the kitchen in the middle of the night. She stops because she feels she does not belong in the place where her sister is.

But is that really the reason? For she knows something more now, deep in her guts, something she never wanted to know about what happened in that kitchen between a man and a little girl. Is it Dragon's powerful male presence, perhaps, that frightens Mira and keeps her inhuman? Or is it this thing still unspoken between Mira and Delilah? For in Delilah's heart, there nags the thought that in their youth, as much as she swore to defend Mira and begged her to speak her secrets, still there was a question that Delilah never asked. A question she would never have acknowledged then, but which she is forced to acknowledge now. In Delilah's heart, there nags the persistent possibility that rescuing Mira was not the final great act of courage after all. There is something still to be done, something Delilah is more than afraid to do, because it would require rebuilding the entire structure of her memories. It implicates her in a guilt greater than, as a child, she ever knew.

There is something else haunting Delilah, too, with every step she takes toward the mountains and away from the desert forever. It isn't her painful and surprising nostalgia for the cave she called home for so many years, or the proud survival she staked in that place, or even the wind and the space of that freedom—that home, that land of outcast animals, that brutal place that loved her against all odds and that she misses against all odds now. No, it is what's beyond the desert that haunts her. It is that forest of her dreams and all her nourishment, the forest of her father, which she promised to burn down and could not. Maybe she told herself that after her search for Mira, she would return to do it. But of course that was never going to happen. And the pine forest, be it a dream or not, is still there: she knows because she dreams of it almost every night, and she wakes with a coldness in her bones, for in the dreams there are no animals, no sign of life. There is only a sad, empty blowing through the abandoned spaces between the trees, like a song of loss, like the sound of betrayal.

Who has been betrayed? Her father, Mira, the forest, Delilah herself? Sitting on the ridge in the evening while the boys insist on cooking her food, she stares out toward the desert and toward that cliff she knows is out there. It is impossible for her to go there now. She'll be lucky if she makes it alive to Kite's house, with the little strength that's left in her.

One night when the moon is full, with her head against a dusty, soft rock that reminds her of the desert, she dreams she hears the cicadas breathing in their cocoons where they nurse patiently from the nourishing roots of trees. This year they are going to sing, after seventeen years of growing in the dark truth of the earth. This year they have finally learned their song. In the dream she hears the silence of that shrill song before it is sung, and she knows you have to wait for age, you have to wait for wisdom, but if you keep drinking from the roots of things it will come. Then Delilah knows she will survive after all, and she knows the older she gets, the stronger she will be. She can feel spring breathing up from the ground.

In the dream the cicadas are telling her a story, which she cannot remember immediately when she wakes. But like the morning she woke from a dream in the desert where she slept in hopelessness at the river's end, she wakes with a fierce clarity, and that clarity contains Mira's name.

She creeps to the Unicorn, who is lying white in the grey, cold grass, eyes open. She kneels down. She grips the base of its neck between the shoulder blades and whispers sharply in its silken ear.

"Mira," she says. She watches its eyes. "There is a pine forest beyond the desert. If you know where it is, take me there."

With a jolt, the Unicorn stands. The hairs of its mane bristle like the hairs on a human's cold skin. Delilah lets go. They breathe together for a moment of awkward silence, Delilah staring at the body of this animal, wondering at the lands it has traveled, remembering her father in the body of a boar with two white horns bursting out of his face. The Unicorn stands unmoving. It takes a great mental shift for Delilah to realize that she is not being proud or distant, but simply waiting for Delilah to get on.

Delilah hoists herself up easily; the Unicorn is small. Delilah has never ridden a horse before. She feels the animal's belly contract with breath between her thighs. She wonders how they will get there. Will they run? Fly?

But while she is wondering, they are already there.

For the Unicorn moves the way dreams move. Or the way cars move. You are here in one place, and then all of the sudden, while you are thinking about something else, you are in another place. There is no memory of the between-here-and-there that connects the two places. For a dream is like a road, where we cannot feel the passing of the landscape, and the City, with its disconnected spaces, is and always was a kind of dream.

They are already here. Delilah slides off the Unicorn's back and lets go. The Unicorn glows in the dead silence of the pine shadows, a glow that seems to communicate directly with the moon. Delilah feels the old sorrow and horror of the hunt fly like a distant scream through her bones.

"Mira," she says, and Mira the Unicorn turns and looks into her eyes. "I killed a doe here once, Mira," she says. "With eyes like yours."

Then she realizes that she doesn't have to figure out how to explain why they are here. Mira is the one person in the world who will understand without any disclaimers or explanations, the one person to whom she can tell a dream without apologizing for the disjointed elements, the confusion, the senselessness, the beings that changed form and the places that were more than one place. Because Mira is crazy.

So Delilah says without any preamble, "Our father came to me here, Mira. He came in the form of a boar. He took me to the heart of the forest, after I had hunted here for ten years. He told me I had to burn this forest down. But I could not do it. Do you know why?"

The Unicorn is frozen. She might actually be made of ice, she holds so still. Delilah cannot see her breathing. She is not still the way she was when Delilah came toward her questioningly in the night, back on the ridge with the boys. She is still like something so terrified that it hopes stillness alone will keep it from being seen. Yet how ridiculous it is to see this stillness in one whose light shines so brightly, so beautifully, that the trees seem to sigh in its presence and the whole forest rests with relief inside it. Filled with tenderness, Delilah rises up and wraps her arms around the Unicorn's neck.

"I just remembered," she whispers. "I remembered the story I dreamed. The story the cicadas have been drinking from the trees."

The Unicorn twitches. Delilah is startled, suddenly, by the mirror light of her horn. If she looks at it closely, it seems to reflect rivers, forests, meadows....

"It goes like this," she says, trying not to think, breathing into the Unicorn's trembling shoulder. "A hundred years ago, Hanum, a desperate and lonely man, destroyed the heart of the world and built a City on top of it. He cleared forests all around it for wood, and he sucked the earth dry for the magic fuel of the ancestors that would make the City run. The peoples who lived in the magical places were all driven out. Without their land, they could not make sustenance or meaning, and they lost each other. The only way they could survive was by finding jobs in the City and making money." Delilah presses her forehead to the Unicorn's back, for she feels foolish. She's no story-teller. She's no healer. Everything she's saying, so simple and child-like, is nothing more than the basic history she and Mira have always known. In fact, Mira probably knows far more, more that their father revealed only to her....

But beneath her head, something is changing in the fur of the animal. It is thinning. The Unicorn's body is baring its vulnerable skin—the way a man bares his head to the heavens as he ages, or the way baby animals are born bare, or the way humans bared their bodies to the Universe and gave themselves up, long ago, saying *I will make my own protection or I will die.* The Unicorn is evolving into a human being.

So Delilah keeps going. "A man who was once a shaman of his people, who once had direct communication with their Goddess, and knew the Unicorn by name, now lost himself in the anonymous monotony of factory work. Then one day, twenty-five years ago, it rained, one last time, over the buildings and the pavement, and when the man felt the tears of the sky he almost remembered. He wept for joy. He saw a beautiful woman coming toward him, and she reminded him of what he had lost. He thought that if he could have her, he might be able to begin again. He thought, *This woman will embody for me all of the universe, all of the spirit which I have lost. I will worship this woman, and in her I will hide the secret of my faith.* And so they fell in love, or thought they did, Mira. They got married. But they did not understand each other. The woman could no longer see in him the shaman she thought she had found. For he was beaten down, day after day, by the soulless work in the soulless factory. Then the man could no longer see the light in her. Instead, he saw only his own failure. Then they had two daughters, Mira—"

Such a simple story, a story they both know and could have told a thousand times, and yet Delilah stops because she cannot go on. The white mane is turning black, the Unicorn is falling to her knees, and the horn is blinding. No, she must go on. There is no choice now.

"The older daughter could see from the first that there was only pain and cruelty in this marriage. She decided not to believe in love and never to go seeking after it. She left her parents as early as she could and fought her own way. She built a hardness around her heart. But the younger daughter's heart bled when she saw her father's sorrow, from the time she was old enough to see. She alone could see through the defenses of each person in her family, and she alone grew up to love each one's real heart with her own pure heart.

"But Mira, her father betrayed that love. Her father used the younger sister's love to keep her silent, while he—" Delilah pauses again, afraid. But she can feel her sister's hair now, in her fingers, and the damp heat of it. She can feel the body of the girl sweating against her own. She can feel that Mira doesn't know what she is or where she is, that she is helpless inside this story, helpless in Delilah's arms—and that she, Delilah, has all the power. She, the predator. So she has to be brave. "While he violated her. While he hurt her. He thought that he could save himself in her. He was selfish. And yes, he was selfish because he was suffering, but he was still wrong. He was still wrong and Mira, I'm so sorry—" Delilah presses her tears gently, like an offering, into her sister's now horn-less head. "We all betrayed you. All three of us. I left you for the boys. I thought it was the only way I could be loved."

"I thought so, too," says Mira.

It's a voice Delilah has never heard. Not the voice of madness or the voice of the wise child, but the voice of an elder whom Delilah has never seen. Delilah pulls back and looks into her face—a child's face baffled by its own womanhood, eyes afraid but determined inside their own beauty.

"Tell me your story now," she whispers to Mira. "If you want to, I want to hear it."

Mira shakes her head. She swallows several times, as the words seem to crawl up her throat, trying to emerge. "You—" she begins hoarsely. "You've seen it. What they did—what they did to the earth."

"I know," says Delilah. "I've seen that. But you are not the earth, Miri. You are not the whole world. You are only one girl, one woman. He was looking for the universe inside you, and he never found it, because it's not there. At least, not for someone who doesn't truly love you."

"But he did love me," sobs Mira, and then she seems to break, enfolding her face in her hands like something she has decided to wrap up again forever. Delilah reaches for her.

"It's okay, little sister," she says. "Of course he did. And he's sorry, Miri. He told me to tell you so. He told me to tell you he's sorry, before he died."

Mira keeps sobbing. The moon inches across the sky above them, as slowly as if they have all the time in the world. Delilah, holding her, has never felt such peace.

"Do you know this place?" she asks Mira after a long time, when Mira is quieter and her body sags lightly against Delilah's. "How did you know where it was?"

"Of course I knew," Mira sighs, her breath clearing a little, her voice sweet as if beyond all the rage and pain of her past, through all the years of numb forgetting, she can pick out some little pebble of beauty. "He told me all about it. Where he came from."

"So you can see it, too?" asks Delilah, suddenly excited, pulling back again, to search her sister's face—as if she could see the forest she walked so alone in for so many years in her sister's eyes. "The boar—our father said it was only a dream."

"He must have meant," says Mira, "because it's all gone now."

"What do you mean, all gone?" asks Delilah quietly, but a shiver passes through her and roots her to the ground. She looks past Mira's shoulder. She jumps backward and grips the dirt. The dust. She looks out into the air.

There is no forest here, only a vast area of clearcut land, most of the stumps already rotting or gone. The land is so barren that not even a crow remains to pick through the pieces. There is nothing but moon and sky and earth.

"But where is it?" she murmurs stupidly.

"You said it yourself," says Mira. "They cut it all down, and that's why Father had to leave."

"So it was never here? I only dreamed it?"

Mira leans forward and kisses Delilah's face, in a gesture so strange, confusing, and beautiful that Delilah almost doesn't care about anything else. "Not 'only'," says Mira.

"But why did he want me to burn——?"

"Because it takes a fire to make the pines grow again."

Delilah stares at her. What part is so difficult for her to understand? She doesn't know, but she feels lost. Suddenly Mira is the wise one, like always.

"See, sister," says Mira. "There is nothing to be lost. Now make a fire."

With hurried and desperate hands, as if dumbly obeying orders in an emergency that is too much for her own mind to handle, Delilah rips off pieces of the stumps and twists them fast. This she can do. She makes a fire. She thrusts the torch at Mira.

"May this heal you," she says at the last minute, because she knows that long ago—in her father's time—people made rituals to transform their lives and their world, and those rituals had blessings and words that held power. She doesn't know how to make a ritual, but as she hands her sister the fire, she feels that it is making itself.

Mira lights the dry peeling layers of the stumps. She lights the decaying twigs upon the ground and the dead pine needles of a hundred years ago. They ignite as if by magic, as if they had been waiting, as if the fire had been inside them all along. They light like jewels behind Mira's human feet; they hesitate, then dart forward, as she walks around and around in a widening spiral of flame. Delilah closes her eyes.

It's okay, she thinks. *Give in. Let the hunger take you, for once. Be the awful, uncontrollable thing you are—be free.*

And she is so relieved by the fire's rage, by its wild forgiveness as it devours and rises and roars around her, that not until the smoke makes her cough does she remember her own humanness.

She opens her eyes, still without fear, and the Unicorn emerges from the flames like moving stone. Delilah, a dark and laughing spider, clambers on and, wrapping her arms around the humanly warm white neck, allows herself to be borne away.

She wakes to the sound of rain and does not open her eyes.

In that rain she feels Moon's kisses all over her skin. She feels his nostalgia for being human, and she knows he is reminding her how delicious it is to be alive in this body. She feels the comfort of his love that encloses both her and Mira, and she knows that Mira is sleeping nearby, in this meadow—this new meadow that dawns in this new day, where she is traveling with the people who love her to the first real home she has ever been to.

She listens to Yora's voice in the river that runs nearby, and the old woman inside her remembers a time that the child Delilah never knew—a time when everyone understood the language of water, though it did not speak in words. Everyone wanted to eat near water; everyone wanted to build their homes near it, not only for drinking, bathing, and washing but also because it spoke to them. When families gathered by lakes or coves, their voices softened, their laughter was easier, and they forgot their petty quarrels. When lonely people sat down beside babbling brooks, their sadness felt peaceful instead of painful. When lovers lay beside waterfalls, they were transported into fairy tales. Poets got their poetry from that music, and story-tellers their stories. The water spoke every language, and could cure every ailment. The ocean helped people forget. The rivers helped people remember. And the rain was something personal and tender, someone you knew by name and longed for.

Now within the sound of the rain, Moon is calling Delilah's attention, gently, lovingly—knowing she is ready for it—to something else.

When she realizes it is the sound of Dragon crying, and looks up through the kaleidescope of the rain to see the terrible twistedness of Dragon's boyish face gazing down at her in tears, she isn't angry or afraid. She looks back at him, feeling older than she is. *You are wiser than he,* Moon seems to say. *Be kind.*

She still feels that strange deep peace, unlike anything she has ever felt in her life.

"What is it?" she asks.

"Delilah, I have to know," Dragon sniffs. "I have to know."

"What?" But she knows. It is time to tell him. How could she have waited so long? How could she have been so selfish with the life within her, which belongs to them both and which, truly, belongs to neither of them? "Okay."

"You'll tell me the truth?"

She looks at him, confused. "Of course."

"You love him, don't you? Tell me—has he touched you? How long have you known him? When did it start? How long have you known each other?"

Startled into complete wakefulness, she pushes herself up, pushes him off of her. "Known *who?*"

"Malachite."

"*What?*"

"Tell me the truth, you promised you would."

It takes her several moments to take this in. Then she knows it's true, that he is still the same Dragon after all. She has to struggle not to laugh. He is the crazy one, after all, so much crazier than Mira ever was.

"Dragon, listen to me. *I just met Kite.* When you introduced him to me half a moon ago. He's a child. Of course I don't want him, love him, like that. *Of course* I've never touched him!" She tries to keep her voice low, hoping Kite hasn't overheard. She's not sure exactly how far away he is sleeping.

To her surprise Dragon seems at least tempted to believe her. He looks hard at her. She realizes then what will help, and when she finally says it, she says it for that reason—to help him. "Dragon, this child is yours. This child I'm carrying. I haven't touched anyone since we—since we last made love."

To her great embarrassment, he flings his arms around her then and begins to fully weep. She wraps her tired arms back around him. Sometimes he can be her god, it is true—sometimes the force of her own desire for him has allowed him to own her almost completely, for a few delirious moments—but at other times, he is that same ridiculous boy after all.

"Dragon, when you say you want to be the lover of the world, how can you expect me to be yours...?"

"I know," he sniffs into her shoulder. "I know."

"It's okay." But she can't hold him up any more. She unwraps his hands, unwinds his arms, and leans into him so that he falls a little back from her body. Then, because she doesn't know what else to do with them, she lays his hands down on her belly. She watches him slowly smile into her eyes; she recognizes the pride there. And she can't help but smile back, a smile that cracks her dry lips.

"Feel this, Coyote," Dragon whispers. "Feel this. *Mother*."

They sit there, quietly and foolishly smiling at each other. Two clumsy, broken halves of a miracle that neither of them will ever be able to explain.

Thank you, thinks Delilah. *Thank you, Mira, for rescuing me.*

"It feels good to be a woman again."

"Do you like being a woman?"

"Yes. Do you like being a man?"

"I don't know. Right now I do."

When they stop speaking, the water murmurs between them, as if they still speak. How long have they been here? They cannot see anything, nor smell. They continue to hold each other. There are no boundaries around them, no walls. The water fills them peacefully; there is only touch.

"I wish we could stay here," says Sky.

"I wonder if we're under the sea," says Lonely. "I wonder how we're speaking?"

Sky doesn't answer.

"Are you human now?" she whispers.

"I don't know. I don't remember, any more, how that felt. I don't feel hungry."

"We're both awake now, at least."

"Yes."

"Have you ever killed anything?" she asks. "Did you hunt for food, where you lived?"

"We fished," he answers thoughtfully. "But with fish it's different. You're not really killing them, in a violent, personal way. You're just moving them from one world to another: water to air. That change kills them, all by itself. Isn't it strange?"

"Yes." She thinks a moment. "Sky?"

"Yes?"

"We need to go back to the City, I think."

He is silent.

"I mean not in a dream form, not in some other form, but as we are now."

He is silent, like a little boy. She strokes his head. "Are you afraid?"

He seems to melt a little into her chest; he allows himself to melt, which moves her. "I'm only a dream, Lonely," he murmurs.

"No," she insists. "Sometimes the dream and the real worlds merge. Like you and me. That's when things really do change."

When he doesn't answer, she adds in a deeper whisper, "I have to do something, Sky. Those people need to see me as I am, finally, and I need to see them. I owe it to them. I owe it to my father, or he'll drift for all eternity, regretting. Don't you know that?"

It's what Sky has always wanted her to do, she thought. Isn't this her destiny? She thinks he will be proud of her now, that he will respond with that stiff opinion in his voice like he did long ago on the mountain, when he told her she must follow her own destiny and not get attached to personal loves. Truly it does not matter now, she tells herself, if he comes with her or not. She will hate to leave him, but she will do it anyway.

Yet he only asks, "And you, Lonely, are you human now?" The question is so gentle, almost teasing in its irony, but also so sad.

"Almost," she says. "But my name isn't Lonely any more. I forgot my real name, so I'll need to think of a new one, at least for now. Will you come outside and help me find one?"

He pulls away and strokes her floating hair. "You're not lonely any more?"

"No, it's not that. It's just that everyone is lonely. That's what I learned, when I came through the City in the other form I was in. If everyone is lonely, it isn't right for me to take that name for mine alone."

Sky nods, and that distant look passes over his eyes, like a mist. "I guess not," he says thoughtfully.

For a moment, she wishes he hadn't accepted it so easily. Her heart pulls childishly in her for a moment, wishing he would take her in his arms and tell her he understands how truly lonely she has been, how she has suffered as no one else has, and how he is here for her now, rescuing her from that loneliness. But she knows it is better this way.

"Come on," she says.

She takes his hands.

"Lonely." He looks at her. "I don't know how. How do we wake up?"

Lonely smiles, remembering how once he taught her to fly. *You have to imagine it first,* he'd said. *Imagine the ground is gone.* She stretches her limbs. "Put your feet on the ground," she says. "This is our dream, so let's dream the stone."

They do.

"Now stand," says Lonely.

They do. A wave of water cascades from their heads, over their bodies, and crashes to the stone. They stand dripping. What was the fountain is only a puddle at their feet, and it is dawn on the island, where they stand out in the open again, under the grey sky and the wheeling gulls. There is no hole, no darkness below. Nor is there a tower. Only the two of them, naked on the surface of the world. He shivers in the wind. She buries her face in his chest, her eyes shut against the pain of the sun.

"I knew you'd come," she says.

"I didn't," he says, still shivering. "I didn't know."

"But you told me, remember? You said the world is round. So I knew we'd come back to each other."

"I know. But there are things that I knew in my mind, but not in my heart. I told you so many things that I knew, but I did not really know. Maybe I was only telling you all those things to remind you of what *you* already knew, because I knew if you could remember, you could help me."

"But I didn't," she says sadly. "I didn't help you."

He thrusts her away from his body and holds her there, so he can see her face. "You did," he cries softly. "You rescued me!"

She looks into his eyes, searching, and begins to smile.

"What is your name?" he laughs. "What is the name of my rescuer? Aren't you going to tell me who you are?"

She laughs, too, but she is afraid. She turns aside. "Okay." *Get it over with,* she thinks. *Don't make a big deal of it. You can always change it later.* "Maybe a word in your language, in my mother's language."

"Ah," he says, still teasing. "So you will make me guess? It's only fair, I suppose, after all I made you guess about me."

"How do you say 'wind'?" she asks.

He makes a sound with his breath that she finds impossible to imitate.

"Never mind. How about 'love'?"

He makes a deep sound, like the song of the oldest whale, that takes her breath away. "That kind of love?"

"Never mind," she says again. It has to be an easy word for other people to speak, not something that takes your whole being to make it every time.

"Maybe it's not something so big and universal like that," says Sky more gently, seeing her fear. "You're only one woman, after all. Even if perhaps you are the most beautiful woman in the world." He smiles a sincere, elegant smile that neither hurts nor flatters.

"You're right!" cries Lonely. "Here I am, doing it again. I'm wasting all this time on my big idea of myself, when out there so many people are suffering, and we don't have much time." She turns and begins to walk in looping circles, as if with intention. "We'll just look around. I'll find something that feels right." She turns her eyes to the ground, acting casual, and then she scans the air. Yet inside of her things are being wrenched apart. She feels like she is killing herself. She feels like crying out, *But it has to be big! It is my NAME!* Yet she stumbles forward, trying to find something beautiful. She picks up a lovely pebble, striated turquoise and pink, but it has no name. She looks up at the sky, and finds the frayed wing shape of a pretty cloud that will never come again, but it has no name either. She bends down and touches the cold layers of the water, and feels the shadows in between them, but they, too, have no names. So many beautiful things in this world have no name.

Suddenly she feels the warm shape of her only love enclosing her from behind. He squats, bending his knees around her thighs where she kneels. "Close your eyes, Beloved," he says softly.

She does. She hears the jeering cry of the gulls, angry, happy, and wild, and she feels the precious breath of Sky on her cheek. She remembers all her other names, the names this life gave to her: *Princess, Beloved, Yora, Meadow, Daughter,* and that name in her mother's language, which no one but she ever heard or ever would. But she wants a new name, one she doesn't associate with any one person or loss, one that everyone can speak..

She smells the lusciousness, the depth, the pain of the sea. What is that smell? That smell that makes the sea more than water, more than just the cold nameless element from which the first heartless, soulless life was born. It reminds her of the first time she breathed the fresh air through a hole her own breath and body had made in the ice of her tower wall. It reminds her of her own sex, hungry and delirious with pleasure. It reminds her of the taste of Sky's human skin. It reminds her of everything human. It even reminds her of being born.

"Salt," she whispers.

"Salt," he whispers back.

She opens her eyes and looks out over the silver nothingness. "But is it wrong of me to claim such an important word? Isn't it as important as the wind and love and loneliness?" She bites her lip, holding back the thrill of it, feeling selfish.

"I guess so. But you came to it in a different way. Not from your mind. Not from imagining yourself bigger than you are, but from your body, your heart, and from being here in my arms."

"But someone else could be Salt too. How could I claim it for mine?"

"Someone else *can* be named Salt. I'm sure someone is. You *don't* claim it. That's not what a name is. A name is something that claims you. A name is what you give of yourself to the world."

She sighs. The breaking apart inside her, the stretching she felt, is happening, but the collapse she expected never comes. It doesn't hurt so badly after all. She feels like she's done this before. Her new name grows gently over her, like fur.

When she opens her eyes, the name has taken a physical form, a new gown around her: simple, a little rough but flowing, nudging alive her most sensitive places, protecting her bare skin.

"You look older," he says, and she remembers the way he first saw her, at the spring at the top of the world. How far they have come! Now they stand close together, broken and cleansed, at the other end of the water's journey—the deep end of that long fall.

He takes her hands. "Salt," he says.

She smiles, full of joy.

Then he says, "Salt," again, and she realizes it is the beginning of a sentence, that he wants to tell her something. "I will come with you to the City. It is my path, too, I know. Coyote was right. I must face the nightmares."

Not understanding the suffering in his face, she reaches to touch it, and opens her mouth as if to speak, but doesn't know what to say.

"Salt," he says again, and he grips her shoulders in his hands. His eyes are such a pale and wild blue, not cold after all, but so crystal-bright they are like fire—like the extreme heat at the center of a flame. "I want you to understand. I—"

She freezes, waiting in the flame of those eyes, for never before has he hesitated over words like this; never before has his voice stumbled through his body like this, as if that body were some unexplored, rocky terrain.

"I want you to understand that, if we stay here on this island forever, I think we will be happy. I would stay with you forever. I could keep us alive in some magical way. We would speak with the gulls and the terns, the passing migrations. We would learn about the sky, and we would listen to the sea all our days, and a long time from now, we would even be able to understand the language of the stars. There would be only us, inside our love."

"But," cries Lonely, forgetting her new name, alarmed by how quickly she can feel herself falling into the temptation of such a dream, "I thought you said we couldn't live only for ourselves—"

"I know," he whispers, and he pulls her swiftly against his chest and holds her tight there. "But I would now. I would live only for us. I would."

She sinks into the deep bliss of that holding and allows herself for a moment to think nothing, only to rest in her own longing. But the song of the wind around them sounds sad. Beyond his shoulder, she sees the others, the others who woke with her. They are mostly still for now. They sit in a daze, huddled apart from each other in the wind, their eyes white and bright. They look like the stones. Slowly, slowly, they will wake and remember. She has not truly looked at them yet. Soon she will have to. And so will Sky.

"If we leave here," Sky says, his lips close to her ear, "I don't know what will happen to me. I want you to know that. I can't promise anything. I can't even promise I will stay with you."

"Why not?" she cries, pulling away and looking at him. "What difference does it make, where we are?"

But the anguish in his eyes is so powerful, it brushes that little bit of anger away from her heart like dust. "I'm trying to tell you the truth," he pleads. "I'm sorry to give you this choice, but I don't know what will happen to me if we enter that world."

She lets her hands fall from his arms. She feels the old weight all over her. "I know what is right," she sighs, looking down. "I know what I have to do. We are not the only ones who woke, Sky. You do not know, still, the darkness that is part of me. They are like my own blood, these people who woke with me. They are nothing but human. They are hungry, thirsty, cold, lonely...."

But he lifts her chin in his hand, and for the rest of her life she will remember the tenderness, the utterly selfless urgency in his eyes as he answers, "I do know them. I do see them. You mistake me—and them. Don't you see the wisdom that is in them? Don't you believe yet in magic? Listen to me, Lonely—Salt—don't do what you think you should do. Do what you long to do. It is more important than anything—for you, for me, and for the whole world. Follow your longing, and things will come right for everyone. You are the goddess of longing. Without your longing, I wouldn't be here. I would be in a place so distant, so unreal, so unattached to anything, forever—" He stops, his voice full of tears, and shakes his head. "Far worse than anything that could happen to me in the City. Worse than death."

So she takes him back into her arms again. She strokes his back, crying with the memory of his silent tears in the meadow, his heavy walk across the lake to her, all the invisible worlds she could not see, that he had to break through in order to get to her. The name *Lonely*, too, will always be a part of her, and she sees that. But she imagines this life now: whole in their aloneness together, alone with the whole universe singing to them, forever. His heart forever warm and human, beating against hers. Finally.

"This isn't a decision I can make," he says. "I have made the decisions I have needed to make, and I surrender now. Whatever you choose, I promise, will be right."

We were born into a world that had no story.

It had no reason for being. It had a Creator, but we did not know the story of that Creator, why He had created this place, or if He had ever loved us.

Every people, the Prince told us in the end, must have a story to sustain it. We must have a story to teach us how to live, why we matter, where the beginning and the end lie, and how to resurrect ourselves when we fall. The animals, he told us, all come into this world with stories already given to them, stories their ancestors have lived out forever. They know what to do. But we, the people, are gifted with the ability to write our own stories.

Our human story, he said, must have gods in it. Gods are not separate from us, he said. Gods are simply what we call the heroes of our stories, so that those people can be larger than life, so that their actions will live on and keep teaching us forever.

We, the children of the City, came into this world without a story. So we, who are still young but will one day be old—who will one day, ourselves, be the ancestors of the young— write this Chronicle now, of what happened when the Princess came to our City, and our City was reborn. This will be our Creation Story.

Our story begins with destruction. Everything that came before was broken.

We had what we called a series of natural disasters.

People will tell it differently, the order in which they came. It may be that the wind came first. We had hurricanes. Anything lighter than a building or a car was torn from the ground, and traffic swerved off of bridges. Pieces of our houses flew through the air and wounded us; some of us were killed by flying trash. Streets were so scattered with debris, we could not drive on most of them. It was dangerous to walk out of doors. Yet we were desperate to get out, for we discovered that within our houses we had almost nothing that we needed.

There were studies that had predicted for a long time the coming of windstorms over clearcut forests where the roots were torn out. But there were other studies that said these studies were meaningless, that the winds worked differently, that our cycle of winds always came from the sea. There were other studies that said hurricanes were not possible in the valley we lived in, because of the shapes of the land around us, and so on. In the end, none of those studies turned out to be important.

Sometime during or after the first storms, we ran out of fuel. We did not know such a thing was possible. Our cars stopped running and our machines stopped working. Our houses went dark and our supermarkets stopped receiving food. We became very afraid. It was rumored that groups of men who had once worked directly for Hanum, who knew about the fuel and where it came from, were making expeditions into the mountains to get more of it. It was rumored that for a price, food could be bought from the City Center, and that price was the fuel itself. People began searching for these secret expeditions in the mountains, killing each other over whatever that secret stuff was.

While officials dispatched from the City Center, along with many other people whose names were never known, were still cleaning up from the chaos of the hurricanes, the earthquakes began. There were three quakes over a period of four and a half days, and the first was the biggest. Entire houses were swallowed into the earth. Bridges fell. Roads fractured and factories collapsed into heaps of rubble. Thousands of people were killed or never found. There had been no preparation for such a thing. No one had ever imagined it. Each person or family fought only for their own survival, and there was no count of the dead, and no help coming from anywhere. There were no more officials. The City Center was closed.

We never knew or thought about what energy passed through the wires that wove our City together, or how it worked or what it meant, but as things began to fall, the wires fell and broke and tangled, and the energy inside them sparked out and turned to flame. At the same time, lightning struck and lit our structures—so dry after so many years without rain—on fire. The wind fueled the fire, and the fire began to eat the City alive.

Then the flood came. The sea, which most of us had never seen, rocked back in response to the quake, and then came tearing forward. It washed over the City, drowning the fire and many of our people and everything that was left to us. When the waters finally receded, our City was unrecognizable, and there was no one alive who did not know great grief.

All that we had made, both beautiful and ugly, was destroyed. Sewage flooded the streets. There were so many bodies, we had to pile them in pieces of houses and send them out to sea to stop the spread of disease. But disease came anyway, and it killed half the people who were left, and many of the others died from drinking filthy water, for there was no fresh water to be found. The rats attacked us in our sleep, and children died from their bites.

What these events did to us, and what they made of us, is hard to describe. We are not who we were before all this happened. These disasters created who we are now more powerfully than our old god Hanum ever did. They made us question who we were and what the City meant to us. They made us feel things we had never felt before; they made us value our lives and our families as we had never valued them before.

This, then, is the beginning of our Creation Story.

In the Beginning, there was only chaos and death.

In the Beginning, the people of the City were barely human yet. We had grief, despair, anger, and lust; we had desire and even moments of joy—such as when one of us found a loved one who was thought dead. But these feelings ruled us; we did not rule them. We did not yet seem to have souls. We crawled the earth in search of food, and sometimes we killed each other for it when we found it. We ate animals that had once been our pets. We disowned our friends in order to justify not sharing what we had. We did not yet know what food was or where it came from. We only knew that we needed it.

But there came a time, in the early days, when we reached a sort of savage stability, a plateau of survival, in which tiny groups of family members or friends scraped together the barest of livings in various pockets of the City. We built fortresses out of rubble, or slept under tarps or out in the fields. It was spring, and growing warmer, and the question of surviving in the cold had not yet presented itself. It turned out that the City Center had not held all the keys to survival after all. There were people who had once worked there but had left or been fired, and there were smaller, secret groups who had raised food animals on their own and who were now willing to provide it to others at a price. Of course, there was not enough for everyone. But we found other ways. Some of us found food out in the fields around the City. The rains were coming regularly now, and that made things grow, and since we didn't know what could be eaten, we ate everything out of desperation. Then more of us died, from poisoning and malnourishment. Many of the most sensitive, the most gentle people died first. But some of us lived.

There were strange tales being told at this time. One told of a god-like, fire-breathing man who needed neither food nor water, and who helped to pull people from the rubble after the quakes—and who healed them with his touch. Another told of a boy—back when the entire populace was gathered around the gates of the City Center, begging for their survival—who did not seem to care, and who roasted a rat over a fire, which he then ate. Some said he was a god, and they thrust him then toward the locked doors. And where no one had ever before been allowed inside, he was let in. When he emerged, he brought nothing with him—no food, no aid. Yet the moment he stepped outside, it was said, the first rains fell. This was seen by some as a sign of renewal from the heavens. Though no one at that time would admit to believing in gods before all this happened, many people fell on their knees in gratitude. They filled whatever containers they could find and had water to drink. In their momentary hope, they even shared with one another. But nothing came after that. They were still hungry, and the gates never opened. When the initial joy of the rains had faded, the questions and demands came flooding forth again, but the boy was nowhere to be found. He had slipped away.

No one knew what to make of these tales, but they were something to tell, and had something different in them than the daily misery that everyone knew. They had at least a hint of miracles in them, and that kept some of us hoping. And people learned from these stories. We started hunting the animals of the City the best we could, and we tried to cook and eat them. This was very difficult, and we did it at first with anger and frustration, without gratitude or knowledge.

There is disagreement over when this change began, and to this day no one knows how it happened, but by some miracle, the river at some point, for no reason, became pure. Then we drank of it, and we did not die.

It was during this time of early human life, this time when we had almost won our daily survival but still lived in brutal darkness, that another stranger came to the City. We did not know at first that she was a woman. Before we heard of her, we heard of the people she came with. These people were monsters, or so we thought. We thought they were our own shadows, come to draw us down finally into the evil darkness that seemed to be overtaking the world. For most of us still thought we were living at the End of Days. We did not yet know that this was the Beginning.

They came quietly and secretly through forgotten streets, and their voices were like growls, and they spoke terrifying words or no words at all. They had a kind of horror in their eyes that mirrored our own, and they were filthy and smelled of decay.

It is hard to define what frightened us so much about them. There was something eerily unprotected in their faces and in the way they held their bodies. That was what made us turn away, cover our mouths and our eyes, and whisper "don't look" to our children. They stood with such helplessness, looking back at us. The oldest ones among them lifted their shaking hands toward us and tried to form words. The young ones hopped excitedly from foot to foot and clutched at the others near them. Even the frightened ones were frightening in their stiffness, their eyes devouring us from within their senseless skulls. These people reached out to us with gestures so innocent in their blatant need, that they filled us with a pity verging on disgust.

Hope, longing, glee, fear—these were things we had all felt, but one did not show them so unselfconsciously, like an animal! One did not fling them out so desperately where anyone could see, like a weak animal that stands out from the herd for the predator's watchful eye. We told ourselves we had never looked like that, and we felt that something awful would see us if we ever did. We kept our dignity and turned away from these newcomers.

They were called the Mad Ones. We would not yet admit that we remembered them.

But it was rumored, in terrified whispers, that they were searching for certain people. They would stop at the encampments in the meadows or by the river, and ask for people by name. They were led by someone whose face remained hidden beneath the hood of a dark cloak, and it was said that this leader was Death itself.

But what was not known then, and not until much later, was that the mad people were searching for their families. And many of their families were found. And because everyone had lost so much, and had grieved the death of so many loved ones, no one was any longer in a position to deny a long-lost relative, lover, or friend, because he or she smelled badly or did not speak as people once had spoken. None of that mattered now. What those families realized then, before the rest of us did, was that we were all mad—and we all had those desperate looks in our faces. And they accepted their loved ones back among them.

The leader of those mad people did not show herself at first. Perhaps she did not want to startle us. She remained inside her dark cloak, and she gathered some of us—the families of these Mad Ones, who had been given new hope now, and who had rediscovered some of the goodness and humanity in themselves by accepting the Mad Ones into their arms again—to the First Council.

There were not many. Only a small crowd gathered on that grey day—what we would later know as the first day of Spring—in a hidden pocket of the rubble where the City Center had once stood. Stronger than any other building in the City, it had stood for longer than the rest, and no one knew what material made it. But something in that material was weakened drastically by the salt water of the sea, and after the sea came it had begun to sink, until its supports collapsed, and piece by piece it fell.

Nothing grew there, in that dusty, crumbled place. The woman in the cloak gathered us there that day, and she did not give wisdom, advice, hope, or answers. She simply told us a story that she would tell over and over throughout the following moons, at every Council that was held thereafter. And those of us there that day were so hungry for a story, so hungry for anything to make our minds wonder again and our hearts rise up in curiosity, so hungry for words with meaning, that we listened. She did not tell the story of the City or what had come before. We weren't ready for that yet. Instead, she told the story of herself.

She told how she'd lived trapped all alone in a tower for more years than she knew, and about the faraway winds and seas that swirled around that forgotten place. She told how the only person who loved her had left her and never come back, and how she had come down from the tower and been sent out alone across the sea. She told of her long, long journey, the beautiful places she had come through, and how she had longed to reach the heart of that one who would love her and whom she could love. She told of finding him and losing him again, of getting lost in the great pointless cycle of time, and of becoming the wind. She told the great myth of Loneliness.

Her voice was child-like and light, but it comforted us the way the sound of the rain comforted us when we first heard it fall on the pavement. We who were ready to believe anything, who were ready for any kind of magic—even magic we had never heard of—cried when we heard her story. We cried because we knew what that felt like, to be trapped all alone in an empty abyss in a tower of our own illusions, not to know why we were there or how long we had been there, and not to know if we could ever be loved. We knew what it felt like to travel all alone and to long for something or someone like that. We knew all about Loneliness. When we cried, we began to feel a little more human again for the first time. And the great miracle was that after telling her story, this woman asked us to tell ours.

All that day we told our stories! She made a space somehow there, so that we could. We told stories we never thought we would tell. We told how we had killed the people we found inside this very building, when we found they had no answers and nothing for us. We told about the loved ones we had not been able to save, or whom we had been too selfish to save. We told about the dark parts of ourselves, and we told of the shape that Loneliness took for each one of us. For some it had happened when alone all day in a house with nothing but machines to talk to, and for others it happened when standing in a crowd that was forever pushing onward and past us. For some it had happened most before the City was destroyed, when we sat at our desks at our jobs, and for others it happened afterward, when everyone we knew was gone and we walked like ghosts in a wasteland we did not recognize and could never get out of. She made it so that every one of us got a chance to speak, even if we thought we could never speak, even if we thought we could never be heard.

When that was done, there was, for some of us, a feeling of great relief, but for others there was a feeling of such weight and despair that we could not go on. How could you bring this out of us? we cried. Before, we were at least able to survive in this terrible world, day to day just focusing on living, not thinking of the horrors we suffered or committed. But now you have made us remember all this, admit to it, and speak of it. How will we live with this now?

And she listened to our despair, and she spoke the names of our feelings, so that we could meet them face to face for the first time. She introduced them to us. Grief. Fury. Horror. Numbness.

She said to us, "You do not have to hold all of this alone. It is part of the World. It is part of everything."

Then she took us to the river, and she let us listen to its song. She called the river Yora, and she told us that, because the goddess of this river had returned to it, we could once again understand its language. We found that she was right. It was not so much a language of words, not a language we could write here. But it was a language that listened, that already knew all of our stories. It was a song language, something we could sing to our children.

She took us to the meadows and bade us listen to the wind. She took us to the earth and showed us what plants would make our bodies feel better. She lit a fire as the night came on, gathered us around it, and told us to look into its center. All of that took a long time, and we cannot put into words now what happened to us during that time. But as we sat around the fire that evening, we felt a little better. It felt as if the world, instead of fighting us as we had always believed, was actually cradling us in its hands. As if it could absorb and understand everything we felt, because it was made of the same stuff we were. We hadn't any idea of that before. We hadn't any idea that we were loved.

And that day, though many people did not even know of it yet, was the day the City was reborn.

This woman was spoken of differently then. The people who had been at the Council spoke of her to others, and others came when she held the next Council. She traveled around the City, and many people wanted to see her. We wanted to hear the story she told. We wanted to tell our own stories. As the Councils grew larger and larger, not all were able to tell their story to her. But once she had begun the story-telling, we everywhere began to emerge from our state of shock, and we began to tell each other stories, even when she wasn't there. We began to gather for story-telling at places where our stories would be reflected back to us by the mirrors of the world: by the river, under the open sky, or around a fire.

Gradually, like a bubble rising to the surface, the truth of the Princess' identity was becoming clear to us. At first that identity had never occurred to us. The old myths of the Princess were even less remembered than the myths of Hanum, and, besides, in the old days we had never imagined the Princess like this. We had never imagined her in a dark cloak with such a laughing voice, such ease in speaking with us, and such suffering in her story. Or perhaps we had never imagined relating to her at all. We had never thought of such a thing. Long ago boys had spoken of rescuing her. No one had ever imagined that she would come to us.

But once the idea was spoken aloud—the idea that she was here—then that bubble burst, and all of the sudden everyone knew it and everyone spoke it. Word traveled instantaneously, faster than cars had ever traveled. The Princess was here. The Princess had come to lead us, to save us.

Whether it happened before or after this realization, we cannot say now, but the Princess cast off her cloak more and more often, and when she came among us, she allowed her beauty to shine. It was dazzling. Birds often flew near her, as if simply to bathe in that beauty. Each curve of her face was as delicately shaped as the edges of a fine grain of sand. Her body flowed forth through the rainbow dreamscape of her dress. Her hands lay open against the air, and windows of light opened around her. The more she admitted to and revealed her beauty, the more magic seemed to follow in her wake. Green grass exploded through the pavement around her feet. Polluted skies melted into clear blue above her.

For a little while we remembered the sacredness of beauty for the sake of beauty alone. For a little while that beauty fed and inspired us, and we remembered that beauty is the only thing that saves us from the dismal realities of life. But soon it became clear why she had hidden herself from us before. For we were still starving and homeless, and we did not know how to rebuild our lives or be happy. It was hard for us to see such beauty and not expect something of it for ourselves. Now that she had come to us and proven herself magical, we expected her to save us or at least to give us answers.

We men felt a furious hunger when we saw her. We felt our ugliness and stench in the filth we lived in. We felt our weakness, when we saw her power—and we resented it. We women felt the raw burning of every loss we'd ever been dealt, the breathless cold in our chests where our youth had once lived, and the trembling fury of all the passions we'd held back all those years—and we resented her, and did not trust her. Our children looked at her long soft dress and felt its untouchable distance; they thought of all the things they no longer had and which they had learned not even to ask for.

There was no place for such beauty, such abundance of life as flowed from her, in this bitter wasteland that our lives had become. Or so we began to feel, watching her. We will not try to say who started it or to find who hurled the first angry words, but at one great Council that she held by the river, the darkness finally rose out of us.

It began with angry questions and then angry demands. Would she not help us? What good were stories? Where did she come from, and if she wasn't one of us, then who was she? What did she know of our suffering? Then we were coming toward her, and a bony hand reached out like claws and tore at her dress. Then as if that hand had given permission, other hands rose up around it, clawing and pulling. If the Princess cried out, we could not hear. We were no longer ourselves. We just wanted so much to touch her, and we wanted so much to have what she had.

That was when the Prince appeared.

There was no clear record of him before this. Some claimed later that they had seen him all along, but that before this he had been like a ghost that followed her, never speaking and not in solid form. Most of us did not remember ever seeing him before, and yet since we had always seen her in a crowd, we could not be sure that she had always been alone. If he was present to us before, he had not become truly real until this moment.

But suddenly he was real, and his sword made a circle around her, so that everyone stepped back, though no one was hurt. This giant crowd of people went absolutely silent. This man of shadowy golden skin, as fluid and graceful as the wind, as beautiful as the Princess herself, stood tensely before her, his legs braced against the ground, and continued to hold out his sword. Even those of us at the back of the crowd who could barely see his face could see the flashing in his eyes. He was tall and bird-like, and yet his muscles and his gaze held as much determination as ours did.

"What do you fight for?" he cried out, so that all of us could hear. "If you are going to fight me, you'd better know what you are fighting for. Because what you fight for makes you what you are, and you will have to live with that forever."

When we still remained silent, he added, "And you have to know who and what you are fighting."

When we didn't move, he dropped his sword, and then he stood there beside her, and they were so beautiful together that all we could do was look. Our hearts ached. He spoke to us that day, more than he would ever speak to us thereafter except at the very last Council, the last time we ever saw him. But he did not say many things. He asked us only a few simple questions, about who we wanted to be. He asked us if we wanted anything more than just to survive, and if there was anything we valued more than our lives. He asked us how we wanted to remember these days, and how we wanted our children to remember us.

Then he told us that this was the beginning of our story, and that any people who becomes truly human, in the most holy sense of the word, must begin with a story. He told us that we must find our story and tell it, and that in every moment of our lives we must live the stories we believe in. He told us there is a sacred order to things and a way that things must be done.

At every Council after, of which there were still many more held that Summer, both the Prince and the Princess were present. There was no more anger and rebellion toward the Princess, though the Prince had never actually fought anyone, and no one actually feared that he would. They simply respected him and her. Though we could not explain it to ourselves, we trusted the Princess more now, now that we knew she wasn't acting alone. The power she brought felt more balanced, somehow, in that two-ness.

At every Council, the Prince first saw that things were in order. First he spoke with the elements and with the animals and plants that were present. It took us a long time to see that this is what he did, for he would walk silently around us and face outward, and we would see saplings or weeds that grew from the pavement trembling in the breeze as they faced him, and we would see small rodents move before him and then seem to freeze as if attending, and we would see the birds land on the rooftops and listen. Sometimes he made soft sounds or seemed to sing, but he did not speak to us or tell us what he was doing. He never taught us anything in words. But simply by watching him, we began to notice how the life around us spoke and listened. We began to see the beauty of the things around us, and as we sat in that silence we began to imagine the new world we might create, a City that would reflect such beauty.

We were a little in awe of him, a little afraid. The winds seemed to murmur in response to his voice. Then he would go around the crowd, whisper to the children, and look into each person's eyes—not in a stern or commanding way, but in a way that made us shiver, a way that forced us to remember the promises we'd made to ourselves about who we really wanted to be. It was as if he knew that about us, as if he'd seen our dreams.

So the Prince made and kept the order of things, while the Princess spoke and listened to us. They did not actually lead. They only allowed us to speak, so that we could begin to think about how we would rebuild, what we would build, and who would do it. They helped us find elders who remembered the skills we'd forgotten, people who had secretly grown gardens and knew what food was; these people had been hiding until now, afraid the others would find them and steal everything they had. The Princess asked the elders of different peoples among us, people of different colors who came from different landscapes long ago, what they could remember. And gradually, gently, as if afraid to hurt us, the Princess told the story of Hanum and how the City was born. But we felt, by now, as if we already knew that story. We found that we remembered more than we had ever admitted to.

This was a time of miracles, and that is why we chronicle the coming of the Princess and the Prince as our Creation Story. But the miracles were not performed directly by them. The miracles happened within us, in their presence. We became good again. We began to help each other. We began to look to each other for answers, for there are many, many people in this place, and we have had many experiences, and we have learned wisdom of untold variety from our families, our schools, our jobs, and our lives, and together we have unimaginable intelligence. So we began to respect ourselves again.

This magical couple, whom we now call gods, never gave us answers. But the Prince was like a firm hand that held us steady, and the Princess was like a mirror of water that the hand held up for us to see ourselves within. In that mirror, finally—because she saw it—we saw our own beauty. We remembered our dreams. Perhaps she was shy at first, but over time that shyness seemed to melt away, and sometimes, instead of standing before us, she would walk quietly among us, touch us, and let us touch her. When we saw her up close, we saw that she was only a person like us, smiling and a little awkward, her lips parted often in surprise and question, laughing easily in the presence of children. Though the Prince never spoke to us individually, and remained always a little distant, communing with forces we could not see, we could feel his kindness and also his love for her. And though later no one could agree on exactly what either of them looked like—their exact features or even the exact shade of their skin —we began to feel that we knew them intimately.

The Princess spoke of how grateful she was, finally, to be one of us. She told of how when she'd first come into the City, she had never seen so many people in her whole life. How, when she saw us for the first time, she wept with joy to know that there were so many faces on this earth, so many possibilities—and with sorrow to know that her father, in all his brilliance and magic, had somehow never seen the potential that we ourselves held within us.

13th MOON

●

Mira will always remember the night of this full moon, on the equinox of spring. It is the night when time starts moving for her again.

Every night now for a little while, she has been taking human form. And though she is silent with everyone else, sometimes she lies with her sister in the evening and practices speaking. At first she thought that the Unicorn was her real self, the immortal self—and that this human body was one she could soon give up forever, too used up and broken to survive—but now she is beginning to wonder if she might have gotten that mixed up. Now it seems to her that the Unicorn body is the one that is old and tired, yearning toward its own death and the time when it will be reborn. Mira feels sad to notice how it fades from her, how it feels less and less natural, how it begins to lift from her again like a dream, while she remains here on the earth with the human body that will live on. But in the mountains where they walk these days, enclosed in the silent rooms of trees and the earth old, old under their feet, Mira feels safer than she did before. The trees talk to her and tell her stories that make her laugh and sigh inside, stories that make her own story seem like simply one more story—and not necessarily one she has to keep. Even if she feels afraid of this change that's happening to her, when she stays near her sister she feels better, because her sister knows exactly how painful it is to be human.

But on this night, Lilah and Dragon are having sex. Mira, left alone, watches them from the high branch of a tree. This tree called her up here. *Come on,* it smiled, knowingly, gently, *come on up. But you have to be a girl to come up here—no Unicorn can climb, you know.* Mira is fascinated as she watches Lilah climb on top of Dragon, watches her ride him gently even as she holds her pregnant belly with one protective hand, her lips hanging over his. Mira watches Dragon lie helpless like that, allowing Lilah to overtake him, even though Mira knows he could grab her if he wanted to, and push her back under. Mira doesn't know what she herself feels as she watches, and the numbness that sits like a rock inside that not-knowing is so painful that she tries to think of something else to distract herself. Something that will take some thought to figure out, to pass the time until they're done.

I am eighteen years old, is the thought that comes to mind first. That's what Lilah told her today, or maybe it was yesterday. She tries to understand what that means. It seems like such a random number: so much older than the lifespan of a grasshopper, for example, but nothing compared to the lifespan of a mountain. It's older than she was when her father died, older than she was when they went away to school—and yet if she feels older now, she is not aware of it. How can people measure age like that? What does it mean, that she is eighteen? Is there something she should be capable of now, something she should be responsible for, something she should feel? These questions make her anxious. Like something is happening to her that other people can see but that she does not know about. It has always been this way for Mira.

She wonders how old Kite is. She knows he is younger than all of them, because of something Lilah said once. She called him a child. But he does not seem like a child to her. The way he looks at her, he doesn't look like a child. Yet he doesn't look at her the way men look at women either. It's somewhere in between.

She has not gone to Kite since the night she and Lilah burned the land of their father. But somewhere inside herself she knows that she is human every night also for this: that she will go to him again. And when she goes to him, she wants to be in this form. She wants him to see her. For the first time she can remember, she wants to be seen, and she doesn't know why. It's something about his seeing, and something about the way he lays his body down—almost mentally, like a blanket he's unfolding, like a thing he knows well and has under control but does not relate to anyone else—that feels safe to her.

I'll go and ask him, she thinks suddenly, *how old he is.* It seems like an easy question, something she should be able to put into words. It shouldn't put her in any danger to ask that. It should be simple, and the answer will be simple, even if it doesn't mean anything to her. At least she will have said something. It will be a beginning.

She hurries down the tree, but she stops every few feet to catch her breath—not from moving but from fear—and to press her chest to the tree, pressing into it like a camouflaged moth, telling herself it's okay. *It's okay if I change my mind. I don't have to ask him. I'll go and sit beside him like before and see if the words come.*

She gets to the bottom of the tree and realizes that what she really fears is not speaking but finding out that she can't speak, finding out that silence is no longer a decision after all, but something she trapped herself inside so long ago that she can no longer get out of it.

Mirr, Mirr, Mirr.

It's darker under the trees and she has to crawl very slowly in order to find him. In some places that almost never get sun, in the damp corners of tree roots and behind the cold faces of stone, a little snow remains, crusted and glowing. But elsewhere the earth sinks a little beneath her knees, and she can feel the first green leaves at once bitter and tender against her palms.

He is still sleeping but something else is awake tonight that hasn't been awake the other nights. It's that part of him. Mira can see the little tower of it beneath the blanket, can see his hands twitch a little in his sleep as if something is alive in him that makes that tower rise and possesses his consciousness and moves him without his knowing. Without realizing it, she grips the earth with her hands and her mouth goes dry, and she is prepared to bolt like an animal. She recognizes that terrible possession. She remembers how there is nothing a man can do to control it. She hears Delilah cry out in distant ecstasy in the dark behind her, and she feels like she did a hundred times in her childhood: so eerily, abysmally alone. She wants to run, but it's like a dream, and all she can do is fall, her own body a bottomless shadow thing that drops her spirit through a trap-door into chaos without a thought.

It was Lilah's presence that protected her those other nights, she realizes. It was Lilah, somehow, who kept Kite safe for her. But Lilah, back there with Dragon, is lost to her now—and Mira, *Mia,* wants to run, run, run….

But then he opens his eyes. The strangest thing happens. As soon as he opens his eyes, she is okay. Or almost okay. She looks into those blue windows, peaceful as a snowflake or smoke on a winter evening, and remembers he is not her father, not some demon possessing him, but just this boy—this mystery of a boy. She sees the longing there, brilliant as an oncoming rain, and yet it does not frighten her, because there is no intention in it. It's simply there. It is so sincere, so helplessly huge, that it makes her eyes tear.

"What?" he whispers, and she knows this night is different, because he has never spoken to her before. "What do you want? What can I give you?"

Mira looks down. She doesn't understand the question. But then she finds herself looking at the tower again, still alive and tall under the blanket. It's dark but a shadow outlines it faintly. She knows it is there. Suddenly Lilah's cries seem so loud she thinks they will engulf her; they are like a roaring in her ears, something so loud, so horribly loud that her whole body shakes with the sound of them. They crescendo and then keep rising inside her head, until she thinks her eardrums will break. She does not know what's happening in her body, or even that her body is still there, but when the cries break off—leaving a sudden, wild silence behind in which she wonders if maybe she imagined them—she finds that the blanket has been torn away. And she knows by the placement of her hand that it was she who did it.

She gasps. Slowly, all the while staring into her eyes as if she herself is willing this to happen, Kite is now undoing the cloth that surrounds the tower, and the thing is being set free. Naked now, it glows in the dark, and she worries about it, bobbing alone there in the cold. He starts to reach for it but then pulls his own hands away. He keeps staring at her face—she can feel his gaze—but she keeps staring at the thing and cannot look away. She can hear his controlled but urgent breathing, his in-breaths tight and his out-breaths weak and fast, as if he is climbing a mountainside with the last of his strength. She starts to back away, then glances back quickly at his face.

"It's okay," he whispers. "I won't touch you." And so she can look back at the thing again, which is what she wants to do—feeling his gentleness, knowing he won't hurt her. She needs to look at it. She needs to watch it for a long, long time. She needs to keep an eye on it. She needs to know what it is, what it will do, what it wants, why it longs for her.

Or maybe she doesn't need to know any of that. Maybe she just needs to sit here and be okay. She tries to concentrate on her breath, which sounds too loud—loud like he's going to find her, he's going to capture her—but no, she remembers, he is right here, she has found him, and he is not doing anything to her. The night isn't that cold. A breeze she knows and trusts encircles her face, and then the rest of her body—a white warm breeze that has always protected her. It asks gently,

What's happening in there?

In where? wonders Mira.

In your body.

I wouldn't know, thinks Mira quickly, but then she realizes that she needs to know, because if she doesn't find out, what if someone else does? She needs to know exactly what she is, exactly what she owns still, so that no one can ever steal it from her again. Eyes still enraptured by the rearing thing, the naked tower, and by his hands clenched near it, she tries to get inside some part of her body. She starts with where her knees feel warm, where his body lies close to them. She travels her attention up her knees, up her thighs—but then she gets lost, and looks quickly back to his face, afraid.

Oh no, she thinks helplessly, *oh no*. But she doesn't know why she thinks that. Such kindness in his eyes! Surprised, she watches one of his hands unfold from where it lies, watches him open it above his prone body, open it up. He is asking her for something, or he is giving her something; she can't tell which. She tries to remember. It's a language she knew once, long long ago. She closes her eyes tight, trying to think. Everything, she feels, depends on her remembering this. If she can't remember, she will be alone forever. She will never be able to be a sister to her sister, never be able to express love, never be able to touch anyone without pain. She has to remember. Tears roll down her face with the effort.

"It's okay," he says again, more loudly now, and she opens her eyes to his again and sees such compassion there that suddenly she remembers easily, without even trying. He is offering her his hand. He is offering to hold her hand. That's what the gesture means.

Smiling a little, relieved, she lays her hand inside of his. It hurts, but that's okay. She still has the other hand free, in case she needs it. He isn't holding her hand hard. She could still pull it away, if she needed to. It doesn't hurt so much, actually, this touch. She couldn't say what it feels like. Something other than pain, and every feeling other than pain is the same to her, because it has no name and is unfamiliar. If she thinks about it too much, it starts to feel like pain after all, because that is the only feeling she knows. But their two hands, entwined like that, float gracefully to the earth between them, and lie there, warm in each other.

She will always remember the embrace of that hand. If only she could tell him, what it means to her! At first it is only her hand that feels it, but then it's as if her whole body fills out, bit by bit, around the flesh of that hand, so that he is cradling more and more of her, without ever moving, until she can feel up from her knees, feel down from her chest, feel down her arms and into her hips and her belly and down. Bit by bit she can feel, and all he is doing is looking into her eyes, and that tower that stands up for her—he is just leaving it there for her to see.

With her other hand, like it's the most natural thing, she reaches down to feel for something between her legs. Something is going on down there. Something really important, that she's been ignoring. When she touches it, she is surprised at the icy sting of her fingers. She can hear Kite's breathing intensify, and she hopes she isn't hurting him somehow by doing this, but now that she's doing it she doesn't want to stop.

Melted and jelly-like, soft as an eye.

She couldn't say exactly what she feels down there but she feels her finger moving and she hears her own breath now along with Kite's, so that she can hardly tell the difference. She's looking into his eyes and something in her knows what he knows, and it is something she has never known before. When she looks back at the tower, she sees it for what it is—not good, not bad, but simply alive with its own particular song, like any other creature in the forest. And because she doesn't know what it is that she's touching, because she doesn't know what she's feeling or whether it's good or bad—only that it makes her tremble, only that it makes her own lips taste sweet, only that she is breathing harder and she doesn't know why, only that it is so, so *important*— she wants to express it to him somehow. So she brings her fingers out from inside of her, as if from out of the ocean, and then touches the tower, sliding the wetness from inside her along its delicate, newborn skin. She looks back at his eyes as he cries out, and then she sees the little fountain jumping out of it, and pulls away as he grabs it suddenly with his own hand and rubs the fountain out.

The fountain is familiar. Maybe she did something like this before, a long time ago. Maybe that time, long ago, was terrible. She isn't sure. But what happens here doesn't feel like anything to do with that. It feels like the first time for Mira. She isn't afraid. She wraps her hands back inside her cloak and looks back at Kite. Always, she will remember the vulnerable, helpless explosion of that naked creature under her hand. Always, she will remember to feel compassion for that creature, and for the gasping in his breath. She feels that she understands something she didn't understand before: something about power and the reasons behind what people do. Most of all, she understands something that lives inside her own body, that has nothing to do with her father or anything that happened to her before: something that simply lives there, that she never knew about before. And she wants to keep it alive. Someday, she wants to bring it out like that again. She had no idea that voice comes not only from the throat and the mouth but also from down there. No wonder she could not speak before. Because she has two mouths, and both of them have to be open.

"Sorry," Kite is saying, covering himself.

But she leans down low so that her face is close to his, and she closes her eyes to feel his breathless wonder. And she says out loud, but gently, into the little spiral fetus of his ear, "Thank you."

Love used to seem simple to Dragon. It was the thing he did not have.

He knew that love was something he needed, and so he used that word to describe whatever attracted him: woman, sex, Kite's friendship, the acceptance of the City, even Coyote's haunting attention. Love was the same as need. Whatever he loved, he needed, and whatever he needed, he loved. Love was absolute and unquestionable and holy and better than him. It felt the same in his loins as it did in his heart: desperate and beautiful and the only thing worth living for, and yet so painful it might kill him.

But now, as he walks into the mountains with Delilah at his side, now as the subtle, ever-changing trees curve their touch around him, now he feels for the first time how complicated love is. Or perhaps the feeling of love is still simple, but knowing what to do with it is not.

The spring earth sinks, delicate and damp, beneath his bare feet. Once, a year ago, he came plummeting down these mountainsides like a fallen bird, dragging his heart behind him, crying out to an empty universe. But that seems like a lifetime ago—another person, hollow and selfish and alone, that he pities now. Now he listens to the wordless words the newly arrived birds and their mates have to say to each other: in the forest their calls are occasional, important, and slow. He has more time in himself now to listen. Things are simple for them. They seem the way he once was: made of pure instinct. They only want to make love, and what comes after that they have not yet imagined and do not need to.

But for him, now, there are so many loves. And though he knows he should be grateful, finally, they make him anxious too.

Here is Delilah, walking beside him in silence—a silence they share comfortably now, that fills him with pride and warmth. He knows that he loves her. Yes, that is real love. He feels it every time he glances at the stiff lift of her chin, and at the swell of her belly, and every time she sighs and he knows she is getting tired even though she won't admit to it, and he curls his arm around her back so gently she can't resist. He remembers when they made love again, finally, and again— the last time only last night. How their fire twined together so easily now. Just like that last time in the desert, when she sat in his arms and melted into him, they spiral up together into the sky now, only now more slowly, more sweetly. Now when they make love, he gets to watch her face, and she lets him watch. Now he understands, finally, that the fire he was trying to raise up inside himself all those years—in the Garden, in the desert, so lonely—needed the fire of another to raise it. It needed to weave back and forth between them, sex to sex and belly to belly, heart to heart and throat to throat; it needed that rhythm of longing and retreat, reaching and releasing, to make it go.

He loves the baby inside of Delilah, the baby she says will be a girl, with a mysterious and protective fierceness that frightens him. That baby belongs to him. The thought of any other man raising that child but him makes the blood pound in his head.

Yet he doesn't want to stay with Delilah. Not always. He wants to be with her sometimes; he wants to care for her; he wants to be her man—and yet at the same time he misses the friends he made in the City, who were surprising, creative, and abundant, who loved his art and made him feel like a god. There are so many women out there that he hasn't even met yet, and he loves that look they will give to him, when he first catches their eyes.

And Mira. Does he love her, too? He wants to know what she thinks of him, because somehow knowing that will determine for sure if he is the man he feels he has become. But he hates needing that from her. And though in that moment under the wave, when she was the Unicorn, he did understand—for a moment—their oneness, now that experience is only something he can describe, not actually feel. Now they are separate again, and he fears her a little. Because he can tell that Delilah would defend her from him with tooth and claw, he is afraid that he might want her, even though he isn't sure that he does want her, any more than he wants any woman.

He would like to look at Mira more, now that she has taken the form of a girl most of the time—at least for the last couple of days. He wishes she could know that he knows what it feels like, to enter into your body for the first time and feel so bewildered by its sensations, so frightened by its powers. How he wanted to reach out to her when she first appeared before them in human form, holding her hands at her sides like objects that frightened her, stepping carefully as if she might spill. *I know*, he wanted to tell her. *I know*. But she always walks behind him with Kite, the two of them whispering together occasionally like new sweethearts, shy and fascinated—even though they are not lovers, because, as Kite explained to him, she is much older than Kite, and anyway Kite feels he is not yet worthy of her. Some nights, now, Delilah sleeps holding her, and Dragon cannot get close to either one of them, but it's okay, because these late-night talks with Kite might be the last talks they ever have, for all he knows.

He loves Kite, for sure. Loves him like his brother, like his son, even like an elder. Kite is sacred to him. How, then, can Dragon also envy him? How is it that he constantly wishes him gone, for fear of losing the love of women? He doesn't want to feel that way. He wants to be loyal to Kite, because that is the only way to be loyal to the man in himself—the only way to be a real man.

And still, always, there is the question of loving Yora. She waits for him in the bottom of his soul, in the corners of his mind, in the unseen, unformed layers of his dreams. Always he is aware of Her voice, Her knowing, as they walk beside the river toward its source. And on the last night before reaching Kite's home, he needs to be with Her. He feels that something is about to happen. He doesn't know why, but he feels it deep down, that he is not going to go all the way with them. Whatever Kite's home is, with its food gardens and its family and its warm beds, is not for him. He feels that something is about to change forever, and it is not—it has never been—under his control.

It's the first time he has tried to speak with Her, since he lost Her in the desert so many moons ago. He has boasted to Kite of Her presence, how their love continues despite all his humanness, how he has learned to understand Her love now, how he has learned to take it as it is. But as he wades into Her slow moonlit waters this night, comes to Her center and stands facing the slick froth of Her, he does not know for sure if the love he's convinced himself of is real, and he realizes that all this time he has avoided finding out.

He kneels, immersing that lower half—that tragic, ever-difficult, ever-yearning half of himself—into Her blurry depths. She's still as cold as the winter, and he closes his eyes, feeling that familiar loneliness—how She winds around him as if he were an obstacle, winds around him like fast snakes more important and knowing than he.

But when he opens his hands under the water, he feels Her fall in.

Yora, do you forgive me? Do I still belong to you? Do you still love me?

And again he remembers his mother, whom he cannot remember—a bitter emptying of hands, the echo of her cry.

She—whoever She is—does not answer him, at least not in words.

But other things happen in this night. Dragon listens to the river as it rolls past him, ahead of him and behind him and forever. He feels the dew taking form and clinging to the bodies of solid things. He feels his great father, the sky, watching him from inside the darkness—and as the sky soundlessly, formlessly, ceaselessly makes love to the earth all night long with His black airy body, so too does the water wait for her lover, the fire, to return. In the morning he will rise in the east, clearing away all memory, all the suffering she carries, all the color that history creates. The sun will rise and make a new world. He will blaze down upon the river and drink her up, and she will lose herself in him and rise up into the sky, where everything is pure and fresh and eternally young. Then he will let her go, and everyone in the world will come together in the shared sorrow of rain.

Dragon listens to the river and feels her cold comfort. He listens to the river and feels how his flame inspires her, how her droplets climb his skin, how he drinks her in and rises inside her and bursts her back out again. All night, he and the river make love, as all night the world makes love with itself all around them, without fanfare, without speaking, without promises, without end.

In the morning he walks back toward his friends, full of gratitude, full of peace, dripping and naked, but when he sees them in the thicket, he suddenly wraps his body in a dark cloak—for Mira's sake. His compassion for her overcomes him now, and overcomes everything else he feels. They are standing in the thicket: Mira and Delilah. They are holding each other silently, rocking ever so slightly, like seaweed at the surface of the sea. When Delilah pulls away and faces him, he can see she has been crying, though her eyes are dry now.

"Before we go on," she says, "my sister wants to say something."

He sees Kite now, sitting by himself in the clearing, with an uncharacteristic fog of sorrow in his eyes. Dragon sits down in the clearing, too, and the women sit with them, and they all wait, while bands of rose-yellow sunlight loop over their legs and arms like rope. Mira closes her eyes and opens them again, her face contorting and rearranging itself as if she were only now being born. Dragon longs to tell her that whatever she says is going to be okay, because she is surrounded by love.

"I will go a different way now," she announces finally. Then she pauses, looking down at her hands as if seeking the next words there.

Dragon glances at Delilah and Kite. They are both perfectly still.

"The people of the City need now the wisdom of animals, and the plants, and the elements. They are missing this." Again the struggle inside; Dragon glimpses black aching space, as if he can see and feel inside her mind. "I must go and gather them. There will be a Council. This is the last task of the Unicorn."

In Delilah's eyes, gazing fixedly at Mira, there is some tired question pulsing, some question perhaps that she has asked many times, and wants to ask yet again, but finds futile. Maybe it is the sound of the river so deeply embedded in his mind, or the fluidity of his Goddess lover in his body, but somehow Dragon feels like he knows what everyone is feeling, with only the briefest glance. Then suddenly, he knows what he is feeling, too. It is not love but something else that feels equally good. It is a feeling of being absolutely certain of what is right—so certain that this knowing is like a river carrying him, so certain that he can relax inside himself with absolute faith, finally, and accept himself without question. It feels exhilarating, like freedom.

"Mira," he says, standing. "I will go with you. I will be your protector."

He says it without asking first, because he knows it is right, and nothing else but this can happen. It is the only thing that can happen. He knows his intentions are true. Mira looks at Delilah. Delilah smiles at Mira.

Then Delilah stands up and walks to Dragon. Trembling, Dragon stands, too. He doesn't know what will happen. He is sure she will test him somehow. But she only looks into his eyes, her face strangely frozen.

"Come back," she says in a small voice. "Come back to me someday,

Dragon. If you want to."

Dragon reels. Then with predatory fierceness, he pulls her against him and kisses her. He loves her. His body flushes hot with gratitude. With the force of the ocean, he realizes how much more he could love her even than he already does, how close he could come to staying with her forever. But for now, all he can do is let her go, hold tightly to her eyes with his own, and nod.

When he looks back at Mira, she is already changing. She does not rise up into the form of the Unicorn, as he expects. Instead she falls down into it, surrendering into a pool of white light, from which the body of a horse struggles through.

The Unicorn looks into Dragon's eyes.

And in this moment, Yora answers him, after all. Dragon knows he's been forgiven.

Perhaps we thought that this time of miracles would last forever. It never occurred to us that our pain, finally, would be healed not by happy miracles but by another kind of pain—a sweeter pain, a pain that made us believe in our humanity again.

This was the pain of watching a god die.

When we first saw the Prince, his hair was as black as sleep, his skin smooth as morning, his limbs as flexible as late-day sunbeams. He leapt from wall to wall as easily as if he could fly, and his rare thoughtless smile, when it came, made women forget themselves—and then remember themselves again. Sometimes he would take the Princess's hand and they would run over the ruins like goats, and we would chase them laughing like children into the fields. We loved to see the two of them together, young, brave, and beautiful.

But that time did not last for long. Within only a few days, he seemed to move somehow more slowly than at first, and once we saw the Princess catch his arm as his legs buckled under him for a moment, and he almost fell.

Within a couple of weeks, his hair was grey, and within one moon, it was white.

By the summer solstice, his skin wrinkled around his eyes and his mouth, making him look kinder somehow, more experienced, and more like one of us. His muscles were thinner, and he often walked leaning on the Princess's arm instead of holding her hand. But she never showed surprise at this change. We never knew anything of their relationship. We did not know where they slept or what they did when they were not with us. We only saw them when they appeared, more and more in the same places, by the river or in the fields. Sometimes many days went by when we would not see them. But we were holding our own Councils now, trying to form some kind of government, trying to decide how to direct our energies in an organized way to rebuild, trying to teach each other what little we knew of how to survive.

The Prince aged faster than it is possible for a human being to age, and yet the more he aged, the more human he seemed. The men among us were astounded by the courage of his vulnerability, the way he walked just as proudly even when he could barely walk at all, and smiled just as broadly and more frequently. The elders who had emerged among us, the ones who had admitted themselves to be shamans of the various peoples of old, nodded their heads knowingly. They said this was a human being once turned god, and now turning back human again. He was catching up for all the years he had missed. Now that he had come among us and accepted this human life, his lifespan would pass all in a moment, they said, and would soon be over.

Yet we could not quite believe this. The Prince and Princess seemed eternal to us, because of the love we could see between them—an innocent kind of love that, prior to their coming, we thought we had forgotten. This beautiful summer, which in retrospect we see as the time of the Prince's dying, was the most magical time we had ever known. We felt more alive than we had ever felt. Though we still had nothing, though we still did not know how to find or create enough food to keep our children healthy or even to keep everyone alive, time seemed to pause in the middle of the year and take a deep breath; it seemed to cradle us in some forgiving embrace. An awed silence moved with the Prince wherever he went. Though we knew there was so much we needed to do to fix our lives and our City, many of us spent days and weeks simply following the Prince and Princess through oceanic fields, overcome with the beauty we saw, as if for the first time, everywhere they led us. The closer the Prince came to the end of his life, the more a light seemed to radiate around them both, and it engulfed all of us, so that for a brief time, we, too, felt like gods and barely seemed to need food or water. When they passed the trees, the trees seemed to sing, and when they passed through the grasses, we saw animals hiding there that we had not seen before, and instead of killing them for food, we heard them whispering to each other. We were comforted because we could hear in those voices that what we had experienced was not so terrible and had always been going on, in some form or another, since the beginning of time. We could hear hints of those stories that came before us, and they gave us a sense of belonging to the world, after all.

It was a strange time, a time that our children, upon hearing of it, may not be able to imagine. It was as if all the knowledge of the world lay open to us, and the doors of other worlds lay open, too. We stood in the fields and opened our eyes, and we could see through the wind to things we had never seen before. We heard voices, as if all of us were the Mad Ones. Deer, lizard, owl, weasel, raven, butterfly—these were like the voices of elders we had never known were there for us, gentle examples of how to live in a wilderness we had once thought alien and inhospitable. By listening to their stories, we learned that hunger, death, loss and fear could all be borne and had their right place among us.

What made it so? What made it such that, during that brief time, we could understand the other beings of the world and feel compassion for them, as if we all spoke the same language? Perhaps it was the magical sphere which the love of the Prince and the Princess for each other created, or perhaps it was the transformation of the Prince's dying—a dying that taught us, finally, the magic that can come after everything is destroyed. Or perhaps it was that time between times, when we had lost everything of the past but had not yet built the future, when we were more present than we had ever been or will ever be again.

All of us began to remember our dreams then, as if they were lit up in our sleep, too brilliant to forget upon waking, even brighter than the day. We spoke of them to each other. We held whole Councils on nothing but our dreams, for it seemed to us that they held messages of great importance. We were dreaming of the lands beyond the City. We were dreaming of the places we had not thought of for many, many years, except in nightmares or in fairy tales, or as places where the reckless young might go for adventure, or as distant views for people on some brief, protected vacation. It seemed as if we recognized those landscapes now, as if they were in fact within us.

We wanted to see those great lands that we saw in our dreams. We thought of exploring, and we thought of spreading out and forming new communities in other places, but we were still afraid. Besides, we knew somehow that this time of miracles was nearly over, and we could not leave yet, for we felt that we were needed here.

The Prince could have gone off on his own somewhere to die. He could have disappeared like our old god Hanum did, hidden himself away in his suffering or simply chosen to be alone in his last moments. Given that the Prince had always seemed so private, mysterious, and other, that is what we expected.

Yet the closer he came to the end of his life, the closer the Prince seemed to come to us. When we were bent with sorrow over the loss we had suffered or the people we missed or the hopelessness of the abyss that seemed to lie between us and any kind of future, he would come and sit beside us. He would rarely touch us or speak a word, but we felt his soft presence and the way he cried with us inside; we felt his compassion so deeply that it brought tears even to those of us who could not remember ever crying. When our children were sick, he would come and whisper to them, and sometimes the joy that suffused their faces at whatever words he spoke —whatever secret worlds he described—would revive them. When we lingered at the places we once knew, seeking again and again for the things we had lost in the rubble, sometimes he would come and search with us, or he would pray with us over the people we had buried and the little monuments to those who were never found.

We knew the Princess came from a lonely tower and was the daughter of Hanum. But we did not know where the Prince came from. We only knew that when he died, he died among us, on purpose, and for that we will always be grateful.

We followed him beyond the fields that we knew, over the hills, and into a young forest north of the City that no one ever knew was there. Maybe fifty years or so ago, it had been cut down for building and paper, and then abandoned, but it had since regrown. On his last day, the first day of Autumn, we followed the Prince and the Princess through that forest. We gathered the plants they showed us to gather, and in the evening we had a small feast of leaves and berries, which would not have sustained us had we not been under the spell of that strange, miraculous, brightly lit time.

The Princess sat beside him with her head bowed. We had seen her walk beside him with her arms around him, as if he were still her young lover, though his youth was gone and his back bent and his limbs crooked like the old trees. We had seen her sit proudly beside him as if he had never changed. But we had never seen this sorrow in her. We had never seen her hide her eyes from us as she did now.

The evening was gentle and the sky seemed to lower its hazy, blue-grey mirror right through the treetops and into our midst. The thrushes were calling in careful, unhurried voices, as if lowering a fragile song leaf by leaf in secret down into our minds. There was a deep peace among us. We could hardly remember who we had been even six moons ago, and yet we remembered things from far before that now, things from before we were even born. The Prince looked out at us and said, "I want to tell you three things."

"First, I want to tell you to remember your dreams, and to keep them by you, even if you do not know why.

"Second, I want to show you what is beautiful here in the forest and fields. I want to tell you, when you build your City again, to build it like this. Build it in this language, because then it will always feed you. Build it in a sacred language, because I am telling you a truth you have forgotten: this, your City, is the heart of this world.

"And, third, I want to tell you that you are not the only City or the only world. Perhaps you will meet the peoples of other cities one day. You will travel to other lands and meet other creatures, beings, and gods. And you must have a story by which to know yourselves. You must have a story, with gods and miracles in it, to guide your choices, keep you anchored, and remind you how to be human."

Then he turned to the Princess and took her hands in his. They were sitting on the ground. It was the end of the day. Only one bird was still singing, trilling up and trilling down, as if it sang both a question and an answer. He whispered to her, but everyone heard him.

He said, "I am yours, Beloved. Thank you for bringing me back to the world. I am alive again."

Then the Princess put her face in her hands and began to weep. Though it seemed perfectly natural, given what would happen, we at first felt a great fear. Though we had all seen loved ones die, and though we had spent the last season telling our stories and accepting the feelings we felt, the Princess's tears came as a shock to us, as if even now we thought she would save us by being above the things we felt. We did not know, at first, what to do. She sobbed and sobbed as if she would never stop, and the Prince just held her in his bony, frail arms.

Then some of us came to our senses and began to gather in, so that we made a circle around them instead of a crowd before them. Children picked up pretty things from the forest floor—fallen flowers, fantastically shaped seed cones, and lichen-laced branches—and wove them in a sort of wreath around the two of them, like a little nest, the way the Prince had always woven a safe space around our Councils by speaking with the winds and the *other beings. When all of this was done, the Princess was finally quiet. The Prince was weak and had lain down on the earth, and the Princess, in order to keep her face close to his, had lain down beside him. We looked at their faces, as they looked into each other's eyes, and we could not see inside the secret of their love. Yet we recognized this moment in our hearts, and we cried for them, and it did not feel strange to us that we stood present at such an intimate, personal time.*

"But what is your real name?" we heard her beg. "Leave me with that, at least."

"It is the name you knew me by," he answered. "That is my real name. This life with you—this has been my real life."

She was hiccuping with the tears again, like a child.

"Tell them," he whispered to her, as if he could no longer find the voice to speak aloud to such a great multitude—and yet all of us heard. All of us. "Tell them I forgive them."

Then he closed his eyes.

We never knew what he meant, exactly, by those words, but we sighed when we heard them, as if we had been holding our breaths. We no longer felt afraid of what was happening or of what would happen next. We no longer felt afraid to travel beyond into the other lands of our dreams.

From the Prince we learned not to be afraid, as our old god Hanum had taught us to be afraid, of aging and dying. We learned that through age, one becomes deeper with love and closer to what one loves, and that through dying, one gives and is reborn.

We stayed there through the night, and the Princess did not move from the ground, though he was clearly gone. We did not move from where we were. Some of us slept and some of us stayed awake with our heads bowed, in respect for him and in wonder at the feelings we felt, which we could name now.

When the morning came, and she still had not moved, an old woman came forward and laid a hand on her shoulder. Then a few others came around her and gently shook her. As if waking for the first time, she gazed around at us like a child. For a moment, we thought she was lost to us. But then she reached out her hands and clasped at ours. We reached back—not the way we had reached for her in the beginning, grabbing and clawing, but with tenderness now, with love. How she needed us then! We did not know that she could need us as much as we had ever needed her. We caressed her head; we let her cry on our shoulders; we wrapped our arms and bodies around her to comfort her. And it seemed as if she had never known this comfort before. As if she had not known that, when he died, we would be there to catch her: that this is what community is for. She had not known that she could touch us in this way, nor had we known that she would let us touch her.

Something changed that morning. Already, she was becoming like one of us. Already, we were seeing that the power, the healing, and the light they had seemed to carry was really ours. We had this to give, with merely the touch of our human hands, which was already magic.

We helped her to her feet. She stood with that joyless, determined strength that we had all had to find in ourselves this past year—that would make her go on and do what she had to do. We walked close beside her and helped her to carry his body all the way back through the forest and fields, walking all day and into the next night.

For though we thought we should bury him there, in that nest of beauty made by children, among the trees who seemed to know him so well, the Princess said no, that he must be buried in the City. That seemed wrong to us at first, for there were so many dead there already who had not even been buried properly. But we did as she asked. We carried him all the way back.

As we walked, she told us of the place he came from. She told of it as if she had been there, though she said she never had, and the love she seemed to feel in telling of it must have given her the strength to go on.

She told us of animals we had never seen and a color green we had only seen in dreams. She told us of a deep underwater darkness and a sweet, rising light—both of which we knew and remembered, or so it seemed to us. Then she told us that this place used to lie where the City Center was built. She said we had to bury him there. And when we protested that we could never clear so much rubble and concrete away, she insisted with a kind of fury in her eyes; she said that it would be so, even if she had to do it alone.

Of course we could not let her do it alone. And truly, after all the years that great steel building had stood in silence, forbidden to us and yet holding our very life's blood in its tight fists, we found some fascination in wondering what forgotten land might have lain beneath it—that we now, at least through memory, would discover.

So we did it. We dug up the crumbled pavement with our hands and the most basic of tools, and we lifted away the rusted steel, and we dug into the forgotten earth beneath it. We did it even though we were starving, even though we were almost dying ourselves, because we felt that if we did not do something meaningful, if we did not do one thing truly good right now, we could not bear all the trials that would come after. We needed to know that we could count on our own hearts.

We helped her to bury him, and when we had done, she turned to us with her radiant face and said simply, "Thank you."

Then she walked into the crowd.

But we did not feel her warm, beautiful passage as we had in the past; we did not part around her light. Instead she seemed to fade, as soon as she entered in among us, into one of us. Almost immediately, we lost her. We had seen her walk in among us, and all eyes had followed her, and yet, suddenly, she could not be identified. We turned every which way in confusion. We knew she was here, that she had not disappeared. But we could not recognize her now. Each of us started after someone different, thinking it was her, until that person turned around and we were unsure now of the face. She could have been any one of us. We no longer knew.

We know that dreams are real now. We know there are gods walking among us and begetting our children, though we can only guess at who they are, and perhaps by the time you read this we will all be a little bit god and a little bit human.

None of us ever saw the Princess again. Yet most of us believe that we see her every day and simply do not know that we see her.

For we see such beauty, every day, that we never saw before.

Through the Story that the Princess and Prince gave to us, we learned the seasons for the first time—the seasons by which we would structure our lives, and survive, and keep this sacred place, the Heart of the World.

Spring was when the Princess first arrived: she tore away our old prejudices and gave us loved ones we had lost—and hope.

Summer was the time when miracles sustained us, when we followed in the wake of beauty; we discovered that, when we dared to look within ourselves, we found not emptiness after all, but riches.

Autumn was the time of harvest, when we buried the Prince's body in that land where he was born. In that deep earth which we never knew was there, we planted the Prince like a seed. And afterward, every vegetable and fruit and living thing that could sustain us magically bloomed. When we saw it growing, we cleared away the rest of the debris. We cleared away many city blocks' worth of land where the City Center once stood, and this was our new Center now: this garden of food, which began from the body of a god and which, over the years that would follow, we would keep alive with the work of our human hands.

Winter was the time of dreams, when we reflected on what had happened and on what we had done, when we felt the safety and pride of the new home we had begun to build for ourselves, and when we sat in gratitude for the final gift the Prince and Princess had left for us—from which, in their absence, we were able to begin again. It was the time of writing down the story of Spring, Summer, and Fall, a story that will be told over and over by the generations that come after us, when we who are now young become elders, and then the ancestors of the future.

I was not included in the Story; I was not written in any Chronicle.

The Prince from the swamp, where long ago the sea and the earth made love, did not speak of me to you. How I wish, sometimes, that you could see me. Yet he could not call upon me with only words, nor could he decide for you when you were ready to see me. So he protected me with his silence. Indeed, he never spoke of me to anyone but his love, who at that time—long ago on a mountaintop—was called Lonely.

Some things are so silent that they are continually forgotten and lost between the cracks of eras, like the truth that Unicorns existed, and what we were for. It is right that I am forgotten. It is in the forgetting that I am released, so that I may one day be reborn.

My first duty, when I left that human form for the last time, was to the elements, from which life is made. I went up on the mountaintop again and spoke with the sun. I spoke with Fire, and Fire was angry. It had been mis-used, mishandled, and forgotten. It was hungry. I asked it what it wanted, and it said it wanted food. It wanted to give life even as it took life, and after it died, it wanted to be remembered and brought back to life, over and over again. So I said that I would carry that message.

I went into the valley and spoke with the ground. The Earth was afraid, for it had been beaten and gutted and shamed. I asked what it wanted. And the Earth wanted to give, and it wanted for that giving to be honored, the way the heart wants its love to be taken. It wanted the security of seasons. It wanted peace and to be fed with the remains of the dead. So I said that I would carry that message.

I wandered throughout the many landscapes and spoke constantly with the wind. I asked the Air what it wanted. It said it wanted nothing. But when I stopped asking and only listened, for many, many days, it said it wanted freedom. It wanted to bring empty purity with every breath, and nothing more. So I said that I would carry that message.

I went back to the sea, and asked the Water what it wanted. The Water was sad, for it wanted to remain pure, so that it could give life. It wanted the joy of running, and the peace of stillness. But it did not ask for anything. It only wanted to fall deeper and deeper toward the center, and never stop. So I said that I would carry that message.

I dipped my horn into the sea and into the wind, and into the earth and into the sun, and I made them pure again, at least for now. I made them whole again; I made them new. Now everyone could receive the gifts of these elements again; now all creatures would be able to trust the Fire, the Water, the Air, and the Earth to give them the life they were meant to have—with-out poison hidden within it. I purified the elements so that even the people could receive these gifts again, like forgiveness.

My next duty was to the plants, who are the first life. The mosses, the ferns, the grasses, the flowers, the trees. They had little to say, and of course they did not ask for anything. But their language, after so many years of taking poison from the elements, had begun to change from the original language. It had become a language of suffering, anger, and fear. Trees grew in uglier shapes, and were stunted; flowers forgot to yield fruit. Fields were thorny and spoke a monotone of brambles, and forests were shallow, with only two scrubby levels of life. So I had to teach them the original languages again: the languages of beauty. That took a long time.

I gave my whole being to these healings. And in between these conversations, I would have died without Dragon.

The stories that are told throughout time, where the Unicorn encounters the Dragon, and every time one slays the other, are not true. Great wars and injustices are perpetrated in the name of this misunderstanding.

The truth is that I needed Dragon, and we were part of each other. Dragon was the very source, the very energy with which I made my healing. He was the life force that I transformed into whatever was needed, to heal the pieces of this world. He was also, at the same time, that which reminded me to feel compassion in spite of everything; without him, I would not have felt the motivation to go on, to give light not only to all the elements and beings of the world, but also to the human beings.

Dragon was also, of course, as he wished to be, my protector.

He came steadily with me as I traveled from one land to another. He walked by my side over field and forest, desert and plain, river and barren cliff. Because in my new activity everywhere, I was more vulnerable than ever before, he stayed by me during those times in between, when someone might see me and not understand, when someone might try to steal the light. This partnership was a healing for both of us, for in order to exist and act in the world, we had also both come from mortal selves. Besides being the Dragon, he was once also the boy who had not known how to love, and besides being the Unicorn, I was once also the girl who had not been able to receive it. So we needed each other now.

When I returned from my last Council, the Council of Animals, Dragon was sleeping. The last thing he remembered was Coyote walking toward us—the last animal to be found and called to the circle. Coyote was laughing, the black hole of his mouth smelling of swamplands.

Now I stood over Dragon, and he scrambled to his knees, and almost cried out at the sight of me. I know why. My horn was nearly gone—only the palest strand of light echoing where it once was. I was blind. My fur was rough and ragged, my legs fleshless and trembling, my body scarred, bleeding, and cold, my neck bald and my tail gone. All my beauty, all my magic—gone. Poor Dragon: it was a nightmare for him.

"What has happened to you?!" he roared, feeling like a child all over again, with the Mother once again stolen from him. "Why didn't you take me with you?"

It's all right, I said to him in my voiceless voice, my breath labored. *No human or god came to this Council. Not even you.*

But Dragon had felt so needed, and now, at the last moment, he felt betrayed.

Don't be angry, I said. *Did you come for pride? Did you come to prove something?*

"No, I came to help you. I came for you!" His voice sounded desperate, reminding him terribly of the lonely boy he used to be.

I am grateful, Dragon. Please stay with me. Now comes the hardest part for me.

For in that Council, each of the animals had come forward to the Unicorn for healing.

They came forth to me one by one from the great circle, to where I lay in the center. Each confessed the wounds that he or she had suffered at the hands of humanity.

The wolf, hanging his head, whispered his humiliation. His ancient clan, his power and respect among all the animal world, his friendship with the moon, all meant nothing to the human hunters. All his stealth and physical wisdom were reduced to startled whines of pain at the shot of a gun, and wolf children left their burrows to find their great elders—their heroes—dead.

The frog told of the poison in his skin, how he could not breathe. The honey bee told of hives without dances, without food, without flowers. The birds told of landing in parking lots— exhausted, disoriented, hungry— where lakes used to be. The deer's senses were confused by the cacophony of sounds and the broken shapes of the forest; she had lost her grace and her memory.

The dog admitted that, after all, he had never been loved back. The cat described a harsh world where hunger and fear disabled all instincts for friendship.

The spider's spirit was wounded by the endless hatred aimed at her, her webs all destroyed whenever they were found, and her babies killed by poison. The turtle had been mishandled by scores of angrily bored children, and she could not cross the road fast enough. The snake had been hated again and again, beaten, skinned.

The whale could no longer communicate with her family under the water, could not find them. Their calls were lost in the terrible noise. The seal had swallowed plastic. The owl flew and flew against the moon on cloudy wings and would die without ever finding a piece of forest wide enough to raise her children in.

I could not change the shape of this world but I could help them remember the truth of their own beauty and their roles in this world, for, as you now know, once you lose those truths you have nothing. So to each of the animals I said, "Please forgive. Please help them anyway, though it seems impossible, though they have treated you cruelly. You are the only ones who can show them the way home."

The wolf I allowed to embrace me, felt his great muscles and steel claws, felt the howl in his breath. I let him drink of my blood. I said to him, "You must teach them to be humble."

The frog I bathed in my tears, spilling clean into his delicate body, and I said, "You must teach them the magic of spring. You must sing them your song, so that they will feel the rain again."

The honey bees I allowed to drink sweetness from the spiral of my horn, a sweetness I could never taste myself, and told them, "You must carry their love. You must sting them even, to wake them up to themselves."

To the birds I gave my white light and said, "You must fly in the formations of beauty; you must remind them."

To the deer I gave my beauty and my eye, saying, "You must bring them your gentleness and compassion. You must bring them back their silence."

The dog I kissed on the mouth; I gave him the heat of my body and said, "You must keep loving anyway, as I know you will."

To the cat I gave the softness of my fur and said, "You must let them touch you, you must allow them the gift of you; you must purr, for it heals them."

For the spider I wove a web in the sky with the white silk strands of my mane and tail, and said, "You must remind them of that other, truer language: the more subtle, the more patterned language."

The turtle's shell I hardened with the bone of my horn itself, and I said, "You must teach them to be still and go inward."

The snake coiled around me, taking my very breath, and I said, "You must remind them of the dark womb of earth."

To the whale I sang my knowing, echoing her feelings back to her so that she felt heard. I said to her, "You must keep the memories."

With the seal I surrendered and played with what little body was left to me, and said, "You must remind them of fairy tales."

To the owl I gave my other eye and said, "You must keep their secrets, until they are ready again to own them."

To all of them, I gave these gifts of myself. To each of them, I said, "Teach them. Appear to them when they despair, when they feel alone. Nestle up to them when they are lonely. Stalk them when they feel afraid of themselves, and call out in the night when they forget. Make constellations of beauty around them."

But then they said to me, "It is you who must begin for us. You must go back and tell them, or they will never listen. You must call to them as you have called to us, so that their hearing will change, and they will hear our voices again. We have always known you, but they do not know, and they are afraid, and their fear hurts us. You must use your voice. You must speak."

By the time I reached the City, I was no longer female or male.

Dragon walked with me. As we came closer, I could feel his heart beating faster, in tune with that faster world that the City is. He felt the thrill of you burning in his mind and his body, the thrill of the unknown. He found it more and more difficult to remain focused. Yet he felt pride, too, in being the protector of the Unicorn, though most of you could not see me. This was in the beginning of spring—you remember?—when the Prince and Princess were just arriving.

The problem, I told him as we walked through the outskirts of the City in the early morning, through the graveyards and alleys, among the same homeless men and women who had always lived there and for whom nothing had changed yet. *The problem, the great Council has decided, is that the people cannot find their souls. They have forgotten where they put them.*

That morning we stood in a quiet spring rain that fell on the rubble of buildings, useless wires, broken lights, a rusted truck that had long forgotten what it was. The sun was patient behind clouds. A mother and her son crossed the street ahead of us with some pieces of wood in their arms, and they did not have to look both ways for cars. A couple of old men sat on the edge of the sidewalk and looked out blankly, aware of each other's presence and yet not knowing what to do with that awareness. A beautiful young woman in rags drank water from a metal pipe. And the water was pure now, because I had touched all the rivers of the world with this simple horn— which once, long ago, my mortal self had wished to cast away.

It's okay, I said to Dragon beside me, feeling his fire. *Only stay with me for one last moment, while I try to speak the first word.*

Dragon stood steady, and I believed in him, and he believed in me. He knew he belonged to the City; he knew he would never truly leave it. For fire, though you did not invent it, belongs to you, the people, now. Only people, of all the animals, can begin it, and only you can use it, and only you can end it. Dragon will never tire of burning among you, burning you alive with his determined gaze of desire, touching you with his hot fingers, reminding you of your original fire, your original life—forcing you to awaken.

I cried out. Only Dragon was not startled, and his presence kept me from being afraid of my own sound.

It was the same cry that I made before the Council, after which, for many days, every being on the earth came to me, in response to that call which reverberated through air and water and earth for great distances all around. It is a call the animals recognized but which the human beings, now, did not. It is terrible and unearthly, as if the moon had a cry, as if the moon—all this time—had something to say.

It sounded like this.

You stopped what you were doing.

You were not aware of hearing anything. But suddenly you were listening, in a way you had not listened in a long time. Perhaps you had never listened in this way.

You heard your own breaths, echoing, as if each of you were enclosed in your own small room. As if your cars were still moving faster than you, isolating you from every other person. Yet you were still. You heard the clouds floating above you—rubbing like fur against the sky. You heard the ancient, hungry minds of insects whirring. You heard slow water moving in its forgotten veins beneath the pavement. You heard the pattern of the rain.

That was the beginning. That was how I introduced the rebirth of the world, and the time that was coming.

I let Dragon go then, to find joy in his world. May he release the responsibility of any guilt or the heaviness of any past thing.

Then I went quiet for a little while. I walked in the shadows and felt the fear and the suffering that you were feeling; I felt it with you, so that your burden would be a little less. I walked in the hidden places of the City and let myself get caught in the river of a ragged people who were moving anew through the streets—people who were called Mad. I walked with them, so that the focus turned toward them again, and so that this time you would see their light.

You did not see me at the Councils the lovers called, where they spoke with you—as I had spoken with the elements and the other beings of the world—about what you wanted. But I walked with this man and woman, whom you called "Prince" and "Princess", wherever they went that spring and summer, so that they would not be alone in the solitude that these names forced upon them.

I walked with the Princess when the Prince was living his last days more and more among you, wanting to understand you and to be as human as he could be. I knew these would be the loneliest times for her. For though she laughed at the fires where you gathered in the evenings, still she was not yet one of you. Only after he died, when she would be forced to join you and feel the understanding, forgiveness, and humility of so many hundreds of others who lost as much or more than she had, would she finally belong. Only when she had lost the love she spent her whole life longing for, would she finally cease to be lonely.

So I stayed with her now and gave her the old, simple comforts. I pressed my animal warmth to hers in the night. I let her rest her hand on my back as she walked beside me, to anchor herself and quiet her thoughts. I listened to her desperate questions. I gave her my enduring, wordless love.

And I thanked her: for her friendship and for reminding me what love is, so that this new story could be born.

As the Prince grew nearer to his death, I spent more and more time by his side also, so that he began to glow so brightly that you almost saw me. In my presence, he was able to connect with you as he had never done before. In my presence, you were able to see his gestures and their meaning; you were able to understand the language of all the beings of the world and hear the messages I had carried from the elements. Those messages were for your hearts—for it is you, despite everything you have done, that the world longs to love. So I gave those messages to you, though most of you—at least the adults among you—did not know I was there.

I listened to what Sky would not tell anyone, even his beloved. How he never knew that, all those years he had tried to help you in your dreams, he had also hated you. How he never knew how angry he still was, for the destruction of his homeland. How, until now, his love for you had been selfish: he had wanted for you to change. How he understood now, the way Hanum had felt: alone and without a people. He understood the bitterness, and he did not want to keep that in his heart any longer or continue to pass it on. He told me that he saw, now, how much you had lost. How you had lost your homes, too, and yet at the same time had never had a real home or even known what home was. How he pitied you. And how gradually, with all the effort of his being—and then later with relief and no effort at all—he forgave you.

I kept speaking to you, in a language you only heard through the words and presence of Prince and Princess, and through the words of the animals and trees which you had never before understood. With every word I spoke, I gave a little bit of myself, until I had entered and become the world, and there was nothing of me left.

Now I am only a memory, which will soon fade as well. I am the memory of that first moment when you felt your souls again, when the whole world changed.

It was morning, and a quiet rain was falling. Do you remember? You stopped what you were doing. You remembered the promise of childhood—a certain taste, a certain smell, a certain way that molecules seemed to sparkle, a certain delicious ease in your belly. Pigeons alighted around you and bowed their smooth little heads. Two rats were speaking together in a gutter. A dog leaned against your legs, joyously breathing. A cat, to whom you had given a little scrap of that meager food you had, licked your hand.

Then you looked at the person next to you, and you saw a god.

$$\mathbb{C}$$

Kite will dream of Mira, the girl, for a long time to come. But she is never again as pure and humanly close as she was in those nights she came to him in the forest for real, when he did not yet even know that she was real, and when he looked into her as into a deep well under a full moon on a wide black night. In his later dreams, which are only dreams after all, she keeps changing, and she touches him as she would never actually have done. She becomes less and less herself, and more and more a part of Kite and his dream of what woman will become to him in the future.

Yet on his last night in the forest, less than a day's walk from home, Kite dreams not of Mira but of a man he has never seen before.

All day he has walked in near total silence with Delilah. This final ascent into the mountains is especially steep, and all her focus has lain in carrying herself forward step by step. Their way has been terribly slow since Dragon and Mira left them, for her exhaustion has weakened her so much, she no longer has the strength to pretend it isn't killing her. She spoke to Kite only once on the first day, but with kindness in her voice, as if she could feel his sorrow and confusion.

"We'll see them again, Kite," she said, and Kite was ashamed to feel tears break in tiny waves under his eyes, and he turned away. "So many times I've lost the ones I loved most, and it seems like they always have a way of coming back to me. It's just been hard for me to realize I can't control when or how."

Kite nodded, not trusting his voice. For days after, they hardly spoke, except to communicate the bare necessities of survival. Sometimes Kite, feeling helpless in the presence of her weakness, and not wanting to embarrass her by exposing her breathlessness with questions she would have to answer, tried to distract her with a few encouraging words about his home. But since he is not naturally much of a talker, he managed to fill only a few moments of the silence. Mira was constantly on his mind, and he knew now that Mira was Delilah's sister, yet he could not bring himself to speak of her, nor could he imagine what he would say. So he distracted himself by listening to the forest and checking their direction again and again in his mind to make sure they were going the right way. He would never have doubted himself alone, but somehow the responsibility of getting Delilah home before she collapsed made him unsure.

In between worrying about Delilah and wishing he could glance at his map again without worrying her, Kite thought about Mira some more. He thought about what she told him in those few precious days when she walked beside him, and proved to him that she was no dream. Each of her hesitant words was so carefully tongued, he could taste their edges; he could hear the shapes her lips made in pronouncing them. She did not speak many words to him, but each one felt like a gift whose joy would keep him awake all night. She told him she had been hiding in the form of a magical creature, but that he had helped her to release that form and be human again. She said it without any pride or drama, so that Kite could not help but believe her. She told him that, when he saw the white horse, she was there in that presence: that animal held her soul in safekeeping. Kite did not understand what she meant by that, but in the glow of her anything seemed possible to him. That this animal which was connected with her should also be connected with his memory of Lonely made utter sense to him. For in both of those women, those two mysteries—though he had lost them and would perhaps never see either one of them again—there lay, for him, all the potential of his own future and the future of the world. That was something which he could not explain but knew, and he did not mind that.

Tonight he and Delilah bed down by a great waterfall that Kite has never seen before. He did not come this way, on his way down. He knows they are not far from home now, but the way from here is not obvious, and Delilah does not have the strength or the will for walking along the bottom of the ridge in search of some steep path up. So they stop, though the sun has not yet set. Kite leaves her, though it makes him uneasy to do so, and goes in search of food. He returns after dark with a rabbit, terrified for some reason that something might have happened to her in his absence, but he finds her in a deep sleep right where he left her. He cooks and eats alone and saves the rest to give her later, for when he nudges her she only murmurs fitfully and falls straight back into oblivion.

Though it's very late now, Kite cannot sleep for a long time. He watches the moon rise, almost full. He thinks of his family, and wonders what they will say when they see him. Will he seem as different as he feels? He is happy to be coming home, and yet he is frightened too, as if once he enters again into the daily life of his family, he might lose everything he gained. Nor can he even cannot define what he's gained. It feels elusive, and he is not entirely sure that it even belongs to him.

In his dream, he is frustrated and mad like he felt sometimes when he was a boy, before he went to the City. But in the dream he is outside the City Center walls, pounding on the doors.

"Let me in!" he cries. "I know something. I have something to tell you."

The voice on the other side of the wall—a serious, quiet male voice—asks,

"What is your name?"

"Kite."

"But your mother," says the voice, "named you Malachite."

And Kite's heart falls with the disappointment of a child, as if he has been told that his great journey to the City was all in his head and never happened at all. It seems to him that this is the reason he cannot get in, that his mother insists on this name she gave him, will not let him change it, and will not let him free. "No!" he yells, pounding his fist on the door in fury. "I am Kite! Why won't she listen? Why does she still call me Malachite? Why?"

Then the door opens, and this tall young man steps out, whom Kite has never seen. Yet he looks as real as Mira did, when Mira appeared, and turned out not to be a dream after all.

"Because your mother holds to the past," answers the man calmly. "Because she wants to honor what is given from our past, from our ancestors."

The man is wearing a skirt of long black and white bird feathers, and his slim chest is bare. When Kite looks into his eyes, he can see the sky, and it frightens him. The man does not look fully human, and yet his voice, now, is kind. Kite is surprised because he realizes, in the dream, that this man is the true inhabitant of the City Center, and he wonders how he never saw this before. Of course those voices in the dark were not real. Of course they were not the answer.

"We hold onto our past," the man continues, "because we have lost so much."

Then he turns around, and beyond him, Kite sees now not the steel building but a field of green water, and the shadows of giant trees.

"I thought," says the man, "that by holding my past a secret, closing my heart even to the one I loved most, I could somehow keep part of it for myself and not lose everything. I thought that the way we lived long ago was the only right way to live, and that no one else would ever understand. But now I see that change comes, whether I will it or not."

And as Kite looks at the curves of the trees, they seem also to be the walls of strange buildings—buildings at once earthy and richly textured like his own home, and shiny and grand like the buildings of the City. What he thought were rivers of water through avenues of reeds seem at once to be the streets of a city he has never seen, intimate and full of secret passageways into gardens, and what he thought were wading white birds seem at once to be white lanterns carried by dancing people. Suddenly he feels a great urgency to enter into that green growing place, into that darkness and into that light. For in its depths he thinks he sees that white horse wandering, and he wants to follow her, for the greatest magic he has known in his life is carried somehow within her, and she is his guide into the future.

"I see now," says the man beside him, "that the job of the original people was simply to guard our wisdom until the next people were ready for it, and that these new people will do what they will with it. They will carry it on into a future we cannot control or dictate—any more than a mother can dictate the future of her child."

He turns toward Kite, and the sorrow Kite sees there he will remember for the rest of his days. He will carry it with him wherever he goes, and no matter what he does, no matter what he tries to create, he will always respect it. "This is the first time I have appeared to anyone in a dream as myself," says the man. "I was waiting, for so long, for the world to turn back to the way it was. But it is never going to turn back. I must surrender to the future. There is something beyond what the City was, and also beyond what my world was. It goes on and on. And you are the bridge, Malachite and Kite. You stand in between."

Kite looks back and sees his mother's house and the fields of his childhood behind him, and he looks forward and sees the ruins of the City and the people picking through the remains, trying to begin again. The man with the sky in his eyes is gone now, and in that disappearance, Kite feels the soft weight of the man's surrender. As he breathes out and wakes, he feels at once the relief and the gentle burden of finally being free.

That freedom he longed for so deeply as he sat in the oak tree and looked out at the City far away—that freedom finally came, at a price. The price was the sad, irreversible wisdom that comes with remembering the suffering of the City, that he will always have to carry now.

He wakes knowing, with a clarity that will not leave him, that he will return to the City. That he is not yet finished there. And that the next time he goes, he will go not to find answers, but to give.

Now Delilah is awake and eating the food he left for her. She has the wherewithal to share a little of what remains with him for breakfast, but he is frightened by the look in her eyes. He cannot even see the Delilah he knows there; her pupils are like lean, focused fists of determination floating in a sea of glazed delirium. She says nothing as he helps her to her feet.

But as they wander along the base of the cliff, he begins to recognize the plants he knows, which also grow around his home. He picks the ones that can be eaten and offers them to her. Looking a little amazed, she takes them from his hands with docile clumsiness and chews them slowly—and then more quickly. He keeps picking them. He sees the warmth return to her face, and when, after a while, she turns to him and he sees her familiar grin, he is so relieved he exhales audibly.

"How do you know all these plants, little mountain boy?" she asks him teasingly, and of course he does not mind her calling him that, though coming from anyone else it would infuriate him.

He shrugs. "I'm not stupid."

"But who taught you?" she insists, looking at him more intently.

"I don't know. My grandmother, I guess." He reflects a moment, and then adds, "I think you'll like my grandmother."

Then they see, at the same moment, the way up. It's a dusty, slippery path made by deer, twining through brambles to the unseen top. Kite looks at Delilah uncertainly, but she braces her shoulders in that familiar way and says, "All right, then."

So they start up, Kite climbing protectively behind Delilah, though he cannot imagine catching her if she falls. He watches her focused, cat-like limbs grip and turn slowly with the extra weight of her belly, and her bare calloused heels poking out from her broken shoes. She's told him she lived alone in the desert for more than seven years. That is all he knows about her.

When they reach the top, she is avoiding his eyes again, as if she intends to keep her energy to herself for a while and simply endure. They walk on in that familiar silence. As they rise higher into the mountains, the air turns refreshingly cool, and the world turns back in time: the trees here are still beginning their spring blooming, and the early lilies are just now opening in their shade. A light wind blows a feeling of mingled suspense and quiet through the evergreen branches and over their skin, and brushes long clouds across the sky. Kite recognizes the rotting trunk of a giant poplar that fell in a storm two years ago, and he recognizes the slope that rises up from it, and the angle with which the sound of the river finds his ear. He veers toward it. When the brush gets close and difficult, he walks ahead and breaks a path for Delilah the best he can.

By the afternoon they are following the familiar creek again, but have been unable to find anything to eat except for greens. Kite glances at Delilah constantly out of the corner of his eye.

"We're almost there, Delilah," he says quietly.

She doesn't say anything for a moment, and then responds just as quietly, "What does that mean? Almost."

"We're really close," he says. "I know where I am. We'll be there way before nightfall. We'll eat when we get there." He feels a surge of surprising joy.

Delilah doesn't say anything, but he notices she walks a little faster now, as if with renewed strength.

"Kite," she says.

"What?"

"Do you think they'll like me? Your family?"

He looks at her abruptly, but she's watching her feet, and then she looks up at the sky with a tight expression as if she's trying to figure it out.

"Of course!" he cries. "Why wouldn't they like you?" He realizes how proud he is to know her.

She shrugs and gives him an unconvincing half-smile. "I'm just a City girl, after all."

Kite looks down. He knows what she means. She is another world from his family. He cannot imagine her settling anywhere, working food quietly up from the ground, or sitting at the same table every night. He cannot imagine her sitting at his table. But she has to have her baby somewhere safe.

"Don't you have a family?" he asks.

"No. Only Mira."

While he wonders what to say next, she changes the subject.

"Why did you go to the City, Kite? Why did you leave your family?"

"I wanted to know what it was like."

"And what is it like, do you think? What will you tell them?"

Kite shakes his head and smiles to himself. "I don't know."

But he keeps thinking about the question. It makes him anxious, not knowing how he will put it into words for his family. It feels to him essential that he do so, if he is to remain independent of them, and not lose the clarity of his memories and impressions over time. He wishes he still had the journal he kept, though he can't remember now if he wrote anything of importance there. There is something he must express to them, something he wants them to know about the City. But at this moment, the intensity of Dragon's presence, the beauty of Mira, and the mystery of Delilah beside him all seem more tangible than his own opinions of what he has seen.

Delilah says nothing more, and he is left to think on her question for a long time. He lets that question float along beside him in the wind as he walks, and fit its shape to the shapes of the trees and slopes he recognizes, which gradually fill their surroundings the closer they get to home, like an image coming into focus around him.

At the crest of a hill, he stops and turns to Delilah. She stops, too, and he looks into her eyes, which is hard to do. He is surprised to see in those eyes not that sweet, mocking confidence which first impressed him, but a nervous reticence, and beneath that, fear. For the first time, he understands that where they are headed now, which is to him a comfort he takes for granted and even tires of, is to her a place of dark unknown where she cannot imagine belonging. For the first time he understands what Dragon always told him: how lucky he is to be so loved he never even thought to imagine what it would feel like not to be.

"It's the same," he says suddenly.

"What?" she says.

"I mean, what you asked me. What I thought of the City. I think it's the same or, at least, not so different from here."

"What are you talking about?"

"I've realized something about community. We humans are so vulnerable—just skin and bones, you know?—and when we're all alone in the wilderness, we get scared. We try to stay safe by keeping to ourselves, being suspicious of anyone we don't know. And the people of the City, they have the same fear. They just learned to deal with that fear differently—by trying to control the elements, trying to conquer them. But that was an illusion. You can't be in control like that. Long ago people didn't survive that way. They survived just by depending on each other and working together the best they could. Right? That's what we all need to do."

Delilah sighs and looks down.

"I'm going back to the City one day, Delilah. But first I'm going to go and find the other people here in the mountains, the other farmers who are left. Our people. Our community right here. We have a kind of wisdom, here, about how things are connected—something they've forgotten in the City. But the City people have another kind of knowledge, and if we could put that wisdom and knowledge together, we could do anything, Delilah." It seems so much clearer to him now. He can think better, now that he's back in the quiet, light air of the forest he knows.

But Delilah still won't look at him. She looks into the wind coming from the valley they rose out of, as if she can still see the City from here. "Kite," she says, with a gentleness that irritates him—the first time she has ever irritated him. "The City is falling apart. There are people headed up here right now, coming up the mountains in search of food, in search of a new life, desperate. People who went mad long ago are trying to get sane again, trying to remember what's real. Everyone is going to want to live like you do now, don't you see? Everyone will clear a bunch of forest to make a farm or a home. Trust me, I know that desperation. People live by destroying."

"No, you don't know," interrupts Kite passionately. "You lived there, but you missed it. You missed seeing all that people can do. You missed the art, you missed the books, you missed the great beautiful buildings and the magic people create, you missed the wonder of it all, all the choices people have. You forgot to be amazed."

Delilah shakes her head. "I didn't miss it, Kite. I just—" Then she looks at him and smiles, and he sees the caring in that smile and forgets his irritation.

"Sorry," she says. But he feels sad, to think how hard he has had to fight everyone to get them to see what he sees. Only Dragon understood.

"Why did we stop?" she asks after a moment.

"Because," says Kite, turning to look down the slope ahead of them, "we're here."

He feels Delilah freeze beside him and, impulsively, he takes her hand. "Come on."

They inch down the steep hill together, grabbing the trunks of saplings to steady themselves, until the grade becomes more level and they can see the meadow ahead of them. They pause to peer through a row of birch trees which are all that separate them from the view of the house, like white columns rising into the sky. They are familiar to Kite, but he sees them differently now. They remind him, for an instant, of the columns on the deck of the great, marble-laced building in the center of the college, through whose doors endless rivers of young students came and went.

From a long distance away, Kite can see his father, a figure in a mist of tall grass striding swiftly from the gardens toward the house with his quiet, decided gate, swinging a bucket in each hand.

Then much closer, suddenly, but as if in slow motion, he sees his sister and mother leave the house with bowls of food in their hands. His sister moves more slowly than she used to, not without energy but as if with more thought, or heavier thoughts. She looks entirely like a grown woman. His mother, to his surprise, looks much smaller than he remembered. When he sees her bend over the outdoor table with the food, the tired slope of her shoulders pains him. She looks so old.

But for some reason Delilah says, catching her breath, "Is your mother a goddess?"

Kite laughs. "My *mother?*"

They stand still for another moment, watching. Chelya, with her efficient grace, turns immediately back toward the house after laying down her load, but his mother remains at the table a little longer, quietly arranging things. Before she goes, for no reason, she looks up toward the forest where he and Delilah stand.

In that moment—when he cannot yet see the expression on his mother's face, but only her hand dropping to her side and her body leaning toward him, and she is calling out the name he chose for himself—he hears Delilah's voice again beside him.

"But I think she is a goddess," she says with the same breathlessness. "The goddess of this mountain, maybe. I—I know her, somehow."

As they go forward from the trees, and Fawn begins to run, Delilah laughs a quiet, amazed little laugh. "Kite," she says. "You're right. Maybe everything is going to be okay, after all."

FIRST SUN

One morning a woman is sitting dreamily on a ledge that was once the wall of a great building, overlooking a garden where five children play. Around her, walls of crumbling concrete keep crumbling, their helpless greyness that has never meant anything to anyone turning slowly over the years into oblivion. She is thinking how beautiful these once heartless walls look now that they're in pieces, now that the grass sprouts from their cracks, moss covers their flanks, and their dying forms assume the shapes of natural things—asymmetrical, unpredictable.

But she doesn't have much time to think, because it is her turn to watch the children. The people living in this part of the City take turns watching each other's children while the others work on building, planting, and holding meetings to discuss the future and how to handle the immediate needs of the people. They have barely emerged past a state of emergency. People are still learning to talk to each other and work together. There is a lot of anger and a lot of confusion, even amidst the wonder of new life. It tires this woman, who prefers to watch the children now, even though she has no children of her own, nor wants any for now.

At this moment, the oldest boy is explaining to her why the youngest girl is crying: her sister won't share the seeds and let her plant some. So the woman goes to the girls and kneels beside them, but even as she does so, she sighs. She notices the detachment of the boy, his awkwardness in explaining the girls' feelings, the way his eyes wander over the edges of the buildings and beyond them to unknown people, unknown questions, unknown skies, as if he dreams of being a man already and following a path beyond all this silliness. She knows how he feels. As the children continue on with their careful, clumsy planting, and the shy, rough pats of their hands against the soil, she remembers two little boys long ago to whom she told a story, and how that story was her own after all.

She remembers their uncle, kneeling across from her in a field high in the mountains, and how he said, "What would you do if you had no obligations to anyone, if you could do anything?"

But for this moment she only kneels to work as she did then, now beside these children, gathering what they scatter behind them in their playfulness—the trampled tools, the spilled bucket of compost. As she works, she feels the happiness of her lover who lives now within the deep ground. She remembers the promise the earth made her long ago: *I am always with you. You cannot leave me.* It is the only promise that has ever been kept.

The first food that grew from his bones, from his blood, from his breath, was not like any food the people remembered. It nourished their bodies down to the core, right down to their spirits. And they dreamed delicious dreams.

When the woman who loved that god lost him and began to live among the people, they asked her her name. When she said it for the first time, it made her cry. Her own tears washed over her, as if she knelt beneath Moon's waterfall all over again, and the rainbow finally overcame her and she was drowned. For when she had discovered that name like a gift for the first time in the private embrace of her beloved's arms, she had never imagined that she would only come to use it at a time when he was gone from this world forever, a time when she had shapeshifted yet again, into a princess, and then into a simple person among the crowd. This last was the greatest transformation she had experienced yet. And what was a name, after all? It seemed nothing to her when she first spoke it to a stranger. It did not make her special. It did not save her from loss. It did not give her any answers. It only made her ordinary. It only made her one of the rest.

Yet it was something to hold onto, too. Even now, it keeps her anchored amidst the storms of her grief, which have not yet abated. She longs for Sky every day. She longs for every moment she remembers, and every lifetime they will live together that has not yet come. Only her name still belongs to her and cannot be taken. It has given her this place among the community of people and of life. Every day she is grateful for that community, with a gratitude as unconscious and necessary as her own legs.

Yet also, she has begun to think again, lately, of solitude.

She has begun to think again of a time before people, a time before Sky was anything but a dream, a time when she and her horse and her own longing were her whole world. The voice of the wind was clearer to her then. She did not notice back then, long ago, how natural that solitude felt. Those moments, now, feel like the most solid happiness she ever knew.

She has begun to speak to the wind again, bit by bit. Sometimes, she does not wait for it to find her. She catches it unaware, teases it back, and wakes it even before it has woken.

"I know you're there," she whispers to it now, sitting apart again, as the children play. And a breeze snakes over the dust and shimmies against her leg.

"I keep asking myself," she murmurs to it vaguely, "I keep asking myself, what is next for me?" Then she pauses, smiling at a memory. "I saw Dragon the other day. He did not recognize me. He seems very happy here, and very loved."

Dragon, dressed in bright colors, was surrounded by children. He was making little flames for them—making them dance in his hands—and they were awed. He was talking about dragons, how they breathed fire like that, how they came in all different colors and were very powerful but would not hurt people if people respected them. In an outer, less cohesive circle around the children, adults stood listening, though some of them pretended they were not listening. The children were asking if Dragon could show them the dragons, if they promised to be very respectful. They were asking where the dragons had all gone.

The wind, never impatient, ripples without direction through her hair. "But am I happy?" she asks it. "What do I want, I wonder?"

That was my question to you once, says the wind, *a long time ago.*

Then as it hurries off into its freedom, over heads, over walls, over anything, it leaves her attention upon a shaggy old dog running toward her.

She holds out her hand.

i know you! cries the dog, pressing his paws against her chest. *i know you!*

She presses his shaggy ears back with her palms and looks into his face. "It *is* you," she says. "How you comforted me so long ago, when I was terrified of this place and could not come in. You remember me!"

He sits panting and closes his eyes, letting her hands rake over him. There is nothing more to be said. He is happy.

"Oh," she says now. "Do you belong to that woman?"

The dog stands up excitedly. *no,* he pants, *but i brought her here, for you.*

Then he trots off, as if hurrying on to his next ecstatic mission. Now the woman comes toward her silently, stepping over the near rock wall: a woman with dark hair like nightfall. So many of the City people are pale, and many of the darker ones have had to be encouraged, over time, out of hiding. But this woman is half dark, half light.

"Can I help?" the unknown woman asks in a small voice.

The woman who was speaking with the wind looks up and smiles at a memory she sees in the other's face. "Of course."

"There will be a garden here?" the darker woman asks. She speaks as if she isn't from this place—as if she does not even know what has happened. "We're trying to plant food everywhere," the first woman explains slowly, curiously, looking into her eyes. Then she says, "I'm Salt."

"I'm Mira," says Mira.

"You look a little like someone I once knew."

Mira kneels. Salt stares at her, feeling at once startled and foolish, as if she is missing something obvious. This girl is not just any girl. She feels so important. Or she reminds Salt of something important—a dream she had?

The impression seems to come from more than her uncanny resemblance to Delilah. But then Salt worries that her stare is frightening the girl.

"You can turn up that row there with your hands," she says to Mira. "Loosen up the soil. I'm sorry I have no other tools to work with right now."

Mira begins obediently. But Salt keeps staring, in spite of her intention not to.

"Something has happened to you," she says suddenly, reaching out to touch Mira's hand. She can't help herself. Every motion of the girl's pained, hesitant body is like a careful attempt to repair the wound of a soul. That wound, too, feels familiar to Salt.

But Mira pulls back sharply, then sits still and lowers her head. Salt immediately regrets her gesture and her words. She begins to think through some apology, feeling an old loneliness rise up inside her that she thought she had conquered. Lost in thought, she unknowingly picks up a fallen leaf and tears it to pieces in her hands.

"My father died," Mira says finally, long after Salt has given up hope of an answer, "when I was young."

"Mine, too," says Salt, and Mira looks up.

"My mother," she says, shaking her head, and stops.

"She could not rescue you," whispers Salt, and Mira nods.

"Whhhooooooh!" roars the youngest boy with his breath, interrupting them. He is running toward the older boy and the older girl who are building a play house out of sticks. It may be the only house they have in this world right now. But the younger boy is pretending to be fire, and will tear it all down. Salt stands, anticipating more tears.

"I came to you," Mira is saying to her, oblivious to the commotion, "because I thought I recognized you, but now I'm not sure."

Salt glances back at her.

"Anyway, something about you— I'm still so new, but you seem safe. Oh, I can't explain anything. Are you old?"

Salt laughs. "Old?" But the little girl comes running to her now, tearing at her skirts.

"He tore down our house!"

Salt sighs. What can she tell them? The truth is that the house was important, but the fire, too, was a true thing. It was something that happened. The boy is only re-enacting the drama of reality. How else can it be understood? But she doesn't know what to tell them. She doesn't know what to do with children, really.

"Hush," says Mira gently, and holds her fragile arms out to the girl. And the girl, not even knowing her, falls into them, and lets Mira caress her back.

"I know," murmurs Mira. "It's so sad. So sad."

Smiling, Salt watches the girl's shoulders relax, and then the girl pulls away and runs back to her friends—everything okay now, forgotten. Mira looks back up at Salt.

"Once I was a different creature," she says thoughtfully, "and that creature was the oldest creature in the world, and I knew so much more than I know now: I was wise. But I gave that form up. I gave it back to the world, to whom it belongs. It never belonged to me, Salt. And now I am only this—this woman, and I feel so young, so unknowing. I don't know what to do, what to say, what to feel. And you seem old to me!"

Salt sits down again, sifts soil between her fingers, dusts a thin layer over the shivering seeds, and thinks. It seems to her that she can speak the truth to this girl, and Mira will not think it strange. So she allows herself to look into her feelings a little more deeply than she would ordinarily do with a stranger present. "In a way I do feel old," she says. "I've seen many worlds, and I've lived many lives, and I've lost what I love most over and over again. That makes me feel old. But at the same time I feel younger than I've ever been. I mean, in my lives before this one, there was always something I had to be, some plan laid out for me, some dream I was for someone else. I was chasing—I didn't even know, Mira—I was chasing a ghost." She pauses, staring into the air. "Now I get to start all over—with no one wanting me, expecting me, or challenging me, no one even truly knowing me. I can go anywhere in the world. I can do anything, meet anyone, and make any choice I want to at any moment."

She smiles at Mira now with the revelation of what she's saying, feeling for the first time since Sky died that she is waking up—and it is a good waking, not like waking from a nightmare. Mira is staring back at her. Her eyes are indigo, her neck long and curved, her shoulders brown and narrow. Like a brand new creature.

"It's that way for me, too," Mira says.

"Have you ever been out in those fields?" Salt asks Mira in a rush. "Out beyond the City, toward the desert and the mountains—those fields that are like the sky, the way it feels to walk through them? Have you been there?"

Mira nods. "I have been there." For an instant she looks not young at all, but very old, much older than Salt. Salt feels the air lift her right up from inside; she feels lighter than she can remember feeling for a long time. Suddenly, as if it were perfectly natural, she imagines traveling with Mira through those fields, laughing with her, discovering and speaking with all the creatures together, talking of their dreams and their longings and knowing that they both have felt all of the same things. She imagines it as if it has already happened. Or as if they have already traveled all those lands together but did not have the language with which to speak of it to each other, until now.

She reaches across the seed beds again for Mira's hand. This time, Mira's fingers close around hers.

"There are other people out there, Mira," she whispers, "in the mountains and the desert and all the lands where I've never even been. And there are great wildernesses where you don't see anyone at all."

Mira nods. "I know people who live in the mountains."

"So do I." Salt smiles to remember, for it feels so long ago that she knew them, and yet they feel so close she could almost touch them. She looks down at her own hand clasped in Mira's, and her heart is beating so alive.

"Salt," says Mira very quietly, "I wish I could see those fields again. I would walk tall in those fields now. I would run. If you—"

She looks up, and Salt looks up too. "If you will come with me. As my friend."

They gaze at each other, as the children cry out and laugh and spill the soil around them, and they try to remember. Because it seems to each one as if she knows the other from somewhere. As if their story already began in some other lifetime, when they stood lost and separate by the sea, and the wind called out a single, restless word, whose gift no one yet knew.

Acknowledgments

Thank you to my publisher, Steve Crimi, for putting all your heart into making this book happen, because you believe in it and for no other reason. Thank you to Krys Crimi, for doing the same, and for your calligraphy. Thank you to my husband, whose honest feedback on my earliest draft was the catalyst for my best revisions. Thank you to my editor, Judy Hogan, for bolstering my faith when I most needed it. Thank you to Susan Yost for cover design and layout, and to Chiwa for your artwork. Thank you to Brian Mashburn for permission to use your beautiful painting, and to Utah Green for permission to use your beautiful song. Thank you to the fox who appeared at the edge of the field, at a time in the very middle of the story when I wondered if it was worth going on, and stared at me long and hard, until I didn't anymore.

Mindi Meltz has worked in many landscapes as a writer, counselor and teacher, and holds an MA in Transpersonal Psychology. She grew up on the coast of Maine, and now lives with her husband in the mountains of Western North Carolina. This is her second novel.

She can be reached at www.mindimeltz.com